Praise for Ken Follett and
The Pillars of the Earth

"Follett is a master."—*The Washington Post*

"A towering tale . . . a ripping read . . . there's murder, arson, treachery, torture, love, and lust."
—*New York Daily News*

"Very good . . . fine detail . . . fast-paced, engaging—an enjoyable historical thriller, well told."
—*Chicago Tribune*

"An extraordinary epic buttressed by suspense . . . a mystifying puzzle involving the execution of an innocent man . . . the erection of a magnificent cathedral . . . romance, rivalry, and spectacle. A monumental masterpiece . . . a towering triumph from a major talent."
—*ALA Booklist*

Ken Follett is the international bestselling author of suspense thrillers and the nonfiction *On Wings of Eagles*. He lives in England. Visit Ken Follett's official Web site at www.ken-follett.com.

ALSO BY KEN FOLLETT

The Modigliani Scandal
Paper Money
Eye of the Needle
Triple
The Key to Rebecca
The Man from St. Petersburg
On Wings of Eagles
Lie Down with Lions
Night over Water
A Dangerous Fortune
A Place Called Freedom
The Third Twin
The Hammer of Eden
Code to Zero
Jackdaws
Hornet Flight
Whiteout
World Without End

The PILLARS OF THE EARTH

KEN FOLLETT

NEW AMERICAN LIBRARY

To Marie-Claire, the apple of my eye

New American Library
Published by New American Library, a division of
Penguin Group (USA) Inc., 375 Hudson Street,
New York, New York 10014, USA
Penguin Group (Canada), 90 Eglinton Avenue East, Suite 700, Toronto,
Ontario M4P 2Y3, Canada (a division of Pearson Penguin Canada Inc.)
Penguin Books Ltd., 80 Strand, London WC2R 0RL, England
Penguin Ireland, 25 St. Stephen's Green, Dublin 2,
Ireland (a division of Penguin Books Ltd.)
Penguin Group (Australia), 250 Camberwell Road, Camberwell, Victoria 3124,
Australia (a division of Pearson Australia Group Pty. Ltd.)
Penguin Books India Pvt. Ltd., 11 Community Centre, Panchsheel Park,
New Delhi - 110 017, India
Penguin Group (NZ), 67 Apollo Drive, Rosedale, North Shore 0632,
New Zealand (a division of Pearson New Zealand Ltd.)
Penguin Books (South Africa) (Pty.) Ltd., 24 Sturdee Avenue,
Rosebank, Johannesburg 2196, South Africa

Penguin Books Ltd., Registered Offices:
80 Strand, London WC2R 0RL, England

Published by New American Library, a division of Penguin Group (USA) Inc. Original
hardcover edition published by William Morrow and Company, Inc. Previously published
in a Plume edition.

First New American Library Printing, February 2002
First New American Library Printing (Deluxe Edition), October 2007
10 9 8 7 6 5 4 3 2 1

Copyright © Ken Follett, 1989
Illustrations by Petra Röhr-Rouendaal, assisted by John Wormald
All rights reserved

NAL REGISTERED TRADEMARK—MARCA REGISTRADA

New American Library Deluxe Edition ISBN: 978-0-451-22524-5

The Library of Congress has catalogued the hardcover edition of this title as follows:

Follett, Ken.
    The pillars of the earth/Ken Follett.
      p. cm.
    ISBN 0-688-04659-2
    1. Great Britain—History—Stephen, 1123–1154—Fiction.   I. Title.
PR6056.O45P55   1989
823'.914—dc20   89-9405

Book design by Oksana Kushnir

Printed in the United States of America

Without limiting the rights under copyright reserved above, no part of this publication may
be reproduced, stored in or introduced into a retrieval system, or transmitted, in any form, or
by any means (electronic, mechanical, photocopying, recording, or otherwise), without the
prior written permission of both the copyright owner and the above publisher of this book.

PUBLISHER'S NOTE
This is a work of fiction. Names, characters, places, and incidents either are the product of
the author's imagination or are used fictitiously, and any resemblance to actual persons, living or dead, business establishments, events, or locales is entirely coincidental.
    The publisher does not have any control over and does not assume any responsibility for
author or third-party Web sites or their content.

The scanning, uploading, and distribution of this book via the Internet or via any other
means without the permission of the publisher is illegal and punishable by law. Please purchase only authorized electronic editions, and do not participate in or encourage electronic piracy of copyrighted materials. Your support of the author's rights is appreciated.

Preface

NOTHING HAPPENS the way you plan it.

A lot of people were surprised by *The Pillars of the Earth,* including me. I was known as a thriller writer. In the book business, when you have had a success, the smart thing to do is write the same sort of thing once a year for the rest of your life. Clowns should not try to play Hamlet; pop stars should not write symphonies. I should not have risked my reputation by writing something out of character and overambitious.

What's more, I don't believe in God. I'm not what you would call a spiritual person. According to my agent, my greatest problem as a writer is that I'm not a tortured soul. The last thing anyone would have expected from me was a story about building a church.

So *Pillars* was an unlikely book for me to write—and I almost didn't. I started it, then dropped it, and did not look at it again for ten years.

This is how it happened.

When I was a boy, all my family belonged to a Puritan religious group called the Plymouth Brethren. For us, a church was a bare room with rows of chairs around a central table. Paintings, statues, and all forms of decoration were banned. The sect also discouraged members from visiting rival churches. So I grew up pretty much ignorant of Europe's wealth of gorgeous church architecture.

I started trying to write novels in my middle twenties, while working as a reporter on London's *Evening News.* I realized then that I had never taken much interest in the cityscape around me, and I had no vocabulary to describe the buildings in which my characters had their adventures. So I bought *An Outline of European Architecture* by Nikolaus Pevsner. That book gave me eyes with which to look at buildings in general and churches in particular. Pevsner got really passionate when he wrote about Gothic cathedrals. The invention of the pointed arch, he wrote, was a rare event in history, when the solution to a technical problem—how to build a taller church—was also sublimely beautiful.

Soon after I read Pevsner's book, my newspaper sent me to the East Anglian city of Peterborough. I have long forgotten what story I was covering, but I shall always remember what I did after filing it. I had to wait an hour for a train back to London, so, remembering Pevsner's fascinating and passionate descriptions of medieval architecture, I went to see Peterborough Cathedral.

It was one of those moments.

The west front of Peterborough has three huge Gothic arches, like doorways for giants. The inside is older than the façade, with arcades of regular round Norman arches in stately procession up the aisle. Like all great churches, it is both tranquil and beautiful. But it was more than that. Because of Pevsner's book, I had some inkling of the effort that had gone into this. I knew the story of humankind's attempts to build ever taller and more beautiful churches. I understood the place of this building in history, my history.

I was enraptured by Peterborough Cathedral.

Cathedral visiting became a hobby for me. Every few months I would drive to one of England's old cities, check into a hotel, and study the church. This way I saw Canterbury, Salisbury, Winchester, Gloucester, and Lincoln, each one unique, each with an intriguing story to tell. Most people take an hour or two to "do" a cathedral, but I like to have a couple of days.

The stones themselves reveal the construction history: stops and starts, damage and rebuilding, extensions in times of prosperity, and stained-glass tributes to the wealthy men who generally paid the bills. Another story is told by the way the church is sited in the town. Lincoln faces the castle across the street, religious and military power nose to nose. Winchester stands amid a neat grid of streets, laid out by a medieval bishop who fancied himself a town planner. Salisbury moved, in the thirteenth century, from a defensive hilltop site—where the ruins of the old cathedral are still visible—to an open meadow, showing that permanent peace had arrived.

But all the while a question nagged at me: Why were these churches built?

There are simple answers—for the glory of God, the vanity of bishops, and so on—but those were not enough for me. The building of the medieval cathedrals is an astonishing European phenomenon. The builders had no power tools, they did not understand the mathematics of structural engineering, and they were poor: the richest of princes did not live as well as, say, a prisoner in a modern jail. Yet they put up the most beautiful buildings that have ever existed, and they built them so well that they are still here, hundreds of years later, for us to study and marvel at.

I began to read about these churches, but I found the books unsatisfactory. There was a great deal of aesthetic guff about elevations, but not much about the living buildings. Then I came across *The Cathedral Builders* by Jean Gimpel. Gimpel, the black sheep of a family of French art dealers, was as impatient as I with discussions about whether a clerestory "worked" aesthetically. His book was about the dirt-poor hovel dwellers who actually put up these fabulous buildings. He read the payroll records of French monasteries and took an interest in who the builders were and how much money they made. He was the first person to notice, for example, that a significant minority of the names were female. The medieval church was sexist, but women as well as men built the cathedrals.

Another work of Gimpel's, *The Medieval Machine*, taught me that the Middle Ages were a time of rapid high-tech innovation, during which the power of water mills was harnessed for a wide variety of industrial applications. Soon I was taking an interest in medieval life in general. And I began to get a picture of how the building of the great cathedrals must have seemed like the right thing to do for medieval people.

The explanation is not simple. It is a little like trying to understand why twentieth-century people spent so much money exploring outer space. In both cases, a whole network of influences operated: scientific curiosity, commercial interests, political rivalries, and the spiritual aspirations of earthbound people. And it seemed to me there was only one way to map that network: by writing a novel.

Sometime in 1976 I wrote an outline and about four chapters of the novel. I sent it to my agent, Al Zuckerman, who wrote, "You have created a tapestry. What you need is a series of linked melodramas."

Looking back, I can see that at the age of twenty-seven I was not capable of writing such a novel. I was like an apprentice watercolor painter planning a vast canvas in oils. To do justice to its subject, the book would have to be very long, cover a period of several decades, and bring alive the great sweep of medieval Europe. I was writing much less ambitious books, and even so, I had not yet mastered the craft.

I dropped the cathedral book and came up with another idea, a thriller about a German spy in wartime England. Happily, that was within my powers, and under the title *Eye of the Needle*, it became my first bestseller.

For the next decade I wrote thrillers, but I continued to visit cathedrals, and the idea of my cathedral novel never went away. I resurrected it in January 1986, having finished my sixth thriller, *Lie Down with Lions*.

My publishers were nervous. They wanted another spy story. My friends were also apprehensive. They know that I enjoy success. I'm not the kind of writer who would deal with a failure by saying that the book was good but the readers were inadequate. I write to entertain, and I'm happy doing so. A failure would make me miserable. No one tried to talk me out of it, but lots of people expressed anxious reservations.

However, I did not plan a "difficult" book. I would write an adventure story, full of colorful characters who were ambitious, wicked, sexy, heroic, and smart. I wanted ordinary readers to be as enraptured as I was by the romance of the medieval cathedrals.

By then I had developed the method of working that I continue to use to this day. I begin by writing an outline of the story, saying what happens in each chapter, and giving thumbnail sketches of the characters. But this book was not like my others. The beginning came easily, but, as the story unwound over the decades and the people grew from youth to maturity, I found it more and more difficult to invent new twists and turns in their lives. I realized that one long book is much more of a challenge than three short ones.

The hero of the story had to be some kind of man of God. This was difficult for me. I would find it hard to get interested in a character who was focused on the afterlife (and so would many readers). To make Prior Philip more sympathetic, I gave him a very practical, down-to-earth religious belief, a concern for people's souls here on earth, not just in heaven.

Philip's sexuality was also a problem. All monks and priests were supposed to be celibate in the Middle Ages. The obvious drama would be that of a man fighting a terrible battle with his lusts. But I could not work up any enthusiasm for that theme. I grew up in the 1960s, and my heart is always with those who deal with temptation by giving in to it. In the end I made him one of that minority of people for whom sex really is no big deal. He is the only cheerfully celibate character I have ever created.

I got in contact with Jean Gimpel, who had inspired me a decade earlier, and was astonished to learn that not only did he live in London but on my street. I hired him as a consultant, and we became friends and table-tennis opponents until his death.

By March of the following year, 1987, I had outlined only the first two thirds of the book. I decided that would have to be sufficient. I began to write.

By December I had a couple hundred pages.

This was pretty disastrous. I had been working on the story for two years, and all I had was an incomplete outline and a few chapters. I couldn't spend the rest of my life on this book. But what was to be done? Well, I could drop it and write another thriller. Or I could work harder. In those days I used to write Monday to Friday, then deal with my business correspondence on Saturday morning. From around January 1988, I began to write Monday through Saturday, and do letters on Sunday. My output increased dramatically, partly because of the extra day, but mainly because of the intensity I was bringing to my work. The problem of the end of the book, which I had not outlined, was solved by a flash of inspiration, when I thought of involving the principal characters in the notorious real-life murder of Thomas Becket.

As I recall, I finished a first draft around the middle of that year. A combination of excitement and impatience impelled me to work even harder on the rewrite, and I began to work seven days a week. My business correspondence was neglected, but I finished the book in March 1989, three years and three months after starting it.

I was exhausted but happy. I felt I had written something special, not just another bestseller, but maybe a great popular novel.

Not many people agreed.

My American hardcover publisher, William Morrow & Co., printed around the same number of copies as they had of *Lie Down with Lions,* and when they sold the same number they were content. My London publishers were more excited, and *Pillars* sold better there than any of my previous books. But the initial reaction among publishers worldwide was a sigh of relief that Follett had completed his crazy project and got away with it. The book won no prizes—it was not even nominated. A few critics adored it, but most were unimpressed. It was a No. 1 bestseller in Italy, where readers have always been kind to me. The paperback was No. 1 for a week in Britain.

I began to think I had been wrong. Maybe the book *was* just another page-tuner, good but not great.

However, one person believed passionately that this book was special. My German editor, Walter Fritzsche, at Gustav Luebbe Verlag, had long dreamed of publishing a novel about the building of a cathedral. He had even spoken to some of his German authors about the idea, but nothing ever came of it. So he was very excited about what I was writing, and when the typescript came in he felt his hopes had been fulfilled.

Until this point, my work had been only modestly successful in Germany. (The villains in my books were often Germans, so I could hardly complain.) Fritzsche was so enthusiastic that he thought *Pillars* could be a breakthrough book, one that would make me the single most popular writer in Germany.

Even I didn't believe that.

But he was right.

Luebbe published the book brilliantly. They hired a young artist, Achim Kiel, to do the cover, but when he insisted on designing the whole book, treating it as an art object, Luebbe had the courage to go with his concept. He was expensive, but he succeeded in communicating to the buyer Fritzsche's feeling that there was something special about this book. (He went on to design all my German editions for many years, creating a look that Luebbe used again and again.)

The first intimation I had that *readers* saw the book as something special came when Luebbe took an advertisement to celebrate the sale of 100,000 copies. I had never sold that many hardcovers in any country other than the United States (which has three times as many people as Germany).

After a couple of years, *Pillars* began to appear on the list of longest-selling books, having made some eighty appearances on the German bestseller list. As time went by, it just stayed there. (To date, it has made more than three hundred weekly appearances.)

One day I was checking my royalty statement from New American Library, my U.S. paperback publisher. These statements are carefully designed to prevent the author from knowing what is really happening to his book, but after decades of persistence I have learned to read them. And I noticed that *Pillars* was selling around 50,000 copies every six months. By comparison, *Eye of the Needle* was selling around 25,000, as were most of my other books.

I checked my U.K. sales and found the same pattern: *Pillars* sold about double.

I began to notice that *Pillars* was mentioned more than any other book in my fan mail. Signing in bookshops, I found that more and more readers told me *Pillars* was their favorite. Many people asked me to write a sequel. (I will, one day.) Some said it was the best book they had ever read, a compliment I had not received for any other book. A British travel company approached me about creating a Pillars of the Earth holiday. This was beginning to look like a cult hit.

Eventually I figured out what was happening. This was a word-of-mouth book. It's a truism of the book business that the best advertising is the kind you can't buy: the personal recommendation of one reader to another. That was what was selling *Pillars*. You did it, dear reader. Publishers, agents, critics, and the people who gave out literary prizes generally overlooked this book, but *you* did not. You noticed that it was different and special, and you told your friends; and in the end the word got around.

And so it happened. It seemed like the wrong book; I seemed like the wrong writer; and I almost didn't do it. But it is my best book, and you honored it.

I appreciate that. Thank you.

—Ken Follett
Stevenage, Hertfordshire
January 1999

On the night of 25 November 1120 the White Ship set out for England and floundered off Barfleur with all hands save one. . . . The vessel was the latest thing in marine transport, fitted with all the devices known to the ship-builder of the time. . . . The notoriety of this wreck is due to the very large number of distinguished persons on board; beside the king's son and heir, there were two royal bastards, several earls and barons, and most of the royal household . . . its historical significance is that it left Henry without an obvious heir . . . its ultimate result was the disputed succession and the period of anarchy which followed Henry's death.

—A. L. Poole,
From Domesday Book to Magna Carta

PROLOGUE

1123

THE SMALL BOYS came early to the hanging.

It was still dark when the first three or four of them sidled out of the hovels, quiet as cats in their felt boots. A thin layer of fresh snow covered the little town like a new coat of paint, and theirs were the first footprints to blemish its perfect surface. They picked their way through the huddled wooden huts and along the streets of frozen mud to the silent marketplace, where the gallows stood waiting.

The boys despised everything their elders valued. They scorned beauty and mocked goodness. They would hoot with laughter at the sight of a cripple, and if they saw a wounded animal they would stone it to death. They boasted of injuries and wore their scars with pride, and they reserved their special admiration for mutilation: a boy with a finger missing could be their king. They loved violence; they would run miles to see bloodshed; and they never missed a hanging.

One of the boys piddled on the base of the scaffold. Another mounted the steps, put his thumbs to his throat and slumped, twisting his face into a grisly parody of strangulation: the others whooped in admiration, and two dogs came running into the marketplace, barking. A very young boy recklessly began to eat an apple, and one of the older ones punched his nose and took his apple. The young boy relieved his feelings by throwing a sharp stone at a dog, sending the animal howling home. Then there was nothing else to do, so they all squatted on the dry pavement in the porch of the big church, waiting for something to happen.

Candlelight flickered behind the shutters of the substantial wood and stone houses around the square, the homes of prosperous craftsmen and traders, as scullery maids and apprentice boys lit fires and heated water and made porridge. The color of the sky turned from black to gray. The townspeople came ducking out of their low doorways, swathed in heavy cloaks of coarse wool, and went shivering down to the river to fetch water.

Soon a group of young men, grooms and laborers and apprentices, swaggered into the marketplace. They turned the small boys out of the church porch with cuffs and kicks, then leaned against the carved stone arches, scratching themselves and spitting on the ground and talking with studied confidence about death by hanging. If he's lucky, said one, his neck breaks as soon as he falls, a quick death, and painless; but if not he hangs there turning red, his mouth opening and shutting like a fish out of water, until he chokes to death; and another said that dying like that can take the time a man takes to walk a mile; and a third said it could be worse than that, he had seen one where by the time the man died his neck was a foot long.

The old women formed a group on the opposite side of the marketplace, as far as possible from the young men, who were liable to shout vulgar remarks at their grandmothers. They always woke up early, the old women, even though they no longer had babies and children to worry over; and they were the first to get their fires lit and their hearths swept. Their acknowledged leader, the muscular Widow Brewster, joined them, rolling a barrel of beer as easily as a child rolls a hoop. Before she could get the lid off there was a small crowd of customers waiting with jugs and buckets.

The sheriff's bailiff opened the main gate, admitting the peasants who lived in the suburb, in the lean-to houses against the town wall. Some brought eggs and milk and fresh butter to sell, some came to buy beer or bread, and some stood in the marketplace and waited for the hanging.

Every now and again people would cock their heads, like wary sparrows, and glance up at the castle on the hilltop above the town. They saw smoke rising steadily from the kitchen, and the occasional flare of a torch behind the arrow-slit windows of the stone keep. Then, at about the time the sun must have started to rise behind the thick gray cloud, the mighty wooden doors opened in the gatehouse and a small group came out. The sheriff was first, riding a fine black courser, followed by an ox cart carrying the bound prisoner. Behind the cart rode three men, and although their faces could not be seen at that distance, their clothes revealed that they were a knight, a priest and a monk. Two men-at-arms brought up the rear of the procession.

They had all been at the shire court, held in the nave of the church, the day before. The priest had caught the thief red-handed; the monk had identified the silver chalice as belonging to the monastery; the knight was the thief's lord, and had identified him as a runaway; and the sheriff had condemned him to death.

While they came slowly down the hill, the rest of the town gathered around the gallows. Among the last to arrive were the leading citizens: the butcher, the baker, two leather tanners, two smiths, the cutler and the fletcher, all with their wives.

The mood of the crowd was odd. Normally they enjoyed a hanging. The prisoner was usually a thief, and they hated thieves with the passion of people whose possessions are hard-earned. But this thief was different. Nobody knew who he was or where he came from. He had not stolen from them, but from a monastery twenty miles away. And he had stolen a jeweled chalice, something whose value was so great that it would be virtually impossible to sell—which was not like stealing a ham or a new knife or a good belt, the loss of which would hurt someone. They could not hate a man for a crime so pointless. There were a few jeers and catcalls as the prisoner entered the marketplace, but the abuse was half-hearted, and only the small boys mocked him with any enthusiasm.

Most of the townspeople had not been in court, for court days were not holidays and they all had to make a living, so this was the first time they had seen the thief. He was quite young, somewhere between twenty and thirty years of age, and of normal height and build, but otherwise his appearance was strange. His skin was as white as the snow on the roofs, he had protuberant eyes of startling bright green, and his hair was the color of a peeled carrot. The maids thought he was ugly; the old women felt sorry for him; and the small boys laughed until they fell down.

The sheriff was a familiar figure, but the other three men who had sealed the thief's doom were strangers. The knight, a fleshy man with yellow hair, was clearly a person of some importance, for he rode a war-horse, a huge beast that cost as much as a carpenter earned in ten years. The monk was much older, perhaps fifty or more, a tall, thin man who sat slumped in his saddle as if life were a wearisome burden to him. Most striking was the priest, a young man with a sharp nose and lank black hair, wearing black robes and riding a chestnut stallion. He had an alert, dangerous look, like a black cat that could smell a nest of baby mice.

A small boy took careful aim and spat at the prisoner. It was a good shot and caught him between the eyes. He snarled a curse and lunged at the spitter, but he was restrained by the ropes attaching him to the sides of the cart. The incident was not remarkable except that the words he spoke were Norman French, the language of the lords. Was he high-born, then? Or just a long way from home? Nobody knew.

The ox cart stopped beneath the gallows. The sheriff's bailiff climbed onto the flatbed of the cart with the noose in his hand. The prisoner started to struggle. The boys cheered—they would have been disappointed if the prisoner had remained calm. The man's movements were restricted by the ropes tied to his wrists and ankles, but he jerked his head from side to side, evading the noose. After a moment the bailiff, a huge man, stepped back and punched the prisoner in the stomach. The man doubled over, winded, and the bailiff slipped the rope over his head and tightened the knot. Then he jumped down to the ground and pulled the rope taut, securing its other end to a hook in the base of the gallows.

This was the turning point. If the prisoner struggled now, he would only die sooner.

The men-at-arms untied the prisoner's legs and left him standing alone on the bed of the cart, his hands bound behind his back. A hush fell on the crowd.

There was often a disturbance at this point: the prisoner's mother would have a screaming fit, or his wife would pull out a knife and rush the platform in a last-minute attempt to rescue him. Sometimes the prisoner called upon God for forgiveness or pronounced blood-curdling curses on his executioners. The men-at-arms now stationed themselves on either side of the scaffold, ready to deal with any incident.

That was when the prisoner began to sing.

He had a high tenor voice, very pure. The words were French, but even those who could not understand the language could tell by its plaintive melody that it was a song of sadness and loss.

> A lark, caught in a hunter's net
> Sang sweeter then than ever,
> As if the falling melody
> Might wing and net dissever.

As he sang he looked directly at someone in the crowd. Gradually a space formed around the person, and everyone could see her.

She was a girl of about fifteen. When people looked at her they wondered why they had not noticed her before. She had long dark-brown hair, thick and rich, which came to a point on her wide forehead in what people called a devil's peak. She had regular features and a sensual, full-lipped mouth. The old women noticed her thick waist and heavy breasts, concluded that she was pregnant, and guessed that the prisoner was the father of her unborn child. But everyone else noticed nothing except her eyes. She might have been pretty, but she had deep-set, intense eyes of a startling golden color, so luminous and penetrating that when she looked at you, you felt she could see right into your heart, and you averted your eyes, scared that she would discover your secrets. She was dressed in rags, and tears streamed down her soft cheeks.

The driver of the cart looked expectantly at the bailiff. The bailiff looked at the sheriff, waiting for the nod. The young priest with the sinister air nudged the sheriff impatiently, but the sheriff took no notice. He let the thief carry on singing. There was a dreadful pause while the ugly man's lovely voice held death at bay.

> *At dusk the hunter took his prey,*
> *The lark his freedom never.*
> *All birds and men are sure to die*
> *But songs may live forever.*

When the song ended the sheriff looked at the bailiff and nodded. The bailiff shouted "Hup!" and lashed the ox's flank with a length of rope. The carter cracked his whip at the same time. The ox stepped forward, the prisoner standing in the cart staggered, the ox pulled the cart away, and the prisoner dropped into midair. The rope straightened and the thief's neck broke with a snap.

There was a scream, and everyone looked at the girl.

It was not she who had screamed, but the cutler's wife beside her. But the girl was the cause of the scream. She had sunk to her knees in front of the gallows, with her arms stretched out in front of her, the position adopted to utter a curse. The people shrank from her in fear: everyone knew that the curses of those who had suffered injustice were particularly effective, and they had all suspected that something was not quite right about this hanging. The small boys were terrified.

The girl turned her hypnotic golden eyes on the three strangers, the knight, the monk and the priest; and then she pronounced her curse, calling out the terrible words in ringing tones: "I curse you with sickness and sorrow, with hunger and pain; your house shall be consumed by fire, and your children shall die on the gallows; your enemies shall prosper, and you shall grow old in sadness and regret, and die in foulness and agony. . . ." As she spoke the last words the girl reached into a sack on the ground beside her and pulled out a live cockerel. A knife appeared in her hand from nowhere, and with one slice she cut off the head of the cock.

While the blood was still spurting from the severed neck she threw the beheaded cock at the priest with the black hair. It fell short, but the blood sprayed over him, and over the monk and the knight on either side of him. The three men twisted away in loathing, but blood landed on each of them, spattering their faces and staining their garments.

The girl turned and ran.

The crowd opened in front of her and closed behind her. For a few moments there was pandemonium. At last the sheriff caught the attention of his men-at-arms and angrily told them to chase her. They began to struggle through the crowd, roughly pushing men and women and children out of the way, but the girl was out of sight in a twinkling, and though the sheriff would search for her, he knew he would not find her.

He turned away in disgust. The knight, the monk and the priest had not watched the flight of the girl. They were still staring at the gallows. The sheriff followed their gaze. The dead thief hung at the end of the rope, his pale young face already turning bluish, while beneath his gently swinging corpse the cock, headless but not quite dead, ran around in a ragged circle on the bloodstained snow.

PART ONE

1135 - 1136

Chapter 1

IN A BROAD VALLEY, at the foot of a sloping hillside, beside a clear bubbling stream, Tom was building a house.

The walls were already three feet high and rising fast. The two masons Tom had engaged were working steadily in the sunshine, their trowels going *scrape, slap* and then *tap, tap* while their laborer sweated under the weight of the big stone blocks. Tom's son Alfred was mixing mortar, counting aloud as he scooped sand onto a board. There was also a carpenter, working at the bench beside Tom, carefully shaping a length of beech wood with an adz.

Alfred was fourteen years old, and tall like Tom. Tom was a head higher than most men, and Alfred was only a couple of inches less, and still growing. They looked alike, too: both had light-brown hair and greenish eyes with brown flecks. People said they were a handsome pair. The main difference between them was that Tom had a curly brown beard, whereas Alfred had only a fine blond fluff. The hair on Alfred's head had been that color once, Tom remembered fondly. Now that Alfred was becoming a man, Tom wished he would take a more intelligent interest in his work, for he had a lot to learn if he was to be a mason like his father; but so far Alfred remained bored and baffled by the principles of building.

When the house was finished it would be the most luxurious home for miles around. The ground floor would be a spacious undercroft, for storage, with a curved vault for a ceiling, so that it would not catch fire. The hall, where people actually lived, would be above, reached by an outside staircase, its height making it hard to attack and easy to defend. Against the hall wall there would be a chimney, to take away the smoke of the fire. This was a radical innovation: Tom had only ever seen one house with a chimney, but it had struck him as such a good idea that he was determined to copy it. At one end of the house, over the hall, there would be a small bedroom, for that was what earls' daughters demanded nowadays—they were too fine to sleep in the hall with the men and the serving wenches and the hunting dogs. The kitchen would be a separate building, for every kitchen caught fire sooner or later, and there was nothing for it but to build them far away from everything else and put up with lukewarm food.

Tom was making the doorway of the house. The doorposts would be rounded to look like columns—a touch of distinction for the noble newlyweds who were to live here. With his eye on the shaped wooden template he was using as a guide, Tom set his iron chisel obliquely against the stone and tapped it gently with the big wooden hammer. A small shower of fragments fell away from the surface, leaving the shape a little rounder. He did it again. Smooth enough for a cathedral.

He had worked on a cathedral once—Exeter. At first he had treated it like any other job. He had been angry and resentful when the master builder had warned him that his work was not quite up to standard: he knew himself to be rather more careful than the average mason. But then he realized that the walls of a cathedral had to be not just good, but *perfect*. This was because the cathedral was for God, and also because the building was so *big* that the slightest lean in the walls, the merest variation from the absolutely true and level, could weaken the structure fatally. Tom's resentment turned to fascination. The combination of a hugely ambitious building with merciless attention to the smallest detail opened Tom's eyes to the wonder of his craft. He learned from the Exeter master about the importance of proportion, the symbolism of various numbers, and the almost magical formulas for working out the correct width of a wall or the angle of a step in a spiral staircase. Such things captivated him. He was surprised to learn that many masons found them incomprehensible.

After a while Tom had become the master builder's right-hand man, and that was when he began to see the master's shortcomings. The man was a great craftsman and an incompetent organizer. He was completely baffled by the problems of obtaining the right quantity of stone to keep pace with the masons, making sure that the blacksmith made enough of the right tools, burning lime and carting sand for the mortar makers, felling trees for the carpenters, and getting enough money from the cathedral chapter to pay for everything.

If Tom had stayed at Exeter until the master builder died, he might have become master himself; but the chapter ran out of money—partly because of the master's mismanagement—and the craftsmen had to move on, looking for work elsewhere. Tom had been offered the post of builder to the Exeter castellan, repairing and improving the city's fortifications. It would have been a lifetime job, barring accidents. But Tom had turned it down, for he wanted to build another cathedral.

His wife, Agnes, had never understood that decision. They might have had a good stone house, and servants, and their own stables, and meat on the table every dinnertime; and she had never forgiven Tom for turning down the opportunity. She could not comprehend the irresistible attraction of building a cathedral: the absorbing complexity of organization, the intellectual challenge of the calculations, the sheer size of the walls, and the breathtaking beauty and grandeur of the finished building. Once he had tasted that wine, Tom was never satisfied with anything less.

That had been ten years ago. Since then they had never stayed anywhere for very long. He would design a new chapter house for a monastery, work for a year or two on a castle, or build a town house for a rich merchant; but as soon as he had some money saved he would leave, with his wife and children, and take to the road, looking for another cathedral.

He glanced up from his bench and saw Agnes standing at the edge of the building site, holding a basket of food in one hand and resting a big jug of beer on the opposite hip. It was midday. He looked at her fondly. No one would ever call her pretty, but her face was full of strength: a broad forehead, large brown eyes, a straight nose, a strong jaw. Her dark, wiry hair was parted in the middle and tied behind. She was Tom's soul mate.

She poured beer for Tom and Alfred. They stood there for a moment, the two big men and the strong woman, drinking beer from wooden cups; and then the fourth member of the family came skipping out of the wheat field: Martha, seven years old and as pretty as a daffodil, but a daffodil with a petal missing, for she had a gap where two milk teeth had fallen out and the new ones had not yet grown. She ran to Tom, kissed his dusty beard, and begged a sip of his beer. He hugged her bony body. "Don't drink too much, or you'll fall into a ditch," he said. She staggered around in a circle, pretending to be drunk.

They all sat down on the woodpile. Agnes handed Tom a hunk

of wheat bread, a thick slice of boiled bacon and a small onion. He took a bite of the meat and started to peel the onion. Agnes gave the children food and began to eat her own. Perhaps it was irresponsible, Tom thought, to turn down that dull job in Exeter and go looking for a cathedral to build; but I've always been able to feed them all, despite my recklessness.

He took his eating knife from the front pocket of his leather apron, cut a slice off the onion, and ate it with a bite of bread. The onion was sweet and stinging in his mouth. Agnes said: "I'm with child again."

Tom stopped chewing and stared at her. A thrill of delight took hold of him. Not knowing what to say, he just smiled foolishly at her. After a few moments she blushed, and said: "It isn't *that* surprising."

Tom hugged her. "Well, well," he said, still grinning with pleasure. "A babe to pull my beard. And I thought the next would be Alfred's."

"Don't get too happy yet," Agnes cautioned. "It's bad luck to name the child before it's born."

Tom nodded assent. Agnes had had several miscarriages and one stillborn baby, and there had been another little girl, Matilda, who had lived only two years. "I'd like a boy, though," he said. "Now that Alfred's so big. When is it due?"

"After Christmas."

Tom began to calculate. The shell of the house would be finished by first frost, then the stonework would have to be covered with straw to protect it through the winter. The masons would spend the cold months cutting stones for windows, vaults, doorcases and the fireplace, while the carpenter made floorboards and doors and shutters and Tom built the scaffolding for the upstairs work. Then in spring they would vault the undercroft, floor the hall above it, and put on the roof. The job would feed the family until Whitsun, by which time the baby would be half a year old. Then they would move on. "Good," he said contentedly. "This is good." He ate another slice of onion.

"I'm too old to bear children," Agnes said. "This must be my last."

Tom thought about that. He was not sure how old she was, in numbers, but plenty of women bore children at her time of life. However, it was true they suffered more as they grew older, and the babies were not so strong. No doubt she was right. But how would she make certain that she would not conceive again? he wondered. Then he realized how, and a cloud shadowed his sunny mood.

"I may get a good job, in a town," he said, trying to mollify her. "A cathedral, or a palace. Then we might have a big house with wood floors, and a maid to help you with the baby."

Her face hardened, and she said skeptically: "It may be." She did not like to hear talk of cathedrals. If Tom had never worked on a cathedral, her face said, she might be living in a town house now, with money saved up and buried under the fireplace, and nothing to worry about.

Tom looked away and took another bite of bacon. They had something to celebrate, but they were in disharmony. He felt let down. He chewed the tough meat for a while, then he heard a horse. He cocked his head to listen. The rider was coming through the trees from the direction of the road, taking a short cut and avoiding the village.

A moment later, a young man on a pony trotted up and dismounted. He looked like a squire, a kind of apprentice knight. "Your lord is coming," he said.

Tom stood up. "You mean Lord Percy?" Percy Hamleigh was one of the most important men in the country. He owned this valley, and many others, and he was paying for the house.

"His son," said the squire.

"Young William." Percy's son, William, was to occupy this house after his marriage. He was engaged to Lady Aliena, the daughter of the earl of Shiring.

"The same," said the squire. "And in a rage."

Tom's heart sank. At the best of times it could be difficult to deal with the owner of a house under construction. An owner in a rage was impossible. "What's he angry about?"

"His bride rejected him."

"The earl's daughter?" said Tom in surprise. He felt a pang of fear: he had just been thinking how secure his future was. "I thought that was settled."

"So did we all—except the Lady Aliena, it seems," the squire said. "The moment she met him, she announced that she wouldn't marry him for all the world and a woodcock."

Tom frowned worriedly. He did not want this to be true. "But the boy's not bad-looking, as I recall."

Agnes said: "As if that made any difference, in her position. If earls' daughters were allowed to marry whom they please, we'd all be ruled by strolling minstrels and dark-eyed outlaws."

"The girl may yet change her mind," Tom said hopefully.

"She will if her mother takes a birch rod to her," Agnes said.

The squire said: "Her mother's dead."

Agnes nodded. "That explains why she doesn't know the facts of life. But I don't see why her father can't compel her."

The squire said: "It seems he once promised he would never marry her to someone she hated."

"A foolish pledge!" Tom said angrily. How could a powerful man tie himself to the whim of a girl in that way? Her marriage could affect military alliances, baronial finances . . . even the building of this house.

The squire said: "She has a brother, so it's not *so* important whom she marries."

"Even so . . ."

"And the earl is an unbending man," the squire went on. "He won't go back on a promise, even one made to a child." He shrugged. "So they say."

Tom looked at the low stone walls of the house-to-be. He had not yet saved enough money to keep the family through the winter, he realized with a chill. "Perhaps the lad will find another bride to share this place with him. He's got the whole county to choose from."

Alfred spoke in a cracked adolescent voice. "By Christ, I think this is him." Following his gaze, they all looked across the field. A horse was coming from the village at a gallop, kicking up a cloud of dust and earth from the pathway. Alfred's oath was prompted by the size as well as the speed of the horse: it was huge. Tom had seen beasts like it before, but perhaps Alfred had not. It was a war-horse, as high at the wither as a man's chin, and broad in proportion. Such war-horses were not bred in England, but came from overseas, and were enormously costly.

Tom dropped the remains of his bread in the pocket of his apron, then narrowed his eyes against the sun and gazed across the field. The horse had its ears back and nostrils flared, but it seemed to Tom that its head was well up, a sign that it was not completely out of control. Sure enough, as it came closer the rider leaned back, hauling on the reins, and the huge animal seemed to slow a little. Now Tom could feel the drumming of its hooves in the ground beneath his feet. He looked around for Martha, thinking to pick her up and put her out of harm's way. Agnes had the same thought. But Martha was nowhere to be seen.

"In the wheat," Agnes said, but Tom had already figured that out and was striding across the site to the edge of the field. He scanned the waving wheat with fear in his heart but he could not see the child.

The only thing he could think of was to try to slow the horse.

He stepped into the path and began to walk toward the charging beast, holding his arms wide. The horse saw him, raised its head for a better look, and slowed perceptibly. Then, to Tom's horror, the rider spurred it on.

"You damned fool!" Tom roared, although the rider could not hear.

That was when Martha stepped out of the field and into the pathway a few yards in front of Tom.

For an instant Tom stood still in a sick panic. Then he leaped forward, shouting and waving his arms; but this was a war-horse, trained to charge at yelling hordes, and it did not flinch. Martha stood in the middle of the narrow path, staring as if transfixed by the huge beast bearing down on her. There was a moment when Tom realized desperately that he could not get to her before the horse did. He swerved to one side, his arm touching the standing wheat; and at the last instant the horse swerved to the other side. The rider's stirrup brushed Martha's fine hair; a hoof stamped a round hole in the ground beside her bare foot; then the horse had gone by, spraying them both with dirt, and Tom snatched her up in his arms and held her tight to his pounding heart.

He stood still for a moment, awash with relief, his limbs weak, his insides watery. Then he felt a surge of fury at the recklessness of the stupid youth on his massive war-horse. He looked up angrily. Lord William was slowing the horse now, sitting back in the saddle, with his feet pushed forward in the stirrups, sawing on the reins. The horse swerved to avoid the building site. It tossed its head and then bucked, but William stayed on. He slowed it to a canter and then a trot as he guided it around in a wide circle.

Martha was crying. Tom handed her to Agnes and waited for William. The young lord was a tall, well-built fellow of about twenty years, with yellow hair and narrow eyes which made him look as if he were always peering into the sun. He wore a short black tunic with black hose, and leather shoes with straps crisscrossed up to his knees. He sat well on the horse and did not seem shaken by what had happened. *The foolish boy doesn't even know what he's done,* Tom thought bitterly. *I'd like to wring his neck.*

William halted the horse in front of the woodpile and looked down at the builders. "Who's in charge here?" he said.

Tom wanted to say *If you had hurt my little girl, I would have killed you,* but he suppressed his rage. It was like swallowing a bitter mouthful. He approached the horse and held its bridle. "I'm the master builder," he said tightly. "My name is Tom."

"This house is no longer needed," said William. "Dismiss your men."

It was what Tom had been dreading. But he held on to the hope that William was being impetuous in his anger, and might be persuaded to change his mind. With an effort, he made his voice friendly and reasonable. "But so much work has been done," he said. "Why waste what you've spent? You'll need the house one day."

"Don't tell me how to manage my affairs, Tom Builder," said William. "You're all dismissed." He twitched a rein, but Tom had hold of the bridle. "Let go of my horse," William said dangerously.

Tom swallowed. In a moment William would try to get the horse's head up. Tom felt in his apron pocket and brought out the crust of bread he had been eating. He showed it to the horse, which dipped its head and took a bite. "There's more to be said, before you leave, my lord," he said mildly.

William said: "Let my horse go, or I'll take your head off." Tom looked directly at him, trying not to show his fear. He was bigger than William, but that would make no difference if the young lord drew his sword.

Agnes muttered fearfully: "Do as the lord says, husband."

There was dead silence. The other workmen stood as still as statues, watching. Tom knew that the prudent thing would be to give in. But William had nearly trampled Tom's little girl, and that made Tom mad, so with a racing heart he said: "You have to pay us."

William pulled on the reins, but Tom held the bridle tight, and the horse was distracted, nuzzling in Tom's apron pocket for more food. "Apply to my father for your wages!" William said angrily.

Tom heard the carpenter say in a terrified voice: "We'll do that, my lord, thanking you very much."

Wretched coward, Tom thought, but he was trembling himself. Nevertheless he forced himself to say: "If you want to dismiss us, you must pay us, according to the custom. Your father's house is two days' walk from here, and when we arrive he may not be there."

"Men have died for less than this," William said. His cheeks reddened with anger.

Out of the corner of his eye, Tom saw the squire drop his hand to the hilt of his sword. He knew he should give up now, and humble himself, but there was an obstinate knot of anger in his belly, and as scared as he was he could not bring himself to release the bridle. "Pay us first, then kill me," he said recklessly. "You may hang for it, or you may not; but you'll die sooner or later, and then I will be in heaven and you will be in hell."

The sneer froze on William's face and he paled. Tom was surprised: what had frightened the boy? Not the mention of hanging, surely: it was not really likely that a lord would be hanged for the murder of a craftsman. Was he terrified of hell?

They stared at one another for a few moments. Tom watched with amazement and relief as William's set expression of anger and contempt melted away, to be replaced by a panicky anxiety. At last William took a leather purse from his belt and tossed it to his squire, saying: "Pay them."

At that point Tom pushed his luck. When William pulled on the reins again, and the horse lifted its strong head and stepped sideways, Tom moved with the horse and held on to the bridle, and said: "A full week's wages on dismissal, that is the custom." He heard a sharp intake of breath from Agnes, just behind him, and he knew she thought he was crazy to prolong the confrontation. But he plowed on. "That's sixpence for the laborer, twelve for the carpenter and each of the masons, and twenty-four pence for me. Sixty-six pence in all." He could add pennies faster than anyone he knew.

The squire was looking inquiringly at his master. William said angrily: "Very *well*."

Tom released the bridle and stepped back.

William turned the horse and kicked it hard, and it bounded forward onto the path through the wheat field.

Tom sat down suddenly on the woodpile. He wondered what had got into him. It had been mad to defy Lord William like that. He felt lucky to be alive.

The hoofbeats of William's war-horse faded to a distant thunder, and his squire emptied the purse onto a board. Tom felt a surge of triumph as the silver pennies tumbled out into the sunshine. It had been mad, but it had worked: he had secured just payment for himself and the men working under him. "Even lords ought to follow the customs," he said, half to himself.

Agnes heard him. "Just hope you're never in want of work from Lord William," she said sourly.

Tom smiled at her. He understood that she was churlish because she had been frightened. "Don't frown too much, or you'll have nothing but curdled milk in your breasts when that baby is born."

"I won't be able to feed any of us unless you find work for the winter."

"The winter's a long way off," said Tom.

II

They stayed at the village through the summer. Later, they came to regard this decision as a terrible mistake, but at the time it seemed sensible enough, for Tom and Agnes and Alfred could each earn a penny a day working in the fields during the harvest. When autumn came, and they had to move on, they had a heavy bag of silver pennies and a fat pig.

They spent the first night in the porch of a village church, but on the second they found a country priory and took advantage of monastic hospitality. On the third day they found themselves in the heart of the Chute Forest, a vast expanse of scrub and rough woodland, on a road not much broader than the width of an ox cart, with the luxuriant growth of summer dying between the oaks on either side.

Tom carried his smaller tools in a satchel and slung his hammers from his belt. He had his cloak in a bundle under his left arm and he carried his iron spike in his right hand, using it as a walking stick. He was happy to be on the road again. His next job might be working on a cathedral. He might become master mason and stay there the rest of his life, and build a church so wonderful it would guarantee that he went to heaven.

Agnes had their few household possessions inside the cooking pot which she carried strapped to her back. Alfred carried the tools they would use to make a new home somewhere: an ax, an adz, a saw, a small hammer, a bradawl for making holes in leather and wood, and a spade. Martha was too small to carry anything but her own bowl and eating knife tied to her belt and her winter cloak strapped to her back. However, she had the duty of driving the pig until they could sell it at a market.

Tom kept a close eye on Agnes as they walked through the endless woods. She was more than halfway through her term now, and carrying a considerable weight in her belly as well as the burden on her back. But she seemed tireless. Alfred, too, was all right: he was at the age when boys have more energy than they know what to do with. Only Martha was tiring. Her thin legs were made for the playful scamper, not the long march, and she dropped behind constantly, so that the others had to stop and wait for her and the pig to catch up.

As he walked Tom thought about the cathedral he would build one day. He began, as always, by picturing an archway. It was very simple: two uprights supporting a semicircle. Then he imagined a second, just the same as the first. He pushed the two together, in his mind, to form one deep archway. Then he added another, and another, then a lot more, until he had a whole row of them, all stuck together, forming a tunnel. This was the essence of a building, for it had a roof to keep the rain off and two walls to hold up the roof. A church was just a tunnel, with refinements.

A tunnel was dark, so the first refinements were windows. If the wall was strong enough, it could have holes in it. The holes would be round at the top, with straight sides and a flat sill—the same shape as the original archway. Using similar shapes for arches and windows and doors was one of the things that made a building beautiful. Regularity was another, and Tom visualized twelve identical windows, evenly spaced, along each wall of the tunnel.

Tom tried to visualize the moldings over the windows, but his concentration kept slipping because he had the feeling that he was being watched. It was a foolish notion, he thought, if only because of course he *was* being observed by the birds, foxes, cats, squirrels, rats, mice, weasels, stoats and voles which thronged the forest.

They sat down by a stream at midday. They drank the pure water and ate cold bacon and crab apples which they picked up from the forest floor.

In the afternoon Martha was tired. At one point she was a hundred yards behind them. Standing waiting for her to catch up, Tom remembered Alfred at that age. He had been a beautiful, golden-haired boy, sturdy and bold. Fondness mingled with irritation in Tom as he watched Martha scolding the pig for being so slow. Then a figure stepped out of the undergrowth just ahead of her. What happened next was so quick that Tom could hardly believe it. The man who had appeared so suddenly on the road raised a club over his shoulder. A horrified shout rose in Tom's throat, but before he could utter it the man swung the club at Martha. It struck her full on the side of the head, and Tom heard the sickening sound of the blow connecting. She fell to the ground like a dropped doll.

Tom found himself running back along the road toward them, his feet pounding the hard earth like the hooves of William's warhorse, willing his legs to carry him faster. As he ran, he watched what was happening, and it was like looking at a picture painted high on a church wall, for he could see it but there was nothing he could do to change it. The attacker was undoubtedly an outlaw. He was a short, thickset man in a brown tunic, with bare feet. For an instant he looked straight at Tom, and Tom could see that the man's face was hideously mutilated: his lips had been cut off, presumably as a punishment for a crime involving lying, and his mouth was now a repulsive permanent grin surrounded by twisted scar tissue. The horrid sight would have stopped Tom in his tracks, had it not been for the prone body of Martha lying on the ground.

The outlaw looked away from Tom and fixed his gaze on the pig. In a flash he bent down, picked it up, tucked the squirming animal under his arm and darted back into the tangled undergrowth, taking with him Tom's family's only valuable possession.

Then Tom was on his knees beside Martha. He put his broad hand on her tiny chest and felt her heartbeat, steady and strong, and his worst fear subsided; but her eyes were closed and there was bright red blood in her blond hair.

Agnes knelt beside him a moment later. She touched Martha's chest, wrist and forehead, then she gave Tom a hard, level look. "She will live," she said in a tight voice. "Fetch back that pig."

Tom quickly unslung his satchel of tools and dropped it on the ground. With his left hand he took his big iron-headed hammer from his belt. He still had his spike in his right. He could see the trampled bushes where the thief had come and gone, and he could hear the pig squealing in the woods. He plunged into the undergrowth.

The trail was easy to follow. The outlaw was a heavily built man, running with a wriggling pig under his arm, and he cut a wide path through the vegetation, flattening flowers and bushes and young trees alike. Tom charged after him, full of a savage desire to get his hands on the man and beat him senseless. He crashed through a thicket of birch saplings, hurtled down a slope, and splashed across a patch of bog to a narrow pathway. There he stopped. The thief might have gone left or right, and now there was no crushed vegetation to show the way; but Tom listened, and heard the pig squealing somewhere to his left. He could also hear someone rushing through the forest behind him—Alfred, presumably. He went after the pig.

The path led him down into a dip, then turned sharply and began to rise. He could hear the pig clearly now. He ran uphill, breathing hard—the years of inhaling stone dust had weakened his lungs. Suddenly the path leveled and he saw the thief, only twenty or thirty yards away, running as if the devil were behind him. Tom put on a spurt and started to gain. He was bound to catch up, if only he could keep going, for a man with a pig cannot run as fast as a man without one. But now his chest hurt. The thief was fifteen yards away, then twelve. Tom raised the spike above his head like a spear. Just a little closer and he would throw it. Eleven yards, ten—

Before the spike left his hand he glimpsed, out of the corner of his eye, a thin face in a green cap emerging from the bushes beside the path. It was too late to swerve. A heavy stick was thrust out in front of him, he stumbled on it as was intended, and he fell to the ground.

He had dropped his spike but he still had hold of the hammer. He rolled over and raised himself on one knee. There were two of them, he saw: the one in the green hat and a bald man with a matted white beard. They ran at Tom.

He stepped to one side and swung his hammer at the green hat. The man dodged, but the big iron hammerhead came down hard on his shoulder and he gave a screech of agony and sank to the ground, holding his arm as if it were broken. Tom did not have time to raise the hammer for another crushing blow before the bald man closed with him, so he thrust the iron head at the man's face and split his cheek.

Both men backed off clutching their wounds. Tom could see that there was no fight left in either one. He turned around. The thief was still running away along the path. Tom went after him again, ignoring the pain in his chest. But he had covered only a few yards when he heard a shout from behind in a familiar voice.

Alfred.

He stopped and looked back.

Alfred was fighting them both, using his fists and his feet. He punched the one in the green hat about the head three or four times, then kicked the bald man's shins. But the two men swarmed him, getting inside his reach so that he could no longer punch or kick hard enough to hurt. Tom hesitated, torn between chasing the pig and rescuing his son. Then the bald one got his foot behind Alfred's leg and tripped him, and as the boy hit the ground the two men fell on him, raining blows on his face and body.

Tom ran back. He charged the bald one bodily, sending the man flying into the bushes, then turned and swung his hammer at the green hat. This man had felt the weight of the hammer once before and was still using only one arm. He dodged the first swing, then turned and dived into the undergrowth before Tom could swing again.

Tom turned and saw the bald man running away down the

path. He looked in the opposite direction: the thief with the pig was nowhere in sight. He breathed a bitter, blasphemous curse: that pig represented half of what he had saved this summer. He sank to the ground, breathing hard.

"We beat three of them!" Alfred said excitedly.

Tom looked at him. "But they got our pig," he said. Anger burned his stomach like sour cider. They had bought the pig in the spring, as soon as they had saved enough pennies, and they had been fattening it all summer. A fat pig could be sold for sixty pence. With a few cabbages and a sack of grain it could feed a family all winter and make a pair of leather shoes and a purse or two. Its loss was a catastrophe.

Tom looked enviously at Alfred, who had already recovered from the chase and the fight, and was waiting impatiently. How long ago was it, Tom thought, when I could run like the wind and hardly feel my heart race? Since I was that age . . . twenty years. Twenty years. It seemed like yesterday.

He got to his feet.

He put his arm around Alfred's broad shoulders as they walked back along the path. The boy was still shorter than his father by the span of a man's hand, but soon he would catch up, and he might grow even bigger. I hope his wit grows too, Tom thought. He said: "Any fool can get into a fight, but a wise man knows how to stay out of them." Alfred gave him a blank look.

They turned off the path, crossed the boggy patch, and began to climb the slope, following in reverse the trail the thief had made. As they pushed through the birch thicket, Tom thought of Martha, and once again rage curdled in his belly. The outlaw had lashed out at her senselessly, for she had been no threat to him.

Tom quickened his pace, and a moment later he and Alfred emerged onto the road. Martha lay there in the same place, not having moved. Her eyes were closed and the blood was drying in her hair. Agnes knelt beside her—and with them, to Tom's surprise, were another woman and a boy. The thought struck him that it was no wonder he had felt watched, earlier in the day, for the forest seemed to be teeming with people. He bent down and rested his hand on Martha's chest again. She was breathing normally.

"She will wake up soon," said the strange woman in an authoritative voice. "Then she will puke. After that she'll be all right."

Tom looked at her curiously. She was kneeling over Martha. She was quite young, perhaps a dozen years younger than Tom. Her short leather tunic revealed lithe brown limbs. She had a pretty face, with dark brown hair that came to a devil's peak on her forehead. Tom felt a pang of desire. Then she raised her glance to look at him, and he gave a start: she had intense, deep-set eyes of an unusual honey-gold color that gave her whole face a magical look, and he felt sure that she knew what he had been thinking.

He looked away from her to cover his embarrassment, and he caught Agnes's eye. She was looking resentful. She said: "Where's the pig?"

"There were two more outlaws," Tom said.

Alfred said: "We beat them, but the one with the pig got away."

Agnes looked grim, but said nothing more.

The strange woman said: "We could move the girl into the shade, if we're gentle." She stood up, and Tom realized that she was quite small, at least a foot shorter than he. He bent down and picked Martha up carefully. Her childish body was almost weightless in his arms. He carried her a few yards along the road and put her down on a patch of grass in the shadow of an old oak. She was still quite limp.

Alfred was picking up the tools that had been scattered on the road during the fracas. The strange woman's boy was watching, his eyes wide and his mouth open, not speaking. He was about three years younger than Alfred, and a peculiar-looking child, Tom observed, with none of his mother's sensual beauty. He had very pale skin, orange-red hair, and blue eyes that bulged slightly. He had the alertly stupid look of a dullard, Tom thought; the kind of child that either dies young or grows up to be the village idiot. Alfred was visibly uncomfortable under his stare.

As Tom watched, the child snatched the saw from Alfred's hand, without saying anything, and examined it as if it were something amazing. Alfred, offended by the discourtesy, snatched it back, and the child let it go with indifference. The mother said: "Jack! Behave yourself." She seemed embarrassed.

Tom looked at her. The boy did not resemble her at all. "Are you his mother?" Tom asked.

"Yes. My name is Ellen."

"Where's your husband?"

"Dead."

Tom was surprised. "You're traveling alone?" he said incredulously. The forest was dangerous enough for a man such as he: a woman alone could hardly hope to survive.

"We're not traveling," said Ellen. "We live in the forest."

Tom was shocked. "You mean you're—" He stopped, not wanting to offend her.

"Outlaws," she said. "Yes. Did you think that all outlaws were like Faramond Openmouth, who stole your pig?"

"Yes," said Tom, although what he wanted to say was *I never thought an outlaw might be a beautiful woman.* Unable to restrain his curiosity, he asked: "What was your crime?"

"I cursed a priest," she said, and looked away.

It did not sound like much of a crime to Tom, but perhaps the priest had been very powerful, or very touchy; or perhaps Ellen just did not want to tell the truth.

He looked at Martha. A moment later she opened her eyes. She was confused and a little frightened. Agnes knelt beside her. "You're safe," she said. "Everything's all right."

Martha said upright and vomited. Agnes hugged her until the spasms passed. Tom was impressed: Ellen's prediction had come true. She had also said that Martha would be all right, and presumably that was reliable too. Relief washed over him, and he was a little surprised at the strength of his own emotion. I couldn't bear to lose my little girl, he thought; and he had to fight back tears. He caught a look of sympathy from Ellen, and once again he felt that her pale gold eyes could see into his heart.

He broke off an oak twig, stripped its leaves, and used them to wipe Martha's face. She still looked pale.

"She needs to rest," said Ellen. "Let her lie down for as long as it takes a man to walk three miles."

Tom glanced at the sun. There was plenty of daylight left. He settled down to wait. Agnes rocked Martha gently in her arms. The boy Jack now switched his attention to Martha, and stared at her with the same idiot intensity. Tom wanted to know more about Ellen. He wondered whether she might be persuaded to tell her story. He did not want her to go away. "How did it all come about?" he asked her vaguely.

She looked into his eyes again, and then she began to talk.

Her father had been a knight, she told them; a big, strong, violent man who wanted sons with whom he could ride and hunt and wrestle, companions to drink and carouse into the night with him. In these matters he was as unlucky as a man could be, for he got Ellen, and then his wife died; and he married again, but his second wife was barren. He came to despise Ellen's stepmother, and eventually sent her away. He must have been a cruel man, but he never seemed so to Ellen, who adored him and shared his scorn for his second wife. When the stepmother left, Ellen stayed, and grew up in what was almost an all-male household. She cut her hair short and carried a dagger, and learned not to play with kittens or care for blind old dogs. By the time she was Martha's age she could spit on the ground and eat apple cores and kick a horse in the belly so hard that it would draw in its breath, allowing her to tighten its girth one more notch. She knew that all men who were not part of her father's band were called cocksuckers and all women who would not go with them were called pigfuckers, although she was not quite sure—and did not much care—what these insults really meant.

Listening to her voice in the mild air of an autumn afternoon, Tom closed his eyes and pictured her as a flat-chested girl with a dirty face, sitting at the long table with her father's thuggish comrades, drinking strong ale and belching and singing songs about battle and looting and rape, horses and castles and virgins, until she fell asleep with her little cropped head on the rough board.

If only she could have stayed flat-chested forever she would have lived a happy life. But the time came when the men looked at her differently. They no longer laughed uproariously when she said: "Get out of my way or I'll cut off your balls and feed them to the pigs." Some of them stared at her when she took off her wool tunic and lay down to sleep in her long linen undershirt. When relieving themselves in the woods, they would turn their backs to her, which they never had before.

One day she saw her father deep in conversation with the parish priest—a rare event—and the two of them kept looking at her, as if they were talking about her. On the following morning her father said to her: "Go with Henry and Everard and do as they tell you." Then he kissed her forehead. She wondered what on earth had come over him—was he going soft in his old age? She saddled her gray courser—she refused to ride the ladylike palfrey or a child's pony—and set off with the two men-at-arms.

They took her to a nunnery and left her there.

The whole place rang with her obscene curses as the two men rode away. She knifed the abbess and walked all the way back to her father's house. He sent her back, bound hand and foot and tied to the saddle of a donkey. They put her in the punishment cell until the abbess's wound healed. It was cold and damp and as black as the night, and there was water to drink but nothing to eat. When they let her out she walked home again. Her father sent her back again, and this time she was flogged before being put in the cell.

They broke her eventually, of course, and she donned the novice's habit, obeyed the rules and learned the prayers, even if in her heart she hated the nuns and despised the saints and disbelieved everything anyone told her about God on principle. But she learned to read and write, she mastered music and numbers and drawing, and she added Latin to the French and English she had spoken in her father's household.

Life in the convent was not so bad, in the end. It was a single-sex community with its own peculiar rules and rituals, and that was exactly what she was used to. All the nuns had to do some physical labor, and Ellen soon got assigned to work with the horses. Before long she was in charge of the stables.

Poverty never worried her. Obedience did not come easily, but it did come, eventually. The third rule, chastity, never troubled her much, although now and again, just to spite the abbess, she would introduce one of the other novice nuns to the pleasures of—

Agnes interrupted Ellen's tale at this point and, taking Martha with her, went off to find a stream in which to wash the child's face and clean up her tunic. She took Alfred too, for protection, although she said she would not go out of earshot. Jack got up to follow them, but Agnes told him firmly to stay behind, and he appeared to understand, for he sat down again. Tom noted that Agnes had succeeded in taking her children where they could not hear any more of this impious and indecent story, while leaving Tom chaperoned.

One day, Ellen went on, the abbess's palfrey went lame when she was several days away from the convent. Kingsbridge Priory happened to be nearby, so the abbess borrowed another horse from the prior there. After she got home, she told Ellen to return the borrowed horse to the priory and bring the lame palfrey back.

There, in the monastery stable within sight of the crumbling old cathedral of Kingsbridge, Ellen met a young man who looked like a whipped puppy. He had the loose-limbed grace of a pup, and the twitching-nosed alertness, but he was cowed and frightened, as if all the playfulness had been beaten out of him. When she spoke to him he did not understand. She tried Latin, but he was not a monk. Finally she said something in French, and his face was suffused with joy and he replied in the same language.

Ellen never went back to the convent.

From that day on she lived in the forest, first in a rough shelter of branches and leaves, later in a dry cave. She had not forgotten the masculine skills she had learned in her father's house: she could still hunt deer, trap rabbits and shoot swans with a bow; she could gut and clean and cook the meat; and she even knew how to scrape and cure the hides and furs for her clothes. As well as game, she ate wild fruits, nuts and vegetables. Anything else she needed—salt, woolen clothing, an ax or a new knife—she had to steal.

The worst time was when Jack was born. . . .

But what about the Frenchman? Tom wanted to ask. Was he Jack's father? And if so, when did he die? And how? But he could tell, from her face, that she was not going to talk about that part of the story, and she seemed the type of person who would not be persuaded against her will, so he kept his questions to himself.

By this time her father had died and his band of men had dispersed, so she had no relatives or friends in the world. When Jack was about to be born she built an all-night fire at the mouth of her cave. She had food and water on hand, and her bow and arrows and knives to ward off the wolves and wild dogs; and she even had a heavy red cloak, stolen from a bishop, to wrap the baby in. But she had not been prepared for the pain and fear of childbirth, and for a long time she thought she was going to die. Nevertheless the baby was born healthy and strong, and she survived.

Ellen and Jack lived a simple, frugal life for the next eleven years. The forest gave them all they needed, as long as they were careful to store enough apples and nuts and salted or smoked venison for the winter months. Ellen often thought that if there were no kings and lords and bishops and sheriffs, then everyone could live like this and be perfectly happy.

Tom asked her how she dealt with the other outlaws, men such as Faramond Openmouth. What would happen if they crept up on her at night and tried to rape her? he wondered, and his loins stirred at the thought, although he had never taken a woman against her will, not even his wife.

The other outlaws were afraid of Ellen, she told Tom, looking at him with her luminous pale eyes, and he knew why: they thought she was a witch. As for law-abiding people traveling through the forest, people who knew they could rob and rape and murder an outlaw without fear of punishment—Ellen just hid from them. Why then had she not hidden from Tom? Because she had seen a wounded child, and wanted to help. She had a child herself.

She had taught Jack everything she had learned in her father's household about weapons and hunting. Then she had taught him all she had learned from the nuns: reading and writing, music and numbers, French and Latin, how to draw, even the Bible stories. Finally, in the long winter evenings, she had passed on the legacy of the Frenchman, who knew more stories and poems and songs than anyone else in the world—

Tom did not believe that the boy Jack could read and write. Tom could write his name, and a handful of words such as *pence* and *yards* and *bushels*; and Agnes, being the daughter of a priest, could do more, although she wrote slowly and laboriously with her tongue poking out of the corner of her mouth; but Alfred could not write a word, and could barely recognize his own name; and Martha could not even do that. Was it possible that this half-witted child was more literate than Tom's whole family?

Ellen told Jack to write something, and he smoothed a patch of earth and scratched letters in it. Tom recognized the first word, *Alfred,* but not the others, and he felt a fool; then Ellen saved his embarrassment by reading the whole thing aloud: "Alfred is bigger than Jack." The boy quickly drew two figures, one bigger than the other, and although they were crude, one had broad shoulders and a rather bovine expression and the other was small and grinning. Tom, who himself had a talent for sketching, was astonished at the simplicity and strength of the picture scratched in the dust.

But the child seemed an idiot.

Ellen had lately begun to realize this, she confessed, guessing Tom's thoughts. Jack had never had the company of other children, or indeed of other human beings except for his mother, and the result was that he was growing up like a wild animal. For all his learning he did not know how to behave with people. That was why he was silent, and stared, and snatched.

As she said this she looked vulnerable for the first time. Her air of impregnable self-sufficiency vanished, and Tom saw her as troubled and rather desperate. For Jack's sake, she needed to rejoin society; but how? If she had been a man, she might conceivably have persuaded some lord to give her a farm, especially if she had lied convincingly and said she was back from a pilgrimage to Jerusalem or Santiago de Compostela. There were some women farmers, but they were invariably widows with grown sons. No lord would give a farm to a woman with one small child. Nobody would hire her as a laborer, either in town or country; besides, she had no place to live, and unskilled work rarely came with accommodation provided. She had no identity.

Tom felt for her. She had given her child everything she could, and it was not enough. But he could see no way out of her dilemma. Beautiful, resourceful, and formidable though she was, she was doomed to spend the rest of her days hiding in the forest with her weird son.

Agnes, Martha and Alfred came back. Tom gazed anxiously at Martha, but she looked as if the worst thing that had ever happened to her was having her face scrubbed. For a while Tom had been absorbed in Ellen's problems, but now he remembered his own plight: he was out of work and his pig had been stolen. The afternoon was wearing on. He began to pick up their remaining possessions.

Ellen said: "Where are you headed?"

"Winchester," Tom told her. Winchester had a castle, a palace, several monasteries, and—most important of all—a cathedral.

"Salisbury is closer," Ellen said. "And last time I was there, they were rebuilding the cathedral—making it bigger."

Tom's heart leaped. This was what he was looking for. If only he could get a job on a cathedral building project he believed he had the ability to become master builder eventually. "Which way is Salisbury?" he said eagerly.

"Back the way you came, for three or four miles. Do you remember a fork in the road, where you went left?"

"Yes—by a pond of foul water."

"That's it. The right fork leads to Salisbury."

They took their leave. Agnes had not liked Ellen, but managed nevertheless to say graciously: "Thank you for helping me take care of Martha."

Ellen smiled and looked wistful as they left.

When they had walked along the road for a few minutes Tom looked back. Ellen was still watching them, standing in the road with her legs apart, shading her eyes with her hand, the peculiar boy standing beside her. Tom waved, and she waved back.

"An interesting woman," he said to Agnes.

Agnes said nothing.

Alfred said: "That boy was *strange*."

They walked into the low autumn sun. Tom wondered what Salisbury was like: he had never been there. He felt excited. Of course, his dream was to build a new cathedral from the ground up, but that almost never happened: it was much more common to find an old building being improved or extended, or partly rebuilt. But that would be good enough for him, as long as it offered the prospect of building to his own designs eventually.

Martha said: "Why did the man hit me?"

"Because he wanted to steal our pig," Agnes told her.

"He should get his *own* pig," Martha said indignantly, as if she had only just realized that the outlaw had done something wrong.

Ellen's problem would have been solved if she had had a craft, Tom reflected. A mason, a carpenter, a weaver or a tanner would not have found himself in her position. He could always go to a town and look for work. There were a few craftswomen, but they were generally the wives or widows of craftsmen. "What she needs," Tom said aloud, "is a husband."

Agnes said crisply: "Well, she can't have mine."

III

The day they lost the pig was also the last day of mild weather. They spent that night in a barn, and when they came out in the morning the sky was the color of a lead roof, and there was a cold wind with gusts of driving rain. They unbundled their cloaks of thick, felted cloth and put them on, fastening them tight under their chins and pulling the hoods well forward to keep the rain off their faces. They set off in a grim mood, four gloomy ghosts in a rainstorm, their wooden clogs splashing along the puddled, muddy road.

Tom wondered what Salisbury cathedral would be like. A cathedral was a church like any other, in principle: it was simply the church where the bishop had his throne. But in practice cathedral churches were the biggest, richest, grandest and most elaborate. A cathedral was rarely a tunnel with windows. Most were three tunnels, a tall one flanked by two smaller ones in a head-and-shoulders shape, forming a nave with side aisles. The side walls of the central tunnel were reduced to two lines of pillars linked by arches, forming an arcade. The aisles were used for processions—which could be spectacular in cathedral churches—and might also provide space for small side chapels dedicated to particular saints, which attracted important extra donations. Cathedrals were the most costly buildings in the world, far more so than palaces or castles, and they had to earn their keep.

Salisbury was closer than Tom had thought. Around midmorning they crested a rise, and found the road falling away gently before them in a long curve; and across the rainswept fields, rising out of the flat plain like a boat on a lake, they saw the fortified hill town of Salisbury. Its details were veiled by the rain, but Tom could make out several towers, four or five, soaring high above the city walls. His spirits lifted at the sight of so much stonework.

A cold wind whipped across the plain, freezing their faces and hands as they followed the road toward the east gate. Four roads met at the foot of the hill, amid a scatter of houses spilled over from the town, and there they were joined by other travelers, walking with hunched shoulders and lowered heads, butting through the weather to the shelter of the walls.

On the slope leading to the gate they came up with an ox cart bearing a load of stone—a very hopeful sign for Tom. The carter was bent down behind the crude wooden vehicle, pushing with his shoulder, adding his strength to that of the two oxen as they inched uphill. Tom saw a chance to make a friend. He beckoned to Alfred, and they both put their shoulders to the back of the cart and helped push.

The huge wooden wheels rumbled onto a timber bridge that spanned an enormous dry moat. The earthworks were formidable: digging that moat, and throwing up the soil to form the town wall, must have taken hundreds of men, Tom thought; a much bigger job even than digging the foundations for a cathedral. The bridge that crossed the moat rattled and creaked under the weight of the cart and the two mighty beasts that were pulling it.

The slope leveled and the cart moved more easily as they approached the gateway. The carter straightened up, and Tom and Alfred did likewise. "I thank you kindly," the carter said.

Tom asked: "What's the stone for?"

"The new cathedral."

"New? I heard they were just enlarging the old one."

The carter nodded. "That's what they said, ten years ago. But there's more new than old, now."

This was further good news. "Who's the master builder?"

"John of Shaftesbury, though Bishop Roger has a lot to do with the designs."

That was normal. Bishops rarely left builders alone to do the job. One of the master builder's problems was often to calm the fevered imaginations of the clerics and set practical limits to their soaring fantasies. But it would be John of Shaftesbury who hired men.

The carter nodded at Tom's satchel of tools. "Mason?"

"Yes. Looking for work."

"You may find it," the carter said neutrally. "If not on the cathedral, perhaps on the castle."

"And who governs the castle?"

"The same Roger is both bishop and castellan."

Of course, Tom thought. He had heard of the powerful Roger of Salisbury, who had been close to the king for as long as anyone could remember.

They passed through the gateway into the town. The place was crammed so full of buildings, people and animals that it seemed in danger of bursting its circular ramparts and spilling out into the moat. The wooden houses were jammed together shoulder to shoulder, jostling for space like spectators at a hanging. Every tiny piece of land was used for something. Where two houses had been built with an alleyway between them, someone had put up a half-size dwelling in the alley, with no windows because its door took up almost all the frontage. Wherever a site was too small even for the narrowest of houses, there was a stall on it selling ale or bread or apples; and if there was not even room for that, then there would be a stable, a pigsty, a dunghill or a water barrel.

It was noisy, too. The rain did little to deaden the clamor of craftsmen's workshops, hawkers calling their wares, people greeting one another and bargaining and quarreling, animals neighing and barking and fighting.

Raising her voice above the noise, Martha said: "What's that stink?"

Tom smiled. She had not been in a town for a couple of years. "That's the smell of people," he told her.

The street was only a little wider than the ox cart, but the carter would not let his beasts stop, for fear they might not start again; so he whipped them on, ignoring all obstacles, and they shouldered their dumb way through the multitude, indiscriminately shoving aside a knight on a war-horse, a forester with a bow, a fat monk on a pony, men-at-arms and beggars and housewives and whores.

The cart came up behind an old shepherd struggling to keep a small flock together. It must be market day, Tom realized. As the cart went by, one of the sheep plunged through the open door of an alehouse, and in a moment the whole flock was in the house, bleating and panicking and upsetting tables and stools and alepots.

The ground underfoot was a sea of mud and rubbish. Tom had an eye for the fall of rain on a roof, and the width of gutter required to take the rain away; and he could see that all the rain falling on all the roofs of this half of the town was draining away through this street. In a bad storm, he thought, you would need a boat to cross the street.

As they approached the castle at the summit of the hill, the street widened. Here there were stone houses, one or two of them in need of a little repair. They belonged to craftsmen and traders, who had their shops and stores on the ground floor and living quarters above. Looking with a practiced eye at what was on sale, Tom could tell that this was a prosperous town. Everyone had to have knives and pots, but only prosperous people bought embroidered shawls, decorated belts and silver clasps.

In front of the castle the carter turned his ox team to the right, and Tom and his family followed. The street led around a quarter-circle, skirting the castle ramparts. Passing through another gate they left the hurly-burly of the town as quickly as they had entered it, and walked into a different kind of maelstrom: the hectic but ordered diversity of a major building site.

They were inside the walled cathedral close, which occupied the entire northwest quarter of the circular town. Tom stood for a moment taking it in. Just seeing and hearing and smelling it gave him a thrill like a sunny day. As they arrived behind the cartload of stone, two more carts were leaving empty. In lean-to sheds all along the side walls of the church, masons could be seen sculpting the stone blocks, with iron chisels and big wooden hammers, into the shapes that would be put together to form plinths, columns, capitals, shafts, buttresses, arches, windows, sills, pinnacles and parapets. In the middle of the close, well away from other buildings, stood the smithy, the glow of its fire visible through the open door-way; and the clang of hammer on anvil carried across the close as the smith made new tools to replace the ones the masons were wearing down. To most people it was a scene of chaos, but Tom saw a large and complex mechanism which he itched to control. He knew what each man was doing and he could see instantly how far the work had progressed. They were building the east facade.

There was a run of scaffolding across the east end at a height of twenty-five or thirty feet. The masons were in the porch, waiting for the rain to ease up, but their laborers were running up and down the ladders with stones on their shoulders. Higher up, on the timber framework of the roof, were the plumbers, like spiders creeping across a giant wooden web, nailing sheets of lead to the struts and installing the drainpipes and gutters.

Tom realized regretfully that the building was almost finished. If he did get hired here the work would not last more than a couple of years—hardly enough time for him to rise to the position of master mason, let alone master builder. Nevertheless he would take the job, if he were offered it, for winter was coming. He and his family could have survived a winter without work if they had still had the pig, but without it Tom had to get a job.

They followed the cart across the close to where the stones were stacked. The oxen gratefully dipped their heads to the water trough. The carter called to a passing mason: "Where's the master builder?"

"In the castle," the mason replied.

The carter nodded and turned to Tom. "You'll find him in the bishop's palace, I expect."

"Thanks."

"Mine to you."

Tom left the close with Agnes and the children following. They retraced their steps through the thronged, narrow streets to the front of the castle. Here was another dry moat and a second huge earthen rampart surrounding the central stronghold. They walked across the drawbridge. In a guardhouse to one side of the gateway, a thickset man in a leather tunic sat on a stool, looking out at the rain. He was wearing a sword. Tom addressed him. "Good day. I'm called Tom Builder. I want to see the master builder, John of Shaftesbury."

"With the bishop," the guard said indifferently.

They went inside. Like most castles, this was a collection of miscellaneous buildings inside a wall of earth. The courtyard was about a hundred yards across. Opposite the gateway, on the far side, was the massive keep, the last stronghold in time of attack, rising high above the ramparts to provide a lookout. On their left was a clutter of low buildings, mostly wooden: a long stable, a kitchen, a bakery and several storehouses. There was a well in the middle. On the right, taking up most of the northern half of the compound, was a large stone house that was obviously the palace. It was built in the same style as the new cathedral, with small roundheaded doorways and windows, and it had two stories. It was new—indeed, masons were still working on one corner of it, apparently building a tower. Despite the rain there were plenty of people in the courtyard, coming in and going out or hurrying through the rain from one building to another: men-at-arms, priests, tradesmen, construction workers and palace servants.

Tom could see several doorways in the palace, all open despite the rain. He was not quite sure what to do next. If the master builder was with the bishop, perhaps he ought not to interrupt. On the other hand, a bishop was not a king; and Tom was a free man and a mason on legitimate business, not some groveling serf with a complaint. He decided to be bold. Leaving Agnes and Martha, he walked with Alfred across the muddy courtyard to the palace and went through the nearest door.

They found themselves in a small chapel with a vaulted ceiling and a window in the far end over the altar. Near the doorway a priest sat at a high desk, writing rapidly on vellum. He looked up.

Tom said briskly: "Where's Master John?"

"In the vestry," said the priest, jerking his head toward a door in the side wall.

Tom did not ask to see the master. He found that if he acted as if he were expected he was less likely to waste time waiting around. He crossed the little chapel in a couple of strides and entered the vestry.

It was a small, square chamber lit by many candles. Most of the floor space was taken up by a shallow sandpit. The fine sand had been smoothed perfectly level with a rule. There were two men in the room. Both glanced briefly at Tom, then returned their attention to the sand. The bishop, a wrinkled old man with flashing black eyes, was drawing in the sand with a pointed stick. The master builder, wearing a leather apron, watched him with a patient air and a skeptical expression.

Tom waited in anxious silence. He must make a good impression: be courteous but not groveling and show his knowledge without being cocky. A master craftsman wanted his subordinates to be obedient as well as skillful, Tom knew from his own experience of being the hirer.

Bishop Roger was sketching a two-story building with large windows in three sides. He was a good draftsman, making straight lines and true right angles. He drew a plan and a side view of the building. Tom could see that it would never be built.

The bishop finished it and said: "There."

John turned to Tom and said: "What is it?"

Tom pretended to think he was being asked for his opinion of the drawing. He said: "You can't have windows that big in an undercroft."

The bishop looked at him with irritation. "It's a writing room, not an undercroft."

"It will fall down just the same."

John said: "He's right."

"But they must have light to write by."

John shrugged and turned to Tom. "Who are you?"

"My name is Tom and I'm a mason."

"I guessed that. What brings you here?"

"I'm looking for work." Tom held his breath.

John shook his head immediately. "I can't hire you."

Tom's heart sank. He felt like turning on his heel, but he waited politely to hear the reasons.

"We've been building for ten years here," John went on. "Most of the masons have houses in the town. We're coming to the end, and now I have more masons on the site than I really need."

Tom knew it was hopeless, but he said: "And the palace?"

"Same thing," said John. "This is where I'm using my surplus men. If it weren't for this, and Bishop Roger's other castles, I'd be laying masons off already."

Tom nodded. In a neutral voice, trying not to sound desperate, he said: "Do you hear of work anywhere?"

"They were building at the monastery in Shaftesbury earlier in the year. Perhaps they still are. It's a day's journey away."

"Thanks." Tom turned to go.

"I'm sorry," John called after him. "You seem like a good man."

Tom went out without replying. He felt let down. He had allowed his hopes to rise too early: there was nothing unusual about being turned down. But he had been excited at the prospect of working on a cathedral again. Now he might have to work on a monotonous town wall or an ugly house for a silversmith.

He squared his shoulders as he walked back across the castle courtyard to where Agnes waited with Martha. He never showed his disappointment to her. He always tried to give the impression that all was well, he was in control of the situation, and it was of no great consequence if there was no work here because there was sure to be something in the next town, or the one after that. He knew that if he showed any sign of distress Agnes would urge him to find a place to settle down, and he did not want to do that, not unless he could settle in a town where there was a cathedral to be built.

"There's nothing for me here," he said to Agnes. "Let's move on."

She looked crestfallen. "You'd think, with a cathedral *and* a palace under construction, there would be room for one more mason."

"Both buildings are almost finished," Tom explained. "They've got more men than they want."

The family crossed the drawbridge and plunged back into the crowded streets of the town. They had entered Salisbury by the east gate, and they would leave by the west, for that way led to Shaftesbury. Tom turned right, leading them through the part of the town they had not so far seen.

He stopped outside a stone house that looked in dire need of repair. The mortar used in building it had been too weak, and was now crumbling and falling out. Frost had got into the holes, cracking some of the stones. If it were left for another winter the damage would be worse. Tom decided to point this out to the owner.

The ground-floor entrance was a wide arch. The wooden door was open, and in the doorway a craftsman sat with a hammer in his right hand and a bradawl, a small metal tool with a sharp point, in his left. He was carving a complex design on a wooden saddle which sat on the bench before him. In the background Tom could see stores of wood and leather, and a boy with a broom sweeping shavings.

Tom said: "Good day, Master Saddler."

The saddler looked up, classified Tom as the kind of man who would make his own saddle if he needed one, and gave a curt nod.

"I'm a builder," Tom went on. "I see you're in need of my services."

"Why?"

"Your mortar is crumbling, your stones are cracking and your house may not last another winter."

The saddler shook his head. "This town is full of masons. Why would I employ a stranger?"

"Very well." Tom turned away. "God be with you."

"I hope so," said the saddler.

"An ill-mannered fellow," Agnes muttered to Tom as they walked away.

The street led them to a marketplace. Here in a half-acre sea of mud, peasants from the surrounding countryside exchanged what little surplus they might have of meat or grain, milk or eggs, for the things they needed and could not make themselves—pots, plowshares, ropes and salt. Markets were usually colorful and rather boisterous. There was a lot of good-natured haggling, mock rivalry between adjacent stall holders, cheap cakes for the children, sometimes a minstrel or a group of tumblers, lots of painted whores, and perhaps a crippled soldier with tales of eastern deserts and berserk Saracen hordes. Those who made a good bargain often succumbed to the temptation to celebrate, and spent their profit on strong ale, so that there was always a rowdy atmosphere by midday. Others would lose their pennies at dice, and that led to fighting. But now, on a wet day in the morning, with the year's harvest sold or stored, the market was subdued. Rain-soaked peasants made taciturn bargains with shivering stall holders, and everyone looked forward to going home to a blazing fireplace.

Tom's family pushed through the disconsolate crowd, ignoring the halfhearted blandishments of the sausage seller and the knife sharpener. They had almost reached the far side of the marketplace when Tom saw his pig.

He was so surprised that at first he could not believe his eyes. Then Agnes hissed: "Tom! Look!" and he knew she had seen it too.

There was no doubt about it: he knew that pig as well as he knew Alfred or Martha. It was being held, in an expert grip, by a man who had the florid complexion and broad girth of one who eats as much meat as he needs and then some more: a butcher, without doubt. Both Tom and Agnes stood and stared at him, and since they blocked his path he could not help but notice them.

"Well?" he said, puzzled by their stares and impatient to get by.

It was Martha who broke the silence. "That's our pig!" she said excitedly.

"So it is," said Tom, looking levely at the butcher.

For an instant a furtive look crossed the man's face, and Tom realized he knew the pig was stolen. But he said: "I've just paid fifty pence for it, and that makes it my pig."

"Whoever you gave your money to, the pig was not his to sell. No doubt that was why you got it so cheaply. Who did you buy it from?"

"A peasant."

"One you know?"

"No. Listen, I'm butcher to the garrison. I can't ask every farmer who sells me a pig or a cow to produce twelve men to swear the animal is his to sell."

The man turned aside as if to go away, but Tom caught him by the arm and stopped him. For a moment the man looked angry, but then he realized that if he got into a scuffle he would have to drop the pig, and that if one of Tom's family managed to pick it up, the balance of power would change and it would be the butcher who had to prove ownership. So he restrained himself and said: "If you want to make an accusation, go to the sheriff."

Tom considered that briefly and dismissed it. He had no proof. Instead he said: "What did he look like—the man who sold you my pig?"

The butcher looked shifty and said: "Like anyone else."

"Did he keep his mouth covered?"

"Now that I think of it, he did."

"He was an outlaw, concealing a mutilation," Tom said bitterly. "I suppose you didn't think of that."

"It's pissing with rain!" the butcher protested. "Everyone's muffled up."

"Just tell me how long ago he left you."

"Just now."

"And where was he headed?"

"To an alehouse, I'd guess."

"To spend my money," Tom said disgustedly. "Go on, clear off. You may be robbed yourself, one day, and then you'll wish there were not so many people eager to buy a bargain without asking questions."

The butcher looked angry, and hesitated as if he wanted to make some rejoinder; then he thought better of it and disappeared.

Agnes said: "Why did you let him go?"

"Because he's known here and I'm not," Tom said. "If I fight with him I'll be blamed. And because the pig doesn't have my name written on its arse, so who is to say whether it is mine or not?"

"But all our savings—"

"We may get the money for the pig, yet," said Tom. "Shut up and let me think." The altercation with the butcher had angered him, and it relieved his frustration to speak harshly to Agnes. "Somewhere in this town there is a man with no lips and fifty silver pennies in his pocket. All we have to do is find him and take the money from him."

"Right," said Agnes determinedly.

"You walk back the way we've come. Go as far as the cathedral close. I'll walk on, and come to the cathedral from the other direction. Then we'll return by the next street, and so on. If he's not on the streets he's in an alehouse. When you see him, stay by him and send Martha to find me. I'll take Alfred. Try not to let the outlaw see you."

"Don't worry," Agnes said grimly. "I want that money, to feed my children."

Tom touched her arm and smiled. "You're a lion, Agnes."

She looked into his eyes for a moment, then suddenly stood on her toes and kissed his mouth, briefly but hard. Then she turned and went back across the marketplace with Martha in tow. Tom watched her out of sight, feeling anxious for her despite her courage; then he went in the opposite direction with Alfred.

The thief seemed to think he was perfectly safe. Of course, when he stole the pig, Tom had been heading for Winchester. The thief had gone in the opposite direction, to sell the pig in Salisbury. But the outlaw woman, Ellen, had told Tom that Salisbury cathedral was being rebuilt, and he had changed his plans, and inadvertently caught up with the thief. However, the man thought he would never see Tom again, which gave Tom a chance to catch him unawares.

Tom walked slowly along the muddy street, trying to seem casual as he glanced in at open doorways. He wanted to remain unobtrusive, for this episode could end in violence, and he did not want people to remember a tall mason searching the town. Most of the houses were ordinary hovels of wood, mud and thatch, with straw on the floor, a fireplace in the middle, and a few bits of home-made furniture. A barrel and some benches made an alehouse; a bed in the corner with a curtain to screen it meant a whore; a noisy crowd around a single table signified a game of dice.

A woman with red-stained lips bared her breasts to him, and he shook his head and hurried past. He was secretly intrigued by the idea of doing it with a total stranger, in daylight, and paying for it, but in all his life he had never tried it.

He thought again of Ellen, the outlaw woman. There was something intriguing about her, too. She was powerfully attractive, but those deep-set, intense eyes were intimidating. An invitation from a whore made Tom feel discontented for a few moments, but the spell cast by Ellen had not yet worn off, and he had a sudden foolish desire to run back into the forest and find her and fall on her.

He arrived at the cathedral close without seeing the outlaw. He looked at the plumbers nailing the lead to the triangular timber roof over the nave. They had not yet begun to cover the lean-to roofs on the side aisles of the church, and it was still possible to see the supporting half-arches which connected the outside edge of the aisle with the main nave wall, propping up the top half of the church. He pointed them out to Alfred. "Without those supports, the nave wall would bow outward and buckle, because of the weight of the stone vaults inside," he explained. "See how the half-arches line up with the buttresses in the aisle wall? They also line up with the pillars of the nave arcade inside. And the aisle windows line up with the arches of the arcade. Strong lines up with strong, and weak with weak." Alfred looked baffled and resentful. Tom sighed.

He saw Agnes coming from the opposite side, and his mind returned to his immediate problem. Agnes's hood concealed her face, but he recognized her chin-forward, sure-footed walk. Broad-shouldered laborers stepped aside to let her pass. If she were to run into the outlaw, and there was a fight, he thought grimly, it would be a fairly even match.

"Did you see him?" she said.

"No. Obviously you didn't either." Tom hoped the thief had not left the town already. Surely he would not go without spending some of his pennies? Money was no use in the forest.

Agnes was thinking the same. "He's here somewhere. Let's keep looking."

"We'll go back by different streets and meet again in the marketplace."

Tom and Alfred retraced their steps across the close and went out through the gateway. The rain was soaking through their cloaks now, and Tom thought fleetingly of a pot of beer and a bowl of beef broth beside an alehouse fire. Then he thought how hard he had worked to buy the pig, and he saw again the man with no lips swinging his club at Martha's innocent head, and his anger warmed him.

It was difficult to search systematically because there was no order to the streets. They wandered here and there, according to where people had built houses, and there were many sharp turns and blind alleys. The only straight street was the one that led from the east gate to the castle drawbridge. On his first sweep Tom had stayed close to the ramparts of the castle. Now he searched the outskirts, zigzagging to the town wall and back into the interior. These were the poorer quarters, with the most ramshackle buildings, the noisiest alehouses and the oldest whores. The edge of the town was downhill from the center, so the refuse from the wealthier neighborhood was washed down the streets to lodge beneath the walls. Something similar seemed to happen to the people, for this district had more than its share of cripples and beggars, hungry children and bruised women and helpless drunks.

But the man with no lips was nowhere to be seen.

Twice Tom spotted a man of about the right build and general appearance, and took a closer look, only to see that the man's face was normal.

He ended his search at the marketplace, and there was Agnes waiting for him impatiently, her body tense and her eyes gleaming. "I've found him!" she hissed.

Tom felt a surge of excitement mingled with apprehension. "Where?"

"He went into a cookshop down by the east gate."

"Lead me there."

They circled the castle to the drawbridge, went down the straight street to the east gate, then turned into a maze of alleys beneath the walls. Tom saw the cookshop a moment later. It was not even a house, just a sloping roof on four posts, up against the town wall, with a huge fire at the back over which a sheep turned on a spit and a cauldron bubbled. It was now about noon and the little place was full of people, mostly men. The smell of the meat made Tom's stomach rumble. He raked the little crowd with his eyes, fearful that the outlaw might have left in the short time it had taken them to get here. He spotted the man immediately, sitting on a stool a little apart from the crowd, eating a bowl of stew with a spoon, holding his scarf in front of his face to hide his mouth.

Tom turned away quickly so that the man should not see him. Now he had to decide how to handle this. He was angry enough to knock the outlaw down and take his purse. But the crowd would not let him walk away. He would have to explain himself, not just to bystanders but to the sheriff. Tom was within his rights, and the fact that the thief was an outlaw meant that he would not have anyone to vouch for his honesty; whereas Tom was evidently a respectable man and a mason. But establishing all that would take time, possibly weeks if the sheriff happened to be away in another part of the county; and there might still be an accusation of breaking the king's peace, if a brawl should result.

No. It would be wiser to get the thief alone.

The man could not stay in the town overnight, for he had no home here, and he could not get lodgings without establishing himself as a respectable man somehow. Therefore he had to leave before the gates closed at nightfall.

And there were only two gates.

"He'll probably go back the way he came," Tom said to Agnes. "I'll wait outside the east gate. Let Alfred watch the west gate. You stay in the town and see what the thief does. Keep Martha with you, but don't let him see her. If you need to send a message to me or Alfred, use Martha."

"Right," Agnes said tersely.

Alfred said: "What should I do if he comes out my way?" He sounded excited.

"Nothing," Tom said firmly. "Watch which road he takes, then wait. Martha will fetch me, and we'll overtake him together." Alfred looked disappointed, and Tom said: "You do as I say. I don't want to lose my son as well as my pig."

Alfred nodded reluctant assent.

"Let's break up, before he notices us huddling together and plotting. Go."

Tom left them immediately, not looking back. He could rely on Agnes to carry out the plan. He hurried to the east gate and left the town, crossing the rickety wooden bridge over which he had pushed the ox cart that morning. Directly ahead of him was the Winchester road, going east, dead straight, like a long carpet unrolled over the hills and valleys. To his left, the road by which Tom—and presumably the thief—had come to Salisbury, the Portway, curled up over a hill and disappeared. The thief would almost certainly take the Portway.

Tom went down the hill and through the cluster of houses at the crossroads, then turned onto the Portway. He needed to hide himself. He walked along the road looking for a suitable spot. He went two hundred yards without finding anything. Looking back, he realized that this was too far: he could no longer see the faces of people at the crossroads, so that he would not know if the man with no lips came along and took the Winchester road. He scanned the landscape again. The road was bordered on either side by ditches, which might have offered concealment in dry weather, but today were running with water. Beyond each ditch the land rose in a hump. In the field on the south side of the road a few cows were grazing the stubble. Tom noticed that one of the cows was lying down at the raised edge of the field, overlooking the road, partly concealed by the hump. With a sigh, he retraced his steps. He jumped the ditch and kicked the cow. It got up and went away. Tom lay down in the warm, dry patch it had left. He pulled his hood over his face and settled to wait, wishing he had had the foresight to buy some bread before leaving the town.

He was anxious and a little scared. The outlaw was a smaller man, but he was fast-moving and vicious, as he had shown when he clubbed Martha and stole the pig. Tom was a little afraid of being hurt but much more worried that he might not get his money.

He hoped Agnes and Martha were all right. Agnes could look after herself, he knew; and even if the outlaw spotted her, what could the man do? He would just be on his guard, that was all.

From where he lay Tom could see the towers of the cathedral. He wished he had had a moment to look inside. He was curious about the treatment of the piers of the arcade. These were usually fat pillars, each with arches sprouting from its top: two arches going north and south, to connect with the neighboring pillars in the arcade; and one going east or west, across the side aisle. It was an ugly effect, for there was something not quite right about an arch that sprang from the top of a round column. When Tom built his cathedral each pier would be a cluster of shafts, with an arch springing from the top of each shaft—an elegantly logical arrangement.

He began to visualize the decoration of the arches. Geometric shapes were the commonest forms—it did not take much skill to carve zigzags and lozenges—but Tom liked foliage, which lent softness and a touch of nature to the hard regularity of the stones.

The imaginary cathedral occupied his mind until midafternoon, when he saw the slight figure and blond head of Martha come skipping across the bridge and through the houses. She hesitated at the crossing, then picked the right road. Tom watched her walk toward him, seeing her frown as she began to wonder where he could be. As she drew level with him he called her softly. "Martha."

She gave a little squeal, then saw him and ran to him, jumping over the ditch. "Mummy sent you this," she said, and took something from inside her cloak.

It was a hot meat pie. "By the cross, your mother's a good woman!" said Tom, and took a mammoth bite. It was made with beef and onions, and it tasted heavenly.

Martha squatted beside Tom on the grass. "This is what

happened to the man who stole our pig," she said. She screwed up her nose and concentrated on remembering what she had been told to say. She was so sweet that she took Tom's breath away. "He came out of the cookshop and met a lady with a painted face, and went to her house. We waited outside."

While the outlaw spent our money on a whore, Tom thought bitterly. "Go on."

"He was not long in the lady's house, and when he came out he went to an alehouse. He's there now. He doesn't drink much but he plays at dice."

"I hope he wins," Tom said grimly. "Is that it?"

"That's all."

"Are you hungry?"

"I had a bun."

"Have you told Alfred all this?"

"Not yet. I'm to go to him next."

"Tell him he must try to stay dry."

"Try to stay dry," she repeated. "Shall I say that before or after telling him about the man who stole our pig?"

It did not matter, of course. "After," Tom said, as she wanted a definite answer. He smiled at her. "You're a clever girl. Off you go."

"I like this game," she said. She waved and left, her girlish legs twinkling as she jumped the ditch daintily and ran back toward the town. Tom watched her with love and anger in his heart. He and Agnes had worked hard to get money to feed their children, and he was ready to kill to get back what had been stolen from them.

Perhaps the outlaw would be ready to kill, too. Outlaws were outside the law, as the name implied: they lived in unconstrained violence. This might not be the first time Faramond Openmouth had come up against one of his victims. He was nothing if not dangerous.

The daylight began to fade surprisingly early, as it sometimes did on wet autumn afternoons. Tom started to worry whether he would recognize the thief in the rain. As evening closed in, the traffic to and from the town thinned out, for most visitors had left in time to reach their home villages by nightfall. The lights of candles and lanterns began to flicker in the higher houses of the town and in the suburban hovels. Tom wondered pessimistically if the thief might stay overnight after all. Perhaps he had dishonest friends in the town who would put him up even though they knew he was an outlaw. Perhaps—

Then Tom saw a man with a scarf across his mouth.

He was walking across the wooden bridge close to two other

men. It suddenly occurred to Tom that the thief's two accomplices, the bald one and the man in the green hat, might have come to Salisbury with him. Tom had not seen either of them in the town but the three might have separated for a while and then joined up again for the return journey. Tom cursed under his breath: he did not think he could fight three men. But as they came closer the group separated, and Tom realized with relief that they were not together after all.

The first two were father and son, two peasants with dark, close-set eyes and hooked noses. They took the Portway, and the man with the scarf followed.

He studied the thief's gait as he came closer. He appeared sober. That was a pity.

Glancing back to the town he saw a woman and a girl emerge onto the bridge: Agnes and Martha. He was dismayed. He had not envisaged their being present when he confronted the thief. However, he realized that he had given no instructions to the contrary.

He tensed as they all came up the road toward him. Tom was so big that most people gave in to him in a confrontation; but outlaws were desperate, and there was no telling what might happen in a fight.

The two peasants went by, mildly merry, talking about horses. Tom took his iron-headed hammer from his belt and hefted it in his right hand. He hated thieves, who did no work but took the bread from good people. He would have no qualms about hitting this one with a hammer.

The thief seemed to slow down as he came near, almost as if he sensed danger. Tom waited until he was four or five yards away— too near to run back, too far to run past. Then Tom rolled over the bank, sprang across the ditch, and stood in his way.

The man stopped dead and stared at him. "What's this?" he said nervously.

He doesn't recognize me, Tom thought. He said: "You stole my pig yesterday and sold it to a butcher today."

"I never—"

"Don't deny it," Tom said. "Just give me the money you got for it, and I won't hurt you."

For a moment he thought the thief was going to do just that. He felt a sense of anticlimax as the man hesitated. Then the thief turned on his heel and ran—straight into Agnes.

He was not traveling fast enough to knock her over—and she was a woman who took a lot of knocking over—and the two of them staggered from side to side for a moment in a clumsy dance.

Then he realized she was deliberately obstructing him, and he pushed her aside. She stuck out her leg as he went past her. Her foot got between his knees and both of them fell down.

Tom's heart was in his mouth as he raced to her side. The thief was getting up with one knee on her back. Tom grabbed his collar and yanked him off her. He hauled him to the side of the road before he could regain his balance, then threw him into the ditch.

Agnes stood up. Martha ran to her. Tom said rapidly: "All right?"

"Yes," Agnes answered.

The two peasants had stopped and turned around, and they were staring at the scene, wondering what was going on. The thief was on his knees in the ditch. "He's an outlaw," Agnes called out to them, to discourage them from interfering. "He stole our pig." The peasants made no reply, but waited to see what would happen next.

Tom spoke to the thief again. "Give me my money and I'll let you go."

The man came up out of the ditch with a knife in his hand, fast as a rat, and went for Tom's throat. Agnes screamed. Tom dodged. The knife flashed across his face and he felt a burning pain along his jaw.

He stepped back and swung his hammer as the knife flashed again. The thief jumped back, and both knife and hammer swished through the damp evening air without connecting.

For an instant the two men stood still, facing one another, breathing hard. Tom's cheek hurt. He realized they were evenly matched, for although Tom was bigger, the thief had a knife, which was a deadlier weapon than a mason's hammer. He felt the cold grasp of fear as he realized he might be about to die. He suddenly felt he could not breathe.

From the corner of his eye he saw a sudden movement. The thief saw it too, and darted a glance at Agnes, then ducked his head as a stone came flying at him from her hand.

Tom reacted with the speed of a man in fear of his life, and swung his hammer at the thief's bent head.

It connected just as the man was looking up again. The iron hammer struck his forehead at the hairline. It was a hasty blow, and did not have all of Tom's considerable strength behind it. The thief staggered but did not fall.

Tom hit him again.

This blow was harder. He had time to lift the hammer above his head and aim it, as the dazed thief tried to focus his eyes. Tom thought of Martha as he swung the hammer down. It struck with all his force, and the thief fell to the ground like a dropped doll.

Tom was wound up too tightly to feel any relief. He knelt beside the thief, searching him. "Where's his purse? Where's his purse, damnation!" The limp body was difficult to move. Finally Tom laid him flat on his back and opened his cloak. There was a big leather purse hanging from his belt. Tom undid its clasp. Inside was a soft wool bag with a drawstring. Tom pulled it out. It was light. "Empty!" Tom said. "He must have another."

He pulled the cloak from under the man and carefully felt it all over. There were no concealed pockets, no hard parts. He pulled off the boots. There was nothing inside them. He drew his eating knife from his belt and slit the soles: nothing.

Impatiently, he slipped his knife inside the neck of the thief's woolen tunic and ripped it to the hem. There was no hidden money belt.

The thief lay in the middle of the mud road, naked but for his stockings. The two peasants were staring at Tom as if he were mad. Furiously, Tom said to Agnes: "He hasn't any money!"

"He must have lost it all at dice," she said bitterly.

"I hope he burns in the fires of hell," Tom said.

Agnes knelt down and felt the thief's chest. "That's where he is now," she said. "You've killed him."

IV

By Christmas they were starving.

The winter came early, and it was as cold and hard and unyielding as a stonemason's iron chisel. There were still apples on the trees when the first frost dusted the fields. People called it a cold snap, thinking it would be brief, but it was not. Villages that left the autumn plowing a little late broke their plowshares on the rock-hard earth. The peasants hastened to kill their pigs and salt them for the winter, and the lords slaughtered their cattle, because winter grazing would not support the same number of livestock as summer. But the endless freeze withered the grass, and some of the remaining animals died anyway. Wolves became desperate, and came into villages at dusk to snatch away scraggy chickens and listless children.

On building sites all over the country, as soon as the first frost struck, the walls that had been built that summer were hastily covered with straw and dung to insulate them from the worst cold, because the mortar in them was not yet completely dry, and if it were to freeze it would crack. No further mortar work would be done until spring. Some of the masons had been hired for the summer only, and they went back to their home villages, where they were known as wrights rather than masons, and they would spend the winter making plows, saddles, harness, carts, shovels, doors, and anything else that required a skilled hand with hammer and chisel and saw. The other masons moved into the lean-to lodges on the site and cut stones in intricate shapes all the hours of daylight. But because the frost was early, the work progressed too fast; and because the peasants were starving, the bishops and castellans and lords had less money to spend on building than they had hoped; and so as the winter wore on some of the masons were dismissed.

Tom and his family walked from Salisbury to Shaftesbury, and from there to Sherborne, Wells, Bath, Bristol, Gloucester, Oxford, Wallingford and Windsor. Everywhere the fires inside the lodges burned, and the churchyards and castle walls rang with the song of iron on stone, and the master builders made small precise models of arches and vaults with their clever hands encased in fingerless gloves. Some masters were impatient, abrupt or discourteous; others looked sadly at Tom's thin children and pregnant wife and spoke kindly and regretfully; but they all said the same thing: No, there's no work for you here.

Whenever they could, they imposed upon the hospitality of monasteries, where travelers could always get a meal of some kind and a place to sleep—strictly for one night only. When the blackberries ripened in the bramble thickets, they lived on those for days on end, like the birds. In the forest, Agnes would light a fire under the iron cooking pot and boil porridge. But still, much of the time, they were obliged to buy bread from bakers and pickled herrings from fishmongers, or to eat in alehouses and cookshops, which was more expensive than preparing their own food; and so their money inexorably drained away.

Martha was naturally skinny but she became even thinner. Alfred was still getting taller, like a weed growing in shallow soil, and he became lanky. Agnes ate sparingly, but the baby growing inside her was greedy, and Tom could see that she was tormented by hunger. Sometimes he ordered her to eat more, and then even her iron will yielded to the combined authority of her husband and her unborn child. Still she did not grow plump and rosy, as she had during other pregnancies. Instead she looked gaunt despite her swollen belly, like a starving child in a famine.

Since leaving Salisbury they had walked around three quarters of a big circle, and by the end of the year they were back in the vast forest that stretched from Windsor to Southampton. They were heading for Winchester. Tom had sold his mason's tools, and all but a few pennies of that money had been spent: he would have to borrow tools, or the money to buy them, as soon as he found employment. If he did not get work in Winchester he did not know what he would do. He had brothers, back in his hometown; but that was in the north, a journey of several weeks, and the family would starve before they got there. Agnes was an only child and her parents were dead. There was no agricultural work in midwinter. Perhaps Agnes could scrape a few pennies as a scullery maid in a rich house in Winchester. She certainly could not tramp the roads much longer, for her time was near.

But Winchester was three days away and they were hungry now. The blackberries were gone, there was no monastery in prospect, and Agnes had no oats left in the cooking pot which she carried on her back. The previous night they had traded a knife for a loaf of rye bread, four bowls of broth with no meat in it, and a place to sleep by the fire in a peasant's hovel. They had not seen a village since. But toward the end of the afternoon Tom saw smoke rising above the trees, and they found the home of a solitary verderer, one of the king's forest police. He gave them a sack of turnips in exchange for Tom's small ax.

They had walked only three miles farther when Agnes said she was too tired to go on. Tom was surprised. In all their years together he had never known her to say she was too tired for anything.

She sat down in the shelter of a big horse-chestnut tree beside the road. Tom dug a shallow pit for a fire, using a worn wooden shovel—one of the few tools they had left, for nobody would want to buy it. The children gathered twigs and Tom started the fire, then he took the cooking pot and went to find a stream. He returned with the pot full of icy water and set it at the edge of the fire. Agnes sliced some turnips. Martha collected the conkers that had dropped from the tree, and Agnes showed her how to peel them and grind the soft insides into a coarse flour to thicken the turnip soup. Tom sent Alfred to find more firewood, while he himself took a stick and went poking around in the dead leaves on the forest floor, hoping to find a hibernating hedgehog or squirrel to put in the broth. He was unlucky.

He sat down beside Agnes while darkness fell and the soup cooked. "Have we any salt left?" he asked her.

She shook her head. "You've been eating porridge without salt for weeks," she said. "Haven't you noticed?"

"No."

"Hunger is the best seasoning."

"Well, we've plenty of that." Tom was suddenly terribly tired. He felt the crushing burden of the piled-up disappointments of the last four months and he could not be brave any longer. In a defeated voice he said: "What went wrong, Agnes?"

"Everything," she said. "You had no work last winter. You got a job in the spring; then the earl's daughter canceled the wedding and Lord William canceled the house. Then we decided to stay and work in the harvest—that was a mistake."

"For sure it would have been easier for me to find a building job in the summer than it was in the autumn."

"And the winter came early. And for all that, we would still have been all right, but then our pig was stolen."

Tom nodded wearily. "My only consolation is knowing that the thief is even now suffering all the torments of hell."

"I hope so."

"Do you doubt it?"

"Priests don't know as much as they pretend to. My father was one, remember."

Tom remembered very well. One wall of her father's parish church had crumbled beyond repair, and Tom had been hired to rebuild it. Priests were not allowed to marry, but this priest had a housekeeper, and the housekeeper had a daughter, and it was an open secret in the village that the priest was the father of the girl. Agnes had not been beautiful, even then, but her skin had had a glow of youth, and she had seemed to be bursting with energy. She would talk to Tom while he was working, and sometimes the wind would flatten her dress against her so that Tom could see the curves of her body, even her navel, almost as clearly as if she had been naked. One night she came to the little hut where he slept, and put a hand over his mouth to tell him not to speak, and pulled off her dress so that he could see her nude in the moonlight, and then he took her strong young body in his arms and they made love.

"We were both virgins," he said aloud.

She knew what he was thinking about. She smiled, then her face saddened again, and she said: "It seems so long ago."

Martha said: "Can we eat now?"

The smell of the soup was making Tom's stomach rumble. He dipped his bowl into the bubbling cauldron and brought out a few slices of turnip in a thin gruel. He used the blunt edge of his knife to test the turnip. It was not cooked all the way through, but he decided not to make them wait. He gave a bowlful to each child, then took one to Agnes.

She looked drawn and thoughtful. She blew on her soup to cool it, then raised the bowl to her lips.

The children quickly drained theirs and wanted more. Tom took the pot out of the fire, using the hem of his cloak to avoid burning his hands, and emptied the remaining soup into the children's bowls.

When he returned to Agnes's side she said: "What about you?"

"I'll eat tomorrow," he said.

She seemed too tired to argue.

Tom and Alfred built the fire high and gathered enough wood to last the night. Then they all rolled up in their cloaks and lay down on the leaves to sleep.

Tom slept lightly, and when Agnes groaned he woke up instantly. "What is it?" he whispered.

She groaned again. Her face was pale and her eyes were closed. After a moment she said: "The baby is coming."

Tom's heart missed a beat. Not here, he thought; not here on the frozen ground in the depths of a forest. "But it's not due," he said.

"It's early."

Tom made his voice calm. "Have the waters broken?"

"Soon after we left the verderer's hut," Agnes panted, not opening her eyes.

Tom remembered her suddenly diving into the bushes as if to answer an urgent call of nature. "And the pains?"

"Ever since."

It was like her to keep quiet about it.

Alfred and Martha were awake. Alfred said: "What's happening?"

"The baby is coming," Tom said.

Martha burst into tears.

Tom frowned. "Could you make it back to the verderer's hut?" he asked Agnes. There they would at least have a roof, and straw to lie on, and someone to help.

Agnes shook her head. "The baby has dropped already."

"It won't be long, then!" They were in the most deserted part of the forest. They had not seen a village since morning, and the verderer had said they would not see one all day tomorrow. That meant there was no possibility of finding a woman to act as midwife. Tom would have to deliver the baby himself, in the cold, with only the children to help, and if anything should go wrong he had no medicines, no knowledge. . . .

This is my fault, Tom thought; I got her with child, and I brought her into destitution. She trusted me to provide for her, and now she is giving birth in the open air in the middle of winter. He had always despised men who fathered children and then left them to starve; and now he was no better than they. He felt ashamed.

"I'm so tired," Agnes said. "I don't believe I can bring this baby into the world. I want to rest." Her face glistened, in the firelight, with a thin film of sweat.

Tom realized he must pull himself together. He was going to have to give Agnes strength. "I'll help you," he said. There was nothing mysterious or complicated about what was going to happen. He had watched the births of several children. The work was normally done by women, for they knew how the mother felt, and that enabled them to be more helpful; but there was no reason why a man should not do it if necessary. He must first make her comfortable; then find out how far advanced the birth was; then make sensible preparations; then calm her and reassure her while they waited.

"How do you feel?" he asked her.

"Cold," she replied.

"Come closer to the fire," he said. He took off his cloak and spread it on the ground a yard from the blaze. Agnes tried to struggle to her feet. Tom lifted her easily, and set her down gently on his cloak.

He knelt beside her. The wool tunic she was wearing underneath her own cloak had buttons all the way down the front. He undid two of them and put his hands inside. Agnes gasped.

"Does it hurt?" he said, surprised and worried.

"No," she said with a brief smile. "Your hands are cold."

He felt the outline of her belly. The swelling was higher and more pointed than it had been last night, when the two of them had slept together in the straw on the floor of a peasant's hovel. Tom pressed a little harder, feeling the shape of the unborn baby. He found one end of the body, just beneath Agnes's navel; but he could not locate the other end. He said: "I can feel its bottom, but not its head."

"That's because it's on the way out," she said.

He covered her and tucked her cloak around her. He would need to make his preparations quickly. He looked at the children. Martha was snuffling. Alfred just looked scared. It would be good to give them something to do.

"Alfred, take that cooking pot to the stream. Wash it clean and bring it back full of fresh water. Martha, collect some reeds and make me two lengths of string, each big enough for a necklace. Quick, now. You're going to have another brother or sister by daybreak."

They went off. Tom took out his eating knife and a small hard stone and began to sharpen the blade. Agnes groaned again. Tom put down his knife and held her hand.

He had sat with her like this when the others were born: Alfred; then Matilda, who had died after two years; and Martha; and the child who had been born dead, a boy whom Tom had secretly planned to name Harold. But each time there had been someone else to give help and reassurance—Agnes' mother for Alfred, a village midwife for Matilda and Harold, and the lady of the manor, no less, for Martha. This time he would have to do it alone. But he must not show his anxiety: he must make her feel happy and confident.

She relaxed as the spasm passed. Tom said: "Remember when Martha was born, and the Lady Isabella acted as midwife?"

Agnes smiled. "You were building a chapel for the lord, and

you asked her to send her maid to fetch the midwife from the village. . . ."

"And she said: 'That drunken old witch? I wouldn't let her deliver a litter of wolfhound pups!' And she took us to her own chamber, and Lord Robert could not go to bed until Martha was born."

"She was a good woman."

"There aren't many ladies like her."

Alfred returned with the pot full of cold water. Tom set it down near the fire, not close enough to boil, so there would be warm water. Agnes reached inside her cloak and took out a small linen bag containing clean rags which she had ready.

Martha came back with her hands full of reeds and sat down to plait them. "What do you need strings for?" she asked.

"Something very important, you'll see," Tom said. "Make them well."

Alfred looked restless and embarrassed. "Go and collect more wood," Tom told him. "Let's have a bigger fire." The boy went off, glad to have something to do.

Agnes's face tautened with strain as she began to bear down again, pushing the baby out of her womb, making a low noise like a tree creaking in a gale. Tom could see that the effort was costing her dear, using up her last reserves of strength; and he wished with all his heart that he could bear down for her, and take the strain himself, to give her some relief. At last the pain seemed to ease, and Tom breathed again. Agnes seemed to drift off into a doze.

Alfred returned with his arms full of sticks.

Agnes became alert again and said: "I'm so cold."

Tom said: "Alfred, build up the fire. Martha, lie down beside your mother and keep her warm." They both obeyed with worried looks. Agnes put her arms around Martha and held her close, shivering.

Tom was sick with worry. The fire was roaring, but the air was getting colder. It might be so cold that it would kill the baby with its first breath. It was not unknown for children to be born out-of-doors; in fact it happened often at harvesttime, when everyone was so busy and the women worked up until the last minute; but at harvest the ground was dry and the grass was soft and the air was balmy. He had never heard of a woman giving birth outside in winter.

Agnes raised herself on her elbows and spread her legs wider.

"What is it?" Tom said in a frightened voice.

She was straining too hard to reply.

Tom said: "Alfred, kneel down behind your mother and let her lean on you."

When Alfred was in position, Tom opened Agnes's cloak and unbuttoned the skirt of her dress. Kneeling between her legs, he could see that the birth opening was beginning to dilate a little already. "Not long now, my darling," he murmured, struggling to keep the tremor of fear out of his voice.

She relaxed again, closing her eyes and resting her weight on Alfred. The opening seemed to shrink a little. The forest was silent but for the crackling of the big fire. Suddenly Tom thought of how the outlaw woman, Ellen, had given birth in the forest alone. It must have been terrifying. She had feared that a wolf would come upon her while she was helpless and steal the newborn baby away, she had said. This year the wolves were bolder than usual, people said, but surely they would not attack a group of four people.

Agnes tensed again, and fresh beads of sweat appeared on her contorted face. This is it, thought Tom. He was frightened. He watched the opening widen again, and this time he could see, by the light of the fire, the damp black hair of the baby's head pushing through. He thought of praying but there was no time now. Agnes began to breathe in short, fast gasps. The opening stretched wider— impossibly wide—and then the head began to come through, face-down. A moment later Tom saw the wrinkled ears flat against the side of the baby's head; then he saw the folded skin of the neck. He could not yet see whether the baby was normal.

"The head is out," he said, but Agnes knew that already, of course, for she could feel it; and she had relaxed again. Slowly the baby turned, so that Tom could see the closed eyes and mouth, wet with blood and the slippery fluids of the womb.

Martha cried: "Oh! Look at its little face!"

Agnes heard her and smiled briefly, then began to strain again. Tom leaned forward between her thighs and supported the tiny head with his left hand as the shoulders came out, first one then the other. Then the rest of the body emerged in a rush, and Tom put his right hand under the baby's hips and held it as the tiny legs slithered into the cold world.

Agnes's opening immediately started to close around the pulsing blue cord that came from the baby's navel.

Tom lifted the baby and scrutinized it anxiously. There was a lot of blood, and at first he feared something was terribly wrong; but on closer examination he could see no injury. He looked between its legs. It was a boy.

"It looks horrible!" said Martha.

"He's perfect," Tom said, and he felt weak with relief. "A perfect boy."

The baby opened its mouth and cried.

Tom looked at Agnes. Their eyes met, and they both smiled.

Tom held the tiny baby close to his chest. "Martha, fetch me a bowl of water out of that pot." She jumped up to do his bidding. "Where are those rags, Agnes?" Agnes pointed to the linen bag lying on the ground beside her shoulder. Alfred passed it to Tom. The boy's face was running with tears. It was the first time he had seen a child born.

Tom dipped a rag into a bowl of warm water and gently washed the blood and mucus off the baby's face. Agnes unbuttoned the front of her tunic and Tom put the baby in her arms. He was still squalling. As Tom watched, the blue cord that went from the baby's belly to Agnes's groin stopped pulsing and shriveled, turning white.

Tom said to Martha: "Give me those strings you made. Now you'll see what they're for."

She passed him the two lengths of plaited reeds. He tied them around the birth cord in two places, pulling the knots tight. Then he used his knife to cut the cord between the knots.

He sat back on his haunches. They had done it. The worst was over and the baby was well. He felt proud.

Agnes moved the baby so that his face was at her breast. His tiny mouth found her enlarged nipple, and he stopped crying and started to suck.

Martha said in an amazed voice: "How does he know he should do that?"

"It's a mystery," said Tom. He handed the bowl to her and said: "Get your mother some fresh water to drink."

"Oh, yes," said Agnes gratefully, as if she had just realized she was desperately thirsty. Martha brought the water and Agnes drank the bowl dry. "That was wonderful," she said. "Thank you."

She looked down at the suckling baby, then up at Tom. "You're a good man," she said quietly. "I love you."

Tom felt tears come to his eyes. He smiled at her, then dropped his gaze. He saw that she was still bleeding a lot. The shriveled birth cord, which was still slowly coming out, lay curled in a pool of blood on Tom's cloak between Agnes's legs.

He looked up again. The baby had stopped sucking and fallen asleep. Agnes pulled her cloak over him, then her own eyes closed.

After a moment, Martha said to Tom: "Are you waiting for something?"

"The afterbirth," Tom told her.

"What's that?"

"You'll see."

Mother and baby dozed for a while, then Agnes opened her eyes again. Her muscles tensed, her opening dilated a little, and the placenta emerged. Tom picked it up in his hands and looked at it. It was like something on a butcher's slab. Looking more closely, he saw that it seemed to be torn, as if there were a piece missing. But he had never looked this closely at an afterbirth, and he supposed they were always like this, for they must always have broken away from the womb. He put the thing on the fire. It made an unpleasant smell as it burned, but if he had thrown it away it might have attracted foxes, or even a wolf.

Agnes was still bleeding. Tom remembered that there was always a rush of blood with the afterbirth, but he did not recall so much. He realized that the crisis was not yet over. He felt faint for a moment, from strain and lack of food; but the spell passed and he pulled himself together.

"You're still bleeding, a little," he said to Agnes, trying not to sound as worried as he was.

"It will stop soon," she said. "Cover me."

Tom buttoned the skirt of her dress, then wrapped her cloak around her legs.

Alfred said: "Can I have a rest now?"

He was still kneeling behind Agnes, supporting her. He must be numb, Tom thought, from staying so long in the same position. "I'll take your place," Tom said. Agnes would be more comfortable with the baby if she could stay half-upright, he thought; and also a body behind her would keep her back warm and shield her from the wind. He changed places with Alfred. Alfred grunted with pain as he stretched his young legs. Tom wrapped his arms around Agnes and the baby. "How do you feel?" he asked her.

"Just tired."

The baby cried. Agnes moved him so that he could find her nipple. As he suckled, she seemed to sleep.

Tom was uneasy. It was normal to be tired, but there was a lethargy about Agnes that bothered him. She was too weak.

The baby slept, and after a while the other two children fell asleep, Martha curled up beside Agnes, and Alfred stretched out on the far side of the fire. Tom held Agnes in his arms, stroking her gently. Every now and again he would kiss the top of her head. He felt her body relax as she fell into a deeper and deeper sleep. It was probably the best thing for her, he decided. He touched her cheek. Her skin was clammy, despite all his efforts to keep her warm. He reached inside her cloak and touched the baby's chest. The child was warm and his heart was beating strongly. Tom smiled. A tough baby, he thought; a survivor.

Agnes stirred. "Tom?"

"Yes."

"Do you remember the night I came to you, in your lodge, when you were working on my father's church?"

"Of course," he said, patting her. "How could I ever forget?"

"I never regretted giving myself to you. Never, for one moment. Every time I think of that night, I feel so glad."

He smiled. That was good to know. "Me, too," he said. "I'm glad you did."

She dozed for a while, then spoke again. "I hope you build your cathedral," she said.

He was surprised. "I thought you were against it."

"I was, but I was wrong. You deserve something beautiful."

He did not know what she meant.

"Build a beautiful cathedral for me," she said.

She was not making sense. He was glad when she fell asleep again. This time her body went quite limp, and her head leaned sideways. Tom had to support the baby to prevent him falling off her chest.

They lay like that for a long time. Eventually the baby woke again and cried. Agnes did not respond. The crying woke Alfred, and he rolled over and looked at his baby brother.

Tom shook Agnes gently. "Wake up," he said. "The baby wants to feed."

"Father!" said Alfred in a scared voice. "Look at her face!"

Tom was filled with foreboding. She had bled too much. "Agnes!" he said. "Wake up!" There was no response. She was unconscious. He got up, easing her back until she lay flat on the ground. Her face was ghastly white.

Dreading what he would see, he unwrapped the folds of the cloak from around her thighs.

There was blood *everywhere*.

Alfred gasped and turned away.

Tom whispered: "Christ Jesus save us."

The baby's crying woke Martha. She saw the blood and began to scream. Tom picked her up and smacked her face. She became silent. "Don't scream," he said calmly, and put her down again.

Alfred said: "Is Mother dying?"

Tom put his hand on Agnes's chest, just underneath her left breast. There was no heartbeat.

No heartbeat.

He pressed harder. Her flesh was warm, and the underside of her heavy breast touched his hand, but she was not breathing, and there was no heartbeat.

A numb coldness settled over Tom like a fog. She was gone. He stared at her face. How could she not be there? He willed her to move, to open her eyes, to draw breath. He kept his hand on her chest. Sometimes a heart might start again, people said—but she had lost so much blood. . . .

He looked at Alfred. "Mother is dead," he whispered.

Alfred stared at him dumbly. Martha began to cry. The new baby was crying too. I must take care of them, Tom thought. I must be strong for them.

But he wanted to weep, to put his arms around her and hold her body while it cooled, and remember her as a girl, and laughing, and making love. He wanted to sob with rage and shake his fist at the merciless heavens. He hardened his heart. He had to stay controlled, he had to be strong for the children.

No tears came to his eyes.

He thought: What do I do first?

Dig a grave.

I must dig a deep hole, and lay her in it, to keep the wolves off, and preserve her bones until the Day of Judgment; and then say a prayer for her soul. Oh, Agnes, why have you left me alone?

The new baby was still crying. His eyes were screwed tightly shut and his mouth opened and closed rhythmically, as if he could get sustenance from the air. He needed feeding. Agnes's breasts were full of warm milk. Why not? thought Tom. He shifted the baby toward her breast. The child found a nipple and sucked. Tom pulled Agnes's cloak tighter around the baby.

Martha was watching, wide-eyed, sucking her thumb. Tom said to her: "Could you hold the baby there, so he doesn't fall?"

She nodded and knelt beside the dead woman and the baby.

Tom picked up the spade. She had chosen this spot to rest, and she had sat under the branches of the chestnut tree. Let this be her last resting-place, then. He swallowed hard, fighting an urge to sit on the ground and weep. He marked a rectangle on the ground some yards from the trunk of the tree, where there would be no roots near the surface; then he began to dig.

He found it helped. When he concentrated on driving his shovel into the hard ground and lifting the earth, the rest of his mind went blank and he was able to retain his composure. He took turns with Alfred, for he too could take comfort in repetitious physical labor. They dug fast, driving themselves hard, and despite the bitter cold air they both sweated as if it were noon.

A time came when Alfred said: "Isn't this enough?"

Tom realized that he was standing in a hole almost as deep as he was tall. He did not want the job to be finished. He nodded reluctantly. "It will do," he said. He clambered out.

Dawn had broken while he was digging. Martha had picked up the baby and was sitting by the fire, rocking it. Tom went to Agnes and knelt down. He wrapped her cloak tightly around her, leaving her face visible, then picked her up. He walked over to the grave and put her down beside it. Then he climbed into the hole.

He lifted her down and laid her gently on the earth. He looked at her for a long moment, kneeling there beside her in her cold grave. He kissed her lips once, softly. Then he closed her eyes.

He climbed out of the grave. "Come here, children," he said. Alfred and Martha came and stood either side of him, Martha holding the baby. Tom put an arm around each of them. They looked into the grave. Tom said: "Say: 'God bless Mother.'"

They both said: "God bless Mother."

Martha was sobbing, and there were tears in Alfred's eyes. Tom hugged them both and swallowed his tears.

He released them and picked up the shovel. Martha screamed when he threw the first shovelful of earth into the grave. Alfred put his arms around his sister. Tom kept on shoveling. He could not bear to throw earth on her face, so he covered her feet, then her legs and body, and piled the earth high so that it formed a mound, and every shovelful slid downward, until at last there was earth on her neck, then over the mouth he had kissed, and finally her face disappeared, never to be seen again.

He filled the grave up quickly.

When it was done he stood looking at the mound. "Goodbye, dear," he whispered. "You were a good wife, and I love you."

With an effort he turned away.

His cloak was still on the ground where Agnes had lain on it to give birth. The lower half of it was sodden with congealed and drying blood. He took his knife and roughly cut the cloak in half. He threw the bloodied portion on the fire.

Martha was still holding the baby. "Give him to me," Tom said. She gazed at him with fear in her eyes. He wrapped the naked baby in the clean half of the cloak and laid it on the grave. The baby cried.

He turned to the children. They were staring at him dumbly. He said: "We have no milk, to keep the baby alive, so he must lie here with his mother."

Martha said: "But he'll die!"

"Yes," Tom said, controlling his voice tightly. "Whatever we do, he will die." He wished the baby would stop crying.

He collected their possessions and put them in the cooking pot, then strapped the pot to his back the way Agnes always did.

"Let's go," he said.

Martha began to sob. Alfred was white-faced. They set off down the road in the gray light of a cold morning. Eventually the sound of the baby crying faded to nothing.

It was no good to stay by the grave, for the children would be unable to sleep there and no purpose would be served by an all-night vigil. Besides, it would do them all good to keep moving.

Tom set a fast pace, but his thoughts were now free, and he could no longer control them. There was nothing to do but walk: no arrangements to make, no jobs to do, nothing to be organized, nothing to look at but the gloomy forest and the shadows fidgeting in the light of the torches. He would think of Agnes, and follow the trail of some memory, and smile to himself, then turn to tell her what he had remembered; then the shock of realizing that she was dead would strike like a physical pain. He felt bewildered, as if something totally incomprehensible had happened, although of course it was the most ordinary thing in the world for a woman of her age to die in childbirth, and for a man of his age to be left a widower. But the sense of loss was like a wound. He had heard that people who had the toes chopped off one foot could not stand up, but fell over constantly until they learned to walk again. He felt like that, as if part of him had been amputated, and he could not get used to the idea that it was gone forever.

He tried not to think about her, but he kept remembering how she had looked before she died. It seemed incredible that she had been alive just a few hours ago, and now she was gone. He pictured her face as she strained to give birth, and then her proud smile as she looked at the baby boy. He recalled what she had said to him afterward: *I hope you build your cathedral;* and then, *Build a beautiful cathedral for me.* She had spoken as if she knew she was dying.

As he walked on, he thought more and more about the baby he had left, wrapped in half a cloak, lying on top of a new grave. He was probably still alive, unless a fox had smelled him already. He would die before morning, however. He would cry for a while, then close his eyes, and his life would slip away as he grew cold in his sleep.

Unless a fox smelled him.

There was nothing Tom could do for the baby. He needed milk

to survive, and there was none: no villages where Tom could seek a wet-nurse, no sheep or goat or cow that could provide the nearest equivalent. All Tom had to give him were turnips, and they would kill him as surely as the fox.

As the night wore on, it seemed to him more and more dreadful that he had abandoned the baby. It was a common enough thing, he knew: peasants with large families and small farms often exposed babies to die, and sometimes the priest turned a blind eye; but Tom did not belong to that kind of people. He should have carried it in his arms until it died, and then buried it. There was no purpose to that, of course, but all the same it would have been the right thing to do.

He realized that it was daylight.

He stopped suddenly.

The children stood still and stared at him, waiting. They were ready for anything; nothing was normal anymore.

"I shouldn't have left the baby," Tom said.

Alfred said: "But we can't feed him. He's bound to die."

"Still I shouldn't have left him," Tom said.

Martha said: "Let's go back."

Still Tom hesitated. To go back now would be to admit he had done wrong to abandon the baby.

But it was true. He had done wrong.

He turned around. "All right," he said. "We'll go back."

Now all the dangers which he had earlier tried to discount suddenly seemed more probable. For sure a fox had smelled the baby by now, and dragged him off to its lair. Or even a wolf. The wild boars were dangerous, even though they did not eat meat. And what about owls? An owl could not carry off a baby, but it might peck out its eyes—

He walked faster, feeling light-headed with exhaustion and starvation. Martha had to run to keep up with him, but she did not complain.

He dreaded what he might see when he returned to the grave. Predators were merciless, and they could tell when a living creature was helpless.

He was not sure how far they had walked: he had lost his sense of time. The forest on either side looked unfamiliar, even though he had just passed through it. He looked anxiously for the place where the grave was. Surely the fire could not have gone out yet—they had built it so high. . . . He scrutinized the trees, looking for the distinctive leaves of the horse chestnut. They passed a side turning which he did not remember, and he began to wonder crazily whether he could possibly have passed the grave already and not seen it; then he thought he saw a faint orange glow ahead.

His heart seemed to falter. He quickened his step and narrowed his eyes. Yes, it was a fire. He broke into a run. He heard Martha cry out, as if she thought he was leaving her, and he called over his shoulder: "We're there!" and heard the two children running after him.

He drew level with the horse-chestnut tree, his heart pounding in his chest. The fire was burning merrily. There was the pile of firewood. There was the bloodstained patch of ground where Agnes had bled to death. There was the grave, a mound of freshly dug earth, under which she now lay. And on the grave was—nothing.

Tom looked around frantically, his mind in a turmoil. There was no sign of the baby. Tears of frustration came to Tom's eyes. Even the half a cloak the baby had been wrapped in had disappeared. Yet the grave was undisturbed—there were no animal tracks in the soft earth, no blood, no marks to indicate that the baby had been dragged away. . . .

Tom began to feel as if he could not see very clearly. It became difficult to think straight. He knew now that he had done a dreadful thing in leaving the baby while it was still alive. When he knew it was dead he would be able to rest. But it might still be alive some-where—somewhere nearby. He decided to circle around and look.

Alfred said: "Where are you going?"

"We must search for the baby," he said, without looking back. He walked around the edge of the little clearing, looking under the bushes, still feeling slightly dizzy and faint. He saw nothing, not even a clue to the direction in which the wolf might have taken the baby. He was now sure it was a wolf. The creature's lair might be nearby.

"We must circle wider," he said to the children.

He led them around again, moving farther from the fire, push-ing through bushes and undergrowth. He was beginning to feel confused, but he managed to keep his mind focused on one thing, the imperative need to find the baby. He felt no grief now, just a fierce, raging determination, and in the back of his mind the appall-ing knowledge that all of this was his fault. He blundered through the forest, raking the ground with his eyes, stopping every few paces to listen for the unmistakable wailing monotone of a newborn baby; but when he and the children were quiet, the forest was silent.

He lost track of time. His ever-increasing circles brought him back to the road at intervals for a while, but later he realized that it seemed a long time since they crossed it. At one point he wondered why he had not come across the verderer's cottage. It occurred to him vaguely that he had lost his way, and might no longer be circling around the grave, but instead wandering through the forest more or less at random; but it did not really matter, so long as he kept searching.

"Father," Alfred said.

Tom looked at him, irritated by the interruption of his concentration. Alfred was carrying Martha, who appeared to be fast asleep on his back. Tom said: "What?"

"Can we rest?" Alfred said.

Tom hesitated. He did not want to stop, but Alfred looked about to collapse. "All right," he said reluctantly. "But not for long."

They were on a slope. There might be a stream at its foot. He was thirsty. He took Martha from Alfred and picked his way down the slope, cradling her in his arms. As he expected, he found a small clear stream, with ice at its edges. He put Martha down on the bank. She did not wake. He and Alfred knelt and scooped up the cold water in their hands.

Alfred lay down next to Martha and closed his eyes. Tom looked around him. He was in a clearing carpeted with fallen leaves. The trees all around were low, stout oaks, their bare branches intertwining overhead. Tom crossed the clearing, thinking of looking for the baby behind the trees, but when he reached the other side his legs went weak and he was obliged to sit down abruptly.

It was full daylight now, but misty, and it seemed no warmer than midnight. He was shivering uncontrollably. He realized he had been walking around wearing only his undertunic. He wondered what had happened to his cloak, but he could not remember. Either the mist thickened, or something strange happened to his vision, for he could not see the children on the far side of the clearing any longer. He wanted to get up and go to them but there was something wrong with his legs.

After a while a weak sun broke through the cloud, and soon after that the angel came.

She walked across the clearing from the east, dressed in a long winter cloak of blanched wool, almost white. He watched her approach without surprise or curiosity. He was beyond wonder or fear. He looked at her with the dull, vacant, emotionless gaze he had bestowed upon the massive trunks of the surrounding oaks. Her oval face was framed with rich dark hair, and her cloak hid her feet, so that she might have been gliding over the dead leaves. She stopped right in front of him, and her pale gold eyes seemed to see into his soul and understand his pain. She looked familiar, as if he might have seen a picture of this very angel in some church he had attended recently. Then she opened her cloak. Underneath it she was naked. She had the body of an earthly woman in her middle twenties, with pale skin and pink nipples. Tom had always assumed angels' bodies to be immaculately hairless, but this one was not.

She went down on one knee in front of him where he sat cross-legged by the oak tree. Leaning toward him, she kissed his mouth. He was too stunned by previous shocks to feel surprise even at this. She pushed him back gently until he was lying flat, then she opened her cloak and lay on top of him with her naked body pressed against him. He felt the heat of her body through his undertunic. After a few moments he stopped shivering.

She took his bearded face in her hands and kissed him again, thirstily, like someone drinking cool water after a long, dry day. After a moment she ran her hands down his arms to his wrists, then lifted his hands to her breasts. He grasped them reflexively. They were soft and yielding, and her nipples swelled under his fingertips.

In the back of his mind he conceived the idea that he was dead. Heaven was not supposed to be like this, he knew, but he hardly cared. His critical faculties had been disengaged for hours. What little capacity he had left for rational thought vanished, and he let his body take charge. He strained upward, pressing his body against hers, drawing strength from her heat and her nakedness. She opened her mouth and thrust her tongue inside his mouth, seeking his tongue, and he responded eagerly.

She pulled away from him briefly, raising her body off his. He watched, dazed, as she pushed up the skirt of his undertunic until it was around his waist, then she straddled his hips. She looked into his eyes, with her all-seeing gaze, as she lowered herself. There was a tantalizing moment when their bodies touched, and she hesitated; then he felt himself enter her. The sensation was so thrilling he felt he might burst with pleasure. She moved her hips, smiling at him and kissing his face.

After a while she closed her eyes and started to pant, and he understood that she was losing control. He watched in delighted fascination. She uttered small rhythmic cries, moving faster and faster, and her ecstasy moved Tom to the depths of his wounded soul, so that he did not know whether he wanted to weep with despair or shout for joy or laugh hysterically; and then an explosion of delight shook them both like trees in a gale, again and again; until at last their passion subsided, and she slumped on his chest.

They lay like that for a long time. The heat of her body warmed
him right through. He drifted into a kind of light sleep. It seemed
short, and more like daydreaming than real sleep; but when he
opened his eyes his mind was clear.

He looked at the beautiful young woman lying on top of him,
and he knew immediately that she was not an angel, but the outlaw
woman Ellen, whom he had met in this part of the forest on the day
the pig was stolen. She felt him stir and opened her eyes, regarding
him with an expression of mingled affection and anxiety.
He suddenly thought of his children. He rolled Ellen off him gently
and sat up. Alfred and Martha lay on the leaves, wrapped in their
cloaks, with the sun shining on their sleeping faces. Then the events
of the night came back to him in a rush of horror, and he remembered that Agnes was dead, and the baby—his son!—was gone; and
he buried his face in his hands.

He heard Ellen give a strange two-tone whistle. He looked up.
A figure emerged from the forest, and Tom recognized her peculiar-
looking son, Jack, with his dead-white skin and orange hair and
bright bird-like blue eyes. Tom got up, rearranging his clothing, and
Ellen stood and closed up her cloak.

The boy was carrying something, and he brought it across and
showed it to Tom. Tom recognized it. It was the half of his cloak in
which he had wrapped the baby before placing it on Agnes's grave.

Uncomprehending, Tom stared at the boy and then at Ellen.
She took his hands in hers, looked into his eyes, and said: "Your
baby is alive."

Tom did not dare to believe her. It would be too wonderful, too
happy for this world. "He can't be," he said.

"He is."

Tom began to hope. "Truly?" he said. "Truly?"

She nodded. "Truly. I will take you to him."

Tom realized she meant it. A flood of relief and happiness
washed over him. He fell to his knees on the ground; and then, at
last, like the opening of a floodgate, he wept.

V

"Jack heard the baby cry," Ellen explained. "He was on his way to the river, to a place north of here where you can kill ducks with stones, if you're a good shot. He didn't know what to do, so he ran home to fetch me. But while we were on our way back to the spot, we saw a priest, riding a palfrey, carrying the baby."

Tom said: "I must find him—"

"Don't panic," Ellen said. "I know where he is. He took a side turning, quite near the grave; a path that leads to a little monastery hidden in the forest."

"The baby needs milk."

"The monks have goats."

"Thank God," Tom said fervently.

"I'll take you there, after you've had something to eat," she said. "But . . ." She frowned. "Don't tell your children about the monastery just yet."

Tom glanced across the clearing. Alfred and Martha slept on. Jack had drifted across to where they lay, and was staring at them in his vacant way. "Why not?"

"I'm not sure . . . I just think it might be wiser to wait."

"But your son will tell them."

She shook her head. "He saw the priest, but I don't think he's worked out the rest of it."

"All right." Tom felt solemn. "If I'd known you were nearby, you might have saved my Agnes."

Ellen shook her head, and her dark hair danced around her face. "There's nothing to be done, except keep the woman warm, and you did that. When a woman is bleeding inside, either it stops, and she gets better, or it doesn't, and she dies." Tears came to Tom's eyes, and Ellen said: "I'm sorry."

Tom nodded dumbly.

She said: "But the living must take care of the living, and you need hot food and a new coat." She stood up.

They woke the children. Tom told them that the baby was all right, that Ellen and Jack had seen a priest carrying him; and that Tom and Ellen were going to go looking for the priest later, but first

Ellen was going to give them food. They accepted the startling news calmly: nothing could shock them now. Tom was no less bemused. Life was moving too fast for him to take in all the changes. It was like being on the back of a runaway horse: everything happened so quickly that there was no time to react to events, and all he could do was hold on tightly and try to stay sane. Agnes had given birth in the cold night air; the baby had been born miraculously healthy; everything had seemed all right and then Agnes, Tom's soul mate, had bled to death in his arms, and he had lost his mind; the baby had been doomed, and left for dead; then they had tried to find it, and failed; then Ellen had appeared, and Tom had taken her for an angel, and they had made love as if in a dream; and she had said the baby was alive and well. Would life ever slow down enough to let Tom think about these awful events?

They set off. Tom had always assumed that outlaws lived in squalor, but there was nothing squalid about Ellen, and Tom wondered what her home would be like. She led them on a zigzag course through the forest. There was no path, but she never hesitated as she stepped over streams, ducked low branches, and negotiated a frozen swamp, a mass of shrubbery, and the enormous trunk of a fallen oak. Finally she walked toward a bramble thicket and seemed to vanish into it. Following her, Tom saw that, contrary to his first impression, there was a narrow passageway winding through the thicket. He followed her. The brambles closed over his head and he found himself in semi-darkness. He stood still, waiting for his eyes to adjust to the gloom. Gradually he realized he was in a cave.

The air was warm. Ahead of him a fire glowed on a hearth of flat stones. The smoke was going straight upward: there was a natural chimney somewhere. On either side of him were animal skins, a wolf and a deer, fixed to the walls of the cave with wooden pegs. A haunch of smoked venison hung from the roof above him. He saw a homemade box full of crab apples, rushlights on ledges, and dry reeds on the floor. At the edge of the fire was a cooking pot, just as there would be in any ordinary household; and, judging by the smell, it contained the same kind of pottage as everyone else ate— vegetables boiled with meat bones and herbs. Tom was astonished. This was a home more comfortable than those of many serfs.

Beyond the fire were two mattresses made of deerskin and stuffed, presumably, with reeds; and neatly rolled on top of each was a wolf fur. Ellen and Jack would sleep there, with the fire between them and the mouth of the cave. At the back of the cave was a formidable collection of weapons and hunting gear: a bow, some arrows, nets, rabbit traps, several wicked daggers, a carefully made wooden lance with its tip sharpened and fire-hardened; and, among all those primitive implements, three books. Tom was flabbergasted: he had never seen books in a *house*, let alone a cave; books belonged in church.

The boy Jack picked up a wooden bowl, dipped it into the pot, and began to drink. Alfred and Martha watched him hungrily. Ellen gave Tom an apologetic look and said: "Jack, when there are strangers, we give them food first, before we eat."

The boy stared at her, mystified. "Why?"

"Because it's a gentle thing to do. Give the children some pottage."

Jack was not convinced, but he obeyed his mother. Ellen gave some soup to Tom. He sat down on the floor and drank. It tasted meaty, and warmed him from the inside. Ellen put a fur around his shoulders. When he had drunk the juice he fished out the vegetables and meat with his fingers. It was weeks since he had tasted meat. This seemed to be duck—shot by Jack with stones and a sling, presumably.

They ate until the pot was empty; then Alfred and Martha lay down on the rushes. Before they fell asleep, Tom told them that he and Ellen were going to look for the priest, and Ellen said Jack would stay here and take care of them until the parents returned. The two exhausted children nodded assent and closed their eyes.

Tom and Ellen went out, Tom wearing the fur Ellen had given him draped over his shoulders to keep him warm. As soon as they were out of the bramble thicket, Ellen stopped, turned to Tom, pulled his head down to hers, and kissed his mouth.

"I love you," she said fiercely. "I loved you from the moment I saw you. I always wanted a man who would be strong and gentle, and I thought there was no such thing. Then I saw you. I wanted you. But I could see you loved your wife. My God, how I envied her. I'm sorry she died, truly sorry, because I can see the grief in your eyes, and all the tears waiting to be shed, and it breaks my heart to see you so sad. But now that she's gone, I want you for myself."

Tom did not know what to say. It was hard to believe that a woman so beautiful and resourceful and self-sufficient should have fallen in love with him at first sight; harder still to know how he felt. He was devastated by the loss of Agnes—Ellen was right to say that he had unshed tears, he could feel their weight behind his eyes. But he was also consumed by desire for Ellen, with her wonderful hot body and her golden eyes and her shameless lust. He felt dreadfully guilty about wanting Ellen so badly when Agnes was only hours in her grave.

He stared back at her, and once again her eyes saw into his heart, and she said: "Don't say anything. You don't have to feel ashamed. I know you loved her. She knew it too, I could tell. You still love her—of course you do. You always will."

She had told him not to say anything, and in any case he had nothing to say. He was struck dumb by this extraordinary woman. She seemed to make everything all right. Somehow, the fact that she appeared to know everything that was in his heart made him feel better, as if now he had nothing more to be ashamed of. He sighed.

"That's better," she said. She took him by the hand, and they walked away from the cave together.

They pushed through the virgin forest for almost a mile, then came to the road. As they walked along, Tom kept looking at Ellen's face beside him. He recalled that when he first met her he had thought she fell short of being beautiful, because of her strange eyes. Now he could not understand how he had ever felt that. He now saw those astonishing eyes as the perfect expression of her unique self. Now she seemed absolutely perfect, and the only puzzle was why she was with him.

They walked for three or four miles. Tom was still tired but the pottage had given him strength; and although he trusted Ellen completely he was still anxious to see the baby with his own eyes.

When they could see the monastery through the trees, Ellen said: "Let's not reveal ourselves to the monks at first."

Tom was mystified. "Why?"

"You abandoned a baby. It counts as murder. Let's spy on the place from the woods and see what kind of people they are."

Tom did not think he was going to be in trouble, given the circumstances, but there was no harm in being cautious, so he nodded assent and followed Ellen into the undergrowth. A few moments later they were lying at the edge of the clearing.

It was a very small monastery. Tom had built monasteries, and he guessed this one must be what they called a cell, a branch or outpost of a large priory or abbey. There were only two stone buildings, the chapel and the dormitory. The rest were made of wood and wattle-and-daub: a kitchen, stables, a barn, and a range of smaller agricultural buildings. The place had a clean, well-kept look, and gave the impression that the monks did as much farming as praying.

There were not many people about. "Most of the monks have

gone to work," Ellen said. "They're building a barn at the top of the hill." She glanced up at the sky. "They'll be back around noon for their dinner."

Tom scanned the clearing. Over to their right, partly concealed by a small herd of tethered goats, he saw two figures. "Look," he said, pointing. As they studied the two figures he saw something else. "The man sitting down is a priest, and . . ."

"And he's holding something in his lap."

"Let's go closer."

They moved through the woods, skirting the clearing, and emerged at a point close to the goats. Tom's heart was in his mouth as he looked at the priest sitting on a stool. He had a baby in his lap, and the baby was Tom's. There was a lump in Tom's throat. It was true, it really was; the baby had lived. He felt like throwing his arms around the priest and hugging him.

There was a young monk with the priest. Looking closely, Tom saw that the youngster was dipping a rag into a pail of milk—goat's milk, presumably—and then putting the sodden corner of the rag into the baby's mouth. That was ingenious.

"Well," Tom said apprehensively, "I'd better go and own up to what I've done, and take my son back."

Ellen looked at him levelly. "Think for a moment, Tom," she said. "What are you going to do then?"

He was not sure what she was getting at. "Ask the monks for milk," he said. "They can see I'm poor. They give alms."

"And then?"

"Well, I hope they'll give me enough milk to keep him alive for three days, until I get to Winchester."

"And after that?" she persisted. "How will you feed the baby then?"

"Well, I'll look for work—"

"You've been looking for work since last time I met you, at the end of the summer," she said. She seemed to be a little angry with Tom, he could not see why. "You've no money and no tools," she went on. "What will happen to the baby if there's no work in Winchester?"

"I don't know," Tom said. He felt hurt that she should speak so harshly to him. "What am I to do—live like you? I can't shoot ducks with a stone—I'm a mason."

"You could leave the baby here," she said.

Tom was thunderstruck. "Leave him?" he said. "When I've only just found him?"

"You'd be sure he'd be warm and fed. You wouldn't have to

carry him while you look for work. And when you do find something, you can come back here and fetch the child."

Tom's instinct rebelled against the whole idea. "I don't know," he said. "What would the monks think of my abandoning the baby?"

"They already know you did that," she said impatiently. "It's just a question of whether you confess now or later."

"Do monks know how to take care of babies?"

"They know as much about it as you do."

"I doubt it."

"Well, they've worked out how to feed a newborn who can only suck."

Tom began to see that she was right. Much as he longed to hold the tiny bundle in his arms, he could not deny that the monks were better able to care for the baby than he was. He had no food and no money and no sure prospect of getting work. "Leave him again," he said sadly. "I suppose I must." He stayed where he was, gazing across the clearing at the small figure in the priest's lap. It had dark hair, like Agnes's hair. Tom had made up his mind, but now he could not tear himself away.

Then a large group of monks appeared on the far side of the clearing, fifteen or twenty of them, carrying axes and saws, and suddenly there was a danger that Tom and Ellen would be seen. They ducked back into the undergrowth. Now Tom could no longer see the baby.

They crept away through the bushes. When they came to the road they broke into a run. They ran for three or four hundred yards, holding hands; then Tom was exhausted. They were at a safe distance, however. They stepped off the road and found a place to rest out of sight.

They sat down on a grassy bank lit by dappled sunlight. Tom looked at Ellen, lying on her back, breathing hard, her cheeks flushed, her lips smiling up at him. Her robe had fallen open at the neck, revealing her throat and the swell of one breast. Suddenly he felt a compulsion to look at her nakedness again, and the desire was much stronger than the guilt he felt. He leaned over to kiss her, then hesitated, because she was so lovely to look at. When he spoke, it was unpremeditated, and his own words took him by surprise. "Ellen," he said, "will you be my wife?"

Chapter 2

PETER OF WAREHAM was a born troublemaker.

He had been transferred to the little cell in the forest from the mother house at Kingsbridge, and it was easy to see why the prior of Kingsbridge had been anxious to get rid of him. A tall, rangy man in his late twenties, he had a powerful intellect and a scornful manner, and he lived in a permanent state of righteous indignation. When he first arrived and started working in the fields he had set a furious pace and then accused others of laziness. However, to his surprise most of the monks had been able to keep up with him, and eventually the younger ones had tired him out. He had then looked for a vice other than idleness, and his second choice had been gluttony.

He began by eating only half his bread and none of his meat. He drank water from streams during the day, diluted his beer, and refused wine. He reprimanded a healthy young monk who asked for more porridge, and reduced to tears a boy who playfully drank another's wine.

The monks showed little evidence of gluttony, Prior Philip thought as they walked back from the hilltop to the monastery at dinnertime. The youngsters were lean and muscular, and the older men were sunburned and wiry. Not one of them had the pale, soft roundness that came from having plenty to eat and nothing to do. Philip thought all monks should be thin. Fat monks provoked poor men to envy and hatred of God's servants.

Characteristically, Peter had disguised his accusation as a confession. "I have been guilty of the sin of gluttony," he had said this morning, when they were taking a break, sitting on the trees they had felled, eating rye bread and drinking beer. "I have disobeyed the Rule of Saint Benedict, which says that monks must not eat meat nor drink wine." He looked around at the others, his head high and his dark eyes blazing with pride, and he let his gaze rest finally on Philip. "And every one here is guilty of the same sin," he finished.

It was very sad that Peter should be like this, Philip thought. The man was dedicated to God's work, and he had a fine mind and great strength of purpose. But he seemed to have a compelling need to feel special and be noticed by others all the time; and this drove him to create scenes. He was a real nuisance, but Philip loved him as much as any of them, for Philip could see, behind the arrogance and the scorn, a troubled soul who did not really believe that anyone could possibly care for him.

Philip had said: "This gives us an opportunity to recall what Saint Benedict said on this topic. Do you remember his exact words, Peter?"

"He says: 'All but the sick should abstain from meat,' and then: 'Wine is not the drink of monks at all,'" Peter replied.

Philip nodded. As he had suspected, Peter did not know the rule as well as Philip. "Almost correct, Peter," he said. "The saint did not refer to meat, but to 'the flesh of four-footed animals,' and even so he made exceptions, not just for the sick, but also for the weak. What did he mean by 'the weak'? Here in our little community, we take the view that men who have been weakened by strenuous work in the fields may need to eat beef now and then to keep up their strength."

Peter had listened to this in sullen silence, his brow creased with disapproval, his heavy black eyebrows drawn together over the bridge of his large curved nose, his face a mask of suppressed defiance.

Philip had gone on: "On the subject of wine, the saint says: 'We read that wine is not the drink of monks at all.' The use of the words *we read* implies that he does not wholly endorse the proscription. He also says that a pint of wine a day should be sufficient for anyone. And he warns us not to drink to satiety. It is clear, is it not, that he does not expect monks to abstain totally?"

"But he says that frugality should be maintained in everything," Peter said.

"And you say we are not frugal here?" Philip asked him.

"I do," he said in a ringing voice.

"'Let those to whom God gives the gift of abstinence know that they shall receive their proper reward,'" Philip quoted. "If you feel that the food here is too generous, you may eat less. But remember what else the saint says. He quotes the first epistle to the Corinthians, in which Saint Paul says: 'Every one has his proper gift from God, one thus, another thus.' And then the saint tells us: 'For this reason, the amount of other people's food cannot be determined without some misgiving.' Please remember that, Peter, as you fast and meditate upon the sin of gluttony."

They had gone back to work then, Peter wearing a martyred air. He was not going to be silenced so easily, Philip realized. Of the monks' three vows, of poverty, chastity and obedience, the one that gave Peter trouble was obedience.

There were ways of dealing with disobedient monks, of course: solitary confinement, bread and water, flogging, and ultimately excommunication and expulsion from the house. Philip did not normally hesitate to use such punishments, especially when a monk seemed to be testing Philip's authority. Consequently he was thought of as a tough disciplinarian. But in fact he hated meting out punishment—it brought disharmony into the monastic brotherhood and made everyone unhappy. Anyway, in the case of Peter, punishment would do no good at all—indeed, it would serve to make the man more prideful and unforgiving. Philip had to find a way to control Peter and soften him at the same time. It would not be easy. But then, he thought, if everything were easy, men would not need God's guidance.

They reached the clearing in the forest where the monastery was. As they walked across the open space, Philip saw Brother John waving energetically at them from the goat pen. He was called Johnny Eightpence, and he was a little soft in the head. Philip wondered what he was excited about now. With Johnny was a man in priest's robes. He looked vaguely familiar, and Philip hurried toward him.

The priest was a short, compact man in his middle twenties, with close-cropped black hair and bright blue eyes that twinkled with alert intelligence. Looking at him was for Philip like looking in a mirror. The priest, he realized with a shock, was his younger brother Francis.

And Francis was holding a newborn baby.

Philip did not know which was more surprising, Francis or the baby. The monks all crowded around. Francis stood up and handed the baby to Johnny; then Philip embraced him. "What are you doing here?" Philip said delightedly. "And why have you got a baby?"

"I'll tell you later why I'm here," Francis said. "As for the baby,

I found him in the woods, all alone, lying near a blazing fire." Francis stopped.

"And . . ." Philip prompted him.

Francis shrugged. "I can't tell you any more than that, because that's all I know. I was hoping to get here last night, but I didn't quite make it, so I spent the night in a verderer's hut. I left at dawn this morning, and I was riding along the road when I heard a baby cry. A moment later I saw it. I picked it up and brought it here. That's the whole tale."

Philip looked incredulously at the tiny bundle in Johnny's arms. He reached out a hand tentatively, and lifted a corner of the blanket. He saw a wrinkled pink face, an open toothless mouth and a little bald head—a miniature of an aging monk. He unwrapped the bundle a little more and saw tiny fragile shoulders, waving arms, and tight-clenched fists. He looked closely at the stump of the umbilical cord which hung from the baby's navel. It was faintly disgusting. Was this natural? Philip wondered. It looked like a wound that was healing well, and would be best left alone. He pulled the blanket down farther still. "A boy," he said with an embarrassed cough, and covered it up again. One of the novices giggled.

Philip suddenly felt helpless. What on earth am I to do with it? he thought. Feed it?

The baby cried, and the sound tugged at his heartstrings like a well-loved hymn. "It's hungry," he said, and he thought in the back of his mind: How did I know that?

One of the monks said: "We can't feed it."

Philip was about to say: Why not? Then he realized why not: there were no women for miles.

However, Johnny had already solved that problem, Philip now saw. Johnny sat down on the stool with the baby in his lap. He had in his hand a towel with one corner twisted into a spiral. He dipped the corner into a pail of milk, let the towel soak up some of the liquid, then put the cloth to the baby's mouth. The baby opened its mouth, sucked on the towel, and swallowed.

Philip felt like cheering. "That was clever, Johnny," he said in surprise.

Johnny grinned. "I've done it before, when a nanny goat died before her kid was weaned," he said proudly.

All the monks watched intently as Johnny repeated the simple action of dipping the towel and letting the baby suck. As he touched the towel to the baby's lips, some of the monks would open their own mouths, Philip saw with amusement. It was a slow way of feeding the baby, but no doubt feeding babies was a slow business anyway.

Peter of Wareham, who had succumbed to the general fascination with the baby and consequently had forgotten to be critical of anything for some time, now recovered himself and said: "It would be less trouble to find the child's mother."

Francis said: "I doubt it. The mother is probably unmarried, and was overtaken in moral transgression. I imagine she is young. Perhaps she managed to keep her pregnancy secret; then, when her time was near, she came out into the forest, and built a fire; gave birth alone, then abandoned the child to the wolves and went back to wherever she came from. She will make sure she can't be found."

The baby had fallen asleep. On impulse, Philip took it from Johnny. He held it to his chest, supporting it with his hand, and rocked it. "The poor thing," he said. "The poor, poor thing." The urge to protect and care for the baby suffused him like a flush. He noticed that the monks were staring at him, astonished at his sudden display of tenderness. They had never seen him caress anyone, of course, for physical affection was strictly prohibited in the monastery. Obviously they had thought him incapable of it. Well, he thought, they know the truth now.

Peter of Wareham spoke again. "We'll have to take the child to Winchester, then, and try to find a foster mother."

If this had been said by anyone else, Philip might not have been so quick to contradict it; but Peter said it, and Philip spoke hastily, and his life was never quite the same afterward. "We're not going to give him to a foster mother," he said decisively. "This child is a gift from God." He looked around at them all. The monks gazed back at him wide-eyed, hanging on his words. "We'll take care of him ourselves," he went on. "We'll feed him, and teach him, and bring him up in the ways of God. Then, when he is a man, he will become a monk himself, and that way we will give him back to God."

There was a stunned silence.

Then Peter said angrily: "It's impossible! A baby cannot be brought up by monks!"

Philip caught his brother's eye, and they both smiled, sharing memories. When Philip spoke again, his voice was heavy with the weight of the past. "Impossible? No, Peter. On the contrary, I'm quite sure it can be done, and so is my brother. We know from experience. Don't we, Francis?"

On the day Philip now thought of as the last day, his father had come home wounded.

Philip had been the first to see him, riding up the twisting hill-side path to the little hamlet in mountainous North Wales. Six-year-old Philip ran out to meet him, as usual; but this time Da did not swing his little boy up onto the horse in front of him. He was riding slowly, slumped in the saddle, holding the reins in his right hand, his left arm hanging limp. His face was pale and his clothes were splashed with blood. Philip was at once intrigued and scared, for he had never seen his father appear weak.

Da said: "Fetch your mother."

When they got him into the house, Mam cut off his shirt. Philip was horrified: the sight of his thrifty mother willfully ruining good clothes was more shocking than the blood. "Don't worry about me now," Da had said, but his normal bark had weakened to a murmur and nobody took any notice—another shocking event, for normally his word was law. "Leave me, and get everyone up to the monas-tery," he said. "The damned English will be here soon." There was a monastery with a church at the top of the hill, but Philip could not understand why they should go there when it was not even Sun-day. Mam said: "If you lose any more blood you won't be able to go anywhere, ever." But Auntie Gwen said she would raise the alarm, and went out.

Years later, when he thought about the events that followed, Philip realized that at this moment everyone had forgotten about him and his four-year-old brother, Francis, and nobody thought to take them to the safety of the monastery. People were thinking of their own children, and assumed that Philip and Francis were all right because they were with their parents; but Da was bleeding to death and Mam was trying to save him, and so it happened that the English caught all four of them.

Nothing in Philip's short experience of life had prepared him for the appearance of the two men-at-arms as they kicked the door open and burst into the one-room house. In other circumstances they would not have been frightening, for they were the kind of big, clumsy adolescents who mocked old women and abused Jews and got into fistfights outside alehouses at midnight. But now (Philip understood years later, when at last he was able to think objectively about that day) the two young men were possessed by bloodlust. They had been in a battle, they had heard men scream in agony and seen friends fall down dead, and they had been scared, literally, out of their wits. But they had won the battle and survived, and now they were in hot pursuit of their enemies, and nothing could satisfy them but more blood, more screaming, more wounds and more death; and all this was written on their twisted faces as they came into the room like foxes into a henhouse.

They moved very fast, but Philip could remember each step forever afterward, as if it had all taken a very long time. Both men wore light armor, just a short vest of chain mail and a leather helmet with iron bands. Both had their swords drawn. One was ugly, with a big bent nose and a squint, and his teeth were bared in a dreadful ape-like grin. The other had a luxuriant beard that was matted with blood—someone else's, presumably, for he did not seem to be wounded. Both men scanned the room without breaking stride. Their merciless, calculating eyes dismissed Philip and Francis, noted Mam, and focused on Da. They were almost upon him before anyone else could move.

Mam had been bending over him, tying a bandage to his left arm. She straightened up and turned on the intruders, her eyes blazing with hopeless courage. Da sprang to his feet and got his good hand to the hilt of his sword. Philip let out a cry of terror.

The ugly man raised his sword above his head and brought it down hilt-first on Mam's head, then pushed her aside without stabbing her, probably because he did not want to risk getting his blade stuck in a body while Da was still alive. Philip figured that out years later: at the time he just ran to his mother, not understanding that she could no longer protect him. Mam stumbled, stunned, and the ugly man went by her, raising his sword again. Philip clung to his mother's skirts as she staggered, dazed; but he could not help looking at his father.

Da got his weapon clear of its scabbard and raised it defensively. The ugly man struck downward and the two blades clashed, ringing like a bell. Like all small boys, Philip thought his father was invincible; and this was the moment when he learned the truth. Da was weak from loss of blood. When the two swords met, his dropped; and the attacker lifted his blade just a little and struck again quickly. The blow landed where the big muscles of Da's neck grew out of his broad shoulders. Philip began to scream when he saw the sharp blade slice into his father's body. The ugly man drew his arm back for a stab, and thrust the point of the sword into Da's belly.

Paralyzed with terror, Philip looked up at his mother. His eyes met hers just as the other man, the bearded one, struck her down. She fell to the floor beside Philip with blood streaming from a head wound. The bearded man changed his grip on his sword, reversing it so that it pointed downward and holding it in both hands; then he raised it high, almost like a man about to stab himself, and brought it down hard. There was a sickening crack of breaking bone as the point entered Mam's chest. The blade went in deep; so deep (Philip noted, even then when he was consumed by blind hysterical fear) that it must have come through her back and stuck in the ground, fixing her to the floor like a nail.

Philip looked wildly for his father again. He saw him slump forward over the ugly man's sword and spew out a huge gout of blood. His assailant stepped back and jerked at the sword, trying to disengage it. Da stumbled another step and stayed with him. The ugly man gave a cry of rage and twisted his sword in Da's belly. This time it came out. Da fell to the floor and his hands went to his open abdomen, as if to cover the gaping wound. Philip had always imagined people's insides to be more or less solid, and he was mystified and nauseated by the ugly tubes and organs that were falling out of his father. The attacker lifted his sword high, point downward, over Da's body, as the bearded man had over Mam, and delivered the final blow in the same way.

The two Englishmen looked at one another, and quite unexpectedly Philip read relief on their faces. Together, they turned and looked at him and Francis. One nodded and the other shrugged, and Philip realized they were going to kill him and his brother by cutting them open with those sharp swords, and when he realized how much it was going to *hurt,* the terror boiled up inside him until he felt as if his head would burst.

The man with blood in his beard stooped swiftly and picked Francis up by one ankle. He held him upside-down in the air while the little boy screamed for his mother, not understanding that she was dead. The ugly man pulled his sword out of Da's body and brought his arm back ready to stab Francis through the heart.

The blow was never struck. A commanding voice rang out, and the two men froze. The screaming stopped, and Philip realized it was he who had been doing it. He looked at the door and saw Abbot Peter, standing there in his homespun robe, with the wrath of God in his eyes, holding a wooden cross in his hand like a sword.

When Philip relived that day in his nightmares, and woke up sweating and screaming in the dark, he would always be able to calm himself, and eventually relax into sleep again, by bringing to mind that final tableau, and the way the screaming and the wounds had been swept aside by the unarmed man with the cross.

Abbot Peter spoke again. Philip did not understand the language he used—it was English, of course—but the meaning was clear, for the two men looked ashamed, and the bearded one put Francis down quite gently. Still talking, the monk strode confidently into the room. The men-at-arms backed off a step, almost as if they were afraid of him—they with their swords and armor, and him with a wool robe and a cross! He turned his back on them, a gesture of contempt, and crouched to speak to Philip. His voice was matter-of-fact. "What's your name?"

"Philip."

"Ah, yes, I remember. And your brother's?"

"Francis."

"That's right." The abbot looked at the bleeding bodies on the earth floor. "That's your Mam, isn't it?"

"Yes," said Philip, and he felt panic come over him as he pointed to the mutilated body of his father and said: "And that's my Da!"

"I know," the monk said soothingly. "You mustn't scream anymore, you must answer my questions. Do you understand that they're dead?"

"I don't know," Philip said miserably. He knew what it meant when animals died, but how could that happen to Mam and Da?

Abbot Peter said: "It's like going to sleep."

"But their eyes are open!" Philip yelled.

"Hush. We'd better close them, then."

"Yes," Philip said. He felt as if that would resolve something.

Abbot Peter stood up, took Philip and Francis by the hand, and led them across the floor to their father's body. He knelt down and took Philip's right hand in his. "I'll show you how," he said. He moved Philip's hand over his father's face, but suddenly Philip was afraid to touch his father, because the body looked so strange, pale and slack and hideously wounded, and he snatched his hand away. Then he looked anxiously at Abbot Peter—a man no one disobeyed—but the abbot was not angry with him. "Come," he said gently, and took Philip's hand again. This time Philip did not resist. Holding Philip's forefinger between his own thumb and finger, the monk made the boy touch his father's eyelid and bring it down until it covered the dreadfully staring eyeball. Then the abbot released Philip's hand and said: "Close his other eye." Unaided now, Philip reached out, touched his father's eyelid, and closed it. Then he felt better.

Abbot Peter said: "Shall we close your Mam's eyes, too?"

"Yes."

They knelt beside her body. The abbot wiped blood off her face with his sleeve. Philip said: "What about Francis?"

"Perhaps he should help, too," said the abbot.

"Do what I did, Francis," Philip said to his brother. "Close Mam's eyes, like I closed Da's, so she can sleep."

"Are they asleep?" said Francis.

"No, but it's *like* sleeping," Philip said authoritatively, "so she should have her eyes shut."

"All right, then," said Francis, and without hesitation he reached out a chubby hand and carefully closed his mother's eyes.

Then the abbot picked them both up, one in each arm, and without another glance at the men-at-arms he carried them out of the house and all the way up the steep hillside path to the sanctuary of the monastery.

He fed them in the monastery kitchen; then, so that they should not be left idle with their thoughts, he told them to help the cook prepare the monks' supper. On the following day he took them to see their parents' bodies, washed and dressed and with the wounds cleaned and repaired and partly concealed, lying in coffins side by side in the nave of the church. There too were several of their relatives, for not all the villagers had made it to the monastery in time to escape the invading army. Abbot Peter took them to the funeral, and made sure they watched the two coffins being lowered into the single grave. When Philip cried, Francis cried too. Someone hushed them, but Abbot Peter said: "Let them weep." Only after that, when they had taken to their hearts the knowledge that their parents had really gone and were never coming back, did he at last talk about the future.

Among their relatives there was not a single family left entire: in every case, either the father or the mother had been killed. There were no relations to look after the boys. That left two options. They could be given, or even sold, to a farmer who would use them as slave labor until they grew old enough and big enough to run away. Or they could be given to God.

It was not unknown for small boys to enter a monastery. The usual age was about eleven, and the lower limit around five, for the monks were not set up to cope with babies. Sometimes the boys were orphans, sometimes they had lost just one parent, and sometimes their parents had too many sons. Normally the family would give the monastery a substantial gift along with the child—a farm, a church or even a whole village. In cases of direst poverty the gift might be waived. However, Philip's father had left a modest hill farm, so the boys were not a charity case. Abbot Peter proposed that the monastery should take over the boys and the farm; the surviving relatives agreed; and the deal was sanctioned by the Prince of Gwynedd, Gruffyd ap Cynan, who was temporarily humbled but not permanently deposed by the invading army of King Henry, which had killed Philip's father.

The abbot knew a lot about grief, but for all his wisdom he was not prepared for what happened to Philip. After a year or so, when grief had seemed to pass, and the two boys had settled into the life of the monastery, Philip became possessed by a kind of implacable rage. Conditions in the hilltop community were not bad enough to justify his anger: there was food, and clothing, and a fire in the dormitory in winter, and even a little love and affection; and the strict discipline and tedious rituals at least made for order and stability; but Philip began to act as if he had been unjustly imprisoned. He disobeyed orders, subverted the authority of monastic officers at every opportunity, stole food, broke eggs, loosed horses, mocked the infirm and insulted his elders. The one offense he stopped short of was sacrilege, and because of that the abbot forgave him everything else. And in the end he simply grew out of it. One Christmas he looked back over the past twelve months and realized that he had not spent a single night in the punishment cell all year.

There was no single reason for his return to normality. The fact that he got interested in his lessons probably helped. The mathematical theory of music fascinated him, and even the way Latin verbs were conjugated had a certain satisfying logic. He had been put to work helping the cellarer, the monk who had to provide all the supplies the monastery needed, from sandals to seed; and that, too, compelled his interest. He developed a hero-worshiping attachment for Brother John, a handsome, muscular young monk who seemed the epitome of learning, holiness, wisdom and kindness. Either in imitation of John, or from his own inclination, or both, he began to find some kind of solace in the daily round of prayers and services. And so he slipped into adolescence with the organization of the monastery on his mind and the holy harmonies in his ears.

In their studies both Philip and Francis were far ahead of any boys of their own age that they knew, but they assumed this was because they lived in the monastery and had been educated more intensively. At this stage they did not realize they were exceptional. Even when they began to do much of the teaching in the little school, and take their own lessons from the abbot himself instead of the pedantic old novice master, they thought they were ahead only because they had got such an early start.

When he looked back on his youth, it seemed to Philip that there had been a brief Golden Age, a year or perhaps less, between the end of his rebellion and the onslaught of fleshly lust. Then came the agonizing era of impure thoughts, nocturnal emissions, dreadfully embarrassing sessions with his confessor (who was the abbot), endless penances and mortification of the flesh with scourges.

Lust never completely ceased to afflict him, but it did eventually become less important, so that it bothered him only now and again, on the rare occasions when his mind and body were idle; like an old injury that still hurts in wet weather.

Francis had fought this battle a little later, and although he had not confided to Philip on the subject, Philip had the impression that Francis had struggled less bravely against evil desires, and had taken his defeats rather too cheerfully. However, the main thing was that they had both made their peace with the passions that were the greatest enemy of the monastic life.

As Philip worked with the cellarer, so Francis worked for the prior, Abbot Peter's deputy. When the cellarer died, Philip was twenty-one, and despite his youth he took over the job. And when Francis reached the age of twenty-one the abbot proposed to create a new post for him, that of sub-prior. But this proposal precipitated a crisis. Francis begged to be excused the responsibility, and while he was at it he asked to be released from the monastery. He wanted to be ordained as a priest and serve God in the world outside.

Philip was astonished and horrified. The idea that one of them might leave the monastery had never occurred to him, and now it was as disconcerting as if he had learned that he was the heir to the throne. But, after much hand-wringing and heart-searching, it happened, and Francis went off into the world, before long to become chaplain to the earl of Gloucester.

Before this happened Philip had seen his future very simply, when he had thought of it at all: he would be a monk, live a humble and obedient life, and in his old age, perhaps, become abbot, and strive to live up to the example set by Peter. Now he wondered whether God intended some other destiny for him. He remembered the parable of the talents: God expected his servants to increase his kingdom, not merely to conserve it. With some trepidation he shared these thoughts with Abbot Peter, fully aware that he risked a reprimand for being puffed up with pride.

To his surprise, the abbot said: "I've been wondering how long it would take you to realize this. Of *course* you're destined for something else. Born within sight of a monastery, orphaned at six, raised by monks, made cellarer at twenty-one—God does not take that much trouble over the formation of a man who is going to spend his life in a small monastery on a bleak hilltop in a remote mountain principality. There isn't enough scope for you here. You must leave this place."

Philip was stunned by this, but before leaving the abbot a question occurred to him, and he blurted it out. "If this monastery is so unimportant, why did God put *you* here?"

Abbot Peter smiled. "Perhaps to take care of you."

Later that year the abbot went to Canterbury to pay his respects to the archbishop, and when he came back he said to Philip: "I have given you to the prior of Kingsbridge."

Philip was daunted. Kingsbridge Priory was one of the biggest and most important monasteries in the land. It was a cathedral priory: its church was a cathedral church, the seat of a bishop, and the bishop was technically the abbot of the monastery, although in practice it was ruled by its prior.

"Prior James is an old friend," Abbot Peter told Philip. "In the last few years he has become rather dispirited, I don't know why. Anyway, Kingsbridge needs young blood. In particular, James is having trouble with one of his cells, a little place in the forest, and he desperately needs a completely reliable man to take over the cell and set it back on the path of godliness."

"So I'm to be prior of the cell?" Philip said in surprise.

The abbot nodded. "And if we're right in thinking that God has much work for you to do, we can expect that he will help you to resolve whatever problems this cell has."

"And if we're wrong?"

"You can always come back here and be my cellarer. But we're not wrong, my son; you'll see."

His farewells were tearful. He had spent seventeen years here, and the monks were his family, more real to him now than the parents who had been savagely taken from him. He would probably never see these monks again, and he was sad.

Kingsbridge overawed him at first. The walled monastery was bigger than many villages; the cathedral church was a vast, gloomy cavern; the prior's house a small palace. But once he got used to its sheer size he saw the signs of that dispiritedness that Abbot Peter had noted in his old friend the prior. The church was visibly in need of major repairs; the prayers were gabbled hastily; the rules of silence were breached constantly; and there were too many servants, more servants than monks. Philip quickly got over being awed and became angry. He wanted to take Prior James by the throat and shake him and say: "How *dare* you do this? How dare you give hasty prayers to God? How dare you allow novices to play at dice and monks to keep pet dogs? How dare you live in a palace, surrounded by servants, while God's church is falling into ruin?" He said nothing of the kind, of course. He had a brief, formal interview with Prior James, a tall, thin, stooped man who seemed to have the weight of the world's troubles on his rounded shoulders. Then he talked to the sub-prior, Remigius. At the start of the conversation Philip hinted that he thought the priory might be overdue for some changes, expecting that its deputy leader would agree wholeheartedly; but Remigius looked down his nose at Philip, as if to say *Who do you think you are?*, and changed the subject.

Remigius said that the cell of St-John-in-the-Forest had been established three years earlier with some land and property, and it should have been self-supporting by now, but in fact it was still dependent on supplies from the mother house. There were other problems: a deacon who happened to spend the night there had criticized the conduct of services; travelers alleged they had been robbed by monks in that area; there were rumors of impurity. . . . The fact that Remigius was unable or unwilling to give exact details was just another sign of the indolent way the whole organization was being run. Philip left trembling with rage. A monastery was supposed to glorify God. If it failed to do that, it was nothing. Kingsbridge Priory was worse than nothing. It shamed God by its slothfulness. But Philip could do nothing about it. The best he could hope for was to reform one of Kingsbridge's cells.

On the two-day ride to the cell in the forest he mulled over the scanty information he had been given and prayerfully considered his approach. He would do well to tread softly at first, he decided. Normally a prior was elected by the monks; but in the case of a cell, which was just an outpost of the main monastery, the prior of the mother house might simply choose. So Philip had not been asked to submit himself for election, and that meant he could not count on the goodwill of the monks. He would have to feel his way cautiously. He needed to learn more about the problems afflicting the place before he could decide how best to solve them. He had to win the respect and trust of the monks, especially those who were older than he and who might resent his position. Then, when his information was complete and his leadership secure, he would take firm action.

It did not work out that way.

The light was fading on the second day when he reined in his pony on the edge of a clearing and inspected his new home. There was only one stone building, the chapel, in those days. (Philip had built the new stone dormitory the following year.) The other, wooden buildings looked ramshackle. Philip disapproved: everything made by monks was supposed to last, and that meant pigsties as well as cathedrals. As he looked around he noted further evidence of the kind of laxity that had shocked him at Kingsbridge: there were no fences, the hay was spilling out of the barn door, and there was a dunghill next to the fishpond. He felt his face go tense with suppressed reproof, and he said to himself: Softly, softly.

At first he saw no one. This was as it should be, for it was time for vespers and most of the monks would be in the chapel. He touched the pony's flank with his whip and crossed the clearing to a hut that looked like a stable. A youth with straw in his hair and a vacant look on his face popped his head over the door and stared at Philip in surprise.

"What's your name?" Philip said, and then, after a moment's shyness, he added: "My son."

"They call me Johnny Eightpence," the youngster said.

Philip dismounted and handed him the reins. "Well, Johnny Eightpence, you can unsaddle my horse."

"Yes, Father." He looped the reins over a rail and moved away.

"Where are you going?" Philip said sharply.

"To tell the brothers that a stranger is here."

"You must practice obedience, Johnny. Unsaddle my horse. I will tell the brothers that I'm here."

"Yes, Father." Looking frightened, Johnny bent to his task.

Philip looked around. In the middle of the clearing was a long building like a great hall. Near it was a small round building with smoke rising from a hole in its roof. That would be the kitchen. He decided to see what was for supper. In strict monasteries only one meal was served each day, dinner at noon; but this was evidently not a strict establishment, and there would be a light supper after vespers, some bread with cheese or salt fish, or perhaps a bowl of barley broth made with herbs. However, as he approached the kitchen he smelled the unmistakable, mouth-watering aroma of roasting meat. He stopped, frowning, then went in.

Two monks and a boy were sitting around the central hearth. As Philip watched, one of the monks passed a jug to the other, who drank from it. The boy was turning a spit, and on the spit was a small pig.

They looked up in surprise as Philip stepped into the light. Without speaking, he took the jug from the monk and sniffed it. Then he said: "Why are you drinking wine?"

"Because it makes my heart glad, stranger," said the monk. "Have some—drink deep."

Clearly they had not been warned to expect their new prior. Equally clearly they had no fear of the consequences if a passing monk should report their behavior to Kingsbridge. Philip had an urge to break the wine jug over the man's head, but he took a deep breath and spoke mildly. "Poor men's children go hungry to provide meat and drink for us," he said. "This is done for the glory of God, not to make our hearts glad. No more wine for you tonight." He turned away, carrying the jug.

As he walked out he heard the monk say: "Who do you think you are?" He made no reply. They would find out soon enough.

He left the jug on the ground outside the kitchen and walked across the clearing toward the chapel, clenching and unclenching his fists, trying to control his anger. Don't be precipitate, he told himself. Be cautious. Take your time.

He paused for a moment in the little porch of the chapel, calming himself, then softly pushed the big oak door and went silently in.

A dozen or so monks and a few novices stood with their backs to him in ragged rows. Facing them was the sacrist, reading from an open book. He spoke the service rapidly and the monks muttered the responses perfunctorily. Three candles of uneven length sputtered on a dirty altarcloth.

At the back, two young monks were holding a conversation, ignoring the service and discussing something in an animated fashion. As Philip drew level, one said something funny, and the other laughed aloud, drowning the gabbled words of the sacrist. This was the last straw for Philip, and all thought of treading softly disappeared from his mind. He opened his mouth and shouted at the top of his voice: "BE SILENT!"

The laughter was cut off. The sacrist stopped reading. The chapel fell silent, and the monks turned around and stared at Philip.

He reached out to the monk who had laughed and grabbed him by the ear. He was about Philip's age, and taller, but he was too surprised to resist as Philip pulled his head down. "On your knees!" Philip yelled. For a moment it looked as if the monk might try to struggle free; but he knew he was in the wrong, and, as Philip had anticipated, his resistance was sapped by his guilty conscience; and when Philip tugged harder on his ear the young man knelt.

"All of you," Philip commanded. "On your knees!"

They had all taken vows of obedience, and the scandalous indiscipline under which they had evidently been living recently was not enough to erase the habit of years. Half the monks and all the novices knelt.

"You've all broken your vows," Philip said, letting his contempt show. "You're blasphemers, every one." He looked around, meeting their eyes. "Your repentance begins now," he said finally.

Slowly they knelt, one by one, until only the sacrist was left standing. He was a fleshy, sleepy-eyed man about twenty years older than Philip. Philip approached him, stepping around the kneeling monks. "Give me the book," he said.

The sacrist stared defiantly back and said nothing.

Philip reached out and lightly grasped the big volume. The sacrist tightened his grip. Philip hesitated. He had spent two days deciding to be cautious and move slowly, yet here he was, with the dust of the road still on his feet, risking everything in a stand-up confrontation with a man he knew nothing about. "Give me the book, and get down on your knees," he repeated.

There was the hint of a sneer on the sacrist's face. "Who are you?" he said.

Philip hesitated again. It was obvious that he was a monk, from his robes and his haircut; and they all must have guessed, from his behavior, that he was in a position of authority; but it was not yet clear whether his rank placed him over the sacrist. All he had to say was *I am your new prior,* but he did not want to. Suddenly it seemed very important that he should prevail by sheer weight of moral authority.

The sacrist sensed his uncertainty and took advantage of it. "Tell us all, please," he said with mock courtesy. "Who is it that commands us to kneel in his presence?"

All hesitation left Philip in a rush, and he thought: God is with me, so what am I afraid of? He took a deep breath, and his words came out in a roar that echoed from the paved floor to the stone-vaulted ceiling. "It is God who commands you to kneel in *his* presence!" he thundered.

The sacrist looked a fraction less confident. Philip seized his chance and snatched the book. The sacrist had lost all authority now, and at last, reluctantly, he knelt.

Hiding his relief, Philip looked around at them all and said: "I am your new prior."

He made them remain kneeling while he read the service. It took a long time, because he made them repeat the responses again and again until they could speak them in perfect unison. Then he led them in silence out of the chapel and across the clearing to the refectory. He sent the roast pork back to the kitchen and ordered bread and weak beer, and he nominated a monk to read aloud while they ate. As soon as they had finished he led them, still in silence, to the dormitory.

He ordered the prior's bedding brought in from the separate prior's house: he would sleep in the same room as the monks. It was the simplest and most effective way to prevent sins of impurity.

He did not sleep at all the first night, but sat up with a candle, praying silently, until it was midnight and time to wake the monks for matins. He went through that service quickly, to let them know he was not completely merciless. They went back to bed, but Philip did not sleep.

He went out at dawn, before they woke, and looked around, thinking about the day ahead. One of the fields had recently been reclaimed from the forest, and right in the middle of it was the huge stump of what must have been a massive oak tree. That gave him an idea.

After the service of prime, and breakfast, he took them all out into the field with ropes and axes, and they spent the morning uprooting the enormous stump, half of them heaving on the ropes while the other half attacked the roots with axes, all saying "He-ee-eave" together. When the stump finally came up, Philip gave them all beer, bread, and a slice of the pork he had denied them at supper.

That was not the end of the problems, but it was the beginning of solutions. From the start he refused to ask the mother house for anything but grain for bread and candles for the chapel. The knowledge that they would get no meat other than what they raised or trapped themselves turned the monks into meticulous livestock husbandmen and bird-snarers; and whereas they had previously looked upon the services as a way of escaping work, they now were glad when Philip cut down the hours spent in chapel so that they could have more time in the fields.

After two years they were self-sufficient, and after another two they were supplying Kingsbridge Priory with meat, game, and a cheese made from goat's milk which became a coveted delicacy. The cell prospered, the services were irreproachable, and the brothers were healthy and happy.

Philip would have been content—but the mother house, Kingsbridge Priory, was going from bad to worse.

It should have been one of the leading religious centers in the kingdom, bustling with activity, its library visited by foreign scholars, its prior consulted by barons, its shrines attracting pilgrims from all over the country, its hospitality renowned by the nobility, its charity famous among the poor. But the church was crumbling, half the monastic buildings were empty, and the priory was in debt to moneylenders. Philip went to Kingsbridge at least once a year, and each time he came back seething with anger at the way in which wealth, which had been given by devout worshipers and increased by dedicated monks, was being dissipated carelessly like the inheritance of the prodigal son.

Part of the problem was the location of the priory. Kingsbridge was a small village on a back road that led nowhere. Since the time of the first King William—who had been called the Conqueror, or the Bastard, depending on who was speaking—most cathedrals had been transferred to large towns; but Kingsbridge had escaped this shake-up. However, that was not an insuperable problem, in Philip's view: a busy monastery with a cathedral church should be a town in itself.

The real trouble was the lethargy of old Prior James. With a limp hand on the tiller, the ship was blown about at hazard and went nowhere.

And, to Philip's bitter regret, Kingsbridge Priory would continue to decline while Prior James was still alive.

They wrapped the baby in clean linen and laid him in a large bread-basket for a cradle. With his tiny belly full of goat's milk he fell asleep. Philip put Johnny Eightpence in charge of him, for despite being somewhat half-witted, Johnny had a gentle touch with creatures that were small and frail.

Philip was agog to know what had brought Francis to the monastery. He dropped hints during dinner, but Francis did not respond, and Philip had to suppress his curiosity.

After dinner it was study hour. They had no proper cloisters here, but the monks could sit in the porch of the chapel and read, or walk up and down the clearing. They were allowed to go into the kitchen from time to time to warm themselves by the fire, as was the custom. Philip and Francis walked around the edge of the clearing, side by side, as they had often walked in the cloisters at the monastery in Wales; and Francis began to speak.

"King Henry has always treated the Church as if it were a subordinate part of his kingdom," he began. "He has issued orders to bishops, imposed taxes, and prevented the direct exercise of papal authority."

"I know," Philip said. "So what?"

"King Henry is dead."

Philip stopped in his tracks. He had not expected *that*.

Francis went on: "He died at his hunting lodge at Lyons-la-Forêt, in Normandy, after a meal of lampreys, which he loved, although they always disagreed with him."

"When?"

"Today is the first day of the year, so it was a month ago exactly."

Philip was quite shocked. Henry had been king since before Philip was born. He had never lived through the death of a king, but he knew it meant trouble, and possibly war. "What happens now?" he said anxiously.

They resumed walking. Francis said: "The problem is that the king's heir was killed at sea, many years ago—you may remember it."

"I do." Philip had been twelve years old. It was the first event of national importance to penetrate his boyish consciousness, and it had made him aware of the world outside the monastery. The king's son had died in the wreck of a vessel called the White Ship, just off Cherbourg. Abbot Peter, who told young Philip all this, had been worried that war and anarchy would follow the death of the heir; but in the event, King Henry kept control, and life went on undisturbed for Philip and Francis.

"The king had many other children, of course," Francis went on. "At least twenty of them, including my own lord, Earl Robert of Gloucester; but as you know, they are all bastards. Despite his rampant fecundity he managed to father only one other legitimate child—and that was a girl, Maud. A bastard can't inherit the throne, but a woman is almost as bad."

"Didn't King Henry nominate an heir?" Philip said.

"Yes, he chose Maud. She has a son, also called Henry. It was the old king's dearest wish that his grandson should inherit the throne. But the boy is not yet three years old. So the king made the barons swear fealty to Maud."

Philip was puzzled. "If the king made Maud his heir, and the barons have already sworn loyalty to her . . . what's the problem?"

"Court life is never that simple," Francis said. "Maud is married to Geoffrey of Anjou. Anjou and Normandy have been rivals for generations. Our Norman overlords hate the Angevins. Frankly, it was very optimistic of the old king to expect that a crowd of Anglo-Norman barons would hand over England and Normandy to an Angevin, oath or no oath."

Philip was somewhat bemused by his younger brother's knowing and disrespectful attitude to the most important men in the land. "How do you know all this?"

"The barons gathered at Le Neubourg to decide what to do. Needless to say, my own lord, Earl Robert, was there; and I went with him to write his letters."

Philip looked quizzically at his brother, thinking how different Francis's life must be from his own. Then he remembered something. "Earl Robert is the eldest son of the old king, isn't he?"

"Yes, and he is *very* ambitious; but he accepts the general view, that bastards have to conquer their kingdoms, not inherit them."

"Who else is there?"

"King Henry had three nephews, the sons of his sister. The eldest is Theobald of Blois; then there is Stephen, much loved by the dead king and endowed by him with vast estates here in England; and the baby of the family, Henry, whom you know as the bishop of Winchester. The barons favored the eldest, Theobald, according to a tradition which you probably think perfectly reasonable." Francis looked at Philip and grinned.

"Perfectly reasonable," Philip said with a smile. "So Theobald is our new king?"

Francis shook his head. "He thought he was, but we younger sons have a way of pushing ourselves to the fore." They reached the farthest corner of the clearing and turned. "While Theobald was graciously accepting the homage of the barons, Stephen crossed the Channel to England and dashed to Winchester, and with the help of baby brother Henry, the bishop, he seized the castle there and— most important of all—the royal treasury."

Philip was about to say: So *Stephen* is our new ruler. But he bit his tongue: he had said that about Maud and Theobald and had been wrong both times.

Francis went on: "Stephen needed only one more thing to make his victory secure: the support of the Church. For until he could be crowned at Westminster by the archbishop he would not *really* be king."

"But surely that was easy," Philip said. "His brother Henry is one of the most important priests in the land—bishop of Winchester, abbot of Glastonbury, as rich as Solomon and almost as powerful as the archbishop of Canterbury. And if Bishop Henry wasn't intending to support him, why had he helped him take Winchester?"

Francis nodded. "I must say that Bishop Henry's operations throughout this crisis have been brilliant. You see, he wasn't helping Stephen out of brotherly love."

"Then what was his motivation?"

"A few minutes ago I reminded you of how the late King Henry had treated the Church as if it were just another part of his kingdom. Bishop Henry wants to ensure that our new king, whoever he may be, will treat the Church better. So before he would guarantee support, *Henry made Stephen swear a solemn oath to preserve the rights and privileges of the Church.*"

Philip was impressed. Stephen's relationship with the Church had been defined, right at the start of his reign, on the Church's terms. But perhaps even more important was the precedent. The Church had to crown kings but until now it had not had the right to lay down conditions. The time might come when no king could come to power without first striking a deal with the Church. "This could mean a lot to us," Philip said.

"Stephen may break his promises, of course," Francis said. "But all the same you're right. He will never be able to be quite as ruthless with the Church as Henry was. But there's another danger. Two of the barons were bitterly aggrieved by what Stephen did. One was Bartholomew, the earl of Shiring."

"I know of him. Shiring is only a day's journey from here. Bartholomew is said to be a devout man."

"Perhaps he is. All I know is that he is a self-righteous and stiff-necked baron who will not renege on his loyalty oath to Maud, despite the promise of a pardon."

"And the other discontented baron?"

"My own Robert of Gloucester. I told you he was ambitious. His soul is tormented by the thought that if only he were legitimate, he would be king. He wants to put his half sister on the throne, believing that she will rely so heavily on her brother for guidance and advice that he will be king in everything but name."

"Is he going to do anything about it?"

"I'm afraid so." Francis lowered his voice, although there was no one near. "Robert and Bartholomew, together with Maud and her husband, are going to foment a rebellion. They plan to unseat Stephen and put Maud on the throne."

Philip stopped walking. "Which would undo everything the bishop of Winchester has achieved!" He grasped his brother's arm. "But, Francis . . ."

"I know what you're thinking." Suddenly all Francis's cockiness left him, and he looked anxious and frightened. "If Earl Robert knew I'd even told you, he would hang me. He trusts me completely. But my ultimate loyalty is to the Church—it has to be."

"But what can you do?"

"I thought of seeking an audience with the new king, and telling him everything. Of course, the two rebel earls would deny it all, and I would be hanged for treachery; but the rebellion would be frustrated and I would go to heaven."

Philip shook his head. "We're taught that it's vain to *seek* martyrdom."

"And I think God has more work for me to do here on earth. I'm in a position of trust in the household of a great baron, and if I stay there and advance myself by hard work, there's a lot I could do to promote the rights of the Church and the rule of law."

"Is there any other way . . . ?"

Francis looked Philip in the eye. "That's why I'm here."

Philip felt a shiver of fear. Francis was going to ask him to get involved, of course; there was no other reason for him to reveal this dreadful secret.

Francis went on: "I can't betray the rebellion, but *you* can."

Philip said: "Jesus Christ and all the saints, preserve me."

"If the plot is uncovered here, in the south, no suspicion will fall on the Gloucester household. Nobody knows I'm here; nobody even knows you're my brother. You could think of some plausible explanation of how you came by the information: you might have seen men-at-arms assembling, or it might be that someone in Earl Bartholomew's household revealed the plot while confessing his sins to a priest you know."

Philip pulled his cloak closer around him, shivering. It seemed to have turned colder suddenly. This was dangerous, very dangerous. They were talking about meddling in royal politics, which regularly killed experienced practitioners. Outsiders such as Philip were foolish to get involved.

But there was so much at stake. Philip could not stand by and see a rebellion against a king chosen by the Church, not when he had a chance to prevent it. And dangerous though it would be for Philip, it would be suicidal for Francis to expose the plot.

Philip said: "What's the rebels' plan?"

"Earl Bartholomew is on his way back to Shiring right now. From there he will send out messages to his followers all over the south of England. Earl Robert will arrive in Gloucester a day or two later and muster his forces in the West Country. Finally Brian Fitzcount, who holds Wallingford Castle, will close its gates; and the whole of southwest England will belong to the rebels without a fight."

"Then it's almost too late!" Philip said.

"Not really. We've got about a week. But you'll have to act quickly."

Philip realized with a sinking feeling that he had more or less made up his mind to do it. "I don't know whom to tell," he said. "One would normally go to the earl, but in this case he's the culprit. The sheriff is probably on his side. We have to think of someone who is certain to be on our side."

"The prior of Kingsbridge?"

"My prior is old and tired. The likelihood is that he would do nothing."

"There must be someone."

"There's the bishop." Philip had never actually spoken to the bishop of Kingsbridge, but he would be sure to receive Philip and listen to him; he would automatically side with Stephen because Stephen was the Church's choice; and he was powerful enough to do something about it.

Francis said: "Where does the bishop live?"

"It's a day and a half from here."

"You'd better leave today."

"Yes," Philip said with a heavy heart.

Francis looked remorseful. "I wish it were someone else."

"So do I," Philip said feelingly. "So do I."

Philip called the monks into the little chapel and told them that the king had died. "We must pray for a peaceful succession and a new king who will love the Church more than the late Henry," he said. But he did not tell them that the key to a peaceful succession had somehow fallen into his own hands. Instead he said: "There is other news that obliges me to visit our mother house at Kingsbridge. I must leave right away."

The sub-prior would read the services and the cellarer would run the farm, but neither of them was a match for Peter of Wareham, and Philip was afraid that if he stayed away long Peter might make so much trouble that there would be no monastery left when he returned. He had not been able to think up a way of controlling Peter without bruising his self-esteem, and now there was no time left, so he had to do the best he could.

"Earlier today we talked about gluttony," he said after a pause. "Brother Peter deserves our thanks for reminding us that when God blesses our farm and gives us wealth, it is not so that we should become fat and comfortable, but for his greater glory. It is part of our holy duty to share our riches with the poor. Until now we have neglected this duty, mainly because here in the forest we don't have anybody to share with. Brother Peter has reminded us that it's our duty to go out and seek the poor, so that we may bring them relief."

The monks were surprised: they had imagined that the subject of gluttony had been closed. Peter himself was looking uncertain. He was pleased to be the center of attention again, but he was wary of what Philip might have up his sleeve—quite rightly.

"I have decided," Philip went on, "that each week we will give to the poor one penny for every monk in our community. If this means we all have to eat a little less, we will rejoice in the prospect of our heavenly reward. More important, we must make sure that our pennies are well spent. When you give a poor man a penny to buy bread for his family, he may go straight to the alehouse and get drunk, then go home and beat his wife, who would therefore have been better off without your charity. Better to give him the bread; better still to give the bread to his children. Giving alms is a holy task that must be done with as much diligence as healing the sick or educating the young. For this reason, many monastic houses appoint an almoner, to be responsible for almsgiving. We will do the same."

Philip looked around. They were all alert and interested. Peter wore a gratified look, evidently having decided that this was a victory for him. No one had guessed what was coming.

"The almoner's job is hard work. He will have to walk to the nearest towns and villages, frequently to Winchester. There he will go among the meanest, dirtiest, ugliest and most vicious classes of people, for such are the poor. He must pray for them when they blaspheme, visit them when they're sick, and forgive them when they try to cheat and rob him. He will need strength, humility and endless patience. He will miss the comfort of this community, for he will be away more than he is with us."

He looked around once again. Now they were all wary, for none of them wanted this job. He let his gaze rest on Peter of Wareham. Peter realized what was coming, and his face fell.

"It was Peter who drew our attention to our shortcomings in this area," Philip said slowly, "so I have decided that it shall be Peter who has the honor of being our almoner." He smiled. "You can begin today."

Peter's face was as black as thunder.

You'll be away too much to cause trouble, Philip thought; and close contact with the vile, verminous poor of Winchester's stinking alleyways will temper your scorn of soft living.

However, Peter evidently saw this as a punishment, pure and simple, and he looked at Philip with an expression of such hatred that for a moment Philip quailed.

He tore his gaze away and looked at the others. "After the death of a king there is always danger and uncertainty," he said. "Pray for me while I'm away."

II

At noon on the second day of his journey, Prior Philip was within a few miles of the bishop's palace. His bowels felt watery as he got nearer. He had thought of a story to explain how he came to know of the planned rebellion. But the bishop might not believe his story; or, believing it, he might demand proof. Worse still—and this possibility had not occurred to Philip until after he parted company with Francis—it was conceivable, albeit unlikely, that the bishop was one of the conspirators, and supported the rebellion. He might be a crony of the earl of Shiring. It was not unknown for bishops to put their own interests before those of the Church.

The bishop could torture Philip to make him reveal his source of information. Of course he had no right to, but then he had no right to plot against the king, either. Philip recalled the instruments of torture depicted in paintings of hell. Such paintings were inspired by what went on in the dungeons of barons and bishops. Philip did not feel he had the strength for a martyr's death.

When he saw a group of travelers on foot in the road ahead of him his first instinct was to rein in to avoid passing them, for he was alone, and there were plenty of footpads who would not scruple to rob a monk. Then he saw that two of the figures were children, and another was a woman. A family group was usually safe. He trotted to catch them.

As he drew nearer he could see them more clearly. They were a tall man, a small woman, a youth almost as big as the man, and two children. They were visibly poor: they carried no little bundles of precious possessions and they were dressed in rags. The man was big-boned, but emaciated, as if he were dying of a wasting disease— or just starving. He looked warily at Philip, and drew the children closer to him with a touch and a murmured word. Philip had at first guessed his age at fifty, but now he saw that the man was in his thirties, although his face was lined with care.

The woman said: "What ho, monk."

Philip looked sharply at her. It was unusual for a woman to speak before her husband did, and while *monk* was not exactly impolite, it would have been more respectful to say *brother* or *father*.

The woman was younger than the man by about ten years, and she had deep-set eyes of an unusual pale gold color that gave her a rather arresting appearance. Philip felt she was dangerous.

"Good day, Father," the man said, as if to apologize for his wife's brusqueness.

"God bless you," said Philip, slowing his mare. "Who are you?"

"Tom, a master builder, seeking work."

"And not finding any, I'd guess."

"That's the truth."

Philip nodded. It was a common story. Building craftsmen normally wandered in search of work, and sometimes they did not find it, either through bad luck or because not many people were building. Such men often took advantage of the hospitality of monasteries. If they had recently been in work they gave generous donations when they left, although after they had been on the road a while they might have nothing to offer. Giving an equally warm welcome to both kinds was sometimes a trial of monastic charity.

This builder was definitely the penniless kind, although his wife looked well enough. Philip said: "Well, I have food in my saddle-bag, and it is dinnertime, and charity is a holy duty; so if you and your family will eat with me, I shall get a reward in heaven, as well as some company while I dine."

"That's good of you," said Tom. He looked at the woman. She gave the slightest of shrugs, then a little nod. Almost without pause the man said: "We'll accept your charity, and thank you."

"Thank God, not me," Philip said automatically.

The woman said: "Thank the peasants whose tithes provided the food."

Here's a sharp one, Philip thought; but he said nothing.

They stopped at a small clearing where Philip's pony could graze the tired winter grass. Philip was secretly glad of the excuse to postpone his arrival at the palace and delay the dreaded interview with the bishop. The builder said that he too was heading for the bishop's palace, hoping that the bishop might want to make repairs or even build an extension. While they were talking, Philip surreptitiously studied the family. The woman seemed too young to be the mother of the older boy. He was like a calf, strong and awkward and stupid-looking. The other boy was small and odd, with carrot-colored hair, snow-white skin and protuberant bright-blue eyes; and he had a way of staring intently at things, with an absent expression that reminded Philip of poor Johnny Eightpence, except that unlike Johnny this boy would give you a very adult, knowing look when you caught his eye. In his way he was as disturbing as his mother, Philip found. The third child was a girl of about six years. She was crying intermittently, and her father watched her constantly with affectionate concern, and gave her a comforting pat from time to time, although he said nothing to her. He was evidently very fond of her. He also touched his wife, once, and Philip saw a look of lust flash between them when their eyes met.

The woman sent the children to find broad leaves to use as platters. Philip opened his saddlebags. Tom said: "Where is your monastery, Father?"

"In the forest, a day's journey from here, to the west." The woman looked up sharply, and Tom raised his eyebrows. "Do you know it?" Philip asked.

For some reason Tom looked awkward. "We must have passed near it on the way from Salisbury," he said.

"Oh, yes, you would have, but it's a long way off the main road, so you wouldn't have seen it, unless you knew where it was and went to find it."

"Ah, I see," said Tom, but his mind seemed to be elsewhere.

Philip was struck by a thought. "Tell me something—did you come across a woman on the road? Probably very young, alone, and, ah, with child?"

"No," said Tom. His tone was casual but Philip had the feeling he was intensely interested. "Why do you ask?"

Philip smiled. "I'll tell you. Early yesterday a baby was found in the forest and brought to my monastery. It's a boy, and I don't think he was even as much as a day old. He must have been born that night. So the mother must have been in the area at the same time as you."

"We didn't see anyone," Tom repeated. "What did you do with the baby?"

"Fed him goat's milk. He seems to be thriving on it."

They were both looking at Philip intently. It was, he thought, a story to touch anyone's heart. After a moment Tom said: "And you're searching for the mother?"

"Oh, no. My question was casual. If I came across her, of course, I would give the baby back to her; but it's clear she doesn't want it, and she'll make sure she can't be found."

"Then what will happen to the boy?"

"We'll raise him at the monastery. He'll be a child of God. That's how I myself was brought up, and my brother too. Our parents were taken from us when we were young, and after that the abbot was our father, and the monks were our family. We were fed, we were warm, and we learned our letters."

The woman said: "And you both became monks." She said it with a touch of irony, as if it proved that the monastery's charity was ultimately self-interested.

Philip was glad to be able to contradict her. "No, my brother left the order."

The children came back. They had not found any broad leaves—it was not easy in winter—so they would eat without platters. Philip gave them all bread and cheese. They tore into the food like starving animals. "We make this cheese at my monastery," he said. "Most people like it when it's new, like this, but it's even better if you leave it to ripen." They were too hungry to care. They finished the bread and cheese in no time. Philip had three pears. He fished them out of his bag and gave them to Tom. Tom gave one to each of the children.

Philip got to his feet. "I'll pray that you find work."

Tom said: "If you think of it, Father, mention me to the bishop. You know our need, and you've found us honest."

"I will."

Tom held the horse while Philip mounted. "You're a good man, father," he said, and Philip saw to his surprise that there were tears in Tom's eyes.

"God be with you," Philip said.

Tom held the horse's head a moment longer. "The baby you told us about—the foundling." He spoke softly, as if he did not want the children to hear. "Did you . . . have you named him yet?"

"Yes. We call him Jonathan, which means a gift from God."

"Jonathan. I like that." Tom released the horse.

Philip looked at him curiously for a moment, then kicked his horse and trotted away.

The bishop of Kingsbridge did not live at Kingsbridge. His palace stood on a south-facing hillside in a lush valley a full day's journey from the cold stone cathedral and its mournful monks. He preferred it this way, for too much churchgoing would get in the way of his other duties of collecting rents, dispensing justice and maneuvering at the royal court. It suited the monks, too, for the farther away the bishop was, the less he interfered with them.

It was cold enough for snow on the afternoon that Philip arrived there. A bitter wind whipped across the bishop's valley, and low gray clouds frowned on his hillside manor house. It was not a castle, but it was nonetheless well defended. The woodland had been cleared for a hundred yards all around. The house was enclosed by a stout wooden fence the height of a man, with a rainwater ditch outside it. The guard at the gate had a slovenly manner but his sword was heavy.

The palace was a fine stone house built in the shape of the letter E. The ground floor was an undercroft, its stout walls pierced by several heavy doors but no windows. One door was open, and through it Philip could see barrels and sacks in the gloom. The other doors were closed and chained. Philip wondered what was behind them: when the bishop had prisoners, that was where they would languish.

The short stroke of the E was an exterior staircase leading to the living quarters above the undercroft. The main room, the upright stroke of the E, would be the hall. The two rooms forming the head and foot of the E would be a chapel and a bedroom, Philip guessed. There were small shuttered windows like beady eyes looking suspiciously out at the world.

Within the compound were a kitchen and a bakehouse of stone as well as wooden stables and a barn. All the buildings were in good repair—which was unfortunate for Tom Builder, Philip thought.

There were several good horses in the stable, including a couple of chargers, and a handful of men-at-arms were scattered around, killing time. Perhaps the bishop had visitors.

Philip left his horse with a stableboy and climbed the steps with a sense of foreboding. The whole place had a distressingly military feel. Where were the queues of petitioners with grievances, the mothers with babies to be blessed? He was entering an unfamiliar world, and he was in possession of a dangerous secret. It might be a long time before I leave here, he thought fearfully. I wish Francis had not come to me.

He reached the top of the stairs. Such unworthy thoughts, he told himself. Here I have a chance to serve God and the Church, and I react by worrying about my own safety. Some men face danger every day, in battle, at sea, and on hazardous pilgrimages or crusades. Even a monk must suffer a little fear and trembling sometimes.

He took a deep breath and went in.

The hall was dim and smoky. Philip closed the door quickly to keep out the cold air, then peered into the gloom. A big fire blazed on the opposite side of the room. That and the small windows provided the only light. Around the fireplace was a group of men, some in clerical clothes and others in the expensive but well-worn garments of minor gentry. They were involved in a serious discussion, their voices low and businesslike. Their seats were scattered randomly, but they all looked at and spoke to a priest who sat in the middle of the group like a spider at the center of a web. He was a thin man, and the way his long legs were splayed apart and his long arms draped over the arms of the chair made him look as if he were about to spring. He had lank, jet-black hair and a pale face with a sharp nose, and his black clothes made him at once handsome and menacing.

He was not the bishop.

A steward got up from a seat beside the door and said to Philip: "Good day, Father. Who do you want to see?" At the same time a hound lying by the fire raised its head and growled. The man in black looked up quickly, saw Philip, and stopped the conversation instantly with a raised hand. "What is it?" he said brusquely.

"Good day," Philip said politely. "I've come to see the bishop."

"He's not here," the priest said dismissively.

Philip's heart sank. He had been dreading the interview and its dangers, but now he felt let down. What was he going to do with his awful secret? He said to the priest: "When do you expect him back?"

"We don't know. What's your business with him?"

The priest's tone was a little abrupt, and Philip was stung. "God's business," he said sharply. "Who are you?"

The priest raised his eyebrows, as if surprised to be challenged, and the other men became suddenly quiet, like people expecting an explosion; but after a pause he replied mildly enough. "I'm his archdeacon. My name is Waleran Bigod."

A good name for a priest, Philip thought. He said: "My name is Philip. I'm the prior of the monastery of St-John-in-the-Forest. It's a cell of Kingsbridge Priory."

"I've heard of you," said Waleran. "You're Philip of Gwynedd."

Philip was surprised. He could not imagine why an actual archdeacon should know the name of someone as lowly as himself. But his rank, modest though it was, was enough to change Waleran's attitude. The irritated look went from the archdeacon's face. "Come to the fire," he said. "You'll take a draft of hot wine to warm your blood?" He gestured to someone sitting on a bench against the wall, and a ragged figure sprang up to do his bidding.

Philip approached the fire. Waleran said something in a low voice and the other men got to their feet and began to take their leave. Philip sat down and warmed his hands while Waleran went to the door with his guests. Philip wondered what they had been discussing, and why the archdeacon had not closed the meeting with a prayer.

The ragged servant handed him a wooden cup. He sipped hot, spiced wine and considered his next move. If the bishop was not available, whom could Philip turn to? He thought of going to Earl Bartholomew and simply begging him to reconsider his rebellion. The idea was ludicrous: the earl would put him in a dungeon and throw away the key. That left the sheriff, who was in theory the king's representative in the county. But there was no telling which side the sheriff might take while there was still some doubt about who was going to be king. Still, Philip thought, I might just have to take that risk, in the end. He longed to return to the simple life of the monastery, where his most dangerous enemy was Peter of Wareham.

Waleran's guests departed, and the door closed on the noise of horses in the yard. Waleran returned to the fireside and pulled up a big chair.

Philip was preoccupied with his problem and did not really want to talk to the archdeacon, but he felt obliged to be civil. "I hope I didn't break up your meeting," he said.

Waleran made a deprecatory gesture. "It was due to end," he said. "These things always go on longer than they need to. We were discussing the renewal of leases of diocesan land—the kind of thing that could be settled in a few moments if only people would be decisive." He fluttered a bony hand as if to dismiss all diocesan leases and their holders. "Now, I hear you've done good work at that little cell in the forest."

"I'm surprised you know about it," Philip replied.

"The bishop is *ex officio* abbot of Kingsbridge, so he's bound to take an interest."

Or he has a well-informed archdeacon, Philip thought. He said: "Well, God has blessed us."

"Indeed."

They were speaking Norman French, the language Waleran and his guests had been using, the language of government; but something about Waleran's accent was a little strange, and after a few moments Philip realized that Waleran had the inflections of one who had been brought up to speak English. That meant he was not a Norman aristocrat, but a native who had risen by his own efforts—like Philip.

A moment later this was confirmed when Waleran switched to English to say: "I wish God would confer similar blessings on Kingsbridge Priory."

Philip was not the only one to be troubled by the state of affairs at Kingsbridge, then. Waleran probably knew more about events there than Philip did. Philip said: "How is Prior James?"

"Sick," Waleran replied succinctly.

Then he definitely would not be able to do anything about Earl Bartholomew's insurrection, Philip thought gloomily. He was going to have to go to Shiring and take his chance with the sheriff.

It occurred to him that Waleran was the kind of man who would know everyone of importance in the county. "What is the sheriff of Shiring like?" he asked.

Waleran shrugged. "Ungodly, arrogant, grasping and corrupt. So are all sheriffs. Why do you ask?"

"If I can't talk to the bishop I probably should go and see the sheriff."

"I am in the bishop's confidence, you know," said Waleran with a little smile. "If I can help . . ." He made an openhanded gesture, like a man who is being generous but knows he may be refused.

Philip had relaxed a little, thinking that the moment of crisis had been postponed for a day or two, but now he was filled with trepidation again. Could he trust Archdeacon Waleran? Waleran's nonchalance was studied, he thought: the archdeacon appeared diffident, but in truth he was probably bursting to know what Philip had to say that was so important. However, that was no reason to mistrust him. He seemed a judicious fellow. Was he powerful enough to do anything about the rebellion? If he could not do it himself, he might be able to locate the bishop. It struck Philip that in fact there was a major advantage to the idea of confiding in Waleran; for whereas the bishop might insist on knowing the real source of Philip's information, the archdeacon did not have the authority to do that, and would have to be content with the story Philip told him, whether he believed it or not.

Waleran gave his little smile again. "If you think about it any longer, I shall begin to believe that you mistrust me!"

Philip felt he understood Waleran. Waleran was a man something like himself: young, well-educated, low-born, and intelligent. He was a little too worldly for Philip's taste, pehaps, but this was pardonable in a priest who was obliged to spend so much of his time with lords and ladies, and did not have the benefit of a monk's protected life. Waleran was a devout man at heart, Philip thought. He would do the right thing for the Church.

Philip hesitated on the edge of decision. Until now only he and Francis had known the secret. Once he told a third person, anything could happen. He took a deep breath.

"Three days ago, an injured man came to my monastery in the forest," he began, silently praying forgiveness for lying. "He was an armed man on a fine, fast horse, and he had taken a fall a mile or two away. He must have been riding hard when he fell, for his arm was broken and his ribs were crushed. We set his arm, but there was nothing we could do about his ribs, and he was coughing blood, a sign of internal damage." As he spoke, Philip was watching Waleran's face. So far it showed nothing more than polite interest. "I advised him to confess his sins, for he was in danger of death. He told me a secret."

He hesitated, not sure how much Waleran might have heard of the political news. "I expect you know that Stephen of Blois has claimed the throne of England with the blessing of the Church."

Waleran knew more than Philip. "And he was crowned at Westminster three days before Christmas," he said.

"Already!" Francis had not known that.

"What was the secret?" Waleran said with a touch of impatience.

Philip took the plunge. "Before he died, the horseman told me that his master Bartholomew, earl of Shiring, had conspired with Robert of Gloucester to raise a rebellion against Stephen." He studied Waleran's face, holding his breath.

Waleran's pale cheeks went a shade whiter. He leaned forward in his chair. "Do you think he was telling the truth?" he said urgently.

"A dying man usually tells the truth to his confessor."

"Perhaps he was repeating a rumor that was current in the earl's household."

Philip had not expected Waleran to be skeptical. He improvised hastily. "Oh, no," he said. "He was a messenger sent by Earl Bartholomew to muster the earl's forces in Hampshire."

Waleran's intelligent eyes raked Philip's expression. "Did he have the message in writing?"

"No."

"Any seal, or token of the earl's authority?"

"Nothing." Philip began to perspire slightly. "I gathered he was well known, by the people he was going to see, as an authorized representative of the earl."

"What was his name?"

"Francis," Philip said stupidly, and wanted to bite his tongue. "Just that?"

"He didn't tell me what else he was called." Philip had the feeling that his story was coming unraveled under Waleran's interrogation.

"His weapons and his armor may identify him."

"He had no armor," Philip said desperately. "We buried his

weapons with him—monks have no use for swords. We could dig them up, but I can tell you that they were plain and undistinguished—I don't think you would find clues there. . . ." He had to divert Waleran from this line of inquiry. "What do you think can be done?"

Waleran frowned. "It's hard to know what to do without proof. The conspirators can simply deny the charge, and then the accuser stands condemned." He did not say *especially if the story turns out to be false,* but Philip guessed that was what he was thinking. Waleran went on: "Have you told anyone else?"

Philip shook his head.

"Where are you going when you leave here?"

"Kingsbridge. I had to invent a reason for leaving the cell, so I said I would visit the priory; and now I must do so, to make the lie true."

"Don't speak of this to anyone there."

"I shan't." Philip had not intended to, but he wondered why Waleran was insisting on the point. Perhaps it was self-interest: if he was going to take the risk of exposing the conspiracy, he wanted to be sure to get the credit. He was ambitious. So much the better, for Philip's purpose.

"Leave this with me." Waleran was suddenly brusque again, and the contrast with his previous manner made Philip realize that his amiability could be put on and taken off like a coat. Waleran went on: "You'll go to Kingsbridge Priory now, and forget about the sheriff, won't you."

"Yes." Philip realized it was going to be all right, at least for a while, and a weight rolled off his back. He was not going to be thrown into a dungeon, interrogated by a torturer, or accused of sedition. He had also handed the responsibility to someone else— someone who appeared quite happy to take it on.

He got up and went to the nearest window. It was mid-afternoon, and there was plenty of daylight left. He had an urge to get away from here and leave the secret behind him. "If I go now I can cover eight or ten miles before nightfall," he said.

Waleran did not press him to stay. "That will take you to the village of Bassingbourn. You'll find a bed there. If you set out early in the morning you can be at Kingsbridge by midday."

"Yes." Philip turned from the window and looked at Waleran. The archdeacon was frowning into the fire, deep in thought. Philip watched him for a moment. Waleran did not share his thoughts. Philip wished he knew what was going on in that clever head. "I'll go right away," he said.

Waleran came out of his reverie and grew charming again. He smiled and stood up. "All right," he said. He walked with Philip to the door and then followed him down the stairs to the yard.

A stableboy brought Philip's horse and saddled it. Waleran might have said goodbye then and returned to his fire, but he waited. Philip guessed that he wanted to make sure Philip took the road to Kingsbridge, not the road to Shiring.

Philip mounted, feeling happier than he had when he had arrived. He was about to take his leave when he saw Tom Builder come through the gate with his family in tow. Philip said to Waleran: "This man is a builder I met on the road. He seems like an honest fellow fallen on hard times. If you need any repairs you'll be glad of him."

Waleran made no reply. He was staring at the family as they walked across the compound. All his poise and composure had deserted him. His mouth was open and his eyes were staring. He looked like a man suffering a shock.

"What is it?" Philip said anxiously.

"That woman!" Waleran's voice was just above a whisper.

Philip looked at her. "She's rather beautiful," he said, realizing it for the first time. "But we're taught that it is better for a priest to be chaste. Turn your eyes away, Archdeacon."

Waleran was not listening. "I thought she was dead," he muttered. He seemed to remember Philip suddenly. He tore his gaze from the woman and looked up at Philip, collecting his wits. "Give my regards to the prior of Kingsbridge," he said. Then he slapped Philip's horse's rump, and the animal sprang forward and trotted out through the gate; and by the time Philip had shortened his reins and got the horse under control he was too far away to say goodbye.

III

Philip came within sight of Kingsbridge at about noon on the following day, as Archdeacon Waleran had forecast. He emerged from a wooded hillside and looked out across a landscape of lifeless, frozen fields relieved only by the occasional bare skeleton of a tree. There were no people to be seen, for in the dead of winter there was no work to do on the land. A couple of miles away across the cold countryside, Kingsbridge Cathedral stood on a rise; a huge, squat building like a tomb on a burial mound.

Philip followed the road into a dip and Kingsbridge disappeared from view. His placid pony picked her way carefully along the frosted ruts. Philip was thinking about Archdeacon Waleran. Waleran was so poised and confident and capable that he made Philip feel young and naïve, although there was not much difference in age between them. Waleran had effortlessly controlled the whole meeting: he had got rid of his guests graciously, listened attentively to Philip's tale, homed in immediately on the crucial problem of lack of evidence, swiftly realized that that line of inquiry was fruitless, and then promptly sent Philip on his way—without, Philip now realized, any guarantee that action would be taken.

Philip grinned ruefully as he saw how well he had been manipulated. Waleran had not even promised to tell the bishop what Philip had reported. But Philip felt confident that the large vein of ambition he detected in Waleran would ensure that the information was used somehow. He even had a notion that Waleran might feel a little indebted to him.

Because he was impressed by Waleran, he was all the more intrigued by the archdeacon's single sign of weakness—his reaction to the wife of Tom Builder. To Philip she had seemed obscurely dangerous. Apparently Waleran found her desirable—which might amount to the same thing, of course. However, there was more to it than that. Waleran must have met her before, for he had said *I thought she was dead*. It sounded as if he had sinned with her in the distant past. He certainly had *something* to feel guilty about, judging by the way he had made sure Philip did not stay around to learn more.

Even this guilty secret did not much reduce Philip's opinion of Waleran. Waleran was a priest, not a monk. Chastity had always been an essential part of the monastic way of life, but it had never been enforced for priests. Bishops had mistresses and parish priests had housekeepers. Like the prohibition against evil thoughts, clerical celibacy was a law too harsh to be obeyed. If God could not forgive lascivious priests, there would be very few clergy in heaven.

Kingsbridge reappeared as Philip crested the next rise. The landscape was dominated by the massive church, with its round-headed arches and small, deep windows, just as the village was dominated by the monastery. The west end of the church, which faced Philip, had stubby twin towers, one of which had fallen in a thunderstorm four years ago. It still had not been rebuilt, and the facade had a reproachful look. This view never failed to anger Philip, for the pile of rubble at the entrance of the church was a shameful reminder of the collapse of monastic rectitude at the priory. The monastery buildings, made of the same pale limestone, stood near the church in groups, like conspirators around a throne. Outside the low wall that enclosed the priory was a scatter of ordinary hovels made of timber and mud with thatched roofs, occupied by the peasants who tilled the fields round about and the servants who worked for the monks. A narrow, impatient river hurried across the southwest corner of the village, bringing fresh water to the monastery.

Philip was already feeling bilious as he crossed the river by an old wooden bridge. Kingsbridge Priory brought shame on God's church and the monastic movement, but there was nothing Philip could do about it; and anger and impotence together turned sour in his stomach.

The priory owned the bridge and charged a toll, and as the woodwork creaked with the weight of Philip and his horse, an elderly monk emerged from a shelter on the opposite bank and came forward to move the willow branch that served as a barrier. He recognized Philip and waved. Philip noticed that he was limping, and said: "What's wrong with your foot, Brother Paul?"

"Just a chilblain. It will ease when the spring comes."

He had nothing on his feet but sandals, Philip saw. Paul was a tough old bird but he was too far gone in years to be spending the whole day out-of-doors in this weather. "You should have a fire," Philip said.

"It would be a mercy," said Paul. "But Brother Remigius says the fire would cost more money than the toll brings."

"How much do we charge?"

"A penny for a horse, and a farthing for a man."

"Do many people use the bridge?"

"Oh, yes, plenty."

"Then how is it that we can't afford a fire?"

"Well, the monks don't pay, of course, nor do the priory servants, nor the villagers. So it's just a traveling knight or a tinker every day or two. Then on holy days, when people come from all over the country to hear the services in the cathedral, we gather farthings galore."

"It seems to me we might man the bridge on holy days only, and give you a fire out of the proceeds," said Philip.

Paul looked anxious. "Don't say anything to Remigius, will you? If he thinks I've been complaining he'll be displeased."

"Don't worry," said Philip. He kicked his horse on so that Paul should not see the expression on his face. This kind of foolishness infuriated him. Paul had given his life to the service of God and the monastery, and now in his declining years he was made to suffer pain and cold for the sake of a farthing or two a day. It was not just cruel, it was wasteful, for a patient old man such as Paul could be set to work at some productive task—raising chickens, perhaps— and the priory would benefit by much more than a few farthings. But the prior of Kingsbridge was too old and lethargic to see that, and it seemed that the same must be true of Remigius, the sub-prior. It was a grave sin, Philip thought bitterly, to waste so carelessly the human and material assets that had been given to God in loving piety.

He was in an unforgiving mood as he guided his pony through the spaces between the hovels to the priory gate. The priory was a rectangular enclosure with the church in the middle. The buildings were laid out so that everything to the north and west of the church was public, worldly, secular and practical, whereas what was to the south and east was private, spiritual and holy.

The entrance to the close was therefore at the northwest corner of the rectangle. The gate stood open, and the young monk in the gatehouse waved as Philip trotted through. Just inside the gate, up against the west wall of the enclosure, was the stable, a stout wooden structure rather better built than some of the dwellings for people on the other side of the wall. Two stable hands sat inside on bales of straw. They were not monks, but employees of the priory. They got reluctantly to their feet as if they resented a visitor coming to cause them extra work. The acrid air stung Philip's nostrils, and he could see that the stalls had not been mucked out for three or four weeks. He was not disposed to overlook the negligence of stable lads today. As he handed over the reins he said: "Before you stable my pony you can clean out one of the stalls and put down fresh straw. Then do the same for the other horses. If their litter becomes permanently wet, they get hoof rot. You don't have so much to do that you can't keep this stable clean." They both looked sullen, so he added: "Do as I say, or I'll make sure you both lose a day's pay for idleness." He was about to leave when he remembered something. "There's a cheese in my saddlebag. Take it to the kitchen and give it to Brother Milius."

He went out without waiting for a reply. The priory had sixty employees to look after its forty-five monks, a shameful excess of servants in Philip's opinion. People who did not have enough to do could easily become so lazy that they skimped what little work they did have, as had clearly happened to the two stable hands. It was just another example of Prior James's slackness.

Philip walked along the west wall of the priory close, past the guesthouse, curious to see whether the priory had any visitors. But the big one-room building was cold and disused, with a windblown drift of last year's dead leaves covering its threshold. He turned left and started across the broad expanse of sparse grass that separated the guesthouse—which sometimes lodged ungodly people and even women—from the church. He approached the west end of the church, the public entrance. The broken stones of the collapsed tower lay where they had fallen, in a big heap twice the height of a man.

Like most churches, Kingsbridge Cathedral was built in the shape of a cross. The west end opened into the nave, which formed the long stem of the cross. The crosspiece consisted of the two transepts which stuck out to the north and south either side of the altar. Beyond the crossing, the east end of the church was called the chancel, and was mainly reserved for the monks. At the farthest extremity of the east end was the tomb of Saint Adolphus, which still attracted occasional pilgrims.

Philip stepped into the nave and looked down the avenue of round arches and mighty columns. The sight further depressed his mood. It was a dank, gloomy building, and it had deteriorated since he last saw it. The windows in the low aisles either side of the nave were like narrow tunnels in the immensely thick walls. Up in the roof, the larger windows of the clerestory illuminated the painted timber ceiling only to show how badly it was fading, the apostles and saints and prophets growing dim and blending inexorably with their background. Despite the cold air blowing in—for there was no glass in the windows—a faint smell of rotting vestments tainted the atmosphere. From the other end of the church came the sound of the service of high mass, the Latin phrases spoken in a singsong voice, and the chanted responses. Philip walked down the nave. The floor had never been paved, so moss grew on the bare earth in the corners where peasant clogs and monkish sandals rarely trod. The carved spirals and flutes of the massive columns, and the incised chevrons that decorated the arches between them, had once been painted and gilded; but now all that remained were a few flakes of papery gold leaf and a patchwork of stains where the paint had been. The mortar between the stones was crumbling and falling out, and gathering in little heaps by the walls. Philip felt the familiar anger rise in him again. When people came here they were supposed to be awestruck by the majesty of Almighty God. But peasants were simple people who judged by appearances, and coming here they would think that God was a careless, indifferent deity unlikely to appreciate their worship or take note of their sins. In the end the peasants paid for the church with the sweat of their brows, and it was outrageous that they were rewarded with this crumbling mausoleum.

Philip knelt before the altar and stayed there a moment, conscious that righteous indignation was not the appropriate state of mind for a worshiper. When he had cooled down a little he rose and passed on.

The eastern arm of the church, the chancel, was divided into two. Nearest the crossing was the quire, with wooden stalls where the monks sat and stood during the services. Beyond the quire was the sanctuary that housed the tomb of the saint. Philip moved behind the altar, intending to take a place in the quire; then he was brought up short by a coffin.

He stopped, surprised. Nobody had told him that a monk was dead. But, of course, he had spoken to only three people: Paul, who was old and a little absentminded; and the two stable hands, to whom he had given no chance to make conversation. He approached the coffin to see who it was. He looked inside, and his heart missed a beat.

It was Prior James.

Philip stared openmouthed. Now everything was changed. There would be a new prior, new hope—

This jubilation was not the right response to the death of a venerable brother, no matter what his faults had been. Philip composed his face and his mind in an attitude of mourning. He studied the dead man. The prior had been white-haired and thin-faced, and he had had a stoop. Now his perpetually weary expression had gone, and instead of looking troubled and disconsolate, he seemed at peace. As Philip knelt beside the bier and murmured a prayer, he wondered if some great trouble had weighed on the old man's heart in the latter years of his life: a sin unconfessed, a woman regretted, or a wrong done to an innocent man. Whatever it was, he would not speak of it now until the Day of Judgment.

Despite his resolution Philip could not prevent his mind from turning to the future. Prior James, indecisive, anxious and spineless, had touched the monastery with a dead hand. Now there would be someone new, someone who would discipline the lazy servants, repair the tumbledown church, and harness the great wealth of property, making the priory a powerful force for good. Philip was too excited to stay still. He got up from the coffin and walked, with a new lightness in his step, to the quire and took an empty place at the back of the stalls.

The service was being conducted by the sacrist, Andrew of York, an irascible, red-faced man who seemed permanently on the verge of apoplexy. He was one of the obedientiaries, the senior officers of the monastery. His area of responsibility was everything holy: the services, the books, the sacred relics, the vestments and the ornaments, and most of all the fabric of the church building. Working under his orders were a cantor to supervise the music and a treasurer to take care of the jeweled gold and silver candlesticks, chalices and other sacred vessels. There was no one in authority over the sacrist except the prior and the sub-prior, Remigius, who was a great crony of Andrew's.

Andrew was reading the service in his usual tone of barely controlled ire. Philip's mind was in a turmoil, and it was some time before he noticed that the service was not proceeding in a seemly way. A group of younger monks were making a noise, talking and laughing. Philip saw that they were making fun of the old novice-master, who had fallen asleep in his place. The young monks—most of whom had been novices under the old master until quite recently, and probably still smarted from the sting of his switch—were flicking pellets of dirt at him. Each time one hit his face he would jerk and move, but would not wake up. Andrew seemed oblivious to what was going on. Philip looked around for the circuitor, the monk responsible for discipline. He was on the far side of the quire, deep in conversation with another monk, taking no notice of the service or the behavior of the youngsters.

Philip watched a moment longer. He had no patience for this kind of thing at the best of times. One of the monks seemed to be a ringleader, a good-looking lad of about twenty-one years with an impish grin. Philip saw him dip the end of his eating knife into the top of a burning candle and flick melted grease at the novice-master's bald pate. As the hot fat landed on his scalp the old monk woke up with a yelp, and the youngsters dissolved in laughter.

With a sigh, Philip left his place. He approached the lad from behind, took him by the ear and ungently hauled him out of the quire and into the south transept. Andrew looked up from the service book and frowned at Philip as they went: he had not seen any of the commotion.

When they were out of earshot of the other monks, Philip stopped, released the lad's ear, and said: "Name?"

"William Beauvis."

"And what devil possessed you during high mass?"

William looked sulky. "I was weary of the service," he said.

Monks who complained of their lot never got any sympathy from Philip. "Weary?" he said, raising his voice a little. "What have you done today?"

William said defiantly: "Matins and lauds in the middle of the night, prime before breakfast, then terce, chapter mass, study, and now high mass."

"And have you eaten?"

"I had breakfast."

"And you expect to have dinner."

"Yes."

"Most people your age do backbreaking work in the fields from sunrise to sunset in order to get their breakfast and their dinner— and still they give some of their bread to you! Do you know why they do this?"

"Yes," said William, shuffling his feet and looking at the ground.

"Go on."

"They do it because they want the monks to sing the services for them."

"Correct. Hardworking peasants give you bread and meat and a stone-built dormitory with a fire in winter—and you are so *weary* that you will not sit still through high mass for them!"

"I'm sorry, brother."

Philip looked at William a moment longer. There was no great harm in him. The real fault lay with his superiors, who were lax enough to permit horseplay in the church. Philip said gently: "If services weary you, why did you become a monk?"

"I'm my father's fifth son."

Philip nodded. "And no doubt he gave the priory some land on condition we took you?"

"Yes—a farm."

It was a common story: a man who had a superfluity of sons gave one to God, ensuring that God would not reject the gift by also giving a piece of property sufficient to support the son in monastic poverty. In that way many men who did not have a vocation became disobedient monks.

Philip said: "If you were moved—to a grange, say, or to my little cell of St-John-in-the-Forest, where there is a good deal of work to be done out-of-doors, and rather less time is spent at worship—do you think that might help you to take part in the services in a proper pious manner?"

William's face lit up. "Yes, Brother, I think it would!"

"I thought so. I'll see what can be done. But don't become too excited—you may have to wait until we have a new prior, and ask him to transfer you."

"Thank you, anyhow!"

The service ended, and the monks began to leave the church in procession. Philip put a finger to his lips to end the conversation. As the monks filed through the south transept, Philip and William joined the line, and went out into the cloisters, the arcaded quadrangle adjacent to the south side of the nave. There the procession broke up. Philip turned toward the kitchen, but his way was barred by the sacrist, who struck an aggressive pose in front of him, with his feet apart and his hands on his hips. "Brother Philip," he said.

"Brother Andrew," Philip said, thinking: What's got into him?

"What do you mean by disrupting the service of high mass?"

Philip was flabbergasted. "Disrupting the service?" he said incredulously. "The lad was misbehaving. He—"

"I am quite capable of dealing with misbehavior in my own services!" said Andrew in a raised voice. The movement of dispersal among the monks was arrested, and they all stayed near to hear what was said.

Philip could not understand the fuss. Young monks and novices occasionally had to be disciplined by their more senior brothers during the services, and there was no rule to say that only the sacrist could do this. Philip said: "But you didn't see what was happening—"

"Or perhaps I did see, but decided to deal with it later."

Philip was quite sure he had not seen anything. "What did you see, then?" he challenged.

"Don't you presume to question me!" Andrew shouted. His red face became purplish. "You may be prior of a little cell in the forest, but I have been sacrist here for twelve years, and I will conduct the cathedral services as I think fit—without assistance from outsiders half my age!"

Philip began to think that perhaps he really had done wrong—otherwise why was Andrew so furious? But more important, a quarrel in the cloisters was not an edifying spectacle for the other monks, and it must be brought to an end. Philip swallowed his pride, gritted his teeth, and bowed his head submissively. "I stand corrected, brother, and I humbly beg your pardon," he said.

Andrew was wound up for a shouting match, and this early withdrawal by his opponent was not satisfying. "Don't let it happen again, then," he said ungraciously.

Philip made no reply. Andrew would have to have the last word, so any further remark by Philip would only draw another rejoinder. He stood looking at the floor and biting his tongue, while Andrew glared at him for several moments. At last the sacrist turned on his heel and walked away with his head held high.

The other monks were staring at Philip. It irked him to be humiliated by Andrew, but he had to take it, for a proud monk was a bad monk. Without speaking to anyone else he left the cloisters.

The monks' domestic quarters were to the south of the cloister square, the dormitory on the southeast corner and the refectory on the southwest. Philip went out to the west, passing through the refectory and emerging once more at the public end of the priory close, within view of the guesthouse and the stables. Here in the southwest corner of the close was the kitchen courtyard, surrounded on three sides by the refectory, the kitchen itself, and the bakehouse and brewery. A cart piled high with turnips stood in the yard waiting to be unloaded. Philip climbed the steps to the kitchen door and went in.

The atmosphere struck him like a blow. The air was hot and heavy with the smell of cooking fish, and there was a raucous din of clattering pans and shouted orders. Three cooks, all red with heat and hurry, were preparing the dinner with the aid of six or seven young kitchen hands. There were two vast fireplaces, one at either end of the room, both blazing fiercely, and at each fireplace twenty or more fish were cooking on a spit turned by a perspiring boy. The smell of the fish made Philip's mouth water. Whole carrots were being boiled in great iron pots of water which hung over the flames. Two young men stood at a chopping block, cutting yard-long loaves of white bread into thick slices to be used as trenchers—edible plates. Overseeing the apparent chaos was one monk: Brother Milius, the kitchener, a man of about Philip's age. He sat on a high stool, watching the frenetic activity all about him with an unper-

turbed smile, as if everything were orderly and perfectly organized—which it probably was to his experienced eye. He smiled at
Philip and said: "Thank you for the cheese."

"Ah, yes." Philip had forgotten about that, so much had
happened since he arrived. "It's made of milk from the morning
milking only—you'll find it tastes subtly different."

"My mouth is watering already. But you look glum. Is something wrong?"

"It's nothing. I had harsh words with Andrew." Philip made a
deprecatory gesture, as if to wave Andrew away. "May I take a hot
stone from your fire?"

"Of course."

There were always several stones in the kitchen fires, ready to
be taken out and used for rapid heating of small amounts of water
or soup. Philip explained: "Brother Paul, on the bridge, has a
chilblain, and Remigius won't give him a fire." He picked up a pair
of long-handled tongs and removed a hot stone from the hearth.

Milius opened a cupboard and took out a piece of old leather
that had once been some kind of apron. "Here—wrap it in this."

"Thanks." Philip put the hot stone in the middle of the leather
and picked up the corners gingerly.

"Be quick," Milius said. "Dinner's ready."

Philip left the kitchen with a wave. He crossed the kitchen
courtyard and headed for the gate. To his left, just inside the west
wall, was the mill. A channel had been dug, upstream of the priory,
many years ago, to bring water from the river to the millpond. After
driving the mill wheel the water ran by an underground channel to
the brewery, the kitchen, the fountain in the cloisters where the
monks washed their hands before meals, and finally the latrine next
to the dormitory, after which it turned south and rejoined the river.
One of the early priors had been an intelligent planner.

There was a pile of dirty straw outside the stable, Philip noted:
the hands were following his orders and mucking out the stalls. He
went out through the gate and walked through the village toward
the bridge.

Was it presumptuous of me to reprove young William Beauvis?
he asked himself as he passed among the shacks. He thought not,
on reflection. In fact it would have been wrong to *ignore* such a dis-
ruption during the service.

He reached the bridge and put his head inside Paul's little shelter. "Warm your feet on this," he said, handing over the hot stone
wrapped in leather. "When it cools a bit, take the leather off and put
your feet directly on the stone. It should last until nightfall."

Brother Paul was pathetically grateful. He slipped off his sandals and put his feet on the bundle immediately. "I can feel the pain easing already," he said.

"If you put the stone back in the kitchen fire tonight it will be hot again by morning," Philip said.

"Brother Milius won't mind?" Paul said nervously.

"I guarantee it."

"You're very good to me, Brother Philip."

"It's nothing." Philip left before Paul's thanks became embarrassing. It was only a hot stone.

He returned to the priory. He went into the cloisters and washed his hands in the stone basin in the south walk, then entered the refectory. One of the monks was reading aloud at a lectern. Dinner was supposed to be taken in silence, apart from the reading, but the noise of forty-odd monks eating amounted to a constant undertone, and there was also a good deal of whispering despite the rule. Philip slipped into an empty place at one of the long tables. The monk next to him was eating with enormous relish. He caught Philip's eye and murmured: "Fresh fish today."

Philip nodded. He had seen it in the kitchen. His stomach rumbled.

The monk said: "We hear you have fresh fish every day at your cell in the forest." There was envy in his voice.

Philip shook his head. "Every other day we have poultry," he whispered.

The monk looked even more envious. "Salt fish here, six times a week."

A servant placed a thick bread trencher in front of Philip, then put on it a fish fragrant with Brother Milius's herbs. Philip's mouth watered. He was about to attack the fish with his eating knife when a monk at the far end of the table stood up and pointed at him. It was the circuitor, the monk responsible for discipline. Philip thought: What now?

The circuitor broke the rule of silence, as was his right. "Brother Philip!"

The other monks stopped eating and the room went quiet.

Philip paused with his knife over the fish and looked up expectantly.

The circuitor said: "The rule is, no dinner for latecomers."

Philip sighed. It seemed he could do nothing right today. He put away his knife, handed the trencher and the fish back to the servant, and bowed his head to listen to the reading.

*   *   *

During the rest period after dinner Philip went to the storeroom beneath the kitchen to talk to Cuthbert Whitehead, the cellarer. The storeroom was a big, dark cavern with short thick pillars and tiny windows. The air was dry and full of the scents of the stores: hops and honey, old apples and dried herbs, cheese and vinegar. Brother Cuthbert was usually to be found here, for his job did not leave him much time for services, which suited his inclination: he was a clever, down-to-earth fellow with little interest in the spiritual life. The cellarer was the material counterpart of the sacrist: Cuthbert had to provide for all the monks' practical needs, gathering in the produce of the monastery's farms and granges and going to market to buy what the monks and their employees could not provide themselves. The job required careful forethought and calculation. Cuthbert did not do it alone: Milius the kitchener was responsible for the preparation of the meals, and there was a chamberlain who took care of the monks' clothing. These two worked under Cuthbert's orders, and there were three more officials who were nominally under his control but had a degree of independence: the guest-master; the infirmarer, who looked after old and sick monks in a separate building; and the almoner. Even with people working under him, Cuthbert had a formidable task; yet he kept it all in his head, saying it was a shame to waste parchment and ink. Philip suspected that Cuthbert had never learned to read and write very well. Cuthbert's hair had been white since he was young, hence the surname Whitehead, but he was now past sixty, and the only hair he had left grew in thick white tufts from his ears and nostrils, as if to compensate for his baldness. As Philip had been a cellarer himself at his first monastery, he understood Cuthbert's problems and sympathized with his grouches. Consequently Cuthbert was fond of Philip. Now, knowing that Philip had missed his dinner, Cuthbert picked out half a dozen pears from a barrel. They were somewhat shriveled, but tasty, and Philip ate them gratefully while Cuthbert grumbled about the monastery's finances.

"I can't understand how the priory can be in debt," Philip said through a mouthful of fruit.

"It shouldn't be," Cuthbert said. "It owns more land, and collects tithes from more parish churches, than ever before."

"So why aren't we rich?"

"You know the system we have here—the monastery's property is mostly divided up among the obedientiaries. The sacrist has his lands, I have mine, and there are smaller endowments for the novice-master, the guest-master, the infirmarer and the almoner.

The rest belongs to the prior. Each uses the income from his property to fulfill his obligations."

"What's wrong with that?"

"Well, all this property should be taken care of. For example, suppose we have some land, and we let it for a cash rent. We shouldn't just give it to the highest bidder and collect the money. We ought to take care to find a good tenant, and supervise him to make sure he farms well; otherwise the pastures become waterlogged, the soil is exhausted, and the tenant is unable to pay the rent so he gives the land back to us in poor condition. Or take a grange, farmed by our employees and managed by monks: if nobody visits the grange except to take away its produce, the monks become slothful and depraved, the employees steal the crops, and the grange produces less and less as the years go by. Even a church needs to be looked after. We shouldn't just take the tithes. We should put in a good priest who knows the Latin and leads a holy life. Otherwise the people descend into ungodliness, marrying and giving birth and dying without the blessing of the Church, and cheating on their tithes."

"The obedientaries should manage their property carefully," Philip said as he finished the last pear.

Cuthbert drew a cup of wine from a barrel. "They should, but they have other things on their minds. Anyway, what does the novice-master know about farming? Why should the infirmarer be a capable estate manager? Of course, a strong prior will force them to husband their resources, to some extent. But we've had a weak prior for thirteen years, and now we have no money to repair the cathedral church, and we eat salt fish six days a week, and the school is almost empty of novices, and no one comes to the guesthouse."

Philip sipped his wine in gloomy silence. He found it difficult to think coolly about such appalling dissipation of God's assets. He wanted to get hold of whoever was responsible and shake him until he saw sense. But in this case the person responsible was lying in a coffin behind the altar. There, at least, was a glimmer of hope. "Soon we'll have a new prior," Philip said. "He ought to put things right."

Cuthbert shot him a peculiar look. "Remigius? Put things right?"

Philip was not sure what Cuthbert meant. "Remigius isn't going to be the new prior, is he?"

"It's likely."

Philip was dismayed. "But he's no better than Prior James! Why would the brothers vote for him?"

"Well, they're suspicious of strangers, so they won't vote for anyone they don't know. That means it has to be one of us. And Remigius is the sub-prior, the most senior monk here."

"But there's no rule that says we have to choose the most senior monk," Philip protested. "It could be another one of the obedientaries. It could be you."

Cuthbert nodded. "I've already been asked. I refused."

"But why?"

"I'm getting old, Philip. The job I have now would defeat me, except that I'm so used to it I can do it automatically. Any more responsibility would be too much. I certainly haven't got the energy to take a slack monastery and reform it. In the end I'd be no better than Remigius."

Philip still could not believe it. "There are others—the sacrist, the circuitor, the novice-master . . ."

"The novice-master is old and more tired than I am. The guest-master is a glutton and a drunkard. And the sacrist and the circuitor are pledged to vote for Remigius. Why? I don't know, but I'll guess. I'd say Remigius has promised to promote the sacrist to sub-prior and make the circuitor the sacrist, as a reward for their support."

Philip slumped back on the sacks of flour that formed his seat. "You're telling me that Remigius already has the election sewn up."

Cuthbert did not reply immediately. He stood up and went to the other side of the storeroom, where he had arranged in line a wooden bath full of live eels, a bucket of clean water, and a barrel one-third full of brine. "Help me with this," he said. He took out a knife. He selected an eel from the bath, banged its head on the stone floor, then gutted it with the knife. He handed the fish, still feebly wriggling, to Philip. "Wash it in the bucket, then drop it in the barrel," he said. "These will deaden our appetites during Lent."

Philip rinsed the half-dead eel as carefully as he could in the bucket, then tossed it into the salt water.

Cuthbert gutted another eel and said: "There is one other possibility: a candidate who would be a good reforming prior and whose rank, although below that of the sub-prior, is the same as that of the sacrist or the cellarer."

Philip plunged the eel into the bucket. "Who?"

"You."

"Me!" Philip was so surprised he dropped the eel on the floor. He did, technically, rank as an obedientary of the priory, but he never thought of himself as being equal to the sacrist and the others because they were all so much older than he. "I'm too young—"

"Think about it," Cuthbert said. "You've spent your whole life in monasteries. You were a cellarer at the age of twenty-one. You've been prior of a small place for four or five years—and you've reformed it. It's clear to everyone that the hand of God is on you."

Philip retrieved the escaped eel and dropped it into the barrel of brine. "The hand of God is on us all," he said noncommittally. He was somewhat stunned by Cuthbert's suggestion. He wanted an energetic new prior for Kingsbridge but he had not thought of himself for the job. "It's true that I'd make a better prior than Remigius," he said thoughtfully.

Cuthbert looked satisfied. "If you have a fault, Philip, it's your innocence."

Philip did not think of himself as innocent. "What do you mean?"

"You don't look for base motives in people. Most of us do. For example, the whole monastery already assumes that you're a candidate and that you've come here to solicit their votes."

Philip was indignant. "On what grounds do they say that?"

"Try to look at your own behavior the way a low suspicious mind would see it. You've arrived within days of the death of Prior James, as if you had someone here primed to send you a secret message."

"But how do they imagine I organized that?"

"They don't know—but they believe you're cleverer than they are." Cuthbert resumed disemboweling eels. "And look how you've behaved today. You walked in and ordered the stables mucked out. Then you dealt with that horseplay during high mass. You talked of transferring young William Beauvis to another house, when everyone knows that transferring monks from one place to another is a prior's privilege. You implicitly criticized Remigius by taking a hot stone out to Brother Paul on the bridge. And finally you brought a delicious cheese to the kitchen, and we all had a morsel after dinner—and although nobody *said* where it came from, not one of us could mistake the flavor of a cheese from St-John-in-the-Forest."

Philip was embarrassed to think that his actions had been so misinterpreted. "Anybody might have done those things."

"Any senior monk might have done *one* of them. Nobody else would have done them all. You walked in and took charge! You've already started reforming the place. And, of course, Remigius's cronies are already fighting back. That's why Andrew Sacrist berated you in the cloisters."

"So that's the explanation! I wondered what had got into him." Philip rinsed an eel thoughtfully. "And I suppose that when the circuitor made me forgo my dinner, that was for the same reason."

"Exactly. A way to humiliate you in front of the monks. I suspect that both moves backfired, by the way: neither reproof was justified, yet you accepted both gracefully. In fact you managed to look quite saintly."

"I didn't do it for effect."

"Nor did the saints. There goes the bell for nones. You'd better leave the rest of the eels to me. After the service it's study hour, and discussion is permitted in the cloisters. A lot of brothers will want to talk to you."

"Not so fast!" Philip said anxiously. "Just because people assume I want to be prior doesn't mean I'm going to stand for election." He was daunted by the prospect of an electoral contest and not at all sure that he wanted to abandon his well-organized forest cell and take on the formidable problems of Kingsbridge Priory. "I need time to think," he pleaded.

"I know." Cuthbert drew himself upright and looked Philip in the eye. "When you're thinking, please remember this: excessive pride is a familiar sin, but a man may just as easily frustrate the will of God through excessive humility."

Philip nodded. "I'll remember. Thank you."

He left the storeroom and hurried to the cloisters. His mind was in a turmoil as he joined the other monks and filed into the church. He was violently excited at the prospect of becoming prior of Kingsbridge, he realized. He had been angry for years about the disgraceful way the priory was run, and now he had a chance to set all those things right himself. Suddenly he was not sure he could. It was not just a question of seeing what ought to be done and ordering that it should be so. People had to be persuaded, property had to be managed, money had to be found. It was a job for a wise head. The responsibility would be heavy.

The church calmed him, as it always did. After this morning's misbehavior the monks were quiet and solemn. As he listened to the familiar phrases of the service, and murmured the responses as he had for so many years, he felt able to think clearly once again.

Do I want to be prior of Kingsbridge? he asked himself, and the answer came back immediately: Yes! To take charge of this crumbling church, to repair it and repaint it and fill it with the song of a hundred monks and the voices of a thousand worshipers saying the Our Father—for that alone he wanted the job. Then there was the monastery's property, to be reorganized and revitalized and made healthy and productive again. He wanted to see a crowd of small boys learning to read and write in a corner of the cloisters. He wanted the guesthouse full of light and warmth, so that barons and bishops would come to visit, and endow the priory with precious gifts before leaving. He wanted to have a special room set aside as a library, and fill it with books of wisdom and beauty. Yes, he wanted to be prior of Kingsbridge.

Are there any other reasons? he asked. When I picture myself as prior, making these improvements for the glory of God, is there any pride in my heart?

Oh, yes.

He could not deceive himself in the cold and holy atmosphere of the church. His aim was the glory of God, but the glory of Philip pleased him too. He liked the idea of giving orders which no one could countermand. He saw himself making decisions, dispensing justice, giving out advice and encouragement, issuing penances and pardons, just as he saw fit. He imagined people saying: "Philip of Gwynedd reformed that place. It was a disgrace until he took over, and just look at it now!"

But I *would* be good, he thought. God gave me the brains to manage property and the ability to lead groups of men. I've proved that, as cellarer in Gwynedd and as prior of St-John-in-the-Forest. And when I run a place the monks are happy. In my priory the old men don't get chilblains and the young men don't get frustrated for lack of work. I take care of people.

On the other hand, both Gwynedd and St-John-in-the-Forest were easy by comparison with Kingsbridge Priory. The Gwynedd place was always well run. The forest cell had been in trouble when he took it over, but it was tiny, and easy to control. The reform of Kingsbridge was the challege of a lifetime. It could take weeks just to find out what its resources were—how much land, and where, and what was on the land, whether forests or pastures or wheat fields. To take control of the scattered properties, to find out what was wrong and put it right, and to knit the parts into a thriving whole would be the work of years. All Philip had done at the forest cell was to make a dozen or so young men work hard in the fields and pray solemnly in church.

All right, he admitted, my motives are tainted and my ability is in doubt. Perhaps I should refuse to stand. At least I could be sure to avoid the sin of pride. But what was it that Cuthbert had said? "A man may just as easily frustrate the will of God through excessive humility."

What does God want? he asked himself finally. Does he want Remigius? Remigius's abilities are less than mine and his motives are probably no more pure. Is there another candidate? Not at present. Until God reveals a third possibility we must assume that the choice is between me and Remigius. It's clear that Remigius would run the monastery the way he ran it while Prior James was ill, which is to say that he would be idle and negligent and he would permit its decline to continue. And me? I'm full of pride and my talents are unproved—but I will *try* to reform the monastery, and if God gives me strength I shall succeed.

All right, then, he said to God as the service came to an end; all right. I'm going to accept nomination, and I'm going to fight with all the strength I have to win the election; and if you don't want me, for some reason that you've chosen not to reveal to me, well, then, you'll just have to stop me any way you can.

Although Philip had spent twenty-two years in monasteries, he had served under long-lived priors, so he had never known an election. It was a unique event in monastic life, for in casting their votes the brothers were not obliged to be obedient—suddenly they were all equal.

Once upon a time, if the legends were true, the monks had been equal in everything. A group of men would decide to turn their backs on the world of fleshly lust and build a sanctuary in the wilderness where they could live lives of worship and self-denial; and they would take over a patch of barren land, clearing the forest and draining the swamp, and they would till the soil and build their church together. In those days they really had been like brothers. The prior was, as his title implied, only the first among equals, and they swore obedience to the Rule of Saint Benedict, not to monastic officials. But all that was now left of that primitive democracy was the election of the prior and the abbot.

Some of the monks were uncomfortable with their power. They wanted to be told how to vote, or they suggested that the decision be referred to a committee of senior monks. Others abused the privilege and became insolent, or demanded favors in return for their support. Most were simply anxious to make the right decision.

In the cloisters that afternoon, Philip spoke to most of them, singly or in little groups, and told them all candidly that he wanted the job and he felt he could do it better than Remigius despite his youth. He answered their questions, most of which were about rations of food and drink. He ended each conversation by saying: "If each of us makes the decision thoughtfully and prayerfully, God will surely bless the outcome." It was the prudent thing to say and he also believed it.

"We're winning," said Milius the kitchener next morning, as Philip and he took their breakfast of horsebread and small beer while the kitchen hands were stoking the fires.

Philip bit off a hunk of the coarse dark bread and took a mouthful of beer to soften it. Milius was a sharp-witted, ebullient young man, a protégé of Cuthbert's and an admirer of Philip. He had dark straight hair and a small face with neat, regular features. Like Cuthbert, he was happy to serve God in practical ways and miss most of the services. Philip was suspicious of his optimism. "How do you come to that conclusion?" he asked skeptically.

"All of Cuthbert's side of the monstery support you—the chamberlain, the infirmarer, the novice-master, myself—because we know you're a good provider, and provisions are the big problem under the present regime. Many of the ordinary monks will vote for you for a similar reason: they think you will manage the priory's wealth better, and that will result in more comfort and better food."

Philip frowned. "I wouldn't like to mislead anyone. My first priority would be to repair the church and smarten up the services. That comes before food."

"Quite so, and they know that," Milius said a little hastily. "That's why the guest-master and one or two others will still vote for Remigius—they prefer a slack regime and a quiet life. The others who support him are all cronies of his who anticipate special privileges when he's in charge—the sacrist, the circuitor, the treasurer and so on. The cantor is a friend of the sacrist, but I think he could be won over to our side, especially if you promise to appoint a librarian."

Philip nodded. The cantor was in charge of the music, and felt he should not have to take care of the books on top of his other duties. "It's a good idea anyway," Philip said. "We need a librarian to build up our collection of books."

Milius got off his stool and began to sharpen a kitchen knife. He had too much energy and had to be doing something with his hands, Philip decided. "There are forty-four monks entitled to vote," Milius said. There had been forty-five, of course, but one was dead. "My best estimate is that eighteen are with us and ten are with Remigius, leaving sixteen undecided. We need twenty-three for a majority. That means you have to win over five waverers."

"When you put it that way, it seems easy," Philip said. "How long have we got?"

"Can't tell. The brothers call the election, but if we do it too early the bishop may refuse to confirm our choice. And if we delay too long he can order us to call it. He also has the right to nominate a candidate. Right now he probably hasn't even heard that the old prior is dead."

"It could be a long time, then."

"Yes. And as soon as we're confident of a majority, you must go back to your cell, and stay away from here until it's all over."

Philip was puzzled by this proposal. "Why?"

"Familiarity breeds contempt." Milius waved the sharpened knife enthusiastically. "Forgive me if I sound disrespectful, but you did ask. At the moment you've got an aura. You're a remote, sanctified figure, especially to us younger monks. You worked a miracle at that little cell, reforming it and making it self-sufficient. You're a tough disciplinarian but you feed your monks well. You're a born leader but you can bow your head and accept rebuke like the youngest novice. You know the Scriptures and you make the best cheese in the country."

"And *you* exaggerate."

"Not much."

"I can't believe people think of me like that—it's not natural."

"Indeed it's not," Milius acknowledged with another little shrug. "And it won't last once they get to know you. If you stayed here you'd lose that aura. They'd see you pick your teeth and scratch your arse, they'd hear you snore and fart, they'd find out what you're like when you're bad-tempered or your pride is hurt or your head aches. We don't want them to do that. Let them watch Remigius blunder and bungle from day to day while your image remains shining and perfect in their minds."

"I don't like this," Philip said in a troubled voice. "It has a deceitful feeling to it."

"There's nothing dishonest about it," Milius protested. "It's a true reflection of how well you would serve God and the monastery if you were prior—and how badly Remigius would rule."

Philip shook his head. "I refuse to pretend to be an angel. All right, I won't stay here—I have to go back to the forest anyway. But we must be straightforward with the brothers. We're asking them to elect a fallible, imperfect man, who will need their help and their prayers."

"Tell them that!" said Milius enthusiastically. "That's perfect—they'll love it."

He was incorrigible, Philip thought. He changed the subject. "What's your impression of the waverers—the brothers who haven't yet made up their minds?"

"They're conservative," Milius said without hesitation. "They see Remigius as the older man, the one who will make fewer changes, the predictable one, the man who is effectively in charge at the moment."

Philip nodded agreement. "And they look at me warily, like a strange dog that may bite."

The bell rang for chapter. Milius swallowed the last of his beer. "There'll be some kind of attack on you now, Philip. I can't forecast what form it will take, but they will be trying to portray you as youthful, inexperienced, headstrong and unreliable. You must appear calm, cautious and judicious, but leave it to me and Cuthbert to defend you."

Philip began to feel apprehensive. This was a new way of thinking—to weigh his every move and calculate how others would interpret and judge it. A slightly disapproving tone crept into his voice as he said: "Normally, I only think about how God would view my behavior."

"I know, I know," Milius said impatiently. "But it's not a sin to help simpler folk see your actions in the right light."

Philip frowned. Milius was distressingly plausible.

They left the kitchen and walked through the refectory to the cloisters. Philip was highly anxious. Attack? What did that mean, an *attack*? Would they tell lies about him? How should he react? If people told lies about him he would be angry. Should he suppress his anger, in order to appear calm and conservative and all the rest? But if he did that, wouldn't the brothers think the lies were true? He was going to be his normal self, he decided; perhaps just a *little* more grave and dignified.

The chapter house was a small round building attached to the east walk of the cloisters. It was furnished with benches arranged in concentric rings. There was no fire, and it was cold after the kitchen. The light came from tall windows set above eye level, so there was nothing to look at but the other monks around the room.

Philip did just that. Almost the whole monastery was present. They were all ages from seventeen to seventy; tall and short, dark and fair; all dressed in the coarse homespun robe of unbleached wool and shod in leather sandals. The guest-master was there, his round belly and red nose revealing his vices—vices that might be pardonable, Philip thought, if he ever had any guests. There was the chamberlain, who forced the monks to change their robes and shave at Christmas and Whitsun (a bath at the same time was recommended but not compulsory). Leaning against the far wall was the oldest brother, a slight, thoughtful, unflappable old man whose hair was still gray rather than white; a man who spoke rarely but effectively; a man who probably should have been prior if he had not been so self-effacing. There was Brother Simon, with his furtive look and restless hands, a man who confessed to sins of impurity so often that (as Milius whispered to Philip) it seemed likely that he enjoyed the confession, not the sin. There was William Beauvis, behaving himself; Brother Paul, hardly limping at all; Cuthbert Whitehead looking self-possessed; John Small, the diminutive treasurer; and Pierre, the circuitor, the mean-mouthed man who had denied Philip his dinner yesterday. As Philip looked around he realized they were all looking at him, and he dropped his eyes, embarrassed.

Remigius came in with Andrew, the sacrist, and they sat by John Small and Pierre. So, Philip thought, they're not going to pretend to be anything other than a faction.

Chapter began with a reading about Simeon Stylites, the saint whose feast day it was. He was a hermit who had spent most of his life on top of a pillar, and while there could be no doubt about his capacity for self-denial, Philip had always harbored a secret doubt about the real value of his testimony. Crowds had flocked to see him, but had they come to be spiritually uplifted, or to look at a freak?

After the prayers came the reading of a chapter of Saint Benedict's book. It was from this reading of a daily chapter that the meeting, and the little building in which it took place, got their names. Remigius stood up to read, and as he paused with the book in front of him, Philip looked intently at his profile, seeing him for the first time through the eyes of a rival. Remigius had a brisk, efficient manner of moving and speaking which gave him an air of competence entirely at variance with his true character. Closer observation revealed clues to what was beneath the facade: his rather prominent blue eyes shifted about rapidly in an anxious way, his weak-looking mouth worked hesitantly two or three times before he spoke, and his hands clenched and opened repeatedly even though he was otherwise still. What authority he had came from arrogance, petulance and a dismissive way with subordinates.

Philip wondered why he had chosen to read the chapter himself. A moment later he understood. "'The first degree of humility is prompt obedience,'" Remigius read. He had chosen Chapter Five, which was about obedience, to remind everyone of his seniority and their subordination. It was a tactic of intimidation. Remigius was nothing if not sly. "'They live not as they themselves will, neither do they obey their own desires and pleasures; but following the command and direction of another and abiding in their monasteries, their desire is to be ruled by an abbot,'" he read. "'Without doubt such as these carry out the saying of our Lord, *I came not to do my own will, but the will of Him Who sent me.*'" Remigius was drawing the battle lines in the expected way: in this contest he was to represent established authority.

The chapter was followed by the necrology, and today of course all prayers were for the soul of Prior James. The liveliest part of chapter was kept to the end: discussion of business, confession of faults and accusations of misconduct.

Remigius began by saying: "There was a disturbance during high mass yesterday."

Philip felt almost relieved. Now he knew how he was going to be attacked. He was not sure that his action yesterday had been right, but he knew why he had done it and he was ready to defend himself.

Remigius went on: "I myself was not present—I was detained in the prior's house, dealing with urgent business—but the sacrist has told me what occurred."

He was interrupted by Cuthbert Whitehead. "Don't reproach yourself on that account, Brother Remigius," he said in a soothing voice. "We know that, in principle, monastery business should never take precedence over high mass, but we understand that the death of our beloved prior has meant that you have to deal with many matters which are outside your normal competence. I feel sure we all agree that no penance is necessary."

The wily old fox, Philip thought. Of course, Remigius had had no intention of confessing a fault. Nevertheless, Cuthbert had pardoned him, thereby making everyone feel that a fault had indeed been admitted. Now, even if Philip were to be convicted of an error, it would do no more than put him on the same level as Remigius. In addition, Cuthbert had planted the suggestion that Remigius was having difficulty coping with the prior's duties. Cuthbert had completely undermined Remigius's authority with a few kindly-sounding words. Remigius looked furious. Philip felt the thrill of triumph tighten his throat.

Andrew Sacrist glared accusingly at Cuthbert. "I'm sure none of us would wish to criticize our revered sub-prior," he said. "The disturbance referred to was caused by Brother Philip, who is visiting us from the cell of St-John-in-the-Forest. Philip took young William Beauvis out of his place in the quire, hauled him over to the south transept, and there reprimanded him while I was conducting the service."

Remigius composed his face in a mask of sorrowful reproof. "We may all agree that Philip should have waited until the end of the service."

Philip examined the expressions of the other monks. They seemed neither to agree nor disagree with what was being said. They were following the proceedings with the air of spectators at a tournament, in which there is no right or wrong and the only interest is in who will triumph.

Philip wanted to protest *If I had waited, the misbehavior would have gone on all through the service,* but he remembered Milius's advice, and remained silent; and Milius spoke up for him. "I too missed high mass, as is frequently my misfortune, for high mass comes just before dinner; so perhaps you could tell me, Brother Andrew, what was happening in the quire before Brother Philip took this action. Was everything orderly and becoming?"

"There was some fidgeting among the youngsters," the sacrist replied sulkily. "I intended to speak to them about it later."

"It's understandable that you should be vague about the details— your mind was on the service," Milius said charitably. "Fortunately, we have a circuitor whose particular duty it is to attend to misbehavior among us. Tell us, Brother Pierre, what *you* observed."

The circuitor looked hostile. "Just what the sacrist has already told you."

Milius said: "It seems we'll have to ask Brother Philip himself for the details."

Milius had been very clever, Philip thought. He had established that neither the sacrist nor the circuitor had seen what the young monks were doing during the service. But although Philip admired Milius's dialectical skill, he was reluctant to play the game. Choosing a prior was not a contest of wits, it was a matter of seeking to know the will of God. He hesitated. Milius was giving him a look that said *Now's your chance!* But there was a stubborn streak in Philip, and it showed most clearly when someone tried to push him into a morally dubious position. He looked Milius in the eye and said: "It was as my brothers have described."

Milius's face fell. He stared incredulously at Philip. He opened his mouth, but visibly did not know what to say. Philip felt guilty about letting him down. I'll explain myself to him afterward, he thought, unless he's too angry.

Remigius was about to press on with the indictment when another voice said: "I would like to confess."

Everyone looked. It was William Beauvis, the original offender, standing up and looking shamefaced. "I was flicking pellets of mud at the novice-master and laughing," he said in a low, clear voice. "Brother Philip made me ashamed. I beg God's forgiveness and ask the brothers to give me a penance." He sat down abruptly.

Before Remigius could react, another youngster stood up and said: "I have a confession. I did the same. I ask for a penance." He sat down again. This sudden access of guilty conscience was infectious: a third monk confessed, then a fourth, then a fifth.

The truth was out, despite Philip's scruples, and he could not help feeling pleased. He saw that Milius was struggling to suppress a triumphant smile. The confession left no doubt that there had been a minor riot going on under the noses of the sacrist and the circuitor.

The culprits were sentenced, by a highly displeased Remigius, to a week of total silence: they were not to speak and no one was to speak to them. It was a harsher punishment than it sounded. Philip had suffered it when he was young. Even for one day the isolation was oppressive, and a whole week of it was utterly miserable.

But Remigius was merely giving vent to his anger at having been outmaneuvered. Once they had confessed he had no option but to punish them, although in punishing them he was conceding that Philip had been right in the first place. His attack on Philip had gone badly wrong, and Philip was triumphant. Despite a guilty pang, he relished the moment.

But Remigius's humiliation was not yet complete.

Cuthbert spoke again. "There was another disturbance that we ought to discuss. It took place in the cloisters just after high mass." Philip wondered what on earth was coming next. "Brother Andrew confronted Brother Philip and accused him of misconduct." Of course he did, Philip was thinking; everyone knows that. Cuthbert went on: "Now, we all know that the time and place for such accusations is here and now, in chapter. And there are good reasons why our forebears ordained it so. Tempers cool overnight, and grievances can be discussed the next morning in an atmosphere of calm and moderation; and the whole community can bring its collective wisdom to bear on the problem. But, I regret to say, Andrew flouted this sensible rule, and made a scene in the cloisters, disturbing everyone and speaking intemperately. To let such misbehavior pass would be unfair on the younger brothers who have been punished for what they have done."

It was merciless, and it was brilliant, Philip thought happily. The question of whether Philip had been right to take William out of the quire during the service had never actually been discussed. Every attempt to raise it had been turned into an inquiry into the behavior of the accuser. And that was as it should be, for Andrew's complaint against Philip had been insincere. Between them Cuthbert and Milius had now discredited Remigius and his two main allies, Andrew and Pierre.

Andrew's normally red face was purple with fury, and Remigius looked almost frightened. Philip was pleased—they deserved it—but now he worried that their humiliation was in danger of going too far. "It's unseemly for junior brothers to discuss the punishment of their

seniors," he said. "Let the sub-prior deal with this matter privately."
Looking around, he saw that the monks approved of his magna-
nimity, and he realized that unintentionally he had scored yet
another point.

It seemed to be all over. The mood of the meeting was with
Philip, and he felt sure he had won over most of the waverers. Then
Remigius said: "There is another matter I have to raise."

Philip studied the sub-prior's face. He looked desperate. Philip
glanced at Andrew Sacrist and Pierre Circuitor and saw that they
both looked surprised. This was something unplanned, then. Was
Remigius going to plead for the job, perhaps?

"Most of you know that the bishop has a right to nominate
candidates for our consideration," Remigius began. "He may also
refuse to confirm our choice. This division of powers can lead to
quarreling between bishop and monastery, as some older brothers
know from experience. In the end, the bishop cannot force us to
accept his candidate, nor can we insist on ours; and where there is
conflict, it has to be resolved by negotiation. In that case, the outcome depends a good deal on the determination and unity of the
brothers—especially their *unity*."

Philip had a bad feeling about this. Remigius had suppressed
his rage and was once again calm and haughty. Philip still did not
know what was coming, but his triumphant feeling evaporated.

"The reason I mention all this today is that two important items
of information have come to my notice," Remigius went on. "The
first is that there may be more than one candidate nominated from
among us here in this room." That didn't surprise anyone, Philip
thought. "The second is that the bishop will also nominate a candidate."

There was a pregnant pause. This was bad news for both
parties. Someone said: "Do you know *whom* the bishop wants?"

"Yes," Remigius said, and in that instant Philip felt sure the
man was lying. "The bishop's choice is Brother Osbert of New-
bury."

One or two of the monks gasped. They were all horrified. They
knew Osbert, for he had been circuitor at Kingsbridge for a while.
He was the bishop's illegitimate son, and he regarded the Church
purely as a means whereby he could live a life of idleness and
plenty. He had never made any serious attempt to abide by his
vows, but kept up a semi-transparent sham and relied upon his
paternity to keep him out of trouble. The prospect of having him as
prior was appalling, even to Remigius's friends. Only the guest-
master and one or two of his irredeemably depraved cronies might

favor Osbert in anticipation of a regime of slack discipline and slovenly indulgence.

Remigius plowed on. "If we nominate two candidates, brothers, the bishop may say that we are divided and cannot make up our collective mind, so therefore he must decide for us, and we should accept his choice. If we want to resist Osbert, we would do well to put forward one candidate only; and, perhaps I should add, we should make sure that our candidate cannot easily be faulted, for example on grounds of youth or inexperience."

There was a murmur of assent. Philip was devastated. A moment ago he had been sure of victory, but it had been snatched from his grasp. Now all the monks were with Remigius, seeing him as the safe candidate, the unity candidate, the man to beat Osbert. Philip felt sure Remigius was lying about Osbert, but it would make no difference. The monks were scared now, and they would back Remigius; and that meant more years of decline for Kingsbridge Priory.

Before anyone could comment, Remigius said: "Let us now dismiss, and think and pray about this problem as we do God's work today." He stood up and went out, followed by Andrew, Pierre and John Small, these three looking dazed but triumphant.

As soon as they had gone, a buzz of conversation broke out among the others. Milius said to Philip: "I never thought Remigius had it in him to pull a trick like that."

"He's lying," Philip said bitterly. "I'm sure of it."

Cuthbert joined them and heard Philip's remark. "It doesn't really matter if he's lying, does it?" he said. "The threat is enough."

"The truth will come out eventually," Philip said.

"Not necessarily," Milius replied. "Suppose the bishop doesn't nominate Osbert. Remigius will just say the bishop yielded before the prospect of a battle with a united priory."

"I'm not ready to give in," Philip said stubbornly.

Milius said: "What else will we do?"

"We must find out the truth," Philip said.

"We can't," said Milius.

Philip racked his brains. The frustration was agony. "Why can't we just ask?" he said.

"Ask? What do you mean?"

"Ask the bishop what his intentions are."

"How?"

"We could send a message to the bishop's palace, couldn't we?" Philip said, thinking aloud. He looked at Cuthbert.

Cuthbert was thoughtful. "Yes. I send messengers out all the time. I can send one to the palace."

Milius said skeptically: "And ask the bishop what his intentions are?"

Philip frowned. That was the problem.

Cuthbert agreed with Milius. "The bishop won't tell us," he said.

Philip was struck by an inspiration. His brow cleared, and he punched his palm excitedly as he saw the solution. "No," he said. "The bishop won't tell us. But his archdeacon will."

That night Philip dreamed about Jonathan, the abandoned baby. In his dream the child was in the porch of the chapel at St-John-in-the-Forest and Philip was inside, reading the service of prime, when a wolf came slinking out of the woods and crossed the field, smooth as a snake, heading for the baby. Philip was afraid to move for fear of causing a disturbance during the service and being reprimanded by Remigius and Andrew, both of whom were there (although in reality neither of them had ever been to the cell). He decided to shout, but although he tried, no sound would come, as often happened in dreams. At last he made such an effort to call out that he woke himself up, and lay in the dark trembling while he listened to the breathing of the sleeping monks all around him and slowly convinced himself that the wolf was not real.

He had hardly thought of the baby since arriving at Kingsbridge. He wondered what he would do with the child if he were to become prior. Everything would be different then. A baby in a little monastery hidden in the forest was of no consequence, however unusual. The same baby at Kingsbridge Priory would cause a stir. On the other hand, what was wrong with that? It was not a sin to give people something to talk about. He would be prior, so he could do as he pleased. He could bring Johnny Eightpence to Kingsbridge to take care of the baby. The idea pleased him inordinately. That's just what I'll do, he thought. Then he remembered that in all probability he would not become prior.

He lay awake until dawn, in a fever of impatience. There was nothing he could do now to press his case. It was useless to talk to the monks, for their thinking was dominated by the threat of Osbert. A few of them had even approached Philip and told him they were sorry he had lost, as if the election had already been held. He had resisted the temptation to call them faithless cowards. He just smiled and told them they might yet be surprised. But his own faith was not strong. Archdeacon Waleran might not be at the bishop's palace; or he might be there but have some reason for not wanting to tell Philip the bishop's plans; or—most likely of all, given the archdeacon's character—he might have plans of his own.

Philip got up at dawn with the other monks and went into the church for prime, the first service of the day. Afterward he headed for the refectory, intending to take his breakfast with the others, but Milius intercepted him and beckoned him, with a furtive gesture, to the kitchen. Philip followed him, his nerves wound taut. The messenger must be back: that was quick. He must have got his reply immediately and started back yesterday afternoon. Even so he had been fast. Philip did not know a horse in the priory stable that was capable of doing the journey so rapidly. But what would the answer be?

It was not the messenger who was waiting in the kitchen—it was the archdeacon himself, Waleran Bigod.

Philip stared at him in surprise. The thin, black-draped form of the archdeacon was perched on a stool like a crow on a tree stump. The end of his beaky nose was red with cold. He was warming his bony white hands around a cup of hot spiced wine.

"It's good of you to come!" Philip blurted out.

"I'm glad you wrote to me," Waleran said coolly.

"Is it true?" Philip asked impatiently. "Will the bishop nominate Osbert?"

Waleran held up a hand to stop him. "I'll get to that. Cuthbert here is just telling me of yesterday's events."

Philip concealed his disappointment. This was not a straightforward answer. He studied Waleran's face, trying to read his mind. Waleran did indeed have plans of his own, but Philip could not guess what they were.

Cuthbert—whom Philip had not at first noticed, sitting by the fire dipping his horsebread into his beer to soften it for his elderly teeth—resumed an account of yesterday's chapter. Philip fidgeted restlessly, trying to guess what Waleran might be up to. He tried a morsel of bread but found he was too tense to swallow. He drank some of the watery beer, just to have something to do with his hands.

"And so," Cuthbert said at last, "it seemed that our only chance was to try to verify the bishop's intentions; and fortunately Philip felt able to presume upon his acquaintanceship with yourself; so we sent you the message."

Philip said impatiently: "And now will you tell us what we want to know?"

"Yes, I'll tell you." Waleran put down his wine untasted. "The bishop would like his son to be prior of Kingsbridge."

Philip's heart sank. "So Remigius told the truth."

Waleran went on: "However, the bishop is not willing to risk a quarrel with the monks."

Philip frowned. This was more or less what Remigius had forecast—but something was not quite right. Philip said to Waleran: "You didn't come all this way just to tell us that."

Waleran shot a look of respect at Philip, and Philip knew he had guessed right. "No," Waleran said. "The bishop has asked me to test the mood of the monastery. And he has empowered me to make a nomination on his behalf. Indeed, I have with me the bishop's seal, so that I can write a letter of nomination, to make the matter formal and binding. I have his full authority, you see."

Philip took a moment to digest that. Waleran was empowered to make a nomination and seal it with the bishop's seal. That meant the bishop had put the whole matter in Waleran's hands. He now spoke with the bishop's authority.

Philip took a deep breath and said: "Do you accept what Cuthbert has told you—that if Osbert were to be nominated, it would cause the quarrel the bishop wants to avoid?"

"Yes, I understand that," said Waleran.

"Then you won't nominate Osbert."

"No."

Philip felt wound up tight enough to snap. The monks would be so glad to escape the threat of Osbert that they would gratefully vote for whoever Waleran might nominate.

Waleran now had the power to choose the new prior.

Philip said: "Then whom will you nominate?"

Waleran said: "You . . . or Remigius."

"Remigius's ability to run the priory—"

"I know his abilities, and yours," Waleran interrupted, once again holding up a thin white hand to stop Philip. "I know which of you would make the best prior." He paused. "But there is another matter."

What now? wondered Philip. What else was there to consider, other than who would make the best prior? He looked at the others. Milius was also mystified, but old Cuthbert had a slight smile, as if he knew what was coming.

Waleran said: "Like you, I'm anxious that important posts in the Church should go to energetic and capable men, regardless of age, rather than being handed out as rewards for long service to senior men whose holiness may be greater than their administrative ability."

"Of course," Philip said impatiently. He did not see the relevance of this lecture.

"We should work together to this end—you three, and me."

Milius said: "I don't know what you're getting at."

"I do," said Cuthbert.

Waleran gave Cuthbert a thin smile, then returned his attention to Philip. "Let me be plain," he said. "The bishop himself is old. One day he will die, and then we will need a new bishop, just as today we need a new prior. The monks of Kingsbridge have the right to elect the new bishop, for the bishop of Kingsbridge is also the abbot of the priory."

Philip frowned. All this was irrelevant. They were electing a prior, not a bishop.

But Waleran went on. "Of course, the monks will not be completely free to choose whom they like to be bishop, for the archbishop and the king will have their views; but in the end it is the monks who legitimize the appointment. And when that time comes, you three will have a powerful influence on the decision."

Cuthbert was nodding as if his guess had turned out to be right, and now Philip, too, had an inkling of what was coming.

Waleran finished: "You want me to make you prior of Kingsbridge. I want you to make me bishop."

So that was it!

Philip stared in silence at Waleran. It was very simple. The archdeacon wanted to make a deal.

Philip was shocked. It was not quite the same as buying and selling a clerical office, which was known as the sin of simony; but it had an unpleasantly commercial feeling about it.

He tried to think objectively about the proposal. It would mean that Philip would become prior. His heart beat faster at the thought. He was reluctant to quibble with anything that would give him the priory.

It would mean that Waleran would probably become bishop at some point. Would he be a good bishop? He would certainly be competent. He appeared to have no serious vices. He had a rather worldly, practical approach to the service of God, but then so did Philip. Philip sensed that Waleran had a ruthless edge that he himself lacked, but he also sensed that it was based on a genuine determination to protect and nurture the interests of the Church.

Who else might be a candidate, when the bishop eventually died? Probably Osbert. It was not unknown for religious offices to be passed from father to son, despite the official requirement of clerical celibacy. Osbert, of course, would be even more of a liability to the Church as bishop than he would be as prior. It would be worth supporting a much worse candidate than Waleran just to keep Osbert out.

Would anyone else be in the running? It was impossible to guess. It might be years yet before the bishop died.

Cuthbert said to Waleran: "We couldn't guarantee to get you elected."

"I know," said Waleran. "I'm asking only for your nomination. Appropriately, that's exactly what I have to offer you in return—a nomination."

Cuthbert nodded. "I'll agree to that," he said solemnly.

"So will I," said Milius.

The archdeacon and the two monks looked at Philip. He hesitated, torn. This was not the way to choose a bishop, he knew; but the priory was within his grasp. It could not be right to barter one holy office for another, like horse traders—but if he refused, the result might be that Remigius became prior and Osbert became bishop!

However, the rational arguments now seemed academic. The desire to be prior was like an irresistible force within him, and he could not refuse, regardless of the pros and cons. He recalled the prayer he had sent up yesterday, telling God that he intended to fight for the job. He raised his eyes now, and sent up another: *If you don't want this to happen, then still my tongue, and paralyze my mouth, and stop my breath in my throat, and prevent me from speaking.*

Then he looked at Waleran and said: "I accept."

The prior's bed was huge, three times the width of any bed Philip had ever slept in. The wooden base stood half the height of a man, and there was a feather mattress on top of that. It had curtains all around to keep out drafts, and on the curtains biblical scenes had been embroidered by the patient hands of a pious woman. Philip examined it with some misgivings. It seemed to him enough of an extravagance that the prior should have a bedroom all to himself— Philip had never in his life had his own bedroom, and tonight would be the first time he had ever slept alone. The bed was too much. He considered having a straw mattress brought over from the dormitory, and moving the bed into the infirmary, where it would ease an ailing monk's old bones. But of course the bed was not just for Philip. When the priory had an especially distinguished guest, a bishop or a great lord or even a king, then the guest would have this bedroom and the prior would shift as best he could somewhere else. So Philip could not really get rid of it.

"You'll sleep soundly tonight," said Waleran Bigod, not without a hint of envy.

"I suppose I shall," Philip said dubiously.

Everything had happened very quickly. Waleran had written a letter to the priory, right there in the kitchen, ordering the monks to hold an immediate election and nominating Philip. He had signed the letter with the bishop's name and sealed it with the bishop's seal. Then the four of them had gone into chapter.

As soon as Remigius saw them enter he knew the battle was over. Waleran read the letter, and the monks cheered when he got to Philip's name. Remigius had the wit to dispense with the formality of the vote and concede defeat.

And Philip was prior.

He had conducted the rest of chapter in something of a daze, and then had walked across the lawns to the prior's house, in the southeast corner of the priory close, to take up residence.

When he saw the bed he realized that his life had changed utterly and irrevocably. He was different, special, set apart from other monks. He had power and privilege. And he had responsibility. He alone had to make sure that this little community of forty-five men survived and prospered. If they starved, it would be his fault; if they became depraved, he would be to blame; if they disgraced God's Church, God would hold Philip responsible. He had sought this burden, he reminded himself; now he must bear it.

His first duty as prior would be to lead the monks into church for high mass. Today was Epiphany, the twelfth day of Christmas, and a holiday. All the villagers would be at the service, and more people would come from the surrounding district. A good cathedral with a strong body of monks and a reputation for spectacular services could attract a thousand people or more. Even dreary Kingsbridge would draw most of the local gentry, for the service was a social occasion too, when they could meet their neighbors and talk business.

But before the service Philip had something else to discuss with Waleran, now that they were alone at last. "That information I passed you," he began. "About the earl of Shiring . . ."

Waleran nodded. "I haven't forgotten—indeed, that could be more important than the question of who is prior or bishop. Earl Bartholomew has arrived in England already. They expect him at Shiring tomorrow."

"What are you going to do?" Philip said anxiously.

"I'm going to make use of Sir Percy Hamleigh. In fact, I'm hoping he'll be in the congregation today."

"I've heard of him, but I've never seen him," Philip said.

"Look for a fat lord with a hideous wife and a handsome son. You can't miss the wife—she's an eyesore."

"What makes you think they will take King Stephen's side against Earl Bartholomew?"

"They hate the earl passionately."

"Why?"

"The son, William, was engaged to marry the earl's daughter, but she took against him, and the marriage was called off, much to the humiliation of the Hamleighs. They're still smarting from the insult, and they'll jump at any chance to strike back at Bartholomew."

Philip nodded, satisfied. He was glad to have shed that responsibility: he had a full quota. Kingsbridge Priory was a big enough problem for him to manage. Waleran could take care of the world outside.

They left the prior's house and walked back to the cloisters. The monks were waiting. Philip took his place at the head of the line and the procession moved off.

It was a good moment when he walked into the church with the monks singing behind him. He liked it more than he had anticipated. He told himself that his new eminence symbolized the power he now had to do good, and that was why he was so profoundly thrilled. He wished Abbot Peter from Gwynedd could see him—the old man would be so proud.

He led the monks into the quire stalls. A major service such as this one was often taken by the bishop. Today it would be led by the bishop's deputy, Archdeacon Waleran. As Waleran began, Philip scanned the congregation, looking for the family Waleran had described. There were about a hundred and fifty people standing in the nave, the wealthy in their heavy winter cloaks and leather shoes, the peasants in their rough jackets and felt boots or wooden clogs. Philip had no trouble picking out the Hamleighs. They were near the front, close to the altar. He saw the woman first. Waleran had not exaggerated—she was repulsive. She wore a hood, but most of her face was visible, and he could see that her skin was covered with unsightly boils which she touched nervously all the time. Beside her was a heavy man of about forty years: that would be Percy. His clothes showed him to be a man of considerable wealth and power, but not in the top rank of barons and earls. The son was leaning against one of the massive columns of the nave. He was a fine figure of a man, with very yellow hair and narrow, haughty eyes. A marriage with an earl's family would have enabled the Hamleighs to cross the line that divided county gentry from the nobility of the kingdom. It was no wonder they were angry about the cancellation of the wedding.

Philip returned his mind to the service. Waleran was going through it a little too fast for Philip's taste. He wondered again whether he had been right to agree to nominate Waleran as bishop when the present bishop should die. Waleran was a dedicated man, but he appeared to undervalue the importance of worship. The prosperity and power of the Church were only means to an end, after all: the ultimate object was the salvation of souls. Philip decided that he must not worry about Waleran too much. The thing was done, now; and anyway, the bishop would probably frustrate Waleran's ambition by living another twenty years.

The congregation was noisy. None of them knew the responses, of course; only priests and monks were expected to take part, except in the most familiar prayers and the amens. Some of the congregation watched in reverent silence, but others wandered around, greeting one another and chatting. They're simple people, Philip thought; you have to *do* something to keep their attention.

The service drew to a close, and Archdeacon Waleran addressed them. "Most of you know that the beloved prior of Kingsbridge has died. His body, which lies here with us in church, will be laid to rest in the priory graveyard today after dinner. The bishop and the monks have chosen as his successor Brother Philip of Gwynedd, who led us into church this morning."

He stopped, and Philip stood up to lead the procession out. Then Waleran said: "I have another sad announcement."

Philip was taken by surprise. He sat down promptly.

"I have just received a message," Waleran said.

He had received no messages, Philip knew. They had been together all morning. What was the sly archdeacon up to now?

"The message tells me of a loss which will grieve us all deeply." He paused again.

Someone was dead—but who? Waleran had known about it before he arrived, but he had kept it a secret, and he was going to pretend that he had only just heard the news. Why?

Philip could think of only one possibility—and if Philip's suspicion were right, Waleran was much more ambitious and unscrupulous than Philip had imagined. Had he really deceived and manipulated them all? Had Philip been a mere pawn in Waleran's game?

Waleran's final words confirmed that he had. "Dearly beloved," he said solemnly, "the bishop of Kingsbridge is dead."

Chapter 3

"THAT BITCH WILL BE THERE," said William's mother. "I'm sure she will."

William looked at the looming facade of Kingsbridge Cathedral with mingled dread and longing. If the Lady Aliena were to be at the Epiphany service it would be painfully embarrassing for them all, but nevertheless his heart quickened at the thought of seeing her again.

They were trotting along the road to Kingsbridge, William and his father on war-horses and his mother on a fine courser, with three knights and three grooms following. They made an impressive and even fearsome party, which pleased William; and the peasants walking on the road scattered before their powerful horses; but Mother was seething.

"They all know, even these wretched serfs," she said through her teeth. "They even tell jokes about us. 'When is a bride not a bride? When the groom is Will Hamleigh!' I had a man flogged for that but it did no good. I'd like to get hold of that bitch, I'd flay her alive, and hang her skin on a nail, and let the birds peck her flesh."

William wished she would not go on about it. The family had been humiliated, and it had been William's fault—or so Mother said—and he did not want to be reminded of it.

They clattered over the rickety wooden bridge that led to Kingsbridge village and urged their horses up the sloping main street to the priory. There were already twenty or thirty horses cropping the sparse grass of the graveyard on the north side of the church, but none as fine as those of the Hamleighs. They rode up to the stable and left their mounts with the priory grooms.

They crossed the green in formation, William and his father on either side of Mother, then the knights behind them, and the grooms bringing up the rear. People stood aside for them, but William could see them nudging one another and pointing, and he felt sure they were whispering about the canceled wedding. He risked a glance at Mother, and he could tell by the thunderous look on her face that she thought the same.

They went into the church.

William hated churches. They were cold and dim even in fine weather, and there was always that faintly corrupt smell lingering in the dark corners and the low tunnels of the aisles. Worst of all, churches made him think of the torments of hell, and he was frightened of hell.

He raked the congregation with his eyes. At first he could hardly distinguish people's faces because of the gloom. After a few moments his eyes adjusted. He could not see Aliena. They progressed up the aisle. She did not seem to be here. He felt both relieved and let down. Then he saw her, and his heart missed a beat.

She was on the south side of the nave near the front, escorted by a knight William did not know, surrounded by men-at-arms and ladies-in-waiting. She had her back to him, but her mass of dark curly hair was unmistakable. As he spotted her she turned, showing a soft curved cheek and a straight, imperious nose. Her eyes, so dark they were almost black, met William's. He stopped breathing. Those dark eyes, already large, widened when she saw him. He wanted to look past her carelessly, as if he had not seen her, but he could not tear his gaze away. He wanted her to smile at him, even if it was only the merest curving of her full lips, no more than a polite acknowledgment. He inclined his head to her, only slightly—it was more of a nod than a bow. Her face set in stiff lines, and she turned away to face the front.

William winced as if he was in pain. He felt like a dog that had been kicked out of the way, and he wanted to curl up in a corner where no one would notice him. He glanced to either side, wondering whether anyone had seen the exchange of looks. As he walked farther up the aisle with his parents, he realized that people were looking from him to Aliena and back again, nudging one another and whispering. He stared straight ahead to avoid meeting anybody's eyes. He had to force himself to hold his head high. How has she done this to us? he thought. We're one of the proudest families in southern England, and she's made us feel small. The thought infuriated him, and he longed to draw his sword and attack some-one, anyone.

The sheriff of Shiring greeted William's father and they shook hands. People looked away, searching for something new to murmur about. William was still seething. Young noblemen approached Aliena and bowed to her in a constant stream. She was willing to smile at *them*.

The service began. William wondered how everything had gone so badly wrong. Earl Bartholomew had a son to inherit his title and his fortune, so the only use he had for a daughter was to form an alliance. Aliena was sixteen years old and a virgin, and showed no inclination to become a nun, so it was assumed she would be delighted to marry a healthy nineteen-year-old nobleman. After all, political considerations might just as easily have led her father to marry her to a fat gouty forty-year-old earl or even a balding baron of sixty.

Once the deal had been agreed, William and his parents had not been reticent about it. They had proudly broadcast the news all over the surrounding counties. The meeting between William and Aliena had been considered a formality by everyone—except Aliena, as it turned out.

They were not strangers, of course. He remembered her as a little girl. She had had an impish face with a snub nose then, and her unruly hair had been kept short. She had been bossy, head-strong, pugnacious, and daring. She always organized the children's games, deciding what they should play, and who should be on which team, adjudicating disputes and keeping score. He had been fascinated by her while at the same time resenting the way she dominated the children's play. It had always been possible to spoil her games, and make himself the center of attention for a while, simply by starting a fight; but that did not last long, and in the end she would resume control, leaving him feeling baffled, defeated, spurned, angry, and yet enchanted—just as he felt now.

After her mother died she had traveled with her father a lot and William had seen less of her. However, he met her often enough to know that she was growing into a ravishingly beautiful young woman, and he had been delighted when he was told she was to be his bride. He assumed she had to marry him whether she liked him or not, but he went along to meet her intending to do all he could to smooth the path to the altar.

She might be a virgin but he was not. Some of the girls he had charmed were almost as pretty as Aliena, almost, although none of them was as high-born. In his experience a lot of girls were impressed by his fine clothes, his spirited horses, and the casual way he had of spending money on sweet wine and ribbons; and if he could get them alone in a barn they generally submitted to him, more or less willingly, in the end.

His usual approach to girls was a little offhand. At first he would let them think he was not particularly interested in them. But when he found himself alone with Aliena his diffidence deserted him. She was wearing a bright blue silk gown, loose and flowing, but all he could think about was the body underneath it, which he would soon be able to see naked whenever he liked. He had found her reading a book, which was a peculiar occupation for a woman who was not a nun. He had asked her what it was, in an attempt to take his mind off the way her breasts moved under the blue silk.

"It's called 'The Romance of Alexander.' It's the story of a king called Alexander the Great, and how he conquered wonderful lands in the east where precious stones grow on grapevines and plants can talk."

William could not imagine why a person would want to waste time on such foolishness, but he had not said so. He had told her about his horses, his dogs, and his achievements in hunting, wrestling and jousting. She had not been as impressed as he had hoped. He had told her about the house his father was building for them, and, to help her prepare for the time when she would be running his household, he gave her an outline of the way he wanted things done. He had felt he was losing her attention, though he could not say why. He sat as close to her as possible, for he wanted to get her in a clinch, and feel her up, and find out whether those tits were as big as he fancied they were; but she leaned away from him, folding her arms and crossing her legs, looking so forbidding that he was reluctantly forced to abandon the idea, and console himself with the thought that soon he would be able to do anything he liked to her.

However, while he was with her she gave no indication of the fuss she was going to make later. She had said, rather quietly, "I don't think we're well suited," but he had taken this for a piece of charming modesty on her part, and had assured her that she would suit him very well. He had no idea that as soon as he was off the premises she would storm in to her father and announce that she would not marry him, nothing would persuade her, she would rather go into a convent, and they could drag her to the altar in chains but she would not speak the vows. The bitch, William thought; the bitch. But he could not summon the kind of venom that Mother spat when she spoke of Aliena. He did not want to flay

Aliena alive. He wanted to lie on top of her hot body and kiss her mouth.

The Epiphany service ended with the announcement of the death of the bishop. William hoped this news would at last overshadow the sensation of the canceled marriage. The monks left in procession, and there was a buzz of excited conversation as the congregation headed for the exits. Many of them had material as well as spiritual ties to the bishop—as his tenants, or subtenants, or as employees on his lands—and everyone was interested in the question of who would succeed him, and whether the successor would make any changes. The death of a great lord was always perilous for those ruled by him.

As William followed his parents down the nave he was surprised to see Archdeacon Waleran coming toward them. He moved briskly through the congregation, like a big black dog in a field of cows; and like cows the people looked nervously over their shoulders at him and moved a step or two out of his way. He ignored the peasants, but spoke a few words to each of the gentry. When he reached the Hamleighs he greeted William's father, ignored William, and turned his attention on Mother. "Such a shame about the marriage," he said.

William flushed. Did the fool think he was being *polite* with his commiserations?

Mother was no more keen to talk about it than William was. "I'm not one to bear a grudge," she lied.

Waleran ignored that. "I've heard something about Earl Bartholomew that may interest you," he said. His voice went quieter, so that he could not be overheard, and William had to strain to catch his words. "It seems the earl will not renege on his vows to the dead king."

Father said: "Bartholomew always was a stiff-necked hypocrite."

Waleran looked pained. He wanted them to listen, not comment. "Bartholomew and Earl Robert of Gloucester will not accept King Stephen, who is the choice of the Church and the barons, as you know."

William wondered why an archdeacon was telling a lord about this routine baronial squabble. Father was thinking the same thought, for he said: "But there's nothing the earls can do about it."

Mother shared Waleran's impatience with Father's interjected comments. *"Listen,"* she hissed at him.

Waleran said: "What I hear is that they're planning to mount a rebellion and make Maud queen."

William could not believe his ears. Had the archdeacon really made that foolhardy statement, in his quiet, matter-of-fact murmur, right here in the nave of Kingsbridge Cathedral? A man could be hanged for it, true or false.

Father was startled, too, but Mother said thoughtfully: "Robert of Gloucester is the half brother of Maud. . . . It makes sense."

William wondered how she could be so down-to-earth about such a scandalous piece of news. But she was very clever, and she was almost always right about everything.

Waleran said: "Anyone who could get rid of Earl Bartholomew, and stop the rebellion before it gets started, would earn the eternal gratitude of King Stephen and the Holy Mother Church."

"Indeed?" said Father in a dazed tone, but Mother was nodding wisely.

"Bartholomew is expected back at home tomorrow." Waleran looked up as he said this, and caught someone's eye. He looked back at Mother and said: "I thought you, of all people, would be interested." Then he moved away and greeted someone else.

William stared after him. Was that really all he was going to say?

William's parents moved on, and he followed them through the great arched doorway into the open air. All three of them were silent. William had heard a good deal of talk, over the past five weeks, about who would be king, but the matter had seemed to be settled when Stephen was crowned at Westminster Abbey three days before Christmas. Now, if Waleran was right, the matter was an open question once again. But why had Waleran made a point of telling the Hamleighs?

They started across the green to the stables. As soon as they got clear of the crowd outside the church porch, and could no longer be overheard, Father said excitedly: "What a piece of good fortune— the very man who insulted the family, caught out in high treason!"

William did not see why that was such good fortune, but Mother obviously did, for she nodded agreement.

Father went on: "We can arrest him at the point of a sword, and hang him from the nearest tree."

William had not thought of that, but now he saw it in a flash. If Bartholomew was a traitor, it was all right to kill him. "We can take our revenge," William burst out. "And instead of being punished for it we'll get a reward from the king!" They would be able to hold their heads high again, and—

"You stupid fools," Mother said with sudden viciousness. "You blind, brainless idiots. So you would hang Bartholomew from the nearest tree. Shall I tell you what would happen then?"

Neither of them said anything. It was wiser not to respond to her questions when she was in this frame of mind.

She said: "Robert of Gloucester would deny there had been any plot, and he would embrace King Stephen and swear loyalty; and there would be the end of it, except that you two would be hanged as murderers."

William shuddered. The idea of being hanged terrified him. He had nightmares about it. However, he could see that Mother was right: the king might believe, or pretend to believe, that no one could have the temerity to rebel against him; and he would think nothing of sacrificing a couple of lives for credibility.

Father said: "You're right. We'll truss him up like a pig for the slaughter, and carry him alive to the king at Winchester, and denounce him there, and claim our reward."

"Why don't you *think*?" said Mother contemptuously. She was very tense, and William could see that she was as excited about all this as Father was, but in a different way. "Wouldn't Archdeacon Waleran like to take a traitor trussed to the king?" she said. "Doesn't he want a reward for himself—don't you know that he lusts with all his heart to be bishop of Kingsbridge? Why has he given you the privilege of making the arrest? Why did he contrive to meet us in church, as if by accident, instead of coming to see us at Hamleigh? Why was our conversation so short and indirect?"

She paused rhetorically, as if for an answer, but both William and Father knew that she did not really want one. William recalled that priests were not supposed to see bloodshed, and considered the possibility that perhaps that might be why Waleran did not want to be involved in arresting Bartholomew; but on further reflection he realized that Waleran had no such scruples.

"I'll tell you why," Mother went on. "Because he's not sure that Bartholomew *is* a traitor. His information is unreliable. I can't guess where he got it—perhaps he overheard a drunken conversation, or intercepted an ambiguous message, or spoke with an untrustworthy spy. In any case he's not willing to stick his neck out. He won't accuse Earl Bartholomew of treason openly, in case the charge should turn out to be false, and Waleran himself be branded a slanderer. He wants someone else to take the risk, and do the dirty work for him; and then when it is over, if treason should be proved, he will step forward and take his share of the credit; but if Bartholomew should turn out to be innocent, Waleran will simply never admit that he said what he said to us today."

It seemed obvious when she put it like that. But without her, William and his father would have fallen right into Waleran's trap. They would have willingly acted as Waleran's agents and taken the risks for him. Mother's political judgment was acute.

Father said: "Do you mean we must just forget about this?"

"Certainly not." Her eyes glittered. "It's still a chance to destroy the people who have humiliated us." A groom held her horse ready. She took the reins and waved him away, but she did not mount immediately. She stood beside the horse, patting its neck reflectively, and spoke in a low voice. "We need evidence of the conspiracy, so that no one will be able to deny it after we've made our accusation. We'll have to get that evidence by stealth, without revealing what we're looking for. Then, when we have it, we can arrest Earl Bartholomew and take him to the king. Confronted with proof, Bartholomew will confess, and beg for mercy. Then we ask for our reward."

"And deny that Waleran helped us," added Father.

Mother shook her head. "Let him have his share of the glory, and his reward. Then he will be indebted to us. That can't do us anything but good."

"But how shall we go about finding evidence of the plot?" said Father anxiously.

"We'll have to find a way to look around Bartholomew's castle," Mother said with a frown. "It won't be easy. Nobody would credit us making a social call—everyone knows we hate Bartholomew."

William was struck by a thought. "I could go," he said.

His parents were both a little startled. Mother said: "You'd arouse less suspicion than your father, I suppose. But what pretext would you have?"

William had thought of that. "I could go to see Aliena," he said, and his pulse raced at the idea. "I could beg her to reconsider her decision. After all, she doesn't really know me. She misjudged me when we met. I could make her a good husband. Perhaps she just needs to be wooed a little harder." He gave what he hoped was a cynical smile, so that they would not know that he meant every word.

"A perfectly credible excuse," said Mother. She looked hard at William. "By Christ, I wonder whether the boy might have some of his mother's brains after all."

William felt optimistic, for the first time in months, when he set out for Earlscastle on the day after Epiphany. It was a clear, cold morning. The north wind stung his ears and the frosted grass crunched under the hooves of his war-horse. He wore a gray cloak of fine Flanders cloth trimmed with rabbit fur over a scarlet tunic.

He was accompanied by Walter, his groom. When William was twelve years old Walter had become his tutor in arms, and had taught him to ride, hunt, fence and wrestle. Now Walter was his groom, companion and bodyguard. He was as tall as William but broader, a formidable barrel of a man. Nine or ten years older than William, he was young enough to go drinking and chasing girls but old enough to keep the boy out of trouble when necessary. He was William's closest friend.

William was strangely excited by the prospect of seeing Aliena again, even though he knew he faced rejection and humiliation once more. That glimpse of her in Kingsbridge Cathedral, when for an instant he had looked into her dark, dark eyes, had rekindled his desire for her. He looked forward eagerly to talking to her, getting close to her, seeing her mass of curls tumble and shake as she talked, watching her body move under her dress.

At the same time, the opportunity for revenge had sharpened William's hatred. He was tense with excitement at the thought that now he might wipe out the humiliation he and his family had suffered.

He wished he had a clearer idea of what he was looking for. He was fairly confident he would find out whether Waleran's story was true, for there would surely be signs of preparation for war at the castle—horses being mustered, weapons being cleaned, food being stockpiled—even though the activity would naturally be masked as something else, preparations for an expedition perhaps, to deceive the casual observer. However, convincing himself of the existence of a plot was not the same as finding proof. William could not think of anything that would count as proof. He planned to keep his eyes open and hope that something would suggest itself. This was not much of a plan, however, and he suffered a nagging worry that the opportunity for revenge might yet slip through his fingers.

As he came nearer he began to feel tense. He wondered whether he might be refused admittance to the castle, and he suffered a moment of panic, until he realized how unlikely it was: the castle was a public place, and for the earl to close it to the local gentry would be as good as an announcement that treachery was afoot.

Earl Bartholomew lived a few miles from the town of Shiring. The castle of Shiring itself was occupied by the sheriff of the county, so the earl had a castle of his own outside the town. The small village that had grown up around the castle walls was known as Earlscastle. William had been there before, but now he looked at it through the eyes of an attacker.

There was a wide, deep moat in the shape of the number eight, with the upper circle smaller than the lower. The earth that had been dug out to form the moat was piled up inside the twin circles, forming ramparts.

At the foot of the eight was a bridge across the moat and a gap in the earth wall, giving admittance to the lower circle. This was the only entrance. There was no way into the upper circle except by going through the lower circle and crossing another bridge over the moat that divided the two circles. The upper circle was the inner sanctum.

As William and Walter trotted across the open fields that surrounded the castle they could see a lot of coming and going. Two men-at-arms crossed the bridge on fast horses and rode off in different directions, and a group of four horsemen preceded William across the bridge as he and Walter entered.

William noted that the last section of the bridge could be drawn up into the massive stone gatehouse that formed the entrance to the castle. There were stone towers at intervals all around the earth wall, so that every part of the perimeter could be covered by defending archers. To take this castle by frontal assault would be a long and bloody business, and the Hamleighs could not muster enough men to be sure of success, William concluded gloomily.

Today, of course, the castle was open for business. William gave his name to the sentry in the gatehouse and was admitted without further ado. Within the lower circle, shielded from the outside world by the earth walls, was the usual range of domestic buildings: stables, kitchens, workshops, a privy tower and a chapel. A sense of excitement was in the air. The grooms, squires, servants and maids all walked briskly and talked loudly, calling greetings to one another and making jokes. To an unsuspecting mind the excitement and the coming and going might be no more than a normal reaction to the return of the master, but to William it seemed more than that.

He left Walter at the stable with the horses and crossed to the far side of the compound where, exactly opposite the gatehouse, there was a bridge across the moat to the upper circle. When he had crossed the bridge he was challenged by another guard in another gatehouse. This time he was asked his business, and he said: "I've come to see the Lady Aliena."

The guard did not know him, but he looked him up and down, noting his fine cloak and red tunic, and took him at face value, as a hopeful suitor. "You may find the young lady in the great hall," he said with a smirk.

In the center of the upper circle was a square stone building, three stories high, with thick walls. This was the keep. As usual the ground floor was a store. The great hall was above the store, reached by a wooden exterior staircase which could be drawn up into the building. On the top floor would be the earl's bedroom, and that was where he would make his last stand when the Hamleighs came to get him.

The whole layout presented a formidable series of obstacles to the attacker. That was the point, of course, but now that William was trying to work out how to get past the obstacles he saw the function of the different elements of the design very clearly. Even if the attackers gained the lower circle, they still had to pass another bridge and another gatehouse, and then assault the sturdy keep. They would have to get to the upper floor somehow—presumably by building their own staircase—and even then there would be yet another fight, in all probability, to get from the hall up the stairs to the earl's bedroom. The only way to take this castle was by stealth, William realized, and he began to toy with ideas of sneaking in somehow.

He mounted the stairs and entered the hall. It was full of people, but the earl was not among them. In the far left-hand corner was the staircase leading to his bedroom, and fifteen or twenty knights and men-at-arms sat around the foot of the stairs, talking together in low tones. This was unusual. Knights and men-at-arms formed separate social classes. The knights were landowners who supported themselves by rents, whereas the men-at-arms were paid by the day. The two groups became comradely only when the smell of war was in the wind.

William recognized some of them: there was Gilbert Catface, a bad-tempered old fighter with an unfashionable beard and long whiskers, past forty years but still tough; Ralph of Lyme, who spent more on clothes than on a bride, today wearing a blue cloak with a red silk lining; Jack fitz Guillaume, already a knight although hardly older than William; and several others whose faces were vaguely familiar. He nodded in their general direction, but they took little notice of him—he was well known, but he was too young to be important.

He turned and looked around the other side of the hall, and saw Aliena immediately.

She looked quite different today. Yesterday she had been dressed up for the cathedral, in silk and fine wool and linen, with rings and ribbons and pointed boots. Today she wore the short tunic of a peasant woman or a child, and her feet were bare. She was sitting on a bench, studying a game board on which were counters of different colors. As William watched, she hitched up her tunic and crossed her legs, revealing her knees, and then wrinkled her nose in a frown. Yesterday she had been formidably sophisticated; today she was a vulnerable child, and William found her even more desirable. He suddenly felt ashamed that this child had been able to cause him so much distress, and he yearned for some way of showing her that he could master her. It was a feeling almost like lust.

She was playing with a boy three years or so younger than she. He had a restless, impatient look: he did not like the game. William could see a family resemblance between the two players. Indeed, the boy looked like Aliena as William remembered her from childhood, with a snub nose and short hair. This must be her younger brother Richard, the heir to the earldom.

William went closer. Richard glanced up at him, then returned his attention to the board. Aliena was concentrating. Their painted wooden board was shaped like a cross and divided into squares of different colors. The counters appeared to be made of ivory, white and black. The game was obviously a variant of merels, or nine-men's morris, and probably a gift brought back from Normandy by Aliena's father. William was more interested in Aliena. When she leaned forward over the board, the neck of her tunic bowed out, and he could see the tops of her breasts. They were as large as he had imagined. His mouth went dry.

Richard moved a counter on the board, and Aliena said: "No, you can't do that."

The boy was put out. "Why not?"

"Because it's against the rules, stupid."

"I don't *like* the rules," Richard said petulantly.

Aliena flared up. "You have to obey the rules!"

"Why do I?"

"You just do, that's why!"

"Well, I don't," he said, and he tipped the board off the bench onto the floor, sending the counters flying.

Quick as a flash, Aliena slapped his face.

He cried out, his pride as well as his face stung. "You—" He hesitated. "You devil-fucker," he shouted. He turned and ran away—but after three steps he cannoned into William.

William picked him up by one arm and held him in midair. "Don't let the priest hear you call your sister such names," he said.

Richard wriggled and squealed. "You're hurting me—let me go!"

William held him a little longer. Richard stopped struggling and began to cry. William put him down, and he ran off in tears.

Aliena was staring at William, her game forgotten, a puzzled frown wrinkling her brow. "Why are you here?" she said. Her voice was low and calm, the voice of an older person.

William sat on the bench, feeling rather pleased about the masterful way he had dealt with Richard. "I've come to see you," he said.

A wary look came over her face. "Why?"

William positioned himself so that he could watch the staircase. He saw, coming down into the hall, a man in his forties dressed like a high-ranking servant, in a round cap and a short tunic of fine cloth. The servant gestured to someone, and a knight and a man-at-arms went up the stairs together. William looked at Aliena again. "I want to talk to you."

"About what?"

"About you and me." Over her shoulder he saw the servant approaching them. There was something a little effeminate about the man's walk. In one hand he carried a loaf of sugar, dirty-brown in color and cone-shaped. In his other hand was a twisted root that looked like ginger. The man was obviously the household steward, and he had been to the spice safe, a locked cupboard in the earl's bedroom, for the day's supplies of precious ingredients, which he was now taking to the cook: sugar to sweeten a crab-apple tart, perhaps, and ginger to flavor lampreys.

Aliena followed William's gaze. "Oh, hello, Matthew."

The steward smiled and broke off a piece of sugar for her. William had a feeling that Matthew was very fond of Aliena. Something in her demeanor must have told him that she was uncomfortable, for his smile turned to a concerned frown and he said: "Is everything all right?" His voice was soft.

"Yes, thank you."

Matthew looked at William and his face registered surprise. "Young William Hamleigh, isn't it?"

William was embarrassed to be recognized, even though it was inevitable. "Keep your sugar for the children," he said, although he had not been offered any. "I don't care for it."

"Very well, lord." Matthew's look said that he had not got where he was today by making trouble for the sons of the gentry. He turned back to Aliena. "Your father brought back some wonderful soft silk—I'll show you later."

"Thank you," she said.

Matthew went away.

William said: "Effeminate fool."

Aliena said: "Why were you so rude to him?"

"I don't let servants call me 'Young William.'" This was not a good way to begin wooing a lady. William realized with a sinking feeling that he had got off to a bad start. He had to be charming. He smiled and said: "If you were my wife, my servants would call you lady."

"Did you come here to talk about marriage?" she said, and William thought he detected a note of incredulity in her voice.

"You don't know me," William said in a tone of protest. He was failing to keep this conversation under control, he realized miserably. He had planned a little small talk before getting down to business, but she was so direct and candid that he was forced to blurt out his message. "You misjudged me. I don't know what I did, last time we met, to make you dislike me; but whatever your reason, you were too hasty."

She looked away, considering her reply. Behind her, William saw the knight and the man-at-arms come down the stairs and go out through the door, looking purposeful. A moment later a man in clerical robes—presumably the earl's secretary—appeared from above and beckoned. Two knights got up and went upstairs: Ralph of Lyme, flashing the red lining of his cloak, and an older man with a bald head. Clearly the men waiting in the hall were seeing the earl, in ones and twos, in his chamber. But why?

"After all this time?" Aliena was saying. She was suppressing some emotion. It might have been anger, but William had a sneaking feeling it was laughter. "After all the trouble, and anger, and scandal; just when it's dying down at last, *now* you tell me I made a mistake?"

When she put it that way it did seem a bit implausible, William realized. "It hasn't died down at all—people are still talking about it, my mother is still furious and my father can't hold his head up in public," he said wildly. "It's not over for us."

"This is all about family honor for you, isn't it?"

There was a dangerous note in her voice, but William ignored it. He had just realized what the earl must be doing with all these knights and men-at-arms: he was sending messages. "Family honor?" he said distractedly. "Yes."

"I know I ought to think about honor, and alliances between families, and all that," Aliena said. "But that's not all there is to marriage." She seemed to ponder for a moment, then reach a decision. "Perhaps I should tell you about my mother. She hated my father. My father isn't a bad man, in fact he's a great man, and I love him, but he's dreadfully solemn and strict, and he never understood Mother. She was a happy, lighthearted person who loved to laugh and tell stories and have music, and Father made her miserable." There were tears in Aliena's eyes, William noted vaguely, but he was thinking about messages. "That's why she died—because he wouldn't let her be happy. I know it. And he knows it too, you see. That's why he promised he would never make me marry someone I don't like. Do you understand, now?"

Those messages are orders, William was thinking; orders to Earl Bartholomew's friends and allies, warning them to get ready to fight. And the messengers are *evidence*.

He realized Aliena was staring at him. "Marry someone you don't like?" he said, echoing her final words. "Don't you like me?"

Her eyes flashed anger. "You haven't been listening," she said. "You're so self-centered that you can't think about anyone else's feelings for a moment. Last time you came here, what did you do? You talked and talked about yourself and never asked me one question!"

Her voice had risen to a shout, and when she stopped, William noticed that the men on the other side of the room had fallen silent, listening. He felt embarrassed. "Not so loud," he said to her.

She took no notice. "You want to know why I don't like you? All right, I'll tell you. I don't like you because you have no refinement. I don't like you because you can hardly read. I don't like you because you're only interested in your *dogs* and your *horses* and your *self*."

Gilbert Catface and Jack fitz Guillaume were laughing aloud now. William felt his face reddening. Those men were *nobodies*, they were *knights*, and they were laughing at *him*, the son of Lord Percy Hamleigh. He stood up. "All *right*," he said urgently, trying to stop Aliena.

It was no good. "I don't like you because you're selfish, dull and stupid," she yelled. All the knights were laughing now. "I dislike you, I despise you, I hate you and I loathe you. And *that's* why I won't marry you!"

The knights cheered and applauded. William cringed inside. Their laughter made him feel small, weak and helpless, like a little boy, and when he was a little boy he had been frightened all the time. He turned away from Aliena, fighting to control his facial expression and hide his feelings. He crossed the room as fast as he could without running, while the laughter grew louder. At last he reached the door, flung it open, and stumbled out. He slammed it behind him and ran down the stairs, choking with shame; and the fading sound of their derisive laughter rang in his ears all the way across the muddy courtyard to the gate.

*   *   *

The path from Earlscastle to Shiring crossed a main road after about a mile. At the crossroads a traveler could turn north, for Gloucester and the Welsh border, or south, for Winchester and the coast. William and Walter turned south.

William's anguish had turned to rage. He was too furious to speak. He wanted to hurt Aliena and kill all those knights. He would have liked to thrust his sword into each laughing mouth and drive it down each throat. And he had thought of a way to avenge himself on at least one of them. If it worked, he would get the proof he needed at the same time. The prospect gave him savage consolation.

First he had to catch one of them. As soon as the road ran into woodland, William dismounted and began to walk, leading his horse. Walter followed in silence, respecting his mood. William came to a narrower stretch of track and stopped. He turned to Walter and said: "Who's better with a knife, you or me?"

"Fighting at close quarters, I'm better," Walter said guardedly. "But you throw more accurately, lord." They all called him lord when he was angry.

"I suppose you can trip a bolting horse, and make him fall?" William said.

"Yes, with a good stout pole."

"Go and find a small tree, then, and pull it up and trim it; then you'll have a good stout pole."

Walter went off.

William led the two horses through the woods and tied them up in a clearing a good way from the road. He took off their saddles and removed some of the cords and straps from the tack—enough to bind a man hand and foot, with a little over. His plan was crude, but there was no time to devise something more elaborate, so he would have to hope for the best.

On his way back to the road he found a stout piece of oak deadfall, dry and hard, to use as a club.

Walter was waiting with his pole. William selected the place where the groom would lie in wait, behind the broad trunk of a beech tree that grew close to the path. "Don't shove the pole out too soon, or the horse will jump over it," he cautioned. "But don't leave it too late, because you can't trip him by his back legs. The ideal is to push it between his forelegs. And try to stick the end into the ground so he doesn't kick it aside."

Walter nodded. "I've seen this done before."

William walked about thirty yards back toward Earlscastle. His role would be to make sure the horse bolted, so that it would be going too fast to avoid Walter's pole. He hid himself as close to the road as he could. Sooner or later one of Earl Bartholomew's messengers would come along. William hoped it would be soon. He was anxious about whether this was going to work, and he was impatient to get it over with.

Those knights had no idea, while they were laughing at me, that I was spying on them, he thought, and it soothed him a little. But one of them is about to find out. And then he'll be sorry he laughed. Then he'll wish he had gone down on his knees and kissed my boots, instead of laughing. He's going to weep and beg and plead with me to forgive him, and I'm just going to hurt him all the more.

He had other consolations. If his plan worked out, it might ultimately bring about the downfall of Earl Bartholomew and the resurrection of the Hamleighs. Then all those who had snickered at the canceled wedding would tremble in fear, and some of them would suffer more than fear.

The downfall of Bartholomew would also be the downfall of Aliena, and that was the best part. Her swollen pride and her superior manner would have to change after her father had been hanged as a traitor. If she wanted soft silk and sugar cones then, she would have to marry William to get them. He imagined her, humble and contrite, bringing him a hot pastry from the kitchen, looking up at him with those big dark eyes, eager to please him, hoping for a caress, her soft mouth slightly open, begging to be kissed.

His fantasy was disturbed by hoofbeats on the winter-hard mud of the road. He drew his knife and hefted it, reminding himself of its weight and balance. At the point, it was sharpened on both sides, for better penetration. He stood upright, flattened his back against the tree that concealed him, held the knife by the blade, and waited, hardly breathing. He was nervous. He was afraid he might miss with the knife, or the horse might not fall, or the rider might kill Walter with a lucky stroke, so that William would have to fight him alone. . . . Something bothered him about the hoofbeats as they came closer. He saw Walter peering at him through the vegetation with a worried frown: he had heard it too. Then William realized what it was. There was more than one horse. He had to make a quick decision. Would they attack two people? That might be too much like a fair fight. He decided to let them go, and wait for a lone rider. It was disappointing, but this was the wisest course. He waved a hand at Walter in a wiping-out gesture. Walter nodded understanding and sank back under cover.

A moment later two horses came into view. William saw a flash of red silk: Ralph of Lyme. Then he saw the bald head of Ralph's companion. The two men trotted past and disappeared from view.

Despite the sense of anticlimax, William was gratified to have confirmation of his theory that the earl was sending these men out on errands. However, he wondered anxiously whether Bartholomew might have a policy of sending them in pairs. It would be a natural precaution. Everyone traveled in groups when possible, for safety. On the other hand, Bartholomew had a lot of messages and a limited number of men, and he might see it as an extravagance to use two knights to take one message. Furthermore, the knights were violent men who could be relied upon to give the average outlaw a hard fight—a fight from which the outlaw would gain little, because a knight did not have much worth stealing, other than his sword, which was hard to sell without answering awkward questions, and his horse, which was liable to be crippled in the ambush. A knight was safer than most people in the forest.

William scratched his head with the hilt of his knife. It could go either way.

He settled down to wait. The forest was quiet. A feeble winter sun came out, shone fitfully through the dense greenery for a while, and then disappeared. William's belly reminded him that it was past dinnertime. A deer crossed the path a few yards away, unaware that she was watched by a hungry man. William became impatient.

If another pair of riders came along, he decided, he would have to attack. It was risky, but he had the advantage of surprise, and he had Walter, who was a formidable fighter. Besides, it might be his last chance. He knew he could get killed, and he was afraid, but that might be better than living on in constant humiliation. At least it was an honorable end to die in a fight.

What would be best of all, he thought, would be for Aliena to appear, all alone, cantering on a white pony. She would come crashing off the horse, bruising her arms and legs, and tumble into a bramble thicket. The thorns would scratch her soft skin, drawing blood. William would jump on top of her and pin her to the ground. She would be mortified.

He played with that idea, elaborating her injuries, relishing the way her chest heaved up and down as he sat astride her, and imagining the expression of abject terror on her face when she realized she was completely in his power; and then he heard hoofbeats again.

This time there was only one horse.

He straightened up, took out his knife, pressed his back against the tree, and listened again.

It was a good, fast horse, not a war-horse but probably a solid courser. It was carrying a moderate weight, such as a man with no armor, and coming at a steady all-day trot, not even breathing hard. William caught Walter's eye and nodded: this was the one, here was the evidence. He raised his right arm, holding the knife by the tip of the blade.

In the distance, William's own horse whinnied.

The sound carried clearly through the still forest and was perfectly audible over the light tattoo of the approaching horse. The horse heard it, and broke its stride. Its rider said "Whoa," and slowed it to a walk. William cursed under his breath. The rider would be wary now, and that would make everything more difficult. Too late, William wished he had taken his own horse farther away.

He could not tell how far away the approaching horse was now that it was walking. Everything was going wrong. He resisted the temptation to look out from behind his tree. He listened hard, taut with strain. Suddenly he heard the horse snort, shockingly close, and then it appeared a yard from where he stood. It saw him a moment after he saw it. It shied, and the rider let out a grunt of surprise.

William cursed. He realized instantly that the horse might turn and bolt the wrong way. He ducked back behind the tree and came out on the other side, behind the horse, with his throwing arm raised. He caught a glimpse of the rider, bearded and frowning as he tugged at the reins: it was tough old Gilbert Catface. William threw the knife.

It was a perfect throw. The knife struck the horse's rump point-first and sank an inch or more into its flesh.

The horse seemed to start, as a man does when shocked; then, before Gilbert could react, it broke into a panic-stricken gallop and took off at top speed—heading straight for Walter's ambush.

William ran after it. The horse covered the distance to where Walter was in a few moments. Gilbert was making no effort to control his mount—he was too busy trying to stay in the saddle. They drew level with Walter's position, and William thought: Now, Walter, now!

Walter timed his move so finely that William never actually saw the pole shoot out from behind the tree. He just saw the horse's forelegs crumple, as if all the strength had left them suddenly. Then its hind legs seemed to catch up with its forelegs, so that they all became entangled. Finally its head went down, its hindquarters went up, and it fell heavily.

Gilbert flew through the air. Going after him, William was brought up short by the fallen horse.

Gilbert landed well, rolled over and got to his knees. For a moment William was afraid he might run off and escape. Then Walter came out of the undergrowth, launched himself through the air, and cannoned into Gilbert's back, knocking him flat.

Both men hit the ground hard. They recovered their balance at the same time, and William saw to his horror that the wily Gilbert had come up with a knife in his hand. William leaped over the fallen horse and swung the oak club at Gilbert just as Gilbert raised his knife. The club hit the side of Gilbert's head.

Gilbert staggered but got to his feet. William damned him for being so *tough*. William drew back the club for another swing but Gilbert was faster, and lunged at William with the knife. William was dressed for courting, not fighting, and the sharp blade sliced through his fine wool cloak; but he jumped back quickly enough to save his skin. Gilbert continued coming at him, keeping him off balance so that he could not wield the club. Each time Gilbert lunged, William jumped back; but William never had quite enough time to recover, and Gilbert rapidly closed on him. Suddenly William was afraid for his life. Then Walter came up behind Gilbert and kicked his legs from under him.

William sagged with relief. For a moment there he had thought he was going to die. He thanked God for Walter.

Gilbert tried to get up but Walter kicked him in the face. William hit him with the club twice for good measure, and after that Gilbert lay still.

They rolled him onto his front, and Walter sat on his head while William tied his hands behind his back. Then William took off Gilbert's long black boots and bound his bare ankles together with a strong piece of leather harness.

He stood up. He grinned at Walter, and Walter smiled. It was a relief to have this slippery old fighter securely tied up.

The next step was to make Gilbert confess.

He was coming round. Walter turned him over. When Gilbert saw William he registered recognition, then surprise, then fear. William was gratified. Gilbert was already regretting his laughter, William thought. In a while he was going to regret it even more.

Gilbert's horse was on its feet, remarkably. It had run a few yards off, but had stopped and was now looking back, breathing hard and starting every time the wind rustled in the trees. William's knife had fallen out of its rump. William picked up his knife and Walter went to catch the horse.

William was listening for the sound of riders. Another messenger might come along at any moment. If that happened Gilbert would have to be dragged out of sight and kept quiet. But no riders came, and Walter was able to catch Gilbert's horse without too much difficulty.

They slung Gilbert across the back of his horse, then led it through the forest to where William had left their own mounts. The other horses became agitated when they smelled the blood seeping from the wound in Gilbert's horse's rump, so William tethered it a little way off.

He looked around for a tree suitable to his purpose. He located an elm with a stout branch protruding at a height of eight or nine feet off the ground. He pointed it out to Walter. "I want to suspend Gilbert from this bough," he said.

Walter grinned sadistically. "What are you going to do to him, lord?"

"You'll see."

Gilbert's leathery face was white with fear. William passed a rope under the man's armpits, tied it behind his back, and looped it over the branch.

"Lift him," he said to Walter.

Walter hoisted Gilbert. Gilbert wriggled and got free of Walter's grasp, falling on the ground. Walter picked up William's club and beat Gilbert about the head until he was groggy, then picked him up again. William threw the loose end of the rope over the branch several times and pulled it tight. Walter released Gilbert and he swung gently from the branch with his feet a yard off the ground.

"Collect some firewood," William said.

They built a fire under Gilbert, and William lit it with a spark from a flint. After a few moments the flames began to rise. The heat brought Gilbert out of his daze.

When he realized what was happening to him he began to moan in terror. "Please," he said. "Please let me down. I'm sorry I laughed at you, please have mercy."

William was silent. Gilbert's groveling was very satisfying, but it was not what William was after.

When the heat began to hurt Gilbert's bare toes, he bent his legs at the knee to take his feet out of the fire. His face was running with sweat, and there was a faint smell of scorching as his clothes got hot. William judged it was time to start the interrogation. He said: "Why did you go to the castle today?"

Gilbert stared wide-eyed at him. "To pay my respects," he said. "Does it matter?"

"Why did you go to pay your respects?"

"The earl has just returned from Normandy."

"You weren't summoned especially?"

"No."

It might be true, William reflected. Interrogating a prisoner was not as straightforward as he had imagined. He thought again. "What did the earl say to you when you went up to his chamber?"

"He greeted me, and thanked me for coming to welcome him home."

Was there a look of wary comprehension in Gilbert's eyes? William was not sure. He said: "What else?"

"He asked after my family and my village."

"Nothing else?"

"Nothing. Why do you care what he said?"

"What did he say to you about King Stephen and the Empress Maud?"

"Nothing, I tell you!"

Gilbert could not keep his knees bent any longer, and his feet fell back into the growing flames. After a second, a yell of agony burst from him, and his body convulsed. The spasm took his feet out of the flames momentarily. He realized then that he could ease the pain by swinging to and fro. With each swing, however, he passed through the flames and cried out again.

Once more William wondered whether Gilbert might be telling the truth. There was no way of knowing. At some point, presumably, he would be in so much agony that he would say whatever he thought William wanted him to say, in a desperate attempt to get some relief; so it was important not to give him too clear an idea of what was wanted, William thought worriedly. Who would have thought that torturing people could be so difficult?

He made his voice calm and almost conversational. "Where are you going now?"

Gilbert screamed in pain and frustration: "What does it matter?"

"Where are you going?"

"Home!"

The man was losing his grip. William knew where he lived, and it was north of here. He had been heading in the wrong direction.

"Where are you going?" William said again.

"What do you want from me?"

"I know when you're lying," William said. "Just tell me the truth." He heard Walter give a low grunt of approval, and he thought: I'm getting better at this. "Where are you going?" he said for the fourth time.

Gilbert became too exhausted to swing himself anymore. Groaning in pain, he came to a stop over the fire, and once more bent his legs to take his feet out of the flames. But now the fire was burning high enough to singe his knees. William noticed a smell, vaguely familiar but also slightly sickening; and after a moment he realized it was the smell of burning flesh, and it was familiar because it was like the smell of dinner. The skin of Gilbert's legs and feet was turning brown and cracking, the hairs on his shins going black; and fat from his flesh dripped into the fire and sizzled. Watching his agony mesmerized William. Every time Gilbert cried out, William felt a profound thrill. He had the power of pain over a man, and it made him feel good. It was a bit like the way he felt when he got a girl alone, in a place where nobody could hear her protest, and pinned her to the ground, pulling her skirts up around her waist, and knew that nothing could now stop him from having her.

Almost reluctantly, he said again: "Where are you going?"

In a voice that was a suppressed scream, Gilbert said: "To Sherborne."

"Why?"

"Cut me down, for the love of Christ Jesus, and I'll tell you everything."

William sensed victory within his grasp. It was deeply satisfying. But he was not quite there yet. He said to Walter: "Just pull his feet out of the fire."

Walter grabbed Gilbert's tunic and pulled on it so that his legs were clear of the flames.

"Now," William said.

"Earl Bartholomew has fifty knights in and around Sherborne," Gilbert said in a strangled cry. "I am to muster them and bring them to Earlscastle."

William smiled. All his guesses were proving gratifyingly accurate. "And what is the earl planning to do with these knights?"

"He didn't say."

William said to Walter: "Let him burn a little more."

"No!" Gilbert screamed. "I'll tell you!"

Walter hesitated.

"Quickly," William warned.

"They are to fight for the Empress Maud, against Stephen," Gilbert said at last.

That was it: that was the proof. William savored his success.

"And when I ask you this in front of my father, will you answer the same?" he said.

"Yes, yes."

"And when my father asks you in front of the king, will you still tell the truth?"

"Yes!"

"Swear by the cross."

"I swear by the cross, I'll tell the truth!"

"Amen," William said contentedly, and he began to stamp out the fire.

They tied Gilbert to his saddle and put his horse on a leading rein, then rode on at a walk. The knight was barely able to stay upright, and William did not want him to die, for he was no use dead, so he tried not to treat him too roughly. Next time they passed a stream he threw cold water over the knight's burned feet. Gilbert screamed in pain, but it probably did him good.

William felt a wonderful sense of triumph mingled with an odd kind of frustration. He had never killed a man, and he wished he could kill Gilbert. Torturing a man without killing him was like stripping a girl naked without raping her. The more he thought about that, the more he felt the need of a woman.

Perhaps when he got home . . . no, there would be no time. He would have to tell his parents what had happened, and they would want Gilbert to repeat his confession in front of a priest and perhaps some other witnesses; and then they would have to plan the capture of Earl Bartholomew, which would surely have to take place tomorrow, before Bartholomew mustered too many fighting men. And still William had not thought of a way to take that castle by stealth, without a prolonged siege. . . .

He was thinking with frustration that it might be a long time before he even *saw* an attractive woman when one appeared on the road ahead.

There were five people in a group, walking toward William. One of them was a dark-haired woman of about twenty-five years, not exactly a girl, but young enough. As she came closer William became more interested: she was quite beautiful, with dark brown hair that came to a devil's peak on her brow, and deep-set eyes of an intense golden color. She had a trim, lithe figure and smooth tanned skin.

"Stay back," William said to Walter. "Keep the knight behind you while I talk to them."

The group stopped and looked warily at him. They were a

family, obviously: there was a tall man who was presumably the husband, a lad who was full-grown but not yet bearded, and a couple of sprats. The man looked familiar, William realized with a start. 'Do I know you?' he said.

"I know you," the man said. "And I know your horse, for together you almost killed my daughter."

It began to come back to William. His horse had not touched the child, but it had been close. "You were building my house," he said. "And when I dismissed you, you demanded payment, and almost threatened me."

The man looked defiant, and did not deny it.

"You're not so cocky now," William said with a sneer. The whole family appeared to be starving. It was turning out to be a good day for settling accounts with people who had offended William Hamleigh. "Are you hungry?"

"Yes, we're hungry," said the builder in a tone of sullen anger.

William looked again at the woman. She stood with her feet a little apart and her chin up, staring at him fearlessly. He had been inflamed by Aliena and now he wanted to slake his lust with this one. She would be lively, he felt sure: she would wriggle and scratch. All the better.

"You're not married to this girl, are you, builder?" he said. "I remember your wife—an ugly cow."

The shadow of pain crossed the builder's face, and he said: "My wife died."

"And you haven't taken this one to church, have you? You haven't got a penny to pay the priest." Behind William, Walter coughed and the horses moved impatiently. "Suppose I give you money for food," William said to the builder, to tantalize him.

"I'll accept it gratefully," the man said, although William could tell it hurt him to be subservient.

"I'm not talking about a gift. I'll buy your woman."

The woman herself spoke. "I'm not for sale, boy."

Her scorn was well directed, and William was angered. I'll show you whether I'm a man or a boy, he thought, when I get you alone. He spoke to the builder. "I'll give you a pound of silver for her."

"She's not for sale."

William's anger grew. It was infuriating to offer a fortune to a starving man and be turned down. He said: "You fool, if you don't take the money I'll run you through with my sword and fuck her in front of the children!"

The builder's arm moved under his cloak. He must have some

kind of weapon, William thought. He was also very big, and although he was as thin as a knife he might put up a mean fight to save his woman. The woman moved her cloak aside and rested her hand on the hilt of a surprisingly long dagger at her belt. The older boy was big enough to cause trouble, too.

Walter spoke in a low but carrying voice. "Lord, there's no time for this."

William nodded reluctantly. He had to get Gilbert back to the Hamleigh manor house. It was too important to delay with a brawl over a woman. He would just have to suffer.

He looked at the little family of five ragged, hungry people, ready to fight to the finish against two beefy men with horses and swords. He could not understand them. "All right, then, starve to death," he said. He kicked his horse and trotted on, and a few moments later they were out of sight.

II

When they were a mile or so from the place where they had encountered William Hamleigh, Ellen said: "Can we slow down now?"

Tom realized he had been setting a fierce pace. He had been frightened: for a moment, back there, it had looked as if he and Alfred would have to fight two armed men on horseback. Tom did not even have a weapon. He had reached under his cloak for his mason's hammer and then remembered, painfully, that he had sold it weeks ago for a sack of oats. He was not sure why William had backed off in the end, but he wanted to put as much distance as possible between them in case the young lord changed his evil little mind.

Tom had failed to find work at the palace of the bishop of Kingsbridge and at every other place he had tried. However, there was a quarry in the vicinity of Shiring, and a quarry—unlike a building site—employed as many men in winter as it did in summer. Of course, Tom's usual work was more skilled and better paid than quarrying, but he was a long way past caring about that. He just wanted to feed his family. The quarry at Shiring was owned by Earl Bartholomew, and Tom had been told that the earl could be found at his castle a few miles to the west of the town.

Now that he had Ellen he was even more desperate than before. He knew that she had thrown her lot in with him for love, and had not weighed the consequences carefully. In particular, she did not have a clear idea of how difficult it might be for Tom to get work. She had not really confronted the possibility that they might not survive the winter, and Tom had held back from disillusioning her, for he wanted her to stay with him. But a woman was liable to put her child before everything else, in the end, and Tom was afraid Ellen would leave him.

They had been together a week: seven days of despair and seven nights of joy. Every morning Tom woke up feeling happy and optimistic. As the day wore on he would get hungry, the children would tire and Ellen would become morose. Some days they got fed—like the time they met the monk with the cheese—and some days they chewed on strips of sun-dried venison from Ellen's reserve. It was like eating deer hide but it was better than nothing, just. But when it got dark they would lie down, cold and miserable, and hold one another close for warmth; then after a while they would start stroking and kissing. At first Tom had always wanted to enter her immediately, but she refused him gently: she wanted to play and kiss much longer. He did it her way and was enchanted. He explored her body boldly, caressing her in places where he had never touched Agnes, her armpits and her ears and the cleft of her buttocks. Some nights they giggled together with their heads beneath their cloaks. At other times they felt very tender. One night when they were alone in the guesthouse of a monastery, and the children were in an exhausted sleep, she was dominant and insistent, commanding him to do things to her, showing him how to excite her with his fingers, and he complied, feeling bemused and inflamed by her shamelessness. When it was all over they would fall into a deep, restful sleep, with the day's fear and anger washed away by love.

It was now midday. Tom judged that William Hamleigh was far away, so he decided to stop for a rest. They had no food other than the dried venison. However, this morning they had begged some bread at a lonely farmhouse, and the woman had given them some ale in a big wooden bottle with no stopper, and told them to keep the bottle. Ellen had saved half the ale for dinner.

Tom sat on the edge of a broad old tree stump and Ellen sat beside him. She took a long draft of the ale and passed it to him. "Do you want some meat as well?" she asked.

He shook his head and drank some ale. He could easily have swallowed it all, but he left some for the children. "Save the meat," he said to Ellen. "We may get supper at the castle."

Alfred put the bottle to his mouth and drained it.

Jack looked crestfallen and Martha burst into tears. Alfred gave an odd little grin.

Ellen looked at Tom. After a few moments she said: "You shouldn't let Alfred get away with that."

Tom shrugged. "He's bigger than they are—he needs it more."

"He always gets a large share anyway. The little ones must have *something*."

"It's a waste of time to interfere in children's quarrels," Tom said.

Ellen's voice became harsh. "You're saying that Alfred can bully the younger children as much as he likes and you will do nothing about it."

"He doesn't bully them," Tom said. "Children always fight."

She shook her head, seeming bewildered. "I don't understand you. In every other way you're a kind man. But where Alfred is concerned, you're just blind."

She was exaggerating, Tom felt, but he did not want to displease her, so he said: "Give the little ones some meat, then."

Ellen opened her bag. She still looked cross. She cut off a strip of dried venison for Martha and another for Jack. Alfred held out his hand for some, but Ellen ignored him. Tom thought she should have given him some. There was nothing wrong with Alfred. Ellen just did not understand him. He was a big boy, Tom thought proudly, and he had a big appetite and a quick temper, and if that was a sin, then half the adolescent boys in the world were damned.

They rested for a while and then walked on. Jack and Martha went ahead, still chewing the leathery meat. The two young ones got on well, despite the difference in their ages—Martha was six and Jack was probably eleven or twelve. But Martha thought Jack was utterly fascinating, and Jack seemed to be enjoying the novel experience of having another child to play with. It was a pity that Alfred did not like Jack. This surprised Tom: he would have expected that Jack, who was not yet becoming a man, would be beneath Alfred's contempt; but it was not so. Alfred was the stronger, of course, but little Jack was clever.

Tom refused to worry about it. They were just boys. He had too much on his mind to waste time fretting over children's squabbles. Sometimes he wondered secretly whether he would ever get work again. He might go on tramping the roads day after day until one by one they died off: a child found cold and lifeless one frosty morning, another too weak to fight off a fever, Ellen ravished and killed by a passing thug like William Hamleigh, and Tom himself becoming thinner and thinner until one day he was too weak to stand up in the morning, and lay on the forest floor until he slipped into unconsciousness.

Ellen would leave him before that happened, of course. She would return to her cave, where there was still a barrel of apples and a sack of nuts, enough to keep two people alive until the spring, but not enough for five. Tom would be heartbroken if she did that.

He wondered how the baby was. The monks had called him Jonathan. Tom liked the name. It meant a gift from God, according to the monk with the cheese. Tom pictured little Jonathan, red and wrinkled and bald, the way he was born. He would be different now: a week was a long time for a newborn baby. He would be bigger already, and his eyes would open wider. Now he would no longer be oblivious to the world around him: a loud noise would make him jump and a lullaby would soothe him. When he needed to burp, his mouth would curl up at the corners. The monks probably would not know that it was wind, and would take it for a real smile.

Tom hoped they were caring for him well. The monk with the cheese had given the impression that they were kindly and capable men. Anyway, they were certainly better able to look after the baby than Tom, who was homeless and penniless. If I ever become master of a really big construction project, and earn forty-eight pence a week plus allowances, I'll give money to that monastery, he thought.

They emerged from the forest and soon afterward they came within sight of the castle.

Tom's spirits lifted, but he repressed his enthusiasm fiercely: he had suffered months of disappointment, and he had learned that the more hopeful he was at the start, the more painful was the rejection at the end.

They approached the castle on a path through bare fields. Martha and Jack came upon an injured bird, and they all stopped to look. It was a wren, so small that they might easily have missed it. Martha stooped over it, and it hopped away, apparently unable to fly. She caught it and picked it up, cradling the tiny creature in her cupped hands.

"It's trembling!" she said. "I can feel it. It must be frightened."

The bird made no further attempt to escape, but sat still in Martha's hands, its bright eyes gazing at the people all around. Jack said: "I think it's got a broken wing."

Alfred said: "Let me see." He took the bird from her.

"We could take care of it," Martha said. "Perhaps it will get better."

"No, it won't," Alfred said. With a quick motion of his big hands he wrung the bird's neck.

Ellen said: "Oh, for God's *sake*."

Martha burst into tears for the second time that day.

Alfred laughed and dropped the bird on the ground.

Jack picked it up. "Dead," he said.

Ellen said: "What is *wrong* with you, Alfred?"

Tom said: "Nothing's wrong with him. The bird was going to die."

He walked on, and the others followed. Ellen was angry with Alfred again, and it made Tom cross. Why make a fuss about a damned wren? Tom remembered what it was like to be fourteen years old, a boy with the body of a man: life was frustrating. Ellen had said *Where Alfred is concerned, you're just blind*, but she did not understand.

The wooden bridge that led over the moat to the gatehouse was flimsy and ramshackle, but that was probably how the earl liked it: a bridge was a means of access for attackers, and the more readily it fell down, the safer the castle was. The perimeter walls were of earth with stone towers at intervals. Ahead of them as they crossed the bridge was a stone gatehouse, like two towers with a connecting walkway. Plenty of stonework here, Tom thought; not one of these castles that are all mud and wood. Tomorrow I could be working. He remembered the feel of good tools in his hands, the scrape of the chisel across a block of stone as he squared its sides and smoothed its face, the dry feel of the dust in his nostrils. Tomorrow night my belly may be full—with food I've earned, not begged.

Coming closer, he noticed with his mason's eye that the battlements on top of the gatehouse were in bad condition. Some of the big stones had fallen, leaving the parapet quite level in parts. There were also loose stones in the arch of the gateway.

There were two sentries at the gate, and both looked alert. Perhaps they were expecting trouble. One of them asked Tom his business.

"Stonemason, hoping to be hired to work in the earl's quarry," he replied.

"Look for the earl's steward," the sentry said helpfully. "His name is Matthew. You'll probably find him in the great hall."

"Thanks," Tom said. "What kind of a man is he?"

The guard grinned at his colleague and said: "Not much of a man at all," and they both laughed.

Tom supposed he would soon find out what that meant. He went in, and Ellen and the children followed. The buildings within the walls were mostly wooden, though some were raised on stone skirtings, and there was one built all of stone that was probably the chapel. As they crossed the compound Tom noticed that the towers around the perimeter all had loose stones and damaged battlements. They crossed the second moat to the upper circle, and stopped at the second gatehouse. Tom told the guard he was looking for Matthew Steward. They all went on into the upper compound and approached the square stone keep. The wooden door at ground level clearly opened into the undercroft. They went up the wooden steps to the hall.

Tom saw both the steward and the earl as soon as he went in. He knew who they were by their clothes. Earl Bartholomew wore a long tunic with flared cuffs on the sleeves and embroidery on the hem. Matthew Steward wore a short tunic, in the same style as the one Tom was wearing, but made of a softer cloth, and he had a little round cap. They were near the fireplace, the earl sitting and the steward standing. Tom approached the two men and stood just out of earshot, waiting for them to notice him. Earl Bartholomew was a tall man of over fifty, with white hair and a pale, thin, haughty face. He did not look like a man of generous spirit. The steward was younger. He stood in a way that reminded Tom of the guard's remark: it looked feminine. Tom was not sure what to make of him.

There were several other people in the hall, but none of them took any notice of Tom. He waited, feeling hopeful and fearful by turns. The earl's conversation with his steward seemed to take forever. At last it ended, and the steward bowed and turned aside. Tom stepped forward with his heart in his mouth. "Are you Matthew?" he said.

"Yes."

"My name is Tom. Master mason. I'm a good craftsman, and my children are starving. I hear you have a quarry." He held his breath.

"We have a quarry, but I don't think we need any more quarrymen," Matthew said. He glanced back at the earl, who shook his head almost imperceptibly. "No," Matthew said. "We can't hire you."

It was the speed of the decision that broke Tom's heart. If people were solemn, and thought hard about it, and rejected him regretfully, he could bear it more easily. Matthew was not a cruel man, Tom could tell, but he was busy, and Tom and his starving family were just another item to be disposed of as quickly as possible.

Tom said desperately: "I could do some repairs here at the castle."

"We have a wright who does all that kind of work for us," Matthew said.

A wright was a jack-of-all-trades, usually trained as a carpenter. "I'm a mason," Tom said. "My walls are strong."

Matthew was annoyed with him for arguing, and seemed about to say something angry; then he looked at the children and his face softened again. "I'd like to give you work, but we don't need you."

Tom nodded. He should now humbly accept what the steward had said, put on a pitiful look, and beg for a meal and a place to sleep for one night. But Ellen was with him, and he was afraid she would leave, so he gave it one more try. He said in a voice loud enough for the earl to hear: "I just hope you're not expecting to do battle soon."

The effect was much more dramatic than he had expected. Matthew gave a start, and the earl got to his feet and said sharply: "Why do you say that?"

Tom perceived he had touched a nerve. "Because your defenses are in bad repair," he said.

"In what way?" the earl said. "Be specific, man!"

Tom took a deep breath. The earl was irritated but attentive. Tom would not get another chance after this. "The mortar in the gatehouse walls has come away in places. This leaves an opening for a crowbar. An enemy could easily pry out a stone or two; and once there's a hole it's easy to pull the wall down. Also"—he hurried on breathlessly, before anyone could comment or argue—"also, all your battlements are damaged. They're level in places. This leaves your archers and knights unprotected from—"

"I know what battlements are for," the earl interrupted tetchily. "Anything else?"

"Yes. The keep has an undercroft with a wooden door. If I were attacking the keep I'd go through that door and start a fire in the stores."

"And if you were the earl, how would you prevent that?"

"I'd have a pile of stones, ready shaped, and a supply of sand and lime for mortar, and a mason standing by ready to block up that doorway in times of danger."

Earl Bartholomew stared at Tom. His pale blue eyes were narrowed and there was a frown on his white forehead. Tom could not read his expression. Was he angry with Tom for being so critical of the castle defenses? You could never tell how a lord would react to criticism. By and large it was best to let them make their own mistakes. But Tom was a desperate man.

At last the earl seemed to reach a conclusion. He turned to Matthew and said: "Hire this man."

A whoop of jubilation rose in Tom's throat and he had to choke it back. He could hardly believe it. He looked at Ellen and they both smiled happily. Martha, who did not suffer from adult inhibitions, shouted: "Horray!"

Earl Bartholomew turned away and spoke to a knight standing nearby. Matthew smiled at Tom. "Have you had dinner today?" he said.

Tom swallowed. He was so happy he felt close to tears. "No, we haven't."

"I'll take you to the kitchen."

Eagerly, they followed the steward out of the hall and across the bridge to the lower compound. The kitchen was a large wood building with a stone skirting. Matthew told them to wait outside. There was a sweet smell in the air: they were baking pastries in there. Tom's belly rumbled and his mouth watered so much it hurt. After a moment Matthew emerged with a big pot of ale and handed it to Tom. "They'll bring out some bread and cold bacon in a moment," he said. He left them.

Tom took a swallow of the ale and passed the pot to Ellen. She gave some to Martha, then took a drink herself and passed it to Jack. Alfred made a grab for it before Jack could drink. Jack turned away, keeping the pot out of Alfred's reach. Tom did not want another quarrel between the children, not now when everything had turned out all right at last. He was about to intervene—thereby breaking his own rule about interference in children's squabbles—when Jack turned around again and meekly handed the pot to Alfred.

Alfred put the pot to his mouth and began to drink. Tom had only taken a swallow, and he thought the pot would come around to him again; but Alfred looked set to drain it. Then a strange thing happened. As Alfred upended the pot to drink the last of the ale, something like a small animal fell out onto his face.

Alfred gave a frightened yell and dropped the pot. He brushed the furry thing off his face, jumping back. "What is it?" he screeched. The thing fell to the floor. He stared down at it, white-faced and trembling with disgust.

They all looked. It was the dead wren.

Tom caught Ellen's eye, and they both looked at Jack. Jack had taken the pot from Ellen, then turned his back for a moment, as if trying to evade Alfred, then handed the pot to Alfred with surprising willingness. . . .

Now he stood quietly, looking at the horrified Alfred with a faint smile of satisfaction on his clever young-old face.

Jack knew he would suffer for that.

Alfred would take his revenge somehow. When the others were not looking, Alfred would punch him in the stomach, perhaps. This was a favorite blow, for it was very painful but left no marks. Jack had seen him do it to Martha several times.

But it had been worth a punch in the stomach just to see the shock and fear on Alfred's face when the dead bird fell out of his beer.

Alfred hated Jack. This was a new experience for Jack. His

mother had always loved him and no one else had had any feelings for him. There was no apparent reason for Alfred's hostility. He seemed to feel much the same about Martha. He was always pinching her, pulling her hair and tripping her, and he relished any opportunity to spoil something she valued. Jack's mother saw what was going on, and hated it, but Alfred's father seemed to think it was all perfectly normal, even though he himself was a kind and gentle man who obviously loved Martha. The whole thing was baffling, but nonetheless fascinating.

Everything was fascinating. Jack had never had such an exciting time in the whole of his life. Despite Alfred, despite feeling hungry most of the time, despite being hurt by the way his mother constantly paid attention to Tom instead of to him, Jack was spellbound by a constant stream of strange phenomena and new experiences.

The castle was the latest in a series of wonders. He had heard about castles: in the long winter evenings in the forest, his mother had taught him to recite *chansons*, narrative poems in French about knights and magicians, most of them thousands of lines long; and castles featured in those stories as places of refuge and romance. Never having seen a castle, he imagined it would be a slightly larger version of the cave in which he lived. The real thing was amazing: it was so big, with so many buildings and such a host of people, all of them so *busy*—shoeing horses, drawing water, feeding chickens, baking bread, and carrying things, always carrying things, straw for the floors, wood for the fires, sacks of flour, bales of cloth, swords and saddles and suits of mail. Tom told him that the moat and the wall were not natural parts of the landscape, but had actually been dug and built by dozens of men all working together. Jack did not disbelieve Tom, but he found it impossible to imagine how it had been done.

At the end of the afternoon, when it became too dark to work, all the busy people gravitated to the great hall of the keep. Rushlights were lit and the fire was built higher, and all the dogs came in from the cold. Some of the men and women took boards and trestles from a stack at the side of the room and set up tables in the shape of the letter T, then ranged chairs along the top of the T and benches down the sides. Jack had never seen people working together in large numbers, and he was struck by how much they enjoyed it. They smiled and laughed as they lifted the heavy boards, calling "Hup!" and "To me, to me," and "Down easy, now." Jack envied their camaraderie, and wondered whether he might share it one day.

After a while everyone sat on the benches. One of the castle servants distributed big wooden bowls and wooden spoons, counting aloud as he gave them out; then he went around again and put a thick slice of stale brown bread in the bottom of each bowl. Another servant brought wooden cups and filled them with ale from a series of big jugs. Jack and Martha and Alfred, all sitting together at the bottom end of the T, got a cup of ale each, so there was nothing to fight over. Jack picked up his cup, but his mother told him to wait for a moment.

When the ale had been poured the hall went quiet. Jack waited, fascinated as always, to see what would happen next. After a moment Earl Bartholomew appeared on the staircase that led down from his bedroom. He came down into the hall, followed by Matthew Steward, three or four other well-dressed men, a boy, and the most beautiful creature Jack had ever set eyes upon.

It was a girl or a woman, he was not sure which. She was dressed in white, and her tunic had amazing flared sleeves which trailed on the ground behind her as she glided down the stairs. Her hair was a mass of dark curls tumbling around her face, and she had dark, dark eyes. Jack realized that this was what the *chansons* meant when they referred to a beautiful princess in a castle. No wonder the knights all wept when the princess died.

When she reached the foot of the stairs Jack saw that she was quite young, just a few years older than himself; but she held her head high and walked to the head of the table like a queen. She sat down beside Earl Bartholomew.

"Who is she?" Jack whispered.

Martha replied: "She must be the earl's daughter."

"What's her name?"

Martha shrugged, but a dirty-faced girl sitting next to Jack said: "She's called Aliena. She's wonderful."

The earl raised his cup to Aliena, then looked slowly all around the table, and drank. That was the signal everyone had been waiting for. They all followed suit, raising their cups before drinking.

The supper was brought in in huge steaming cauldrons. The earl was served first; then his daughter, the boy, and the men with them at the head of the table; then everyone else helped themselves. It was salt fish in a spicy stew. Jack filled his bowl and ate it all, then ate the bread trencher at the bottom of the bowl, soaked with oily soup. In between mouthfuls he watched Aliena, riveted by everything she did, from the dainty way she speared bits of fish on the end of her knife and delicately put them between her white teeth, to the commanding voice in which she called servants and gave them orders. They all seemed to like her. They came quickly when she called, smiled when she spoke, and hurried to do her bidding. The young men around the table looked at her a lot, Jack observed, and some of them showed off when they thought she was looking their way. But she was concerned mainly with the older men with her father, making sure they had enough bread and wine, asking them questions and listening attentively to their answers. Jack wondered what it would be like to have a beautiful princess speak to you, then look at you with big dark eyes while you replied.

After supper there was music. Two men and a woman played tunes with sheep bells, a drum, and pipes made from the bones of animals and birds. The earl closed his eyes and seemed to become lost in the music, but Jack did not like the haunting, melancholy tunes they played. He preferred the cheerful songs his mother sang. The other people in the hall seemed to feel the same way, for they fidgeted and shuffled, and there was a general sense of relief when the music ended.

Jack was hoping to get a closer look at Aliena, but to his disappointment she left the room after the music, and went up the stairs. She must have her own bedroom on the top floor, he realized.

The children and some of the adults played chess and nine-men's morris to while away the evening, and the more industrious people made belts, caps, socks, gloves, bowls, whistles, dice, shovels and horsewhips. Jack played several games of chess, winning them all; but a man-at-arms was angry at being defeated by a child and after that Jack's mother made him stop playing. He moved around the hall, listening to the different conversations. Some people talked sensibly, he found, about the fields and the animals, or about bishops and kings, while others only teased one another, and boasted, and told funny stories. He found them all equally intriguing.

Eventually the rushlights burned down, the earl retired, and the other sixty or seventy people wrapped their cloaks around them and lay down on the straw-covered floor to sleep.

As usual, his mother and Tom lay down together, under Tom's big cloak, and she hugged him the way she used to hug Jack when he was small. He watched enviously. He could hear them talking quietly, and his mother gave a low, intimate laugh. After a while their bodies began to move rhythmically under the cloak. The first time he had seen them do this, Jack had been terribly worried, thinking that whatever it was, it must hurt; but they kissed one another while they were doing it, and although sometimes his mother moaned, he could tell it was a moan of pleasure. He was reluctant to ask her about it, he was not sure why. Now, however, as the fire burned lower, he saw another couple doing the same sort of thing, and he was forced to conclude that it must be normal. It was just another mystery, he thought, and soon after that he fell asleep.

The children were awake early in the morning, but breakfast could not be served until mass had been said, and mass could not be said until the earl got up, so they had to wait. An early-rising servant conscripted them to bring in firewood for the day. The adults started to wake as the cold morning air came in through the door. When the children had finished bringing in the wood, they met Aliena.

She came down the stairs, as she had last night, but now she looked different. She wore a short tunic and felt boots. Her massed curls were tied back with a ribbon, showing the graceful line of her jaw, her small ears and her white neck. Her big dark eyes, which had seemed grave and adult last night, now sparkled with fun, and she was smiling. She was followed by the boy who had sat at the head of the table with her and the earl last night. He looked a year or two older than Jack, but he was not full-grown like Alfred. He looked curiously at Jack, Martha and Alfred, but it was the girl who spoke. "Who are you?" she said.

Alfred replied. "My father is the stonemason who's going to repair this castle. I'm Alfred. My sister's name is Martha. That's Jack."

When she came close Jack could smell lavender, and he was awestruck. How could a person smell of flowers?

"How old are you?" she said to Alfred.

"Fourteen." Alfred was also overawed by her, Jack could tell. After a moment Alfred blurted: "How old are you?"

"Fifteen. Do you want something to eat?"

"Yes."

"Come with me."

They all followed her out of the hall and down the steps. Alfred said: "But they don't serve breakfast before mass."

"They do what I tell them," Aliena said with a toss of her head.

She led them across the bridge to the lower compound and told them to wait outside the kitchen while she went in. Martha whispered to Jack: "Isn't she pretty?" He nodded dumbly. A few moments later Aliena came out with a pot of beer and a loaf of wheat bread. She broke the bread into hunks and handed it out, then she passed the pot around.

After a while Martha said shyly: "Where's your mother?"

"My mother died," Aliena said briskly.

"Aren't you sad?" Martha said.

"I was, but it was a long time ago." She indicated the boy beside her with a jerk of her head. "Richard can't even remember it."

Richard must be her brother, Jack concluded.

"My mother's dead, too," Martha said, and tears came to her eyes.

"When did she die?" Aliena asked.

"Last week."

Aliena did not seem much moved by Martha's tears, Jack observed; unless she was being matter-of-fact to hide her own grief. She said abruptly: "Well, who's that woman with you, then?"

Jack said eagerly: "That's *my* mother." He was thrilled to have something to say to her.

She turned to him as if seeing him for the first time. "Well, where's *your* father?"

"I haven't got one," he said. He felt excited just to have her looking at him.

"Did he die, too?"

"No," Jack said. "I never had a father."

There was a moment of silence, then Aliena, Richard and Alfred all burst out laughing. Jack was puzzled, and looked blankly at them; and their laughter increased, until he began to feel mortified. What was so funny about never having had a father? Even Martha was smiling, her tears forgotten.

Alfred said in a jeering tone: "Where did you come from, then, if you didn't have a father?"

"From my mother—all young things come from their mothers," Jack said, mystified. "What have fathers got to do with it?"

They all laughed even more. Richard jumped up and down with glee, pointing a mocking finger at Jack. Alfred said to Aliena: "He doesn't know anything—we found him in the forest."

Jack's cheeks burned with shame. He had been so happy to be talking to Aliena, and now she thought he was a complete fool, a forest ignoramus; and the worst of it was he still did not know what he had said wrong. He wanted to cry, and that made it worse. The bread stuck in his throat and he could not swallow. He looked at Aliena, her lovely face alive with amusement, and he could not stand it, so he threw his bread on the ground and walked away.

Not caring where he went, he walked until he came to the bank of the castle wall, and scrambled up the steep slope to the top. There he sat down on the cold earth, looking outward, feeling sorry for himself, hating Alfred and Richard and even Martha and Aliena. Princesses were heartless, he decided.

The bell rang for mass. Religious services were yet another mystery to him. Speaking a language that was neither English nor French, the priests sang and talked to statues, to pictures, and even to beings that were completely invisible. Jack's mother avoided going to services whenever she could. As the inhabitants of the castle made their way to the chapel, Jack scooted over the top of the wall and sat out of sight on the far side.

The castle was surrounded by flat, bare fields, with woodland in the distance. Two early visitors were walking across the level ground toward the castle. The sky was full of low gray cloud. Jack wondered if it might snow.

Two more early visitors appeared within Jack's view. These two were on horseback. They rode rapidly to the castle, overtaking the first pair. They walked their horses across the wooden bridge to the gatehouse. All four visitors would have to wait until after mass before they could get on with whatever business brought them here, for everyone attended the service except for the sentries on duty.

A sudden voice close by made Jack jump. "So there you are." It was his mother. He turned to her, and she saw immediately that he was upset. "What's the matter?"

He wanted to take comfort from her, but he hardened his heart and said: "Did I have a father?"

"Yes," she said. "Everyone has a father." She knelt beside him.

He turned his face away. His humiliation had been her fault, for not telling him about his father. "What happened to him?"

"He died."

"When I was small?"

"Before you were born."

"How could he be my father, if he died before I was born?"

"Babies grow from a seed. The seed comes out of a man's prick and is planted in a woman's cunny. Then the seed grows into a baby in her belly, and when it's ready it comes out."

Jack was silent for a moment, digesting this information. He had a suspicion that it was connected with what they did in the night. "Is Tom going to plant a seed in you?" he said.

"Maybe."

"Then you'll have a new baby."

She nodded. "A brother for you. Would you like that?"

"I don't care," he said. "Tom has taken you away from me already. A brother wouldn't make any difference."

She put her arm around him and hugged him. "Nobody will ever take me away from you," she said.

That made him feel a bit better.

They sat together for a while, then she said: "It's cold here. Let's go and sit by the fire until breakfast."

He nodded. They got up and went back over the castle wall, running down the bank into the compound. There was no sign of the four visitors. Perhaps they had gone into the chapel.

As Jack and his mother walked over the bridge to the upper compound, Jack said: "What was my father's name?"

"Jack, the same as you," she said. "They called him Jack Shareburg."

That pleased him. He had the same name as his father. "So, if there's another Jack, I can tell people that I'm Jack Jackson."

"You can. People don't always call you what you want them to, but you can try."

Jack nodded. He felt better. He would think of himself as Jack Jackson. He was not so ashamed now. At least he knew about fathers, and he knew the name of his own. Jack Shareburg.

They reached the gatehouse of the upper compound. There were no sentries there. Jack's mother stopped, frowning. "I've got the oddest feeling that something strange is going on," she said. Her voice was calm and even, but there was a note of fear that chilled Jack, and he had a premonition of disaster.

His mother stepped into the small guardroom in the base of the guardhouse. A moment later Jack heard her gasp. He went in behind her. She was standing in an attitude of shock, her hand up to her mouth, staring down at the floor.

The sentry was lying flat on his back, his arms limp at his sides. His throat was cut, there was a pool of fresh blood on the ground beside him, and he was unquestionably dead.

III

William Hamleigh and his father had set off in the middle of the night, with almost a hundred knights and men-at-arms on horse-back, and Mother in the rearguard. The torchlit army, their faces muffled against the cold night air, must have terrified the inhabitants of the villages through which they thundered on their way to Earlscastle. They had reached the crossroads while it was still pitch-dark. From there they had walked their horses, to give them a rest and to minimize the noise. As dawn cracked the sky they concealed themselves in the woods across the fields from the castle of Earl Bartholomew.

William had not actually counted the number of fighting men he had seen in the castle—an omission for which Mother had berated him mercilessly, even though, as he had tried to point out, many of the men he saw there were waiting to be sent on errands, and others might have arrived after William left, so a count would not be reliable. But it would have been better than nothing, as Father had said. However, he estimated he had seen about forty men; so if there had been no great change in the few hours since, the Hamleighs would have an advantage of better than two to one.

It was nowhere near enough to besiege the castle, of course. However, they had devised a plan for taking the castle without a siege. The problem was that the attacking army would be seen by lookouts, and the castle would be closed up long before they arrived. The answer was to find some way to keep the castle open for the time it took the army to get there from its place of conceal-ment in the woods.

It had been Mother who solved the problem, of course.

"We need a diversion," she had said, scratching a boil on her chin. "Something to panic them, so that they don't notice the army until it's too late. Like a fire."

Father said: "If a stranger walks in and starts a fire, that will alert them anyway."

"It would have to be done on the sly," William said.

"Of course it would," said Mother impatiently. "You'll have to do it while they're at mass."

"Me?" William had said.

He had been put in charge of the advance party.

The morning sky lightened with painful slowness. William was nervously impatient. During the night, he and Mother and Father had added refinements to the basic idea, but still there was a great deal that could go wrong: the advance party might not get into the castle for some reason, or they might be viewed with suspicion and be unable to act surreptitiously, or they might be caught before they could achieve anything. Even if the plan worked, there would be a battle, William's first real fight. Men would be wounded and killed, and William might be one of the unlucky ones. His bowels tightened with fear. Aliena would be there, and she would know if he were vanquished. On the other hand, she would be there to see it if he triumphed. He pictured himself bursting into her bedroom with a bloody sword in his hand. Then she would wish she had not laughed at him.

From the castle came the sound of the bell for morning mass.

William nodded, and two men detached themselves from the group and began to walk across the fields toward the castle. They were Raymond and Ranulf, two hard-faced, hard-muscled men some years older than William. William had picked them himself: his father had given him complete control. Father himself would lead the main assault.

William watched Raymond and Ranulf walk briskly across the frozen fields. Before they reached the castle, he looked at Walter, then kicked his horse, and he and Walter set off across the fields at a trot. The sentries on the battlements would see two separate pairs of people, one on foot and one on horseback, approaching the castle first thing in the morning: it looked perfectly innocent.

William's timing was good. He and Walter passed Raymond and Ranulf about a hundred yards from the castle. At the bridge they dismounted. William's heart was in his mouth. If he messed up this part, the whole attack would be ruined.

There were two sentries at the gate. William had a nightmarish suspicion that there would be an ambush, and a dozen men-at-arms would spring out of concealment and hack him to pieces. The sentries looked alert but not anxious. They were not wearing armor. William and Walter had chain mail under their cloaks.

William's guts seemed to have turned to water. He could not swallow. One of the sentries recognized him. "Hello, Lord William," he said jovially. "Come courting again, have you?"

William said "Oh, my God," in a weak voice, then plunged a dagger into the sentry's belly, jabbing it up under the rib cage to the heart.

The man gasped, sagged, and opened his mouth as if to scream. A noise could spoil everything. Panicking, not knowing what to do, William pulled out the dagger and stuck it into the man's open mouth, shoving the blade into his throat to shut him up. Instead of a scream, blood flowed out of his mouth. The man's eyes closed. William pulled the dagger out as the man fell to the ground.

William's horse had sidestepped away, frightened by the sudden movements. William caught its bridle, then looked at Walter, who had taken the other sentry. Walter had knifed his man more efficiently, slitting his throat, so that he died in silence. I must remember that, William thought, next time I have to silence a man. Then he thought: I've done it! I've killed a man!

He realized he was no longer scared.

He handed his reins to Walter and ran up the spiral staircase to the gatehouse tower. On the upper level was a winding room for pulling up the drawbridge. With his sword, William hacked at the thick hawser. Two blows were sufficient to sever it. He dropped the loose end out of the window. It fell on the bank and slid softly into the moat, hardly making a splash. Now the drawbridge could not be raised against Father's attacking force. This was one of the refinements they had thought of last night.

Raymond and Ranulf arrived at the gatehouse just as William reached the foot of the stairs. Their first job was to wreck the huge ironbound oak gates which closed the arch leading from the bridge into the compound. They each took out a wooden hammer and a chisel and began to chip out the mortar surrounding the mighty iron hinges. The striking of hammer on chisel made a dull thud which sounded terribly loud to William.

William dragged the two dead sentries into the guardroom quickly. With everyone at mass, there was a strong chance the bodies would not be seen until it was too late.

He took his reins from Walter and the two of them walked out from under the arch and headed across the compound toward the stable. William forced his legs to move at a normal, unhurried pace, and glanced surreptitiously up at the sentries on the watchtowers. Had one of them seen the drawbridge rope fall into the moat? Were they wondering about the sound of hammering? Some of them were looking at William and Walter, but they did not seem agitated, and the hammering, which was already fading in William's ears, must have been inaudible from the tops of the towers. William felt relieved. The plan was working.

They reached the stables and went inside. They both draped their horses' reins loosely over a bar, so the beasts could escape.

Then William took out his flint and scraped a spark, setting fire to the straw on the floor. It was soiled and damp in patches, but nevertheless it began to smolder. He lit three more small fires, and Walter did the same. They stood watching for a moment. The horses caught a whiff of smoke, and moved nervously in the stalls. William stayed a moment longer. The fire was under way, and so was the plan.

He and Walter left the stable and went out into the open compound. At the gateway, hidden under the arch, Raymond and Ranulf were still chipping away at the mortar around the hinges. William and Walter turned toward the kitchen, to give the impression that they might be going to get something to eat, which would be natural. There was no one else in the compound: everyone was at mass. Casually looking up at the battlements, William observed that the sentries were not looking into the castle, but out across the fields, as of course they were supposed to. Nevertheless William expected someone to emerge from one of the buildings at any moment and challenge them; and then they would have to kill him right here in the open, and if that were seen the game would be up.

They skirted the kitchen and headed for the bridge leading to the upper compound. They heard the muted sounds of the service as they passed the chapel. Earl Bartholomew was in there, all unsuspecting, William thought with a thrill; he had no idea that there was an army a mile away, four of the enemy were already inside his stronghold, and his stables were on fire. Aliena was in the chapel too, praying on her knees. Soon she'll be on her knees to me, William thought, and the blood pounded in his head giddily.

They reached the bridge and started across. They had ensured that the first bridge remained passable, by cutting the drawbridge rope and disabling the gate, so that their army could get in. But the earl could still flee across the bridge and take refuge in the upper compound. William's next task was to prevent this by raising the drawbridge to make the second bridge impassable. The earl would then be isolated and vulnerable in the lower compound.

They reached the second gatehouse and a sentry stepped out of the guardroom. "You're early," he said.

William said: "We've been summoned to see the earl." He approached the sentry, but the man stepped back a pace. William did not want him to back away too far, for if he stepped out from under the arch he would be visible to the sentries on the ramparts of the upper circle.

"The earl's in chapel," the sentry said.

"We'll have to wait." This guard had to be killed quickly and quietly, but William did not know how to get close enough. He glanced at Walter for guidance, but Walter was just waiting patiently, looking imperturbable.

"There's a fire in the keep," the guard said. "Go and warm yourselves." William hesitated, and the guard began to look wary. "What are you waiting for?" he said with a trace of irritation.

William cast around desperately for something to say. "Can we get something to eat?" he said at last.

"Not until after mass," the sentry said. "Then they'll serve breakfast in the keep."

Now William saw that Walter had been edging imperceptibly to one side. If the guard would only turn a little, Walter could get behind him. William took a few casual steps in the opposite direction, going past the sentry, saying, "I'm not impressed by your earl's hospitality." The sentry was turning. William said: "We've come a long way—"

Then Walter pounced.

He stepped behind the sentry and put his arms over the man's shoulders. With his left hand he jerked the sentry's chin back, and with the knife in his right hand he slit the man's throat. William breathed a sigh of relief. It was done in a moment.

Between them, William and Walter had killed three men before breakfast. William felt a thrilling sense of power. Nobody will laugh at me after today! he thought.

Walter dragged the body into the guardroom. The plan of this gatehouse was exactly the same as that of the first one, with a spiral staircase up to the winding room. William went up the stairs and Walter followed.

William had not reconnoitered this room when he was at the castle yesterday. He had not thought to, but in any case it would have been hard to think of a plausible pretext. He had assumed that there would be a winding wheel, or at least a reel with a handle, for lifting the drawbridge; but now he saw that there was no winding gear at all, just a rope and a capstan. The only way to lift the drawbridge was to heave on the rope. William and Walter grasped it and pulled together, but the bridge did not even creak. It was a task for ten men.

William was puzzled for a moment. The other drawbridge, the one leading to the castle entrance, had a big wheel. He and Walter could have lifted that one. Then he realized that the outer drawbridge would be raised every night, whereas this one was only lifted in an emergency.

There was nothing to be gained by pondering over it, anyway. The question was what to do next. If he could not raise the drawbridge, he could at least close the gates, which would certainly delay the earl.

He ran back down the staircase with Walter close behind. As he reached the foot of the stairs he had a shock. Not everyone was at mass, it seemed. He saw a woman and a child come out of the guardroom.

William's step faltered. He recognized the woman immediately. She was the builder's wife, the one he had tried to buy yesterday for a pound. She saw him, and her penetrating honey-colored eyes looked straight through him. William did not even consider pretending to be an innocent visitor waiting for the earl: he knew she would not be deceived. He had to prevent her from giving the alarm. And the way to do that was to kill her, quickly and silently, as they had killed the sentries.

Her all-seeing eyes read his intentions in his face. She grabbed her child's hand and turned away. William made a grab for her but she was too quick for him. She ran into the compound, heading for the keep. William and Walter ran after her.

She was very light on her feet, and they were wearing chain mail and carrying heavy weapons. She reached the staircase that led up to the great hall. As she ran up the steps, she screamed. William looked up at the ramparts all around. The scream had alerted at least two sentries. The game was up. William stopped running and stood at the foot of the steps, breathing hard. Walter did the same. Two sentries, then three, then four were running down the ramparts into the compound. The woman disappeared into the keep, still hand in hand with the boy. She was no longer important: now that the sentries had been alerted there was no point in killing her.

He and Walter drew their swords and stood side by side, ready to fight for their lives.

The priest was elevating the Host over the altar when Tom realized there was something wrong with the horses. He could hear a lot of neighing and stamping, much more than was normal. A moment later someone interrupted the priest's quiet Latin chant by saying loudly: "I smell smoke!"

Tom smelled it too, then, and so did everyone else. Tom was taller than the rest and could see out of the chapel windows if he stood on tiptoe. He stepped to the side and looked out. The stables were blazing fiercely.

"Fire!" he said, and before he could say any more his voice was drowned by the shouts of the others. There was a rush for the door. The service was forgotten. Tom held Martha back, for fear she would be hurt in the crush, and told Alfred to stay with them. He wondered where Ellen and Jack were.

A moment later there was no one in the chapel but the three of them and an annoyed priest.

Tom took the children outside. Some people were releasing the horses to save them from harm, and others were drawing water from the well to throw on the flames. Tom could not see Ellen. The freed horses charged around the compound, terrified by the fire and the running, shouting people. The drumming of hooves was tremendous. Tom listened hard for a moment, and frowned: it was really *too* tremendous—it sounded more like a hundred horses than twenty or thirty. Suddenly he was struck by a frightening apprehension. "Stay right here for a moment, Martha," he said. "Alfred, you look after her." He ran up the embankment to the top of the ramparts. It was a steep slope, and he had to slow down before he reached the top. At the summit, breathing hard, he looked out.

His apprehension had been right, and now his heart was seized in the cold grip of fear. An army of horsemen, eighty to a hundred strong, was charging across the brown fields toward the castle. It was a fearsome sight. Tom could see the metallic glint of their chain mail and their drawn swords. The horses were galloping flat out, and a fog of warm breath rose from their nostrils. The riders were hunched in their saddles, grimly purposeful. There was no yelling and screaming, just the deafening thunder of hundreds of pounding hooves.

Tom looked back into the castle compound. Why could nobody else hear the army? Because the sound of the hooves was muffled by the castle walls and merged with the noise of panic in the compound. Why had the sentries seen nothing? Because they had all left their posts to fight the fire. This attack had been masterminded by someone clever. Now it was up to Tom to give the alarm.

And where was Ellen?

His eyes raked the compound as the attackers pounded nearer. Much of it was obscured by thick white smoke from the burning stables. He could not see Ellen.

He spotted Earl Bartholomew, beside the well, trying to organize the carrying of water to the fire. Tom ran down the embankment and rushed across the compound to the well. He grabbed the earl's shoulder, none too gently, and yelled in his ear to make himself heard above the din. "It's an attack!"

"What?"

"We're being attacked!"

The earl was thinking about the fire. "Attacked? Who by?"

"Listen!" Tom yelled. "A hundred horses!"

The earl cocked his head. Tom watched as realization dawned on the pale, aristocratic face. "You're right—by the cross!" He suddenly looked afraid. "Have you seen them?"

"Yes."

"Who— Never mind who! A hundred horses?"

"Yes—"

"Peter! Ralph!" The earl turned from Tom and summoned his lieutenants. "It's a raid—this fire is a diversion—we're under attack!" Like the earl, they were at first uncomprehending, then they listened, and finally they showed fear. The earl yelled: "Tell the men to get their swords—hurry, hurry!" He turned back to Tom. "Come with me, stonemason—you're strong, we can close the gates." He ran off across the compound and Tom followed him. If they could close the gates and raise the drawbridge in time, they could hold off a hundred men.

They reached the gatehouse. They could see the army through the arch. It was less than a mile away now, and spreading out, Tom observed, the faster horses in front and the stragglers behind. "Look at the gates!" the earl yelled.

Tom looked. The two great iron-banded oak gates lay flat on the ground. Their hinges had been chiseled out of the wall, he could see. Some of the enemy had been here earlier, he thought. His stomach churned with fear.

He looked back into the compound, still searching for Ellen. He could not see her. What had become of her? Anything could happen now. He needed to be with her and protect her.

"The drawbridge!" said the earl.

The best way to protect Ellen was to keep the attackers out, Tom realized. The earl ran up the spiral staircase that led to the winding room, and with an effort Tom made himself follow. If they could lift the drawbridge, a few men could hold the gatehouse. But when he reached the winding room his heart sank. The rope had been cut. There was no way to lift the drawbridge.

Earl Bartholomew cursed bitterly. "Whoever planned this is as cunning as Lucifer," he said.

It struck Tom that whoever had wrecked the gates, cut the drawbridge rope and started the fire must still be inside the castle somewhere, and he looked around fearfully, wondering where the intruders might be.

The earl glanced out of an arrow-slit window. "Dear God, they're almost here." He ran down the stairs.

Tom was close on his heels. In the gateway, several knights were hastily buckling their sword belts and putting on helmets. Earl Bartholomew started to give orders. "Ralph and John—drive some loose horses across the bridge to get in the enemy's way. Richard—Peter—Robin—get some others and make a stand here." The gateway was narrow, and a few men could hold off the attackers for a little while at least. "You—stonemason—get the servants and children across the bridge to the upper compound."

Tom was glad to have an excuse to look for Ellen. He ran to the chapel first. Alfred and Martha were where he had left them a few moments earlier, looking scared. "Go to the keep," he shouted to them. "Any other children or women you pass, tell them to go with you—orders of the earl. Run!" They ran off immediately.

Tom looked around. He would follow them soon: he was determined not to get caught in the lower compound. But he had a few moments to spare in which he could carry out the earl's order. He ran to the stable, where people were still throwing buckets of water over the flames. "Forget the fire, the castle is being attacked," he yelled. "Take your children to the keep."

Smoke got in his eyes and his vision blurred with tears. He rubbed his eyes and ran to a small crowd who were standing watching the fire consume the stables. He repeated his message to them, and to a group of stable hands who had rounded up some of the loose horses. Ellen was nowhere to be seen.

The smoke made him cough. Choking, he ran back across the compound to the bridge that led to the upper circle. He paused there, gasping for air, and looked back. People were streaming across the bridge. He was almost sure that Ellen and Jack must have gone to the keep already, but he was terrified that he might have missed them. He could see a tightly packed knot of knights engaged in fierce hand-to-hand fighting at the lower gatehouse. Otherwise there was nothing to see but smoke. Suddenly Earl Bartholomew appeared at his side, with blood on his sword and tears on his face from the smoke. "Save yourself!" the earl shouted at Tom. At that moment the attackers burst through the arch of the lower gatehouse, scattering the defending knights. Tom turned and ran across the bridge.

Fifteen or twenty of the earl's men stood at the second gatehouse, ready to defend the upper compound. They parted to let Tom and the earl through. As their ranks closed again, Tom heard hooves hammering on the wooden bridge behind him. The defenders had no chance now. At the back of his mind Tom realized that this had been a cleverly planned and perfectly executed raid. But his main thought was fear for Ellen and the children. A hundred bloodthirsty armed men were about to burst in on them. He ran across the upper compound to the keep.

Halfway up the wooden steps leading to the great hall he glanced back. The defenders of the second gatehouse were overcome almost immediately by the charging horsemen. Earl Bartholomew was on the steps behind Tom. There was just time for them both to get into the keep and lift the staircase inside. Tom ran the rest of the way up the steps and leaped into the hall—and then he saw that the attackers had been cleverer yet.

The attackers' advance party, who had wrecked the gates, and cut the rope of the drawbridge, and set fire to the stables, had performed one more task: they had come to the keep and ambushed all who took refuge there.

They were now standing just inside the great hall, four grim-faced men in chain mail. All around them were the bleeding bodies of dead and wounded knights of the earl's, who had been slaughtered as they stepped inside. And the leader of the advance party, Tom saw with a shock, was William Hamleigh.

Tom stared, stunned by surprise. William's eyes were wide with bloodlust. Tom thought William was going to kill him, but before he had time to be scared, one of William's henchmen seized Tom's arm, pulled him inside and shoved him out of the way.

So it was the Hamleighs who were attacking Earl Bartholomew's castle. But why?

All the servants and children were in a frightened huddle on the far side of the hall. Only the armed men were being killed, then. Tom scanned the faces in the hall, and, to his overwhelming relief and gratitude, he saw Alfred, Martha, Ellen and Jack, all in a group, looking terrified but alive and apparently unhurt.

Before he could go to them a fight started in the doorway. Earl Bartholomew and two knights charged in and were ambushed by the waiting Hamleigh knights. One of the earl's men was struck down immediately, but the other protected the earl with his raised sword. Several more of Bartholomew's knights came in behind the earl, and suddenly there was a tremendous skirmish at close quarters, with knives and fists being used because there was no room to deploy a long sword. For a moment it looked as if the earl's men would overcome William's; then some of Bartholomew's men turned and began to defend themselves from behind: clearly the attacking army had penetrated the upper compound and was now mounting the steps and attacking the keep.

A powerful voice bellowed: "HOLD!"

The men on both sides took defensive positions, and the fighting stopped.

The same voice called: "Bartholomew of Shiring, will you surrender?"

Tom saw the earl turn and look out through the door. Knights stepped aside to get out of his line of vision. "Hamleigh," the earl murmured in a quietly incredulous tone. Then he raised his voice and said: "Will you leave my family and servants unharmed?"

"Yes."

"Will you swear it?"

"I swear it, by the cross, if you surrender."

"I surrender," said Earl Bartholomew.

There was a great cheer from outside.

Tom turned away. Martha ran across the room to him. He picked her up, then embraced Ellen.

"We're safe," Ellen said with tears in her eyes. "All of us—all safe."

"Safe," said Tom bitterly, "but destitute again."

William stopped cheering suddenly. He was the son of Lord Percy, and it was undignified for him to yell and whoop like the men-at-arms. He composed his face in an expression of lordly satisfaction.

They had won. He had carried out the plan, not without some setbacks, but it had worked, and the attack had succeeded largely because of his advance work. He had lost count of the men he had killed and maimed, yet he was unharmed. He was struck by a thought: there was a lot of blood on his face for one who was un-injured. When he wiped it away, more came. It must be his own. He put his hand to his face, then to his head. Some of his hair had gone, and when he touched his scalp it hurt like fire. He had not been wearing a helmet, for that would have looked suspicious. Now that he was aware of the wound it started to hurt. He did not mind. An injury was a badge of courage.

His father came up the steps and confronted Earl Bartholomew in the doorway. Bartholomew held out his sword, hilt first, in a gesture of surrender. Percy took it, and his men cheered again.

As the noise died down William heard Bartholomew say: "Why have you done this?"

Father replied: "You plotted against the king."

Bartholomew was astonished that Father knew this, and the shock showed on his face. William held his breath, wondering whether Bartholomew, in the despair of defeat, would admit the conspiracy in front of all these people. But he recovered his composure, drew himself upright, and said: "I'll defend my honor in front of the king, not here."

Father nodded. "As you wish. Tell your men to lay down their arms and leave the castle."

The earl murmured a command to his knights, and one by one they approached Father and dropped their swords on the floor in front of him. William enjoyed watching that. Look at them all, humbled before my father, he thought proudly. Father was talking to one of his knights. "Round up the loose horses and put them in the stable. Have some men go around and disarm the dead and wounded." The weapons and horses of the defeated belonged to the victors, of course: Bartholomew's knights would disperse unarmed and on foot. The Hamleighs' men would also empty the castle's stores. The confiscated horses would be loaded with goods and driven back to Hamleigh, the village from which the family took its name. Father beckoned another knight and said: "Sort out the kitchen staff and have them make dinner. Send the rest of the servants away." Men were hungry after a battle: now there would be a feast. Earl Bartholomew's best food and wine would be eaten and drunk here before the army rode home.

A moment later, the knights around Father and Bartholomew divided, making a passage, and Mother swept in.

She looked very small among all the hefty fighting men, but when she unwound the scarf that had covered her face, those who had not seen her before started back, shocked, as people always were, by her disfigurement. She looked at Father. "A great triumph," she said in a satisfied tone.

William wanted to say: *That was because of good advance work, wasn't it, Mother?*

He bit his tongue, but his father spoke for him. "It was William who got us in."

Mother turned to him, and he waited eagerly for her to congratulate him. "Did he?" she said.

"Yes," Father said. "The boy did a good job."

Mother nodded. "Perhaps he did," she said.

William's heart was warmed by her praise, and he grinned foolishly.

She looked at Earl Bartholomew. "The earl should bow to me," she said.

The earl said: "No."

Mother said: "Fetch the daughter."

William looked around. For a moment he had forgotten about Aliena. He scanned the faces of the servants and children, and spotted her right away, standing with Matthew, the effeminate household steward. William went to her, took her arm, and brought her to his mother. Matthew followed them.

Mother said: "Cut off her ears."

Aliena screamed.

William felt a strange stirring in his loins.

Bartholomew's face turned gray. "You promised you wouldn't harm her if I surrendered," he said. "You swore it."

Mother said: "And our protection will be as complete as your surrender."

That was clever, William thought.

Still Bartholomew looked defiant.

William wondered who would be chosen to cut off Aliena's ears. Perhaps Mother would give him the task. The idea was peculiarly exciting.

Mother said to Bartholomew: "Kneel."

Slowly, Bartholomew went down on one knee and bowed his head.

William felt faintly disappointed.

Mother raised her voice. "Look at this!" she shouted to the assembled company. "Never forget the fate of a man who insults the Hamleighs!" She looked around defiantly, and William's heart swelled with pride. The family honor was restored.

Mother turned away, and Father took over. "Take him to his bedroom," he said. "Guard him well."

Bartholomew got to his feet.

Father said to William: "Take the girl as well."

William took Aliena's arm in a hard grip. He liked touching her. He was going to take her up to the bedroom. There was no telling what might happen. If he were left alone with her, he would be able to do anything he wanted to her. He could rip her clothes off and look at her nakedness. He could—

The earl said: "Let Matthew Steward come with us, to take care of my daughter."

Father glanced at Matthew. "He looks safe enough," he said with a grin. "All right."

William looked at Aliena's face. She was still white, but she was even more beautiful when she was frightened. It was so exciting to see her in this vulnerable state. He wanted to crush her ripe body beneath his, and see the fear in her face as he forced her thighs apart. On impulse, he put his face close to hers and said in a low voice: "I still want to marry you."

She drew away from him. "Marry?" she said in a loud voice full of scorn. "I'd rather die than marry you, you loathsome puffed-up toad!"

All the knights smiled broadly, and a few of the servants sniggered. William felt his face flush bright red.

Mother took a sudden step forward and slapped Aliena's face. Bartholomew moved to defend her but the knights restrained him. "Shut up," Mother said to Aliena. "You're not a fine lady anymore—you're the daughter of a traitor, and soon you'll be destitute and starving. You're not good enough for my son now. Get out of my sight, and don't speak another word."

Aliena turned away. William released her arm, and she followed her father. As he watched her go, William realized that the sweet taste of revenge had turned bitter in his mouth.

She was a real heroine, just like a princess in a poem, Jack thought. He watched, awestruck, as she climbed the stairs with her head held high. The whole room was silent until she disappeared from sight. When she went it was like a lamp going out. Jack stared at the place where she had been.

One of the knights came over and said: "Who's the cook?"

The cook himself was too wary to volunteer, but someone else pointed him out.

"You're going to make dinner," the knight told him. "Take your helpers and go to the kitchen." The cook picked half a dozen people out of the crowd. The knight raised his voice. "The rest of you—clear off. Get out of the castle. Go quickly and don't try to take anything that's not yours, if you value your lives. We've all got blood on our swords and a little more won't show. Get moving!"

They all shuffled through the door. Jack's mother took his hand and Tom held Martha's. Alfred stayed close. They were all wearing their cloaks, and they had no possessions other than their clothes and their eating knives. With the crowd they went down the steps, over the bridge, across the lower compound, and through the gatehouse, stepping over the useless gates, leaving the castle without a pause. When they stepped off the bridge onto the field on the far side of the moat, the tension snapped like a cut bowstring, and they all began to talk about their ordeal in loud, excited voices. Jack listened idly as he walked along. Everybody was recalling how brave they had been. He had not been brave—he had simply run away.

Aliena was the only one who had been brave. When she came into the keep and found that instead of being a place of safety it was a trap, she had taken charge of the servants and children, telling them to sit down and keep quiet and stay out of the way of the fighting men, screaming at the Hamleighs' knights when they were rough with their prisoners or raised their swords against unarmed men and women, acting as if she were completely invulnerable.

His mother ruffled his hair. "What are you thinking about?"

"I was wondering what will happen to the princess."

She knew what he meant. "The Lady Aliena."

"She's like a princess in a poem, living in a castle. But knights aren't as virtuous as the poems say."

"That's true," Mother said grimly.

"What will become of her?"

She shook her head. "I really don't know."

"Her mother's dead."

"Then she'll have a hard time."

"I thought so." Jack paused. "She laughed at me because I didn't know about fathers. But I liked her all the same."

Mother put her arm around him. "I'm sorry I didn't tell you about fathers."

He touched her hand, accepting her apology. They walked on in silence. From time to time a family would leave the road and head across the fields, making for the home of relatives or friends where they might beg some breakfast and think about what to do next. Most of the crowd stayed together as far as the crossroads, then they split up, some going north or south, some continuing straight on toward the market town of Shiring. Mother detached herself from Jack and put a hand on Tom's arm, making him stop. "Where shall we go?" she said.

He looked faintly surprised to be asked, as if he expected them all to follow wherever he led without asking questions. Jack had noticed that Mother often brought that surprised look to Tom's face. Perhaps his previous wife had been a different sort of person.

"We're going to Kingsbridge Priory," Tom said.

"Kingsbridge!" Mother seemed shaken. Jack wondered why.

Tom did not notice. "Last night I heard there's a new prior," he went on. "Usually a new man wants to make some repairs or alterations to the church."

"The old prior is dead?"

"Yes."

For some reason Mother was soothed by that news. She must have known the old prior, Jack thought, and disliked him.

Tom heard the troubled note in her voice at last. "Is there something wrong with Kingsbridge?" he asked her.

"I've been there. It's more than a day's journey."

Jack knew that it was not the length of the journey that bothered Mother, but Tom did not. "A little more," he said. "We can get there by midday tomorrow."

"All right."

They walked on.

A little later Jack began to feel a pain in his belly. For a while he wondered what it was. He had not been hurt at the castle and Alfred had not punched him for two days. But eventually he realized what it was.

He was hungry again.

Chapter 4

KINGSBRIDGE CATHEDRAL was not a welcoming sight. It was a low, squat, massive structure with thick walls and tiny windows. It had been built long before Tom's time, in the days when builders had not realized the importance of proportion. Tom's generation knew that a straight, true wall was stronger than a thick one, and that walls could be pierced with large windows so long as the arch of the window was a perfect half-circle. From a distance the church looked lopsided, and when Tom got closer he saw why: one of the twin towers at the west end had fallen down. He was delighted. The new prior was likely to want it rebuilt. Hope quickened his pace. To have been hired, as he had been at Earlscastle, and then to see his new employer defeated in battle and captured was heart-breaking. He felt he could not take another disappointment like that.

He glanced at Ellen. He was afraid that any day now she would decide that he was not going to find work before they all starved to death, and then she would leave him. She smiled at him, then she frowned again as she looked at the looming hulk of the cathedral. She was always uncomfortable with priests and monks, he had observed. He wondered if she felt guilty because the two of them were not actually married in the eyes of the Church.

The priory close was full of bustle and industry. Tom had seen sleepy monasteries and busy ones, but Kingsbridge was exceptional. It looked as if it were being spring-cleaned three months early. Outside the stable, two monks were grooming horses and a third was cleaning harness while novices mucked out the stalls. More monks were sweeping and scrubbing the guesthouse, which was next to the stable, and a cartload of straw stood outside ready to be strewn on the clean floor.

However, no one was working on the fallen tower. Tom studied the pile of stones that was all that remained of it. The collapse had to have occurred some years ago, for the broken edges of the stones had been blunted by frost and rain, the crushed mortar had been washed away, and the pile of masonry had sunk an inch or two into the soft earth. It was remarkable that the repair had been left undone for so long, for cathedral churches were supposed to be prestigious. The old prior must have been idle or incompetent, or both. Tom had probably arrived just when the monks were planning the rebuilding. He was overdue for some luck.

"No one recognizes me," Ellen said.

"When were you here?" Tom asked her.

"Thirteen years ago."

"No wonder they've forgotten you."

As they passed the west front of the church Tom opened one of the big wooden doors and looked inside. The nave was dark and gloomy, with thick columns and an ancient wooden ceiling. However, several monks were whitewashing the walls with long-handled brushes, and others were sweeping the beaten-earth floor. The new prior was evidently getting the whole place smartened up. That was a hopeful sign. Tom closed the door.

Beyond the church, in the kitchen courtyard, a team of novices stood around a trough of filthy water, scraping the accumulated soot and grease off cooking pots and kitchen utensils with sharp stones. Their knuckles were raw and red from constant immersion in the icy water. When they saw Ellen they giggled and looked away.

Tom asked a blushing novice where the cellarer was to be found. Strictly speaking, it was the sacrist he should have asked for, because the fabric of the church was the sacrist's responsibility; but cellarers as a class were more approachable. In the end the prior would make the decision, anyway. The novice directed him to the undercroft of one of the buildings around the courtyard. Tom went in through an open doorway, and Ellen and the children followed. They all paused inside the door to peer into the gloom.

This building was newer and more soundly constructed than the church, Tom could tell at once. The air was dry and there was no smell of rot. Indeed, the mixed aromas of the stored food gave him painful stomach pangs, for he had not eaten in two days. As his eyes adjusted he saw that the undercroft had a good flagstone floor, short thick pillars, and a tunnel-vaulted ceiling. A moment later he noticed a tall, bald man spooning salt from a barrel into a pot. "Are you the cellarer?" said Tom, but the man held up a hand for silence, and Tom saw that he was counting. They all waited in silence for him to finish. At last he said: "Two score and nineteen, three score," and put the spoon down.

Tom said: "I'm Tom, master builder, and I'd like to rebuild your northwest tower."

"I'm Cuthbert, called Whitehead, the cellarer, and I'd like to see it done," the man replied. "But we'll have to ask Prior Philip. You'll have heard that we have a new prior?"

"Yes." Cuthbert was the friendly sort of monk, Tom decided; worldly and easygoing. He would be happy to chat. "And the new man seems intent on improving the appearance of the monastery."

Cuthbert nodded. "But he's not so keen on paying for it. Did you notice that all the work is being done by monks? He won't hire any workmen—says the priory already has too many servants."

That was bad news. "How do the monks feel about that?" Tom asked delicately.

Cuthbert laughed, and his wrinkled face creased up even more. "You're a tactful man, Tom Builder. You're thinking that you don't often see monks working so hard. Well, the new prior's not forcing anyone. But he interprets the Rule of Saint Benedict in such a way that those who do physical labor may eat red meat and drink wine, whereas those who merely study and pray must live on salt fish and weak beer. He can show you an elaborate theoretical justification for it, too, but the upshot is that he has plenty of volunteers for the hard work, especially among the youngsters." Cuthbert did not seem disapproving, just bemused.

Tom said: "But monks can't build stone walls, no matter how well they eat." As he spoke, he heard a baby cry. The sound tugged at his heartstrings. It took him a moment to realize how odd it was that there should be a baby in a monastery.

"We'll ask the prior," Cuthbert was saying, but Tom hardly heard. It sounded like the cry of a very small baby, just a week or two old, and it was coming nearer. Tom caught Ellen's eye. She looked startled too. Then there was a shadow in the door. Tom had a lump in his throat. A monk walked in carrying the baby. Tom looked at its face. It was his child.

Tom swallowed hard. The baby's face was red, its fists were clenched, and its mouth was open, showing toothless gums. Its cry was not the cry of pain or sickness, just a simple demand for food. It was the healthy, lusty yell of a normal baby, and Tom felt weak with relief to see his son looking so well.

The monk carrying him was a cheerful-looking boy of about twenty years, with unruly hair and a big, rather stupid grin. Unlike most of the monks, he did not react to the presence of a woman. He smiled at everyone and then spoke to Cuthbert. "Jonathan needs more milk."

Tom wanted to take the child in his arms. He tried to freeze his face so that his expression would not betray his emotions. He threw a furtive glance at the children. All they knew was that the abandoned baby had been found by a traveling priest. They did not even know that the priest had taken him to the little monastery in the forest. Now their faces showed nothing but mild curiosity. They had not connected this baby with the one they had left behind.

Cuthbert picked up a ladle and a small jug, and filled the jug from a bucket of milk. Ellen said to the young monk: "May I hold the baby?" She held out her arms and the monk handed the child to her. Tom envied her. He longed to hold that tiny hot bundle close to his heart. Ellen rocked the baby, and he was quiet for a moment.

Cuthbert looked up and said: "Ah. Johnny Eightpence is a fair nursemaid, but he doesn't have the woman's touch."

Ellen smiled at the boy. "Why do they call you Johnny Eight-pence?"

Cuthbert answered for him. "Because he's only eight pence to the shilling," he said, tapping the side of his head to indicate that Johnny was half-witted. "But he seems to understand the needs of poor dumb creatures better than us wise folk. All part of God's wider purpose, I'm sure," he finished vaguely.

Ellen had edged over to Tom, and now she held the baby out to him. She had read his thoughts. He gave her a look of profound gratitude, and took the tiny child in his big hands. He could feel the baby's heartbeat through the blanket in which it was wrapped. The material was fine: he wondered briefly where the monks had got such soft wool. He held the baby to his chest and rocked. His technique was not as good as Ellen's, and the child started to cry again, but Tom did not mind: that loud, insistent yell was music to his ears, for it meant that the child he had abandoned was fit and strong. Hard though it was, he felt he had made the right decision in leaving the baby at the monastery.

Ellen asked Johnny: "Where does he sleep?"

Johnny answered for himself this time. "He has a crib in the dormitory with the rest of us."

"He must wake you all in the night."

"We get up at midnight anyway, for matins," Johnny said.

"Of course! I was forgetting that monks' nights are as sleepless as mothers'."

Cuthbert handed Johnny the jug of milk. Johnny took the baby from Tom with a practiced one-arm movement. Tom was not ready to give the baby up, but in the monks' eyes he had no rights at all, so he had to let him go. A moment later Johnny and the baby were gone, and Tom had to resist the impulse to go after them and say *Wait, stop, that's my son, give him back to me.* Ellen stood beside him and squeezed his arm in a discreet gesture of sympathy.

Tom realized he had new reason to hope. If he could get work here, he could see baby Jonathan all the time, and it would be almost as if he had never abandoned him. It seemed almost too good to be true, and he did not dare to wish for it.

Cuthbert was looking shrewdly at Martha and Jack, who had both gone big-eyed at the sight of the jug full of creamy milk that Johnny had taken away. "Would the children like some milk?" he asked.

"Yes, please, Father, they would," Tom said. He would have liked some himself.

Cuthbert ladled milk into two wooden bowls and gave them to Martha and Jack. They both drank quickly, leaving big white rings around their mouths. "Some more?" Cuthbert offered.

"Yes, please," they replied in unison. Tom looked at Ellen, knowing that she must feel as he did, deeply thankful to see the little ones fed at last.

As Cuthbert refilled the bowls he said casually: "Where have you folks come from?"

"Earlscastle, near Shiring," said Tom. "We left there yesterday morning."

"Have you eaten since?"

"No," Tom said flatly. He knew that Cuthbert's inquiry was kindly, but he hated to admit that he had been unable to feed his children himself.

"Have some apples to keep you going until suppertime, then," Cuthbert said, pointing to the barrel near the door.

Alfred, Ellen and Tom went to the barrel while Martha and Jack were drinking their second bowl of milk. Alfred tried to fill his arms with apples. Tom smacked them out of his hands and said in a low voice: "Just take two or three." He took three.

Tom ate his apples gratefully, and his belly felt a little better, but he could not help wondering how soon supper would be served. Monks generally ate before dark, to save candles, he recalled happily.

Cuthbert was looking hard at Ellen. "Do I know you?" he said eventually.

She looked uneasy. "I don't think so."

"You seem familiar," he said uncertainly.

"I used to live near here as a child," she said.

"That would be it," he said. "That's why I have this feeling that you look older than you should."

"You must have a very good memory."

He frowned at her. "Not quite good enough," he said. "I'm sure there's something else. . . . No matter. Why did you leave Earlscastle?"

"It was attacked, yesterday at dawn, and taken," Tom replied. "Earl Bartholomew is accused of treason."

Cuthbert was shocked. "Saints preserve us!" he exclaimed, and suddenly he looked like an old maid frightened by a bull. "Treason!"

There was a footstep outside. Tom turned and saw another monk walk in. Cuthbert said: "This is our new prior."

Tom recognized the prior. It was Philip, the monk they had met on their way to the bishop's palace, the one who had given them the delicious cheese. Now everything fell into place: the new prior of Kingsbridge was the old prior of the little cell in the forest, and he had brought Jonathan with him when he came here. Tom's heart leaped with optimism. Philip was a kindly man, and he had seemed to like and trust Tom. Surely he would give him a job.

Philip recognized him. "Hello, Master Builder," he said. "You didn't get much work at the bishop's palace, then?"

"No, Father. The archdeacon wouldn't hire me, and the bishop wasn't there."

"Indeed he wasn't—he was in heaven, though we didn't know it at the time."

"The bishop is dead?"

"Yes."

"That's old news," Cuthbert butted in impatiently. "Tom and his family have just come from Earlscastle. Earl Bartholomew has been captured and his castle overrun!"

Philip was very still. "Already!" he murmured.

"Already?" Cuthbert repeated. "Why do you say 'already'?" He seemed fond of Philip but wary of him, like a father whose son has been away to war and has come home with a sword in his belt and a slightly dangerous look in his eye. "Did you know this was going to happen?"

Philip was slightly flustered. "No, not exactly," he said uncertainly. "I had heard a rumor that Earl Bartholomew was opposed to King Stephen." He recovered his composure. "We can all be thankful for this," he announced. "Stephen has promised to protect the Church, whereas Maud might have oppressed us as much as her late father did. Yes, indeed. This is good news." He looked as pleased as if he had done it himself.

Tom did not want to talk about Earl Bartholomew. "It isn't good news for me," he said. "The earl had hired me, the day before, to strengthen the castle's defenses. I didn't even get a single day's pay."

"What a shame," said Philip. "Who was it that attacked the castle?"

"Lord Percy Hamleigh."

"Ah." Philip nodded, and once again Tom felt his news was only confirming Philip's expectations.

"You're making some improvements here, then," Tom said, trying to bring the subject around to his own interest.

"I'm trying," Philip said.

"You'll want to rebuild the tower, I'm sure."

"Rebuild the tower, repair the roof, pave the floor—yes, I want to do all of that. And you want the job, of course," he added, apparently having just realized why Tom was here. "I wasn't thinking. I wish I could hire you. But I couldn't pay you, I'm afraid. This monastery is penniless."

Tom felt as if he had been struck by a fist. He had been confident of getting work here—everything had pointed to it. He could hardly believe his ears. He stared at Philip. It really was not credible that the priory had no money. The cellarer had said it was monks doing all the extra work, but even so, a monastery could always borrow money from the Jews. Tom felt as if this were the end of the road for him. Whatever it was that had kept him going all winter now seemed to drain out of him, and he felt weak and spineless. I can't go on, he thought; I'm finished.

Philip saw his distress. "I can offer you supper, and a place to sleep, and some breakfast in the morning," he said.

Tom felt bitterly angry. "I'll accept it," he said, "but I'd rather earn it."

Philip raised his eyebrows at the note of anger, but he spoke mildly. "Ask God—that's not begging, it's prayer." Then he went out.

The others looked a little scared, and Tom realized that his anger must be showing. Their staring at him annoyed him. He went out of the storeroom a few steps behind Philip, and stood in the courtyard, looking at the big old church, trying to control his feelings.

After a moment Ellen and the children followed him out. Ellen put her arm around his waist in a comforting gesture, which made the novices whisper and nudge one another. Tom ignored them. "I'll pray," he said sourly. "I'll pray for a thunderbolt to strike the church and level it to the ground."

In the last two days Jack had learned to fear the future.

During his short life he had never had to think farther ahead than tomorrow; but if he had, he would have known what to expect. One day was much like another in the forest, and the seasons changed slowly. Now he did not know, from day to day, where he would be, what he would do or whether he would eat.

The worst part of it was feeling hungry. Jack had been secretly eating grass and leaves, to try to ease the pangs, but they gave him a different kind of stomachache and made him feel peculiar. Martha often cried because she was so hungry. Jack and Martha always walked together. She looked up to him, and nobody had ever done that before. Being helpless to relieve her suffering was worse than his own hunger.

If they had still been living in the cave he would have known where to go to kill ducks, or find nuts, or steal eggs; but in towns and villages, and on the unfamiliar roads between them, he was at a loss. All he knew was that Tom had to find work.

They spent the afternoon in the guesthouse. It was a simple one-room building with a dirt floor and a fireplace in the middle, exactly like the houses peasants lived in, but Jack, who had always lived in a cave, thought it was marvelous. He was curious about how the house was made, and Tom told him. Two young trees had been chopped down, trimmed, and leaned against one another at an angle; then two more had been placed in the same way at four yards distance; and the two triangles thus formed were linked, at their tops, by a ridgepole. Parallel with the ridgepole, light slats were fixed, joining the trees, forming a sloping roof that reached to the ground. Rectangular frames of woven reeds, called hurdles, were laid over the slats, and made waterproof with mud. The gable ends were made of stakes driven into the ground, the chinks between them filled with mud. There was a door in one gable end. There were no windows.

Jack's mother spread fresh straw on the floor and Jack lit a fire with the flint he always carried. When the others were out of earshot he asked Mother why the prior would not hire Tom, when there was obviously work to be done. "It seems he would rather save his money, so long as the church is still usable," she said. "If the whole church had fallen down, they would be forced to rebuild it, but as it's just the tower, they can live with the damage."

When the daylight began to soften into dusk, a kitchen hand came to the guesthouse with a cauldron of pottage and a loaf as long as a man is tall, all just for them. The pottage was made with vegetables and herbs and meat bones, and its surface glistened with fat. The loaf was horsebread, made with all kinds of grain, rye and barley and oats, plus dried peas and beans; it was the cheapest bread, Alfred said, but to Jack, who had never eaten bread until a few days ago, it was delicious. Jack ate until his belly ached. Alfred ate until there was nothing left.

As they sat by the fire trying to digest their feast, Jack said to Alfred: "Why did the tower fall down, anyway?"

"Probably it was struck by lightning," said Alfred. "Or there might have been a fire."

"But there's nothing to burn," Jack said. "It's all made of stone."

"The *roof* isn't stone, stupid," Alfred said scornfully. "The roof is made of wood."

Jack thought about that for a moment. "And if the roof burns, does the building always fall down?"

Alfred shrugged. "Sometimes."

They sat in silence for a while. Tom and Jack's mother were talking in low voices on the other side of the fireplace. Jack said: "It's funny about that baby."

"What's funny?" Alfred said after a moment.

"Well, your baby was lost in the forest, miles away, and now here's a baby at the priory."

Neither Alfred nor Martha seemed to think the coincidence very remarkable, and Jack promptly forgot about it.

The monks all went to bed immediately after supper, and they did not provide candles for the humbler sort of guest, so Tom's family sat and looked at the fire until it went out, then lay down on the straw.

Jack stayed awake, thinking. It had occurred to him that if the cathedral were to burn down tonight, all their problems would be solved. The prior would hire Tom to rebuild the church, they would all live here in this fine house, and they would have meat-bone pottage and horsebread for ever and ever.

If I were Tom, he thought, I'd set fire to the church myself. I'd get up quietly while everyone else was sleeping, and sneak into the church, and start a fire with my flint, then creep back here while it was spreading, and pretend to be asleep when the alarm was raised. And when the people started throwing buckets of water on the flames, as they did when the stables burned at Earl Bartholomew's castle, I'd join in with them, as if I wanted to put out the fire just as much as they did.

Alfred and Martha were asleep—Jack could tell by their breathing. Tom and Ellen did what they usually did under Tom's cloak (Alfred said it was called "fucking") then they, too, fell asleep. It seemed that Tom was not going to get up and set fire to the cathedral.

But what *was* he going to do? Would the family walk the roads until they starved to death?

When they were all asleep, and he could hear the four of them breathing in the slow, regular rhythm that indicated deep slumber, it occurred to Jack that *he* could set the cathedral on fire.

The thought made his heart race with fear.

He would have to get up very quietly. He could probably unbar the door and slip out without waking anyone. The church doors might be locked, but there would surely be a way to get in, especially for someone small.

Once inside, he knew how he would reach the roof. He had learned a lot in two weeks with Tom. Tom talked about buildings all the time, mostly addressing his remarks to Alfred; and although Alfred was not interested, Jack was. He had found out, among other things, that all large churches had staircases built into the walls to give access to the higher parts for repair work. He would find a staircase and climb up to the roof.

He sat up in the dark, listening to the breathing of the others. He could distinguish Tom's by its slightly chesty wheeze, caused (Mother said) by years of inhaling stone dust. Alfred snored once, loudly, then turned over and was silent again.

Once he had set the fire, he would have to get back to the guesthouse quickly. What would the monks do if they caught him? In Shiring Jack had seen a boy of his own age tied up and flogged for stealing a cone of sugar from a spice shop. The boy had screamed and the springy switch had made his bottom bleed. It had seemed much worse than men killing one another in a battle as they had at Earlscastle, and the vision of the bleeding boy had haunted Jack. He was terrified of the same happening to him.

If I do this, he thought, I'll never tell a soul.

He lay down again, pulled his cloak around him, and closed his eyes.

He wondered if the church door was locked. If it was, he could get in through the windows. Nobody would see him if he stayed on the north side of the close. The monks' dormitory was south of the church, masked by the cloisters, and there was nothing on this side except the graveyard.

He decided just to go and have a look, to see if it was possible.

He hesitated a moment longer, then he stood up.

The new straw crunched under his feet. He listened again to the breathing of the four sleeping people. It was very silent: the mice had stopped moving in the straw. He took a step, and listened again. The others slept on. He lost patience and took three rapid steps to the door. When he stopped, the mice had decided they had nothing to fear, and started scrabbling again, but the people slept on.

He touched the door with his fingertips, then ran his hands down to the bar. It was an oak beam resting in paired brackets. He got his hands under it, gripped, and lifted. It was heavier than he had expected, and after lifting it less than an inch he had to drop it. The thud it made when it hit the brackets sounded very loud. He froze, listening. Tom's wheezy breathing faltered. What will I say if I'm caught? thought Jack desperately. I'll say I was going outside . . . going outside . . . I know, I'll say I was going to relieve myself. He relaxed now that he had an excuse. He heard Tom turn over, and waited for the deep, dusty voice, but it did not come, and Tom began to breathe evenly again.

The edges of the door were outlined with ghostly silver. There must be a moon, Jack thought. He gripped the bar again, took a deep breath, and strained to lift it. This time he was ready for its weight. He raised it and pulled it toward himself, but he had not lifted it high enough, and it failed to clear the brackets. He raised it an inch more, and it came free. He held it against his chest, relieving the strain on his arms a little; then he slowly went down on one knee, then on both, and lowered the bar to the floor. He stayed in that position for a few moments, trying to quiet his breathing, while the ache in his arms eased. There was no sound from the others except the noises of sleep.

Gingerly, Jack opened the door a crack. Its iron hinge squeaked, and a cold draft came through the opening. He shivered. He wrapped his cloak closer around him and opened the door a little more. He slipped out and closed it behind him.

The cloud was breaking up, and the moon came and went in

the restless sky. There was a cold wind. Jack was momentarily tempted to return to the stuffy warmth of the house. The enormous church with its fallen tower loomed over the rest of the priory, silver and black in the moonlight, its mighty walls and tiny windows making it look more like a castle. It was ugly.

All was quiet. Outside the priory walls, in the village, there might be a few people sitting up late, drinking ale by the glow of the fireside or sewing by rushlights, but here nothing moved. Still Jack hesitated, looking at the church. It looked back at him accusingly, as if it knew what was on his mind. He shook off the spooky feeling with a shrug, and walked across the broad green to the west end.

The door was locked.

He walked around to the north side and looked at the cathedral windows. Some church windows had lengths of translucent linen stretched across them, to keep out the cold, but these seemed to have nothing. They were big enough for him to crawl through, but they were too high to reach. He explored the stonework with his fingers, feeling the cracks in the wall where the mortar had worn away, but they were not big enough to give him toeholds. He needed something to use as a ladder.

He considered fetching stones from the fallen tower and constructing an improvised staircase, but the unbroken stones were too heavy, and the broken ones were too uneven. He had a feeling that he had seen something, during the course of the day, that would serve his purpose exactly, and he racked his brains to remember it. It was like trying to see something out of the corner of his eye: it always remained just out of sight. Then he glanced across the moonlit grave-yard to the stable, and it came back to him: a little wooden mounting block, with two or three steps, to help short people climb on large horses. One of the monks had been standing on it to comb a horse's mane.

He made his way across to the stable. It was the kind of thing that might not get put away at night, since it was hardly worth stealing. He walked quietly, but the horses heard him all the same, and one or two of them snorted and coughed. He stopped, frightened. There might be grooms sleeping in the stable. He stood still for a moment, listening for the sound of human movement, but none came, and the horses went quiet.

He could not see the mounting block. Perhaps it was up against the wall. Jack peered into the moon-shadows. It was hard to see anything. Cautiously, he went right up to the stable and walked along its length. The horses heard him again, and now his closeness made them nervous: one of them whinnied. Jack froze. A man's voice called out: "Quiet, quiet." As he stood there like a scared statue, he saw the mounting block right under his nose, so close that he would have fallen over it with one more step. He waited a few moments. There was no more noise from the stable. He bent down, picked it up, and hefted it on his shoulder. He turned around and padded back across the grass to the church. The stable was quiet.

When he climbed to the top step of the block he was still not high enough to reach the windows. It was irritating: he could not even look in. He had not finally made up his mind to do the deed, but he did not want to be prevented by practical considerations: he wanted to decide for himself. He wished he were as tall as Alfred.

There was one more thing to try. He stood back, took a short run, jumped one-footed onto the block, then sprang up. He reached the windowsill easily, and got a grip on the stone frame. With a jerk he pulled himself up until he could half-sit on the sill. But when he tried to crawl through the opening he had a surprise. The window was blocked by iron latticework which he had not seen from outside, presumably because it was black. Jack examined it with both hands, kneeling on the sill. There was no way through: it was probably there specifically to prevent people from getting in when the church was shut.

Disappointed, he jumped down to the ground. He picked up the mounting block and carried it back to where he had found it. This time the horses made no noise.

He looked at the fallen northwest tower, on the left-hand side of the main door. He climbed carefully over the stones at the edge of the heap, peering toward the interior of the church, looking for a way through the rubble. When the moon went behind a cloud he waited, shivering, for it to come out again. He was worried that his weight, small though it was, might shift the balance of the stones and cause a landslide, which would wake everyone even if it did not kill him. As the moon reappeared he scanned the pile and decided to risk it. He began to ascend with his heart in his mouth. Most of the stones were firm but one or two wobbled precariously under his weight. It was the kind of climb he would have enjoyed in daylight, with help near at hand and nothing on his conscience; but now he was too anxious, and his normal surefootedness left him. He slipped on a smooth surface and almost fell down; and there he decided to stop.

He was high enough to look down on the roof of the aisle that ran along the north side of the nave. He was hoping that there might be a hole in the roof, or perhaps a gap between the roof and the pile of rubble, but it was not so: the roof continued unbroken into the ruins of the tower, and there appeared to be nowhere to slip through. Jack was half disappointed and half relieved.

He climbed down again, backward, looking over his shoulder to find a foothold. The closer he got to the ground, the better he felt. He jumped the last few feet and landed gratefully on the grass.

He returned to the north side of the church and walked on around. He had seen several churches in the last two weeks and all of them were roughly the same shape. The largest part was the nave, which was always to the west. Then there were two arms, which Tom called transepts, sticking out to the north and south. The east end was called the chancel and it was shorter than the nave. Kingsbridge was individual only in that its west end had two towers, one on each side of the entrance, as it were to match the transepts.

There was a door in the north transept. Jack tried it and found it locked. He walked on, around the east end: no door there at all. He paused to look across the grassed courtyard. In the far southeast corner of the priory close there were two houses, the infirmary and the prior's house. Both were dark and silent. He went on, around the east end and along the south side of the chancel until he came to the out-jutting south transept. At the end of the transept, like a hand on an arm, was the round building they called the chapter house. Between the transept and the chapter house was a narrow alley leading into the cloisters. Jack went through the alley.

He found himself in a square quadrangle, with a lawn in the middle and a covered walkway all around. The pale stone of the arches was ghostly white in the moonlight, and the shadowed walkway was impenetrably dark. Jack waited a moment to let his eyes adjust.

He had emerged onto the east side of the square. To his left he could make out the door to the chapter house. Farther to his left, at the southern end of the east walk, he could see, facing him, another door, which he thought probably led to the monks' dormitory. To his right, another door led into the south transept of the church. He tried it. It was locked.

He went along the north walk. There he found a door leading into the nave of the church. It, too, was locked.

On the west walk there was nothing until he came to the southwest corner, where he found the door to the refectory. What a lot of food had to be found, he thought, to feed all those monks every day. Nearby was a fountain with a basin: the monks washed their hands before meals.

He continued along the south walk. Halfway along there was an arch. Jack turned through it and found himself in a little passage, with the refectory on his right and the dormitory on his left. He imagined all the monks fast asleep on the floor just the other side of the stone wall. At the end of the passage there was nothing but a muddy slope leading down to the river. Jack stood there for a moment, looking at the water a hundred yards away. For no particular reason, he remembered a story about a knight who had his head cut off but lived on; and involuntarily he imagined the headless knight coming out of the river and walking up the slope toward him. There was nothing there, but still he was scared. He turned around and hurried back to the cloisters. He felt safer there.

He hesitated under the arch, looking into the moonlit quadrangle. There must be a way to sneak into such a big building, he felt, but he could not think where else to look. In a way he was glad. He had been contemplating doing something appallingly dangerous, and if it turned out to be impossible, so much the better. On the other hand, he dreaded the thought of leaving this priory and taking to the road again in the morning: the endless walking, the hunger, Tom's disappointment and anger, Martha's tears. It could all be avoided, just by one little spark from the flint he carried in the little pouch hanging from his belt!

Something moved at the corner of his vision. He started, and his heart beat faster. He turned his head and saw, to his horror, a ghostly figure, carrying a candle, gliding silently along the east walk toward the church. A scream rose in his throat and he fought it down. Another figure followed the first. Jack stepped back into the archway, out of sight, and put his fist in his mouth, biting his skin to stop himself from crying aloud. He heard an eerie moaning sound. He stared in sheer terror. Then realization dawned: what he was seeing was a procession of monks going from the dormitory to the church for the midnight service, singing a hymn as they went. The panicky feeling persisted for a moment, even when he had understood what he was looking at; then relief washed over him, and he began to shake uncontrollably.

The monk at the head of the procession unlocked the door to the church with a huge iron key. The monks filed in. No one turned around to look in Jack's direction. Most of them appeared to be half asleep. They did not close the church door behind them.

When he had recovered his composure Jack realized that now he could get into the church.

His legs felt too weak to walk.

I could just go in, he thought. I don't have to do anything when

I'm inside. I'll look and see whether it is possible to get up to the roof. I might not set fire to it. I'll just take a look.

He took a deep breath, then stepped out of the archway and padded across the quadrangle. He hesitated at the open door and peeped in. There were candles on the altar, and in the quire where the monks stood in their stalls, but the light merely made small pools in the middle of the big empty space, leaving the walls and the aisles in deep gloom. One of the monks was doing something incomprehensible at the altar, and the others would occasionally chant a few phrases of mumbo jumbo. It seemed incredible to Jack that people should get up out of warm beds in the middle of the night to do something like this.

He slipped through the door and stood close to the wall.

He was inside. The darkness concealed him. However, he could not stay right there, for they would see him on their way out. He sidled farther in. The flickering candles threw restless shadows. The monk at the altar might have seen Jack, if he had looked up, but he seemed completely absorbed in what he was doing. Jack moved quickly from the cover of one mighty pillar to the next, pausing in between so that his movements would be irregular, like the shifting of the shadows. The light became brighter as he neared the crossing. He was afraid the monk at the altar would look up suddenly, see him, bound across to the transept, pick him up by the scruff of the neck—

He reached the corner and turned gratefully into the deeper shadows of the nave.

He paused for a moment, feeling relieved. Then he retreated along the aisle toward the west end of the church, still pausing irregularly, as he would if he were stalking a deer. When he was in the farthest, darkest part of the church, he sat down on the plinth of a column to wait for the service to end.

He put his chin down inside his cloak and breathed on his chest to warm himself. His life had changed so much in the last two weeks that it seemed years ago that he had lived contentedly in the forest with his mother. He knew he would never feel as safe again. Now that he knew about hunger, and cold, and danger, and desperation, he would always be afraid of them.

He peeped around the pillar. Above the altar, where the candles were brightest, he could just make out the high wooden ceiling. Newer churches had stone vaults, he knew, but Kingsbridge was old. That wooden ceiling would burn well.

I'm not going to do it, he thought.

Tom would be so happy if the cathedral burned down. Jack was not sure he liked Tom—he was too forceful, commanding and harsh. Jack was used to his mother's milder ways. But Jack was impressed by Tom, even awestruck. The only other men Jack had come across were outlaws; dangerous, brutish men who respected only violence and cunning, men for whom the ultimate achievement was to knife someone in the back. Tom was a new type of being, proud and fearless even without a weapon. Jack would never forget the way Tom had faced up to William Hamleigh, the time when Lord William had offered to buy Mother for a pound. What struck Jack so vividly was that *Lord William had been scared.* Jack told his mother that he had never imagined a man could be as brave as Tom was, and she said: "That was why we had to leave the forest. You need a man to look up to."

Jack was puzzled by that remark, but it was true that he would like to do something to impress Tom. Setting fire to the cathedral was not the thing, though. It would be better if nobody knew about that, at least not for many years. But perhaps a day would come when Jack would say to Tom: "You remember the night Kingsbridge Cathedral burned down, and the prior hired you to rebuild it, and we all had food and shelter and security at last? Well, I've got something to tell you about how that fire started. . . ." What a great moment that would be.

But I don't dare do it, he thought.

The singing stopped, and there was a scuffling sound as the monks left their places. The service was over. Jack shifted his position to stay out of sight while they filed out.

They snuffed the candles in the quire stalls as they went, but they left one burning on the altar. The door banged shut. Jack waited a little longer, in case there was still someone inside. There was no sound for a long time. At last he came out from behind his pillar.

He walked up the nave. It was an odd feeling, to be alone in this big, cold, empty building. This is what it must be like to be a mouse, he thought, hiding in corners when the big people are around and then coming out when they have gone. He reached the altar and took the fat, bright candle, and that made him feel better.

Carrying the candle, he began to inspect the inside of the church. At the corner where the nave met the south transept, the place where he had most feared being spotted by the monk at the altar, there was a door in the wall with a simple latch. He tried the latch. The door opened.

His candle revealed a spiral staircase, so narrow that a fat man could not have passed through it, so low that Tom would have had to bend double. He went up the steps.

He emerged in a narrow gallery. On one side, a row of small arches looked out into the nave. The ceiling sloped from the tops of the arches down to the floor on the other side. The floor itself was not flat, but curved down at either side. It took Jack a moment to realize where he was. He was above the aisle on the south side of the nave. The tunnel-vaulted ceiling of the aisle was the curved floor on which Jack was standing. From the outside of the church the aisle could be seen to have a lean-to roof, and that was the sloping ceiling under which Jack was standing. The aisle was much lower than the nave, so he was still a long way from the main roof of the building.

He walked west along the gallery, exploring. It was quite thrilling, now that the monks had gone and he was no longer in fear of being spotted. It was as if he had climbed a tree and found that at the very top, hidden from view by the lower branches, all the trees were connected, and you could walk around in a secret world a few feet above the earth.

At the end of the gallery was another small door. He went through it and found himself on the inside of the southwest tower, the one that had not fallen down. The space he was in was obviously not meant to be seen, for it was rough and unfinished, and instead of a floor there were rafters with wide gaps between them. However, around the inside of the wall ran a flight of wooden steps, a staircase without a handrail. Jack went up.

Halfway up one wall was a small arched opening. The staircase passed right by it. Jack put his head inside and held up his candle. He was in the roof space, above the timber ceiling and below the lead roof.

At first he could see no pattern in the tangle of wooden beams, but after a moment he perceived the structure. Huge oak timbers, each of them a foot wide and two feet deep, spanned the width of the nave from north to south. Above each beam were two mighty rafters, forming a triangle. The regular row of triangles stretched away beyond the light of the candle. Looking down, between the beams, he could see the back of the painted wooden ceiling of the nave, which was fixed to the lower edges of the crossbeams.

At the edge of the roof space, in the corner at the base of the triangle, was a catwalk. Jack crawled through the little opening and onto the catwalk. There was just enough headroom for him to stand up: a man would have had to stoop. He walked along it a little way. There was enough timber here for a conflagration. He sniffed, trying to identify the odd smell in the air. He decided it was pitch. The roof timbers were tarred. They would burn like straw.

A sudden movement on the floor startled him and made his heart race. He thought of the headless knight in the river and the ghostly monks in the cloisters. Then he thought of mice, and felt better. But when he looked carefully he saw that it was birds: there were nests under the eaves.

The roof space followed the pattern of the church below, branching out over the transepts. Jack went as far as the crossing and stood at the corner. He realized he must be directly above the little spiral staircase that had brought him from ground level up to the gallery. If he had been planning to start a fire, this was where he would do it. From here it could spread four ways: west along the nave, south along the south transept, and through the crossing to the chancel and the north transept.

The main timbers of the roof were made of heart-of-oak, and although they were tarred they might not catch fire from a candle flame. However, under the eaves was a litter of ancient wood chips and shavings, discarded bits of rope and sacking, and abandoned birds' nests, which would make perfect kindling. All he would have to do would be to collect it and pile it up.

His candle was burning low.

It seemed so easy. Collect up the litter, touch the candle flame to it, and leave. Cross the close like a ghost, slip into the guesthouse, bar the door, curl up in the straw and wait for the alarm.

But if he were seen . . .

If he should be caught now, he could say he was harmlessly exploring the cathedral, and he would suffer no worse than a spanking. But if they caught him setting fire to the church they would do more than spank him. He remembered the sugar thief in Shiring, and the way his bottom bled. He recalled some of the punishments the outlaws had suffered: Farad Openmouth had had his lips cut off, Jack Flathat had lost his hand, and Alan Catface had been put in the stocks and stoned and had never been able to talk properly since. Even worse were the stories of those who had not survived their punishments: a murderer who had been tied to a barrel studded with spikes and then rolled downhill so that all the spikes went through his body; a horse thief who had been burned alive; a thieving whore who had been impaled on a pointed stake. What would they do to a boy who set fire to a church?

Thoughtfully, he began to collect the inflammable rubbish from under the eaves and pile it up on the catwalk exactly below one of the mighty rafters.

When he had a pile a foot high he sat down and looked at it.

His candle guttered. In a few moments he would have lost his chance.

With a quick motion he touched the candle flame to a piece of sacking. It caught fire. The flame spread immediately to some wood shavings, then a dried, crumbling bird's nest; and then the little fire was blazing cheerfully.

I could still put it out, Jack thought.

The kindling was burning a little too quickly: at this rate it would be used up before the roof timber began to smolder. Jack hurriedly collected more rubbish and piled it on. The flames rose higher. I could still put it out, he thought. The pitch with which the beam was coated began to blacken and smoke. The rubbish burned up. I could just let the fire go out, now, he thought. Then he saw that the catwalk itself was burning. I could probably smother the fire with my cloak, still, he thought. Instead he threw more litter onto the fire and watched it burn higher.

The atmosphere became hot and smoky in the little angle of the eaves, even though the freezing night air was only an inch away on the other side of the roof. Some of the smaller timbers, to which the lead sheets of the roof were nailed, began to burn. Then, at last, a small flame flickered up from the massive main beam.

The cathedral was on fire.

It was done now. There was no turning back.

Jack felt scared. Suddenly he wanted to get out fast, and return to the guesthouse. He wanted to be rolled up in his cloak, nestling in a little hollow in the straw, with his eyes shut tight, and the others breathing evenly all around him.

He retreated along the catwalk.

When he reached the end he looked back. The fire was spreading surprisingly quickly, perhaps because of the pitch with which the wood was coated. All the small timbers were ablaze, the main beams were beginning to burn, and the fire was spreading along the catwalk. Jack turned his back on it.

He ducked into the tower and went down the stairs, then ran along the gallery over the aisle and hurried down the spiral staircase to the floor of the nave. He ran to the door by which he had come in.

It was locked.

He realized he had been stupid. The monks had unlocked the door when they came in, so of course they had locked it again as they left.

Fear rose in his throat like bile. He had set the church on fire and now he was locked inside.

He fought down panic and tried to think. He had tried every door from the outside, and found them all locked; but perhaps some of them were fastened with bars, rather than locks, so that they could be opened from the inside.

He hurried across the crossing to the north transept and examined the door in the north porch. It had a lock.

He ran down the dark nave to the west end and tried each of the great public entrances. All three doors were locked with keys. Finally he tried the little door that led into the south aisle from the north walk of the cloister square. That, too, was locked.

Jack wanted to cry, but that would do no good. He looked up at the wooden ceiling. Was it his imagination, or could he see, by the faint moonlight, a little smoke drifting out from the ceiling near the corner of the south transept?

He thought: What am I going to do?

Would the monks wake up, and come rushing in to put out the fire, in such a panic that they hardly noticed one small boy slipping out through the door? Or would they see him immediately, and grab him, screaming accusations? Or would they stay asleep, all unconscious, until the whole building had collapsed, and Jack lay crushed under a huge pile of stones?

Tears came to his eyes, and he wished he had never touched the candle flame to that pile of litter.

He looked around wildly. If he went to a window and screamed, would anybody hear?

There was a crash from above. He looked up and saw that a hole had appeared in the wooden ceiling, where a beam had fallen and poked through. The hole appeared as a patch of red on a black background. A moment later there was another crash, and a huge timber smashed right through the ceiling and fell, turning over once in the air, to hit the ground with a thump that shook the mighty columns of the nave. A shower of sparks and burning embers drifted down after it. Jack listened, waiting for shouts, cries for help, or the ringing of a bell; but nothing happened. The crash had not been heard. And if that had not awakened them, they certainly would not hear him screaming.

I'm going to die here, he thought hysterically; I'm going to burn or be crushed, unless I can think of a way out!

He thought of the fallen tower. He had examined it from the outside, and he had not seen a way in, but then he had been timid, for fear of falling and causing a landslide. Perhaps if he looked again, from the inside this time, he would see something he had missed; and perhaps desperation would help him squeeze through where before he had seen no gap.

He ran to the west end. The glow of the fire coming through the hole in the ceiling, combined with the flames licking up from the beam that had fallen to the floor of the nave, now gave a stronger light than the moon, and the arcade of the nave was edged with gold instead of silver. Jack examined the pile of stones that had once been the northwest tower. They appeared to form a solid wall. There was no way through. Foolishly, he opened his mouth and yelled "Mother!" at the top of his voice, even though he knew she could not hear.

He fought down his panic once again. There was something in the back of his mind about this collapsed tower. He had been able to get inside the other tower, the one that was still standing, by going along the gallery over the south aisle. If he now went along the gallery over the north aisle, he might see a gap in this pile of rubble, a gap that was not visible from ground level.

He ran back to the crossing, staying under the shelter of the north aisle in case more burning beams should come crashing through the ceiling. There should be a little door and a spiral staircase on this side, just as there was on the other. He came to the corner of the nave and the north transept. He could not see the door. He looked around the corner: it was not on the other side either. He could not believe his bad luck. It was crazy: there had to be a way into the gallery!

He thought hard, fighting to stay calm. There was a way into the fallen tower, he just had to find it. I could get back into the roof space, via the good, southwest tower, he thought. I could cross to the other side of the roof space. There should be a little opening on that side, giving access to the collapsed northwest tower. That may provide me with a way out.

He looked up at the ceiling fearfully. The fire would now be an inferno. But he could not think of any alternative.

First he had to cross the nave. He looked up again. As far as he could tell, there was nothing about to come down immediately. He took a deep breath and dashed across to the other side. Nothing fell on him.

In the south aisle, he pulled open the little door and ran up the spiral staircase. When he reached the top and stepped into the gallery he could feel the warmth of the fire above. He ran along the gallery, went through the door into the good tower, and raced up the stairs.

He ducked his head and crawled through the little arch into the roof space. It was full of smoke and heat. All the uppermost timbers were ablaze, and at the far end the biggest beams were burning strongly. The tarry smell made Jack cough. He hesitated only a moment, then stepped onto one of the big beams that spanned the nave and began to walk across. In moments he was wet with perspiration because of the heat, and his eyes began to water so that he could hardly see where he was going. He coughed, and then his foot slipped off the beam and he stumbled sideways. He fell with one foot on the beam and one foot off. His right foot landed on the ceiling, and to his horror it went straight through the rotten wood. A picture flashed into his mind of the height of the nave, and how far he would drop if he fell right through the ceiling; and he screamed as he tumbled forward, putting his arms out in front of him, imagining himself turning over and over in the air as the falling beam had done. But the wood held his weight.

He remained frozen still, shocked, resting on his hands and one knee, with the other leg sticking through the ceiling. Then the fierce heat of the fire brought him out of his shock. Gently he extracted his foot from the hole. He got on his hands and knees and crawled forward.

As he neared the other side, several large beams fell into the nave. The whole building seemed to shake, and the beam under Jack quivered like a bowstring. He stopped and held on tight. The tremor passed. He crawled on, and a moment later he reached the catwalk on the north side.

If his guess turned out to be wrong, and there was no opening from here into the ruins of the northwest tower, he would have to go back.

As he stood upright, he got a breath of cold night air. There must be some kind of gap. But would it be big enough for a small boy?

He took three paces to the west and stopped an instant before he would have stepped out into nothingness.

He found himself looking through a large hole out onto the moonlit ruins of the fallen tower. His knees went weak with relief. He was out of the inferno.

But he was high up, at roof level, and the top of the rubble pile was a long way below him, too far to jump. He could escape the flames now, but could he reach the ground without breaking his neck? Behind him, the flames were rapidly coming closer, and smoke was billowing out of the opening in which he stood.

This tower had once had a staircase around its inner wall, just as the other one still did, but most of this staircase had been destroyed in the collapse. However, where the wooden treads had been set into the wall with mortar, there were stumps of wood sticking out, sometimes just an inch or two long, sometimes more. Jack wondered whether he could climb down the stumps. It would be a precarious descent. He noticed a smell of scorching: his cloak was getting hot. In a moment it would catch fire. He had no choice.

He sat down, reached out for the nearest stump, held on with both hands, then eased one leg down until he found a foothold. Then he put the other foot down. Feeling his way with his feet, he eased himself down one step. The stumps held. He reached down once again, testing the strength of the next stump before putting his weight on it. This one felt a little loose. He trod gingerly, holding on tightly in case he should find himself swinging by his hands. Each perilous step down brought him nearer to the top of the rubble pile. As he descended, the stumps seemed to get smaller, as if the lower ones had suffered more severe damage. He put one foot, in its felt boot, on a stump no wider than his toe; and when he rested his weight on it his foot slipped. His other foot was on a larger stump, but when suddenly he put his full weight on it the other stump broke. He tried to hold on with his hands, but the stumps were so small that he could not grip hard, and he slipped, terrified, from his precarious perch and fell through the air.

He landed hard on his hands and knees on the top of the pile of rubble. For an instant he was so shocked and frightened he thought he must be dead; then he realized that he had been lucky enough to fall well. His hands stung and his knees would be massively bruised, but he was all right.

After a moment he climbed down the pile of rubble and jumped the last few feet to the ground.

He was safe. He felt weak with relief. He wanted to cry again. He had escaped. He felt proud: what an adventure he had had!

But it was not yet over. Out here there was only a whiff of smoke, and the noise of the fire, so deafening inside the roof space, now sounded like a distant wind. Only the reddish glow behind the windows proved that the church was on fire. Nevertheless, those last tremors must have disturbed someone's sleep, and any moment now a bleary-eyed monk would come stumbling out of the dormitory, wondering whether the earthquake he had felt had been real or only a dream. Jack had set fire to the church—a heinous crime in the eyes of a monk. He had to get away quickly.

He ran across the grass to the guesthouse. All was quiet and still. He stopped outside, panting. If he went in breathing like this he would wake them all. He tried to control his breathing but that seemed to make it worse. He would just have to stay here until it became normal again.

A bell rang, piercing the quiet, and went on, pealing urgently, an unmistakable alarm. Jack froze. If he went inside now they would know. But if he did not—

The door of the guesthouse opened, and Martha came out. Jack just stared at her, terrified.

"Where have you been?" she said softly. "You smell of smoke."

A plausible lie came into Jack's head. "I've only just stepped out," he said desperately. "I heard that bell."

"Liar," Martha said. "You've been gone for ages. I know, I was awake."

He realized there was no fooling her. "Was anyone else awake?" he said fearfully.

"No, only me."

"Don't tell them I was gone. Please?"

She heard the fear in his voice and spoke soothingly. "All right, I'll keep it a secret. Don't worry."

"Thank you!"

At that moment Tom stepped out, scratching his head.

Jack was frightened. What would Tom think?

"What's going on?" Tom said sleepily. He sniffed. "I smell smoke."

Jack pointed at the cathedral with a trembling arm. "I think . . ." he said, and then swallowed. It was going to be all right, he realized, with a grateful sense of relief. Tom would just assume that Jack had got up a moment earlier, as Martha had. Jack spoke again, more confidently this time. "Look at the church," he said to Tom. "I think it's on fire."

II

Philip had not yet got used to sleeping alone. He missed the stuffy air of the dormitory, the sound of other people shifting and snoring, the disturbance when one of the older monks got up to go to the latrine (followed, usually, by the other older ones, a regular procession which always amused the youngsters). Being alone did not bother Philip at nightfall, when he was always dead tired; but in the middle of the night, when he had been thoroughly roused by the service, he now found it difficult to go back to sleep. Instead of getting back into the big soft bed (it was a little embarrassing how quickly he had got used to *that*), he would build up the fire and read by candlelight, or kneel down and pray, or just sit thinking.

He had plenty to think about. The priory's finances were worse than he had anticipated. The main reason probably was that the whole organization generated very little cash. It owned vast acreages, but many farms were let at low rents on long leases, and some of them paid rent in kind—so many sacks of flour, so many barrels of apples, so many cartloads of turnips. Those farms that were not rented out were run by monks, but they never seemed to be able to produce a surplus of food for sale. The priory's other main asset was the churches it owned, and from which it received the tithes. Unfortunately, most of these were under the control of the sacrist, and Philip was having trouble finding out exactly how much he received and how he spent it. There were no written accounts. However, it was clear that the sacrist's income was too small, or his management of it too bad, to maintain the cathedral church in good repair; although over the years the sacrist had built up an impressive collection of jeweled vessels and ornaments.

Philip could not get all the details until he had time to tour the monastery's far-flung properties, but the outline was already clear; and the old prior had for some years been borrowing from moneylenders in Winchester and London just to meet everyday expenses. Philip had become quite depressed when he realized how bad it was.

However, as he thought and prayed about it, the solution became clear. Philip had a three-stage plan. He would begin by taking control of the priory's finances personally. At present, each of the monastic officials controlled parts of the property, and fulfilled his responsibility with the income from that property: the cellarer, the sacrist, the guest-master, the novice-master and the infirmarer all had "their" farms and churches. Naturally, none of them would ever confess to having too much money, and if they had any surplus they took care to spend it, for fear that something would be taken away from them. Philip had decided to appoint a new official, called the purser, whose job it would be to receive all monies due to the priory, with no exceptions, and then give out to each official just what he needed.

The purser would naturally be someone Philip trusted. His first inclination had been to give the job to Cuthbert Whitehead, the cellarer; but then he had recalled Cuthbert's aversion to writing things down. That was no good. From now on all income and outgoings were to be written in a great book. Philip had decided to appoint the young kitchener, Brother Milius, as purser. The other monastic officials would not like the idea no matter who got the job, but Philip was the boss, and anyway the majority of monks, who knew or suspected that the priory was in trouble, would support reforms.

When he had control of the money, Philip would implement stage two of his plan.

All the distant farms would be leased for cash rents. This would put an end to expensive transportation of goods across long distances. There was a property of the priory's in Yorkshire that paid a "rent" of twelve lambs, and faithfully sent them all the way to Kingsbridge each year, even though the cost of transport was more than the value of the lambs, and anyway half of them always died en route. In future, only the nearest farms would produce food for the priory.

He also planned to change the present system under which each farm produced a little of everything—some grain, some meat, some milk and so on. Philip had thought for years that this was wasteful. Every farm managed to produce only enough of each item for its own needs—or perhaps it would be truer to say that every farm always managed to consume just about everything it produced. Philip wanted each farm to concentrate on one thing. All the grain would be grown in a group of villages in Somerset, where the priory also owned several mills. The lush hillsides of Wiltshire would graze cattle for butter and beef. The little cell of St-John-in-the-Forest would breed goats and make cheese.

But Philip's most important scheme was to convert all the middle-ranking farms—those with poor or indifferent soil, especially the hill properties—to sheep farming.

He had spent his boyhood in a monastery that farmed sheep (everyone farmed sheep in that part of Wales), and he had seen the price of wool rise slowly but steadily, year by year, ever since he could remember, right up to the present. Sheep would solve the priory's cash problem permanently, in time.

That was stage two of the plan. Stage three was to demolish the cathedral church and build a new one.

The present church was old, ugly and impractical; and the fact that the northwest tower had fallen down was a sign that the whole structure might be weak. Modern churches were taller, longer, and—most important—lighter. They were also designed to display the important tombs and saintly relics that pilgrims came to see. These days, more and more, cathedrals had additional small altars and special chapels dedicated to particular saints. A well-designed church that catered to the multiplying demands of today's congregations would draw many more worshipers and pilgrims than Kingsbridge could attract at the moment; and by doing so it could pay for itself, in the long run. When Philip had put the priory's finances on a sound footing, he would build a new church which would symbolize the regeneration of Kingsbridge.

It would be his crowning achievement.

He thought he would have enough money to begin rebuilding in about ten years' time. It was a rather daunting thought—he would be almost forty! However, within a year or so he hoped to be able to afford a program of repairs which would make the present building respectable, if not impressive, by the Whitsun after next.

Now that he had a plan he felt cheerful and optimistic again. Mulling over the details, he dimly heard a distant bang, like the slamming of a big door. He wondered vaguely whether someone was up and about in the dormitory or the cloisters. He supposed that if there were trouble he would find out about it soon enough, and his thoughts drifted back to rents and tithes. Another important source of wealth for monasteries was gifts from the parents of boys who became novices, but to attract the right sort of novices the monastery needed a flourishing school—

His reflections were interrupted again, this time by a louder bang that actually made his house shake slightly. That was definitely *not* a door slamming, he thought. Whatever is going on over there? He went to the window and opened the shutter. The cold night blew in, making him shiver. He looked out over the church, the chapter house, the cloisters, the dormitory and the kitchen buildings beyond. They all appeared peaceful in the moonlight. The air was so frosty that his teeth hurt when he breathed. But there was something else about the air. He sniffed. He could smell smoke.

He frowned anxiously, but he could see no fire.

He drew his head into the room and sniffed again, thinking that he might be smelling smoke from his own fireplace, but it was not so.

Mystified and alarmed, he pulled on his boots rapidly, picked up his cloak, and ran out of the house.

The smell of smoke became stronger as he hurried across the green toward the cloisters. There was no doubt that some part of the priory was on fire. His first thought was that it must be the kitchen—nearly all fires started in kitchens. He ran through the passage between the south transept and the chapter house and across the cloister square. In daytime he would have gone through the refectory to the kitchen courtyard, but at night it was locked, so he went out through the arch in the south walk and turned right to the back of the kitchen. There was no sign of fire here, nor in the brewery or the bakehouse, and the smell of smoke now seemed a little less. He ran a little farther, and looked past the corner of the brewery, across the green to the guesthouse and the stables. All seemed quiet over there.

Could the fire be in the dormitory? The dormitory was the only other building with a fireplace. The thought was horrifying. As he ran back into the cloisters he had a grisly vision of all the monks in their beds, overcome by smoke, unconscious as the dormitory blazed. He ran to the dormitory door. As he reached it, it opened, and Cuthbert Whitehead stepped out, carrying a rushlight.

Cuthbert said immediately: "Can you smell it?"

"Yes—are the monks all right?"

"There's no fire here."

Philip was relieved. At least his flock was safe. "Where, then?"

"What about the kitchen?" Cuthbert said.

"No—I've checked." Now that he knew nobody was in danger, he began to worry about his property. He had just been thinking about finances, and he knew he could not afford repairs to buildings right now. He looked at the church. Was there a faint red glow behind the windows?

Philip said: "Cuthbert, get the church key from the sacrist."

Cuthbert was ahead of him. "I have it here."

"Good man!"

They hurried along the east walk to the door in the south transept. Cuthbert unlocked it hastily. As soon as the door swung open, smoke billowed out.

Philip's heart missed a beat. How could his church be on fire?

He stepped inside. At first the scene was confusing. On the floor of the church, around the altar and here in the south transept, several huge pieces of wood were burning. Where had they come from? How had they produced so much smoke? And what was the roaring noise that sounded like a much bigger fire?

Cuthbert shouted: "Look up!"

Philip looked up, and his questions were answered. The ceiling was blazing furiously. He stared at it, horrified: it looked like the underside of hell. Most of the painted ceiling had already gone, revealing the timber triangles of the roof, blackened and blazing, the flames and smoke leaping and swirling in a fiendish dance. Philip stood still, shocked into immobility, until his neck started to hurt from looking up; then he gathered his wits.

He ran to the middle of the crossing, stood in front of the altar, and looked around the whole church. The entire roof was ablaze, from the west door to the east end and all across both transepts. For a panicky moment he thought *How are we going to get water up there?* He imagined a line of monks running along the gallery with buckets, and he realized immediately that it was impossible: even if he had a hundred people for the job, they could not carry up to the roof a quantity of water sufficient to put out this roaring inferno. The whole roof was going to be destroyed, he realized with a sinking heart; and the rain and snow would fall into the church until he could find the money for a new roof.

A crashing sound made him look up. Immediately above him, an enormous timber was moving slowly sideways. It was going to fall on top of him. He dashed back into the south transept, where Cuthbert stood looking scared.

A whole section of the roof, three triangles of beam-and-rafter plus the lead sheets nailed to them, was falling in. Philip and Cuthbert watched, transfixed, quite forgetting their own safety. The roof fell on one of the big round arches of the crossing. The enormous weight of the falling wood and lead cracked the stonework of the arch with a prolonged explosive sound like thunder. Everything happened slowly: the beams fell slowly, the arch broke up slowly, and the smashed masonry fell slowly through the air. More roof beams came free, and then, with a noise like a long slow peal of thunder, a whole section of the north wall of the chancel shuddered and slid sideways into the north transept.

Philip was appalled. The sight of such a mighty building being destroyed was strangely shocking. It was like watching a mountain fall down or a river run dry: he had never really thought it could happen. He could hardly believe his eyes. It made him feel disoriented, and he did not know what to do.

Cuthbert was tugging at his sleeve. "Come out!" he yelled.

Philip could not tear himself away. He remembered that he

had been anticipating ten years of austerity and hard work to put the monastery back on a sound financial footing. Now, suddenly, he had to build a new roof *and* a new north wall, and perhaps more if the destruction went on. . . . This is the devil's work, he thought. How else could the roof have caught fire on a freezing night in January?

"We'll be killed!" Cuthbert shouted, and the note of human fear in his voice touched Philip's heart. He turned away from the blaze, and they both ran out of the church into the cloisters.

The monks had been alerted and were filing out of the dormitory. As they came out they naturally wanted to stop and look at the church. Milius Kitchener was standing at the door hurrying them along to avoid a logjam, directing them away from the church and along the south walk of the cloisters. Halfway along the walk Tom Builder stood, telling them to turn under the arch and escape that way. Philip heard Tom saying: "Go to the guesthouse—stay well clear of the church!"

He was overreacting, Philip thought: surely they would have been safe enough here in the cloisters? But there was no harm done, and perhaps it was a sensible precaution. In fact, he reflected, I probably should have thought of it myself.

But Tom's caution made him wonder how far the destruction might spread. If the cloisters were not absolutely safe, what about the chapter house? There, in a little side room with thick stone walls and no windows, they kept the ironbound oak chest containing what little money they had, plus the sacrist's jeweled vessels and all the priory's precious charters and deeds of ownership. A moment later he saw Alan the treasurer, a young monk who worked with the sacrist and took care of the ornaments. Philip called him. "The treasure must be taken from the chapter house—where's the sacrist?"

"He's gone, Father."

"Go and find him and get the keys, then take the treasure out of the chapter house and carry it to the guesthouse. Run!"

Alan ran off. Philip turned to Cuthbert. "You'd better make sure he does it." Cuthbert nodded and followed Alan.

Philip looked back at the church. In the few moments his attention had been elsewhere, the fire had become fiercer, and now the light of the flames shone brightly in all the windows. The sacrist should have thought of the treasure, instead of saving his own skin so hastily. Was there anything else that had been overlooked? Philip found it hard to think systematically when everything was happening so quickly. The monks were moving to safety, the treasury was being taken care of—

He had forgotten the saint.

At the far east end of the church, beyond the bishop's throne, was the stone tomb of Saint Adolphus, an early English martyr. Inside the tomb was a wooden coffin containing the skeleton of the saint. Periodically the lid of the tomb was lifted to display the coffin. Adolphus was not as popular now as he had once been, but in the old days sick people had been miraculously cured by touching the tomb. A saint's remains could be a big attraction in a church, promoting worship and pilgrimages. They brought in so much money that, shamefully, it was not unknown for monks actually to steal holy relics from other churches. Philip had planned to revive interest in Adolphus. He had to save the skeleton.

He would need help to lift the lid of the tomb and carry the coffin. The sacrist should have thought about this, too. But he was nowhere to be seen. The next monk to emerge from the dormitory was Remigius, the haughty sub-prior. He would have to do. Philip called him over and said: "Help me rescue the bones of the saint."

Remigius's pale green eyes looked fearfully at the burning church, but after a moment's hesitation he followed Philip along the east walk and through the door.

Philip paused inside. It was only a few moments since he had run out, but the fire had progressed very fast. There was a sting in his nostrils that reminded him of burning tar, and he realized that the roof timbers must have been coated with pitch to prevent their rotting. Despite the flames there seemed to be a cold wind: the smoke was escaping through gaping holes in the roof, and the fire was drawing cold air into the church through the windows. The updraft fanned the blaze. Glowing embers rained down on the church floor, and several larger timbers, burning up in the roof, looked as if they could fall at any time. Until this moment Philip had been worried first about the monks and second about priory property, but now for the first time he was afraid for himself, and he hesitated to go farther into the inferno.

The longer he waited, the greater the risk; and if he thought about it too much he would lose his nerve entirely. He hitched up the skirts of his robe, shouted "Follow me!" and ran into the transept. He dodged around the small bonfires on the floor, expecting at any moment to be flattened by a falling roof beam. He ran with his heart in his mouth, feeling as if he wanted to scream with tension. Then, suddenly, he reached the safety of the aisle on the other side.

He paused there for a moment. The aisles were stone-vaulted and there was no fire here. Remigius was right beside him. Philip panted and coughed as smoke caught in his throat. Crossing the transept had taken only a few moments but it had seemed longer than a midnight mass.

"We shall be killed!" Remigius said.

"God will preserve us," Philip said. Then he thought: So why am I frightened?

This was no time for theology.

He went along the transept and turned the corner into the chancel, still keeping to the side aisle. He could feel the heat from the wooden stalls, which were burning merrily in the middle of the quire, and he suffered a pang of loss: the stalls had been expensively made and covered with beautiful carvings. He put them out of his mind and concentrated on the task at hand. He ran on up the chancel to the east end.

The tomb of the saint was halfway across the church. It was a big stone box standing on a low plinth. Philip and Remigius would have to raise the stone lid, put it to one side, lift the coffin out of the tomb, and carry it to the aisle, while the roof above them disintegrated. Philip looked at Remigius. The sub-prior's prominent green eyes were wide with fear. Philip concealed his own dread for Remigius's sake. "You take that end, I'll take this," he said, pointing, and without waiting for agreement he ran to the tomb.

Remigius followed.

They stood at opposite ends and grasped the stone lid. They both heaved.

The lid did not move.

Philip realized he should have brought more monks. He had not paused to think. But it was too late now: if he went out and summoned more help, the transept might be impassable when he tried to return. But he could not leave the saint's remains here. A beam would fall and smash the tomb; then the wooden coffin would catch fire, and the ashes would be scattered in the wind, a dreadful sacrilege and a terrible loss to the cathedral.

He had an idea. He moved around to the side of the tomb and beckoned Remigius to stand beside him. He knelt down, put both hands to the overhanging edge of the lid, and pushed up with all his might. When Remigius copied him, the lid lifted. Slowly they raised it higher. Philip had to go up on one knee, and Remigius followed suit; then they both stood. When the lid was vertical they gave it one more shove and it toppled over, fell on the floor on the other side of the tomb, and cracked in two.

Philip looked inside the tomb. The coffin was in good condition, its wood still apparently sound and its iron handles only superficially tarnished. Philip stood at one end, leaned in, and grasped two handles. Remigius did the same at the other end. They lifted the coffin a few inches, but it was much heavier than Philip had expected, and after a moment Remigius let his end fall, saying: "I can't do it—I'm older than you."

Philip suppressed an angry retort. The coffin was probably lined with lead. But now that they had broken the lid of the tomb, the coffin was even more vulnerable than before. "Come here," Philip shouted to Remigius. "We'll try to stand it on end."

Remigius came around the tomb and stood beside Philip. They each took one protruding iron handle and heaved. The end came up relatively easily. They got it above the level of the top of the tomb, then they both walked forward, one on either side, raising the coffin as they went, until it stood on end. They paused for a moment. Philip realized they had lifted the foot of the coffin, so the saint was now standing on his head. Philip sent him a silent apology. Small pieces of burning wood fell around them constantly. Every time a few sparks landed on Remigius's robe he would slap at them frantically until they disappeared, and whenever he got the chance he would steal a frightened look at the burning roof. Philip could see that the man's courage was rapidly running out.

They tipped the coffin so that it was leaning against the inside of the tomb, then pushed a little more. The other end came up off the ground and the coffin seesawed on the edge of the tomb; then they eased it down until the other end hit the ground. They tipped it end-over-end once more, so that it lay on the ground the right way up. The holy bones must be rattling around in there like dice in a cup, Philip thought; this is the closest thing to sacrilege that I've ever done, but there's nothing else for it.

Standing at one end of the coffin, they each took a handle, lifted, and began to drag it across the church toward the relative safety of the aisle. Its iron corners plowed small furrows in the beaten earth. They had almost reached the aisle when a section of the roof, blazing timbers and hot lead, came crashing down right on the saint's now-empty tomb. The bang was deafening, the floor trembled with the impact, and the stone tomb was smashed to smithereens. A big beam bounced onto the coffin, missing Philip and Remigius by inches and knocking the coffin out of their grasp. It was too much for Remigius. "This is the devil's work!" he shouted hysterically, and he ran away.

Philip almost followed him. If the devil really were at work in here tonight, there was no telling what might happen. Philip had never seen a fiend but he had heard plenty of tales of people who had. But monks are made to oppose Satan, not flee from him, Philip told himself sternly. He glanced longingly at the shelter of the aisle, then steeled himself, grabbed the coffin handles, and heaved.

He managed to drag it out from under the fallen beam. The wood of the coffin was dented and splintered but not actually broken, remarkably. He dragged it a little farther. A shower of small glowing embers fell around him. He glanced up at the roof. Was that a two-legged figure, dancing a mocking jig up there in the flames, or was it just a wisp of smoke? He looked down again, and saw that the skirt of his robe had caught fire. He knelt down and smacked at the flames with his hands, flattening the burning fabric against the floor, and the flames died instantly; then he heard a noise that was either the screech of tortured wood or the mad mocking laugh of an imp. "Saint Adolphus preserve me," he gasped, and he took hold of the coffin handles again.

Inch by inch he dragged the coffin across the ground. The devil left him alone for a moment. He did not look up—better not to gaze upon the fiend. At last he reached the shelter of the aisle, and felt a little safer. His aching back forced him to stop and straighten up for a moment.

It was a long way to the nearest door, which was in the south transept. He was not sure he could drag the coffin all that way before the whole roof fell in. Perhaps that was what the devil was counting on. Philip could not stop himself from looking up into the flames again. The smoky two-legged figure darted behind a blackened beam just as Philip caught sight of it. He knows I can't make it, Philip thought. He looked along the aisle, tempted to abandon the saint and run for his life—and there he saw, coming toward him, Brother Milius, Cuthbert Whitehead, and Tom Builder, three very corporeal forms rushing to his aid. His heart leaped for joy, and suddenly he was not sure there was a fiend in the roof at all.

"Thank God!" he said. "Help me with this," he added unnecessarily.

Tom Builder took one swift appraising look at the burning roof. He did not appear to see any fiends, but he said: "Let's make it quick."

They each took a corner and lifted the coffin onto their shoulders. It was a strain even with four of them. Philip called: "Forward!" They walked along the aisle as fast as they could, bowed down by the heavy burden.

When they reached the south transept, Tom called: "Wait." The floor was an obstacle course of small fires, and more fragments of burning wood fell continuously. Philip peered across the gap, trying to map a route through the flames. During the few moments that they paused, a rumble began at the west end of the church. Philip looked up, full of dread. The rumble grew to a thunder.

Tom Builder said enigmatically: "It's weak, like the other one."

"What is?" Philip shouted.

"The southwest tower."

"Oh, no!"

The thunder became even louder. Philip looked, horrified, as the entire west end of the church seemed to move forward a yard, as if the hand of God had struck it. Ten or more yards of roof fell down into the nave with the impact of an earthquake. Then the whole of the southwest tower seemed to crumble and fall, like a landslide, into the church.

Philip was paralyzed with shock. His church was disintegrating in front of his eyes. The damage would take years to repair even if he could find the money. What would he do? How would the monastery continue? Was this the end of Kingsbridge Priory?

He was jerked out of his paralysis by the movement of the coffin on his shoulder when the other three men pressed forward. Philip followed where it took him. Tom negotiated a way through the maze of fires. A burning brand fell on top of the coffin but fortunately it slipped to the floor without touching any of them. A moment later they reached the opposite side and passed through the door, out of the church into the cool night air.

Philip was so devastated by the destruction of the church that he felt no relief at his own escape. They hurried around the cloisters to the south arch and passed through. When they were well clear of the buildings Tom said: "This will do." Thankfully, they lowered the coffin to the frosty ground.

Philip took a few moments to catch his breath. In that pause he realized that this was no time to act stunned. He was the prior, he was in charge here. What should he do next? It might be wise to make sure all the monks had escaped safely. He took one more deep breath, then straightened his shoulders and looked at the other men. "Cuthbert, you stay here and guard the saint's coffin," he said. "The rest of you, follow me."

He led them around the back of the kitchen buildings, passed between the brewery and the mill, and crossed the green to the guesthouse. The monks, Tom's family, and most of the villagers were standing around in groups, talking in subdued tones and staring wide-eyed at the blazing church. Philip turned to look at it before speaking to them. The sight was painful. The entire west end was a pile of rubble, and huge flames were shooting up from what remained of the roof.

He tore his gaze away. "Is everyone here?" he called out. "If you can think of anyone who's missing, call out his name."

Someone said: "Cuthbert Whitehead."

"He's guarding the bones of the saint. Anyone else?"

There was no one else.

Philip said to Milius: "Count the monks, to make sure. There should be forty-five including you and me." Knowing he could trust Milius, he put that out of his mind and turned to Tom Builder. "Is all your family here?"

Tom nodded and pointed. They were standing by the guesthouse wall; the woman, the grown son and the two little ones. The small boy gave Philip a frightened look. This must be a terrifying experience for them, Philip thought.

The sacrist was sitting on the ironbound box that contained the treasure. Philip had forgotten about that: he was relieved to see it safe. He addressed the sacrist. "Brother Andrew, the coffin of Saint Adolphus is behind the refectory. Take some brothers to help you, and carry it . . ." He thought for a moment. The safest place was probably the prior's residence. "Take it to my house."

"To your house?" Andrew said argumentatively. "The relics should be in my care, not yours."

"Then you should have rescued them from the church!" Philip flared. "Do as I say, without another word!"

The sacrist got up reluctantly, looking furious.

Philip said: "Make haste, man, or I'll strip you of your office here and now!" He turned his back on Andrew and spoke to Milius. "How many?"

"Forty-four, plus Cuthbert. Eleven novices. Five guests. Everyone is accounted for."

"That's a mercy." Philip looked at the raging fire. It seemed almost miraculous that they were all alive and no one had even been hurt. He realized he was exhausted, but he was too worried to sit down and rest. "Is there anything else of value that we should rescue?" he said. "We have the treasure and the relics. . . ."

Alan, the young treasurer, spoke up. "What about the books?"

Philip groaned. Of course—the books. They were kept in a locked cupboard in the east cloister, next to the door of the chapter house, where the monks could get them during study periods. It would take a dangerously long time to empty the cupboard book by book. Perhaps a few strong youngsters could pick up the whole cupboard and carry it to safety. Philip looked around. The sacrist had chosen half a dozen monks to deal with the coffin, and they were already making their way across the green. Now Philip selected three young monks and three of the older novices, and told them to follow him.

He retraced his steps across the open space in front of the burning church. He was too tired to run. They passed between the mill and the brewery, and went around the back of the kitchen and refectory. Cuthbert Whitehead and the sacrist were organizing the removal of the coffin. Philip led his group along the passage that ran between the refectory and the dormitory and under the south archway into the cloisters.

He could feel the heat of the fire. The big book cupboard had carvings on its doors depicting Moses and the tablets of stone. Philip directed the young men to tip the cupboard forward and hoist it on their shoulders. They carried it around the cloisters to the south archway. There Philip paused and looked back while they went on. His heart filled with grief at the sight of the ruined church. There was less smoke and more flame now. Whole stretches of the roof had disappeared. As he watched, the roof over the crossing seemed to sag, and he realized it was going to go next. There was a thunderous crash, louder than anything that had gone before, and the roof of the south transept fell in. Philip felt a pain that was almost physical, as if his own body were burning. A moment later the wall of the transept seemed to bulge out over the cloisters. God help us, it's going to fall down, Philip thought. As the stonework began to crumble and scatter he realized it was falling toward him, and he turned to flee; but before he had taken three steps something hit the back of his head and he lost consciousness.

For Tom, the raging fire that was destroying Kingsbridge Cathedral was a beacon of hope.

He looked across the green at the huge flames that leaped high in the air from the ruins of the church, and all he could think was: This means work!

The thought had been hiding in the back of his mind, ever since he had emerged, bleary-eyed, from the guesthouse, and seen the faint red glow in the church windows. All the time he had been hurrying the monks out of danger, and rushing into the burning church to find Prior Philip, and carrying the saint's coffin out, his heart had been bursting with shameless, happy optimism.

Now that he had a moment to reflect, it occurred to him that he ought not to be happy about the burning of a church; but then, he thought, no one had been hurt, and the priory's treasure had been saved, and the church was old and crumbling anyway; so why not rejoice?

The young monks came back across the green, carrying the heavy book cupboard. All I have to do now, Tom thought, is make sure that I get the job of rebuilding this church. And the time to speak to Prior Philip about it is now.

However, Philip was not with the monks carrying the book cupboard. They reached the guesthouse and lowered the cupboard to the ground. "Where's your prior?" Tom said to them.

The eldest of them looked back in surprise. "I don't know," he said. "I thought he was behind us."

Perhaps he had stayed back to watch the blaze, Tom thought; but perhaps he was in trouble.

Without further ado Tom ran across the green and around the back of the kitchen. He hoped Philip was all right, not just because Philip seemed such a good man, but because he was Jonathan's protector. Without Philip there was no knowing what might happen to the baby.

Tom found Philip in the passage between the refectory and the dormitory. To his relief, the prior was sitting upright, looking dazed but unhurt. Tom helped him to his feet.

"Something hit my head," Philip said groggily.

Tom looked past him. The south transept had fallen into the cloisters. "You're fortunate to be alive," Tom said. "God must have a purpose for you."

Philip shook his head to clear it. "I passed out for a moment. I'm all right now. Where are the books?"

"They took them to the guesthouse."

"Let's go back there."

Tom took Philip's arm as they walked. The prior was not badly hurt but he was upset, Tom could see.

By the time they got back to the guesthouse, the fire in the church was past its peak, and the flames were dying down a little; but nevertheless Tom could see people's faces quite clearly, and he realized with a little shock that it was daybreak.

Philip started organizing things again. He told Milius Kitchener to make porridge for everyone and authorized Cuthbert Whitehead to open a barrel of strong wine to warm them up in the meantime. He ordered the fire lit in the guesthouse, and the older monks went in out of the cold. It started to rain, wind-driven sheets of water, freezing cold, and the flames in the ruined church faded fast.

When everyone was busy again, Prior Philip walked away from the guesthouse, on his own, and headed for the church. Tom saw him and followed. This was his chance. If he could handle this right he could work here for years.

Philip stood staring at what had been the west end of the church, shaking his head sadly at the wreckage, looking as if it were his life that was in ruins. Tom stood beside him in silence. After a while Philip moved on, walking along the north side of the nave, through the graveyard. Tom walked with him, surveying the damage.

The north wall of the nave was still standing, but the north transept and part of the north wall of the chancel had fallen. The church still had an east end. They turned around the end and looked at the south side. Most of the south wall had come down and the south transept had collapsed into the cloisters. The chapter house was still standing.

They walked to the archway that led into the east walk of the cloisters. There they were halted by the pile of rubble. It looked a mess, but Tom's trained eye could see that the cloister walks themselves were not badly damaged, just buried under the fallen ruins. He climbed over the broken stones until he could see into the church. Just behind the altar there was a semi-concealed staircase that led down into the crypt. The crypt itself was beneath the quire. Tom peered in, studying the stone floor over the crypt for signs of cracking. He could see none. There was a good chance the crypt had survived intact. He would not tell Philip yet: he would save the news for a crucial moment.

Philip had walked on, around the back of the dormitory. Tom hurried to catch him. They found the dormitory unmarked. Going on, they found the other monastic buildings more or less unharmed: the refectory, the kitchen, the bakehouse and the brewery. Philip might have taken some consolation in that, but his expression remained glum.

They ended up where they had started, in front of the ruined west end, having completed a full circuit of the priory close without speaking a word. Philip sighed heavily and broke the silence. "The devil did this," he said.

Tom thought: This is my moment. He took a deep breath and said: "It might be God's work."

Philip looked up at him in surprise. "How so?"

Tom said carefully: "No one has been hurt. The books, the treasure and the bones of the saint were saved. Only the church has been destroyed. Perhaps God wanted a new church."

Philip smiled skeptically. "And I suppose God wanted you to build it." He was not too stunned to see that Tom's line of thought might be self-interested.

Tom stood his ground. "It may be so," he said stubbornly. "It was not the devil who sent a master builder here on the night the church burned down."

Philip looked away. "Well, there will be a new church, but I don't know when. And what am I to do meanwhile? How can the life of the monastery go on? All we're here for is worship and study."

Philip was deep in despair. This was the moment for Tom to offer him new hope. "My boy and I could have the cloisters cleared and ready for use in a week," he said, making his voice sound more confident than he felt.

Philip was surprised. "Could you?" Then his expression changed once more, and he looked defeated again. "But what will we use for a church?"

"What about the crypt? You can hold services there, couldn't you?"

"Yes—it would do very well."

"I'm sure the crypt is not badly damaged," Tom said. It was almost true: he was almost sure.

Philip was looking at him as if he were the angel of mercy.

"It won't take long to clear a path through the debris from the cloisters to the crypt stairs," Tom went on. "Most of the church on that side has been completely destroyed, which is fortunate, oddly enough, because it means there's no further danger from falling masonry. I'd have to survey the walls that are still standing, and it might be necessary to shore some of them up. Then they should be checked every day for cracks, and even so you ought not to enter the church in a gale." All of this was important, but Tom could see that Philip was not taking it in. What Philip wanted from Tom now was positive news, something to lift his spirits. And the way to get hired was to give him what he wanted. Tom changed his tone. "With some of your younger monks laboring for me, I could fix things up so that you're able to resume normal monastic life, after a fashion, within two weeks."

Philip was staring at him. "Two weeks?"

"Give me food and lodging for my family, and you can pay my wages when you have the money."

"You could give me back my priory in two weeks?" Philip repeated incredulously.

Tom was not sure he could, but if it took three no one would die of it. "Two weeks," he said firmly. "After that, we can knock down the remaining walls—that's a skilled job, mind you, if it's to be done safely—then clear the rubble, stacking the stones for reuse. Meanwhile we can plan the new cathedral." Tom held his breath. He had done his best. Surely Philip would hire him now!

Philip nodded, smiling for the first time. "I think God did send you," he said. "Let's have some breakfast, then we can start work."

Tom breathed a shaky sigh of relief. "Thank you," he said. There was a quaver in his voice that he could not quite control, but suddenly he did not care, and with a barely suppressed sob, he said: "I can't tell you how much it means to me."

After breakfast Philip held an impromptu chapter in Cuthbert's store-room beneath the kitchen. The monks were nervously excited. They were men who had chosen, or had reconciled themselves to, a life of security, predictability and tedium, and most of them were badly disoriented. Their bewilderment touched Philip's heart. He felt more than ever like a shepherd, whose job it is to care for foolish and helpless creatures; except that these were not dumb animals, they were his brothers, and he loved them. The way to comfort them, he had decided, was to tell them what was going to happen, use up their nervous energy in hard work, and return to a semblance of normal routine as soon as possible.

Despite the unusual surroundings, Philip did not abbreviate the ritual of chapter. He ordered the reading of the martyrology for the day, followed by the memorial prayers. This was what monasteries were for: prayer was the justification of their existence. Nevertheless, some of the monks were restive, so he chose Chapter Twenty of Saint Benedict's Rule, the section called "On Reverence at Prayer." The necrology followed. The familiar ritual calmed their nerves, and he noticed that the scared look was slowly leaving the faces around him as the monks realized that their world was not coming to an end after all.

At the end Philip rose to address them. "The catastrophe that struck us last night is, after all, only physical," he began, putting into his voice as much warmth and reassurance as he could. "Our life is spiritual; our work is prayer, worship and contemplation." He looked all around the room for a moment, catching as many eyes as he could, making sure he had their concentrated attention; then he said: "We will resume that work within a few days, that I promise you."

He paused to let those words sink in, and the easing of tension in the room was almost tangible. He gave them a moment, then went on. "God in his wisdom sent us a master builder yesterday to help us through this crisis. He has assured me that if we work under his direction we can have the cloisters ready for normal use within a week."

There was a subdued murmur of pleased surprise.

"I'm afraid our church will never be used for services again—it will have to be built anew, and that will take many years, of course.

However, Tom Builder believes the crypt to be undamaged. The crypt is consecrated, so we can hold services there. Tom says he can make it safe within a week after finishing the cloisters. So, you see, we can resume normal worship in time for Quinquagesima Sunday."

Once again their relief was audible. Philip saw that he had succeeded in soothing and reassuring them. At the beginning of this chapter they had been frightened and confused; now they were calm and hopeful. Philip added: "Brothers who feel themselves too frail to undertake physical labor will be excused. Brothers who work all day with Tom Builder will be allowed red meat and wine."

Philip sat down. Remigius was the first to speak. "How much will we have to pay this builder?" he asked suspiciously.

You could trust Remigius to try to find fault. "Nothing, yet," Philip replied. "Tom knows our poverty. He will work for food and lodging for himself and his family, until we can afford his wages." That was ambiguous, Philip realized: it might mean that Tom would not be entitled to wages until the priory could afford it, whereas the reality was that the priory would owe him wages for every day he worked, starting today. But before Philip could clarify the agreement, Remigius spoke again.

"And where will they lodge?"

"I have given them the guesthouse."

"They could lodge with one of the village families."

"Tom has made us a generous offer," Philip said impatiently. "We're fortunate to have him. I don't want to make him sleep crowded in with someone's goats and pigs when we have a decent house standing empty."

"There are two women in that family—"

"A woman and a girl," Philip corrected him.

"One woman, then. We don't want a woman living in the priory!"

The monks muttered restively: they did not like Remigius's quibbling. Philip said: "It's perfectly normal for women to stay in the guesthouse."

"Not *that* woman!" Remigius blurted, then he immediately looked as if he regretted it.

Philip frowned. "Do you know the woman, Brother?"

"She once inhabited these parts," Remigius said reluctantly.

Philip was intrigued. It was the second time something of this sort had happened in connection with the builder's wife: Waleran Bigod had also been disturbed by the sight of her. Philip said: "What's wrong with her?"

Before Remigius could answer, Brother Paul, the old monk who kept the bridge, spoke up. "I remember," he said rather dreamily. "There was a wild forest girl used to live around here—oh, it must be fifteen year ago. That's who she reminds me of—probably it's the same girl, grown up."

"People said she was a witch," Remigius said. "We can't have a witch living in the priory!"

"I don't know about that," said Brother Paul in the same slow, meditative voice. "Any woman who lives wild gets called a witch sooner or later. People saying a thing doesn't make it so. I'm content to leave it to Prior Philip to judge, in his wisdom, whether she's a danger."

"Wisdom doesn't come immediately with the assumption of monastic office," Remigius snapped.

"Indeed not," said Brother Paul slowly. He looked directly at Remigius and said: "Sometimes it doesn't come at all."

The monks laughed at that riposte, which was all the funnier for coming from an unexpected source. Philip had to pretend to be displeased. He clapped his hands for silence. "Enough!" he said. "These matters are solemn. I will question the woman. Now let us go about our duties. Those who wish to be excused from labor may retire to the infirmary for prayer and meditation. The rest, follow me."

He left the storeroom and walked around the back of the kitchen buildings to the south archway which led into the cloisters. A few monks left the group and headed for the infirmary, among them Remigius and Andrew Sacrist. There was nothing frail about either of them, Philip thought, but they would probably cause trouble if they joined the labor force, so he was happy to see them go. Most of the monks followed Philip.

Tom had already marshaled the priory servants and started work. He stood on the pile of rubble in the cloister square with a large piece of chalk in his hand, marking stones with the letter T, his initial.

For the first time ever, it occurred to Philip to wonder how such large stones could be moved. They were certainly too big for a man to lift. He saw the answer immediately. A pair of poles were laid side by side on the ground, and a stone was rolled along until it rested across the poles. Then two people would take the ends of the poles and lift. Tom Builder must have shown them how to do that.

The work was proceeding rapidly, with most of the priory's sixty servants helping, making a stream of people carrying stones away and coming back for more. The sight lifted Philip's spirits, and he gave up a silent prayer of thanks for Tom Builder.

Tom saw him and came down off the pile. Before speaking to Philip he addressed one of the servants, the tailor who sewed the monks' clothes. "Start the monks carrying stones," he instructed the man. "Make sure they take only the stones I've marked, otherwise the pile may slip and kill someone." He turned to Philip. "I've marked enough to keep them going for a while."

"Where are they taking the stones?" Philip asked.

"Come and I'll show you. I want to check that they're stacking them properly."

Philip went with Tom. The stones were being taken to the east side of the priory close. "Some of the servants will still have to do their normal duties," Philip said as they walked. "The stable hands must still care for the horses, the cooks have to prepare meals, someone must fetch firewood and feed the chickens and go to market. But they're none of them overworked, and I can spare half of them. In addition, you'll have about thirty monks."

Tom nodded. "That'll do."

They passed the east end of the church. The laborers were stacking the still-warm stones up against the east wall of the priory close, a few yards from the infirmary and the prior's house. Tom said: "The old stones must be saved for the new church. They won't be used for walls, because secondhand stones don't weather well; but they'll do for foundations. All the broken stones must be kept, too. They'll be mixed with mortar and poured into the cavity between the inner and outer skins of the new walls, forming the rubble core."

"I see." Philip watched while Tom instructed the workers how to stack stones in an interlocking pattern so that the pile would not topple. It was already clear that Tom's expertise was indispensable.

When Tom was satisfied, Philip took his arm and led him on around the church, to the graveyard on the north side. The rain had stopped, but the gravestones were still wet. Monks were buried at the east end of the graveyard, villagers at the west end. The dividing line was the out-jutting north transept of the church, now in ruins. Philip and Tom stopped in front of it. A weak sun broke through the clouds. There was nothing sinister about the blackened timbers in daylight, and Philip felt almost ashamed that he had thought he had seen a devil last night.

He said: "Some of the monks are uneasy about having a woman live within the precincts of the priory." The look that came over Tom's face was more intense than anxiety: he seemed scared, even panicked. He really loves her, Philip thought. He went on hastily: "But I don't want you to have to live in the village and share a hovel with another family. To avoid trouble, it would be wise for your wife to be circumspect. Tell her to stay away from the monks as much as possible, especially the young ones. She should keep her face covered if she has to walk about the priory. Most of all, she mustn't do anything which could incur the suspicion of witchcraft."

"It shall be done," said Tom. There was a note of determination in his voice, and he looked a little daunted. Philip recalled that the wife was a sharp-witted woman with a mind of her own. She might not take kindly to being told to make herself inconspicuous. However, her family had been destitute yesterday, so she was likely to see these restraints as a small price to pay for shelter and security.

They walked on. Last night Philip had seen all this destruction as a supernatural tragedy, a terrible defeat for the forces of civilization and true religion, a body blow to his life's work. Now it just seemed like a problem he had to solve—formidable, yes; even daunting; but not superhuman. The change was mainly due to Tom. Philip felt very grateful to him.

They reached the west end. Philip saw a fast horse being saddled at the stable, and wondered who was going on a journey today, of all days. He left Tom to return to the cloisters while he himself went over to the stable to investigate.

One of the sacrist's helpers had ordered the horse: young Alan, who had rescued the treasure chest from the chapter house. "And where are you off to, my son?" said Philip.

"To the bishop's palace," Alan replied. "Brother Andrew has sent me to fetch candles, holy water and the Host, as we lost all those things in the fire and we are to have services again as soon as possible."

That made sense. All such supplies had been kept in a locked box in the quire, and the box was sure to have been burned. Philip was glad the sacrist was well organized for a change. "That's good," he said. "But wait a while. If you're going to the palace, you can take a letter from me to Bishop Waleran." Sly Waleran Bigod was now bishop-elect, thanks to some rather disreputable maneuvering; but Philip could not now withdraw his support, and was obliged to treat Waleran as his bishop. "I ought to give him a report on the fire."

"Yes, Father," Alan replied, "but I already have a letter to the bishop from Remigius."

"Oh!" Philip was surprised. That was very enterprising of Remigius, he thought. "All right," he said to Alan. "Travel cautiously, and may God go with you."

"Thank you, Father."

Philip walked back toward the church. Remigius had been *very* quick off the mark. Why had he and the sacrist been in such a hurry? It was enough to make Philip a little uneasy. Was the letter just about the burning of the church? Or was there something else in it?

Philip stopped halfway across the green and turned to look back. He would be perfectly within his rights to take the letter from Alan and read it. But he was too late: Alan was trotting through the gate. Philip stared after him, feeling mildly frustrated. At that moment, Tom's wife stepped out of the guesthouse, carrying a scuttle which presumably contained ashes from the fireplace. She turned toward the dunghill near the stable. Philip watched her. The way she walked was pleasing, like the gait of a good horse.

He thought again about Remigius's letter to Waleran. Somehow he could not shake off an intuitive, but nonetheless worrying, suspicion that the main burden of the message was not, in fact, the fire.

For no very good reason he felt sure the letter was about the stonemason's wife.

III

Jack woke up at first cockcrow. He opened his eyes and saw Tom getting up. He lay still and listened to Tom pissing on the ground outside the door. He longed to move to the warm place Tom had vacated and cuddle up to his mother, but he knew Alfred would mock him mercilessly if he did, so he stayed where he was. Tom came back in and shook Alfred awake.

Tom and Alfred drank the ale remaining from last night's dinner and ate some stale horsebread, then they went out. There was some bread left over, and Jack hoped that today they would leave it behind, but he was disappointed: Alfred took it with him, as usual.

Alfred worked all day on the site with Tom. Jack and his mother sometimes went into the forest for the day. Mother would set traps while Jack went after duck with his slingshot. Whatever they caught they would sell to villagers or to the cellarer, Cuthbert. This was their only source of cash, since Tom was not being paid. With the money, they bought cloth or leather or tallow, and on the days when they did not go into the forest Mother would make shoes, undershirts, candles or a cap while Jack and Martha played with the village children. On Sundays, after the service, Tom and Mother liked to sit by the fire, talking. Sometimes they would start kissing, and Tom would put his hand inside Mother's robe, and then they would send the children out for a while and bar the door. This was the worst time of the entire week, for Alfred would be bad-tempered and would persecute the younger ones.

Today was an ordinary day, however, and Alfred would be busy from dawn to dusk. Jack got up and went outside. It was cold but dry. Martha came out a few moments later. The cathedral ruins were already aswarm with workers carrying stones, shoveling rubble, building wooden supports for unsteady walls and demolishing those which were too far gone to save.

There was general agreement, among the villagers and monks, that the fire had been started by the devil, and for long periods Jack actually forgot that he had started it himself. When he remembered, he would be brought up with a start, and then he would feel extraordinarily pleased with himself. He had taken a terrible risk, but he had got away with it, and he had saved the family from starvation.

The monks had their breakfast first, and the lay workers got nothing until the monks went into chapter. It was an awfully long wait for Martha and Jack. Jack always woke up hungry, and the cold morning air increased his appetite.

"Let's go to the kitchen courtyard," Jack said. The kitchen hands might give them some scraps. Martha agreed readily: she thought Jack was wonderful, and would go along with anything he suggested.

When they got to the kitchen area they found that Brother Bernard, who was in charge of the bakehouse, was making bread today. Because his helpers were all working on the site, he was carrying firewood for himself. He was a young man, but rather fat, and he was puffing and sweating under a load of logs. "We'll fetch your wood, brother," Jack offered.

Bernard dumped the load beside his oven and handed Jack the broad, flat basket. "There's good children," he panted. "God will bless you."

Jack took the basket and the two of them ran to the firewood pile behind the kitchen. They loaded the basket with logs, then carried the heavy load between them.

When they got back the oven was already hot, and Bernard emptied their basket directly onto the fire and sent them back for more. Jack's arms ached but his stomach hurt more, and he hurried to load the basket again.

The second time they returned Bernard was putting tiny loaves of dough on a tray. "Fetch me one more basket, and you shall have hot buns," he said. Jack's mouth watered.

They filled the basket extra high the third time, and staggered back, each holding one handle. As they approached the courtyard they met Alfred, walking with a bucket, presumably on his way to fetch water from the channel that ran from the millpond across the green before disappearing underground by the brewery. Alfred hated Jack even more since Jack had put the dead bird in Alfred's beer. Normally Jack would casually turn and walk the other way when he saw Alfred. Now he wondered whether to drop the basket and run, but that would look cowardly, and besides, he could smell the fragrance of new bread from the bakehouse, and he was ravenous; so he pressed on, with his heart in his mouth.

Alfred laughed at them struggling under a weight he could easily have carried alone. They gave him a wide berth, but he took a couple of steps toward them and gave Jack a shove, knocking him off his feet. Jack fell hard on his bottom, jarring his spine painfully. He dropped his side of the basket and all the firewood tipped out onto the ground. Tears welled up in his eyes, caused by rage rather than pain. It was so unfair that Alfred should be able to do that, without provocation, and get away with it. Jack got up and patiently put the wood back into the basket, pretending for Martha's benefit not to care. They picked up the basket again and continued on to the bakehouse.

There they had their reward. The tray of buns was cooling on a stone shelf. When they came in Bernard took one, stuffed it in his mouth, and said: "They're all right. Help yourselves. But careful— they're hot."

Jack and Martha each took a bun. Jack bit into his tentatively, afraid of burning his mouth, but it was so delicious that he ate it all in a moment. He looked at the remaining buns. There were nine left. He glanced up at Brother Bernard, who was grinning at him. "I know what you want," the monk said. "Go on, take the lot."

Jack lifted the skirt of his cloak and wrapped the rest of the buns in it. "We'll take them to Mother," he said to Martha.

"There's a good boy you are," Bernard said. "Off you go, then."

"Thank you, Brother," Jack said.

They left the bakery and headed for the guesthouse. Jack was thrilled. Mother would be pleased with him for providing such a treat. He was tempted to eat another bun before he handed them over, but he resisted the temptation: it would be so nice to give her such a lot.

As they were crossing the green, they met Alfred again.

He had evidently filled his bucket, returned to the site, and emptied it, and he was now coming back for a refill. Jack decided to look nonchalant and hope that Alfred would ignore him. But the way he was carrying the buns, wrapped in the skirt of his cloak, was too obvious to conceal; and once again Alfred turned toward them.

Jack would have given him a bun willingly, but he knew Alfred would take them all if he got the chance. Jack broke into a run.

Alfred gave chase and soon caught up with him. Alfred stuck out one long leg and tripped Jack, and Jack went flying. The hot buns scattered all over the ground.

Alfred picked one up, wiped a smear of mud off it, and popped it into his mouth. His eyes widened with surprise. "New bread!" he said. He began to pick up the others.

Jack scrambled to his feet and tried to grab one of the fallen buns, but Alfred hit him a hefty swipe with the flat of his hand, knocking him down again. Alfred quickly scooped up the rest of the buns and walked off, munching. Jack burst into tears.

Martha looked sympathetic, but Jack did not want sympathy: he was suffering from humiliation as much as anything else. He walked off, and when Martha followed he turned on her and said: "Go away!" She looked hurt, but she stopped and let him go.

He walked toward the ruins, drying his tears on his sleeve. There was murder in his heart. I destroyed the cathedral, he thought; I could kill Alfred.

Around the ruins there was a good deal of sweeping and tidying this morning. Some ecclesiastical dignitary was coming to inspect the damage, Jack recalled.

It was Alfred's physical superiority that was so maddening: he could do anything he liked just because he was so big. Jack walked around for a while, seething, wishing Alfred had been in the church when all these stones fell.

Eventually he saw Alfred again. He was in the north transept, shoveling stone chips into a cart, and he was gray with dust. Near the cart was a roof timber that had survived almost undamaged, merely singed and blackened with soot. Jack rubbed the surface of the beam with a finger: it left a whitish line. Inspired, Jack wrote in the soot: "Alfred is a pig."

Some of the laborers noticed. They were surprised Jack could write. One young man said: "What does it say?"

"Ask Alfred," Jack replied.

Alfred peered at the writing and frowned in annoyance. He could read his own name, Jack knew, but not the rest. He was riled. He knew he was being insulted but he did not know what had been said, and that was humiliating in itself. He looked rather foolish. Jack's anger was a little soothed. Alfred might be bigger, but Jack was smarter.

Still nobody knew what the words said. Then a novice monk walked past, read the writing, and smiled. "Who's Alfred?" he said.

"Him," said Jack with a jerk of the thumb. Alfred looked angrier, but he still did not know what to do, so he leaned on his shovel, looking stupid.

The novice laughed. "A pig, eh? What's he digging for— acorns?" he said.

"Must be!" said Jack, delighted to have an ally.

Alfred dropped his shovel and made a grab for Jack.

Jack was ready for him, and went off like an arrow from a bow. The novice stuck out a foot to trip Jack—as if to be evenhandedly nasty to both sides—but Jack nimbly leaped over it. He raced along what had been the chancel, dodging around piles of rubble and jumping over fallen roof timbers. He could hear the heavy steps and grunting breath of Alfred right behind him, and fear lent him speed.

A moment later he realized he had run the wrong way. There was no way out of that end of the cathedral. He had made a mistake. He realized, with a sinking heart, that he was going to get hurt.

The upper half of the east end had fallen in, and the stones were piled up against what remained of the wall. Having nowhere else to go, Jack scrambled up the pile with Alfred hot on his heels. He reached the top and saw in front of him a sheer drop of about fifteen feet. He teetered fearfully on the edge. It was too far to jump without hurting himself. Alfred made a grab for his ankle. Jack lost his balance. For a moment he stood with one foot on the wall and the other in the air, windmilling his arms in an attempt to regain his footing. Alfred kept hold of his ankle. Jack felt himself falling inexorably the wrong way. Alfred held on a moment longer, unbalancing Jack further, then let go. Jack fell through the air, unable to right himself, and he heard himself scream. He landed on his left side. The impact was terrific. By an unlucky chance his face hit a stone. Everything went black for a moment.

When he opened his eyes Alfred was standing over him—he must have clambered down the wall somehow—and beside him was one of the older monks. Jack recognized the monk: it was Remigius, the sub-prior. Remigius caught his eye and said: "Get up, lad."

Jack was not sure he could. He could not move his left arm. The left side of his face was numb. He sat upright. He had thought he was going to die, and it surprised him to be able to move at all. Using his right arm to push himself up, he struggled painfully to his feet, putting most of his weight on his right leg. As the numbness went he began to hurt.

Remigius took him by the left arm. Jack cried out in pain. Remigius ignored him and grabbed Alfred's ear. He would probably issue some dire punishment to both of them, Jack thought. Jack hurt too much to care.

Remigius spoke to Alfred. "Now, my lad, why are you trying to kill your brother?"

"He's not my brother," Alfred said.

Remigius's expression changed. "Not your brother?" he said. "Don't you have the same mother and father?"

"*She's* not my mother," Alfred said. "My mother's dead."

A crafty look came over Remigius's face. "When did your mother die?"

"At Christmas."

"*Last* Christmas?"

"Yes."

Despite his pain, Jack could see that Remigius was intensely interested in this, for some reason. The monk's voice quivered with suppressed excitement as he said: "So your father has only lately met this boy's mother?"

"Yes."

"And since they have been . . . together, have they been to see a priest, to have their union solemnized?"

"Uh . . . I don't know." Alfred did not understand the words being used, Jack could tell. For that matter neither did Jack.

Remigius said impatiently: "Well, have they had a wedding?"

"No."

"I see." Remigius looked pleased about this, although Jack would have thought he would be cross. There was a rather satisfied look on the monk's face. He was silent and thoughtful for a moment, then he seemed to remember the two boys. "Well, if you want to stay in the priory and eat the monks' bread, don't fight, even if you aren't brothers. We men of God must not see blood-shed—that is one of the reasons we live a life of withdrawal from the world." With that little speech Remigius released them both and turned away, and at last Jack could run to his mother.

It had taken three weeks, not two, but Tom had got the crypt ready for use as a makeshift church, and today the bishop-elect was coming to hold the first service in it. The cloisters had been cleared of rubble, and Tom had repaired the damaged parts: cloisters were simple structures, just covered walkways, and the work had been easy. Most of the rest of the church was just heaps of ruins, and some of the walls that were still standing were in danger of falling, but Tom had cleared a passage from the cloisters, through what had been the south transept, to the crypt stairs.

Tom looked around him. The crypt was a good size, about fifty feet square, plenty big enough for the monks' services. It was a rather dark room, with heavy pillars and a low vaulted ceiling, but it was stoutly constructed, which was why it had survived the fire. They had brought in a trestle table to be used as an altar, and the benches from the refectory would serve as stalls for the monks. When the sacrist brought in his embroidered altar cloths and jeweled candlesticks, it would look just fine.

With the resumption of services Tom's work force would shrink. Most of the monks would return to their lives of worship, and many of those who did labor would resume their agricultural or administrative tasks. Tom would still have about half the priory servants as laborers, however. Prior Philip had taken a tough line with them. He felt there had been too many of them, and if any were unwilling to transfer from their duties as grooms or kitchen hands he was quite ready to dismiss them. A few had gone, but most remained.

The priory already owed Tom three weeks' wages. At the full master builder's rate of fourpence a day, that came to seventy-two pence. As each day went by the debt mounted, and it would become more and more difficult for Prior Philip to pay Tom off. After about half a year Tom would ask the prior to start paying him. By then he would be owed two and a half pounds of silver, which Philip would have to find before he could dismiss Tom. The debt made Tom feel secure.

There was even a chance—he hardly dared to think it—that this job would last him the rest of his life. It was, after all, a cathedral church; and if the powers-that-be were to decide to commission a prestigious new building, and if they could find the money to pay for it, it could be the largest construction project in the kingdom, employing dozens of masons for several decades.

This was too much to hope for, really. Talking to the monks and the villagers, Tom had learned that Kingsbridge had never been an important cathedral. Tucked away in a quiet village, it had had a series of unambitious bishops and was clearly undergoing a slow decline. The priory was undistinguished and penniless. Some monasteries attracted the attention of kings and archbishops by their lavish hospitality, their excellent schools, their great libraries,the researches of their philosopher-monks or the erudition of their priors and abbots; but Kingsbridge had none of those marks. The likelihood was that Prior Philip would build a small church, constructed simply and fitted out modestly; and that might take no more than ten years.

However, that suited Tom perfectly.

He had realized, even before the fire-blackened ruins were cold, that this was his chance to build his own cathedral.

Prior Philip was already convinced that God had sent Tom to Kingsbridge. Tom knew he had won Philip's trust by the efficient way he had begun the process of clearing up and made the priory viable again. When the moment was right he would begin talking to Philip about designs for the new building. If he handled the situation carefully, there was every chance that Philip would ask him to draw the designs. The fact that the new church was likely to be fairly modest made it more probable that the planning might be entrusted to Tom, rather than to a master with more experience of cathedral building. Tom's hopes were high.

The bell rang for chapter. This was also the sign that the lay workers should go in for breakfast. Tom left the crypt and headed for the refectory. On his way he was confronted by Ellen.

She stood aggressively in front of him, as if to bar his way, and there was an odd look in her eye. Martha and Jack were with her. Jack looked terrible: one eye was closed, the left side of his face was bruised and swollen, and he leaned on his right leg, as if his left could not take any weight. Tom felt sorry for the little chap. "What happened to you?" he said.

Ellen said: "Alfred did this."

Tom groaned inwardly. For a moment he felt ashamed of Alfred, who was so much bigger than Jack. But Jack was no angel. Perhaps Alfred had been provoked. Tom looked around for his son, and caught sight of him walking toward the refectory, covered with dust. "Alfred!" he bellowed. "Come here."

Alfred turned around, saw the family group, and approached slowly, looking guilty.

Tom said to him: "Did you do this?"

"He fell off a wall," Alfred said sullenly.

"Did you push him?"

"I was chasing him."

"Who started it?"

"Jack called me a name."

Jack, speaking through swollen lips, said: "I called him a pig because he took our bread."

"Bread?" said Tom. "Where did you get bread before breakfast?"

"Bernard Baker gave it to us. We fetched firewood for him."

"You should have shared it with Alfred," Tom said.

"I would have."

Alfred said: "Then why did you run away?"

"I was taking it home to Mother," Jack protested. "Then Alfred ate it all!"

Fourteen years of raising children had taught Tom that there was no prospect of discovering the rights and wrongs of a childish quarrel. "Go to breakfast, all three of you, and if there's any more fighting today, you, Alfred, will end up with a face like Jack's, and I'll be the one who does it to you. Now clear off."

The children went away.

Tom and Ellen followed at a slower pace. After a moment Ellen said: "Is that all you're going to say?"

Tom glanced at her. She was still angry, but there was nothing he could do about it. He shrugged. "As usual, both parties are guilty."

"Tom! How can you say that?"

"One's as bad as the other."

"Alfred took their bread. Jack called him a pig. That doesn't draw blood!"

Tom shook his head. "Boys always fight. You could spend your whole life adjudicating their quarrels. Best to leave them to it."

"That won't do, Tom," she said in a dangerous tone. "Look at Jack's face, then look at Alfred's. That's not the result of a childish fight. That's a vicious attack by a grown man on a small boy."

Tom resented her attitude. Alfred was not perfect, he knew, but neither was Jack. Tom did not want Jack to become the pampered favorite in this family. "Alfred's not a grown man, he's fourteen years old. But he *is* working. He's making a contribution to the support of the family, and Jack isn't. Jack plays all day, like a child. In my book that means Jack ought to show Alfred respect. He does no such thing, as you will have noticed."

"I don't care!" Ellen flared. "You can say what you like, but my son is badly bruised, and might have been seriously injured, and *I will not allow it!*" She began to cry. In a quieter voice, but still angry, she said: "He's my child and I can't bear to see him like that."

Tom sympathized with her, and he was tempted to comfort her, but he was afraid to give in. He had a feeling that this conversation might be a turning point. Living with his mother and no one else, Jack had always been overprotected. Tom did not want to concede that Jack ought to be cushioned against the normal knocks of everyday life. That would set a precedent that could cause endless trouble in years to come. Tom knew, in truth, that Alfred had gone too far this time, and he was secretly resolved to make the boy leave Jack alone; but it would be a bad thing to say so. "Beatings are a part of life," he said to Ellen. "Jack must learn to take them or avoid them. I can't spend my life protecting him."

"You could protect him from that bullying son of yours!"

Tom winced. He hated to hear her call Alfred a bully. "I might, but I shan't," he said angrily. "Jack must learn to protect himself."

"Oh, go to hell!" Ellen said, and she turned and walked away.

Tom entered the refectory. The wooden hut where the lay workers normally ate had been damaged by the fall of the southwest tower, so they took their meals in the refectory after the monks had finished and gone. Tom sat apart from everyone else, feeling unsociable. A kitchen hand brought him a jug of ale and some slices of bread in a basket. He dipped a piece of bread in the ale to soften it and began to eat.

Alfred was a big lad with too much energy, Tom thought fondly. He sighed into his beer. The boy *was* something of a bully, Tom knew in his heart; but he would calm down in time. Meanwhile, Tom was not going to make his own children give special treatment to a newcomer. They had had too much to put up with already. They had lost their mother, they had been forced to tramp the roads, they had come near to starving to death. He was not going to impose any more burdens on them if he could help it. They were due for a little indulgence. Jack would just have to keep out of Alfred's way. It would not kill him.

A disagreement with Ellen always left Tom heavyhearted. They had quarreled several times, usually about the children, although this was their worst dispute so far. When she was hard-faced and hostile he could not remember what it had been like, just a little while earlier, to feel passionately in love with her: she seemed like an angry stranger who had intruded into his peaceful life.

He had never had such furious, bitter quarrels with his first wife. Looking back, it seemed to him that he and Agnes had agreed about everything important, and that when they disagreed it had not made them angry. That was how it should be between man and wife, and Ellen would have to realize that she could not be part of a family and yet have all her own way.

Even when Ellen was at her most infuriating he never quite wished that she would go away, but all the same he often thought of Agnes with regret. Agnes had been with him for most of his adult life, and now he had a constant sense of there being something missing. While she was alive he had never thought that he was particularly fortunate to have her, nor had he felt thankful for her; but now that she was dead he missed her, and he felt ashamed that he had taken her for granted.

At quiet moments in the day, when all his laborers had their instructions and were busy about the site, and Tom was able to get down to a skilled task, rebuilding a bit of wall in the cloisters or repairing a pillar in the crypt, he sometimes held imaginary conversations with Agnes. Mostly he told her about Jonathan, their baby son. Tom saw the child most days, being fed in the kitchen or walked in the cloisters or put to bed in the monks' dormitory. He seemed perfectly healthy and happy, and no one but Ellen knew or even suspected that Tom had a special interest in him. Tom also talked to Agnes about Alfred and Prior Philip and even Ellen, explaining his feelings about them, just as he would have done (except in the case of Ellen) if Agnes had been alive. He told her of his practical plans for the future, too: his hope that he would be employed here for years to come, and his dream of designing and building the new cathedral himself. In his head he heard her replies and questions. She was at different times pleased, encouraging, fascinated, suspicious, or disapproving. Sometimes he felt she was right, sometimes wrong. If he had told anyone of these conversations, they would have said he was communing with a ghost, and there would have been a flurry of priests and holy water and exorcism; but he knew there was nothing supernatural about what was happening. It was just that he knew her so well that he could imagine how she would feel and what she would say in just about any situation.

She came into his mind unbidden at odd times. When he peeled a pear with his eating knife for little Martha, he remembered how Agnes had always laughed at him because he would take pains to remove the peel in once continuous strip. Whenever he had to write something he would think of her, for she had taught him everything she had learned from her father, the priest; and he would remember her teaching him how to trim a quill or how to spell *caementarius*, the Latin word for "mason." As he washed his face on Sundays he would rub soap into his beard and recall how, when they were young, she had taught him that washing his beard would keep his face free from lice and boils. Never a day went by without some such little incident bringing her vividly to mind.

He knew he was lucky to have Ellen. There was no danger of his taking *her* for granted. She was unique: there was something abnormal about her, and it was that abnormal something that made her magnetic. He was grateful to her for consoling him in his grief, the morning after Agnes died; but sometimes he wished he had met her a few days—instead of a few hours—after he had buried his wife, just so that he would have had time to be heartbroken alone. He would not have observed a period of mourning—that was for lords and monks, not ordinary folk—but he would have had time to become accustomed to the absence of Agnes before he started to get used to living with Ellen. Such thoughts had not occurred to him during the early days, when the threat of starvation had combined with the sexual excitement of Ellen to produce a kind of hysterical end-of-the-world elation. But since he had found work and security, he had begun to feel pangs of regret. And sometimes it seemed that when he thought like this about Agnes, he was not only missing her, but mourning the passing of his own youth. Never again would he be as naive, as aggressive, as hungry or as strong as he had been when he had first fallen in love with Agnes.

He finished his bread and left the refectory ahead of the others. He went into the cloisters. He was pleased with his work here: it was now hard to imagine that the quadrangle had been buried under a mass of rubble three weeks earlier. The only remaining signs of the catastrophe were some cracked paving stones for which he had been unable to find replacements.

There was a lot of dust about, though. He would have the cloisters swept again and then sprinkled with water. He walked through the ruined church. In the north transept he saw a blackened beam with words written in the soot. Tom read it slowly. It said: "Alfred is a pig." So that was what had infuriated Alfred. Quite a lot of the wood from the roof had not burned to ashes, and there were blackened beams like this lying all around. Tom decided he would detail a group of workers to collect all the timber and take it to the firewood store. "Make the site look tidy," Agnes would say when someone important was coming to visit. "You want them to feel glad that Tom's in charge." Yes, dear, Tom thought, and he smiled to himself as he went about his work.

Waleran Bigod's party was sighted a mile or so away across the fields. There were three of them, riding quite hard. Waleran himself was in the lead, on a black horse, his black cloak flying behind. Philip and the senior monastic officials waited by the stable to welcome them.

Philip was not sure how to treat Waleran. Waleran had deceived him, indisputably, by not telling him that the bishop was dead; but when the truth came out Waleran had not appeared in the least ashamed; and Philip had not known what to say to him. He still did not know, but he suspected that there was nothing to be gained by complaining. Anyway, that whole episode had been overshadowed by the catastrophe of the fire. Philip would just be extremely wary of Waleran in future.

Waleran's horse was a stallion, skittish and excitable despite having been ridden several miles. He held its head down hard as he walked it to the stable. Philip disapproved: there was no need for a clergyman to cut a dash on horseback, and most men of God chose quieter mounts.

Waleran swung off the horse with a fluid motion and gave the reins to a stable hand. Philip greeted him formally. Waleran turned and surveyed the ruins. A bleak look came into his eyes, and he said: "This was an expensive fire, Philip." He seemed genuinely distressed, somewhat to Philip's surprise.

Before Philip could reply, Remigius spoke up. "The devil's work, my lord bishop," he said.

"Was it, now?" said Waleran. "In my experience, the devil is usually assisted in such work by monks who light fires in church to take the chill off matins, or carelessly leave burning candles in the bell tower."

Philip was amused to see Remigius crushed, but he could not let Waleran's insinuations pass. "I've held an investigation into possible causes of the conflagration," he said. "No one lit a fire in the church that night—I can be sure because I was present at matins myself. And no one had been up in the roof for months beforehand."

"So what is your explanation—lightning?" Waleran said skeptically.

Philip shook his head. "There was no storm. The fire seems to have started in the vicinity of the crossing. We did leave a candle burning on the altar after the service, as usual. It's possible that the altar cloth caught fire, and a spark was taken by an updraft to the wooden ceiling, which was very old and dry." Philip shrugged. "It's not a very satisfactory explanation, but it's the best we have."

Waleran nodded. "Let's have a closer look at the damage."

They moved off toward the church. Waleran's two companions were a man-at-arms and a young priest. The man-at-arms stayed behind to see to the horse. The priest accompanied Waleran, and was introduced to Philip as Dean Baldwin. As they all crossed the green to the church, Remigius put a hand on Waleran's arm, stopping him, and said: "The guesthouse is undamaged, as you can see."

Everyone stopped and turned around. Philip wondered irritably what Remigius was thinking of. If the guesthouse was undamaged, why make everyone stop and look at it? The builder's wife was walking up from the kitchens, and they all watched her enter the house. Philip glanced at Waleran. He was looking slightly shocked. Philip remembered the moment, back at the bishop's palace, when Waleran had seen the builder's wife, and had looked almost frightened. What was it about that woman?

Waleran gave Remigius a swift look and an almost imperceptible nod, then he turned to Philip and said: "Who is living there?"

Philip was quite sure Waleran had recognized her, but he said: "A master builder and his family."

Waleran nodded and they all moved on. Philip knew now why Remigius had called attention to the guesthouse: he had wanted to make sure Waleran saw the woman. Philip made up his mind to question her at the earliest opportunity.

They went into the ruins. A group of seven or eight men, made up of monks and priory servants in about equal numbers, was lifting a half-burned roof beam under the supervision of Tom. The whole site looked busy but tidy. Philip felt that the air of bustling efficiency did him credit, although Tom was responsible.

Tom came to meet them. He towered over everyone else. Philip said to Waleran: "This is our master builder, Tom. He's managed to make the cloisters and the crypt usable again already. We're very grateful to him."

"I remember you," Waleran said to Tom. "You came to me just after Christmas. I didn't have any work for you."

"That's right," Tom said in his deep, dusty voice. "Perhaps God was saving me to help Prior Philip in his time of trouble."

"A theological builder," Waleran mocked.

Tom reddened faintly under his dusty skin. Philip thought that Waleran must have a strong nerve, to make fun of such a big man, even thought Waleran was a bishop and Tom only a mason.

"What is your next step here?" Waleran asked.

"We must make the place safe by knocking down the remaining walls, before they fall on someone," Tom replied, meekly enough. "Then we should clear the site ready for the building of the new church. As soon as possible we should find tall trees for the timbers of the new roof—the longer the wood is seasoned, the better the roof will be."

Philip said hastily: "Before we start felling trees we must find the money to pay for them."

"We'll speak about that later," Waleran said enigmatically.

That remark intrigued Philip. He hoped Waleran had a scheme for raising the money to build the new church. If the priory had to rely on its own resources it would not be able to begin for many years. Philip had been agonizing over this for the past three weeks, and he still had not come up with a solution.

He led the group along the path that had been cleared through the rubble to the cloisters. One glance was sufficient for Waleran to see that this area had been set to rights. They moved on from there and crossed the green to the prior's house in the southeast corner of the close.

Once inside, Waleran took off his cloak and sat down, holding his pale hands out to the fire. Brother Milius, the kitchener, served hot spiced wine in small wooden bowls. Waleran sipped his and said to Philip: "Has it occurred to you that Tom Builder might have started the fire to provide himself with work?"

"Yes, it has," Philip said. "But I don't think he did. He would have had to get inside the church, which was securely locked up."

"He might have gone in during the day and hidden himself away."

"Then he would have been unable to get out after he started the fire." He shook his head. This was not the real reason he was sure Tom was innocent. "Anyway, I don't believe him capable of such a thing. He's an intelligent man—much more so than you might think at first—but he's not sly. If he were guilty, I think I would have seen it in his face, when I looked him in the eye and asked him how he thought the fire might have started."

Somewhat to Philip's surprise, Waleran agreed immediately. "I believe you're right," he said. "I can't see him setting fire to a church, somehow. He's just not the type."

"We may never know for sure how the fire started," Philip said. "But we must face the problem of raising the money to build a new church. I don't know—"

"Yes," Waleran interrupted, and held up a hand to stop Philip. He turned to the others in the room. "I must speak to Prior Philip alone," he said. "The rest of you may leave us."

Philip was intrigued. He could not imagine why Waleran had to speak to him alone about this.

Remigius said: "Before we go, lord bishop, there is something the brothers have asked me to say to you."

Philip thought: What now?

Waleran raised a skeptical eyebrow. "And why should they ask *you,* rather than your prior, to raise a matter with me?"

"Because Prior Philip is deaf to their complaint."

Philip was angry and mystified. There had been no complaint. Remigius was just trying to embarrass Philip by creating a scene in front of the bishop-elect. Philip caught an inquiring glance from Waleran. He shrugged and tried to look unconcerned. "I can't wait to hear what the complaint is," he said. "Please go ahead, Brother Remigius—if you're *quite* sure the matter is important enough to require the attention of the bishop."

Remigius said: "There is a woman living in the priory."

"Not that again," Philip said with exasperation. "She's the builder's wife, and she lives in the guesthouse."

"She's a witch," said Remigius.

Philip wondered why Remigius was doing this. Remigius had

mounted this particular horse once already, and it would not run. The point was moot, but the prior was the authority, and Waleran was bound to support Philip, unless he wanted to be called in every time Remigius disagreed with his superior. Wearily, Philip said: "She's not a witch."

"Have you interrogated the woman?" Remigius demanded.

Philip recalled that he had promised to question her. He had never done so: he had seen the husband, and told him to tell her to be circumspect, but he had not actually spoken to the woman himself. That was a pity, for it permitted Remigius to score a point; but it was not much of a point, and Philip felt sure it would not cause Waleran to take Remigius's side. "I haven't interrogated her," Philip admitted. "But there is no evidence of witchcraft, and the whole family is perfectly honest and Christian."

"She's a witch and a fornicator," Remigius said, flushing with righteous indignation.

"*What?*" Philip exploded. "With whom does she fornicate?"

"With the builder."

"He's her husband, you fool!"

"No, he's not," Remigius said triumphantly. "They're not married, and they've only known one another a month."

Philip was bowled over. He had never suspected this. Remigius had taken him completely by surprise.

If Remigius was telling the truth, the woman was a fornicator, technically. It was a type of fornication that was normally overlooked, for many couples did not get around to having their union blessed by a priest until they had been together for a while, often until the first child was conceived. Indeed, in very poor or remote parts of the country, couples often lived as man and wife for decades, and brought up children, and then startled a visiting priest by asking him to solemnize their marriage around the time their grandchildren were being born. However, it was one thing for a parish priest to be indulgent among poor peasants on the outskirts of Christendom, and quite another when an important employee of a priory was committing the same act within the precincts of the monastery.

"What makes you think they aren't married?" Philip said skeptically, although he felt sure Remigius would have checked the facts before speaking up in front of Waleran.

"I found the sons fighting, and they told me they aren't brothers. Then the whole story came out."

Philip was disappointed with Tom. Fornication was a common enough sin, but it was particularly abhorrent to monks, who forsook all carnality. How could Tom do this? He should have known it was hateful to Philip. Philip felt angrier with Tom than he did with Remigius. But Remigius had been sneaky. Philip asked him: "Why did you not tell me, your prior, about this?"

"It was only this morning that I heard it."

Philip sat back in his seat, defeated. Remigius had caught him out. Philip looked foolish. This was Remigius's revenge for his defeat in the election. Philip looked at Waleran. The complaint had been made to Waleran: now Waleran could pronounce judgment.

Waleran did not hesitate. "The case is clear enough," he said. "The woman must confess her sin, and do public penance for it. She must leave the priory, and live in chastity, apart from the builder, for a year. Then they may be married."

A year apart was a harsh sentence. Philip felt she deserved it, for defiling the monastery. But he was anxious about how she would receive it. "She may not submit to your judgment," he said.

Waleran shrugged. "Then she will burn in hell."

"If she leaves Kingsbridge, I'm afraid Tom may go with her."

"There are other builders."

"Of course." Philip would be sorry to lose Tom. But he could tell, from Waleran's expression, that Waleran would not mind if Tom and his woman were to leave Kingsbridge and never come back; and he wondered again why she was so important.

Waleran said: "Now clear out, all of you, and let me speak to your prior."

"Just a minute," Philip said sharply. It was his house, and they were his monks, after all; he would summon and dismiss them, not Waleran. "I will speak to the builder myself about this matter. None of you is to mention it to anyone, do you hear? There'll be a harsh punishment for you if you disobey me over this. Is that clear, Remigius?"

"Yes," said Remigius.

Philip looked inquiringly at Remigius and said nothing. There was a pregnant silence.

"Yes, *Father*," Remigius said at last.

"All right, off you go."

Remigius, Andrew, Milius, Cuthbert and Dean Baldwin all trooped out. Waleran helped himself to a little more hot wine and stretched his feet out to the fire. "Women always cause trouble," he said. "When there's a mare in heat in the stables, all the stallions start nipping the grooms, kicking their stalls and generally causing trouble. Even the geldings start to misbehave. Monks are like geldings: physical passion is denied them, but they can still smell cunt."

Philip was embarrassed. There was no need for such explicit talk, he felt. He looked at his hands. "What about rebuilding the church?" he said.

"Yes. You must have heard that that business you came to see me about—Earl Bartholomew and the conspiracy against King Stephen—turned out well for us."

"Yes." It seemed a long time ago that Philip had gone to the bishop's palace, in fear and trembling, to tell of the plot against the king whom the Church had chosen. "I heard that Percy Hamleigh attacked the earl's castle and took him prisoner."

"That's right—Bartholomew is now in a dungeon at Winchester, waiting to hear his fate," Waleran said with satisfaction.

"And Earl Robert of Gloucester? He was the more powerful conspirator."

"And therefore gets the lighter punishment. In fact no punishment at all. He has pledged allegiance to King Stephen, and his part in the plot has been . . . overlooked."

"But what has this got to do with our cathedral?"

Waleran stood up and went to the window. When he looked out at the ruined church, there was real sadness in his eyes, and Philip realized that there was a core of genuine piety in Waleran, for all his worldly ways. "Our part in the defeat of Bartholomew puts King Stephen in our debt. Before too long, you and I will go and see him."

"See the king!" Philip said. He was a little intimidated by the prospect.

"He will ask us what we want as our reward."

Philip saw what Waleran was getting at, and he was thrilled to the core. "And we'll tell him . . ."

Waleran turned back from the window and looked at Philip, and his eyes looked like black jewels, glittering with ambition. "We'll tell him we want a new cathedral for Kingsbridge," he said.

Tom knew Ellen was going to hit the roof.

She was already angry about what had happened to Jack. Tom needed to soothe her. But the news of her "penance" was going to inflame her. He wished he could postpone telling her for a day or two, to give her time to cool off; but he could not, for Prior Philip had said she must be off the premises by nightfall. He had to tell her immediately, and since it was midday when Philip told Tom, Tom told Ellen at dinner.

They went into the refectory with the other priory employees when the monks had finished their dinner and gone. The tables were crowded, but Tom thought that might not be a bad thing: the presence of other people might restrain her a little, he thought.

He was wrong about that, he soon learned.

He tried to break the news gradually. First he said: "They know we're not married."

"Who told them?" she said angrily. "Some troublemaker?"

"Alfred. Don't blame him—that sly monk Remigius got it out of him. Anyway, we never told the children to keep it secret."

"I don't blame the boy," she said more calmly. "So what do they say?"

He leaned across the table and spoke in a low voice. "They say you're a fornicator," he said, hoping no one else would hear.

"A fornicator?" she said loudly. "What about you? Don't these monks know that it takes two to fornicate?"

The people sitting nearby started to laugh.

"Hush," Tom said. "They say we have to get married."

She looked at him hard. "If that was all, you wouldn't be looking so hangdog, Tom Builder. Tell me the rest."

"They want you to confess your sin."

"Hypocritical perverts," she said disgustedly. "They spend all night up one another's arseholes and then they have the nerve to call what we're doing a sin."

There was more laughter at that. People stopped their own conversations to listen to Ellen.

"Just talk quietly," Tom pleaded.

"I suppose they want me to do penance, too. Humiliation is all part of it. What do they want me to do? Come on, tell the truth, you can't lie to a *witch*."

"Don't say that!" Tom hissed. "It makes things worse."

"Then tell me."

"We have to live apart for a year, and you have to remain chaste—"

"Piss on that!" Ellen shouted.

Now everyone was looking.

"Piss on you, Tom Builder!" she said. She realized she had an audience. "Piss on all of you, too," she said. Most people grinned. It was hard to take offense, perhaps because she looked so lovely with her face flushed red and her golden eyes wide. She stood up. "Piss on Kingsbridge Priory!" She jumped up on to the table, and there was a burst of applause. She walked along the board. The diners snatched their bowls of soup and mugs of ale out of her way and sat back, laughing. "Piss on the prior!" she said. "Piss on the sub-prior, and the sacrist, and the cantor and the treasurer, and all their deeds and charters, and their chests full of silver pennies!" She reached the end of the table. Beyond it was another, smaller table where someone would sit and read aloud during the monks' dinner. There was an open book on the table. Ellen jumped from the dining table to the reading table.

Suddenly Tom knew what she was going to do. "Ellen!" he called. "Don't, please—"

"Piss on the Rule of Saint Benedict!" she yelled at the top of her voice. Then she hitched up her skirt, bent her knees, and urinated on the open book.

The men roared with laughter, banged on the tables, hooted and whistled and cheered. Tom was not sure whether they shared Ellen's contempt for the Rule or they just enjoyed seeing a beautiful woman expose herself. There was something erotic about her shameless vulgarity, but it was also exciting to see someone openly abuse the book that the monks were so tediously solemn about. Whatever the reason, they loved it.

She jumped off the table and, amid a thunder of applause, ran out of the door.

Everyone began to talk at the same time. No one had ever seen anything quite like that before. Tom was horrified and embarrassed: the consequences would be dire, he knew. Yet a part of him was thinking: What a woman!

Jack got up after a moment and followed his mother out, with the trace of a grin on his swollen face.

Tom looked at Alfred and Martha. Alfred had a bewildered air but Martha was giggling. "Come on, you two," Tom said, and the three of them left the refectory.

When they got outside Ellen was nowhere to be seen. They went across the green to the guesthouse and found her there. She was sitting in the chair waiting for him. She was wearing her cloak, and holding her big leather satchel. She looked cool, calm and collected. Tom's heart went cold when he saw the bag, but he pretended not to have noticed it. "There's going to be hell to pay," he said.

"I don't believe in hell," she said.

"I hope they'll let you confess, and do penance."

"I'm not going to confess."

His self-control broke. "Ellen, don't leave!"

She looked sad. "Listen, Tom. Before I met you I had food to eat and a place to live. I was safe and secure and self-sufficient: I needed nobody. Since I've been with you I've come closer to starvation than at any time in my life. You've got work now, but there's no security in it: the priory has no money to build a new church, and you could be on the road again next winter."

"Philip will raise the money somehow," Tom said. "I'm sure he will."

"You can't be sure," she said.

"You don't believe," Tom said bitterly. Then, before he could stop himself, he added: "You're just like Agnes, you don't believe in my cathedral."

"Oh, Tom, if it was just me, I'd stay," she said sadly. "But look at my son."

Tom looked at Jack. His face was purple with bruising, his ear was swollen to twice its normal size, his nostrils were full of dried blood and he had a broken front tooth.

Ellen said: "I was afraid he would grow up like an animal if we stayed in the forest. But if this is the price of teaching him to live with other people, it's too much to pay. So I'm going back to the forest."

"Don't say that," Tom said desperately. "Let's talk about it. Don't make a rash decision—"

"It's not rash, it's not rash, Tom," she said sorrowfully. "I'm so sad that I can't even be angry anymore. I really wanted to be your wife. But not at any cost."

If Alfred had not chased Jack, none of this would have happened, Tom thought. But it was only a boyish scrap, wasn't it? Or was Ellen right when she said Tom had a blind spot about Alfred? Tom began to feel he had been wrong. Perhaps he should have taken a firmer line with Alfred. Boys fighting was one thing, but Jack and Martha were smaller than Alfred. Perhaps he was a bully.

But it was too late to change that now. "Stay in the village," Tom said desperately. "Wait a while and see what happens."

"I don't suppose the monks will let me, now."

He realized she was right. The village was owned by the priory and all the householders paid rent to the monks—usually in the form of days of work—and the monks could refuse to house anyone they did not like. They could hardly be blamed if they rejected Ellen. She had made her decision and she had literally pissed on her chances of retracting it.

"I'll go with you, then," he said. "The monastery owes me seventy-two pennies already. We'll go on the road again. We survived before. . . ."

"What about your children?" she said gently.

Tom remembered how Martha had cried from hunger. He knew he could not make her go through that again. And there was his baby son, Jonathan, living here with the monks. I don't want to leave him again, Tom thought; I did it once, and hated myself for it.

But he could not bear the thought of losing Ellen.

"Don't tear yourself apart," she said. "I won't tramp the roads with you again. That's no solution—we'd be worse off than we are now, in every way. I'm going back to the forest, and you're not coming with me."

He stared at her. He wanted to believe that she did not mean it, but the look on her face told him she did. He could not think of anything more to say to stop her. He opened his mouth to speak, but no words came. He felt helpless. She was breathing hard, her bosom rising and falling with emotion. He wanted to touch her, but he felt she did not want him to. I may never embrace her again, he thought. It was hard to believe. For weeks he had lain with her every night, and touched her as familiarly as he would touch himself; and now suddenly it was forbidden, and she was like a stranger.

"Don't look so sad," she said. Her eyes were full of tears.

"I can't help it," he said. "I am sad."

"I'm sorry I've made you so unhappy."

"Don't be sorry for that. Be sorry that you made me so happy. That's what hurts, woman. That you made me so happy."

A sob escaped from her lips. She turned away and left without another word.

Jack and Martha went out after her. Alfred hesitated, looking awkward, then followed them.

Tom stood staring at the chair she had left. No, he thought, it can't be true, she isn't leaving me.

He sat down in the chair. It was still warm from her body, the body he loved so much. He stiffened his face to stop the tears.

He knew she would not change her mind now. She never vacillated: she was a person who made a decision and then carried it through.

She might regret it eventually, though.

He seized on that shred of hope. He knew she loved him. That had not changed. Only last night she had made love frantically, like someone slaking a terrible thirst; and after he was satisfied she had rolled on top of him and carried on, kissing him hungrily, gasping into his beard as she came time and time again, until she was too exhausted with pleasure to go on. And it was not just the fucking that she liked. They enjoyed being together all the time. They talked constantly, much more than he and Agnes had talked even in the early days. She's going to miss me as much as I'll miss her, he thought. After a while, when her anger has died down, and she has settled into a new routine, she'll hanker for someone to talk to, a hard body to touch, a bearded face to kiss. Then she'll think of me.

But she was proud. She might be too proud to come back even if she wanted to.

He sprang out of his chair. He had to tell her what was on his mind. He left the house. She was at the priory gate, saying goodbye to Martha. Tom ran past the stable and caught up with her.

She gave him a sad smile. "Goodbye, Tom."

He took her hands. "Will you come back, one day? Just to see us? If I know you're not going away forever, that I will see you again sometime, if only for a little while—if I know that I can bear it."

She hesitated.

"Please?"

"All right," she said.

"Swear it."

"I don't believe in oaths."

"But I do."

"All right. I swear it."

"Thank you." He pulled her gently to him. She did not resist him. He hugged her, and his control broke. Tears poured down his face. At last she drew away. Reluctantly he let her go. She turned toward the gate.

At that moment there was a noise from the stable, the sound of a spirited horse being disobedient, stamping and snorting. Automatically, they all looked round. The horse was Waleran Bigod's black stallion, and the bishop was about to mount. His eyes met Ellen's, and he froze.

At that moment she started to sing.

Tom did not know the song, although he had heard her sing often. The melody was terribly sad. The words were French, but he could understand them well enough.

> *A lark, caught in a hunter's net*
> *Sang sweeter then than ever,*
> *As if the falling melody*
> *Might wing and net dissever.*

Tom looked from her to the bishop. Waleran was terrified: his mouth was open, his eyes wide, his face as white as death. Tom was astonished: why did a simple song have the power to scare such a man?

At dusk the hunter took his prey,
The lark his freedom never.
All birds and men are sure to die
But songs may live forever.

Ellen called out: "Goodbye, Waleran Bigod. I'm leaving Kingsbridge, but I'm not leaving you. I'll be with you in your dreams."

And mine, Tom thought.

For a moment no one moved.

Ellen turned away, holding Jack's hand; and they all watched in silence as she marched out through the priory gates and disappeared into the gathering dusk.

II

PART TWO

1136–1137

Chapter 5

AFTER ELLEN HAD GONE, Sundays were very quiet at the guesthouse. Alfred played football with the village boys in the meadow on the other side of the river. Martha, who missed Jack, played pretend games, gathering vegetables and making pottage and dressing a doll. Tom worked on his cathedral design.

He had hinted to Philip, once or twice, that he should think about what kind of church he wanted to build, but Philip had not noticed, or had chosen to ignore the implication. He had a lot on his mind. But Tom thought about little else, especially on Sundays.

He liked to sit just inside the door of the guesthouse and look across the green at the cathedral ruins. He made sketches on a piece of slate sometimes, but most of the work was in his head. He knew that it was hard for most people to visualize solid objects and complex spaces, but he had always found it easy.

He had won Philip's trust and gratitude for the way he had dealt with the ruins; but Philip still saw him as a jobbing mason. He had to convince Philip that he was capable of designing and building a cathedral.

One Sunday about two months after Ellen left, he felt ready to begin drawing.

He made a mat of woven reeds and pliable twigs, about three feet by two. He made neat wooden sides to the mat so that it had raised edges, like a tray. Then he burned some chalk for lime, mixed up a small quantity of strong plaster, and filled the tray with the mixture. As the mortar began to harden, he drew lines in it with a needle. He used his iron foot rule for straight lines, his set square for right angles and his compasses for curves.

He would do three drawings: a section, to explain how the church was constructed; an elevation, to illustrate its beautiful proportions; and a floor plan to show the accommodation. He began with the section.

He imagined that the cathedral was like a long loaf of bread, then he cut off the crust at the west end, to see inside, and he began to draw.

It was very simple. He drew a tall flat-topped archway. That was the nave, seen from the end. It would have a flat wooden ceiling, like the old church. Tom would have greatly preferred to build a curved stone vault, but he knew Philip could not afford it.

On top of the nave he drew a triangular roof. The width of the building was determined by the width of the roof, and that in turn was limited by the timber available. It was difficult to get hold of beams longer than about thirty-five feet—and they were fiercely expensive. (Good timber was so valuable that a fine tree was liable to be chopped down and sold by its owner long before it was that high.) The nave of Tom's cathedral would probably be thirty-two feet wide, or twice the length of Tom's iron pole.

The nave he had drawn was high, impossibly high. But a cathedral had to be a dramatic building, awe-inspiring in its size, pulling the eye heavenward with its loftiness. One reason people came to them was that cathedrals were the largest buildings in the world: a man who never went to a cathedral could go through life without seeing a building much bigger than the hovel he lived in.

Unfortunately, the building Tom had drawn would fall down. The weight of lead and timber in the roof would be too much for the walls, which would buckle outward and collapse. They had to be propped up.

For that purpose Tom drew two roundtopped archways, half the height of the nave, one on either side. These were the aisles. They would have curved stone ceilings: since the aisles were lower and narrower, the expense of stone vaults was not so great. Each aisle would have a sloping lean-to roof.

The side aisles, joined to the nave by their stone vaults, provided some support, but they did not reach quite high enough. Tom would build extra supports, at intervals, in the roof space of the side aisles, above the vaulted ceiling and below the lean-to roof. He drew one of them, a stone arch rising from the top of the aisle wall across to the nave wall. Where the support rested on the aisle wall, Tom braced it further with a massive buttress jutting out from the side of the church. He put a turret on top of the buttress, to add weight and make it look nicer.

You could not have an awesomely tall church without the strengthening elements of aisles, supports and buttresses; but this might be difficult to explain to a monk, and Tom had drawn the sketch to help make it clear.

He also drew the foundations, going far underground beneath the walls. Laymen were always surprised at how deep foundations were.

It was a simple drawing, too simple to be of much use to builders; but it should be right for showing to Prior Philip. Tom wanted him to understand what was being proposed, visualize the building, and get excited about it. It was hard to imagine a big, solid church when what was in front of you was a few lines scratched in plaster. Philip would need all the help Tom could give him.

The walls he had drawn looked solid, seen end on, but they would not be. Tom now began to draw the side view of the nave wall, as seen from inside the church. It was pierced at three levels. The bottom half was hardly a wall at all: it was just a row of columns, their tops joined by semicircular arches. It was called the arcade. Through the archways of the arcade could be seen the round-headed windows of the aisles. The windows would be neatly lined up with the archways, so that light from outside could fall, unobstructed, into the nave. The columns in between would be lined up with the buttresses on the outside walls.

Above each arch of the arcade was a row of three small arches, forming the tribune gallery. No light would come through these, for behind them was the lean-to roof of the side aisle.

Above the gallery was the clerestory, so called because it was pierced with windows which lit the upper half of the nave.

In the days when the old Kingsbridge Cathedral had been built, masons had relied on thick walls for strength, and had nervously inserted mean little windows that let in hardly any light. Modern builders understood that a building would be strong enough if its walls were straight and true.

Tom designed the three levels of the nave wall—arcade, gallery and clerestory—strictly in the proportions 3:1:2. The arcade was half the height of the wall, and the gallery was one third of the rest. Proportion was everything in a church: it gave a subliminal feeling of rightness to the whole building. Studying the finished drawing, Tom thought it looked perfectly graceful. But would Philip think so? Tom could see the tiers of arches marching down the length of the church, with their moldings and carvings picked out by an after-noon sun . . . but would Philip see the same?

He began his third drawing. This was a floor plan of the church. In his imagination he saw twelve arches in the arcade. The church was therefore divided into twelve sections, called bays. The nave would be six bays long, the chancel four. In between, taking up the space of the seventh and eighth bays, would be the crossing, with the transepts sticking out either side and the tower rising above.

All cathedrals and nearly all churches were cross-shaped. The cross was the single most important symbol of Christianity, of course, but there was a practical reason too: the transepts provided useful space for extra chapels and offices such as the sacristy and the vestry.

When he had drawn a simple floor plan Tom returned to the central drawing, which showed the interior of the church viewed from the west end. Now he drew the tower rising above and behind the nave.

The tower should be either one and a half times the height of the nave, or double it. The lower alternative gave the building an attractively regular profile, with the aisles, the nave and the tower rising in equal steps, 1:2:3. The higher tower would be more dramatic, for then the nave would be double the size of the aisles, and the tower double the nave, the proportions being 1:2:4. Tom had chosen the dramatic: this was the only cathedral he would ever build, and he wanted it to reach for the sky. He hoped Philip would feel the same.

If Philip accepted the design, Tom would have to draw it again, of course, more carefully and exactly to scale. And there would be many more drawings, hundreds of them: plinths, columns, capitals, corbels, doorcases, turrets, stairs, gargoyles, and countless other details—Tom would be drawing for years. But what he had in front of him was the essence of the building, and it was good: simple, inexpensive, graceful and perfectly proportioned.

He could not wait to show it to someone.

He had planned to find a suitable moment to take it to Prior Philip; but now that it was done he wanted Philip to see it right away.

Would Philip think him presumptuous? The prior had not asked him to prepare a design. He might have another master builder in mind, someone he had heard of who had worked for another monastery and had done a good job. He might scorn Tom's aspirations.

On the other hand, if Tom did not show him something, Philip might assume Tom was not capable of designing, and might hire someone else without even considering Tom. Tom was not prepared to risk that: he would rather be thought presumptuous.

The afternoon was still light. It would be study time in the cloisters. Philip would be at the prior's house, reading his Bible. Tom decided to go and knock at his door.

Carrying his board carefully, he left the house.

As he walked past the ruins, the prospect of building a new cathedral suddenly seemed daunting: all that stone, all that timber, all those craftsmen, all those *years*. He would have to control it all, make sure there was a steady supply of materials, monitor the quality of timber and stone, hire and fire men, tirelessly check their work with his plumb line and level, make templates for the moldings, design and build lifting machines . . . He wondered if he really was capable of it.

Then he thought what a thrill it would be to create something from nothing; to see, one day in the future, a new church here where now there was nothing but rubble, and to say: I made this.

There was another thought in his mind, hidden away in a dusty corner; something he was hardly willing to admit to himself. Agnes had died without a priest, and she was buried in unconsecrated ground. He would have liked to go back to her grave, and get a priest to say prayers over it, and perhaps put up a small headstone; but he was afraid that if he called attention to her burying place in any way, somehow the whole story of abandoning the baby would come out. Leaving a baby to die still counted as murder. As the weeks went by he had worried more and more about Agnes's soul, and whether it was in a good place or not. He was afraid to ask a priest about it because he did not want to give details. But he had consoled himself with the thought that if he built a cathedral, God would surely favor him; and he wondered whether he could ask that Agnes receive the benefit of that favor instead of himself. If he could dedicate his work on the cathedral to Agnes, he would feel that her soul was safe, and he could rest easy.

He reached the prior's house. It was a small stone building on one level. The door stood open, although it was a cold day. He hesitated for a moment. Calm, competent, knowledgeable, expert, he said to himself. A master of every aspect of modern building. Just the man you'd cheerfully trust.

He stepped inside. There was only one room. At one end was a big bed with luxurious hangings; at the other a small altar with a crucifix and a candlestick. Prior Philip stood by a window, reading from a vellum sheet with a worried frown. He looked up and smiled at Tom. "What's that you've got?"

"Drawings, Father," Tom said, making his voice deep and reassuring. "For a new cathedral. May I show you?"

Philip looked surprised but intrigued. "By all means."

There was a large lectern in a corner. Tom brought it into the light by the window and put his plaster frame on its angled rest. Philip looked at the drawing. Tom watched Philip's face. He could tell that Philip had never seen an elevation drawing, a floor plan or a section through a building. The prior's face wore a puzzled frown.

Tom began to explain. He pointed to the elevation. "You're standing in the center of the nave, looking at the wall," he said. "Here are the pillars of the arcade. They're joined by arches. Through the archways you can see the windows in the aisle. Above the arcade is the tribune gallery, and above that, the clerestory windows."

Philip's expression cleared as he understood. He was a quick learner. He looked at the floor plan, and Tom could see he was equally puzzled by that.

Tom said: "When we walk around the site, and mark where the walls will be built, and where the pillars meet the ground, and the positions of the doors and buttresses, we will have a plan like this, and it will tell us where to place our pegs and strings."

Enlightenment dawned on Philip's face again. It was no bad thing, Tom thought, that Philip had trouble understanding the drawings: it gave Tom a chance to be confident and expert. Finally Philip looked at the section. Tom explained: "Here is the nave, in the middle, with a timber ceiling. Behind the nave is the tower. Here are the aisles, on either side of the nave. At the outer edges of the aisles are the buttresses."

"It looks splendid," Philip said. Tom could tell that the section drawing particularly impressed him, with the inside of the church open to view, as if the west end had been swung aside like a cupboard door to reveal the interior.

Philip looked at the floor plan again. "Are there only six bays to the nave?"

"Yes, and four to the chancel."

"Isn't that rather small?"

"Can you afford to build it bigger?"

"I can't afford to build it at all," Philip said. "I don't suppose you have any idea how much this would cost."

"I know exactly how much it would cost," Tom said. He saw surprise on Philip's face: Philip had not realized Tom could do figure work. He had spent many hours calculating the cost of his design to the last penny. However, he gave Philip a round figure. "It would be no more than three thousand pounds."

Philip laughed hollowly. "I've spent the last few weeks working out the annual income of the priory." He waved the sheet of vellum that he had been reading so anxiously when Tom walked in. "Here's the answer. Three hundred pounds a year. And we spend every penny."

Tom was not surprised. It was obvious that the priory had been badly managed in the past. He had faith that Philip would reform its finances. "You'll find the money, Father," he said. "With God's help," he added piously.

Philip returned his attention to the drawings, looking unconvinced. "How long would this take to build?"

"That depends on how many people you employ," Tom said. "If you hire thirty masons, with enough laborers, apprentices, carpenters and smiths to service them, it might take fifteen years: one year for the foundations, four years for the chancel, four years for the transepts, and six years for the nave."

Once again Philip looked impressed. "I wish my monastic officials had your ability to think ahead and calculate," he said. He studied the drawings wistfully. "So I need to find two hundred pounds a year. It doesn't sound so bad when you put it that way." He looked thoughtful. Tom felt excited: Philip was beginning to think of this as a workable project, not just an abstract design. "Suppose I could afford more—could we build faster?"

"Up to a point," Tom replied guardedly. He did not want Philip to become overoptimistic: that might lead to disillusionment. "You could employ sixty masons, and build the whole church at once, instead of working from east to west; and that might take eight or ten years. Any more than sixty, on a building this size, and they would start getting in one another's way, and slow the work down."

Philip nodded: he appeared to understand that without difficulty. "Still, even with just thirty masons, I could have the east end completed after five years."

"Yes, and you could use it for services, and set up a new shrine for the bones of Saint Adolphus."

"Indeed." Philip was really excited now. "I had been thinking it would be decades before we could have a new church." He looked shrewdly at Tom. "Have you ever built a cathedral before?"

"No, though I've designed and built smaller churches. But I

worked on Exeter cathedral, for several years, finishing up as deputy master builder."

"You want to build this cathedral yourself, don't you?"

Tom hesitated. It was as well to be candid with Philip: the man had no patience for prevarication. "Yes, Father. I want you to appoint me master builder," he said as calmly as he could.

"Why?"

Tom had not expected that question. There were so many reasons. *Because I've seen it done badly, and I know I could do it well,* he thought. *Because there is nothing more satisfying, to a master craftsman, than to exercise his skill, except perhaps to make love to a beautiful woman. Because something like this gives meaning to a man's life.* Which answer did Philip want? The prior would probably like him to say something pious. Recklessly, he decided to tell the real truth. "Because it will be beautiful," he said.

Philip looked at him strangely. Tom could not tell whether he was angry, or something else. "Because it will be beautiful," Philip repeated. Tom began to feel that was a silly reason, and decided to say something more, but he could not decide what. Then he realized that Philip was not skeptical at all—he was moved. Tom's words had touched his heart. Finally Philip nodded, as if agreeing after some reflection. "Yes. And what could be better than to make something beautiful for God?" he said.

Tom remained silent. Philip had not said Yes, you shall be master builder. Tom waited.

Philip seemed to reach a decision. "I'm going with Bishop Waleran to see the king in Winchester in three days' time," he said. "I don't know exactly what the bishop plans, but I'm sure we will be asking King Stephen to help us pay for a new cathedral church for Kingsbridge."

"Let's hope he grants your wish," Tom said.

"He owes us a favor," Philip said with an enigmatic smile. "He ought to help us."

"And if he does?" Tom said.

"I think God sent you to me with a purpose, Tom Builder," said Philip. "If King Stephen gives us the money, you can build the church."

It was Tom's turn to be moved. He hardly knew what to say. He had been granted his life's wish—but conditionally. Everything depended on Philip's getting help from the king. He nodded, accepting the promise and the risk. "Thank you, Father," he said.

The bell rang for vespers. Tom picked up his board.

"Do you need that?" Philip said.

Tom realized it would be a good idea to leave it here. It would be a constant reminder to Philip. "No, I don't need it," he said. "I have it all in my head."

"Good. I'd like to keep it here."

Tom nodded and went to the door.

It occurred to him that if he did not ask about Agnes now he probably never would. He turned back. "Father?"

"Yes?"

"My first wife . . . Agnes, her name was . . . she died without a priest, and she's buried in unconsecrated ground. She hadn't sinned, it was just . . . the circumstances. I wondered . . . Sometimes a man builds a chapel, or founds a monastery, in the hope that in the afterlife, God will remember his piety. Do you think my design might serve to protect Agnes's soul?"

Philip frowned. "Abraham was asked to sacrifice his only son. God no longer asks for blood sacrifices, for the ultimate sacrifice has been made. But the lesson of Abraham's story is that God demands the best we have to offer, that which is most precious to us. Is this design the best thing you could offer God?"

"Except for my children, yes."

"Then rest easy, Tom Builder. God will accept it."

II

Philip had no idea why Waleran Bigod wanted to meet him in the ruins of Earl Bartholomew's castle.

He had been obliged to travel to the town of Shiring and spend the night there, then set off this morning for Earlscastle. Now, as the horse jogged toward the castle looming up out of the morning mist ahead of him, he decided it was probably a matter of convenience: Waleran was on his way from one place to another, passing no nearer to Kingsbridge than here, and the castle was a handy landmark.

Philip wished he knew more about what Waleran was planning. He had not seen the bishop-elect since the day he had inspected the cathedral ruins. Waleran did not know how much money Philip needed to build the church, and Philip did not know what Waleran was planning to ask from the king. Waleran liked to keep his plans to himself. It made Philip highly nervous.

He was glad to have learned, from Tom Builder, exactly what it would take to build the new cathedral, depressing though the news was. Once again he was glad Tom was around. Tom was a man of surprising depths. He could hardly read or write, but he could design a cathedral, draw plans, calculate the numbers of men and the time it would take to build, *and* figure out how much all that would cost. He was a quiet man, but despite that he was a formidable presence: he was very tall, with a bearded, weather-beaten face, keen eyes and a high forehead. Philip sometimes felt slightly intimidated by him, and tried to conceal it by adopting a hearty tone. But Tom was very earnest, and anyway he had no idea that Philip found him daunting. The conversation about his wife had been touching, and had revealed a piety that had not previously been apparent. Tom was one of those people who kept his religion deep in his heart. Sometimes they were the best kind.

As Philip approached Earlscastle he felt increasingly uncomfortable. This had once been a thriving castle, defending the countryside all around, employing and feeding large numbers of people. Now it was ruined, and the hovels clustered about it were deserted, like empty nests in the bare branches of a tree in winter. And Philip was responsible for this. He had revealed the conspiracy being hatched here, and had brought down the wrath of God, in the shape of Percy Hamleigh, upon the castle and its inhabitants.

The walls and the gatehouse had not been badly damaged in the fighting, he noted. That meant the attackers had probably got inside before the gates could be shut. He walked his horse across the wooden bridge and entered the first of two compounds. Here the evidence of battle was clearer: apart from the stone chapel, all that remained of the castle buildings was a few charred stumps of wood sticking up out of the ground, and a small whirlwind of ashes blowing along the base of the castle wall.

There was no sign of the bishop. Philip rode through the compound, crossed the bridge at the far side, and entered the upper compound. Here there was a massive stone keep, with an unsteady-looking wooden staircase leading up to its second-floor entrance. Philip gazed up at the forbidding stonework with its mean arrow-slit windows: mighty though it was, it had not protected Earl Bartholomew.

From those windows he would be able to look over the castle walls and watch for the bishop. He tied his horse to the handrail of the staircase and went up.

The door opened to his touch. He stepped inside. The great hall was dark and dusty, and the rushes on the floor were dry as bones. There was a cold fireplace and a spiral stair leading up. Philip went to a window. The dust made him sneeze. He could not see much from the window so he decided to go up to the next floor.

At the top of the spiral stairs he faced two doors. He guessed that the smaller one led to the latrine, the larger one to the earl's bedroom. He went through the larger door.

The room was not empty.

Philip stopped dead, shocked rigid. There in the middle of the room, facing him, was a young woman of extraordinary beauty. For a moment he thought he was seeing a vision, and his heart raced. She had a cloud of dark curls around a bewitching face. She stared back at him out of large dark eyes, and he realized she was as star-tled as he. He relaxed, and was about to take another step into the room, when he was seized from behind and felt the cold blade of a long knife at his throat; and a male voice said: "And who the devil are you?"

The girl moved toward him. "Say your name, or Matthew will kill you," she said regally.

Her manner showed her to be of noble birth, but even nobles were not allowed to threaten monks. "Tell Matthew to take his hands off the prior of Kingsbridge, or it may be the worse for him," Philip said calmly.

He was released. He glanced back over his shoulder and saw a slight man of about his own age. This Matthew had presumably come out of the latrine.

He turned back to the girl. She appeared to be about seventeen years old. Despite her haughty manner she was shabbily dressed. As he studied her, a chest against the wall behind her opened up, and a teenaged boy got out, looking sheepish. He held a sword. He had been lying in wait, or hiding, Philip could not tell which.

"And who are you?" Philip said.

"I am the daughter of the earl of Shiring, and my name is Aliena."

The daughter! thought Philip. I didn't know she was still living here. He looked at the boy. He was about fifteen, and resembled the girl except for a snub nose and short hair. Philip raised an inquiring eyebrow at him.

"I am Richard, the heir to the earldom," the boy said in a cracked adolescent voice.

Behind Philip, the man said: "And I am Matthew, the steward of the castle."

The three of them had been hiding here since Earl Bartholomew was captured, Philip realized. The steward was taking care of the children: he must have a store of food or money hidden away. Philip addressed the girl. "I know where your father is, but what about your mother?"

"She died many years ago."

Philip felt a stab of guilt. The children were virtually orphans, and it was partly his doing. "But haven't you got relatives to look after you?"

"I'm looking after the castle until my father returns," she said.

They were living in a dream world, Philip realized. She was trying to live as if she still belonged to a rich and powerful family. With her father imprisoned and in disgrace, she was just another girl. The boy was heir to nothing at all. Earl Bartholomew was never coming back to this castle, unless the king decided to hang him here. He pitied the girl, but in a way he also admired the strength of will that sustained the fantasy and made two other people share it. She might have been a queen, he thought.

From outside came a clatter of hooves on wood: several horses were crossing the bridge. Aliena said to Philip: "Why have you come here?"

"It's just a rendezvous," Philip said. He turned around and

took a step toward the door. Matthew was in his way. For a moment they stood still, facing one another. The four people in the room made a frozen tableau. Philip wondered if they were going to try to stop him from leaving. Then the steward stood aside.

Philip went out. He held up the skirt of his robe and hurried down the spiral stairs. When he reached the bottom he heard footsteps behind him. Matthew caught him up.

"Don't tell anyone we're here," he said.

Philip saw that Matthew understood the unreality of their position. "How long will you stay here?" he asked.

"As long as we can," the steward replied.

"And when you have to leave? What will you do then?"

"I don't know."

Philip nodded. "I'll keep your secret," he said.

"Thank you, Father."

Philip crossed the dusty hall and stepped outside. Looking down, he saw Bishop Waleran and two others reining in their horses near his own. Waleran wore a heavy cloak trimmed with black fur, and a black fur cap. He looked up, and Philip met his pale eyes. "My lord bishop," said Philip respectfully. He went down the wooden steps. The image of the virginal girl upstairs was still vivid in his mind, and he felt like shaking his head to get rid of her.

Waleran dismounted. He had the same two companions, Philip saw: Dean Baldwin and the man-at-arms. He nodded to them, then knelt and kissed Waleran's hand.

Waleran accepted his homage but did not wallow in it: he withdrew his hand after a moment. It was power itself, not its trappings, that Waleran loved.

"On your own, Philip?" Waleran said.

"Yes. The priory is poor, and an escort for me is an unnecessary expense. When I was prior of St-John-in-the-Forest I never had an escort, and I'm still alive."

Waleran shrugged. "Come with me," he said. "I want to show you something." He marched off across the courtyard to the nearest tower. Philip followed. Waleran entered the low doorway at the foot of the tower and climbed the staircase inside. There were bats clustered under the low ceiling, and Philip ducked his head to avoid brushing against them.

They emerged at the top of the tower and stood at the battlements, looking out over the land all around. "This is one of the smaller earldoms in the land," Waleran said.

"Indeed." Philip shivered. There was a cold, damp wind up

here, and his cloak was not as thick as Waleran's. He wondered what the bishop was leading up to.

"Some of this land is good, but much is forest and stony hill-sides."

"Yes." On a clear day they might have seen many acres of forest and farmland, but now, although the early mist had gone, they could barely make out the near edge of the forest to the south, and the flat fields around the castle.

"This earldom also has a huge quarry which produces first-class limestone," Waleran went on. "Its forests contain many acres of good timber. And its farms generate considerable wealth. If we had this earldom, Philip, we could build our cathedral."

"If pigs had wings they could fly," Philip said.

"Oh, thou of little faith!"

Philip stared at Waleran. "Are you serious?"

"Very."

Philip was skeptical, but despite himself he felt a tiny spurt of hope. If only this could come true! But he said: "The king needs military support. He'll give the earldom to someone who can lead knights into battle."

"The king owes his crown to the Church, and his victory over Bartholomew to you and me. Knights aren't all he needs."

Waleran *was* serious, Philip saw. Was it possible? Would the king hand over the earldom of Shiring to the Church, to finance the rebuilding of Kingsbridge Cathedral? It was hardly believable, despite Waleran's arguments. But Philip could not help thinking how marvelous it would be to have the stone, the timber *and* the money to pay the craftsmen, all handed to him on a plate; and he remembered that Tom Builder had said he could hire sixty masons, and finish the church in eight to ten years. The mere thought was enthralling.

"But what about the former earl?" he said.

"Bartholomew has confessed his treason. He has never denied the plot, but for some time he maintained that what he did was not treason, on the grounds that Stephen was a usurper. However, the king's torturer has finally broken him."

Philip shuddered and tried not to think about what they had done to Bartholomew to make that rigid man yield.

He put the thought out of his mind. "The earldom of Shiring," he murmured to himself. It was an incredibly ambitious demand. But the idea was thrilling. He felt full of irrational optimism.

Waleran glanced up at the sky. "Let's get moving," he said. "The king expects us the day after tomorrow."

*   *   *

William Hamleigh studied the two men of God from his hiding place behind the battlements of the next tower. He knew them both. The tall one, who looked like a blackbird with his pointed nose and his black cloak, was the new bishop of Kingsbridge. The small, energetic one with the shaved head and the bright blue eyes was Prior Philip. William wondered what they were doing here.

He had watched the monk arrive, look around as though he expected to see people here, and then go into the keep. William could not guess whether Philip had met the three people who lived in the keep—he had been inside only a few moments, and they might have hidden from him. As soon as the bishop arrived, Prior Philip had come out of the keep and the two of them had climbed the tower. Now the bishop was gesturing at the land all around the castle with a somewhat proprietorial air. William could tell by the way they were standing and their gestures that the bishop was being ebullient and the prior skeptical. They were hatching a plot, he felt sure.

However, he had not come here to spy on them. He had come to spy on Aliena.

He did this more and more often. She preyed on his mind all the time, and he suffered involuntary daydreams in which he came across her tied up and naked in a wheat field, or cowering like a frightened puppy in a corner of his bedroom, or lost in the forest late in the evening. It got so that he had to see her in the flesh. He would ride to Earlscastle early in the morning. He left Walter, his groom, looking after the horses in the forest, and he walked across the fields to the castle. He sneaked inside and found a hiding place from which he could observe the keep and the upper compound. Sometimes he had to wait a long time to see her. His patience would be sorely tried, but the thought of going away again without even a glimpse of her was insupportable, so he always stayed. Then, when at last she did appear, his throat dried, and his heart beat faster, and the palms of his hands became damp. Often she was with her brother or the effeminate steward, but sometimes she was alone. One afternoon, in the summer, when he had waited for her since early morning, she had gone to the well, drawn some water, and taken off her clothes to wash. Just the memory of that sight inflamed him all over again. She had deep, proud breasts that moved in a teasing way when she lifted her arms to rub soap into her hair. Her nipples had puckered delightfully when she splashed cold water over herself. There was a surprisingly big bush of dark curly hair between her legs, and when she washed herself there, rubbing vigorously with a soapy hand, William had lost control and ejaculated in his clothes.

Nothing so nice had happened since, and she certainly would not wash herself in winter, but there had been lesser delights. When she was alone she would sing, or even talk to herself. William had seen her braid her hair, and dance, and chase pigeons off the ramparts like a small child. Clandestinely watching her do these little private things, William felt a sense of power over her that was quite delicious.

She would not come out while the bishop and the monk were here, of course. Fortunately they did not stay long. They left the battlements quite quickly, and a few moments later they and their attendants rode out of the castle. Had they come here just to see the view from the battlements? If so, they had been somewhat frustrated by the weather.

The steward had come out for firewood earlier, before the visitors arrived. He did the cooking in the keep. Soon he would come out again and fetch water from the well. William guessed they ate porridge, for they had no oven to bake bread. Later in the day the steward would leave the castle, sometimes taking the boy with him. Once they had gone it was only a matter of time before Aliena emerged.

When he got bored with waiting, William would conjure up the vision of her washing herself. The memory was almost as good as the real thing. But today he was unsettled. The visit of the bishop and the prior seemed to have tainted the atmosphere. Until today there had been an enchanted air about the castle and its three inhabitants, but the arrival of those thoroughly unmagical men on their muddy horses had broken the spell. It was like being disturbed by a noise when in the middle of a wonderful dream: try as he might, he could not stay asleep.

For a while he tried guessing what the visitors had been up to, but he could not fathom it. Nevertheless he felt sure they were scheming something. There was one person who probably could work it out: his mother. He decided to abandon Aliena for today, and ride home to report what he had seen.

They arrived in Winchester at nightfall on the second day. They entered by the King's Gate, in the south wall of the city, and went directly into the cathedral close. There they parted company. Waleran went to the residence of the bishop of Winchester, a palace in its own grounds adjacent to the cathedral close. Philip went to pay his respects to the prior and beg for a mattress in the monks' dormitory.

After three days on the road, Philip found the calm and quiet of the monastery as refreshing as a fountain on a hot day. The Winchester prior was a plump, easygoing man with pink skin and white hair. He invited Philip to have supper with him in his house. While they ate they talked about their respective bishops. The Winchester prior was clearly in awe of Bishop Henry and completely subservient to him. Philip surmised that when your bishop was as wealthy and powerful as Henry, there was nothing to be gained by quarreling with him. All the same, Philip did not intend to be so much under the thumb of *his* bishop.

He slept like a top and got up at midnight for matins.

When he went into Winchester Cathedral for the first time he began to feel intimidated.

The prior had told him that it was the biggest church in the world, and when he saw it he believed it was. It was an eighth of a mile long: Philip had seen villages that could fit inside it. It had two great towers, one over the crossing and the other at the west end. The central tower had collapsed, thirty years earlier, onto the tomb of William Rufus, an ungodly king who probably should not have been buried in a church in the first place; but it had since been rebuilt. Standing directly beneath the new tower, singing matins, Philip felt the whole building had an air of immense dignity and strength. The cathedral Tom had designed would be modest by comparison—if it got built at all. He now realized that he was moving in the very highest of circles, and he felt nervous. He was only a boy from a Welsh hill village who had had the good fortune to become a monk. Today he would speak to the king. What gave him the right?

He went back to bed with the other monks, but he lay awake worrying. He was afraid he might say or do something that would offend King Stephen or Bishop Henry and turn them against Kingsbridge. French-born people often mocked the way the English spoke their language: what would they think of a Welsh accent? In the monastic world, Philip had always been judged by his piety, obedience, and devotion to God's work. Those things counted for nothing here, in the capital city of one of the greatest kingdoms in the world. Philip was out of his depth. He became oppressed by the feeling that he was some kind of impostor, a nobody pretending to be a somebody, and that he was sure to be found out in no time and sent home in disgrace.

He got up at dawn, went to prime, then took breakfast in the refectory. The monks had strong beer and white bread: this was a wealthy monastery. After breakfast, when the monks went in to chapter, Philip walked over to the bishop's palace, a fine stone building with large windows, surrounded by several acres of walled garden.

Waleran was confident of getting Bishop Henry's support in his outrageous scheme. Henry was so powerful that his help might even make the whole thing possible. He was Henry of Blois, the king's younger brother. As well as being the most well-connected clergyman in England, he was the richest, for he was also abbot of the wealthy monastery of Glastonbury. He was expected to be the next archbishop of Canterbury. Kingsbridge could not have a more powerful ally. Perhaps it really will happen, Philip thought; perhaps the king will enable us to build a new cathedral. When he thought about that he felt as if his heart would burst with hope.

A household steward told Philip that Bishop Henry was not likely to appear before midmorning. Philip was much too wound up to return to the monastery. Feeling impatient, he set out to look at the biggest town he had ever seen.

The bishop's palace was in the southeast corner of the city. Philip walked along the east wall, through the grounds of yet another monastery, St. Mary's Abbey, and emerged in a neighborhood that appeared to be devoted to leather and wool. The area was crisscrossed with little streams. Looking closely, Philip realized they were not natural, but man-made channels, diverting part of the River Itchen to flow through the streets and supply the great quantities of water needed for tanning hides and washing fleeces. Such industries were normally established beside a river, and Philip marveled at the audacity of men who could bring the river to their workshops instead of the other way around.

Despite the industry, the town was quieter and less crowded than any other Philip had seen. A place such as Salisbury, or Hereford, seemed constricted by its walls, like a fat man in a tight tunic: the houses were too close together, the backyards too small, the marketplace too crowded, the streets too narrow; and as people and animals jostled for space, there was a feeling that fights could break out at any moment. But Winchester was so big that there seemed to be room for everyone. As he walked around, Philip gradually realized that part of the reason for the spacious feel was that the streets were laid out on a square grid pattern. They were mostly straight and intersected at right angles. He had never seen that before. The town must have been built according to a plan.

There were dozens of churches. They were all shapes and sizes, some of wood and others of stone, each serving its own small neighborhood. The city had to be very rich to support so many priests.

Walking along Fleshmonger Street made him feel faintly ill. He had never seen so much raw meat all in one place. Blood flowed out of the butchers' shops into the street, and fat rats dodged between the feet of the people who came to buy.

The south end of Fleshmonger Street opened out on to the middle of the High Street, opposite the old royal palace. The palace had not been used by kings since the new keep had been built in the castle, Philip had been told, but the royal moneyers still minted silver pennies in the undercroft of the building, protected by thick walls and iron-barred gates. Philip stood at the bars for a while, watching the sparks fly as the hammers pounded the dies, awe-struck by the sheer wealth in front of his eyes.

There was a handful of other people watching the same sight. No doubt it was something all visitors to Winchester looked at. A young woman standing nearby smiled at Philip, and he smiled back. She said: "You can do anything you like for a penny."

He wondered what she meant, and smiled vaguely again. Then she opened her cloak, and he saw to his horror that under-neath it she was completely naked. "Anything you like, for a silver penny," she said.

He felt a faint stirring of desire, like the ghost of a memory long submerged; then he realized that she was a whore. He felt his face go bright red with embarrassment. He turned quickly and hurried away. "Don't be afraid," she called. "I like a nice round head." Her mocking laughter followed him.

Feeling hot and bothered, he turned down an alley off the High Street and found himself in the marketplace. He could see the towers of the cathedral rising above the market stalls. He hurried through the crowds, oblivious to the blandishments of the vendors, and found his way back into the close.

He felt the ordered calm of the church precincts like a cool breeze. He paused in the graveyard to collect his thoughts. He felt ashamed and outraged. How dare she tempt a man in monk's robes? She had obviously identified him as a visitor. . . . Was it possible that monks who were away from their home monastery could be customers of hers? Of course it was, he realized. Monks committed all the same sins that ordinary people did. He had just been shocked by the woman's shamelessness. The sight of her nakedness remained with him, the way the hot heart of a candle flame, stared at for a few moments, would burn on behind closed eyelids.

He sighed. It had been a morning of vivid images: the man-made streams, the rats in the butchers' shops, the stacks of new-minted silver pennies, and then the woman's private parts. For a while, he knew, those pictures would come back to him to unsettle his meditations.

He went into the cathedral. He felt too grubby to kneel and pray, but just walking down the nave and out through the south door purified him somewhat. He passed through the priory and went to the bishop's palace.

The ground floor was a chapel. Philip went up the stairs to the hall and stepped inside. There was a small group of servants and young clergymen near the door, standing around or sitting on the bench up against the wall. At the far end of the room Waleran and Bishop Henry were sitting at a table. Philip was stopped by a steward who said: "The bishops are at breakfast," as if that meant Philip could not see them.

"I'll join them at table," Philip said.

"You'd better wait," the steward said.

Philip decided that the steward had taken him for an ordinary monk. "I'm the prior of Kingsbridge," he said.

The steward shrugged and stood aside.

Philip approached the table. Bishop Henry was at the head, with Waleran on his right. Henry was a short, broad-shouldered man with a pugnacious face. He was about the same age as Waleran, a year or two older than Philip; no more than thirty. However, by contrast with Waleran's dead-white skin and Philip's own bony frame, Henry had the florid complexion and rounded limbs of a hearty eater. His eyes were alert and intelligent, and his face seemed set in a determined expression. As the youngest of four brothers, he had probably had to fight for everything all his life. Philip was surprised to see that Henry's head was shaved, a sign that he had at one time taken monastic vows and still considered himself a monk. However, he was not wearing homespun; in fact, he was dressed in the most gorgeous tunic made of purple silk. Waleran was wearing a spotless white linen shirt under his usual black tunic, and Philip realized that both men were dressed up for their audience with the king. They were eating cold beef and drinking red wine. Philip was hungry after his walk, and his mouth watered.

Waleran looked up and saw him, and a look of faint irritation crossed his face.

"Good morning," Philip said.

Waleran said to Henry: "This is my prior."

Philip did not much like being described as Waleran's prior. He said: "Philip of Gwynedd, prior of Kingsbridge, my lord bishop."

He anticipated kissing the bishop's beringed hand, but Henry merely said, "Splendid," and ate another mouthful of beef. Philip stood there rather awkwardly. Were they not going to ask him to sit down?

Waleran said: "We'll join you shortly, Philip."

Philip realized he was being dismissed. He turned away, feeling humiliated. He returned to the group around the door. The steward who had tried to turn him back now smirked at him with a look that said *I told you so*. Philip stood apart from the others. He suddenly felt ashamed of the stained brown robe he had been wearing day and night for half a year. Benedictine monks often dyed their habits black, but Kingsbridge had given that up, years ago, to save money. Philip had always believed that dressing up in fine clothes was sheer vanity, entirely inappropriate for any man of God, no matter how high his rank; but now he saw the point of it. He might not have been treated so dismissively if he had come dressed in silk and furs.

Ah, well, he thought, a monk should be humble, so this must be good for my soul.

The two bishops rose from the table and came to the door. An attendant produced a scarlet robe edged with fine embroidery and silk fringes for Henry. As he was putting it on, Henry said: "You won't have to say much today, Philip."

Waleran added: "Leave the talking to us."

Henry said: "Leave the talking to me," with the faintest emphasis on the *me*. "If the king asks you a question or two, answer plainly, and don't try to dress up the facts too much. He'll understand your need for a new church without any weeping and wailing on your part."

Philip did not need to be told that. Henry was being unpleasantly condescending. However, Philip nodded assent and concealed his resentment.

"We'd better go," Henry said. "My brother is an early riser, and he's liable to conclude the day's business rapidly, then go hunting in the New Forest."

They went out. A man-at-arms, wearing a sword and carrying a staff, went in front of Henry as they walked to the High Street and then up the hill toward the West Gate. People stood aside for the two bishops, but not for Philip, so he ended up walking behind. Now and again someone would call out for a blessing, and Henry would make the sign of the cross in the air without pausing in his stride. Just before the gatehouse they turned aside and walked over a wooden bridge that spanned the castle moat. Despite being assured that he would not have to say much, Philip had a fluttery fear in his belly: he was about to see the king.

The castle occupied the southwest corner of the city. Its western and southern walls were part of the city wall. But the walls that separated the back of the castle from the city were no less high and strong than its outer defenses, as if the king needed protection against the citizens just as much as against the outside world.

They entered by a low gateway in the wall and immediately came upon the massive keep which dominated this end of the compound. It was a formidable square tower. Counting the arrow-slit windows, Philip reckoned it must have four floors. As usual, the ground floor consisted of storerooms, and an outside staircase led to an upstairs entrance. A pair of sentries at the foot of the stairs bowed as Henry passed.

They went into the hall. There were rushes on the floor, a few seats recessed into the stone walls, some wooden benches and a fireplace. In a corner two men-at-arms guarded a staircase, set into the wall, leading up. One of the men met Bishop Henry's eye immediately. He nodded and went up the stairs, presumably to tell the king that his brother was waiting.

Philip felt nauseated with anxiety. In the next few minutes his whole future might be decided. He wished he felt better about his allies. He wished he had spent the early morning hours praying for success instead of wandering around Winchester. He wished he had worn a clean robe.

There were twenty or thirty other people in the room, nearly all of them men. They seemed to be a mixture of knights, priests and prosperous townspeople. Suddenly Philip started, surprised: over by the fire, talking to a woman and a young man, was Percy Hamleigh. What was he doing here? The two people with him were his ugly wife and his brutish son. They had been Waleran's collaborators, as it were, in the downfall of Bartholomew: it could hardly be a coincidence that they were here today. Philip wondered whether Waleran had expected them.

Philip said to Waleran: "Do you see—"

"I see them," Waleran snapped, visibly displeased.

Philip felt their presence here was ominous, though he could not have said just why. He studied them. The father and son were alike: big, beefy men with yellow hair and sullen faces. The wife looked like the kind of demon that tortured sinners in paintings of hell. She touched the sores on her face constantly, her skeletal hands moving restlessly. She wore a yellow gown that made her look even uglier. She shifted from one foot to another, darting glances around the room all the time. She met Philip's eyes, and he looked away quickly.

Bishop Henry was moving around, greeting the people he knew and blessing those he did not, but he must have been keeping an eye on the stairs, for as soon as the sentry came down again, Henry looked across at him, saw the man nod, and abandoned his conversation in midsentence.

Waleran followed Henry up the stairs and Philip brought up the rear with his heart in his mouth.

The upstairs room was the same size and shape as the entrance hall, but it felt completely different. There were tapestries on the walls and sheepskin rugs on the scrubbed floorboards. The fire blazed strongly and the room was brightly lit by dozens of candles. Near the door was an oak table with pens, ink and a stack of vellum sheets for letters, and a cleric sat waiting to take the king's dictation. Near the fireplace, in a big wooden chair covered with fur, sat the king.

The first thing Philip noticed was that he was not wearing a crown. He had on a purple tunic over leather leggings, as if he were about to go out on horseback. Two big hunting dogs lay at his feet like favored courtiers. He resembled his brother Bishop Henry, but Stephen's features were a little finer, making him more handsome, and he had a lot of tawny hair. However, there was the same look of intelligence about the eyes. He sat back in his big chair—Philip supposed it was a throne—looking relaxed, with his legs stretched out in front of him and his elbows on the arms of the seat, but despite his posture there was an air of tension in the room. The king was the only one at ease.

As the bishops and Philip entered, a big man in expensive clothes was leaving. He nodded in a familiar way to Bishop Henry and ignored Waleran. He was probably a powerful baron, Philip thought.

Bishop Henry approached the king, bowed, and said: "Good morning, Stephen."

"I still haven't seen that bastard Ranulf," said King Stephen. "If he doesn't show up soon I'm going to cut his fingers off."

Henry said: "He'll be here any day, I promise you, but perhaps you should cut his fingers off anyway."

Philip had no idea who Ranulf was or why the king wanted to see him, but he got the impression that although Stephen was displeased, he was not serious about mutilating the man.

Before Philip could give it any further thought, Waleran stepped forward and bowed, and Henry said: "You remember Waleran Bigod, the new bishop of Kingsbridge."

"Yes," Stephen said, "but who's this?" He looked at Philip.

Waleran said: "This is my prior."

Waleran did not say his name, so Philip supplied it. "Philip of Gwynedd, prior of Kingsbridge." His voice sounded louder than he had intended. He bowed.

"Come forward, father prior," Stephen said. "You seem afraid. What are you worried about?"

Philip could not think how to answer that. He was worried about so many things. In desperation he said: "I'm worried because I don't have a clean robe to wear."

Stephen laughed, but not unkindly. "Then stop worrying," he said. With a glance at his well-dressed brother he added: "I like a monk to look like a monk, not like a king."

Philip felt a little better.

Stephen said: "I heard about the fire. How are you managing?"

Philip said: "On the day of the fire, God sent us a builder. He repaired the cloisters very quickly, and we use the crypt for services. With his help, we're clearing the ruins ready for rebuilding; and he has drawn plans for a new church."

Waleran raised his eyebrows at that: he did not know about the plans. Philip would have told him, if he had asked; but he had not. The king said: "Commendably prompt. When will you begin to build?"

"As soon as I can find the money."

Bishop Henry cut in: "That's why I've brought Prior Philip and Bishop Waleran to see you. Neither the priory nor the diocese has the resources to finance a project this big."

"Nor does the Crown, my dear brother," said Stephen.

Philip was discouraged: that was not a promising beginning.

Henry said: "I know. That's why I've looked for a way in which you could make it possible for them to rebuild Kingsbridge, but at no cost to yourself."

Stephen looked skeptical. "And did you succeed in devising such an ingenious, not to say magical, scheme?"

"Yes. My suggestion is that you should give the earl of Shiring's lands to the diocese to finance the building program."

Philip held his breath.

The king looked thoughtful.

Waleran opened his mouth to speak, but Henry silenced him with a gesture.

The king said: "It's a clever idea. I'd like to do it."

Philip's heart leaped.

The king said: "Unfortunately, I've just virtually promised the earldom to Percy Hamleigh."

A groan escaped Philip's lips. He had thought the king was going to say yes. The disappointment was like a knife wound.

Henry and Waleran were dumbstruck. No one had anticipated this.

Henry was the first to speak. He said: "Virtually?"

The king shrugged. "I might wriggle out of it, although not without considerable embarrassment. But after all, it was Percy who brought the traitor Bartholomew to justice."

Waleran burst out: "Not without help, my lord!"

"I knew you had played some part in it. . . ."

"It was I who told Percy Hamleigh of the plot against you."

"Yes. By the way, how did *you* learn of it?"

Philip shuffled his feet. They were on dangerous ground. No one must know that the information had come originally from his brother, Francis, for Francis was still working for Robert of Gloucester, who had been forgiven for his part in the plot.

Waleran said: "The information came from a deathbed confession."

Philip was relieved. Waleran was repeating the lie Philip had told him, but speaking as if the "confession" had been made to him rather than to Philip. Philip was more than content to have attention drawn away from his own role in this.

The king said: "Still, it was Percy, not you, who attacked Bartholomew's castle, risking life and limb, and arrested the traitor."

"You could reward Percy some other way," Henry put in.

"Shiring is what Percy wants," the king said. "He knows the area. And he'll rule effectively there. I could give him Cambridgeshire, but would the fenmen follow him?"

Henry said: "You ought to give thanks to God first, men second. It was God who made you king."

"But it was Percy who arrested Bartholomew."

Henry bridled at this irreverence. "God controls all things—"

"Don't press me on this," Stephen said, holding up his right hand.

"Of course," Henry said submissively.

It was a vivid demonstration of royal power. For a moment there they had been arguing almost like equals, but Stephen had been able to regain the upper hand with a word.

Philip was bitterly disappointed. At the start he had thought this an impossible demand, but he had gradually come to hope it would be granted, even to fantasize about how he would use the wealth. Now he had been brought back to reality with a hard bump.

Waleran said: "My lord king, I thank you for being willing to reconsider the future of the Shiring earldom, and I will await your decision anxiously and prayerfully."

That was neat, Philip thought. It sounded as if Waleran was giving in gracefully. In fact he was summing up by saying that the question was still open. The king had not said that. If anything, his response had been negative. But there was nothing offensive about insisting that the king could still decide one way or the other. I must remember that, Philip thought: when you're about to be turned down, go for a postponement.

Stephen hesitated a moment, as if entertaining a faint suspicion that he was being manipulated; then he seemed to dismiss any doubts. "Thank you all for coming to see me," he said.

Philip and Waleran turned to leave, but Henry stood his ground and said: "When shall we hear your decision?"

Stephen once again looked somewhat cornered. "The day after tomorrow," he said.

Henry bowed, and the three of them went out.

The uncertainty was almost as bad as a negative decision. Philip found the waiting unbearable. He spent the afternoon with the Winchester priory's marvelous collection of books, but they could not distract him from wondering what was going on in the king's mind. Could the king renege on his promise to Percy Hamleigh? How important was Percy? He was a member of the gentry who aspired to an earldom—surely Stephen had no reason to fear offending him. But how badly did Stephen want to help Kingsbridge? Notoriously, kings became pious as they aged. Stephen was young.

Philip was turning the possibilities over and over in his mind, and looking at but not reading Boethius's *The Consolation of Philosophy*, when a novice came tiptoeing along the cloister walk and approached him shyly. "There's someone asking for you in the outer court, father," the lad whispered.

If the visitor had been made to wait outside, that meant he was not a monk. "Who is it?" Philip said.

"It's a woman."

Philip's first, horrified thought was that it was the whore who had accosted him outside the mint; but something in the novice's expression told him otherwise. There was another woman whose eyes had met his today. "What does she look like?"

The boy made a disgusted face.

Philip nodded, understanding. "Regan Hamleigh." What mischief was she up to now? "I'll come at once."

He walked slowly and thoughtfully around the cloisters and out to the courtyard. He would need his wits about him to deal with this woman.

She was standing outside the cellarer's parlor, wrapped in a heavy cloak, hiding her face in a hood. She gave Philip a look of such naked malevolence that he had half a mind to turn around and go back in immediately; but he was ashamed to run from a woman, so he stood his ground and said: "What do you want with me?"

"You foolish monk," she spat. "How can you be so stupid?"

He felt his face redden. "I'm the prior of Kingsbridge, and you'd better call me Father," he said; but to his chagrin he sounded petulant rather than authoritative.

"All right, *Father*—how can you just let yourself be *used* by those two greedy bishops?"

Philip took a deep breath. "Speak plainly," he said angrily.

"It's hard to find words plain enough for someone as witless as you, but I'll try. Waleran is using the burned-down church as a pretext for getting the lands of the Shiring earldom for himself. Is that plain speaking? Have you grasped that concept?"

Her contemptuous tone continued to rile Philip, but he could not resist the temptation to defend himself. "There's nothing underhand about it," he said. "The income from the lands is to be used to rebuild the cathedral."

"What makes you think so?"

"That's the whole idea!" Philip protested; but at the back of his mind he already felt the first stirrings of doubt.

Regan's scornful tone changed and she became sly. "Will the new lands belong to the priory?" she said. "Or to the diocese?"

Philip stared at her for a moment, then turned away: her face was too revolting to look at. He had been working on the assumption that the lands would belong to the priory, and be under his control, rather than to the diocese, where they would be under Waleran's control. But he now recalled that when they had been with the king, Bishop Henry had specifically asked for the lands to be given to the diocese. Philip had assumed that was a slip of the tongue. But it had not been corrected, then or later.

He eyed Regan suspiciously. She could not possibly have known what Henry was going to say to the king. She might be right about this. On the other hand, she could simply be trying to make trouble. She had everything to gain from a quarrel between Philip and Waleran at this point. Philip said: "Waleran is the bishop—he has to have a cathedral."

"He has to have a lot of things," she rejoined. She became less malevolent and more human as she began to reason, but Philip still could not bear to look at her for long. "For some bishops, a fine cathedral would be the first priority. For Waleran there are other necessities. Anyway, as long as he controls the purse strings, he will be able to dole out as much or as little as he likes to you and your builders."

Philip realized she was right about that, at least. If Waleran was collecting the rents, he would naturally retain a portion for his expenses. He alone would be able to say what that portion should be. There would be nothing to stop him from diverting the funds to purposes having nothing to do with the cathedral, if he so chose. And Philip would never know, from one month to the next, whether he was going to be able to pay the builders.

There was no doubt it would be better if the priory owned the land. But Philip was sure Waleran would resist that idea, and Bishop Henry would back Waleran. Then Philip's only hope would be to appeal to the king. And King Stephen, seeing the churchmen divided, might solve the problem by giving the earldom to Percy Hamleigh.

Which was what Regan wanted, of course.

Philip shook his head. "If Waleran is trying to deceive me, why did he bring me here at all? He could have come on his own, and made the same plea."

She nodded. "He could have. But the king might have asked himself how sincere Waleran was, saying that he only wanted the earldom in order to build a cathedral. You've lulled any suspicions Stephen might have had, by appearing here in support of Waleran's claim." Her tone became contemptuous again. "And you look so pathetic, in your dirty robe, that the king pities you. No, Waleran was clever to bring you."

Philip had a horrible feeling she might be right, but he was not willing to admit it. "You just want the earldom for your husband," he said.

"If I could show you proof, would you ride half a day to see it?"

The last thing Philip wanted was to be sucked into Regan Hamleigh's scheming. But he had to find out whether her allegation was true. Reluctantly, he said: "Yes, I'll ride half a day."

"Tomorrow?"

"Yes."

"Be ready at dawn."

It was William Hamleigh, the son of Percy and Regan, who was waiting for Philip in the outer courtyard the following morning as the monks began to sing prime. Philip and William left Winchester by the West Gate, then immediately turned north on Athelynge Street. Bishop Waleran's palace was in this direction, Philip realized; and it was about half a day's ride. So that was where they were going. But why? He was deeply suspicious. He decided to be alert for trickery. The Hamleighs might well be trying to use him. He speculated about how. There might be a document in Waleran's possession that the Hamleighs wanted to see or even steal—some kind of deed or charter. Young Lord William could tell the bishop's staff that the two of them had been sent to fetch the document: they might believe him because Philip was with him. William could easily have some such little scheme up his sleeve. Philip would have to be on his guard.

It was a gloomy, gray morning with drizzling rain. William set a brisk pace for the first few miles, then slowed to a walk to rest the horses. After a while he said: "So, monk, you want to take the earldom away from me."

Philip was taken aback by his hostile tone: he had done nothing to deserve it, and he resented it. Consequently his reply was sharp. "From you?" he said. "You aren't going to get it, boy. I might get it, or your father might, or Bishop Waleran might. But nobody has asked the king to give it to *you*. The very idea is a joke."

"I shall inherit it."

"We'll see." Philip decided there was no point in quarreling with William. "I don't mean you any harm," he said in a conciliatory tone. "I just want to build a new cathedral."

"Then take someone else's earldom," William said. "Why do people always pick on us?"

There was a lot of bitterness in the boy's voice, Philip noted. He said: "Do people always pick on you?"

"You'd think they'd learn a lesson from what happened to Bartholomew. He insulted our family, and look where he is now."

"I thought it was his daughter who was responsible for the insult."

"The bitch is as proud and arrogant as her father. But she'll suffer, too. They'll all kneel to us in the end, you'll see."

These were not the usual emotions of a twenty-year-old, Philip thought. William sounded more like an envious and venomous middle-aged woman. Philip was not enjoying the conversation. Most people would dress up their naked hatred in reasonable clothes, but William was too naïve to do that. Philip said: "Revenge is best left until the Day of Judgment."

"Why don't you wait until the Day of Judgment to build your church?"

"Because by then it will be too late to save the souls of sinners from the torments of hell."

"Don't start on about that!" William said, and there was a note of hysteria in his voice. "Save it for your sermons."

Philip was tempted to make another sharp retort, but he bit it back. There was something very odd about this boy. Philip had the feeling that William could fly into an uncontrollable rage at any moment, and that when enraged he would be lethally violent. Philip was not afraid of him. He had no fear of violent men, perhaps because as a child he had seen the worst they could do and survived it. But there was nothing to be gained by infuriating William with reprimands, so he said gently: "Heaven and hell is what I deal in. Virtue and sin, forgiveness and punishment, good and evil. I'm afraid I can't shut up about them."

"Then talk to yourself," William said, and he spurred his horse into a trot and pulled ahead.

When he was forty or fifty yards in front he slowed down again. Philip wondered whether the boy would relent and return to ride side by side, but he did not, and for the rest of the morning they traveled apart.

Philip felt anxious and somewhat depressed. He had lost control of his destiny. He had let Waleran Bigod take charge in Winchester, and now he was letting William Hamleigh take him on a mystery journey. They're all trying to manipulate me, he thought; why am I letting them? It's time I started to take the initiative. But there was nothing he could do, right away, except turn around and go back to Winchester, and that seemed like a futile gesture, so he continued to follow William, staring gloomily at William's horse's rear end as they jogged along.

A little before noon they reached the valley where the bishop's palace was. Philip recalled coming here at the beginning of the year, full of trepidation, bringing with him a deadly secret. An awful lot had changed since then.

To his surprise, William rode past the palace and on up the hill. The road narrowed to a simple path between fields: it led nowhere important, Philip knew. As they approached the top of the hill, Philip saw that some kind of building work was going on. A little below the summit they were stopped by a bank of earth that looked as if it had been dug up recently. Philip was struck by an awful suspicion.

They turned aside and rode alongside the bank until they found a gap. They went through. Inside the bank was a dry moat, filled in at this point to allow people to cross.

Philip said: "Is this what we came to see?"

William just nodded.

Philip's suspicion was confirmed. Waleran was building a castle. He was devastated.

He kicked his horse forward and crossed the ditch, with William following. The ditch and the bank encircled the top of the hill. On the inside rim of the ditch a thick stone wall had been built to a height of two or three feet. The wall was clearly unfinished, and judging by its thickness it was intended to be very high.

Waleran was building a castle, but there were no workmen on the site, no tools to be seen, and no stacks of stone or timber. A great deal had been done in a short time; then work had stopped suddenly. Obviously Waleran had run out of money.

Philip said to William: "I suppose there's no doubt that it is the bishop who is building this castle."

William said: "Would Waleran Bigod allow anyone *else* to build a castle next to his palace?"

Philip felt hurt and humiliated. The picture was crystal clear: Bishop Waleran wanted the Shiring earldom, with its quarry and its timber, to build his own castle, not the cathedral. Philip was merely a tool, the burning of Kingsbridge Cathedral just a convenient excuse. Their role was to enliven the king's piety so that he would grant Waleran the earldom.

Philip saw himself as Waleran and Henry must see him: naïve, compliant, smiling and nodding as he was led to the slaughter. They had judged him so well! He had trusted them and deferred to them, he had even borne their slights with a brave smile, because he thought they were helping him, when all the time they were double-crossing him.

He was shocked by Waleran's unscrupulousness. He recalled the look of sadness in Waleran's eyes as he looked at the ruined cathedral. Philip had glimpsed the deep-rooted piety in Waleran at that moment. Waleran must think that pious ends justified dishonest means in the service of the Church. Philip had never believed that. I would never do to Waleran what Waleran is trying to do to me, he thought.

He had never before thought of himself as gullible. He wondered where he had gone wrong. It occurred to him that he had let himself be overawed—by Bishop Henry and his silk robes, by the magnificence of Winchester and its cathedral, by the piles of silver in the mint and the heaps of meat in the butchers' shops, and by the thought of seeing the king. He had forgotten that God saw through the silk robes to the sinful heart, that the only wealth worth having was treasure in heaven, and that even the king had to kneel down in church. Feeling that everyone else was so much more powerful and sophisticated than he was, he had lost sight of his true values, suspended his critical faculties, and placed his trust in his superiors. His reward had been treachery.

He took one more look around the rainswept building site, then turned his horse and rode away, feeling wounded. William followed. "What about that, then, monk?" William jeered. Philip did not reply.

He recalled that he had helped Waleran become bishop. Waleran had said: "You want me to make you prior of Kingsbridge. I want you to make me bishop." Of course, Waleran had not revealed that the bishop was already dead, so the promise had seemed somewhat insubstantial. And it had seemed that Philip was obliged to give the promise in order to secure his election as prior. But these were just excuses. The truth was that he should have left the choice of prior *and* bishop in the hands of God.

He had not made that pious decision, and his punishment was that he had to contend with Bishop Waleran.

When he thought about how he had been slighted, condescended to, manipulated and deceived, he became angry. Obedience was a monastic virtue, but outside the cloisters it had its drawbacks, he thought bitterly. The world of power and property required that a man be suspicious, demanding, and insistent.

"Those lying bishops made a fool of you, didn't they?" William said.

Philip reined in his horse. Shaking with rage, he pointed a finger at William. "Shut your mouth, boy. You're speaking of God's holy priests. If you say another word you'll burn for it, I promise you."

William went white with fear.

Philip kicked his horse on. William's sneer reminded him that the Hamleighs had an ulterior motive in taking him to see Waleran's castle. They wanted to cause a quarrel between Philip and Waleran to ensure that the disputed earldom would go to neither the prior nor the bishop, but to Percy. Well, Philip was not going to be manipulated by them, either. He had finished being manipulated. From now on he would do the manipulating.

That was all very well, but what could be done? If Philip quarreled with Waleran, Percy would get the lands; and if Philip did nothing, Waleran would get them.

What did the king want? He wanted to help build the new cathedral: that kind of thing was appropriately kingly, and would benefit his soul in the afterlife. But he needed to reward Percy's loyalty, too. Oddly enough, there was no particular pressure on him to please the more powerful men, the two bishops. It occurred to Philip that there might be a solution to the dilemma that would solve the king's problem by satisfying both himself and Percy Hamleigh.

Now there was a thought.

The idea pleased him. An alliance between himself and the Hamleighs was the last thing anyone expected—and for that reason it just might work. The bishops would be completely unprepared for it. They would be caught wrong-footed.

That would be a delightful reversal.

But could he negotiate a deal with the grasping Hamleighs? Percy wanted the rich farmland of Shiring, the title of earl, and the power and prestige of a force of knights under his command. Philip, too, wanted the rich farmland, but he did not want the title or the knights: he was more interested in the quarry and the forest.

The form of a compromise began to take shape in Philip's mind. He began to think that all was not yet lost.

How sweet it would be to win now, after all that had happened.

With mounting excitement, he considered his approach to the Hamleighs. He was determined he would not play the role of supplicant. He would have to make his proposal seem irresistible.

By the time they reached Winchester, Philip's cloak was soaked through, and his horse was bad-tempered, but he thought he had the answer.

As they passed under the arch of the West Gate he said to William: "Let's go and see your mother."

William was surprised. "I thought you would want to see Bishop Waleran right away."

No doubt that was what Regan had told William to expect. "Don't bother to tell me what you thought, lad," Philip snapped. "Just take me to your mother." He felt very ready for a confrontation with Lady Regan. He had been passive too long.

William turned south and led Philip to a house in Gold Street, between the castle and the cathedral. It was a large dwelling with stone walls to waist level and a timber frame above. Inside was an entrance hall with several apartments off it. The Hamleighs were probably lodging here: many Winchester citizens rented rooms to people who were attending the royal court. If Percy became earl he would have his own town house.

William showed Philip into a front room with a big bed in it and a fireplace. Regan was sitting by the fire and Percy was standing near her. Regan looked up at Philip with an expression of surprise, but she recovered quickly enough, and said: "Well, monk—was I right?"

"You were as wrong as you could be, you foolish woman," Philip said harshly.

She was shocked into silence by his angry tone.

He was gratified by the effect of giving her a taste of her own medicine. He went on in the same tone. "You thought you could cause a quarrel between me and Waleran. Did you imagine I wouldn't see what you were up to? You're a sly vixen but you're not the only person in the world who can *think*."

He could see by her face that she realized her plan had not worked, and she was thinking furiously what to do next. He pressed on while she was disconcerted.

"You've failed, Regan. You've got two options now. One is to sit tight and hope for the best. Wait for the king's decision. Take your chances on his mood tomorrow morning." He paused.

She spoke reluctantly. "And the alternative?"

"The alternative is that we make a deal, you and I. We divide the earldom between us, leaving nothing for Waleran. We go to the king privately and tell him we've reached a compromise, and get his blessing for it before the bishops can object." Philip sat down on a bench and pretended a casual air. "It's your best chance. You've got no real choice." He looked into the fire, not wanting her to see how tense he was. The idea had to appeal to them, he thought. It was the certainty of getting something weighed against the possibility of getting nothing. But they were greedy—they might prefer an all-or-nothing gamble.

It was Percy who spoke first. "Divide the earldom? How?"

They were interested, at least, Philip thought with relief. "I'm going to propose a division so generous that you would be mad to turn it down," Philip said to him. He turned back to Regan. "I'm offering you the best half."

They looked at him, waiting for him to elaborate, but he said no more. Regan said: "What do you mean, the best half?"

"What is more valuable—arable land or forest?"

"Arable land, certainly."

"Then you shall have the arable and I'll have the forest."

Regan narrowed her eyes. "That will give you timber for your cathedral."

"Correct."

"What about pasture?"

"Which do you want—the cattle pastures or the sheep grazing?"

"The pasture."

"Then I'll have the hill farms with their sheep. Would you like the income from markets, or the quarry?"

Percy said: "The market inc—"

Regan interrupted him. "Suppose we said the quarry?"

Philip knew she had understood what was on his mind. He wanted the stone from the quarry for his cathedral. He knew she did not want the quarry. The markets made more money for less effort. He said confidently: "You won't, though, will you?"

She shook her head. "No. We'll take the markets."

Percy tried to look as if he were being fleeced. "I need the forest to hunt," he said. "An earl must have some hunting."

"You can hunt there," Philip said quickly. "I just want the timber."

"That's agreeable," Regan said. Her agreement came a little too quickly for Philip's comfort. He felt a pang of anxiety. Had he given something important away without knowing it? Or was she simply impatient to dispose of a trifling detail? Before he could give it much thought she went on: "Suppose we go through the deeds and charters in Earl Bartholomew's old treasury and find there are some lands that we think should be ours and you think should be yours?"

The fact that she was getting down to such details encouraged Philip to think she was going to accept his proposal. He concealed his excitement and spoke coolly. "We'll have to agree on an arbitrator. How about Bishop Henry?"

"A priest?" she said with a touch of her habitual scorn. "Would he be objective? No. How about the sheriff of Shiring?"

He would be no more objective than the bishop, Philip thought; but he could not think of anyone who would satisfy both sides, so he said: "Agreed—on condition that if we dispute *his* decision we have the right to appeal to the king." That ought to be a sufficient safeguard.

"Agreed," Regan said; then she glanced at Percy and added: "If my husband pleases."

Percy said: "Yes, yes."

Philip knew he was close to success. He took a deep breath and said: "If the overall proposal is agreed, then—"

"Wait a moment." Regan stopped him. "It's not agreed."

"But I've given you everything you want."

"We might yet get the whole earldom, no division."

"And you might get nothing at all."

Regan hesitated. "How do you propose to handle this, if we do agree?"

Philip had thought of that. He looked at Percy. "Could you get to see the king tonight?"

Percy looked anxious, but he said: "If I had a good reason—yes."

"Go to him and tell him we've reached an agreement. Ask him to announce it as his decision tomorrow morning. Assure him that you and I will declare ourselves satisfied with it."

"What if he asks whether the bishops have agreed to it?"

"Say there hasn't been time to put it to them. Remind him that it is the prior, not the bishop, who has to build the cathedral. Imply that if I am satisfied the bishops must be too."

"But what if the bishops complain when the deal is announced?"

"How can they?" Philip said. "They're pretending to ask for the earldom solely in order to finance the cathedral. Waleran can hardly protest on the grounds that he will now be unable to divert funds to other purposes."

Regan gave a short cackle. Philip's cunning appealed to her. "It's a good plan," she said.

"There's an important condition," Philip said, and he looked her in the eye. "The king must announce that my share goes to the *priory*. If he doesn't make that clear, I'll ask him to. If he says anything else—the diocese, the sacrist, the archbishop, anything—I'll repudiate the whole deal. I don't want you to be in any doubt about that."

"I understand," said Regan, a little tetchily.

Her irritation made Philip suspect that she had been toying with the idea of presenting to the king a slightly different version of the agreement. He was glad he had made the point firmly.

He got up to leave, but he wanted to set the seal on their pact somehow. "We are agreed, then," he said, with just the hint of a question in his voice. "We have a solemn pact." He looked at them both.

Regan gave a slight nod, and Percy said: "We have a pact."

Philip's heart beat faster. "Good," he said tightly. "I'll see you tomorrow morning at the castle." He kept his face expressionless as he left the room, but when he reached the dark street he relaxed his control and permitted himself a broad, triumphant grin.

Philip fell into a troubled, anxious sleep after supper. He got up at midnight for matins, then lay awake on his straw mattress, wondering what would happen tomorrow.

He felt King Stephen ought to consent to the proposal. It solved the king's problem: it gave him an earl *and* a cathedral. He was not so sure that Waleran would take it lying down, despite what he had said to Lady Regan. Waleran might find an excuse to object to the arrangement. He might, if he thought fast enough, protest that the deal did not provide the money to build the impressive, prestigious, richly decorated cathedral he wanted. The king might be persuaded to think again.

A different hazard occurred to Philip shortly before dawn: Regan might double-cross him. She could do a deal with Waleran. Suppose she offered the bishop the same compromise? Waleran would have the stone and timber he needed for his castle. This possibility agitated Philip and he turned restlessly in his bed. He wished he could have gone to the king himself, but the king probably would not have received him—and anyway, Waleran might have learned of it and become suspicious. No, there was no action he could have taken to guard against the risk of a double-cross. All he could do now was pray.

He did that until dawn.

He took breakfast with the monks. He found that their white bread did not keep the stomach full as long as horsebread; but even so he could not eat much of it today. He went early to the castle, although he knew the king would not be receiving people at that hour. He entered the hall and sat on one of the stone wall-seats to wait.

The room slowly filled up with petitioners and courtiers. Some of them were very brightly dressed, with yellow and blue and pink tunics and lush fur trimmings on their cloaks. The famous Domesday Book was kept somewhere in this castle, Philip recalled. It was probably in the hall above, where the king had received Philip and the two bishops: Philip had not noticed it, but he had been too tense to notice much. The royal treasury was here, too, but that was presumably on the top floor, in a vault off the king's bedroom. Once again Philip found himself somewhat awestruck by his surroundings, but he had resolved not to be intimidated any longer. These people in their fine robes, knights and lords and merchants and bishops, were just men. Most of them could not write much more than their own names. Furthermore, they were all here to get something for themselves, but he, Philip, was here on behalf of God. His mission, and his dirty brown robe, put him above the other petitioners, not below them.

That thought gave him courage.

A ripple of tension ran through the room as a priest appeared on the stairs leading to the upper hall. Everyone hoped that meant the king was receiving. The priest exchanged a few murmured words with one of the armed guards, then disappeared back up the stairs. The guard picked out a knight from the crowd. The knight left his sword with the guards and went up the stairs.

Philip thought what an odd life the king's clergymen must lead. The king had to have clergy, of course, not just to say mass, but to do the vast amount of reading and writing involved in governing the kingdom. There was nobody else to do it, other than clergy: those few laymen who were literate could not read or write fast enough. But there was nothing very holy about the life of the king's clergy. Philip's own brother, Francis, had chosen that life, and worked for Robert of Gloucester. I must ask him what it's like, Philip thought, if I ever see him again.

Soon after the first petitioner went up the stairs, the Hamleighs came in.

Philip resisted the impulse to go to them straightaway: he did not want the world to know they were in collusion, not yet. He stared at them intently, studying their expressions, trying to read their thoughts. He decided that William looked hopeful, Percy seemed anxious, and Regan was as taut as a bowstring. After a few moments, Philip stood up and crossed the room, as casually as he could manage. He greeted them politely, then said to Percy: "Did you see him?"

"Yes."

"And?"

"He said he would think about it overnight."

"But *why*?" Philip said. He was disappointed and cross. "What is there to think about?"

Percy shrugged. "Ask him."

Philip was exasperated. "Well, how did he *seem*—pleased, or what?"

Regan answered. "My guess is that he liked the idea of being released from his dilemma but felt suspicious that it all sounded too easy."

That made sense, but Philip was still annoyed that King Stephen had not seized the opportunity with both hands. "We'd better not talk any longer," he said after a moment. "We don't want the bishops to guess that we're colluding against them—not before the king makes his announcement." He nodded politely and moved away.

He returned to his stone seat. He tried to pass the time by thinking about what he would do if his plan worked. How soon could work start on the new cathedral? It depended on how quickly he could get some cash out of his new property. There would be quite a lot of sheep: he would have fleeces to sell in the summer.

Some of the hill farms would be rented, and most rents fell due soon after harvesttime. By the autumn there might be enough money to hire a forester and a master quarryman and begin stock-piling timber and stone. At the same time, laborers could start to dig the foundations, under the supervision of Tom Builder. They might be ready to start stonework sometime next year.

It was a fine dream.

Courtiers went up and down the stairs with alarming rapidity: King Stephen was working fast today. Philip began to worry that the king might finish his day's work and go hunting before the bishops arrived.

At last they came. Philip got to his feet slowly as they walked in. Waleran looked tense, but Henry just looked bored. To Henry this was a minor matter: he owed support to his fellow bishop, but the outcome would make little difference to him. For Waleran, however, the outcome was crucial to his plan to build a castle—and a castle was only a step in Waleran's upward progress on the ladder of power.

Philip was not sure how to treat them. They had tried to trick him, and he wanted to rail at them, to tell them that he had discovered their treachery; but that would alert them that something was up, and he wanted them all unsuspecting, so that the compro-mise would be endorsed by the king before they could gather their wits. So he concealed his feelings and smiled politely. He need not have bothered: they ignored him completely.

It was not long before the guards called them. Henry and Waleran went up the stairs first, followed by Philip. The Hamleighs brought up the rear. Philip's heart was in his mouth.

King Stephen was standing in front of the fire. Today he seemed to have a more brisk and businesslike air. That was good: he would be impatient of any quibbling by the bishops. Bishop Henry went and stood beside his brother at the fire, and the others all stood in a line in the middle of the room. Philip felt a pain in his hands, and realized he was pressing his fingernails into his palms. He forced his fingers to relax.

The king spoke to Bishop Henry in a low voice that no one else could hear. Henry frowned and said something equally inaudible. They talked for a few moments, then Stephen held up a hand to silence his brother. He looked at Philip.

Philip reminded himself that the king had spoken kindly to him last time, joshing him about being nervous and saying he liked a monk to dress like a monk.

There were no pleasantries today, however. The king coughed

and began. "My loyal subject, Percy Hamleigh, today becomes the earl of Shiring."

From the corner of his eye, Philip saw Waleran start forward, as if to protest; but Bishop Henry stopped him with a quick, forbidding gesture.

The king went on: "Of the former earl's possessions, Percy shall have the castle, all the land that is tenanted to knights, plus all other arable land and low-lying pasture."

Philip could hardly contain his excitement. It looked as if the king had accepted the deal! He stole another look at Waleran, whose face was a picture of frustration.

Percy knelt in front of the king and held his hands together in an attitude of prayer. The king placed his hands over Percy's. "I make you, Percy, earl of Shiring, to have and enjoy the lands and revenues aforesaid."

Percy said: "I swear by all that is holy to be your liege man and to fight for you against any other."

Stephen released Percy's hands, and Percy stood up.

Stephen turned to the rest of them. "All other farmlands belonging to the former earl, I give"—he paused for a moment, looking from Philip to Waleran and back again—"I give to the *priory* of Kingsbridge, for the building of the new cathedral."

Philip suppressed a whoop of joy—he had won! He could not stop himself from beaming with pleasure at the king. He looked at Waleran. Waleran was shocked to the core. He was making no pretense of equanimity: his mouth was open, his eyes were wide, and he was staring at the king with frank incredulity. His gaze swiveled to Philip. Waleran knew he had failed, somehow, and that Philip was the beneficiary of his failure; but he could not imagine how it had happened.

King Stephen said: "Kingsbridge Priory shall also have the right to take stone from the earl's quarry and timber from his forest, without limit, for the building of the new cathedral."

Philip's throat went dry. That was not the deal! The quarry and the forest were supposed to *belong* to the priory, and Percy was only to have hunting rights. Regan *had* altered the terms after all. Now Percy was to own the property and the priory merely had the right to take timber and stone. Philip had only a few seconds to decide whether to repudiate the whole deal. The king was saying: "In the event of a disagreement, the sheriff of Shiring shall adjudicate, but the parties have the right to appeal to me as a last resort." Philip was thinking: Regan has behaved outrageously, but what difference does it make? The deal still gives me most of what I wanted.

Then the king said: "I believe this arrangement had already been approved by both sides here." And there was no time left.

Percy said: "Yes, lord king."

Waleran opened his mouth to deny that he had approved the compromise, but Philip got in first. "Yes, lord king," he said.

Bishop Henry and Bishop Waleran both turned their heads to Philip and stared at him. Their expressions showed utter astonishment as they realized that Philip, the youthful prior who did not even know enough to wear a clean habit to the king's court, had negotiated a deal with the king behind their backs. After a moment, Henry's face relaxed into amusement, like one who is beaten at nine-men's morris by a nimble-witted child; but Waleran's gaze became malevolent. Philip felt he could read Waleran's mind. Waleran was realizing that he had made the cardinal error of underestimating his opponent, and he was humiliated. For Philip, this moment made up for everything: the treachery, the humiliation, the slights. Philip lifted his chin, risking committing the sin of pride, and gave Waleran a look that said: You'll have to try harder than that to outwit Philip of Gwynedd.

The king said: "Let the former earl, Bartholomew, be told of my decision."

Bartholomew was in a dungeon somewhere nearby, Philip presumed. He remembered those children, living with their servant in the ruined castle, and he felt a pang of guilt as he wondered what would happen to them now.

The king dismissed everyone except Bishop Henry. Philip crossed the room floating on air. He reached the top of the staircase at the same time as Waleran, and stopped to let Waleran go first. Waleran shot him a look of poisonous fury. When he spoke his voice was like bile, and despite Philip's elation, Waleran's words chilled him to the bone. The mask of hatred opened its mouth, and Waleran hissed: "I swear by all that's holy, you'll never build your church." Then he pulled his black robes around his shoulders and went down the stairs.

Philip realized he had made an enemy for life.

III

William Hamleigh could hardly contain his excitement when Earls-castle came into sight.

It was the afternoon of the day after the king had made his decision. William and Walter had ridden for most of two days but William did not feel tired. He felt as if his heart was swelling up in his chest and blocking his throat. He was about to see Aliena again.

He had once hoped to marry her because she was the daughter of an earl, and she had rejected him, three times. He winced as he remembered her scorn. She had made him feel like a nobody, a peasant; she had acted as if the Hamleighs were a family of no account. But the tables had turned. It was her family that was of no account, now. He was the son of an earl, and she was nothing. She had no title, no position, no land, no wealth. He was going to take possession of the castle, and he was going to throw her out, and then she would have no home either. It was almost too good to be true.

He slowed his horse as they approached the castle. He did not want Aliena to have any warning of his arrival: he wanted her to have a sudden, horrible, devastating shock.

Earl Percy and Countess Regan had returned to their old manor house at Hamleigh, to arrange for the treasure, the best horses, and the household servants to be moved to the castle. William's job was to hire some local people to clean up the castle, light fires, and make the place habitable.

Low iron-gray clouds boiled across the sky, so close they seemed almost to touch the battlements. There would be rain tonight. That made it even better. He would be throwing Aliena out into a storm.

He and Walter dismounted and walked their horses over the wooden drawbridge. Last time I was here I captured the place, William thought proudly. The grass was already growing in the lower compound. They tied up their horses and left them to graze. William gave his war-horse a handful of grain. They stowed their saddles in the stone chapel, as there was no stable. The horses snorted and stamped, but a wind was blowing up, and the sounds were lost. William and Walter crossed the second bridge to the upper compound.

There was no sign of life. William suddenly thought that Aliena might have gone. What a disappointment that would be! He and Walter would have to spend a dreary, hungry night in a cold and dirty castle. They went up the outside steps to the hall door. "Quietly," William said to Walter. "If they're here, I want to give them a shock."

He pushed open the door. The great hall was empty and dark, and smelled as if it had not been used for months: as he had expected, they had been living on the top floor. William trod softly as he walked across the hall to the stairs. Dry reeds rustled under his feet. Walter followed close behind.

They climbed the stairs. They could hear nothing: the thick stone walls of the keep muffled all sound. Halfway up, William stopped, turned to Walter, put his finger to his lips, and pointed. There was a light shining under the door at the top of the stairs. Someone was here.

They went on up the stairs and paused outside the door. From inside came the sound of a girlish laugh. William smiled happily. He found the handle, turned it gently, then kicked the door open. The laugh turned into a scream of fright.

The scene in the room made a pretty picture. Aliena and her younger brother, Richard, were sitting at a small table, close to the fire, playing a board game of some kind, and Matthew the steward was standing behind her, looking over her shoulder. Aliena's face was rose-colored in the glow of the fire, and her dark curls glinted with auburn lights. She wore a pale linen tunic. She was looking up at William with her red lips in a big O of surprise. William watched her, enjoying her fright, saying nothing. After a moment she recovered, stood up, and said: "What do you want?"

William had rehearsed this scene many times in his imagination. He walked slowly into the room and stood by the fire, warming his hands; then he said: "I live here. What do *you* want?"

Aliena looked from him to Walter. She was scared and confused, but nevertheless her tone was challenging. "This castle belongs to the earl of Shiring. State your business and then clear out."

William smiled triumphantly. "The earl of Shiring is my father," he said. The steward grunted, as if he had been afraid of this. Aliena looked bewildered. William went on: "The king made my father earl yesterday, at Winchester. The castle now belongs to us. I'm the master here until my father arrives." He snapped his fingers at the steward. "And I'm hungry, so bring me bread and meat and wine."

The steward hesitated. He threw a worried look at Aliena. He was afraid to leave her. But he had no choice. He went to the door.

Aliena took a step toward the door, as if to follow him.

"Stay here," William ordered her.

Walter stood between her and the door, barring her way.

"You have no right to command me!" Aliena said, with a touch of her old imperiousness.

Matthew spoke in a scared tone. "Stay, my lady. Don't anger them. I'll be quick."

Aliena frowned at him, but she stayed where she was. Matthew went out.

William sat in Aliena's chair. She moved to her brother's side. William studied them. There was a similarity between them, but all the strength was in the girl's face. Richard was a tall, awkward adolescent, with no beard yet. William liked the sensation of having them in his power. He said: "How old are you, Richard?"

"Fourteen years," the boy said sullenly.

"Ever killed a man?"

"No," he answered, then with a little attempt at bravado he added: "Not yet."

You'll suffer too, you pompous little prick, William thought. He turned his attention to Aliena. "How old are you?"

At first she looked as if she would not speak to him, but then she appeared to change her mind, perhaps remembering that Matthew had said *Don't anger them.* "Seventeen," she said.

"My, my, the whole family can count," William said. "Are you a virgin, Aliena?"

"Of course!" she blazed.

Suddenly William reached forward and grabbed her breast. It filled his big hand. He squeezed: it felt firm but yielding. She jerked back, and it slipped from his grasp.

Richard stepped forward, too late, and knocked William's arm aside. Nothing could have pleased William more. He came out of his chair fast and hit Richard in the face with a swinging punch. As he had suspected, Richard was soft: he cried out and his hands flew to his face.

"Leave him alone!" Aliena cried.

William looked at her with surprise. She seemed more concerned about her brother than about herself. That might be worth remembering.

Matthew came back in carrying a wooden platter with a loaf of bread, a side of ham and a jug of wine on it. He paled when he saw Richard holding his hands to his face. He put the platter down on the table and went to the boy. Taking Richard's hands away gently, he looked at the boy's face. It was already red and puffy around the eye. "I *told* you not to anger them," he muttered, but he seemed relieved that it was no worse. William was disappointed: he had hoped Matthew would fly into a rage. The steward threatened to be a killjoy.

The sight of the food made William's mouth water. He pulled his chair up to the table, took out his eating knife, and cut a thick slice of ham. Walter sat opposite him. Through a mouthful of bread and ham, William said to Aliena: "Bring some cups and pour the wine." Matthew moved to do it. William said: "Not you—her." Aliena hesitated. Matthew looked at her anxiously and nodded. She came across to the table and picked up the jug.

As she leaned over, William reached down, slipped his hand under the hem of her tunic, and rapidly ran his fingers up her leg. His fingertips felt slender calves with soft hair, then the muscles behind her knee, and then the soft skin of the inside of her thigh; then she jerked away, spun around, and swung the heavy wine jug at his head.

William warded off the blow with his left hand and slapped her face with his right. He put all his force into the slap. His hand stung in a very satisfying way. Aliena screamed. Out of the corner of his eye William saw Richard move. He had been hoping for that. He pushed Aliena aside forcefully, and she fell to the floor with a thud. Richard came at William like a deer charging the hunter. William dodged Richard's first wild blow, then punched him in the stomach. As the boy doubled over, William hit him several times in rapid succession about the eyes and nose. It was not as exciting as hitting Aliena, but it was gratifying enough, and within moments Richard's face was covered with blood.

Suddenly Walter gave a warning cry and sprang to his feet, looking past William's shoulder. William spun round to see Matthew coming at him with a knife held high ready to stab. William was taken by surprise—he had not expected bravery from the effeminate steward. Walter could not reach him in time to prevent the stroke. All William could do was to hold up both arms to protect himself, and for a terrible moment he thought he was going to be killed in his moment of triumph. A stronger attacker would have knocked William's arms aside, but Matthew was a slight figure softened by indoor living, and the knife did not quite reach William's neck. He felt a sudden surge of relief, but he was not yet safe. Matthew lifted his arm for another blow. William took a step back and reached for his sword. Then Walter came around the table with a long pointed dagger in his hand and stabbed Matthew in the back.

An expression of terror came over Matthew's face. William saw the point of Walter's dagger emerge from Matthew's chest, tearing a slit in his tunic. Matthew's own knife fell from his hand and bounced on the floorboards. He tried to draw breath in a gasp, but a gurgling noise came from his throat and he seemed unable to breathe. He sagged; blood came from his mouth; his eyes closed; and he fell. Walter withdrew the long dagger as the body sank to the floor. For a moment blood spurted from the wound, but almost immediately the flow slowed to a trickle.

They all looked at the corpse on the floor: Walter, William, Aliena and Richard. William was light-headed after his close brush with death. He felt as if he could do anything. He reached out and grabbed the neck of Aliena's tunic. The linen was soft and fine, very expensive. He gave a sharp jerk. The tunic ripped. He kept on pulling, so that it tore all the way down the front. A strip a foot wide came away in his hand. Aliena screamed, then tried to pull the remnants of the garment together over her front. The torn edges would not meet. William's throat went dry. Her sudden vulnerability was thrilling. It was much more exciting than when he had watched her washing, for now she knew he was looking, and she felt ashamed, and her shame inflamed him all the more. She covered her breasts with one arm and her triangle with the other hand. William dropped the strip of linen and grabbed her by the hair. He jerked her toward him, spun her around, and ripped the rest of the tunic from her back.

She had delicate white shoulders, a small waist, and surprisingly full hips. He pulled her to him, pressing himself against her back, grinding his hips against her buttocks. He bent his head and bit her soft neck hard, until he tasted blood and she screamed again. He saw Richard move.

"Hold the boy," he said to Walter.

Walter grabbed Richard and put him in an armlock.

Holding Aliena hard against him with one arm, William explored her body with the other hand. He felt her breasts, weighing and then squeezing them, and he pinched her small nipples; then he ran his hand over her stomach and into the triangle of hair between her legs, bushy and curly like the hair on her head. He prodded her roughly with his fingers. She began to cry. His prick was so stiff he felt it would burst.

He stepped away from her and jerked her backward over his outstretched leg. She fell on her back with a crash. The fall winded her and she gasped for breath.

William had not planned this, and he was not quite sure how it had happened, but nothing in the world could stop him now.

He lifted his tunic and showed her his prick. She looked horrified: she had probably never seen a stiff one. She was a real virgin. All the better.

"Bring the boy here," William said to Walter. "I want him to see it all." For some reason, the thought of doing it in front of Richard's eyes was intensely piquant.

Walter pushed Richard forward and forced him to his knees.

William knelt on the floor and prized Aliena's legs apart. She began to struggle. He fell on top of her, trying to crush her into submission, but still she resisted, and he could not get inside her. He was irritated: this was spoiling everything. He raised himself on one elbow and hit her across the face with his fist. She cried out and her cheek turned an angry red, but as soon as he tried to enter her, she began to resist him again.

Walter could have held her still, but he had the boy.

Suddenly William was inspired. "Cut the boy's ear off, Walter," he said.

Aliena went still. "No!" she said hoarsely. "Leave him alone—don't hurt him anymore."

"Open your legs, then," William said.

She stared at him, wide-eyed with horror at the dreadful choice forced upon her. William enjoyed her anguish. Walter, playing the game perfectly, drew his knife and put it to Richard's right ear. He hesitated, then with a movement that was almost tender, he sliced off the boy's earlobe.

Richard screamed. Blood spurted from the small wound. The piece of flesh fell on Aliena's heaving chest.

"Stop!" she screamed. "All right. I'll do it." She opened her legs.

William spat on his hand, then rubbed the moisture between her legs. He pushed his fingers inside her. She cried out with pain. That excited him more. He lowered himself on top of her. She lay still, tense. Her eyes were closed. Her body was slick with sweat from the struggle, but she shivered. William adjusted his position, then hesitated, enjoying the anticipation and her dread. He looked at the others. Richard was looking on with horror. Walter was watching greedily.

William said: "Your turn next, Walter."

Aliena groaned in despair.

Suddenly he shoved inside her roughly, pushing as hard and far as he could. He felt the resistance of her maidenhead—a real virgin!—and he shoved again, brutally. It hurt him but it hurt her more. She screamed. He shoved once more, harder still, and he felt it break. Aliena's face turned white, her head slumped to one side, and she fell into a faint; then at last William spurted his seed inside her, laughing and laughing with triumph and pleasure until he was drained dry.

The storm raged for most of the night, then toward dawn it stopped. The sudden quiet woke Tom Builder. As he lay in the dark, listening to the heavy breathing of Alfred beside him and the quieter sound of Martha on his other side, he calculated that it might be a clear morning, which would mean he could see the sun rise for the first time in two or three cloudy weeks. He had been waiting for this.

He got up and opened the door. It was still dark: there was plenty of time. He prodded his son with a foot. "Alfred! Wake up! There's going to be a sunrise."

Alfred groaned and sat upright. Martha turned over without waking. Tom went to the table and took the lid off a pottery crock. He removed a half-eaten loaf and cut off two thick slices, one for himself and one for Alfred. They sat down on the bench and ate breakfast.

There was ale in the jug. Tom took a long swallow and passed it to Alfred. Agnes would have made them use cups, and so would Ellen, but there was no woman in the house now. When Alfred had drunk his fill from the jug they left the house.

The sky was turning from black to gray as they crossed the priory close. Tom had intended to go to the prior's house and wake Philip. However, Philip's thoughts had followed the same lines as Tom's, and he was already there in the ruins of the cathedral, wearing a heavy cloak, kneeling on the wet ground, saying prayers.

Their task was to establish an accurate east-west line, which would form the axis around which the new cathedral would be built.

Tom had prepared everything some time ago. In the ground at the east end he had planted an iron spike with a small loop in its top like the eye of a needle. The spike was almost as tall as Tom, so that its "eye" was at the level of Tom's eyes. He had fixed it in place with a mixture of rubble and mortar, so that it could not be shifted accidentally. This morning he would plant another such spike, dead west of the first one, at the opposite end of the site.

"Mix up some mortar, Alfred," he said.

Alfred went to fetch sand and lime. Tom went to his tool shed near the cloisters and got a small mallet and the second spike. Then he went to the west end of the site and stood waiting for the sun to rise. Philip finished his prayers and joined him, while Alfred mixed sand and lime with water on a mortarboard.

The sky grew brighter. The three men became tense. They were all watching the east wall of the priory close. At last the red disk of the sun showed over the top of the wall.

Tom shifted his position until he could see the edge of the sun through the small loop in the spike at the far end. Then, as Philip began to pray aloud in Latin, Tom held the second spike in front of him so that it blocked his view of the sun. Steadily, he lowered it to the ground and pressed its pointed end into the damp earth, always keeping it precisely between his eye and the sun. He drew the mallet from his belt and carefully tapped the spike into the ground until its "eye" was level with his eyes. Now, if he had done the job properly, and if his hands had not trembled, the sun should shine through the eyes of both spikes.

He closed one eye and looked through the near spike at the far one. The sun still shone into his eye through the two loops. The two spikes lay on a perfect east-west line. That line would provide the orientation of the new cathedral.

He had explained this to Philip, and he now stood aside and let the prior look through the loops himself, to check.

"Perfect," Philip said.

Tom nodded. "It is."

"Do you know what day it is?" Philip said.

"Friday."

"It's also the day of the martyrdom of Saint Adolphus. God sent us a sunrise so that we could orient the church on our patron's day. Isn't that a good sign?"

Tom smiled. In his experience good workmanship was more important than good omens in the building industry. But he was happy for Philip. "Yes, indeed," he said. "It's a very good sign."

Chapter 6

ALIENA WAS DETERMINED not to think about it.

She sat all night on the cold stone floor of the chapel, with her back to the wall, staring into the darkness. At first she could think of nothing but the hellish scene she had been through, but gradually the pain eased a little, and she was able to concentrate her mind on the sounds of the storm, the rain falling on the roof of the chapel and the wind howling around the ramparts of the deserted castle.

She had been naked at first. After the two men had . . . When they had finished, they had gone back to the table, leaving her lying on the floor, and Richard bleeding beside her. The men had begun eating and drinking as if they had forgotten about her, and then she and Richard had taken their chance and fled from the room. The storm had started by then, and they had run across the bridge in torrential rain and taken refuge in the chapel. But Richard had gone back to the keep almost immediately. He must have gone into the room where the men were, and snatched his cloak and Aliena's from the hook by the door, and run away again before William and his groom had time to react.

But still he would not speak to her. He gave her her cloak, and wrapped his own around him; then he sat on the floor a yard away from her, with his back to the same wall. She longed for someone who loved her to put his arms around her and comfort her, but Richard acted as if she had done something terribly shameful; and the worst of it was that she felt the same way. She felt as guilty as if *she* had committed a sin. She quite understood his not comforting her, his not wanting to touch her.

She was glad it was cold. It helped her to feel withdrawn from the world, isolated; and it seemed to dull the pain. She did not sleep, but at some point in the night they both went into a kind of trance, and sat as still as death for a long time.

The sudden ending of the storm broke the spell. Aliena realized she could see the chapel windows, small gray patches in what had previously been unrelieved blankness. Richard stood up and went to the door. She watched him, feeling annoyed by the disturbance: she wanted to sit there against the wall until she froze to death or starved, for she could think of nothing more appealing than to slip peacefully into permanent unconsciousness. Then he opened the door, and the faint light of dawn illuminated his face.

Aliena was shocked out of her trance. Richard was barely recognizable. His face was swollen out of shape and covered with dried blood and bruises. It made Aliena want to cry. Richard had always been full of empty bravado. As a small boy he had dashed around the castle on an imaginary horse, pretending to stab people with an imaginary lance. Father's knights would always encourage him by pretending to be frightened of his wooden sword. In reality Richard could be scared off by a hissing cat. But he had done his best, last night, and he had been badly beaten for it. Now she would have to take care of him.

Slowly she got to her feet. Her body ached, but the pain was not as bad as it had been last night. She considered what might be happening in the keep. William and his groom would have finished the jug of wine at some point during the night and then they would have fallen asleep. They would probably wake at sunrise.

By then she and Richard must be gone.

She went to the other end of the chapel, to the altar. It was a simple wooden box, painted white, bare of ornament. She leaned against it and then, with a sudden shove, pushed it over.

"What are you doing?" said Richard in a frightened voice.

"This was Father's secret hiding place," she said. "He told me about it before he went away." On the floor where the altar had been was a cloth bundle. Aliena unwrapped it to reveal a full-size sword, complete with scabbard and belt, and a vicious-looking dagger a foot long.

Richard came over to look. He had little skill with a sword. He had been taking lessons for a year but he was still clumsy. However, Aliena certainly could not wield it, so she handed it to him. He buckled the belt around his waist.

Aliena looked at the dagger. She had never carried a weapon. All her life she had had someone to protect her. Realizing that she needed the deadly knife for her own protection, she felt utterly abandoned. She was not sure she could ever use it. I've stuck a wooden lance into a wild pig, she thought; why couldn't I stick this into a man—someone like William Hamleigh? She recoiled from the thought.

The dagger had a leather sheath with a loop for attaching it to a belt. The loop was big enough to go around Aliena's slim wrist like a bracelet. She eased it over her left hand and pushed the knife up her sleeve. It was long—it reached past her elbow. Even if she could not stab someone, perhaps she could use it to frighten people.

Richard said: "Let's get away, quickly."

Aliena nodded, but as she was making for the door, she stopped. The day was rapidly becoming lighter, and she could see on the chapel floor two shadowy objects she had not noticed before. Looking closely, she saw that they were saddles, one of average size and one truly enormous. She visualized William and his groom, arriving here last night, flushed with their triumph at Winchester and wearied by their journey, carelessly lifting the saddles from their horses and dumping them in here before hurrying to the keep. They would not imagine that anyone would dare steal from them. But desperate people find courage.

Aliena went to the door and looked out. The light was clear but weak, and there were no colors. The wind had dropped and the sky was cloudless. Several wooden shingles had fallen from the roof of the chapel in the night. The compound was empty except for the two horses grazing the wet grass. They both looked up at Aliena, then put their heads down again. One of them was a huge war-horse: that explained the oversized saddle. The other was a dappled stallion, not good-looking but compact and solid. Aliena stared at them, then at the saddles, then back at the horses.

"What are we waiting for?" Richard said anxiously.

Aliena made up her mind. "Let's take their horses," she said decisively.

Richard looked scared. "They'll kill us."

"They won't be able to catch us. If we *don't* take their horses they might come after us and kill us."

"What if they catch us before we get away?"

"We'll just have to be quick." She was not as confident as she pretended, but she had to encourage Richard. "Let's saddle the courser first—he looks more friendly. Bring the regular saddle."

She hurried across the compound. Both horses were tied by long ropes to the stumps of burned buildings. Aliena picked up the courser's rope and pulled gently. This would be the groom's horse, of course. Aliena would have preferred something smaller and more timid, but she thought she could handle this one. Richard would have to take the war-horse.

The courser looked suspiciously at Aliena and laid back its ears. She was desperately impatient, but she forced herself to talk softly and pull gently on the rope, and the horse calmed down. She held its head and stroked its nose; then Richard slipped the bridle on and pushed the bit into its mouth. Aliena was relieved. Richard lifted the smaller of the two saddles onto its back and secured it with rapid, sure movements. Both of them had been used to horses from an early age.

There were bags attached to both sides of the groom's saddle. Aliena hoped they might contain something useful—a flint, some food, or a little horse grain—but there was no time to investigate now. She glanced nervously across the compound toward the bridge that led to the keep. There was nobody there.

The war-horse had watched the courser being saddled, and knew what was coming, but it was not keen to cooperate with total strangers. It snorted and resisted the pull of the rope. "Hush!" Aliena said. She held the rope tightly, pulling steadily, and the horse came to her reluctantly. But it was very strong, and if it made a determined effort to resist, there would be trouble. Aliena wondered whether the courser could carry her and Richard. But then William would be able to come after them on the war-horse.

When she had the horse close, she looped the rope around the stump so that it could not move away. But when Richard tried to put the bridle on, the horse tossed its head and evaded it.

"Try putting the saddle on first," Aliena said. She talked to the beast and patted its mighty neck while Richard hefted the massive saddle and tied it on. The horse began to look somewhat defeated. "Now, you be good," Aliena said in a firm voice, but the horse was not fooled: it sensed the panic just beneath the surface. Richard approached with the bridle and the horse snorted and tried to move away. "I've got something for you," Aliena said, and reached into the empty pocket of her cloak. The horse was deceived. She brought out a handful of nothing, but the horse dipped his head and nuzzled her hand, looking for food. She felt the rough skin of its tongue on her palm. While its head was down and its mouth was open, Richard slipped the bridle on.

Aliena shot another fearful glance toward the keep. All was quiet.

"Get on," she said to Richard.

He put one foot in a high stirrup—not without difficulty—and swung himself up onto the huge horse. Aliena untied the rope from the stump.

The horse neighed loudly.

Aliena's heart raced. That sound might have carried to the keep. A man such as William would know the voice of his own horse, especially a horse as expensive as this one. He might have woken up.

She hurried to untie the other horse. Her cold fingers fumbled with the knot. The thought of William waking up had made her lose her nerve. He would open his eyes, sit up, look around him, remember where he was, and wonder why his horse had called. He was sure to come. She felt she could not face him again. The shameful, brutal, agonizing thing he had done to her came back in all its horror.

Richard said urgently: "Come on, Allie!" His horse was jittery and impatient now. He was working hard to make it stay still. He needed to gallop it for a mile or two, to tire it; then it would be more tractable. It neighed again, and started moving sideways.

At last Aliena got the knot undone. She was tempted to drop the rope, but then she would have had no way to tie the horse up again, so she coiled it hastily and messily and tied it to a saddle strap. She needed to adjust the stirrups: they were the right length for William's groom, who was several inches taller than she was, so they would be too low for her to reach when she was in the saddle. But she could picture William coming down the stairs, crossing the hall, coming out into the air—

"I can't hold this horse much longer," Richard said in a strained voice.

Aliena was as jittery as the war-horse. She swung herself up on the stallion. Sitting on the saddle hurt her, inside, and it was all she could do to stay on. Richard moved his horse toward the gate, and Aliena's horse followed without any prompting from her. The stirrups were out of reach, as she had expected, and she had to grip with her knees. As they moved off she heard a shout from somewhere behind her, and she groaned aloud: "Oh, no." She saw Richard kick his horse. The huge beast lumbered into a trot. Her own followed suit. She was grateful that it always did what the war-horse did, for she was in no state to control it herself. Richard kicked the war-horse again and it picked up speed as they passed under the arch of the gatehouse. Aliena heard another shout, much closer. She looked over her shoulder to see William and his groom pounding across the compound after her.

Richard's horse was nervous, and as soon as it saw open fields in front of it, it put its head down and broke into a gallop. They thundered across the wooden drawbridge. Aliena felt something tug at her thigh, and saw, out of the corner of her eye, a man's hand reaching for her saddle straps; but an instant later it was gone, and she knew they had escaped. Relief flooded her; but then she felt the pain again. As the horse galloped across the field she felt stabbed inside, as she had when the foul William had penetrated her; and there was a warm trickle on her thigh. She gave the horse its head and shut her eyes tight against the pain. But the horror of the night before came back to her, and she saw it all behind her closed eyelids. As they raced across the field she chanted in time with the horse's hoofbeats: "I can't re*member* I can't re*member* I *can't* I *can't* I *can't.*"

Her horse angled to the right and she sensed that it was going up a slight slope. She opened her eyes and saw that Richard had turned off the mud path and was taking a long route to the woods. She thought he probably wanted to make sure the war-horse was good and tired before letting it slow down. Both beasts would be easier to manage after being ridden hard. Soon she felt her own mount starting to flag. She sat back in the saddle. The horse slowed to a canter, then a trot, then a walk. Richard's horse still had energy to burn, and it pulled away.

Aliena looked back across the fields. The castle was a mile away, and she was not sure whether or not she could see two figures standing on the drawbridge looking toward her. They would have to walk a long way to find replacement horses, she thought. She felt safe for a while.

Her hands and feet tingled as they warmed up. Heat rose from the horse as from a fire, and wrapped her in a hot-air cocoon. Richard let his horse slow down at last, and turned back toward her, his horse walking and blowing hard. They turned into the trees. They both knew these woods well, for they had lived here most of their lives.

"Where are we going?" asked Richard.

Aliena frowned. Where *were* they going? What were they going to do? They had no food, nothing to drink, and no money. She had no clothes except for the cloak she was wearing—no tunic, no undershirt, no hat, no shoes. She intended to take care of her brother—but how?

She could see now that for the past three months she had been living in a dream. She had known, in the back of her mind, that the old life was over, but she had refused to face it. William Hamleigh had woken her up. She had no doubt that his story was true, and

King Stephen had made Percy Hamleigh the earl of Shiring; but perhaps there was more to it. Perhaps the king had made some provision for her and Richard. If not, he should have, and they could certainly petition him. Either way, they had to go to Winchester. There they could at least find out what had happened to their father.

She suddenly thought: Oh, Father, where did it all go wrong?

Ever since her mother had died, her father had taken special care of her. She knew he paid more attention to her than other fathers did to their daughters. He felt bad that he had not married again, to give her a new mother; and he had explained that he was happier with the memory of his wife than he ever could be with a substitute. Aliena had never wanted another mother anyway. Her father had looked after her, and she had looked after Richard, and that way no harm could ever come to any of them.

Those days were gone forever.

"Where are we going?" Richard said again.

"To Winchester," she said. "We'll go and see the king."

Richard was enthusiastic. "Yes! And when we report what William and his groom did last night, the king will surely—"

In a flash, Aliena was possessed by uncontrollable rage. "Shut your mouth!" she screamed. The horses started nervously. She pulled viciously on her reins. "Don't ever say that!" She was choking with fury and could hardly spit out the words. "We're not going to tell anyone what they did—not anyone! Never! Never! Never!"

The groom's saddlebags contained a large lump of hard cheese, some dregs of wine in a leather bottle, a flint and some kindling, and a pound or two of mixed grains which Aliena imagined were for the horses. She and Richard ate the cheese and drank the wine at noon, while the horses grazed the sparse grass and evergreen shrubs and drank from a clear stream. She had stopped bleeding and the lower half of her torso felt numb.

They had seen some other travelers, but Aliena had told Richard to speak to no one. To the casual observer they appeared a formidable couple, Richard in particular, on his huge horse, with his sword; but a few moments' conversation would reveal them to be a pair of kids with no one to take care of them, and then they might be vulnerable. So they steered clear of other people.

As the day began to fade they looked for somewhere to spend the night. They found a clearing near a stream a hundred yards or so from the road. Aliena gave the horses some grain while Richard made a fire. If they had had a cooking pot they could have made porridge with the horse grain. As it was, they would just have to chew the grains raw, unless they could find some sweet chestnuts and roast them.

While she was pondering that, and Richard was out of sight gathering firewood, she was scared by a deep voice close to her. "And who would you be, my lass?"

She screamed. The horse backed away, frightened. Aliena turned and saw a dirty, bearded man all dressed in brown leather. He took a step toward her. "Keep away from me!" she shrieked.

"No need to be afraid," he said.

Out of the corner of her eye she saw Richard step into the clearing behind the stranger, his arms full of wood. He stood looking at the two of them. *Draw your sword!* thought Aliena, but he looked too scared and uncertain to do anything. She stepped back, trying to get the horse between herself and the stranger. "We've got no money," she said. "We've got nothing."

"I'm the king's verderer," he said.

Aliena almost collapsed with relief. A verderer was a royal servant paid to enforce the forest laws. "Why didn't you say so, you foolish man?" she said, angry at having been scared. "I took you for an outlaw!"

He looked startled, and rather offended, as if she had said something impolite; but all he said was: "You'll be a high-born lady, then."

"I am the daughter of the earl of Shiring."

"And the boy will be his son," said the verderer, although he had not seemed to see Richard.

Richard now stepped forward and dropped his firewood. "That's right," he said. "What's your name?"

"Brian. Are you planning to spend the night here?"

"Yes."

"All alone?"

"Yes." Aliena knew he was wondering why they had no escort, but she was not going to tell him.

"And you've no money, you say."

Aliena frowned at him. "Do you doubt me?"

"Oh, no. I can tell you're nobility, by your manners." Was there a hint of irony in his voice? "If you're alone and penniless, perhaps you'd prefer to spend the night at my house. It's not far."

Aliena had no intention of putting herself at the mercy of this rough character. She was about to refuse when he spoke again.

"My wife would be glad to give you supper. And I've a warm outhouse where you could sleep, if you prefer to sleep alone."

The wife made a difference. Accepting the hospitality of a respectable family should be safe enough. Still Aliena hesitated. Then she thought of a fireplace, a bowl of hot pottage, a cup of wine, and a bed of straw with a roof over it. "We'd be grateful," she said. "We've nothing to give you—I told the truth about having no money—but we'll come back and reward you one day."

"Good enough," said the verderer. He went over to the fire and kicked it out.

Aliena and Richard mounted—they had not yet unsaddled the horses. The verderer came over and said: "Give me the reins." Not sure what he wanted to do, Aliena gave him the reins, and Richard did likewise. The man set off through the forest, leading the horses. Aliena would have preferred to hold the reins herself, but she decided to let him have his way.

It was farther than he had indicated. They had traveled three or four miles, and it was dark, by the time they reached a small wood house with a thatched roof on the edge of a field. But there was light shining through the shutters and a smell of cooking, and Aliena dismounted gratefully.

The verderer's wife heard the horses and came to the door. The man said to her: "A young lord and lady, alone in the forest. Give them something to drink." He turned to Aliena. "In you go. I'll see to the horses."

Aliena did not like his peremptory tone—she would have preferred it if she were the one giving instructions—but she had no wish to unsaddle her own horse, so she went inside. Richard followed. The house was smoky and smelly, but warm. There was a cow tethered in one corner. Aliena was glad the man had mentioned an outhouse: she had never slept with cattle. A pot bubbled on the fire. They sat on a bench, and the wife gave them each a bowl of soup from the pot. It tasted gamey. When she saw Richard's face in the light she was shocked. "What happened to you?" she said.

Richard opened his mouth to reply but Aliena forestalled him. "We've had a series of misfortunes," she said. "We're on our way to see the king."

"I see," said the wife. She was a small, brown-skinned woman with a guarded look. She did not persist in her questioning.

Aliena ate her soup quickly and wanted more. She held out her bowl. The woman looked away. Aliena was puzzled. Did she not know what Aliena wanted? Or did she not have any more? Aliena was about to speak to her sharply when the verderer came in. "I'll show you the barn, where you can sleep," he said. He took a lamp from a hook by the door. "Come with me."

Aliena and Richard stood up. Aliena said to the wife: "There is one thing more I need. Can you give me an old dress? I've got nothing on under this cloak."

The woman looked annoyed for some reason. "I'll see what I can find," she muttered.

Aliena went to the door. The verderer was giving her a strange look, staring at her cloak as if he might be able to see through it if he looked hard enough. "Lead the way!" she said sharply. He turned and went through the door.

He led them around to the back of the house and through a vegetable patch. The shifting light of the lamp revealed a small wooden building, more of a shed than a barn. He opened the door. It banged against a water butt that collected the rain from the roof. "Take a look," he said. "See if it suits you."

Richard went in first. "Bring the light, Allie," he said. Aliena turned to take the lamp from the verderer. As she did so, he gave her a powerful shove. She fell sideways, through the doorway and into the barn, cannoning off her brother. They both ended up in a tangle on the floor. It went dark and the door banged shut. There was a peculiar noise outside, as of something heavy being moved in front of the door.

Aliena could not believe this was happening.

"What's going on, Allie?" Richard cried.

She sat up. Was the man really a verderer, or was he an outlaw? He could not be an outlaw—his house was too substantial. But if he really was a verderer, why had he locked them up? Had they broken a law? Did he guess that the horses were not theirs? Or did he have some dishonest motive?

"Allie, why did he do that?" Richard said.

"I don't know," she said wearily. She had no energy left to be upset or angry. She got up and pushed at the door. It would not move. She guessed that the verderer had put the water butt up against it. In the dark, she felt the walls of the barn. She could reach the lower slopes of the roof, too. The building was made of close-set timbers. It had been carefully constructed. It was the verderer's jail, where he kept offenders before taking them to the sheriff. "We can't get out," she said.

She sat down. The floor was dry and covered with straw. "We're stuck here until he lets us out," she said resignedly. Richard sat beside her. After a while they lay down back to back. Aliena felt she was too battered and frightened and tense to go to sleep, but she was also exhausted, and within a few moments she fell into a healing slumber.

*   *   *

She woke up when the door opened and daylight fell on her face. She sat up immediately, feeling frightened, not knowing where she was or why she was sleeping on the hard ground. Then she remembered, and was still more frightened: what was the verderer going to do to them? However, it was not the verderer who came in but his small brown wife; and although her face was as set and closed as it had been last night, she was carrying a hunk of bread and two cups.

Richard sat up too. They both eyed the woman warily. She said nothing, but handed them each a cup, then broke the bread in two and gave half to each of them. Aliena suddenly realized she was starving. She dipped her bread in her beer and began to eat.

The woman stood in the doorway, watching them, while they finished off the bread and beer. Then she handed Aliena what looked like a length of worn, yellowing linen, folded up. Aliena unfolded it. It was an old dress.

The woman said: "Put that on and get out of here."

Aliena was mystified by the combination of kindness and hard words, but she did not hesitate to take the dress. She turned her back, dropped her cloak, pulled the dress over her head quickly, and put the cloak back on.

She felt better.

The woman handed her a pair of worn wooden clogs, too big.

Aliena said: "I can't ride with clogs on."

The woman laughed harshly. "You won't be riding."

"Why not?"

"He's taken your horses."

Aliena's heart sank. It was too unfair that they should suffer more bad luck. "Where's he taken them?"

"He doesn't tell me these things, but I'd guess he's gone to Shiring. He'll sell the beasts, then find out who you are, and whether there's anything more to be made out of you than the price of your horseflesh."

"So why are you letting us go?"

The woman looked Aliena up and down. "Because I didn't like the way he looked at you when you told him you were naked under your cloak. You may not understand that now, but you will when you're a wife."

Aliena understood it already, but she did not say so.

Richard said: "Won't he kill you when he finds you've let us go?"

She gave a cynical smile. "He doesn't scare me as much as he scares others. Now be off."

They went out. Aliena understood that this woman had learned how to live with a brutal and heartless man, and had even managed to preserve a minimum of decency and compassion. "Thank you for the dress," she said awkwardly.

The woman did not want her thanks. She pointed down the path and said: "Winchester is that way."

They walked away and did not look back.

Aliena had never worn clogs—people of her class always had leather boots or sandals—and she found them clumsy and uncomfortable. However, they were better than nothing when the ground was cold.

When they were out of sight of the verderer's house, Richard said: "Allie, why are these things happening to us?"

The question demoralized Aliena. Everyone was cruel to them. People were allowed to beat them and rob them as if they were horses or dogs. There was nobody to protect them. We've been too trusting, she thought. They had lived for three months in the castle without ever barring the doors. She resolved to trust nobody in the future. Never again would she let someone else take the reins of her horse, even if she had to be rude to prevent it. Never again would she let someone get behind her the way the verderer had last night, when he pushed her into the shed. She would never accept the hospitality of a stranger, never leave her door unlocked at night, never take kindness at face value.

"Let's walk faster," she said to Richard. "Perhaps we can reach Winchester by nightfall."

They followed the path to the clearing where they had met the verderer. The remains of their fire were still there. From there they easily found the road to Winchester. They had been to Winchester before, many times, and they knew the way. Once they were on the road they could move faster. Frost had hardened the mud since the storm two nights ago.

Richard's face was returning to normal. He had washed it yesterday, in a cold brook in the woods, and most of the dried blood had gone. There was an ugly scab where his right earlobe had been. His lips were still swollen but the puffiness had gone from the rest of his face. However, he was still badly bruised, and the angry color of the bruises gave him a rather frightening appearance. Still, that would do no harm.

Aliena missed the heat of the horse beneath her. Her hands and feet were painfully cold, even though her body was warm from the exertion of walking. The weather remained cold all morning, then at midday the temperature rose a little. By then she was hungry. She remembered that only yesterday she had felt as if she did not care whether she ever got warm or ate food again. But she did not want to think about that.

Whenever they heard horses or saw people in the distance they darted into the woods and hid until the other travelers had passed by. They hurried through villages, speaking to no one. Richard wanted to beg for food but Aliena would not let him.

By the middle of the afternoon they were within a few miles of their destination and no one had bothered them. Aliena was thinking that it was not so difficult to avoid trouble, after all. Then, on a particularly desolate stretch of the road, a man suddenly stepped out of the bushes and stood in front of them.

They had no time to hide. "Keep walking," Aliena said to Richard, but the man moved to block their way, and they had to stop. Aliena looked behind, thinking of running that way; but another fellow had materialized out of the forest and was standing ten or fifteen yards away, blocking their escape.

"What have we here?" said the man in front, in a loud voice. He was a fat, red-faced man with a big swollen belly and a filthy matted beard, and he carried a heavy club. He was almost certainly an outlaw. Aliena could tell from his face that he was the kind of man who would commit violence readily, and her heart filled with dread.

"Leave us alone," she said in a pleading tone. "We've got nothing for you to steal."

"I'm not so sure," said the man. He took a step toward Richard. "This looks like a fine sword, worth several shillings."

"It's mine!" Richard protested, but he just sounded like a scared child.

It's no use, Aliena thought. We're powerless. I'm a woman and he's a boy, and people can do anything they like with us.

With a surprisingly agile movement the fat man suddenly raised his club and struck at Richard. Richard tried to dodge. The blow was aimed at his head but it hit his shoulder. The fat man was strong, and the blow knocked Richard down.

Suddenly Aliena lost her temper. She had been treated unjustly, vilely abused, and robbed, and she was cold and hungry and hardly in control of herself. Her little brother had been beaten half to death less than two days ago and now the sight of someone clubbing him maddened her. She lost all sense of reason or caution. Without even thinking, she pulled the dagger from her sleeve, flew at the fat outlaw, and jabbed the knife at his great belly, screaming: "Leave him alone, you dog!"

She took him completely by surprise. His cloak had come open when he hit Richard, and his hands were still occupied with the club. He was completely off guard: no doubt he had thought himself safe from attack by a young girl who appeared unarmed. The point of the knife went through the wool of his tunic and the linen of his undershirt and was stopped by the taut skin of his belly. Aliena experienced a flash of revulsion, a moment of sheer horror at the thought of breaking human skin and penetrating the flesh of a real person; but fear stiffened her resolve, and she shoved the knife through his skin and into the soft organs of his abdomen; and then she became terrified that she might not kill him, that he might stay alive to take his revenge, and so she kept on pushing until the long knife was inside him up to the hilt and would not go in any farther.

Suddenly the fearsome, arrogant, cruel man was a frightened wounded animal. He cried out in pain, dropped his club, and stared down at the knife sticking into him. Aliena understood in a flash that he knew it was a mortal wound. She snatched her hand away in horror. The outlaw staggered back. Aliena remembered that there was another thief behind her, and panic seized her: he would surely take a terrible revenge for the death of his accomplice. She grabbed the hilt of the knife again and jerked. The wounded man had turned slightly away from her, and she had to pull the knife sideways. She felt it slice through his soft insides as it came out of his fat belly. Blood spurted on her hand and the man screamed like an animal and fell to the ground. She spun round, knife in bloody hand, and faced the other man. As she did so, Richard struggled to his feet and drew his sword.

The second thief looked from one of them to the other, then at his dying friend, and without further ado he turned and ran into the woods.

Aliena watched, incredulous. They had scared him off. It was hard to take in.

She looked at the man on the ground. He lay flat on his back with his guts falling out of the great tear in his belly. His eyes were wide open and his face was twisted with pain and fear.

Aliena felt no relief, no pride in having defended herself and her brother from ruthless men: she was too disgusted and repelled by the hideous sight.

Richard felt no such qualms. "You stabbed him, Allie!" he said in a voice between excitement and hysteria. "You did for them!"

Aliena looked at him. He had to be taught a lesson. "Kill this one," she said.

Richard stared at her. "What?"

"Kill him," she repeated. "Put him out of his misery. Finish him off!"

"Why me?"

She deliberately made her voice harsh. "Because you act like a boy and I need a man. Because you've never done anything with a sword except play at war, and you have to start somewhere. What's the matter with you? What are you afraid of? He's dying anyway. He can't hurt you. Use your sword. Get some practice. Kill him!"

Richard held his sword in both hands and looked uncertain. "How?"

The man screamed again.

Aliena yelled at Richard: "I don't know how! Cut off his head, or stab him in the heart! Anything! Just shut him up!"

Richard looked cornered. He lifted his sword and lowered it again.

Aliena said: "If you don't do this I'll leave you alone, I swear by all the saints. I'll get up one night and go away and when you wake up in the morning I won't be there and you'll be all on your own. Now kill him!"

Richard raised his sword again. Then, incredibly, the dying man stopped screaming and tried to get up. He rolled to one side and raised himself on one elbow. Richard gave a shout that was half a yell of fear and half a battle cry, and brought his sword down hard on the man's exposed neck. The weapon was heavy and the blade was sharp, and the blow sliced more than halfway through the fat neck. Blood spurted like a fountain and the head leaned grotesquely to one side. The body slumped to the earth.

Aliena and Richard stared at it. Steam rose from the hot blood in the winter air. They were both stunned by what they had done. Suddenly Aliena wanted to get away from there. She started to run. Richard followed.

She stopped when she could run no more, and that was when she realized she was sobbing. She walked on slowly, no longer caring if Richard saw her in tears. He seemed unaffected anyway.

Gradually she calmed down. The wooden clogs were hurting her. She stopped and took them off. She walked on in her bare feet, carrying the clogs. Soon they would reach Winchester.

After a while Richard said: "We're fools."

"Why?"

"That man. We just left him there. We should have taken his boots."

Aliena stopped and stared, horrified, at her brother.

He looked back at her and gave a little laugh. "There's nothing wrong with that, is there?" he said.

II

Aliena began to feel hopeful again as she walked through the West Gate to Winchester High Street at nightfall. In the forest she had felt that she might be murdered and no one would ever know what had happened, but now she was back in civilization. Of course, the city was full of thieves and cutthroats, but they could not commit their crimes in broad daylight with impunity. In the city there were laws, and lawbreakers were banished, mutilated or hanged.

She remembered going down this street with her father only a year or so ago. They had been on horseback, naturally; he on a highly strung chestnut courser and she on a beautiful gray palfrey. People made way for them as they rode through the broad streets. They owned a house in the south of the city, and when they arrived they were welcomed by eight or ten servants. The house had been cleaned, there was fresh straw on the floor, and all the fires were lit. During their stay Aliena had worn beautiful clothes every day: fine linen, silk, and soft wool, all dyed gorgeous colors; boots and belts of calf leather; and jeweled brooches and bracelets. It had been her job to make sure there was always a welcome for anyone who came to see the earl: meat and wine for the wealthy, bread and ale for the poorer sort, a smile and a place by the fire for either. Her father was punctilious about hospitality, but he was not good at doing it personally—people found him cool, remote, and even high-handed. Aliena supplied the lack.

Everyone respected her father, and the very highest had called on him: the bishop, the prior, the sheriff, the royal chancellor, and the barons at the court. She wondered how many of those people would recognize her now, walking barefoot through the mud and filth of that same High Street. The thought did not dampen her optimism. The important thing was that she no longer felt like a victim. She was back in a world where there were rules and laws, and she had a chance to regain control of her life.

They walked past their house. It was empty and locked up: the Hamleighs had not yet taken it over. For a moment Aliena was tempted to try to get in. It's my house! she thought. But it was not, of course, and the idea of spending the night there reminded her of the way she had lived in the castle, closing her eyes to reality. She walked on determinedly.

The other good thing about being in the city was that there was a monastery here. The monks would always provide a bed for anyone who begged it. She and Richard would sleep under a roof tonight, safe and dry.

She found the cathedral and went into the priory courtyard. Two monks stood at a trestle table doling out horsebread and beer to a hundred or more people. It had not occurred to Aliena that there would be so many others begging the monks' hospitality. She and Richard joined the queue. It was amazing, she thought, how people who would normally jostle and shove one another to get at free food could be made to stand quietly in an orderly line just because a monk told them to.

They got their supper and took it into the guesthouse. This was a big wooden building like a barn, bare of furniture, dimly lit by rushlights, smelling strongly of many people crowded closely together. They sat on the ground to eat. The floor was covered with rushes that were none too fresh. Aliena wondered whether she should tell the monks who she was. The prior might remember her. In such a large priory there would naturally be a superior guesthouse for high-born visitors. But she found herself reluctant to do that. Perhaps it was that she was afraid of being spurned; but she also felt she would be putting herself in someone else's power again, and although she had nothing to fear from a prior, nevertheless she felt more comfortable remaining anonymous and unnoticed.

The other guests were mostly pilgrims, with a sprinkling of traveling craftsmen—identifiable by the tools they carried—and some hawkers, men who went from village to village selling things that peasants could not make for themselves, pins and knives and cooking pots and spices. Some of them had their wives and children with them. The children were noisy and excited, rushing around and fighting and falling over. Every now and again one would cannon into an adult, get a smack on the head, and burst into tears. Some of them were not perfectly house-trained, and Aliena saw several children urinating into the rushes on the floor. Such things were probably of no consequence in a house where the livestock slept in the same room as the people, but in a crowded hall it was rather disgusting, Aliena thought: they all had to sleep on those rushes later.

She began to get the feeling that people were looking at her as if they knew she had been deflowered. It was ridiculous, of course, but the feeling would not go away. She kept checking to see whether she was bleeding. She was not. But every time she turned around she caught someone giving her a hard, penetrating stare. As soon as she met their eyes they would look away, but a little while later she would catch someone else doing it. She kept telling herself that this was foolish, they weren't staring at her, they were just looking curiously around a crowded room. There was nothing to look at, anyway: she was no different from them in appearance— she was as dirty, badly dressed and tired as they were. But the feeling persisted, and against her will she got angry. There was one man who kept catching her eye, a middle-aged pilgrim with a large family. Eventually she lost her temper and yelled at him: "What are you looking at? Stop staring at me!" He seemed embarrassed and averted his eyes without replying.

Richard said quietly: "Why did you do that, Allie?"

She told him to shut up and he did.

The monks came around and took away the lights soon after supper. They liked people to go to sleep early: it kept them out of the alehouses and brothels of the city at night, and in the morning it made it easier for the monks to get the visitors off the premises early. Several of the single men left the hall when the lights went out, headed no doubt for the fleshpots, but most people curled up in their cloaks on the floor.

It was many years since Aliena had slept in a hall like this. As a child she had always envied the people downstairs, lying side by side in front of the dying fire, in a room full of smoke and the smell of dinner, with the dogs to guard them: there had been a sense of togetherness in the hall which was absent from the spacious, empty chambers of the lord's family. In those days she had sometimes left her own bed and tiptoed down the stairs to sleep alongside one of her favorite servants, Madge Laundry or Old Joan.

Drifting off to sleep with the smell of her childhood in her nostrils, she dreamed about her mother. Normally she had trouble remembering what her mother had looked like, but now, to her surprise, she could see Mama's face clearly, in every detail: the small features, the timid smile, the slight frame, the look of anxiety in the eyes. She saw her mother's walk, leaning slightly to one side as if she were always trying to get close to the wall, with the opposite arm extended a little for balance. She could hear her mother's laugh, that unexpectedly rich contralto, always ready to break into song or laughter but usually afraid to do so. She knew, in the dream, something that had never been clear to her awake: that her father had so frightened her mother and suppressed her sense of the joy of life that she had shriveled up and died like a flower in a drought. All this came into Aliena's mind like something very familiar, something she had always known. However, what was shocking was that Aliena was pregnant. Mother seemed pleased. They sat together in a bedroom, and Aliena's belly was so distended that she had to sit with her legs slightly apart and her hands crossed over her bump, in the age-old pose of the mother-to-be. Then William Hamleigh burst into the room, carrying in his hand the dagger with the long blade, and Aliena knew he was going to stab her belly the way she had stabbed the fat outlaw in the forest, and she screamed so loud she woke up sitting upright; and then she realized that William was not here and she had not even screamed, the noise had only been in her head.

After that she lay awake wondering if she really was pregnant.

The thought had not occurred to her before, and now it terrified her. How disgusting it would be to have William Hamleigh's baby. It might not be his—it might be the groom's. She might never know. How could she love the baby? Every time she looked at it, it would remind her of that dreadful night. She would have the baby in secret, she vowed, and leave it out in the cold to die as soon as it was born, the way the peasants did when they had too many children. With that resolve she drifted off to sleep again.

It was barely light when the monks brought breakfast. The noise woke Aliena. Most of the other guests were awake already, because they had gone to sleep so early, but Aliena had slept on: she had been very tired.

Breakfast was hot gruel with salt. Aliena and Richard ate hungrily and wished there were bread to go with it. Aliena thought over what she would say to King Stephen. She felt sure that he had simply forgotten that the earl of Shiring had two children. As soon as they appeared and reminded him, he would willingly make provision for them, she thought. However, in case he needed persuading she ought to have a few words ready. She would not insist that her father was innocent, she decided, for that would imply that the king's judgment had been at fault, and he would be offended. Nor would she protest about Percy Hamleigh being made earl. Men of affairs hated to have past decisions disputed. "For better or worse, that's been settled," her father would say. No, she would simply point out that she and her brother were innocent, and ask the king to give them a knight's estate, so that they could support themselves modestly, and Richard could prepare to become one of the king's fighting men in a few years' time. A small estate would enable her to take care of her father, when the king pleased to release him from jail. He was no longer a threat: he had no title, no followers and no money. She would remind the king that her father had faithfully served the old king, Henry, who had been Stephen's uncle. She would not be forceful, just humbly firm, clear and simple.

After breakfast she asked a monk where she could wash her face. He looked startled: evidently it was an unusual request. However, monks were in favor of cleanliness, and he showed her an open conduit where clean cold water ran into the priory grounds, and warned her not to wash "indecently," as he put it, in case one of the brothers should accidentally see her and thereby soil his soul. Monks did a lot of good but their attitudes could be irritating.

When she and Richard had washed the dirt of the road off their faces they left the priory and walked uphill along the High Street to the castle, which stood to one side of the West Gate. By coming early Aliena hoped to befriend or charm whoever was in charge of admitting petitioners, and ensure that she was not forgotten in the crowd of important people who would arrive later. However, the atmosphere within the castle walls was even quieter than she had hoped. Had King Stephen been here so long that few people needed to see him? She was not sure when he might have come. The king was normally at Winchester throughout Lent, she thought, but she was not sure when Lent had begun, for she had lost track of dates, living in the castle with Richard and Matthew and no priest.

There was a burly guard with a gray beard standing at the foot of the keep steps. Aliena made to walk past him, as she had when she came here with her father, but the guard lowered his spear across her path. She looked at him imperiously and said: "Yes?"

"And where do you think you're going, my girl?" said the guard.

Aliena saw, with a sinking feeling, that he was the type of person who liked being a guard because it gave him the chance to stop people from going where they wanted to go. "We're here to petition the king," she said frostily. "Now let us pass."

"You?" the guard said with a sneer. "Wearing a pair of clogs that my wife would be ashamed of? Clear off."

"Get out of my way, guard," said Aliena. "Every citizen has the right to petition the king."

"But the poorer sort generally are not foolish enough to try to exercise that right—"

"We are not the poorer sort!" Aliena blazed. "I am the daughter of the earl of Shiring, and my brother is his son, so let us pass, or you'll end up rotting in a dungeon."

The guard looked a little less bumptious, but he said smugly: "You can't petition the king, because he's not here. He's at Westminster, as you ought to know if you are who you say you are."

Aliena was thunderstruck. "But why has he gone to Westminster? He should be here for Easter!"

The guard realized she was not a street urchin. "Easter court is at Westminster. It seems he's not going to do everything exactly the same as the old king did, and why should he?"

He was right, of course, but the idea that a new king would follow a different timetable had never occurred to Aliena, who was too young to remember when Henry had been the new king. Despair washed over her. She had thought she knew what to do, and she had been so wrong. She felt like giving up.

She shook her head to dispel the sense of doom. This was a setback, not a defeat. Appealing to the king was not the only way to take care of her brother and herself. She had come to Winchester with two purposes, and the second was to find out what had happened to her father. He would know what she should do next.

"Who *is* here, then?" she said to the guard. "There must be some royal officials. I just want to see my father."

"There's a clerk and a steward up there," the guard replied. "Did you say the earl of Shiring was your father?"

"Yes." Her heart missed a beat. "Do you know anything about him?"

"I know where he is."

"Where?"

"In the jail right here at the castle."

So close! "Where's the jail?"

The guard jerked a thumb over his shoulder. "Down the hill, past the chapel, opposite the main gate." Excluding them from the keep had gratified his mean streak and now he was willing to be informative. "You'd better see the jailer. His name is Odo, and he's got deep pockets."

Aliena did not understand the remark about deep pockets but she was too agitated to clarify it. Until this moment her father had been in a vague, distant place called "prison," but now, suddenly, he was right here in this very castle. She forgot all about appealing to the king. All she wanted to do was see Father. The thought that he was close by, ready to help her, made her feel the danger and uncertainty of the last few months more acutely. She wanted to run into his arms and hear him say: "It's all right, now. Everything's going to be all right."

The keep stood on a rise in one corner of the compound. Aliena turned and looked down at the rest of the castle. It was a motley collection of stone and wood buildings enclosed by high walls. Down the hill, the guard had said; past the chapel—she spotted a neat stone building that looked like a chapel—and opposite the main gate. The main entrance was a gate in the outer wall, permitting the king to come into his castle without first having to enter the city. Opposite that entrance, close to the back wall that separated the castle from the city, was a small stone building that could be the jail.

Aliena and Richard hurried down the slope. Aliena wondered how he would be. Did they give people proper food in jail? Her father's own prisoners had always got horsebread and pottage at Earlscastle, but she had heard that prisoners were sometimes ill-treated elsewhere. She hoped Father was all right.

Her heart was in her mouth as she crossed the compound. It was a big castle but it was crowded with buildings: kitchens, stables, and barracks. There were two chapels. Now that she knew the king was away, Aliena could see the signs of his absence, and she noted them distractedly as she wove her way toward the jail: stray pigs and sheep had wandered in from the suburbs just outside the gate and were rooting around in the rubbish tips, men-at-arms were lolling about with nothing to do but call out insolent remarks to passing women, and there was some kind of betting game going on in the porch of one of the chapels. The atmosphere of laxity bothered Aliena. She was afraid it might mean her father was not looked after properly. She began to dread what she might find.

The jail was a semi-derelict stone building that looked as if it might once have been a house for a royal official, a chancellor or bailiff of some kind, before it fell into disrepair. The upper story, which had once been the hall, was completely ruined, having lost most of its roof. Only the undercroft remained whole. Here there were no windows, just a big wooden door with iron studs. The door stood slightly ajar. As Aliena hesitated outside, a handsome middle-aged woman in a good-quality cloak passed her, opened the door and went in. Aliena and Richard followed her.

The gloomy interior smelled of old dirt and corruption. The undercroft had once been an open storeroom, but it had later been divided into small compartments by hastily built rubble walls. Somewhere in the depths of the building a man was moaning monotonously, like a monk chanting services alone in a church. The area just inside the door formed a small lobby, with a chair, a table and a fire in the middle of the floor. A big, stupid-looking man with a sword at his belt was lackadaisically sweeping the floor. He looked up and greeted the handsome woman. "Good morning, Meg." She gave him a penny and disappeared into the gloom. He looked at Aliena and Richard. "What do you want?"

"I'm here to see my father," Aliena said. "He is the earl of Shiring."

"No, he's not," said the jailer. "He's just plain Bartholomew now."

"To hell with your distinctions, jailer. Where is he?"

"How much have you got?"

"I've no money, so don't bother asking for a bribe."

"If you've no money, you can't see your father." He resumed sweeping.

Aliena wanted to scream. She was within a few yards of her father and she was being kept from him. The jailer was big and he was armed: there was no chance of defying him. But she did not have any money. She had been afraid of this when she saw the woman Meg give him a penny, but that might have been for some special privilege. Obviously not: a penny must be the price of admission.

She said: "I'll get a penny, and bring it to you as soon as I can. But won't you let us see him now, just for a few moments?"

"Get the penny first," the jailer said. He turned his back and went on sweeping.

Aliena was fighting back tears. She was tempted to yell out a message in the hope that her father would hear her; but she realized that a garbled message might frighten and demoralize him: it would make him anxious without giving him any information. She went to the door, feeling maddeningly impotent.

She turned around on the threshold. "How is he? Just tell me that—please? Is he all right?"

"No, he's not," the jailer said. "He's dying. Now get out of here."

Aliena's vision blurred with tears and she stumbled through the door. She walked away, not seeing where she was going, and bumped into something—a sheep or a pig—and almost fell. She began to sob. Richard took her arm, and she let him guide her. They went out of the castle by the main gate, into the scattered hovels and small fields of the suburbs, and eventually came to a meadow and sat on a tree stump.

"I hate it when you cry, Allie," said Richard pathetically.

She tried to pull herself together. She had located her father—that was something. She had learned that he was sick: the jailer was a cruel man who was probably exaggerating the seriousness of the illness. All she had to do was find a penny, and she would be able to talk to him, and see for herself, and ask him what she should do—for Richard and for Father.

"How are we going to get a penny, Richard?" she said.

"I don't know."

"We've nothing to sell. No one would lend to us. You're not tough enough to steal. . . ."

"We could beg," he said.

That was an idea. There was a prosperous-looking peasant coming down the hill toward the castle on a sturdy black cob. Aliena sprang to her feet and ran to the road. As he drew near she said: "Sir, will you give me a penny?"

"Piss off," the man snarled, and kicked his horse into a trot.

She walked back to the tree stump. "Beggars usually ask for food or old clothes," she said dejectedly. "I never heard of anyone giving them money."

"Well, how *do* people get money?" Richard said. The question had obviously never occurred to him before.

Aliena said: "The king gets money from taxes. Lords have rents. Priests have tithes. Shopkeepers have something to sell. Craftsmen get wages. Peasants don't need money because they have fields."

"Apprentices get wages."

"So do laborers. We could work."

"Who for?"

"Winchester is full of little manufactories where they make leather and cloth," Aliena said. She began to feel optimistic again. "A city is a good place to find work." She sprang to her feet. "Come on, let's get started!"

Richard still hesitated. "I can't work like a common man," he said. "I'm the son of an earl."

"Not anymore," Aliena said harshly. "You heard what the jailer said. You'd better realize that you're no better than anyone else, now."

He looked sulky and said nothing.

"Well, I'm going," she said. "Stay here if you like." She walked away from him, toward the West Gate. She knew his sulks: they never lasted.

Sure enough, he caught her up before she reached the city. "Don't be cross, Allie," he said. "I'll work. I'm pretty strong, actually—I'll make a very good laborer."

She smiled at him. "I'm sure you will." It was not true, but there was no point in discouraging him.

They walked down the High Street. Aliena recalled that Winchester was laid out and divided up in a very logical way. The southern half, on their right as they walked, was divided into three parts: first there was the castle, then a district of wealthy homes, then the cathedral close and the bishop's palace in the southeast corner. The northern half, on their left, was also divided into three: the Jews' neighborhood, the middle part where the shops were, and the manufactories in the northeast corner.

Aliena led the way down the High Street to the eastern end of the city, then they turned left, into a street that had a brook running along it. On one side were normal houses, mostly wooden, a few partly of stone. On the other side was a jumble of improvised buildings, many of them no more than a roof supported by poles, most of them looking as if they might fall down at any minute. In some cases a little bridge, or a few planks, led across the brook to the building, but some of the buildings actually straddled the brook. In every building or yard, men and woman were doing something that required large quantities of water: washing wool, tanning leather, fulling and dyeing cloth, brewing ale, and other operations that Aliena did not recognize. A variety of unfamiliar smells pricked her nostrils, acrid and yeasty, sulfurous and smoky, woody and rotten. The people all looked terribly *busy*. Of course, peasants also had a great deal to do, and they worked very hard, but they went about their tasks at a measured pace, and they always had time to stop and examine some curiosity or talk to passersby. The people in the manufactories never looked up. Their work seemed to take all their concentration and energy. They moved quickly, whether they were carrying sacks or pouring great buckets of water or pounding leather or cloth. As they went about their mysterious tasks in the gloom of their ramshackle huts, they made Aliena think of the demons stirring their cauldrons in pictures of hell.

She stopped outside a place where they were doing something she understood: fulling cloth. A muscular-looking woman was drawing water from the brook and pouring it into a huge stone trough lined with lead, stopping every now and again to add a measure of fuller's earth from a sack. Lying in the bottom of the trough, completely submerged, was a length of cloth. Two men with large wooden clubs—called fuller's bats, Aliena recollected— were pounding the cloth in the trough. The process caused the cloth to shrink and thicken, making it more waterproof; and the fuller's earth leached out the oils from the wool. At the back of the premises were stacked bales of untreated cloth, new and loosely woven, and sacks of fuller's earth.

Aliena crossed the brook and approached the people working at the trough. They glanced at her and continued working. The ground was wet all around them, and they worked with their feet bare, she noticed. When she realized they were not going to stop and ask her what she wanted, she said loudly: "Is your master here?"

The woman replied by jerking her head toward the back of the premises.

Aliena beckoned Richard to follow and went through a gate to a yard where lengths of cloth were drying on wooden frames. She saw the figure of a man bent over one of the frames, arranging the cloth. "I'm looking for the master," she said.

He straightened up and looked at her. He was an ugly man with one eye and a slightly hunched back, as if he had been bending over drying frames for so many years that he could no longer stand quite upright. "What is it?" he said.

"Are you the master fuller?"

"I've been working at it nigh on forty year, man and boy, so I hope I'm master," he said. "What do you want?"

Aliena realized she was dealing with the type of man who always had to prove how smart he was. She adopted a humble tone and said: "My brother and I want to work. Will you employ us?"

There was a pause while he looked her up and down. "Christ Jesus and all the saints, what would I do with you?"

"We'll do anything," Aliena said resolutely. "We need some money."

"You're no good to me," the man said contemptuously, and he turned away to resume his work.

Aliena was not going to content herself with that. "Why not?" she said angrily. "We're not scrounging, we want to *earn* something."

He turned to her again.

"Please?" she said, although she hated to beg.

He regarded her impatiently, as he might have looked at a dog, wondering whether to make the effort of kicking it; but she could tell that he was tempted to show her how stupid she was being and how clever he was by contrast. "All right," he said with a sigh. "I'll explain it to you. Come with me."

He led them to the trough. The men and the woman were pulling the length of cloth out of the water, rolling it as it emerged. The master spoke to the woman. "Come here, Lizzie. Show us your hands."

The woman obediently came over and held out her hands. They

were rough and red, with open sores where they had got chapped and the skin had broken.

"Feel those," the master said to Aliena.

Aliena touched the woman's hands. They were as cold as snow, and very rough, but what was most striking was how hard they were. She looked at her own hands, holding the woman's: they suddenly looked soft and white and very small.

The master said: "She's had her hands in water since she was a little 'un, so she's used to it. You're different. You wouldn't last the morning at this work."

Aliena wanted to argue with him, and say that she would get used to it, but she was not sure it was true. Before she could say anything, Richard spoke up. "What about me?" he said. "I'm bigger than both those men—I could do that work."

It was true that Richard was actually taller and broader than the men who had been wielding the fuller's bats. And he could handle a war-horse, Aliena recalled, so he should be able to pound cloth.

The two men finished rolling up the wet cloth, and one of them hoisted the roll onto his shoulder, ready to take it to the yard for drying. The master stopped him. "Let the young lord feel the weight of the cloth, Harry."

The man called Harry lifted the cloth off his shoulder and put it on Richard's. Richard sagged under the weight, straightened up with a mighty effort, paled, and then sank to his knees so that the ends of the roll rested on the ground. "I can't carry it," he said breathlessly.

The men laughed, the master looked triumphant, and the one called Harry took the cloth back, hoisted it onto his own shoulder with a practiced movement, and carried it away. The master said: "It's a different kind of strength, one that comes from *having* to work."

Aliena was angry. They were mocking her when all she wanted was to find an honest way to earn a penny. The master was thoroughly enjoying making a fool of her, she knew. He would probably keep it up as long as she let him. But he would never employ her or Richard. "Thank you for your courtesy," she said with heavy sarcasm, and she turned and walked away.

Richard was upset. "It was heavy because it was so wet!" he said. "I wasn't expecting that."

Aliena realized she had to stay cheerful, to keep Richard's morale up. "That's not the only kind of work there is," she said as she strode along the muddy street.

"What else could we do?"

Aliena did not answer immediately. They reached the north wall of the city and turned left, heading west. The poorest houses were here, built up against the wall, often no more than lean-to shacks; and because they had no backyards the street was filthy. Eventually Aliena said: "Remember how girls used to come to the castle, sometimes, when there was no room for them at home anymore and they had no husband yet? Father would always take them in. They worked in the kitchens or the laundry or the stables, and Father used to give them a penny on saint's days."

"Do you think we could live at Winchester Castle?" Richard said dubiously.

"No. They won't take people in while the king's away—they must have more people than they need. But there are lots of rich folk in the city. Some of them must want servants."

"It's not man's work."

Aliena wanted to say *Why don't you come up with some ideas yourself, instead of just finding fault with everything I say?* But she bit her tongue and said: "It only wants one of us to work long enough to get a penny, then we can see Father and ask him what we should do next."

"All right." Richard was not averse to the idea of only one of them working, especially if the one was likely to be Aliena.

They turned left again and entered the section of the city called the Jewry. Aliena stopped outside a big house. "They must have servants in there," she said.

Richard was shocked. "You wouldn't work for Jews, would you?"

"Why not? You don't catch people's heresy the way you catch their fleas, you know."

Richard shrugged and followed her inside.

It was a stone house. Like most city homes, it had a narrow frontage but reached back a long way. They were in an entrance hall that was the full width of the house. There was a fire and some benches. The smell from the kitchen made Aliena's mouth water, although it was different from regular cooking, with a hint of alien spices. A young girl came from the back of the house and greeted them. She had dark skin and brown eyes, and she spoke respectfully. "Do you want to see the goldsmith?"

So that was what he was. "Yes, please," said Aliena. The girl disappeared again and Aliena looked around. A goldsmith would need a stone house, of course, to protect his gold. The door between this room and the back of the house was made of heavy oak planks banded with iron. The windows were narrow, too small for anyone to climb through, even a child. Aliena thought how nerve-racking it must be to have all your wealth in gold or silver, which could be stolen in an instant, leaving you destitute. Then she reflected that Father had been rich with a more normal kind of wealth—land and a title—and yet he had lost everything in a day.

The goldsmith came out. He was a small, dark man, and he peered at them, frowning, as if he were examining a small piece of jewelry and assessing its worth. After a moment he seemed to sum them up, and he said: "You have something you would like to sell?"

"You've judged us well, goldsmith," Aliena said. "You've guessed we're high-born people who now find themselves destitute. But we have nothing to sell."

The man looked worried. "If you're looking for a loan, I fear—"

"We don't expect anyone to lend us money," Aliena broke in. "Just as we have nothing to sell, so we have nothing to pawn."

He looked relieved. "Then how can I help you?"

"Would you take me on as a servant?"

He was shocked. "A Christian? Certainly not!" He actually shrank back at the thought.

Aliena was disappointed. "Why not?" she said plaintively.

"It would never do."

She felt rather offended. The idea that someone should find *her* religion distasteful was demeaning. She remembered the clever phrase she had used to Richard. "You don't catch people's religions the way you catch their fleas," she said.

"The people of the town would object."

Aliena felt sure he was using public opinion as an excuse, but it was probably true all the same. "I suppose we'd better seek out a rich Christian, then," she said.

"It's worth a try," the goldsmith said doubtfully. "Let me tell you something candidly. A wise man would not employ you as a servant. You're used to giving orders, and you would find it very hard to be on the receiving end." Aliena opened her mouth to protest, but he held up his hand to stop her. "Oh, I know you're willing. But all your life others have served you, and even now you feel in your heart of hearts that things should be arranged to please you. High-born people make poor servants. They are disobedient, resentful, thoughtless, touchy, and they think they're working hard even though they do less than everyone else—so they cause trouble among the rest of the staff." He shrugged. "This is my experience."

Aliena forgot that she had been offended by his distaste for her religion. He was the first kindly person she had met since she left the castle. She said: "But what *can* we do?"

"I can only tell you what a Jew would do. He would find something to sell. When I came to this city I began by buying jewelry from people who needed cash, then melting the silver and selling it to the coiners."

"But where did you get the money to buy the jewelry?"

"I borrowed from my uncle—and paid him interest, by the way."

"But nobody will lend to us!"

He looked thoughtful. "What would I have done if I had no uncle? I think I would have gone into the forest and collected nuts, then brought them into the town and sold them to the housewives who do not have the time to go to the forest and cannot grow trees in their backyards because the yards are so full of refuse and filth."

"It's the wrong time of year," Aliena said. "There's nothing growing now."

The goldsmith smiled. "The impatience of youth," he said. "Wait a while."

"All right." There was no point in explaining about Father. The goldsmith had done his best to be helpful. "Thank you for your advice."

"Farewell." The goldsmith returned to the back of the house and closed the massive ironbound door.

Aliena and Richard went out. The goldsmith had been kind but nevertheless they had spent half a day being turned away from places, and Aliena could not help feeling dejected. Not knowing where to go next, they wandered through the Jewry and emerged in the High Street again. Aliena was beginning to feel hungry—it was dinnertime—and she knew that if she was hungry, Richard would be ravenous. They walked aimlessly along the High Street, envying the well-fed rats that swarmed in the refuse, until they came to the old royal palace. There they stopped, as all out-of-towners did, to look through the bars at the coiners manufacturing money. Aliena stared at the stacks of silver pennies, thinking that she wanted only one of those, and she could not get it.

After a while she noticed a girl of about her own age standing nearby, smiling at Richard. The girl looked friendly. Aliena hesitated, saw her smile again, and spoke to her. "Do you live here?"

"Yes," the girl said. It was Richard she was interested in, not Aliena.

Aliena blurted out: "Our father's in the jailhouse, and we're trying to find some way to make a living and get some money to bribe the jailer. Do you know what we might do?"

The girl turned her attention from Richard back to Aliena.

"You're penniless, and you want to know how to make some money?"

"That's right. We're willing to work hard. We'll do anything. Can you think of something?"

The girl gave Aliena a long, assessing look. "Yes, I can," she said at last. "I know someone who might help you."

Aliena was thrilled: this was the first person to say *Yes* to her all day. "When can we see him?" she said eagerly.

"Her."

"What?"

"It's a woman. And you can probably see her right away, if you come with me."

Aliena and Richard exchanged a delighted look. Aliena could hardly believe the change in their luck.

The girl turned away, and they followed. She led them to a large wooden house on the south side of the High Street. Most of the house was at ground level but it had a small upper story. The girl went up an outside staircase and beckoned them to follow her.

The upstairs was a bedchamber. Aliena looked around her with wide eyes: it was more richly decorated and furnished than any of the rooms at the castle had been, even when Mother was alive. The walls were hung with tapestries, the floor was covered with fur rugs, and the bed was surrounded by embroidered curtains. On a chair like a throne sat a middle-aged woman in a gorgeous gown. She had been beautiful when she was young, Aliena guessed, although now her face was lined and her hair thin.

"This is Mistress Kate," said the girl. "Kate, this girl is penniless and her father's in the jailhouse."

Kate smiled. Aliena smiled back, but she had to force herself: there was something about Kate that she disliked. Kate said: "Take the boy to the kitchen and give him a cup of beer while we talk."

The girl took Richard out. Aliena was glad he would get some beer—perhaps they would give him something to eat as well.

Kate said: "What's your name?"

"Aliena."

"That's unusual. But I like it." She stood up and came close, a little too close. She took Aliena's chin in her hand. "You've got a *very* pretty face." Her breath smelled of wine. "Take off your cloak."

Aliena was puzzled by this inspection, but she submitted to it: it seemed harmless, and after this morning's rejections she did not want to throw away her first decent chance by seeming uncooperative. She shrugged off her cloak, dropped it on a bench, and stood there in the old linen dress the verderer's wife had given her.

Kate walked around her. For some reason she seemed impressed. "My dear girl, you need never want for money, or anything else. If you work for me we'll both be rich."

Aliena frowned. This sounded crazy. All she wanted to do was help with laundry, or cooking, or sewing: she did not see how she could make anybody rich. "What sort of work are you talking about?" she said.

Kate was behind her. She ran her hands down Aliena's sides, feeling her hips, and stood close so that Aliena could feel Kate's breasts pressing against her back. "You've got a beautiful figure," Kate said. "And your skin is lovely. You're high-born, aren't you?"

"My father was the earl of Shiring."

"Bartholomew! Well, well. I remember him—not that he was ever a customer of mine. A very virtuous man, your father. Well, I understand why you're destitute."

So Kate had customers. "What do you sell?" Aliena asked.

Kate did not answer directly. She came around in front of Aliena again, looking at her face. "Are you a virgin, dear?"

Aliena flushed with shame.

"Don't be shy," said Kate. "I see you're not. Well, no matter. Virgins are worth a lot but they don't last, of course." She put her hands on Aliena's hips, leaned forward, and kissed her forehead. "You're so voluptuous, although you don't know it. By the saints, you're irresistible." She slid her hand up from Aliena's hip to her bosom, and gently took one breast in her hand, weighing it and squeezing it slightly, then she leaned forward and kissed Aliena's lips.

Aliena understood everything in a flash: why the girl had smiled at Richard outside the mint, where Kate got her money, what Aliena would have to do if she worked for Kate, and what kind of woman Kate was. She felt foolish for not having understood earlier. For a moment she let Kate kiss her—it was so different from what William Hamleigh had done that she was not in the least repelled—but this was not it, this was not what she would have to do to earn money. She pulled away from Kate's embrace. "You want me to become a whore," she said.

"A lady of pleasure, my dear," said Kate. "Get up late, wear beautiful clothes every day, make men happy, and become rich. You'd be one of the best. There's a look about you. . . . You could charge anything, anything. Believe me, I know."

Aliena shuddered. There had always been a whore or two at the castle—it was necessary in a place where there were so many men without their wives—and they had been regarded as the lowest of the low, the humblest of the womenfolk, below even the sweepers. But it was not the low status that made Aliena tremble with disgust. It was the idea of men such as William Hamleigh walking in and fucking her for a penny. The thought brought back the memory of his big body poised over her, as she lay on the floor with her legs apart, shaking with terror and loathing, waiting for him to penetrate her. The scene came back to her with renewed horror and took away all her poise and confidence. She felt that if she stayed in this house a moment longer it would all happen to her again. She was overcome by a panicky urge to get outside. She backed toward the door. She was frightened of offending Kate, frightened that anyone should be angry with her. "I'm sorry," she mumbled. "Please forgive me, but I couldn't do that, really. . . ."

"Think about it!" Kate said cheerfully. "Come back if you change your mind. I'll still be here."

"Thank you," Aliena said unsteadily. She found the door at last. She opened it and scuttled out. Still upset, she ran down the stairs into the street and went to the front door of the house. She pushed it open but she was frightened to go in. "Richard!" she called. "Richard, come out!" There was no reply. The interior was dimly lit, and she could see nothing but a few vague female figures inside. "Richard, where are you?" she screamed hysterically.

She realized that passersby were staring at her, and that made her more anxious. Suddenly Richard appeared, with a cup of ale in one hand and a chicken leg in the other. "What's the matter?" he said through a mouthful of meat. His tone indicated that he was annoyed at having been disturbed.

She grabbed his arm and pulled. "Come out of there," she said. "It's a whorehouse!"

Several bystanders laughed loudly at this, and one or two called out jeering remarks.

"They might give you some meat," Richard said.

"They want me to be a whore!" she blazed.

"All right, all right," Richard said. He downed his beer, put the cup on the floor inside the door, and stuffed the remains of the chicken leg inside his shirt.

"Come on," Aliena said impatiently, though once again the need to deal with her younger brother had the effect of calming her. He did not seem angered by the idea that someone wanted his sister to become a whore, but he did look regretful at having to leave a place where there was chicken and beer to be had for the asking.

Most of the bystanders walked on, seeing that the fun was over, but one remained. It was the well-dressed woman they had seen in the jailhouse. She had given the jailer a penny, and he had called her Meg. She was looking at Aliena with an expression of curiosity mingled with compassion. Aliena had developed an aversion to being stared at, and she looked away angrily; then the woman spoke to her. "You're in trouble, aren't you?" she said.

A note of kindness in Meg's voice made Aliena turn back. "Yes," she said after a pause. "We're in trouble."

"I saw you at the jailhouse. My husband is in prison—I visit him every day. Why were you there?"

"Our father is there."

"But you didn't go inside."

"We haven't any money to pay the jailer."

Meg looked over Aliena's shoulder at the whorehouse door. "Is that what you're doing here—trying to get money?"

"Yes, but I didn't know what it was until . . ."

"You poor thing," Meg said. "My Annie would have been your age, if she'd lived. . . . Why don't you come to the jailhouse with me tomorrow morning, and between us we'll see if we can persuade Odo to act like a Christian and take pity on two destitute children."

"Oh, that would be wonderful," Aliena said. She was touched. There was no guarantee of success, but the fact that someone was willing to help brought tears to her eyes.

Meg was still looking hard at her. "Have you had any dinner?"

"No. Richard got something in . . . that place."

"You'd better come to my house. I'll give you some bread and meat." She noticed Aliena's wary look, and added: "And you don't have to do anything for it."

Aliena believed her. "Thank you," she said. "You're very kind. Not many people have been kind to us. I don't know how to thank you."

"No need," she said. "Come with me."

Meg's husband was a wool merchant. At his house in the south of town, at his stall in the market on market days, and at the great annual fair held on St. Giles's Hill, he bought fleeces brought to him by peasants from the surrounding countryside. He crammed them into great woolsacks, each holding the fleece of two hundred and forty sheep, and stored them in the barn at the back of his house. Once a year, when the Flemish weavers sent their agents to buy the soft, strong English wool, Meg's husband would sell it all and arrange for the sacks to be shipped via Dover and Boulogne to Bruges and Ghent, where the fleece would be turned into top-quality cloth and sold all over the world at prices far too high for the peasants who kept the sheep. So Meg told Aliena and Richard over dinner, with that warm smile which said that whatever happens, there's no need for people to be unkind to one another.

Her husband had been accused of selling short weight, a crime the city took very seriously, for its prosperity was based on a reputation for honest dealing. Judging by the way Meg spoke of it, Aliena thought he was probably guilty. His absence had made little different to the business, though. Meg had simply taken his place. In winter there was not much to do anyway: she had made a trip to Flanders; assured all her husband's agents that the enterprise was functioning normally; and carried out repairs to the barn, enlarging it a little at the same time. When shearing began she would buy wool just as he had done. She knew how to judge its quality and set a price. She had already been admitted into the merchant's guild of the city, despite the stain on her husband's reputation, for there was a tradition of merchants helping each other's families in times of trouble, and anyway he had not yet been proved guilty.

Richard and Aliena ate her food and drank her wine and sat by her fire talking until it began to get dark outside; then they went back to the priory to sleep. Aliena had nightmares again. This time she dreamed about her father. In the dream he was sitting on a throne in the prison, as tall and pale and authoritative as ever, and when she went to see him she had to bow as if he were the king. Then he spoke to her accusingly, saying she had abandoned him here in prison and gone to live in a whorehouse. She was outraged by the injustice of the charge, and said angrily that *he* had abandoned *her*. She was going to add that he had left her to the mercy of William Hamleigh, but she was reluctant to tell her father what William had done to her; then she saw that William was also in the room, sitting on a bed and eating cherries from a bowl. He spat a cherry pip at her and it hit her cheek, stinging her. Her father smiled and then William started throwing soft cherries at her. They splattered her face and dress, and she began to cry, because although the dress was old it was the only one she had, and now it was blotched all over with cherry juice like bloodstains.

She felt so unbearably sad in the dream that when she woke up and discovered it was not real she felt an enormous sense of relief, even though the reality—that she was homeless and penniless— was much worse than being pelted with soft cherries.

The light of dawn was seeping through the cracks in the walls of the guesthouse. All around her people were waking up and beginning to move around. Soon the monks came in, opened the doors and the shutters, and called everyone to breakfast.

Aliena and Richard ate hurriedly, then went to Meg's house. She was ready to leave. She had made a spicy beef stew to warm up for her husband's dinner, and Aliena told Richard to carry the heavy pot for her. Aliena wished they had something to give Father. She had not thought of it, but even if she had, she could not have bought anything. It was awful to think they could do nothing for him.

They walked up the High Street, entered the castle by the back gate, and then walked past the keep and down the hill to the jail. Aliena recalled what Odo had told her yesterday, when she had asked whether Father was all right. "No, he's not," the jailer had said. "He's dying." She had thought he was exaggerating to be cruel, but now she began to worry. She said to Meg: "Is there anything wrong with my father?"

"I don't know, dear," Meg said. "I've never seen him."

"The jailer said he was dying."

"That man is as mean as a cat. He probably said it just to make you miserable. Anyway, you'll know in a moment."

Aliena was not comforted, despite Meg's good intentions, and she was full of dread as she walked through the doorway into the evil-smelling gloom of the jail.

Odo was warming his hands at the fire in the middle of the lobby. He nodded at Meg and looked at Aliena. "Have you got the money?" he said.

"I'll pay for them," Meg said. "Here's two pennies, one for me and one for them."

A crafty look came over Odo's stupid face, and he said: "It's twopence for them—a penny for each."

"Don't be such a dog," Meg said. "You let them both in, or I'll make trouble for you with the merchant guild, and you'll lose the job."

"All right, all right, no need for threats," he said grumpily. He pointed to an archway in the stone wall to their right. "Bartholomew is that way."

Meg said: "You'll need a light." She drew two candles from the pocket of her cloak and lit them at the fire, then gave one to Aliena. Her face looked troubled. "I hope all will be well," she said, and she kissed Aliena. Then she went quickly through the opposite arch.

"Thank you for the penny," Aliena called after her, but Meg had disappeared into the gloom.

Aliena peered apprehensively in the direction Odo had indicated. Holding the candle up high, she went through the archway, and found herself in a tiny square vestibule. The light of the candle showed three heavy doors, each barred on the outside. Odo called out: "Straight in front of you."

Aliena said: "Lift the bar, Richard."

Richard took the heavy wooden bar out of its brackets and stood it up against the wall. Aliena pushed the door open and sent up a quick silent prayer.

The cell was dark but for the light of her candle. She hesitated in the doorway, peering into the moving shadows. The place smelled like a privy. A voice said: "Who is it?"

Aliena said: "Father?" She made out a dark figure sitting on the straw-covered floor.

"Aliena?" There was incredulity in the voice. "Is that Aliena?" It sounded like Father's voice, but older.

Aliena went closer, holding the candle up. He looked up at her, the candlelight caught his face, and she gasped in horror.

He was hardly recognizable.

He had always been a thin man, but now he looked like a skeleton. He was filthy dirty and dressed in rags. "Aliena!" he said. "It is you!" His face twisted into a smile, and it was like the grin of a skull.

Aliena burst into tears. Nothing could have prepared her for the shock of seeing him so transformed. It was the most dreadful thing imaginable. She knew instantly that he was dying: the vile Odo had told the truth. But he was still alive, still suffering, and painfully pleased to see her. She had been determined to stay calm, but now she lost control completely, and fell to her knees in front of him, weeping with great racking sobs that came from deep inside her.

He leaned forward and put his arms around her, patting her back as if he were comforting a child over a grazed knee or a broken toy. "Don't cry," he said gently. "Not when you've made your father so happy."

Aliena felt the candle taken from her hand. Father said: "And is that tall young man my Richard?"

"Yes, Father," Richard said stiffly.

Aliena put her arms around Father, and felt his bones like sticks in a sack. He was wasting away: there was no flesh beneath his skin. She wanted to say something to him, some words of love or comfort, but she could not speak for sobbing.

"Richard," he was saying, "you've grown! Have you got a beard yet?"

"It's just started, Father, but it's very fair."

Aliena realized that Richard was on the edge of tears and struggling to maintain his composure. He would feel humiliated if he broke down in front of Father, and Father would probably tell him to snap out of it and be a man, which would make it worse. Worrying about Richard, she stopped crying. With an effort she pulled herself together. She hugged Father's appallingly thin body once more; then she withdrew from his embrace, wiped her eyes, and blew her nose on her sleeve.

"Are you both all right?" Father said. His voice was slower than it used to be, and it quavered occasionally. "How have you managed? Where have you been living? They wouldn't tell me anything about you—it was the worst torture they could have devised. But you seem fine—fit and healthy! This is wonderful!"

Mention of torture made Aliena wonder whether he had suffered physical torments, but she did not ask him: she was afraid of what he might tell her. Instead she answered his question with a lie. "We're fine, Father." She knew that the truth would be devastating to him. It would destroy this moment of happiness and fill the last days of his life with an agony of self-reproach. "We've been living at the castle and Matthew has been taking care of us."

"But you can't live there anymore," he said. "The king has made that fat oaf Percy Hamleigh the earl now—he'll have the castle."

So he knew about that. "It's all right," she said. "We've moved out."

He touched her dress, the old linen shift that the verderer's wife had given her. "What's this?" he said sharply. "Have you sold your clothes?"

He was still perceptive, Aliena noted. It would not be easy to deceive him. She decided to tell him part of the truth. "We left the castle in a hurry, and we haven't any clothes."

"Where's Matthew now? Why isn't he with you?"

She had been afraid of this question. She hesitated.

It was only a momentary pause, but he noticed it. "Come! Don't try to hide anything from me!" he said with something of his old authority. "Where's Matthew?"

"He was killed by the Hamleighs," she said. "But they did us no harm." She held her breath. Would he believe her?

"Poor Matthew," he said sorrowfully. "He was never a fighting man. I hope he went straight to heaven."

He had accepted her story. She was relieved. She moved the conversation off this dangerous ground. "We decided to come to Winchester to ask the king to make some provision for us, but he—"

"No use," Father interrupted briskly, before she could explain why they had failed to see the king. "He wouldn't do anything for you."

Aliena was hurt by his dismissive tone. She had done her best, against the odds, and she wanted him to say *Well done*, not *That was a waste of time*. He had always been quick to correct and slow to praise. I ought to be used to it, she thought. Submissively she said: "What should we do now, Father?"

He shifted his sitting position, and there was a clanking noise. Aliena realized with a shock that he was in chains. He said: "I had one chance to hide some money away. It wasn't much of a chance, but I had to take it. I had fifty bezants in a belt under my shirt. I gave the belt to a priest."

"Fifty!" Aliena was surprised. A bezant was a gold coin. They were not minted in England, but came from Byzantium. She had never seen more than one at a time. A bezant was worth twenty-four silver pennies. Fifty were worth . . . she could not figure it out.

"Which priest?" said Richard practically.

"Father Ralph, of the church of St. Michael near the North Gate."

"Is he a good man?" Aliena asked.

"I hope so. I really don't know. On the day the Hamleighs brought me to Winchester, before they locked me up in here, I found myself alone with him, just for a few moments, and I knew it would be my only chance. I gave him the belt, and begged him to keep it for you. Fifty bezants is worth five pounds of silver."

Five pounds. As this news sank in Aliena realized that the money would transform their existence. They would not be destitute; they would no longer have to live from hand to mouth. They could buy bread, and a pair of boots to replace those painful clogs, and even a couple of cheap ponies if they needed to travel. It did not solve all their problems, but it took away that frightening feeling of living constantly on the edge of a life-or-death crisis. She would not have to be thinking all the time of how they were going to survive. Instead she could turn her attention to something constructive—like getting Father out of this awful place. She said: "When we've got the money, what shall we do? We must get you freed."

"I'm not coming out," he said harshly. "Forget about that. If I weren't dying already they'd have hanged me."

Aliena gasped. How could he talk that way?

"Why are you shocked?" he said. "The king has to get rid of me, but this way I won't be on his conscience."

Richard said: "Father, this place is not well guarded while the king is away. With a few men I believe I could break you out."

Aliena knew that was not going to happen. Richard did not have the ability or the experience to organize a rescue, and he was too young to persuade men to follow him. She was afraid Father would wound Richard by pouring scorn on the proposal, but all he said was: "Don't even think about it. If you break in here I'll refuse to go out with you."

Aliena knew there was no point in arguing with him once he had made up his mind. But it broke her heart to think of him ending his days in this stinking jail. However, it occurred to her that there was a lot she could do to make him more comfortable here. She said: "Well, if you're going to stay here, we can clean the place up and get fresh rushes. We'll bring hot food in for you every day. We'll get some candles, and perhaps we could borrow a Bible for you to read. You can have a fire—"

"Stop!" he said. "You're not going to do any of that. I will not have my children wasting their lives hanging around a jailhouse waiting for an old man to die."

Tears came to Aliena's eyes again. "But we can't leave you like this!"

He ignored her, which was his normal response to people who foolishly contradicted him. "Your dear mother had a sister, your Aunt Edith. She lives in the village of Huntleigh, on the road to Gloucester, with her husband, who is a knight. You are to go there."

It occurred to Aliena that they could still see Father at intervals. And perhaps he would permit his in-laws to make him more comfortable. She tried to remember Aunt Edith and Uncle Simon. She had not seen them since Mama died. She had a vague recollection of a thin, nervous woman like her mother and a big, hearty man who ate and drank a lot. "Will they look after us?" she said uncertainly.

"Of course. They're your kin."

Aliena wondered whether that was sufficient reason for a modest knightly family to welcome two large and hungry youngsters into their home; but Father said it would be all right, and she trusted him. "What will we do?" she said.

"Richard will be a squire to his uncle and learn the arts of knighthood. You will be lady-in-waiting to Aunt Edith until you marry."

As they talked, Aliena felt as if she had been carrying a heavy weight for miles, and had not noticed the pain in her back until she put the burden down. Now that Father was taking charge, it seemed to her that the responsibility of the last few days had been far too much for her to bear. And his authority and ability to control the situation, even when he was sick in jail, gave her comfort and took the edge off her sorrow, for it seemed unnecessary to worry about the person who was in charge.

Now he became even more magisterial. "Before you leave me, I want you both to swear an oath."

Aliena was shocked. He had always counseled against oath-taking. *To swear an oath is to put your soul at risk,* he would say. *Never take an oath unless you're sure you would rather die than break it.* And he was here because of an oath: the other barons had broken their word and accepted Stephen as king, but Papa had refused. He would rather die than break his oath, and here he was dying.

"Give me your sword," he said to Richard.

Richard drew his sword and handed it over.

Father took it and reversed it, holding out the hilt. "Kneel down."

Richard knelt in front of Father.

"Put your hand on the hilt." Father paused, as if gathering his strength; then his voice rang out like a peal of bells. "Swear by Almighty God, and Jesus Christ, and all the saints, that you will not rest until you are earl of Shiring and lord of all the lands I ruled."

Aliena was surprised and somewhat awestruck. She had expected Father to demand some general promise, such as to tell the truth always and fear God; but no, he was giving Richard a very specific task, one that might take a lifetime.

Richard took a deep breath and spoke with a shake in his voice. "I swear by Almighty God, and Jesus Christ, and all the saints, that I will not rest until I am earl of Shiring, and lord of all the lands you ruled."

Papa sighed, as if he had completed an onerous task. Then he surprised Aliena again. He turned and proffered the hilt of the sword to her. "Swear by Almighty God, and Jesus Christ, and all the saints, that you will take care of your brother Richard until he has fulfilled his vow."

A sense of doom swamped Aliena. This was to be their fate, then: Richard would avenge Father, and she would take care of Richard. For her it would be a mission of revenge, for if Richard became earl, William Hamleigh would lose his inheritance. It flashed across her mind that no one had asked *her* how she wanted to spend her life; but the foolish thought was gone as fast as it came. This was her destiny, and it was a fit and proper one. She was not unwilling, but she knew this was a fateful moment, and she had a sense of doors closing behind her and the path of her life being fixed irrevocably. She put her hand on the hilt of the sword and took the oath. Her voice surprised her by its strength and resolution. "I swear by Almighty God, and Jesus Christ, and all the saints, that I will take care of my brother Richard until he has fulfilled his vow." She crossed herself. It was done. I've sworn an oath, she thought, and I must die rather than break my word. The thought gave her a kind of angry satisfaction.

"There," Father said, and his voice sounded weak again. "Now you need never come to this place again."

Aliena could not believe he meant it. "Uncle Simon can bring us to see you now and again, and we can make sure you're warm and fed—"

"No," he said sternly. "You have a task to fulfill. You're not going to waste your energies visiting a jail."

She heard that don't-argue note in his voice again, but she could not help protesting against the harshness of his decision. "Then let us come again just once, to bring you a few comforts!"

"I want no comforts."

"Please . . ."

"Never."

She gave up. He was always at least as hard on himself as he was on everyone else. "Very well," she said, and it came out in a sob.

"Now you'd better go," he said.

"Already?"

"Yes. This is a place of despair and corruption and death. Now that I've seen you, and I know you're well, and you've promised to rebuild what we have lost, I'm content. The only thing that could destroy my happiness would be to see you wasting your time visiting a jailhouse. Now go."

"Papa, no!" she protested, although she knew it was no use.

"Listen," he said, and his voice softened at last. "I've lived an honorable life, and now I'm going to die. I've confessed my sins. I'm ready for eternity. Pray for my soul. Go."

Aliena leaned forward and kissed his brow. Her tears fell freely on his face. "Goodbye, Father dear," she whispered. She got to her feet.

Richard bent down and kissed him. "Goodbye, Father," he said unsteadily.

"May God bless you both, and help you keep your vows," Father said.

Richard left him the candle. They went to the door. At the threshold Aliena turned and looked back at him in the unsteady light. His fleshless face was set in an expression of calm determination that was very familiar. She looked at him until tears obscured her vision. Then she turned away, went through the lobby of the jailhouse, and stumbled out into the open air.

III

Richard led the way. Aliena was stunned with grief. It was as if Father had already died; but it was worse, for he was still suffering. She heard Richard asking for directions but she paid no attention. She gave no thought to where they were going until he stopped outside a small wooden church with a lean-to hovel beside it. Looking around, Aliena saw that they were in a poor district of small tumbledown houses and filthy streets in which fierce dogs chased rats through the refuse and barefoot children played in the mud. "This must be St. Michael's," Richard said.

The lean-to at the side of the church had to be the priest's house. It had one shuttered window. The door stood open. They went in.

There was a fire in the middle of the single room. The place was furnished with a roughhewn table, a few stools, and a beer barrel in the corner. The floor was strewn with rushes. Near the fire a man sat on a chair drinking from a large cup. He was a small, thin man of about fifty years, with a red nose and wispy gray hair. He wore ordinary everyday clothes, a dirty undershirt with a brown tunic, and clogs.

"Father Ralph?" said Richard dubiously.

"What if I am?" he replied.

Aliena sighed. Why did people manufacture trouble when there was already so much of it in the world? But she had no energy left for dealing with bad temper, so she left it to Richard, who said: "Does that mean yes?"

The question was answered for them. A voice from outside called: "Ralph? Are you in?" A moment later a middle-aged woman came in and gave the priest a hunk of bread and a large bowl of something that smelled like meat stew. For once the smell of meat did not make Aliena's mouth water: she was too numb even to be hungry. The woman was probably one of Ralph's parishioners, for her clothes were of the same poor quality as his own. He took the food from her without a word and began to eat. She glanced incuriously at Aliena and Richard and went out again.

Richard said: "Well, *Father* Ralph, I am the son of Bartholomew, the former earl of Shiring."

The man paused in his eating and looked up at them. There

was hostility in his face, and something else Aliena could not read—fear? Guilt? He returned his attention to his dinner, but mumbled: "What do you want with me?"

Aliena felt a tug of fear.

"You know what I want," Richard said. "My money. Fifty bezants."

"I don't know what you're talking about," Ralph said.

Aliena stared at him incredulously. This could not be happening. Father had left money for them with this priest—he had said so! Father did not make mistakes about such things.

Richard had gone white. He said: "What do you mean?"

"I mean, I don't know what you're talking about. Now piss off." He took another spoonful of stew.

The man was lying, of course; but what could they do about it? Richard pressed on stubbornly. "My father left money with you—fifty bezants. He told you to give it to me. Where is it?"

"Your father gave me nothing."

"He said he did—"

"He lied, then."

That was one thing you could be sure Father had not done. Aliena spoke for the first time. "You're the liar, and we know it."

Ralph shrugged. "Complain to the sheriff."

"You'll be in trouble if we do. They cut off the hands of thieves in this city."

The shadow of fear briefly crossed the priest's face, but it was gone in a moment, and his reply was defiant. "It will be my word against the word of a jailed traitor—if your father lives long enough to give evidence."

Aliena realized he was right. There would be no independent witnesses to say that Father had given him the money, for the whole idea was that it was a secret, money that could not be taken away by the king or Percy Hamleigh or any of the other carrion crows who flocked around the possessions of a ruined man. Things were just as they had been in the forest, Aliena realized bitterly. People could rob her and Richard with impunity, because they were the children of a fallen noble. Why am I frightened of these men? she asked herself angrily. Why aren't they frightened of me?

Richard looked at her and said in a low voice: "He's right, isn't he?"

"Yes," she said venomously. "There's no point in our complaining to the sheriff." She was thinking of the one time men had been afraid of her: in the forest, when she had stabbed the fat outlaw, and the other one had run away in fear. This priest was no better than the outlaw. But he was old and quite feeble, and he had probably counted on never having to face his victims. Perhaps he could be frightened.

Richard said: "What shall we do, then?"

Aliena gave in to a sudden furious impulse. "Burn down his house," she said. She stepped to the middle of the room and kicked the fire with her wooden clogs, scattering burning logs. The rushes around the fireplace caught immediately.

"Hey!" Ralph yelled. He half rose from his seat, dropping his bread and spilling the stew in his lap; but before he could get to his feet Aliena was on him. She felt completely out of control; she acted without thinking. She pushed him, and he slipped off the chair and tumbled to the floor. She was astonished at how easy it was to knock him down. She fell on him, landing with her knees on his chest and winding him. Mad with rage, she thrust her face close to his and screamed: "You lying thieving godless heathen, I'm going to burn you to death!"

His eyes flicked to one side and he looked even more terrified. Following his glance, Aliena saw that Richard had drawn his sword and was holding it ready to strike. The priest's dirty face went pale, and he whispered: "You're a devil. . . ."

"You're the one who steals money from poor children!" Our of the corner of her eye she saw a stick with one end burning brightly. She picked it up and held the hot end close to his face. "Now I'm going to burn out your eyes, one by one. First the left eye—"

"No, please," he whispered. "Please don't hurt me."

Aliena was thrown by the rapidity with which he crumbled. She realized that the rushes were burning all around her. "Where's the money, then?" she said in a voice which suddenly sounded normal.

The priest was still terrified. "In the church."

"Where exactly?"

"Under the stone behind the altar."

Aliena looked up at Richard. "Guard him while I go and look," she said. "If he moves, kill him."

Richard said: "Allie, the house will burn down."

Aliena went to the corner and lifted the lid of the barrel. It was half full of beer. She grasped the rim and pulled it over. Beer flowed all over the floor, soaking the rushes and putting out the flames.

Aliena walked out of the house. She knew she really had been ready to put out the priest's eyes, but instead of feeling ashamed she was overwhelmed by a sense of her own power. She had resolved not to let people make her a victim, and she had proved she could keep her resolution. She strode up to the front of the church and tried the door. It was fastened with a small lock. She could have gone back to the priest for the key, but instead she drew the dagger from her sleeve, inserted the blade in the crack of the door, and broke the lock. The door swung open and she marched inside.

It was the poorest kind of church. There was no furniture other than the altar and no decoration except for some crude paintings on the limewashed wood of the walls. In one corner, a single candle flickered beneath a small wooden effigy which presumably represented Saint Michael. Aliena's triumph was disturbed for a moment by the realization that five pounds presented a terrible temptation to a man as poor as Father Ralph. Then she put sympathy out of her mind.

The floor was earth but there was a single large stone slab behind the altar. It made a rather obvious hiding place, but of course no one would bother to rob a church as visibly poor as this. Aliena went down on one knee and pushed the stone. It was very heavy and did not move. She began to feel anxious. Richard could not be relied upon to keep Ralph quiet indefinitely. The priest might get away and call for help, and then Aliena would have to prove that the money was hers. Indeed, that might be the least of her worries now that she had attacked a priest and broken into a church. She felt a chill of anxiety as she realized that she was on the wrong side of the law now.

That frisson of fear gave her extra strength. With a mighty heave she moved the stone an inch or two. It covered a hole about a foot deep. She managed to move the stone a little farther. Inside the hole was a wide leather belt. She put her hand in and drew the belt out.

"There!" she said aloud. "I've got it." It gave her great satisfaction to think that she had defeated the dishonest priest and retrieved her father's money. Then, as she stood up, she realized that her victory was qualified: the belt felt suspiciously light. She unfastened the end and tipped out the coins. There were only ten of them. Ten bezants were worth a pound of silver.

What had happened to the rest? Father Ralph had spent it! She became enraged again. Her father's money was all she had in the world and a thieving priest had taken four fifths of it. She marched out of the church, swinging the belt. On the street, a passerby looked startled when he caught her eye, as if there was something odd about her expression. She took no notice and went into the priest's house.

Richard was standing over Father Ralph, with his sword at the priest's throat. As Aliena came through the door she screamed: "Where's the rest of my father's money?"

"Gone," the priest whispered.

She knelt by his head and put her knife to his face. "Gone where?"

"I spent it," he confessed in a voice hoarse with fear.

Aliena wanted to stab him, or beat him, or throw him into a river;

but none of it would do any good. He was telling the truth. She looked at the overturned barrel: a drinking man could get through a great deal of beer. She felt as if she might explode with frustration. "I'd cut off your ear if I could sell it for a penny," she hissed at him. He looked as if he thought she might cut it off anyway.

Richard said anxiously: "He's spent the money. Let's take what we've got and go."

He was right, Aliena realized reluctantly. Her anger began to evaporate, leaving behind a residue of bitterness. There was nothing to be gained by frightening the priest anymore, and the longer they stayed, the more chance there was that someone would come in and cause trouble. She stood up. "All right," she said. She put the gold coins back in the belt and buckled it around her waist beneath her cloak. She pointed a finger at the priest. "I may come back one day and kill you," she spat.

She went out.

She strode away along the narrow street. Richard caught up with her, hurrying. "You were wonderful, Allie!" he said excitedly. "You scared him half to death—and you got the money!"

She nodded. "Yes, I did," she said sourly. She was still tense, but now that her fury had abated she felt deflated and unhappy.

"What shall we buy?" he said eagerly.

"Just a little food for our journey."

"Shan't we buy horses?"

"Not with a pound."

"Still, we could get you some boots."

She considered that. The clogs tortured her but the ground was too cold for bare feet. However, boots were expensive and she was reluctant to spend the money so quickly. "No," she decided. "I'll live a few more days without boots. We'll keep the money for now."

He was disappointed, but he did not dispute her authority. "What food shall we get?"

"Horsebread, hard cheese and wine."

"Let's get some pies."

"They cost too much."

"Oh." He was silent for a moment, then he said: "You're awfully grumpy, Allie."

Aliena sighed. "I know." She thought: Why do I feel this way? I should be proud. I brought us here from the castle, I defended my brother, I found my father, I got our money.

Yes, and I stuck a knife into a fat man's belly, and made my brother kill him, and I held a burning stick to a priest's face, and I was ready to put his eyes out.

"Is it because of Father?" said Richard sympathetically.

"No, it's not," Aliena replied. "It's because of me."

Aliena regretted not buying the boots.

On the road to Gloucester she wore the clogs until they made her feet bleed, then she walked barefoot until she could no longer stand the cold, whereupon she put the clogs on again. She found it helped not to look at her feet: they hurt more when she could see the sores and the blood.

In the hill country there were a lot of poor smallholdings where peasants grew an acre or so of oats or rye and kept a few scrawny animals. Aliena stopped on the outskirts of a village, when she thought they must be near Huntleigh, to speak to a peasant who was shearing a sheep in a fenced yard next to a low, wattle-and-daub farmhouse. He had the sheep's head trapped in a wooden fixture like a stocks, and was cutting its wool with a long-bladed knife. Two more sheep waited uneasily nearby, and one that was already shorn was grazing in the field, looking naked in the cold air.

"It's early for shearing," Aliena said.

The peasant looked up at her and grinned good-humoredly. He was a young man with red hair and freckles, and his sleeves were rolled up, showing hairy arms. "Ah, but I need the money. Better the sheep go cold than I go hungry."

"How much do you get?"

"Penny a fleece. But I have to go to Gloucester to get it, so I lose a day in the field, just when it's spring and there's a lot to do." He was cheerful enough, despite his grumbling.

"What's this village?" Aliena asked him.

"Strangers call it Huntleigh," he said. Peasants never used the name of their village—to them it was just the village. Names were for outsiders. "Who are you?" he asked with frank curiosity. "What brings you here?"

"I'm the niece of Simon of Huntleigh," Aliena said.

"Indeed. Well, you'll find him in the big house. Go back along this road a few yards, then take the path through the fields."

"Thank you."

The village sat in the middle of its plowed fields like a pig in a wallow. There were twenty or so small dwellings clustered around the manor house, which was not much bigger than the home of a prosperous peasant. Aunt Edith and Uncle Simon were not very wealthy, it seemed. A group of men stood outside the manor house with a couple of horses. One of them appeared to be the lord: he wore a scarlet coat. Aliena looked at him more closely. It was twelve or thirteen years since she had seen her Uncle Simon, but she thought this was he. She remembered him as a big man, and now he looked smaller, but no doubt that was because Aliena had grown. His hair was thinning and he had a double chin which she did not recall. Then she heard him say: "He's very high in the wither, this beast," and she recognized the rasping, slightly breathy voice.

She began to relax. From now on they would be fed and clothed and cared for and protected: no more horsebread and hard cheese, no more sleeping in barns, no more walking the roads with one hand on her knife. She would have a soft bed and a new dress and a dinner of roast beef.

Uncle Simon caught her eye. At first he did not know who she was. "Look at this," he said to his men. "A handsome wench and a boy soldier to visit us." Then something else came into his eyes, and Aliena knew he had realized they were not total strangers. "I know you, don't I?" he said.

Aliena said: "Yes, Uncle Simon, you do."

He jumped, as if scared by something. "By the saints! The voice of a ghost!"

Aliena did not understand that, but a moment later he explained. He came over to her, peering hard at her, as if he were about to look at her teeth like a horse; and he said: "Your mother had the same voice, like honey pouring out of a jar. You're as beautiful as she was too, by Christ." He put out his hand to touch her face, and she quickly stepped back out of reach. "But you're as stiff-necked as your damned father, I can see that. I suppose he sent you here, did he?"

Aliena bristled. She did not like to hear Father referred to as "your damned father." But if she protested, he would take it as further proof that she was stiff-necked; so she bit her tongue and answered him submissively. "Yes. He said Aunt Edith would take care of us."

"Well, he was wrong," Uncle Simon said. "Aunt Edith is dead. What's more, since your father's disgrace, I've lost half of my lands to that fat rogue Percy Hamleigh. It's hard times here. So you can turn right around and go back to Winchester. I'm not taking you in."

Aliena was shaken. He seemed so hard. "But we're your kin!" she said.

He had the grace to look slightly ashamed, but his reply was harsh. "You're not my kin. You used to be my first wife's niece. Even when Edith was alive she never saw her sister, because of that pompous ass your mother married."

"We'll work," Aliena pleaded. "We're both willing—"

"Don't waste your breath," he said. "I'm not having you."

Aliena was shocked. He was so definite. It was clear there was no point in arguing with him or begging. But she had suffered so many disappointments and reverses of this kind that she felt bitter rather than sad. A week ago something like this would have made her burst into tears. Now she felt like spitting at him. She said: "I'll remember this when Richard is the earl and we take the castle back."

He laughed. "Shall I live so long?"

Aliena decided not to stay and be humiliated any longer. "Let's go," she said to Richard. "We'll look after ourselves." Uncle Simon had already turned away and was looking at the horse with the high wither. The men with him were a little embarrassed. Aliena and Richard walked away.

When they were out of earshot, Richard said plaintively: "What are we going to do, Allie?"

"We're going to show these heartless people that we're better than they are," she said grimly, but she did not feel brave, she was just full of hatred, for Uncle Simon, for Father Ralph, for Odo Jailer, for the outlaws, for the verderer, and most of all for William Hamleigh.

"It's a good thing we've got some money," Richard said.

It was. But the money would not last forever. "We can't just spend it," she said as they walked along the path that led back to the main road. "If we use it all up on food and things like that, we'll just be destitute again when it's all gone. We've got to *do* something with it."

"I don't see why," Richard said. "I think we should buy a pony."

She stared at him. Was he joking? There was no smile on his face. He simply did not understand. "We've got no position, no title, and no land," she said patiently. "The king won't help us. We can't get ourselves hired as laborers—we tried, in Winchester, and no one would take us on. But somehow we have to make a living and turn you into a knight."

"Oh," he said. "I see."

She could tell that he did not really see. "We need to establish ourselves in some occupation that will feed us and give us at least a chance of making enough money to buy you a good horse."

"You mean I should become an apprentice to a craftsman?"

Aliena shook her head. "You have to become a knight, not a carpenter. Have we ever met anyone who had an independent livelihood but no skills?"

"Yes," Richard said unexpectedly. "Meg in Winchester."

He was right. Meg was a wool merchant although she had never been an apprentice. "But Meg has a market stall." They passed the red-haired peasant who had given them directions. His four shorn sheep were grazing in the field, and he was tying their fleeces into bundles with cord made of reeds. He looked up from his work and waved. It was people such as he who took their wool into the towns and sold it to wool merchants. But the merchant had to have a place of business. . . .

Or did he?

An idea was forming in Aliena's mind.

She turned back abruptly.

Richard said: "Where are you going?"

She was too excited to answer him. She leaned on the peasant's fence. "How much did you say you could get for your wool?"

"Penny a fleece," he said.

"But you have to spend all day going to Gloucester and back."

"That's the trouble."

"Suppose I buy your wool? That would save you the journey."

Richard said: "Allie! We don't need wool!"

"Shut up, Richard." She did not want to explain her idea to him now—she was impatient to try it out on the peasant.

The peasant said: "That would be a kindness." But he looked dubious, as if he suspected trickery.

"I couldn't offer you a penny a fleece, though."

"Aha! I thought there'd be a snag."

"I could give you twopence for four fleeces."

"But they're worth a penny each!" he protested.

"In Gloucester. This is Huntleigh."

He shook his head. "I'd rather have fourpence and lose a day in the field than have twopence and gain a day."

"Suppose I offer you threepence for four fleeces."

"I lose a penny."

"And save a day's journey."

He looked bewildered. "I never heard of nothing like this before."

"It's as if I were a carter, and you paid me a penny to take your wool to market." She found his slowness exasperating. "The question is, is an extra day in the fields worth a penny to you, or not?"

"It depends what I do with the day," he said thoughtfully.

Richard said: "Allie, what are we going to do with four fleeces?"

"Sell them to Meg," she said impatiently. "For a penny each. That way we're a penny better off."

"But we have to go all the way to Winchester for a penny!"

"No, stupid. We buy wool from fifty peasants and take the whole lot to Winchester. Don't you see? We could make fifty pennies! We could feed ourselves *and* save up for a good horse for you!"

She turned back to the peasant. His cheerful grin had gone, and he was scratching his ginger-colored head. Aliena was sorry she had perplexed him, but she wanted him to accept her offer. If he did, she would know it was possible for her to fulfill her vow to her father. But peasants were stubborn. She felt like taking him by the collar and shaking him. Instead, she reached inside her cloak and fumbled in her purse. They had changed the gold bezants for silver pennies at the goldsmith's house in Winchester, and now she took out three pennies and showed them to the peasant. "Here," she said. "Take it or leave it."

The sight of the silver helped the peasant make up his mind. "Done," he said, and took the money.

Aliena smiled. It looked as if she might have found the answer.

That night she used a bundled fleece for a pillow. The smell of sheep reminded her of Meg's house.

When she woke up in the morning she discovered that she was not pregnant.

Things were looking up.

Four weeks after Easter, Aliena and Richard entered Winchester with an old horse pulling a homemade cart bearing a huge sack which contained two hundred and forty fleeces—the precise number which made up a standard woolsack.

At that point they discovered taxes.

Previously they had always entered the city without attracting any attention, but now they learned why city gates were narrow and constantly manned by customs officers. There was a toll of one penny for every cartload of goods taken into Winchester. Fortunately, they still had a few pennies left, and they were able to pay; otherwise they would have been turned away.

Most of the fleeces had cost them between one half and three quarters of a penny each. They had paid seventy-two pence for the old horse, and the rickety cart had been thrown in. Most of the rest of the money had been spent on food. But tonight they would have a pound of silver *and* a horse and cart.

Aliena's plan was then to go out again and buy another sackful of fleeces, and to do the same again and again until all the sheep were shorn. By the end of the summer she wanted to have the money to buy a strong horse and a new cart.

She felt very excited as she led their old nag through the streets toward Meg's house. By the end of the day she would have proved that she could take care of herself and her brother without any help from anyone. It made her feel very mature and independent. She was in charge of her own destiny. She had had nothing from the king, she did not need relatives, and she had no use for a husband.

She was looking forward to seeing Meg, who had been her inspiration. Meg was one of the few people who had helped Aliena without trying to rob, rape or exploit her. Aliena had a lot of questions to ask her about business in general and the wool trade in particular.

It was market day, so it took them some time to drive their cart through the crowded city to Meg's street. At last they arrived at her house. Aliena stepped into the hall. A woman she had never seen before was standing there. "Oh!" said Aliena, and she stopped short.

"What is it?" said the woman.

"I'm a friend of Meg's."

"She doesn't live here anymore," the woman said curtly.

"Oh, dear." Aliena saw no need for her to be so brusque. "Where has she moved to?"

"She's gone with her husband, who left this city in disgrace," the woman said.

Aliena was disappointed and afraid. She had been counting on Meg to make the sale of the wool easy. "That's terrible news!"

"He was a dishonest tradesman, and if I were you I wouldn't boast about being a friend of hers. Now clear off."

Aliena was outraged that someone should speak ill of Meg. "I don't care what her husband may have done, Meg was a fine woman and greatly superior to the thieves and whores that inhabit this stinking city," she said, and she went out before the woman could think of a rejoinder.

Her verbal victory gave her only momentary consolation. "Bad news," she said to Richard. "Meg has left Winchester."

"Is the person who lives there now a wool merchant?" he said.

"I didn't ask. I was too busy telling her off." Now she felt foolish.

"What shall we do, Allie?"

"We've got to sell these fleeces," she said anxiously. "We'd better go to the marketplace."

They turned the horse around and retraced their steps to the High Street, then threaded their way through the crowds to the market, which was between the High Street and the cathedral. Aliena led the horse and Richard walked behind the cart, pushing it when the horse needed help, which was most of the time. The marketplace was a seething mass of people squeezing along the narrow aisles between the stalls, their progress constantly delayed by carts such as Aliena's. She stopped and stood on top of her sack of wool and looked for wool merchants. She could see only one. She got down and headed the horse in that direction.

The man was doing good business. He had a large space roped off with a shed behind it. The shed was made of hurdles, light timber frames filled in with woven twigs and reeds, and it was obviously a temporary structure erected each market day. The merchant was a swarthy man whose left arm ended at the elbow. Attached to his stump he had a wooden comb, and whenever a fleece was offered to him he would put his arm into the wool, tease out a portion with the comb, and feel it with his right hand before giving a price. Then he would use the comb and his right hand together to count out the number of pennies he had agreed to pay. For large purchases he weighed the pennies in a balance.

Aliena pushed her way through the crowd to the bench. A peasant offered the merchant three rather thin fleeces tied together with a leather belt. "A bit sparse," said the merchant. "Three farthings each." A farthing was a quarter of a penny. He counted out two pennies, then took a small hatchet and with a quick, practiced stroke cut a third penny into quarters. He gave the peasant the two pennies and one of the quarters. "Three times three farthings is twopence and a farthing." The peasant took the belt off the fleeces and handed them over.

Next, two young men dragged a whole sack of wool up to the counter. The merchant examined it carefully. "It's a full sack, but the quality's poor," he said. "I'll give you a pound."

Aliena wondered how he could be so sure the sack was full. Perhaps you could tell with practice. She watched him weigh out a pound of silver pennies.

Some monks were approaching with a huge cart piled high with sacks of wool. Aliena decided to get her business done before the monks. She beckoned to Richard, and he dragged their sack of wool off the cart and brought it up to the counter.

The merchant examined the wool. "Mixed quality," he said. "Half a pound."

"What?" Aliena said incredulously.

"A hundred and twenty pennies," he said.

Aliena was horrified. "But you just paid a pound for a sack!"

"It's because of the quality."

"You paid a pound for poor quality!"

"Half a pound," he repeated stubbornly.

The monks arrived and crowded the stall, but Aliena was not going to move: her livelihood was at stake, and she was more frightened of destitution than she was of the merchant. "Tell me why," she insisted. "There's nothing wrong with the wool, is there?"

"No."

"Then give me what you paid those two men."

"No."

"Why not?" she almost screamed.

"Because nobody pays a girl what they would pay a man."

She wanted to strangle him. He was offering her less than she had paid. It was outrageous. If she accepted his price, all her work would have been for nothing. Worse than that, her scheme for providing a livelihood for herself and her brother would have failed, and her brief period of independence and self-sufficiency would be over. And why? Because he would not pay a girl the same as he paid a man!

The leader of the monks was looking at her. She hated people to stare at her. "Stop staring!" she said rudely. "Just do your business with this godless peasant."

"All right," the monk said mildly. He beckoned to his colleagues and they dragged up a sack.

Richard said: "Take the ten shillings, Allie. Otherwise we'll have nothing but a sack of wool!"

Aliena stared angrily at the merchant as he examined the monks' wool. "Mixed quality," he said. She wondered if he ever pronounced wool good quality. "A pound and twelvepence a sack."

Why did it have to happen that Meg went away? thought Aliena bitterly. Everything would have been all right if she had stayed.

"How many sacks have you got?" said the merchant.

A young monk in novice's robes said: "Ten," but the leader said: "No, eleven." The novice looked as if he was inclined to argue, but he said nothing.

"That's eleven and a half pounds of silver, plus twelvepence." The merchant began to weigh out the money.

"I won't give in," Aliena said to Richard. "We'll take the wool somewhere else—Shiring, perhaps, or Gloucester."

"All that way! And what if we can't sell it there?"

He was right—they might have the same trouble elsewhere. The real difficulty was that they had no status, no support, no protection. The merchant would not dare to insult the monks, and even the poor peasants could probably cause trouble for him if he dealt unfairly with them, but there was no risk to a man who tried to cheat two children with nobody in the world to help them.

The monks were dragging their sacks into the merchant's shed. As each one was stashed, the merchant handed to the chief monk a weighed pound of silver and twelve pennies. When all the sacks were in, there was a bag of silver still on the counter.

"That's only ten sacks," said the merchant.

"I told you there was only ten," the novice said to the chief monk.

"This is the eleventh," said the chief monk, and he put his hand on Aliena's sack.

She stared at him in astonishment.

The merchant was equally surprised. "I've offered her half a pound," he said.

"I've bought it from her," the monk said. "And I've sold it to you." He nodded to the other monks and they dragged Aliena's sack into the shed.

The merchant looked disgruntled, but he handed over the last pound bag and twelve more pennies. The monk gave the money to Aliena.

She was dumbstruck. Everything had been going wrong and now this complete stranger had rescued her—after she had been rude to him, too!

Richard said: "Thank you for helping us, Father."

"Give thanks to God," said the monk.

Aliena did not know what to say. She was thrilled. She hugged the money to her chest. How could she thank him? She stared at her savior. He was a small, slight, intense-looking man. His movements were quick and he looked alert, like a small bird with dull plumage but bright eyes. His eyes were blue, in fact. The fringe of hair around his shaved pate was black streaked with gray, but his face was young. Aliena began to realize that he was vaguely familiar. Where had she seen him before?

The monk's mind was going along the same path. "You don't remember me, but I know you," he said. "You're the children of Bartholomew, the former earl of Shiring. I know you've suffered great misfortunes, and I'm glad to have a chance to help you. I'll buy your wool anytime."

Aliena wanted to kiss him. Not only had he saved her today, he was prepared to guarantee her future! She found her tongue at last. "I don't know how to thank you," she said. "God knows, we need a protector."

"Well, now you have two," he said. "God, and me."

Aliena was profoundly moved. "You've saved my life, and I don't even know who you are," she said.

"My name is Philip," he said. "I'm the prior of Kingsbridge."

Chapter 7

I T WAS A GREAT DAY when Tom Builder took the stonecutters to the quarry.

They went a few days before Easter, fifteen months after the old cathedral burned down. It had taken this long for Prior Philip to amass enough cash to hire craftsmen.

Tom had found a forester and a master quarryman in Salisbury, where the Bishop Roger's palace was almost complete. The forester and his men had now been at work for two weeks, finding and felling tall pine trees and mature oaks. They were concentrating their efforts on the woods near the river, upstream from Kingsbridge, for it was very costly to transport materials on the winding mud roads, and a lot of money could be saved by simply floating the wood downstream to the building site. The timber would be roughly lopped for scaffolding poles, carefully shaped into templates to guide the masons and stonecarvers, or—in the case of the tallest trees—set aside for future use as roof beams. Good wood was now arriving in Kingsbridge at a steady rate and all Tom had to do was pay the foresters every Saturday evening.

The quarrymen had arrived over the last few days. The master quarryman, Otto Blackface, had brought with him his two sons, both of whom were stonecutters; four grandsons, all apprentices; and two laborers, one his cousin and the other his brother-in-law. Such nepotism was normal, and Tom had no objection to it: a family group usually made a good team.

As yet there were no craftsmen working in Kingsbridge, on the site itself, other than Tom and the priory's carpenter. It was a good idea to stockpile some materials. But soon Tom would hire the people who formed the backbone of the building team, the masons. They were the men who put one stone on another and made the walls rise. Then the great enterprise would begin. Tom walked with a spring in his step: this was what he had hoped for and worked toward for ten years.

The first mason to be hired, he had decided, would be his own son Alfred. Alfred was sixteen years old, approximately, and had acquired the basic skills of a mason: he could cut stones square and build a true wall. As soon as hiring began, Alfred would get full wages.

Tom's other son, Jonathan, was fifteen months old and growing fast. A sturdy child, he was the pampered pet of the whole monastery. Tom had worried a little, at first, about the baby being looked after by the half-witted Johnny Eightpence, but Johnny was as attentive as any mother and had more time than most mothers to devote to his charge. The monks still did not suspect that Tom was Jonathan's father, and now they probably never would.

Seven-year-old Martha had a gap in her front teeth and she missed Jack. She was the one who worried Tom most, for she needed a mother.

There was no shortage of women who would like to marry Tom and take care of his little daughter. He was not an unattractive man, he knew, and his livelihood looked secure now that Prior Philip was starting to build in earnest. Tom had moved out of the guesthouse and had built himself a fine two-room house, with a chimney, in the village. Eventually, as master builder in charge of the whole project, he could expect a salary and benefits that would be the envy of many minor gentry. But he could not conceive of marrying anyone but Ellen. He was like a man who has got used to drinking the finest wine, and now finds that everyday wine tastes like vinegar. There was a widow in the village, a plump, pretty woman with a smiling face and a generous bosom and two well-behaved children, who had baked several pies for him and kissed him longingly at the Christmas feast, and would marry him as quick as he liked. But he knew that he would be unhappy with her, for he would always hanker after the excitement of being married to the unpredictable, infuriating, bewitching, passionate Ellen.

Ellen had promised to come back, one day, to visit. Tom felt fiercely certain that she would keep that promise, and he clung to it stubbornly, even though it was more than a year since she had walked out. And when she did come back he was going to ask her to marry him.

He thought she might accept him now. He was no longer destitute: he could feed his own family and hers too. He felt that Alfred and Jack could be prevented from fighting, if they were handled right. If Jack were made to work, Alfred would not resent him so badly, Tom thought. He was going to offer to take Jack as an apprentice. The lad had shown an interest in building, he was as bright as a button, and in a year or so he would be big enough for the heavy work. Then Alfred would not be able to say that Jack was idle. The other problem was that Jack could read and Alfred could not. Tom was going to ask Ellen to teach Alfred to read and write. She could give him lessons every Sunday. Then Alfred would be able to feel every bit as good as Jack. The boys would be equal, both educated, both working, and before long much the same size.

He knew Ellen had really liked living with him, despite all their trials. She liked his body and she liked his mind. She would want to come back to him.

Whether he would be able to square things with Prior Philip was another matter. Ellen had insulted Philip's religion rather decisively. It was hard to imagine anything more offensive to a prior than what she had done. Tom had not yet solved that problem.

Meanwhile, all his intellectual energy was employed in planning the cathedral. Otto and his team of stonecutters would build a rough lodge for themselves at the quarry, where they could sleep at night. When they were settled in, they would build real houses, and those who were married would bring their families to live with them.

Of all the building crafts, quarrying required the least skill and the most muscle. The master quarryman did the brainwork: he decided which zones would be mined and in what order; he arranged for ladders and lifting gear; if a sheer face was to be worked he would design scaffolding; he made sure there was a constant supply of tools coming from the smithy. Actually digging out the stones was relatively simple. The quarryman would use an iron-headed pickax to make an initial groove in the rock, then deepen it with a hammer and chisel. When the groove was big enough to weaken the rock, he would drive a wooden wedge into it. If he had judged his rock rightly, it would split exactly where he wanted.

Laborers removed the stones from the quarry, either carrying them on stretchers or lifting them with a rope attached to a huge winding wheel. In the lodge, stonecutters with axes would hack the stones roughly into the shape specified by the master builder. Accurate carving and shaping would be done at Kingsbridge, of course.

The biggest problem would be transport. The quarry was a day's journey from the building site, and a carter would probably charge fourpence a trip—and he could not carry more than eight or nine of the big stones without breaking his cart or killing his horse. As soon as the quarrymen were settled in, Tom had to explore the area and see whether there were any waterways that could be used to shorten the journey.

They had set off from Kingsbridge at daybreak. As they walked through the forest, the trees arching over the road made Tom think of the piers of the cathedral he would build. The new leaves were just coming out. Tom had always been taught to decorate the cushion capitals on top of the piers with scrolls or zigzags, but now it occurred to him that decorations in the shape of leaves would look rather striking.

They made good time, so that by midafternoon they were in the vicinity of the quarry. To his surprise, Tom heard in the distance the sound of metal clanging on rock, as if someone was working there. Technically the quarry belonged to the earl of Shiring, Percy Hamleigh, but the king had given Kingsbridge Priory the right to mine it for the cathedral. Perhaps, Tom speculated, Earl Percy intended to work the quarry for his own benefit at the same time as the priory worked it. The king probably had not specifically prohibited that, but it would cause a lot of inconvenience.

As they drew nearer, Otto, a dark-skinned man with a rough manner, frowned at the sound, but he said nothing. The other men muttered to one another uneasily. Tom ignored them but he walked faster, impatient to find out what was going on.

The road curved through a patch of woodland and ended at the base of a hill. The hill itself was the quarry, and a huge bite had been taken out of its side by past quarrymen. Tom's initial impression was that it would be easy to work: a hill was bound to be better than a pit, for it was always less trouble to lower stones from a height than to lift them out of a hole.

The quarry was being worked, no question of that. There was a lodge at the foot of the hill, a sturdy scaffold reaching twenty feet or more up the scarred hillside, and a stack of stones waiting to be collected. Tom could see at least ten quarrymen. Ominously, there were a couple of hard-faced men-at-arms lounging outside the lodge, throwing stones at a barrel.

"I don't like the look of this," said Otto.

Tom did not like it either, but he pretended to be unperturbed. He marched into the quarry as if he owned it, and walked swiftly toward the two men-at-arms. They scrambled to their feet with the startled, faintly guilty air of sentries who have been on guard for too many uneventful days. Tom quickly looked over their weapons: each had a sword and a dagger, and they wore heavy leather jerkins, but they had no armor. Tom himself had a mason's hammer hanging from his belt. He was in no position to get into a fight. He walked straight at the two men without speaking, then at the last minute turned aside and walked around them, and continued on to the lodge. They looked at one another, unsure what to do: if Tom had been smaller, or had not had a hammer, they might have been quicker to stop him, but now it was too late.

Tom went into the lodge. It was a spacious wood building with a fireplace. Clean tools hung around the walls and there was a big stone in the corner for sharpening them. Two stonecutters stood at a massive wooden bench called a banker, trimming stones with axes. "Greetings, brothers," Tom said, using the form of address of one craftsman to another. "Who's the master here?"

"I'm the master quarryman," said one of them. "I'm Harold of Shiring."

"I'm the master builder at Kingsbridge Cathedral. My name is Tom."

"Greetings, Tom Builder. What are you here for?"

Tom studied Harold for a moment before answering. He was a pale, dusty man with small dusty-green eyes, which he narrowed when he spoke, as if he were always blinking away stone dust. He leaned casually on the banker, but he was not as relaxed as he pretended. He was nervous, wary and apprehensive. He knows exactly why I'm here, Tom thought. "I've brought my master quarryman to work here, of course."

The two men-at-arms had followed Tom in, and Otto and his team had come in behind them. Now one or two of Harold's men also crowded in, curious to see what the fuss was about.

Harold said: "The quarry is owned by the earl. If you want to take stone you'll have to see him."

"No, I won't," Tom said. "When the king gave the quarry to Earl Percy, he also gave Kingsbridge Priory the right to take stone. We don't need any further permission."

"Well, we can't all work it, can we?"

"Perhaps we can," said Tom. "I wouldn't want to deprive your men of employment. There's a whole hill of rock—enough for two cathedrals and more. We should be able to find a way to manage the quarry so that we can all cut stone here."

"I can't agree to that," said Harold. "I'm employed by the earl."

"Well, I'm employed by the prior of Kingsbridge, and my men start work here tomorrow morning, whether you like it or not."

One of the men-at-arms spoke up then. "You won't be working here tomorrow or any other day."

Until this moment Tom had been clinging to the idea that

although Percy was violating the spirit of the royal edict by mining the quarry himself, if he was pushed he would adhere to the letter of the agreement, and permit the priory to take stone. But this man-at-arms had obviously been instructed to turn the priory's quarrymen away. That was a different matter. Tom realized, with sinking spirits, that he was not going to get any stone without a fight.

The man-at-arms who had spoken was a short, stocky fellow of about twenty-five years, with a pugnacious expression. He looked stupid but stubborn—the hardest type to reason with. Tom gave him a challenging look and said: "Who are you?"

"I'm a bailiff for the earl of Shiring. He's told me to guard this quarry, and that's what I'm going to do."

"And how do you propose to do it?"

"With this sword." He touched the hilt of the weapon at his belt.

"And what do you think the king will do to you when you're brought before him for breaking his peace?"

"I'll take my chances."

"But there are only two of you," Tom said in a reasonable tone of voice. "We're seven men and four boys, and we have the king's permission to work here. If we kill you, we won't hang."

Both men-at-arms looked thoughtful, but before Tom could press his advantage, Otto spoke. "Just a minute," he said to Tom. "I brought my people here to cut stones, not fight."

Tom's heart sank. If the quarrymen were not prepared to make a stand, there was no hope. "Don't be so timid!" he said. "Are you going to let yourselves be deprived of work by a couple of bully-boys?"

Otto looked surly. "I'm not going to fight armed men," he replied. "I've been earning steadily for ten years and I'm not that desperate for work. Besides, *I* don't know the rights and wrongs of this—as far as I'm concerned it's your word against theirs."

Tom looked at the rest of Otto's team. Both the stonecutters wore the same obstinate look as Otto. Of course, they would follow his lead: he was their father as well as their master. And Tom could see Otto's point. Indeed, if he were in Otto's position he would probably take the same line. He would not get into a brawl with armed men unless he was desperate.

But knowing that Otto was being reasonable gave Tom no comfort; in fact it made him even more frustrated. He decided to give it one more try. "There won't be any fighting," he said. "They know the king will hang them if they hurt us. Let's just make our fire, and settle down for the night, and start work in the morning."

Mentioning the night was a mistake. One of Otto's sons said: "How could we sleep, with these murdering villains nearby?"

The others murmured agreement.

"We'll set watches," Tom said desperately.

Otto shook his head decisively. "We're leaving tonight. Now."

Tom looked around at the men and saw that he was defeated. He had set out this morning with such high hopes, and he could hardly believe that his plans had been frustrated by these petty thugs. It was too galling for words. He could not resist a bitter parting shot. "You're going against the king, and that's a dangerous business," he said to Harold. "You tell the earl of Shiring that. And tell him that I'm Tom Builder of Kingsbridge, and if I ever get my hands around his fat neck I might just squeeze it until he chokes."

Johnny Eightpence made a miniature monk's robe for little Jonathan, complete with wide sleeves and a hood. The tiny figure looked so fetching in it that he melted everyone's heart, but it was not very practical: the hood kept falling forward, obscuring his vision, and when he crawled the robe got in the way of his knees.

In the middle of the afternoon, when Jonathan had had his nap (and the monks had had theirs), Prior Philip came across the baby, with Johnny Eightpence, in what had been the nave of the church, and was now the novices' playground. This was the time of day when the novices were allowed to let off steam, and Johnny was watching them play tag while Jonathan investigated the network of pegs and cord with which Tom Builder had laid out the ground plan of the east end of the new cathedral.

Philip stood beside Johnny for a few moments in companionable silence, watching the youngsters race around. Philip was very fond of Johnny, who made up for his lack of brains by having an extraordinarily good heart.

Jonathan was on his feet now, leaning against a stake Tom had driven into the ground where the north porch would be. He held on to the cord attached to the stake, and with that unsteady support took a couple of awkward, deliberate steps. "He'll be walking soon," Philip said to Johnny.

"He keeps trying, Father, but he generally falls on his bottom."

Philip crouched down and reached out his hands to Jonathan. "Walk to me," he said. "Come on."

Jonathan grinned, showing miscellaneous teeth. He took another step holding on to Tom's cord. Then he pointed at Philip, as if that would help, and with a sudden access of boldness, he crossed the intervening space with three rapid, decisive steps.

Philip caught him in his arms and said: "Well done!" He

hugged him, feeling as proud as if the achievement were his, not the baby's.

Johnny was equally excited. "He walked! He walked!"

Jonathan struggled to be put down. Philip set him on his feet, to see if he would walk again; but he had had enough for one day, and he immediately dropped to his knees and crawled to Johnny.

Some of the monks had been scandalized, Philip recalled, when he had brought Johnny and baby Jonathan to Kingsbridge; but Johnny was easy to deal with so long as you did not forget that he was essentially a child in a man's body; and Jonathan had overcome all opposition by sheer force of personal charm.

Jonathan had not been the only cause of unrest during that first year. Having voted for a good provider, the monks felt cheated when Philip introduced an austerity drive to reduce the priory's day-to-day expenses. Philip had been a little hurt: he felt he had made it clear that his top priority would be the new cathedral. The monastic officers had also resisted his plan to take away their financial independence, even though they knew perfectly well that without reforms the priory was headed for ruin. And when he had spent money on enlarging the monastery's flocks of sheep there had almost been a mutiny. But monks were essentially people who wanted to be told what to do; and Bishop Waleran, who might have encouraged the rebels, had spent most of the year going to Rome and coming back; so in the end muttering was as far as the monks had got.

Philip had suffered some lonely moments, but he was sure results would vindicate him. His policies were already bearing fruit in a very satisfying way. The price of wool had risen again, and Philip had already started shearing: that was why he could afford to hire foresters and quarrymen. As the financial position improved and cathedral building progressed, his position as prior would become unassailable.

He gave Johnny Eightpence an affectionate pat on the head and walked through the building site. With some help from priory servants and younger monks, Tom and Alfred had made a start on digging the foundations. However, they were only five or six feet deep as yet. Tom had told Philip that the foundation holes would have to be twenty-five feet deep in places. He would need a large force of laborers, plus some lifting gear, to dig so far down.

The new church would be bigger than the old one, but it would still be small for a cathedral. A part of Philip wanted it to be the longest, highest, richest and most beautiful cathedral in the kingdom, but he suppressed the wish, and told himself to be grateful for any kind of church.

He went into Tom's shed and looked at the woodwork on the bench. The builder had spent most of the winter in here, working with an iron measuring stick and a set of fine chisels, making what he called templates—wooden models for the masons to use as guides when they were cutting stones into shape. Philip had watched with admiration while Tom, a big man with big hands, precisely and painstakingly carved the wood into perfect curves and square corners and exact angles. Now Philip picked up one of the templates and examined it. It was shaped like the edge of a daisy, a quarter-circle with several round projections like petals. What sort of stone needed to be that shape? He found that these things were hard to visualize, and he was constantly impressed by the power of Tom's imagination. He looked at Tom's drawings, engraved on plaster in wooden frames, and eventually he decided that he was holding a template for the piers of the arcade, which would look like clusters of shafts. Philip had thought they would actually be clusters of shafts, but now he realized that would be an illusion: the piers would be solid stone columns with shaft-like decorations.

Five years, Tom had said, and the east end would be finished. Five years, and Philip would be able to hold services in a cathedral again. All he had to do was find the money. This year it had been hard to scrape together enough cash to make a modest start, because his reforms were slow to take effect; but next year, after he had sold the new spring's wool, he would be able to hire more craftsmen and begin to build in earnest.

The bell rang for vespers. Philip left the little shed and walked to the crypt entrance. Glancing over at the priory gate, he was astonished to see Tom Builder coming in with all the quarrymen. Why were they back? Tom had said he would be away for a week and the quarrymen were to have stayed there indefinitely. Philip hurried to meet them.

As he came close he saw that they looked tired and dispirited, as if something terribly discouraging had happened. "What is it?" he said. "Why are you here?"

"Bad news," said Tom Builder.

Philip simmered with fury all through vespers. What Earl Percy had done was outrageous. There was no doubt about the rights and wrongs of the case, no ambiguity about the king's instructions: the earl had been there himself when the announcement was made, and the priory's right to mine the quarry was enshrined in a charter. Philip's right foot tapped the stone floor of the crypt in an urgent, angry rhythm. He was being robbed. Percy might as well steal pennies from a church treasury. There was no shred of an excuse for it. Percy was flagrantly defying both God and the king. But the worst of it was that Philip could not build the new cathedral unless he got the stone for nothing from that quarry. He was already working with a bare-minimum budget, and if he had to pay the market price for his stone, and transport it from even farther away, he could not build at all. He would have to wait another year or more, and then it would be six or seven years before he could hold services in a cathedral again. The thought was too much to bear.

He held an emergency chapter immediately after vespers and told the monks the news.

He had developed a technique for handling chapter meetings. Remigius, the sub-prior, still bore a grudge against Philip for defeating him in the election, and he often let his resentment show when monastery business was discussed. He was a conservative, unimaginative, pedantic man, and his whole approach to the running of the priory conflicted with Philip's. The brothers who had supported Remigius in the election tended to back him in chapter: Andrew, the apoplectic sacrist; Pierre, the circuitor, who was responsible for discipline and had the narrow-minded attitudes that seemed to go with the job; and John Small, the lazy treasurer. Similarly, Philip's closest colleagues were the men who had campaigned for him: Cuthbert Whitehead, the old cellarer; and young Milius, to whom Philip had given the newly created post of bursar, controller of the priory's finances. Philip always let Milius argue with Remigius. Philip had normally discussed anything important with Milius before the meeting, and when he had not, Milius could be relied on to present a point of view close to Philip's own. Then Philip could sum up like an impartial arbiter, and although Remigius rarely got his way, Philip would often accept some of his arguments, or adopt part of his proposal, to maintain the feeling of consensus government.

The monks were enraged by what Earl Percy had done. They had all rejoiced when King Stephen had given the priory unlimited free timber and stone, and now they were scandalized that Percy should defy the king's order.

When the protests died down, however, Remigius had another point to make. "I remember saying this a year ago," he began. "The pact according to which the quarry is owned by the earl but we have quarrying rights was always unsatisfactory. We should have held out for total ownership."

The fact that there was some justice in this remark did not make it any easier for Philip to swallow. Total ownership was what he had agreed with Lady Regan, but she had cheated him out of it at the last minute. He was tempted to say that he had got the best deal he could, and he would like to see Remigius do any better in the treacherous maze of the royal court; but he bit his tongue, for he was, after all, the prior, and he had to take responsibility when things went wrong.

Milius came to his rescue. "It's all very well to wish the king had given us outright ownership of the quarry, but he didn't, and the main question is, what do we do now?"

"I should think that's fairly obvious," Remigius said immediately. "We can't expel the earl's men ourselves, so we'll have to get the king to do it. We must send a deputation to him and ask him to enforce his charter."

There was a murmur of agreement. Andrew, the sacrist, said: "We should send our wisest and most fluent speakers."

Philip realized that Remigius and Andrew saw themselves as leading the delegation.

Remigius said: "After the king hears what has happened, I don't think Percy Hamleigh will be earl of Shiring much longer."

Philip was not so sure of that.

"Where is the king?" Andrew said as an afterthought. "Does anybody know?"

Philip had recently been to Winchester, and had heard there of the king's movements. "He's gone to Normandy," he said.

Milius quickly said: "It will take a long time to catch up with him."

"The pursuit of justice always requires patience," Remigius intoned pompously.

"But every day we spend pursuing justice, we're not building our new cathedral," Milius replied. His tone of voice showed that he was exasperated by Remigius's ready acceptance of a delay to the building program. Philip shared that feeling. Milius went on: "And that's not our only problem. Once we've found the king, we have to persuade him to hear us. That can take weeks. Then he may give Percy the chance to defend himself—more delay. . . ."

"How could Percy possibly defend himself?" Remigius said testily.

Milius replied: "I don't know, but I'm sure he'll think of something."

"But in the end the king is bound to stand by his word."

A new voice was heard, saying: "Don't be so sure." Everyone turned to look. The speaker was Brother Timothy, the oldest monk in the priory. A small, modest man, he spoke rarely, but when he did he was worth listening to. Philip occasionally thought Timothy should have been prior. He normally sat through chapter looking half asleep, but now he was leaning forward, his eyes bright with conviction. "A king is a creature of the moment," he went on. "He's constantly under threat, from rebels within his own kingdom and from neighboring monarchs. He needs allies. Earl Percy is a powerful man with a lot of knights. If the king needs Percy at the moment when we present our petition, we will be refused, quite regardless of the justice of our case. The king is not perfect. There is only one true judge, and that is God." He sat back, leaning against the wall and half closing his eyes, as if he were not in the least interested in how his speech was received. Philip concealed a smile: Timothy had precisely formulated Philip's own misgivings about going to the king for justice.

Remigius was reluctant to give up the prospect of a long, exciting trip to France and a sojourn at the royal court; but at the same time he could not contradict Timothy's logic. "What else can we do, then?" he said.

Philip was not sure. The sheriff would not be able to intervene in this case: Percy was too powerful to be controlled by a mere sheriff. And the bishop could not be relied upon either. It was frustrating. But Philip was not willing to sit back and accept defeat. He would take over that quarry if he had to do it himself. . . .

Now there was an idea.

"Just a minute," he said.

It would involve all the able-bodied brothers in the monastery . . . it would have to be carefully organized, like a military operation without weapons . . . they would need food for two days. . . .

"I don't know if this will work, but it's worth a try," he said. "Listen."

He told them his plan.

They set out almost immediately: thirty monks, ten novices, Otto Blackface and his team of quarrymen, Tom Builder and Alfred, two horses and a cart. When darkness fell they lit lanterns to show them the road. At midnight they stopped to rest and eat the picnic the kitchen had hastily prepared: chicken, white bread and red wine. Philip had always believed that hard work should be rewarded by good food. When they marched on, they sang the service they should have been performing back at the priory.

At some point during the darkest hour, Tom Builder, who was leading the way, held up a hand to stop them. He said to Philip: "Only a mile more to the quarry."

"Good," said Philip. He turned to the monks. "Take off your clogs and sandals, and put on the felt boots." He took off his own sandals and pulled on a pair of the soft felt boots that peasants wore in winter.

He singled out two novices. "Edward and Philemon, stay here

with the horses and the cart. Keep quiet, and wait until full daylight; then join us. Is that clear?"

"Yes, Father," they said together.

"All right, the rest of you," Philip said. "Follow Tom Builder, now, in *complete silence*, please."

They all walked on.

There was a light west wind blowing, and the rustling of the trees covered the sound of fifty men breathing and fifty pairs of felt boots shuffling. Philip began to feel tense. His plan seemed a little crazy now that he was about to put it into operation. He said a silent prayer for success.

The road curved to the left, and then the flickering lanterns dimly showed a wooden lodge, a stack of part-finished stone blocks, some ladders and scaffolding, and in the background a dark hillside disfigured by the white scars of quarrying. Philip suddenly wondered whether the men asleep in the lodge had dogs. If they did, Philip would lose the element of surprise, and the whole scheme would be jeopardized. But it was too late to back out now.

The whole crowd shuffled past the lodge. Philip held his breath, expecting at any moment to hear a cacophony of barking. But there were no dogs.

He brought his people to a halt around the base of the scaffolding. He was proud of them for being so quiet. It was difficult for people to stay silent even in church. Perhaps they were too frightened to make a noise.

Tom Builder and Otto Blackface began silently to place the quarrymen around the site. They divided them into two groups. One group gathered near the rock face at ground level. The others mounted the scaffolding. When they were all in position, Philip directed the monks, with gestures, to stand or sit around the workmen. He himself stayed apart from the rest, at a point halfway between the lodge and the rock face.

Their timing was perfect. Dawn came a few moments after Philip made his final dispositions. He took a candle from inside his cloak and lit it from a lantern, then he faced the monks and lifted the candle. It was a prearranged signal. Each of the forty monks and novices took out a candle and lit it from one of the three lanterns. The effect was dramatic. Day broke over a quarry occupied by silent, ghostly figures each holding a small, flickering light.

Philip turned again to face the lodge. As yet there was no sign of life. He settled down to wait. Monks were good at that. Standing still for hours was part of their everyday life. The workmen were not so used to it, however, and they began to get impatient after a while, shuffling their feet and murmuring to one another in low voices; but it did not matter now.

Either the muttering or the strengthening daylight woke the inhabitants of the lodge. Philip heard someone cough and spit, then there was a scraping noise as of a bar being lifted from behind a door. He held up his hand for dead silence.

The door of the lodge swung open. Philip kept his hand in the air. A man came out rubbing his eyes. Philip knew him, from Tom's description, to be Harold of Shiring, the master quarryman. Harold did not see anything unusual at first. He leaned against the door-post and coughed again, the deep, bubbling cough of a man who has too much stone dust in his lungs. Philip dropped his hand. Somewhere behind him, the cantor hit a note, and immediately all the monks began to sing. The quarry was flooded with eerie harmonies.

The effect on Harold was devastating. His head jerked up as if it had been pulled by a string. His eyes widened and his jaw dropped as he saw the spectral choir that had appeared, as if by magic, in his quarry. A cry of fear escaped from his open mouth. He staggered back through the door of the lodge.

Philip permitted himself a satisfied smile. It was a good start.

However, the supernatural dread would not last very long. He lifted his hand again and waved it without turning around. In response to his signal the quarrymen started to work and the clang of iron on rock punctuated the music of the choir.

Two or three faces peeped fearfully from the doorway. The men soon realized they were looking at ordinary, corporeal monks and workmen, not visions or spirits, and they stepped out of the lodge for a better view. Two men-at-arms came out, buckling their sword belts, and stood staring. This was the crucial moment for Philip: what would the men-at-arms do?

The sight of them, big and bearded and dirty, with their chain-link belts, their swords and daggers, and their heavy leather jerkins, brought back to Philip a vivid, crystal-clear memory of the two soldiers who had burst into his home when he was six years old and killed his mother and father. He was stabbed, suddenly and unexpectedly, by grief for the parents he hardly remembered. He stared with loathing at Earl Percy's men, not seeing them but seeing instead an ugly man with a bent nose and a dark man with blood in his beard; and he was filled with rage and disgust and a fierce determination that such mindless, godless ruffians should be defeated.

For a while they did nothing. Gradually all the earl's quarrymen came out of the lodge. Philip counted them: there were twelve workmen plus the men-at-arms.

The sun peeped over the horizon.

The Kingsbridge quarrymen were already digging out stones. If the men-at-arms wanted to stop them, they would have to lay hands on the monks who surrounded and protected the workers. Philip had gambled that the men-at-arms would hesitate to do violence to praying monks.

So far he was right: they were hesitating.

The two novices who had been left behind now arrived, leading the horses and the cart. They looked around fearfully. Philip indicated with a gesture where they should pull up. Then he turned, met Tom Builder's eye, and nodded.

Several stones had been cut by this time, and now Tom directed some of the younger monks to pick up the stones and carry them to the cart. The earl's men watched this new development with interest. The stones were too heavy to be lifted by one man, so they had to be lowered from the scaffolding by ropes, then carried across the ground on stretchers. As the first stone was manhandled into the cart, the men-at-arms went into a huddle with Harold. Another stone was put into the cart. The two men-at-arms separated from the crowd around the lodge and walked over to the cart. One of the novices, Philemon, climbed into the cart and sat on the stones, looking defiant. Brave lad! thought Philip, but he was afraid.

The men approached the cart. The four monks who had carried the two stones stood in front of it, forming a barrier. Philip tensed. The men stopped and stood face to face with the monks. They both put their hands to the hilts of their swords. The singing stopped as everyone watched with bated breath.

Surely, Philip thought, they won't be able to bring themselves to put defenseless monks to the sword. Then he thought how easy it would be for them, big strong men who were accustomed to the slaughter of the battlefield, to run their sharp swords through these people from whom they had nothing to fear, not even retaliation. Then again, they must consider the divine punishment they would risk by murdering men of God. Even thugs such as these must know that eventually they would stand at the Day of Judgment. Were they afraid of the eternal fire? Perhaps; but they were also afraid of their employer, Earl Percy. Philip guessed that the thought uppermost in their minds must be whether he would consider they had an adequate excuse for their failure to keep the Kingsbridge men out of the quarry. He watched them, hesitating in front of a handful of young monks, hands on their swords, and imagined them weighing the danger of failing Percy against the wrath of God.

The two men looked at one another. One shook his head. The other shrugged. Together, they walked out of the quarry.

The cantor hit a new note and the monks burst into a triumphant hymn. A shout of victory went up from the quarrymen. Philip sagged with relief. For a moment it had looked dreadfully dangerous. He could not help beaming with pleasure. The quarry was his.

He blew out his candle and went over to the cart. He embraced each of the four monks who had faced the men-at-arms, and the two novices who had brought the cart. "I'm proud of you," he said warmly. "And I believe God is too."

The monks and the quarrymen were all shaking hands and congratulating one another. Otto Blackface came over to Philip and said: "That was well done, Father Philip. You're a brave man, if I may say so."

"God protected us," Philip said. His eye fell on the earl's quarrymen, standing in a disconsolate group around the door of their lodge. He did not want to make enemies of them, for while they were at a loose end there would always be a danger that Percy would use them to make further trouble. Philip decided to speak to them.

He took Otto's arm and led him over to the lodge. "God's will has been done here today," he said to Harold. "I hope there are no hard feelings."

"We're out of work," Harold said. "That's a hard feeling."

Philip suddenly saw a way to get Harold's men on his side. Impulsively he said: "You can be back in work today, if you want. Work for me. I'll hire your whole team. You won't even have to move out of your lodge."

Harold was surprised at this turn of events. He looked startled, then recovered his composure and said: "At what wages?"

"Standard rates," Philip replied promptly. "Twopence a day for craftsmen, a penny a day for laborers, fourpence for yourself, and you pay your own apprentices."

Harold turned away and looked at his colleagues. Philip drew Otto away to let them discuss the proposal in private. Philip could not really afford twelve more men, and if they accepted his offer he would have to postpone further the day when he could hire masons. That meant he would be cutting stone faster than he could use it. He would build up a stockpile, but it would be bad for his flow of cash. However, having all Percy's quarrymen on the priory payroll would be a good defensive move. If Percy wanted to try again to work the quarry himself, he would first have to hire a team of quarrymen; which might be difficult, once the news of today's events got around. And if at some future date Percy should try another stratagem to close the quarry, Philip would have a stockpile of stone.

Harold appeared to be arguing with his men. After a few moments he left them and approached Philip again. "Who's to be in charge, if we work for you?" he said. "Me, or your own master quarryman?"

"Otto here is in charge," Philip said without hesitation. Harold certainly could not be in charge, in case his loyalty should be won back by Percy. And there could not be two masters, for that would lead to disputes. "You can still run your own team," Philip said to Harold. "But Otto will be over you."

Harold looked disappointed and returned to his men. The discussion continued. Tom Builder joined Philip and Otto. "Your plan worked, Father," he said with a broad grin. "We repossessed the quarry without shedding a drop of blood. You're amazing."

Philip was inclined to agree, and realized he was guilty of the sin of pride. "It was God who worked the miracle," he said, reminding himself as well as Tom.

Otto said: "Father Philip has offered to hire Harold and his men to work with me."

"Really!" Tom looked displeased. It was the master builder who was supposed to recruit craftsmen, not the prior. "I shouldn't have thought he could afford it."

"I can't," Philip admitted. "But I don't want these men hanging around with nothing to do, waiting for Percy to think of another way to get the quarry back."

Tom looked thoughtful, then he nodded. "And it will do no harm to have a reserve of stone in case Percy succeeds."

Philip was glad Tom saw the sense of what he had done.

Harold seemed to be reaching agreement with his men. He came back to Philip and said: "Will you pay the wages to me, and leave me to distribute the money as I think fit?"

Philip was dubious. That meant the master could take more than his share. But he said: "It's up to the master builder."

"It's common enough," Tom said. "If that's what your team wants, I'm willing."

"In that case, we accept," Harold said.

Harold and Tom shook hands. Philip said: "So everyone gets what they want. Good!"

"There's one who hasn't got what they want," Harold said.

"Who's that?" said Philip.

"Earl Percy's wife, Regan," Harold said lugubriously. "When she finds out what's happened here there's going to be blood all over the floor."

II

There was no hunting today, so the young men at Earlscastle played one of William Hamleigh's favorite games, stoning the cat.

There were always plenty of cats in the castle, and one more or less made no difference. The men closed the doors and shuttered the windows of the hall of the keep, and pushed the furniture up against the wall so that the cat could not hide behind anything; then they made a pile of stones in the middle of the room. The cat, an aging mouser with gray in its fur, sensed the bloodlust in the air and sat near the door, hoping to get out.

Each man had to put a penny into the pot for each stone he threw, and the man who threw the fatal stone took the pot.

As they drew lots to determine the order of throwing, the cat became agitated, pacing up and down in front of the door.

Walter threw first. This was lucky, for although the cat was wary it did not know the nature of the game, and might be taken by surprise. With his back to the animal, Walter picked a stone from the pile and concealed it in his hand; then he turned around slowly and threw suddenly.

He missed. The stone thudded into the door and the cat jumped and ran. The others jeered.

It was unlucky to throw second, for the cat was fresh and light on its feet, whereas later it would be tired and possibly injured. A young squire was next. He watched the cat run around the room, looking for a way out, and waited until it slowed down; then he threw. It was a good shot but the cat saw it coming and dodged it. The men groaned.

It ran around the room again, faster now, getting panicky, jumping up onto the trestles and boards that were stacked against the wall, jumping back down to the floor. An older knight threw next. He feinted a throw, to see which way the cat would jump, then threw for real when it was running, aiming a little ahead of it. The others applauded his cunning, but the cat saw the stone coming and stopped suddenly, avoiding it.

In desperation the cat tried to squeeze behind an oak chest in a corner. The next thrower saw an opportunity and seized it: he threw quickly, while the cat was stationary, and struck its rump. A great cheer went up. The cat gave up trying to squeeze behind the chest and ran on around the room, but now it was limping and it moved more slowly.

It was William's turn next.

He thought he could probably kill the cat if he was careful. In order to tire it a little more he yelled at it, making it run faster for a moment; then he feinted a throw, with the same effect. If one of the others had delayed like this he would have been booed, but William was the earl's son, so they waited patiently. The cat slowed down, obviously in pain. It approached the door hopefully. William drew back his arm. Unexpectedly the cat stopped against the wall beside the door. William began to throw. Before the stone left his hand the door was flung open, and a priest in black stood there. William threw, but the cat sprang like an arrow from a bow, howling triumphantly. The priest in the doorway gave a frightened, high-pitched shriek, and clutched at the skirts of his robes. The young men burst out laughing. The cat cannoned into the priest's legs, then landed on its feet and shot out through the door. The priest stood frozen in an attitude of fright, like an old woman scared by a mouse, and the young men roared with laughter.

William recognized the priest. It was Bishop Waleran.

He laughed all the more. The fact that the womanish priest who had been frightened by a cat was also a rival of the family made it even better.

The bishop recovered his composure very quickly. He flushed red, pointed an accusing finger at William, and said in a grating voice: "You'll suffer eternal torment in the lowest depths of hell."

William's laughter turned to terror in a flash. His mother had given him nightmares, when he was small, by telling him what the devils did to people in hell, burning them in the flames and poking their eyes out and cutting off their private parts with sharp knives, and ever since then he hated to hear talk of it. "Shut up!" he screamed at the bishop. The room fell silent. William drew his knife and walked toward Waleran. "Don't you come here preaching, you snake!" Waleran did not look frightened at all, just intrigued, as if he was interested to have discovered William's weakness; and that made William angrier still. "I'll swing for you, so help me—"

He was mad enough to knife the bishop, but he was stopped by a voice from the staircase behind him. "William! Enough!"

It was his father.

William stopped and, after a moment, sheathed his knife.

Waleran came into the hall. Another priest followed him and shut the door behind him: Dean Baldwin.

Father said: "I'm surprised to see you, Bishop."

"Because last time we met, you induced the prior of Kingsbridge to double-cross me? Yes, I suppose you would be surprised. I'm not normally a forgiving man." He turned his icy gaze on William again for a moment, then looked back at Father. "But I don't bear a grudge when it's against my interest. We need to talk."

Father nodded thoughtfully. "You'd better come upstairs. You too, William."

Bishop Waleran and Dean Baldwin climbed the stairs to the earl's quarters, and William followed. He felt let down because the cat had escaped. On the other hand, he realized that he too had had a lucky escape: if he had touched the bishop he probably would have been hanged for it. But there was something about Waleran's delicacy, his preciousness, that William hated.

They went into Father's chamber, the room where William had raped Aliena. He remembered that scene every time he was here: her lush white body, the fear on her face, the way she had screamed, the twisted expression on her little brother's face as he had been forced to look on, and then—William's masterstroke—the way he had let Walter enjoy her afterward. He wished he had kept her here, a prisoner, so that he could have her anytime he wanted.

He had thought about her obsessively ever since. He had even tried to track her down. A verderer had been caught trying to sell William's war-horse in Shiring, and had confessed, under torture, that he had stolen it from a girl answering to the description of Aliena. William had learned from the Winchester jailer that she had visited her father before he died. And his friend Mistress Kate, the owner of a brothel he frequented, had told him she had offered Aliena a place in her house. But the trail had petered out. "Don't let her prey on your mind, Willy-boy," Kate had said sympathetically. "You want big tits and long hair? We've got it. Take Betty and Millie together, tonight, four big breasts all to yourself, why don't you?" But Betty and Millie had not been innocent, and white-skinned, and frightened half to death; and they had not pleased him. In fact, he had not achieved real satisfaction with a woman since that night with Aliena here in the earl's chamber.

He put the thought of her out of his mind. Bishop Waleran was speaking to Mother. "I suppose you know that the prior of Kingsbridge has taken possession of your quarry?"

They did not know. William was astonished, and Mother was furious. "What?" she said. "How?"

"Apparently your men-at-arms succeeded in turning away the quarrymen, but the next day when they woke up they found the quarry overrun with monks singing hymns, and they were afraid to lay hands on men of God. Prior Philip then hired your quarrymen, and now they're all working together in perfect harmony. I'm surprised the men-at-arms didn't come back to you to report."

"Where are they, the cowards?" Mother screeched. She was red in the face. "I'll see to them—I'll make them cut off their own balls—"

"I see why they didn't come back," Waleran said.

"Never mind the men-at-arms," Father said. "They're just soldiers. That sly prior is the one responsible. I never imagined he could pull a trick like this. He's outwitted us, that's all."

"Exactly," said Waleran. "For all his air of saintly innocence, he's got the cunning of a house rat."

William thought that Waleran, too, was like a rat, a black one with a pointed snout and sleek black hair, sitting in a corner with a crust in its paws, darting wary glances around the room as it nibbled its dinner. Why was he interested in who occupied the quarry? He was as cunning as Prior Philip: he, too, was plotting something.

Mother said: "We can't let him get away with this. The Hamleighs must not be seen to be defeated. That prior must be humiliated."

Father was not so sure. "It's only a quarry," he said. "And the king did—"

"It's not just the quarry, it's the family's honor," Mother interrupted. "Never mind what the king said."

William agreed with Mother. Philip of Kingsbridge had defied the Hamleighs, and he had to be crushed. If people were not afraid of you, you had nothing. But he did not see what the problem was. "Why don't we go in with some men and just throw the prior's quarrymen out?"

Father shook his head. "It's one thing to obstruct the king's wishes passively, as we did by working the quarry ourselves; but quite another to send armed men to expel workmen who are there by express permission of the king. I could lose the earldom for that."

William reluctantly saw his point of view. Father was always cautious, but he was usually justified.

Bishop Waleran said: "I have a suggestion." William had felt sure he had something up his embroidered black sleeve. "I believe this cathedral should not be built at Kingsbridge."

William was mystified by this remark. He did not see its relevance. Nor did Father. But Mother's eyes widened, she stopped scratching her face for a moment, and she said thoughtfully: "That's an interesting idea."

"In the old days most cathedrals were in villages such as Kingsbridge," Waleran went on. "Many of them were moved to towns sixty or seventy years ago, during the time of the first King William. Kingsbridge is a small village in the middle of nowhere. There's nothing there but a run-down monastery that isn't rich enough to maintain a cathedral, let alone build one."

Mother said: "And where would *you* wish it built?"

"Shiring," said Waleran. "It's a big town—the population must be a thousand or more—and it has a market and an annual fleece fair. And it's on a main road. Shiring makes sense. And if we both campaign for it—the bishop and the earl united—we could push it through."

Father said: "But if the cathedral were at Shiring, the Kingsbridge monks would not be able to look after it."

"That's the *point*," Mother said impatiently. "Without the cathedral, Kingsbridge would be nothing, the priory would sink back into obscurity, and Philip would once again be a nonentity, which is what he deserves."

"So who would look after the new cathedral?" Father persisted.

"A new chapter of canons," Waleran said. "Appointed by me."

William had been as puzzled as his father, but now he began to see Waleran's thinking: in moving the cathedral to Shiring, Waleran would also take personal control of it.

"What about the money?" said Father. "Who would pay for the new cathedral, if not Kingsbridge Priory?"

"I think we'd find that most of the priory's property is dedicated to the cathedral," Waleran said. "If the cathedral moves, the property goes with it. For example, when King Stephen divided up the old earldom of Shiring, he gave the hill farms to Kingsbridge Priory, as we know only too well; but he did that in order to help finance the new cathedral. If we told him that someone else was building the new cathedral, he would expect the priory to release those lands to the new builders. The monks would put up a fight, of course; but examination of their charters would settle the matter."

The picture was becoming clearer to William. Not only would Waleran get control of the cathedral by this stratagem; he would also get his hands on most of the priory's wealth.

Father was thinking the same thing. "It's a grand scheme for you, Bishop, but what's in it for me?"

It was Mother who answered him. "Can't you see?" she said tetchily. "You own Shiring. Think how much prosperity would come to the town along with the cathedral. There would be hundreds of craftsmen and laborers building the church for years:

they all have to live somewhere and pay you rent, and buy food and clothing at your market. Then there will be the canons who run the cathedral; and the worshipers who will come to Shiring instead of Kingsbridge at Easter and Whitsun for the big services; and the pilgrims who come to visit the shrines. . . . They all spend money." Her eyes were bright with greed. William could not remember seeing her so enthusiastic for a long time. "If we handle this right, we could turn Shiring into one of the most important cities in the kingdom!"

And it will be mine, William thought. When Father dies I will be the earl.

"All right," said Father. "It will ruin Philip, it will bring power to you, Bishop, and it will make me rich. How could it be done?"

"The decision to move the location of the cathedral must be made by the archbishop of Canterbury, theoretically."

Mother looked at him sharply. "Why 'theoretically'?"

"Because there is no archbishop just now. William of Corbeil died at Christmas and King Stephen has not yet nominated his successor. However, we know who is likely to get the job: our old friend Henry of Winchester. He wants the job; the pope has already given him interim control; and his brother is the king."

"How much of a friend is he?" said Father. "He didn't do much for you when you were trying to get this earldom."

Waleran shrugged. "He'll help me if he can. We'll have to make a convincing case."

Mother said: "He won't want to make powerful enemies, just now, if he's hoping to be made archbishop."

"Correct. But Philip isn't powerful enough to matter. He's not likely to be consulted about the choice of archbishop."

"So why shouldn't Henry just give us what we want?" William asked.

"Because he's *not* the archbishop, not yet; and he knows that people are watching him to see how he behaves during his care-takership. He wants to be seen making judicious decisions, not just handing out favors to his friends. Plenty of time for that *after* the election."

Mother said reflectively: "So the best that can be said is that he will listen sympathetically to our case. What is our case?"

"That Philip can't build a cathedral, and we can."

"And how shall we persuade him of that?"

"Have you been to Kingsbridge lately?"

"No."

"I was there at Easter." Waleran smiled. "They haven't started building yet. All they've got is a flat piece of ground with a few stakes banged into the soil and some ropes marking where they hope to build. They've started digging foundations, but they've only gone down a few feet. There's a mason working there with his apprentice, and the priory carpenter, and occasionally a monk or two doing some laboring. It's a very unimpressive sight, especially in the rain. I'd like Bishop Henry to see it."

Mother nodded sagely. William could see that the plan was good, even though he hated the thought of collaborating with the loathsome Waleran Bigod.

Waleran went on: "We'll brief Henry beforehand on what a small and insignificant place Kingsbridge is, and how poor the monastery is; then we'll show him the site where it has taken them more than a year to dig a few shallow holes; then we'll take him to Shiring and impress him with how fast we could build a cathedral there, with the bishop and the earl and the townspeople all putting their maximum energies into the project."

"Will Henry come?" Mother said anxiously.

"All we can do is ask," Waleran replied. "I'll invite him to visit on Whitsunday in his archiepiscopal role. That will flatter him by implying that we already consider him to be the archbishop."

Father said: "We must keep this secret from Prior Philip."

"I don't think that will be possible," Waleran said. "The bishop can't make a surprise visit to Kingsbridge—it would look very odd."

"But if Philip knows in advance that Bishop Henry is coming, he might make a big effort to advance the building program."

"What with? He hasn't any money, especially now that he's hired all your quarrymen. Quarrymen can't build walls." Waleran shook his head from side to side with a satisfied smile. "In fact, there isn't a thing he can do except hope the sun shines on Whitsunday."

At first Philip was pleased that the bishop of Winchester was to come to Kingsbridge. It would mean an open-air service, of course, but that was all right. They would hold it where the old cathedral used to be. In case of rain, the priory carpenter would build a temporary shelter over the altar and the area immediately around it, to keep the bishop dry; and the congregation could just get wet. The visit seemed like an act of faith on Bishop Henry's part, as if he were saying that he still considered Kingsbridge to be a cathedral, and the lack of a real church was just a temporary problem.

However, it occurred to him to wonder what Henry's motive was. The usual reason for a bishop to visit a monastery was to get free food, drink and lodging for himself and his entourage; but Kingsbridge was famous—not to say notorious—for the plainness of its food and the austerity of its accommodation, and Philip's reforms had merely raised its standard from dreadful to barely adequate. Henry was also the richest clergyman in the kingdom, so he certainly was not coming to Kingsbridge for its food and drink. But he had struck Philip as a man who did nothing without a reason.

The more Philip thought about it, the more he suspected that Bishop Waleran had something to do with it. He had expected Waleran to arrive at Kingsbridge within a day or two of the letter, to discuss arrangements for the service and hospitality for Henry, and to make sure Henry would be pleased and impressed with Kingsbridge; and as the days went by and Waleran did not show up, Philip's misgivings deepened.

However, even in his most mistrustful moments he had not dreamed of the treachery that was revealed, ten days before Whitsun, by a letter from the prior of Canterbury Cathedral. Like Kingsbridge, Canterbury was a cathedral run by Benedictine monks, and monks always helped one another if they could. The prior of Canterbury, who naturally worked closely with the acting archbishop, had learned that Waleran had invited Henry to Kingsbridge for the express purpose of persuading him to move the diocese, and the new cathedral, to Shiring.

Philip was shocked. His heart beat faster and the hand holding the letter trembled. It was a fiendishly clever move by Waleran, and Philip had not anticipated it, had not imagined anything like it.

It was his own lack of foresight that shook him. He knew how treacherous Waleran was. The bishop had tried to double-cross him, a year ago, over the Shiring earldom. And he would never forget how angry Waleran had been when Philip had outwitted him. He could picture Waleran's face, suffused with rage, as he said *I swear by all that's holy, you'll never build your church.* But as time went by the menace of that oath had faded, and Philip's guard had slipped. Now here was a brutal reminder that Waleran had a long memory.

"Bishop Waleran says you have no money, and in fifteen months you have built nothing," the prior of Canterbury wrote. "He says that Bishop Henry will see for himself that the cathedral will never get built if it is left to Kingsbridge Priory to build it. He argues that the time to make the move is now, before any real progress is made."

Waleran was too cunning to get caught in an outright lie, so he was purveying a gross exaggeration. Philip had in fact achieved a great deal. He had cleared the ruins, approved the plans, laid out the new east end, made a start on the foundations, and begun felling trees and quarrying stone. But he did not have much to show a visitor. And he had overcome terrific obstacles to achieve this much—reforming the priory's finances, winning a major grant of lands from the king, and defeating Earl Percy over the quarry. It was not fair!

With the letter from Canterbury in his hand, he went to his window and looked out over the building site. Spring rains had turned it into a sea of mud. Two young monks with their hoods pulled over their heads were carrying timber up from the riverside. Tom Builder had made a contraption with a rope and a pulley for lifting barrels of earth out of the foundation hole, and he was operating the winding wheel while his son Alfred, down in the hole, filled the barrels with wet mud. They looked as though they could work at that pace forever and never make any difference. Anyone but a professional would see this scene and conclude that no cathedral would be built here this side of the Day of Judgment.

Philip left the window and returned to his writing desk. What could be done? For a moment he was tempted to do nothing. Let Bishop Henry come and look, and make his own decision, he thought. If the cathedral is to be built at Shiring, so be it. Let Bishop Waleran take control of it and use it for his own ends; let it bring prosperity to the town of Shiring and the evil Hamleigh dynasty. God's will be done.

He knew that would not do, of course. Having faith in God did not mean sitting back and doing nothing. It meant believing that you would find success if you did your best honestly and energetically. Philip's holy duty was to do all he could to prevent the cathedral from falling into the hands of cynical and immoral people who would exploit it for their own aggrandizement. That meant showing Bishop Henry that his building program was well under way and Kingsbridge had the energy and determination to finish it.

Was it true? The fact was that Philip was going to find it mortally difficult to build a cathedral here. Already he had almost been forced to abandon the project just because the earl refused him access to the quarry. But he knew he would succeed, in the end, because God would help him. However, his own conviction would not be enough to persuade Bishop Henry.

He decided he would do his best to make the site look more impressive, for what it was worth. He would set all the monks to work for the ten days remaining before Whitsun. Perhaps they could get part of the foundation hole dug to its full depth, so that Tom and Alfred could begin laying the foundation stones. Perhaps a part of the foundation could be completed up to ground level, so that Tom could start building a wall. That would be a little better than the present scene, but not much. What Philip really needed was a hundred laborers, but he did not have the money even for ten.

Bishop Henry would arrive on a Sunday, of course, so nobody would be working, unless Philip were to co-opt the congregation. That would provide a hundred laborers. He imagined himself standing up in front of them and announcing a new kind of Whitsun service: instead of singing hymns and saying prayers, we're going to dig holes and carry stones. They would be astonished. They would . . .

What would they do, actually?

They would probably cooperate wholeheartedly.

He frowned. Either I'm crazy, he thought, or this idea could actually work.

He thought about it some more. I get up at the end of the service, and I say that today's penance for forgiveness of all sins is half a day's labor on the cathedral building site. Bread and ale will be provided at dinnertime.

They would do it. Of course they would.

He felt the need to try the idea out on someone else. He considered Milius, but rejected him: Milius's thought processes were too similar to his own. He needed someone with a slightly different outlook. He decided to talk to Cuthbert Whitehead, the cellarer. He pulled on his cloak, drew the hood forward to keep the rain off his face, and went out.

He hurried across the muddy building site, passing Tom with a perfunctory wave, and made for the kitchen courtyard. This range of buildings now included a hen house, a cow shed and a dairy, for Philip did not like to spend scarce cash on simple commodities that the monks could provide for themselves, such as eggs and butter.

He entered the cellarer's storeroom in the undercroft below the kitchen. He inhaled the dry, fragrant air, full of the herbs and spices Cuthbert had stored. Cuthbert was counting garlic, peering at the strings of bulbs and muttering numbers in an undertone. Philip saw with a small shock that Cuthbert was getting old: his flesh seemed to be wasting away beneath his skin.

"Thirty-seven," Cuthbert said aloud. "Would you like a cup of wine?"

"No, thank you." Philip found that wine in the daytime made him lazy and short-tempered. No doubt that was why Saint Benedict counseled monks to drink in moderation. "I want your advice, not your victuals. Come and sit down."

Negotiating a path through the boxes and barrels, Cuthbert stumbled over a sack and almost fell before sitting on a three-legged stool in front of Philip. The storeroom was not as tidy as it had once been, Philip noted. He was struck by a thought. "Are you having trouble with your eyesight, Cuthbert?"

"It's not what it was, but it will do," Cuthbert said shortly.

His eyes had probably been poor for years—that might even be why he had never learned to read very well. However, he was obviously touchy about it, so Philip said no more, but made a mental note to begin grooming a replacement cellarer. "I've had a very disturbing letter from the prior of Canterbury," he said, and he told Cuthbert about Bishop Waleran's scheming. He concluded by saying: "The only way to make the site look like a hive of activity is to get the congregation to work on it. Can you think of any reason why I shouldn't do that?"

Cuthbert did not even think about it. "On the contrary, it's a good idea," he said immediately.

"It's a little unorthodox, isn't it?" Philip said.

"It's been done before."

"Really?" Philip was surprised and pleased. "Where?"

"I've heard of it in several places."

Philip was excited. "Does it work?"

"Sometimes. It probably depends on the weather."

"How is it managed? Does the priest make an announcement at the end of the service, or what?"

"It's more organized than that. The bishop, or prior, sends out messengers to the parish churches, announcing that forgiveness for sins may be had in return for work on the building site."

"That's a grand idea," Philip said enthusiastically. "We might get a bigger congregation than usual, attracted by the novelty."

"Or a smaller one," Cuthbert said. "Some people would rather give money to the priest, or light a candle to a saint, than spend all day wading in mud and carrying heavy stones."

"I never thought of that," Philip said, suddenly deflated. "Perhaps this isn't such a good idea after all."

"What other ideas have you got?"

"Not one."

"Then you'll have to try this, and hope for the best, won't you?"

"Yes," said Philip. "Hope for the best."

III

Philip did not sleep at all during the night before Whitsunday.

There had been a week of sunshine, perfect for his plan—more people would volunteer in fine weather—but as darkness fell on the Saturday, it began to rain. He lay awake listening disconsolately to the raindrops on the roof and the wind in the trees. He felt he had prayed enough. God must be fully aware of the circumstances now.

On the previous Sunday, every monk in the priory had visited one or more churches to speak to the congregations and tell them they could obtain forgiveness for their sins by working on the cathedral building site on Sundays. On Whitsunday they would get forgiveness for the past year, and thereafter a day of labor was worth a week of routine sins, excluding murder and sacrilege. Philip himself had gone to the town of Shiring, and had spoken at each of its four parish churches. He had sent two monks to Winchester to visit as many as possible of the multitude of small churches in that city. Winchester was two days' journey away, but Whitsun was a six-day holiday, and people would make such a trip for a big fair or a spectacular service. In total, many thousands of people had heard the message. There was no knowing how many might respond.

For the rest of the time they had all been working on the site. The good weather and the long days of early summer had helped, and they had achieved most of what Philip had hoped for. The foundation had been laid for the wall at the easternmost end of the chancel. Some of the foundation for the north wall had been dug to its full depth, ready for foundation stones to be laid; and Tom had built enough lifting mechanisms to keep scores of people busy digging the rest of the vast hole, if scores of people should turn up. In addition, the riverbank was crowded with timber sent downstream by the foresters and with stones from the quarry, all of which had to be carried up the slope to the cathedral site. There was work here for hundreds.

But would anyone come?

At midnight Philip got up and walked through the rain to the crypt for matins. When he returned after the service, the rain had stopped. He did not go back to bed, but sat up reading. Nowadays this period between midnight and dawn was the only time he had for study and meditation, for the whole of the day was always taken up with the administration of the monastery.

Tonight, however, he had trouble concentrating, and his mind kept returning to the prospect of the day ahead, and the chances of success or failure. Tomorrow he could lose everything he had worked for over the past year and more. It occurred to him, perhaps because he was feeling fatalistic, that he ought not to want success for its own sake. Was it his pride that was at stake here? Pride was the sin he was most vulnerable to. Then he thought of all the people who depended on him for support, protection and employment: the monks, the priory servants, the quarrymen, Tom and Alfred, the villagers of Kingsbridge and the worshipers of the whole county. Bishop Waleran would not care for them the way Philip did. Waleran seemed to think he was entitled to use people any way he chose in the service of God. Philip believed that caring for people *was* the service of God. That was what salvation was about. No, it could not be God's will that Bishop Waleran should win this contest. Perhaps my pride is at stake, a little bit, Philip admitted to himself; but there are men's souls in the balance too.

At last dawn cracked the night, and once again he walked to the crypt, this time for the service of prime. The monks were restless and excited: they knew that today was crucial to their future. The sacrist hurried through the service, and for once Philip forgave him.

When they left the crypt and headed toward the refectory for breakfast it was fully light, and there was a clear blue sky. God had sent the weather they had prayed for, at least. It was a good start.

Tom Builder knew that his future was at stake today.

Philip had shown him the letter from the prior of Canterbury. Tom was sure that if the cathedral was built at Shiring, Waleran would hire his own master builder. He would not want to use a design Philip had approved, nor would he risk employing someone who might be loyal to Philip. For Tom, it was Kingsbridge or nothing. This was the only opportunity he would ever get to build a cathedral, and it was in jeopardy today.

He was invited to attend chapter with the monks in the morning. This happened occasionally. Usually it was because they were going to discuss the building program and might need his expert opinion on questions of design, cost or timetabling. Today he was going to make arrangements for employing the volunteer workers, if any came. He wanted the site to be a hive of busy, efficient activity when Bishop Henry arrived.

He sat patiently through the readings and the prayers, not understanding the Latin words, thinking about his plans for the day; then Philip switched to English and called on him to outline the organization of the work.

"I shall be building the east wall of the cathedral and Alfred will be laying stone in the foundations," Tom began. "The aim, in both cases, is to show Bishop Henry how far advanced the building is."

"How many men will the two of you need to help you?" Philip asked.

"Alfred will need two laborers to bring the stones to him. He'll be using material from the ruins of the old church. He'll also need someone to make mortar. I'll also need a mortar maker and two laborers. Alfred can use misshapen stones in the foundations, as long as they're flat top and bottom; but my stones will have to be properly dressed, since they will be visible aboveground, so I've brought two stonecutters back from the quarry to help me."

Philip said: "All that is very important for impressing Bishop Henry, but most of the volunteers will be digging the foundations."

"That's right. The foundations are marked out for the whole of the chancel of the cathedral, and most of them are still only a few feet deep. Monks must man the winding gear—I've instructed several of you how to do it—and the volunteers can fill the barrels."

Remigius said: "What if we get more volunteers than we can use?"

"We can employ just about any number," Tom said. "If we haven't enough lifting devices, people can carry earth out of the holes in buckets and baskets. The carpenter will have to stand by to make extra ladders—we've got the timber."

"But there's a limit to the number of people who can get down in that foundation hole," Remigius persisted.

Tom had the feeling that Remigius was just argumentative. "It will take several hundred," he said testily. "It's a big hole."

Philip said: "And there's other work to be done, besides digging."

"Indeed," Tom said. "The other main area of work is carrying timber and stone up to the site from the riverside. You monks must make sure the materials are stacked in the right places on the site. The stones should go beside the foundation holes, but on the *outside* of the church, where they won't get in the way. The carpenter will tell you where to put the timber."

Philip said: "Will all the volunteers be unskilled?"

"Not necessarily. If we get people from the towns, there may be some craftsmen among them—I hope so. We must find out who they are and use them. Carpenters can build lodges for winter work. Any masons can cut stones and lay foundations. If there's a blacksmith, we'll put him to work in the village forge, making tools. All that sort of thing will be tremendously useful."

Milius the bursar said: "That's all quite clear. I'd like to get started. Some of the villagers are here already, waiting to be told what to do."

There was something else Tom needed to tell them, something important but subtle, and he was searching for the right words. Monks could be arrogant, and might alienate the volunteers. Tom wanted today's operation to be easygoing and cheerful. "I've worked with volunteers before," he began. "It's important not to . . . not to treat them like servants. We may feel that they are laboring to obtain a heavenly reward, and should therefore work harder than they would for money; but they don't necessarily take that attitude. They feel they're working for nothing, and doing a great kindness to us thereby; and if we seem ungrateful they will work slowly and make mistakes. It will be best to rule them with a light touch."

He caught Philip's eye and saw that the prior was suppressing a smile, as if he knew what misgivings underlay Tom's honeyed words. "A good point," Philip said. "If we handle them right, these people will feel happy and uplifted, and that will create a good atmosphere, which will make a positive impression on Bishop Henry." He looked around at the assembled monks. "If there are no more questions, let's begin."

Aliena had enjoyed a year of security and prosperity under the wing of Prior Philip.

All her plans had worked. She and Richard had toured the countryside buying fleeces from peasants all last spring and summer, selling to Philip every time they had a standard woolsack. They had ended the season with five pounds of silver.

Father had died just a few days after they saw him, although Aliena did not find out until Christmas. She had located his grave, after spending much hard-earned silver on bribes, in a pauper's cemetery in Winchester. She cried hard, not just for him but for the life they had lived together, secure and carefree, the life that would never come back. In a way she had said goodbye to him before he died: when she left the jail she knew she would never see him again. In another way he was still with her, for she was bound by the oath he had made her swear, and she was resigned to spending her life doing his will.

During the winter she and Richard lived in a small house up against the wall of Kingsbridge Priory. They had built a cart, buying the wheels from the Kingsbridge cartwright, and in the spring they had bought a young ox to pull it. The shearing season was now in full swing and already they had made more than the cost of the ox and the new cart. Next year, perhaps she would employ a man to help her, and find Richard a place as a page in the household of a minor noble, so that he could begin his knightly training.

But it was all dependent on Prior Philip.

As an eighteen-year-old girl on her own, she was still considered fair game by every thief and many legitimate traders. She had tried to sell a sack of wool to merchants in Shiring and Gloucester, just to see what would happen, and both times she had been offered half price. There was never more than one merchant in a town so they knew she had no alternative. Eventually she would have her own storehouse, and sell her entire stock to the Flemish buyers; but that time was a long way off. Meanwhile she was dependent on Philip.

And Philip's position had suddenly become precarious.

She was constantly alert to danger from outlaws and thieves, but it had come as a great shock to her, when everything was going smoothly, to have her whole livelihood threatened in such an unexpected way.

Richard had not wanted to work on the cathedral building site on Whitsunday—he was nothing if not ungrateful—but Aliena had bullied him into agreeing, and the two of them walked the few yards to the priory close soon after sunrise. Almost the whole village had turned out: thirty or forty men, some of them with their wives and children. Aliena was surprised, until she reflected that Prior Philip was their lord, and when your lord asked for volunteers it was probably unwise to refuse. In the past year she had gained a startling new perspective on the lives of ordinary people.

Tom Builder was giving the villagers their assignments. Richard immediately went to speak to Tom's son Alfred. They were almost the same age—Richard was fifteen and Alfred about a year older—and they played football with the other boys in the village every Sunday. The little girl, Martha, was here too, but the woman, Ellen, and the funny-looking boy with red hair had disappeared, no one knew where. Aliena remembered when Tom's family had come to Earlscastle. They had been destitute then. Like Aliena, they had been saved by Prior Philip.

Aliena and Richard were given a shovel each and told to dig foundations. The ground was damp but the sun was out and it would soon dry the surface. Aliena began to dig energetically. Even with fifty people working, it took a long time to make the holes noticeably deeper. Richard rested on his shovel rather frequently. One time Aliena said: "If you ever want to be a knight, dig!" But it made no difference.

She was thinner and stronger than she had been a year ago, thanks to tramping the roads and lifting heavy loads of raw wool, but now she found that digging could still make her back ache. She was grateful when Prior Philip rang a bell and declared a break. Monks brought hot bread from the kitchen and served weak beer. The sun was growing stronger, and some of the men stripped to the waist.

While they were resting, a group of strangers came through the gate. Aliena looked at them hopefully. There were just a handful of them, but perhaps they were the forerunners of a large crowd. They came over to the table where the bread and beer was being handed out, and Prior Philip welcomed them.

"Where are you from?" he asked as they gulped gratefully at their pots of beer.

"From Horsted," one of them replied, wiping his mouth on his sleeve. That was promising: Horsted was a village of two or three hundred people a few miles west of Kingsbridge. They might hope for another hundred volunteers from there, with luck.

"And how many of you are coming, in all?" Philip asked.

The man looked surprised at the question. "Just us four," he replied.

During the next hour people trickled through the priory gate until, by midmorning, there were seventy or eighty volunteers at work, including the villagers. Then the flow stopped altogether.

It was not enough.

Philip stood at the east end, watching Tom build a wall. He had already constructed the bases of two buttresses up to the level of the third course of stones, and now he was building the wall between. It would probably never be finished, Philip thought despondently.

The first thing Tom did, when the laborers brought him a stone, was to take out an iron instrument shaped like the letter L and use it to check that the edges of the stone were square. Then he would shovel a layer of mortar on to the wall, furrow the mortar with the point of his trowel, put the new stone on, and scrape off the surplus mortar. In placing the stone he was guided by a taut string which was stretched between the two buttresses.

Philip noticed that the stone was almost as smooth on the top and bottom, where the mortar was, as on the side that would show. This surprised him, and he asked Tom the reason. "A stone must never touch the ones above or below," Tom replied. "That's what the mortar's for."

"Why must they not touch?"

"It causes cracks." Tom stood upright to explain. "If you tread on a slate roof, your foot will go through it; but if you put a plank across the roof, you can walk on it without damaging the slates. The plank spreads the weight, and that's what mortar does."

Philip had never thought of that. Building was an intriguing business, especially with someone like Tom, who was able to explain what he was doing.

The roughest face of the stone was the back. Surely, Philip thought, that face would be visible from inside the church? Then he recalled that Tom was in fact building a double-skinned wall with a cavity between, so that the back of each stone would be hidden.

When Tom had laid the stone on the bed of mortar, he picked up his level. This was an iron triangle with a leather thong attached to its apex and some markings on its base. The thong had a lead weight attached to it so that it always hung straight down. He put the base of the instrument on the stone and watched how the leather thong fell. If it hung to one side or the other of the center line, he would tap the stone with his hammer until it was exactly level. Then he would move the instrument until it straddled the join between the two adjacent stones, to check that the tops of the stones were exactly in line. Finally he turned the instrument sideways on the stone to make sure it was not leaning one way or the other. Before picking up a new stone he would snap the taut string to satisfy himself that the faces of the stones were in a straight line. Philip had not realized it was so important that stone walls should be precisely straight and true.

He lifted his gaze to the rest of the building site. It was so big that eighty men and women and a few children were lost in it. They were working away cheerfully in the sunshine, but they were so few that it seemed to him there was an air of futility about their efforts. He had originally hoped for a hundred people, but now he saw that even that would not have been enough.

Another little group came through the gateway, and Philip forced himself to go to greet them with a smile. There was no need for them to know that their efforts would be wasted. They would gain forgiveness for their sins, anyway.

It was a large group, he saw as he approached them. He counted twelve, and then two more came in. Perhaps after all he would have a hundred people by midday, when the bishop was expected. "God bless you all," he said to them. He was about to tell them where to start digging when he was interrupted by a loud shout. "Philip!"

He frowned disapprovingly. The voice belonged to Brother Milius. Even Milius was supposed to call Philip "Father" in public. Philip looked in the direction from which the voice came. Milius was balancing on the priory wall in a somewhat undignified stance. In a calm but carrying voice, Philip said: "Brother Milius, get off the wall."

To his astonishment Milius stayed there and shouted: "Come and look at this!"

The new arrivals were getting a poor impression of monastic obedience, Philip thought, but he could not help wondering what it was that had got Milius so excited that he had forgotten all his manners. "Come here and tell me about it, Milius," he said in a voice he normally reserved for noisy novices.

"You must look!" Milius yelled.

He'd better have a very good reason for this, Philip thought crossly; but since he did not want to give his closest colleague a telling-off in front of all these strangers, he was obliged to smile and do as Milius asked. Feeling irritated to the point of anger, he walked across the muddy ground in front of the stable and jumped up onto the low wall. "What is the *meaning* of this behavior?" he hissed.

"Just look!" Milius said, pointing.

Following his gesture, Philip looked out, over the roofs of the village, past the river, to the road that followed the rise and fall of the land to the west. At first he could not believe his eyes. Between the fields of green crops, the undulating road was a solid mass of people, hundreds of them, all walking toward Kingsbridge. "What is it?" he said uncomprehendingly. "An army?" And then he realized that, of course, they were his volunteers. His heart leaped for joy. "Look at them!" he shouted. "There must be five hundred—a thousand—more!"

"That's right!" Milius said happily. "They came, after all!"

"We're saved." Philip was too thrilled to remember why he was supposed to be angry with Milius. The mass of people filled the road all the way to the bridge, and the line wound through the village all the way to the priory gate. The people he had greeted were the head of a phalanx. They were pouring through the gate now, and milling about at the western end of the building site, waiting for someone to tell them what to do. "Hallelujah!" he yelled recklessly.

It was not enough to rejoice—he had to use these people. He jumped down off the wall. "Come on!" he shouted to Milius. "Call all the monks off laboring—we're going to need them as marshals. Tell the kitchener to bake all the bread he can and roll out some more barrels of beer. We'll need more buckets and shovels. We must get all these people working before Bishop Henry arrives!"

For the next hour Philip was frantically busy. At first, just to get people out of the way, he assigned a hundred or more to the task of bringing materials up from the riverbank. As soon as Milius had assembled a supervisory group of monks, he began sending the volunteers down into the foundations. They soon ran out of shovels, barrels and buckets. Philip ordered all the cooking pots brought from the kitchen, and set some of the volunteers to making rough timber boxes and basketwork platters for carrying earth. There were not enough ladders or lifting devices, so they made a long slope at one end of the largest foundation hole so that people could walk into and out of it. He realized he had not given sufficient thought to the question of where he was going to put the vast quantity of earth that was coming out of the foundations. Now it was too late to mull it over: he made a snap decision, and ordered the earth dumped on a patch of rocky ground near the river. Perhaps it might become cultivable. While he was giving that order, Bernard Kitchener came to him in a panic, saying he had only catered for two hundred people at most, and there seemed to be at least a thousand here. "Build a fire in the kitchen courtyard and make soup in an iron bath," Philip said. "Water the beer. Use all the stores. Get some of the villagers to prepare food on their own hearths. Improvise!" He turned away from the kitchener and resumed organizing laborers.

He was still giving orders when someone tapped him on the shoulder and said in French: "Prior Philip, may I have your attention for a moment?" It was Dean Baldwin, Waleran Bigod's associate.

Philip turned around and saw the entire visiting party, all on horseback and gorgeously dressed, gazing in astonishment at the scene around them. There was Bishop Henry, a short, thickset man with a pugnacious look about him, his monkish haircut contrasting strangely with his embroidered scarlet coat. Beside him was Bishop Waleran, dressed in black as always, his dismay not quite concealed by his habitual look of frozen disdain. There was fat Percy Hamleigh, his strapping son, William, and his hideous wife, Regan:

Percy and William were looking bemused, but Regan understood exactly what Philip had done and she was furious.

Philip returned his attention to Bishop Henry, and found to his surprise that the bishop was favoring him with a look of intense interest. Philip returned his gaze frankly. Bishop Henry's expression showed surprise, curiosity and a kind of amused respect. After a moment Philip approached the bishop, held his horse's head, and kissed the beringed hand that Henry proffered.

Henry dismounted with a smooth, agile movement, and the rest of his party followed suit. Philip called a couple of monks to stable the horses. Henry was the same age as Philip, approximately, but his florid complexion and well-covered frame made him look older. "Well, Father Philip," he said. "I came to verify reports that you were not capable of getting a new cathedral built here at Kingsbridge." He paused, looked around at the hundreds of workers, then returned his gaze to Philip. "It seems I was misinformed."

Philip's heart missed a beat. Henry could hardly make it plainer: Philip had won.

Philip turned to Bishop Waleran. Waleran's face was a mask of suppressed fury. He knew he had been defeated again. Philip knelt, bowing his head to hide the look of triumphant delight on his face, and kissed Waleran's hand.

Tom was enjoying building the wall. It was so long since he had done this that he had forgotten the deep tranquillity that came from laying one stone upon another in perfect straight lines and watching the structure grow.

When the volunteers started to arrive by the hundred, and he realized that Philip's scheme was going to work, he enjoyed it all the more. These stones would be part of Tom's cathedral; and this wall that was now only a foot high would eventually reach for the sky. Tom felt he was at the beginning of the rest of his life.

He knew when Bishop Henry arrived. Like a stone dropped into a pond, the bishop sent a ripple through the mass of laborers, as people stopped work for a moment to look up at the richly dressed figures picking their dainty way through the mud. Tom continued to lay stones. The bishop must be bowled over by the sight of a thousand volunteers cheerfully and enthusiastically laboring to build their new cathedral. Now Tom needed to make an equally good impression. He was never at ease with well-dressed people, but he needed to appear competent and wise, calm and self-assured, the kind of man to whom you would gratefully entrust the worrisome complexities of a vast and costly building project.

He kept a lookout for the visitors and put down his trowel as the party approached him. Prior Philip led Bishop Henry up to Tom, and Tom knelt and kissed the bishop's hand. Philip said: "Tom is our builder, sent to us by God on the day the old church burned down."

Tom knelt again to Bishop Waleran, then looked at the rest of the party. He reminded himself that he was the master builder, and should not be overly subservient. He recognized Percy Hamleigh, for whom he had once built half a house. "My Lord Percy," he said with a small bow. He spotted Percy's hideous wife. "My Lady Regan." Then his eye fell on the son. He remembered how William had almost run Martha down on his great war-horse; and how William had tried to buy Ellen in the forest. That young man was a nasty piece of work. But Tom made his face a polite mask. "And young Lord William. Greetings."

Bishop Henry was looking keenly at Tom. "Have you drawn your plans, Tom Builder?"

"Yes, my lord bishop. Would you like to see them?"

"Most certainly."

"Perhaps you will step this way."

Henry nodded, and Tom led the way to his shed, a few yards away. He stepped inside the little wooden building and brought out the ground plan, drawn in plaster on a large wooden frame four feet long. He leaned it against the wall of the shed and stepped back.

This was a delicate moment. Most people could not read a plan, but bishops and lords hated to admit it, so it was necessary to explain the concept to them in a way that did not reveal their ignorance to the rest of the world. Some bishops did understand it, of course, and then they were insulted when a mere builder presumed to instruct them.

Nervously, Tom pointed at the plan and said: "This is the wall I'm building."

"Yes, the eastern facade, obviously," said Henry. That answered the question: he could read a plan perfectly well. "Why aren't the transepts aisled?"

"For economy," Tom answered promptly. "However, we won't start building them for another five years, and if the monastery continues to prosper as it has done in the first year under Prior Philip, it may well be that by then we will be able to afford aisled transepts." He had praised Philip and answered the question at the same time, and he felt rather clever.

Henry nodded approval. "Sensible to plan modestly and leave room for expansion. Show me the elevation."

Tom got out the elevation. He made no comment on it, now that he knew Henry was able to understand what he was looking at. This was confirmed when Henry said: "The proportions are pleasing."

"Thank you," Tom said. The bishop seemed pleased with everything. Tom added: "It's a modest cathedral, but it will be lighter and more beautiful than the old one."

"And how long will it take to complete?"

"Fifteen years, if the work is uninterrupted."

"Which it never is. However. Can you show us what it will *look* like—I mean, to someone standing outside?"

Tom understood him. "You want to see a sketch."

"Yes."

"Certainly." Tom returned to his wall, with the bishop's party in tow. He knelt over his mortarboard and spread the mortar in a uniform layer, smoothing the surface. Then, with the point of his trowel, he drew a sketch of the west end of the church in the mortar. He knew he was good at this. The bishop, his party, and all the monks and volunteer workers nearby watched in fascination. Drawing always seemed a miracle to people who could not do it. In a few moments Tom had created a line drawing of the west facade, with its three arched doorways, its big window, and its flanking turrets. It was a simple trick, but it never failed to impress.

"Remarkable," said Bishop Henry when the drawing was done. "May God's blessing be added to your skill."

Tom smiled. That amounted to a powerful endorsement of his appointment.

Prior Philip said: "My lord bishop, will you take some refreshment before you conduct the service?"

"Gladly."

Tom was relieved. His test was over and he had passed it.

"Perhaps you would step into the prior's house, just across here," Philip said to the bishop. The party began to move off. Philip squeezed Tom's arm and said in a murmur of restrained jubilation: "We've done it!"

Tom breathed a sigh of relief as the dignitaries left him. He felt pleased and proud. Yes, he thought, we've done it. Bishop Henry was more than impressed: he was flabbergasted, despite his composure. Obviously Waleran had primed him to expect a scene of lethargy and inactivity, so the reality had been even more striking. In the end Waleran's malice had worked against him and heightened the triumph of Philip and Tom.

Just as he was basking in the glow of an honest victory, he heard a familiar voice. "Hello, Tom Builder."

He turned around and saw Ellen.

It was Tom's turn to be flabbergasted. The cathedral crisis had so filled his mind that he had not thought about her all day. He gazed at her happily. She looked just the same as the day she had walked away: slender, brown-skinned, with dark hair that moved like waves on a beach, and those deep-set luminous golden eyes. She smiled at him with that full-lipped mouth that always made him think of kissing.

He was seized by an urge to take her in his arms but he fought it down. With some difficulty he managed to say: "Hello, Ellen."

A young man beside her said: "Hello, Tom."

Tom looked at him curiously.

Ellen said: "Don't you remember Jack?"

"Jack!" he said, startled. The lad had changed. He was a little taller than his mother now, and he had the bony physique that made grandmothers say that a boy had outgrown his strength. He still had bright red hair, white skin and blue eyes, but his features had resolved into more attractive proportions, and one day he might even be handsome.

Tom looked back at Ellen. For a moment he just enjoyed staring at her. He wanted to say *I've missed you, I can't tell you how much I've missed you*, and he almost did, but then he lost his nerve, and instead he said: "Well, where have you been?"

"We've been living where we always lived, in the forest," she said.

"And what made you come back today, of all days?"

"We heard about the appeal for volunteers, and we were curious to know how you were getting along. And I haven't forgotten that I promised to come back one day."

"I'm so glad you did," Tom said. "I've been longing to see you."

She looked guarded. "Oh?"

This was the moment for which he had been waiting and planning for a year, and now that it had come he was scared. Until now he had been able to live in hope, but if she turned him down today he would know he had lost her forever. He was frightened to begin. The silence dragged out. He took a deep breath. "Listen," he said. "I want you to come back to me. Now, please don't say anything until you've heard what I have to say—please?"

"All right," she said neutrally.

"Philip is a very good prior. The monastery is getting wealthier all the time, thanks to his good management. My job here is secure. We won't have to tramp the roads again, ever, I promise."

"It wasn't that—"

"I know, but I want to tell you everything."

"All right."

"I've built a house in the village, with two rooms and a chimney, and I can make it bigger. We wouldn't have to live in the priory."

"But Philip owns the village."

"Philip is indebted to me right now." Tom waved an arm to indicate the scene all around. "He knows he couldn't have done this without me. If I ask him to forgive you for what you did, and to regard your year of exile as penance enough, he'll agree. He couldn't deny me that, today of all days."

"What about the boys?" she said. "Am I supposed to watch Alfred spill Jack's blood every time he feels irritable?"

"I think I've got the answer to that, really," Tom said. "Alfred is a mason now. I'll take Jack as my apprentice. That way, Alfred won't be resentful of Jack's idleness. And you can teach Alfred to read and write, so that the two boys will be equal—both working-men, both literate."

"You've thought about this a lot, haven't you?" she said.

"Yes."

He waited for her reaction. He was no good at being persuasive. All he could do was set out the situation. If only he could have drawn her a sketch! He felt he had dealt with every possible objection. She must agree now! But still she hesitated. "I'm not sure," she said.

His self-control broke. "Oh, Ellen, don't say that." He was afraid of crying in front of all these people, and he was so choked up that he could hardly speak. "I love you so much, please don't go away again," he begged. "The only thing that's kept me going is the hope that you'd come back. I just can't bear to live without you. Don't close the gates of paradise. Can't you see that I love you with all my heart?"

Her manner changed instantly. "Why didn't you say so, then?" she whispered, and she came to him. He wrapped his arms around her. "I love you, too, you silly fool," she said.

He felt weak with joy. She *does* love me, she *does*, he thought. He hugged her hard, then he looked at her face. "Will you marry me, Ellen?"

There were tears in her eyes, but she was smiling too. "Yes, Tom, I'll marry you," she said. She lifted her face.

He pulled her to him and kissed her mouth. He had dreamed of this for a year. He closed his eyes and concentrated on the delightful touch of her full lips on his. Her mouth was slightly open and her lips were moist. The kiss was so delicious that for a moment he forgot himself. Then someone nearby said: "Don't swallow her, man!"

He pulled away from her and said: "We're in a church!"

"I don't care," she said merrily, and she kissed him again.

Prior Philip had outwitted them again, William thought bitterly as he sat in the prior's house, drinking Philip's watery wine and eating sweetmeats from the priory kitchen. It had taken William a while to appreciate the brilliance and completeness of Philip's victory. There had been nothing wrong with Bishop Waleran's original assessment of the situation: it was true that Philip was short of money and would have great difficulty building a cathedral at Kingsbridge. But despite that, the wily monk had made dogged progress, hired a master builder, started the building and then, out of nothing, conjured a vast work force to bamboozle Bishop Henry. And Henry had been duly impressed, all the more so because Waleran had painted such a bleak picture in advance.

That damned monk knew he had won, too. He could not keep the triumphant smile off his face. Now he was deep in conversation with Bishop Henry, talking animatedly about breeds of sheep and the price of wool, and Henry was listening carefully, almost respectfully, meanwhile rudely ignoring William's mother and father, who were far more important than a mere prior.

Philip was going to regret this day. Nobody was allowed to best the Hamleighs and get away with it. They had not reached the position they enjoyed today by allowing monks to get the better of them. Bartholomew of Shiring had insulted them and had died in a traitor's jail. Philip would fare no better.

Tom Builder was another man who was going to regret crossing the Hamleighs. William had not forgotten how Tom had defied him at Durstead, holding his horse's head and forcing him to pay the workmen. Today Tom had disrespectfully called him "young Lord William." He was obviously hand in glove with Philip now, building cathedrals, not manor houses. He would learn that it was better to take your chances with the Hamleighs than to join forces with their enemies.

William sat quietly fuming until Bishop Henry got to his feet and said he was ready to hold the service. Prior Philip gestured to a novice, who went running from the room, and a few moments later a bell began to ring.

They all left the house, Bishop Henry first, Bishop Waleran second, then Prior Philip, then the lay people. All the monks were waiting outside, and they fell into line behind Philip, forming a procession. The Hamleighs had to bring up the rear.

The volunteers filled the entire western half of the priory close, sitting on walls and roofs. Henry mounted a platform in the middle of the building site. The monks formed up in rows behind him, where the quire of the new cathedral would be. The Hamleighs and the other lay members of the bishop's entourage made their way to what would become the nave.

As they took their places, William saw Aliena.

She looked very different. She wore rough, cheap clothing and wooden clogs, and the mass of curls that framed her head was damp with sweat. But it was definitely Aliena, and she was still so beautiful that his throat went dry and he stared at her, unable to tear his gaze away, while the service began and the priory close filled with the sound of a thousand voices saying the Our Father.

She seemed to feel his intense look, for she appeared troubled, shifting from foot to foot and then glancing around as if searching. Finally she met his eyes. An expression of horror and fear came over her face, and she shrank back, although she was already ten yards or more away and separated from him by dozens of people. Her fear made her all the more desirable to him, and he felt his body respond in a way it had not done for a year. His lust for her was mingled with resentment because of the spell she had cast over him. She flushed and dropped her gaze, as if she were ashamed. She spoke briefly to a boy next to her—that was the brother, of course, William thought, recalling the face in a flash of erotic memory—and then she turned away and disappeared into the crowd.

William felt let down. He was tempted to follow her, but of course he could not, not in the middle of a service, in front of his parents, two bishops, forty monks and a thousand worshipers. So he turned back to face the front, disappointed. He had lost his chance to find out where she lived.

Although she had gone, she still filled his mind. He wondered if it was a sin to have an erection in church.

He noticed that Father was looking agitated. "Look!" he was saying to Mother. "Look at that woman!"

At first William thought Father must be talking about Aliena. But she was nowhere in sight, and when he followed his father's stare, he saw a woman nearer to thirty years of age, not as voluptuous as Aliena but with an agile, untamed look that made her interesting. She was standing some distance away with Tom, the master builder, and William thought it was probably the builder's wife, the woman he had tried to buy in the forest one day a year or so ago. But why would his father know her?

"Is it her?" Father said.

The woman turned her head, almost as if she had heard them, and looked straight at them, and William saw again her pale, penetrating golden eyes.

"It *is* her, by God," Mother hissed.

The woman's stare shook Father. His red face paled and his hands trembled. "Jesus Christ preserve us," he said. "I thought she was dead."

And William thought: Now what the devil is that all about?

Jack had been dreading this.

For a whole year he had known that his mother missed Tom Builder. She was less even-tempered than she used to be; she often had a dreamy, faraway look; and in the night she sometimes made the panting noises, as if she were dreaming or imagining that she was making love to Tom. Jack had known, all along, that she would come back. And now she had agreed to stay.

He hated the idea.

The two of them had always been happy together. He loved his mother and his mother loved him, and there was no one else to interfere.

Life in the forest was somewhat uninteresting, it was true. He had missed the fascination of the crowds and the cities he had seen in his brief sojourn with Tom's family. He missed Martha. Oddly enough, he had relieved the boredom of the forest by daydreaming about the girl he thought of as the Princess, although he knew her name was Aliena. And he would be interested to work with Tom, and find out how buildings were constructed. But he would no longer be free. People would tell him what to do. He would have to work whether he wanted to or not. And he would have to share his mother with the rest of the world.

As he sat on the wall near the priory gate, ruminating disconsolately, he was astonished to see the Princess.

He blinked. She was pushing her way through the crowd, heading for the gate, looking distressed. She was even more beautiful than he remembered. In those days she had had a rounded, voluptuous, girlish body dressed in costly clothes. Now she looked thinner and more like a woman than a girl. The sweat-soaked linen shift she wore clung to her body, showing her full breasts and the ribs beneath, a flat belly, narrow hips and long legs. Her face was smeared with mud and her massed curls were untidy. She was upset about something, frightened and distressed, but the emotion only made her face more radiant. Jack was captivated by the sight of her. He felt a peculiar stirring in his loins that he had never experienced before.

He followed her. There was no conscious decision. One moment he was sitting on the wall gaping at her and the next he was hurrying through the gate behind her. He caught up with her on the street outside. She had a musky scent, as though she had been working hard. He remembered that she used to smell of flowers. "Is anything wrong?" he said.

"No, nothing's wrong," she said curtly, and she quickened her step.

Jack kept pace with her. "You don't remember me. Last time we met, you explained to me how babies were conceived."

"Oh, shut up and go away!" she shouted.

He stopped and let her walk on. He felt disappointed. Obviously he had said the wrong thing.

She had treated him like an irritating child. He was thirteen years old, but that probably seemed like childhood to her, from the lofty height of eighteen or so years.

He saw her go up to a house, take out a key that hung from a thong around her neck, and unlock the door.

She lived right here!

That made everything different.

Suddenly the prospect of leaving the forest and living in Kingsbridge did not seem so bad. He would see the Princess every day. That would compensate for a lot.

He stayed where he was, watching the door, but she did not reemerge. It was an odd thing to do, to stand in a street in the hope of seeing someone who hardly knew him; but he did not want to move. He was seething inside with a new emotion. Nothing seemed very important anymore except the Princess. He was single-minded about her. He was enchanted. He was possessed.

He was in love.

PART THREE

1140-1142

Chapter 8

T HE WHORE WILLIAM PICKED was not very pretty but she had big breasts and her mass of curly hair appealed to him. She sauntered over to him, swaying her hips, and he saw that she was a little older than he had thought, maybe twenty-five or thirty, and while her mouth smiled innocently her eyes were hard and calculating. Walter chose next. He selected a small, vulnerable-looking girl with a boyish, flat-chested figure. When William and Walter had made their selection the other four knights moved in.

William had brought them to the whorehouse because they needed some kind of release. They had not had a battle for months and they were becoming discontented and quarrelsome.

The civil war that had broken out a year ago, between King Stephen and his rival, Maud, the so-called Empress, was now in a lull. William and his men had followed Stephen all over southwest England. His strategy was energetic but erratic. He would attack one of Maud's strongholds with tremendous enthusiasm; but if he did not win an early victory, he swiftly tired of the siege, and would move on. The military leader of the rebels was not Maud herself, but her half brother Robert, earl of Gloucester; and so far Stephen had failed to force him into a confrontation. It was an indecisive war, with much movement and little actual fighting; and so the men were restless.

The whorehouse was divided by screens into small rooms, each with a straw mattress. William and his knights took their chosen women behind the screens. William's whore adjusted the screen for privacy, then pulled down the top of her shift, exposing her breasts. They were big, as William had seen, but they had the large nipples and visible veins of a woman who has suckled children, and William was a little disappointed. Nevertheless, he pulled her to him and took her breasts in his hands, squeezing them and pinching the nipples. "Gently," she said in a tone of mild protest. She put her arms around him and pulled his hips forward, rubbing herself against him. After a few moments she pushed her hand between their bodies and felt for his groin.

He muttered a curse. His body was not responding.

"Don't worry," she murmured. Her condescending tone angered him, but he said nothing as she disengaged herself from his embrace, knelt down, lifted the front of his tunic and went to work with her mouth.

At first the sensation pleased him, and he thought everything was going to be all right, but after the initial surge he lost interest again. He watched her face, as that sometimes inflamed him, but now he was only reminded of how unimpressive he appeared. He began to feel angry, and that made him shrivel even more.

She stopped and said: "Try to relax." When she started again she sucked so hard that she hurt him. He pulled away, and her teeth scraped his sensitive skin, making him cry out. He struck her backhanded across the face. She gasped and fell sideways.

"Clumsy bitch," he snarled. She lay on the mattress at his feet, looking up at him fearfully. He threw a random kick at her, more in irritation than malice. It caught her in the belly. It was harder than he had really intended, and she doubled up in pain.

He realized that his body was responding at last.

He knelt down, rolled her on to her back, and straddled her. She stared up at him with pain and fear in her eyes. He pulled up the skirt of her dress until it was around her waist. The hair between her legs was thick and curly. He liked that. He fondled himself as he looked at her body. He was not quite stiff enough. The fear was going from her eyes. It occurred to him that she could be deliberately putting him off, trying to deflate his desire so that she would not have to service him. The thought infuriated him. He made a fist and punched her face hard.

She screamed and tried to get out from under him. He rested his weight on her, pinning her down, but she continued to struggle and yell. Now he was fully erect. He tried to force her thighs apart, but she resisted him.

The screen was jerked aside and Walter came in, wearing only his boots and undershirt, with his prick sticking out in front of him like a flagpole. Two more knights came in behind him: Ugly Gervase and Hugh Axe.

"Hold her down for me, lads," William said to them.

The three knights knelt down around the whore and held her still.

William positioned himself to enter her, then paused, enjoying the anticipation.

Walter said: "What happened, lord?"

"Changed her mind when she saw the size of it," William said with a grin.

They all roared with laughter. William penetrated her. He liked it when there were people watching. He started to move in and out.

Walter said: "You interrupted me just as I was getting mine in."

William could see that Walter had not yet been satisfied. "Stick it in this one's mouth," he said. "She likes that."

"I'll give it a try." Walter changed his position and grabbed the woman by the hair, lifting her head. By now she was frightened enough to do anything, and she cooperated readily. Gervase and Hugh were no longer needed to hold her down, but they stayed and watched. They looked fascinated: they had probably never seen a woman done by two men at the same time. William had never seen it either. There was something curiously exciting about it. Walter seemed to feel the same, for after just a few moments he began to breathe heavily and move convulsively, and then he came. Watching him, William did the same a second or two later.

After a moment, they got to their feet. William still felt excited. "Why don't you two do her?" he said to Gervase and Hugh. He liked the idea of watching a repeat performance.

However, they were not keen. "I've got a little darling waiting," said Hugh, and Gervase said: "Me, too."

The whore stood up and rearranged her dress. Her face was unreadable. William said to her: "That wasn't so bad, was it?"

She stood in front of him and stared at him for a moment, then she pursed her lips and spat. He felt his face covered with a warm, sticky fluid: she had retained Walter's semen in her mouth. The stuff blurred his vision. Angry, he raised a hand to strike her, but she ducked out between the screens. Walter and the other knights burst out laughing. William did not think it was funny, but he could not chase after the girl with semen all over his face, and he realized that the only way to retain his dignity was to pretend not to care, so he laughed too.

Ugly Gervase said: "Well, lord, I hope you don't have Walter's baby, now!" and they roared. Even William thought that was funny.

They all walked out of the little booth together, leaning on one another and wiping their eyes. The other girls were staring at them, looking anxious: they had heard William's whore scream and were afraid of trouble. One or two customers peeped out curiously from the other booths. Walter said: "First time I ever saw that stuff spurt out of a girl!" and they started laughing again.

One of William's squires was standing by the door, looking anxious. He was only a lad and he had probably never been inside a brothel before. He smiled nervously, not sure whether he was entitled to join in the hilarity. William said to him: "What are you doing here, you po-faced idiot?"

"There's a message come for you, lord," the squire said.

"Well, don't waste time, tell me what it is!"

"I'm very sorry, lord," said the boy. He looked so frightened that William thought he was going to turn around and run out of the house.

"What are you sorry for, you turd?" William roared. "Give me the message!"

"Your father's dead, lord," the boy blurted out, and he burst into tears.

William stared, dumbstruck. Dead? he thought. Dead? "But he's in perfectly good health!" he shouted stupidly. It was true that Father was not able to fight on the battlefield anymore, but that was not surprising in a man almost fifty years old. The squire continued to cry. William recalled the way Father had looked last time he saw him: stout, red-faced, hearty and choleric, as full of life as a man could be, and that was only . . . He realized, with a small shock, that it was nearly a year since he had seen his father. "What happened?" he said to the squire. "What happened to him?"

"He had a seizure, lord," the squire sobbed.

A seizure. The news began to sink in. Father was dead. That big, strong, blustering, irascible man was lying helpless and cold on a stone slab somewhere—

"I'll have to go home," William said suddenly.

Walter said gently: "You must first ask the king to release you."

"Yes, that's right," William said vaguely. "I must ask permission." His mind was in a turmoil.

"Shall I tip the brothel keeper?" said Walter.

"Yes." William handed Walter his purse. Someone put William's cloak over his shoulders. Walter murmured something to the woman who ran the whorehouse and gave her some money. Hugh Axe opened the door for William. They all went out.

They walked through the streets of the small town in silence.

William felt peculiarly detached, as if he were watching everything from above. He could not take in the fact that his father no longer existed. As they approached headquarters he tried to pull himself together.

King Stephen was holding court in the church, for there was no castle or guildhall here. It was a small, simple stone church with its inside walls painted bright red, blue and orange. A fire had been lit in the middle of the floor, and the handsome, tawny-haired king sat near it on a wooden throne, with his legs stretched out before him in his usual relaxed position. He wore soldier's clothes, high boots and a leather tunic, but he had a crown instead of a helmet. William and Walter pushed through the crowd of petitioners near the church door, nodded at the guards who were keeping the general public back, and strode into the inner circle. Stephen was talking to a newly arrived earl, but he noticed William and broke off immediately. "William, my friend. You've heard."

William bowed. "My lord king."

Stephen stood up. "I mourn with you," he said. He put his arms around William and held him for a moment before releasing him.

His sympathy brought the first tears to William's eyes. "I must ask you for leave to go home," he said.

"Granted willingly, though not gladly," said the king. "We'll miss your strong right arm."

"Thank you, lord."

"I also grant you custody of the earldom of Shiring, and all the revenues from it, until the question of the succession is decided. Go home, and bury your father, and come back to us as soon as you can."

William bowed again and withdrew. The king resumed his conversation. Courtiers gathered around William to commiserate. As he accepted their condolences, the significance of what the king had said hit him. He had given William custody of the earldom *until the question of the succession is decided*. What question? William was the only child of his father. How could there be a question? He looked at the faces around him and his eye lit upon a young priest who was one of the more knowledgeable of the king's clerics. He drew the priest to him and said quietly: "What the devil did he mean about the 'question' of the succession, Joseph?"

"There's another claimant to the earldom," Joseph replied.

"Another claimant?" William repeated in astonishment. He had no half brothers, illegitimate brothers, cousins. . . . "Who is it?"

Joseph pointed to a figure standing with his back to them. He was with the new arrivals. He was wearing the clothing of a squire.

"But he's not even a knight!" William said loudly. "My father was the earl of Shiring!"

The squire heard him, and turned around. "My father was also the earl of Shiring."

At first William did not recognize him. He saw a handsome, broad-shouldered young man of about eighteen years, well-dressed for a squire, and carrying a fine sword. There was confidence and even arrogance in the way he stood. Most striking of all, he gazed at William with a look of such pure hatred that William shrank back.

The face was very familiar, but changed. Still William could not place it. Then his saw that there was an angry scar on the squire's right ear, where the earlobe had been cut off. In a vivid flash of memory he saw a small piece of white flesh fall onto the heaving chest of a terrified virgin, and heard a boy scream in pain. This was Richard, the son of the traitor Bartholomew, the brother of Aliena. The little boy who had been forced to watch while two men raped his sister had grown into a formidable man with the light of vengeance in his light blue eyes. William was suddenly terribly afraid.

"You remember, don't you?" Richard said, in a light drawl that did not quite mask the cold fury underneath.

William nodded. "I remember."

"So do I, William Hamleigh," said Richard. "So do I."

William sat in the big chair at the head of the table, where his father used to sit. He had always known he would occupy this seat one day. He had imagined he would feel immensely powerful when he did so, but in reality he was a little frightened. He was afraid that people would say he was not the man his father had been, and that they would disrespect him.

His mother sat on his right. He had often watched her, when his father was in this chair, and observed the way she played on Father's fears and weaknesses to get her own way. He was determined not to let her do the same to him.

On his left sat Arthur, a mild-mannered, gray-headed man who had been Earl Bartholomew's reeve. After becoming earl, Father had hired Arthur, because Arthur had a good knowledge of the estate. William had always been dubious about that reasoning. Other people's servants sometimes clung to the ways of their former employer.

"King Stephen can't *possibly* make Richard the earl," Mother was saying angrily. "He's just a squire!"

"I don't understand how he even managed that," William said irritably. "I thought they had been left penniless. But he had fine clothes and a good sword. Where did he get the money?"

"He set himself up as a wool merchant," Mother said. "He's got all the money he needs. Or rather, his sister has—I hear Aliena runs the business."

Aliena. So she was behind this. William had never quite forgotten her, but she had not preyed on his mind so much, after the war broke out, until he had met Richard. Since then she had been in his thoughts continually, as fresh and beautiful, as vulnerable and desirable as ever. He hated her for the hold she had over him.

"So Aliena is rich now?" he said with an affectation of detachment.

"Yes. But you've been fighting for the king for a year. He cannot refuse you your inheritance."

"Richard has fought bravely too, apparently," William said. "I made some inquiries. Worse still, his courage has come to the notice of the king."

Mother's expression changed from angry scorn to thoughtfulness. "So he really has a chance."

"I fear so."

"Right. We must fight him off."

Automatically, William said: "How?" He had resolved not to let his mother take charge but now he had done it.

"You must go back to the king with a bigger force of knights, new weapons and better horses, and plenty of squires and men-at-arms."

William would have liked to disagree with her but he knew she was right. In the end the king would probably give the earldom to the man who promised to be the most effective supporter, regardless of the rights and wrongs of the case.

"That's not all," Mother went on. "You must take care to look and act like an earl. That way the king will start to think of the appointment as a foregone conclusion."

Despite himself William was intrigued. "How should an earl look and act?"

"Speak your mind more. Have an opinion about everything: how the king should prosecute the war, the best tactics for each battle, the political situation in the north, and—especially this—the abilities and loyalty of other earls. Talk to one man about another. Tell the earl of Huntingdon that the count of Warenne is a great fighter; tell the bishop of Ely that you don't trust the sheriff of Lincoln. People will say to the king: 'William of Shiring is in the count of Warenne's faction,' or 'William of Shiring and his followers are against the sheriff of Lincoln.' If you appear powerful, the king will feel comfortable about giving you more power."

William had little faith in such subtlety. "I think the size of my army will count for more," he said. He turned to the reeve. "How much is there in my treasury, Arthur?"

"Nothing, lord," said Arthur.

"What the devil are you talking about?" said William harshly. "There must be something. How much is it?"

Arthur had a slightly superior air, as if he had nothing to fear from William. "Lord, there's no money at all in the treasury."

William wanted to strangle him. "This is the earldom of Shiring!" he said, loud enough to make the knights and castle officials farther down the table look up. "There must be money!"

"Money comes in all the time, lord, of course," Arthur said smoothly. "But it goes out again, especially in wartime."

William studied the pale, clean-shaven face. Arthur was far too complacent. Was he honest? There was no way of telling. William wished for eyes that could see into a man's heart.

Mother knew what William was thinking. "Arthur is honest," she said, not caring that the man was right there. "He's old, and lazy and set in his ways, but he's honest."

William was stricken. He had only just sat in the chair and already his power was shriveling, as if by magic. He felt cursed. There seemed to be a law that William would always be a boy among men, no matter how old he grew. Weakly, he said: "How has this happened?"

Mother said: "Your father was ill for the best part of a year before he died. I could see he was letting things slip, but I couldn't get him to do anything about it."

It was news to William that his mother was not omnipotent. He had never before known her unable to get her way. He turned to Arthur. "We have some of the best farmland in the kingdom here. How can we be penniless?"

"Some of the farms are in trouble, and several tenants are in arrears with their rents."

"But why?"

"One reason I hear frequently is that the young men won't work on the land, but leave for the towns."

"Then we must stop them!"

Arthur shrugged. "Once a serf has lived in a town for a year, he becomes a freeman. It's the law."

"And what about the tenants who haven't paid? What have you done to them?"

"What can one do?" said Arthur. "If we take away their livelihood, they'll never be able to pay. So we must be patient, and hope
for a good harvest which will enable them to catch up."

Arthur was altogether too cheerful about his inability to solve
any of these problems, William thought angrily; but he reined in his
temper for the moment. "Well, if all the young men are going to the
towns, what about our rents from house property in Shiring? That
should have brought in some cash."

"Oddly enough, it hasn't," said Arthur. "There are a lot of
empty houses in Shiring. The young men must be going elsewhere."

"Or people are lying to you," William said. "I suppose you're
going to say that the income from the Shiring market and the fleece
fair is down too?"

"Yes—"

"Then why don't you increase the rents and taxes?"

"We have, lord, on the orders of your late father, but the
income has gone down nonetheless."

"With such an unproductive estate, how did Bartholomew keep
body and soul together?" William said in exasperation.

Arthur even had an answer for that. "He had the quarry, also.
That brought in a great deal of money, in the old days."

"And now it's in the hands of that damned monk." William
was shaken. Just when he needed to make an ostentatious display
he was being told that he was penniless. The situation was very
dangerous for him. The king had just granted him custody of an
earldom. It was a kind of probation. If he returned to court with a
diminutive army it would seem ungrateful, even disloyal.

Besides, the picture Arthur had painted could not be entirely
true. William felt sure people were cheating him—and they were
probably laughing about it behind his back, too. The thought made
him angry. He was not going to tolerate it. He would show them.
There would be bloodshed before he accepted defeat.

"You've got an excuse for everything," he said to Arthur. "The
fact is, you've let this estate run to seed during my father's illness,
which is when you ought to have been most vigilant."

"But, lord—"

William raised his voice. "Shut your mouth or I'll have you
flogged."

Arthur paled and went silent.

William said: "Starting tomorrow, we're going on a tour of the
earldom. We're going to visit every village I own, and shake them
all up. You may not know how to deal with whining, lying peasants, but I do. We'll soon find out how impoverished my earldom

is. And if you've lied to me, I swear to God you'll be the first of many hangings."

As well as Arthur, he took his groom, Walter, and the other four knights who had fought beside him for the past year: Ugly Gervase, Hugh Axe, Gilbert de Rennes and Miles Dice. They were all big, violent men, quick to anger and always ready to fight. They rode their best horses and went armed to the teeth, to scare the peasantry. William believed that a man was helpless unless people were afraid of him.

It was a hot day in late summer, and the wheat stood in fat sheaves in the fields. The abundance of visible wealth made William all the more angry that he had no money. Someone *must* be robbing him. They ought to be too frightened to dare. His family had won the earldom when Bartholomew was disgraced, and yet he was penniless while Bartholomew's son had plenty! The idea that people were stealing from him, and laughing at his unsuspecting ignorance, gnawed at him like a stomachache, and he got angrier as he rode along.

He had decided to begin at Northbrook, a small village somewhat remote from the castle. The villagers were a mixture of serfs and freemen. The serfs were William's property, and could not do anything without his permission. They owed him so many days' work at certain times of year, plus a share of their own crops. The freemen just paid him rent, in cash or in kind. Five of them were in arrears. William had a notion they thought they could get away with it because they were far from the castle. It might be a good place to begin the shake-up.

It was a long ride, and the sun was high when they approached the village. There were twenty or thirty houses surrounded by three big fields, all of them now stubble. Near the houses, at the edge of one of the fields, were three large oak trees in a group. As William and his men drew near, he saw that most of the villagers appeared to be sitting in the shade of the oaks, eating their dinner. He spurred his horse into a canter for the last few hundred yards, and the others followed suit. They halted in front of the villagers in a cloud of dust.

As the villagers were scrambling to their feet, swallowing their horsebread and trying to keep the dust out of their eyes, William's mistrustful gaze observed a curious little drama. A middle-aged man with a black beard spoke quietly but urgently to a plump red-cheeked girl with a plump, red-cheeked baby. A young man joined them and was hastily shooed away by the older man. Then the girl walked off toward the houses, apparently under protest, and disappeared in the dust. William was intrigued. There was something furtive about the whole scene, and he wished Mother were here to interpret it.

He decided to do nothing about it for the moment. He addressed Arthur in a voice loud enough for them all to hear. "Five of my free tenants here are in arrears, is that right?"

"Yes, lord."

"Who is the worst?"

"Athelstan hasn't paid for two years, but he was very unlucky with his pigs—"

William spoke over Arthur, cutting him off. "Which one of you is Athelstan?"

A tall, stoop-shouldered man of about forty-five years stepped forward. He had thinning hair and watery eyes.

William said: "Why don't you pay me rent?"

"Lord, it's a small holding, and I've no one to help me, now that my boys have gone to work in the town, and then there was the swine fever—"

"Just a moment," William said. "Where did your sons go?"

"To Kingsbridge, lord, to work on the new cathedral there, for they want to marry, as young men must, and my land won't support three families."

William tucked away in his memory, for future reflection, the information that the young men had gone to work on Kingsbridge Cathedral. "Your holding is big enough to support one family, at any rate, but still you don't pay your rent."

Athelstan began to talk about his pigs again. William stared malevolently at him without listening. I know why you haven't paid, he thought; you knew your lord was ill and you decided to cheat him while he was incapable of enforcing his rights. The other four delinquents thought the same. You rob us when we're weak!

For a moment he was full of self-pity. The five of them had been chuckling over their cleverness, he felt sure. Well, now they would learn their lesson. "Gilbert and Hugh, take this peasant and hold him still," he said quietly.

Athelstan was still talking. The two knights dismounted and approached him. His tale of swine fever tailed off into nothing. The knights took him by the arms. He turned pale with fear.

William spoke to Walter in the same quiet voice. "Have you got your chain-mail gloves?"

"Yes, lord."

"Put them on. Teach Athelstan a lesson. But make sure he lives to spread the word."

"Yes, lord." Walter took from his saddlebag a pair of leather gauntlets with fine chain mail sewn to the knuckles and the backs of the fingers. He pulled them on slowly. All the villagers watched in dread, and Athelstan began to moan with terror.

Walter got off his horse, walked over to Athelstan and punched him in the stomach with one mailed fist. The thud as the blow landed was sickeningly loud. Athelstan doubled over, too winded to cry out. Gilbert and Hugh pulled him upright, and Walter punched his face. Blood spurted from his mouth and nose. One of the onlookers, a woman who was presumably his wife, screamed out and jumped on Walter, yelling: "Stop! Leave him! Don't kill him!"

Walter brushed her off, and two other women grabbed her and pulled her back. She continued to scream and struggle. The other peasants watched in mutinous silence as Walter beat Athelstan systematically until his body was limp, his face covered with blood and his eyes closed in unconsciousness.

"Let him go," William said at last.

Gilbert and Hugh released Athelstan. He slumped to the ground and lay still. The women released the wife and she ran to him, sobbing, and knelt beside him. Walter took off the gauntlets and wiped the blood and pieces of flesh off the chain mail.

William had already lost interest in Athelstan. Looking around the village, he saw a new-looking two-story wooden structure built on the edge of the brook. He pointed to it and said to Arthur: "What's that?"

"I haven't seen it before, lord," Arthur said nervously.

William thought he was lying. "It's a water mill, isn't it?"

Arthur shrugged, but his indifference was unconvincing. "I can't imagine what else it would be, right there by the stream."

How could he be so insolent, when he had just seen a peasant beaten half to death on William's orders? Almost desperately, William said: "Are my serfs allowed to build mills without my permission?"

"No, lord."

"Do you know *why* this is prohibited?"

"So that they will bring their grain to the lord's mills and pay him to grind it for them."

"And the lord will profit."

"Yes, lord." Arthur spoke in the condescending tone of one who explains something elementary to a child. "But if they pay a fine for building a mill, the lord will profit just the same."

William found his tone maddening. "No, he won't profit just the same. The fine is never as much as the peasants would otherwise have to pay. That's why they love to build mills. And that's why my father would never let them." Without giving Arthur the chance to reply, he kicked his horse and rode over to the mill. His knights followed, and the villagers tailed along behind them in a ragged crowd.

William dismounted. There was no doubt about what the building was. A large waterwheel was turning under the pressure of the fast-flowing stream. The wheel turned a shaft which went through the side wall of the mill. It was a solid wooden construction, made to last. Whoever built it had clearly expected to be free to use it for years.

The miller stood outside the open door, wearing a prepared expression of injured innocence. In the room behind him were sacks of grain in neat stacks. William dismounted. The miller bowed to him politely, but was there not a hint of scorn in his look? Once again William had the painful sense that these people thought he was a nobody, and his inability to impose his will on them made him feel impotent. Indignation and frustration welled up in him, and he yelled at the miller furiously. "Whatever made you think you could get away with this? Do you imagine that I'm stupid? Is that it? Is that what you think?" Then he punched the man in the face.

The miller gave an exaggerated cry of pain and fell to the ground quite unnecessarily.

William stepped over him and went inside. The shaft of the waterwheel was connected, by a set of wooden gears, to the shaft of the grindstone on the upper floor. The milled grain fell through a chute to the threshing floor at ground level. The second floor, which had to bear the weight of the grindstone, was supported by four stout timbers (taken from William's forest without permission, undoubtedly). If the timbers were cut the whole building would fall.

William went outside. Hugh Axe carried the weapon from which he got his name strapped to his saddle. William said: "Give me your battle-ax." Hugh obliged. William went back inside and began to attack the timber supports of the upper floor.

It gave him great satisfaction to feel the blade of the ax thud into the building that the peasants had so carefully constructed in their attempt to cheat him of his milling fees. They aren't laughing at me now, he thought savagely.

Walter came in and stood watching. William hacked a deep notch in one of the supports and then cut halfway through a second. The platform above, which carried the enormous weight of the millstone, began to tremble. William said: "Get a rope." Walter went out.

William cut into the other two timbers as deeply as he dared. The building was ready to collapse. Walter came back with some rope. William tied the rope to one of the timbers, then carried the other end outside and tied it around the neck of his war-horse.

The peasants watched in sullen silence.

When the rope was fixed, William said: "Where's the miller?"

The miller approached, still trying to look like one who is being unjustly dealt with.

William said: "Gervase, tie him up and put him inside."

The miller made a break for it, but Gilbert tripped him and sat on him, and Gervase tied his hands and feet with leather thongs. The two knights picked him up. He began to struggle and plead for mercy.

One of the villagers stepped out of the crowd and said: "You can't do this. It's murder. Even a lord can't murder people."

William pointed a trembling finger at him. "If you open your mouth again I'll put you inside with him."

For a moment the man looked defiant; then he thought better of it and turned away.

The knights came out of the mill. William walked his horse forward until it had taken up the slack in the rope. He slapped its rump, and it took the strain.

Inside the building, the miller began to scream. The noise was bloodcurdling. It was the sound of a man in mortal terror, a man who knew that within the next few moments he was going to be crushed to death.

The horse tossed its head, trying to slacken the rope around its neck. William yelled at it and kicked its rump to make it pull, then shouted at his knights: "Heave on the rope, you men!" The four knights grabbed the taut rope and pulled with the horse. The villagers' voices were raised in protest, but they were all too frightened to interfere. Arthur was standing to one side, looking sick.

The miller's screams became more shrill. William imagined the blind terror that must be possessing the man as he waited for his dreadful death. None of these peasants will ever forget the revenge of the Hamleighs, he thought.

The timber creaked loudly; then there was a loud crack as it broke. The horse bounded forward and the knights let go of the rope. A corner of the roof sagged. The women began to wail. The wooden walls of the mill seemed to shudder; the miller's screams rose higher; there was a mighty crash as the upper floor gave way; the screaming was cut off abruptly; and the ground shook as the grindstone landed on the threshing floor. The walls splintered, the roof caved in, and in a moment the mill was nothing but a pile of firewood with a dead man inside it.

William began to feel better.

Some of the villagers ran forward and began to dig into the debris frantically. If they were hoping to find the miller alive they would be disappointed. His body would be a grisly sight. That was all to the good.

Looking around, William spotted the red-cheeked girl with the red-cheeked baby, standing at the back of the crowd, as if she were trying to be inconspicuous. He remembered how the man with the black beard—presumably her father—had been keen to keep her out of sight. He decided to solve that mystery before leaving the village. He caught her eye and beckoned her. She looked behind her, hoping he was pointing at someone else. "You," William said. "Come here."

The man with the black beard saw her and gave a grunt of exasperation.

William said: "Who's your husband, wench?"

The father said: "She has no—"

He was too late, however, for the girl said: "Edmund."

"So you *are* married. But who's your father?"

"I am," said the man with the black beard. "Theobald."

William turned to Arthur. "Is Theobald a freeman?"

"He's a serf, lord."

"And when a serf's daughter marries, is it not the lord's right, as her owner, to enjoy her on the wedding night?"

Arthur was shocked. "Lord! That primitive custom has not been enforced in this part of the world in living memory!"

"True," said William. "The father pays a fine, instead. How much did Theobald pay?"

"He hasn't paid yet, lord, but—"

"Not paid! And she with a fat red-cheeked child!"

Theobald said: "We never had the money, lord, and she was with child by Edmund, and wanted to be wed, but we can pay now, for we've got the crop in."

William smiled at the girl. "Let me see the baby."

She stared at him fearfully.

"Come. Give it to me."

She was afraid but she could not bring herself to hand over her baby. William stepped closer and gently took the child from her. Her eyes filled with terror but she did not resist him.

The baby began to squall. William held it for a moment, then grasped both its ankles in one hand and with a swift motion threw it into the air as high as he could.

The girl screamed like a banshee and gazed into the air as the baby flew upward.

The father ran forward with his arms outstretched to catch it as it fell.

While the girl was looking up and screaming, William took a handful of her dress and ripped it. She had a pink, rounded young body.

The father caught the baby safely.

The girl turned to run, but William caught her and threw her to the ground.

The father handed the baby to a woman and turned to look at William.

William said: "As I wasn't given my due on the wedding night, and the fine hasn't been paid, I'll take what's owed me now."

The father rushed at him.

William drew his sword.

The father stopped.

William looked at the girl, lying on the ground, trying to cover her nakedness with her hands. Her fear aroused him. "And when I've done, my knights will have her too," he said with a contented smile.

II

In three years Kingsbridge had changed beyond recognition.

William had not been here since the Whitsunday when Philip and his army of volunteers had frustrated Waleran Bigod's scheme. Then it had been forty or fifty wooden houses clustered around the priory gate and scattered along the muddy footpath that led to the bridge. Now, he saw as he approached the village across the undulating fields, there were three times as many houses, at least. They formed a brown fringe all around the gray stone wall of the priory and completely filled the space between the priory and the river. Several of the houses looked large. Within the priory close there were new stone buildings, and the walls of the church seemed to be going up fast. There were two new quays beside the river. Kingsbridge had become a town.

The appearance of the place confirmed a suspicion that had been growing in his mind since he had come home from the war. As he had toured around, collecting arrears of rent and terrorizing disobedient serfs, he had continually heard talk of Kingsbridge. Landless young men were going there to work; prosperous families were sending their sons to school at the priory; smallholders would sell their eggs and cheese to the men working on the building site; and everyone who could went there on holy days, even though there was no cathedral. Today was a holy day—Michaelmas Day, which fell on a Sunday this year. It was a mild early-autumn morning, nice weather for traveling, so there should be a good crowd. William expected to find out what drew them to Kingsbridge.

His five henchmen rode with him. They had done sterling work in the villages. The news of William's tour had spread with uncanny speed, and after the first few days people knew what to expect. At William's approach they would send the children and young women to hide in the woods. It pleased William to strike fear into people's hearts: it kept them in their place. They certainly knew he was in command now!

As his group came closer to Kingsbridge, he kicked his horse into a trot, and the others followed suit. Arriving at speed was always more impressive. Other people shrank back to the sides of the road, or jumped into the fields, to get out of the way of the big horses.

They clattered over the wooden bridge, making a loud noise and ignoring the tollhouse keeper, but the narrow street ahead of them was blocked by a cart loaded with barrels of lime and pulled by two huge, slow-moving oxen; and the knights' horses were forced to slow abruptly.

William looked around as they followed the cart up the hill. New houses, hastily built, filled the spaces between the old ones. He noticed a cookshop, an alehouse, a smithy and a shoemaker's. The air of prosperity was unmistakable. William was envious.

There were not many people in the streets, however. Perhaps they were all up at the priory.

With his knights behind him he followed the ox cart through the priory gates. It was not the kind of entrance he liked to make, and he had a pang of anxiety that people would notice and laugh at him, but happily nobody even looked.

By contrast with the deserted town outside the walls, the priory close was humming with activity.

William reined in and looked around, trying to take it all in. There were so many people, and there was so much going on, that at first he found it somewhat bewildering. Then the scene resolved into three sections.

Nearest him, at the western end of the priory close, there was a market. The stalls were set up in neat north-south rows, and several hundred people were milling about in the aisles, buying food and drink, hats and shoes, knives, belts, ducklings, puppies, pots, earrings, wool, thread, rope, and dozens of other necessities and luxuries. The market was clearly thriving, and all the pennies, half-pennies and farthings that were changing hands must add up to a great deal of money.

It was no wonder, William thought bitterly, that the market at Shiring was in decline, when there was a flourishing alternative here at Kingsbridge. The rents from stall holders, tolls on suppliers, and taxes on sales that should have been going into the earl of Shiring's treasury were instead filling the coffers of Kingsbridge Priory.

But a market needed a license from the king, and William was sure Prior Philip did not have one. He was probably planning to apply as soon as he was caught, like the Northbrook miller. Unfortunately it would not be so easy for William to teach Philip a lesson.

Beyond the market was a zone of tranquillity. Adjacent to the cloisters, where the crossing of the old church used to be, there was an altar under a canopy, with a white-haired monk standing in front of it reading from a book. On the far side of the altar, monks in neat rows were singing hymns, although at this distance their music was drowned by the noise of the marketplace. There was a small congregation. This was probably nones, a service conducted for the benefit of the monks, William thought: all work and marketing would stop for the main Michaelmas service, of course.

At the far side of the priory close, the east end of the cathedral was being built. This was where Prior Philip was spending his rake-off from the market, William thought sourly. The walls were thirty or forty feet high, and it was already possible to see the outlines of the windows and the arches of the arcade. Workers swarmed all over the site. William thought there was something odd about the way they looked, and realized after a moment that it was their colorful dress. They were not regular laborers, of course— the paid work force would be on holiday today. These people were volunteers.

He had not expected that there would be so *many* of them. Hundreds of men and women were carrying stones and splitting timber and rolling barrels and heaving cartloads of sand up from the river, all working for nothing but forgiveness of their sins.

The sly prior had a crafty setup, William observed enviously. The people who came to work on the cathedral would spend money at the market. People who came to the market would give a few hours to the cathedral, for their sins. Each hand washed the other.

He kicked his horse forward and rode across the graveyard to the building site, curious to see it more closely.

The eight massive piers of the arcade marched down either side of the site in four opposed pairs. From a distance, William had thought he could see the round arches joining one pier with the next, but now he realized the arches were not built yet—what he had seen was the wooden falsework, made in the same shape, upon which the stones would rest while the arches were being constructed and the mortar was drying. The falsework did not rest on the ground, but was supported on the out-jutting moldings of the capitals on top of the piers.

Parallel with the arcade, the outer walls of the aisles were going up, with regular spaces for the windows. Midway between each window opening, a buttress jutted out from the line of the wall. Looking at the open ends of the unfinished walls, William could see that they were not solid stone: they were in fact double walls with a space in between. The cavity appeared to be filled with rubble and mortar.

The scaffolding was made of stout poles roped together, with trestles of flexible saplings and woven reeds laid across the poles.

A lot of money had been spent here, William noted.

He rode on around the outside of the chancel, followed by his knights. Against the walls were wooden lean-to huts, workshops and lodges for the craftsmen. Most of them were locked shut now, for there were no masons laying stones or carpenters making falsework today. However, the supervising craftsmen—the master masons and the master carpenter—were directing the volunteer laborers, telling them where to stack the stones, timber, sand and lime they were carrying up from the riverside.

William rode around the east end of the church to the south side, where his way was blocked by the monastic buildings. Then he turned back, marveling at the cunning of Prior Philip, who had his master craftsmen busy on a Sunday and his laborers working for no pay.

As he reflected on what he was seeing, it seemed devastatingly clear that Prior Philip was largely responsible for the decline in the fortunes of the Shiring earldom. The farms were losing their young men to the building site, and Shiring—jewel of the earldom—was being eclipsed by the growing new town of Kingsbridge. Residents here paid rent to Philip, not William, and people who bought and sold goods at this market generated income for the priory, not the earldom. And Philip had the timber, the sheep farms and the quarry that had once enriched the earl.

William and his men rode back across the close to the market. He decided to take a closer look. He urged his horse into the crowd. It inched forward. The people did not scatter fearfully out of his path. When the horse nudged them, they looked up at William with irritation or annoyance rather than dread, and moved out of the way in their own good time, with a somewhat condescending air. Nobody here was frightened of him. It made him nervous. If people were not scared there was no telling what they might do.

He went down one row and back up the next, with his knights trailing behind him. He became frustrated with the slow movement of the crowd. It would have been quicker to walk; but then, he felt sure, these insubordinate Kingsbridge people would probably have been cocky enough to jostle him.

He was halfway along the return aisle when he saw Aliena.

He reined in abruptly and stared at her, transfixed.

She was no longer the thin, strained, frightened girl in clogs that he had seen here on Whitsunday three years ago. Her face, then drawn with tension, had filled out again, and she had a happy, healthy look. Her dark eyes flashed with humor and her curls tumbled about her face when she shook her head.

She was so beautiful that she made William's head swim with desire.

She was wearing a scarlet robe, richly embroidered, and her expressive hands glinted with rings. There was an older woman with her, standing a little to one side, like a servant. Plenty of money, Mother had said; that was how Richard had been able to become a squire and join King Stephen's army equipped with fine weapons. Damn her. She had been destitute, a penniless, powerless girl—how had she done it?

She was at a stall that carried bone needles, silk thread, wooden thimbles and other sewing necessities, discussing the goods animatedly with the short, dark-haired Jew who was selling them. Her stance was assertive, and she was relaxed and self-confident. She had recovered the poise she had possessed as daughter of the earl.

She looked much older. She *was* older, of course: William was twenty-four, so she must be twenty-one now. But she looked more than that. There was nothing of the child in her now. She was mature.

She looked up and met his eye.

Last time he had locked glances with her, she had blushed for shame, and run away. This time she stood her ground and stared back at him.

He tried a knowing smile.

An expression of scathing contempt came over her face.

William felt himself flush red. She was as haughty as ever, and she scorned him now as she had five years ago. He had humiliated and ravished her, but she was no longer terrified of him. He wanted to speak to her, and tell her that he could do again what he had done to her before; but he was not willing to shout it over the heads of the crowd. Her unflinching gaze made him feel small. He tried to sneer at her, but he could not, and he knew he was making a foolish grimace. In an agony of embarrassment he turned away and kicked his horse on; but even then the crowd slowed him down, and her withering look burned into the back of his neck as he moved away from her by painful inches.

When at last he emerged from the marketplace he was confronted by Prior Philip.

The short Welshman stood with his hands on his hips and his chin thrust aggressively forward. He was not quite as thin as he used to be, and what little hair he had was turning prematurely from black to gray, William saw. He no longer looked too young for his job. Now his blue eyes were bright with anger. "Lord William!" he called in a challenging tone.

William tore his mind away from the thought of Aliena and remembered that he had a charge to make against Philip. "I'm glad to come across you, Prior."

"And I you," Philip said angrily, but the shadow of a doubtful frown crossed his brow.

"You're holding a market here," William said accusingly.

"So what?"

"I don't believe King Stephen ever licensed a market in Kingsbridge. Nor did any other king, to my knowledge."

"How dare you?" said Philip.

"I or anybody—"

"You!" Philip shouted, overriding him. "How dare you come in here and talk about a license—you, who in the past month have gone through this county committing arson, theft, rape, and at least one murder!"

"That's nothing to do—"

"How dare you come into a monastery and talk about a license!" Philip yelled. He stepped forward, wagging his finger at William, and William's horse sidestepped nervously. Somehow Philip's voice was more penetrating than William's and William could not get a word in. A crowd of monks, volunteer workers and market customers was gathering around, watching the row. Philip was unstoppable. "After what you've done, there is only *one* thing you should say: 'Father, I have sinned!' You should get down on your *knees* in this priory! You should beg for forgiveness, if you want to escape the fires of hell."

William blanched. Talk of hell filled him with uncontrollable terror. He tried desperately to interrupt Philip's flow, saying: "What about your market? What about your market?"

Philip hardly heard. He was in a fury of indignation. "Beg forgiveness for the awful things you have done!" he shouted. "On your knees! On your knees, or you'll burn in hell!"

William was almost frightened enough to believe that he would suffer hellfire unless he knelt and prayed in front of Philip right now. He knew he was overdue for confession, for he had killed many men in the war, on top of the sins he had committed during his tour of the earldom. What if he were to die before he confessed? He began to feel shaky at the thought of the eternal flames and the devils with their sharp knives.

Philip advanced on him, pointing his finger and shouting: "On your knees!"

William backed his horse. He looked around desperately. The crowd hemmed him in. His knights were behind him, looking bemused: they could not decide how to cope with a spiritual threat from an unarmed monk. William could not take any more humiliation. After Aliena, this was too much. He pulled on the reins, making his massive war-horse rear dangerously. The crowd parted in front of its mighty hooves. When its forefeet hit the ground again he kicked it hard, and it lunged forward. The onlookers scattered. He kicked it again, and it broke into a canter. Burning with shame, he fled out through the priory gate, with his knights following, like a pack of snarling dogs chased off by an old woman with a broom.

William confessed his sins, in fear and trembling, on the cold stone floor of the little chapel at the bishop's palace. Bishop Waleran listened in silence, his face a mask of distaste, as William catalogued the killings, the beatings and the rapes he was guilty of. Even while he confessed, William was filled with loathing for the supercilious bishop, with his clean white hands folded over his heart, and his translucent white nostrils slightly flared, as if there were a bad smell in the dusty air. It tormented William to beg Waleran for absolution, but his sins were so heavy that no ordinary priest could forgive them. So he knelt, possessed by fear, while Waleran commanded him to light a candle in perpetuity in the chapel at Earlscastle, and then told him his sins were absolved.

The fear lifted slowly, like a fog.

They came out of the chapel into the smoky atmosphere of the great hall and sat by the fire. Autumn was turning to winter and it was cold in the big stone house. A kitchen hand brought hot spiced bread made with honey and ginger. William began to feel all right at last.

Then he remembered his other problems. Bartholomew's son Richard was making a bid for the earldom, and William was too poor to raise an army big enough to impress the king. He had raked in considerable cash in the past month, but it was still not sufficient. He sighed, and said: "That damned monk is drinking the blood of the Shiring earldom."

Waleran took some bread with a pale, long-fingered hand like a claw. "I've been wondering how long it would take you to reach that conclusion."

Of course, Waleran would have worked it all out long before William. He was so superior. William would rather not talk to him. But he wanted the bishop's opinion on a legal point. "The king has never licensed a market in Kingsbridge, has he?"

"To my certain knowledge, no."

"Then Philip is breaking the law."

Waleran shrugged his bony, black-draped shoulders. "For what it's worth, yes."

Waleran seemed uninterested but William plowed on. "He ought to be stopped."

Waleran gave a fastidious smile. "You can't deal with him the way you deal with a serf who's married off his daughter without permission."

William reddened: Waleran was referring to one of the sins he had just confessed. "How can you deal with him, then?"

Waleran considered. "Markets are the king's prerogative. In more peaceful times he would probably handle this himself."

William gave a scornful laugh. For all his cleverness, Waleran did not know the king as well as William did. "Even in peacetime he wouldn't thank me for complaining to him about an unlicensed market."

"Well, then, his deputy, to deal with local matters, is the sheriff of Shiring."

"What can he do?"

"He could bring a writ against the priory in the county court."

William shook his head. "That's the last thing I want. The court would impose a fine, the priory would pay it, and the market would continue. It's almost like giving a license."

"The trouble is, there are really no grounds for refusing to let Kingsbridge have a market."

"Yes, there are!" said William indignantly. "It takes trade away from the market at Shiring."

"Shiring is a full day's journey from Kingsbridge."

"People will walk a long way."

Waleran shrugged again. William realized he shrugged when he disagreed. Waleran said: "Tradition says a man will spend a third of a day walking to the market, a third of a day at the market, and a third of a day walking home. Therefore, a market serves the people within a third of a day's journey, which is reckoned to be seven miles. If two markets are more than fourteen miles apart, their catchment areas do not overlap. Shiring is twenty miles from Kingsbridge. According to the rule, Kingsbridge is entitled to a market, and the king should grant it."

"The king does what he likes," William blustered, but he was bothered. He had not known about this rule. It put Prior Philip in a stronger position.

Waleran said: "Anyway, we won't be dealing with the king,

we'll be dealing with the sheriff." He frowned. "The sheriff could just order the priory to desist from holding an unlicensed market."

"That's a waste of time," William said contemptuously. "Who takes any notice of an order that isn't backed up by a threat?"

"Philip might."

William did not believe that. "Why would he?"

A mocking smile played around Waleran's bloodless lips. "I'm not sure I can explain it to you," he said. "Philip believes that the law should be king."

"Stupid idea," said William impatiently. "The king is king."

"I said you wouldn't understand."

Waleran's knowing air infuriated William. He got up and went to the window. Looking out, he could see, at the top of the nearby hill, the earthworks where Waleran had started to build a castle four years ago. Waleran had hoped to pay for it out of the income from the Shiring earldom. Philip had frustrated his plans, and now the grass had grown back over the mounds of earth, and brambles filled the dry ditch. William recalled that Waleran had hoped to build with stone from the earl of Shiring's quarry. Now Philip had the quarry. William mused: "If I had my quarry back, I could use it as a surety, and borrow money to raise an army."

"Then why don't you take it back?" said Waleran.

William shook his head. "I tried, once."

"And Philip outmaneuvered you. But there are no monks there now. You could send a squad of men to evict the stonecutters."

"And how would I stop Philip from moving back in, the way he did last time?"

"Build a high fence around the quarry and leave a permanent guard."

It was possible, William thought eagerly. And it would solve his problem at a stroke. But what was Waleran's motive in suggesting it? Mother had warned him to beware of the unscrupulous bishop. "The only thing you need to know about Waleran Bigod," she had said, "is that everything he does is carefully calculated. Nothing spontaneous, nothing careless, nothing casual, nothing superfluous. Above all, nothing generous." But Waleran hated Philip, and had sworn to prevent him from building his cathedral. That was motive enough.

William looked thoughtfully at Waleran. His career was in a stall. He had become bishop very young, but Kingsbridge was an insignificant and impoverished diocese and Waleran had surely intended it to be a stepping-stone to higher things. However, it was the prior, not the bishop, who was winning wealth and fame.

Waleran was withering in Philip's shadow much as William was. They both had reason to want to destroy him.

William decided, yet again, to overcome his loathing of Waleran for the sake of his own long-term interests.

"All right," he said. "This could work. But suppose Philip then complains to the king?"

Waleran said: "You'll say you did it as a reprisal for Philip's unlicensed market."

William nodded. "Any excuse will do, so long as I go back to the war with a big enough army."

Waleran's eyes glinted with malice. "I have a feeling Philip can't build that cathedral if he has to buy stone at a market price. And if he stops building, Kingsbridge could go into decline. This could solve all your problems, William."

William was not going to show gratitude. "You really hate Philip, don't you?"

"He's in my way," Waleran said, but for a moment William had glimpsed the naked savagery beneath the bishop's cool, calculating manner.

William returned to practical matters. "There must be thirty quarrymen there, some with their wives and children," he said.

"So what?"

"There may be bloodshed."

Waleran raised his black eyebrows. "Indeed?" he said. "Then I shall give you absolution."

III

They set out while it was still dark, in order to arrive at dawn. They carried flaming torches, which made the horses jumpy. As well as Walter and the other four knights, William took six men-at-arms. Trailing behind them were a dozen peasants who would dig the ditch and put up the fence.

William believed firmly in careful military planning—which was why he and his men were so useful to King Stephen—but on this occasion he had no battle plan. It was such an easy operation that it would have been demeaning to make preparations as if it were a real fight. A few stonecutters and their families could not put up much opposition; and anyway, William remembered being told how the stonecutters' leader—was his name Otto? Yes, Otto Blackface— had refused to fight, on the first day Tom Builder had taken his men to the quarry.

A chill December morning dawned, with rags and tatters of mist hanging on the trees like poor people's washing. William disliked this time of year. It was cold in the morning and dark in the evening, and the castle was always damp. Too much salt meat and salt fish was served. His mother was bad-tempered and the servants were surly. His knights became quarrelsome. This little fight would be good for them. It would also be good for him: he had already arranged to borrow two hundred pounds from the Jews of London against the surety of the quarry. By the end of today his future would be secure.

When they were about a mile from the quarry William stopped, picked out two men, and sent them ahead, on foot. "There may be a sentry, or some dogs," he warned. "Have a bow out ready with an arrow at the string."

A little later the road curved to the left, then ended suddenly at the sheer side of a mutilated hill. This was the quarry. All was quiet. Beside the road, William's men were holding a scared boy—presumably an apprentice who had been on sentry duty—and at his feet was a dog bleeding to death with an arrow through its neck.

The raiding party drew up, making no particular effort to be silent. William reined in and studied the scene. Much of the hill had disappeared since last he saw it. The scaffolding ran up the hillside to inaccessible areas and down into a deep pit which had been opened up at the foot of the hill. Stone blocks of different shapes and sizes were stacked near the road, and two massive wooden carts with huge wheels were loaded with stone ready to go. Everything was covered with gray dust, even the bushes and trees. A large area of woodland had been cleared—*my* woodland, William thought angrily—and there were ten or twelve wooden buildings, some with small vegetable gardens, one with a pigsty. It was a little village.

The sentry had probably been asleep—and his dog, too. William spoke to him. "How many men are here, lad?"

The boy looked scared but brave. "You're Lord William, aren't you?"

"Answer the question, boy, or I'll take off your head with this sword."

He went white with fear, but replied in a voice of quavering defiance. "Are you trying to steal this quarry away from Prior Philip?"

What's the matter with me, William thought? I can't even frighten a skinny child with no beard! Why do people think they can defy me? "This quarry is mine!" he hissed. "Forget about Prior Philip—he can't do anything for you now. How many men?"

Instead of replying the boy threw back his head and began to yell. "Help! Look out! Attack! Attack!"

William's hand went to his sword. He hesitated, looking across at the houses. A scared face peered out from a doorway. He decided to forget about the apprentice. He snatched a blazing torch from one of his men and kicked his horse.

He rode at the houses, carrying the torch high, and heard his men behind him. The door of the nearest hut opened and a bleary-eyed man in an undershirt looked out. William threw the burning torch over the man's head. It landed on the floor behind him in the straw, which caught fire immediately. William gave a whoop of triumph and rode past.

He went on through the little cluster of houses. Behind him, his men charged, yelling and throwing their torches at the thatched roofs. All the doors opened, and terrified men, women and children began to pour out, screaming and trying to dodge the hammering hooves. They milled about in a panic while the flames took hold. William reined in at the edge of the melee and watched for a moment. The domestic animals got loose, and a frantic pig charged around blindly while a cow stood still in the middle of it all, its stupid head weaving from side to side in bewilderment. Even the young men, normally the most belligerent group, were confused and scared. Dawn was definitely the best time for this sort of thing: there was something about being half naked that took away people's aggression.

A dark-skinned man with a thatch of black hair came out of one of the huts with his boots on and started giving orders. This must be Otto Blackface. William could not hear what he was saying. He could guess from the gestures that Otto was telling the women to pick up the children and hide in the woods, but what was he saying to the men? A moment later William found out. Two young men ran to a hut set apart from the others and opened its door, which was locked from the outside. They stepped in and re-emerged with heavy stonecutters' hammers. Otto directed other men to the same hut, which was obviously a tool shed. They were going to make a fight of it.

Three years ago Otto had refused to fight for Philip. What had changed his mind?

Whatever it was, it was going to kill him. William smiled grimly and drew his sword.

There were now six or eight men armed with sledgehammers and long-handled axes. William spurred his horse and charged at the group around the door of the tool shed. They scattered out of his way, but he swung his sword and managed to catch one of them with a deep cut to the upper arm. The man dropped his ax.

William galloped away, then turned his horse. He was breathing hard and feeling good: in the heat of a battle there was no fear, only excitement. Some of his men had seen what was happening and looked to William for guidance. He beckoned them to follow him, then charged the stonecutters again. They could not dodge six knights as easily as they could dodge one. William struck down two of them, and several more fell to the swords of his men, although he was moving too fast to count how many or see whether they were dead or just wounded.

When he turned again, Otto was rallying his forces. As the knights charged, the stonecutters dispersed into the cluster of burning houses. It was a clever tactic, William realized regretfully. The knights followed, but it was easier for the stonecutters to dodge when they were split up, and the horses shied away from the blazing buildings. William chased a gray-haired man with a hammer, and just missed him several times before the man evaded him by running through a house with a burning roof.

William realized that Otto was the problem. He was giving the stonecutters courage as well as organizing them. As soon as he fell, the others would give up. William reined in his horse and looked for the dark-skinned man. Most of the women and children had disappeared, except for two five-year-olds standing in the middle of the battlefield, holding hands and crying. William's knights were charging between the houses, chasing the stonecutters. To his surprise, William saw that one of his men-at-arms had fallen to a hammer, and lay on the ground, groaning and bleeding. William was dismayed: he had not anticipated any casualties on his own side.

A distraught woman was running in and out of burning houses, calling out something William could not hear. She was searching for someone. Finally she saw the two five-year-olds, and picked them up one in each arm. As she ran away she almost collided with one of William's knights, Gilbert de Rennes. Gilbert raised his sword to strike her. Suddenly Otto sprang out from behind a hut and swung a long-handled ax. His handling of the weapon was skillful and its blade sliced right through Gilbert's thigh and bit into the wood of the saddle. The severed leg dropped to the ground, and Gilbert screamed and fell off his horse.

He would never fight again.

Gilbert was a valuable knight. Angry, William spurred his horse forward. The woman with the children vanished. Otto was struggling to pull the blade of his ax from Gilbert's saddle. He looked up and saw William coming. If he had run at that moment he might have escaped, but he stayed and tugged at his ax. It came free when William was almost on him. William raised his sword. Otto stood his ground and lifted the ax. At the last moment William realized the ax was going to be used on the horse, and the stonecutter could cripple the animal before William was close enough to strike him down. William hauled on the reins desperately, and the horse skidded to a halt and reared up, turning its head away from Otto. The blow fell on the horse's neck, and the edge of the ax bit deeply into the powerful muscles. Blood spurted like a fountain, and the horse fell. William was off its back before the huge body hit the ground.

He was enraged. The war-horse had cost a fortune and had survived with him through a year of civil war, and it was maddening to lose it to a quarryman's ax. He jumped over its body and lunged furiously at Otto with the sword.

Otto was no easy victim. He held his ax in both hands and used its heart-of-oak handle to parry William's sword. William struck harder and harder, driving him back. Despite his age Otto was powerfully muscled, and William's blows hardly jarred him. William took his sword in both hands and struck harder. Once again the handle of the ax intervened, but this time William's blade stuck in the wood. Then Otto was advancing and William was retreating. William tugged hard at his sword and his blade came unstuck, but now Otto was almost on him.

Suddenly William was afraid for his life.

Otto raised the ax. William dodged back. His heel connected with something and he stumbled and fell backward over the body of his horse. He landed in a puddle of warm blood but managed to keep hold of his sword. Otto stood over him with his ax raised. As the weapon came down, William rolled frantically sideways. He felt the wind as the blade sliced the air next to his face; then he sprang to his feet and thrust at the stonecutter with his sword.

A soldier would have moved sideways before pulling his weapon out of the ground, knowing that a man is at his most vulnerable when he has just struck a blow and missed; but Otto was no soldier, just a brave fool, and he was standing with one hand on the haft of the ax and the other arm stretched out for balance, leaving the whole of his body an easy target. William's hasty thrust was almost blind, but nevertheless it connected. The point of the sword pierced Otto's chest. William pushed harder and the blade slid between the man's ribs. Otto released his hold on the ax, and over his face came an expression William knew well. His eyes showed surprise, his mouth opened as if to scream, although no sound came, and his skin suddenly looked gray. It was the look of a man who has received a mortal wound. William thrust the blade home harder, just to make sure, then pulled it out. Otto's eyes rolled up in his head, a bright red stain appeared on his shirt front and instantly grew large, and he fell.

William spun round, scanning the whole scene. He saw two stonecutters running away, presumably having seen their leader killed. As they ran they shouted to the others. The fight turned into a retreat. The knights chased the runaways.

William stood still, breathing hard. The damned quarrymen had fought back! He looked at Gilbert. He lay still, in a pool of blood, with his eyes closed. William put a hand on his chest: there was no heartbeat. Gilbert was dead.

William walked around the still-burning houses, counting bodies. Three stonecutters lay dead, plus a woman and a child who both looked as if they had been trampled by horses. Three of William's men-at-arms were wounded, and four horses were dead or crippled.

When he had completed his count he stood by the corpse of his war-horse. He had liked that horse better than he liked most people.

After a battle he usually felt exhilarated, but now he was depressed. It was a shambles. This should have been a simple operation to chase off a group of helpless workmen, and it had turned into a pitched battle with high casualties.

The knights chased the stonecutters as far as the woods, but there the horses could not catch the men, so they turned back. Walter rode up to where William stood and saw Gilbert dead on the ground. He crossed himself and said: "Gilbert has killed more men than I have."

"There aren't so many like him, that I can afford to lose one in a squabble with a damned monk," William said bitterly. "To say nothing of the horses."

"What a turnup," Walter said. "These people put up more of a fight than Robert of Gloucester's rebels!"

William shook his head in disgust. "I don't know," he said, looking around at the bodies. "What the devil did they think they were fighting for?"

Chapter 9

JUST AFTER DAWN, when most of the brothers were in the crypt for the service of prime, there were only two people in the dormitory: Johnny Eightpence, sweeping the floor at one end of the long room, and Jonathan, playing school at the other.

Prior Philip paused in the doorway and watched Jonathan. He was almost five years old, an alert, confident boy with a childish gravity that charmed everyone. Johnny still dressed him in a miniature monk's habit. Today Jonathan was pretending to be the novicemaster, giving lessons to an imaginary row of pupils. "That's wrong, Godfrey!" he said sternly to the empty bench. "No dinner for you if you don't learn your berves!" He meant *verbs*. Philip smiled fondly. He could not have loved a son more deeply. Jonathan was the one thing in life that gave him sheer unadulterated joy.

The child ran around the priory like a puppy, petted and spoiled by all the monks. To most of them he was just like a pet, an amusing plaything; but to Philip and Johnny he was something more. Johnny loved him like a mother; and Philip, though he tried to conceal it, felt like the boy's father. Philip himself had been raised, from a young age, by a kindly abbot, and it seemed the most natural thing in the world for him to play the same role with Jonathan. He did not tickle or chase him the way the monks did, but he told him Bible stories, and played counting games with him, and kept an eye on Johnny.

He went into the room, smiled at Johnny, and sat on the bench with the imaginary schoolboys.

"Good morning, Father," Jonathan said solemnly. Johnny had taught him to be scrupulously polite.

Philip said: "How would you like to go to school?"

"I know Latin already," Jonathan boasted.

"Really?"

"Yes. Listen. Omnius pluvius buvius tuvius nomine patri amen."

Philip tried not to laugh. "That *sounds* like Latin, but it's not *quite* right. Brother Osmund, the novice-master, will teach you to speak it properly."

Jonathan was a little cast down to discover that he did not know Latin after all. He said: "Anyway, I can run fast and fast, look!" He ran at top speed from one side of the room to the other.

"Wonderful!" said Philip. "That really is fast."

"Yes—and I can go even faster—"

"Not just now," Philip said. "Listen to me for a moment. I'm going away for a while."

"Will you be back tomorrow?"

"No, not that soon."

"Next week?"

"Not even then."

Jonathan looked blank. He could not conceive of a time farther ahead than next week. Another mystery occurred to him. "But why?"

"I have to see the king."

"Oh." That did not mean much to Jonathan either.

"And I'd like you to go to school while I'm away. Would you like that?"

"Yes!"

"You're almost five years old. Your birthday is next week. You came to us on the first day of the year."

"Where did I come from?"

"From God. All things come from God."

Jonathan knew that was no answer. "But where was I *before*?" he persisted.

"I don't know."

Jonathan frowned. A frown looked funny on such a carefree young face. "I must have been *somewhere*."

One day, Philip realized, someone would have to tell Jonathan how babies were born. He grimaced at the thought. Well, this was not the time, happily. He changed the subject. "While I'm away, I want you to learn to count up to a hundred."

"I can count," Jonathan said. "One two three four five six seven eight nine ten eleven twelve thirteen fourteen porteen scorteen horteen—"

"Not bad," said Philip, "but Brother Osmund will teach you more. You must sit still in the schoolroom and do everything he tells you to."

"I'm going to be the best in the school!" said Jonathan.

"We'll see." Philip studied him for a moment longer. Philip was fascinated by the child's development, the way he learned things and the phases through which he passed. This current insistence on being able to speak Latin, or count, or run fast, was curious: was it a necessary prelude to real learning? It must serve some purpose in God's plan. And one day Jonathan would be a man. What would he be like then? The thought made Philip impatient for Jonathan to grow up. But that would take as long as the building of the cathedral.

"Give me a kiss, then, and say goodbye," Philip said.

Jonathan lifted his face and Philip kissed the soft cheek. "Goodbye, Father," said Jonathan.

"Goodbye, my son," Philip said.

He gave Johnny Eightpence's arm an affectionate squeeze and went out.

The monks were coming out of the crypt and heading for the refectory. Philip went the opposite way, and entered the crypt to pray for success on his mission.

He had been heartbroken when they told him what had happened at the quarry. Five people killed, one of them a little girl! He had hidden himself in his house and cried like a child. Five of his flock, struck down by William Hamleigh and his pack of brutes. Philip had known them all: Harry of Shiring, who had once been Lord Percy's quarryman; Otto Blackface, the dark-skinned man who had been in charge of the quarry since the very beginning; Otto's handsome son Mark; Mark's wife, Alwen, who played tunes on sheep bells in the evenings; and little Norma, Otto's seven-year-old granddaughter, his favorite. Good-hearted, God-fearing, hardworking people, who had a right to expect peace and justice from their lords. William had slaughtered them like a fox killing chickens. It was enough to make the angels weep.

Philip had grieved for them, and then he had gone to Shiring to demand justice. The sheriff had refused point-blank to take any action. "Lord William has a small army—how should I arrest him?" Sheriff Eustace had said. "The king needs knights to fight against Maud—what will he say if I incarcerate one of his best men? If I brought a charge of murder against William, I'd either be killed immediately by his knights or hanged for a traitor later by King Stephen."

The first casualty of a civil war was justice, Philip had realized.

Then the sheriff had told him that William had made a formal complaint about the Kingsbridge market.

It was ludicrous, of course, that William could get away with murder and at the same time charge Philip on a technicality; but Philip felt helpless. It was true that he did not have permission to hold a market, and he was in the wrong, strictly speaking. But he could not remain in the wrong. He was the prior of Kingsbridge. All he had was his moral authority. William could call up an army of knights; Bishop Waleran could use his contacts in high places; the sheriff could claim royal authority; but all Philip could do was to say *this* is right and *that* is wrong; and if he were to forfeit that position he really would be helpless. So he had ordered the market to cease.

That left him in a truly desperate position.

The priory's finances had improved dramatically, thanks to stricter controls on the one hand, and on the other, ever-rising earnings from the market and from sheep farming; but Philip always spent every penny on the building, and he had borrowed heavily from the Jews of Winchester, a loan he had yet to repay. Now, at a stroke, he had lost his supply of cost-free stone, his income from the market had dried up, and his volunteer laborers—many of whom came mainly for the market—were likely to dwindle. He would have to lay off half the builders, and abandon hope of finishing the cathedral in his own lifetime. He was not prepared to do that.

He wondered if the crisis was his own fault. Had he been too confident, too ambitious? Sheriff Eustace had said as much. "You're too big for your boots, Philip," he had said angrily. "You run a little monastery, and you're a little prior, but you want to rule the bishop and the earl and the sheriff. Well, you can't. We're too powerful for you. All you do is cause trouble." Eustace was an ugly man with uneven teeth and a cast in one eye, and he was wearing a dirty yellow robe; but unimpressive though he was, his words had stabbed Philip's heart. He was painfully aware that the quarrymen would not have died if he had not made an enemy of William Hamleigh. But he could not do other than be William's enemy. If he gave up, even more people would suffer, people such as the miller William had killed and the serf's daughter he and his knights had raped. Philip had to fight on.

And that meant he had to go to see the king.

He hated the idea. He had approached the king once before, at Winchester four years ago, and although he had got what he wanted, he had been dreadfully ill-at-ease at the royal court. The king was surrounded by wily and unscrupulous people jostling for his attention and squabbling over his favors, and Philip found such people contemptible. They were trying to acquire wealth and position they did not merit. He did not really understand the game they were playing: in his world, the best way to get something was to deserve it, not to toady to the giver. But now he had no alternative but to enter their world and play their game. Only the king could grant Philip permission to hold a market. Only the king could now save the cathedral.

He finished his prayers and left the crypt. The sun was coming up, and there was a pink flush on the gray stone walls of the rising cathedral. The builders, who worked from sunrise to sunset, were just beginning, opening their lodges and sharpening their tools and mixing up the first batch of mortar. The loss of the quarry had not yet affected the building: they had always quarried stone faster than they could use it, from the beginning, and now they had a stockpile that would last many months.

It was time for Philip to leave. All the arrangements were made. The king was at Lincoln. Philip would have a traveling companion: Richard, the brother of Aliena. After fighting for a year as a squire, Richard had been knighted by the king. He had come home to re-equip himself and was now going to rejoin the royal army.

Aliena had done astonishingly well as a wool merchant. She no longer sold her wool to Philip, but dealt directly with the Flemish buyers herself. Indeed, this year she had wanted to buy the entire fleece production of the priory. She would have paid less than the Flemish, but Philip would have got the money earlier. He had turned her down. However, it was a measure of her success that she could even make the offer.

She was at the stable with her brother now, Philip saw as he walked across. A crowd had gathered to say goodbye to the travelers. Richard was sitting on a chestnut war-horse that must have cost Aliena twenty pounds. He had grown into a handsome, broad-shouldered young man, his regular features marred only by an angry scar on his right ear: the earlobe had been cut off, no doubt in some fencing accident. He was splendidly dressed in red and green and outfitted with a new sword, lance, battle-ax and dagger. His baggage was carried by a second horse which he had on a leading-rein. With him were two men-at-arms on coursers and a squire on a cob.

Aliena was in tears, although Philip could not tell whether she was sorry to see her brother go, proud that he looked so fine, or frightened that he might never come back. All three, perhaps. Some of the villagers had come to say goodbye, including most of the young men and boys. No doubt Richard was their hero. All the monks were here, too, to wish their prior a safe journey.

The stable hands brought out two horses, a palfrey saddled ready for Philip and a cob loaded with his modest baggage—mainly food for the journey. The builders put down their tools and came over, led by bearded Tom and his redheaded stepson, Jack.

Philip formally embraced Remigius, his sub-prior, and took a warmer farewell of Milius and Cuthbert, then mounted the palfrey. He would be sitting in this hard saddle a long time, he realized grimly. From his raised position he blessed them all. The monks, builders and villagers waved and called out their goodbyes as he and Richard rode side by side through the priory gates.

They went down the narrow street through the village, waving to people who looked out of their doorways, then clattered across the wooden bridge and onto the road through the fields. A little later, Philip glanced back over his shoulder, and saw the rising sun shining through the window space in the half-built east end of the new cathedral. If he failed in his mission, it might never be finished. After all he had been through to get this far, he could not bear to contemplate the idea of defeat now. He turned back and concentrated on the road ahead.

Lincoln was a city on a hill. Philip and Richard approached it from the south, on an ancient and busy road called Ermine Street. Even from a distance they could see, at the top of the hill, the towers of the cathedral and the battlements of the castle. But they were still three or four miles away when, to Philip's astonishment, they came to a city gate. The suburbs must be *vast*, he thought; the population must run to *thousands*.

At Christmas the city had been seized by Ranulf of Chester, the most powerful man in the north of England and a relative of the Empress Maud. King Stephen had since retaken the city, but Ranulf's forces still held the castle. Now, Philip and Richard had learned as they drew nearer, Lincoln was in the peculiar position of having two rival armies camped within its walls.

Philip had not warmed to Richard in their four weeks together. Aliena's brother was an angry youth, who hated the Hamleighs and was set on revenge; and he talked as if Philip felt the same. But there was a difference. Philip hated the Hamleighs for what they did to their subjects: getting rid of them would make the world a better place. Richard could not feel good about himself until he had defeated the Hamleighs: his motive was entirely selfish.

Richard was physically brave, always ready for a fight; but in other ways he was weak. He confused his men-at-arms by sometimes treating them as equals and sometimes ordering them around like servants. In taverns he would try to make an impression by buying beer for strangers. He pretended to know the way when he was not really sure, and sometimes led the party far astray because he could not admit that he had made a mistake. By the time they reached Lincoln, Philip knew that Aliena was worth ten of Richard.

They passed a large lake teeming with ships; then at the foot of the hill they crossed the river that formed the southern boundary of the city proper. Lincoln obviously lived by shipping. Beside the bridge there was a fish market. They went through another guarded gate. Now they left behind the sprawl of the suburbs and entered the teeming city. A narrow, impossibly crowded street ran steeply up the hill directly in front of them. The houses that jostled shoulder to shoulder on either side were made partly or wholly of stone, a sign of considerable wealth. The hill was so steep that most houses had their main floor several feet above ground level at one end and below the surface at the other. The area underneath the downhill end was invariably a craftsman's workplace or a shop. The only open spaces were the graveyards next to the churches, and on each of these there was a market: grain, poultry, wool, leather and others. Philip and Richard, with Richard's small entourage, fought their way through the dense crowd of townspeople, men-at-arms, animals and carts. Philip realized with astonishment that there were stones beneath his feet. The whole street was paved! What wealth there must be here, he thought, for stones to be laid in the street as if it were a palace or a cathedral. The way was still slippery with refuse and animal dung, but it was much better than the river of mud that constituted most city streets in winter.

They reached the crest of the hill and passed through yet another gate. Now they entered the inner city, and the atmosphere was suddenly different: quieter, but very tense. Immediately to their left was the entrance to the castle. The great ironbound door in the archway was shut tight. Dim figures moved behind the arrow-slit windows in the gatehouse, and sentries in armor patrolled the castellated ramparts, the feeble sunshine glinting off their burnished helmets. Philip watched them pacing to and fro. There was no conversation between them, no joshing and laughter, no leaning on the balustrade to whistle at passing girls: they were upright, eagle-eyed, and fearful.

To Philip's right, no more than a quarter of a mile from the castle gate, was the west front of the cathedral, and Philip saw instantly that despite its proximity to the castle it had been taken over as the king's military headquarters. A line of sentries barred the narrow road that led between the canons' houses to the church. Beyond the sentries, knights and men-at-arms were passing in and out through the three doorways to the cathedral. The graveyard was an army camp, with tents and cooking fires and horses grazing the turf. There were no monastic buildings: Lincoln Cathedral was not run by monks, but by priests called canons, who lived in ordinary town houses near the church.

The space between the cathedral and the castle was empty

except for Philip and his companions. Philip suddenly realized that they had the full attention of the guards on the king's side and the sentries on the opposing ramparts. He was in the no-man's-land between the two armed camps, probably the most dangerous spot in Lincoln. Looking around, he saw that Richard and the others had already moved on, and he followed them hastily.

The king's sentries let them through immediately: Richard was well known. Philip admired the west facade of the cathedral. It had an enormously tall entrance arch, and subsidiary arches on either side, half the size of the central one but still awesome. It looked like the gateway to heaven—which it was, of course, in a way. Philip immediately decided he wanted tall arches in the west front of Kingsbridge Cathedral.

Leaving the horses with the squire, Philip and Richard made their way through the encampment and entered the cathedral. It was even more crowded inside than out. The aisles had been turned into stables, and hundreds of horses were tied to the columns of the arcade. Armed men thronged the nave, and here too there were cooking fires and bedding. Some spoke English, some French, and a few spoke Flemish, the guttural tongue of the wool merchants of Flanders. By and large the knights were in here and the men-at-arms were outside. Philip was sorry to see several men playing at nine-men's morris for money, and he was even more disturbed by the appearance of some of the women, who were dressed very skimpily for winter and appeared to be flirting with the men—almost, he thought, as if they were sinful women, or even, God forbid, whores.

To avoid looking at them he raised his eyes to the ceiling. It was of wood, and beautifully painted in glowing colors, but it was a terrible fire risk with all those people cooking in the nave. He followed Richard through the crowd. Richard seemed at ease here, assured and confident, calling out greetings to barons and lords, and slapping knights on the back.

The crossing and the east end of the cathedral had been roped off. The east end appeared to have been reserved for the priests—I should think so, too, Philip thought—and the crossing had become the king's quarters.

There was another line of guards behind the rope, then a crowd of courtiers, then an inner circle of earls, with King Stephen at the center on a wooden throne. The king had aged since the last time Philip saw him, five years ago in Winchester. There were lines of anxiety on his handsome face and a little gray in his tawny hair, and a year of fighting had made him thinner. He seemed to be having an amiable argument with his earls, disagreeing without anger. Richard went to the edge of the inner circle and made a deep ceremonial bow. The king glanced over, recognized him, and said in a booming voice: "Richard of Kingsbridge! Glad to have you back!"

"Thank you, my lord king," said Richard.

Philip stepped up beside him and bowed in the same way.

Stephen said: "Have you brought a monk as your squire?" All the courtiers laughed.

"This is the prior of Kingsbridge, lord," said Richard.

Stephen looked again, and Philip saw the light of recognition in his eye. "Of course, I know Prior . . . Philip," he said, but his tone was not as warm as when he greeted Richard. "Have you come to fight for me?" The courtiers laughed again.

Philip was pleased the king had remembered his name. "I'm here because God's work of rebuilding Kingsbridge Cathedral needs urgent help from my lord king."

"I must hear all about it," Stephen interrupted hastily. "Come and see me tomorrow, when I'll have more time." He turned back to the earls, and resumed his conversation in a lower voice.

Richard bowed and withdrew, and Philip did the same.

Philip did not speak to King Stephen on the following day, nor the day after, nor the day after that.

On the first night he stayed at an alehouse, but he felt oppressed by the constant smell of roasting meat and the laughter of loose women. Unfortunately, there was no monastery in the town. Normally the bishop would have offered him accommodation, but the king was living in the bishop's palace and all the houses around the cathedral were crammed full with members of Stephen's entourage. On the second night Philip went right outside the town, beyond the suburb of Wigford, where there was a monastery that ran a home for lepers. There he got horsebread and weak beer for supper, a hard mattress on the floor, silence from sundown to midnight, services in the small hours of the morning, and a breakfast of thin porridge without salt; and he was happy.

He went to the cathedral early every morning, carrying the precious charter that gave the priory the right to take stone from the quarry. Day after day the king failed to notice him. When the other petitioners talked among themselves, discussing who was in favor and who was out, Philip remained aloof.

He knew why he was being kept waiting. The entire Church was at odds with the king. Stephen had not kept the generous promises that had been extracted from him at the start of his reign. He had made an enemy of his brother, the wily Bishop Henry of Winchester, by supporting someone else for the job of archbishop of Canterbury; a move which had also disappointed Waleran Bigod, who wanted to rise on Henry's coattails. But Stephen's greatest sin, in the eyes of the Church, had been to arrest Bishop Roger of Salisbury and Roger's two nephews, who were bishops of Lincoln and Ely, all on one day, on charges of unlicensed castle building. A chorus of outrage had gone up from cathedrals and monasteries all over the country at this act of sacrilege. Stephen was hurt. As men of God the bishops had no need of castles, he said; and if they built castles they could not expect to be treated purely as men of God. He was sincere, but naïve.

The split had been patched up, but King Stephen was no longer eager to hear the petitions of holy men, so Philip had to wait. He used the opportunity to meditate. It was something he had little time for as prior, and he missed it. Now, suddenly, he had nothing to do for hours on end, and he spent the time lost in thought.

Eventually the other courtiers left a space around him, making him quite conspicuous, and it must have been increasingly difficult for Stephen to ignore him. He was deep in contemplation of the sublime mystery of the Trinity on the morning of his seventh day in Lincoln when he realized that someone was standing right in front of him, looking at him and speaking to him, and that person was the king.

"Are you asleep with your eyes open, man?" Stephen was saying in a tone halfway between amusement and irritation.

"I'm sorry, lord, I was thinking," Philip said, and bowed belatedly.

"Never mind. I want to borrow your clothes."

"What?" Philip was too surprised to mind his manners.

"I want to take a look around the castle, and if I'm dressed as a monk they won't shoot arrows at me. Come on—go into one of the chapels and take off your robe."

Philip had only an undershirt on beneath his robe. "But, lord, what shall I wear?"

"I forget how modest you monks are." Stephen clicked his fingers at a young knight. "Robert—lend me your tunic, quick."

The knight, who was talking to a girl, took off his tunic with a swift motion, gave it to the king with a bow, then made a vulgar gesture to the girl. His friends laughed and cheered.

King Stephen gave the tunic to Philip.

Philip slipped into the tiny chapel of St. Dunstan, asked the saint's pardon with a hasty prayer, then took off his habit and put on the knight's short-skirted scarlet tunic. It seemed very strange indeed: he had been wearing monastic clothing since the age of six, and he could not have felt more odd if he had been dressed as a woman. He emerged and handed his monkish robe to Stephen, who pulled it over his head swiftly.

Then the king astonished him by saying: "Come with me, if you like. You can tell me about Kingsbridge Cathedral."

Philip was taken aback. His first instinct was to refuse. A sentry on the castle ramparts might be tempted to take a shot at him, and he would not be protected by religious garments. But he was being offered an opportunity to be totally alone with the king, with plenty of time to explain about the quarry and the market. He might never get another chance like this.

Stephen picked up his own cloak, which was purple with white fur at the collar and hem. "Wear this," he said to Philip. "You'll draw their fire away from me."

The other courtiers had gone quiet, watching, wondering what would happen.

The king was making a point, Philip realized. He was saying that Philip had no business here in an armed camp, and could not expect to be granted privileges at the expense of men who risked their lives for the king. This was not unfair. But Philip knew that if he accepted this point of view he might as well go home and give up all hope of repossessing the quarry or reopening the market. He had to accept the challenge. He drew a deep breath and said: "Perhaps it is God's will that I should die to save the king." Then he took the purple cloak and put it on.

There was a murmur of surprise from the crowd; and King Stephen himself looked quite startled. Everyone had expected Philip to back down. Almost immediately he wished he had. But he had committed himself now.

Stephen turned and walked toward the north door. Philip followed him. Several courtiers made to go with them, but Stephen waved them back, saying: "Even a monk might attract suspicion if he is attended by the entire royal court." He pulled the cowl of Philip's robe over his head and they passed out into the graveyard.

Philip's costly cloak drew curious glances as they picked their way across the campsite: men assumed he was a baron and were puzzled not to recognize him. The glances made him feel guilty, as if he were some kind of impostor. Nobody looked at Stephen.

They did not go directly to the main gate of the castle, but made their way through a maze of narrow lanes and came out by the church of St.-Paul-in-the-Bail, across from the northeast corner of the castle. The castle walls were built on top of massive earth ramparts and surrounded by a dry moat. There was a swath of open space fifty yards wide between the edge of the moat and the nearest buildings. Stephen stepped onto the grass and began to walk west, studying the north wall of the castle, staying close to the backs of the houses on the outer rim of the cleared area. Philip went with him. Stephen made Philip walk on his left, between him and the castle. The open space was there to give bowmen a clear shot at anyone who approached the walls, of course. Philip was not afraid to die but he was afraid of pain, and the thought uppermost in his mind was how much an arrow would *hurt*.

"Scared, Philip?" said Stephen.

"Terrified," Philip replied candidly; and then, made reckless by fear, he added cheekily: "How about you?"

The king laughed at his nerve. "A little," he admitted.

Philip remembered that this was his chance to talk about the cathedral. But he could not concentrate while his life was in such peril. His eyes went constantly to the castle, and he raked the ramparts, watching for a man drawing a bow.

The castle occupied the entire southwest corner of the inner city, its west wall being part of the city wall, so to walk all the way around it one had to go out of the city. Stephen led Philip through the west gate, and they passed out into the suburb called Newland. Here the houses were like peasant hovels, made of wattle-and-daub, with large gardens such as village houses had. A bitter cold wind whipped across the open fields beyond the houses. Stephen turned south, still skirting the castle. He pointed to a little door in the castle wall. "That's where Ranulf of Chester sneaked out to make his escape when I took the city, I suspect," he said.

Philip was less frightened here. There were other people on the pathway, and the ramparts on this side were less heavily guarded, for the occupants of the castle were afraid of an attack from the city, not from the countryside. Philip took a deep breath and then blurted out: "If I am killed, will you give Kingsbridge a market and make William Hamleigh give back the quarry?"

Stephen did not answer immediately. They walked downhill to the southwest corner of the castle and looked up at the keep. From their position it appeared loftily impregnable. Just below that corner they turned into another gateway and entered the lower city to walk along the castle's south side. Philip felt in danger again. It would not be too difficult for someone inside the castle to deduce that the two men who were making a circuit of the walls must be on a scouting expedition, and therefore they were fair game, especially the one in the purple cloak. To distract himself from his fear he studied the keep. There were small holes in the wall which served as outlets for the latrines, and the refuse and filth which was washed out simply fell on the walls and the mound below and stayed there until it rotted away. No wonder there was a stink. Philip tried not to breathe too deeply, and they hurried past.

There was another, smaller tower at the southeast corner. Now Philip and Stephen had walked around three sides of the square. Philip wondered if Stephen had forgotten his question. He was apprehensive about asking it again. The king might feel he was being pushed, and take offense.

They reached the main street that went through the middle of the town and turned again, but before Philip had time to feel relieved they passed through another gate into the inner city, and a few moments later they were in the no-man's-land between cathedral and castle. To Philip's horror the king stopped there.

He turned to talk to Philip, positioning himself in such a way that he could scrutinize the castle over Philip's shoulder. Philip's vulnerable back, clad in ermine and purple, was exposed to the gatehouse which was bristling with sentries and archers. He went as stiff as a statue, expecting an arrow or a spear in his back at any moment. He began to perspire despite the freezing cold wind.

"I gave you that quarry years ago, didn't I?" said King Stephen.

"Not exactly," Philip replied through gritted teeth. "You gave us the right to take stone for the cathedral. But you gave the quarry to Percy Hamleigh. Now Percy's son, William, has thrown out my stonecutters, killing five people—including a woman and a child—and he refuses us access."

"He shouldn't do things like that, especially if he wants me to make him earl of Shiring," Stephen said thoughtfully. Philip was encouraged. But a moment later the king said: "I'm damned if I can see a way to get into this castle."

"Please make William reopen the quarry," Philip said. "He is defying you and stealing from God."

Stephen seemed not to hear. "I don't think they've got many men in there," he said in the same musing tone. "I suspect nearly all of them are on the ramparts, to make a show of strength. What was that about a market?"

This was all part of the test, Philip decided; making him stand out in the open with his back to a host of archers. He wiped his brow with the fur cuff of the king's cloak. "My lord king, every Sunday people come from all over the county to worship at Kingsbridge and labor, for no wages, on the cathedral building site. When we first began, a few enterprising men and women would come to the site and sell meat pies, and wine, and hats, and knives, to the volunteer workers. So, gradually, a market grew up. And now I am asking you to license it."

"Will you pay for your license?"

A payment was normal, Philip knew, but he also knew that it might be waived for a religious body. "Yes, lord, I will pay—unless you would wish to give us the license without payment, for the greater glory of God."

Stephen looked directly into Philip's eyes for the first time. "You're a brave man, to stand there, with the enemy behind you, and bargain with me."

Philip gave back an equally frank stare. "If God decides my life is over, nothing can save me," he said, sounding braver than he felt. "But if God wants me to live on and build Kingsbridge Cathedral, ten thousand archers cannot strike me down."

"Well said!" Stephen remarked, and, clapping a hand on Philip's shoulder, he turned toward the cathedral. Weak with relief, Philip walked beside him, feeling better for every step away from the castle. He seemed to have passed the test. But it was important to get an unambiguous commitment from the king. Any moment now he would be engulfed by courtiers again. As they passed through the line of sentries, Philip took his courage in both hands and said: "My lord king, if you would write a letter to the sheriff of Shiring—"

He was interrupted. One of the earls rushed up, looking flustered, and said: "Robert of Gloucester is on his way here, my lord king."

"What? How far away?"

"Close. A day at most—"

"Why haven't I been warned? I posted men all around!"

"They came by the Fosse Way, then turned off the road to approach across open country."

"Who is with him?"

"All the earls and knights on his side who have lost their lands in the last two years. Ranulf of Chester is also with him—"

"Of course. Treacherous dog."

"He has brought all his knights from Chester, plus a horde of wild rapacious Welshmen."

"How many men altogether?"

"About a thousand."

"Damn—that's a hundred more than we have."

By this time several barons had gathered around, and now another one spoke. "Lord, if he's coming across open country, he'll have to cross the river at the ford—"

"Good thinking, Edward!" Stephen said. "Take your men down to that ford and see if you can hold it. You'll need archers, too."

"How far are they now, does anybody know?" asked Edward.

The first earl said: "Very close, the scout said. They could reach the ford before you."

"I'll go right away," Edward said.

"Good man!" said King Stephen. He made a fist with his right hand and punched his left palm. "I shall meet Robert of Gloucester on the battlefield at last. I wish I had more men. Still—an advantage of a hundred men isn't much."

Philip listened to it all in grim silence. He was sure he had been on the point of getting Stephen's agreement. Now the king's mind was elsewhere. But Philip was not ready to give up. He was still wearing the king's purple robe. He slipped it off his shoulders and held it out, saying: "Perhaps we should both revert to type, my lord king."

Stephen nodded absently. A courtier stepped behind the king and helped him take off the monkish habit. Philip handed over the royal robe and said: "Lord, you seemed well disposed to my request."

Stephen looked irritated to be reminded. He shrugged on his robe and was about to speak when a new voice was heard.

"My lord king!"

Philip recognized the voice. His heart sank. He turned and saw William Hamleigh.

"William, my boy!" said the king, in the hearty voice he used with fighting men. "You've arrived just in time!"

William bowed and said: "My lord, I've brought fifty knights and two hundred men from my earldom."

Philip's hopes turned to dust.

Stephen was visibly delighted. "What a good man you are!" he said warmly. "That gives us the advantage over the enemy!" He put his arm around William's shoulders and walked with him into the cathedral.

Philip stood where he was and watched them go. He had been agonizingly close to success, but in the end William's army had counted for more than justice, he thought bitterly. The courtier who had helped the king take off the monk's habit now held the robe out to Philip. Philip took it. The courtier followed the king and his entourage into the cathedral. Philip put on his monastic robe. He was deeply disappointed. He looked at the three huge arched doorways of the cathedral. He had hoped to build archways like that at Kingsbridge. But King Stephen had taken the side of William Hamleigh. The king had been faced with a straight choice: the justice of Philip's case against the advantage of William's army. He had failed his test.

Philip was left with only one hope: that King Stephen would be defeated in the forthcoming battle.

II

The bishop said mass in the cathedral when the sky was beginning to change from black to gray. By then the horses were saddled, the knights were wearing their chain mail, the men-at-arms had been fed, and a measure of strong wine had been served to give them all heart.

William Hamleigh knelt in the nave with the other knights and earls, while the war-horses stamped and snorted in the aisles, and was forgiven in advance for the killing he would do that day.

Fear and excitement made William light-headed. If the king won a victory today, William's name would forever be associated with it, for men would say that he had brought the reinforcements that tipped the balance. If the king should lose . . . anything could happen. He shivered on the cold stone floor.

The king was at the front, in a fresh white robe, with a candle in his hand. As the Host was elevated, the candle broke, and the flame went out. William trembled with dread: it was a bad omen. A priest brought a new candle and took away the broken one, and Stephen smiled nonchalantly, but the feeling of supernatural horror stayed with William, and when he looked around he could tell that others felt the same.

After the service the king put on his armor, helped by a valet. He had a knee-length mail coat made of leather with iron rings sewn to it. The coat was slit up to the waist in front and behind so that he could ride in it. The valet laced it tightly at the throat. He then put on a close-fitting cap with a long mail hood attached, covering his tawny hair and protecting his neck. Over the cap he wore an iron helmet with a nosepiece. His leather boots had mail trimmings and pointed spurs.

As he put on his armor, the earls gathered around him. William followed his mother's advice and acted as if he were already one of them, pushing through the crowd to join the group around the king. After listening for a moment he realized they were trying to persuade Stephen to withdraw and leave Lincoln to the rebels.

"You hold more territory than Maud—you can raise a larger army," said an older man whom William recognized as Lord Hugh. "Go south, get reinforcements, come back and outnumber them."

After the portent of the broken candle, William almost wished for withdrawal himself; but the king had no time for such talk. "We're strong enough to defeat them now," he said cheerfully. "Where's your spirit?" He strapped on a belt with a sword on one side and a dagger on the other, both of them in wood-and-leather scabbards.

"The armies are too evenly matched," said a tall man with short, grizzled hair and a close-trimmed beard: the earl of Surrey. "It's too risky."

This was a poor argument to use with Stephen, William knew: the king was nothing if not chivalrous. "Too evenly matched?" he repeated scornfully. "I prefer a fair fight." He pulled on the leather gauntlets with mail on the backs of the fingers. The valet handed him a long wooden shield covered with leather. He hooked its strap around his neck and held it in his left hand.

"We've little to lose by withdrawing at this point," Hugh persisted. "We aren't even in possession of the castle."

"I would lose my chance of meeting Robert of Gloucester on the battlefield," Stephen said. "For two years he's been avoiding me. Now that I have an opportunity to deal with the traitor once and for all, I'm not going to pull out just because we're evenly matched!"

A groom brought his horse, saddled ready. As Stephen was about to mount, there was a flurry of activity around the door at the west end of the cathedral, and a knight came running up the nave, muddy and bleeding. William had a doomy premonition that this would be bad news. As the man bowed to the king, William recognized him as one of Edward's men who had been sent to guard the ford. "We were too late, lord," the man said hoarsely, breathing hard. "The enemy has crossed the river."

It was another bad sign. William suddenly felt colder. Now there was nothing but open fields between the enemy and Lincoln.

Stephen too looked struck down for an instant, but he recovered his composure swiftly. "No matter!" he said. "We will meet them all the sooner!" He mounted his war-horse.

He had a battle-ax strapped to his saddle. The valet handed him a wooden lance with a bright iron point, completing his weaponry. Stephen clicked his tongue, and the horse obediently moved forward.

As he rode down the nave of the cathedral, the earls, barons and knights mounted and fell in behind him, and they left the cathedral in procession. In the grounds the men-at-arms joined them. This was when men began to feel scared and look for a chance to slip away; but their dignified pace, and the almost ceremonial atmosphere, with the townspeople looking on, meant it would be very difficult for the fainthearted to escape.

Their numbers were augmented by a hundred or more townsmen, fat bakers and shortsighted weavers and red-faced brewers, poorly armored and riding their cobs and palfreys. Their presence was a sign of the unpopularity of Ranulf.

The army could not pass the castle, for they would have been exposed to archery fire from its battlements, so they left the town by the north gate, which was called Newport Arch, and turned west. This was where the battle would be fought.

William studied the terrain with a keen eye. Although the hill on the south side of the town sloped steeply to the river, here on the west there was a long ridge which fell gently to the plain. William saw immediately that Stephen had chosen the right spot from which to defend the town, for no matter how the enemy approached they would always be downhill from the king's army.

When Stephen was a quarter of a mile or so out of the city two scouts came up the slope, riding fast. They spotted the king and went straight to him. William crowded closer to hear their report.

"The enemy is approaching fast, lord," said one of the scouts.

William looked across the plain. Sure enough, he could see a black mass in the distance, moving slowly toward him: the enemy. He felt a shiver of fear. He shook himself, but the fear persisted. It would go when the fighting started.

King Stephen said: "What are their dispositions?"

"Ranulf and the knights of Chester form the middle, lord," the scout began. "They are on foot."

William wondered how the scout knew this. He must have gone right into the enemy camp and listened while marching orders were given. That took a cool nerve.

"Ranulf in the center?" said Stephen. "As if he were the leader, rather than Robert!"

"Robert of Gloucester is on his left flank, with an army of men who call themselves The Disinherited," the scout went on. William knew why they used that name—they had all lost lands since the civil war began.

"Robert has given Ranulf command of the operation, then," Stephen said thoughtfully. "A pity. I know Robert well—I practically grew up with him—and I could guess his tactics. But Ranulf is a stranger to me. No matter. Who's on their right?"

"The Welsh, lord."

"Archers, I suppose." The men of South Wales had a reputation for bowmanship.

"Not these," the scout said. "They are a raving mob, with their faces painted, singing barbaric songs, and armed with hammers and clubs. Very few have horses."

"They must be from North Wales," Stephen mused. "Ranulf has promised them pillage, I expect. God help Lincoln if they get inside the walls. But they won't! What's your name, scout?"

"Roger, called Lackland," the man said.

"Lackland? You shall have ten acres for this work."

The man was thrilled. "Thank you, lord!"

"Now." Stephen turned and looked at his earls. He was about to make his dispositions. William tensed, wondering what role the king would assign to him. "Where is my lord Alan of Brittany?"

Alan edged his horse forward. He was the leader of a force of Breton mercenaries, rootless men who fought for pay and whose only loyalty was to themselves.

Stephen said to Alan: "I'll have you and your brave Bretons in the front line on my left."

William saw the wisdom of that: Breton mercenaries against Welsh adventurers, the untrustworthy versus the undisciplined.

"William of Ypres!" Stephen called.

"My lord king." A dark man on a black war-horse raised his lance. This William was the leader of another force of mercenaries, Flemish men, a shade more reliable than the Bretons, it was said.

Stephen said: "You on my left also, but behind Alan's Bretons."

The two mercenary leaders wheeled about and rode back into the army to organize their men. William wondered where he would be placed. He had no wish to be in the front line. He had already done enough to distinguish himself, by bringing his army. A safe, uneventful rearguard position would suit him today.

King Stephen said: "My lords of Worcester, Surrey, Northampton, York and Hertford, with your knights, form my right flank."

Once again William saw the sense of Stephen's dispositions. The earls and their knights, mostly mounted, would face Robert of Gloucester and the "disinherited" nobles who supported him, most of whom would also be on horseback. But William was disappointed not to have been included with the earls. Surely the king could not have forgotten about him?

"I will hold the middle ground, dismounted, with foot soldiers," Stephen said.

For the first time William disapproved of a decision. It was always better to stay on horseback as long as you could. But Ranulf, at the head of the opposing army, was said to be on foot, and

Stephen's overwrought sense of fair play compelled him to meet his enemy on equal terms.

"With me in the center I will have William of Shiring and his men," the king said.

William did not know whether to be thrilled or terrified. It was a great honor to be chosen to stand with the king—Mother would be gratified—but it put him in the most dangerous position. Worse still, he would be on foot. It also meant the king would be able to see him and judge his performance. He would have to appear fearless and take the fight to the enemy, as opposed to keeping out of trouble and fighting only when forced to, which was the tactic he preferred.

"The loyal citizens of Lincoln will bring up the rear," Stephen said. This was a mixture of compassion and military good sense. The citizens would not be much use anywhere, but in the rear they could do little damage and would suffer fewer casualties.

William raised the banner of the earl of Shiring. This was another idea of Mother's. He was not entitled to the banner, strictly speaking, because he was not the earl; but the men with him were used to following the Shiring banner—or so he would argue if challenged. And by the end of the day, if the battle went well, he might be earl.

His men gathered around him. Walter was by his side, as always, a solid, reassuring presence. So were Ugly Gervase, Hugh Axe and Miles Dice. Gilbert, who had died at the quarry, had been replaced by Guillaume de St. Clair, a fresh-faced young man with a vicious streak.

Looking around, William was infuriated to see Richard of Kingsbridge, wearing bright new armor and riding a splendid war-horse. He was with the earl of Surrey. He had not brought an army for the king, as William had, but he looked impressive—fresh-faced, vigorous, and brave—and if he did great things today he might win royal favor. Battles were unpredictable, and so were kings.

On the other hand, perhaps Richard would be killed today. What a stroke of luck *that* would be. William lusted for it more than he had ever lusted for a woman.

He looked to the west. The enemy was closer.

Philip was on the roof of the cathedral, and he could see Lincoln laid out like a map. The old city surrounded the cathedral on the hilltop. It had straight streets and neat gardens and the castle in the southwest corner. The newer part, noisy and overcrowded, occupied the steep hillside to the south, between the old city and the River Witham. This district was normally bustling with commercial activity, but today it was covered with a fearful silence like a pall, and the people were standing on their rooftops to watch the battle. The river came in from the east, ran along the foot of the hill, then widened into a big natural harbor called Brayfield Pool, which was surrounded by quays and full of ships and boats. A canal called the Fosdyke ran west from Brayfield Pool—all the way to the River Trent, Philip had been told. Seeing it from a height, Philip marveled at how it ran straight for miles. People said it had been built in ancient times.

The canal formed the edge of the battlefield. Philip watched King Stephen's army march out of the city in a ragged crowd and slowly form up in three orderly columns on the ridge. Philip knew that Stephen had placed the earls on his right for they were the most colorful, with their tunics of red and yellow and their bright banners. They were also the most active, riding up and down, giving orders and holding consultations and making plans. The group to the king's left, on the slope of the ridge that went down to the canal, were dressed in dull gray and brown, had fewer horses, and were less busy, conserving their energies: they would be the mercenaries.

Beyond Stephen's army, where the line of the canal became indistinct and merged with the hedgerows, the rebel army covered the fields like a swarm of bees. At first they had appeared to be stationary; then, when he looked again after a while, they were closer; and now, if he concentrated, he could just discern their motion. He wondered how strong they were. All indications were that the two sides were evenly matched.

There was nothing Philip could do to influence the outcome—a situation he hated. He tried to quiet his spirit and be fatalistic. If God wanted a new cathedral at Kingsbridge, he would cause Robert of Gloucester to defeat King Stephen today, so that Philip could ask the victorious Empress Maud to let him repossess the quarry and reopen the market. And if Stephen should defeat Robert, Philip would have to accept God's will, give up his ambitious plans, and let Kingsbridge once more decline into sleepy obscurity.

Try as he might, Philip could not think that way. He wanted Robert to *win*.

A strong wind buffeted the towers of the cathedral and threatened to blow the more frail spectators off the leads and hurl them to the graveyard below. The wind was bitterly cold. Philip shivered and pulled his cloak tighter around him.

The two armies were now about a mile apart.

* * *

The rebel army halted when it was about a mile from the king's front line. It was tantalizing to be able to see their mass but not make out any details. William wanted to know how well armed they were, whether they were cheerful and aggressive or tired and reluctant, even how tall they were. They continued to advance at a slow creep, as those in the rear, motivated by the same anxiety that William was suffering, pressed forward to get a look at the enemy.

In Stephen's army the earls and their knights lined up on their horses, with their lances at the ready, as if they were at a tournament and about to begin the jousting. William reluctantly sent all the horses in his contingent to the rear. He told the squires not to go back to the city but to hold the horses there in case they were needed—for flight, he meant, although he did not say so. If a battle was lost it was better to run than die.

There was a lull, when it seemed as if the fighting would never begin. The wind dropped and the horses calmed down, although the men did not. King Stephen took off his helmet and scratched his head. William became fretful. Fighting was all right but thinking about it made him feel nauseated.

Then, for no apparent reason, the atmosphere became tense again. A battle cry went up from somewhere. All the horses suddenly turned skittish. A cheer began, and was drowned, almost instantly, by the thunder of hooves. The battle was on. William smelled the sour, sweaty odor of fear.

He looked around, trying desperately to figure out what was happening, but all was confusion, and being on foot he could see only his immediate surroundings. The earls on the right seemed to have started the battle by charging the enemy. Presumably the forces opposite them, Earl Robert's army of disinherited nobles, were responding in like manner, charging in formation. Almost immediately, a cry went up from the left, and William turned to see that the mounted men among the Breton mercenaries were spurring their horses forward. At that, a bloodcurdling cacophony arose from the corresponding section of the enemy army—the Welsh mob, presumably. He could not see who had the advantage.

He had lost sight of Richard.

Dozens of arrows rose like a flock of birds from behind the enemy lines and began to fall all around. William held his shield over his head. He loathed arrows—they killed at random.

King Stephen roared a war cry and charged. William drew his sword and ran forward, calling his men to follow. But the horsemen on his left and right had fanned out as they charged forward, and they came between him and the enemy.

On his right, there was a deafening clash of iron on iron, and the air filled with a metallic smell he knew well. The earls and the disinherited had joined battle. All he could see was men and horses colliding, wheeling, charging and falling. The neighing of the beasts was indistinguishable from the men's battle cries, and somewhere in that noise William could already hear the bone-chilling, dreadful screams of wounded men in agony. He hoped Richard was one of those screaming.

William looked left and was horrified to see that the Bretons were falling back before the clubs and axes of the wild Welsh tribesmen. The Welsh were bersesrk, yelling and screaming and trampling one another in their eagerness to get at the enemy. Perhaps they were greedy to loot the rich city. The Bretons, with nothing more than the prospect of another week's pay to spur them on, were fighting defensively and giving ground. William was disgusted.

He was frustrated that he had not yet struck a single blow. He was surrounded by his knights, and ahead of him were the horses of the earls and the Bretons. He pushed forward, slightly ahead and to one side of the king. There was combat all around: fallen horses, men fighting hand to hand with the ferocity of cats, the deafening ring of swords, and the sickly smell of blood; but William and King Stephen were, for the moment, stuck in a dead zone.

Philip could see everything, but he understood nothing. He had no idea what was going on. All was confusion: flashing blades, charging horses, banners flying and falling, and the sounds of battle, carried on the wind, muted by distance. It was maddeningly frustrating. Some men fell and died, others overcame and fought on, but he could not tell who was winning and who losing.

A cathedral priest standing nearby in a fur coat looked at Philip and said: "What's going on?"

Philip shook his head and said: "I can't tell."

But even as he spoke he discerned a movement. To the left of the battlefield, some men were running away down the hill toward the canal. They were drab-dressed mercenaries, and as far as Philip could tell, it was the king's men who were fleeing and the painted tribesmen of the attacking army who were in pursuit. The victorious whooping of the Welsh could be heard from here. Philip's hopes lifted: the rebels were winning already!

Then there was a sea change on the other side. To the right, where the mounted men were engaged, the king's army seemed to be falling back. The movement was at first slight, then steady, then rapid; and even as Philip watched, the retreat turned into a rout, and scores of the king's men turned their horses and began to flee from the battlefield.

Philip was elated: this must be God's will!

Could it really be over so quickly? The rebels were advancing on both flanks, but the center was still holding steady. The men around King Stephen were fighting more fiercely than those to either side. Would they be able to stem the flow? Perhaps Stephen and Robert of Gloucester would fight it out personally: single combat between two leaders could sometimes settle the issue regardless of what was happening elsewhere on the field. It was not yet over.

The tide turned with horrifying speed. At one moment the two armies were even, both sides fighting fiercely; and at the next, the king's men were falling back fast. William was deeply disheartened. On his left, the Breton mercenaries were running away down the hill and being chased into the canal by the Welsh; and on his right, the earls with their war-horses and banners were turning from the fight and trying to escape back toward Lincoln. Only the middle was holding: King Stephen was in the thick of it, laying about him with his massive sword, and the Shiring men were fighting like pack-wolves all around him. But the situation was unstable. If the flanks continued to retreat the king would end up surrounded. William wanted Stephen to fall back. But the king was more brave than wise, and he fought on.

William felt the entire battle take a lurch to the left. Looking around, he saw the Flemish mercenaries coming from behind and falling on the Welsh, who were forced to stop chasing the Bretons down the hill and turn to defend themselves. For a moment there was a melee. Then Ranulf of Chester's men, in the middle of the enemy front line, attacked the Flemish, who now found themselves squeezed between the men from Chester and the Welsh.

Seeing the rally, King Stephen urged his men to press forward. William thought Ranulf might have made a mistake. If the king's forces could close with Ranulf's men now, Ranulf would be the one who was squeezed on two sides.

One of William's knights fell in front of him and suddenly he was in the midst of the fighting.

A beefy northerner with blood on his sword lunged at him. William parried the thrust easily: he was fresh and his antagonist was already tired. William thrust at the man's face, missed, and parried another jab. He raised his sword high, deliberately opening himself to a stab; then, when the other man predictably stepped forward with another thrust, William dodged it and brought his sword down, two-handed, on the other man's shoulder. The blow split the man's armor and broke his collarbone, and he fell.

William enjoyed a moment of elation. His fear had gone. He roared: "Come on, you dogs!"

Two more men took the place of the fallen knight and attacked William simultaneously. He held them off but he was forced to give ground.

There was a surge on his right, and one of his opponents had to turn aside to defend himself against a red-faced man armed with a cleaver, who looked like a crazed butcher. That left only one for William to deal with. He grinned savagely and pressed forward. His opponent panicked and slashed wildly at William's head. William ducked and stabbed the man in the thigh, just below the fringe of his short mail jacket. The leg buckled and the man fell.

Once again William had no one to fight. He stood still, breathing hard. For a moment he had thought the king's army was going to be routed, but they had rallied, and now neither side appeared to have the advantage. He looked to his right, wondering what had caused the surge that had distracted one of his antagonists. To his astonishment he saw that the citizens of Lincoln were giving the enemy a hard fight. Perhaps it was because they were defending their own homes. But who had rallied them, after the earls on that flank had fled? His question was answered: to his dismay he saw Richard of Kingsbridge on his war-horse, urging the townsmen on. William's heart sank. If the king saw Richard being brave it could undo all William's work. William looked over at Stephen. At that moment the king caught Richard's eye and waved encouragement. William let out a resentful curse.

The townsmen's rally relieved the pressure on the king, but only for a moment. To the left, Ranulf's men had routed the Flemish mercenaries, and now Ranulf turned toward the center of the defending forces. At the same time the so-called Disinherited rallied against Richard and the townsmen, and the fighting became furious.

William was attacked by a huge man with a battle-ax. He dodged desperately, suddenly afraid for his life. With each swing of the ax he leaped back, and he realized fearfully that the whole of the king's army was falling back at much the same pace. To his left, the Welsh came back up the hill and, incredibly, started throwing stones. It was ridiculous but effective, for now William had to keep an eye out for flying rocks as well as defend himself against the giant with the battle-ax. There seemed to be a lot more of the enemy than before, and William felt, with a sense of despair, that the king's men were outnumbered. Hysterical fear rose in his throat as he realized that the battle was very nearly lost and he was in mortal danger. The king should flee now. Why was he fighting on? It was insane—he would be killed—they would all be killed! William's antagonist raised his ax high. William's fighting instincts took over for an instant, and instead of falling back as he had before, he leaped forward and lunged at the big man's face. His sword point went into the man's neck just under the chin. William thrust it home hard. The man's eyes closed. William felt a moment of grateful relief. He pulled the sword out and darted back to dodge the ax that now fell from the man's dead hands.

He snatched a look at the king, just a few yards to his left. As he looked, the king brought his sword down hard on a man's helmet, and the sword snapped in two like a twig. That was it, William thought with relief; the battle was over. The king would flee and save himself to fight another day. But the hope was premature. William had half turned, ready to run, when a townsman offered the king a long-handled woodsman's ax. To William's dismay, Stephen grabbed the weapon and fought on.

William was tempted to run anyway. Looking to his right, he saw Richard on foot, fighting like a madman, pressing forward, laying about him with his sword, striking men down left, right and center. William could not flee when his rival was still fighting.

William was attacked again, this time by a short man with light armor who moved very quickly, his sword flashing in the sunlight. As their weapons clashed William realized he was up against a formidable fighter. Once again he found himself on the defensive and afraid for his life, and his knowledge that the battle was lost sapped his will to fight. He parried the rapid thrusts and slashes that were aimed at him, wishing he could get in the one strong blow that would smash through the man's armor. He saw a chance and swung his sword. The other man dodged and thrust, and William felt his left arm go numb. He was wounded. He felt sick with fear. He continued to fall back under the assault, feeling oddly unbalanced, as if the ground was shifting beneath him. His shield hung loose from his neck: he was unable to hold it steady with his useless left arm. The small man sensed victory and pressed his attack. William saw death and was filled with mortal dread.

Suddenly Walter appeared at his side.

William stepped back. Walter swung his sword two-handed. Catching the small man by surprise, he cut him down like a sapling. William suddenly felt dizzy with relief. He put a hand on Walter's shoulder.

"We've lost it!" Walter shouted at him. "Let's get out!"

William pulled himself together. The king was still fighting, even though the battle was lost. If only he would give up now, and try to get away, he could return to the south and muster another army. But the longer he fought on, the greater the probability that he could be captured or killed, and that could mean only one thing: Maud would be queen.

William and Walter edged back together. Why was the king so foolish? He had to prove his courage. Gallantry would be the death of him. Once again William was tempted to abandon the king. But Richard of Kingsbridge was still there, holding the right flank like a rock, swinging his sword and mowing men down like a reaper. "Not yet!" William said to Walter. "Watch the king!"

They retreated step by step. The fighting became less fierce as men realized that the issue had been decided and there was no point in taking risks. William and Walter crossed swords with two knights, but the knights were content to drive them back, and William and Walter fought defensively. Hard blows were struck but no one exposed himself to danger.

William stepped back two paces and chanced a look at the king. At that moment a huge rock came flying across the field and struck Stephen's helmet. The king staggered and fell to his knees. William's antagonist paused and turned his head to see what William was looking at. The battle-ax dropped from King Stephen's hands. An enemy knight ran to him and pulled off the helmet. "The king!" he shouted triumphantly. "I have the king!"

William, Walter and the entire royal army turned and ran.

Philip was jubilant. The retreat started in the middle of the king's army and spread like a ripple to the flanks. Within a few heartbeats the entire royal army was on the run. This was King Stephen's reward for injustice.

The attackers gave chase. There were forty or fifty riderless horses in the rear of the king's army, being held by squires, and some of the fleeing men leaped on them and made their escape, heading not for the city of Lincoln but for the open country.

Philip wondered what had happened to the king.

The citizens of Lincoln were hurriedly leaving their rooftops. Children and animals were rounded up. Some families disappeared into their houses, closing the shutters and barring the doors. There was a flurry of movement among the boats on the lake: some citizens were trying to get away by river. People began to arrive at the cathedral, to take refuge there.

At each entrance to the city, people rushed to close the huge ironbound doors. Suddenly Ranulf of Chester's men burst out of the castle. They divided into groups, evidently following a prearranged plan, and one group went to each city gate. They waded in among the citizens, striking them down to left and right, and reopened the doors to admit the conquering rebels.

Philip decided to get off the cathedral roof. The others with him, mostly cathedral canons, had the same thought. They all ducked through the low doorway that led into the turret. There they met the bishop and the archdeacons, who had been higher up in the tower. Philip thought Bishop Alexander looked frightened. That was a pity: the bishop would need courage to share today.

They all went carefully down the long, narrow spiral staircase and emerged in the nave of the church at the west end. There were already a hundred or so citizens in the church, and more pouring through the three great doorways. As Philip looked out, two knights came into the cathedral courtyard, bloodstained and muddy, riding hard, obviously having come from the battle. They rode straight into the church without dismounting. When they saw the bishop one of them shouted: "The king is captured!"

Philip's heart leaped. King Stephen was not just beaten, he was taken prisoner! The royalist forces throughout the kingdom would surely collapse now. The implications tumbled over one another in Philip's imagination, but before he could sort them out he heard Bishop Alexander shout: "Close the doors!"

Philip could hardly believe his ears. "No!" he shouted. "You can't do that!"

The bishop stared at him, white with fear and panic. He was not sure who Philip was. Philip had made a formal call on him, out of courtesy, but they had not spoken since. Now, with a visible effort, Alexander remembered him. "This is not your cathedral, Prior Philip, it's mine. Close the doors!" Several priests went to do his bidding.

Philip was horrified at this display of naked self-interest by a clergyman. "You can't lock people out," he shouted angrily. "They might be killed!"

"If we don't lock the doors we'll all be killed!" Alexander screeched hysterically.

Philip grabbed him by the front of the robe. "Remember who you are," he hissed. "We're not supposed to be afraid—especially of death. Pull yourself together."

"Get him off me!" Alexander screamed.

Several canons pulled Philip away.

Philip shouted at them: "Don't you see what he's doing?"

A canon said: "If you're so brave, why don't you go out there and protect them yourself?"

Philip tore himself free. "That's exactly what I'm going to do," he said.

He turned around. The big central door was just closing. He dashed across the nave. Three priests were pushing it shut as more people fought to get through the narrowing gap. Philip squeezed out just before the door closed.

In the next few moments a small crowd gathered in the porch. Men and women banged on the door and screamed to be let in, but there was no response from inside the church.

Suddenly Philip was afraid. The panic on the faces of the people locked out scared him. He felt himself trembling. He had encountered a victorious army once before, at the age of six, and the horror he had felt then returned to him now. The moment when the men-at-arms had burst into his parents' house came back as vividly as if it had happened yesterday. He stood rooted to the spot, and tried to stop shaking, while the crowd boiled around him. It was a long time since he had been tormented by this nightmare. He saw the bloodlust on the men's faces, and the way the sword had transfixed his mother, and the awful sight of his father's guts spilling out of his belly; and he felt again that uncomprehending, overwhelming, insane hysterical terror. Then he saw a monk come through the door with a cross in his hand, and the screaming stopped. The monk showed him and his brother how to close the eyes of his mother and father, so that they could sleep the long sleep. He remembered, as if he had just awakened from a dream, that he was not a frightened child anymore, he was a grown man and a monk; and just as Abbot Peter had rescued him and his brother on that dreadful day twenty-seven years ago, so today the grown-up Philip, strengthened by faith and protected by God, would come to the help of those in fear of their lives.

He forced himself to take a single step forward; and once he had done that the second was a little less difficult, and the third was almost easy.

When he reached the street that led to the west gate he was almost knocked over by a mob of fleeing townspeople: men and boys running with bundles of precious possessions, old people gasping for breath, screaming girls, women carrying squalling children in their arms. The rush carried him back several yards, then he fought against the flow. They were heading for the cathedral. He wanted to tell them it was closed, and they should stay quietly in their own homes and bar the doors; but everyone was shouting and no one was listening.

He progressed slowly along the street, moving against the flood of people. He had gained only a few yards when a group of four horsemen came charging along the street. They were the cause of the stampede. Some people flattened themselves against house walls, but others could not get out of the way in time, and many fell beneath the flailing hooves. Philip was horrified but there was nothing he could do, and he dodged into an alleyway to avoid becoming a victim himself. A moment later the horsemen had passed by and the street was deserted.

Several bodies were left lying on the ground. As Philip stepped out of his alley he saw one of them move: a middle-aged man in a scarlet cloak was trying to crawl along the ground despite an injured leg. Philip crossed the street, intending to try to carry the man; but before he got there, two men with iron helmets and wooden shields appeared. One of them said: "This one's alive, Jake."

Philip shuddered. It seemed to him that their demeanor, their voices, their clothes and even their faces were the same as those of the two men who had killed his parents.

The one called Jake said: "He'll fetch a ransom—look at that red cloak." He turned, put his fingers in his mouth, and whistled. A third man came running up. "Take Redcoat here into the castle and tie him up."

The third man put his arms around the wounded citizen's chest and dragged him off. The injured man screamed in pain as his legs bumped over the stones. Philip shouted: "Stop!" They all stopped for a moment, looked at him, and laughed; then they carried on with what they were doing.

Philip shouted again but they ignored him. He watched helplessly as the wounded man was dragged off. Another man-at-arms came out of a house, wearing a long fur coat and carrying six silver plates under his arm. Jake saw him and took note of the booty. "These are rich houses," he said to his comrade. "We ought to get into one of them. See what we can find." They went up to the locked door of a stone house and attacked it with a battle-ax.

Philip felt useless but he was not willing to give up. However, God had not put him in this position to defend rich men's property, so he left Jake and his companions and hurried toward the west gate. More men-at-arms came running along the street. Mingled with them were several short, dark men with painted faces, dressed in sheepskin coats and armed with clubs. They were the Welsh tribesmen, Philip realized, and he felt ashamed that he came from the same country as these savages. He clung to the wall of a house and tried to look inconspicuous.

Two men emerged from a stone house dragging by the legs a white-bearded man in a skullcap. One of them held a knife to the man's throat and said: "Where's your money, Jew?"

"I have no money," the man said plaintively.

Nobody would believe that, Philip thought. The wealth of the Jews of Lincoln was famous; and anyway, the man had been living in a stone house.

Another man-at-arms came out dragging a woman by the hair. The woman was middle-aged and presumably the Jew's wife. The first man shouted: "Tell us where the money is, or she'll have my sword up her cunt." He lifted the woman's skirt, exposing her graying pubic hair, and held a long dagger pointing at her groin.

Philip was about to intervene, but the old man gave in immediately. "Don't hurt her, the money's in the back," he said urgently. "It's buried in the garden, by the woodpile—please, let her go."

The three men ran back into the house. The woman helped the man to his feet. Another group of horsemen thundered down the narrow street, and Philip flung himself out of the way. When he got up again, the two Jews had disappeared.

A young man in armor came down the street, running for his life, with three or four Welshmen in pursuit. They caught him just as he drew level with Philip. The foremost pursuer swung with his sword and touched the fugitive's calf. It did not seem to Philip like a deep wound but it was enough to make the young man stumble and fall to the ground. Another pursuer reached the fallen man and hefted a battle-ax.

With his heart in his mouth, Philip stepped forward and shouted: "Stop!"

The man raised his ax.

Philip rushed at him.

The man swung the ax, but Philip pushed him at the last minute. The blade of the ax clanged on the stone pavement a foot from the victim's head. The attacker recovered his balance and stared at Philip in amazement. Philip stared back at him, trying not to tremble, wishing he could remember a word or two of Welsh. Before either of them moved, the other two pursuers caught up, and one of them cannoned into Philip, sending him sprawling. That probably saved his life, he realized a moment later. When he recovered, everyone had forgotten him. They were butchering the poor young man on the ground with unbelievable savagery. Philip scrambled to his feet, but he was already too late: their hammers and axes were thudding into a corpse. He looked up at the sky and shouted angrily: "If I can't save anyone, why did you send me here?"

As if in reply, he heard a scream from a nearby house. It was a one-story building of stone and wood, not as costly as those around it. The door stood open. Philip ran inside. There were two rooms with an arch between, and straw on the floor. A woman with two small children huddled in a corner, terrified. Three men-at-arms were in the middle of the house, confronting one small, bald man. A young woman of about eighteen years was on the floor. Her dress was ripped and one of the three men-at-arms was kneeling on her chest, holding her thighs apart. The bald man was clearly trying to stop them from raping his daughter. As Philip came in, the father flung himself at one of the men-at-arms. The soldier threw him off. The father staggered back. The soldier plunged his sword into the father's abdomen. The woman in the corner screamed like a lost soul.

Philip yelled: "Stop!"

They all looked at him as if he were mad.

In his most authoritative voice he said: "You'll all go to hell if you do this!"

The one who had killed the father raised his sword to strike Philip.

"Just a minute," said the man on the ground, still holding the girl's legs. "Who are you, monk?"

"I am Philip of Gwynedd, prior of Kingsbridge, and I command you in God's name to leave that girl alone, if you care for your immortal souls."

"A prior—I thought so," said the man on the ground. "He's worth a ransom."

The first man sheathed his sword and said: "Get over in the corner with the woman, where you belong."

Philip said: "Don't lay hands on a monk's robes." He was trying to sound dangerous but he could hear the note of desperation in his voice.

"Take him to the castle, John," said the man on the ground, who was still sitting on the girl. He seemed to be the leader.

"Go to hell," said John. "I want to fuck her first." He grabbed Philip's arms and, before Philip could resist, flung him into the corner. Philip tumbled onto the floor beside the mother.

The man called John lifted the front of his tunic and fell on the girl.

The mother turned her head aside and began to sob.

Philip said: "I will not watch this!" He stood up and grabbed the rapist by the hair, pulling him off the girl. The rapist roared with pain.

The third man raised a club. Philip saw the blow coming, but he was too late. The club landed on his head. He felt a moment of agonizing pain, then everything went black and he lost consciousness before he hit the ground.

The prisoners were taken to the castle and locked in cages. These were stout wooden structures like miniature houses, six feet long and three feet wide, and only a little higher than a man's head. Instead of solid walls they had close-spaced vertical posts, which enabled the jailer to see inside. In normal times, when they were used to confine thieves and murderers and heretics, there would be only one or two people to a cage. Today the rebels put eight or ten in each, and still there were more prisoners. The surplus captives were tied together with ropes and herded into a corner of the compound. They could have escaped fairly easily, but they did not, probably because they were safer here than outside in the town.

Philip sat in one corner of a cage, nursing a splitting headache, feeling a fool and a failure. In the end he had been as useless as the cowardly Bishop Alexander. He had not saved a single life; he had not even prevented one blow. The citizens of Lincoln would have been no worse off without him. Unlike Abbot Peter, he had been powerless to stop the violence. I'm just not the man Father Peter was, he thought.

Worse still, in his vain attempt to help the townspeople he had probably thrown away his chance of winning concessions from the Empress Maud when she became queen. He was now a prisoner of her army. It would be assumed, therefore, that he had been with King Stephen's forces. Kingsbridge Priory would have to pay a ransom for Philip's release. It was quite likely that the whole thing would come to Maud's notice; and then she would be prejudiced against Philip. He felt sick, disappointed, and full of remorse.

More prisoners were brought in through the day. The influx ended around nightfall, but the sacking of the city went on outside the castle walls: Philip could hear the shouts and screams and sounds of destruction. Toward midnight the noise died down, presumably as the soldiers became so drunk on stolen wine and sated with rape and violence that they could do no more damage. A few of them staggered into the castle, boasting of their triumphs, quarreling among themselves and vomiting on the grass; and eventually fell down insensible and slept.

Philip slept, too, although he did not have enough room to lie down, and had to slump in the corner with his back against the wooden bars of his cage. He woke at dawn, shivering with cold, but the pain in his head had softened, mercifully, to a dull ache. He stood up to stretch his legs, and slapped his arms against his sides to warm himself. All the castle buildings were overflowing with people. The open-fronted stables revealed men sleeping in the stalls, while the horses were tied up outside. Pairs of legs stuck out of the bakehouse door and the kitchen undercroft. The small minority of sober soldiers had pitched tents. There were horses everywhere. In the southeast corner of the castle compound was the keep, a castle within a castle, built on a high mound, its mighty stone walls encircling half a dozen or more wooden buildings. The earls and knights of the winning side would be in there, sleeping off their own celebration.

Philip's mind turned to the implications of yesterday's battle. Did it mean the war was over? Probably. Stephen had a wife, Queen Matilda, who might fight on: she was countess of Boulogne, and with her French knights she had taken Dover Castle early in the war and now controlled much of Kent on her husband's behalf. However, she would find it difficult to gather support from the barons while Stephen was in prison. She might hold on to Kent for a while but she was unlikely to make any gains.

Nevertheless, Maud's problems were not yet over. She had to consolidate her military victory, gain the approval of the Church and be crowned at Westminster. However, given determination and a little wisdom she would probably succeed.

And that was good news for Kingsbridge; or it would be, if Philip could get out of here without being branded a supporter of Stephen.

There was no sun, but the air warmed a little as the day got brighter. Philip's fellow-prisoners awoke gradually, groaning with aches and pains: most of them had been at least bruised, and they felt worse after a cold night, with only the minimal shelter of the roof and bars of the cage. Some were wealthy citizens and others were knights who had been captured in battle. When most of them were awake Philip asked: "Did anyone see what happened to Richard of Kingsbridge?" He was hoping Richard had survived, for Aliena's sake.

A man with a bloodstained bandage around his head said: "He fought like a lion—he rallied the townsmen when things got bad."

"Did he live or die?"

The man shook his wounded head slowly. "I didn't see him at the end."

"What about William Hamleigh?" It would be a blessed relief if William had fallen.

"He was with the king for most of the battle. But he got away at the end—I saw him on a horse, flying across the field, well ahead of the pack."

"Ah." The faint hope faded. Philip's problems were not to be solved that easily.

The conversation lapsed and the cage fell silent. Outside, the soldiers were on the move, nursing their hangovers, checking their booty, making sure their hostages were still in captivity, and getting breakfast from the kitchen. Philip wondered whether prisoners got fed. They must, he thought, for otherwise they would die and there would be no ransoms; but who would take the responsibility for feeding all these people? That started him wondering how long he would be here. His captors would have to send a message to Kingsbridge, demanding a ransom. The brothers would send one of their number to negotiate his release. Who would it be? Milius would be the best, but Remigius, who as sub-prior was in charge in Philip's absence, might send one of his cronies, or even come himself. Remigius would do everything slowly: he was incapable of prompt and decisive action even in his own interest. It could take months. Philip became gloomier.

Other prisoners were luckier. Soon after sunrise, wives and children and relatives of the captives began to trickle into the castle, fearfully and hesitantly at first, then with more confidence, to negotiate the ransom of their loved ones. They would bargain with the captors for a while, protesting their lack of money, offering cheap jewelry or other valuables; then they would reach an agreement, depart, and return a little later with whatever ransom had been agreed, usually cash. The piles of booty grew higher and the cages emptied out.

By midday half the prisoners had gone. They were the local people, Philip assumed. Those remaining must be from distant towns, and were probably all knights who had been taken during the battle. This impression was confirmed when the constable of the castle came around the cages and asked the names of everyone remaining: most of them were knights from the south. Philip noticed that in one of the cages there was only one man, and he was confined in stocks, as if someone wanted to be doubly sure he could not escape. After staring at the special prisoner for a few minutes Philip realized who it was.

"Look!" he said to the three men in his own cage. "That man on his own. Is it who I think it is?"

The others looked. "By Christ, it's the king," said one, and the others agreed.

Philip stared at the muddy, tawny-haired man with his hands and feet confined uncomfortably in the wooden vise of the stocks. He looked just like all the rest of them. Yesterday he had been king of England. Yesterday he had refused Kingsbridge a market license. Today he could not stand up without someone else's leave. The king had got his just deserts, but all the same Philip felt sorry for him.

Early in the afternoon the prisoners were given food. It was lukewarm leftovers from the dinner provided for the fighting men, but they fell on it ravenously. Philip hung back and let the others have most of it, for he regarded hunger as a base weakness that ought to be resisted from time to time, and considered any enforced fast to be an opportunity to mortify the flesh.

While they were scraping the bowl there was a flurry of activity over at the keep, and a group of earls came out. As they walked down the steps of the keep and across the castle compound, Philip observed that two of them went a little in front of the others, and were treated with deference. They had to be Ranulf of Chester and Robert of Gloucester, but Philip did not know which was which. They approached Stephen's cage.

"Good day, Cousin Robert," Stephen said, heavily emphasizing the word *cousin*.

The taller of the two men replied. "I didn't intend for you to spend the night in the stocks. I ordered that you be moved, but the order wasn't obeyed. However, you seem to have survived."

A man in priest's clothing detached himself from the group and came toward Philip's cage. At first Philip paid him no attention, for Stephen was asking what was to be done with him, and Philip wanted to hear the answer; but the priest said: "Which one of you is the prior of Kingsbridge?"

"I am," Philip said.

The priest spoke to one of the men-at-arms who had brought Philip here. "Release that man."

Philip was mystified. He had never seen the priest in his life. Clearly his name had been picked out of the list compiled earlier by the castle constable. But why? He would be glad to get out of the cage, but he was not ready to rejoice—he did not know what was in store for him.

The man-at-arms protested: "He's my prisoner!"

"Not anymore," said the priest. "Let him go."

"Why should I release him without a ransom?" the man said belligerently.

The priest replied equally forcefully. "First, because he's neither a fighting man in the king's army nor a citizen of this town, so you have committed a crime by imprisoning him. Second, because he's a monk, and you are guilty of sacrilege by laying hands on a man of God. Third, because Queen Maud's secretary says you have to release him, and if you refuse you'll end up inside that cage yourself, faster than you can blink, so *jump to it.*"

"All right," the man grumbled.

Philip was dismayed. He had been nursing a faint hope that Maud would never get to know of his imprisonment here. If Maud's secretary had asked to see him, that hope was now dashed. Feeling as if he had hit rock bottom, he stepped out of the cage.

"Come with me," said the priest.

Philip followed him. "Am I to be set free?" he said.

"I imagine so." The priest looked surprised by the question. "Don't you know whom you're going to see?"

"I haven't an inkling."

The priest smiled. "I'll let him surprise you."

They crossed the compound to the keep and climbed the long flight of steps that led up the mound to the gate. Philip racked his brains but could not guess why a secretary of Maud's should have an interest in him.

He followed the priest through the gate. The circular stone keep was lined with two-story houses built against the wall. In the middle was a tiny courtyard with a well. The priest led Philip into one of the houses.

Inside the house was another priest, standing in front of the fire with his back to the door. He had the same build as Philip, short and slight, and the same black hair, but his head was not shaved and his hair was not graying. It was a very familiar back. Philip could hardly believe his luck. A broad grin spread across his face.

The priest turned. He had bright blue eyes just like Philip's and he, too, was grinning. He held out his arms. "Philip," he said.

"Well, God be praised!" Philip said in astonishment. "Francis!"

The two brothers embraced, and Philip's eyes filled with tears.

III

The royal reception hall at Winchester Castle looked very different. The dogs had gone, and so had King Stephen's plain wooden throne, the benches, and the animal skins from the walls. Instead there were embroidered hangings, richly colored carpets, bowls of sweetmeats, and painted chairs. The room smelled of flowers.

Philip was never at ease at the royal court, and a *feminine* royal court was enough to put him in a state of quivering anxiety. The Empress Maud was his only hope of getting the quarry back and reopening the market, but he had no confidence that this haughty, willful woman would make a just decision.

The Empress sat on a delicately carved gilded throne, wearing a dress the color of bluebells. She was tall and thin, with proud dark eyes and straight, glossy black hair. Over her gown she wore a pelisse, a knee-length silk coat with a tight waist and flared skirt; a style that had not been seen in England until she arrived, but was now much imitated. She had been married to her first husband for eleven years and her second for fourteen, but she still looked less than forty years old. People raved about her beauty. To Philip she looked rather angular and unfriendly; but he was a poor judge of feminine attraction, being more or less immune to it.

Philip, Francis, William Hamleigh and Bishop Waleran bowed to her and stood waiting. She ignored them for a while and continued talking to a lady-in-waiting. The conversation seemed to be rather trifling, for they both laughed prettily; but Maud did not interrupt it to greet her visitors.

Francis worked closely with her, and saw her almost every day, but they were not great friends. Her brother Robert, Francis's former employer, had given him to her when she arrived in England, because she needed a first-class secretary. However, this was not the only motive. Francis acted as link man between brother and sister, and kept an eye on the impetuous Maud. It was nothing for brothers and sisters to betray one another, in the treacherous life of the royal court, and Francis's real role was to make it difficult for Maud to do anything underhand. Maud knew this and accepted it, but her relationship with Francis was nevertheless an uneasy one.

It was two months since the battle of Lincoln, and in that time all had gone well for Maud. Bishop Henry had welcomed her to Winchester (thereby betraying *his* brother King Stephen) and had convened a great council of bishops and abbots which had elected her queen; and she was now negotiating with the commune of London to arrange her coronation at Westminster. King David of Scotland, who happened to be her uncle, was on his way to pay her a formal royal visit, one sovereign to another.

Bishop Henry was strongly supported by Bishop Waleran of Kingsbridge; and, according to Francis, Waleran had persuaded William Hamleigh to switch sides, and pledge allegiance to Maud. Now William had come for his reward.

The four men stood waiting: William with his backer, Bishop Waleran, and Prior Philip with his sponsor, Francis. This was the first time Philip had set eyes on Maud. Her appearance did not reassure him: despite her regal air he thought she looked flighty.

When Maud finished chatting she turned to them with a triumphant look, as if to say: See how unimportant you are, even my lady-in-waiting has priority over you. She looked at Philip steadily for a few moments, until he became embarrassed, then she said: "Well, Francis. Have you brought me your twin?"

Francis said: "My brother, Philip, lady, the prior of Kingsbridge."

Philip bowed again and said: "Somewhat too old and gray to be a twin, lady." It was the kind of trivial, self-deprecating remark that courtiers seemed to find amusing, but she gave him a frozen look and ignored it. He decided to abandon any attempt to be charming.

She turned to William. "And Sir William Hamleigh, who fought bravely against my army at the battle of Lincoln, but has now seen the error of his ways."

William bowed and wisely kept his mouth shut.

She turned back to Philip. "You ask me to grant you a license to hold a market."

"Yes, my lady."

Francis said: "The income from the market will all be spent on building the cathedral, lady."

"On what day of the week do you want to hold your market?" she asked.

"Sunday."

She raised her plucked eyebrows. "You holy men are generally opposed to Sunday markets. Don't they keep people from church?"

"Not in our case," Philip said. "People come to labor on the building and attend a service, and they do their buying and selling as well."

"So you're already holding this market?" she said sharply.

Philip realized he had blundered. He felt like kicking himself.

Francis rescued him. "No, lady, they are not holding the market at present," he said. "It began informally, but Prior Philip ordered it to cease until he was granted a license."

That was the truth, but not the whole truth. However, Maud seemed to accept it. Philip silently prayed for forgiveness for Francis.

Maud said: "Is there no other market in the area?"

William spoke up. "Yes, there is, at Shiring; and the Kingsbridge market has been taking business away."

Philip said: "But Shiring is twenty miles from Kingsbridge!"

Francis said: "My lady, the rule is that markets must be at least fourteen miles apart. By that criterion Kingsbridge and Shiring do not compete."

She nodded, apparently willing to accept Francis's ruling on a point of law. So far, thought Philip, it's going our way.

Maud said: "You also ask for the right to take stone from the earl of Shiring's quarry."

"We have had that right for many years, but William lately threw out our quarrymen, killing five—"

"Who gave you the right to take stone?" she interrupted.

"King Stephen—"

"The usurper!"

Francis hastily said: "My lady, Prior Philip naturally accepts that all edicts of the pretender Stephen are invalid unless ratified by you."

Philip accepted no such thing but he saw that it would be unwise to say so.

William blurted out: "I closed the quarry in retaliation for his illegal market!"

It was amazing, Philip thought, how a clear case of injustice could come to seem evenly balanced when argued at the court.

Maud said: "This entire squabble came about because Stephen's original ruling was foolish."

Bishop Waleran spoke for the first time. "There, lady, I heartily agree with you," he said oilily.

"It was asking for trouble, to give the quarry to one person but let another mine it," she said. "The quarry must belong to one or the other."

That was true, Philip thought. And if she were to follow the spirit of Stephen's original ruling, it would belong to Kingsbridge.

She went on: "My decision is that it shall belong to my noble ally, Sir William."

Philip's heart sank. The cathedral building could not have come on so well without free access to that quarry. It would have to slow right down while Philip tried to find the money to buy stone. And all because of the whim of this capricious woman! It made him fume.

William said: "Thank you, lady."

Maud said: "However, Kingsbridge shall have market rights as at Shiring."

Philip's spirits rose again. The market would not quite pay for the stone but it was a big help. It meant he would be scraping around for money again, just as he had at the beginning, but he could carry on.

Maud had given each one a part of what he wanted. Perhaps she was not so empty-headed after all.

Francis said: "Market rights as at Shiring, lady?"

"That's what I said."

Philip was not sure why Francis had repeated it. It was common for licenses to refer to the rights enjoyed by another town: it was evenhanded and saved writing. Philip would have to check exactly what Shiring's charter said. There might be restrictions, or extra privileges.

Maud said: "So you have both got something. William gets the quarry and Prior Philip gets the market. And in return, each of you will pay me one hundred pounds. That is all." She turned away.

Philip was flabbergasted. A hundred pounds! The priory did not have a hundred pennies at the moment. How was he to raise this money? The market would take years to earn a hundred pounds. It was a devastating blow that would set the building program back permanently. He stood staring at Maud, but she was apparently deep in conversation with her lady-in-waiting again. Francis nudged him. Philip opened his mouth to speak. Francis held a finger to his lips. Philip said: "But . . ." Francis shook his head urgently.

Philip knew Francis was right. He let his shoulders slump in defeat. Helplessly, he turned away and walked out of the royal presence.

Francis was impressed when Philip showed him around Kingsbridge Priory. "I was here ten years ago, and it was a dump," he said irreverently. "You've really brought it to life."

He was very taken with the writing room, which Tom had

finished while Philip was in Lincoln. A small building next to the chapter house, it had large windows, a fireplace with a chimney, a row of writing desks, and a big oak cupboard for the books. Four of the brothers were at work there already, standing at the high desks, writing on parchment sheets with quill pens. Three were copying: one the Psalms of David, one Saint Matthew's Gospel, and one the Rule of Saint Benedict. In addition, Brother Timothy was writing a history of England, although as he had begun with the creation of the world Philip was afraid the old boy might never finish it. The writing room was small—Philip had not wanted to divert much stone from the cathedral—but it was a warm, dry, well-lit place, just what was needed. "The priory has disgracefully few books, and as they're iniquitously expensive to buy, this is the only way to build our collection," Philip explained.

In the undercroft was a workshop where an old monk was teaching two youngsters how to stretch the skin of a sheep for parchment, how to make ink, and how to bind the sheets into a book. Francis said: "You'll be able to sell books, too."

"Oh, yes—the writing room will pay for itself many times over."

They left the building and walked through the cloisters. It was the study hour. Most of the monks were reading. A few were meditating, an activity that was suspiciously similar to dozing, as Francis remarked skeptically. In the northwest corner were twenty schoolboys reciting Latin verbs. Philip stopped and pointed. "See the little boy at the end of the bench?"

Francis said: "Writing on a slate, with his tongue sticking out?"

"That's the baby you found in the forest."

"But he's so big!"

"Five and a half years old, and precocious."

Francis shook his head in wonderment. "Time goes by so fast. How is he?"

"He's spoiled by the monks, but he'll survive. You and I did."

"Who are the other pupils?"

"Either novice monks, or the sons of merchants and local gentry learning to write and figure."

They left the cloisters and passed on to the building site. The eastern limb of the new cathedral was now more than half built. The great double row of mighty columns was forty feet high, and all the arches in between had been completed. Above the arcade, the tribune gallery was taking shape. Either side of the arcade, the lower walls of the aisle had been built, with their out-jutting buttresses. As they walked around, Philip saw that the masons were constructing the half-arches that would connect the tops of those buttresses with the top of the tribune gallery, allowing the buttresses to take the weight of the roof.

Francis was almost awestruck. "You've done all this, Philip," he said. "The writing room, the school, the new church, even all these new houses in the town—it's all come about because you made it happen."

Philip was touched. No one had ever said that to him. If asked, he would say that God had blessed his efforts. But in his heart of hearts he knew that what Francis said was true: this thriving, busy town was his creation. Recognition gave him a warm glow, especially coming as it did from his sophisticated, cynical younger brother.

Tom Builder saw them and came over. "You've made marvelous progress," Philip said to him.

"Yes, but look at that." Tom pointed to the northeast corner of the priory close, where stone from the quarry was stockpiled. There were normally hundreds of stones stacked in rows, but now there were only about twenty-five scattered on the ground. "Unfortunately, our marvelous progress means we've used up our stock of stone."

Philip's elation evaporated. Everything he had achieved here was at risk, because of Maud's harsh ruling.

They walked along the north side of the site, where the most skilled masons were working at their benches, carving the stones into shape with hammers and chisels. Philip stopped behind one craftsman and studied his work. It was a capital, the large, jutting-out stone that always stood on top of a column. Using a light hammer and a small chisel, the mason was carving a pattern of leaves on the capital. The leaves were deeply undercut and the work was delicate. To Philip's surprise, he saw that the craftsman was young Jack, Tom's stepson. "I thought Jack was still a learner," he said.

"He is." Tom moved on, and when they were out of earshot he said: "The boy is remarkable. There are men here who have been carving stone since before he was born, and none of them can match his work." He gave a slightly embarrassed laugh. "And he isn't even my own son!"

Tom's real son, Alfred, was a master mason and had his own gang of apprentices and laborers, but Philip knew that Alfred and his gang did not do the delicate work. Philip wondered how Tom felt about that in his heart.

Tom's mind had returned to the problem of paying for the market license. "Surely the market will bring in a lot of money," he said.

"Yes, but not enough. It should raise about fifty pounds a year at the start."

Tom nodded gloomily. "That will just about pay for the stone."

"We could manage if I didn't have to pay Maud a hundred pounds."

"What about the wool?"

The wool that was piling up in Philip's barns would be sold at the Shiring Fleece Fair in a few weeks' time, and would fetch about a hundred pounds. "That's what I'm going to use to pay Maud. But then I'll have nothing left for the craftsmen's wages for the next twelve months."

"Can't you borrow?"

"I already have. The Jews won't lend me any more. I asked, while I was in Winchester. They won't lend you money if they don't think you can pay it back."

"What about Aliena?"

Philip was startled. He had never thought of borrowing from her. She had even more wool in her barns. After the fleece fair she might have two hundred pounds. "But she needs the money to make her living. And Christians can't charge interest. If she lent her money to me she would have nothing to trade with. Although . . ." Even as he spoke, he was turning over a new idea. He remembered that Aliena had wanted to buy his entire wool production for the year. Perhaps they could work something out. . . . "I think I'll talk to her anyway," he said. "Is she at home at the moment?"

"I think so—I saw her this morning."

"Come, Francis—you're about to meet a remarkable young woman." They left Tom and hurried out of the close into the town. Aliena had two houses side by side up against the west wall of the priory. She lived in one and used the other as a barn. She was very wealthy. There had to be a way she could help the priory pay Maud's extortionate fee for the market license. A vague idea was taking shape in Philip's mind.

Aliena was in the barn, supervising the unloading of an ox cart stacked high with sacks of wool. She wore a brocade pelisse, like the one the Empress Maud had worn, and her hair was done up in a white linen coif. She looked authoritative, as always, and the two men unloading the cart obeyed her instructions without question. Everyone respected her, although—strangely—she had no close friends. She greeted Philip warmly. "When we heard about the battle of Lincoln we were afraid you might have been killed!" she said. There was real concern in her eyes, and Philip was moved to think that people had been worried about him. He introduced her to Francis.

"Did you get justice at Winchester?" Aliena asked.

"Not exactly," Philip replied. "The Empress Maud granted us a market but denied us the quarry. The one more or less compensates for the other. But she charged me a hundred pounds for the market license."

Aliena was shocked. "That's terrible! Did you tell her the income from the market goes to the cathedral building?"

"Oh, yes."

"But where will you find a hundred pounds?"

"I thought you might be able to help."

"Me?" Aliena was taken aback.

"In a few weeks' time, after you've sold your wool to the Flemish, you'll have two hundred pounds or more."

Aliena looked troubled. "And I'd give it to you, gladly, but I need it to buy more wool next year."

"Remember you wanted to buy my wool?"

"Yes, but it's too late now. I wanted to buy it early in the season. Besides, you can sell it yourself soon."

"I was thinking," Philip said. "Could I sell you *next* year's wool?"

She frowned. "But you haven't got it."

"Could I sell it to you before I've got it?"

"I don't see how."

"Simple. You give me the money now. I give you the wool next year."

Aliena clearly did not know how to take this proposal: it was unlike any known way of doing business. It was new to Philip, too: he had just made it up.

Aliena spoke slowly and thoughtfully. "I would have to offer you a slightly lower price than you could get by waiting. Moreover, the price of wool might go up between now and next summer—it has every year I've been in the business."

"So I lose a little and you gain a little," Philip said. "But I'll be able to carry on building for another year."

"And what will you do next year?"

"I don't know. Perhaps I'll sell you the following year's wool."

Aliena nodded. "It makes sense."

Philip took her hands and looked into her eyes. "If you do this, Aliena, you'll save the cathedral," he said fervently.

Aliena looked very solemn. "You saved me, once, didn't you?"

"I did."

"Then I'll do the same for you."

"God bless you!" In an excess of gratitude he hugged her; then he remembered she was a woman and detached himself hastily. "I don't know how to thank you," he said. "I was at my wits' end."

Aliena laughed. "I'm not sure I deserve this much gratitude. I'll probably do very well out of the arrangement."

"I hope so."

"Let's drink a cup of wine together to seal the bargain," she said. "I'll just pay the carter."

The ox cart was empty and the wool stacked neatly. Philip and Francis stepped outside while Aliena settled up with the carter. The sun was going down and the building workers were walking back to their homes. Philip's elation returned. He had found a way to carry on, despite all the setbacks. "Thank God for Aliena!" he said.

"You didn't tell me she was so beautiful," Francis said.

"Beautiful? I suppose she is."

Francis laughed. "Philip, you're blind! She's one of the most beautiful women I've ever seen. She's enough to make a man give up the priesthood."

Philip looked sharply at Francis. "You ought not to talk like that."

"Sorry."

Aliena came out and locked the barn; then they went into her home. It was a large house with a main room and a separate bedroom. There was a beer barrel in the corner, a whole ham hanging from the ceiling, and a white linen cloth on the table. A middle-aged woman servant poured wine from a flask into silver goblets for the guests. Aliena lived comfortably. If she's so beautiful, Philip wondered, why hasn't she got a husband? There was no shortage of aspirants: she had been courted by every eligible young man in the county, but she had turned them all down. He felt so grateful to her that he wanted her to be happy.

Her mind was still on practicalities. "I won't have the money until after the Shiring Fleece Fair," she said when they had toasted their agreement.

Philip turned to Francis. "Will Maud wait?"

"How long?"

"The fair is three weeks from Thursday."

Francis nodded. "I'll tell her. She'll wait."

Aliena untied her headdress and shook out her curly dark hair. She gave a tired sigh. "The days are too short," she said. "I can't get everything done. I want to buy more wool but I've got to find enough carters to take it all to Shiring."

Philip said: "And next year you'll have even more."

"I wish we could make the Flemish come here to buy. It would be so much easier for us than taking all our wool to Shiring."

Francis interjected: "But you can."

They both looked at him. Philip said: "How?"

"Hold your own fleece fair."

Philip began to see what he was driving at. "Can we?"

"Maud gave you exactly the same rights as Shiring. I wrote your charter myself. If Shiring can hold a fleece fair, so can you."

Aliena said: "Why, that would be wonderful—we wouldn't have to cart all these sacks to Shiring. We could do the business here, and ship the wool directly to Flanders."

"That's the least of it," Philip said excitedly. "A fleece fair makes as much in a week as a Sunday market makes in a whole year. We can't do it this year, of course—nobody will know about it. But we can spread the news, at this year's Shiring Fleece Fair, that we're going to hold our own next year, and make sure all the buyers know the date. . . ."

Aliena said: "It will make a big difference to Shiring. You and I are the biggest sellers of wool in the county, and if we both withdraw, the Shiring fair will be less than half its usual size."

Francis said: "William Hamleigh will lose money. He'll be as mad as a bull."

Philip could not help a shudder of revulsion. A mad bull was just what William was like.

"So what?" said Aliena. "If Maud has given us permission, we can go ahead. There's nothing William can do about it, is there?"

"I hope not," Philip said fervently. "I certainly hope not."

Chapter 10

WORK STOPPED AT NOON on Saint Augustine's Day. Most of the builders greeted the midday bell with a sigh of relief. They normally worked from sunrise to sunset, six days a week, so they needed the rest they got on holy days. However, Jack was too absorbed in his work to hear the bell.

He was mesmerized by the challenge of making soft, round shapes out of hard rock. The stone had a will of its own, and if he tried to make it do something it did not want to do, it would fight him, and his chisel would slip, or dig in too deeply, spoiling the shapes. But once he had got to know the lump of rock in front of him he could transform it. The more difficult the task, the more fascinated he was. He was beginning to feel that the decorative carving demanded by Tom was too easy. Zigzags, lozenges, dogtooth, spirals and plain roll moldings bored him, and even these leaves were rather stiff and repetitive. He wanted to carve natural-looking foliage, pliable and irregular, and copy the different shapes of real leaves, oak and ash and birch, but Tom would not let him. Most of all he wanted to carve scenes from stories, Adam and Eve, David and Goliath, and the Day of Judgment, with monsters and devils and naked people, but he did not dare to ask.

Eventually Tom made him stop work. "It's a holiday, lad," he said. "Besides, you're still my apprentice, and I want you to help me clear up. All tools must be locked away before dinner."

Jack put away his hammer and chisels, and carefully deposited the stone on which he had been working in Tom's shed; then he went around the site with Tom. The other apprentices were tidying up and sweeping away the stone chips, sand, lumps of dried mortar and wood shavings that littered the site. Tom picked up his compasses and level while Jack collected his yardsticks and plumb lines, and they took everything to the shed.

In the shed Tom kept his poles. These were long iron rods, square in cross-section and dead straight, all exactly the same length. They were kept in a special wooden rack which was locked. They were measuring sticks.

As they continued around the site, picking up mortarboards and shovels, Jack was thinking about the poles. "How long is a pole?" he asked.

Some of the masons heard him and laughed. They often found his questions amusing. Edward Short, a diminutive old mason with leathery skin and a twisted nose, said: "A pole is a pole," and they laughed again.

They enjoyed teasing the apprentices, especially if it gave them a chance to show off their superior knowledge. Jack hated to be laughed at for his ignorance but he put up with it because he was so curious. "I don't understand," he said patiently.

"An inch is an inch, a foot is a foot, and a pole is a pole," said Edward.

A pole was a unit of measurement, then. "So how many feet are there in a pole?"

"Aha! That depends. Eighteen, in Lincoln. Sixteen in East Anglia."

Tom interrupted to give a sensible answer. "On this site there are fifteen feet to a pole."

A middle-aged woman mason said: "In Paris they don't use the pole at all—just the yardstick."

Tom said to Jack: "The whole plan of the church is based on poles. Fetch me one and I'll show you. It's time you understood these things." He gave Jack a key.

Jack went to the shed and took a pole from the rack. It was quite heavy. Tom liked to explain things, and Jack loved to listen. The organization of the building site made an intriguing pattern, like the weaving on a brocade coat, and the more he understood, the more fascinated he became.

Tom was standing in the aisle at the open end of the half-built chancel, where the crossing would be. He took the pole and laid it on the ground so that it spanned the aisle. "From the outside wall to the middle of the pier of the arcade is a pole." He turned the pole end over end. "From there to the middle of the nave is a pole." He turned it over again, and it reached the middle of the opposite pier. "The nave is two poles wide." He turned it over again, and it reached to the wall of the far aisle. "The whole church is four poles wide."

"Yes," said Jack. "And each bay must be a pole long."

Tom looked faintly annoyed. "Who told you that?"

"Nobody. The bays of the aisles are square, so if they're a pole wide they must be a pole long. And the bays of the nave are the same length as the bays of the aisles, obviously."

"Obviously," said Tom. "You should be a philosopher." In his voice was a mixture of pride and irritation. He was pleased that Jack was quick to understand, irritated that the mysteries of masonry should be so easily grasped by a mere boy.

Jack was too caught up in the splendid logic of it all to pay attention to Tom's sensitivities. "The chancel is four poles long, then," he said. "And the whole church will be twelve poles when it's finished." He was struck by another thought. "How high will it be?"

"Six poles high. Three for the arcade, one for the gallery, and two for the clerestory."

"But what's the point of having everything measured by poles? Why not build it all higgledy-piggledy, like a house?"

"First, because it's cheaper this way. All the arches of the arcade are identical, so we can reuse the falsework arches. The fewer different sizes and shapes of stone we need, the fewer templates I have to make. And so on. Second, it simplifies every aspect of what we're doing, from the original laying-out—everything is based on a pole square—to painting the walls—it's easier to estimate how much whitewash we'll need. And when things are simple, fewer mistakes are made. The most expensive part of a building is the mistakes. Third, when everything is based on a pole measure, the church just looks right. Proportion is the heart of beauty."

Jack nodded, enchanted. The struggle to control an operation as ambitious and intricate as building a cathedral was endlessly fascinating. The notion that the principles of regularity and repetition could both simplify the construction and result in a harmonious building was a seductive idea. But he was not sure whether proportion was the heart of beauty. He had a taste for wild, spreading, disorderly things: high mountains, aged oaks, and Aliena's hair.

He ate his dinner ravenously but quickly, then he left the village, heading north. It was a warm early-summer day, and he was barefoot. Ever since he and his mother had come to live in Kingsbridge for good, and he had become a worker, he had enjoyed returning to the forest periodically. At first he had spent the time getting rid of surplus energy, running and jumping, climbing trees and shooting ducks with his sling. That was when he was getting used to the new, taller, stronger body he now had. The novelty of that had worn off. Now when he walked in the forest he thought about things: why proportion should be beautiful, how buildings stayed standing, and what it would be like to stroke Aliena's breasts.

He had worshiped her from a distance for years. His abiding picture of her was from the first time he had seen her, as she came down the stairs to the hall at Earlscastle, and he had thought she must a princess in a story. She had continued to be a remote figure. She talked to Prior Philip, and Tom Builder, and Malachi the Jew, and the other wealthy and powerful people of Kingsbridge; and Jack never had a reason to address her. He just looked at her, praying in church or riding her palfrey across the bridge, or sitting in the sun outside her house; wearing costly furs in winter and the finest linen in summer, her wild hair framing her beautiful face. Before he went to sleep he would think about what it would be like to take those clothes off her, and see her naked, and kiss her soft mouth gently.

In the last few weeks he had become dissatisfied and depressed with this hopeless daydreaming. Seeing her from a distance and overhearing her conversations with other people and imagining making love to her were no longer enough. He needed the real thing.

There were several girls his own age who might have given him the real thing. Among the apprentices there was much talk about which of the young women in Kingsbridge were randy and exactly what each of them would let a young man do. Most of them were determined to remain virgins until they were married, according to the teachings of the Church, but there were certain things you could do and still remain a virgin, or so the apprentices said. The girls all thought Jack was a little strange—they were probably right, he felt—but one or two of them found his strangeness appealing. One Sunday after church he had struck up a conversation with Edith, the sister of a fellow apprentice; but when he had talked about how he loved to carve stone, she had started to giggle. The following Sunday he had gone walking in the fields with Ann, the blond daughter of the tailor. He had not said much to her, but he had kissed her, and then suggested they lie down in a field of green barley. He had kissed her again and touched her breasts, and she had kissed him back, enthusiastically; but after a while she had pulled away from him and said: "Who is she?" Jack had been thinking about Aliena at that very moment and he was thunderstruck. He had tried to brush it aside, and kiss her again, but she turned her face away, and said: "Whoever she is, she's a lucky girl." They had walked back to Kingsbridge together, and when they separated Ann had said: "Don't waste time trying to forget her. It's a lost cause. She's the one you want, so you'd better try and get her." She had smiled at him fondly and added: "You've got a nice face. It might not be as difficult as you think."

Her kindness made him feel bad, the more so because she was one of the girls the apprentices said were randy, and he had told everyone that he was going to try to feel her up. Now such talk seemed so juvenile that it made him squirm. But if he had told her the name of the woman who was on his mind, Ann might not have been so encouraging. Jack and Aliena were about the most unlikely match conceivable. Aliena was twenty-two years old and he was seventeen; she was the daughter of an earl and he was a bastard; she was a wealthy wool merchant and he was a penniless apprentice. Worse still, she was famous for the number of suitors she had rejected. Every presentable young lord in the county, and every prosperous merchant's eldest son, had come to Kingsbridge to pay court to her, and all had gone away disappointed. What chance was there for Jack, who had nothing to offer, unless it was "a nice face"?

He and Aliena had one thing in common: they liked the forest. They were peculiar in this: most people preferred the safety of the fields and villages, and stayed away from the forest. But Aliena often walked in the woodlands near Kingsbridge, and there was a particular secluded spot where she liked to stop and sit down. He had seen her there once or twice. She had not seen him: he walked silently, as he had learned to in childhood, when he had had to find his dinner in the forest.

He was heading for her clearing without any idea of what he would do if he found her there. He knew what he would like to do: lie down beside her and stroke her body. He could talk to her, but what would he say? It was easy to talk to girls of his own age. He had teased Edith, saying: "I don't believe *any* of the terrible things your brother says about you," and of course she had wanted to know what the terrible things were. With Ann he had been direct: "Would you like to walk in the fields with me this afternoon?" But when he tried to come up with an opening line for Aliena his mind went blank. He could not help thinking of her as belonging to the older generation. She was so grave and responsible. She had not always been like that, he knew: at seventeen she had been quite playful. She had suffered terrible troubles since then, but the playful girl must still be there somewhere inside the solemn woman. For Jack that made her even more fascinating.

He was getting near her spot. The forest was quiet in the heat of the day. He moved silently through the undergrowth. He wanted to see her before she saw him. He was still not sure he had the nerve to approach her. Most of all he was afraid of putting her off. He had spoken to her on the very first day he returned to Kingsbridge, the Whitsunday that all the volunteers had come to work on the cathedral, and he had said the wrong thing then, with the result that he had hardly talked to her for four years. He did not want to make a similar blunder now.

A few moments later he peeped around the trunk of a beech tree and saw her.

She had picked an extraordinarily pretty place. There was a little waterfall trickling into a deep pool surrounded by mossy stones. The sun shone on the banks of the pool, but a yard or two back there was shade beneath the beech trees. Aliena sat in the dappled sunlight reading a book.

Jack was astonished. A woman? Reading a book? In the open air? The only people who read books were monks, and not many of them read anything except the services. It was an unusual book, too—much smaller than the tomes in the priory library, as if it had been made especially for a woman, or for someone who wanted to carry it around. He was so surprised that he forgot to be shy. He pushed his way through the bushes and came out into her clearing, saying: "What are you reading?"

She jumped, and looked up at him with terror in her eyes. He realized he had frightened her. He felt very clumsy, and was afraid he had once again started off on the wrong foot. Her right hand flew to her left sleeve. He recalled that she had once carried a knife in her sleeve—perhaps she did still. A moment later she recognized him, and her fear went as quickly as it had come. She looked relieved, and then—to his chagrin—faintly irritated. He felt unwelcome, and he would have liked to turn right around and disappear back into the forest. But that would have made it difficult to speak to her another time, so he stayed, and faced her rather unfriendly look, and said: "Sorry I frightened you."

"You didn't *frighten* me," she said quickly.

He knew that was not true, but he was not going to argue with her. He repeated his initial question. "What are you reading?"

She glanced down at the bound volume on her knee, and her expression changed again: now she looked wistful. "My father got this book on his last trip to Normandy. He brought it home for me. A few days later he was put in jail."

Jack edged closer and looked at the open page. "It's in French!" he said.

"How do you know?" she said in astonishment. "Can you read?"

"Yes—but I thought all books were in Latin."

"Nearly all. But this is different. It's a poem called 'The Romance of Alexander.'"

Jack was thinking: I'm really doing it—I'm talking to her! This is wonderful! But what am I going to say next? How can I keep this going? He said: "Um . . . well, what's it about?"

"It's the story of a king called Alexander the Great, and how he conquered wonderful lands in the east where precious stones grow on grapevines and plants can talk."

Jack was sufficiently intrigued to forget his anxiety. "How do the plants talk? Do they have mouths?"

"It doesn't say."

"Do you think the story is true?"

She looked at him with interest, and he stared into her beautiful dark eyes. "I don't know," she said. "I always wonder whether stories are true. Most people don't care—they just like the stories."

"Except for the priests. They always think the sacred stories are true."

"Well of course *they* are true."

Jack was as skeptical of the sacred stories as he was of all the others; but his mother, who had taught him skepticism, had also taught him to be discreet, so he did not argue. He was trying not to look at Aliena's bosom, which was just at the edge of his vision: he knew that if he dropped his eyes she would know what he was looking at. He tried to think of something else to say. "I know a lot of stories," he said. "I know 'The Song of Roland,' and 'The Pilgrimage of William of Orange'—"

"What do you mean, you *know* them?"

"I can recite them."

"Like a jongleur?"

"What's a jongleur?"

"A man who goes around telling stories."

That was a new concept to Jack. "I never heard of such a man."

"There are lots in France. I used to go overseas with my father when I was a child. I loved the jongleurs."

"But what do they do? Just stand on the street and speak?"

"It depends. They come into the lord's hall on feast days. They perform at markets and fairs. They entertain pilgrims outside churches. Great barons sometimes have their own jongleur."

It occurred to Jack that not only was he talking to her, but he was having a conversation he could not have had with any other girl in Kingsbridge. He and Aliena were the only people in the town, apart from his mother, who knew about French romance poems, he was sure. They had an interest in common, and they were discussing it. The thought was so exciting that he lost track of what they were saying and he felt confused and stupid.

Fortunately she carried on. "Usually the jongleur plays the fiddle while he recites the story. He plays fast and high when there's a battle, slow and sweet when two people are in love, jerky for a funny part."

Jack liked that idea: background music to enhance the high points of the story. "I wish I could play the fiddle," he said.

"Can you really recite stories?" she said.

He could hardly believe she was really interested in him, asking him questions about himself! And her face was even lovelier when it was animated by curiosity. "My mother taught me," he said. "We used to live in the forest, just the two of us. She told me the stories again and again."

"But how can you remember them? Some of them take *days* to tell."

"I don't know. It's like knowing your way through the forest. You don't keep the whole forest in your mind, but wherever you are, you know where to go next." Glancing at the text of her book again, he was struck by something. He sat on the grass next to her to look more closely. "The rhymes are different," he said.

She was not sure what he meant. "In what way?"

"They're better. In 'The Song of Roland,' the word *sword* rhymes with *horse*, or *lost*, or with *ball*. In your book, *sword* rhymes with *horde* but not with *horse*; *lord* but not *loss*; *board* but not *ball*. It's a completely different way of rhyming. But it's better, much better. I like these rhymes."

"Would you . . ." She looked diffident. "Would you tell me some of 'The Song of Roland'?"

Jack shifted his position a little so that he could look at her. The intensity of her look, the sparkle of eagerness in her bewitching eyes, gave him a choking feeling. He swallowed hard, then began.

The lord and king of all France, Charles the Great
Has spent seven long years fighting in Spain.
He has conquered the highlands and the plain.
Before him not a single fort remains,
No town or city wall for him to break,
But Saragossa, on a high mountain
Ruled by King Marsilly the Saracen.
He serves Mahomed, to Apollo prays,
But even there he never will be safe.

Jack paused, and Aliena said: "You know it! You really do! Just like a jongleur!"

"You see what I mean about the rhymes, though."

"Yes, but it's the stories I like, anyway," she said. Her eyes twinkled with delight. "Tell me some more."

Jack felt as if he would faint with happiness. "If you like," he said weakly. He looked into her eyes and began the second verse.

II

The first game of Midsummer Eve was eating the how-many bread. Like many of the games, it had a hint of superstition about it that made Philip uneasy. However, if he tried to ban every rite that smacked of the old religions, half the people's traditions would be prohibited, and they would probably defy him anyway; so he exercised a discreet tolerance of most things, and took a firm line on one or two excesses.

The monks had set up tables on the grass at the western end of the priory close. Kitchen hands were already carrying steaming cauldrons across the courtyard. The prior was lord of the manor, so it was his responsibility to provide a feast for his tenants on important holidays. Philip's policy was to be generous with food and mean with drink, so he served weak beer and no wine. Nevertheless there were five or six incorrigibles who managed to drink themselves insensible every feast day.

The leading citizens of Kingsbridge sat at Philip's table: Tom Builder and his family; the senior master craftsmen, including Tom's elder son, Alfred; and the merchants, including Aliena but not Malachi the Jew, who would join in the festivities later, after the service.

Philip called for silence and said grace; then he handed the how-many loaf to Tom. As the years went by, Philip valued Tom more and more. There were not many people who said what they meant and did what they said. Tom reacted to surprises, crises and disasters by calmly weighing up the consequences, assessing the damage and planning the best response. Philip looked at him fondly. Tom was very different today from the man who had walked into the priory five years ago begging for work. Then he had been exhausted, haggard, and so thin that his bones seemed to be on the point of poking through his weatherbeaten skin. In the intervening years he had filled out, especially since his woman came back. He was not fat, but there was flesh on his big frame, and the desperate look had long gone from his eyes. He was expensively dressed, in a tunic of Lincoln green, and soft leather shoes, and a belt with a silver buckle.

Philip had to ask the question that would be answered by the how-many bread. He said: "How many years will it take to finish the cathedral?"

Tom took a bite of the bread. It was baked with small, hard seeds, and as Tom spat the seeds into his hand, everyone counted aloud. Sometimes when this game was played, and someone got a big mouthful of seeds, it was found that nobody around the table could count high enough; but there was no danger of that today, with all the merchants and craftsmen present. The answer came to thirty. Philip pretended to be dismayed. Tom said: "I should live so long!" and everyone laughed.

Tom passed the bread to his wife, Ellen. Philip was very wary of this woman. Like the Empress Maud, she had power over men, a kind of power Philip could not compete with. The day Ellen was thrown out of the priory, she had done an appalling thing, a thing Philip could still hardly bring himself to think about. He had assumed she would never be seen again, but to his horror she had returned, and Tom had begged Philip to forgive her. Cleverly, Tom had argued that if God could forgive her sin, then Philip had no right to refuse. Philip suspected the woman was not very repentant. But Tom had asked on the day the volunteers had come and saved the cathedral, and Philip had found himself granting Tom's wish against all his instincts. They had been married in the parish church, a small wooden building in the village that had been there longer than the priory. Since then Ellen had behaved herself, and had not given Philip reason to regret his decision. Nevertheless she made him uneasy.

Tom asked her: "How many men love you?"

She took a tiny bite of the bread, which made everyone laugh again. In this game the questions tended to be mildly suggestive. Philip knew that if he had not been present they would have been downright ribald.

Ellen counted three seeds. Tom pretended to be outraged. "I shall tell you who my three lovers are," said Ellen. Philip hoped she was not going to say anything offensive. "The first is Tom. The second is Jack. And the third is Alfred."

There was a round of applause for her wit, and the bread went on around the table. Next it was the turn of Tom's daughter, Martha. She was about twelve years old, and shy. The bread predicted that she would have three husbands, which seemed most unlikely.

Martha passed the bread to Jack, and as she did so Philip saw a light of adoration in her eyes, and realized that she hero-worshiped her stepbrother.

Jack intrigued Philip. He had been an ugly child, with his carrot-colored hair and pale skin and bulging blue eyes, but now that he was a young man his features had composed themselves, as it were, and his face was so strikingly attractive that strangers would turn and stare. But in temperament he was as wild as his mother. He had very little discipline and he had no concept of obedience. As a stonemason's laborer he had been almost useless, for instead of providing a steady stream of mortar and stones he would try to pile up a whole day's supply, then go off and do something else. He was always disappearing. One day he had decided that none of the stones on the site suited the particular carving he had to do, so without telling anyone he had gone all the way to the quarry and picked out a stone he liked. He had brought it back on a borrowed pony two days later. But people forgave him his transgressions, partly because he was a truly exceptional stone carver, and partly because he was so likable—a trait he definitely had not inherited from his mother, in Philip's opinion. Philip had given some thought to what Jack would do with his life. If he went into the Church he could easily end up a bishop.

Martha asked Jack: "How many years before you marry?"

Jack took a small bite: apparently he was keen to wed. Philip wondered if he had anyone in mind. To Jack's evident dismay he got a mouthful of seeds, and as they were counted his face was a picture of indignation. The total came to thirty-one. "I'll be forty-eight years old!" he protested. They all thought that was hilarious, except for Philip, who worked out the calculation, found it correct, and marveled that Jack had been able to figure it out so fast. Even Milius the bursar could not do that.

Jack was sitting next to Aliena. Philip realized he had seen those two together several times this summer. It was probably because they were both so bright. There were not many people in Kingsbridge who could talk to Aliena on her own level; and Jack, for all his ungovernable ways, was more mature than the other apprentices. Still Philip was intrigued by their friendship, for at their age five years was a big difference.

Jack passed the bread to Aliena and asked her the question he had been asked: "How many years until you marry?"

Everyone groaned, for it was too easy to ask the same question again. The game was supposed to be an exercise in wit and raillery. But Aliena, who was famous for the number of suitors she had turned down, made them laugh by taking a huge bite of bread, indicating that she did not want to marry. But her ploy was unsuccessful: she spat out only one seed.

If she was going to marry next year, Philip thought, the groom had not appeared on the scene yet. Of course he did not believe in the predictive power of the bread. The probability was that she would die an old maid—except that she was not a maiden, according to rumor, for she had been seduced, or raped, by William Hamleigh, people said.

Aliena passed the bread to her brother, Richard, but Philip did not hear what she asked him. He was still thinking about Aliena. Unexpectedly, both Aliena and Philip had failed to sell all their wool this year. The surplus was not great—less than a tenth of Philip's stock, and an even smaller proportion for Aliena—but it was somewhat discouraging. After that, Philip had worried that Aliena would back out of the deal for next year's wool, but she had stuck by her bargain, and paid him a hundred and seven pounds.

The big news of the Shiring Fleece Fair had been Philip's announcement that next year Kingsbridge would be holding its own fair. Most people had welcomed the idea, for the rents and tolls charged by William Hamleigh at the Shiring fair were extortionate, and Philip was planning to set much lower rates. So far, Earl William had not made his reaction known.

By and large, Philip felt that the priory's prospects were much brighter than they had seemed six months ago. He had overcome the problem caused by the closing of the quarry and defeated William's attempt to shut down his market. Now his Sunday market was thriving again and paying for expensive stone from a quarry near Marlborough. Throughout the crisis, cathedral building had continued uninterrupted, although it had been a close thing. Philip's only remaining anxiety was that Maud had not yet been crowned. Although she was indisputably in command, and she had been approved by the bishops, her authority rested only on her military might until there was a proper coronation. Stephen's wife still held Kent, and the commune of London was ambivalent. A single stroke of misfortune, or one bad decision, could topple her, as the battle of Lincoln had destroyed Stephen, and then there would be anarchy again.

Philip told himself not to be pessimistic. He looked at the people around the table. The game had ended and they were tucking in to their dinner. They were honest, good-hearted men and women who worked hard and went to church. God would take care of them.

They ate vegetable pottage, baked fish flavored with pepper and ginger, a variety of ducks, and a custard cleverly colored with red and green stripes. After dinner they all carried their benches into the unfinished church for the play.

The carpenters had made two screens, which were placed in the side aisles, at the east end, closing the space between the aisle wall and the first pier of the arcade, so that they effectively hid the last bay of each aisle. The monks who would play the parts were already behind those screens, waiting to walk into the middle of the nave to act out the story. The one who would be Saint Adolphus, a beardless novice with an angelic face, was lying on a table at the far end of the nave, draped in a shroud, pretending to be dead and trying not to giggle.

Philip had mixed feelings about the play, as he did about the how-many bread. It could so easily slip into irreverence and vulgarity. But people loved it so much that if he had not permitted it they would have made their own play, outside the church, and free from his supervision it would have become thoroughly bawdy. Besides, the ones who loved it most were the monks who performed it. Dressing up and pretending to be someone else, and acting outrageously—even sacrilegiously—seemed to give them some kind of release, probably because they spent the rest of their lives being so solemn.

Before the play there was a regular service, which the sacrist kept brief. Philip then gave a short account of the spotless life and miraculous works of Saint Adolphus. Then he took his seat in the audience and settled down to watch the performance.

From behind the left-hand screen came a large figure dressed in what at first looked like shapeless, colorful garments, and on closer examination turned out to be pieces of brightly colored cloth wrapped around him and pinned. His face was painted and he carried a bulging moneybag. This was the rich barbarian. There was a murmur of admiration for his getup, followed by a ripple of laughter as people recognized the actor beneath the costume: it was fat Brother Bernard, the kitchener, whom they all knew and liked.

He paraded up and down several times, to let everyone admire him, and rushed at the little children in the front row, causing squeals of fright; then he crept up to the altar, looking around as if to make sure he was alone, and placed the moneybag behind it. He turned to the audience, leered, and said in a loud voice: "These foolish Christians will fear to steal my silver, for they imagine it is protected by Saint Adolphus. Ha!" He then retired behind the screen.

From the opposite side entered a group of outlaws, dressed in rags, carrying wooden swords and hatchets, their faces smeared with soot and chalk. They stalked around the nave, looking fearsome, until one of them saw the moneybag behind the altar. There followed an argument: should they steal it or not? The Good Outlaw argued that it would surely bring them bad luck; the Bad Outlaw said that a dead saint could do them no harm. In the end they took the money and retired into the corner to count it.

The barbarian reentered, looked everywhere for his money, and flew into a rage. He approached the tomb of Saint Adolphus and cursed the saint for failing to protect his treasure.

At that, the saint rose up from his grave.

The barbarian shuddered violently with terror. The saint ignored him and approached the outlaws. Dramatically, he struck them down one by one just by pointing at them. They simulated agonized death throes, rolling around on the ground, twisting their bodies into grotesque shapes and making hideous faces.

The saint spared only the Good Outlaw, who now put the money back behind the altar. With that the saint turned to the audience and said: "Beware, all you who may doubt the power of Saint Adolphus!"

The audience cheered and clapped. The actors stood in the nave grinning sheepishly for a while. The purpose of the drama was its moral, of course, but Philip knew that the parts people enjoyed most were the grotesqueries, the rage of the barbarian and the death throes of the outlaws.

When the applause died down Philip stood up, thanked the actors, and announced that the races would begin shortly in the pasture by the riverside.

This was the day that five-year-old Jonathan discovered he was not, after all, the faster runner in Kingsbridge. He entered the children's race, wearing his specially made monkish robe, and caused howls of laughter when he hitched it up around his waist and ran with his tiny bottom exposed to the world. However, he was competing with older children, and he finished among the last. His expression when he realized he had lost was so shocked and disappointed that Tom felt heartbroken for him, and picked him up to console him.

The special relationship between Tom and the priory orphan had grown gradually, and no one in the village had thought to wonder if there was a secret reason for it. Tom spent all day within the priory close, where Jonathan ran free, so it was inevitable that they saw a lot of one another; and Tom was at the age when a man's children are too old to be cute but have not yet given him grand-children, and he sometimes takes a fond interest in other people's babies. As far as Tom knew, it had never crossed anyone's mind to suspect that he was Jonathan's father. If anything, people suspected that Philip was the boy's real father. That was a much more natural supposition—though Philip would not doubt be horrified to hear it.

Jonathan spotted Aaron, the eldest son of Malachi, and wriggled out of Tom's arms to go and play with his friend, the disappointment forgotten.

While the apprentices' races were on, Philip came and sat on the grass beside Tom. It was a hot, sunny day, and there was perspiration on Philip's shaved head. Tom's admiration for Philip grew year by year. Looking all around, at the young men running their race, the old people dozing in the shade, and the children splashing in the river, he reflected that it was Philip who kept all this together. He ruled the village, administering justice, deciding where new houses should be built, and settling quarrels; he employed most of the men and many of the women too, either as building workers or priory servants; and he managed the priory, which was the beating heart of the organism. He fought off predatory barons, negotiated with the monarch, and kept the bishop at bay. All these well-fed people sporting in the sunshine owed their prosperity in some measure to Philip. Tom himself was the prime example.

Tom was very conscious of the depth of Philip's clemency in pardoning Ellen. It was quite something for a monk to forgive what she had done. And it meant so much to Tom. When she went away, his joy at building the cathedral had been shadowed by loneliness. Now that she was back, he felt complete. She was still willful, maddening, quarrelsome and intolerant, but somehow these things were trifling: there was a passion inside her that burned like a candle in a lantern, and it lit up his life.

Tom and Philip watched a race in which the boys had to walk on their hands. Jack won it. "That boy is exceptional," Philip said.

"Not many people can walk that fast on their hands," Tom said.

Philip laughed. "Indeed—but I wasn't thinking about his acrobatic skill."

"I know." Jack's cleverness had long been a source of both pleasure and pain to Tom. Jack had a lively curiosity about building— something Alfred had always lacked—and Tom enjoyed teaching Jack the tricks of the trade. But Jack had no sense of tact, and would argue with his elders. It was often better to conceal one's superiority, but Jack had not learned that yet, not even after years of persecution by Alfred.

"The boy should be educated," Philip went on.

Tom frowned. Jack was being educated. He was an apprentice. "What do you mean?"

"He should learn to write a good hand, and study Latin grammar, and read the ancient philosophers."

Tom was even more puzzled. "To what end? He's going to be a mason."

Philip looked him in the eye. "Are you sure?" he said. "He's a boy who doesn't do what he's expected to."

Tom had never considered this. There were youngsters who defied expectations: earls' sons who refused to fight, royal children who entered monasteries, peasants' bastards who became bishops. It was true, Jack was the type. "Well, what do you think he will do?" he said.

"It depends on what he learns," Philip said. "But I want him for the Church."

Tom was surprised: Jack seemed such an unlikely clergyman. Tom was also a little wounded, in a strange way. He was looking forward to Jack's becoming a master mason, and he would be terribly disappointed if the boy chose another course in life.

Philip did not notice Tom's unhappiness. He went on: "God needs the best and the brightest young men to work for him. Look at those apprentices, competing to see who can jump the highest. All of them are capable of being carpenters, or masons, or stone cutters. But how many of them could be a bishop? Only one—Jack."

That was true, Tom thought. If Jack had the chance of a career in the Church, with a powerful patron in Philip, he should probably take it, for it would lead to much greater wealth and power than he could hope for as a mason. Reluctantly Tom said: "What have you got in mind, exactly?"

"I want Jack to become a novice monk."

"A monk!" It seemed an even more unlikely calling than the priesthood for Jack. The boy chafed at the discipline of a building site—how would he cope with the monastic rule?

"He would spend most of his time studying," Philip said. "He would learn everything our novice-master can teach him, and I would give him lessons myself as well."

When a boy became a monk, it was normal for the parents to make a generous donation to the monastery. Tom wondered what this proposal would cost.

Philip guessed his thoughts. "I wouldn't expect you to present a gift to the priory," he said. "It will be enough that you give a son to God."

What Philip did not know was that Tom had already given one son to the priory: little Jonathan, who was now paddling at the edge of the river with his robe once again hoisted up around his waist. However, Tom knew he should suppress his own feelings in this. Philip's proposal was generous: he obviously wanted Jack badly.

The offer was a tremendous opportunity for Jack. A father would give his right arm to be able to set a son on such a career. Tom suffered a twinge of resentment that it was his stepson, rather than Alfred, who was being given this marvelous chance. The feeling was unworthy and he suppressed it. He should be glad, and encourage Jack, and hope the lad would learn to reconcile himself to the monastic regime.

"It should be done soon," Philip added. "Before he falls in love with some girl."

Tom nodded. Across the meadow, the women's race was reaching its climax. Tom watched, thinking. After a moment he realized that Ellen was in the lead. Aliena was hard on her heels, but when they got to the finish line Ellen was still a little ahead. She raised her hands in a victory gesture.

Tom pointed at her. "It's not me who needs to be persuaded," he said to Philip. "It's her."

Aliena was surprised to have been beaten by Ellen. Ellen was very young to be the mother of a seventeen-year-old, but still she had to be at least ten years older than Aliena. They smiled at one another now, as they stood panting and sweating at the finish line. Aliena observed that Ellen had lean, muscular brown legs and a compact figure. All those years of living in the forest had made her tough.

Jack came up to congratulate his mother on winning. They were very fond of one another, Aliena could tell. They looked completely different: Ellen was a tanned brunette, with deep-set golden-brown eyes, and Jack was a redhead with blue eyes. He must be like his father, Aliena thought. Nothing was ever said about Jack's father, Ellen's first husband. Perhaps they were ashamed of him.

As she looked at the two of them together, it occurred to Aliena that Jack must remind Ellen of the husband she had lost. That might be why she was so fond of him. Perhaps the son was, as it were, all she had left of a man she had adored. A physical resemblance could be inordinately powerful in that way. Aliena's brother, Richard, sometimes reminded her of their father, with a look or a gesture, and that was when she felt a surge of affection; although it did not prevent her from wishing that Richard was more like his father in character.

She knew she ought not to be dissatisfied with Richard. He went to war and fought bravely, and that was all that was required of him. But she was dissatisfied a lot these days. She had wealth and security, a home and servants, fine clothes, pretty jewels, and a position of respect in the town. If anyone had asked her she would have said she was happy. But beneath the surface there was an undercurrent of restlessness. She never lost her enthusiasm for her work, but some mornings she wondered if it mattered what gown she put on and whether she wore jewelry. Nobody cared how she looked, so why should she? Paradoxically, she had become more conscious of her body. As she walked around, she could feel her breasts move. When she went down to the women's beach at the riverside to bathe, she felt embarrassed about how hairy she was. Sitting on her horse she was aware of the parts of her body that were touching the saddle. It was quite peculiar. It was as if there were a snooper peeking at her all the time, trying to look through her clothes and see her naked, and the snooper was herself. She was invading her own privacy.

She lay down on the grass, puffed out. Perspiration ran between her breasts and down the insides of her thighs. Impatiently she turned her mind to a more immediate problem. She had not sold all her wool this year. It was not her fault: most of the merchants had been left with unsold fleece, and so had Prior Philip. Philip was very calm about the whole thing but Aliena was anxious. What was she to do with all this wool? She could keep it until next year, of course. But what if she failed to sell it again? She did not know how long it took raw wool to deteriorate. She had a feeling it might dry out, becoming brittle and difficult to work.

If things went badly wrong she would be unable to support Richard. Being a knight was a very expensive business. The warhorse, which had cost twenty pounds, had lost its nerve after the battle of Lincoln and was now next to useless; soon he would want another one. Aliena could afford it, but it made a big dent in her resources. He was embarrassed about being dependent upon her—it was not the usual situation for a knight—and he had hoped to make enough in plunder to support himself, but lately he had been on the losing side. If he was to regain the earldom, Aliena had to continue to prosper.

In her worst nightmare she lost all her money, and the two of them were destitute again, prey to dishonest priests, lecherous noblemen and bloodthirsty outlaws; and they ended up in the stinking dungeon where she had last seen her father, chained to the wall and dying.

To contrast with her nightmare, she had a dream of happiness. In it, she and Richard lived together in the castle, their old home. Richard ruled as wisely as their father had, and Aliena helped him as she had helped Father, welcoming important guests and dispensing hospitality and sitting on his left at the high table for dinner. But lately even that dream had left her discontented.

She shook her head, to dispel this melancholy mood, and thought about wool again. The simplest way to handle the problem was to do nothing. She could store the surplus wool until next year, and then, if she was unable to sell it, she would take the loss. She could bear it. However, that left the remote danger that the same thing would happen again next year, and this might be the beginning of a downward trend; so she cast about for some other solution. She had already tried to sell the wool to a weaver in Kingsbridge, but he had all he needed.

It occurred to her now, looking at the women of Kingsbridge as they recovered from their race, that most of them knew how to make cloth from raw wool. It was a tedious business, but simple: peasants had been doing it since Adam and Eve. The fleece had to be washed, then combed to take out the tangles, then spun into yarn. The yarn was woven into cloth; then the loosely woven fabric was felted, or fulled, to shrink and thicken it into something that could be used to make clothes. The townswomen would probably be willing to do that for a penny a day. But how long would it take? And what price would the finished cloth fetch?

She would have to try the scheme out with a small quantity. Then, if it worked, she could get several people doing the job during the long winter evenings.

She sat up, quite excited by her new idea. Ellen was lying right next to her. Jack was sitting on the other side of Ellen. He caught Aliena's eye, smiled faintly, and looked away, as if he was a little embarrassed at having been caught looking at her. He was a funny boy, with a head full of ideas. Aliena could remember him as a small, peculiar-looking child who did not know how babies were conceived. But she had hardly noticed him when he came to live in Kingsbridge. And now he seemed so different, so completely a new person, that it was as if he had sprung up from nowhere, a flower that appears one morning where the previous day there was nothing but bare earth. For a start he was no longer peculiar-looking. In fact, she thought, regarding him with a faint smile of amusement, the girls probably thought he was terribly handsome. He certainly had a nice smile. She herself paid no attention to his looks, but she was a little intrigued by his astonishing imagination. She had discovered that not only did he know several verse narratives in full—some of them thousands and thousands of lines long—but he could also make them up as he went along, so that she was never sure whether he was remembering or extemporizing. And the stories were not the only surprising thing about him. He was curious about everything and puzzled by things that everyone else took for granted. One day he had asked where all the water in the river came from. "Every hour, thousands and thousands of gallons of water flow past Kingsbridge, night and day, all the year round. It's been going on since before we were born, since before our parents were born, since before *their* parents were born. Where does it all come from? Is there a huge lake somewhere that feeds it? That lake must be as big as all England! What if one day it dries up?" He was always saying things like that, some of them less fanciful, and it made Aliena realize that she was starved of intelligent conversation. Most people in Kingsbridge could talk only about agriculture and adultery, neither of which interested her. Prior Philip was different, of course, but he did not often allow himself to indulge in idle talk: he was always busy, dealing with the building site, the monks, or the town. Aliena suspected that Tom Builder was also highly intelligent, but he was a thinker rather than a talker. Jack was the first real friend she had made. He was a marvelous discovery, despite his youth. Indeed, when she was away from Kingsbridge she had found herself looking forward to returning so that she could talk to him.

She wondered where he got his ideas from. That thought had made her notice Ellen. What a strange woman *she* must be, to raise a child in the forest! Aliena had talked to Ellen and found in her a kindred spirit, an independent and self-sufficient woman somewhat angry at the way life had treated her. Now, on impulse, Aliena said: "Ellen, where did *you* learn the stories?"

"From Jack's father," Ellen said without thinking, and then a guarded look came over her face, and Aliena knew she should not ask any more questions.

Another thought occurred to her. "Do you know how to weave?"

"Of course," Ellen said. "Doesn't everyone?"

"Would you like to do some weaving for money?"

"Perhaps. What have you got in mind?"

Aliena explained. Ellen was not short of money, of course, but it was Tom who earned it, and Aliena had a suspicion that Ellen might like to make some for herself.

The suspicion turned out to be right. "Yes, I'll give that a try," Ellen said.

At that moment Ellen's stepson, Alfred, came along. Like his father, Alfred was something of a giant. Most of his face was concealed behind a bushy beard, but the eyes above it were narrow-set, giving him a cunning look. He could read and write and add up, but despite that he was rather stupid. Nevertheless he had prospered, and he had his own gang of masons, apprentices and laborers. Aliena had observed that big men often gained positions of power regardless of their intelligence. As a ganger Alfred had another advantage, of course: he could always be sure of getting work for his men because his father was the master builder of Kingsbridge Cathedral.

He sat on the grass beside her. He had enormous feet shod in heavy leather boots that were gray with stone dust. She rarely spoke to him. They should have had a lot in common, for they were the only young people among the wealthier class of Kingsbridge, the class that lived in the houses nearest to the priory wall; but Alfred always seemed so dull. After a moment he spoke. "There ought to be a stone church," he said abruptly.

Clearly the rest of them were supposed to figure out the context of this remark for themselves. Aliena thought for a moment then said: "Are you talking about the parish church?"

"Yes," he said as if it was obvious.

The parish church was now used a good deal, for the cathedral crypt, which the monks were using, was cramped and airless, and the population of Kingsbridge had grown. Yet the parish church was an old wooden building with a thatched roof and a dirt floor.

"You're right," Aliena said. "We should have a stone church."

Alfred was looking at her expectantly. She wondered what he wanted her to say.

Ellen, who was probably used to coaxing sense out of him, said: "What's on your mind, Alfred?"

"How do churches get started, anyway?" he asked. "I mean, if we want a stone church, what do we do?"

Ellen shrugged. "No idea."

Aliena frowned. "You could form a parish guild," she suggested. A parish guild was an association of people who held a banquet every now and again and collected money among themselves, usually to buy candles for their local church, or to help widows and orphans in the neighborhood. Small villages never had guilds, but Kingsbridge was no longer a village.

"How would that do it?" Alfred said.

"The members of the guild would pay for the new church," Aliena said.

"Then we should start a guild," Alfred said.

Aliena wondered if she had misjudged him. He had never struck her as the pious type, but here he was trying to raise money to build a new church. Perhaps he had hidden depths. Then she realized that Alfred was the only building contractor in Kingsbridge, so he was sure to get the job of building the church. He might not be intelligent, but he was shrewd enough.

Nevertheless she still liked his idea. Kingsbridge was becoming a town, and towns always had more than one church. With an alternative to the cathedral, the town would not be so completely dominated by the monastery. At the moment Philip was the undisputed lord and master here. He was a benevolent tyrant, but she could foresee a time when it might suit the merchants of the town to have an alternative church.

Alfred said: "Would you explain about the guild to some of the others?"

Aliena had recovered her breath after the race. She was reluctant to exchange the company of Ellen and Jack for that of Alfred, but she was quite enthusiastic about his idea, and anyway it would have been a little churlish to refuse. "I'd be glad to," she said, and she got up and went with him.

The sun was going down. The monks had lit the bonfire and were serving the traditional ale spiced with ginger. Jack wanted to ask his mother a question, now that they were alone, but he was nervous. Then someone started to sing, and he knew she would join in at any moment, so he blurted it out. "Was my father a jongleur?"

She looked at him. She was surprised but not cross. "Who taught you that word?" she said. "You've never seen a jongleur."

"Aliena. She used to go to France with her father."

Mother gazed across the darkling meadow toward the bonfire. "Yes, he was a jongleur. He told me all those poems, just the way I told them to you. And are you now telling them to Aliena?"

"Yes." Jack felt a little bashful.

"You really love her, don't you?"

"Is it so obvious?"

She smiled fondly. "Only to me, I think. She's a lot older than you."

"Five years."

"You'll get her, though. You're like your father. He could have any woman he wanted."

Jack was embarrassed to talk about Aliena but thrilled to hear about his father, and he was eager for more; but to his intense annoyance Tom came up at that moment and sat down with them. He began to speak immediately. "I've been talking to Prior Philip about Jack," he said. His tone was light, but Jack sensed tension underneath, and saw trouble coming. "Philip says the boy should be educated."

Mother's response was predictably indignant. "He is educated," she said. "He can read and write English and French, he knows his numbers, he can recite whole bookfuls of poetry—"

"Now, don't misunderstand me willfully," Tom said firmly. "Philip didn't say that Jack is ignorant. Quite the opposite. He's saying that Jack is so clever he should have *more* education."

Jack was not pleased by these compliments. He shared his mother's suspicion of churchmen. There was sure to be a catch in this somewhere.

"More?" Ellen said scornfully. "What more does that monk want him to learn? I'll tell you. Theology. Latin. Rhetoric. Metaphysics. Cow shit."

"Don't dismiss it so quickly," Tom said mildly. "If Jack takes up Philip's offer, and goes to school, and learns to write at speed in a good secretary's hand, and studies Latin and theology and all the other subjects you call cow shit, he could become a clerk to an earl or a bishop, and eventually he could be a wealthy and powerful man. Not all barons are the sons of barons, as the saying goes."

Ellen's eyes narrowed dangerously. "If he takes up Philip's offer, you said. What is Philip's offer, exactly?"

"That Jack becomes a novice monk—"

"Over my dead body!" Ellen shouted, leaping to her feet. "The damned Church is not having my son! Those treacherous lying priests took his father but they're not taking him, I'll put a knife in Philip's belly first, so help me, I swear by all the gods."

Tom had seen Mother in a tantrum before and he was not as impressed as he might have been. He said calmly: "What the devil is the matter with you, woman? The boy has been offered a magnificent opportunity."

Jack was intrigued most of all by the words *Those treacherous lying priests took his father*. What did she mean by that? He wanted to ask her but he did not get the chance.

"He's not going to be a monk!" she yelled.

"If he doesn't want to be a monk, he doesn't have to."

Mother looked sulky. "That sly prior has a knack of getting his own way in the end," she said.

Tom turned to Jack. "It's about time you said something, lad. What do *you* want to do with your life?"

Jack had never thought about that particular question, but the answer came out with no hesitation, as if he had made up his mind long ago. "I'm going to be a master builder, like you," he said. "I'm going to build the most beautiful cathedral the world has ever seen."

* * *

The red edge of the sun dropped below the horizon and night fell. It was time for the last ritual of Midsummer Eve: floating wishes. Jack had a candle end and a piece of wood ready. He looked at Ellen and Tom. They were both gazing at him, somewhat nonplussed: his certainty about his future had surprised them. Well, no wonder: it had surprised him too.

Seeing that they had no more to say, he jumped to his feet and ran across the meadow to the bonfire. He lit a dry twig at the fire, melted the base of his candle a little, and stuck it to the piece of wood; then he lit the wick. Most of the villagers were doing the same. Those who could not afford a candle made a sort of boat with dried grass and rushes, and twisted the grasses together in the middle to make a wick.

Jack saw Aliena standing quite near him. Her face was outlined by the red glow of the bonfire, and she looked deep in thought. On impulse he said: "What will you wish for, Aliena?"

She answered him without pausing for thought. "Peace," she said. Then, looking somewhat startled, she turned away.

Jack wondered if he were crazy to love her. She liked him well enough—they had become friends—but the idea of lying naked together and kissing one another's hot skin was as far from her heart as it was close to his own.

When everyone was ready, they knelt down beside the river, or waded into the shallows. Holding their flickering lights, they all made a wish. Jack closed his eyes tight and visualized Aliena, lying in a bed with her breasts peeping over the coverlet, holding her arms out to him and saying: "Make love to me, husband." Then they all carefully floated their lights on the water. If the float sank or the flame blew out, it meant you would never get your wish. As soon as Jack let go, and the little craft moved away, the wooden base became invisible, and only the flame could be seen. He watched it intently for a while, then he lost track of it among the hundreds of dancing lights, bobbing on the surface of the water, flickering wishes floating downstream until they disappeared around the bend of the river and were lost from view.

III

All that summer, Jack told Aliena stories.

They met on Sundays, occasionally at first and then regularly, in the glade by the little waterfall. He told her about Charlemagne and his knights, and William of Orange and the Saracens. He became completely absorbed in the stories while he was telling them. Aliena liked to watch the expressions change on his young face. He was indignant about injustice, appalled by treachery, thrilled by the bravery of a knight and moved to tears by a heroic death; and his emotions were catching, so that she too was moved. Some of the poems were too long to recite in one afternoon, and when he had to tell a story in installments he always broke off at a moment of tension, so that Aliena spent all week wondering what would happen next.

She never told anyone about these meetings. She was not sure why. Perhaps it was that they would not understand the fascination of stories. Whatever the reason, she just let people believe that she was going on her usual Sunday afternoon ramble; and without consulting her Jack did the same; then it got to the point where they could not tell anyone without appearing to confess to something they felt guilty about; and so, rather by accident, the meetings became secret.

One Sunday Aliena read "The Romance of Alexander" to him, just for a change. Unlike Jack's poems of courtly intrigue, international politics and sudden death in battle, Aliena's romance featured love affairs and magic. Jack was very taken with these new story-telling elements, and the following Sunday he embarked upon a new romance of his own invention.

It was a hot day in late August. Aliena was wearing sandals and a light linen dress. The forest was still and silent but for the tinkling of the waterfall and the rise and fall of Jack's voice. The story began in a conventional way, with a description of a brave knight, big and strong, mighty in battle, and armed with a magic sword, who was assigned a difficult task: to travel to a far eastern land and bring back a grapevine that grew rubies. But it rapidly deviated from the usual pattern. The knight was killed and the story focused on his squire, a brave but penniless young man of seventeen who was hopelessly in love with the king's daughter, a beautiful princess. The squire vowed to fulfil the task given to his master, even though he was young and inexperienced and had only a piebald pony and a bow.

Instead of vanquishing an enemy with one tremendous blow of a magic sword, as the hero generally did in these stories, the squire fought desperate losing battles and won only by luck or ingenuity, generally escaping death by a hair. He was often scared by the enemies that he faced—unlike Charlemagne's fearless knights—but he never turned back from his mission. All the same, his task, like his love, seemed hopeless.

Aliena found herself more captivated by the pluck of the squire than she had been by the might of his master. She chewed her knuckles in anxiety when he rode into enemy territory, gasped when a giant's sword barely missed him, and sighed when he lay down his lonely head to sleep and dream of the faraway princess. His love for her seemed of a piece with his general indomitability.

In the end, he brought home the grapevine that grew rubies, astonishing the entire court. "But the squire did not care *that* much," Jack said with a contemptuous snap of his fingers, "for all those barons and earls. He was interested in one person only. That night, he stole into her room, evading the guards with a cunning ruse he had learned on his journey east. At last he stood beside her bed and gazed upon her face." Jack looked into Aliena's eyes as he said this. "She woke at once, but she was not afraid. The squire reached out and gently took her hand." Jack mimed the story, reaching for Aliena's hand and holding it in both of his. She was mesmerized by the intensity of his gaze and the power of the young squire's love, and she hardly noticed that Jack was holding her hand. "He said to her, 'I love you dearly,' and kissed her on the lips." Jack leaned over and kissed Aliena. His lips touched hers so gently that she hardly felt it. It happened very quickly, and he resumed the story instantly. "The princess fell asleep," he continued. Aliena thought: Did that really happen? Did Jack kiss me? She could hardly believe it, but she could still feel the touch of his mouth on hers. "The next day, the squire asked the king if he could marry the princess, as his reward for bringing home the jeweled vine." Jack kissed me without thinking, Aliena decided. It was just part of the story. He doesn't even realize what he did. I'll just forget about it. "The king refused him. The squire was heartbroken. All the courtiers laughed. That very day the squire left that land, riding on his piebald pony; but he vowed that one day he would return, and on that day he would marry the beautiful princess." Jack stopped, and let go of Aliena's hand.

"And then what happened?" she said.

"I don't know," Jack replied. "I haven't thought of it yet."

All the important people in Kingsbridge joined the parish guild. It was a new idea to most of them, but they liked the thought that Kingsbridge was now a town, not a village, and their vanity was touched by the appeal to them, as leading citizens, to provide a stone church.

Aliena and Alfred recruited the members and organized the first guild dinner, in mid-September. The major absentees were Prior Philip, who was somewhat hostile to the enterprise, although not enough to prohibit it; Tom Builder, who declined because of Philip's feeling; and Malachi, who was excluded by his religion.

Meanwhile, Ellen had woven a bale of cloth from Aliena's surplus wool. It was coarse and colorless, but it was good enough for monks' robes, and the priory cellarer, Cuthbert Whitehead, had bought it. The price was cheap, but it was still double the cost of the original wool, and even after paying Ellen a penny a day Aliena was better off by half a pound. Cuthbert was keen to buy more cloth at that price, so Aliena bought Philip's surplus wool to add to her own stock, and found a dozen more people, mostly women, to weave it. Ellen agreed to make another bale, but she would not felt it, for she said the work was too hard; and most of the others said the same.

Aliena sympathized. Felting, or fulling, was heavy work. She remembered how she and Richard had gone to a master fuller in Winchester and asked him to employ them. The fuller had had two men pounding cloth with bats in a trough while a woman poured water in. The woman had shown Aliena her raw, red hands, and when the men had put a bale of wet cloth on Richard's shoulder it had brought him to his knees. Most people could manage to felt a small amount, enough to make clothes for themselves and their families, but only strong men could do it all day. Aliena told her weavers to go ahead and make loose-woven cloth, and she would hire men to felt it, or sell it to a master fuller in Winchester.

The guild dinner was held in the wooden church. Aliena organized the food. She parceled out the cooking among the members, most of whom had at least one domestic servant. Alfred and his men constructed a long table made of trestles and boards. They bought strong ale and a barrel of wine.

They sat at either side of the table, with nobody at the head or foot, for all were to be equal within the guild. Aliena wore a deep-red silk dress ornamented by a gold brooch with rubies in it, and a dark gray pelisse with fashionably wide sleeves. The parish priest said grace: he of course was delighted by the idea of the guild, for a new church would increase his prestige and multiply his income.

Alfred presented a budget and timetable for the building of the new church. He spoke as if this were all his own work, but Aliena knew that Tom had done most of it. The building would take two years and cost ninety pounds, and Alfred proposed that the guild's forty members should each pay sixpence a week. It was a little more than some of them had reckoned on, Aliena could tell by their faces. They all agreed to pay it, but Aliena thought the guild could expect one or two to default.

She herself could pay it easily. Looking around the table, she realized she was probably the richest person there. She was in a small minority of women: the only others were a brewster with a reputation for good strong ale, a tailor who employed two seam-stresses and some apprentices, and the widow of a shoemaker, who managed the business her husband had left. Aliena was the youn-gest woman there, and younger than any of the men except Alfred, who was a year or two younger than she.

Aliena missed Jack. She had not yet heard the second install-ment of the story of the young squire. Today was a holiday, and she would have liked to meet him in the glade. Perhaps she still could, later on.

The talk around the table was of the civil war. Stephen's wife, Queen Matilda, had put up more of a fight than anyone expected: she had recently taken the city of Winchester and captured Robert of Gloucester. Robert was the brother of the Empress Maud and the commander in chief of her military forces. Some people said Maud was only a figurehead, and Robert was the true leader of the rebellion. In any event, the capture of Robert was almost as bad for Maud as the capture of Stephen had been for the loyalists, and everyone had an opinion on what direction the war would take next.

The drink at this feast was stronger than that provided by Prior Philip, and as the meal progressed, the revelers became quite raucous. The parish priest failed to act as a restraining influence, probably because he was drinking as much as anyone else. Alfred, who was sitting next to Aliena, seemed preoccupied, but even he became flushed. Aliena herself was not fond of strong drink, and she took a cup of apple cider with her dinner.

When most of the food was finished, someone proposed a toast to Alfred and Aliena. Alfred beamed with pleasure as he acknowl-edged it. After that the singing began, and Aliena started to wonder how soon she could slip away.

Alfred said to her: "We did well, together."

Aliena smiled. "Let's see how many of them are still paying sixpence a week this time next year."

Alfred did not want to hear about misgivings or qualifications today. "We did well," he repeated. "We're a good team." He raised his cup to her and drank. "Don't you think we're a good team?"

"We certainly are," she said, to humor him.

"I've enjoyed it," he went on. "Doing this with you—the guild, I mean."

"I've enjoyed it, too," she said politely.

"Have you? That makes me very happy."

She looked at him more carefully. Why was he laboring the point? His speech was clear and precise, and he showed no signs of real drunkenness. "It's been fine," she said neutrally.

He put a hand on her shoulder. She hated to be touched, but she had trained herself not to flinch, because men became so offended. "Tell me something," he said, lowering his voice to an intimate level. "What are you looking for in a husband?"

Surely he's not going to ask me to marry him, she thought dismally. She gave her standard answer. "I don't need a husband—my brother is trouble enough."

"But you need love," he said.

She groaned inwardly.

She was about to reply when he held up a hand to stop her—a masculine habit she found particularly maddening. "Don't tell me you don't need love," he said. "Everybody needs love."

She gazed at him steadily. She knew there was something peculiar about her: most women were keen to get married; and if they were still single, as she was, at the age of twenty-two, they were more than keen, they were desperate. What's wrong with me? she thought. Alfred was young, fit and prosperous: half the girls in Kingsbridge would like to marry him. For a moment she toyed with the idea of saying yes. But the thought of actually living with Alfred, eating supper with him every night and going to church with him and giving birth to his children, was appalling. She would rather be lonely. She shook her head. "Forget it, Alfred," she said firmly. "I don't need a husband, for love or anything else."

He was not to be discouraged. "I love you, Aliena," he said. "Working with you, I've been truly happy. I need you. Will you be my wife?"

He had said it now. She was sorry, for it meant she had to reject him formally. She had learned that there was no point in trying to do this gently, either: they took a kindly refusal as a sign of indecision, and pressed her all the more. "No, I won't," she said. "I don't love you and I haven't much enjoyed working with you, and I wouldn't marry you if you were the only man on earth."

He was hurt. He must have thought his chances were strong. Aliena was sure she had done nothing to encourage him. She had treated him as an equal partner, listened to him when he spoke, talked to him frankly and directly, fulfilled her responsibilities and expected him to fulfill his. But some men took that for encouragement. "How can you say that?" he spluttered.

She sighed. He was wounded, and she felt sorry for him; but in a moment he would be indignant, and act as if she had made an unfair accusation against him; then finally he would convince himself that she had gratuitously insulted him, and he would become offensive. Not all rejected suitors behaved like that, but a certain type did, and Alfred was that type. She was going to have to leave.

She stood up. "I respect your proposal, and I thank you for the honor you do me," she said. "Please respect my refusal, and don't ask me again."

"I suppose you're running off to see my snotnosed little stepbrother," he said nastily. "I can't imagine he gives you much of a ride."

Aliena flushed with embarrassment. So people were beginning to notice her friendship with Jack. Trust Alfred to put a smutty interpretion on it. Well she *was* running off to see Jack, and she was not going to let Alfred stop her. She bent down and thrust her face into his. He was startled. Quietly and deliberately she said: "Go. To. Hell." Then she turned and went out.

Prior Philip held court in the crypt once a month. In the old days it had been once a year, and even then the business rarely took all day. But when the population trebled, lawbreaking had increased tenfold.

The nature of crime had changed, too. Formerly, most offenses had to do with land, crops or livestock. A greedy peasant would try surreptitiously to move the boundary of a field so as to extend his land at the expense of a neighbor; a laborer would steal a sack of corn from the widow he worked for; a poor woman with too many children would milk a cow that was not hers. Nowadays most of the cases involved money, Philip thought, as he sat through his court on the first day of December. Apprentices stole money from their masters, a husband took his wife's mother's savings, merchants passed dud coinage, and wealthy women underpaid simpleminded servants who could hardly count their weekly wages. There had been no such crimes in Kingsbridge five years ago, because then nobody had much cash.

Philip dealt with nearly all offenses by a fine. He could also have people flogged, or put in the stocks, or imprisoned in the cell beneath the monks' dormitory, but these punishments were rarer, and reserved mainly for crimes of violence. He had the right to hang thieves, and the priory owned a stout wooden gallows; but he had never used it, not yet, and he cherished a secret hope that he never would. The most serious crimes—murder, killing the king's deer, and highway robbery—were dealt with by the king's court at Shiring, presided over by the sheriff, and Sheriff Eustace did more than enough hanging.

Today Philip had seven cases of unauthorized grain grinding. He left them until the end and dealt with them all together. The priory had just built a new water mill to run alongside the old one—Kingsbridge needed two mills now. But the new building had to be paid for, which meant that everyone had to bring their grain to be ground at the priory. Strictly speaking, that had always been the law, as it was in every manor in the country: peasants were not allowed to grind grain at home; they had to pay the lord to do it for them. In recent years, as the town grew and the old mill began to break down frequently, Philip had overlooked a growing amount of illicit grinding; but now he had to clamp down.

He had the names of the offenders scratched on a slate, and he read them out, one by one, beginning with the wealthiest. "Richard Longacre, you had a large grindstone turned by two men, Brother Franciscus says." Franciscus was the priory's miller.

A prosperous-looking yeoman stepped forward. "Yes, my lord prior, but I've broken it now."

"Pay sixty pence. Enid Brewster, you had a handmill in your brewery. Eric Enidson was seen using it, and he is charged too."

"Yes, lord," said Enid, a red-faced woman with powerful shoulders.

"And where is the handmill now?" Philip asked her.

"I threw it in the river, lord."

Philip did not believe her, but there was not much he could do about it. "Fined twenty-four pence, and twelve for your son. Walter Tanner?"

Philip went on down the list, fining people according to the scale of their illegitimate operations, until he came to the last and poorest. "Widow Goda?"

A pinch-faced old woman in faded black clothes stepped forward.

"Brother Franciscus saw you grinding grain with a stone."

"I didn't have a penny for the mill, lord," she said resentfully.

"You had a penny to buy grain, though," Philip said. "You shall be punished like everyone else."

"Would you have me starve?" she said defiantly.

Philip sighed. He wished Brother Franciscus had pretended not to notice Goda breaking the law. "When was the last time someone starved to death in Kingsbridge?" he said. He looked around at the assembled citizens. "Anybody remember the last time someone starved to death in our town?" He paused for a moment, as if waiting for a reply, then said: "I think you'll find it was before my time."

Goda said: "Dick Shorthouse died last winter."

Philip remembered the man, a beggar who slept in pigsties and stables. "Dick fell down drunk in the street at midnight and froze to death when it snowed," he said. "He didn't starve, and if he'd been sober enough to walk to the priory, he wouldn't have been cold either. If you're hungry, don't try to cheat me—come to me for charity. And if you're too proud to do that, and you would rather break the law instead, you must take your punishment like everyone else. Do you hear me?"

"Yes, lord," the old woman said sulkily.

"Fined a farthing," Philip said. "Court is over."

He stood up and went out, climbing the stairs that led up to ground level from the crypt.

Work on the new cathedral had slowed dramatically, as it always did a month or so before Christmas. The exposed edges and tops of the unfinished stonework were covered with straw and dung—the litter from the priory stables—to keep the frost off the new masonry. The masons could not build in the winter, because of the frost, they said. Philip had asked why they could not uncover the walls every morning and cover them again at night: it was not often frosty in the daytime. Tom said that walls built in winter fell down. Philip believed that, but he did not think it was because of the frost. He thought the real reason might be that the mortar took several months to set properly. The winter break allowed it to get really hard before the new year's masonry was built on top. That would also explain the masons' superstition that it was bad luck to build more than twenty feet high in a single year: more than that, and the lower courses might become deformed by the weight on them before the mortar could harden.

Philip was surprised to see all the masons out in the open, in what would be the chancel of the church. He went to see what they were doing.

They had made a semicircular wooden arch and stood it

upright, propped up with poles on both sides. Philip knew that the wooden arch was a piece of what they called falsework: its purpose was to support the stone arch while it was being built. Now, however, the masons were assembling the stone arch at ground level, without mortar, to make sure the stones fit together perfectly. Apprentices and laborers were lifting the stones onto the falsework while the masons looked on critically.

Philip caught Tom's eye and said: "What's this for?"

"It's an arch for the tribune gallery."

Philip looked up reflexively. The arcade had been finished last year and the gallery above it would be completed next year. Then only the top level, the clerestory, would remain to be built before the roof went on. Now that the walls had been covered up for the winter, the masons were cutting the stones ready for next year's work. If this arch was right, the stones for all the others would be cut to the same patterns.

The apprentices, among whom was Tom's stepson, Jack, built the arch up from either side, with the wedge-shaped stones called voussoirs. Although the arch would eventually be built high up in the church, it would have elaborate decorative moldings; so each stone bore, on the surface that would be visible, a line of large dog-tooth carving, another line of small medallions, and a bottom line of simple roll molding. When the stones were put together, the carvings lined up exactly, forming three continuous arcs, one of dog-tooth, one of medallions and one of roll molding. This gave the impression that the arch was constructed of several semicircular hoops of stone one on top of another, whereas, in fact, it was made of wedges placed side by side. However, the stones had to fit together precisely, otherwise the carvings would not line up and the illusion would be spoiled.

Philip watched while Jack lowered the central keystone into place. Now the arch was complete. Four masons picked up sledge-hammers and knocked out the wedges that supported the wooden falsework a few inches above the ground. Dramatically, the wooden support fell. Although there was no mortar between the stones, the arch remained standing. Tom Builder gave a grunt of satisfaction.

Someone pulled at Philip's sleeve. He turned to see a young monk. "You've got a visitor, father. He's waiting in your house."

"Thank you, my son." Philip left the builders. If the monks had put the visitor in the prior's house to wait, that meant it was someone important. He crossed the close and went into his house.

The visitor was his brother, Francis. Philip embraced him

warmly. Francis looked careworn. "Have you been offered something to eat?" Philip said. "You seem weary."

"They gave me some bread and meat, thanks. I've spent the autumn riding between Bristol, where King Stephen was imprisoned, and Rochester, where Earl Robert was held."

"You said *was*."

Francis nodded. "I've been negotiating a swap: Stephen for Robert. It was done on All Saints' Day. King Stephen is now back in Winchester."

Philip was surprised. "It seems to me that the Empress Maud got the worst of the bargain—she gave a king to get an earl."

Francis shook his head. "She was helpless without Robert. Nobody likes her, nobody trusts her. Her support was collapsing. She had to have him back. Queen Matilda was clever. She wouldn't take anything less than King Stephen in exchange. She held out for that and in the end she got it."

Philip went to the window and looked out. It had started to rain, a cold slantwise rain blowing across the building site, darkening the high walls of the cathedral and dripping off the low thatched roofs of the craftsmen's lodges. "What does it mean?" he said.

"It means that Maud is once again just an aspirant to the throne. After all, Stephen has actually been crowned, whereas Maud never was, not quite."

"But it was Maud who licensed my market."

"Yes. That could be a problem."

"Is my license invalid?"

"No. It was properly granted by a legitimate ruler who had been approved by the Church. The fact that she wasn't crowned doesn't make any difference. But Stephen could withdraw it."

"The market is paying for the stone," Philip said anxiously. "I can't build without it. This is bad news indeed."

"I'm sorry."

"What about my hundred pounds?"

Francis shrugged. "Stephen will tell you to get it back from Maud."

Philip felt sick. "All that money," he said. "It was God's money, and I lost it."

"You haven't lost it yet," Francis said. "Stephen may not revoke your license. He's never shown much interest in markets one way or the other."

"Earl William may pressure him."

"William changed allegiance, remember? He threw his lot in with Maud. He won't have much influence with Stephen anymore."

"I hope you're right," Philip said fervently. "I hope to God you're right."

When it got too cold to sit in the glade, Aliena took to visiting Tom Builder's house in the evenings. Alfred was normally at the alehouse, so the family group consisted of Tom, Ellen, Jack and Martha. Now that Tom was doing so well, they had comfortable seats, and a roaring fire, and plenty of candles. Ellen and Aliena would work at the weaving. Tom would draw plans and diagrams, scratching his drawings with a sharp stone onto polished pieces of slate. Jack would pretend to be making a belt, or sharpening knives, or weaving a basket, although he would spend most of the time furtively staring at Aliena's face in the candlelight, watching her lips move as she talked or studying her white throat as she drank a glass of ale. They laughed a lot that winter. Jack loved to make Aliena laugh. She was so controlled and reserved, in general, that it was a joy to see her let herself go, almost like catching a glimpse of her naked. He was constantly thinking of things to say to amuse her. He would do impressions of the craftsmen on the building site, imitating the accent of a Parisian mason or the bowlegged walk of a blacksmith. Once he invented a comical account of life with the monks, giving each of them plausible sins—pride for Remigius, gluttony for Bernard Kitchener, drunkenness for the guest-master, and lust for Pierre Circuitor. Martha was often helpless with laughter and even the taciturn Tom cracked a smile.

It was on one such evening that Aliena said: "I don't know if I'm going to be able to sell all this cloth."

They were somewhat taken aback. Ellen said: "Then why are we weaving it?"

"I haven't given up hope," Aliena said. "I've just got a problem."

Tom looked up from his slate. "I thought the priory was eager to buy it all."

"That's not the problem. I can't find people to do the felting, and the priory doesn't want loose-woven cloth—nor does anyone else."

Ellen said: "Felting is backbreaking work. I'm not surprised no one will do it."

"Can't you get men to do it?" Tom suggested.

"Not in prosperous Kingsbridge. All the men have work enough. In the big towns there are professional fullers, but most of them work for weavers, and they're prohibited from felting for their employer's rivals. Anyway, it would cost too much to cart the cloth to Winchester and back.''

''It's a real problem,'' Tom acknowledged, and went back to his drawing.

Jack was struck by a thought. ''It's a pity we can't get oxen to do it.''

The others laughed. Tom said: ''You might as well try to teach an ox to build churches.''

''Or a mill,'' Jack persisted. ''There are usually easy ways to do the hardest work.''

''She wants to felt the cloth, not grind it,'' Tom said.

Jack was not listening. ''We use lifting gear, and winding wheels, to raise stones up to the high scaffolding.''

Aliena said: ''Oh, if there was some ingenious mechanism to get this cloth felted, it would be wonderful.''

Jack thought how pleased she would be if he could solve this problem for her. He determined to find a way.

Tom said thoughtfully: ''I've heard of a water mill being used to work the bellows in a forge—but I've never seen it.''

''Really!'' Jack said. ''That proves it!''

Tom said: ''A mill wheel goes round and round, and a grindstone goes round and round, so the one can drive the other; but a fuller's bat goes up and down. You can't make a round waterwheel drive an up-and-down bat.''

''But a bellows goes up and down.''

''True, true; but I never saw that forge, I only heard tell of it.''

Jack tried to picture the machinery of a mill. The force of the water drove the mill wheel around. The shaft of the mill wheel was connected to another wheel inside the mill. The inside wheel, which was upright, had teeth that interlocked with the teeth of another wheel which lay flat. The flat wheel turned the millstone. ''An upright wheel can drive a flat wheel,'' Jack muttered, thinking aloud.

Martha laughed. ''Jack, stop! If mills could felt cloth, clever people would have thought of it already.''

Jack ignored her. ''The fuller's bats could be fixed to the shaft of the mill wheel,'' he said. ''The cloth could be laid flat where the bats fall.''

Tom said: ''But the bats would strike once, then get stuck; and the wheel would stop. I told you—wheels go round and round, but bats have to go up and down.''

''There must be a way,'' Jack said stubbornly.

''There's no way,'' Tom said decisively, in the tone of voice he used to close a conversational subject.

"I bet there is, though," Jack muttered rebelliously; and Tom pretended not to hear.

On the following Sunday, Jack disappeared.

He went to church in the morning, and ate his dinner at home, as usual; but he did not appear at suppertime. Aliena was in her own kitchen, making a thick broth of ham and cabbage with pepper in it, when Ellen came looking for Jack.

"I haven't seen him since mass," Aliena said.

"He vanished after dinner," Ellen said. "I assumed he was with you."

Aliena felt a little embarrassed that Ellen should have made that assumption so readily. "Are you worried?"

Ellen shrugged. "A mother is always worried."

"Has he quarreled with Alfred?" Aliena said nervously.

"I asked the same question. Alfred says not." Ellen sighed. "I don't suppose he's come to any harm. He's done this before and I daresay he'll do it again. I never taught him to keep regular hours."

Later in the evening, just before bedtime, Aliena called at Tom's house to see whether Jack had reappeared. He had not. She went to bed worried. Richard was away in Winchester, so she was alone. She kept thinking Jack might have fallen into the river and drowned, or something. How terrible that would be for Ellen: Jack was her only son. Tears came to Aliena's eyes when she imagined Ellen's grief at losing Jack. This is stupid, she thought: I'm crying over someone else's sorrow about something that hasn't happened. She pulled herself together and tried to think of another subject. The surplus cloth was her big problem. Normally she could worry about business half the night, but tonight her mind kept returning to Jack. Suppose he had broken his leg, and was lying in the forest, unable to move?

Eventually she drifted into a restless sleep. She woke at first light, still feeling tired. She threw on her heavy cloak over her nightshirt, and pulled on her fur-lined boots, then went outside to look for him.

He was not in the garden behind the alehouse, where men commonly fell asleep, and were saved from freezing by the heat of the fetid dunghill. She went down to the bridge and walked fearfully along the bank to a bend in the river where debris was washed up. A family of ducks was scavenging among the bits of wood, wornout shoes, rusty discarded knives and rotting meat bones on the beach. Jack was not there, thank God.

She went back up the hill and into the priory close, where the cathedral builders were beginning their day's work. She found Tom in his shed. "Has Jack come back?" she said hopefully.

Tom shook his head. "Not yet."

As she was going out, the master carpenter came up, looking worried. "All our hammers have gone," he said to Tom.

"That's funny," Tom said. "I've been looking for a hammer and can't find one."

Then Alfred put his head around the door and said: "Where are all the masons' bolsters?"

Tom scratched his head. "It seems as if every hammer on the site has disappeared," he said in a baffled voice. Then his expression changed, and he said: "That boy Jack is behind this, I'll bet."

Of course, Aliena thought. Hammers. Felting. The mill.

Without saying what she was thinking, she left Tom's shed and hurried across the priory close, going past the kitchen, to the southwest corner, where a channel diverted from the river drove two mills, one old and the other brand-new. As she had suspected, the wheel of the old mill was turning. She went inside.

What she saw confused and frightened her at first. There was a row of hammers fixed to a horizontal pole. Apparently of their own volition the hammers lifted their heads, like horses looking up from the manger. Then they went down again, all together, and struck simultaneously with a mighty bang that made her heart stop. She gave a cry of shock. The hammers lifted their heads, as if they had heard her cry, then they struck again. They were pounding a length of her loose-woven cloth that lay in an inch or two of water in a shallow wooden trough of the type used by mortar makers on the building site. The hammers were felting the cloth, she realized, and she stopped being frightened, although they still looked disturbingly alive. But how was it done? She saw that the pole on which the hammers were fixed ran parallel with the shaft of the mill wheel. A plank fixed to the shaft went round and round as the shaft turned. When the plank came around, it connected with the handles of the hammers, pushing the handles down so that the heads came up. As the plank continued to turn the handles were released. Then the hammers fell and pounded the cloth in the trough. It was exactly what Jack had talked about that evening: a mill that could felt cloth.

She heard his voice. "The hammers should be weighted so that they fall harder." She turned around and saw him, looking tired but triumphant. "I think I've solved your problem," he said, and grinned sheepishly.

"I'm so glad you're all right—we were worried about you!" she said. Without thinking, she threw her arms around him and kissed him. It was a very brief kiss, not much more than a peck; but then, when their lips separated, his arms went around her waist, holding her body gently but firmly against his own, and she found herself looking into his eyes. All she could think of was how happy she was that he was alive and unhurt. She gave him an affectionate squeeze. She was suddenly aware of her own skin: she could feel the roughness of her linen undershirt and the soft fur of her boots, and her nipples tingled as they pressed against his chest.

"You were worried about me?" he said wonderingly.

"Of course! I hardly slept!"

She was smiling happily, but he looked terribly solemn, and after a moment his mood overcame hers, and she felt strangely moved. She could hear her heart beating, and her breath came faster. Behind her, the hammers thudded in unison, shaking the wooden structure of the mill with each concerted blow, and she seemed to feel the vibration deep inside her.

"I'm all right," he said. "Everything's all right."

"I'm so glad," she repeated, and it came out in a whisper.

She saw him close his eyes and bend his face to hers, and then she felt his mouth on her own. His kiss was gentle. He had full lips and a soft adolescent beard. She closed her eyes to concentrate on the sensation. His mouth moved against hers, and it seemed natural to part her lips. Her mouth had suddenly become ultra-sensitive, so that she could feel the lightest touch, the tiniest movement. The tip of his tongue caressed the inside of her upper lip. She felt so overwhelmed with happiness that she wanted to cry. She pressed her body against his, crushing her soft breasts against his hard chest, feeling the bones of his hips dig into her belly. She was no longer merely relieved that he was safe, and glad to have him here. Now there was a new emotion. His physical presence filled her with an ecstatic sensation that made her slightly dizzy. Holding his body in her arms, she wanted to touch him more, to feel more of him, to get even closer. She rubbed his back with her hands. She wanted to feel his skin, but his clothes frustrated her. Without thinking, she opened her mouth and pushed her tongue between his lips. He made a small animal sound in the back of his throat, like a muffled moan of delight.

The door of the mill banged open. Aliena pulled away from Jack. Suddenly she felt shocked, as if she had been fast asleep and someone had slapped her to wake her up. She was horrified by what they had been doing—kissing and rubbing one another like a whore and a drunk in an alehouse! She stepped back and turned around, mortified with embarrassment. The intruder was Alfred, of all people. That made her feel worse. Alfred had proposed marriage to her, three months ago, and she had refused him haughtily. Now he had seen her acting like a bitch in heat. It seemed somehow hypocritical. She flushed with shame. Alfred was staring at her, his expression a mixture of lust and contempt that reminded her vividly of William Hamleigh. She was disgusted with herself for giving Alfred a reason to look down on her, and furious at Jack for his part in it.

She turned away from Alfred and looked at Jack. When his eyes met hers he registered shock. She realized that her anger was showing in her face but she could not help it. Jack's expression of dazed happiness turned into confusion and hurt. Normally that would have melted her, but now she was too upset. She hated him for what he had made her do. Quick as a flash, she slapped his face. He did not move, but there was agony in his look. His cheek reddened where she had hit him. She could not bear to see the pain in his eyes. She tore her gaze away.

She could not stay there. She ran to the door with the incessant thud of the hammers pounding in her ears. Alfred stepped aside quickly, looking almost frightened. She dashed past him and went through the door. Tom Builder was just outside, with a small crowd of building workers. Everyone was heading for the mill to find out what was going on. Aliena hurried past them without speaking. One or two of them glanced curiously at her, making her burn with shame; but they were more interested in the hammering sound coming from the mill. The coldly logical part of Aliena's mind recalled that Jack had solved the problem of felting her cloth; but the thought that he had been up all night doing something for her only made her feel worse. She ran past the stable, through the priory gate, and along the street, her boots slipping and sliding in the mud, until she reached her house.

When she got inside she found Richard there. He was sitting at the kitchen table with a loaf of bread and a bowl of ale. "King Stephen is on the march," he said. "The war has started again. I need a new horse."

IV

For the next three months Aliena hardly spoke two words in a row to Jack.

He was heartbroken. She had kissed him as if she loved him, there was no mistaking that. When she left the mill he felt sure they would kiss like that again, soon. He walked around in an erotic haze, thinking: Aliena loves me! Aliena loves me! She had stroked his back and put her tongue into his mouth and pressed her breasts against him. When she avoided him he thought at first that she was just embarrassed. She could not possibly pretend not to love him, after that kiss. He waited for her to get over her shyness. With the help of the priory carpenter he made a stronger, more permanent fulling mechanism for the old mill, and Aliena got her cloth felted. She thanked him sincerely, but her voice was cold and her eyes evaded his.

When it had gone on not just for a few days, but for several weeks, he was forced to admit that there was something seriously wrong. A tidal wave of disillusionment engulfed him, and he felt as if he would drown in regret. He was baffled. He wished miserably that he was older, and had more experience with women, so that he could tell whether she was normal or peculiar, whether this was temporary or permanent, and whether he should ignore it or confront her. Being uncertain, and also being terrified of saying the wrong thing and making matters worse, he did nothing; and then the constant feeling of rejection began to get to him, and he felt worthless, stupid, and impotent. He thought how foolish he was, to have imagined that the most desirable and unattainable woman in the county might fall for him, a mere boy. He had amused her for a while, with his stories and his jokes, but as soon as he had kissed her like a man, she had run away. What a fool he was to have hoped for anything else!

After a week or two of telling himself how stupid he was he began to get angry. He was irritable at work, and people started to treat him warily. He was mean to his stepsister, Martha, who was almost as hurt by him as he was by Aliena. On Sunday afternoons he wasted his wages gambling on cockfights. All his passion came out in his work. He was carving corbels, the jutting-out stones that appeared to support arches or shafts that did not reach all the way to the ground. Corbels were often decorated with leaves, but a traditional alternative was to carve a man who appeared to be holding up the arch with his hands or supporting it on his back. Jack altered the customary pattern just a little, but the effect was to show a disturbingly twisted human figure with an expression of pain, condemned, as it were, to an eternity of agony as he held up the vast weight of stone. Jack knew it was brilliant: nobody else could carve a figure that looked as if it were in pain. When Tom saw it he shook his head, unsure whether to marvel at its expressiveness or disapprove of its unorthodoxy. Philip was very taken with it. Jack did not care what they thought: he felt that anyone who disliked it was blind.

One Monday in Lent, when everyone was short-tempered because they had not eaten meat for three weeks, Alfred came to work with a triumphant look on his face. He had been to Shiring the day before. Jack did not know what he had done there but he was clearly pleased about it.

During the midmorning break, when Enid Brewster tapped a barrel of ale in the middle of the chancel and sold it to the builders, Alfred held out a penny and called: "Hey, Jack Tomson, fetch me some ale."

This is going to be about my father, Jack thought. He ignored Alfred.

One of the carpenters, an older man called Peter, said: "You'd better do what you're told, prentice boy." An apprentice was always supposed to obey a master craftsman.

"I'm not Tom's son," Jack said. "Tom is my stepfather, and Alfred knows it."

"Do what he says, all the same," Peter said in a reasonable tone.

Reluctantly, Jack took Alfred's money and joined the line. "My father's name was Jack Shareburg," he said in a loud voice. "You can all call me Jack Jackson, if you want to make a difference between me and Jack Blacksmith."

Alfred said: "Jack Bastard is more like it."

Jack said to the world at large: "Have you ever wondered why Alfred never laces up his boots?" They all looked at Alfred's feet. Sure enough, his heavy, muddy boots, which were designed to be tied at the top with cords, were loosely open. "It's so that he can get at his toes quickly—in case he needs to count above ten." The craftsmen smiled and the apprentices chortled. Jack handed Alfred's penny to Enid and got a jug of ale. He took it to Alfred and handed it to him with a small satirical bow. Alfred was annoyed, but not very; he still had something up his sleeve. Jack moved away and drank his ale with the apprentices, hoping Alfred would lay off.

It was not to be. A few moments later Alfred followed him, and said: "If Jack Shareburg was my father I wouldn't be so quick to claim him. Don't you realize what he was?"

"He was a jongleur," Jack said. He made himself sound confident, but he was afraid of what Alfred was going to say. "I don't suppose you know what a jongleur is."

"He was a thief," said Alfred.

"Oh, shut up, shithead." Jack turned away and sipped his beer, but he could hardly swallow. Alfred had a reason for saying this.

"Don't you know how he died?" Alfred persisted.

This is it, Jack thought; this is what he learned yesterday in Shiring; this is why he's wearing that stupid grin. He turned around reluctantly and faced Alfred. "No, I don't know how my father died, Alfred, but I think you're going to tell me."

"He was hanged by the neck, like the lousy thief he was."

Jack gave an involuntary cry of anguish. He knew intuitively that this was true. Alfred was so completely sure of himself that he could not be making it up. And Jack saw in a flash that this explained his mother's reticence. For years he had secretly dreaded something like this. All the time he had pretended there was nothing wrong, he was not a bastard, he had a real father with a real name. In fact he had always feared that there was a disgrace about his father, that the taunts were valid, that he really did have something to be ashamed of. He was already low: Aliena's rejection had left him feeling worthless and small. Now the truth about his father hit him like a blow.

Alfred stood there smiling, inordinately pleased with himself: the effect of his revelation had delighted him. His expression maddened Jack. It was bad enough, for Jack, that his father had been hanged. That Alfred was happy about it was too much to bear. Without thinking, Jack threw his beer in Alfred's grinning face.

The other apprentices, who had been watching the two stepbrothers and enjoying the altercation, hastily moved a step or two back. Alfred dashed the beer from his eyes, roared with anger, and lashed out with one huge fist, a surprisingly quick movement for such a big man. The blow connected with Jack's cheek, so hard that instead of hurting, it just went numb. Before he had time to react, Alfred's other fist sank into his middle. This punch hurt terribly. Jack felt as if he would never breathe again. He crumpled and fell to the ground. As he landed, Alfred kicked him in the head with one heavy boot, and for a moment he saw nothing but white light.

He rolled over blindly and struggled to his feet. But Alfred was not yet satisfied. As Jack came upright he felt himself grabbed. He began to wriggle. He was frightened now. Alfred would have no mercy. Jack would be beaten to a pulp if he could not escape. For a moment Alfred's grip was too strong and Jack could not get free, but then Alfred drew back one massive fist for a blow, and in that instant Jack slipped out of his grasp.

He darted away and Alfred lunged after him. Jack dodged around a lime barrel, pulling it over so that it fell in Alfred's path, spilling lime on the ground. Alfred jumped over the barrel but cannoned into a water butt and that, too, was upset. When the water came into contact with the lime it boiled and hissed fiercely. Some of the builders, seeing the waste of costly material, shouted protests, but Alfred was deaf to them, and Jack could think of nothing but trying to get away from Alfred. He ran, still doubled up with pain and half blind from the kick in the head.

Hard on his heels, Alfred stuck out a foot and tripped him. Jack fell headlong. I'm going to die, he thought as he rolled over; Alfred will kill me now. He fetched up under a ladder that was leaning against the scaffolding high up on the building. Alfred bore down on him. Jack felt like a cornered rabbit. The ladder saved him. As Alfred ducked behind it, Jack dodged around to the front and catapulted himself up the rungs. He went up the ladder like a rat up a gutter.

He felt the ladder shake as Alfred came up behind him. Normally he could outrun Alfred, but he was still dazed and winded. He reached the top and lurched onto the scaffolding. He stumbled and fell against the wall. The stonework had been laid that morning and the mortar was still wet. As Jack careered into it, a whole section of the wall shifted, and three or four stones slipped sideways and fell over the side. Jack thought he was going with them. He teetered at the edge, and as he looked down he saw the big stones tumbling over and over as they fell eighty feet and landed on the roofs of the lean-to lodges at the foot of the wall. He righted himself and hoped no one was in the lodges. Alfred came up over the top of the ladder and advanced toward him on the flimsy scaffolding.

Alfred was red and panting, and his eyes were full of hate. Jack had no doubt that in this state Alfred could kill. If he gets hold of me, Jack thought, he'll throw me over the side. As Alfred advanced, Jack retreated. He trod in something soft and realized it was a pile of mortar. Inspired, he stooped quickly, picked up a handful, and threw it accurately into Alfred's eyes.

Blinded, Alfred stopped advancing and shook his head, trying to get rid of the mortar. At last Jack had a chance to escape. He ran to the far end of the scaffolding platform, intending to descend, run out of the priory close, and spend the rest of the day hiding in the forest. But to his horror there was no ladder at the other end of the platform. He could not climb down the scaffolding, for it did not reach to the ground—it was built on joists stuck into putlog holes in the wall. He was trapped.

He looked back. Alfred had got his eyesight back and was coming toward him.

There was one other way down.

At the unfinished end of the wall, where the chancel would join on to the transept, each course of masonry was half a stone's length shorter than the one below, creating a steep flight of narrow steps, which was sometimes used by the more daring laborers as an alternative way up to the platform. With his heart in his mouth Jack got on top of the wall and walked along, carefully but quickly, trying not to see how far he would fall if he slipped. He reached the top of the stepped section, paused at the edge, and looked down. He felt faintly sick. He glanced back over his shoulder: Alfred was on the wall behind him. He went down.

Jack could not understand why Alfred was so unafraid: he had never been brave. It was as if hatred had dulled his sense of danger. As they ran down the dizzily steep steps, Alfred was gaining on Jack. They were still more than twelve feet off the ground when Jack realized Alfred was very nearly on him. In desperation he jumped off the side of the wall onto the thatched roof of the carpenters' lodge. He bounced off the roof onto the ground, but he landed badly, twisting his ankle, and he fell to the ground.

He staggered upright. The seconds he lost by falling had enabled Alfred to reach the ground and run to the lodge. For a split second Jack stood with his back to the wall, and Alfred paused, waiting to see which way he would jump. Jack suffered a moment of terrified indecision; then, inspired, he stepped to one side and backed into the lodge.

It was empty of craftsmen, for they were all standing around Enid's barrel. On the benches were the hammers and saws and chisels of the carpenters, and the pieces of wood they had been working on. In the middle of the floor was a large piece of new falsework, to be used in building an arch; and at the back, up against the church wall, was a blazing fire, fed by shavings and off-cuts from the carpenters' raw material.

There was no way out.

Jack turned to face Alfred. He was cornered. For a moment he was paralyzed with fright. Then his fear gave way to anger. I don't care if I get killed, he thought, so long as I make Alfred bleed before I die. He did not wait for Alfred to hit him. He lowered his head and charged. He was too maddened even to use his fists. He simply ran into Alfred full tilt.

It was the last thing Alfred expected. Jack's forehead smashed into his mouth. Jack was two or three inches shorter and a lot lighter, but all the same his charge threw Alfred back. As Jack recovered his balance he saw blood on Alfred's lips, and he was satisfied.

For a moment Alfred was too surprised to react. In that instant, Jack's eye lit on a big wooden sledgehammer leaning against a bench. As Alfred recovered his wits and came at Jack, Jack lifted the hammer and swung it wildly. Alfred dodged back and the hammer missed him. Suddenly Jack had the upper hand. Encouraged, he went after Alfred, already relishing the sensation of solid wood crunching Alfred's bones. This time he put all his strength into the blow. Once again it missed Alfred; but it connected with the pole supporting the roof of the lodge.

The lodge was not solidly constructed. Nobody lived in it. Its only function was to enable the carpenters to work in the rain. When Jack hit the pole with the hammer, the pole moved. The walls were flimsy hurdles of interwoven twigs, and gave no support at all. The thatched roof sagged. Alfred looked up fearfully. Jack hefted the hammer. Alfred backed through the door. Jack swung at him again. Alfred dodged back, tripped over a low stack of timber, and sat down heavily. Jack raised the hammer high for the coup de grâce. His arms were seized in a strong grasp. He looked around and saw Prior Philip, with a face like thunder. Philip wrenched the hammer from Jack's grip.

Behind the prior, the roof of the lodge fell in. Jack and Philip looked. As it fell into the fire, the dry thatch caught alight instantly, and a moment later there was a fierce blaze.

Tom appeared and pointed at the three workmen nearest to him. "You, you and you—bring that water butt from outside the smithy." He turned to three others. "Peter, Rolf, Daniel, fetch buckets. You apprentices, shovel earth over the flames—all of you, and quick about it!"

For the next few minutes everyone concentrated on the fire, and Alfred and Jack were forgotten. Jack got out of the way and stood watching, feeling stunned and helpless. Alfred stood some distance away. Was I really about to smash Alfred's head with a hammer? Jack though incredulously. The whole thing seemed unreal. He was still in a state of dazed shock when the combination of water and earth put out the flames.

Prior Philip stood looking at the mess, breathing hard after his exertions. "Look at that," he said to Tom. He was furious. "A lodge wrecked. Carpenters' work ruined. A barrel of lime wasted and a whole section of new masonry destroyed."

Jack realized that Tom was in trouble: it was his job to keep order on the site and Philip blamed him for the damage. The fact that the culprits were Tom's sons made it even worse.

Tom put his hand on Philip's arm and spoke softly. "The lodge will deal with it," he said.

Philip was not to be mollified. "I will deal with it," he snapped. "I'm the prior and you all work for me."

"Then allow the masons to deliberate before you make any decisions," Tom said in a quiet and reasonable voice. "We may come up with a proposal that will recommend itself to you. If not, you're still free to do what you will."

Philip was visibly reluctant to let the initiative pass from his hands, but tradition was on Tom's side: the masons disciplined themselves. After a pause Philip said: "Very well. But whatever you decide, I will not have both your sons working on this site. One of them must go." Still fuming, he strode away.

With a black look at Jack and Alfred, Tom turned away and went into the largest of the masons' lodges.

Jack realized he was in serious trouble as he followed Tom into the lodge. When the masons disciplined one of their number it was usually for offenses such as drunkenness at work and theft of building materials, and the commonest punishment was a fine. Fighting between apprentices generally resulted in both combatants being put in the stocks for a day, but of course Alfred was not an apprentice, and anyway, fights did not normally do so much damage. The lodge could expel a member who worked for less than the agreed minimum wage. It could also punish a member who committed adultery with another mason's wife, although Jack had never known this. Theoretically, apprentices could be flogged, but although this punishment was sometimes threatened he had never seen it carried out.

The master masons crowded into the wooden lodge, sitting on the benches and leaning against the back wall, which was in fact the side of the cathedral. When they were all inside, Tom said: "Our employer is angry, and with justification. This incident has done a lot of costly damage. Worse, it has brought disgrace on us masons. We must deal firmly with those who are to blame. This is the only way to regain our good reputation as proud and disciplined builders, men who are masters of ourselves as well as masters of our craft."

"Well said," Jack Blacksmith called out, and there was a murmur of agreement.

"I only saw the end of this fight," Tom went on. "Did anyone see it start?"

"Alfred went for the lad," said Peter Carpenter, the one who had advised Jack to be obedient and fetch Alfred's ale.

A young mason called Dan, who worked for Alfred, said: "Jack threw beer in Alfred's face."

"The lad was provoked, though," said Peter. "Alfred insulted Jack's natural father."

Tom looked at Alfred. "Did you?"

"I said his father was a thief," Alfred replied. "It's true. He was hanged for it at Shiring. Sheriff Eustace told me yesterday."

Jack Blacksmith said: "It's a poor thing if a master craftsman has to hold his tongue in case an apprentice doesn't like what he says."

There was a murmur of approval. Jack realized despondently that, whatever happened, he was not going to get off lightly. Perhaps I'm doomed to be a criminal, like my father, he thought; perhaps I'll end up on the gallows too.

Peter Carpenter, who was emerging as Jack's defender, said: "I still say it makes a difference if the craftsman went out of his way to anger the apprentice."

"The apprentice still has to be punished," said Jack Blacksmith.

"I don't deny that," said Peter. "I just think the craftsman ought to be disciplined too. Master craftsmen should use the wisdom of their years to bring about peace and harmony on a building site. If they provoke fights they fail in their duty."

There appeared to be some agreement with that, but Dan, Alfred's supporter, said: "It's a dangerous principle, to forgive the apprentice because the craftsman was unkind. Apprentices always think masters are unkind. If you start arguing that way you'll end up with masters never speaking to their apprentices for fear the apprentices will strike them for discourtesy."

That speech drew warm support, to Jack's disgust. It just showed that the masters' authority had to be bolstered, regardless of the rights and wrongs of the case. He wondered what his punishment would be. He had no money to pay a fine. He hated the thought of being put in the stocks: what would Aliena think of him? But it would be worse to be flogged. He thought he would knife anyone who tried to flog him.

Tom said: "We mustn't forget that our employer also has a strong view about this. He says he will not have both Alfred and Jack working on the site. One of them must go."

"Might he be talked out of that?" said Peter.

Tom looked thoughtful, but after a pause he said: "No."

Jack was shocked. He had not taken Prior Philip's ultimatum seriously. But Tom had.

Dan said: "If one of them has to go, I trust there's no argument about which it will be." Dan was one of the masons working for Alfred, rather than directly for the priory, and if Alfred went Dan would probably have to go too.

Once again Tom looked thoughtful, and once again he said: "No, no argument." He looked at Jack. "Jack must be the one to go."

Jack realized he had fatally underestimated the consequences of the fight. But he could hardly believe they were going to throw him out. What would life be like if he did not work on Kingsbridge Cathedral? Since Aliena had withdrawn into her shell, the cathedral was all he cared about. How could he leave?

Peter Carpenter said: "The priory might accept a compromise. Jack could be suspended for a month."

Yes, please, thought Jack.

"Too weak," said Tom. "We must be seen to act decisively. Prior Philip will not accept anything less."

"So be it," Peter said, giving in. "This cathedral loses the most talented young stone carver most of us have ever seen, all because Alfred can't keep his damn mouth shut." Several masons voiced their approval of that sentiment. Encouraged, Peter went on: "I respect you, Tom Builder, more than I've ever respected any master builder I've worked for, but it must be said that you've got a blind spot about your pigheaded son Alfred."

"No abuse, please," Tom said. "Let's stick to the facts of the case."

"All right," Peter said. "I say Alfred must be punished."

"I agree," Tom said, to everyone's surprise. Jack thought the remark about his blind spot had got to him. "Alfred should be disciplined."

"Why?" Alfred said indignantly. "For beating an apprentice?"

"He's not your apprentice, he's mine," Tom said. "And you did more than beat him. You chased him all over the site. If you had let him run away the lime wouldn't have spilled, the masonry wouldn't have been damaged and the carpenters' lodge wouldn't have

burned down; and you could have dealt with him as soon as he
came back. There was no need for what you did."

The masons agreed.

Dan, who seemed to have become the spokesman for Alfred's
masons, said: "I hope you're not proposing we expel Alfred from
the lodge. I for one will fight against that."

"No," Tom said. "It's bad enough to lose a talented apprentice.
I don't also want to lose a sound mason who runs a reliable gang.
Alfred must stay—but I think he should be fined."

Alfred's men looked relieved.

"A heavy fine," said Peter.

"A week's wages," Dan proposed.

"A month's," said Tom. "I doubt whether Prior Philip will be
satisfied with less."

Several men said: "Aye."

"Are we of one mind on this, brother masons?" Tom said,
using a customary form of words.

"Aye," they all said.

"Then I will tell the prior our decision. The rest of you had
better go back to work."

Jack watched miserably as they all filed out. Alfred shot him a
look of smug triumph. Tom waited until they had all gone, then said
to Jack: "I did my best for you—I hope your mother will see that."

"You've never done anything for me!" Jack burst out. "You
couldn't feed me or clothe me or house me. We were happy until
you came along, and then we starved!"

"But in the end—"

"You won't even protect me from that mindless brute you call
your son!"

"I tried—"

"You wouldn't even have this job if I hadn't burned the old
cathedral down!"

"What did you say?"

"Yes, I burned the old cathedral."

Tom went pale. "That was lightning—"

"There was no lightning. It was a fine night. And no one had
made a fire in the church, either. I set light to the roof."

"But why?"

"So that you would have work. Otherwise my mother would
have died in the forest."

"She wouldn't—"

"Your first wife did, though, didn't she?"

Tom turned white. Suddenly he looked older. Jack realized that he had wounded Tom profoundly. He had won the argument, but he had probably lost a friend. He felt sour and sad.

Tom whispered: "Get out of here."

Jack left.

He walked away from the towering walls of the cathedral, close to tears. His life had been devastated in a few moments. It was incredible that he was going away from this church forever. He turned at the priory gate and looked back. There were so many things he had been planning. He wanted to carve a whole doorway all by himself; he wanted to persuade Tom to have stone angels in the clerestory; he had an innovative design for blind arcading in the transepts which he had not even shown to anyone yet. Now he would never do any of these things. It was so unfair. His eyes filled with tears.

He made his way home, seeing through a blur. Mother and Martha were sitting at the kitchen table. Mother was teaching Martha to write with a sharp stone and a slate. They were surprised to see him. Martha said: "It can't be dinnertime already."

Mother read Jack's face. "What is it?" she said anxiously.

"I had a fight with Alfred and got expelled from the site," he said grimly.

"Wasn't Alfred expelled?" said Martha.

Jack shook his head.

"That's not fair!" Martha said.

Mother said wearily: "What did you fight about this time?"

Jack said: "Was my father hanged at Shiring for thieving?"

Martha gasped.

Mother looked sad. "He wasn't a thief," she said. "But yes, he was hanged at Shiring."

Jack was fed up with enigmatic statements about his father. He said brutally: "Why will you never tell me the truth?"

"Because it makes me so sad!" Mother burst out, and to Jack's horror she began to cry.

He had never seen her cry. She was always so strong. He was close to breaking down himself. He swallowed hard and persisted. "If he wasn't a thief, why was he hanged?"

"I don't know!" Mother cried. "I never knew. He never knew either. They said he stole a jeweled cup."

"From whom?"

"From here—from Kingsbridge Priory."

"Kingsbridge! Did Prior Philip accuse him?"

"No, no, it was long before the time of Philip." She looked at Jack through her tears. "Don't start asking me who accused him and why. Don't get caught in that trap. You could spend the rest of your life trying to put right a wrong done before you were born. I didn't raise you so that you could take revenge. Don't make that your life."

Jack vowed he would learn more sometime, despite what she said; but right now he wanted her to stop crying. He sat beside her on the bench and put his arm around her. "Well, it looks as if the cathedral won't be my life, now."

Martha said: "What will you do, Jack?"

"I don't know. I can't live in Kingsbridge, can I?"

Martha was distraught. "But why not?"

"Alfred tried to kill me and Tom expelled me from the site. I'm not going to live with them. Anyway, I'm a man. I should leave my mother."

"But what will you do?"

Jack shrugged. "The only thing I know about is building."

"You could work on another church."

"I might come to love another cathedral as much as I love this one, I suppose," he said despondently. He was thinking: But I'll never love another woman the way I love Aliena.

Mother said: "How could Tom do this to you?"

Jack sighed. "I don't think he really wanted to. Prior Philip said he wouldn't have me and Alfred both working on the site."

"So that damned monk is at the bottom of this!" Mother said angrily. "I swear—"

"He was very upset about the damage we did."

"I wonder if he could be made to see reason."

"What do you mean?"

"God is supposed to be merciful—perhaps monks should be too."

"You think I should plead with Philip?" Jack asked, somewhat surprised at the direction of Mother's thinking.

"I was thinking I might talk to him," she said.

"You!" That was even more uncharacteristic. Jack was quite shocked. For Mother to be willing to ask Philip for mercy, she must be badly upset.

"What do you think?" she asked him.

Tom had seemed to think Philip would not be merciful, Jack recalled. But then, Tom's overriding concern had been that the lodge should take decisive action. Having promised Philip that they would be firm, Tom could not then plead for mercy. Mother was not in the same position. Jack began to feel a little more hopeful. Perhaps he would not have to leave after all. Perhaps he could stay in Kingsbridge, close to the cathedral and to Aliena. He no longer hoped that she would love him, but nevertheless he hated the thought of going away and never seeing her again.

"All right," he said. "Let's go and plead with Prior Philip. We've got nothing to lose but our pride."

Mother put on her cloak and they went out together, leaving Martha sitting alone at the table, looking anxious.

Jack and his mother did not often walk side by side, and now he was struck by how short she was: he towered over her. He felt suddenly fond of her. She was always ready to fight like a cat for his sake. He put his arm around her and hugged her. She smiled at him as if she knew what he was thinking.

They entered the priory close and went to the prior's house. Mother banged on the door and walked in. Tom was there with Prior Philip. Jack knew immediately, by their faces, that Tom had *not* told Philip about Jack setting fire to the old cathedral. That was a relief. Now he probably never would. That secret was safe.

Tom looked anxious, if not a little scared, when he saw Mother. Jack recalled that he had said *I did my best for you, I hope your mother will see that.* Tom was remembering the last time Jack and Alfred had a fight: Mother had left Tom in consequence. Tom was afraid she would leave now.

Philip was no longer looking angry, Jack thought. Perhaps the lodge's decision had mollified him. He might even be feeling a trifle guilty about his harshness.

Mother said: "I've come here to ask you to be merciful, Prior Philip."

Tom immediately looked relieved.

Philip said: "I'm listening."

Mother said: "You're proposing to send my son away from everything he loves—his home, his family and his work."

And the woman he adores, Jack thought.

Philip said: "Am I? I thought he had simply been dismissed from his work."

"He's never learned any kind of work but building, and there's no other building work in Kingsbridge for him. And the challenge of that vast church has got into his blood. He'll go wherever someone is building a cathedral. He'll go to Jerusalem if there's stone there to be carved into angels and devils." How does she know all this? Jack wondered. He had hardly thought it himself—but it was true. She added: "I might never see him again." Her voice shook a little at the end, and he thought wonderingly how much she must love him. She would never plead like this for herself, he knew.

Philip looked sympathetic, but it was Tom who replied. "We can't have Jack and Alfred working on the same site," he said doggedly. "They'll fight again. You know that."

"Alfred could go," Mother said.

Tom looked sad. "Alfred is *my* son."

"But he's twenty years old, and he's as mean as a bear!" Although Mother's voice was assertive, her cheeks were wet with tears. "He doesn't care for this cathedral any more than I do—he'd be perfectly happy building houses for butchers and bakers in Winchester or Shiring."

"The lodge can't expel Alfred and keep Jack," Tom said. "Besides, the decision is already made."

"But it's the wrong decision!"

Philip spoke. "There might be another answer."

Everyone looked at him.

"There might be a way for Jack to stay in Kingsbridge, and even devote himself to the cathedral, without falling foul of Alfred."

Jack wondered what was coming. This sounded too good to be true.

"I need someone to work with me," Philip went on. "I spend too much time making detail decisions on the building. I need a kind of assistant, who would fulfill the role of clerk of works. He would deal with most of the queries himself, referring only the most important questions to me. He would also keep track of the money and the raw materials, handling payments to suppliers and carters, and wages too. Jack can read and write, and he can add numbers faster than anyone I've ever met—"

"And he understands every aspect of building," Tom put in. "I've seen to that."

Jack's mind was spinning. He could stay after all! He would be clerk of works. He would not be carving stone, but he would be supervising the entire design on Philip's behalf. It was an astonishing proposal. He would have to deal with Tom as an equal. But he knew he was capable of it. And Tom did too.

There was one snag. Jack voiced it. "I can't live with Alfred any longer."

Ellen said: "It's time Alfred had a home of his own, anyway. Perhaps if he left us he'd be more serious about finding a wife."

Tom said angrily: "You keep thinking of reasons for getting rid of Alfred. I'm not going to throw my own son out of my house!"

"You don't understand me, either of you," Philip said. "You haven't completely comprehended my proposal. Jack would not be living with you."

He paused. Jack guessed what was coming next, and it was the last, and biggest, shock of the day.

Philip said: "Jack would have to live here, in the priory." He looked at them with a little frown, as if he could not see why they still had not grasped his meaning.

Jack had understood him. He recalled Mother saying, on Midsummer Eve last year, *That sly prior has a knack of getting his own way in the end.* She had been right. Philip was renewing the offer he had made then. But this time it was different. The choice Jack now faced was stark. He could leave Kingsbridge, and abandon everything he loved. Or he could stay, and lose his freedom.

"My clerk of works can't be a layman, of course," Philip finished, in the tone of one who states the obvious. "Jack will have to become a monk."

V

On the night before the Kingsbridge Fleece Fair, Prior Philip stayed up after the midnight services, as usual; but instead of reading and meditating in his house, he made a tour of the priory close. It was a warm summer night, with a clear sky and a moon, and he could see without the aid of a lantern.

The entire close had been taken over by the fair, with the exception of the monastic buildings and the cloisters, which were sacred. In each of the four corners a huge latrine pit had been dug, so that the rest of the close would not become completely foul, and the latrines had been screened off to safeguard the sensibilities of the monks. Literally hundreds of market stalls had been erected. The simplest were nothing more than crude wooden counters on trestles. Most were a little more elaborate: they had a signboard with the name of the stall holder and a picture of his wares, a separate table for weighing, and a locked cupboard or shed to keep the goods in. Some stalls incorporated tents, either to keep the rain off or so that business could be done in private. The most elaborate stalls were small houses, with large storage areas, several counters, and tables and chairs where the merchant could offer hospitality to his important customers. Philip had been surprised when the first of the merchants' carpenters had arrived a full week before the fair and demanded to be shown where to erect his stall, but the structure that went up had taken four days to build and two to stock.

Philip had originally planned the layout of the stalls in two wide avenues on the west side of the close, in much the same configuration as the stalls of the weekly market; but he had soon realized that that would not be enough. The two avenues of stalls now ran all along the north side of the church as well, and then turned down the east end of the close as far as Philip's house; and there were more stalls actually inside the unfinished church, in the aisles between the piers. The stall holders were not all wool merchants by any means: everything was sold at a fair, from horsebread to rubies.

Philip walked along the moonlit rows. They were all ready now, of course: no stall building would be allowed today. Most of them were also stocked with goods. The priory had already collected more than ten pounds in fees and duties. The only goods that could be brought in on the day of the fair were freshly cooked foods, bread and hot pies and baked apples. Even the barrels of beer had been brought in yesterday.

As Philip walked around, he was watched by dozens of half-open eyes, and greeted by several sleepy grunts. The stall holders would not leave their precious goods unguarded: most of them were sleeping at their stalls, and the wealthier merchants had left servants on guard.

He was not yet certain exactly how much money he would make from the fair, but it was virtually guaranteed to be a success, and he was confident of reaching his original estimate of fifty pounds. There had been moments, in the past few months, when he had feared that the fair would not take place at all. The civil war dragged on, with neither Stephen nor Maud gaining the upper hand, but his license had not been revoked. William Hamleigh had tried to sabotage the fair in various ways. He had told the sheriff to ban it, but the sheriff had asked for authority from one of the two rival monarchs, and it had not been forthcoming. William had forbidden his tenants to sell wool at Kingsbridge; but most of them were anyway in the habit of selling to merchants such as Aliena, rather than marketing the fleeces themselves, so the main effect of the ban was to create more business for her. Finally, he had announced that he was reducing the rents and duties at the Shiring Fleece Fair to the levels Philip was charging; but his announcement came too late to make much difference, for the big buyers and sellers had already made their plans.

Now, with the sky growing perceptibly lighter in the east on the morning of the big day, William could do no more. The sellers were here with their wares, and in a little while the buyers would begin to arrive. Philip thought William would find that in the end the Kingsbridge Fleece Fair damaged the Shiring fair less than he feared. Sales of wool seemed to go up every year without fail: there was enough business for two fairs anyway.

He had walked all the way around the close to the southwest corner, where the mills and the fishpond were. He stood there for a while, watching the water flow past the two silent mills. One was now used exclusively for felting cloth, and it made a lot of money. Young Jack was responsible for that. He had an ingenious mind. He was going to be a tremendous asset to the priory. He seemed to have settled quite well as a novice, although he tended to regard the services as a distraction from cathedral building, rather than the other way around. However, he would learn. The monastic life was a sanctifying influence. Philip thought God had a purpose for Jack. In the very back of Philip's mind was a secret long-term hope: that one day Jack would take his place as prior of Kingsbridge.

Jack got up at dawn and slipped out of the dormitory before the service of prime to make one last inspection tour of the building site. The morning air was cool and clear, like pure water from a spring. It would be a warm, sunny day, good for business, good for the priory.

He walked around the cathedral walls, making sure that all the tools and work-in-progress were safely locked inside the lodges. Tom had built light wooden fences around the stockpiles of timber and stone, to guard the raw materials against accidental damage by careless or drunken visitors. They did not want any daredevils climbing the structure, so all the ladders were safely hidden away, the spiral staircases in the thickness of the walls were closed off with temporary doors, and the stepped ends of the part-built walls were obstructed by wooden blocks. Some of the master craftsmen would be patrolling the site throughout the day to make sure there was no damage.

Jack managed to skip quite a lot of the services, one way or another. There was always something to be done on site. He did not have his mother's hatred of the Christian religion, but he was more or less indifferent to it. He had no enthusiasm for it, but he was willing to go through the motions if it suited his purpose. He made sure to go to one service every day, usually one that was attended either by Prior Philip or the novice-master, who were the two senior monks most likely to notice his presence or absence. He could not have borne it if he had to attend them all. Being a monk was the strangest and most perverted way of life imaginable. Monks spent half their lives putting themselves through pain and discomfort that they could easily avoid, and the other half muttering meaningless mumbo jumbo in empty churches at all hours of the day and night. They deliberately shunned anything good—girls, sports, feasting and family life. However, Jack had noted, the happiest among them had usually found some pursuit that gave deep satisfaction: illustrating manuscripts, writing history, cooking, studying philosophy, or—like Philip—changing Kingsbridge from a sleepy village into a thriving cathedral city.

Jack did not like Philip but he liked working with him. Jack did not warm to professional men of God any more than his mother did. He was embarrassed by Philip's piety; he disliked his single-minded sinlessness; and he mistrusted his tendency to believe that

God would take care of anything that he, Philip, could not cope with. Nevertheless, Philip was good to work for. His orders were clear, he left Jack room to make decisions for himself, and he never blamed his servants for his own mistakes.

Jack had been a novice only three months, so he would not be asked to take vows for another nine months. The three vows were poverty, celibacy and obedience. The vow of poverty was not all it seemed. Monks had no personal possessions and no money of their own, but they lived more like lords than like peasants—they had good food, warm clothes and fine stone buildings to live in. Celibacy was no problem, Jack thought bitterly. He had gained a certain cold satisfaction from telling Aliena personally that he was entering the monastery. She had looked shocked and guilty. Now, whenever he felt the restless irritability that came from the lack of female companionship, he would think of how Aliena had treated him—their secret assignations in the forest, their winter evenings, the two times he had kissed her—and then he would recall how she had suddenly turned as cold and hard as a rock; and thinking of that made him feel that he never wanted to have anything more to do with women. However, the vow of obedience would be difficult to keep, he could tell already. He was happy to take orders from Philip, who was intelligent and organized; but it was hard to obey the foolish sub-prior, Remigius, or the drunken guest-master, or the pompous sacrist.

Nevertheless, he was contemplating taking the vows. He did not have to keep them. All he cared about was building the cathedral. The problems of supply, construction and management were endlessly absorbing. One day he might have to help Tom devise a method of checking that the number of stones arriving at the site was the same as the number leaving the quarry—a complex problem, for the journey time varied between two days and four, so it was not possible to have a simple daily tally. Another day the masons might complain that the carpenters were not making the falsework properly. Most challenging of all were the engineering problems, such as how to lift tons of stone to the top of the walls using makeshift machinery fixed to flimsy scaffolding. Tom Builder discussed these problems with Jack as with an equal. He seemed to have forgiven Jack for that angry speech, in which Jack said that Tom had never done anything for him. And Tom acted as if he had forgotten the revelation that Jack had set fire to the old cathedral. They worked together cheerfully, and the days flew by. Even during the tedious services Jack's mind was occupied by some knotty question of construction or planning. His knowledge was increasing fast.

Instead of spending years carving stones, he was learning cathedral design. There could hardly have been a better training for someone who wanted to be a master builder. For that, Jack was prepared to yawn through any number of midnight matins.

The sun was edging over the east wall of the priory close. Everything was in order on the site. The stall holders who had spent the night with their goods were beginning to fold away their bedding and put out their wares. The first customers would be here soon. A baker walked past Jack carrying a tray of new loaves on her head. The smell of hot fresh bread made Jack's mouth water. He turned and went back to the monastery, heading for the refectory, where they would soon be serving breakfast.

The first customers were the families of the stall holders and the townspeople, all curious to look at the first Kingsbridge Fleece Fair, none very interested in buying. Thrifty people had filled their bellies with horsebread and porridge before leaving home, so that they would not be tempted by the highly spiced and garishly colored confections on the food stalls. The children wandered around wide-eyed, dazzled by the display of desirable things. An optimistic early-rising whore with red lips and red boots sauntered along, smiling hopefully at middle-aged men, but there were no takers at this hour.

Aliena watched it all from her stall, which was one of the biggest. In the last few weeks she had taken delivery of Kingsbridge Priory's entire output of fleece for the year; the wool for which she had paid a hundred and seven pounds last summer. She had also been buying from farmers, as she always did; and this year there had been more sellers than usual, because William Hamleigh had forbidden his tenants to sell at the Kingsbridge fair, so they had all sold to merchants. And of all the merchants, Aliena had got the most business, because she was based at Kingsbridge where the fair was to be held. She had done so well that she had run out of money for buying, and had borrowed forty pounds from Malachi to keep her going. Now, in the warehouse that formed the rear half of her stall, she had a hundred and sixty sacks of raw wool, the product of forty thousand sheep, and it had cost her more than two hundred pounds, but she would sell it for three hundred, which was enough money to pay the wages of a skilled mason for over a century. The sheer scale of her own business amazed her whenever she thought of the numbers.

She did not expect to see her buyers until midday. There would be only five or six of them. They would all know each other, and she would know most of them from previous years. She would give each one a cup of wine, and sit and talk for a while. Then she would show him her wool. He would ask her to open a sack or two—never the top one on the pile, of course. He would plunge his hand deep into the sack and bring out a handful of wool. He would tease out the strands to determine their length, rub them between finger and thumb to test their softness, and sniff them. Finally he would offer to buy her entire stock at a ridiculously low price, and Aliena would refuse him. She would tell him her asking price, and he would shake his head. They would take another glass of wine.

Aliena would go through the same ritual with another buyer. She would give dinner to as many of them as were there at midday. Someone would offer to take a large quantity of wool at a price not much above what Aliena had paid for it. She would counter by dropping her asking price a shade. In the early afternoon she would begin closing deals. Her first deal would be at a lowish price. The other merchants would demand that she deal with them at the same price, but she would refuse. Her price would go up during the course of the afternoon. If it went up too fast, business would be slow, while the merchants calculated how soon they could fill their quotas elsewhere. If she was asking less than they were willing to pay, she would know by the relative haste with which they reached agreement. She would close deals one by one, and their servants would begin loading the huge sacks of wool onto the ox wagons with their enormous wooden wheels, while Aliena weighed the pound bags of silver pennies and guilders.

There was no doubt that today she would rake in more money than ever before. She had twice as much to sell, and wool prices were up. She planned to buy Philip's output a year in advance again, and she had a secret scheme to build herself a stone house, with spacious cellars for storage of wool, an elegant and comfortable hall, and a pretty upstairs bedroom just for herself. Her future was secure, and she was confident of being able to support Richard as long as he needed her. Everything was perfect.

That was why it was so strange that she was completely and utterly miserable.

It was four years, almost to the day, since Ellen had returned to Kingsbridge, and they had been the best four years of Tom's life.

The pain of Agnes's death had dulled to an ache. It was still with him, but he no longer got that embarrassing feeling that he was about to burst into tears every now and again for no apparent reason. He still held imaginary conversations with her, in which he told her about the children, and Prior Philip, and the cathedral; but the conversations were less frequent. The bittersweet memory of her had not blighted his love for Ellen. He was able to live in the present. Seeing Ellen and touching her, talking to her and sleeping with her were daily joys.

He had been deeply wounded, on the day of the fight between Jack and Alfred, by Jack's saying that Tom had never looked after him; and that accusation had overshadowed even the appalling revelation that Jack had set fire to the old cathedral. He had agonized over it for several weeks, but in the end he had decided that Jack was wrong. Tom had done his best, and no man could do any more. Having reached that conclusion he had stopped worrying.

Building Kingsbridge Cathedral was the most profoundly satisfying work he had ever done. He was responsible for the design and the execution. No one interfered with him, and there was no one else to blame if things went wrong. As the mighty walls rose, with their rhythmic arches, their graceful moldings, and their individual carvings, he could look around and think: I did all this, and I did it well.

His nightmare, that one day he would again find himself on the road with no work, no money and no way of feeding his children, seemed very far away, now that there was a stout money chest full to bursting with silver pennies buried under the straw in his kitchen. He still shuddered when he remembered that cold, cold night when Agnes had given birth to Jonathan and died; but he felt sure nothing that bad would ever happen again.

He sometimes wondered why Ellen and he had not had children. They had both been proved fertile in the past, and there was no shortage of opportunities for her to get pregnant—they still made love almost every night, even after four years. However, it was not a cause of deep regret to him. Little Jonathan was the apple of his eye.

He knew, from past experience, that the best way to enjoy a fair was with a small child, so he sought Jonathan out around midmorning, when the crowds began to arrive. Jonathan was almost an attraction in his own right, dressed as he was in his miniature habit. He had lately conceived a desire to have his head shaved, and Philip had indulged him—Philip was as fond of the child as Tom was— with the result that he looked more than ever like a tiny little monk. There were several real midgets in the crowd, performing tricks and begging, and they fascinated Jonathan. Tom had to hurry him away from one who drew a crowd by exposing his full-size penis. There were jugglers, acrobats and musicians performing and passing a hat round; soothsayers and surgeons and whores touting for business; trials of strength, wrestling contests and games of chance. People were wearing their most colorful clothes, and those who could afford it had doused themselves with scent and oiled their hair. Everyone seemed to have money to spend, and the air was full of the jingle of silver.

The bearbaiting was about to begin. Jonathan had never seen a bear, and he was fascinated. The animal's grayish-brown coat was scarred in several places, indicating that it had survived at least one previous contest. A heavy chain around its waist was fixed to a stake driven deep into the ground, and it was padding around on all fours at the limit of the chain, glaring angrily at the waiting crowd. Tom fancied he saw a cunning light in the beast's eye. Had he been a gambling man, he might have bet on the bear.

The sound of frantic barking came from a locked chest to one side. The dogs were in there, and they could smell their enemy. Every now and again the bear would stop his pacing, look at the box, and growl; and the barking would rise to hysteria pitch.

The owner of the animals, the bearward, was taking bets. Jonathan became impatient, and Tom was about to move on when at last the bearward unlocked the box. The bear stood upright at the limit of its chain and snarled. The bearward shouted something and threw the chest open.

Five greyhounds sprang out. They were light and fast-moving, and their gaping mouths showed sharp little teeth. They all went straight for the bear. The bear lashed out at them with its massive paws. It struck one dog and sent it flying; then the others backed off.

The crowd pushed closer. Tom checked on Jonathan: he was at the front, but still well out of the bear's reach. The bear was clever enough to draw back to the stake, letting its chain go loose, so that when it lunged it would not be brought up short. But the dogs were smart, too. After their initial scattered attack they regrouped and then spread out in a circle. The bear swung around in an agitated fashion, trying to see all ways at once.

One of the dogs rushed at it, yapping fiercely. The bear came to meet it and lashed out. The dog quickly retreated, staying out of reach; and the other four rushed in from all sides. The bear swung around, swiping at them. The crowd cheered as three of them sank their teeth into the flesh of its haunches. It rose on its hind legs with a roar of pain, shaking them off, and they scrambled out of reach.

The dogs tried the same tactic once more. Tom thought the bear was going to fall for it again. The first dog darted within its reach, the bear went for it, and the dog backed off; but when the other dogs rushed the bear it was ready for them, and it turned quickly, lunged at the nearest, and swiped the dog's side with its paw. The crowd cheered as much for the bear as they had for the dogs. The bear's sharp claws ripped the dog's silky skin and left three deep bloody tracks. The dog yelped pitifully and retired from the fight to lick its wounds. The crowd jeered and booed.

The remaining four dogs circled the bear warily, making the occasional rush but turning back well before the danger point. Someone started a slow handclap. Then a dog made a frontal attack. It rushed in like a streak of lightning, slipped under the bear's swipe, and leaped for its throat. The crowd went wild. The dog sank its pointed white teeth into the bear's massive neck. The other dogs attacked. The bear reared up, pawing at the dog at its throat, then went down and rolled. For a moment Tom could not tell what was happening: there was just a flurry of fur. Then three dogs jumped clear, and the bear righted itself and stood on all fours, leaving one dog on the ground, crushed to death.

The crowd became tense. The bear had eliminated two dogs, leaving three; but it was bleeding from its back, neck and hind legs, and it looked frightened. The air was full of the smell of blood and the sweat of the crowd. The dogs had stopped yapping, and were circling the bear silently. They too looked scared, but they had the taste of blood in their mouths and they wanted a kill.

Their attack began the same way: one of them rushed in and rushed out again. The bear swiped at it halfheartedly and swung around to meet the second dog. But now this one, too, cut short its rush and retreated out of reach; and then the third dog did the same. The dogs darted in and out, one at a time, keeping the bear constantly shifting and turning. With each rush they got a little closer, and the bear's claws came a little nearer to catching them. The spectators could see what was happening, and the excitement in the crowd grew. Jonathan was still at the front, just a few steps from Tom, looking awestruck and a little frightened. Tom looked back at the fight just in time to see the bear's claws brush one dog while another dashed between the great beast's hind legs and savaged its soft belly. The bear made a sound like a scream. The dog dashed out from under it and escaped. Another dog rushed the bear. The bear slashed at it, missing by inches; and then the same dog went for its underbelly again. This time when the dog escaped it left the bear with a huge bleeding gash in its abdomen. The bear reared up and went down on all fours again. For a moment Tom thought it was finished, but he was wrong: the bear still had some fight left in it. When the next dog rushed in, the bear made a token swipe at it, turned its head, saw the second dog coming, turned surprisingly fast and hit it with a mighty blow that sent it flying through the air. The crowd roared with delight. The dog landed like a bag of meat. Tom watched it for a moment. It was alive, but it seemed unable to move. Perhaps its back was broken. The bear ignored it, for it was out of reach and out of action.

Now there were only two dogs left. They both darted in and out of the bear's reach several times, until its lunges at them became perfunctory; then they began to circle it, moving faster and faster. The bear turned this way and that, trying to keep them both in sight. Exhausted and bleeding copiously, it could hardly stay upright. The dogs went around in ever-decreasing circles. The earth beneath the bear's mighty paws had been turned to mud by all the blood. One way or another, the end was in sight. Finally the two dogs attacked at once. One went for the throat and the other for the belly. With a last desperate swipe, the bear slashed the dog at its throat. There was a grisly fountain of blood. The crowd yelled their approval. At first Tom thought the dog had killed the bear, but it was the other way around: the blood came from the dog, which now fell to the ground with its throat slashed open. Its blood pumped out for a moment longer, then stopped. It was dead. But in the meantime the last dog had ripped open the bear's belly, and now its guts were falling out. The bear swiped feebly at the dog. The dog easily evaded the blow and struck again, savaging the bear's intestines. The bear swayed and seemed about to fall. The roar of the crowd grew to a crescendo. The bear's ripped guts gave out a revolting stench. It gathered its strength and struck at the dog again. The blow connected, and the dog jumped sideways, with blood oozing from a slash along its back; but the wound was super-ficial and the dog knew the bear was finished, so it went right back on the attack, biting at the bear's guts until, at last, the great animal closed its eyes and slumped to the ground, dead.

The bearward came forward and took the victorious dog by the collar. The Kingsbridge butcher and his apprentice stepped out of the crowd and began to cut the bear up for its meat: Tom supposed they had agreed on a price with the bearward in advance. Those who had won their bets demanded to be paid. Everyone wanted to pat the surviving dog. Tom looked for Jonathan. He could not see him.

The child had been just a couple of yards away throughout the bearbaiting. How had he managed to disappear? It must have happened while the sport was at its height, and Tom was concentrating on the spectacle. Now he was cross with himself. He searched the crowd. Tom was a head taller than everyone else, and Jonathan was easy to spot with his monk's habit and shaved head; but he was nowhere to be seen.

The child could not come to much harm in the priory close, but he might come across things that Prior Philip would prefer him not to see: whores servicing their clients up against the priory wall, for example. Looking around, Tom glanced up at the scaffolding high on the cathedral building, and there, to his horror, he saw a small figure in a monastic robe.

He felt a moment of panic. He wanted to yell *Don't move, you'll fall!* but his words would have been lost in the noise of the fair. He pushed through the crowd toward the cathedral. Jonathan was running along the scaffolding, absorbed in some imaginary game, heedless of the danger that he might slip and fall over the edge and tumble eighty feet to his death—

Tom quenched the terror rising like bile in his throat.

The scaffolding did not rest on the ground, but on heavy timbers inserted into purpose-built holes high up in the walls. These timbers jutted out six feet or so. Stout poles were laid across them and roped to them, and then trestles made of flexible saplings and woven reeds were laid on the poles. The scaffolding was normally reached via the spiral stone staircases built into the thickness of the walls. But those staircases had been closed off today. So how had Jonathan climbed up? There were no ladders—Tom had seen to that, and Jack had double-checked. The child must have climbed up the stepped end of the unfinished wall. The ends had been built up with wood, so that they no longer provided easy access; but Jonathan could have clambered over the blocks. The child was full of self-confidence—but all the same he fell over at least once a day.

Tom reached the foot of the wall and looked up fearfully. Jonathan was playing happily eighty feet above. Fear gripped Tom's heart with a cold hand. He shouted at the top of his voice: "Jonathan!"

The people around him were startled, and looked up to see what he was shouting at. As they spotted the child on the scaffolding they pointed him out to their friends. A small crowd gathered.

Jonathan had not heard. Tom cupped his hands around his mouth and shouted again. "Jonathan! Jonathan!"

This time the boy heard. He looked down, saw Tom, and waved.

Tom shouted: "Come down!"

Jonathan seemed about to obey, then he looked at the wall along which he would have to walk, and the steep flight of steps he would have to descend, and he changed his mind. "I can't!" he called back, and his high voice floated down to the people on the ground.

Tom realized he was going to have to go up and get him. "Just stay where you are until I reach you!" he shouted. He pushed the blocks of wood off the lower steps and mounted the wall.

It was four feet wide at the foot, but it narrowed as it went up. Tom climbed steadily. He was tempted to rush, but he forced himself to be calm. When he glanced up he saw Jonathan sitting on the edge of the scaffolding, dangling his short legs over the sheer drop.

At the very top the wall was only two feet thick. Even so, it was plenty wide enough to walk on, provided you had strong nerves, and Tom did. He made his way along the wall, jumped down onto the scaffolding, and took Jonathan in his arms. He was swamped with relief. "You foolish boy," he said, but his voice was full of love, and Jonathan hugged him.

After a moment Tom looked down again. He saw a sea of upturned faces: a hundred or more people were watching. They probably thought it was another show, like the bearbaiting. Tom said to Jonathan: "All right, let's go down now." He set the boy on the wall, and said: "I'll be right behind you, so don't worry."

Jonathan was not convinced. "I'm scared," he said. He held out his arms to be picked up, and when Tom hesitated he burst into tears.

"Never mind, I'll carry you," Tom said. He was not very happy about it, but Jonathan was now too upset to be trusted at this height. Tom clambered onto the wall, knelt beside Jonathan, picked him up, and stood upright.

Jonathan held on tight.

Tom stepped forward. Because he had the child in his arms he could not see the stones immediately beneath his feet. That could not be helped. With his heart in his mouth, he walked gingerly along the wall, placing his feet cautiously. He had no fear for himself, but with the child in his arms he was terrified. At last he came to the beginning of the steps. It was no wider here at first, but somehow it seemed less precipitous, with the steps in front of him. He started down gratefully. With each step he felt calmer. When he reached the level of the gallery, and the wall widened to three feet, he paused to let his heartbeat slow down.

He looked out, past the priory close, over Kingsbridge, to the fields beyond, and there he saw something that puzzled him. There was a cloud of dust on the road leading to Kingsbridge, about half a mile away. After a moment he realized that he was looking at a large troop of men on horseback, approaching the town at a smart trot. He peered into the distance, trying to figure out who they were. At first he thought it must be a very wealthy merchant, or a group of merchants, with a large entourage, but there were too many of them, and somehow they did not look like commercial people. He tried to put his finger on what it was about them that made him think they were something other than merchants. As they came closer he saw that some of them were riding war-horses, most had helmets, and they were armed to the teeth.

Suddenly he felt scared.

"Jesus Christ, who are those people?" he said aloud.

"Don't say 'Christ,'" Jonathan reprimanded him.

Whoever they were, they meant trouble.

Tom hurried down the steps. The crowd cheered as he jumped down to the ground. He ignored them. Where were Ellen and the children? He looked all around, but he could not see them.

Jonathan tried to wriggle out of his arms. Tom held him tight. As he had his youngest child right here, the first thing to do was to put him somewhere safe. Then he could find the others. He pushed through the crowd to the door that led into the cloisters. It was locked from the inside, to preserve the privacy of the monastery during the fair. Tom banged on it and yelled: "Open up! Open up!"

Nothing happened.

Tom was not even sure there was anyone in the cloisters. There was no time to speculate. He stepped back, put Jonathan down, lifted his large booted right foot and kicked at the door. The wood around the lock splintered. He kicked it again, harder. The door flew open. Just the other side of it was an elderly monk, looking astonished. Tom lifted Jonathan and put him inside. "Keep him in there," he said to the old monk. "There's going to be trouble."

The monk nodded dumbly and took Jonathan's hand.

Tom closed the door.

Now he had to find the rest of his family in a crowd of a thousand or more.

The near impossibility of the task scared him. He could not see a single familiar face. He climbed onto an empty beer barrel to get a better view. It was midday, and the fair was at its height. The crowd moved like a slow river along the aisles between the stalls, and there were eddies around the vendors of food and drink as people queued to buy dinner. Tom raked the crowds but he could not see any of his family. He despaired. He looked over the roofs of the houses. The riders were almost at the bridge, and had increased their pace to a gallop. They were men-at-arms, all of them, and they carried firebrands. Tom was horrified. There would be mayhem.

Suddenly he saw Jack right beside him, looking up at him with an expression of amusement. "Why are you standing on a barrel?" he said.

"There's going to be trouble!" Tom said urgently. "Where's your mother?"

"At Aliena's stall. What sort of trouble?"

"Bad. Where are Alfred and Martha?"

"Martha's with Mother. Alfred's watching the cockfighting. What is it?"

"See for yourself." Tom gave Jack a hand up. Jack stood precariously on the rim of the barrel in front of Tom. The riders were pounding across the bridge into the village. Jack said: "Christ Jesus, who are they?"

Tom peered at the leader, a big man on a war-horse. He recognized the yellow hair and heavy build. "It's William Hamleigh," he said.

As the riders reached the houses they touched their torches to the roofs, setting fire to the thatch. "They're burning the town!" Jack exploded.

"It's going to be even worse than I thought," Tom said. "Get down."

They both jumped to the ground.

"I'll get Mother and Martha," Jack said.

"Take them to the cloisters," Tom said urgently. "It will be the only safe place. If the monks object, tell them to go shit."

"What if they lock the door?"

"I just broke the lock. Go quickly! I'll fetch Alfred. Go!"

Jack hurried away. Tom headed for the cockpit, roughly pushing people aside. Several men objected to his shoving but he ignored them and they shut up when they saw his size and the look of stony determination on his face. It was not long before the smoke of the burning houses blew into the priory close. Tom smelled it, and he noticed one or two other people sniffing the air curiously. He had only a few moments left before panic broke out.

The cockpit was near the priory gate. There was a large, noisy crowd around it. Tom shoved through, looking for Alfred. In the middle of the crowd was a shallow hole in the ground a few feet across. In the center of the hole, two cocks were tearing each other to pieces with beaks and spurred claws. There were feathers and blood everywhere. Alfred was near the front, watching intently, yelling at the top of his voice, encouraging one or other of the wretched birds. Tom forced his way between the packed people and grabbed Alfred's shoulder. "Come!" he shouted.

"I've got sixpence on the black one!" Alfred shouted back.

"We've got to get out of here!" Tom yelled. At that moment a drift of smoke blew over the cockpit. "Can't you smell the fire?"

One or two of the spectators heard the word *fire* and looked at Tom curiously. The smell came again, and they picked it up. Alfred smelled it too. "What is it?" he said.

"The town is on fire!" Tom said.

Suddenly everyone wanted to leave. The men dispersed in all directions, pushing and shoving. In the pit, the black cock killed the brown, but nobody cared anymore. Alfred started to go the wrong way. Tom grabbed him. "We'll go to the cloisters," he said. "It's the only safe place."

The smoke began to come over in billows, and fear spread through the crowd. Everyone was agitated but no one knew what to do. Looking over the heads, Tom could see that people were pouring out through the priory gate; but the gate was narrow, and anyway they were no safer out there than in here. Nevertheless, more people got the idea, and he and Alfred found themselves struggling against a tide of people frantically going in the opposite direction. Then, quite suddenly, the tide turned, and everyone was going their way. Tom looked around to discover the reason for the change, and saw the first of the horsemen ride into the close.

At that point the crowd became a mob.

The riders were a terrifying sight. Their huge horses, just as frightened as the crowd, plunged and reared and charged, trampling people left, right and center. The armed and helmeted riders laid about them with clubs and torches, felling men, women and children, and setting fire to stalls, clothes, and people's hair. Everyone was screaming. More riders came through the gate, and more people disappeared beneath the massive hooves. Tom shouted in Alfred's ear: "You go on to the cloisters—I want to make sure the others have got clear. Run!" He gave him a shove. Alfred took off.

Tom headed for Aliena's stall. Almost immediately he tripped over someone and fell to the ground. Cursing, he got to his knees; but before he could stand upright he saw a war-horse bearing down on him. The beast's ears were back and its nostrils were flared, and Tom could see the whites of its terrified eyes. Above the horse's head, Tom saw the beefy face of William Hamleigh, distorted into a grimace of hatred and triumph. The thought flashed through his mind that it would be nice to hold Ellen in his arms once again. Then a massive hoof kicked him in the exact center of his forehead, he felt a dreadful, frightening pain as his skull seemed to burst open, and the whole world went black.

*　　*　　*

The first time Aliena smelled smoke, she thought it was coming from the dinner she was serving.

Three Flemish buyers were sitting at the table in the open air in front of her storehouse. They were corpulent, black-bearded men who spoke English with a heavy Germanic accent and wore clothes of exquisitely fine cloth. Everything was going well. She was close to starting the selling, and had decided to serve lunch first in order to give the buyers time to get anxious. Nevertheless, she would be glad when this vast fortune in wool became someone else's. She put the platter of honey-roast pork chops in front of them and looked critically at it. The meat was done to a turn, with the border of fat just crisp and brown. She poured more wine. One of the buyers sniffed the air, then they all looked around anxiously. Aliena was suddenly fearful. Fire was the wool merchant's nightmare. She looked at Ellen and Martha, who were helping her serve dinner. "Can you smell smoke?" she said.

Before they could reply Jack appeared. Aliena had not got used to seeing him in a monk's habit, with his carrot-colored hair shaved from the top of his head. There was an agitated look on his sweet face. She felt a sudden urge to take him in her arms and kiss away the frown on his forehead. But she turned away quickly, remembering how she had let herself down with him in the old mill six months ago. She still flushed for shame every time she recalled that incident.

"There's trouble," he shouted urgently. "We must all take refuge in the cloisters."

She looked at him. "What's happening—is there a fire?"

"It's Earl William and his men-at-arms," he said.

Aliena suddenly felt as cold as the grave. William. Again.

Jack said: "They've set fire to the town. Tom and Alfred are going to the cloisters. Come with me, please."

Ellen unceremoniously dropped the bowl of greens she was carrying onto the table in front of a startled Flemish buyer. "Right," she said. She grabbed Martha by the arm. "Let's go."

Aliena shot a panicky look at her storehouse. She had hundreds of pounds' worth of raw wool in there that she had to protect from fire—but how? She caught Jack's eye. He was looking at her expectantly. The buyers left the table hurriedly. Aliena said to Jack: "Go. I have to look after my stall."

Ellen said: "Jack—come on!"

"In a moment," he said, and turned back to Aliena.

Aliena saw Ellen hesitate. She was clearly torn between saving Martha and waiting for Jack. Again she said: "Jack! Jack!"

He turned to her. "Mother! Take Martha!"

"All right!" she said. "But *please* hurry!" She and Martha left.

Jack said: "The town is on fire. The cloisters will be the safest place—they're made of stone. Come with me, quickly."

Aliena could hear screams from the direction of the priory gate. The smoke was suddenly everywhere. She looked all around, trying to make out what was happening. Her insides were knotted with fear. Everything she had worked for for over six years was stacked up in the storehouse.

Jack said: "Aliena! Come to the cloisters—we'll be safe there!"

"I can't!" she shouted. "My wool!"

"To hell with your wool!"

"It's all I've got!"

"It's no good to you if you're dead!"

"It's easy for you to say that—but I've spent all these years getting to this position—"

"Aliena! *Please!*"

Suddenly the people right outside the stall were screaming in mortal terror. The riders had entered the priory close and were charging through the crowds, regardless of whom they trampled, setting fire to the stalls. Terror-stricken people were crushing one another in their desperate attempts to get out of the way of the flying hooves and the firebrands. The crowd pressed against the flimsy wooden hurdle that formed the front of Aliena's stall, and it immediately collapsed. People spilled onto the open space in front of the storehouse and upset the table with its plates of food and cups of wine. Jack and Aliena were forced back. Two riders charged into the stall, one swinging a club at random, the other brandishing a flaming torch. Jack pushed himself in front of Aliena, shielding her. The club came down at Aliena's head, but Jack threw a protective arm over her, and the club smashed down on his wrist. She felt the blow but he took the impact. When she looked up she saw the face of the second rider.

It was William Hamleigh.

Aliena screamed.

He looked at her for a moment, with the torch blazing in his hand and the light of triumph glittering in his eyes. Then he kicked his horse and forced it into her storehouse.

"No!" Aliena screamed.

She struggled to escape from the crush, shoving and punching those around her, including Jack. At last she got free and dashed into the storehouse. William was leaning out from the saddle, putting his torch to the piled sacks of wool. "No!" she screamed again. She threw herself at him and tried to pull him off the horse. He brushed her aside and she fell to the ground. He held his torch to the woolsacks again. The wool caught fire with a mighty roar. The horse reared and screamed in terror at the flames. Suddenly Jack was there, pulling Aliena out of the way. William wheeled the horse and went out of the storehouse fast. Aliena got to her feet. She picked up an empty sack and tried to beat the flames out. Jack said: "Aliena, you'll be killed!" The heat became agonizing. She grabbed at a woolsack that was not yet on fire, and tried to pull it free. Suddenly she heard a roaring in her ears and felt intense heat on her face, and she realized in terror that her hair was on fire. An instant later Jack threw himself at her, wrapping his arms around her head and pulling her tightly against his body. They both fell to the ground. He held her hard for a moment, then loosed his hold. She smelled singed hair but it was no longer burning. She could see that Jack's face was burned and his eyebrows had gone. He grabbed her by one ankle and dragged her out through the door. He kept on pulling her, despite her struggles, until they were well clear.

The area of her stall had emptied. Jack released his hold on her. She tried to get up, but he grabbed her and held her down. She continued to struggle, staring madly at the fire that was consuming all her years of work and worry, all her wealth and security, until she had no energy left to fight him. Then she just lay there and screamed.

Philip was in the undercroft beneath the priory kitchen, counting money with Cuthbert Whitehead, when he heard the noise. He and Cuthbert looked at one another, frowning, then got up to see what was going on.

They stepped through the door into a riot.

Philip was horrified. People were running in every direction, pushing and shoving, falling over and treading on one another. Men and women were shouting and children were crying. The air was full of smoke. Everyone seemed to be trying to get out of the priory close. Apart from the main gate, the only exit was through the gap between the kitchen buildings and the mill. There was no wall there, but there was a deep ditch that carried water from the millpond to the brewery. Philip wanted to warn people to be careful of the ditch, but nobody was listening to anyone.

The cause of the rush was obviously a fire, and a very big one. The air was thick with the smoke of it. Philip was full of fear. With this many people all crowded together, the slaughter could be appalling. What could be done?

First he had to find out exactly what was going on. He ran up the steps to the kitchen door, to get a better view. What he saw filled him with dread.

The entire town of Kingsbridge was alight.

A cry of horror and despair escaped his throat.

How could this be happening?

Then he saw the horsemen, charging through the crowd with their burning firebrands, and he realized that it was not an accident. His first thought was that there was a battle going on between the two sides in the civil war, and somehow it had engulfed Kingsbridge. But the men-at-arms were attacking the citizens, not one another. This was no battle: it was a massacre.

He saw a large blond man on a massive war-horse crashing through the crowds of people. It was William Hamleigh.

Hatred rose in Philip's gorge. To think that the slaughter and destruction going on all around had been caused deliberately, for reasons of greed and pride, drove him half mad. He shouted at the top of his voice: "I see you, William Hamleigh!"

William heard his name called over the screams of the crowd. He reined in his horse and met Philip's eye.

Philip yelled: "You'll go to hell for this!"

William's face was suffused with bloodlust. Even the threat of what he feared most had no effect on him today. He was like a madman. He waved his firebrand in the air like a banner. "This is hell, monk!" he shouted back; and he wheeled his horse and rode on.

Suddenly everyone had disappeared, the riders and the crowds. Jack released his hold on Aliena and stood up. His right hand felt numb. He remembered that he had taken the blow aimed at Aliena's head. He was glad his hand hurt. He hoped it would hurt for a long time, to remind him.

The storehouse was an inferno, and smaller fires burned all around. The ground was littered with bodies, some moving, some bleeding, some limp and still. Apart from the crackle of the flames it was quiet. The mob had got out, one way or another, leaving their dead and wounded behind. Jack felt dazed. He had never seen a battlefield but he imagined it must look like this.

Aliena started to cry. Jack put a comforting hand on her shoulder. She pushed it off. He had saved her life, but she did not care for that: she cared only for her damned wool, which was now irretrievably lost in smoke. He looked at her for a moment, feeling sad. Most of her hair had burned away, and she no longer looked beautiful, but he loved her all the same. It hurt him to see her so distraught, and not to be able to comfort her.

He felt sure she would not try to go into the storehouse now. He was worried about the rest of his family, so he left Aliena and went looking for them.

His face hurt. He put a hand to his cheek, and his own touch stung him. He must have got burned too. He looked at the bodies on the ground. He wanted to do something for the wounded, but he did not know where to begin. He searched for familiar faces among the strangers, hoping not to see any. Mother and Martha had gone to the cloisters—they had been well ahead of the mob, he thought. Had Tom found Alfred? He turned toward the cloisters. Then he saw Tom.

His stepfather's tall body was stretched out full length on the muddy ground. It was perfectly still. His face was recognizable, even peaceful-looking, up to the eyebrows; but his forehead was open and his skull was completely smashed. Jack was appalled. He could not take it in. Tom could not be dead. But this thing could not be alive. He looked away, then looked back. It was Tom, and he was dead.

Jack knelt beside the body. He felt the urge to do something, or say something, and for the first time he understood why people liked to pray for the dead. "Mother is going to miss you terribly," he said. He remembered the angry speech he had made to Tom on the day of his fight with Alfred. "Most of that wasn't true," he said, and the tears started to flow. "You didn't fail me. You fed me and took care of me, and you made my mother happy, truly happy." But there was something more important than all that, he thought. What Tom had given him was nothing so commonplace as food and shelter. Tom had given him something unique, something no other man had to give, something even his own father could not have given him; something that was a passion, a skill, an art, and a way of life. "You gave me the cathedral," Jack whispered to the dead man. "Thank you."

PART FOUR

1142 – 1145

Chapter 11

WILLIAM'S TRIUMPH WAS RUINED by Philip's prophecy: instead of feeling satisfied and jubilant, he was terrified that he would go to hell for what he had done.

He had answered Philip bravely enough, jeering "This is hell, monk!" but that had been in the excitement of the attack. When it was over, and he had led his men away from the blazing town; when their horses and their heartbeats had slowed down; when he had time to look back over the raid, and think of how many people he had wounded and burned and killed; then he recalled Philip's angry face, and his finger pointing straight down into the bowels of the earth, and the doom-laden words: "You'll go to hell for this!"

By the time darkness fell he was completely depressed. His men-at-arms wanted to talk over the operation, reliving the high spots and relishing the slaughter, but they soon caught his mood and relapsed into gloomy silence. They spent that night at the manor house of one of William's larger tenants. At supper the men grimly drank themselves senseless. The tenant, knowing how men normally felt after a battle, had brought in some whores from Shiring; but they did poor business. William lay awake all night, terrified that he might die in his sleep and go straight to hell.

The following morning, instead of returning to Earlscastle, he went to see Bishop Waleran. He was not at his palace when they arrived, but Dean Baldwin told William that he was expected that afternoon. William waited in the chapel, staring at the cross on the altar and shivering despite the summer heat.

When Waleran arrived at last, William felt like kissing his feet.

The bishop swept into the chapel in his black robes and said coldly: "What are you doing here?"

William got to his feet, trying to hide his abject terror behind a facade of self-possession. "I've just burned the town of Kingsbridge—"

"I know," Waleran interrupted. "I've been hearing about nothing else all day. What possessed you? Are you mad?"

This reaction took William completely by surprise. He had not discussed the raid with Waleran in advance because he had been so sure Waleran would approve: Waleran hated everything to do with Kingsbridge, especially Prior Philip. William had expected him to be pleased, if not gleeful. William said: "I've just ruined your greatest enemy. Now I need to confess my sins."

"I'm not surprised," Waleran said. "They say more than a hundred people burned to death." He shuddered. "A horrible way to die."

"I'm ready to confess," William said.

Waleran shook his head. "I don't know that I can give you absolution."

A cry of fear escaped William's lips. "Why not?"

"You know that Bishop Henry of Winchester and I have taken the side of King Stephen again. I don't think the king would approve of my giving absolution to a supporter of Queen Maud."

"Damn you, Waleran, it was you who persuaded me to change sides!"

Waleran shrugged. "Change back."

William realized that this was Waleran's objective. He wanted William to switch his allegiance to Stephen. Waleran's horror at the burning of Kingsbridge had been faked: he had simply been establishing a bargaining position. This realization brought enormous relief to William, for it meant that Waleran was not implacably opposed to giving him absolution. But did he want to switch again? For a moment he said nothing as he tried to think about it calmly.

"Stephen has been winning victories all summer," Waleran went on. "Maud is begging her husband to come over from Normandy to help her, but he won't. The tide is flowing our way."

An awful prospect opened up before William: the Church refused to absolve him from his crimes; the sheriff accused him of murder; a victorious King Stephen backed the sheriff and the Church; and William himself was tried and hanged. . . .

"Be like me, and follow Bishop Henry—he knows which way the wind blows," Waleran urged. "If everything works out right,

Winchester will be made an archdiocese, and Henry will be the archbishop of Winchester—on a par with the archbishop of Canterbury. And when Henry dies, who knows? I could be the next archbishop. After that . . . well, there are English cardinals already—one day there may be an English pope. . . ."

William stared at Waleran, mesmerized, despite his own fear, by the naked ambition revealed on the bishop's normally stony face. Waleran as pope? Anything was possible. But the immediate consequences of Waleran's aspirations were more important. William could see that he was a pawn in Waleran's game. Waleran had gained in prestige, with Bishop Henry, by his ability to deliver William and the knights of Shiring to one side or the other in the civil war. That was the price William had to pay for having the Church turn a blind eye to his crimes. "Do you mean . . ." His voice was hoarse. He coughed and tried again. "Do you mean that you will hear my confession if I swear allegiance to Stephen and come over to his side again?"

The glitter went from Waleran's eyes and his face became expressionless again. "That's exactly what I mean," he said.

William had no choice, but in any event he could see no reason to refuse. He had switched to Maud when she appeared to be winning, and he was quite ready to switch back now that Stephen seemed to be gaining the upper hand. Anyway, he would have consented to anything to be free of that awful terror of hell. "Agreed, then," he said without further hesitation. "Only hear my confession, quickly."

"Very well," said Waleran. "Let us pray."

As they went briskly through the service, William felt the load of guilt fall from his back, and he gradually began to be pleased about his triumph. When he emerged from the chapel his men could see that his spirits had lifted, and they cheered up immediately. William told them that they would once again be fighting for King Stephen, in accordance with the will of God as expressed by Bishop Waleran, and they made that the excuse for a celebration. Waleran called for wine.

While they were waiting for dinner, William said: "Stephen ought to confirm me in my earldom now."

"He ought to," Waleran agreed. "But that doesn't mean he will."

"But I've come over to his side!"

"Richard of Kingsbridge never left it."

William permitted himself a smug smile. "I think I've disposed of the threat from Richard."

"Oh? How?"

"Richard has never had any land. The only way he's been able to keep up a knightly entourage is by using his sister's money."

"It's unorthodox, but it's worked so far."

"But now his sister no longer has any money. I set fire to her barn yesterday. She's destitute. And so is Richard."

Waleran nodded acknowledgment. "In that case it's only a matter of time before he disappears from sight. And then, I should think, the earldom is yours."

Dinner was ready. William's men-at-arms sat below the salt and flirted with the palace laundresses. William was at the head of the table with Waleran and his archdeacons. Now that he had relaxed, William rather envied the men with the laundresses: archdeacons made dull company.

Dean Baldwin offered William a dish of peas and said: "Lord William, how will you prevent someone else from doing what Prior Philip tried to do, and starting his own fleece fair?"

William was surprised by this question. "They wouldn't dare!"

"Another monk wouldn't dare, perhaps; but an earl might."

"He'd need a license."

"He might get one, if he fought for Stephen."

"Not in this county."

"Baldwin is right, William," said Bishop Waleran. "All around the borders of your earldom there are towns that could hold a fleece fair: Wilton, Devizes, Wells, Marlborough, Wallingford. . . ."

"I burned Kingsbridge, I can burn any place," William said irritably. He took a swallow of wine. It angered him to have his victory deprecated.

Waleran took a roll of new bread and broke it without eating any. "Kingsbridge is an easy target," he argued. "It has no town wall, no castle, not even a big church for people to take refuge in. And it's run by a monk who has no knights or men-at-arms. Kingsbridge is defenseless. Most towns aren't."

Dean Baldwin added: "And when the civil war is over, whoever wins, you won't even be able to burn a town like Kingsbridge and get away with it. That's breaking the king's peace. No king could overlook it in normal times."

William saw their point and it made him angry. "Then the whole thing might have been for nothing," he said. He put down his knife. His stomach was cramped with tension and he could no longer eat.

Waleran said: "Of course, if Aliena is ruined, that leaves a kind of vacancy."

William did not follow him. "What do you mean?"

"Most of the wool in the county was sold to her this year. What will happen next year?"

"I don't know."

Waleran continued in the same thoughtful manner. "Apart from Prior Philip, all the wool producers for miles around are either tenants of the earl or tenants of the bishop. You're the earl, in every-thing but name, and I'm the bishop. If we forced all our tenants to sell their fleeces to us, we would control two thirds of the wool trade in the county. We would sell at the Shiring Fleece Fair. There wouldn't be enough business left to justify another fair, even if someone got a license."

It was a brilliant idea, William saw immediately. "And we'd make as much money as Aliena did," he pointed out.

"Indeed." Waleran took a delicate bite of the meat in front of him and chewed reflectively. "So you've burned Kingsbridge, ruined your worst enemy, and established a new source of income for yourself. Not a bad day's work."

William took a deep draft of wine, and felt a glow in his belly. He looked down the table, and his eye lit on a plump dark-haired girl who was smiling coquettishly at two of his men. Perhaps he would have her tonight. He knew how it would be. When he got her in a corner, and threw her on the floor, and lifted her skirt, he would remember Aliena's face, and the expression of terror and despair as she saw her wool going up in flames; and then he would be able to do it. He smiled at the prospect, and took another slice off the haunch of venison.

Prior Philip was shaken to the core by the burning of Kingsbridge. The unexpectedness of William's move, the brutality of the attack, the dreadful scenes as the crowd panicked, the awful slaughter, and his own utter impotence, all combined to leave him stunned.

Worst of all was the death of Tom Builder. A man at the height of his skill, and a master of every aspect of his craft, Tom had been expected to continue to manage the building of the cathedral until it was finished. He was also Philip's closest friend outside the cloisters. They had talked at least once a day, and struggled together to find solutions to the endless variety of problems that confronted them in their vast project. Tom had had a rare combination of wisdom and humility that made him a joy to work with. It seemed impossible that he was gone.

Philip felt that he did not understand anything anymore, he had no real power, and he was not competent to be in charge of a cow shed, much less a town the size of Kingsbridge. He had always believed that if he did his honest best and trusted in God, everything would turn out well in the end. The burning of Kingsbridge seemed to have proved him wrong. He lost all motivation, and sat in his house at the priory all day long, watching the candle burn down on the little altar, thinking disconnected, desolate thoughts, doing nothing.

It was young Jack who saw what had to be done. He got the dead bodies taken to the crypt, put the wounded in the monks' dormitory, and organized emergency feeding for the living in the meadow on the other side of the river. The weather was warm, and everyone slept in the open air. The day after the massacre, Jack organized the dazed townspeople into teams of laborers and got them to clear the ashes and debris from the priory close, while Cuthbert Whitehead and Milius Bursar ordered supplies of food from surrounding farms. On the second day they buried their dead in one hundred and ninety-three new graves on the north side of the priory close.

Philip simply issued the orders that Jack proposed. Jack pointed out that most of the citizens who had survived the fire had lost very little of material value—just a hovel and a few sticks of furniture, in most cases. The crops were still in the fields, the livestock were in the pastures, and people's savings were still where they had been buried, usually beneath the hearth of their homes, untouched by the aboveground blaze that had swept the town. The merchants whose stocks had burned were the greatest sufferers: some were ruined, as Aliena was; others had some of their wealth in buried silver, and would be able to start again. Jack proposed rebuilding the town immediately.

At Jack's suggestion, Philip gave extraordinary permission for timber to be cut freely in the priory's forests for the purpose of rebuilding houses, but only for one week. In consequence Kingsbridge was deserted for seven days while every family selected and felled the trees they would use for their new homes. During that week, Jack asked Philip to draw a plan of the new town. The idea caught Philip's imagination and he came out of his depression.

He worked on his plan nonstop for four days. There would be large houses all around the priory walls, for the wealthy craftsmen and shopkeepers. He recalled the grid pattern of Winchester's streets, and planned the new Kingsbridge on the same convenient basis. Straight streets, broad enough for two carts to pass, would run down to the river, with narrower cross streets. He made the standard building plot twenty-four feet wide, which was an ample frontage for a town house. Each plot would be a hundred and twenty feet deep, to make room for a decent backyard with a privy, a vegetable garden, and a stable, cow shed or pigsty. The bridge had burned down and the new one would be built in a more convenient position, at the bottom end of the new main street. The main road through the town would now go from the bridge straight up the hill, past the cathedral and out the far side, as in Lincoln. Another wide street would run from the priory gate to a new quay at the riverside, downstream from the bridge and around the bend in the river. That way, bulk supplies could reach the priory without using the main shopping street. There would be a completely new district of small houses around the new quay: the poor would be downstream of the priory, and their dirty habits would not foul the supply of fresh water to the monastery.

Planning the rebuilding brought Philip out of his helpless trance, but every time he looked up from his drawings he was swept by rage and grief for the people who had been lost. He wondered whether William Hamleigh was in fact the devil incarnate: he caused more misery than seemed humanly possible. Philip saw the same alternation of hope and bereavement on the faces of the townspeople as they arrived back from the forest with their loads of timber. Jack and the other monks had laid out the plan of the new town on the ground with stakes and string, and as the people chose their plots, every now and again someone would say gloomily: "But what's the point? It might be burned again next year." If there had been some hope of justice, some expectation that the evildoers might be punished, perhaps the people would not have been so inconsolable; but although Philip had written to Stephen, Maud, Bishop Henry, the archbishop of Canterbury, and the pope, he knew that in wartime there was little chance that a man as powerful and important as William would be brought to trial.

The larger building plots in Philip's scheme were much in demand, despite higher rents, so he altered his plan to allow for more of them. Almost nobody wanted to build in the poorer quarter, but Philip decided to leave the layout as it was, for future use. Ten days after the fire, new wooden houses were going up on most plots, and another week later most of them were finished. Once the people had built their houses, work started again on the cathedral. The builders got paid and wanted to spend their money; so the shops reopened, and the smallholders brought their eggs and onions into town; and the scullery maids and laundresses recommenced work for the shopkeepers and craftsmen; and so, day by day, material life in Kingsbridge returned to normal.

But there were so many dead that it seemed like a town of ghosts. Every family had lost at least one member: a child, a mother, a husband, a sister. The people wore no badges of mourning but the lines of their faces showed grief as starkly as bare trees show winter. One of the worst hit was six-year-old Jonathan. He moped about the priory close like a lost soul, and eventually Philip realized he was missing Tom, who had, it seemed, spent more time with the boy than anyone had noticed. Once Philip understood this, he took care to set aside an hour each day for Jonathan, to tell him stories, play counting games, and listen to his voluble chatter.

Philip wrote to the abbots of all the major Benedictine monasteries in England and France, asking them if they could recommend a master builder to replace Tom. A prior in Philip's position would normally consult his bishop about this, for bishops traveled widely and were likely to hear of good builders, but Bishop Waleran would not help Philip. The fact that the two of them were permanently at odds made Philip's job lonelier than it should have been.

While Philip waited for replies from the abbots, the craftsmen looked instinctively to Alfred for leadership. Alfred was Tom's son, he was a master mason, and he had for some time been operating his own semi-autonomous team on the site. He did not have Tom's brain, unfortunately, but he was literate and authoritative, and he slipped gradually into the gap left by the death of his father.

There seemed to be a lot more problems and queries about the building than there had been in Tom's time, and Alfred always seemed to come up with a question when Jack was nowhere to be found. No doubt that was natural: everyone in Kingsbridge knew the stepbrothers hated one another. However, the upshot was that Philip found himself once again bothered by endless questions of detail.

But as the weeks went by Alfred gained in confidence, until one day he came to Philip and said: "Wouldn't you rather have the cathedral vaulted?"

Tom's design called for a wooden ceiling over the center of the church, and vaulted stone ceilings over the narrower side aisles. "Yes, I would," Philip said. "But we decided on a wooden ceiling to save money."

Alfred nodded. "The trouble is, a wooden ceiling can burn. A stone vault is fireproof."

Philip studied him for a moment, wondering whether he had underestimated Alfred. Philip would not have expected Alfred to propose a variation on his father's design: that was more the kind of thing Jack would do. But the idea of a fireproof church was very striking, especially since the whole town had burned down.

Thinking along the same lines, Alfred said: "The only building left standing in the town after the fire was the new parish church."

And the new parish church—built by Alfred—had a stone vault, Philip thought. But a snag occurred to him. "Would the existing walls take the extra weight of a stone roof?"

"We'd have to reinforce the buttresses They'd stick out a bit more, that's all."

He had really thought this out, Philip realized. "What about the cost?"

"It will cost more in the long run, of course, and the whole church will take three or four extra years to complete. But it won't make any difference to your annual outlay."

Philip liked the idea more and more. "But will it mean we have to wait another year before we can use the chancel for services?"

"No. Stone or wood, we can't start on the ceiling until next spring, because the clerestory must harden before we put any weight on it. The wood ceiling is quicker to build, by a few months; but either way, the chancel will be roofed by the end of next year."

Philip considered. It was a matter of balancing the advantage of a fireproof roof against the disadvantage of another four years of building—and another four years of cost. The extra cost seemed a long way in the future, and the gain in safety was immediate. "I think I'll discuss it with the brothers in chapter," he said. "But it sounds like a good idea to me."

Alfred thanked him and went out, and after he had gone Philip sat staring at the door, wondering whether he really needed to search for a new master builder after all.

Kingsbridge made a brave show on Lammas Day. In the morning, every household in the town made a loaf—the harvest was just in, so flour was cheap and plentiful. Those who did not have an oven of their own baked their loaf at a neighbor's house, or in the vast ovens belonging to the priory and the town's two bakers, Peggy Baxter and Jack-atte-Noven. By midday the air was full of the smell of new bread, making everyone hungry. The loaves were displayed on tables set up in the meadow across the river, and everyone walked around admiring them. No two were alike. Many had fruit or spices inside: there was plum bread, raisin bread, ginger bread, sugar bread, onion bread, garlic bread, and many more. Others were colored green with parsley, yellow with egg yolk, red with sandalwood or purple with turnsole. There were lots of odd shapes: triangles, cones, balls, stars, ovals, pyramids, flutes, rolls, and even figures of eight. Others were even more ambitious: there were loaves in the shapes of rabbits, bears, monkeys and dragons. There were houses and castles of bread. But the most magnificent, by general agreement, was the loaf made by Ellen and Martha, which was a representation of the cathedral as it would look when finished, based on the design by her late husband, Tom.

Ellen's grief had been terrible to see. She had wailed like a soul in torment, night after night, and no one had been able to comfort her. Even now, two months later, she was haggard and hollow-eyed; but she and Martha seemed able to help one another, and making the bread cathedral had given them some kind of consolation.

Aliena spent a long time staring at Ellen's construction. She wished there was something she could do to find comfort. She had no enthusiasm for anything. When the tasting began, she went from table to table listlessly, not eating. She had not even wanted to build a house for herself, until Prior Philip told her to snap out of it, and Alfred brought her the wood and assigned some of his men to help her. She was still eating at the monastery every day, when she remembered to eat at all. She had no energy. If it occurred to her to do something for herself—make a kitchen bench from leftover timber, or finish the walls of her house by filling in the chinks with mud from the river, or make a snare to catch birds so that she could feed herself—she would remember how hard she had worked to build up her trade as a wool merchant, and how quickly it had all gone to ruin, and she would lose her enthusiasm. So she went on from day to day, getting up late, going to the monastery for dinner if she felt hungry, spending the day watching the river flow by, and going to sleep in the straw on the floor of her new house when darkness fell.

Despite her lassitude, she knew that this Lammas Day festival was no more than a pretense. The town had been rebuilt, and people were going about their business as before, but the massacre threw a long shadow, and she could sense, beneath the facade of well-being, a deep undercurrent of fear. Most people were better than Aliena at acting as if all was well, but in truth they all felt as she did, that this could not last, and whatever they built now would be destroyed again.

While she stood looking vacantly at the piles of bread, her brother, Richard, arrived. He came across the bridge from the deserted town, leading his horse. He had been away, fighting for Stephen, since before the massacre, and he was astonished by what he found. "What the devil happened here?" he said to her. "I can't find our house—the whole town has changed!"

"William Hamleigh came on the day of the fleece fair, with a troop of men-at-arms, and burned the town," Aliena said.

Richard paled with shock, and the scar on his right ear showed livid. "William!" he breathed. "That devil."

"We've got a new house, though," Aliena said expressionlessly. "Alfred's men built it for me. But it's much smaller, and it's down by the new quay."

"What happened to you?" he said, staring at her. "You're practically bald, and you've got no eyebrows."

"My hair caught fire."

"He didn't . . ."

Aliena shook her head. "Not this time."

One of the girls brought Richard some salt bread to taste. He took some but did not eat it. He looked stunned.

"I'm glad you're safe, anyway," Aliena said.

He nodded. "Stephen is marching on Oxford, where Maud is holed up. The war could be over soon. But I need a new sword—I came to get some money." He ate some bread. The color came back to his face. "By God, this tastes good. You can cook me some meat later."

Suddenly she was afraid of him. She knew he was going to be furious with her and she had no strength to stand up to him. "I haven't any meat," she said.

"Well, get some from the butcher, then!"

"Don't be angry, Richard," she said. She began to tremble.

"I'm not angry," he said irritably. "What's the matter with you?"

"All my wool was burned in the fire," she said, and stared at him in fear, waiting for him to explode.

He frowned, looked at her, swallowed, and threw away the crust of his bread. "All of it?"

"All of it."

"But you must have some money still."

"None."

"Why not? You always had a great chest full of pennies buried under the floor—"

"Not in May. I had spent it all on wool—every penny. And I borrowed forty pounds from poor Malachi, which I can't repay. I certainly can't buy you a new sword. I can't even buy a piece of meat for your supper. We're completely penniless."

"Then how am I supposed to carry on?" he shouted angrily. His horse pricked up its ears and fidgeted uneasily.

"I don't know!" Aliena said tearfully. "Don't shout, you're frightening the horse." She began to cry.

"William Hamleigh did this," Richard said through his teeth.

"One of these days I'm going to butcher him like a fat pig, I swear by all the saints."

Alfred came up to them, his bushy beard full of crumbs of bread, with a corner of a plum loaf in his hand. "Try this," he said to Richard.

"I'm not hungry," Richard said ungraciously.

Alfred looked at Aliena and said: "What's the matter?"

Richard answered the question. "She's just told me we're penniless."

Alfred nodded. "Everyone lost something, but Aliena lost everything."

"You realize what this means to me," Richard said, speaking to Alfred but looking accusingly at Aliena. "I'm finished. If I can't replace weapons, and can't pay my men, and can't buy horses, then I can't fight for King Stephen. My career as a knight is over—and I'll never be the earl of Shiring."

Alfred said: "Aliena might marry a wealthy man."

Richard laughed scornfully. "She's turned them all down."

"One of them might ask her again."

"Yes." Richard's face twisted in a cruel smile. "We could send letters to all her rejected suitors, telling them she has lost all her money and is now willing to reconsider—"

"Enough," Alfred said, putting a hand on Richard's arm. Richard shut up. Alfred turned to Aliena. "Do you remember what I said to you, a year ago, at the first dinner of the parish guild?"

Aliena's heart sank. She could hardly believe that Alfred was going to start that again. She had no strength to deal with this. "I remember," she said. "And I hope you remember my reply."

"I still love you," Alfred said.

Richard looked startled.

Alfred went on: "I still want to marry you. Aliena, will you be my wife?"

"No!" Aliena said. She wanted to say more, to add something that would make it final and irreversible, but she felt too tired. She looked from Alfred to Richard and back again, and suddenly she could not take any more. She turned away from them and walked quickly out of the meadow and crossed the bridge to the town.

She was wearily angry with Alfred for repeating his proposal in front of Richard. She would have preferred her brother not to know about it. It was three months since the fire—why had Alfred left it until now? It was as if he had been waiting for Richard, and had made his move the moment Richard arrived.

She walked through the deserted new streets. Everyone was at the priory tasting the bread. Aliena's house was in the new poor quarter, down by the quay. The rents were low there but even so she had no idea how she would pay.

Richard caught her up on horseback, then dismounted and walked beside her. "The whole town smells of new wood," he said conversationally. "And everything is so clean!"

Aliena had got used to the new appearance of the town but he was seeing it for the first time. It *was* unnaturally clean. The fire had swept away the damp, rotten wood of the older buildings, the thatched roofs thick with grime from years of cooking fires, the foul ancient stables and the fetid old dunghills. There was a smell of newness: new wood, new thatch, new rushes on the floors, even new whitewash on the walls of the wealthier dwellings. The fire seemed to have enriched the soil, so that wild flowers grew in odd corners. Someone had remarked how few people had fallen ill since the fire, and this was thought to confirm a theory, held by many philosophers, that disease was spread by evil-smelling vapors.

Her mind was wandering. Richard had said something. "What?" she said.

"I said, I didn't know Alfred proposed marriage to you last year."

"You had more important things on your mind. That was about the time Robert of Gloucester was taken captive."

"Alfred was kind, to build you a house."

"Yes, he was. And here it is." She looked at him while he looked at the house. He was crestfallen. She felt sorry for him: he had come from an earl's castle, and even the large town house they had had before the fire had been a comedown for him. Now he had to get used to the kind of dwelling occupied by laborers and widows.

She took his horse's bridle. "Come. There's room for the horse at the back." She led the huge beast through the one-room house and out through the back door. There were rough low fences separating the yards. She tied the horse to a fence post and began to take off the heavy wooden saddle. From nowhere, grass and weeds had seeded the burned earth. Most people had dug a privy, planted vegetables and built a pigsty or a hen house in their yard, but Aliena's was still untouched.

Richard lingered in the house, but there was not much to look at, and after a moment he followed Aliena into the yard. "The house is a bit bare—no furniture, no pots, no bowls . . ."

"I haven't any money," Aliena said apathetically.

"You haven't done anything to the garden, either," he said, looking around distastefully.

"I haven't got the energy," she said crossly, and she handed him the big saddle and went into the house.

She sat on the floor with her back to the wall. It was cool in here. She could hear Richard dealing with his horse in the yard. After she had been sitting still for a few moments she saw a rat poke its snout up out of the straw. Thousands of rats and mice must have perished in the fire, but now they were beginning to be seen again. She looked around for something to kill it with, but there was nothing to hand, and anyway the creature disappeared again.

What am I going to do? she thought. I can't live like this for the rest of my life. But the mere idea of beginning a new enterprise exhausted her. She had rescued herself and her brother from penury once, but the effort had used up all her reserves, and she could not do it again. She would have to find some passive way of life, controlled by someone else, so that she could live without making decisions or taking initiatives. She thought of Mistress Kate, in Winchester, who had kissed her lips, and squeezed her breast, and said: "My dear girl, you need never want for money, or anything else. If you work for me we'll both be rich." No, she thought, not that; not ever.

Richard came in carrying his saddlebags. "If you can't look after yourself, you'd better find someone else to look after you," he said.

"I've always got you."

"I can't take care of you!" he protested.

"Why not?" A small spark of anger flared in her. "I've looked after you for six long years!"

"I've been fighting a war—all you've done is sell wool."

And knife an outlaw, she thought; and throw a dishonest priest to the floor, and feed and clothe and protect you when you could do nothing but bite your knuckles and look terrified. But the spark had died and the anger had gone, and she merely said: "I was joking, of course."

He grunted, not sure whether to be offended by that remark; then he shook his head irritably and said: "Anyway, you shouldn't be so quick to reject Alfred."

"Oh, for God's sake, shut up," she said.

"What's wrong with him?"

"Nothing's wrong with Alfred. Don't you understand? Something's wrong with *me*."

He put down the saddle and pointed his finger at her. "That's right, and I know what it is. You're completely selfish. You think only of yourself."

It was so monstrously unjust that she was unable to feel angry. Tears came to her eyes. "How can you say that?" she protested miserably.

"Because everything would be all right if only you would marry Alfred, but still you refuse."

"For me to marry Alfred wouldn't help you."

"Yes, it would."

"How?"

"Alfred said he would help me fight on, if I was his brother-in-law. I'd have to cut down a bit—he can't afford all my men-at-arms—but he promised me enough for a war-horse and new weapons, and my own squire."

"When?" Aliena said in astonishment. "When did he say this?"

"Just now. At the priory."

Aliena felt humiliated, and Richard had the grace to look a little shamefaced. The two men had been negotiating over her like horse dealers. She got to her feet, and without another word she left the house.

She walked back up to the priory and entered the close from the south side, jumping across the ditch by the old water mill. The mill was quiet today since it was a holiday. She would not have walked that way if the mill had been working, for the pounding of the hammers as they felted the cloth always gave her a headache.

The priory close was deserted, as she had expected. The building site was quiet. This was the hour when the monks studied or rested; and everyone else was in the meadow today. She wandered across to the cemetery on the north side of the building site. The carefully tended graves, with their neat wooden crosses and bunches of fresh flowers, told the truth: the town had not yet got over the massacre. She stopped beside Tom's stone tomb, adorned with a simple marble angel carved by Jack. Seven years ago, she thought, my father arranged a perfectly reasonable marriage for me. William Hamleigh wasn't old, he wasn't ugly, and he wasn't poor. He would have been accepted with a sigh of relief by any other girl in my position. But I refused him, and look at the trouble that has followed: our castle attacked, my father jailed, my brother and me destitute—even the burning of Kingsbridge and the killing of Tom are consequences of my obstinacy.

Somehow the death of Tom seemed worse than all the other sorrows, perhaps because he had been loved by so many people, perhaps because he was the second father Jack had lost.

And now I'm refusing another perfectly reasonable proposal, she thought. What gives me the right to be so particular? My fastidiousness has caused enough trouble. I should accept Alfred, and be thankful that I don't have to work for Mistress Kate.

She turned away from the grave and walked over to the building site. She stood in what would be the crossing and looked at the chancel. It was finished but for the roof, and the builders were getting ready for the next phase, the transepts: already the plan had been laid out on the ground on either side of her with stakes and string, and the men had started digging the foundations. The towering walls in front of her cast long shadows in the late-afternoon sun. It was a mild day, but the cathedral felt cold. Aliena looked for a long time at the rows of round arches, large at ground level, small above, and mid-sized on top. There was something deeply satisfying about the regular rhythm of arch, pier, arch, pier.

If Alfred really was willing to finance Richard, Aliena still had a chance to fulfill her vow to her father, that she would take care of Richard until he won back the earldom. In her heart she knew she had to marry Alfred. She just could not face it.

She walked along the southern side aisle, dragging her hand along the wall, feeling the rough texture of the stones, running her fingernails over the shallow grooves made by the stone-mason's toothed chisel. Here in the aisles, under the windows, the wall was decorated with blind arcading, like a row of filled-in arches. The arcading served no purpose but it added to the sense of harmony Aliena felt when she looked at the building. Everything in Tom's cathedral looked as if it was meant to be. Perhaps her life was like that, everything foreordained in a grand design, and she was like a foolish builder who wanted a waterfall in the chancel.

In the southeast corner of the church, a low doorway led to a narrow spiral staircase. On impulse Aliena went through the doorway and climbed the stairs. When she lost sight of the doorway, and could not yet see the top of the stairs, she began to feel peculiar, for the passage looked as if it might wind upward forever. Then she saw daylight: there was a small slit window in the turret wall, put there to light the steps. Eventually she emerged onto the wide gallery over the aisle. It had no windows to the outside, but on the inside it looked into the roofless church. She sat on the sill of one of the inner arches, leaning against the pillar. The cold stone caressed her cheek. She wondered whether Jack had carved this one. It occurred to her that if she fell from here she might die. But it was not really high enough: she might just break her legs, and lie in agony until the monks came and found her.

She decided to climb to the clerestory. She returned to the turret staircase and went on up. The next stage was shorter, but still she found it frightening, and her heart was beating loudly by the time she reached the top. She stepped into the clerestory passage, a narrow tunnel in the wall. She edged along the passage until it came out onto the inner sill of a clerestory window. She held on to the pillar that divided the window. When she looked down at the seventy-five-foot drop, she started to shake.

She heard footsteps on the turret stairs. She found herself breathing hard, as if she had been running. There had been no one else in sight. Had someone crept up behind her, trying to sneak up on her? The steps came along the clerestory passage. She let go of the pillar and stood teetering on the edge. A figure appeared on the sill. It was Jack. Her heart beat so loudly she could hear it.

"What are you doing?" he said warily.

"I . . . I was seeing how your cathedral is coming along."

He pointed to the capital above her head. "I did that."

She looked up. The stone was carved with the figure of a man who appeared to be holding the weight of the arch on his back. His body was twisted as if in pain. Aliena stared at it. She had never seen anything quite like it. Without thinking, she said: "That's how I feel."

When she looked back at him he was beside her, holding her arm gently but firmly. "I know," he said.

She looked at the drop. The thought of falling all that way made her sick with fear. He tugged at her arm. She allowed herself to be led into the clerestory passage.

They went all the way down the turret stairs and came out on the ground. Aliena felt weak. Jack turned to her and said in a conversational tone: "I was reading in the cloisters, and looked up and saw you in the clerestory."

She looked at his young face, so full of concern and tenderness; and she remembered why she had run away from everyone else and sought solitude here. She yearned to kiss him, and she saw the answering longing in his eyes. Every fiber of her body told her to throw herself into his arms, but she knew what she had to do. She wanted to say *I love you like a thunderstorm, like a lion, like a helpless rage;* but instead she said: "I think I'm going to marry Alfred."

He stared at her. He looked stunned. Then his face became sad, with an old, wise sadness that was beyond his years. She thought he was going to cry, but he did not. Instead there was anger in his eyes. He opened his mouth to speak, changed his mind, hesitated, then spoke at last.

In a voice like the cold north wind he said: "You would have done better to jump off the clerestory."

He turned from her and walked back into the monastery.

I've lost him forever, Aliena thought; and she felt as if her heart would break.

II

Jack was seen sneaking out of the monastery on Lammas Day. It was not a serious offense in itself, but he had been caught several times before, and the fact that this time he had gone out to speak to an unmarried woman made the whole thing more grave. His transgression was discussed in chapter the following day, and he was ordered to be kept in close confinement. That meant he was restricted to the monastic buildings, the cloisters and the crypt, and any time he went from one building to another he had to be accompanied.

He hardly noticed. He was so devastated by Aliena's announcement that nothing else made much difference. If he had been flogged instead of just confined, he felt, he would have been equally oblivious.

There was now no question of his working on the cathedral, of course; but much of the pleasure had gone out of that since Alfred had taken charge. Now he spent the free afternoons reading. His Latin had improved by leaps and bounds and he could read anything, albeit slowly; and as he was supposed to be reading to improve his Latin, rather than for any other purpose, he was allowed to use any book that took his fancy. Small though the library was, it had several works of philosophy and mathematics, and Jack had plunged into them with enthusiasm.

Much of what he read was disappointing. There were pages of genealogies, repetitive accounts of miracles performed by long-dead saints, and endless theological speculation. The first book that really appealed to Jack told the whole history of the world from the Creation to the founding of Kingsbridge Priory, and when he finished it he felt he knew everything that had ever happened. He realized after a while that the book's claim to tell *all* events was implausible, for after all, things were going on everywhere all the time, not just in Kingsbridge and England, but in Normandy, Anjou, Paris, Rome, Ethiopia, and Jerusalem, so the author must have left a lot out. Nevertheless, the book gave Jack a feeling he had never had before, that the past was like a story, in which one thing led to another, and the world was not a boundless mystery, but a finite thing that could be comprehended.

Even more intriguing were the puzzles. One philosopher asked why a weak man can move a heavy stone with a lever. This had never seemed strange to Jack before, but now the question tormented him. He had spent several weeks at the quarry at one time, and he recalled that when a stone could not be moved with a crowbar a foot long, the solution was generally to use a crowbar two feet long. Why should the same man be unable to move the stone with a short lever yet able to move it with a long one? That question led to others. The cathedral builders used a huge winding wheel to lift large stones and timbers up to the roof. The load at the end of the rope was much too heavy for a man to lift with his hands, but the same man could turn the wheel that wound the rope, and the load would rise. How was that possible?

Such speculations distracted him for a while, but his thoughts returned again and again to Aliena. He would stand in the cloisters, with a heavy book on a lectern in front of him, and recall that morning in the old mill when he had kissed her. He could remember every instant of that kiss, from the first soft touch of lips to the thrilling sensation of her tongue in his mouth. His body had pressed hers from thighs to shoulders, so that he could feel the contours of her breasts and her hips. The memory was so intense that it was like experiencing it all over again.

Why had she changed? He still believed that the kiss was real and her subsequent coldness was false. He felt he knew her. She was loving, sensual, romantic, imaginative, and warm. She was also thoughtless and imperious, and she had learned to be tough; but she was not cold, not cruel, not heartless. It was *not* in character for her to marry for money a man she did not love. She would be unhappy, she would regret it, she would be sick with misery; he knew it and in her heart she must know it too.

One day when he was in the writing room, a priory servant who was sweeping the floor stopped for a rest, leaned on his broom, and said: "Big celebration coming up in your family, then."

Jack was studying a map of the world drawn on a big sheet of vellum. He looked up. The speaker was a gnarled old man too feeble now for heavy work. He probably had Jack confused with someone else. "Why's that, Joseph?"

"Didn't you know? Your brother's getting married."

"I have no brothers," Jack said automatically, but his heart had gone cold.

"Stepbrother, then," said Joseph.

"No, I didn't know." Jack had to ask the question. He gritted his teeth. "Who is he marrying?"

"That Aliena."

So she was determined to go through with it. Jack had been harboring a secret hope that she would change her mind. He looked away so that Joseph should not see the despair on his face. "Well, well," he said, trying to make his voice sound unemotional.

"Yes—her that used to be so high-and-mighty, until she lost everything in the fire."

"Did—did you say when?"

"Tomorrow. They're going to get wed in the new parish church Alfred built."

Tomorrow!

Aliena was going to marry Alfred tomorrow. Until now Jack had never really believed it would happen. Now the reality burst on him like a thunderclap. Aliena was going to get married tomorrow. Jack's life would end tomorrow.

He looked down at the map on the lectern in front of him. What did it matter whether the center of the world was Jerusalem or Wallingford? Would he be happier if he knew how levers worked? He had told Aliena that she should jump from the clerestory rather than marry Alfred. What he should have said was that he, Jack, might as well jump from the clerestory.

He despised the priory. Being a monk was a stupid way of life. If he could not work on the cathedral and Aliena married someone else, he had nothing to live for.

What made it worse was that he knew how thoroughly miserable she would be living with Alfred. This was not just because he hated Alfred. There were some girls who might be more or less contented married to Alfred: for example, Edith, the one who had giggled when Jack talked to her about how he loved to carve stone. Edith would not expect much of Alfred, and she would be glad to flatter him and obey him as long as he continued prosperous and loved their children. But Aliena would hate every minute. She would loathe Alfred's physical coarseness, she would despise him for his bullying ways, she would be disgusted by his meanness, and she would find his slow-wittedness maddening. Marriage to Alfred would be hell for her.

Why could she not see that? Jack was mystified. What was going on in her mind? Surely *anything* would be better than marriage to a man she did not love. She had caused a sensation by refusing to marry William Hamleigh seven years ago, yet now she had passively accepted a proposal from someone equally unsuitable. What was she thinking of?

Jack had to know.

He had to talk to her, and to hell with the monastery.

He rolled up the map, replaced it in the cupboard, and went to the door. Joseph was still leaning on his broomstick. "Are you leaving?" he said to Jack. "I thought you were supposed to stay here until the circuitor comes for you."

"The circuitor can go shit," said Jack, and he stepped out.

As he emerged into the east walk of the cloisters, he caught the eye of Prior Philip, who was coming in from the building site to the north. Jack turned away quickly, but Philip called out: "Jack! What are you doing? You're supposed to be confined."

Jack had no patience for monastic discipline now. He ignored Philip and walked the other way, heading for the passage that led from the south walk down to the small houses around the new quay. But his luck was out. At that moment Brother Pierre, the circuitor, came out of the passage, followed by his two deputies. They saw Jack and stopped dead. A look of astonished indignation spread over Pierre's moon-shaped face.

Philip called out: "Stop that novice, Brother Circuitor!"

Pierre held out a hand to stop Jack. Jack pushed him aside. Pierre reddened and grabbed at Jack's arm. Jack wrenched his arm free and punched Pierre on the nose. Pierre gave a shout, more of outrage than pain. Then his two deputies jumped on Jack.

Jack struggled like a maniac, and almost got free, but when Pierre recovered from the blow to his nose and joined in, the three of them were able to wrestle Jack to the ground and hold him there. He continued to wriggle, furious that this monastic horseshit was now keeping him from something really important, speaking to Aliena. He kept saying: "Let me go, you stupid fools!" The two deputies sat on him. Pierre stood upright, wiping his bleeding nose on the sleeve of his habit. Philip appeared beside him.

Despite his own rage, Jack could see that Philip too was angry, angrier than Jack had ever seen him. "I will not tolerate this behavior from anyone," he said in a voice like iron. "You're a novice monk, and you *will* obey me." He turned to Pierre. "Put him in the obedience room."

"No!" Jack shouted. "You can't!"

"I most certainly can," Philip said wrathfully.

The obedience room was a small, windowless cell in the undercroft beneath the dormitory, at the south end, next to the latrines. It was mainly used to imprison lawbreakers who were waiting to be dealt with at the prior's court, or to be transferred to the sheriff's jail at Shiring; but it did occasional service as a punishment cell for monks who committed serious disciplinary offenses, such as acts of impurity with priory servants.

It was not the solitary confinement that scared Jack—it was the fact that he would not be able to get out to see Aliena. "You don't understand!" he yelled at Philip. "I have to speak to Aliena!"

It was the worst thing he could have said. Philip got angrier. "It was for speaking to her that you were originally punished," he said furiously.

"But I must!"

"The only thing you *must* do is learn to fear God and obey your superiors."

"You're not my superior, you silly ass! You're nothing to me. Let me go, damn you all!"

"Take him away," Philip said grimly.

A little crowd had gathered by now, and several monks lifted Jack by his arms and legs. He wriggled like a fish on a hook but there were too many of them. He could not believe that this was happening. They carried him, kicking and struggling, along the passage to the door of the obedience room. Someone opened it. Brother Pierre's voice said vengefully: "Throw him in!" They swung him back, then he was hurled through the air. He landed in a heap on the stone floor. He scrambled to his feet, numb to his bruises, and rushed at the door, but it slammed shut just as he crashed into it, and a moment later the heavy iron bar thudded down outside and the key turned in the lock.

Jack hammered on the door with all his might. "Let me out!" he yelled hysterically. "I have to stop her from marrying him! Let me out!" There was no sound from outside. He kept on calling, but his demands turned into pleas, and his voice dropped to a whine, then eventually to a whisper, and he wept tears of frustrated rage.

At last his eyes dried up and he could cry no more.

He turned from the door. The cell was not quite pitch-black: a little light came under the door and he could make out his surroundings vaguely. He went around the walls, feeling with his hands. He could tell by the pattern of chisel marks on the stones that the cell had been built a long time ago. The room was almost featureless. It was about six feet square, with a column in one corner and an upward-arching ceiling: clearly it had once been part of a larger room and had been walled off for use as a prison. In one wall there was a space like an opening for a slit window, but it was tightly shuttered, and would have been too small for anyone to crawl through even if it had been open. The stone floor felt damp. Jack became aware of a constant rushing noise, and realized that the water channel, which ran through the priory from the millpond to the latrines, must pass beneath the cell. That would explain why the floor was of stone instead of beaten earth.

He felt drained. He sat on the floor with his back to the wall and stared at the crack of light under the door, the tantalizing reminder of where he wanted to be. How had he got into this fix? He had never believed in the monastery, never intended to dedicate his life to God—he did not really believe in God. He had become a novice as a solution to an immediate problem, a way of staying in Kingsbridge, close to what he loved. He had thought: I can always leave if I want to. But now he did want to leave, wanted to more than he had ever imagined, and he could not: he was a prisoner. I'll strangle Prior Philip as soon as I get out of here, he thought, even if I have to hang for it afterward.

That started him wondering when he *would* be released. He heard the bell ring for supper. They certainly intended to leave him here all night. They were probably discussing him right now. The worst of the monks would argue that he should be shut up for a week—he could just see Pierre and Remigius calling for firm discipline. Others, who liked him, might say one night was sufficient punishment. What would Philip say? He liked Jack, but he would be terribly angry now, especially after Jack had said *You're not my superior, you silly ass, you're nothing to me.* Philip would be tempted to let the hard-liners have their own way. The only hope was that they might want Jack thrown out of the monastery immediately, which in their view would be a harsher sentence. That way he might be able to speak to her before the wedding. But Philip would be against that, Jack was sure. Philip would see expelling Jack as an admission of defeat.

The light under the door was growing fainter. It was getting dark outside. Jack wondered how prisoners were supposed to relieve themselves. There was no pot in the cell. It would not be characteristic of the monks to overlook that particular detail: they believed in cleanliness, even for sinners. He inspected the floor again, inch by inch, and found a small hole close to one corner. The noise of water was louder there, and he guessed it led to the underground channel. This was presumably his latrine.

Shortly after he made this discovery the small shutter opened. Jack sprang to his feet. A bowl and a crust of bread were placed on the sill. Jack could not see the face of the man who put them there. "Who's that?" he said.

"I am not permitted to converse with you," the man said in a monotone. However, Jack recognized the voice: it was an old monk called Luke.

"Luke, have they said how long I have to stay in here?" Jack cried.

He repeated the formula: "I am not permitted to converse with you."

"Please, Luke, tell me if you know!" Jack pleaded, not caring how pathetic he might sound.

Luke replied in a whisper. "Pierre said a week, but Philip made it two days." The shutter slammed.

"Two days!" Jack said desperately. "But she'll be married by then!"

There was no reply.

Jack stood still, staring at nothing. The light coming through the slit had been strong by comparison with the near-dark inside, and he could not see for a few moments, until his sight readjusted to the gloom; then his eyes filled with new tears, and he was blind again.

He lay down on the floor. There was nothing more to be done. He was locked in here until Monday, and by Monday Aliena would be Alfred's wife, waking up in Alfred's bed, with Alfred's seed inside her. The thought nauseated him.

Soon it was pitch-black. He fumbled his way to the sill and drank from the bowl. It contained plain water. He took a small piece of bread and put it in his mouth, but he was not hungry and he could hardly swallow it. He drank the rest of the water and lay down again.

He did not sleep, but he went into a kind of doze, almost like a trance, in which he relived, as in a dream or a vision, the Sunday afternoons he had spent with Aliena last summer, when he had told her the story of the squire who loved the princess, and went in search of the vine that bore jewels.

The midnight bell brought him out of the doze. He was used to the monastic timetable now, and he felt wide awake at midnight, though he often needed to sleep in the afternoons, especially if there had been meat for dinner. The monks would be getting out of their beds and forming up in lines for the procession from dormitory to church. They were immediately above Jack, but he could hear nothing: the cell was soundproof. It seemed very soon afterward that the bell rang again for lauds, which took place an hour after midnight. Time was passing quickly, too quickly, for tomorrow Aliena would be married.

In the small hours, despite his misery, he fell asleep.

He came awake with a start. There was someone in the cell with him.

He was terrified.

The cell was pitch-black. The sound of water seemed louder. "Who is it?" he said in a trembling voice.

"It's me—don't be afraid."

"Mother!" He almost fainted with relief. "How did you know I was in here?"

"Old Joseph came to tell me what had happened," she replied in a normal voice.

"Quiet! The monks will hear you."

"No, they won't. You can sing and shout in here without being heard above. I know—I've done it."

His head was so full of questions that he did not know which to ask first. "How did you get in here? Is the door open?" He moved toward her, holding his hands out in front of him. "Oh—you're wet!"

"The water channel runs right under here. There's a loose stone in the floor."

"How did you know that?"

"Your father spent ten months in this cell," she said, and in her voice there was the bitterness of years.

"My father? *This* cell? Ten months?"

"That's when he taught me all those stories."

"But why was he in here?"

"We never found out," she said resentfully. "He was kidnapped, or arrested—he never knew which—in Normandy, and he was brought here. He didn't speak English or Latin and he had no idea where he was. He worked in the stables for a year or so—that's how I met him." Her voice softened with nostalgia. "I loved him from the moment I set eyes on him. He was so gentle, and he looked so frightened and unhappy, yet he sang like a bird. Nobody had spoken to him for months. He was so pleased when I said a few words in French, I think he fell in love with me just for that." Anger made her voice hard again. "After a while they put him in this cell. That's when I discovered how to get in here."

It occurred to Jack that he must have been conceived right here on the cold stone floor. The thought embarrassed him and he was glad it was too dark for him and his mother to see each other. He said: "But my father must have done something to be arrested like that."

"He couldn't think of anything. And in the end they invented a crime. Someone gave him a jeweled cup and told him he could go. A mile or two away he was arrested, and accused of stealing the cup. They hanged him for it." She was crying.

"Who did all this?"

"The sheriff of Shiring, the prior of Kingsbridge . . . it doesn't matter *who*."

"What about my father's family? He must have had parents, brothers and sisters. . . ."

"Yes, he had a big family, back in France."

"Why didn't he escape, and go back there?"

"He tried, once; and they caught him and brought him back. That was when they put him in the cell. He could have tried again, of course, once we had found out how to get out of here. But he didn't know the way home, he couldn't speak a word of English, and he was penniless. His chances were slim. He should have done it anyway, we know now; but at the time we never thought they'd hang him."

Jack put his arms around her, to comfort her. She was soaking wet and shivering. She needed to get out of here and get dry. He realized, with a shock, that if she could get out, so could he. For a few moments he had almost forgotten about Aliena, as his mother talked about his father; but now he realized that his wish had been granted—he could speak to Aliena before her wedding. "Show me the way out," he said abruptly.

She sniffed and swallowed her tears. "Hold my arm and I'll lead you."

They moved across the cell and then he felt her go down. "Just lower yourself into the channel," she said. "Take a deep breath and put your head under. Then crawl against the flow. Don't go with the flow, or you'll end up in the monks' latrine. You'll get short of breath when you're almost there, but just keep calm and crawl on, and you'll make it." She went lower still, and he lost contact.

He found the hole and eased himself down. His feet touched the water almost immediately. When he stood on the bottom of the channel his shoulders were still in the cell. Before lowering himself farther, he found the stone and replaced it in position, thinking mischievously that the monks would be mystified when they found the cell empty.

The water was cold. He took a deep breath, went down on his hands and knees, and crawled against the flow. He went as fast as he could. As he crawled, he pictured the buildings above him. He was going beneath the passageway, then the refectory, the kitchen and the bakehouse. It was not far, but it seemed to take forever. He tried to surface but banged his head on the roof of the tunnel. He felt panicky, and remembered what his mother had said. He was almost there. A few moments later he saw light ahead of him. Dawn must have broken while they were talking in the cell. He crawled until the light was above him, then he stood upright and gasped the fresh air gratefully. When he had got his breath back he climbed out of the ditch.

His mother had changed her clothes. She was wearing a clean, dry dress, and wringing out the wet one. She had brought dry clothes for him too. There in a neat pile on the bank were the garments he had not worn for half a year: a linen shirt, a green wool tunic, gray hose and leather boots. Mother turned her back and Jack threw off the heavy monastic robe, stepped out of the sandals, and quickly dressed in his own clothes.

He threw the monk's habit into the ditch. He was never going to wear it again.

"What will you do now?" Mother asked.

"Go to Aliena."

"Right away? It's early."

"I can't wait."

She nodded. "Be gentle. She's bruised."

Jack stooped to kiss her, then impulsively threw his arms around her and hugged her. "You got me out of a prison," he said, and he laughed. "What a mother!"

She smiled, but her eyes were moist.

He gave her a farewell squeeze and walked away.

Even though it was now full light, there was nobody about because it was Sunday, and people did not have to work, so they took the opportunity to sleep past sunrise. Jack was not sure whether he should be afraid of being seen. Did Prior Philip have the right to come after a runaway novice and force him to return? Even if he had that right, would he want to? Jack did not know. However, Philip was the law in Kingsbridge, and Jack had defied him, so there was bound to be trouble of some kind. However, Jack was looking no farther ahead than the next few moments.

He reached Aliena's little house. It occurred to him that Richard might be there. He hoped not. However, there was nothing he could do about it. He went up to the door and tapped on it gently.

He cocked his head and listened. Nothing moved inside. He tapped again, harder, and this time he was rewarded by the sound of rustling straw as someone moved. "Aliena!" he said in a loud whisper.

He heard her come to the door. A frightened voice said: "Yes?"

"Open the door!"

"Who is it?"

"It's Jack."

"Jack!"

There was a pause. Jack waited.

* * *

Aliena closed her eyes in despair and slumped forward, leaning against the door with her cheek on the rough woodwork. Not Jack, she thought; not today, not now.

His voice came again, a low, urgent whisper. "Aliena, please, open the door, quickly! If they catch me they'll put me back in the cell!"

She had heard that he had been locked up—it was all over town. Obviously he had escaped. And he had come straight to her. Her heart quickened. She could not turn him away.

She lifted the bar and opened the door.

His red hair was plastered wetly to his head, as if he had bathed. He was wearing ordinary clothes, not his monk's habit. He smiled at her, as if seeing her was the best thing that had ever happened to him. Then he frowned, and said: "You've been crying."

"Why have you come here?" she said.

"I had to see you."

"I'm getting married today."

"I know. Can I come in?"

It would be wrong to let him in, she knew; but then it occurred to her that tomorrow she would be Alfred's wife, so this might be the last time she would ever talk to Jack alone. She thought: I don't care if it is wrong. She opened the door wider. Jack stepped in, and she closed it again and replaced the bar.

They stood facing one another. Now she felt embarrassed. He stared at her with desperate longing, as a man dying of thirst might gaze at a waterfall. "Don't look at me like that," she said, and she turned away.

"Don't marry him," Jack said.

"I must."

"You'll be miserable."

"I'm miserable now."

"Look at me, please?"

She turned to face him and raised her eyes.

"Please tell me why you're doing this," he said.

"Why should I?"

"Because of the way you kissed me in the old mill."

She dropped her gaze and felt herself blush hotly. She had let herself down that day and had been ashamed of herself ever since. Now he was using it against her. She said nothing. She had no defense.

He said: "After that, you turned cold."

She kept her gaze lowered.

"We were such friends," he went on remorselessly. "All that summer, in your glade, by the waterfall . . . my stories . . . we were so happy. I kissed you there, once. Do you remember?"

She did remember, of course, although she had been pretending to herself that it never happened. Now the memory melted her heart, and she looked at him with tearful eyes.

"Then I made the mill do your felting," he said. "I was so pleased that I could help you in your business. You were thrilled when you saw it. Then we kissed again, but that wasn't a little kiss, like the first one. This time it was . . . passionate." Oh, God, yes, it was, she thought, and she blushed again, and began to breathe fast; and wished he would stop, but he would not. "We held each other very tight. We kissed for a long time. You opened your mouth—"

"Stop!" she cried.

"Why?" he said brutally. "What's wrong with it? Why did you turn cold?"

"Because I'm frightened!" she said without thinking, and she burst into tears. She buried her face in her hands and sobbed. A moment later she felt his hands on her heaving shoulders. She did nothing, and after a while he gently enfolded her in his arms. She took her hands from her face and cried on his green tunic.

After a while she put her arms around his waist.

He laid his cheek on her hair—her ugly, short, shapeless hair, not yet grown back after the fire—and stroked her back as if she were a baby. She wanted to stay like that forever. But he pulled away from her so that he could look at her, and he said: "Why does it make you frightened?"

She knew, but she could not tell him. She shook her head and took a step back; but he held her wrists, keeping her near.

"Listen, Aliena," he said. "I want you to know how terrible this has been for me. You seemed to love me, then you seemed to hate me, and now you're going to marry my stepbrother. I don't understand. I don't know anything about these things, I've never been in love before. It's all so *hurtful*. I can't find words for how bad it is. Don't you think you should at least try to explain to me why I have to go through this?"

She felt full of remorse. To think that she had hurt him so badly when she loved him so much. She was ashamed of the way she had treated him. He had done nothing but kind things to her and she had ruined his life. He was entitled to an explanation. She steeled herself. "Jack, something happened to me a long time ago, something truly awful, something I've made myself forget for years. I wanted never to think of it again, but when you kissed me like that it all came back to me, and I couldn't stand it."

"What was it? What was the thing that happened?"

"After my father was imprisoned, we lived in the castle, Richard and I and a servant called Matthew; and one night William Hamleigh came and threw us out."

He narrowed his eyes. "And?"

"They killed poor Matthew."

He knew she was not telling him the whole truth. "Why?"

"What do you mean?"

"Why did they kill your servant?"

"Because he was trying to stop them." Tears were streaming down her face now, and her throat felt constricted every time she tried to speak, as if the words were choking her. She shook her head helplessly, and tried to turn away, but Jack would not let her go.

In a voice as gentle as a kiss he said: "Stop them from doing what?"

Suddenly she knew she could tell him, and it all came out in a rush. "They forced me," she said. "The groom held me down, and William got on top of me, but still I wouldn't let him, and then they cut off a piece of Richard's ear, and they said they would cut him more." She was sobbing with relief now, grateful beyond expression that at last she could say it. She looked into Jack's eyes and said: "So I opened my legs, and William did it to me, while the groom forced Richard to watch."

"I'm so sorry," Jack whispered. "I heard rumors, but I never thought . . . Dear Aliena, how could they?"

She had to tell him everything. "Then, when William had done it to me, the groom did it too."

Jack closed his eyes. His face was white and taut.

Aliena said: "And then, you see, when you and I kissed, I wanted you to do it, and that made me think of William and his groom; and I felt so horrible, and frightened, and I ran away. That's why I was so mean to you, and made you miserable. I'm sorry."

"I forgive you," he whispered. He drew her to him, and she let him put his arms around her again. It was so comforting.

She felt him shudder. Anxiously she said: "Do I disgust you?"

He looked at her. "I adore you," he said. He bent his head and kissed her mouth.

She froze. This was not what she wanted. He pulled away a little, then kissed her again. The touch of his lips on hers was very soft. Feeling grateful, and friendly toward him, she pursed her lips, just a little, then relaxed them again, in a faint echo of his kiss. Encouraged, he moved his lips against hers again. She could feel his breath warm on her face. He opened his mouth a fraction. She pulled away quickly.

He looked hurt. "Is it that bad?"

In truth, she was no longer as frightened as she had been. She had told him the horrible truth about herself and he had not recoiled in disgust; in fact, he was as tender and kind as ever. She tilted her head and he kissed her again. This was not scary. There was nothing threatening, nothing violently uncontrollable, no force or hatred or dominance; just the reverse. This kiss was a shared pleasure.

His lips parted and she felt the tip of his tongue. She went taut. He teased her lips apart. She relaxed again. He sucked gently at her lower lip. She felt a little dizzy.

He said: "Would you do what you did last time?"

"What did I do?"

"I'll show you. Open your mouth, just a little."

She did as he said, and she felt his tongue again, touching her lips, passing between her parted teeth, and probing into her mouth until he found her own tongue. She pulled away.

"There," he said. "That's what you did."

"Did I?" She was shocked.

"Yes." He smiled, then suddenly he looked solemn. "If you would only do it again, that would make up for all the sorrow of the last nine months."

She tilted her face again and closed her eyes. After a moment she felt his mouth on hers. She opened her lips, hesitated, then nervously pushed her tongue into his mouth. As she did so she remembered how she had felt the last time she did it, in the old mill, and that ecstatic sensation came back. She was filled with the need to hold him, to touch his skin and his hair, to feel his muscles and his bones, to be inside him and have him inside her. Her tongue met his, and instead of feeling embarrassed and faintly repelled, she was thrilled to be doing something so intimate as touching his tongue with her own.

They were both breathing hard now. Jack held her head in his hands. She stroked his arms, his back, and then his hips, feeling the taut, bunched muscles. Her heart pounded in her chest. At last she broke the kiss, breathless.

She looked at him. He was flushed and panting, and his face shone with desire. After a moment he bent forward again, but instead of kissing her mouth, he lifted her chin and kissed the delicate skin of her throat. She heard herself moan with pleasure. He moved his head lower, and brushed his lips over the swell of her breast. Her nipples were swollen under the coarse fabric of the linen nightshirt, and they felt unbearably tender. His lips closed over one nipple. She felt the heat of his breath on her skin. "Gently," she whispered fearfully. He kissed her nipple through the linen, and although he was as gentle as could be, she felt a sensation of pleasure as sharp as if he had bitten her, and she gasped.

Then he went down on his knees in front of her.

He pressed his face into her lap. Until this moment all the sensation had been in her breasts, but now, suddenly, she felt the tingling move to her groin. He found the hem of her nightshirt and lifted it to her waist. She watched him, afraid of his reaction: she had always felt ashamed of being so hairy down there. But he was not repelled; in fact he leaned forward and kissed her gently, right there, as if it was the nicest thing in the world.

She sank down on her knees in front of him. Her breath came in gasps now, as if she had run a mile. She wanted him badly. Her throat was dry with desire. She put her hands on his knees, then slid one hand under his tunic. She had never touched a man's cock. It was hot and dry and hard as a board. Jack closed his eyes and groaned deep in his throat as she explored its length with her fingertips. She lifted his tunic, bent down, and kissed it, just as he had kissed her, a gentle brush of the lips. Its end was swollen tight as a drum and wet with some kind of moisture.

She was suddenly possessed by a desire to show him her breasts. She came upright again. He opened his eyes. Watching him, she quickly pulled her nightshirt over her head and discarded it. Now she was completely naked. She felt sharply self-conscious, but it was a good feeling, delightfully indecent. Jack stared, mesmerized, at her breasts. "They're so beautiful," he said.

"Do you really think so?" she said. "I always thought they were too big."

"Too big!" he said as if the suggestion were outrageous. He reached out and touched her left breast with his right hand. He stroked her skin gently with his fingertips. She looked down, watching what he was doing. After a while she wanted him to be firmer. She took both his hands in hers and pressed them to her breasts. "Do it harder," she said hoarsely. "I want to feel you more."

Her words inflamed him. He squeezed her breasts, then took her nipples in his fingers and pinched them, just hard enough to hurt a little. The sensation drove her wild. All thought went out of her mind and she was completely possessed by the feel of his body and her own. "Take off your clothes," she said. "I want to look at you."

He pulled off his tunic and his undershirt, his boots and his hose, and knelt in front of her again. His red hair was drying into undisciplined curls. His body was thin and white, with bony shoulders and hips. He looked wiry and agile, young and fresh. His cock stuck up like a tree out of the auburn hair of his groin. Suddenly she wanted to kiss his chest. She leaned forward and brushed her lips across his flat male nipples. They puckered, just as hers had. She sucked at them gently, wanting him to have the same pleasure he had given her. He stroked her hair.

She wanted him inside her, quickly.

She could see that he was not sure what to do next. "Jack," she said. "Are you a virgin?"

He nodded, looking a little foolish.

"I'm glad," she said fervently. "I'm so glad."

She took his hand and put it between her legs. She was swollen and sensitive there, and his touch was like a shock. "Feel me," she said. He moved his fingers, exploring. "Feel inside," she said. Hesitantly, he pushed a finger inside her. She was slippery with desire. "There," she said with a sigh of satisfaction. "That's where it has to go." She detached his hand and lay back in the straw.

He lay over her, supporting himself on one elbow, and kissed her mouth. She felt him enter her a little way, then stop. "What is it?" she said.

"It feels too small," he said. "I'm afraid of hurting you."

"Push harder," she said. "I want you so much I don't care if it hurts."

She felt him push. It did hurt, more than she had expected, but only for a moment, and then she felt wonderfully filled. She looked at him. He withdrew a little and pushed again, and she pushed back. She smiled at him. "I never knew it was so nice," she said wonderingly. He closed his eyes, as if the happiness was too much to bear.

He began to move rhythmically. The constant strokes set up a pulse of pleasure somewhere in her groin. She heard herself give little gasps of excitement every time their bodies came together. He lowered himself so that his chest was touching her nipples and she could feel his hot breath. She dug her fingers into his hard back. Her regular gasps turned into cries. Suddenly she needed to kiss him. She buried her hands in his curls and pulled his head to hers. She kissed his lips hard, then thrust her tongue into his mouth and moved faster and faster. Having his cock in her cunt and her tongue in his mouth drove her out of her mind with pleasure. She felt a great spasm of joy shake her, so violent that it was like falling off a horse and hitting the ground. It made her cry out loud. She opened her eyes and looked into his eyes and said his name, and then another wave took her, and another; and then she felt his body convulse, and he cried out too, and she felt a hot jet spurt inside her, and that inflamed her even more, so that she shook with pleasure again and again, so many times that she lost count, until at last the feeling began to fade, and gradually she went limp and still.

She was too exhausted to speak or move, but she could feel Jack's weight slumped on top of her, his bony hips on hers, his flat chest squashing her soft breasts, his mouth close to her ear, his fingers entwined in her hair. A part of her mind thought vaguely: That's what it's supposed to be like, between men and women; that's why everyone makes so much fuss about it; that's why husbands and wives love one another so much.

Jack's breathing became light and regular, and his body relaxed until it was completely limp. He was asleep.

She turned her head and kissed his face. He was not too heavy. She wanted him to stay there, asleep on top of her, forever.

That thought made her remember.

Today was her wedding day.

Dear God, she thought, what have I done?

She began to cry.

After a moment, Jack woke up.

He kissed the tears on her cheeks with unbearable tenderness.

She said: "Oh, Jack, I want to marry you."

"Then that's what we'll do," he said in a voice of profound satisfaction.

He had misunderstood her, and that made it even worse. "But we can't," she said, and her tears flowed faster.

"But after this—"

"I know—"

"After this, you must marry me!"

"We can't marry," she said. "I've lost all my money, and you've got nothing."

He raised himself on his elbows. "I've got my hands," he said fiercely. "I'm the best stone carver for miles around."

"You were dismissed—"

"It makes no difference. I could get work on any building site in the world."

She shook her head miserably. "It's not enough. I have to think about Richard."

"Why?" he said indignantly. "What has all this got to do with Richard? He can take care of himself."

Suddenly Jack looked boyish, and Aliena felt the difference in their ages: he was five years younger than she, and he still thought he had a right to be happy. She said: "I swore an oath to my father, when he was dying, that I would look after Richard until he becomes earl of Shiring."

"But that could be never!"

"But an oath is an oath."

Jack looked nonplussed. He rolled off her. His soft penis slipped out of her and she experienced a sense of loss like a pain. I will never feel him inside me again, she thought sorrowfully.

He said: "You can't mean this. An oath is just words! It's nothing by comparison with *this*. This is real, this is you and me." He looked at her breasts, then he reached out and stroked the curly hair between her legs. It was so poignant that she felt his touch like a whiplash. He saw her wince, and stopped.

For a moment she was on the edge of saying *Yes, all right, let's run away together now,* and perhaps if he had carried on stroking her like that she would have; but reason returned, and she said: "I'm going to marry Alfred."

"Don't be ridiculous."

"It's the only way."

He stared at her. "I just don't believe you," he said.

"It's true."

"I can't give you up. I can't, I can't." His voice cracked, and he stifled a sob.

She tried reason, arguing with herself as much as with him. "What's the point of breaking my vow to my father, in order to make a marriage vow to you? If I break the first vow, the second is worthless."

"I don't care. I don't want your vows. I just want us to be together all the time and make love whenever we feel like it."

It was an eighteen-year-old view of marriage, she thought, but she did not say so. She would have accepted it gladly if she had been free. "I can't do what I want," she said sadly. "It's not my destiny."

"What you're doing is wrong," he said. "I mean *evil*. To give up happiness like this is like throwing jewels into the ocean. It's far worse than any sin."

She was unexpectedly struck by the thought that her mother would have agreed with that. She was not sure how she knew. She dismissed the idea. "I could never be happy, even with you, if I had to live with the knowledge that I had broken my promise to my father."

"You care more for your father and your brother than you do for me," he said, sounding faintly petulant for the first time.

"No . . ."

"What, then?"

He was just being argumentative, but she considered the question seriously. "I suppose it means that my oath to my father is more important to me than my love for you."

"Is it?" he said incredulously. "Is it really?"

"Yes, it is," she said with a heavy heart, and her words sounded to her like a funeral bell.

"Then there's nothing more to be said."

"Only . . . that I'm sorry."

He got to his feet. He turned his back to her and picked up his undershirt. She looked at his long, slender body. There was a lot of curly red-gold hair on his legs. He put on his shirt and tunic quickly, then pulled up his socks and stepped into his boots. It all happened much too quickly.

"You're going to be fearfully unhappy," he said.

He was trying to be nasty to her, but the attempt was a failure, for she could hear compassion in his voice.

"Yes, I am," she said. "Would you at least . . . at least say you respect me for my decision?"

"No," he said without hesitation. "I don't. I despise you for it."

She sat there naked, looking at him, and she began to weep.

"I might as well go," he said, and his voice cracked on the last word.

"Yes, go," she sobbed.

He went to the door.

"Jack!"

He turned at the door.

She said: "Wish me luck, Jack?"

He lifted the bar. "Good—" He stopped, unable to speak. He looked down at the floor, then up at her again. This time his voice came out in a whisper. "Good luck," he said.

Then he went out.

The house that had been Tom's house was now Ellen's, but it was also Alfred's home, so this morning it was full of people preparing a wedding feast, organized by Martha, Alfred's thirteen-year-old sister, with Jack's mother looking on disconsolately. Alfred was there with a towel in his hand, about to go down to the river— women bathed once a month, and men at Easter and Michaelmas, but it was traditional to bathe on your wedding morning. The place went quiet when Jack walked in.

Alfred said: "What do you want?"

"I want you to call off the wedding," Jack replied.

"Piss off," Alfred said.

Jack realized he had started badly. He should try not to make a confrontation out of this. What he was proposing was in Alfred's interest, too, if only he could be made to see it. "Alfred, she doesn't love you," he said as gently as he could.

"You don't know anything about it, laddie."

"I do," Jack persisted. "She doesn't love you. She's marrying you for Richard's sake. He's the only one who will be made happy by this marriage."

"Go back to the monastery," Alfred said contemptuously. "Where's your habit, anyway?"

Jack took a deep breath. There was nothing else for it but to tell him the real truth. "Alfred. She loves *me*."

He expected Alfred to be enraged, but instead the shadow of a sly grin appeared on Alfred's face. Jack was nonplussed. What did it mean? Gradually the explanation dawned on him. "You know that already," he said unbelievingly. "You know she loves me, and you don't care! You want her anyway, whether she loves you or not. You just want to have her."

Alfred's furtive smile became more visible and more malicious, and Jack knew that everything he was saying was true; but there was something else, something more to be read in Alfred's face. An incredible suspicion arose in Jack's mind. "Why do you want her?" he said. "Is it . . . Could it be that you only want to marry her to take her away from me?" His voice rose in anger. "That you're marrying her out of *spite*?" A look of cunning triumph spread across Alfred's stupid face, and Jack knew that he was right again. He was devastated. The idea that Alfred was doing all this not out of an understandable lust for Aliena but out of pure malice was too much to bear. "Damn you, you'd better treat her right!" he yelled.

Alfred laughed.

The ultimate malignity of Alfred's purpose struck Jack like a blow. Alfred was not going to treat her well. That would be his final revenge on Jack. Alfred was going to marry Aliena and make her miserable. "You filth," Jack said bitterly. "You slime. You shit. You ugly, stupid, evil, *loathsome* slug."

His contempt finally got to Alfred, who dropped his towel and came at Jack with his hand balled into a fist. Jack was ready for him, and stepped forward to hit him first. Then Jack's mother was between them, and despite being smaller than either of them she stopped them with a word.

"Alfred. Go and bathe."

Alfred calmed down quickly. He realized he had won the day without needing to fight Jack, and his thoughts revealed themselves in a smug look. He left the house.

Mother said: "What are you going to do, Jack?"

Jack found that he was shaking with rage. He breathed in and out several times before he could speak. He could not stop the wedding, he realized. But he could not watch it either. "I have to leave Kingsbridge."

He saw sorrow cross her face, but she nodded. "I was afraid you'd say that. But I think you're right."

A bell began to ring in the priory. Jack said: "Any moment now they'll discover that I've escaped."

She lowered her voice. "Go quickly, but hide down by the river, within sight of the bridge. I'll bring you some things."

"All right." He turned away.

Martha stood between him and the door with tears pouring down her face. He hugged her. She squeezed him hard. Her girlish body was flat and bony, like a boy's. "Come back one day," she said fiercely.

He kissed her once, quickly, and went out.

There were plenty of people about now, fetching water and enjoying the mild autumn morning. Most people knew he had become a novice monk—the town was still small enough for everyone to know everyone else's business—and his layman's clothing drew surprised looks, although nobody actually questioned him. He went quickly down the hill, crossed the bridge, and walked along the bank of the river until he came to a clump of reeds. He crouched down beside the reeds and watched the bridge, waiting for his mother.

He had no idea where he was going to go. Perhaps he would walk in a straight line until he came to a town where they were building a cathedral, and stop there. He had meant what he said to Aliena about finding work: he knew he was good enough to be employed anywhere. Even if the site had a full complement, he would only have to show the master builder how he could carve, and he would get taken on. But there seemed no point to it anymore. He would never love another woman after Aliena, and he felt much the same about Kingsbridge Cathedral. He wanted to build *here*, not just anywhere.

Perhaps he would just walk into the forest and lie down and

die. That seemed to him a nice idea. It was mild weather, the trees were green-and-gold; he could make a peaceful end. His only regret would be that he had not found out more about his father before he died.

He was picturing himself lying on a bed of autumn leaves and passing gently into death, when he saw Mother cross the bridge. She was leading a horse.

He got to his feet and ran to her. The horse was the chestnut mare she always rode. "I want you to take my mare," she said.

He took her hand and squeezed it by way of thanks.

Tears came to her eyes. "I never did look after you very well," she said. "First I brought you up wild, in the forest. Then I let you nearly starve with Tom. Then I made you live with Alfred."

"You looked after me fine, Mother," he said. "I made love to Aliena this morning. Now I can die happy."

"You foolish boy," she said. "You're just like me. If you can't have the lover you want, you won't have anyone else."

"Is that how you are?" he said.

She nodded. "After your father died, I lived alone rather than take second best. I never wanted another man until I saw Tom. That was eleven years later." She detached her hand from his. "I'm telling you this for a reason. It may take eleven years, but you *will* love someone else one day; I promise you."

He shook his head. "It doesn't seem possible."

"I know." She looked nervously back over her shoulder at the town. "You'd better go."

He walked over to the horse. It was loaded with two bulging saddlebags. "What's in the bags?" he asked.

"Some food and money, and a full wineskin, in this one," she replied. "The other contains Tom's tools."

Jack was moved. Mother had insisted on keeping Tom's tools after he died, as a memento. Now she was passing them on to him. He hugged her. "Thank you," he said.

"Where will you go?" she asked him.

He thought again of his father. "Where do jongleurs tell their tales?" he asked.

"On the pilgrim road to Santiago de Compostela."

"Do you think the jongleurs might remember Jack Shareburg?"

"They might. Tell them he looked like you."

"Where's Compostela?"

"In Spain."

"Then I'm going to Spain."

"It's a long way, Jack."

"I've got time."

She put her arms around him and hugged him tight. He wondered how many times she had done that in the last eighteen years, comforting him over a grazed knee, a lost toy, a boyish disappointment—and now a grief that was all too grown-up. He thought of the things she had done, from raising him in the forest to getting him out of the punishment cell. She had always been willing to fight like a cat for her son. It hurt to leave her.

She let him go, and he swung up onto the horse.

He looked back at Kingsbridge. It had been a sleepy village with an old, tumbledown cathedral when he first came here. He had set fire to that old cathedral, although not a soul knew it but him. Now Kingsbridge was a busy, self-important little town. Well, there were other towns. It was a wrench to go, but he was on the edge of the unknown, about to embark on an adventure, and that eased the pain of leaving everything he loved.

Mother said: "Come back, one day, please, Jack."

"I'll come back."

"Promise?"

"I promise."

"If you run out of money before you find work, sell the horse, not the tools," she said.

"I love you, Mother," he said.

Her eyes overflowed. "Take care of yourself, my son."

He kicked the horse, and it walked away. He turned and waved. She waved back. Then he kicked it into a trot, and after that he did not look back.

Richard came home just in time for the wedding.

King Stephen had generously given him two days' leave, he explained. The king's army was at Oxford, laying siege to the castle, where they had Maud trapped, so there was nothing much for the knights to do. "I couldn't miss my sister's wedding day," Richard said, and Aliena sourly thought: You just want to make dead sure the deed is done, so that you get what Alfred has promised you.

Still, she was glad he was there to walk her to the church and give her away. Otherwise she would have had nobody.

She put on a new linen undershirt and a white dress in the latest style. There was not much she could do with her mutilated hair, but she twisted the longest parts into plaits and bound them in fashionable white silk sheaths. A neighbor loaned her a looking-glass. She was pale, and her eyes showed that she had spent a sleepless night. Well, there was nothing she could do about that.

Richard watched her. He wore a faintly sheepish look, as if he felt guilty, and he fidgeted restlessly. Perhaps he was afraid she would call the whole thing off at the last minute.

There were moments when she was sorely tempted to do just that. She imagined herself and Jack walking away from Kingsbridge hand in hand, to start a new life somewhere else, a simple life of straightforward honest work, free from the chains of old vows and dead parents. But it was a foolish dream. She could never be happy if she abandoned her brother.

When she reached that conclusion, she imagined going down to the river and throwing herself in, and she saw her limp body, in a waterlogged wedding dress, drifting downstream, face up, with her hair floating around her head; and then she realized that marriage to Alfred was better than that, and she came back to where she started, regarding the marriage as the best available solution to most of her troubles.

How Jack would pour scorn on that kind of thinking.

The church bell tolled.

Aliena stood up.

She had never visualized her wedding day this way. When she had thought about it, as a girl, she had imagined herself on her father's arm, walking from the castle keep across the drawbridge to the chapel in the lower courtyard, with Papa's knights and men-at-arms, servants and tenants packed into the castle precincts to cheer and wish her well. The young man waiting in the chapel had always been rather indistinct in this daydream, but she knew that he adored her and made her laugh and she thought he was wonderful. Well. Nothing in her life had turned out the way she expected. Richard held the door of the little one-room house and she went out into the street.

To her surprise, some of the neighbors were waiting outside their doors to see her go by. Several people called out "God bless you" and "Good luck!" as she emerged. She felt terribly grateful to them. She was showered with corn as she walked up the street. Corn was for fertility. She would have babies, and they would love her.

The parish church was on the far side of town, in the wealthy quarter, where she would be living from tonight. They walked past the monastery. The monks would be holding their service in the crypt right now, but Prior Philip had promised to put in an appearance at the wedding feast and bless the happy couple. Aliena hoped he would make it. He had been an important force in her life, ever since the day, six years ago, when he had bought her wool at Winchester.

They arrived at the new church, built by Alfred with help from Tom. There was a crowd outside. The wedding would take place in the porch, in English; then there would be a Latin mass afterward inside the church. Everyone who worked for Alfred was there, and so were most of the people who had done weaving for Aliena in the old days. They all cheered when Aliena arrived.

Alfred was waiting with his sister, Martha, and one of his masons, Dan. Alfred was wearing a new scarlet tunic and clean boots. He had long, gleaming dark hair like Ellen's. Aliena realized that Ellen was not here. She was disappointed. She was about to ask Martha where her stepmother was, when the priest came out and the service began.

Aliena reflected that her life had been set on a new course six years ago when she had made a vow to her father, and now a fresh era was beginning with another vow to a man. She rarely did anything for herself. She had made a shocking exception this morning, with Jack. When she recalled what she had done she could hardly believe it. It seemed like a dream, or one of Jack's fanciful tales, something that had no connection with real life. She would never tell a soul. It would be a lovely secret she would hug to herself, and remember once in a while, like a miser counting a hidden hoard in the dead of night.

They were coming to the vows. On the priest's cue, Aliena said: "Alfred the son of Tom Builder, I take you as my husband, and swear to be faithful always." When she had said that she wanted to cry.

Alfred made his vow next. There was a ripple of noise on the outskirts of the crowd as he spoke, and one or two people looked behind. Aliena caught Martha's eye, and Martha whispered: "It's Ellen."

The priest frowned crossly and said: "Alfred and Aliena are now married in the eyes of God, and may the blessing—"

He never finished the sentence. A loud voice rang out from behind Aliena: "I curse this wedding!"

It was Ellen.

A gasp of horror went up from the congregation.

The priest tried to continue. "And may the blessing—" Then he stopped, paled, and made the sign of the cross.

Aliena turned around. Ellen was standing behind her. The crowd had shrunk back from her. She was holding a live cockerel in one hand and a long knife in the other. There was blood on the knife, and blood spurting from the severed neck of the bird. "I curse this marriage with sorrow," she said, and her words chilled Aliena's heart. "I curse this marriage with barrenness," she said. "I curse it with bitterness, and hatred, and bereavement, and regret. I curse it with impotence." As she said the word *impotence* she threw the bloody cockerel up into the air. Several people screamed and cowered back. Aliena stood rooted to the spot. The cock flew through the air, spraying blood, and landed on Alfred. He jumped back, terrified. The grisly object flopped on the ground, still bleeding.

When everyone looked up, Ellen was gone.

Martha had put clean linen sheets and a new wool blanket on the bed, the great feather bed that had belonged to Ellen and Tom and was now to be Alfred's and Aliena's. Ellen had not been seen since the wedding. The feast had been a subdued affair, like a picnic on a cold day, with everyone grimly going through the motions of eating and drinking because there was nothing else to do. The guests had all left at sundown, without any of the usual coarse jokes about the newlyweds' first night. Martha was now in her own little bed in the other room. Richard had returned to Aliena's little house, which would now be his.

Alfred was talking of building a stone house for them next summer. He had been boasting about it to Richard during the feast. "It will have a bedchamber, and a hall, and an undercroft," he had said. "When John Silversmith's wife sees it she'll want one just like it. Pretty soon all the prosperous men in town will want a stone house."

"Have you done a design?" Richard had asked, and Aliena had heard a hint of skepticism, although nobody else seemed to notice.

"I've got some old drawings of my father's, done in ink on vellum. One of them is the house we were building for Aliena and William Hamleigh, all those years ago. I'll base it on that."

Aliena had turned away from them in disgust. How could anyone be so crass as to mention that on her wedding day? Alfred had been full of bluster all afternoon, pouring wine and telling jokes and exchanging sly winks with his workmates. He seemed happy.

Now he was sitting on the edge of the bed taking off his boots. Aliena took the ribbons out of her hair. She did not know what to think about Ellen's curse. It had shocked her, and she had no idea what was going on in Ellen's mind, but somehow she was not frightened by it the way most people were.

This could not be said of Alfred. When the slaughtered cock landed on him he had practically gibbered. Richard had shaken him out of it, literally, holding him by the front of his tunic and jerking him back and forth. He had recovered his wits quickly enough, however, and since then the only sign of his fright had been the relentlessness of his backslapping, beer-swilling good cheer.

Aliena felt oddly calm. She did not relish what she was about to do, but at least she was not being forced to it, and while it might be a little distasteful, it would not be humiliating. There was only one man, and no one else would be watching.

She took off her dress.

Alfred said: "By Christ, that's a long knife."

She undid the strap that held the knife to her left forearm, then got into bed in her undershirt.

Alfred finally got his boots off. He pulled off his hose and stood up. He threw a lewd look at her. "Take off your underclothes," he said. "I'm entitled to see my wife's tits."

Aliena hesitated. She was reluctant to be naked, somehow, but it would be foolish to deny him the first thing he asked. Obediently, she sat up and pulled her undershirt off over her head, fiercely suppressing the memory of how differently she had felt when she did the same thing, this morning, for Jack.

"What a pair of beauties," Alfred said. He came and stood beside the bed and took hold of her right breast. His huge hands were rough-skinned, with dirt under the fingernails. He squeezed too hard, and she winced. He laughed and released her. Stepping back, he took off his tunic and hung it on a hook. Then he returned to the bed and pulled the sheet off her.

Aliena swallowed hard. She felt vulnerable like this, naked under his gaze. He said: "By God, that's a hairy one." He reached down and felt between her legs. She stiffened, and then made herself relax and part her thighs. "Good girl," he said, and thrust a finger inside her. It hurt: she was dry. She could not understand it—this morning, with Jack, she had been wet and slippery. Alfred grunted and forced his finger in farther.

She felt like crying. She had known she would not much enjoy it, but she had not expected him to be so unfeeling. He had not even kissed her yet. He doesn't love me, she thought; he doesn't even like me. I'm a fine young horse that he's about to ride. In fact he would treat a horse better than this—he would pat it and stroke it so that it could get used to him, and he'd talk softly to calm it down. She fought back the tears. I chose this, she thought; nobody made me marry him, so I'll just put up with it now.

"Dry as a sawpit," Alfred muttered.

"I'm sorry," she whispered.

He removed his hand, spat on it twice, and rubbed the spittle between her legs. It seemed a dreadfully contemptuous act. She bit her lip and looked away.

He spread her thighs. She closed her eyes, then opened them and forced herself to look at him, thinking: Get used to this, you're going to be doing it for the rest of your life. He got on the bed and knelt between her legs. The shadow of a frown crossed his face. He put one hand between her thighs, opening her up, and the other hand went beneath his undershirt. She could see the hand moving under the linen. His frown deepened. "Christ Jesus," he muttered. "You're so lifeless, it puts me off, it's like feeling up a corpse."

It seemed so unfair of him to blame her. "I don't know what I'm supposed to do!" she said tearfully.

"Some girls enjoy it," he said.

Enjoy it! she thought. Impossible! Then she remembered how, that very morning, she had groaned and cried with delight. But it was as if there was no connection between what she had done then and what she was doing now.

That was foolish. She sat upright. Alfred was rubbing himself beneath his shirt. "Let me," she said, and she slipped her hand between his legs. It felt limp and lifeless. She was not sure what to do with it. She squeezed it gently, then stroked it with her fingertips. She searched his face for a reaction. He just seemed angry. She carried on, but it made no difference.

"Do it harder," he said.

She began to rub it vigorously. It stayed soft, but he moved his hips, as if he was enjoying it. Encouraged, she rubbed harder. Suddenly he gave a cry of pain and pulled away. She had rubbed too hard. "Stupid cow!" he said, and he slapped her face, backhanded, with a swipe that knocked her sideways.

She lay on the bed, whimpering in pain and fear.

"You're no good, you're cursed!" he said furiously.

"I did my best!"

"You're a dead cunt," he spat. He took her by the arms, lifted her upright, and pushed her off the bed. She fell into the straw on the floor. "That witch Ellen meant this to happen," he said. "She's always hated me."

Aliena rolled over and knelt upright on the floor, staring at him. He did not look as if he would hit her again. He was no longer enraged, just bitter. "You can stay there," he said. "You're no good to me as a wife, so you can keep out of my bed. You can be a dog, and sleep on the floor." He paused. "I can't stand you looking at me!" he said with a note of panic in his voice. He looked around for the candle, spotted it, and put it out with a blow, knocking it to the ground.

Aliena stayed motionless in the darkness. She heard Alfred moving on the feather bed, lying down and pulling up the blanket and shifting the pillows. She was almost afraid to breathe. He was restless for a long time, tossing and turning in the bed, but he did not get up again, nor did he speak to her. Eventually he was still, and his breathing became even. When she was sure he was asleep, she crawled across the room, trying not to make the straw rustle, and found her way into the corner. She curled up and lay there, wide awake. Eventually she began to cry. She tried not to, for fear of waking him, but she could not hold the tears in, so she sobbed quietly. If the noise woke him, he gave no sign of it. She stayed like that, lying on the straw in the corner, crying softly, until eventually she cried herself to sleep.

Chapter 12

ALIENA WAS SICK all that winter.

She slept badly every night, wrapped in her cloak on the floor at the foot of Alfred's bed, and during the day she was possessed by a hopeless lassitude. She often felt nauseated, so she ate very little, but despite that she seemed to put on weight: she was sure her breasts and hips were larger, and her waist thickened.

She was supposed to be running Alfred's house, although Martha actually did most of the work. The three of them lived together in a sorry ménage. Martha had never liked her brother, and Aliena now loathed him with a passion, so it was not surprising that he spent as much time as possible away from the house, at work during the day and in the alehouse every evening. Martha and Aliena bought food and cooked it unenthusiastically, and made clothes in the evenings. Aliena looked forward to the spring, when it would once again be warm enough for her to visit her secret glade on Sunday afternoons. There she could lie in peace and daydream of Jack.

Meanwhile, her consolation was Richard. He had a spirited black courser, a new sword, and a squire with a pony, and he was once again fighting for King Stephen, albeit with a reduced entourage. The war dragged on into the new year: Maud had escaped from Oxford Castle and slipped through Stephen's hands once again, and her brother Robert of Gloucester had retaken Wareham, so the old seesaw continued, with each side gaining a little and then losing it. But Aliena was fulfilling her vow, and she could take satisfaction in that, if in nothing else.

In the first week of the year Martha began to bleed for the first time. Aliena made her a hot drink with herbs and honey to ease the cramps, and answered her questions about the woman's curse, and went to find the box of rags that she kept for her own periods. However, the box was not in the house, and she eventually realized she had not brought it here from her old house when she got married.

But that had been three months ago.

Which meant she had not bled for three months.

Not since her wedding day.

Not since she had made love with Jack.

She left Martha sitting by the kitchen fire, sipping her honey drink and toasting her toes, and went across town to her old house. Richard was not there but she had a key. She found the box without any trouble, but she did not go back right away. Instead she sat by the cold fireplace, wrapped in her cloak, deep in thought.

She had married Alfred at Michaelmas. It was now past Christmas. That was a quarter of a year. There had been three new moons. She should have bled three times. Yet her box of rags had been on the high shelf, alongside the small grindstone Richard used for sharpening kitchen knives. Now she held it in her lap. She ran a finger over the rough wood. Her finger came up dirty. The box was covered with dust.

The worst of it was, she had *never* made love with Alfred.

After that awful first night, he had tried again three times: once the following night, then a week later, and again a month after that when he had come home particularly drunk. But he was always completely incapable. At first Aliena had encouraged him, out of a sense of duty; but each failure made him angrier than the last, and she became frightened. It seemed safer to stay out of his way, and wear unappealing clothes, and make sure he never saw her undressing, and let him forget about it. Now she wondered if she should have tried more. But in truth she knew it would have made no difference. It was hopeless. She was not sure why—perhaps it was Ellen's curse, perhaps Alfred was just impotent, or perhaps it was because of the memory of Jack—but she felt certain Alfred never would make love to her now.

So he was bound to know that the baby was not his.

She stared miserably at the old, cold ashes in Richard's fireplace, wondering why she always had such bad luck. Here she was trying to make the best of a bad marriage and she had the misfortune to be pregnant by another man, after one single act of intercourse.

There was no point in self-pity. She had to decide what to do.

She rested her hand on her stomach. Now she knew why she had been putting on weight, why she kept feeling nauseated, why she was always so tired. There was a little person in there. She smiled to herself. How nice it would be to have a baby.

She shook her head. It would not be nice at all. Alfred would be as mad as a bull. There was no knowing what he would do—kill her, throw her out, kill the baby. . . . She had a sudden, terrible foreboding that he would try to do harm to the unborn baby by kicking her in the stomach. She wiped her brow: she had broken out in a cold sweat.

I won't tell him, she thought.

Could she keep her pregnancy secret? Perhaps. She had already taken to wearing shapeless, baggy clothes. She might not get very big—some women didn't. Alfred was the least observant of men. No doubt the wiser women in the town would guess, but she could probably rely on them to keep it to themselves, or at any rate not to talk to the menfolk about it. Yes, she decided, it might just be possible to keep it from him until after the baby was born.

Then what? Well, at least the little mite would have been brought safely into the world. Alfred would not be able to kill it by kicking Aliena. But he would still know that it was not his. He was sure to hate the poor thing: it would be a permanent slur on his manhood. There would be hell to pay.

Aliena could not think that far ahead. She had decided on the safest course for the next six months. She would try in the meantime to figure out what to do after the baby was born.

I wonder whether it's a boy or a girl, she thought.

She stood up with her box of clean rags for Martha's first monthly period. I pity you, Martha, she thought wearily; you've got all this in front of you.

Philip spent that winter brooding over his troubles.

He had been horrified by Ellen's heathen curse, uttered in the porch of a church during a service. There was no doubt in his mind now that she was a witch. He only regretted his foolishness in ever forgiving her for her insult to the Rule of Saint Benedict, all those years ago. He should have known that a woman who could do that would never really repent. However, one happy consequence of the whole horrifying business was that Ellen had once again left Kingsbridge and had not been seen since. Philip hoped fervently that she would never return.

Aliena was visibly unhappy as Alfred's wife, although Philip did not believe that the curse was the cause of that. Philip knew almost nothing about married life but he could guess that a bright, knowledgeable, lively person such as Aliena would be unhappy living with someone as slow-thinking and narrow-minded as Alfred, whether they were man and wife or anything else.

Aliena should have married Jack, of course. Philip could see that now, and he felt guilty that he had been so committed to his own plans for Jack that he had failed to realize what the boy really needed. Jack was never meant for the cloistered life and Philip had done wrong in pressuring him into it. Now Jack's brilliance and energy had been lost to Kingsbridge.

It seemed that everything had gone wrong since the disaster of the fleece fair. The priory was more in debt than ever. Philip had dismissed half the building work force because he no longer had the money to pay them. In consequence, the population of the town had shrunk, which meant that the Sunday market became smaller and Philip's income from rents fell. Kingsbridge was in a downward spiral.

The heart of the problem was the townspeople's morale. Although they had rebuilt their houses and restarted their small businesses, they had no confidence in the future. Whatever they planned, whatever they might build, could be wiped out in a day by William Hamleigh, if he should choose to attack again. This undercurrent of insecurity ran in everyone's thinking and paralyzed all enterprise.

Eventually Philip realized he had to do something to stop the slide. He needed to make a dramatic gesture to tell the world in general, and the townspeople in particular, that Kingsbridge was fighting back. He spent many hours of prayer and meditation trying to decide just what that gesture should be.

What he really needed was a miracle. If the bones of Saint Adolphus would cure a princess of the plague, or cause a brackish well to give sweet water, people would flood into Kingsbridge on pilgrimage. But the saint had performed no miracles for years. Philip sometimes wondered whether his steady, practical methods of ruling the priory displeased the saint, for miracles seemed to happen more frequently in places where the rule was less sensible and the atmosphere was charged with religious fervor, if not out-and-out hysteria. But Philip had been taught in a more down-to-earth school. Father Peter, the abbot of his first monastery, used to say: "Pray for miracles, but plant cabbages."

The symbol of Kingsbridge's life and vigor was the cathedral. If only it could be finished by a miracle! One time he prayed for such a miracle all night, but in the morning the chancel was still unroofed and open to the weather, and its high walls were ragged-ended where they would meet the transept walls.

Philip had not yet hired a new master builder. He had been shocked to learn how much they demanded in wages: he had never realized how cheap Tom was. Anyway, Alfred was running the reduced work force without much difficulty. Alfred had become rather morose since his marriage, like a man who defeats many rivals to become king and then finds that kingship is a wearisome burden. However, he was authoritative and decisive, and the other men respected him.

But Tom had left a gap that could not be filled. Philip missed him personally, not just as master builder. Tom had been interested in *why* churches had to be built one way rather than another, and Philip had enjoyed sharing speculations with him about what made some buildings stand up while others fell down. Tom had not been an exceptionally devout man, but he had occasionally asked Philip questions about theology which showed that he applied as much intelligence to his religion as he did to his building. Tom's brain had more or less matched Philip's own. Philip had been able to converse with him without talking down. There were too few such people in Philip's life. Jack had been one, despite his youth; Aliena another, but she had disappeared into her sorry marriage. Cuthbert White-head was getting old, now, and Milius Bursar was almost always away from the priory, touring the sheep farms, counting acres and ewes and woolsacks. In time, a lively and busy priory in a prosperous cathedral city would draw scholars the way a conquering army attracted fighting men. Philip looked forward to that time. But it would never come unless he could find a way to re-energize Kingsbridge.

"It's been a mild winter," Alfred said one morning soon after Christmas. "We can begin earlier than usual."

That started Philip thinking. The vault would be built that summer. When it was finished, the chancel would be usable, and Kingsbridge would no longer be a cathedral town without a cathedral. The chancel was the most important part of a church: the high altar and the holy relics were kept at the far east end, called the presbytery, and most of the services took place in the quire, where the monks sat. Only on Sundays and holy days was the rest of a church used. Once the chancel had been dedicated, what had been a building site would become a church, albeit an incomplete one.

It was a pity they would have to wait almost a year before that happened. Alfred had promised to finish the vault by the end of this year's building season, and the season generally finished in November, depending on the weather. But when Alfred said he would be able to start early, Philip began to wonder whether he might finish early too. Everyone would be stunned if the church could be opened this summer. It was the kind of gesture he had been searching for: something that would surprise the whole county, and give out the message that Kingsbridge could not be put down for long.

"Can you finish by Whitsun?" Philip said impulsively.

Alfred sucked his breath in through his teeth and looked doubtful. "Vaulting is the most skilled work of all," he said. "It mustn't be hurried, and you can't let apprentices do it."

His father would have answered yes or no, Philip thought irritably. He said: "Suppose I could give you extra laborers—monks. How much would that help?"

"A little. It's more masons we need, really."

"I might be able to give you one or two more," Philip said rashly. A mild winter meant early shearing, so he could hope to begin selling wool sooner than usual.

"I don't know." Alfred was still looking pessimistic.

"Suppose I offered the masons a bonus?" Philip said. "An extra week's wages if the vault is ready for Whitsunday."

"I've never heard of that before," Alfred said. He looked as if an improper suggestion had been made.

"Well, there's a first time for everything," Philip said testily. Alfred's caution was getting on his nerves. "What do you say?"

"I can't say yes or no to that," Alfred said stolidly. "I'll put it to the men."

"Today?" Philip said impatiently.

"Today."

Philip had to be satisfied with that.

William Hamleigh and his knights arrived at Bishop Waleran's palace just behind an ox cart loaded high with sacks of wool. The new season's shearing had begun. Like William, Waleran was buying wool from farmers at last year's prices and expecting to sell it again for considerably more. Neither of them had had much trouble forcing their tenants to sell to them: a few peasants who defied the rule were evicted and their farmhouses were burned, and after that there were no more rebels.

As William went through the gate he glanced up the hill. The stunted ramparts of the castle the bishop had never built had stood on that hill for seven years, a permanent reminder of how Waleran had been outwitted by Prior Philip. As soon as Waleran began to reap the rewards of the wool business, he would probably recommence building. In the days of old King Henry, a bishop had not needed any more defenses than the flimsy fence of wooden stakes behind a little ditch that surrounded this palace. Now, after five years of civil war, men who were not even earls or bishops were building formidable castles.

Things were going well for Waleran, William thought sourly as he dismounted at the stable. Waleran had remained loyal to Bishop Henry of Winchester through all Henry's switches of allegiance, and as a result had become one of Henry's closest allies. Over the years Waleran had been enriched by a steady stream of properties and privileges, and had visited Rome twice.

William had not been so lucky—hence his sourness. Despite having gone along with each of Waleran's changes of allegiance, and despite having supplied large armies to both sides in the civil war, he still had not been confirmed as earl of Shiring. He had been brooding on this during a lull in the fighting, and had become so angry about it that he had made up his mind to have a confrontation with Waleran.

He went up the steps to the hall entrance, with Walter and the other knights following. The steward on guard inside the door was armed, another sign of the times. Bishop Waleran sat in a big chair in the middle of the room, as always, with his bony arms and legs at all angles as if he had been untidily dropped there. Baldwin, now an archdeacon, was standing beside him, his stance suggesting he might be waiting for instructions. Waleran was staring into the fire, deep in thought, but he looked up sharply when William approached.

William felt the familiar loathing as he greeted Waleran and sat down. Waleran's soft thin hands, his lank black hair, his dead-white skin and his pale malignant eyes made William's skin crawl. He was everything William hated: devious, physically weak, arrogant and clever.

William could tell that Waleran felt much the same about him. Waleran could never quite conceal the distaste he felt when William walked in. He sat upright and folded his arms, his lip curled a little, and he frowned faintly, altogether as if he was suffering from a twinge of indigestion.

They talked of the war for a while. It was a stiff, awkward conversation, and William was relieved when it was broken by a messenger with a letter written on a roll of parchment and sealed with wax. Waleran sent the messenger off to the kitchen to get something to eat. He did not open the letter.

William took the opportunity to change the subject. "I didn't come here to exchange news of battles. I came to tell you that I've run out of patience."

Waleran raised his eyebrows and said nothing. Silence was his response to unpleasant topics.

William plowed on: "It's almost three years since my father died, but King Stephen still hasn't confirmed me as earl. This is outrageous."

"I couldn't agree more," Waleran said languidly. He toyed with his letter, examining the seal and playing with the ribbon.

"That's good," William said, "because you're going to have to do something about it."

"My dear William, I can't make you earl."

William had known that Waleran would take this attitude, and he was determined not to accept it. "You have the ear of the king's brother."

"But what am I to say to him? That William Hamleigh has served the king well? If it is true, the king knows it, and if not, he knows that also."

William was no match for Waleran in logic so he simply ignored the arguments. "You owe it to me, Waleran Bigod."

Waleran looked faintly angered. He pointed at William with the letter. "I owe you nothing. You have always served your own ends even when you did what I wanted. There are no debts of gratitude between us."

"I tell you, I won't wait any longer."

"What will you do?" Waleran said with the hint of a sneer.

"Well, first I'll see Bishop Henry myself."

"And?"

"I'll tell him that you have been deaf to my pleas, and in consequence I'm changing my allegiance to the Empress Maud." William was gratified to see Waleran's expression change: he went a shade paler and looked just a little bit surprised.

"Change again?" Waleran said skeptically.

"Just one more time than you," William responded stoutly.

Waleran's supercilious indifference was shaken, but not much. Waleran's career had benefited greatly from his ability to deliver William and his knights to whichever side Bishop Henry favored at the moment: it would be a blow to him if William suddenly turned independent—but not a fatal blow. William studied Waleran's face as he mulled over this threat. William could read the other man's mind: he was thinking that he wanted to keep William loyal, but wondering how much he should put into the effort.

To gain time Waleran broke the seal on his letter and unrolled it. As he read, a faint flush of anger appeared on his fish-white cheeks. "Damn the man," he hissed.

"What is it?" William asked.

Waleran held it out.

William took it from him and peered at the letters. "To—the—most—holy—gracious—bishop—"

Waleran snatched it back, impatient of William's slow reading. "It's from Prior Philip," he said. "He informs me that the chancel of the new cathedral will be finished by Whitsunday, and he has the nerve to beg me to officiate at the service."

William was surprised. "How has he managed it? I thought he had sacked half his builders!"

Waleran shook his head. "No matter what happens he seems to bounce back." He gave William a speculative look. "He hates you, of course. Thinks you're the devil incarnate."

William wondered what was going on now in Waleran's devious mind. "So what?" he said.

"It would be quite a blow to Philip if you were confirmed as earl on Whitsunday."

"You wouldn't do it for me, but you'd do it to spite Philip," William said grouchily, but in reality he was feeling hopeful.

"I can't do it at all," Waleran said. "But I will speak to Bishop Henry." He looked up at William expectantly.

William hesitated. At last, reluctantly, he muttered: "Thank you."

Spring was cold and dismal that year, and on the morning of Whitsunday it was raining. Aliena had woken up in the night with a backache, and it was still troubling her with a stabbing pain every now and again. She sat in the cold kitchen, plaiting Martha's hair before going to church, while Alfred ate a large breakfast of white bread, soft cheese and strong beer. A particularly sharp twinge in her back made her stop and stand upright for a moment, wincing. Martha noticed and said: "What's the matter?"

"Backache," Aliena said shortly. She did not want to discuss it, for the cause was surely sleeping on the floor in the drafty back room, and nobody knew about that, not even Martha.

Martha stood up and took a hot stone from the fire. Aliena sat down. Martha wrapped the stone in an old scorched piece of leather, and held it against Aliena's back. It gave her immediate relief. Martha started to plait Aliena's hair, which had grown again after being burned away and was once again an undisciplined mass of dark curls. Aliena felt soothed.

She and Martha had become quite close since Ellen left. Poor Martha: she had lost her mother and then her stepmother. Aliena felt herself to be a poor substitute for a mother. Besides, she was only ten years older than Martha. She played the role of older sister, really. Oddly enough, the person Martha missed most was her stepbrother, Jack.

But then, everyone missed Jack.

Aliena wondered where he was. He might be quite close, working on a cathedral in Gloucester or Salisbury. More likely he had gone to Normandy. But he could be much farther afield: Paris, Rome, Jerusalem, or Egypt. Recalling the stories that pilgrims told about such faraway places, she visualized Jack in a sandy desert, carving stones for a Saracen fortress in the blinding sunlight. Was he thinking of her now?

Her thoughts were interrupted by a noise of hooves outside, and a moment later her brother, Richard, walked in, leading his horse. He and the horse were soaking wet and covered with mud. Aliena took some hot water from the fire for him to wash his hands and face, and Martha led the horse out to the backyard. Aliena put bread and cold beef on the kitchen table and poured him a cup of beer.

Alfred said: "What's the news of the war?"

Richard dried his face on a rag and sat down to his breakfast. "We were defeated at Wilton," he said.

"Was Stephen taken?"

"No, he escaped, just as Maud escaped from Oxford. Now Stephen is at Winchester and Maud is at Bristol, and they're both licking their wounds and consolidating their hold on the areas they control."

The news always seemed to be the same, Aliena thought. One side or both had won some small victory or suffered some small loss, but there was never any prospect of the end of the war.

Richard looked at her and said: "You're getting fat."

She nodded and said nothing. She was eight months pregnant, but nobody knew. It was lucky that the weather had been cold, so that she had been able to continue to wear layers of loose winter clothing which concealed her shape. In a few weeks' time the baby would be born, and the truth would come out. She still had no idea what she was going to do then.

The bell rang to summon the townspeople to mass. Alfred pulled on his boots and looked expectantly at Aliena.

"I don't think I can go," she said. "I feel terrible."

He shrugged indifferently and turned to her brother. "You

should come, Richard. Everyone will be there today—it's the first service in the new church."

Richard was surprised. "You've got the ceiling up already? I thought that was going to take the rest of the year."

"We rushed it. Prior Philip offered the men an extra week's wages if they could finish by today. It's amazing how much faster they worked. Even so, we only just made it—we took the falsework down this morning."

"I must see this," Richard said. He stuffed the last of the bread and beef into his mouth and stood up.

Martha said to Aliena: "Do you want me to stay with you?"

"No, thanks. I'm fine. You go. I'll just lie down."

The three of them put on their cloaks and went out. Aliena went into the back room, taking with her the hot stone in its leather wrapping. She lay down on Alfred's bed with the stone under her back. She had become terribly lethargic since her marriage. Previously, she had run a household *and* been the busiest wool merchant in the county; now, she had trouble keeping house for Alfred even though she had nothing else to do.

She lay there feeling sorry for herself for a while, wishing she could fall asleep. Suddenly she felt a trickle of warm water on her inner thigh. She was shocked. It was almost as if she was urinating, but she wasn't, and a moment later the trickle turned into a flood. She sat bolt upright. She knew what it meant. Her waters had broken. The baby was coming.

She felt scared. She needed help. She called to her neighbor at the top of her voice: "Mildred! Mildred, come here!" Then she remembered that nobody was at home—they had all gone to church.

The flow of water slowed, but Alfred's bed was soaked. He was going to be furious, she thought fearfully; and then she remembered that he was going to be furious anyway, for he would know that the baby was not his child, and she thought: Oh, God, what am I going to do?

The back pain came again, and she realized that this must be what they called labor pains. She forgot about Alfred. She was about to give birth. She was too frightened to go through with it alone. She wanted someone to help her. She decided to go to the church.

She swung her legs off the bed. Another spasm took her, and she paused, her face screwed up in pain, until it went away. Then she got off the bed and left the house.

Her mind was in a whirl as she staggered along the muddy street. When she was at the priory gate the pain came again, and she had to lean against the wall and grit her teeth until it passed. Then she went into the priory close.

Most of the population of the town was crowded into the high tunnel of the chancel and the lower tunnels of the two side aisles. The altar was at the far end. The new church was peculiar in appearance: the rounded stone ceiling would eventually have a triangular wooden roof over it, but now it looked unprotected, like a bald man without a hat. The congregation stood with their backs to Aliena.

As she lurched toward the cathedral, the bishop, Waleran Bigod, got up to speak. She saw, as if in a nightmare, that William Hamleigh was standing beside him. Bishop Waleran's words penetrated her distress. ". . . with great pride and pleasure that I have to tell you that the Lord King, Stephen, has confirmed Lord William as the earl of Shiring."

Despite her pain and fear Aliena was horrified to hear this. For six years, ever since the awful day when they had seen their father in the Winchester jailhouse, she had dedicated her life to winning back the family property. She and Richard had survived robbers and rapists, conflagration and civil war. Several times the prize had seemed to be within their grasp. But now they had lost it.

The congregation murmured angrily. They had all suffered at William's hands and they still lived in fear of him. They were not happy to see him honored by the king who was supposed to protect them. Aliena looked around for Richard, to see how he was taking this terminal blow; but she could not locate him.

Prior Philip stood up with a face like thunder and started the hymn. The congregation began halfheartedly to sing. Aliena leaned against a column as another contraction seized her. She was at the back of the crowd and nobody noticed her. Somehow the bad news had calmed her. I'm only having a baby, she thought; it happens every day. I just need to find Martha or Richard, and they will take care of everything.

When the pain passed she pushed her way into the congregation, looking for Martha. There was a group of women in the low tunnel of the north aisle, and she made for them. People looked curiously at her, but their attention was distracted by something else: a strange noise like rumbling. At first it was hardly distinguishable from the singing, but the singing quickly died away as the rumbling got louder.

Aliena reached the group of women. They were looking around anxiously for the source of the noise. Aliena touched one of them on the shoulder and said: "Have you seen Martha, my sister-in-law?"

The woman looked at her, and Aliena recognized the tanner's wife, Hilda. "Martha's on the other side, I think," Hilda said; then the rumbling became deafening and she looked away.

Aliena followed her gaze. In the middle of the church everyone was looking up, toward the top of the walls. The people in the side aisles craned their necks to peer through the arches of the arcade. Someone screamed. Aliena saw a crack appear in the far wall, running between two neighboring windows in the clerestory. As she looked, several huge pieces of masonry dropped from above into the crowd in the middle of the church. There was a cacophony of screaming and shouting, and everyone turned to flee.

The ground beneath her feet shook. Even as she tried to push her way out of the church she was aware that the high walls were spreading apart at the top, and the round barrel of the vault was cracking up. Hilda the tanner's wife fell in front of her, and Aliena tripped over the prone figure and went down herself. A shower of small stones spattered her as she tried to get up. Then the low roof of the aisle cracked and fell in, something hit her head, and everything went black.

Philip had begun the service feeling proud and grateful. It had been a close thing, but the vault was finished in time. In fact, only three of the four bays of the chancel had been vaulted, for the fourth could not be done until the crossing was built and the ragged-ended chancel walls were joined to the transepts. However, three bays were enough. All the builders' equipment had been ruthlessly cleared out: the tools, the piles of stone and timber, the scaffolding poles and hurdles, the heaps of rubble and the rubbish. The chancel had been swept clean. The monks had whitewashed the stonework and painted straight red lines on the mortar, making the pointing look neater than it really was, in accordance with custom. The altar and the bishop's throne had been moved up from the crypt. However, the bones of the saint, in their stone casket, were still down there: moving them was a solemn ceremony, called translation, which was to be the climax of today's service. As the service had begun, with the bishop on his throne, the monks in new robes lined up behind the altar, and the people of the town massed in the body of the church and crowded into the aisles, Philip had felt fulfilled, and he had thanked God for bringing him successfully to the end of the first, crucial stage in the rebuilding of the cathedral.

When Waleran had made his announcement about William, Philip had been furious. It was so obviously timed to mar the triumph of the occasion and remind the townspeople that they were still at the mercy of their savage overlord. Philip had been casting about wildly for some adequate response when the rumbling started.

It was like a nightmare that Philip sometimes had, in which he was walking on the scaffolding, very high up, perfectly confident of his safety, when he noticed a loose knot in the ropes binding the scaffolding poles together—nothing very serious—but when he bent to tighten the knot, the hurdle beneath him tilted a little, not much at first but enough to make him stumble, and then, in a flash, he was falling through the vast space of the chancel of the cathedral, falling sickeningly fast, and he knew he was about to die.

The rumbling was at first mystifying. For a moment or two he thought it was thunder; then it grew too loud, and the people stopped singing. Still Philip thought it was only some strange phenomenon, shortly to be explained, whose worst effect would be to interrupt the service. Then he looked up.

In the third bay, where the falsework had come down only this morning, cracks were appearing in the masonry, high on the walls, at the clerestory level. They appeared suddenly and flashed across the wall from one clerestory window to the next like striking snakes. Philip's first reaction was disappointment: he had been happy that the chancel was finished, but now he would have to undertake repairs, and all the people who had been so impressed with the builders' work would say: "More haste, less speed." Then the tops of the walls seemed to lean outward, and he realized with an awful sense of horror that this was not merely going to interrupt the service, this was going to be a catastrophe.

Cracks appeared in the curved vault. A big stone became detached from the web of masonry and tumbled slowly through the air. People started screaming and trying to get out of its way. Before Philip could see whether anyone was badly hurt, more stones began to fall. The congregation panicked, pushing and shoving and trampling on one another as they tried to dodge the falling stones. Philip had the wild thought that this was another attack of some kind by William Hamleigh; then he saw William, at the front of the congregation, battering people around him in a terrified bid to escape, and realized that William would not have done this to himself.

Most people were trying to move away from the altar, to get out of the cathedral through the open west end. But it was the westernmost part of the building, the open end, that was collapsing. The problem was in the third bay. In the second bay, where Philip was, the vault seemed to be holding; and behind him, in the first bay where the monks were lined up, it looked solid. At that end the opposite walls were held together by the east facade.

He saw little Jonathan, with Johnny Eightpence, both huddled at the far end of the north aisle. They were safer there than anywhere, Philip decided; and then he realized that he should try to get the rest of his flock to safety. "Come this way!" he shouted. "Everybody! Move this way!" Whether they heard him or not, they took no notice.

In the third bay, the tops of the walls crumbled, falling outward, and the entire vault collapsed, large and small stones falling through the air like a lethal hailstorm to land on the hysterical congregation. Philip darted forward and grabbed a citizen. "Go back!" he yelled, and shoved the man toward the east end. The startled man saw the monks huddled against the far wall and dashed to join them. Philip did the same to two women. The people with them realized what he was doing and moved east without being pushed. Other people began to get the idea, and a general move east began among those who had been at the front of the congregation. Looking up for an instant, Philip was appalled to see that the second bay was going to go: the same cracks were snaking across the clerestory and frosting the vault directly over his head. He continued to herd people to the safety of the east end, knowing that every person he moved might be a life saved. A rain of crumbled mortar fell on his shaved head, and then the stones started to come down. The people were scattering. Some had taken refuge in the shelter of the side aisles; some were crowded up against the east wall, among them Bishop Waleran; others were still trying to crowd out of the west end, crawling over the fallen rubble and bodies in the third bay. A stone hit Philip's shoulder. It was a glancing blow but it hurt. He put his hands over his head and looked around wildly. He was alone in the middle of the second bay: everyone else was around the edges of the danger zone. He had done all he could. He ran to the east end.

There he turned again and looked up. The clerestory of the second bay was collapsing now, and the vault was falling into the chancel, in exact replication of what had happened in the third bay; but there were fewer victims, because the people had had a chance to get out of the way, and because the roofs of the side aisles appeared to be holding there, whereas in the third bay they had given way. Everyone in the crowd at the east end moved back, pressing up against the wall, and all faces were turned up, watching the vault, to see whether the collapse would spread to the first bay. The crash of falling masonry seemed to become less loud, but a fog of dust and small stones filled the air and for a few moments no one could see anything. Philip held his breath. The dust cleared and he could see the vault again. It had collapsed right up to the edge of the first bay; but now it seemed to be holding.

The dust settled. Everything went quiet. Philip stared aghast at the ruins of his church. Only the first bay remained intact. The walls of the second bay were standing up to the level of the gallery, but in the third and fourth bays only the side aisles were left, and they were badly damaged. The floor of the church was a pile of rubble littered with the still or feebly moving bodies of the dead and injured. Seven years of work and hundreds of pounds in money had been destroyed, and dozens of people had been killed, maybe hundreds, all in a few terrible moments. Philip's heart ached for the wasted work and the lost people, and for the widows and orphans left behind; and his eyes filled with bitter tears.

A harsh voice spoke in his ear. "This is what comes of your damned arrogance, Philip!"

He turned around to see Bishop Waleran, his black clothes coated with dust, glaring at him triumphantly. Philip felt as if he had been stabbed. To see a tragedy such as this was heartbreaking, but to be *blamed* for it was unbearable. He wanted to say *I only tried to do my best!* but the words would not come: his throat seemed constricted and he could not speak.

His eye lit on Johnny Eightpence and little Jonathan, emerging from the shelter of the aisle, and he suddenly remembered his responsibilities. There would be plenty of time later to agonize over who was to blame. Right now there were scores of people injured and many more trapped in the rubble. He had to organize the rescue operation. He glared at Bishop Waleran and said fiercely: "Get out of my way." The startled bishop stepped aside, and Philip leaped up on the altar.

"Listen to me!" he called out at the top of his voice. "We have to take care of the wounded, rescue people who are trapped, and then bury the dead and pray for their souls. I'm going to appoint three leaders to organize this." He looked at the faces all around him, checking to see who was still alive and well. He spotted Alfred. "Alfred Builder is in charge of moving rubble and rescuing trapped people, and I want all the masons and wrights to work with him." Looking at the monks, he was relieved to see his trusted confidant, Milius, unhurt. "Milius Bursar is responsible for moving the dead and injured out of the church, and he will need strong young helpers. Randolph Infirmarer will take care of the wounded once they're out of this mess, and the older ones can help him, especially the older women. Right—let's begin." He jumped down from the altar. There was a hubbub of speech as people started to give orders and ask questions.

Philip went over to Alfred, who was looking shaken and scared. If anyone was to blame for this it was he, as master builder, but this was no time for recriminations. Philip said: "Divide your people into teams and give them separate areas to work."

Alfred looked blank for a moment; then his face cleared. "Yes. Right. We'll start at the west end and clear rubble out into the open space."

"Good." Philip left him and pushed through the crowd to Milius. He heard Milius say: "Carry the wounded well clear of the church and put them on the grass. Take the dead bodies out to the north side." He moved away, content as always to trust Milius to do the right thing. He saw Randolph Infirmarer clambering over the rubble and hurried after him. They both picked their way across the piles of ruined stonework. Outside the church at the west end was a crowd of people who had managed to get out before the worst of the collapse and so escaped injury. "Use those people," Philip said to Randolph. "Send someone to the infirmary to fetch your equipment and supplies. Have a few of them go to the kitchen for hot water. Ask the cellarer for strong wine for those who need reviving. Make sure you lay the dead and injured out in neat lines with spaces between them, so that your helpers don't fall over the bodies."

He looked around. The survivors were going to work. Many of those who had been sheltered by the intact east end had followed Philip across the rubble and had already started to remove the bodies. One or two of the injured who had only been dazed or stunned were getting to their feet unaided. Philip saw an old woman sitting on the floor looking bewildered. He recognized her as Maud Silver, the widow of a silversmith. He helped her up and led her away from the wreckage. "What happened?" she said, not looking at him. "I don't know what happened."

"Nor do I, Maud," he said.

As he returned to help someone else, Bishop Waleran's words sounded again in his mind: *This is what comes of your damned arrogance, Philip.* The accusation cut him to the quick because he thought it might be true. He was always pushing for more, better, faster. He had pushed Alfred to finish the vault just as he had pushed for a fleece fair and pushed to get the earl of Shiring's quarry. In each case the result had been tragedy: the slaughter of the quarrymen, the burning of Kingsbridge, and now this. Clearly ambition was to blame. Monks did better to live a life of resignation, accepting the tribulations and setbacks of this world as lessons in patience, taught by the Almighty.

As Philip helped to carry the groaning wounded and the unresisting dead out of the ruins of his cathedral, he resolved that in the future he would leave it to God to be ambitious and pushing: he, Philip, would passively accept whatever happened. If God wanted a cathedral, God would provide a quarry; if the town was burned, it should be taken as a sign that God did not want a fleece fair; and now that the church had fallen down, Philip would not rebuild it.

As he reached that decision, he saw William Hamleigh.

The new earl of Shiring was sitting on the floor in the third bay, near the north aisle, ashen-faced and trembling with pain, with his foot trapped under a big stone. Philip wondered, as he helped roll the stone away, why God had chosen to let so many good people die but had spared an animal such as William.

William was making a great fuss about the pain in his foot but was otherwise all right. They helped him to his feet. He leaned on the shoulder of a big man about his own size and began to hop away. Then a baby cried.

Everyone heard it. There were no babies in sight. They all looked around, mystified. The crying came again, and Philip realized it was coming from beneath a massive pile of stones in the aisle. "Over here!" he called. He caught Alfred's eye and beckoned him. "There's a baby alive under all that," he said.

They all listened to the crying. It sounded like a very small baby, not yet a month old. "You're right," Alfred said. "Let's shift some of those big stones." He and his helpers began to move rubble from a pile that completely blocked the arch of the third bay. Philip joined in. He could not think which of the townswomen had given birth in the last few weeks. Of course, a birth might not have come to his attention: although the town had got smaller in the past year, it was still big enough for him to miss such a commonplace event.

The crying stopped suddenly. Everyone stood still and listened, but it did not begin again. Grimly, they recommenced moving the stones. It was a perilous business, for removing one stone might cause others to fall. This was why Philip had put Alfred in charge. However, Alfred was not as cautious as Philip would have wished, and he seemed to be letting everyone do as they pleased, pulling stones away without any overall plan. At one point the whole pile shifted dangerously, and Philip called out: "Wait!"

They all stopped. Alfred was too shocked to organize people properly, Philip realized. He would have to do it himself. He said:

"If there is someone alive under there, something must have protected them; and if we let the pile shift, they could lose their protection, and be killed by our efforts. Let's do this carefully." He pointed to a group of stonemasons standing together. "You three, climb the heap and take stones from the top. Instead of carrying them away yourselves, just pass each stone to one of us and we'll take them away."

They restarted work according to Philip's plan. It seemed quicker as well as safer.

Now that the baby had stopped crying they were not sure exactly where they were heading, so they cleared across a broad area, most of the width of the bay. Some of the rubble was what had fallen from the vault, but the roof of the aisle had partly collapsed, so there were timber and roof slates as well as stones and mortar.

Philip worked tirelessly. He wanted that baby to survive. Even though he knew there were dozens of people dead, somehow the baby seemed more important. If it could be rescued, he felt, there was still hope for the future. As he hefted the stones, coughing and half blind from the dust, he prayed fervently that the baby would be found alive.

Eventually he could see, above the heaped rubble, the outer wall of the aisle and part of one deep-set window. There seemed to be a space behind the pile. Perhaps someone was alive in there. A mason climbed gingerly up the pile and looked down into the space. "Jesus!" he exclaimed.

For once Philip ignored the blasphemy. "Is the babe all right?" he said.

"I can't tell," said the mason.

Philip wanted to ask what the mason had seen, or, better still, take a look for himself, but the man recommenced clearing stones with renewed vigor, and there was nothing for it but to continue to help, in a fever of curiosity.

The level of the pile came down rapidly. There was a large stone near ground level that required three men to move it. As it was rolled aside, Philip saw the baby.

It was naked, and newborn. Its white skin was smeared with blood and building dust, but he could see that it had a head of startling carrot-colored hair. Looking more closely, Philip saw that it was a boy. It was lying on a woman's bosom and sucking at her breast. The child was alive, he saw, and his heart leaped for joy. He looked at the woman. She was alive, too. She caught his eye and gave him a weary, happy smile.

It was Aliena.

*   *   *

Aliena never went back to Alfred's house.

He told everyone that the baby was not his, and as proof pointed to the child's red hair, exactly the same color as Jack's; but he did not try to do any harm either to the baby or Aliena, apart from saying he would not have them in his house.

Aliena moved back into the one-room house in the poor quarter with her brother, Richard. She was relieved that Alfred's revenge was so mild. She was glad that she would no longer have to sleep on the floor at the foot of his bed like a dog. But mainly she was thrilled and proud about her lovely baby. He had red hair and blue eyes and perfect white skin, and he reminded her vividly of Jack.

No one knew why the church had fallen down. There were plenty of theories, however. Some said Alfred was not capable of being master builder. Others blamed Philip, for rushing to get the vault finished by Whitsun. Some of the masons said the falsework had been taken down before the mortar was properly dry. One old mason said the walls had never been intended to bear the weight of a stone vault.

Seventy-nine people had been killed, including those who died of their injuries later. Everyone said it would have been more if Prior Philip had not herded so many people to the east end. The priory graveyard was already full because of the fire at the fleece fair the previous year, and most of the dead were buried at the parish church. A lot of people said the cathedral was under a curse.

Alfred took all his masons off to Shiring, where he was building stone houses for the wealthy townspeople. The other craftsmen drifted away from Kingsbridge. No one was actually dismissed, and Philip continued to pay wages, but there was nothing for the men to do but tidy up the rubble, and after a few weeks they had all gone. No volunteers came to work on Sundays, the market was reduced to a few dispirited stalls, and Malachi packed his family and his possessions onto a huge cart pulled by four oxen and left town, searching for greener pastures.

Richard rented his fine black stallion to a farmer and he and Aliena lived on the proceeds. Without Alfred's support he could not go on as a knight, and in any case there was no point now that William had been made earl. Aliena still felt bound by her vow to her father, but just now there seemed nothing she could do to fulfill it. Richard sank into lethargy. He got up late, sat in the sun most of the day, and spent his evenings in the alehouse.

Martha still lived in the big house, alone except for an elderly woman servant. However, she spent most of her time with Aliena:

she loved to help with the baby, especially as he looked so much like her adored Jack. She wanted Aliena to call him Jack, but Aliena was reluctant to name him, for reasons she herself did not quite understand.

For Aliena the summer went by in a maternal glow. But when the harvest was in, and the weather cooled a little, and the evenings became shorter, she grew discontented.

Whenever she thought about her future, Jack came into her mind. He had gone, she had no idea where, and he would probably never come back, but he was still with her, dominating her thoughts, full of life and energy, as clear and vivid to her as if she had seen him only yesterday. She considered moving to another town and pretending she was a widow; she thought of trying to persuade Richard to earn a living somehow; she contemplated doing some weaving, or taking in washing, or becoming a servant to one of the few townspeople who were still wealthy enough to hire help; and each new scheme was greeted with scornful laughter by the imaginary Jack in her head, who said: "Nothing will be any good without me." Making love to Jack on the morning of her marriage to Alfred had been the greatest sin she had ever committed, and she had no doubt that now she was being punished for it; but still there were times when she felt it was the only good thing she had done in her entire life; and when she looked at her baby, she could not bring herself to regret it. Nevertheless she was restless. A baby was not enough. She felt incomplete, unfulfilled. Her house seemed too small, Kingsbridge seemed half dead, life was too uneventful. She became impatient with the baby and snappish with Martha.

At the end of the summer, the farmer brought the horse back: it was no longer needed, and suddenly Richard and Aliena had no income. One day in early autumn Richard went to Shiring to sell his armor. While he was away, and Aliena was eating apples for dinner to save money, Jack's mother walked into the house.

"Ellen!" Aliena said. She was more than startled. There was consternation in her voice, for Ellen had cursed a church wedding, and Prior Philip might yet have her punished for it.

"I came to see my grandson," Ellen said calmly.

"But how did you know . . . ?"

"You hear things, even in the forest." She went over to the cradle in the corner and looked at the sleeping child. Her face softened. "Well, well. There's no doubt about whose son he is. Does he keep well?"

"Never had anything wrong with him—he's small but tough," Aliena said proudly. She added: "Like his grandmother." She studied Ellen. She was leaner than when she had left, and brown-skinned, and she wore a short leather tunic that revealed her tanned calves. Her feet were bare. She looked young and fit: forest life seemed to suit her. Aliena calculated that she must be thirty-five years old. "You seem very well," she said.

"I miss you all," Ellen said. "I miss you, and Martha, and even your brother Richard. I miss my Jack. And I miss Tom." She looked sad.

Aliena was still worried for her safety. "Did anyone see you coming here? The monks might still want to punish you."

"There isn't a monk in Kingsbridge who's got the guts to arrest me," she said with a grin. "But I was careful anyway—no one saw me." There was a pause. Ellen looked hard at Aliena. Aliena became slightly uncomfortable under the penetrating stare of Ellen's curious honey-colored eyes. At last Ellen said: "You're wasting your life."

"What do you mean?" Aliena said, though Ellen's words had struck a chord instantly.

"You should go and find Jack."

Aliena felt a pang of delicious hope. "But I can't," she said.

"Why not?"

"I don't know where he is, for one thing."

"I do."

Aliena's heart beat faster. She had thought nobody knew where Jack had gone. It was as if he had vanished off the face of the earth. But now she would be able to imagine him in a specific, real place. It changed everything. He might be somewhere nearby. She could show him his baby.

Ellen said: "At least, I know where he was headed."

"Where?" Aliena said urgently.

"Santiago de Compostela."

"Oh, God." Her heart sank. She was desperately disappointed. Compostela was the town in Spain where the Apostle James was buried. It was a journey of several months. Jack might as well have been on the far side of the world.

Ellen said: "He was hoping to speak to the jongleurs on the road and find out something about his father."

Aliena nodded disconsolately. That made sense. Jack had always resented knowing so little about his father. But he might well never return. On such a long journey he was almost certain to find a cathedral he wanted to work on, and then he might settle down. In going to seek his father he had probably lost his son.

"It's so far away," Aliena said. "I wish I could go after him."

"Why not?" Ellen said. "Thousands of people go there on pilgrimage. Why shouldn't you?"

"I made a vow to my father to take care of Richard until he becomes the earl," she told Ellen. "I couldn't leave him."

Ellen looked skeptical. "Just how do you imagine you're helping him at the moment?" she said. "You're penniless and William is the new earl. Richard has lost any chance he might have had of regaining the earldom. You're no more use to him here in Kingsbridge than you would be in Compostela. You dedicated your life to that wretched vow. But now there's nothing more you can do. I don't see how your father could reproach you. If you ask me, the greatest favor you could do Richard would be to abandon him for a while, and give him a chance to learn independence."

It was true, Aliena thought, that she was no use to Richard at the moment, whether she stayed in Kingsbridge or not. Could it be possible that she was now free—free to go and find Jack? The mere idea made her heart race. "But I haven't any money to go on pilgrimage," she said.

"What happened to that great big horse?"

"We still have it—"

"Sell it."

"How can I? It's Richard's."

"For God's sake, who the hell bought it?" Ellen said angrily. "Did Richard work hard for years building up a wool business? Did Richard negotiate with greedy peasants and hard-nosed Flemish buyers? Did Richard collect the wool and store it and set up a market stall and sell it? Don't tell me it's Richard's horse!"

"He would be so angry—"

"Good. Let's hope he gets angry enough to do some work for the first time in his life."

Aliena opened her mouth to argue, then closed it again. Ellen was right. Richard had always relied on her for everything. While he had been fighting for his patrimony she had been obliged to support him. But now he was not fighting for anything. He had no further claim on her.

She imagined meeting Jack again. She visualized his face, smiling at her. They would kiss. She felt a stir of pleasure in her loins. She realized she was getting damp down there at the mere thought of him. She felt embarrassed.

Ellen said: "Traveling is hazardous, of course."

Aliena smiled. "That's one thing I'm not worried about. I've been traveling since I was seventeen years old. I can take care of myself."

"Anyway, there will be hundreds of people on the road to Compostela. You can join with a large pilgrim band. You won't have to travel alone."

Aliena sighed. "You know, if I didn't have Baby I think I'd do it."

"It's because of Baby that you must," Ellen said. "He needs a father."

Aliena had not looked at it that way: she had been thinking of the journey as purely selfish. Now she saw that the baby needed Jack as much as she did. In her obsession with the day-to-day care of the baby she had not thought about his future. Suddenly it seemed terribly unfair that he should grow up not knowing the brilliant, unique, adorable genius who was his father.

She realized she was talking herself into going, and she felt a thrill of apprehension.

A snag occurred to her. "I couldn't take the baby to Compostela."

Ellen shrugged. "He won't know the difference between Spain and England. But you don't have to take him."

"What else could I do?"

"Leave him with me. I'll feed him on goat's milk and wild honey."

Aliena shook her head. "I couldn't bear to be parted from him. I love him too much."

"If you love him," Ellen said, "go and find his father."

Aliena found a ship at Wareham. When she had crossed to France as a girl, with her father, they had gone in one of the Norman warships. These were long, narrow vessels whose sides curved up to a high, sharp point at front and back. They had rows of oars along each side and a square leather sail. The ship that was to take her to Normandy now was similar to those warships, but wider at the waist, and deeper, to take cargo. It had come from Bordeaux, and she had watched the barefoot sailors unload great casks of wine destined for the cellars of the wealthy.

Aliena knew she should leave her baby but she was heartbroken about it. Every time she looked at him she rehearsed all the arguments and decided again that she ought to go; and it made no difference: she did not want to part from him.

Ellen had come to Wareham with her. Here Aliena had joined up with two monks from Glastonbury Abbey who were going to visit their property in Normandy. Three other people would be passengers on the ship: a young squire who had spent four years with an English relative and was returning to his parents in Toulouse, and two young masons who had heard that wages were higher and girls were prettier on the other side of the water. On the morning they were to sail, they all waited in the alehouse while the crew loaded the ship with heavy ingots of Cornish tin. The masons drank several pots of ale but did not appear to get drunk. Aliena hugged the baby and cried silently.

At last the ship was ready to leave. The sturdy gray mare Aliena had bought in Shiring had never seen the sea, and refused to go up the gangplank. However, the squire and the masons collaborated enthusiastically and eventually got the horse on board.

Aliena was blinded by tears as she gave her baby to Ellen. Ellen took the baby, but she said: "You can't do this. I was wrong to suggest it."

Aliena cried even more. "But there's Jack," she sobbed. "I can't live without Jack, I know I can't. I must look for him."

"Oh, yes," Ellen said. "I'm not suggesting you abandon the trip. But you can't leave your baby behind. Take him with you."

Aliena was flooded with gratitude and cried all the more. "Do you really think it will be all right?"

"He's been as happy as could be, all the way here, riding with you. The rest of the trip will only be more of the same. And he doesn't much like goat's milk."

The captain of the vessel said: "Come on, ladies, the tide's on the turn."

Aliena took the baby back and kissed Ellen. "Thank you. I'm so happy."

"Good luck," Ellen said.

Aliena turned and ran up the gangplank onto the ship.

They left immediately. Aliena waved until Ellen was a dot on the quay. As they rowed out of Poole Harbour it began to rain. There was no shelter up above, so Aliena sat in the bottom, with the horses and the cargo. The partial decking on which the oarsmen sat above her head did not completely protect her from the weather, but she was able to keep the baby dry inside her cloak. The motion of the ship seemed to agree with him, and he went to sleep. When darkness fell, and the ship anchored, Aliena joined the monks in their prayers. Afterward she dozed fitfully, sitting upright with the baby in her arms.

They landed at Barfleur the next day and Aliena found lodgings in the nearest town, Cherbourg. She spent another day going around the town, speaking to innkeepers and builders, asking if they recalled a young English mason with flaming red hair. Nobody did. There were lots of redheaded Normans, so they might not have noticed him. Or he might have crossed to a different port.

Aliena had not realistically expected to find traces of Jack so soon, but nevertheless she was disheartened. On the following day she set off, heading south. She traveled with a seller of knives and his cheerful fat wife and four children. They moved quite slowly, and Aliena was happy to keep to their pace and conserve her horse's strength, for it had to carry her a long way. Despite the protection of traveling with a family she kept her sharp, long-bladed knife strapped up her left sleeve. She did not look rich: her clothes were warm but not fancy, and her horse was sturdy rather than spirited. She was careful to keep a few coins handy in a purse, and never show anyone the heavy money belt strapped around her waist underneath her tunic. She fed the baby discreetly, not letting strange men see her breasts.

That night she was immensely cheered by a splendid stroke of luck. They stopped at a tiny village called Lessay, and there Aliena met a monk who vividly remembered a young English mason who had been fascinated by the revolutionary new rib-vaulting in the abbey church. Aliena was exultant. The monk even remembered Jack saying he had landed at Honfleur, which explained why there was no trace of him at Cherbourg. Although it was a year ago, the man talked volubly about Jack, and had obviously been charmed by him. Aliena was thrilled to be talking to someone who had seen him. It was confirmation that she was on the right trail.

Eventually she left the monk and lay down to sleep on the floor of the abbey guesthouse. As she drifted off she hugged the baby tight and whispered into his tiny pink ear: "We're going to find your Daddy."

The baby fell ill at Tours.

The city was wealthy and dirty and crowded. Rats ran in packs around the huge grain stores beside the river Loire. It was full of pilgrims. Tours was a traditional starting point for the pilgrimage to Compostela. In addition, the feast day of Saint Martin, the first bishop of Tours, was imminent, and many had come to the abbey church to visit his tomb. Martin was famous for having cut his cloak in two and given half to a naked beggar. Because of the feast, the inns and lodging houses of Tours were packed. Aliena was obliged to take what she could, and she stayed in a ramshackle dockside tavern run by two elderly sisters who were too old and frail to keep the place clean.

At first she did not spend much time at her lodgings. With her baby in her arms she explored the streets, asking after Jack. She soon realized the city was so constantly full of visitors that the inn-keepers could not even remember their guests of the week before last, so there was no point in asking them about someone who might have been here a year ago. However, she stopped at every building site to ask if they had employed a young English mason with red hair called Jack. Nobody had.

She was disappointed. She had not heard anything of him since Lessay. If he had stuck to his plan of going to Compostela he would almost certainly have come to Tours. She began to fear that he might have changed his mind.

She went to the church of Saint Martin, as everyone did; and there she saw a team of builders engaged on extensive repair work. She sought out the master builder, a small, bad-tempered man with thinning hair, and asked if he had employed an English mason.

"I never employ the English," he said abruptly, before she had finished her sentence. "English masons are no good."

"This one is *very* good," she said. "And he speaks good French, so you might not have known he's English. He has red hair—"

"No, never seen him," the master said rudely, and turned away.

Aliena went back to her lodgings somewhat depressed. To be treated nastily for no reason at all was very dispiriting.

That night she suffered a stomach upset and got no sleep at all. The next day she felt too ill to go out, and spent all day lying in bed in the tavern, with the stink of the river coming in at the window and the smells of spilled wine and cooking oil seeping up the stairs. On the following morning the baby was ill.

He woke her with his crying. It was not his usual lusty, demanding squall, but a thin, weak, sorry complaint. He had the same upset stomach Aliena had, but he was also feverish. His normally alert blue eyes were shut tight in distress, and his tiny hands were clenched into fists. His skin was flushed and blotchy.

He had never been ill before, and Aliena did not know what to do.

She gave him her breast. He sucked thirstily for a while, then cried again, then sucked again. The milk went straight through him, and seemed to give him no comfort.

There was a pleasant young chambermaid working at the tavern, and Aliena asked her to go to the abbey and buy holy water. She considered sending for a doctor, but they always wanted to bleed people, and she could not believe that it would help Baby to be bled.

The maid returned with her mother, who burned a bunch of dried herbs in an iron bowl. They gave off an acrid smoke that seemed to absorb the bad smells of the place. "The baby will be thirsty—give him the breast as often as he wants it," she said. "Have plenty to drink yourself, so that you have enough milk. That's all you can do."

"Will he be all right?" Aliena said anxiously.

The woman looked sympathetic. "I don't know, dear. When they're so small you can't tell. Usually they survive things like this. Sometimes they don't. Is he your first?"

"Yes."

"Just remember that you can always have more."

Aliena thought: But this is Jack's baby, and I've lost Jack. She kept her thoughts to herself, thanked the woman, and paid her for the herbs.

When they had gone she diluted the holy water with ordinary water, dipped a rag in it, and cooled the baby's head.

He seemed to get worse as the day wore on. Aliena gave him her breast when he cried, sang to him when he lay awake, and cooled him with holy water when he slept. He suckled continually but fitfully. Fortunately she had plenty of milk—she always had. She herself was still ill and kept going with dry bread and watered wine. As the hours went by she came to hate the room she was in, with its bare flyblown walls, rough plank floor, ill-fitting door and mean little window. It had precisely four items of furniture: the rickety bed, a three-legged stool, a clothes pole, and a floor-standing candlestick with three prongs but only one candle.

When darkness fell the maid came and lit the candle. She looked at the baby, who was lying on the bed, waving his arms and legs and grizzling plaintively. "Poor little thing," she said. "He doesn't understand why he feels so bad."

Aliena moved from the stool to the bed, but she kept the candle burning, so that she could see the baby. Through the night they both dozed fitfully. Toward dawn the baby's breathing became shallow, and he stopped crying and moving.

Aliena began to cry silently. She had lost Jack's trail, and her baby was going to die here, at a house full of strangers in a city far from home. There would never be another Jack and she would never have another baby. Perhaps she would die too. That might be for the best.

At daybreak she blew out the candle and fell into an exhausted sleep.

A loud noise from downstairs woke her abruptly. The sun was up and the riverside below the window was loudly busy. The baby was dead still, his face peaceful at last. Cold fear gripped her heart. She touched his chest: he was neither hot nor cold. She gasped with fright. Then he gave a deep, shuddering sigh and opened his eyes. Aliena almost fainted with relief.

She snatched him up and hugged him, and he began to cry lustily. He was well again, she realized: his temperature was normal and he was in no distress. She put him to her breast and he sucked hungrily. Instead of turning away after a few mouthfuls he carried on, and when one breast was dry he drained the other. Then he fell into a deep, contented sleep.

Aliena realized that her symptoms had gone, too, although she felt wrung out. She slept beside the baby until midday, then fed him again; then she went down to the public room of the tavern and ate a dinner of goat's cheese and fresh bread with a little bacon.

Perhaps it was the holy water of Saint Martin that had made the baby well. That afternoon she went back to Saint Martin's tomb to give thanks to the saint.

While she was in the great abbey church, she watched the builders at work, thinking about Jack, who might yet see his baby after all. She wondered whether he had got diverted from his intended route. Perhaps he was working in Paris, carving stones for a new cathedral there. While she was thinking about him, her eye lit on a new corbel being installed by the builders. It was carved with a figure of a man who appeared to be holding the weight of the pillar above on his back. She gasped aloud. She knew instantly, without a shadow of doubt, that the twisted, agonized figure had been carved by Jack. So he had been here!

With her heart beating excitedly, she approached the men who were doing the work. "That corbel," she said breathlessly. "The man who carved it was English, wasn't he?"

An old laborer with a broken nose answered her. "That's right—Jack Fitzjack did it. Never seen anything like it in my life."

"When was he here?" Aliena said. She held her breath while the old man scratched his graying head through a greasy cap.

"Must be nearly a year ago, now. He didn't stay long, mind. Master didn't like him." He lowered his voice. "Jack was too good, if you want to know the truth. He showed the master up. So he had to go." He laid a finger alongside his nose in a gesture of confidentiality.

Aliena said excitedly: "Did he say where he was going?"

The old man looked at the baby. "That child is his, if the hair is anything to go by."

"Yes, he is."

"Will Jack be pleased to see you, do you think?"

Aliena realized the laborer thought Jack might have been running away from her. She laughed. "Oh, yes!" she said. "He'll be pleased to see me."

He shrugged. "He said he was going to Compostela, for what it's worth."

"Thank you!" Aliena said happily, and to the old man's astonishment and delight she kissed him.

The pilgrim trails across France converged at Ostabat, in the foothills of the Pyrenees. There the group of twenty or so pilgrims with whom Aliena was traveling swelled to about seventy. They were a footsore but merry bunch: some prosperous citizens, some probably on the run from justice, a few drunks, and several monks and clergymen. The men of God were there for reasons of piety but most of the others seemed bent on having a good time. Several languages were spoken, including Flemish, a German tongue, and a southern French language called Oc. Nevertheless there was no lack of communication among them, and as they crossed the Pyrenees together they sang, played games, told stories, and—in several cases—had love affairs.

After Tours, unfortunately, Aliena did not find any more people who remembered Jack. However, there were not as many jongleurs along her route through France as she had imagined. One of the Flemish pilgrims, a man who had made the journey before, said there would be more of them on the Spanish side of the mountains.

He was right. At Pamplona, Aliena was thrilled to find a jongleur who recalled speaking to a young Englishman with red hair who had been asking about his father.

As the weary pilgrims moved slowly through northern Spain toward the coast, she met several more jongleurs, and most of them remembered Jack. She realized, with mounting excitement, that all of them said he had been going *to* Compostela: no one had encountered him coming back.

Which meant he was still there.

As her body became more sore her spirits lifted higher. She could hardly contain her optimism during the last few days of the journey. It was midwinter, but the weather was mild and sunny. The baby, now six months old, was fit and happy. She felt sure of finding Jack at Compostela.

They arrived there on Christmas Day.

They went straight to the cathedral and attended mass. The church was packed, naturally. Aliena walked round and round the congregation, staring at faces, but Jack was not there. Of course, he was not very devout; in fact he never went to churches except to work. By the time she had found accommodation it was dark. She went to bed, but she could hardly sleep for excitement, knowing that Jack was probably within a few steps of where she lay, and tomorrow she would see him, and kiss him, and show him his baby.

She was up at first light. The baby sensed her impatience and nursed irritably, biting her nipples with his gums. She washed him hastily, then went out, carrying him in her arms.

As she walked the dusty streets she expected to see Jack around every corner. How astonished he would be when he caught sight of her! And how pleased! However, she did not see him on the streets, so she began calling at lodging houses. As soon as people started work she went to building sites and spoke to masons. She knew the words for *mason* and *redhead* in the Castilian dialect, and the inhabitants of Compostela were used to foreigners, so she succeeded in communicating; but she found no trace of Jack. She began to be worried. Surely people should know him. He was not the kind of person you could easily overlook, and he must have been living here for several months. She also kept an eye open for his characteristic carvings, but she saw none.

Around midmorning she met a blowsy, middle-aged woman tavern-keeper who spoke French and remembered Jack.

"A handsome lad—is he yours? None of the local girls made any progress with him, anyway. He was here at midsummer, but he didn't stay long, more's the pity. He wouldn't say where he was going, either. I liked him. If you find him, give him a big kiss from me."

Aliena went back to her lodgings and lay on the bed, staring at the ceiling. The baby grizzled but for once she ignored him. She was exhausted, disappointed, and homesick. It was not fair: she had trailed him all the way to Compostela, but he had gone somewhere else!

Since he had not gone back to the Pyrenees, and as there was nothing to the west of Compostela but a strip of coastline and an ocean that reached to the end of the world, Jack must have gone farther south. She would have to set off again, on her gray mare, with her baby in her arms, into the heart of Spain.

She wondered how far from home she would have to go before her pilgrimage came to an end.

Jack spent Christmas Day with his friend Raschid Alharoun in Toledo. Raschid was a baptized Saracen who had made a fortune importing spices from the East, especially pepper. They met at midday mass in the great cathedral and then strolled back, in the warm winter sunshine, through the narrow streets and the fragrant bazaar to the wealthy quarter.

Raschid's house was made of dazzling white stone and built around a courtyard with a fountain. The shady arcades of the courtyard reminded Jack of the cloisters at Kingsbridge Priory. In England they gave protection from wind and rain, but here their purpose was to deflect the heat of the sun.

Raschid and his guests sat on floor cushions and dined off a low table. The men were waited on by the wives and daughters, and various servant girls whose place in the household was somewhat dubious: as a Christian, Raschid could have only one wife, but Jack suspected that he had quietly overlooked the Church's disapproval of concubines.

The women were the greatest attraction of Raschid's hospitable house. They were all beautiful. His wife was a statuesque, graceful woman with smooth dark-brown skin, lustrous black hair, and liquid brown eyes, and his daughters were slimmer versions of the same type. There were three of them. The eldest was engaged to be married to another dinner guest, the son of a silk merchant in the city. "My Raya is the perfect daughter," Raschid said as she went around the table with a bowl of scented water for the guests to dip their hands in. "She is attentive, obedient and beautiful. Josef is a lucky man." The fiancé bowed his head in acknowledgment of his good fortune.

The second daughter was proud, even haughty. She appeared to resent the praise lavished on her sister. She looked down at Jack while she poured some kind of drink into his goblet from a copper jug. "What is it?" he said.

"Peppermint cordial," she said disdainfully. She disliked waiting on him, for she was the daughter of a great man, and he was a penniless vagabond.

It was the third daughter, Aysha, whom Jack liked most. In the three months he had been here he had got to know her quite well. She was fifteen or sixteen years old, small and lively, always grinning. Although she was three or four years younger than he, she did not seem juvenile. She had a lively, questioning intelligence. She asked him endless questions about England and the different way of life there. She often made fun of Toledo society manners—the snobbery of the Arabs, the fastidiousness of the Jews, and the bad taste of the newly rich Christians—and she sometimes had Jack in fits of laughter. Although she was the youngest, she seemed the least innocent of the three: something about the way she looked at Jack, as she leaned over him to place a dish of spicy prawns on the table, unmistakably revealed a licentious streak. She caught his eye and said "Peppermint cordial" in a perfect imitation of her sister's snooty manner, and Jack giggled. When he was with Aysha he could often forget Aliena for hours at a time.

But when he was away from this house, Aliena was on his mind as much as if he had left her only yesterday. His memories of her were painfully vivid, although he had not seen her for more than a year. He could recall any of her expressions at will: laughing, thoughtful, suspicious, anxious, pleased, astonished, and—clearest of all—passionate. He had forgotten nothing about her body, and he could still see the curve of her breast, feel the soft skin on the inside of her thigh, taste her kiss, and smell the scent of her arousal. He often longed for her.

To cure himself of his fruitless desire he sometimes imagined what Aliena must be doing. In his mind's eye he would see her pulling Alfred's boots off at the end of the day, sitting down to eat with him, kissing him, making love to him, and giving her breast to a baby boy who looked just like Alfred. These visions tortured him but did not stop him from longing for her.

Today, Christmas Day, Aliena would roast a swan and re-dress it with its feathers for the table, and there would be posset to drink, made of ale, eggs, milk, and nutmeg. The food in front of Jack could not have been more different. There were mouth-watering dishes of strangely spiced lamb, rice mixed with nuts, and salads dressed with lemon juice and olive oil. It had taken Jack awhile to get used to Spanish cooking. They never served the great joints of beef, legs of pork and haunches of venison without which no feast was complete in England; nor did they consume thick slabs of bread. They did not have the lush pastures for grazing vast herds of cattle or the rich soil on which to grow fields of waving wheat. They made up for the relatively small quantities of meat by imaginative ways of cooking it with all kinds of spices, and in place of the ubiquitous bread of the English they had a wide variety of vegetables and fruits.

Jack was living with a small group of English clerics in Toledo. They were part of an international community of scholars that included Jews, Muslims and Arab Christians. The Englishmen were occupied translating works of mathematics from Arabic into Latin, so they could be read by Christians. There was an atmosphere of feverish excitement among them as they discovered and explored the treasure-house of Arab learning, and they had casually welcomed Jack as a student: they admitted into their circle anyone who understood what they were doing and shared their enthusiasm for it. They were like peasants who have labored for years to scratch a crop out of poor soil and then suddenly move to a rich alluvial valley. Jack had abandoned building to study mathematics. He had not yet needed to work for money: the clerics casually gave him a bed and any meals he wanted, and they would have provided him with a new robe and sandals if he had needed them.

Raschid was one of their sponsors. As an international trader he was multilingual and cosmopolitan in his attitudes. At home he spoke Castilian, the language of Christian Spain, rather than Mozarabic. His family also all spoke French, the language of the Normans, who were important traders. Although he was a man of commerce, he had a powerful intellect and a wide-ranging curiosity. He loved to talk to scholars about their theories. He had taken a liking to Jack immediately, and Jack dined at his house several times a week.

Now, as they began to eat, Raschid asked Jack: "What have the philosophers taught us this week?"

"I've been reading Euclid." Euclid's *Elements of Geometry* had been one of the first books translated.

"Euclid is a funny name for an Arab," said Ismail, Raschid's brother.

"He was Greek," Jack explained. "He lived before the birth of Christ. His work was lost by the Romans but preserved by the Egyptians—so it comes to us in Arabic."

"And now Englishmen are translating it into Latin!" Raschid said. "This amuses me."

"But what have you learned?" said Josef, the fiancé of Raya.

Jack hesitated. It was hard to explain. He tried to make it practical. "My stepfather, the builder, taught me how to perform certain operations in geometry: how to divide a line exactly in half, how to draw a right angle, and how to draw one square inside another so that the smaller is half the area of the larger."

"What is the purpose of such skills?" Josef interrupted. There was a note of scorn in his voice. He saw Jack as something of an upstart, and was jealous of the attention Raschid paid to Jack's conversation.

"Those operations are essential in planning buildings," Jack replied pleasantly, pretending not to notice Josef's tone. "Take a look at this courtyard. The area of the covered arcades around the edges is exactly the same as the open area in the middle. Most small courtyards are built like that, including the cloisters of monasteries. It's because these proportions are most pleasing. If the middle is bigger, it looks like a marketplace, and if it's smaller, it just looks as if there's a hole in the roof. But to get it exactly right, the builder has to be able to draw the open part in the middle so that it's precisely half the area of the whole thing."

"I never knew that!" Raschid said triumphantly. He liked nothing better than to learn something new.

"Euclid explains why these techniques work," Jack went on. "For example, the two parts of the divided line are equal because they form corresponding sides of congruent triangles."

"Congruent?" Raschid queried.

"It means exactly alike."

"Ah—now I see."

However, no one else did, Jack could tell.

Josef said: "But you could perform all these geometric operations before you read Euclid—so I don't see that you're any better off now."

Raschid protested: "A man is always better off for understanding something!"

Jack said: "Besides, now that I understand the principles of geometry I may be able to devise solutions to new problems that baffled my stepfather." He felt rather frustrated by the conversation: Euclid had come to him like the blinding flash of a revelation, but he was failing to communicate the thrilling importance of these new discoveries. He changed tack somewhat. "It's Euclid's method that is the most interesting," he said. "He takes five axioms—self-evident truths—and deduces everything else logically from them."

"Give me an example of an axiom," Raschid said.

"A line can be prolonged indefinitely."

"No it can't," said Aysha, who was handing round a bowl of figs.

The guests were somewhat startled to hear a girl joining in the argument, but Raschid laughed indulgently: Aysha was his favorite. "And why not?" he said.

"It has to come to an end sometime," she said.

Jack said: "But in your imagination, it could go on indefinitely."

"In my imagination, water could flow uphill and dogs speak Latin," she retorted.

Her mother came into the room and heard that rejoinder. "Aysha!" she said in a steely voice. "Out!"

All the men laughed. Aysha made a face and went out. Josef's father said: "Whoever marries her will have his hands full!" They laughed again. Jack laughed too; then he noticed they were all looking at him, as if the joke was on him.

After dinner, Raschid showed off his collection of mechanical toys. He had a tank in which you could mix water and wine and they would come out separately; a marvelous water-driven clock, which kept track of the hours in the day with phenomenal accuracy; a jug that would refill itself but never overflow; and a small wooden statue of a woman with eyes made of some kind of crystal that absorbed water in the warmth of the day and then shed it in the cool of the evening, so that she appeared to be weeping. Jack shared Raschid's fascination with these toys, but he was most intrigued by the weeping statue, for whereas the mechanisms of the others were simple once they had been explained, no one really understood how the statue worked.

They sat in the arcades around the courtyard in the afternoon, playing games, dozing, or talking idly. Jack wished he belonged to a big family like this one, with sisters and uncles and in-laws, and a family home they could all visit, and a position of respect in a small town. Suddenly he recalled the conversation he had had with his mother the night she rescued him from the priory punishment cell.

He had asked her about his father's relations, and she had said *Yes, he had a big family, back in France.* I have got a family like this one, somewhere, Jack realized. My father's brothers and sisters are my uncles and aunts. I might have cousins of my own age. I wonder if I will ever find them?

He felt adrift. He could survive anywhere but he belonged nowhere. He had been a carver, a builder, a monk and a mathematician, and he did not know which was the real Jack, if any. He sometimes wondered if he should be a jongleur like his father, or an outlaw like his mother. He was nineteen years old, homeless and rootless, with no family and no purpose in life.

He played chess with Josef and won; then Raschid came up and said: "Give me your chair, Josef—I want to hear more about Euclid."

Josef obediently gave up his chair to his prospective father-in-law, then moved away—he had already heard everything he ever wanted to know about Euclid. Raschid sat down and said to Jack: "You're enjoying yourself?"

"Your hospitality is matchless," Jack said smoothly. He had learned courtly manners in Toledo.

"Thank you; but I meant with Euclid."

"Yes. I don't think I succeeded in explaining the importance of this book. You see—"

"I think I understand," Raschid said. "Like you, I love knowledge for its own sake."

"Yes."

"Even so, every man has to make a living."

Jack did not see the relevance of that remark, so he waited for Raschid to say more. However, Raschid sat back with his eyes half closed, apparently content to enjoy a companionable silence. Jack began to wonder whether Raschid was reproaching him for not working at a trade. Eventually Jack said: "I expect I shall go back to building, one day."

"Good."

Jack smiled. "When I left Kingsbridge, riding my mother's horse, with my stepfather's tools in a satchel slung across my shoulder, I thought there was only one way to build a church: thick walls with round arches and small windows topped by a wooden ceiling or a barrel-shaped stone vault. The cathedrals I saw on my way from Kingsbridge to Southampton taught me no different. But Normandy changed my life."

"I can imagine," Raschid said sleepily. He was not very interested, so Jack recalled those days in silence. Within hours of landing at Honfleur he was looking at the abbey church of Jumièges. It was the highest church he had ever seen, but otherwise it had the usual round arches and wooden ceiling—except in the chapter house, where Abbot Urso had built a revolutionary stone ceiling. Instead of a smooth, continuous barrel, or a creased groin vault, this ceiling had ribs which sprang up from the tops of the columns and met at the apex of the roof. The ribs were thick and strong, and the triangular sections of ceiling between the ribs were thin and light. The monk who was keeper of the fabric explained to Jack that it was easier to build that way: the ribs were put up first, and the sections between were then simpler to make. This type of vault was also lighter. The monk was hoping to hear news from Jack of technical innovations in England, and Jack had to disappoint him. However, Jack's evident appreciation of rib-vaulting pleased the monk, and he told Jack that there was a church at Lessay, not far away, that had rib-vaulting throughout.

Jack went to Lessay the next day, and spent all afternoon in the church, staring in wonder at the vault. What was so striking about it, he finally decided, was the way the ribs, coming down from the apex of the vault to the capitals on top of the columns, seemed to *dramatize* the way the weight of the roof was being carried by the strongest members. The ribs made the logic of the building visible.

Jack traveled south, to the county of Anjou, and got a job doing repair work at the abbey church in Tours. He had no trouble persuading the master builder to give him a trial. The tools he had in his possession showed that he was a mason, and after a day at work the master knew he was a good one. His boast to Aliena, that he could get work anywhere in the world, was not entirely vain.

Among the tools he had inherited was Tom's foot rule. Only master builders owned these, and when the others discovered Jack had one, they asked him how he had become a master at such a young age. His first inclination was to explain that he was not really a master builder; but then he decided to say he was. After all, he had effectively run the Kingsbridge site while he was a monk, and he could draw plans just as well as Tom. But the master he was working for was annoyed to discover that he had hired a possible rival. One day Jack suggested a modification to the monk in charge of the building, and drew what he meant on the tracing floor. That was the beginning of his troubles. The master builder became convinced that Jack was after his job. He began to find fault with Jack's work, and put him on the monotonous task of cutting plain blocks.

Soon Jack set off again. He went to the abbey of Cluny, the headquarters of a monastic empire that spread all across Christendom. It was the Cluniac order that had initiated and fostered the now-famous pilgrimage to the tomb of Saint James at Compostela. All along the Compostela road there were churches dedicated to Saint James and Cluniac monasteries to take care of pilgrims. As Jack's father had been a jongleur on the pilgrim road, it seemed likely he had visited Cluny.

However, he had not. There were no jongleurs at Cluny. Jack learned nothing about his father there.

Nevertheless, the journey was by no means wasted. Every arch Jack had ever seen, until the moment he entered the abbey church of Cluny, had been semicircular; and every vault had been either tunnel-shaped, like a long line of round arches all stuck together, or groined, like the crossing where two tunnels met. The arches at Cluny were not semicircular.

They rose to a point.

There were pointed arches in the main arcades; the groined vaults of the side aisles had pointed arches; and—most startling of all—above the nave there was a stone ceiling that could only be described as a pointed barrel vault. Jack had always been taught that a circle was strong because it was perfect, and a round arch was strong because it was part of a circle. He would have thought that pointed arches were weak. In fact, the monks told him, the pointed arches were considerably stronger than the old round ones. The church at Cluny seemed to prove it, for despite the great weight of stonework in its peaked vault, it was very high.

Jack did not stay long at Cluny. He continued south, following the pilgrim road, diverging whenever the whim took him. In the early summer there were jongleurs all along the route, in the larger towns or near the Cluniac monasteries. They recited their verse narratives to crowds of pilgrims in front of churches and shrines, sometimes accompanying themselves on the viol, just the way Aliena had told him. Jack approached every one and asked if he had known Jack Shareburg. They all said no.

The churches he saw on his way through southwest France and northern Spain continued to astonish him. They were all much higher than the English cathedrals. Some of them had banded barrel vaults. The bands, reaching from pier to pier across the vault of the church, made it possible to build in stages, bay by bay, instead of all at once. They also changed the look of a church. By emphasizing the divisions between bays, they revealed that the building was a series of identical units, like a sliced loaf; and this imposed order and logic on the huge interior space.

He was in Compostela at midsummer. He had not known there

were places in the world that were so hot. Santiago was another breathtakingly tall church, and the nave, still under construction, also had a banded barrel vault. From there he went farther south.

The kingdoms of Spain had been under Saracen rule until recently; indeed, most of the country south of Toledo was still Muslim-dominated. The appearance of Saracen buildings fascinated Jack: their high, cool interiors, their arcades of arches, their stonework blinding white in the sun. But most interesting of all was the discovery that both rib-vaulting and pointed arches featured in Muslim architecture. Perhaps this was where the French had got their new ideas.

He could never work on another church like Kingsbridge Cathedral, he thought as he sat in the warm Spanish afternoon, listening vaguely to the laughter of the women somewhere deep in the big cool house. He still wanted to build the most beautiful cathedral in the world, but it would not be a massive, solid, fortress-like structure. He wanted to use the new techniques, the rib-vaults and the pointed arches. However, he thought he would not use them in quite the way they had been used so far. None of the churches he had seen had made the most of the possibilities. A picture of a church was forming in his mind. The details were hazy but the overall feeling was very strong: it was a spacious, airy building, with sunlight pouring through its huge windows, and an arched vault so high it seemed to reach heaven.

"Josef and Raya will need a house," Raschid said suddenly. "If you were to build it, other work would follow."

Jack was startled. One thing he had not thought of building was houses. "Do you think they want me to build their house?" he said.

"They might."

There was another long silence, during which Jack contemplated life as a housebuilder for wealthy merchants in Toledo.

Eventually Raschid seemed to come awake. He sat upright and opened his eyes wide. "I like you, Jack," he said. "You're an honest man, and you're worth talking to, which is more than can be said for most people I've met. I hope we will always be friends."

"So do I," said Jack, somewhat surprised by this unprompted tribute.

"I'm a Christian, so I don't keep my women locked away, as some of my Muslim brothers do. On the other hand, I'm Arab; which means I don't give them quite the . . . forgive me, the license, that other women are used to. I allow them to meet and talk with male guests at the house. I even allow friendships to develop. But at the point where friendship begins to ripen into something more—as happens so naturally among young people—then I expect the man to make a formal move. Anything else would be an insult."

"Of course," Jack said.

"I knew you'd understand." Raschid stood up and put an affectionate hand on Jack's shoulder. "I've never been blessed with a son; but if I had, I think he would have been like you."

On impulse, Jack said: "But darker, I hope."

Raschid looked blank for a moment, then he roared with laughter, startling the other guests around the courtyard. "Yes!" he said merrily. "Darker!" And he went into the house, still guffawing.

The older guests began to take their leave. Jack sat by himself, thinking over what had been said to him, as the afternoon cooled. He was being offered a deal, there was no question of that. If he married Aysha, Raschid would launch him as housebuilder to the wealthy of Toledo. There was also a warning: if he did not intend to marry her, he should stay away. The people of Spain had more elaborate manners than the English, but they could make their meaning plain when necessary.

When Jack reflected on his situation he sometimes found it incredible. Is this me? he thought. Is this Jack Jackson, bastard son of a man who was hanged, brought up in the forest, apprentice mason, escaped monk? Am I really being offered the beautiful daughter of a wealthy Arab merchant, plus a guaranteed living as a builder, in this balmy city? It sounds too good to be true. I even like the girl!

The sun was going down, and the courtyard was in shadow. There were only two people left in the arcade—himself and Josef. He was just wondering whether this situation could have been contrived when Raya and Aysha appeared, proving that it had. Despite the theoretical strictness about physical contact between girls and young men, their mother knew exactly what was happening, and Raschid probably did too. They would give the sweethearts a few moments of solitude; then, before they had time to do anything serious, the mother would come out into the courtyard, pretending to be outraged, and order the girls back inside.

On the other side of the courtyard Raya and Josef immediately started kissing. Jack stood up as Aysha approached him. She was wearing a floor-length white dress of Egyptian cotton, a fabric Jack had never seen before he came to Spain. Softer than wool and finer than linen, it clung to Aysha's limbs as she moved, and its white color seemed to glow in the twilight. It made her brown eyes look almost black. She stood close to him, grinning impishly. "What did he say to you?" she said.

Jack guessed she meant her father. "He offered to set me up as a housebuilder."

"What a dowry!" she said scornfully. "I can't believe it! At least he might have offered you money."

She had no patience with traditional Saracen indirection, Jack observed wryly. He found her frankness refreshing. "I don't think I want to build houses," he said.

She suddenly became solemn. "Do you like me?"

"You know I do."

She took a step forward, lifted her face, closed her eyes, stood on tiptoe and kissed him. She smelled of musk and ambergris. She opened her mouth, and her tongue darted between his lips playfully. His arms went around her almost involuntarily. He rested his hands on her waist. The cotton was very light: it was almost like touching her bare skin. She took his hand and raised it to her breast. Her body was lean and taut, and her breast was shallow, like a small, firm mound, with a tiny hard nipple at its tip. Her chest moved up and down as she became aroused. Jack was shocked to feel her hand moving between his legs. He squeezed her nipple between his fingertips. She gasped, and broke away from him, panting. He dropped his hands.

"Did I hurt you?" he whispered.

"No!" she said.

He thought of Aliena, and felt guilty; then he realized how foolish that was. Why should he feel that he was betraying a woman who had *married* another man?

Aysha looked at him for a moment. It was almost dark, but he could see that her face was suffused with desire. She lifted his hand and put it back on her breast. "Do it again, but harder," she said urgently.

He found her nipple and leaned forward to kiss her, but she pulled her head back and watched his face while he caressed her. He squeezed her nipple gently, then, obediently, pinched it hard. She arched her back so that her flat breasts protruded and her nipples made small hard puckers in the fabric of her dress. Jack bent his head to her breast. His lips closed around her nipple through the cotton. Then, on impulse, he took it between his teeth and bit down. He heard her sharp intake of breath.

He felt a shudder pass through her. She lifted his head from her breast and pressed herself against him. He bent his face to hers. She kissed him frantically, as if she wanted to cover his face with her mouth, and pulled his body to hers, making small panicky sounds in the back of her throat. Jack was aroused, bewildered and even a little scared: he had never known anything like this. He thought she was about to reach a climax. Then they were interrupted.

Her mother's voice came from the doorway. "Raya! Aysha! Come inside at once!"

Aysha looked up at him, panting. After a moment she kissed him again, hard, pressing her lips against his until she bruised him. She broke away. "I love you," she hissed. Then she ran into the house.

Jack watched her go. Raya followed her at a more sedate pace. Their mother flashed a disapproving look at him and Josef and then went in after the girls, shutting the door decisively behind her. Jack stood staring at the closed door, wondering what to make of it all.

Josef crossed the courtyard and interrupted his reverie. "Such beautiful girls—both of them!" he said with a conspiratorial wink.

Jack nodded absently and moved toward the gate. Josef went with him. As they passed under the arch, a servant materialized out of the shadows and closed the gate behind them.

Josef said: "The trouble with being engaged is that it leaves you with an ache between the legs." Jack made no reply. Josef said: "I might go down to Fatima's to get it eased." Fatima's was the whorehouse. Despite its Saracen name, nearly all the girls were light-skinned, and the few Arab whores were very high-priced. "Do you want to come?" Josef said.

"No," Jack replied. "I've got a different kind of ache. Good night." He walked quickly away. Josef was not his favorite companion at the best of times and tonight Jack found himself in an unforgiving mood.

The night air cooled as he headed back toward the college where he had a hard bed in the dormitory. He felt he was at a turning point. He was being offered a life of ease and prosperity, and all he had to do was forget Aliena and abandon his aspiration to build the most beautiful cathedral in the world.

That night he dreamed that Aysha came to him, her naked body slippery with scented oil, and she rubbed herself against him but would not let him make love to her.

When he woke up in the morning he had made his decision.

The servants would not let Aliena into the house of Raschid Alharoun. She probably looked like a beggar, she thought as she stood outside the gate, in her dusty tunic and worn boots, with her baby in her arms. "Tell Raschid Alharoun that I am seeking his friend Jack Fitzjack from England," she said in French, wondering if the dark-skinned servants could understand a single word. After a muttered consultation in some Saracen tongue, one of the servants, a tall man with coaly skin and hair like the fleece of a black sheep, went into the house.

Aliena fidgeted restlessly while the other servants stared at her openly. She had not learned patience, even on this interminable pilgrimage. After her disappointment at Compostela she had followed the road into the interior of Spain, to Salamanca. No one there remembered a redhaired young man interested in cathedrals and jongleurs, but a kindly monk told her that there was a community of English scholars at Toledo. It seemed a faint hope, but Toledo was not much farther down the dusty road, so she pressed on.

Another tantalizing disappointment had been waiting for her here. Yes, Jack had been here—what a stroke of luck!—but alas, he had already left. She was catching up with him: she was now only a month behind him. But, once again, nobody knew where he had gone.

In Compostela she had been able to guess that he must have gone south, because she had come from the east, and there was sea to the north and west. Here, unfortunately, there were more possibilities. He might have gone northeast, back toward France; west to Portugal; or south to Granada; and from the Spanish coast he might have taken ship for Rome, Tunis, Alexandria or Beirut.

Aliena had decided to give up the search if she did not get a strong indication of which way he had gone when he left here. She was bone-weary and a long way from home. She had very little energy or determination left, and she could not face going farther with no more than a faint hope of success. She was ready to turn around and go back to England, and try to forget about Jack forever.

Another servant came out of the white house. This one was dressed in more costly clothes and spoke French. He looked at Aliena warily but addressed her politely. "You are a friend of Mr. Jack?"

"Yes, an old friend from England. I would like to speak with Raschid Alharoun."

The servant glanced at the baby.

Aliena said: "I'm a relative of Jack's." It was not untrue: she was the estranged wife of Jack's stepbrother, and that was a relationship.

The servant opened the gate wider and said: "Please come with me."

Aliena stepped inside gratefully. If she had been turned away here it would have been the end of the road.

She followed the servant across a pleasant courtyard, past a splashing fountain. She wondered what had drawn Jack to the home of this wealthy merchant. It seemed an unlikely friendship. Had Jack recited verse narratives in these shady arcades?

They went into the house. It was a palatial home, with high, cool rooms, floors of stone and marble, and elaborately carved furniture with rich upholstery. They went through two archways and a wooden door, and then Aliena had the feeling they might have entered the women's quarters. The servant held up his hand for her to wait, then coughed gently.

A moment later a tall Saracen woman in a black robe glided into the room, holding a corner of her garment up in front of her mouth in a pose that was insulting in any language. She looked at Aliena and said in French: "Who are you?"

Aliena drew herself up to her full height. "I am the Lady Aliena, daughter of the late earl of Shiring," she said as haughtily as she could. "I take it I have the pleasure of addressing the wife of Raschid the pepper seller." She could play this game as well as anyone.

"What do you want here?"

"I came to see Raschid."

"He doesn't receive women."

Aliena realized she had no hope of gaining this woman's co-operation. However, she had nowhere else to go, so she kept trying. "He may receive a friend of Jack's," she persisted.

"Is Jack your husband?"

"No." Aliena hesitated. "He's my brother-in-law."

The woman looked skeptical. Like most people, she probably assumed that Jack had impregnated Aliena, then abandoned her, and Aliena was pursuing him with the object of forcing him to marry her and support the child.

The woman half turned and called out something in a language Aliena did not understand. A moment later three young women came into the room. It was obvious from their looks that they were her daughters. She spoke to them in the same language, and they all stared at Aliena. There followed a rapid conversation in which the syllable *Jack* recurred often.

Aliena felt humiliated. She was tempted to turn on her heel and walk out; but that would mean giving up her search altogether. These awful people were her last hope. She raised her voice, interrupting their conversation, and said: "Where is Jack?" She intended to be forceful but to her dismay her voice just sounded plaintive.

The daughters fell silent.

The mother said: "We don't know where he is."

"When did you see him last?"

She hesitated. She did not want to answer, but she could hardly pretend not to know when she had seen him last. "He left Toledo the day after Christmas," she said reluctantly.

Aliena forced a friendly smile. "Do you recall his saying anything about where he might be going?"

"I told you, we don't know where he is."

"Perhaps he said something to your husband."

"No, he did not."

Aliena despaired. She had an intuitive feeling that the woman *did* know something. However, it was clear that she was not going to reveal it. Aliena felt suddenly weak and weary. With tears in her eyes she said: "Jack is the father of my child. Don't you think he would like to see his son?"

The youngest of the three daughters started to say something, but the mother interrupted her. There was a short, fierce exchange: mother and daughter had the same fiery temperament. But in the end the daughter shut up.

Aliena waited, but no more was said. The four of them just stared at her. They were unquestionably hostile, but they were so curious that they were in no hurry to see her go. However, there was no point in staying. She might as well get out, go back to her lodgings, and make preparations for the long journey back to Kingsbridge. She took a deep breath and made her voice cool and steady. "I thank you for your hospitality," she said.

The mother had the grace to look slightly ashamed.

Aliena left the room.

The servant was hovering outside. He fell into step beside her and escorted her through the house. She blinked back tears. It was unbearably frustrating to know that her whole journey had failed because of the malice of one woman.

The servant led her across the courtyard. As they reached the gate, Aliena heard running footsteps. She looked back to see the youngest daughter coming after her. She stopped and waited. The servant looked uneasy.

The girl was short and slender, and very pretty, with golden skin and eyes so dark they were nearly black. She wore a white dress and made Aliena feel dusty and unwashed. She spoke broken French. "Do you love him?" she blurted.

Aliena hesitated. She realized she had no more dignity left to lose. "Yes, I love him," she confessed.

"Does he love you?"

Aliena was about to say yes; then she realized she had not seen him for more than a year. "He used to," she said.

"I think he loves you," the girl said.

"What makes you say that?"

The girl's eyes filled with tears. "I wanted him for myself. And I nearly got him." She looked at the baby. "Red hair and blue eyes." The tears ran down her smooth brown cheeks.

Aliena stared at her. This explained her hostile reception. The mother had wanted Jack to marry this girl. She could not have been more than sixteen, but she had a sensual look that made her seem older. Aliena wondered exactly what had happened between them. She said: "You 'nearly' got him?"

"Yes," the girl said defiantly. "I knew he liked me. It broke my heart when he went away. But now I understand." She lost her composure, and her face crumpled in grief.

Aliena could feel for a woman who had loved Jack and lost him. She touched the girl's shoulder in a comforting gesture. But there was something more important than compassion. "Listen," she said urgently. "Do you know where he went?"

The girl looked up and nodded, sobbing.

"Tell me!"

"Paris," she said.

Paris!

Aliena was jubilant. She was back on the trail. Paris was a long way, but the journey would be mostly over familiar ground. And Jack was only a month ahead of her. She felt rejuvenated. I'll find him, in the end, she thought; I know I will!

"Are you going to Paris now?" the girl said.

"Oh, yes," Aliena said. "I've come this far—I won't stop now. Thank you for telling me—thank you."

"I want him to be happy," she said simply.

The servant fidgeted discontentedly. He looked as if he thought he might get into trouble over this. Aliena said to the girl: "Did he say anything else? Which road he would take, or anything that might help me?"

"He wants to go to Paris because someone told him they are building beautiful churches there."

Aliena nodded. She could have guessed that.

"And he took the weeping lady."

Aliena did not know what she meant. "The weeping lady?"

"My father gave him the weeping lady."

"A lady?"

The girl shook her head. "I don't know the right words. A lady. She weeps. From the eyes."

"You mean a picture? A painted lady?"

"I don't understand," the girl said. She looked over her shoulder anxiously. "I have to go."

Whatever the weeping lady was, it did not sound very important. "Thank you for helping me," Aliena said.

The girl bent down and kissed the baby's forehead. Her tears fell on his plump cheeks. She looked up at Aliena. "I wish I were you," she said. Then she turned away and ran back into the house.

Jack's lodgings were in the rue de la Boucherie, in a suburb of Paris on the left bank of the Seine. He saddled his horse at daybreak. At the end of the street he turned right and passed through the tower gate that guarded the Petit Pont, the bridge that led to the island city in the middle of the river.

The wooden houses on either side projected over the edges of the bridge. In the gaps between the houses were stone benches where, later in the morning, famous teachers would hold open-air classes. The bridge took Jack into the Juiverie, the island's main street. The bakeries along the street were packed with students buying their breakfast. Jack got a pastry filled with cooked eel.

He turned left opposite the synagogue, then right at the king's palace, and crossed the Grand Pont, the bridge that led to the right bank. The small, well-built shops of the moneychangers and goldsmiths on either side were beginning to open for business. At the end of the bridge he passed through another gatehouse and entered the fish market, where business was already brisk. He pushed through the crowds and started along the muddy road that led to the town of Saint-Denis.

When he was still in Spain he had heard, from a traveling mason, about Abbot Suger and the new church he was building at Saint-Denis. As he made his way northward through France that spring, working for a few days whenever he needed money, he heard Saint-Denis mentioned often. It seemed the builders were using both of the new techniques, rib-vaulting and pointed arches, and the combination was rather striking.

He rode for more than an hour through fields and vineyards. The road was not paved but it had milestones. It passed the hill of Montmartre, with a ruined Roman temple at its summit, and went through the village of Clignancourt. Three miles after Clignancourt he reached the small walled town of Saint-Denis.

Denis had been the first bishop of Paris. He had been decapitated at Montmartre and then had walked, carrying his severed head in his hands, out into the countryside to this spot, where at last he fell. A pious woman had buried him and a monastery had been erected over his grave. The church had become the burying place for the kings of France. The current abbot, Suger, was a powerful and ambitious man who had reformed the monastery and was now modernizing the church.

Jack entered the town and reined in his horse in the middle of the marketplace to look up at the west front of the church. There was nothing revolutionary here. It was a straightforward old-- fashioned facade with twin towers and three round-arched doorways. He rather liked the aggressive way the piers thrust out from the wall, but he would not have ridden five miles to see that.

He tied his horse to a rail in front of the church and went closer. The sculpture around the three portals was quite good: lively subjects, precisely chiseled. Jack went in.

Inside there was an immediate change. Before the nave proper, there was a low entryway, or narthex. As Jack looked up at the ceiling he experienced a surge of excitement. The builders had used rib-vaulting and pointed arches in combination here, and Jack saw in a flash that the two techniques went together perfectly: the grace of the pointed arch was accentuated by the ribs that followed its line.

There was more to it. In between the ribs, instead of the usual web of mortar-and-rubble, this builder had put cut stones, as in a wall. Being stronger, the layer of stones could probably be thinner, and therefore lighter, Jack realized.

As he stared up, craning his neck until it ached, he understood a further remarkable feature of this combination. Two pointed arches of different widths could be made to reach the same height, merely by adjusting the curve of the arch. This gave the bay a more regular look. It could not be done with round arches, of course: the height of a semicircular arch was always half its width, so a wide one had to be higher than a narrow one. That meant that in a rectangular bay, the narrow arches had to spring from a point higher up the wall than the springing of the wide ones, so that their tops would be at the same level and the ceiling would be even. The result was always lopsided. This problem had now vanished.

Jack lowered his head and gave his neck a rest. He felt as jubilant as if he had just been crowned king. This, he thought, was how he would build his cathedral.

He looked into the main body of the church. The nave itself was clearly quite old, although relatively long and wide: it had been built many years ago, by someone other than the current master, and it was quite conventional. But then, at the crossing, there seemed to be steps down—no doubt leading to the crypt and the royal tombs—and steps up to the chancel. It looked as if the chancel were floating a little way above the ground. The structure was obscured, from this angle, by dazzling sunlight coming through the east windows, so much that Jack supposed the walls must be unfinished, and the sun shining through the gaps.

He walked along the south aisle to the crossing. As he got nearer to the chancel he sensed that something quite remarkable was ahead of him. There was, indeed, sunlight pouring in, but the vault appeared to be complete and there were no gaps in the walls. When Jack stepped out of the aisle into the crossing he saw that the sun was streaming in through rows of tall windows, some of them made of colored glass, and all this sunshine seemed to fill the vast empty vessel of the church with warmth and light. Jack could not understand how they had got so much window area: there seemed to be more window than wall. He was awestruck. How had this been done, if not by magic?

He felt a frisson of superstitious dread as he mounted the steps that led up to the chancel. He stopped at the top of the stair and peered into the confusion of shafts of colored light and stone that was ahead of him. Slowly the realization came over him that he had seen something like this before, but in his imagination. This was the church he had dreamed of building, with its vast windows and surging vaults, a structure of light and air that seemed held up by enchantment.

A moment later he saw it differently. Everything fell into place quite suddenly, and in a lightning flash of revelation, Jack saw what Abbot Suger and his builder had done.

The principle of rib-vaulting was that a ceiling was made of a few strong ribs, with the gaps between the ribs filled in with light material. *They had applied that principle to the whole building.* The wall of the chancel consisted of a few strong piers joined by windows. The arcade separating the chancel from its side aisles was not a wall but a row of piers joined by pointed arches, leaving wide spaces through which the light from the windows could fall into the middle of the church. The aisle itself was divided in two by a row of thin columns.

Pointed arches and rib-vaulting had been combined here, as they had in the narthex, but it was now clear that the narthex had been a cautious trial for the new technology. By comparison with this, the narthex was musclebound, its ribs and moldings too heavy, its arches too small. Here everything was thin, light, delicate and airy. The simple roll moldings were all narrow and the colonettes were long and thin.

It would have looked too fragile to stay upright, except that the ribs showed so clearly how the weight of the building was being carried by the piers and columns. Here was a visible demonstration that a big building did not need thick walls with tiny windows and massive piers. Provided the weight was distributed precisely on a load-bearing skeleton, the rest of the building could be light stonework, glass, or empty space. Jack was spellbound. It was almost like falling in love. Euclid had been a revelation, but this was more than a revelation, for it was beautiful too. He had had visions of a church like this, and now he was actually looking at it, touching it, standing under its sky-high vault.

He walked around the curved east end in a daze, staring at the vaulting of the double aisle. The ribs arched over his head like branches in a forest of perfect stone trees. Here, as in the narthex, the filling between the ceiling ribs was cut stone jointed with mortar, instead of the easier, but heavier, rubble-and-mortar. The outer wall of the aisle had pairs of big windows with pointed tops to match the pointed arches. The revolutionary architecture was perfectly complemented by the colored windows. Jack had never seen colored glass in England, but he had come across several examples in France: however, in the small windows of an old-style church it could not achieve its full potential. Here, the effect of the morning sun pouring through the rich many-colored windows was more than beautiful, it was spellbinding.

Because the church was round-ended, the side aisles curved around to meet at the east end, forming a semicircular ambulatory or walkway. Jack walked all the way around the half circle, then turned and came back, still marveling. He returned to his starting point.

There he saw a woman.

He recognized her.

She smiled.

His heart stood still.

Aliena shaded her eyes. The sunlight coming through the windows at the east end of the church dazzled her. Like a vision, a figure walked toward her out of the blaze of colored sunshine. He looked as if his hair was on fire. He came closer. It was Jack.

Aliena felt faint.

He came to her and stood in front of her. He was thin, terribly thin, but his eyes shone with an intensity of emotion. They stared at one another in silence for a moment.

When he spoke, his voice was hoarse. "Is it really you?"

"Yes," she said. Her voice came out in a whisper. "Yes, Jack. It's really me."

The tension was too much, and she began to cry. He put his arms around her and hugged her, with the baby in her arms between them, and patted her back, saying "There, there," as if she were a child. She leaned against him, breathing his familiar dusty smell, hearing his dear voice as he soothed her, letting her tears fall on his bony shoulder.

Eventually he looked at her face and said: "What are you doing here?"

"Looking for you," she said.

"Looking for me?" he said incredulously. "Then . . . how did you find me?"

She wiped her eyes and sniffed. "I followed you."

"How?"

"I asked people if they had seen you. Masons, mostly, but some monks and lodging-house keepers."

His eyes widened. "You mean—you've been to Spain?"

She nodded. "Compostela, then Salamanca, then Toledo."

"How long have you been traveling?"

"Three fourths of a year."

"But why?"

"Because I love you."

He seemed overwhelmed. His eyes filled with tears. He whispered: "I love you, too."

"Do you? Do you, still?"

"Oh, yes."

She could tell he meant it. She tilted her face up. He leaned forward, over the baby, and kissed her softly. The touch of his mouth on hers made her feel dizzy.

The baby cried.

She broke the kiss and rocked him a little, and he quieted.

Jack said: "What's the baby called?"

"I haven't named him yet."

"Why not? He must be a year old!"

"I wanted to consult you."

"Me?" Jack frowned. "What about Alfred? It's up to the father. . . ." He tailed off. "Why . . . Is he . . . is he mine?"

"Look at him," she said.

Jack looked. "Red hair . . . It must be a year and three quarters since . . ."

Aliena nodded.

"Good God," Jack said. He seemed awestruck. "My son." He swallowed hard.

She watched his face anxiously as he tried to take in the news. Would he see this as the termination of his youth and freedom? His expression became solemn. Normally a man had nine months to get used to the idea of being a father. Jack had to do it all at once. He looked again at the baby, and at last he smiled. "Our son," he said. "I'm so glad."

Aliena sighed happily. Everything was all right at last.

Another thought struck Jack. "What about Alfred? Does he know . . . ?"

"Of course. He only had to look at the child. Besides . . ." She felt embarrassed. "Besides, your mother cursed the marriage, and Alfred was never able to, you know, do anything."

Jack laughed harshly. "There's true justice," he said.

Aliena did not like the relish with which he said it. "It was very hard for me," she said, in a tone of mild reproof.

His face changed quickly. "I'm sorry," he said. "What did Alfred do?"

"When he saw the baby, he threw me out."

Jack looked angry. "Did he hurt you?"

"No."

"He's a pig, all the same."

"I'm glad he threw us out. It was because of that that I came looking for you. And now I've found you. I'm so happy I don't know what to do."

"You were very brave," Jack said. "I still can't take it in. You followed me all that way!"

"I'd do it all again," she said fervently.

He kissed her again. A voice said in French: "If you insist on behaving lewdly in church, please remain in the nave."

It was a young monk. Jack said: "I'm sorry, Father." He took Aliena's arm. They went down the steps and across the south transept. Jack said: "I was a monk for a while—I know how hard it is for them to look at happy lovers kissing."

Happy lovers, Aliena thought. That's what we are.

They walked the length of the church and stepped out into the busy market square. Aliena could hardly believe that she was standing in the sunshine with Jack by her side. It was almost too much happiness to bear.

"Well," he said, "what shall we do?"

"I don't know," she said, smiling.

"Let's get a loaf of bread and a flask of wine, and ride out into the fields to eat our dinner."

"It sounds like paradise."

They went to the baker and the vintner, and then they got a wedge of cheese from a dairywoman in the marketplace. In no time at all they were riding out of the village into the fields. Aliena had to keep looking at Jack to make sure he really was there, riding along beside her, breathing and smiling.

He said: "How is Alfred managing the building site?"

"Oh! I haven't told you!" Aliena had forgotten how long he had been away. "There was a terrible disaster. The roof fell in."

"What!" Jack's loud exclamation startled his horse, and it did a skittish little dance. He calmed it. "How did that happen?"

"Nobody knows. They had three bays vaulted in time for Whitsunday, and then it all fell down during the service. It was dreadful—seventy-nine people were killed."

"That's terrible." Jack was shaken. "How did Prior Philip take it?"

"Badly. He's given up building altogether. He seems to have lost all his energy. He does nothing nowadays."

Philip found it hard to imagine Philip in that state—he had always seemed so full of enthusiasm and determination. "So what happened to the craftsmen?"

"They all drifted away. Alfred lives in Shiring now, and builds houses."

"Kingsbridge must be half empty."

"It's turning back into a village, like it used to be."

"I wonder what Alfred did wrong?" Jack said half to himself. "That stone vault was never in Tom's original plans; but Alfred made the buttresses bigger to take the weight, so it should have been all right."

He was sobered by the news, and they rode on in silence. A mile or so out of Saint-Denis they tied up the horses in the shade of an elm tree and sat down in a corner of a field of green wheat, beside a little brook, to eat their dinner. Jack took a draft of the wine and smacked his lips. "England has nothing to compare with French wine," he said. He broke the loaf and gave Aliena some.

Aliena shyly undid the laced front of her dress and gave her nipple to the baby. She caught Jack looking at her and flushed. She cleared her throat and spoke to cover her embarrassment. "Do you know what you'd like to call him?" she said awkwardly. "Jack, perhaps?"

"I don't know." He looked thoughtful. "Jack was the father I never knew. It might be bad luck to give our son the same name. The nearest I ever had to a real father was Tom Builder."

"Would you like to call him Tom?"

"I think I would."

"Tom was such a big man. How about Tommy?"

Jack nodded. "Tommy it is."

Oblivious of the significance of the moment, Tommy had fallen asleep, having sucked his fill. Aliena put him down on the ground with a kerchief folded under his head for a pillow. Then she looked at Jack. She felt awkward. She wanted him to make love to her, right here on the grass, but she felt sure he would be shocked if she asked him, so she just looked at him and hoped.

He said: "If I tell you something, will you promise not to think badly of me?"

"All right."

He looked embarrassed, and said: "Ever since I saw you, I can hardly think of anything but the naked body under your dress."

She smiled. "I don't think badly of you," she said. "I'm glad."

He stared at her hungrily.

She said: "I love it when you look at me like that."

He swallowed drily.

She held out her arms, and he came to her and embraced her.

It was almost two years since the one and only time they had made love. That morning they had both been swept away by desire and regret. Now they were just two lovers in a field. Aliena suddenly felt anxious. Would it be all right? How terrible if something went wrong, after all this time.

They lay down on the grass side by side and kissed. She closed her eyes and opened her mouth. She felt his eager hand on her body, exploring urgently. There was a quickening in her loins. He kissed her eyelids and the end of her nose, and said: "All this time, I ached for you, every day."

She hugged him hard. "I'm so glad I found you," she said.

They made gentle, happy love in the open air, with the sun beating down on them and the stream burbling beside them; and Tommy slept through it all, and woke up when it was over.

The wooden statue of the lady had not wept since it left Spain. Jack did not understand how it worked, so he could not be sure why it would not weep outside its own country. However, he had an idea that the tears that came at nightfall were caused by the sudden cooling of the air, and he had noticed that sunsets were more gradual in northern territories, so he suspected that the problem had to do with the slower nightfall. He still kept the statue, however. It was rather bulky to carry around, but it was a souvenir of Toledo, and it reminded him of Raschid, and (although he did not tell Aliena this) of Aysha as well. But when a stonemason at Saint-Denis wanted a model for a statue of the Virgin, Jack brought the wooden lady to the masons' lodge, and left it there.

He had been hired by the abbey to work on the rebuilding of the church. The new chancel, which had so devastated him, was not quite complete, and had to be finished in time for the dedication ceremony at midsummer; but the energetic abbot was already preparing to rebuild the nave in the same revolutionary style, and Jack was hired to carve stones in advance for that.

The abbey rented him a house in the village, and he moved in, along with Aliena and Tommy. During the first night they spent in the house they made love five times. Living together as man and wife seemed the most natural thing in the world. After a few days Jack felt as if they had always lived together. Nobody asked whether their union had been blessed by the church.

The master builder at Saint-Denis was the greatest mason Jack had ever met, easily. As they finished the new chancel and prepared to rebuild the nave, Jack watched the master and absorbed everything he did. The technical advances here were his, not the abbot's. Suger was in favor of new ideas, in a general way, but he was more interested in ornament than structure. His pet project was the new tomb for the remains of Saint Denis and his two companions, Rusticus and Eleutherius. The relics were kept in the crypt, but Suger planned to bring them up into the new chancel, so the whole world could see them. The three caskets would rest in a stone tomb veneered with black marble. The top of the tomb was a miniature church made of gilded wood; and in the nave and side aisles of the miniature were three empty coffins, one for each of the martyrs. The tomb would stand in the middle of the new chancel, attached to the back of the new high altar. Both the altar and the base of the tomb were already in place, and the miniature church was in the carpenters' lodge, where a painstaking craftsman was carefully gilding the wood with priceless gold paint. Suger was not a man to do things by halves.

The abbot was a formidable organizer, Jack observed as preparations for the dedication ceremony accelerated. Suger invited everybody who was anybody, and most of them accepted, notably the king and queen of France, and nineteen archbishops and bishops including the archbishop of Canterbury. Such morsels of news were picked up by the craftsmen as they worked in and on the church. Jack often saw Suger himself, in his homespun habit, striding around the monastery giving instructions to a flock of monks who followed him like ducklings. He reminded Jack of Philip of Kingsbridge. Like Philip, Suger came from a poor background and had been brought up in the monastery. Like Philip, he had reorganized the finances and tightened up the management of the monastery's property so that it produced much more income; and like Philip he was spending the extra money on building. Like Philip, he was busy, energetic and decisive.

Except that Philip was none of these things anymore, according to Aliena.

Jack found that hard to imagine. A quiescent Philip seemed as unlikely as a kindly Waleran Bigod. However, Philip had suffered a se ies of terrible disappointments. First there had been the burning of the town. Jack shuddered when he recalled that awful day: the smoke, the fear, the dreadful horsemen with their flaming torches, and the blind panic of the hysterical mob. Perhaps the heart had gone out of Philip then. Certainly the town had lost its nerve afterward. Jack remembered it well: the atmosphere of fear and uncertainty had pervaded the place like a faint but unmistakable odor of decay. No doubt Philip had wanted the opening ceremony for the new chancel to be a symbol of new hope. Then, when it turned into another disaster, he must have given up.

Now the builders had gone away, the market had declined, and the population was shrinking. Young people were beginning to move to Shiring, Aliena said. It was only a problem of morale, of course: the priory still had all its property, including the vast flocks of sheep which brought in hundreds of pounds every year. If it were only a question of money, Philip could surely afford to recommence building, on some scale. It would not be easy, certainly: masons would be superstitious about working on a church that had already fallen down once; and it would be difficult to whip up the enthusiasm of the local people yet again. But the main problem, judging by what Aliena said, was that Philip had lost the will. Jack wished he could do something to help bring it back.

Meanwhile, the bishops, archbishops, dukes and counts began arriving at Saint-Denis two or three days before the ceremony. All the notables were taken on a conducted tour of the building. Suger himself escorted the most distinguished visitors, and lesser dignitaries were taken around by monks or craftsmen. They were all awestruck by the lightness of the new construction and the sunny effect of the huge windows of colored glass. As just about every important church leader in France was seeing this, it struck Jack that the new style was likely to be widely imitated; indeed, masons who could say they had actually worked on Saint-Denis would be in great demand. Coming here had been a clever move, cleverer than he had imagined: it had greatly improved his chances of designing and building a cathedral himself.

King Louis arrived on the Saturday, with his wife and his mother, and they moved into the abbot's house. That night matins were sung from dusk to dawn. By sunrise there was a crowd of peasants and Parisian citizens outside the church, waiting for what promised to be the greatest assemblage of holy and powerful men that most of them would ever see. Jack and Aliena joined the crowd as soon as Tommy had been fed. One day, Jack thought, I'll say to Tommy: "You don't remember it, but when you were just a year old you saw the king of France."

They bought bread and cider for their breakfast and ate while they were waiting for the show to begin. The public was not allowed into the church, of course, and the king's men-at-arms kept them at a distance; but all the doors were open, and people clustered in knots where they could see in. The nave was packed with the lords and ladies of the nobility. Fortunately the chancel was raised several feet, because of the large crypt under it, so Jack could still see the ceremony.

There was a flurry of activity at the far end of the nave, and suddenly all the nobles bowed. Over their lowered heads, Jack saw the king enter the church from the south. He could not see the king's face to make out his features, but his purple tunic made a vivid splash of color as he moved into the center of the crossing and knelt before the main altar.

The bishops and archbishops came in immediately afterward. They were all dressed in dazzling white robes with gold embroidery, and each bishop carried his ceremonial crozier. The crozier was supposed to be a simple shepherd's crook, but so many of them were ornamented with fabulous jewels that the whole procession glittered like a mountain stream in the sunlight.

They all walked slowly across the church and up the steps into the chancel, then took prearranged places around the font in which—Jack knew because he had observed the preparations—there were several gallons of holy water. There followed a lull during which prayers were said and hymns were sung. The crowd became restless, and Tommy got bored. Then the bishops moved off in procession again.

They left the church by the south door and disappeared into the cloisters, much to the disappointment of the spectators; but then they emerged from the monastic buildings and filed across the front of the church. Each bishop carried a small brush called an aspergillum and a vessel of holy water, and as they marched, singing, they dipped the brushes in the water and sprinkled the walls of the church. The crowd surged forward, people begging for a blessing and trying to touch the snow-white robes of the holy men. The king's men-at-arms beat the people back with sticks. Jack stayed well back in the crowd. He did not want a blessing and he preferred to stay away from those sticks.

The procession made its stately way along the north side of the church, and the crowd followed, trampling over the graves in the cemetery. Some spectators had taken up positions here in anticipation, and they resisted the pressure from the newcomers. One or two fights broke out.

The bishops passed the north porch and continued around the half circle of the east end, the new part. This was where the craftsmen's workshops had been built, and now the crowd surged around the huts, threatening to flatten the light wooden buildings. As the leaders of the procession began to disappear back into the abbey, the more hysterical members of the crowd became desperate, and pushed forward more determinedly. The king's men responded with increased violence.

Jack began to feel anxious. "I don't like the look of this," he said to Aliena.

"I was about to say the same," she replied. "Let's get out of this crowd."

Before they could move, a scuffle broke out between the king's men and a group of youths at the front. The men-at-arms laid about them fiercely with their clubs, but the youths, instead of cowering away, fought back. The last of the bishops hurried into the cloisters with a distinctly perfunctory sprinkling of the last part of the chancel. When the holy men were out of sight, the crowd turned its attention on the men-at-arms. Someone threw a stone and hit one of the men square on the forehead. A cheer went up as he fell. The hand-to-hand fighting spread quickly. Men-at-arms came running from the west front of the church to defend their comrades.

It was turning into a riot.

There was no hope of the ceremony providing a distraction in the next few moments. Jack knew that the bishops and the king were now descending into the crypt to fetch the remains of Saint Denis. They would carry them all around the cloisters but would not bring them out of doors. The dignitaries were not due to show themselves again until the service was over. Abbot Suger had not anticipated the size of the crowd of spectators, nor had he made arrangements to keep them happy. Now they were dissatisfied, they were hot—the sun was high by this time—and they wanted to vent their emotions.

The king's men were armed but the spectators were not, and at first the armed men got the better of it; then someone had the bright idea of breaking into the craftsmen's huts for weapons. A pair of youths kicked down the door of the masons' lodge and came out a moment later with bolster hammers in their hands. There were masons in the crowd, and some of them pushed through the throng to the lodge and tried to stop people from going in; but they were unable to stand their ground, and got shoved aside.

Jack and Aliena were trying to retreat out of the crowd, but the people behind them were pressing forward urgently, and they found themselves trapped. Jack kept Tommy hard up against his chest, protecting the baby's back with his arms and covering the little head with his hands, at the same time struggling to stay close to Aliena. He saw a small, furtive-looking man with a black beard emerge from the masons' lodge carrying the wooden statue of the weeping lady. I'll never see that again, he thought with a pang of regret; but he was too busy trying to escape from the crush to worry about being robbed.

The carpenters' lodge was broken open next. The craftsmen had given up hope of protecting their lodges, and they made no attempt to restrain the crowd. The smithy proved too strong, but the crowd burst through the flimsy wall of the roofers' lodge and took the heavy, wickedly sharp tools used for trimming and nailing lead sheets, and Jack thought: Someone is going to be killed before this is over.

Despite all his efforts he was pushed forward, toward the north porch where the fighting was fiercest. The same thing was happening to the black-bearded thief, he noticed: the man was trying to get away with his loot, hugging the wooden statue to his chest the way Jack was hugging Tommy, but he, too, was being forced farther into the melee by the press of the crowd.

Suddenly Jack had a brainwave. He gave Tommy to Aliena, saying: "Stay close to me." Then he grabbed the little thief and wrested the statue away from him. The man resisted for a moment, but Jack was bigger, and anyway the thief was now more worried about saving his skin than stealing the statue, and after a moment he relinquished his hold.

Jack lifted the statue above his head and started to shout: "Revere the Madonna!" At first nobody took any notice. Then one or two people looked at him. "Touch not the Holy Mother!" he shouted at the top of his voice. The people near him backed off superstitiously, making a space around him. He began to warm to his theme. "It is a sin to desecrate the image of the Virgin!" He held the statue high above his head and walked forward, toward the church. This just might work, he thought with a surge of hope. More people stopped fighting to see what was going on.

He glanced behind him. Aliena was following, unable to do anything else because of the press of the crowd. However, the riot was rapidly simmering down. The crowd moved forward with Jack, and people began to repeat his words in an awestruck murmur: "It is the Mother of God. . . . Hail, Mary. . . . Make way for the effigy of the Blessed Maiden. . . ." All they wanted was a show, and now that Jack was giving them one the fighting stopped almost completely, with only two or three continuing scuffles on the fringes. Jack marched forward solemnly. He was rather startled at the ease with which he had stopped a riot. The crowd fell away before him, and he reached the north porch of the church. There he set the statue down, with great reverence, in the cool shade of the doorway. It was a little over two feet high, and seemed less impressive standing on the ground.

The mob gathered around the doorway expectantly. Jack was at a loss to know what to do. They probably wanted a sermon. He had acted like a clergyman, bearing the statue on high and calling out sonorous warnings, but that was the limit of his priestly skills. He felt fearful: what might the crowd do to him if he disappointed them now?

Suddenly they gave a collective gasp.

Jack looked behind him. Some of the nobles from the congregation had gathered in the north transept, looking out, but he could see nothing to justify the crowd's apparent amazement.

"A miracle!" someone said, and others took up the cry: "A miracle! A miracle!"

Jack looked at the statue, and then he understood. Water was dripping from its eyes. At first he was as awestruck as the crowd, but a moment later he recalled his theory that the lady wept when there was a sudden change from warm to cold, as happened at nightfall in southern regions. The statue had just been moved from the heat of the day into the cool of the north porch. That would explain the tears. But the crowd did not know that, of course. All they saw was a statue weeping, and they marveled.

A woman at the front tossed a denier, the French silver penny, at the feet of the statue. Jack felt like laughing aloud. What was the point of giving money to a piece of wood? But the people had been so indoctrinated by the Church that their automatic response to something holy was to give money, and several others in the crowd followed the woman's example.

Jack had never thought that Raschid's toy might make money.

Indeed, it could not make money for Jack—the people would not give if they thought the money was going into Jack's pocket. But it would be worth a fortune to any church.

And when Jack realized that, he suddenly saw what he had to do.

It came to him in a flash, and he began speaking even before he had seen all the implications himself: the words came at the same time as the thoughts. "The Weeping Madonna belongs not to me, but to God," he began. The crowd fell silent. This was the sermon they had been waiting for. Behind Jack, the bishops were singing in the church, but no one was interested in them now. "For hundreds of years, she languished in the land of the Saracens," Jack went on. He had no idea what the history of the statue was, but it did not seem to matter: the priests themselves never inquired too closely into the truth of stories of miracles and holy relics. "She has traveled many miles, but her journey is not yet ended. Her destination is the cathedral church of Kingsbridge, in England."

He caught Aliena's eye. She was staring at him in amazement. He had to resist the temptation to wink at her to let her know he was making it up as he went along.

"It is my holy mission to take her to Kingsbridge. There, she will find her resting place. There, she will be at peace." As he looked at Aliena the final, most brilliant inspiration came to him and he said: "I have been appointed master builder of the new church at Kingsbridge."

Aliena's mouth fell open. Jack looked away from her. "The Weeping Madonna has commanded that a new, more glorious church be built for her at Kingsbridge, and with her help I shall create a shrine for her as beautiful as the new chancel which has been erected here for the sacred remains of Saint Denis."

He glanced down, and the money on the ground gave him the idea for his finishing touch. "Your pennies will be used for the new church," he said. "The Madonna confers a blessing on every man, woman and child who offers a gift to help her build her new home."

There was a moment of silence; then his listeners started to throw pennies on the ground around the base of the statue. Each person called out something as he or she made the offering. Some said "Alleluia" or "Praise God" and others asked for a blessing, or some more specific favor: "Make Robert well," or "Let Anne conceive," or "Give us a good harvest." Jack studied their faces: they were excited, elevated, happy. They pushed forward, jostling one another in their eagerness to give their pennies to the Weeping

Madonna. Jack looked down and watched, marveling, as the money piled up like a snowdrift around his feet.

The Weeping Madonna had the same effect in every town and village on the road to Cherbourg. As they walked in procession along the main street a crowd would gather; and then, after they had paused in front of the church to give time for the entire population to assemble, they would take the statue into the cool of the building, and it would weep, whereupon the people would fall over one another in their eagerness to give money for the building of Kingsbridge Cathedral.

They had almost lost it, right at the start. The bishops and archbishops examined the statue and pronounced it genuinely miraculous, and Abbot Suger wanted to keep it for Saint-Denis. He had offered Jack a pound, then ten pounds, and finally fifty pounds. When he realized Jack was not interested in money he threatened to take the statue away forcibly; but Archbishop Theobald of Canterbury prevented him. Theobald also saw the moneymaking potential of the statue and he wanted it to go to Kingsbridge, which was in his archdiocese. Suger had given in with bad grace, churlishly expressing reservations about the genuineness of the miracle.

Jack had told the craftsmen at Saint-Denis that he would hire any of them who cared to follow him to Kingsbridge. Suger was not pleased about that, either. Most of them would stay where they were, in fact, on the principle that a bird in the hand is worth two in the bush; but there were a few who were from England originally and might be tempted to move back; and the others would spread the word, for it was every mason's duty to tell his brothers about new building sites. Within a few weeks, craftsmen from all over Christendom would begin drifting into Kingsbridge, the way Jack had drifted into six or seven different sites over the past two years. Aliena asked Jack what he would do if Kingsbridge Priory did not make him master builder. Jack had no idea. He had made his announcement on the spur of the moment and he had no contingency plans in case things went wrong.

Archbishop Theobald, having claimed the Weeping Madonna for England, was not willing to let Jack simply walk away with it. He had sent two priests from his entourage, Reynold and Edward, to accompany Jack and Aliena on their journey. Jack had been displeased about this at first, but he quickly got to like them. Reynold was a fresh-faced, argumentative young man with an incisive mind, and he was very interested in the mathematics Jack had learned in Toledo. Edward was a mild-mannered older man who was something of a glutton. Their principal function was to make sure none of the donations went into Jack's purse, of course. In fact, the priests spent freely out of the donations to pay their traveling expenses, whereas Jack and Aliena paid their own, so the archbishop would have done better to trust Jack.

They went to Cherbourg on their way to Barfleur, where they would take ship for Wareham. Jack knew something was wrong long before they reached the heart of the little seaside town. People were not staring at the Madonna.

They were staring at Jack.

The priests noticed it after a while. They were carrying the statue on a wooden trestle, as they always did when entering a town. As the crowd began to follow them, Reynold hissed at Jack: "What's going on?"

"I don't know."

"They're more interested in you than the statue! Have you been here before?"

"Never."

Aliena said: "It's the older ones who look at Jack. The youngsters look at the statue."

She was right. The children and young people were reacting to the statue with normal curiosity. It was the middle-aged who stared at him. He tried staring back, and found that they got scared. One made the Sign of the Cross at him. "What have they got against me?" he wondered aloud.

Their procession attracted followers just as rapidly as always, however, and they reached the marketplace with a large crowd in tow. They put the Madonna down in front of the church. The air smelled of salt water and fresh fish. Several townspeople went into the church. What normally happened next was that the local clergy would come out and talk to Reynold and Edward. There would be a discussion and explanations, and then the statue would be carried inside, where it would weep. The Madonna had only failed once: on a cold day, when Reynold insisted on going through with the procedure despite Jack's warning that it might not work. Now they respected his advice.

The weather was right today, but something else was wrong. There was superstitious fear on the wind-whipped faces of the sailors and fishermen all around. The young sensed the disquiet of their elders, and the whole crowd was suspicious and vaguely hostile. No one approached the little group to ask questions about the statue. They stood at a distance, talking in low voices, waiting for something to happen.

At last the priest emerged. In other towns the priest had approached in a mood of wary curiosity, but this one came out like an exorcist, holding a cross in front of him like a shield and carrying a chalice of holy water in his other hand. Reynold said: "What does he think he's going to do—cast out demons?" The priest walked over, chanting something in Latin, and approached Jack. He said in French: "I command, thee, evil spirit, to return to the Place of Ghosts! In the name—"

"I'm not a ghost, you damn fool!" Jack burst out. He felt unnerved.

The priest went on: "Father, Son and Holy Spirit—"

"We're on a mission for the archbishop of Canterbury," Reynold protested. "We've been blessed by him."

Aliena said: "He's not a ghost; I've known him since he was twelve years old!"

The priest began to look uncertain. "You are the ghost of a man of this town who died twenty-four years ago," he said. Several people in the crowd voiced their agreement, and the priest recommenced his incantation.

"I'm only twenty years old," Jack said. "Perhaps I just resemble the man who died."

Someone stepped out from the crowd. "You don't just resemble him," he said. "You are him—no different from the day you died."

The crowd murmured with superstitious dread. Jack, feeling unnerved, looked at the speaker. He was a gray-bearded man of forty or so years, wearing the clothes of a successful craftsman or small merchant. He was not the hysterical type. Jack addressed him with a voice that faltered somewhat. "My companions know me," he said. "Two of them are priests. The woman is my wife. The baby is my son. Are they ghosts, too?"

The man looked uncertain.

A white-haired woman standing beside him spoke up. "Don't you know me, Jack?"

Jack jumped as if he had been stung. Now he was scared. "How did you know my name?" he said.

"Because I'm your mother," she said.

"You're not!" Aliena said, and Jack heard a note of panic in her voice. "I know his mother, and she's not you! What's happening here?"

"Evil magic!" said the priest.

"Wait a minute," said Reynold. "Jack may be related to the man who died. Did he have any children?"

"No," said the gray-bearded man.

"Are you sure?"

"He never married."

"That's not the same thing."

One or two people snickered. The priest glared at them.

The gray-bearded man said: "But he died twenty-four years ago, and *this* Jack says he's only twenty."

"How did he die?" Reynold asked.

"Drowned."

"Did you see the body?"

There was a silence. Finally the gray-bearded man said: "No, I never saw his body."

"Did *anyone* see it?" Reynold said, his voice rising as he scented victory.

Nobody spoke.

Reynold turned to Jack. "Is your father alive?"

"He died before I was born."

"What was he?"

"A jongleur."

A gasp went up from the crowd, and the white-haired woman said: "My Jack was a jongleur."

"But *this* Jack is a stonemason," Reynold said. "I've seen his work. However, he could be the *son* of Jack the jongleur." He turned to Jack. "What was your father called? Jack Jongleur, I suppose?"

"No. They called him Jack Shareburg."

The priest repeated the name, pronouncing it slightly differently. "Jacques Cherbourg?"

Jack was stunned. He had never understood his father's name, but now it was clear. Like many traveling men, he was called by the name of the town he came from. "Yes," Jack said wonderingly. "Of course. Jacques Cherbourg." He had found traces of his father at last, long after he had given up looking. He had gone all the way to Spain, but what he wanted had been here, on the coast of Normandy. He had fulfilled his quest. He felt wearily satisfied, as if he had put down a heavy burden after carrying it a long way.

"Then everything is clear," Reynold said, looking around triumphantly at the crowd. "Jacques Cherbourg did not drown, he survived. He went to England, lived there a while, made a girl pregnant, and died. The girl gave birth to a boy and named him after the father. Jack here is now twenty, and looks exactly like his father did twenty-four years ago." Reynold looked at the priest. "No need for exorcism here, father. It's just a family reunion."

Aliena put her arm through Jack's and squeezed his hand. He felt stupefied. There were a hundred questions he wanted to ask and he did not know where to start. He blurted one out at random. "Why were you so sure he died?"

"Everyone on the White Ship died," said the gray-bearded man.

"The White Ship?"

"I remember the White Ship," said Edward. "That was a famous disaster. The heir to the throne was drowned. Then Maud became the heir, and that's why we've got Stephen."

Jack said: "But why was he on such a ship?"

The old woman who had spoken earlier answered. "He was to entertain the nobles on the voyage." She looked at Jack. "You must be his boy, then. My grandson. I'm sorry I thought you were a ghost. You look so like him."

"Your father was my brother," said the gray-bearded man. "I'm your Uncle Guillaume."

Jack realized with a glow of pleasure that this was the family he had longed for, his father's relations. He was no longer alone in the world. He had found his roots at last.

"Well, this is my son, Tommy," he said. "Look at his red hair."

The white-haired woman looked fondly at the baby, then said in a shocked voice: "Oh, my soul, I'm a great-grandmother!"

Everyone laughed.

Jack said: "I wonder how my father got to England?"

Chapter 13

"**S**O GOD SAID TO SATAN, 'Look at my man Job. Look at him. There's a good man, if ever I saw one.'" Philip paused for effect. This was not a translation, of course: this was a freestyle retelling of the story. "'Tell me if that isn't a perfect and upright man, who fears God and does no evil.' So Satan said: 'Of course he worships you. You've given him everything. Just look at him. Seven sons and three daughters. Seven thousand sheep, and three thousand camels, and five hundred pairs of oxen, and five hundred asses. That's why he's a good man.' So God said: 'All right. Take it all away from him, and see what happens.' And that's what Satan did."

While Philip was preaching, his mind kept wandering to a mystifying letter he had received that morning from the archbishop of Canterbury. It began by congratulating him on obtaining the miraculous Weeping Madonna. Philip did not know what a weeping madonna was but he was quite sure he did not have one. The archbishop was glad to hear that Philip was recommencing the building of the new cathedral. Philip was doing no such thing. He was waiting for a sign from God before doing anything, and while he waited he was holding Sunday services in the small new parish church. Finally Archbishop Theobald commended his shrewdness in appointing a master builder who had worked on the new chancel at Saint-Denis. Philip had heard of the abbey of Saint-Denis, of course, and the famous Abbot Suger, the most powerful churchman in the kingdom of France; but he knew nothing of the new chancel there and he had not appointed a master builder from anywhere. Philip thought the letter had probably been intended for someone else and sent to him in error.

"Now, what did Job say, when he lost all his wealth, and his children died? Did he curse God? Did he worship Satan? No! He said: 'I was born naked, and I'll die naked. The Lord gives and the Lord takes away—blessed be the name of the Lord.' That's what Job said. And then God said to Satan: 'What did I tell you?' And Satan said: 'All right, but he's still got his health, hasn't he? A man can put up with anything while he's in good health.' And God saw that he had to let Job suffer some more in order to prove his point, so he said: 'Take away his health, then, and see what happens.' So Satan made Job ill, and he had boils from the top of his head to the soles of his feet."

Sermons were becoming more common in churches. They had been rare when Philip was a boy. Abbot Peter had been against them, saying they tempted the priest to indulge himself. The old-fashioned view was that the congregation should be mere spectators, silently witnessing the mysterious holy rites, hearing the Latin words without understanding them, blindly trusting in the efficacy of the priest's intercession. But ideas had changed. Progressive thinkers nowadays no longer saw the congregation as mute observers of a mystical ceremony. The Church was supposed to be an integral part of their everyday existence. It marked the milestones in their lives, from christening, through marriage and the birth of children, to extreme unction and burial in consecrated ground. It might be their landlord, judge, employer or customer. Increasingly, people were expected to be Christians every day, not just on Sundays. They needed more than just rituals, according to the modern view: they wanted explanations, rulings, encouragement, exhortation.

"Now, I believe that Satan had a conversation with God about Kingsbridge," Philip said. "I believe that God said to Satan: 'Look at my people in Kingsbridge. Aren't they good Christians? See how they work hard all week in their fields and workshops, and then spend all day Sunday building me a new cathedral. Tell me they're not good people, if you can!' And Satan said: 'They're good because they're doing well. You've given them good harvests, and fine weather, and customers for their shops, and protection from evil earls. But take all that away from them, and they'll come over to my side.' So God said: 'What do you want to do?' And Satan said: 'Burn the town.' So God said: 'All right, burn it, and see what happens.' So Satan sent William Hamleigh to set fire to our fleece fair."

Philip took great consolation from the story of Job. Like Job,

Philip had worked hard all his life to do God's will to the best of his ability; and, like Job, he had been rewarded with bad luck, failure and ignominy. But the purpose of the sermon was to lift the spirits of the townspeople, and Philip could see that it was not working. However, the story was not yet over.

"And then God said to Satan: 'Look now! You've burned that whole town to the ground, and they're *still* building me a new cathedral. *Now* tell me they're not good people!' But Satan said: 'I was too easy on them. Most of them escaped that fire. And they soon rebuilt their little wooden houses. Let me send a real disaster, then see what happens.' And God sighed, and said: 'What do you want to do now, then?' And Satan said: 'I'm going to bring the roof of that new church down on their heads.' And he did—as we all know."

Looking around the congregation, Philip saw very few people who had not lost a relative in that awful collapse. There was Widow Meg, who had had a good husband and three strapping sons, all of whom had died; she had not spoken a word since, and her hair was white. Others had been mutilated. Peter Pony's right leg had been crushed, and he walked with a limp: he had been a horse catcher before, but now he worked for his brother, making saddles. There was hardly a family in town that had escaped. Sitting on the floor down at the front was a man who had lost the use of his legs. Philip frowned: who was he? He had not been injured in the roof collapse—Philip had never seen him before. Then he recalled being told that there was a cripple begging in the town and sleeping in the ruins of the cathedral. Philip had ordered that he be given a bed in the guesthouse.

His mind was wandering again. He returned to his sermon. "Now, what did Job do? His wife said to him: 'Curse God, and die.' But did he? He did not. Did he lose his faith? He did not. Satan was disappointed in Job. And I tell you"—Philip raised his hand dramatically, to emphasize the point—"I tell you, Satan is going to be disappointed in the people of Kingsbridge! For we continue to worship the true God, just as Job did in all his tribulations."

He paused again, to let them digest that, but he could tell he had failed to move them. The faces that looked up at him were interested, but not inspired. In truth he was not an inspirational preacher. He was a down-to-earth man. He could not captivate a congregation by the force of his personality. People did become intensely loyal to him, it was true, but not instantly: it happened slowly, over time, as they came to understand how he lived and what he achieved. His work sometimes inspired people—or it had, in the old days—but never his words.

However, the best part of the story was to come. "What happened to Job, after Satan had done his worst? Well, God gave him more than he had in the first place—twice as much! Where he had grazed seven thousand sheep, he now had fourteen thousand. The three thousand camels he had lost were replaced by six thousand. And he fathered seven more sons and three more daughters."

They looked indifferent. Philip plowed on. "And Kingsbridge will prosper again, one day. The widows shall marry again, and the widowers find wives; and those whose children died shall conceive again; and our streets will be full of people, and our shops stocked with bread and wine, leather and brass, buckles and shoes; and one day we will rebuild our cathedral."

The trouble was, he was not sure he believed it himself; and so he could not say it with conviction. No wonder the congregation was unmoved.

He looked down at the heavy book in front of him, and translated the Latin into English. "And Job lived a hundred and forty years more, and saw his sons, and his grandsons, and his great-grandsons. And then he died, being old and full of days." He closed the book.

There was a disturbance at the back of the little church. Philip looked up irritably. He was aware that his sermon had not had the effect he hoped for, but nevertheless he wanted a few moments of silence at the end of it. The church door was open, and all those at the back were looking out. Philip could see quite a crowd outside—it must contain everyone in Kingsbridge who was not in the church, he thought. What was going on?

Several possibilities went through his mind—there had been a fight, a fire, someone was dying, a large troop of horsemen was approaching—but he was completely unprepared for what actually happened. First, two priests came in carrying a statue of a woman on a board draped with an embroidered altar cloth. The solemnity of their demeanor suggested that the statue represented a saint, presumably the Virgin. Behind the priests walked two more people, and they provided the bigger surprise: one was Aliena, and the other was Jack.

Philip regarded Jack with affection mingled with exasperation. That boy, he thought: on the day he first came here the old cathedral burned down, and since then nothing connected with him has been normal. But Philip was more pleased than annoyed by Jack's entrance. Despite all the trouble the boy caused, he made life interesting. Boy? Philip looked at him again. Jack was no longer a boy. He had been away two years but he had aged ten, and his eyes were weary and knowing. Where had he been? And how had Aliena found him?

The procession moved up the middle of the church. Philip decided to do nothing and see what happened. A buzz of excitement went around as people recognized Jack and Aliena. Then there was a new sound, rather like a murmur of awe, and someone said: "She weeps!"

Others repeated it like a litany: "She weeps! She weeps!" Philip peered at the statue. Sure enough, there was water coming from the eyes. He suddenly remembered the archbishop's mysterious letter about the miraculous Weeping Madonna. So this was it. As to whether the weeping was a miracle, Philip would suspend judgment. He could see that the eyes appeared to be made of stone, or perhaps some kind of crystal, whereas the rest of the statue was wooden: that might have something to do with it.

The priests turned around and put the board down on the floor so that the Madonna was facing the congregation. Then Jack began to speak.

"The Weeping Madonna came to me in a far, far country," he began. Philip resented his taking over the service but he decided not to act precipitately: he would let Jack have his say. Anyway, he was intrigued. "A baptized Saracen gave her to me," Jack went on. The congregation murmured in surprise: Saracens were usually the barbaric black-faced enemy in such stories, and few people knew that some of them were actually Christians. "At first I wondered why she had been given to me. Nevertheless, I carried her for many miles." Jack had the congregation spellbound. He's a better preacher of sermons than I am, Philip thought ruefully; I can feel the tension building already. "At last I began to realize that she wanted to go home. But where was her home? Finally it came to me: she wanted to go to Kingsbridge."

The congregation broke into a hubbub of amazement. Philip was skeptical. There was a difference between the way God worked and the way Jack worked, and this had the hallmark of Jack. But Philip remained silent.

"But then I thought: What am I taking her to? What shrine will she have at Kingsbridge? In what church will she find her rest?" He looked around at the plain whitewashed interior of the parish church, as if to say: This obviously will not do. "And it was as if she spoke aloud, and said to me: 'You, Jack Jackson, shall make me a shrine, and build me a church.'"

Philip began to see what Jack was up to. The Madonna was to be the spark that reignited the people's enthusiasm for building a new cathedral. It would do what Philip's sermon about Job had failed to do. But still Philip had to ask himself: Is this God's will, or just Jack's?

"So I asked her: 'With what? I have no money.' And she said: 'I will provide the money.' Well, we set off, with the blessing of Archbishop Theobald of Canterbury." Jack glanced up at Philip as he named the archbishop. He's telling me something, Philip thought: he's saying that he's got powerful backing for this.

Jack swung his gaze back to the congregation. "And along the road, from Paris, across Normandy, over the sea, and all the way to Kingsbridge, devout Christians have given money for the building of the shrine of the Weeping Madonna." With that, Jack beckoned to someone outside.

A moment later two beturbaned Saracens marched solemnly into the church, carrying on their shoulders an ironbound chest.

The villagers cowered back from them in fear. Even Philip was astonished. He knew, in theory, that Saracens had brown skin, but he had never seen one, and the reality was amazing. Their swirling, brightly colored robes were equally striking. They strode through the awestruck congregation and knelt before the Madonna, placing the chest reverently on the floor.

There was a breathless silence as Jack unlocked the chest with a huge key and lifted the lid. People craned their necks to look. Suddenly Jack tipped the chest over.

There was a noise like a waterfall, and a stream of silver pennies poured out of the chest, hundreds of them, thousands. People crowded around to stare: none of them had ever seen so much money.

Jack raised his voice to be heard over their exclamations. "I have brought her home, and now I give her to the building of the new cathedral." Then he turned, looked Philip in the eye, and inclined his head in a little bow, as if to say: Over to you.

Philip hated to be manipulated like this but at the same time he was bound to acknowledge that the way it had been done was masterly. However, that did not mean he was going to give in to it. The people might acclaim the Weeping Madonna but only Philip could decide whether she would be allowed to rest in Kingsbridge Cathedral alongside the bones of Saint Adolphus. And he was not yet convinced.

Some of the villagers began questioning the Saracens. Philip stepped down from his pulpit and went closer to listen. "I come from a far, far country," one of them was saying. Philip was surprised to hear that he spoke English just like a Dorset fisherman, but most of the villagers did not even know that Saracens had a language of their own.

"What is your country called?" someone asked.

"My country is called Africa," the Saracen replied. There was more than one country in Africa, of course, as Philip knew—although most of the villagers did not—and Philip wondered which one this Saracen came from. How exciting it would be if it were a place mentioned in the Bible, such as Egypt or Ethiopia.

A little girl reached out a tentative finger and touched his dark-brown hand. The Saracen smiled at her. Apart from his color, Philip thought, he looked no different from anyone else. Encouraged, the girl said: "What's it like in Africa?"

"There are great deserts, and fig trees."

"What's a fig?"

"It's . . . it's a fruit, that looks like a strawberry and tastes like a pear."

Philip was suddenly struck by a horrible suspicion. He said: "Tell me, Saracen, what city were you born in?"

"Damascus," the man said.

Philip's suspicion was confirmed. He was angered. He touched Jack's arm and drew him aside. In a quietly furious voice he said: "What are you playing at?"

"What do you mean?" Jack said, trying to play innocent.

"Those two aren't Saracens. They're fishermen from Wareham with brown dye on their faces and hands."

Jack did not seem bothered about having his deception discovered. He grinned and said: "How did you guess?"

"I don't think that man has ever seen a fig, and Damascus is not in Africa. What is the meaning of this dishonesty?"

"It's a harmless deception," Jack said, and flashed his engaging smile.

"There is no such thing as a harmless deception," Philip said coldly.

"All right." Jack saw that Philip was angry. He became serious. "It serves the same purpose as an illuminated drawing on a page of the Bible. It's not the truth, it's an illustration. My brown-dyed Dorsetshire men dramatize the true fact that the Weeping Madonna comes from a Saracen land."

The two priests and Aliena had detached themselves from the crowd around the Madonna and joined Philip and Jack. Philip ignored them and said to Jack: "You aren't frightened of a drawing of a snake. An illustration isn't a lie. Your Saracens aren't illustrations, they're impostors."

"We collected much more money after we got the Saracens," Jack said.

Philip looked at the pennies heaped on the floor. "The townspeople probably think that's enough to build a whole cathedral," he said. "It looks to me like about a hundred pounds. You know that won't even pay for a year's work."

"The money is like the Saracens," Jack said. "It's symbolic. You know you've got the money to start building."

That was true. There was nothing stopping Philip from building. The Madonna was just the sort of thing needed to bring Kingsbridge back to life. It would attract people to the town—pilgrims and scholars as well as the idly curious. It would put new heart into the townspeople. It would be seen as a good omen. Philip had been waiting for a sign from God, and he wanted very badly to believe that this was it. But this did not have the feel of a sign from God. It had the feel of a stunt by Jack.

The younger of the two priests said: "I'm Reynold and this is Edward—we work for the archbishop of Canterbury. He sent us to accompany the Weeping Madonna."

Philip said: "If you have the archbishop's blessing, why did you need a couple of fairground Saracens to legitimize the Madonna?"

Edward looked a little shamefaced. Reynold said: "It was Jack's idea, but I confess I saw no harm in it. Surely you're not dubious about the Madonna, Philip?"

"You can call me Father," Philip snapped. "Working for the archbishop doesn't give you the right to condescend to your superiors. The answer to your question is yes. I am dubious about the Madonna. I am not going to install this statue in the precincts of Kingsbridge Cathedral until I'm convinced that it is a holy artifact."

"A wooden statue weeps," Reynold said. "How much of a miracle do you want?"

"The weeping is unexplained. That doesn't make it a miracle. The changing of liquid water into solid ice is also inexplicable, but it isn't miraculous."

"The archbishop would be most disappointed if you refused the Madonna. He had a battle to prevent Abbot Suger from commandeering her for Saint-Denis."

Philip knew he was being threatened. Young Reynold will have to work a lot harder than this to intimidate me, he thought. He said smoothly: "I'm quite sure the archbishop would not want me to accept the Madonna without making some routine inquiries about her legitimacy."

There was a movement at their feet. Philip looked down and saw the cripple he had noticed earlier. The unfortunate man was dragging himself across the floor, his paralyzed legs trailing behind him, trying to get close to the statue. Whichever way he turned he was blocked by the crowd. Automatically, Philip stood aside to let him through. The Saracens were preventing people from actually touching the statue, but the cripple escaped their notice. Philip saw the man's hand reach out. Philip would normally have prevented someone from touching a holy relic, but he had not yet accepted that this statue was holy, so he did nothing. The cripple touched the hem of the wooden dress. Suddenly he let out a shout of triumph. "I feel it!" he yelled. "I feel it!"

Everyone looked at him.

"I feel the strength coming back!" he shouted.

Philip stared at the man incredulously, knowing what would happen next. The man bent one leg, then the other. There was a collective gasp from the onlookers. He reached out a hand and someone took it. With an effort, the man pulled himself upright.

The crowd made a noise like a groan of passion.

Someone called out: "Try to walk!"

Still holding the hand of his helper, the man took one tentative step, then another. The people watched in dead silence. On his third step he stumbled, and they sighed. But the man regained his balance and walked on.

They cheered.

He went down the nave with the people following him. After a few more steps he broke into a run. The cheering rose to a crescendo as he went out through the church door into the sunshine, followed by most of the congregation.

Philip looked at the two priests. Reynold was awestruck, and Edward had tears pouring down his face. Obviously they were not in on it. Philip turned to Jack and said furiously: "How dare you pull a trick like that?"

"Trick?" said Jack. "What trick?"

"That man had never been seen in this district until a few days ago. In another day or two he'll disappear, never to be seen again, with his pockets full of your money. I know how these things are done, Jack. You're not the first person to fake a miracle, regrettably. There was never anything wrong with his legs, was there? He's another Wareham fisherman."

The accusation was confirmed by Jack's guilty look.

Aliena said: "Jack, I told you you shouldn't try that."

The two priests were thunderstruck. They had been completely taken in. Reynold was furious. He rounded on Jack. "You had no right!" he spluttered.

Philip felt sad as well as angry. In his heart he had hoped the Madonna would prove legitimate, for he could see just how he would use her to revitalize the priory and the town. But it was not to be. He looked around the little parish church. Only a handful of worshipers remained, still staring at the statue. He said to Jack: "You've gone too far this time."

"The tears are real—there's no trick involved there," Jack said. "But the cripple was a mistake, I admit."

"It was worse than a mistake," Philip said angrily. "When people learn the truth it will shake their faith in *all* miracles."

"Why do they need to learn the truth?"

"Because I'll have to explain to them why the Madonna is not going to be installed in the cathedral. There's no question of my accepting the statue now, of course."

Reynold said: "I think that's a little hasty—"

"When I want your opinion, young man, I'll ask for it," Philip snapped.

Reynold shut up but Jack persisted. "Are you sure you've got the right to deprive your people of the Madonna? Look at them." He indicated the handful of worshipers who had remained behind. Among them was Meg Widow. She was kneeling in front of the statue with tears streaming down her face. Jack did not know, Philip realized, that Meg had lost her entire family in the collapse of Alfred's roof. Her emotion touched Philip's heart, and he wondered if Jack might be right after all. Why take this away from people? Because it's dishonest, he reminded himself sternly. They believed in the statue because they saw a faked miracle. He hardened his heart.

Jack knelt down beside Meg and spoke to her. "Why are you weeping?"

"She's dumb," Philip told him.

Then Meg said: "The Madonna has suffered as I have. She understands."

Philip was thunderstruck.

Jack said: "You see? The statue eases her suffering— What are you staring at?"

"She's dumb," Philip said again. "She hasn't uttered a word for more than a year."

"That's right!" Aliena said. "Meg was struck dumb after her husband and boys died when the roof fell."

"This woman?" Jack said. "But she just . . ."

Reynold looked bewildered. "You mean this is a miracle?" he said. "A *real* one?"

Philip looked at Jack's face. Jack was more shocked than anyone. There was no trickery here.

Philip was profoundly moved. He had seen the hand of God move and work a miracle. He was shaking a little. "Well, Jack," he said in an unsteady voice. "Despite all you have done to discredit the Weeping Madonna, it seems that God intends to work wonders with it anyway."

For once Jack was lost for words.

Philip turned away from him and went to Meg. He took her hands and gently pulled her upright. "God has made you well again, Meg," he said, his voice trembling with emotion. "Now you can start a new life." He recalled that he had preached a sermon on the story of Job. The words came back to him: "So the Lord blessed the latter end of Job more than his beginning. . . ." He had told the people of Kingsbridge that the same would be true of them. I wonder, he thought, looking at the rapture on Meg's tear-stained face, I wonder whether this could be the start of it.

There was an uproar in chapter when Jack presented his design for the new cathedral.

Philip had warned Jack to expect trouble. Philip had seen the drawings previously, of course. Jack had carried them to the prior's house early one morning, a plan and an elevation, drawn on plaster in wooden frames. They had looked at them together in the clear early light, and Philip had said: "Jack, this will be the most beautiful church in England—but we're going to have trouble with the monks."

Jack knew from his time as a novice that Remigius and his cronies still routinely opposed any plan that was dear to Philip's heart, even though it was eight years since Philip had defeated Remigius in the election. They rarely got much support from the broad mass of the brothers, but in this case Philip was uncertain: they were such a conservative lot that they could be scared by the revolutionary design. However, there was nothing for it but to show them the drawings and try to convince them. Philip certainly could not go ahead and build the cathedral without the wholehearted support of the majority of his monks.

On the following day Jack attended chapter and presented his plans. The drawings were propped up on a bench against the wall, and the monks crowded around to look at them. As they took in the details, there was a murmur of discussion which rose rapidly to a hubbub. Jack was discouraged: the tone was disapproving, bordering on outrage. The noise grew louder as they began to argue among themselves, some attacking the design and others defending it.

After a while Philip called for order and they calmed down. Milius Bursar asked a prearranged question. "Why are the arches pointed?"

"It's a new technique they're using in France," Jack replied. "I've seen it in several churches. The pointed arch is stronger. That is what will enable me to build the church so high. It will probably be the tallest nave in England."

They liked that idea, Jack could tell.

Someone else said: "The windows are so *big*."

"Thick walls are unnecessary," Jack said. "They've proved that in France. It's the piers that hold the building up, especially with rib-vaulting. And the effect of the big windows is breathtaking. At Saint-Denis the abbot has put in colored glass with pictures on it. The church becomes a place of sunshine and air, instead of gloom and darkness."

Several of the monks were nodding approval. Perhaps they were not as conservative as he had thought.

But Andrew Sacrist spoke next. "Two years ago you were a novice among us. You were disciplined for striking the prior, and you evaded that discipline and ran away. Now you come back wanting to tell us how to build our church."

Before Jack could speak, one of the younger monks protested: "That's nothing to do with it! We're discussing the design, not Jack's past!"

Several monks tried to speak at the same time, some of them shouting. Philip made them all shut up and asked Jack to answer the question.

Jack had been expecting something like this and he was ready. "I made a pilgrimage to Santiago de Compostela as penance for that sin, Father Andrew, and I hope my bringing the Weeping Madonna to you may count as recompense for my wrongdoing," he said meekly. "I'm not destined to be a monk, but I hope I can serve God in a different way—as his builder."

They seemed to accept that.

However, Andrew had not finished. "How old are you?" he said, although he surely knew the answer.

"Twenty years."

"That's very young to be a master builder."

"Everyone here knows me. I've lived here since I was a boy." Since I burned down your old church, he thought guiltily. "I served my apprenticeship under the original master builder. You've seen my stonework. When I was a novice I worked with Prior Philip and Tom Builder as clerk of the works. I humbly ask the brothers to judge me by my work, not by my age."

It was another prepared speech. He saw one of the monks grin at the word *humbly,* and realized it might have been a small error: they all knew that whatever other qualities he had he was not humble.

Andrew was quick to take advantage of his slip. "Humbly?" he said, and his face began to turn red as he feigned outrage. "It wasn't very *humble* of you to announce to the masons of Paris three months ago that you had *already* been appointed master builder here."

Once again there was a hubbub of indignant reactions from the monks. Jack groaned inwardly. How the devil had Andrew got hold of that little tidbit? Reynold or Edward must have been indiscreet. He tried to shrug it off. "I was hoping to attract some of those craftsmen to Kingsbridge," he said as the noise died down. "They will be useful, no matter who is appointed master here. I don't think my presumption did any harm." He tried an engaging grin. "But I'm sorry I'm not humbler." This did not go down very well.

Milius Bursar got him out of trouble by asking another prearranged question. "What do you propose to do about the existing chancel, which has partly collapsed?"

"I've examined it very carefully," Jack said. "It can be repaired. If you appoint me master builder today I will have it usable again within a year. Furthermore, you can continue to use it while I'm building the transepts and the nave to the new design. Finally, when the nave is finished, I propose demolishing the chancel and building a new one to match the rest of the new church."

Andrew said: "But how do we know the old chancel won't fall down again?"

"The collapse was caused by Alfred's stone vault, which was not in the original plans. The walls weren't strong enough to hold it up. I propose to revert to Tom's design and build a timber ceiling."

There was a murmur of surprise. The question of why the roof had fallen in had been a matter of controversy. Andrew said: "But Alfred increased the size of the buttresses to support the extra weight."

This had puzzled Jack, too, but he thought he had found the answer. "They still weren't strong enough, particularly at the top. If you study the ruins you can see that the part of the structure that gave way was the clerestory. There was very little reinforcement at that level."

They seemed satisfied with that. Jack felt that his ability to give a confident answer had enhanced his status as a master builder.

Remigius stood up. Jack had been wondering when he would make his contribution. "I should like to read a verse of the Holy Scriptures to the brethren in chapter," he said, rather theatrically. He looked at Philip, who nodded consent.

Remigius walked to the lectern and opened the huge Bible. Jack studied the man. His thin mouth was nervously mobile, and his watery blue eyes bulged a little, giving him a permanent expression of indignation. He was a picture of resentment. Years ago he had come to believe that he was destined to be a leader of men, but in truth he was too weak a character, and now he was doomed to live out his life in disappointment, making trouble for better men. "The Book of Exodus," he intoned as he turned the parchment pages. "Chapter Twenty. Verse Fourteen." Jack wondered what on earth was coming. Remigius read: "Thou shalt not commit adultery." He closed the book with a bang and returned to his seat.

In a tone of mild exasperation, Philip said: "Perhaps you would tell us, Brother Remigius, why you chose to read that short verse in the middle of our discussion of building plans?"

Remigius pointed an accusing finger at Jack. "Because the man who wants to be our master builder is living in a state of sin!" he thundered.

Jack could hardly believe he was serious. He said indignantly: "It's true that our union has not been blessed by the Church, because of special circumstances, but we'll get married as soon as you like."

"You can't," Remigius said triumphantly. "Aliena is already married."

"But that union was never consummated."

"Nevertheless, the couple were wed in church."

"But if you won't let me marry her, how can I avoid committing adultery?" Jack said angrily.

"That's enough!" The voice was Philip's. Jack looked at him. He seemed furious. He said: "Jack, are you living in sin with your brother's wife?"

Jack was flabbergasted. "Didn't you know?"

"Of course I didn't!" Philip roared. "Do you think I could have remained silent about it if I had?"

There was a silence. It was unusual for Philip to shout. Jack saw that he was in real trouble. His offense was a technicality, of course, but monks were supposed to be strict about such things. Unfortunately, the fact that Philip had not known that he was living with Aliena made matters much worse. It had enabled Remigius to take Philip by surprise and make a fool of him. Now Philip would have to be firm, to prove that he was strict.

Jack said miserably: "But you can't build the wrong sort of church just to punish me."

Remigius said with relish: "You'll have to leave the woman."

"Piss off, Remigius," Jack said. "She has my child—he's a year old!"

Remigius sat back with a look of satisfaction.

Philip said: "Jack, if you speak like that in chapter you'll have to leave."

Jack knew he should calm down but he could not. "But it's ludicrous!" he said. "You're telling me to abandon my woman and our child! This isn't morality, it's hairsplitting."

Philip's anger abated somewhat, and Jack saw the more familiar light of sympathy in his clear blue eyes. He said: "Jack, you may take a pragmatic approach to God's laws but we prefer to be rigid— that's why we're monks. And we cannot have you as builder while you're living in a state of adultery."

Jack remembered a line of Scripture. "Jesus said: 'He that is without sin among you, let him first cast a stone.'"

Philip said: "Yes, but Jesus said to the adulteress: 'Go, and sin no more.'" He turned to Remigius. "I take it you would withdraw your opposition if the adultery ceased."

"Of course!" said Remigius.

Despite his anger and misery, Jack noticed that Philip had outmaneuvered Remigius neatly. He had made the adultery the decisive question, thereby sidestepping the whole issue of the new design. But Jack was not ready to go along with that. He said: "I'm not going to leave her!"

Philip said: "It might not be for long."

Jack paused. That had taken him by surprise. "What do you mean?"

"You could marry Aliena if her first marriage was annulled."

"Can that be done?"

"It should be automatic, if, as you say, the marriage was never consummated."

"What do I have to do?"

"Apply to an ecclesiastical court. Normally it would be Bishop Waleran's court, but in this case you probably should go straight to the archbishop of Canterbury."

"And is the archbishop bound to agree?"

"In justice, yes."

That was not a totally unequivocal answer, Jack noted. "But we would have to live apart meanwhile?"

"If you want to be appointed master builder of Kingsbridge Cathedral—yes."

Jack said: "You're asking me to choose between the two things I love most in all the world."

Philip said: "Not for long."

His voice made Jack look up sharply: there was real compassion in it. Jack realized Philip was genuinely sorry to have to do this. That made him less angry and more sad. He said: "How long?"

"It could be as much as a year."

"A year!"

"You don't have to live in different towns," Philip said. "You can still see Aliena and the child."

"Do you know she went to Spain to look for me?" Jack said. "Can you imagine that?" But the monks had no conception of what love was about. He said bitterly: "Now I must tell her we've got to live apart."

Philip stood up and put a hand on Jack's shoulder. "The time will go by faster than you think, I promise you," he said. "And you'll be busy—building the new cathedral."

II

The forest had grown and changed in eight years. Jack had thought he could never get lost in territory he had once known like the back of his hand, but he had been wrong. Old trails were overgrown, new ones had been trodden in the undergrowth by the deer and the boar and the wild ponies, streamlets had altered course, old trees had fallen and young ones were taller. Everything was diminished: distances seemed less and hills not so steep. Most striking of all, he felt a stranger here. When a young deer gazed at him, startled, across a glade, Jack could not guess which family the deer belonged to or where its dam was. When a flight of ducks took off, he did not instantly know what stretch of water they had risen from and why. And he was nervous, for he had no idea where the outlaws were.

He had ridden most of the way here from Kingsbridge, but he had to dismount as soon as he left the main road, for the trees grew too low over the trail to permit him to ride. Returning to the haunts of his boyhood made him feel irrationally sad. He had never appreciated, because he had never realized, how simple life had been then. His greatest passion had been for strawberries, and he had known that every summer, for a few days, there would be as many as he could eat, growing on the forest floor. Nowadays everything was problematical: his combative friendship with Prior Philip; his frustrated love for Aliena; his towering ambition to build the most beautiful cathedral in the world; his burning need to find out the truth about his father.

He wondered how much his mother had changed in the two years he had been away. He was looking forward eagerly to seeing her again. He had coped perfectly well on his own, of course, but it was very reassuring to have someone in your life who was always ready to fight for you, and he had missed that comforting feeling.

It had taken him all day to reach the part of the forest where he and she had used to live. Now the short winter afternoon was darkening rapidly. Soon he would have to give up the search for their old cave, and concentrate on finding a sheltered place in which to spend the night. It would be cold. Why am I worried? he thought. I used to spend every night in the forest.

In the end she found him.

He was on the point of giving up. A narrow, almost invisible track through the vegetation, probably used only by badgers and foxes, petered out in a thicket. There was nothing to do but retrace his steps. He turned his horse around and almost walked into her.

"You've forgotten how to move quietly in the forest," she said. "I could hear you crashing around a mile away."

Jack smiled. She had not changed. "Hello, Mother," he said. He kissed her cheek, then, in a rush of affection, he hugged her.

She touched his face. "You're thinner than ever."

He looked at her. She was brown and healthy, her hair still thick and dark, without any gray. Her eyes were the same golden color, and they still seemed to see right through Jack. He said: "You're just the same."

"Where did you go?" she said.

"All the way to Compostela, and even farther, to Toledo."

"Aliena went after you—"

"She found me. Thanks to you."

"I'm glad." She closed her eyes as if sending up a prayer of thanks. "I'm so glad."

She led him through the forest to the cave, which was less than a mile away: his memory had not been so bad after all. She had a blazing log fire and three sputtering rushlights. She gave him a mug of the cider she made with crab apples and wild honey, and they roasted some chestnuts. Jack could remember the items that a forest dweller could not make for herself, and he had brought his mother knives, cord, soap and salt. She began to skin a coney for the cooking pot. He said: "How are you, Mother?"

"Fine," she said; then she looked at him and realized the question was serious. "I grieve for Tom Builder," she said. "But he's dead and I don't care to take another husband."

"And are you happy here, otherwise?"

"Yes and no. I'm used to living in the forest. I like being alone. I never did get used to busybody priests telling me how to behave. But I miss you, and Martha, and Aliena; and I wish I could see more of my grandson." She smiled. "But I can never go back to live in Kingsbridge, not after cursing a Christian wedding. Prior Philip will never forgive me for that. However, it's all worth it if I've brought you and Aliena together at last." She looked up from her work with a pleased smile. "So how do you like married life?"

"Well," he said hesitantly, "we're not married. In the eyes of the Church, Aliena is still married to Alfred."

"Don't be stupid. What does the Church know about it?"

"Well, they know who they've married, and they wouldn't let me build the new cathedral while I was living with another man's wife."

Her eyes flashed anger. "So you've left her?"

"Yes. Until she can get an annulment."

Mother put the rabbit's skin to one side. With a sharp knife in her bloody hands she began to joint the carcass, dropping the pieces into the cooking pot bubbling on the fire. "Prior Philip did that to me, once, when I was with Tom," she said, slicing the raw meat with swift strokes. "I know why he gets so frantic about people making love. It's because he's not allowed to do it himself, and he resents other people's freedom to enjoy what is forbidden to him. Of course, there's nothing he can do about it when they're married by the Church. But if they're not, he gets the chance to spoil things for them, and that makes him feel better." She cut off the rabbit's feet and threw them into a wooden bucket full of rubbish.

Jack nodded. He had accepted the inevitable, but every time he said good night to Aliena and walked away from her door he felt angry with Philip, and he understood his mother's persistent resentment. "It's not forever, though," he said.

"How does Aliena feel about it?"

Jack grimaced. "Not good. But she thinks it's her fault, for marrying Alfred in the first place."

"So it is. And it's your fault for being determined to build churches."

He was sorry that she could not share his vision. "Mother, it's not worth building anything else. Churches are bigger and higher and more beautiful and more difficult to build, and they have more decoration and sculpture than any other kind of building."

"And you won't be satisfied with anything less."

"Right."

She shook her head in perplexity. "I'll never know where you got the idea that you were destined for greatness." She dropped the rest of the rabbit in the pot and began to clean the underside of its skin. She would use the fur. "You certainly didn't inherit it from your forebears."

That was the cue he had been waiting for. "Mother, when I was overseas I learned some more about my forebears."

She stopped scraping and looked at him. "What on earth do you mean?"

"I found my father's family."

"Good God!" She dropped the rabbit skin. "How did you do that? Where are they? What are they like?"

"There's a town in Normandy called Cherbourg. That's where he came from."

"How can you be sure?"

"I look so much like him, they thought I was a ghost."

Mother sat down heavily on a stool. Jack felt guilty about having shocked her so badly, but he had not expected her to be so shaken by the news. She said: "What . . . what are his people like?"

"His father's dead, but his mother's still alive. She was kind, once she was convinced I wasn't the ghost of my father. His older brother is a carpenter with a wife and three children. My cousins." He smiled. "Isn't that nice? We've got relations."

The thought seemed to upset her, and she looked distressed. "Oh, Jack, I'm so sorry I didn't give you a normal upbringing."

"I'm not," he said lightly. He was embarrassed when his mother showed remorse: it was so out of character for her. "But I'm glad I met my cousins. Even if I never see them again, it's good to know they're there."

She nodded sadly. "I understand."

Jack took a deep breath. "They thought my father had drowned in a shipwreck twenty-four years ago. He was aboard a vessel called the White Ship which went down just out of Barfleur. Everyone was thought to have drowned. Obviously my father survived. But somehow they never knew that, because he never went back to Cherbourg."

"He went to Kingsbridge," she said.

"But *why?*"

She sighed. "He clung to a barrel and was washed ashore near a castle," she said. "He went to the castle to report the shipwreck. There were several powerful barons at the castle, and they showed great consternation when he turned up. They took him prisoner and brought him to England. After some weeks or months—he got rather confused—he ended up in Kingsbridge."

"Did he say anything else about the wreck?"

"Only that the ship went down very fast, as if it had been holed."

"It sounds as if they needed to keep him out of the way."

She nodded. "And then, when they realized they couldn't hold him prisoner forever, they killed him."

Jack knelt in front of her and forced her to look at him. In a voice shaking with emotion he said: "But who were *they*, Mother?"

"You've asked me that before."

"And you've never told me."

"Because I don't want you to spend your life trying to avenge the death of your father!"

She was still treating him like a child, withholding information that might not be good for him, he felt. He tried to be calm and adult. "I'm going to spend my life building Kingsbridge Cathedral and making babies with Aliena. But I want to know why they hanged my father. And the only people who have the answer are the men who gave false testimony against him. So I have to know who they were."

"At the time I didn't know their names."

He knew she was being evasive and it made him angry. *"But you know now!"*

"Yes, I do," she said tearfully, and he realized that this was as painful for her as it was for him. "And I'll tell you, because I can see you'll never stop asking." She sniffed and wiped her eyes.

He waited in suspense.

"There were three of them: a monk, a priest and a knight."

Jack looked at her hard. "Their names."

"You're going to ask them why they lied under oath?"

"Yes."

"And you expect them to tell you?"

"Perhaps not. I'll look into their eyes when I ask them, and that may tell me all I need to know."

"Even that may not be possible."

"I want to try, Mother!"

She sighed. "The monk was the prior of Kingsbridge."

"Philip!"

"No, not Philip. This was before Philip's time. It was his predecessor, James."

"But he's dead."

"I told you it might not be possible to question them."

Jack narrowed his eyes. "Who were the others?"

"The knight was Percy Hamleigh, the earl of Shiring."

"William's father!"

"Yes."

"He's dead, too!"

"Yes."

Jack had a terrible feeling that all three would turn out to be dead men, and the secret buried with their bones. "Who was the priest?" he said urgently.

"His name was Waleran Bigod. He's now the bishop of Kingsbridge."

Jack gave a sigh of profound satisfaction. "And he's still alive," he said.

*   *   *

Bishop Waleran's castle was finished at Christmas. William Hamleigh and his mother rode to it on a fine morning early in the new year. They saw it from a distance, across the valley. It was at the highest point of the opposite ridge, overlooking the surrounding countryside with a forbidding regard.

As they crossed the valley they passed the old palace. It was now used as a storehouse for fleeces. Income from wool was paying for much of the new castle.

They trotted up the gentle slope on the far side of the valley and followed the road through a gap in the earth ramparts and across a deep dry moat to a gateway in a stone wall. With ramparts, a moat *and* a stone wall, this was a highly secure castle, superior to William's own and to many of the king's.

The inner courtyard was dominated by a massive square keep three stories high which dwarfed the stone church that stood alongside it. William helped his mother dismount. They left their knights to stable the horses and mounted the steps that led to the hall.

It was midday, and in the hall Waleran's servants were preparing the table. Some of his archdeacons, deans, employees and hangers-on were standing around waiting for dinner. William and Regan waited while a steward went up to the bishop's private quarters to announce their arrival.

William was burning inside with a fierce, agonizing jealousy. Aliena was in love, and the whole county knew it. She had given birth to a love child, and her husband had thrown her out of his house. With her baby in her arms, she had gone off to look for the man she loved, and had found him after searching half of Christendom. The story was being told and retold all over southern England. It made William sick with hatred every time he heard it. But he had thought of a way to get revenge.

They were taken up the stairs and shown into Waleran's chamber. They found him sitting at a table with Baldwin, who was now an archdeacon. The two clerics were counting money on a checkered cloth, building the silver pennies into piles of twelve and moving them from black squares to white. Baldwin stood up and bowed to Lady Regan, then quickly put away the cloth and the coins.

Waleran got up from the table and went to the chair by the fire. He moved quickly, like a spider, and William felt the old familiar loathing. Nevertheless he resolved to be unctuous. He had heard recently of the dreadful death of the earl of Hereford, who had quarreled with the bishop of Hereford and died in a state of excommunication. His body had been buried in unconsecrated ground.

When William imagined his own body lying in undefended earth, vulnerable to all the imps and monsters that inhabited the underworld, he shook with fright. He would never quarrel with *his* bishop.

Waleran was as pale and thin as ever, and his black robes hung on him like laundry drying on a tree. He never seemed to change. William knew that he himself had changed. Food and wine were his principal pleasures, and each year he grew a little stouter, despite the active life he led, so that the expensive chain mail that had been made for him when he turned twenty-one had been replaced twice over in the succeeding seven years.

Waleran was just back from York. He had been away for almost half a year, and William politely asked him: "Did you have a successful trip?"

"No," he replied. "Bishop Henry sent me there to attempt to resolve a four-year-old dispute over who is to be archbishop of York. I failed. The row goes on."

The less said about that the better, William thought. He said: "While you've been away, there have been a lot of changes here. Especially at Kingsbridge."

"At Kingsbridge?" Waleran was surprised. "I thought that problem had been solved once and for all."

William shook his head. "They've got the Weeping Madonna."

Waleran looked irritated. "What the devil are you talking about?"

William's mother answered. "It's a wooden statue of the Virgin that they use in processions. At certain times, water comes from its eyes. The people think it's miraculous."

"It *is* miraculous!" William said. "A statue that weeps!"

Waleran gave him a scornful look.

Regan said: "Miraculous or not, thousands of people have been to see it in the last few months. Meanwhile, Prior Philip has recommenced building. They're repairing the chancel and putting a new timber ceiling on it, and they've started on the rest of the church. The foundations for the crossing have been dug, and some new stonemasons have arrived from Paris."

"Paris?" Waleran said.

Regan said: "The church is now going to be built in the style of Saint-Denis, whatever that is."

Waleran nodded. "Pointed arches. I heard talk of it at York."

William did not care what style Kingsbridge Cathedral would be. He said: "The point is, young men off my farms are moving to Kingsbridge to work as laborers, the Kingsbridge market is open again every Sunday, taking business away from Shiring. . . . It's the same old story!" He glanced uneasily at the other two, wondering whether either of them suspected that he had an ulterior motive; but neither looked suspicious.

Waleran said: "The worst mistake I ever made was to help Philip become prior."

"They're going to have to learn that they just can't do this," William said.

Waleran looked at him thoughtfully. "What do you want to do?"

"I'm going to sack the town again." And when I do, I'll kill Aliena and her lover, he thought; and he looked into the fire, so that his mother should not meet his eyes and read his thoughts.

"I'm not sure you can," Waleran said.

"I've done it before—why shouldn't I do it again?"

"Last time you had a good reason: the fleece fair."

"This time it's the market. They've never had King Stephen's permission for that either."

"It's not quite the same. Philip was pushing his luck by holding a fleece fair, and you attacked it immediately. The Sunday market has been going on at Kingsbridge for six years now, and anyway, it's twenty miles from Shiring so it ought to be licensed."

William suppressed his anger. He wanted to tell Waleran to stop being such a feeble old woman; but that would never do.

While he was swallowing his protest a steward came into the room and stood silently by the door. Waleran said: "What is it?"

"There's a man here who insists on seeing you, my lord bishop. Name of Jack Jackson. A builder, from Kingsbridge. Shall I send him away?"

William's heart raced. It was Aliena's lover. How had the man happened to come here just when William was plotting his death? Perhaps he had supernatural powers. William was possessed by dread.

"From Kingsbridge?" Waleran said with interest.

Regan said: "He's the new master builder there, the one who brought the Weeping Madonna from Spain."

"Interesting," said Waleran. "Let's have a look at him." He said to the steward: "Send him in."

William stared at the door with superstitious terror. He expected a tall, fearsome man in a black cloak to stride in and point directly at him with an accusing finger. But when Jack came through the door, William was shocked by his youth. Jack could not have been much past twenty. He had red hair and alert blue eyes which flickered over William, paused on Regan—whose frightful facial sores arrested the glance of anyone who was not used to them—and came to rest on

Waleran. The builder was not much intimidated by finding himself in the presence of the two most powerful men in the county, but apart from that surprising nonchalance he did not seem very fearsome.

Like William, Waleran sensed the young builder's insubordinate attitude, and reacted with a coldly haughty voice. "Well, lad, what's your business with me?"

"The truth," Jack said. "How many men have you seen hang?"

William caught his breath. It was a shocking and insolent question. He looked at the others. His mother was leaning forward, frowning intently at Jack, as if she might have seen him before and was trying to place him. Waleran was looking coldly amused.

Waleran said: "Is this a riddle? I've seen more men hang than I care to count, and there will be another if you don't speak respectfully."

"I beg your pardon, my lord bishop," Jack said, but he still did not sound frightened. "Do you remember all of them?"

"I think so," Waleran said, and he sounded intrigued despite himself. "I suppose there is a particular one that you're interested in."

"Twenty-two years ago, at Shiring, you watched the hanging of a man called Jack Shareburg."

William heard his mother give a muffled gasp.

"He was a jongleur," Jack continued. "Do you recall him?"

William felt the atmosphere in the room become tense all of a sudden. There *was* something unnaturally frightful about Jack Jackson; there had to be, for him to have this effect on Waleran and Mother. "I think perhaps I do remember," Waleran said, and William heard in his voice the strain of self-control. What was going on here?

"I imagine you do," Jack said, and now he was sounding insolent again. "The man was convicted on the testimony of three people. Two of them are now dead. You were the third."

Waleran nodded. "He had stolen something from Kingsbridge Priory—a jeweled chalice."

A flinty look came into Jack's blue eyes. "He had done nothing of the kind."

"I caught him myself, with the chalice on him."

"You lied."

There was a pause. When Waleran spoke again his tone was mild but his face was as hard as iron. "I may have your tongue ripped out for that," he said.

"I just want to know why you did it," Jack said as if he had not heard the grisly threat. "You can be candid here. William is no threat to you, and his mother seems to know all about it already."

William looked at his mother. It was true, she did have a knowing air. William himself was now completely mystified. It seemed—he hardly dared to hope—that Jack's visit actually had nothing to do with William and his secret plans to kill Aliena's lover.

Regan said to Jack: "You're accusing the bishop of perjury!"

"I shan't repeat the charge in public," Jack said coolly. "I've got no proof, and anyway I'm not interested in revenge. I would just like to understand why you hanged an innocent man."

"Get out of here," Waleran said icily.

Jack nodded as if he had expected no more. Although he had not got answers to his questions, there was a look of satisfaction on his face, as if his suspicions had somehow been confirmed.

William was still baffled by the whole exchange. On impulse, he said: "Wait a moment."

Jack turned at the door and looked at him with those mocking blue eyes.

"What . . ." William swallowed and got his voice under control. "What's your interest in this? Why did you come here and ask these questions?"

"Because the man they hanged was my father," Jack said, and he went out.

There was a silence in the room. So Aliena's lover, the master builder at Kingsbridge, was the son of a thief who had been hanged at Shiring, William thought: so what? But Mother seemed anxious, and Waleran actually looked shaken.

Eventually Waleran said bitterly: "That woman has dogged me for twenty years." He was normally so guarded that William was shocked to see him letting his feelings show.

"She disappeared after the cathedral fell down," Regan said. "I thought we'd seen the last of her."

"Now her son has come to haunt us." There was something like real fear in Waleran's voice.

William said: "Why don't you slap him in irons for accusing you of perjury?"

Waleran threw him a look of scorn, then said: "Your boy's a damn fool, Regan."

William realized the charge of perjury must be true. And if he was able to figure that out, so could Jack. "Does anyone else know?"

Regan said: "Prior James confessed his perjury, before he died, to the sub-prior, Remigius. But Remigius has always been on our side against Philip, so he's no danger. Jack's mother knows some of it, but not all; otherwise she would have used the information by now. But Jack has traveled around—he may have picked up something his mother didn't know."

William saw that this strange story from the past could be used to his advantage. As if it had just occurred to him, he said: "Then let's kill Jack Jackson."

Waleran just shook his head contemptuously.

Regan said: "That would serve to draw attention to him and his charges."

William was disappointed. It had seemed almost providential. He thought about it, while the silence in the room dragged out. Then a new thought came to him, and he said: "Not necessarily."

They both looked at him skeptically.

"Jack might be killed without drawing attention to him," William said doggedly.

"All right, tell us how," Waleran said.

"He could be killed in an attack on Kingsbridge," William said, and he had the satisfaction of seeing the same look of startled respect on both their faces.

Jack walked around the building site with Prior Philip late in the afternoon. The ruins of the chancel had been cleared, and the rubble formed two huge heaps on the north side of the priory close. New scaffolding was up, and the masons were rebuilding the fallen walls. Alongside the infirmary was a large stockpile of timber.

"You're moving along quickly," Philip said.

"Not as fast as I'd like," Jack replied.

They inspected the foundations of the transepts. Forty or fifty laborers were down in the deep holes, shoveling mud into buckets, while others at ground level operated the winches that lifted the buckets out of the holes. Huge rough-cut stone blocks for the foundations were stacked nearby.

Jack took Philip into his own workshop. It was much bigger than Tom's shed had been. One side was completely open, for better light. Half the ground area was occupied by his tracing floor. He had laid planks over the earth, put a wooden border a couple of inches high around the planks, then poured plaster onto the wood until it filled the frame and threatened to overflow the border. When the plaster set, it was hard enough to walk on, but drawings could be scratched on it with a short length of iron wire sharpened to a point. This was where Jack designed the details. He used compasses, a straightedge and a set square. The scratch marks were white and clear when first made, but they faded to gray quite quickly, which meant that new drawings could be made on top of old ones without confusion. It was an idea he had picked up in France.

Most of the rest of the hut was taken up by the bench on which Jack was working in wood, making the templates that would show the masons how to carve the stones. The light was fading: he would do no more woodwork today. He began to put his tools away.

Philip picked up a template. "What's this for?"

"The plinth at the base of a pier."

"You prepare things well in advance."

"I just can't wait to start building properly."

These days all their conversations were terse and factual.

Philip put down the template. "I must go in to compline." He turned away.

"And I shall go and *visit* my family," Jack said acidly.

Philip paused, turned as if he was going to speak, looked sad, and left.

Jack locked his toolbox. That had been a foolish remark. He had accepted the job on Philip's terms and it was pointless to complain about it now. But he felt constantly angry with Philip, and he could not always keep it in.

He left the priory close in twilight and went to the little house in the poor quarter where Aliena lived with her brother, Richard. She smiled happily when Jack walked in, but they did not kiss: they never touched one another nowadays, for fear they would become aroused, and then they would either have to part frustrated or give in to their lust and risk being caught breaking their promise to Prior Philip.

Tommy was playing on the floor. He was now a year and half old, and his current obsession was putting things into other things. He had four or five kitchen bowls in front of him, and he tirelessly put the smaller ones inside the larger and tried to put the larger inside the smaller. Jack was very struck by the idea that Tommy did not know instinctively that a large bowl would not fit inside a small one; that this was something human beings had to learn. Tommy was struggling with spatial relationships just as Jack did when he tried to visualize something like the shape of a stone in a curved vault.

Tommy fascinated Jack and made him feel anxious too. Until now Jack had never worried about his ability to find work, hold down a job, and support himself. He had set out to cross France without giving a moment's thought to the possibility that he might become destitute and starve. But now he wanted security. The need to take care of Tommy was much more compelling than the need to take care of himself. For the first time in his life he had responsibilities.

Aliena put a jug of wine and a spiced cake on the table and sat down opposite Jack. He poured a cup of wine and sipped it gratefully. Aliena put some cake in front of Tommy, but he was not hungry, and he scattered it in the rushes on the floor.

Aliena said: "Jack, I need more money."

Jack was surprised. "I give you twelve pennies a week. I only make twenty-four."

"I'm sorry," she said. "You live alone—you don't need as much."

Jack thought this was rather unreasonable. "But a laborer only gets sixpence a week—and some of them have five or six children!"

Aliena looked cross. "Jack, I don't know how laborers' wives keep house—I never learned. And I don't spend anything on myself. But you have dinner here every day. And there's Richard—"

"Well, what about Richard?" Jack said angrily. "Why doesn't he support himself?"

"He never has done."

Jack felt that Aliena and Tommy were enough of a burden for him. "I don't know that Richard is my responsibility!"

"Well, he's mine," she said quietly. "When you took me on you took him too."

"I don't remember agreeing to that!" he said angrily.

"Don't be cross."

It was too late: Jack was already cross. "Richard is twenty-three years old—two years older than I am. How come I'm keeping him? Why should I eat dry bread for breakfast and pay for Richard's bacon?"

"Anyway, I'm pregnant again."

"What?"

"I'm having another baby."

Jack's anger evaporated. He seized her hand. "That's wonderful!"

"Are you glad?" she said. "I was afraid you'd be angry."

"Angry! I'm thrilled! I never knew Tommy when he was tiny— now I'll find out what I missed."

"But what about the extra responsibility, and the money?"

"Oh, to hell with the money. I'm just bad-tempered because we have to live apart. We've got plenty of money. But another baby! I hope it's a girl." He thought of something, and frowned. "But when . . . ?"

"It must have been just before Prior Philip made us live apart."

"Maybe on Halloween." He grinned. "Do you remember that night? You rode me like a horse—"

"I remember," she said with a blush.

He gazed at her fondly. "I'd like to do you now."

She smiled. "Me too."

They held hands across the table.

Richard came in.

He threw the door open and walked inside, hot and dusty, leading a sweating horse. "I've got bad news," he said, panting.

Aliena picked Tommy up off the floor to get him out of the way of the hooves. Jack said: "What's happened?"

"We must all get out of Kingsbridge tomorrow," he said.

"But why?"

"William Hamleigh is going to burn the town again on Sunday."

"No!" Aliena cried.

Jack went cold. He saw again the scene three years ago, when William's horsemen had invaded the fleece fair, with their blazing torches and brutal clubs. He recalled the panic, the screaming, and the smell of burning flesh. He saw again the corpse of his stepfather, with his forehead smashed. He felt sick at heart.

"How do you know?" he asked Richard.

"I was in Shiring, and I saw some of William's men buying weapons at the armorer's shop."

"That doesn't mean—"

"There's more. I followed them into an alehouse and listened to their talk. One of them asked what defenses Kingsbridge had, and another said none."

Aliena said: "Oh, God, it's true." She looked at Tommy, and her hand went to her stomach, where the new baby was growing. She looked up, and Jack met her eye. They were both thinking the same.

Richard went on: "Later I got talking to some of the younger ones, who don't know me. I told them about the battle of Lincoln, and so on, and said I was looking for a fight. They told me to go to Earlscastle, but it would have to be today, for they were to leave tomorrow, and the fight would be on Sunday."

"Sunday," Jack whispered fearfully.

"I rode out to Earlscastle, to double-check."

Aliena said: "Richard, that was dangerous."

"All the signs are there: messengers coming and going, weapons being sharpened, horses exercised, tack cleaned. . . . There's no doubt of it." In a voice full of hatred, Richard finished: "No amount of evildoing will satisfy that devil William—he always wants more." His hand went to his right ear, and he touched the angry scar there with an unconscious nervous gesture.

Jack studied Richard for a moment. He was an idler and a wastrel, but in one area his judgment was trustworthy: the military. If he said William was planning a raid he was probably right. "This is a catastrophe," Jack said, half to himself. Kingsbridge was just beginning to recover from the slump. Three years ago the fleece fair had burned, two years ago the cathedral had fallen on the congregation, and now this. People would say the bad luck of Kingsbridge had come back. Even if they managed to avoid bloodshed by fleeing, Kingsbridge would be ruined. No one would want to live here, come to the market or work here. It could even stop the building of the cathedral.

Aliena said: "We must tell Prior Philip—right away."

Jack nodded. "The monks will be at supper. Let's go."

Aliena picked up Tommy and they all hurried up the hill toward the monastery in the dusk.

Richard said: "When the cathedral is finished, they can hold the market inside it. That will protect it from raids."

Jack said: "But meanwhile we need the income from the market to pay for the cathedral."

Richard, Aliena and Tommy waited outside while Jack went into the monks' refectory. A young monk was reading aloud in Latin while the others ate in silence. Jack recognized an apocalyptic passage from the Book of Revelation. He stood in the doorway and caught Philip's eye. Philip was surprised to see him, but got up from the table and came out straightaway.

"Bad news," Jack said grimly. "I'll let Richard tell you."

They talked in the cavernous gloom of the repaired chancel. Richard gave Philip the details in a few sentences. When he had finished, Philip said: "But we aren't holding a fleece fair—just a little market!"

Aliena said: "At least we've got the chance to evacuate the town tomorrow. Nobody need get hurt. And we can rebuild our houses, as we did last time."

"Unless William decides to hunt down the evacuees," Richard said grimly. "I wouldn't put it past him."

"Even if we all escape, I think it means the end of the market," Philip said gloomily. "People will be afraid to set up stalls in Kingsbridge after this."

Jack said: "It may mean the end of the cathedral. In the last ten years the church has burned down once and fallen down once, and a lot of masons were killed when the town burned. Another disaster would be the last, I think. People would say it's bad luck."

Philip looked stricken. He was not yet forty years old, Jack reckoned, but his face was becoming lined, and his fringe of hair was now more gray than black. Nevertheless, there was a dangerous light in his clear blue eyes as he said: "I'm not going to accept this. I don't think it's the will of God."

Jack wondered what on earth he was talking about. How could he "not accept" it? The chickens might as well say they refused to accept the fox, for all the difference it would make to their fate. "So what are you going to do?" Jack said skeptically. "Pray that William will fall out of bed tonight and break his neck?"

Richard was excited by the idea of resistance. "Let's fight," he said. "Why not? There are hundreds of us. William will bring fifty men, a hundred at most—we could win by sheer weight of numbers."

Aliena protested: "And how many of our people will be killed?"

Philip was shaking his head. "Monks don't fight," he said regretfully. "And I can't ask townspeople to give their lives when I'm not prepared to risk my own."

Jack said: "Don't count on my masons fighting, either. It's not part of their job."

Philip looked at Richard, who was the nearest they had to a military expert. "Is there any way we can defend the town without a pitched battle?"

"Not without town walls," Richard said. "We've got nothing to put in front of the enemy but bodies."

"Town walls," Jack said thoughtfully.

Richard said: "We could challenge William to settle the issue by single combat—a fight between champions. But I don't suppose he would agree to it."

"Town walls would do it?" Jack said.

Richard said impatiently: "They might save us another time, but not now. We can't build town walls overnight."

"Can't we?"

"Of course not, don't be—"

"Shut up, Richard," Philip said forcefully. He looked expectantly at Jack. "What's on your mind?"

"A wall is not that hard to build," Jack said.

"Go on."

Jack's mind was spinning. The others were listening with bated breath. He said: "There are no arches, no vaults, no windows, no roof. . . . A wall *can* be built overnight, if you've got the men and materials."

"What would we build it of?" Philip said.

"Look around you," Jack said. "Here are ready-cut stone blocks intended for the foundations. There is a stack of timber bigger than a house. In the graveyard is a heap of rubble from the collapse. Down at the riverside there's another huge stack of stone from the quarry. There's no shortage of materials."

"And the town is full of builders," Philip said.

Jack nodded. "The monks can do the organizing. The builders can do the skilled work. And for laborers we'll have the entire population of the town." He was thinking rapidly. "The wall would have to run all along the nearside bank of the river. We'd dismantle the bridge. Then we'd have to take the wall up the hill alongside the poor quarter to join up with the east wall of the priory . . . out to the north . . . and down the hill to the riverbank again. I don't know whether there's enough stone for that. . . ."

Richard said: "It doesn't have to be stone to be effective. A simple ditch, with an earth rampart made of the mud dug out of the ditch, will serve the purpose, especially in a place where the enemy is attacking uphill."

"Surely stone is better," Jack said.

"Better, but not essential. The purpose of a wall is to force a delay on the enemy while he's in an exposed position, and enable the defender to bombard him from a sheltered position."

"Bombard him?" Aliena said. "With what?"

"Stones, boiling oil, arrows—there's a bow in most households in the town—"

Aliena shuddered and said: "So we still end up fighting, after all."

"But not hand to hand, not quite."

Jack felt torn. The safest course, in all probability, was for everyone to take refuge in the forest, in the hope that William would be satisfied with burning the houses. But even then there was a risk that he and his men would hunt the townspeople down. Would the danger be greater if they all stayed here, behind a town wall? If something went wrong, and William and his men found a way to breach the wall, the carnage would be appalling. Jack looked at Aliena and Tommy, and thought of the new child growing inside Aliena. "Is there a middle course?" he said. "We could evacuate the women and children, and the men could stay and defend the walls."

"No, thank you," Aliena said firmly. "That's the worst of both worlds. We would have no town walls and no menfolk to fight for us either."

She was right, Jack realized. Town walls were no good without people to defend them, and the women and children could not be left unguarded in the forest: William might leave the town alone and kill the women.

Philip said: "Jack, you're the builder. Can we put up a town wall in one day?"

"I've never built a town wall," Jack said. "There's no question of drawing plans, of course. We'd have to assign a craftsman to each section and let him use his judgment. The mortar will hardly be set by Sunday morning. It will be the worst-built wall in England. But yes, we can do it."

Philip turned to Richard. "You've seen battles. If we build a wall, can we hold William off?"

"Certainly," Richard said. "He will come prepared for a lightning raid, not a siege. If he finds a fortified town here there will be nothing he can do."

Finally Philip looked at Aliena. "You're one of the vulnerable people, with a child to protect. What do you think? Should we run to the forest, and hope William doesn't come after us, or stay here and build a wall to keep him out?"

Jack held his breath.

"It's not just a question of safety," Aliena said after a pause. "Philip, you've dedicated your life to this priory. Jack, the cathedral is your dream. If we run away, you'll lose everything you've lived for. And as for me . . . Well, I have a special reason for wanting to see William Hamleigh's power curbed. I say we stay."

"All right," Philip said. "We build a wall."

As night fell, Jack, Richard and Philip walked the boundaries of the town with lanterns, deciding where the wall should go. The town was built on a low hill, and the river wound around two sides of it. The riverbanks were too soft to hold a stone wall without good foundations, so Jack proposed a wooden fence there. Richard was quite satisfied with that. The enemy could not attack the fence except from the river, which was almost impossible.

On the other two sides, some stretches of wall would be simple earth ramparts with a ditch. Richard declared that this would be effective where the ground was sloping and the enemy was forced to attack uphill. However, where the ground was level a stone wall would be needed.

Jack then went around the village gathering his builders together, getting them out of their homes—out of their beds, in some cases— and out of the alehouse. He explained the emergency and how the town was going to deal with it; then he walked around the boundaries with them and assigned a section of wall to each man: wooden fencing to carpenters, stone wall to masons, and ramparts to apprentices and laborers. He asked each man to mark out his own section with stakes and string before going to bed, and to give some thought, as he went to sleep, to how he would build it. Soon the perimeter of the town was marked by a dotted line of twinkling lights as the craftsmen did their laying out by lanternshine. The blacksmith lit his fire and settled down to spend the rest of the night making spades. The unusual after-dark activity disturbed the bedtime rituals of most of the townspeople, and the craftsmen spent a good deal of time explaining what they were doing to drowsy inquirers. Only the monks, who had gone to bed at nightfall, slept on in blissful ignorance.

But at midnight, when the craftsmen were finishing their preparations and most of the townspeople had retired—if only to discuss the news in hushed excitement under the blankets—the monks were awakened. Their services were cut short, and they were given bread and ale in the refectory while Philip briefed them. They were to be tomorrow's organizers. They were divided into teams, each team working for one builder. They would take orders from him and supervise the digging, lifting, fetching and carrying. Their first priority, Philip emphasized in his talk, was to make sure that the builder had a never-failing supply of the raw materials he needed: stones and mortar, timber and tools.

As Philip talked, Jack wondered what William Hamleigh was doing. Earlscastle was a day's hard ride from Kingsbridge, but William would not try to do it in a day, for then his army would arrive exhausted. They would set out this morning at sunrise. They would not ride all together, but would separate, and cover their weapons and armor as they traveled, to avoid raising the alarm. They would rendezvous discreetly in the afternoon, somewhere just an hour or two from Kingsbridge, probably at the manor house of one of William's larger tenants. In the evening they would drink beer and sharpen their blades and tell one another grisly stories about previous triumphs, young men mutilated, old men trampled beneath the hooves of warhorses, girls raped and women sodomized, children beheaded and babies spitted on the points of swords while their mothers screamed in anguish. Then they would attack tomorrow morning. Jack shuddered with fear. But this time we're going to stop them, he thought. All the same he was scared.

Each team of monks located its own stretch of wall and its source of raw materials. Then, as the first hint of dawn paled the eastern horizon, they went around their assigned neighborhood, knocking on doors, waking the inhabitants while the monastery bell rang urgently.

By sunrise the operation was in full swing. The younger men and women did the laboring while the older ones supplied food and drink and the children ran errands and carried messages. Jack toured the site constantly, monitoring progress anxiously. He told a mortar maker to use less lime, so that the mortar would set faster. He saw a carpenter making a fence with scaffolding poles, and told his laborers to use cut timber from a different stockpile. He made sure that the different sections of the wall would meet in a clean join. And he joked, smiled, and encouraged people constantly.

The sun came up into a clear blue sky. It was going to be a hot day. The priory kitchen supplied barrels of beer, but Philip ordered it to be watered, and Jack approved, for people who were working hard would drink a lot in this weather, and he did not want them falling asleep.

Despite the awful danger there was an incongruous air of jollity. It was like a holiday, when the whole town did something together, like making bread on Lammas Day or floating candles downstream on Midsummer Eve. People seemed to forget the peril which was the reason for their activity. However, Philip did see a few people discreetly leaving town. Either they were going to take their chances in the forest, or more likely they had relations in out-lying villages who would take them in. Nevertheless, nearly every-one stayed.

At noon Philip rang the bell again, and work stopped for dinner. Philip made a tour of the wall with Jack while the workers were eating. Despite all the activity they did not seem to have achieved much. The stone walls had only reached ground level, the earth ramparts were still low mounds, and there were vast gaps in the wooden fence.

At the end of their tour Philip said: "Are we going to finish in time?"

Jack had been purposely cheerful and optimistic all morning, but now he forced himself to make a realistic assessment. "At this rate, no," he said despondently.

"What can we do to speed things up?"

"The only way to build faster is to build worse, normally."

"Then let's build worse—but how?"

Jack considered. "At the moment we've got masons building walls, carpenters building fences, laborers making earthworks, and townspeople fetching and carrying. But most carpenters can build a straightforward wall, and most laborers can put up a wooden fence. So let's get the carpenters to help the masons with the stonework, have the laborers build the fences, and let the townspeople dig the ditch and throw up the ramparts. And as soon as the operation is running smoothly, the younger monks can forget about organization and help with the laboring."

"All right."

They gave the new orders as people were finishing dinner. Not only would this be the worst-built wall in England, Jack thought; it would probably be the shortest-lived. If all of it was still standing in a week's time, it would be a miracle.

During the afternoon, people began to get tired, especially those who had been up in the night. The holiday atmosphere evaporated and the workers became grimly determined. The stone walls rose, the ditch got deeper, and the gaps in the fence began to close. They stopped work for supper, as the sun dipped toward the western skyline, then began again.

At nightfall the wall was not complete.

Philip set a watch, ordered everyone except the guards to get a few hours of sleep, and said he would ring the bell at midnight. The exhausted townspeople went to their beds.

Jack went to Aliena's house. She and Richard were still awake.

Jack said to Aliena: "I want you to take Tommy and go and hide in the woods."

The thought had been in the back of his mind all day. At first he had rejected the idea; but as time went on he kept returning to the dreadful memory of the day William burned the fleece fair; and in the end he decided to send her away.

"I'd rather stay," she said firmly.

Jack said: "Aliena, I don't know if this is going to work, and I don't want you to be here if William Hamleigh gets past this wall."

"But I can't leave while you're organizing everyone else to stay and fight," she said reasonably.

He was long past worrying about what was reasonable. "If you go now they won't know."

"They'll realize eventually."

"By then it will be over."

"But think about the disgrace."

"To hell with the disgrace!" he shouted. He was mad with frustration at not being able to find the words to persuade her. "I want you to be safe!"

His angry voice woke Tommy, who started to cry. Aliena

picked him up and rocked him. She said: "I'm not even sure I'd be safer in the forest."

"William won't be searching the forest. It's the town he's interested in."

"He might be interested in me."

"You could hide in your glade. Nobody ever goes there."

"William might find it by accident."

"Listen to me. You'll be safer there than here. I know it."

"All the same I want to stay here."

"I don't want you here," he said harshly.

"Well, I'm staying anyway," she replied with a smile, ignoring his deliberate rudeness.

Jack suppressed a curse. There was no arguing with her once she had made up her mind: she was as stubborn as a mule. He pleaded with her instead. "Aliena, I'm scared of what's going to happen tomorrow."

"I'm scared, too," she said. "And I think we should be scared together."

He knew he should give in gracefully, but he was too worried. "Damn you, then," he said angrily, and he stormed out.

He stood outside, breathing the night air. After a few moments he cooled down. He was still terribly worried, but it was foolish to be angry with her: they might both die in the morning.

He went back inside. She was standing where he had left her, looking sad. "I love you," he said. They embraced, and stood like that for a long while.

When he went out again the moon was up. He calmed himself with the thought that Aliena might even be right: she could be safer here than in the woods. At least this way he would know if she was in trouble, and could do his best to protect her.

He knew he would not sleep, even if he went to bed. He had a foolish fear that everyone might sleep past midnight, and nobody would wake until dawn when William's men rode in slashing and burning. He walked restlessly around the edge of the town. It was odd: Kingsbridge had never had a perimeter until today. The stone walls were waist-high, which was not enough. The fences were high but there were still enough gaps for a hundred men to ride through in a few moments. The earth ramparts were not too high for a good horse to surmount. There was a lot to do.

He stopped at the place where the bridge used to be. It had been taken to pieces, and the parts had been stored in the priory. He looked over the moonlit water. He saw a shadowy figure approach along the line of the wooden fence, and felt a shiver of superstitious apprehension, but it was only Prior Philip, as sleepless as Jack.

For the moment Jack's grudge against Philip had been over-shadowed by the threat from William, and Jack did not feel unfriendly toward Philip. He said: "If we survive this, we should rebuild the wall, bit by bit."

"I agree," Philip said fervently. "We should aim to have a stone wall right around the town within a year."

"Just here, where the bridge crosses the river, I would put a gate and a barbican, so that we could keep people out without dis-mantling the bridge."

"It's not the kind of thing we monks are good at—organizing town defenses."

Jack nodded. They were not supposed to be involved in any kind of violence. "But if you don't organize it, who will?"

"How about Aliena's brother, Richard?"

Jack was startled by that idea, but a moment's reflection led him to realize that it was brilliant. "He'd do it well, it would keep him from idleness, and I wouldn't have to support him any longer," he said enthusiastically. He looked at Philip with reluctant admiration. "You never stop, do you?"

Philip shrugged. "I wish all our problems could be solved so simply."

Jack's mind returned to the wall. "I suppose Kingsbridge will now be a fortified town forevermore."

"Not forever, but certainly until Jesus comes again."

"You never know," Jack said speculatively. "There may come a time when savages like William Hamleigh aren't in power; when the laws protect the ordinary people instead of enslaving them; when the king makes peace instead of war. Think of that—a time when towns in England don't need walls!"

Philip shook his head. "What an imagination," he said. "It won't happen before Judgment Day."

"I suppose not."

"It must be almost midnight. Time to start again."

"Philip. Before you go."

"What?"

Jack took a deep breath. "There's still time to change our plan. We could evacuate the town now."

"Are you afraid, Jack?" Philip said, not unkindly.

"Yes. But not for myself. For my family."

Philip nodded. "Look at it this way. If you leave now, you will probably be safe—tomorrow. But William may come another day. If we let him have his way tomorrow, we will *always* live in fear. You, me, Aliena, and little Tommy, too: he'll grow up in fear of William, or someone like William."

He was right, Jack thought. If children such as Tommy were to grow up free, their parents had to stop running away from William.

Jack sighed. "All right."

Philip went off to ring the bell. He was a ruler who kept the peace, dispensed justice, and did not oppress the poor people under him, Jack thought. But did you really have to be celibate to do that?

The bell began to toll. Lamps were lit in the shuttered houses, and the craftsmen stumbled out, rubbing their eyes and yawning. They started work slowly, and there were some bad-tempered exchanges with laborers; but Philip had the priory bakehouse going, and soon there was hot bread and fresh butter, and everyone cheered up.

At dawn Jack made another tour with Philip, both of them anxiously scanning the dark horizon for signs of horsemen. The riverside fence was almost complete, with all the carpenters working together to fill in the last few yards. On the other two sides, the earth ramparts were now as high as a man, and the depth of the ditch on the outside gave it an extra three or four feet: a man might scramble up, with difficulty, but he would have to get off his horse. The wall was also man-height, but the last three or four courses of stone were completely weak, because the mortar had not set. However, the enemy would not learn that until they tried to scale the wall, and at that point it might even serve to distract them.

Apart from those gaps in the wooden fence, the work was done, and Philip issued fresh orders. The older citizens and the children were to go to the monastery and take refuge in the dormitory. Jack was pleased: Aliena would have to stay with Tommy, and the two of them would be well behind the front line. The craftsmen were to continue building, but some of their laborers now became military squadrons, under Richard's leadership. Each group was responsible for defending the section of wall it had built. Those of the townsmen and women who had bows would be ready at the walls to shoot arrows down on the enemy. Those who had no weapons would throw stones, and they were to make stockpiles ready. Boiling water was another useful weapon, and cauldrons were heated ready to be poured down on attackers at strategic points. Several of the townsmen had swords, but they were the least useful of weapons: if it came to hand-to-hand combat, the enemy would have got in, and the building of the wall would have been in vain.

Jack had been awake for forty-eight hours straight. He had a headache and his eyes felt gritty. He sat on the thatched roof of a house near the river and looked out across the fields, while the carpenters rushed to finish the fence. Suddenly he realized that William's men might shoot burning arrows over the wall in an attempt to set fire to the town without having to breach the wall. Wearily he got off the roof and trotted up the hill to the priory close. There he found that Richard had had the same thought, and had already got some of the monks to organize barrels of water and buckets at strategic locations around the outer edges of the town.

He was just leaving the priory when he heard what sounded like warning shouts.

His heart racing, he scrambled up onto the roof of the stable and looked out over the fields to the west. On the road that led to the bridge, a mile or so away, a cloud of dust betrayed the approach of a large group of horsemen.

Until this moment there had been an element of unreality about the whole thing; but now the men who wanted to burn Kingsbridge were right there, riding along the road, and suddenly the danger was hideously real.

Jack felt a sudden urge to find Aliena, but there was no time. He jumped off the roof and ran down the hill to the riverbank. A crowd of men was gathered around the last gap. As he watched, they drove stakes into the ground, filling the space, and hastily nailed the last two bracing members to the back, finishing the job. Most of the townspeople were here, apart from those who had taken refuge in the refectory. A few moments after Jack arrived, Richard came running down, shouting: "There's nobody on the other side of town! There could be another group sneaking up behind us! Go back to your posts, quickly!" As they started to move off, he muttered to Jack: "There's no discipline—no discipline at all!"

Jack stared out across the fields as the dust cloud got closer and the figures of the individual horsemen became visible. They were like fiends from hell, he thought, insanely intent on death and destruction. They existed because earls and kings felt the need of them. Philip may be a damned fool on matters of love and marriage, Jack thought, but at least he's found a way to rule a community without the help of savages like these.

It was an odd moment for such reflections. Was this the kind of thing men thought about when they were about to die?

The horsemen came closer. There were more than the fifty Richard had forecast. Jack reckoned the number was nearer to a hundred. They headed for the place where the bridge had been; then they began to slow down. Jack's spirits rose as they came to a ragged halt and reined in their horses in the meadow on the other side of the river. As they stared across the water at the brand-new town wall, somebody near Jack started to laugh. Someone else joined in, and then the laughter spread like wildfire, so that soon there were fifty, a hundred, two hundred men and women roaring with laughter at the embarrassed men-at-arms stuck on the wrong side of the river with no one to fight.

Several of the horsemen dismounted and went into a huddle. Peering through the faint morning haze, Jack thought he could see the yellow hair and red face of William Hamleigh at the center of the group, but he could not be sure.

After a while they got back on their horses, regrouped, and rode off. The people of Kingsbridge raised a mighty cheer. But Jack did not think William had given up yet. They were not going back the way they had come. Instead they were heading upstream alongside the river. Richard came to Jack's side and said: "They're looking for a ford. They'll cross the river and sweep through the woods to come at us from the other side. Spread the word."

Jack went swiftly around the wall, relaying Richard's forecast. To the north and east, the wall was of earth or stone, but there was no river in the way. On that side the wall incorporated the east wall of the priory close, only a few steps from the refectory where Aliena and Tommy had taken refuge. Richard had stationed Oswald, the horse dealer, and Dick Richards, the son of the tanner, on the roof of the infirmary with their bows and arrows: they were the best shots in town. Jack went to the northeast corner and stood on the earth rampart, looking across the field to the woods from which William's men would emerge.

The sun climbed in the sky. It was another hot, cloudless day. The monks came around the walls with bread and beer. Jack wondered how far upstream William would go. There was a place a mile away where a good horse could swim across, but it would look risky to a stranger, and William would probably go a couple of miles farther, when he would come to a shallow ford.

Jack wondered how Aliena was feeling. He wanted to go to the refectory and see her, but he was reluctant to leave the wall; for if he did it, others would want to, and the wall would be left undefended.

While he was resisting the temptation there was a shout, and the horsemen reappeared.

They came out of the woods to the east, so that Jack had the sun in his eyes when he looked at them: no doubt that was intentional. After a moment he realized they were not just approaching, they were charging. They must have reined in in the woods, out of sight, and spied out the ground, then planned this charge. Jack went taut with fear. They were not going to look at the wall and go away: they were going to try to breach it.

The horses galloped across the field. One or two townspeople shot arrows. Richard, standing near Jack, yelled angrily: "Too early! Too early! Wait until they're in the ditch—then you can't miss!" Few people heard him, and a light shower of wasted arrows fell on the green barley shoots in the field. As a military force we're hopeless, Jack thought; only the wall can save us.

He had a stone in one hand and in the other he held a sling just like the one he had used as a boy to shoot ducks for his dinner. He wondered whether his aim was still good. He realized he was gripping his weapons as hard as he could, and he forced himself to relax his hold. Stones were effective against ducks, but they seemed appallingly feeble against the armored men on big horses who were thundering closer every second. He swallowed drily. Some of the enemy had bows and burning arrows, he saw; and a moment later he realized that the men with bows were heading for the stone walls, and the others for the earth ramparts. That meant William had decided he could not storm the stone wall: he did not realize the mortar was so new that the wall could be pulled down by hand. He had been fooled. Jack enjoyed a small moment of triumph.

Then the attackers were at the walls.

The townspeople shot wildly, and a hail of hasty arrows raked the horsemen. Despite their poor aim they could not fail to claim some victims. The horses reached the ditch. Some balked, and some charged down into the dip and up the other side. Immediately opposite Jack's position, a huge man in battered chain mail jumped his horse across the ditch so that it landed on the lower slope of the rampart and kept coming up. Jack loaded his sling and let fly. His aim was as good as ever: the stone hit the horse full on the end of its nose. Already floundering in the loose earth, it whinnied in pain, reared up, and turned around. It cantered away, but its rider slid off and drew his sword.

Most of the horses had turned back, either of their own volition or because their riders had turned them; but several men were attacking on foot, and the others were turning again ready to make another charge. Glancing back over his shoulder, Jack saw that several thatched roofs were burning, despite the efforts of the firefighters—the younger women of the town—to put out the flames. The dreadful thought flashed through Jack's mind that this was not going to work. Despite the heroic effort of the last thirty-six hours, these savage men would cross the wall, burn the town, and ravage the people.

The prospect of hand-to-hand fighting terrified him. He had never been taught to fight, never used a sword—not that he had one—and his only experience of fighting was when Alfred had beaten him up. He felt helpless.

The horsemen charged again and those of the attackers who had lost their mounts came up the ramparts on foot. Rocks and arrows rained on them. Jack worked his sling systematically, loading and firing, loading and firing like a machine. Several of the attackers fell under the rain of missiles. Right in front of Jack a rider took a fall and lost his helmet, revealing a head of yellow hair: it was William himself.

None of the horses made it to the top of the earth rampart, but some of the men on foot did, and, to Jack's horror, the townsmen were forced to join combat with them, fighting off the swords and lances of the attackers with poles and axes. Some of the enemy made it over the top, and Jack saw three or four townsmen near him fall. His heart was full of horror: the townspeople were losing.

But eight or ten townsmen surrounded every attacker who got across the wall, pounding them with sticks and hacking mercilessly with axes, and although several townsmen were wounded all the attackers were killed rapidly. Then the townsmen began to drive the others back down the slope of the ramparts. The charge petered out. Those attackers still on horseback milled around uncertainly while a few loose skirmishes continued on the ramparts. Jack rested for a moment, breathing hard, grateful for the reprieve, waiting with dread for the enemy's next move.

William raised his sword in the air and yelled to attract the attention of his men. He waved his sword in a circle, to rally them, then pointed it at the walls. They regrouped and prepared to charge the walls once again.

Jack saw an opportunity.

He picked up a stone, loaded his sling, and took careful aim at William.

The stone flew through the air as straight as a mason's line and hit William in the middle of the forehead, so hard that Jack heard the thud of rock on bone.

William fell to the ground.

His men hesitated uncertainly and the charge faltered.

A big dark man jumped from his horse and ran to William's side. Jack thought he recognized William's groom, Walter, who always rode with him. Still holding on to his reins, Walter knelt down by William's prone body. For a moment Jack hoped William might be dead. Then William moved, and Walter helped him to his feet. William was looking dazed. Everyone on both sides of the battle was watching the two of them. For a moment the hail of stones and arrows stopped.

Still looking unsteady, William mounted Walter's horse, assisted by Walter, who then climbed on behind him. There was a moment of hesitation as everyone wondered whether William would be able to carry on. Walter waved his sword in a circle in the rallying gesture; then, to Jack's unspeakable relief, he pointed to the woods.

Walter kicked the horse and they charged off.

The other horsemen followed. Those who were still fighting on the ramparts gave up, backed off, and ran across the field after their leader. A few stones and arrows chased them over the barley.

The townspeople cheered.

Jack looked around him, feeling dazed. Was it all over? He could hardly believe it. The fires were going out—the women had succeeded in keeping them under control. Men were dancing on the ramparts, hugging one another. Richard came up to him and clapped him on the back. "It was the wall that did it, Jack," he said. "Your wall."

Townspeople and monks crowded around the two of them, all wanting to congratulate Jack and each other.

"Have they gone for good?" Jack said.

"Oh, yes," Richard replied. "They won't come back, now that they've discovered we're determined to defend the walls. William knows that you can't take a walled town if the people are resolved to resist you; not without a vast army and a six-month siege."

"So it's over," Jack said stupidly.

Aliena came pushing through the crowd with Tommy in her arms. Jack embraced her gratefully. They were alive and they were together, and he was thankful.

He suddenly felt the effect of his two days without sleep, and he wanted to lie down. But it was not to be. Two young masons grabbed him and lifted him on to their shoulders. A cheer went up. They moved off, taking the crowd with them. Jack wanted to tell them that it was not *he* who had saved them, they had done it themselves; but he knew they would not listen, for they wanted a hero. As the news spread, and the whole town realized they had won, the cheering became thunderous. They've been living in fear of William for years, Jack thought, but today they've won their freedom. He was carried around the town in a triumphal procession, waving and smiling, and longing for the moment when he could lay his head down and close his eyes in blissful sleep.

III

The Shiring Fleece Fair was bigger and better than ever. The square in front of the parish church, where they held markets and executions as well as the annual fair, was crammed with stalls and people. Wool was the main commodity, but there were also displays of everything else that could be bought and sold in England: gleaming new swords, decoratively carved saddles, fat piglets, red boots, ginger cakes and straw hats. As William strolled around the square with Bishop Waleran, he calculated that the market was going to make more money for him than ever before. Yet it gave him no pleasure.

He was still sick with humiliation after his defeat at Kingsbridge. He had expected to charge in unopposed and burn the town, but in the event he had lost men and horses and had been turned back without achieving anything. Worst of all, he knew that the building of the wall had been organized by Jack Jackson, the lover of Aliena, the very man he had wanted to kill.

He had failed to kill Jack, but was still determined to take his revenge.

Waleran was also thinking about Kingsbridge, and he said: "I still don't know how they built the wall so quickly."

"It probably wasn't much of a wall," William said.

Waleran nodded. "But I'm sure Prior Philip is already busy improving it. If I were he, I'd make the wall stronger and higher, build a barbican, and appoint a night watchman. Your days of raiding Kingsbridge are over."

William agreed, but he pretended not to. "I can still besiege the town."

"That's a different affair. A quick raid may be overlooked by the king. A prolonged siege, during which the townspeople can send a message to the king begging him to protect them . . . It can be awkward."

"Stephen won't move against me," William said. "He needs me." He was not arguing out of conviction, however. In the end he planned to concede the bishop's point. But he wanted to make Waleran work hard for it, so that he would feel under a small obligation to William. Then William would make the request that was so heavily on his mind.

A thin, ugly woman stepped out, pushing in front of her a pretty girl of about thirteen years, presumably her daughter. The mother pulled aside the top of the girl's flimsy dress to show her small, immature breasts. "Sixty pence," the mother hissed. William felt a stirring in his loins, but he shook his head in refusal and brushed past.

The child-whore made him think of Aliena. She had been little more than a child when he had ravished her. That was almost a decade ago, but he could not forget her. Perhaps he would never have her for himself now; but he could still stop anyone else from having her.

Waleran was thoughtful. He hardly seemed to look where he was going, but people shrank back out of his way, as if they were afraid even to be touched by the skirts of his black robe. After a moment he said: "Did you hear that the king took Faringdon?"

"I was there." It had been the most decisive victory of the entire long civil war. Stephen had captured hundreds of knights and a great armory, and driven Robert of Gloucester all the way back to the west country. So crucial was the victory that Ranulf of Chester, Stephen's old enemy in the north, had laid down his arms and sworn allegiance to the king.

Waleran said: "Now that Stephen is more secure, he won't be so tolerant of his barons waging their own private wars."

"Perhaps," William said. He wondered if this was the moment to agree with Waleran and make his request. He hesitated: he was embarrassed. In making the request he was going to reveal something of his soul, and he hated to do that to a man as ruthless as Bishop Waleran.

"You should leave Kingsbridge alone, at least for a while," Waleran went on. "You've got the fleece fair. You still have a weekly market, albeit smaller than it once was. You have the wool business. And you've got all the most fertile land in the county, either directly under your control or farmed by your tenants. My situation is also better than it used to be. I've improved my property and rationalized my holdings. I've built my castle. It's becoming less necessary to fight with Prior Philip—at the very moment when it's becoming politically dangerous."

All over the market square people were making and selling food, and the air was full of smells: spicy soup, new bread, sugar confections, boiled ham, frying bacon, apple pie. William felt nauseated. "Let's go to the castle," he said.

The two men left the market square and walked up the hill. The sheriff was going to give them dinner. At the castle gate William stopped.

"Perhaps you're right about Kingsbridge," he said.

"I'm glad you see it."

"But I still want my revenge on Jack Jackson, and you can give it to me, if you will."

Waleran raised an eloquent eyebrow. His expression said he was fascinated to listen but did not consider himself under any obligation.

William plowed on: "Aliena has applied to have her marriage annulled."

"Yes, I know."

"What do you think will be the outcome?"

"Apparently the marriage was never consummated."

"Is that all there is to it?"

"Probably. According to Gratian—a learned man whom I have met myself, actually—what constitutes a marriage is the mutual consent of the two parties; but he also maintains that the act of physical union 'completes' or 'perfects' the marriage. He specifically says that if a man marries a woman but does not copulate with her, then marries a second woman with whom he does copulate, then it is the second of the two marriages that is valid, that is to say, the consummated one. The fascinating Aliena will no doubt have mentioned this in her application, if she had sound advice, which I imagine she got from Prior Philip."

William was impatient of all this theory. "So they will get the annulment."

"Unless someone brings up the argument against Gratian. In fact there are two: one theological and one practical. The theological argument is that Gratian's definition denigrates the marriage of Joseph and Mary, since it was unconsummated. The practical argument is that for political reasons, or to amalgamate two properties, marriages are quite commonly arranged between two children who are physically incapable of consummation. If either bride or groom should die before puberty, the marriage would be invalidated, under Gratian's definition, and that could have very awkward consequences."

William could never follow these convoluted clerical wrangles, but he had a pretty good idea of how they were settled. "What you mean is, it could go either way."

"Yes."

"And which way it goes depends upon who is putting pressure on."

"Yes. In this case, there's nothing hanging on the outcome—no property, no question of allegiance, no military alliance. But if there were more at stake, and someone—an archdeacon, for example—

were to put the argument against Gratian forcefully, they would probably refuse the annulment." Waleran gave William a knowing look that made William want to squirm. "I think I can guess what you're going to ask me next."

"I want you to oppose the annulment."

Waleran narrowed his eyes. "I can't make out whether you love that wretched woman or hate her."

"No," William said. "Nor can I."

Aliena sat on the grass, in the green gloom beneath the mighty beech tree. The waterfall cast droplets like tears onto the rocks at her feet. This was the glade where Jack had told her all those stories. This was where he had given her that first kiss, so casually and quickly that she had pretended that it had never happened. This was where she had fallen in love with him, and refused to admit it, even to herself. Now she wished with all her heart that she had given herself to him then, and married him and had his babies, so that now, whatever else intervened, she would be his wife.

She lay down to rest her aching back. It was the height of summer, and the air was hot and still. This pregnancy was so heavy, and she still had at least six weeks to go. She thought she might be carrying twins, except that she felt kicking in only one place, and when Martha, Jack's stepsister, had listened with her ear right up against Aliena's belly she had heard only one heartbeat.

Martha was looking after Tommy this Sunday afternoon, so that Aliena and Jack could meet in the woods and be alone for a while to talk about their future. The archbishop had refused the annulment, apparently because Bishop Waleran had objected. Philip said they could apply again, but they must live apart meanwhile. Philip agreed that it was unjust, but he said it must be God's will. It seemed more like ill will to Aliena.

The bitterness of regret was a weight she carried around with her, like the pregnancy. Sometimes she was more aware of it, sometimes she almost forgot about it, but it was always there. Often it hurt, but it was a familiar pain. She regretted hurting Jack, she regretted what she had done to herself, she even regretted the sufferings of the contemptible Alfred, who now lived in Shiring and never showed his face in Kingsbridge. She had married Alfred for one reason only, to support Richard in his attempt to win the earldom. She had failed to achieve her purpose and her true love for Jack had been blighted. She was twenty-six years old, her life was ruined, and it was her own fault.

She thought nostalgically of those early days with Jack. When she first met him he had been just a little boy, albeit an unusual one. After he grew up she had continued to think of him as a boy. That was why he had got under her guard. She had turned away every suitor, but she had not thought of Jack as a suitor, and so she had let him get to know her. She wondered why she had been so resistant to love. She adored Jack and there was no pleasure in life like the joy of lying with him; yet once upon a time she had deliberately closed her eyes to such happiness.

When she looked back, her life before Jack seemed empty. She had been frantically busy, building up her wool business, but now those busy days appeared joyless, like an empty palace, or a table laden with silver plates and gold cups but no food.

She heard footsteps and sat up quickly. It was Jack. He was thin and graceful, like a scrawny cat. He sat beside her and kissed her mouth softly. He smelled of perspiration and stone dust. "It's so hot," he said. "Let's bathe in the stream."

The temptation was irresistible.

Jack pulled off his clothes. She watched, staring at him hungrily. She had not seen his naked body for months. He had a lot of red hair on his legs but none on his chest. He looked at her, waiting for her to strip. She felt shy: he had never seen her body when she was pregnant. She unlaced the neck of her linen dress slowly, then pulled it off over her head. She watched his expression anxiously, afraid he would hate her swollen body, but he showed no revulsion: on the contrary, the look that came over his face was one of fondness. I should have known better, she thought; I should have known he would love me just as much.

With a swift movement he knelt on the ground in front of her . and kissed the taut skin of her distended belly. She gave an embarrassed laugh. He touched her navel. "Your belly button sticks out," he said.

"I knew you were going to say that!"

"It used to be like a dimple—now it's like a nipple."

She felt shy. "Let's bathe," she said. She would feel less self-conscious in the water.

The pool by the waterfall was about three feet deep. Aliena slid into the water. It was deliciously cool on her hot skin, and she shivered with delight. Jack got in beside her. There was no room to swim—the pool was only a few feet across. He put his head under the waterfall and washed the stone dust out of his hair. Aliena felt good in the water: it relieved the weight of her pregnancy. She ducked her head under the surface to wash her hair.

When she came up for air, Jack kissed her.

She spluttered and laughed, breathless, rubbing the water out of her eyes. He kissed her again. She put out her arms to hold herself steady, and her hand closed on the hard rod standing upright between Jack's loins like a flagpole. She gasped with pleasure.

"I've missed this," Jack said in her ear, and his voice was hoarse with lust and some other emotion, sadness perhaps.

Aliena's throat was dry with desire. She said: "Are we going to break our promise?"

"Now, and forevermore."

"What do you mean?"

"We're not going to live apart. We're leaving Kingsbridge."

"But what will you do?"

"Go to a different town and build another cathedral."

"But you won't be master. It won't be your design."

"One day I may get another chance. I'm young."

It was possible, but the odds were against it, Aliena knew; and Jack knew it too. The sacrifice he was making for her moved her to tears. Nobody had ever loved her like this; nobody else ever would. But she was not willing to let him give up everything. "I won't do it," she said.

"What do you mean?"

"I'm not going to leave Kingsbridge."

He was angry. "Why not? Anywhere else, we can live as man and wife, and nobody will care. We could even get married in a church."

She touched his face. "I love you too much to take you away from Kingsbridge Cathedral."

"That's for me to decide."

"Jack, I love you for offering. The fact that you're ready to give up your life's work to live with me is . . . it almost breaks my heart that you should love me so much. But I don't want to be the woman who took you away from the work you loved. I'm not willing to go with you that way. It will cast a shadow over our entire lives. You may forgive me for it, but I never will."

Jack looked sad. "I know better than to fight you once you've decided. But what will we do?"

"We'll try again for the annulment. We'll live apart."

He looked miserable.

She finished: "And we'll come here every Sunday and break our promise."

He pressed up against her, and she could feel him becoming aroused again. "Every Sunday?"

"Yes."

"You might get pregnant again."

"We'll take that chance. And I'm going to start manufacturing cloth, as I used to. I've bought Philip's unsold wool again, and I'm going to organize the townspeople to spin and weave it. Then I'll felt it in the fulling mill."

"How did you pay Philip?" Jack said in surprise.

"I haven't, yet. I'm going to pay him in bales of cloth, when it's made."

Jack nodded. He said bitterly: "He agreed to that because he wants you to stay here so that I'll stay."

Aliena nodded. "But he'll still get cheap cloth out of it."

"Damn Philip. He always gets what he wants."

Aliena saw that she had won. She kissed him and said: "I love you."

He kissed her back, running his hands all over her body, greedily feeling her secret places. Then he stopped and said: "But I want to be with you every night, not just on Sundays."

She kissed his ear. "One day we will," she breathed. "I promise you."

He moved behind her, drifting in the water, and pulled her to him, so that his legs were underneath her. She parted her thighs and floated down gently into his lap. He stroked her full breasts with his hands and played with her swollen nipples. Finally he penetrated her, and she shuddered with pleasure.

They made love slowly and gently in the cool pond, with the rush of the waterfall in their ears. Jack put his arms around her bump, and his knowing hands touched her between her legs, pressing and stroking as he went in and out. They had never done this before, made love this way, so that he could caress her most sensitive places at the same time, and it was sharply different, a more intense pleasure, different the way a stabbing pain is different from a dull ache; but perhaps that was because she felt so sad. After a while she abandoned herself to the sensation. Its intensity built up so quickly that the climax took her by surprise, almost frightening her, and she was racked by spasms of pleasure so convulsive that she screamed.

He stayed inside her, hard, unsatisfied, while she caught her breath. He was still, no longer thrusting, but she realized he had not reached a climax. After a while she began to move again, encouragingly, but he did not respond. She turned her head and kissed him over her shoulder. The water on his face was warm. He was weeping.

PART FIVE

1152 - 1155

Chapter 14

AFTER SEVEN YEARS Jack had finished the transepts—the two arms of the cross-shaped church—and they were everything he had hoped for. He had improved on the ideas of Saint-Denis, making everything taller and narrower—windows, arches, and the vault itself. The clustered shafts of the piers rose gracefully through the gallery and became the ribs of the vault, curving over to meet in the middle of the ceiling, and the tall pointed windows flooded the interior with light. The moldings were fine and delicate, and the carved decoration was a riot of stone foliage.

And there were cracks in the clerestory.

He stood in the high clerestory passage, staring out across the chasm of the north transept, brooding on a bright spring morning. He was shocked and baffled. By all the wisdom of the masons the structure was strong; but a crack showed a weakness. His vault was higher than any other he had ever seen, but not by that much. He had not made the mistake of Alfred, and put a stone vault on a structure that was not built to take the weight: his walls had been designed for a stone vault. Yet cracks had appeared in his clerestory in roughly the same place where Alfred's had failed. Alfred had miscalculated but Jack was sure he had not done the same thing. Some new factor was operating in Jack's building and he did not know what it was.

It was not dangerous, not in the short term. The cracks had been filled with mortar and they had not yet reappeared. The building was safe. But it was weak; and for Jack the weakness spoiled it. He wanted his church to last until the Day of Judgment.

He left the clerestory and went down the turret staircase to the gallery, where he had made his tracing floor, in the corner where there was a good light from one of the windows in the north porch. He began to draw the plinth of a nave pier. He drew a diamond, then a square inside the diamond, then a circle inside the square. The main shafts of the pier would spring from the four points of the diamond and rise up the column, eventually branching off north, south, east and west to become arches or ribs. Subsidiary shafts, springing from the corners of the square, would rise to become vaulting ribs, going diagonally across the nave vault on one side and the aisle vault on the other. The circle in the middle represented the core of the pier.

All Jack's designs were based on simple geometrical shapes and some not-so-simple proportions, such as the ratio of the square root of two to the square root of three. Jack had learned how to figure square roots in Toledo, but most masons could not calculate them, and instead used simple geometric constructions. They knew that if a circle was drawn around the four corners of a square, the diameter of the circle was bigger than the side of the square in the ratio of the square root of two to one. That ratio, root-two to one, was the most ancient of the masons' formulas, for in a simple building it was the ratio of the outside width to the inside width, and therefore gave the thickness of the wall.

Jack's task was much complicated by the religious significance of various numbers. Prior Philip was planning to rededicate the church to the Virgin Mary, because the Weeping Madonna worked more miracles than the tomb of Saint Adophus; and in consequence they wanted Jack to use the numbers nine and seven, which were Mary's numbers. He had designed the nave with nine bays and the new chancel, to be built when all else was finished, with seven. The interlocked blind arcading in the side aisles would have seven arches per bay, and the west facade would have nine lancet windows. Jack had no opinion about the theological significance of numbers but he felt instinctively that if the same numbers were used fairly consistently it was bound to add to the harmony of the finished building.

Before he could finish his drawing of the plinth he was interrupted by the master roofer, who had hit a problem and wanted Jack to solve it.

Jack followed the man up the turret staircase, past the clerestory, and into the roof space. They walked across the rounded domes that were the top side of the ribbed vault. Above them, the roofers were unrolling great sheets of lead and nailing them to the rafters, starting at the bottom and working up so that the upper sheets would overlap the lower and keep the rain out.

Jack saw the problem immediately. He had put a decorative pinnacle at the end of a valley between two sloping roofs, but he had left the design to a master mason, and the mason had not made provision for rainwater from the roof to pass through or under the pinnacle. The mason would have to alter it. He told the master roofer to pass this instruction on to the mason, then he returned to his tracing floor.

He was astonished to find Alfred waiting for him there.

He had not spoken to Alfred for ten years. He had seen him at a distance, now and again, in Shiring or Winchester. Aliena had not so much as caught sight of him for nine years, even though they were still married, according to the Church. Martha went to visit him at his house in Shiring about once a year. She always brought back the same report: he was prospering, building houses for the burgers of Shiring; he lived alone; he was the same as ever.

But Alfred did not appear prosperous now. Jack thought he looked tired and defeated. Alfred had always been big and strong, but now he had a lean look: his face was thinner, and the hand with which he pushed the hair out of his eyes was bony where it had once been beefy.

He said: "Hello, Jack."

His expression was aggressive but his tone of voice was ingratiating—an unattractive mixture.

"Hello, Alfred," Jack said warily. "Last time I saw you, you were wearing a silk tunic and running to fat."

"That was three years ago—before the first of the bad harvests."

"So it was." Three bad harvests in a row had caused a famine. Serfs had starved, many tenant farmers were destitute, and presumably the burgers of Shiring could no longer afford splendid new stone houses. Alfred was feeling the pinch. Jack said: "What brings you to Kingsbridge after all this time?"

"I heard about your transepts and came to look." His tone was one of grudging admiration. "Where did you learn to build like this?"

"Paris," Jack said shortly. He did not want to discuss that period of his life with Alfred, who had been the cause of his exile.

"Well." Alfred looked awkward, then said with elaborate indifference: "I'd be willing to work here, just to pick up some of these new tricks."

Jack was flabbergasted. Did Alfred really have the nerve to ask him for a job? Playing for time, he said: "What about your gang?"

"I'm on my own now," Alfred said, still trying to be casual. "There wasn't enough work for a gang."

"We're not hiring, anyway," Jack said, equally casually. "We've got a full complement."

"But you can always use a good mason, can't you?"

Jack heard a faint pleading note and realized that Alfred was desperate. He decided to be honest. "After the life we've had, Alfred, I'm the last person you should come to for help."

"You are the last," Alfred said candidly. "I've tried everywhere. Nobody's hiring. It's the famine."

Jack thought of all the times Alfred had mistreated him, tormented him, and beaten him. Alfred had driven him into the monastery and then had driven him away from his home and family. He had no reason to help Alfred: indeed, he had cause to gloat over Alfred's misfortune. He said: "I wouldn't take you on even if I was needing men."

"I thought you might," Alfred said with bullheaded persistence. "After all, my father taught you everything you know. It's because of him that you're a master builder. Won't you help me for his sake?"

For Tom. Suddenly Jack felt a twinge of conscience. In his own way, Tom had tried to be a good stepfather. He had not been gentle or understanding, but he had treated his own children much the same as Jack, and he had been patient and generous in passing on his knowledge and skills. He had also made Jack's mother happy, most of the time. And after all, Jack thought, here I am, a successful and prosperous master builder, well on the way to achieving my ambition of building the most beautiful cathedral in the world, and there's Alfred, poor and hungry and out of work. Isn't that revenge enough?

No, it's not, he thought.

Then he relented.

"All right," he said. "For Tom's sake, you're hired."

"Thank you," Alfred said. His expression was unreadable. "Shall I start right away?"

Jack nodded. "We're laying foundations in the nave. Just join in."

Alfred held out his hand. Jack hesitated momentarily, then shook it. Alfred's grip was as strong as ever.

Alfred disappeared. Jack stood staring down at his drawing of a nave plinth. It was life-size, so that when it was finished a master carpenter could make a wooden template directly from the drawing. The template would then be used by the masons to mark the stones for carving.

Had he made the right decision? He recalled that Alfred's vault had collapsed. However, he would not use Alfred on difficult work such as vaulting or arches: straightforward walls and floors were his metier.

While Jack was still pondering, the noon bell rang for dinner. He put down his sharpened-wire drawing instrument and went down the turret staircase to ground level.

The married masons went home to dinner and the single ones ate in the lodge. On some building sites dinner was provided, as a way of preventing afternoon lateness, absenteeism and drunkenness; but monks' fare was often Spartan and most building workers preferred to provide their own. Jack was living in Tom Builder's old house with Martha, his stepsister, who acted as his housekeeper. Martha also minded Tommy and Jack's second child, a girl whom they had named Sally, while Aliena was busy. Martha usually made dinner for Jack and the children, and Aliena sometimes joined them.

He left the priory close and walked briskly home. On the way a thought struck him. Would Alfred expect to move back into the house with Martha? She was his natural sister, after all. Jack had not thought of that when he gave Alfred the job.

It was a foolish fear, he decided a moment later. The days when Alfred could bully him were long past. He was the master builder of Kingsbridge, and if he said Alfred could not move into the house, then Alfred would not move into the house.

He half expected to find Alfred at the kitchen table, and was relieved to find he was not. Aliena was watching the children eat, while Martha stirred a pot on the fire. The smell of lamb stew was mouth-watering.

He kissed Aliena's forehead briefly. She was thirty-three years old now, but she looked as she had ten years ago: her hair was still a rich dark-brown mass of curls, and she had the same generous mouth and fine, dark eyes. Only when she was naked did she show the physical effects of time and childbirth: her marvelous deep breasts were lower, her hips were broader, and her belly had never reverted to its original taut flatness.

Jack looked affectionately at the two offspring of Aliena's body: nine-year-old Tommy, a healthy red-haired boy, big for his age, shoveling lamb stew into his mouth as if he had not eaten for a week; and Sally, age seven, with dark curls like her mother's, smiling happily and showing a gap between her front teeth just like the one Martha had had when Jack first saw her seventeen years ago. Tommy went to the school in the priory every morning to learn to read and write, but the monks would not take girls, so Aliena was teaching Sally.

Jack sat down, and Martha took the pot off the fire and set it on the table. Martha was a strange girl. She was past twenty years old, but she showed no interest in getting married. She had always been attached to Jack, and now she seemed perfectly content to be his housekeeper.

Jack presided over the oddest household in the county, without a doubt. He and Aliena were two of the leading citizens of the town: he the master builder at the cathedral and she the largest manufacturer of cloth outside Winchester. Everyone treated them as man and wife, yet they were forbidden to spend nights together, and they lived in separate houses, Aliena with her brother and Jack with his stepsister. Every Sunday afternoon, and on every holiday, they would disappear, and everyone knew what they were doing except, of course, Prior Philip. Meanwhile, Jack's mother lived in a cave in the forest because she was supposed to be a witch.

Every now and again Jack got angry about not being allowed to marry Aliena. He would lie awake, listening to Martha snoring in the next room, and think: I'm twenty-eight years old—why am I sleeping alone? The next day he would be bad-tempered with Prior Philip, rejecting all the chapter's suggestions and requests as impracticable or overexpensive, refusing to discuss alternatives or compromises, as if there were only one way to build a cathedral and that was Jack's way. Then Philip would steer clear of him for a few days and let the storm blow over.

Aliena, too, was unhappy, and she took it out on Jack. She would become impatient and intolerant, criticizing everything he did, putting the children to bed as soon as he came in, saying she was not hungry when he ate. After a day or two of this mood she would burst into tears and say she was sorry, and they would be happy again, until the next time the strain became too much for her.

Jack ladled some stew into a bowl and began to eat. "Guess who came to the site this morning," he said. "Alfred."

Martha dropped an iron pot lid on the hearthstone with a loud clang. Jack looked at her and saw fear on her face. He turned to Aliena and saw that she had turned white.

Aliena said: "What's he doing in Kingsbridge?"

"Looking for work. The famine has impoverished the merchants of Shiring, I guess, and they aren't building stone houses like they used to. He's dismissed his gang and he can't find work."

"I hope you threw him out on his tail," Aliena said.

"He said I should give him a job for Tom's sake," Jack said nervously. He had not anticipated such a strong reaction from the two women. "After all, I owe everything to Tom."

"Cow shit," Aliena said, and Jack thought: she got that expression from my mother.

"Well, I hired him anyway," he said.

"Jack!" Aliena screamed. "How could you? You can't let him come back to Kingsbridge—that devil!"

Sally began to cry. Tommy stared wide-eyed at his mother. Jack said: "Alfred isn't a devil. He's hungry and penniless. I saved him, for the sake of his father's memory."

"You wouldn't feel sorry for him if he'd forced you to sleep on the floor at the foot of his bed like a dog for nine months."

"He's done worse things to me—ask Martha."

Martha said: "And to me."

Jack said: "I just decided that seeing him like that was enough revenge for me."

"Well it's not enough for me!" Aliena stormed. "By Christ, you're a damned fool, Jack Jackson. Sometimes I thank God I'm not married to you."

That hurt. Jack looked away. He knew she did not mean it, but it was bad enough that she should say it, even in anger. He picked up his spoon and started to eat. It was hard to swallow.

Aliena patted Sally's head and put a piece of carrot into her mouth. Sally stopped crying.

Jack looked at Tommy, who was still staring at Aliena with a frightened face. "Eat, Tommy," said Jack. "It's good."

They finished their dinner in silence.

In the spring of the year that the transepts were finished, Prior Philip made a tour of the monastery's property in the south. After three bad years he needed a good harvest, and he wanted to check what state the farms were in.

He took Jonathan with him. The priory orphan was now a tall, awkward, intelligent sixteen-year-old. Like Philip at that age, he did not seem to suffer a moment's doubt about what he wanted to do with his life: he had completed his novitiate and taken his vows, and he was now Brother Jonathan. Also like Philip, he was interested in the material side of God's service, and he worked as deputy to Cuthbert Whitehead, the aging cellarer. Philip was proud of the boy: he was devout, hardworking, and well liked.

Their escort was Richard, the brother of Aliena. Richard had at last found his niche in Kingsbridge. After they built the town wall, Philip had suggested to the parish guild that they appoint Richard as Head of the Watch, responsible for the town's security. He organized the night watchmen and arranged for the maintenance and improvement of the town walls, and on market days and holy days he was empowered to arrest troublemakers and drunks. These tasks, which had become essential as the village had grown into a town, were all things a monk was not supposed to do; so the parish guild, which Philip had at first seen as a threat to his authority, had turned out to be useful after all. And Richard was happy. He was about thirty years old now, but the active life he led kept him looking young.

Philip wished Richard's sister could be as settled. If ever a person had been failed by the Church it was Aliena. Jack was the man she loved and the father of her children, but the Church insisted that she was married to Alfred, even though she had never had carnal knowledge of him; and she was unable to get an annulment because of the ill will of the bishop. It was shameful, and Philip felt guilty, even though he was not responsible.

Toward the end of the trip, when they were riding home through the forest on a bright spring morning, young Jonathan said: "I wonder why God makes people starve."

It was a question every young monk asked sooner or later, and there were lots of answers to it. Philip said: "Don't blame this famine on God."

"But God made the weather that caused the bad harvests."

"The famine is not just due to bad harvests," Philip said. "There are always bad harvests, every few years, but people don't starve. What's special about this crisis is that it comes after so many years of civil war."

"Why does that make a difference?" Jonathan asked.

Richard, the soldier, answered him. "War is bad for farming," he said. "Livestock get slaughtered to feed the armies, crops are burned to deny them to the enemy, and farms are neglected while knights go to war."

Philip added: "And when the future is uncertain, people are not willing to invest time and energy clearing new ground, increasing herds, digging ditches and building barns."

"We haven't stopped doing that sort of work," Jonathan said.

"Monasteries are different. But most ordinary farmers let their farms run down during the fighting, so that when the bad weather came they were not in good shape to ride it out. Monks take a longer view. But we have another problem. The price of wool has slumped because of the famine."

"I don't see the connection," Jonathan said.

"I suppose it's because starving people don't buy clothes." It was the first time in Philip's memory that the price of wool had failed to go up annually. He had been forced to slow the pace of cathedral building, stop taking new novices, and eliminate wine and meat from the monks' diet. "Unfortunately, it means that we're economizing just when more and more destitute people are coming to Kingsbridge looking for work."

Jonathan said: "And so they end up queueing at the priory gate for free horsebread and pottage."

Philip nodded grimly. It broke his heart to see strong men reduced to begging for bread because they could find no work. "But remember, it's caused by war, not bad weather," he said.

With youthful passion Jonathan said: "I hope there's a special place in hell for the earls and kings who cause such misery."

"I hope so— Saints preserve us, what's that?"

A strange figure had burst from the undergrowth and was running full-tilt at Philip. His clothes were ragged, his hair was wild, and his face was black with dirt. Philip thought the poor man must be running away from an enraged boar, or even an escaped bear.

Then the man ran up and threw himself on Philip.

Philip was so surprised that he fell off his horse.

His attacker fell on top of him. The man smelled like an animal, and sounded like one too: he made a constant inarticulate grunting noise. Philip wriggled and kicked. The man seemed to be trying to get hold of the leather satchel that Philip had slung over his shoulder. Philip realized the man was trying to rob him. There was nothing in the satchel but a book, *The Song of Solomon*. Philip struggled desperately to get free, not because he was specially attached to the book, but because the robber was so disgustingly dirty.

But Philip was tangled up in the strap of the satchel and the robber would not let go. They rolled over on the hard ground, Philip trying to get away and the robber trying to keep hold of the satchel. Philip was vaguely aware that his horse had bolted.

Suddenly the robber was jerked away by Richard. Philip rolled over and sat upright, but he did not get to his feet for a moment. He was dazed and winded. He breathed the clean air, relieved to be free of the robber's noxious embrace. He felt his bruises. Nothing was broken. He turned his attention to the others.

Richard had the robber flat on the ground and was standing over him, with one foot between the man's shoulder blades and the point of his sword touching the back of the man's neck. Jonathan was holding the two remaining horses and looking bewildered.

Philip got gingerly to his feet, feeling weak. When I was Jonathan's age, he thought, I could fall off a horse and jump right back on again.

Richard said: "If you keep an eye on this cockroach, I'll catch your horse." He offered Philip his sword.

"All right," Philip said. He waved the sword away. "I shan't need that."

Richard hesitated, then sheathed his sword. The robber lay still. The legs sticking out from under his tunic were as thin as twigs, and the same color; and he was barefoot. Philip had never been in any serious danger: this poor man was too weak to strangle a chicken. Richard walked off after Philip's horse.

The robber saw Richard go, and tensed. Philip knew the man was about to make a break for it. He stopped him by saying: "Would you like something to eat?"

The robber raised his head and looked at Philip as if he thought Philip was mad.

Philip went to Jonathan's horse and opened a saddlebag. He took out a loaf, broke it, and offered half to the robber. The man grabbed it unbelievingly and immediately stuffed most of it into his mouth.

Philip sat on the ground and watched him. The man ate like an animal, trying to swallow as much as possible before the meal could be snatched from him. At first Philip had thought he was an old man, but now that he could see him better he realized that the thief was quite young, perhaps twenty-five.

Richard came back, leading Philip's horse. He was indignant when he saw the robber sitting eating. "Why have you given him our food?" he said to Philip.

"Because he's starving," Philip said.

Richard did not reply, but his expression said that monks were mad.

When the robber had eaten the bread, Philip said: "What's your name?"

The man looked wary. He hesitated. Philip somehow got the idea that the man had not spoken to another human being for a while. At last he said: "David."

He still had his sanity, anyway, Philip thought. He said: "What happened to you, David?"

"I lost my farm after the last harvest."

"Who was your landlord?"

"The earl of Shiring."

William Hamleigh. Philip was not surprised.

Thousands of tenant farmers had been unable to pay their rents after three bad harvests. When Philip's tenants defaulted he simply forgave the rent, since if he made people destitute they would just come to the priory for charity anyway. Other landlords, notably Earl William, took advantage of the crisis to evict tenants and repossess their farms. The result was a huge increase in the number of outlaws living in the forest and preying on travelers. That was why Philip had to take Richard everywhere with him as bodyguard.

"What about your family?" Philip asked the robber.

"My wife took the baby and went back to her mother. But there was no room for me."

It was a familiar story. Philip said: "It's a sin to lay hands on a monk, David, and it's wrong to live by theft."

"But how shall I live?" the man cried.

"If you're going to stay in the forest you'd better catch birds and fish."

"I don't know how!"

"You're a failure as a robber," Philip said. "What chance of success did you have, with no weapon, up against three of us, and Richard here armed to the teeth?"

"I was desperate."

"Well, next time you're desperate, go to a monastery. There's always something for a poor man to eat." Philip got to his feet. The sour taste of hypocrisy was in his mouth. He knew the monasteries could not possibly feed all the outlaws. For most of them there really was no alternative but theft. But his role in life was to counsel virtuous living, not to make excuses for sin.

There was no more he could do for this wretched man. He took the reins of his horse from Richard and climbed into the saddle. He could tell that the bruises from his fall were going to hurt him for days. "Go thy way, and sin no more," he said, quoting Jesus; then he kicked his horse forward.

"You're too good, you are," said Richard as they rode off.

Philip shook his head sadly. "The real trouble is, I'm not good enough."

On the Sunday before Whitsun, William Hamleigh got married.

It was his mother's idea.

Mother had been nagging him for years to find a wife and father an heir, but he had always put it off. Women bored him and, in a way that he did not understand and really did not want to think about, they made him anxious. He kept telling Mother he would marry soon but he never did anything about it.

In the end she found him a bride.

Her name was Elizabeth. She was the daughter of Harold of Weymouth, a wealthy knight and a strong supporter of Stephen. As Mother explained to William, with a little effort he could have made a better match—could have married the daughter of an earl—but as he was not willing to put his mind to it, Elizabeth would do.

William had seen her at the king's court in Winchester, and Mother had noticed him staring at her. She had a pretty face, a mass of light brown curls, a big bust and narrow hips—just William's type.

She was fourteen years old.

When William stared at her, he had been imagining meeting her on a dark night and taking her by force in the back alleys of Winchester: marriage had not crossed his mind. However, Mother swiftly established that the father was agreeable, and the girl herself was an obedient child who would do what she was told. Having reassured William that there would be no repetition of the humiliation Aliena had inflicted on the family, Mother arranged a meeting.

William had been nervous. Last time he had done this, he had been an inexperienced youth of twenty, the son of a knight, meeting an arrogant young lady of the nobility. But now he was a battle-hardened man, thirty-seven years old, and he had been the earl of Shiring for ten years. He was foolish to be nervous about a meeting with a fourteen-year-old girl.

However, she was even more nervous. She was also desperate to please him. She talked excitably about her home and family, her horses and dogs, and her relations and friends. He sat silently, watching her face, imagining what she would look like naked.

Bishop Waleran married them in the chapel at Earlscastle, and there was a big feast that went on for the rest of the day. By custom, everyone of importance in the county had to be invited, and William would have lost face badly if he had not provided a lavish banquet. They roasted three whole oxen and dozens of sheep and pigs in the castle compound, and the guests drank the castle cellars dry of beer, cider and wine. William's mother presided over the festivities with a look of triumph on her disfigured face. Bishop Waleran found vulgar celebrations somewhat distasteful, and he left when the bride's uncle began to tell funny stories about newlyweds.

The bride and groom retired to their chamber at nightfall, leaving the guests to continue reveling. William had been at enough weddings to know the ideas that were passing through the minds of the younger guests, so he stationed Walter outside the room and barred the door to prevent interruption.

Elizabeth took off her tunic and her shoes and stood there in her linen shirt. "I don't know what to do," she said simply. "You'll have to show me."

This was not quite how William had imagined it. He went over to her. She lifted her face, and he kissed her soft lips. Somehow the kiss failed to generate any heat. He said: "Take off your shirt and lie on the bed."

She pulled the undershirt over her head. She was quite plump. Her large breasts had tiny indented nipples. A light brown fuzz of hair covered the triangle between her legs. Obediently she walked to the bed and lay down on her back.

William kicked off his boots. He sat on the bed beside her and squeezed her breasts. Her skin was soft. This sweet, obliging, smiling girl was nothing like the image that had made his throat go dry, of a woman in the grip of passion, moaning and sweating beneath him, and he felt cheated.

He put his hand between her thighs and she parted her legs immediately. He pushed his finger inside her. She gasped, hurt; then quickly said: "It's all right, I don't mind."

He wondered briefly whether he was going about this in completely the wrong way. He had a momentary vision of a different scene in which the two of them lay side by side, touching and talking and getting to know one another gradually. However, desire had at last stirred inside him when she gasped in pain, and he brushed his doubts aside and fingered her more roughly. He watched her face as she struggled to bear the pain silently.

He got on the bed and knelt between her legs. He was not fully aroused. He rubbed himself to make his organ stiffer, but it had little effect. It was her damned smile that was making him impotent, he was sure. He pushed two fingers inside her, and she gave a little cry of pain. That was better. Then the silly bitch started smiling again. He realized he would have to wipe the smile off her face. He slapped her hard. She cried out, and her lip bled. This was more like it.

He hit her again.

She started to cry.

After that it was all right.

The following Sunday happened to be Whitsunday, when a huge crowd would attend the cathedral. Bishop Waleran would take the service. There would be even more people than usual, because everyone was keen to look at the new transepts, which had recently been finished. Rumor said they were amazing. William would show his bride to the ordinary folk of the county at that service. He had not been to Kingsbridge since they built the wall, but Philip could not stop him from going to church.

Two days before Whitsunday, his mother died.

She was about sixty years old. It was quite sudden. She felt breathless after dinner on Friday and went to bed early. Her maid woke William a little before dawn to tell him that his mother was in distress. He got up from his bed and went stumbling into her room, rubbing his face. He found her gasping horribly for breath, unable to speak, a look of terror in her eyes.

William was frightened by her great shuddering gasps and her staring eyes. She kept looking at him, as if she expected him to do something. He was so scared he decided to leave the room, and he turned away; then he saw the maid standing at the door, and he felt ashamed of his fear. He forced himself to look at Mother again. Her face seemed to change shape continually in the inconstant light of the one candle. Her hoarse, ragged breathing got louder and louder until it seemed to fill his head. He could not understand why it had not woken the whole castle. He put his hands over his ears to shut out the noise but he could still hear it. It was as if she was shouting at him, the way she had when he was a boy, a mad furious scolding tirade, and her face looked angry too, the mouth wide, the eyes staring, the hair disarrayed. The conviction that she was demanding something grew, and he felt himself becoming younger and smaller, until he was possessed by a blind terror he had not felt since childhood, a terror that came from knowing that the only person he loved was a raging monster. It had always been like this: she would tell him to come to her, or go away, or get on his pony, or get off; and he would be slow to respond, so she would yell; and then he would be so frightened that he could not understand what she was asking him to do; and there would be a hysterical deadlock, with her screaming louder and louder and him becoming blind, deaf and dumb with terror.

But this time it was different.

This time, she died.

First her eyes closed. William began to feel calmer then. Gradually her breathing became shallower. Her face went grayish despite the boils. Even the candle seemed to burn more weakly, and the moving shadows no longer frightened William. At last her breathing just stopped.

"There," William said, "she's all right, now, isn't she?"

The maid burst into tears.

He sat beside the bed looking at her still face. The maid fetched the priest, who said angrily: "Why didn't you call me earlier?" William hardly heard him. He stayed with her until sunrise; then the women servants asked him to leave so they could "lay her out." William went down to the hall where the inhabitants of the castle—

knights, men-at-arms, clergymen and servants—were eating a subdued breakfast. He sat at the table beside his young wife and drank some wine. One or two of the knights and the household steward spoke to him, but he did not reply. Eventually Walter came in and sat beside him. Walter had been with him for many years and he knew when to be silent.

After a while William said: "Are the horses ready?"

Walter looked surprised. "For what?"

"For the journey to Kingsbridge. It takes two days—we have to leave this morning."

"I didn't think we would go—under the circumstances. . . ."

For some reason this made William angry. "Did I say we wouldn't go?"

"No, lord."

"Then we're going!"

"Yes, lord." Walter stood up. "I'll see to it at once."

They set off at midmorning, William and Elizabeth and the usual entourage of knights and grooms. William felt as if he was in a dream. The landscape seemed to move past him, instead of the other way around. Elizabeth rode beside him, bruised and silent. When they stopped Walter took care of everything. At each meal William ate a little bread and drank several cups of wine. In the night he dozed fitfully.

They could see the cathedral from a distance, across the green fields, as they approached Kingsbridge. The old cathedral had been a squat, broad-shouldered building with small windows like beady eyes under round-arched eyebrows. The new church looked radically different, even though it was not finished yet. It was tall and slender, and the windows seemed impossibly big. As they came closer, William saw that it dwarfed the priory buildings around it in a way that the old cathedral never had.

The road was busy with riders and pedestrians all heading for Kingsbridge: the Whitsunday service was popular, for it took place in early summer when the weather was good and the roads were dry. This year more people than usual had come, attracted by the novelty of the new building.

William and his party cantered the last mile, scattering unwary pedestrians, and clattered onto the wooden drawbridge that crossed the river. Kingsbridge was now one of the most heavily fortified towns in England. It had a stout stone wall with a castellated parapet, and here, where previously the bridge had led straight into the main street, the way was barred by a stone-built barbican with enormously heavy ironbound doors that now stood open but were undoubtedly shut tight at night. I don't suppose I'll ever be able to burn this town again, William thought vaguely.

People stared as he rode up the main street toward the priory. People always stared at William, of course: he was the earl. Today they were also interested in the young bride who rode at his left. On his right was Walter, as always.

They rode into the priory close and dismounted at the stables. William left his horse to Walter and turned to look at the church. The eastern end, the top of the cross, was at the far side of the close and hidden from view. The western end, the tail of the cross, was not yet built, but its shape was marked out on the ground with stakes and string, and some of the foundations had already been laid. Between the two was the new part, the arms of the cross, consisting of the north and south transepts, with the space between them which was called the crossing. The windows *were* as big as they had seemed. William had never seen a building like this in his life.

"It's fantastic," Elizabeth said, breaking her submissive silence.

William wished he had left her behind.

Somewhat awestruck, he walked slowly up the nave, between the lines of stakes and string, with Elizabeth following. The first bay of the nave had been partly built, and looked as if it was supporting the huge pointed arch which formed the western entrance to the crossing. William passed under that incredible arch and found himself in the crowded crossing.

The new building looked unreal: it was too tall, too slender, too graceful and fragile to stand up. It seemed to have no walls, nothing to hold up the roof but a row of willowy piers reaching eloquently upward. Like everyone around him, William craned his neck to look up, and saw that the piers continued into the curved ceiling to meet at the crown of the vault, like the overarching branches of a stand of mature elms in the forest.

The service began. The altar had been set up at the near end of the chancel, with the monks behind it, so that the crossing and both transepts were free for the congregation, but even so the crowd overflowed into the unbuilt nave. William pushed his way to the front, as was his prerogative, and stood near the altar, with the other nobles of the county, who nodded to him and whispered among themselves.

The painted timber ceiling of the old chancel was awkwardly juxtaposed with the tall eastern arch of the crossing, and it was clear that the builder intended eventually to demolish the chancel and rebuild it to match the new work.

A moment after that thought had crossed William's mind his eye fell on the builder in question, Jack Jackson. He was a handsome devil, with his mane of red hair, and he wore a dark red tunic, embroidered at the hem and neckline, just like a nobleman. He looked rather pleased with himself, no doubt because he had built the transepts so fast and everyone was so astonished by his design. He was holding the hand of a boy of about nine years who looked just like him. William realized with a shock that that must be Aliena's child, and he felt a sharp pang of envy. A moment later he caught sight of Aliena herself. She was standing a little behind Jack and to one side, with a faint smile of pride on her face. William's heart leaped: she was as lovely as ever. Elizabeth was a poor substitute, a pallid imitation of the real, red-blooded Aliena. In her arms Aliena held a little girl about seven years old, and William recalled that she had had a second child by Jack even though they were not married.

William looked more closely at Aliena. She was not quite as lovely as ever, after all: there were lines of strain around her eyes, and behind the proud smile was a hint of sadness. After all these years she still could not marry Jack, of course, William thought with satisfaction: Bishop Waleran had kept his promise and had repeatedly blocked the annulment. That thought often gave William consolation.

It was Waleran, William now realized, who was standing at the altar, lifting the Host above his head so that the entire congregation could see it. Hundreds of people went down on their knees. The bread became Christ at that moment, a transformation that struck awe into William even though he had no idea what was involved.

He concentrated on the service for a while, watching the mystical actions of the priests, listening to the meaningless Latin phrases and muttering familiar fragments of the responses. The dazed feeling that had been with him for the last day or so persisted, and the magical new church, with sunlight playing on its impossible columns, served to intensify the sense that he was in a dream.

The service was coming to an end. Bishop Waleran turned to address the congregation. "We will now pray for the soul of Countess Regan Hamleigh, the mother of Earl William of Shiring, who died on Friday night."

There was a buzz of comment as people heard the news, but William was staring at the bishop in horror. He had realized at last what she had been trying to say while she died. She had been asking for the priest—*but William had not sent for him.* He had watched her weaken, he had seen her eyes close, he had heard her breathing stop, and he had let her die unshriven. How could he have done something like that? Ever since Friday night her soul had been in Hell, suffering the torments that she had described to him so graphically many times, with no prayers to relieve her! His heart was so laden with guilt that he seemed to feel it slow its pace and for a moment he felt that he, too, would die. How could he have let her languish in that dread place, her soul disfigured by sins as her face was with boils, while she longed for the peace of Heaven? "What am I going to do?" he said aloud, and the people around him looked at him in surprise.

When the prayer ended and the monks filed out in procession, William remained on his knees in front of the altar. The rest of the congregation drifted out into the sunshine, ignoring him; all except Walter, who stayed nearby, watching and waiting. William was praying with all his might, keeping a picture of his mother in his head while he repeated the Paternoster and all the other bits of prayers and services he could remember. After a while he realized there were other things he could do. He could light candles; he could pay priests and monks to say masses for her regularly; he could even have a special chapel built for the benefit of her soul. But everything he thought of seemed insufficient. It was as if he could see her, shaking her head, looking hurt and disappointed in him, saying: "How long will you let your mother suffer?"

He felt a hand on his shoulder and looked up. Bishop Waleran stood in front of him, still wearing the gorgeous red robe he used for Whitsun. His black eyes looked deep into William's, and William felt as if he had no secrets from that penetrating gaze. Waleran said: "Why do you weep?"

William realized his face was wet with tears. He said: "Where is she?"

"She has gone to be purified by fire."

"Is she in pain?"

"Terrible pain. But we can speed the souls of our loved ones as they pass through that dread place."

"I'll do anything!" William sobbed. "Just tell me what!"

Waleran's eyes glittered with greed. "Build a church," he said. "Just like this one. But in Shiring."

A cold fury possessed Aliena whenever she traveled around the estates that had been part of her father's earldom. All the blocked ditches and broken fences and empty, tumbledown cow sheds angered her; the meadows running to seed made her sad; and the deserted villages broke her heart. It was not just the bad harvests.

The earldom could have fed its people, even this year, if it had been properly run. But William Hamleigh had no notion of husbanding his land. For him, the earldom was a private treasure chest, not an estate that fed thousands of people. When his serfs had no food, they starved. When his tenants could not pay their rents, he threw them out. Since William became earl the acreage under cultivation had shrunk, because the lands of some dispossessed tenants had returned to their natural state. And he did not have the brains to see that this was not even in his own interest in the long term.

The worst of it was, Aliena felt partly responsible. It was her father's estate, and she and Richard had failed to win it back for the family. They had given up, when William became earl and Aliena lost all her money; but the failure still rankled, and she had not forgotten her vow to her father.

On the road from Winchester to Shiring, with a wagonload of yarn and a brawny carter with a sword at his belt, she remembered riding along the very same road with her father. He had constantly brought new land into cultivation, by clearing areas of forest, draining marshland, or plowing hillsides. In bad years he always put aside enough seed to supply the needs of those who were too improvident, or just too hungry, to save their own. He never forced tenants to sell their beasts or their plows to pay rent, for he knew that if they did that, they would be unable to farm the following year. He had treated the land well, maintaining its capacity to produce, the way a good farmer would take care of a dairy cow.

Whenever she thought of those old days, with her clever, proud, rigid father beside her, she felt the pain of loss like a wound. Life had started to go wrong when he had been taken away. Everything she had done since then seemed, in retrospect, to have been hollow: living at the castle with Matthew, in a dreamworld; going to Winchester in the vain hope of seeing the king; even struggling to support Richard while he fought in the civil war. She had achieved what other people saw as success: she had become a prosperous wool merchant. But that had brought her only a semblance of happiness. She had found a way of life and a place in society that gave her security and stability, but in her heart she had still been hurt and lost—until Jack came into her life.

Her inability to marry Jack had blighted everything since. She had come to hate Prior Philip, whom she had once looked up to as her savior and mentor. She had not had a happy, amiable conversation with Philip for years. Of course, it was not his fault that they could not get an annulment; but it was he who had insisted they live apart, and Aliena could not help resenting him for that.

She loved her children, but she worried about them, being

brought up in such an unnatural household, with a father who went away at bedtime. So far, happily, they showed no ill effects: Tommy was a strapping, good-looking boy who liked football, races and playing soldiers; and Sally was a sweet, thoughtful girl who told stories to her dolls and loved to watch Jack at his tracing floor. Their constant needs and their simple love were the one solidly normal element in Aliena's eccentric life.

She still had her work, of course. She had been a merchant of some kind for most of her adult life. At present she had dozens of men and women in scattered villages spinning and weaving for her in their homes. A few years ago there had been hundreds, but she was feeling the effects of the famine like everyone else, and there was no point in making more cloth than she could sell. Even if she were married to Jack she would still want to have her own independent work.

Prior Philip kept saying the annulment could be granted any day, but Aliena and Jack had now been living this infuriating life for seven long years, eating together and bringing up their children and sleeping apart.

She felt Jack's unhappiness more painfully than her own. She adored him. Nobody knew how much she loved him, except perhaps his mother, Ellen, who saw everything. She loved him because he had brought her back to life. She had been like a caterpillar in a cocoon, and he had drawn her out and shown her that she was a butterfly. She would have spent her entire life numb to the joys and pains of love, if he had not walked into her secret glade, and shared his story-poems with her, and kissed her so lightly, and then slowly, gently, awakened the love that lay dormant in her heart. He had been so patient, so tolerant, despite his youth. For that she would always love him.

As she passed through the forest she wondered whether she would run into Jack's mother, Ellen. They saw her occasionally, at a fair in one of the towns; and about once a year she would sneak into Kingsbridge at dusk and spend the night with her grandchildren. Aliena felt an affinity for Ellen: they were both oddities, women who did not fit into the mold. However, she emerged from the forest without seeing Ellen.

As she traveled through farmland she checked the crops ripening in the fields. It would be a fair harvest, she estimated. They had not had a good summer, for there had been some rain and it had been cold. But they had not had the floods and crop diseases which had blighted the last three harvests. Aliena was thankful. There were thousands of people living right on the edge of starvation, and another bad winter would kill most of them.

She stopped to water her oxen at the pond in the middle of a village called Monksfield, which was part of the earl's estate. It was a fairly large place, surrounded by some of the best land in the county, and it had its own priest and a stone church. However, only about half the fields round about had been sown this year. Those that had been were now covered with yellow wheat, and the rest were sprouting weeds.

Two other travelers had stopped at the pond in the middle of the village to water their horses. Aliena looked at them warily. Sometimes it was good to team up with other people, for mutual protection; but it could be risky, too, for a woman. Aliena found that a man such as her carter was perfectly willing to do what she told him when they were alone, but if other men were present he was liable to become insubordinate.

However, one of the two travelers at Monksfield pond was a woman. Aliena looked more closely and revised *woman* to *girl*. Aliena recognized her. She had last seen this girl in Kingsbridge Cathedral on Whitsunday. It was Countess Elizabeth, the wife of William Hamleigh.

She looked miserable and cowed. With her was a surly man-at-arms, obviously her bodyguard. That could have been my fate, Aliena thought, if I had married William. Thank God I rebelled.

The man-at-arms nodded curtly to the carter and ignored Aliena. She decided not to suggest teaming up.

While they were resting, the skies turned black and a sharp wind whipped up. "Summer storm," said Aliena's carter succinctly.

Aliena looked anxiously at the sky. She did not mind getting wet, but the storm would slow their progress, and they might find themselves out in the open at nightfall. A few drops of rain fell. They would have to take shelter, she decided reluctantly.

The young countess said to her guard: "We'd better stay here for a bit."

"Can't do that," the guard said brusquely. "Master's orders."

Aliena was outraged to hear the man speak to the girl that way. "Don't be such a fool!" she said. "You're supposed to look after your mistress!"

The guard looked at her in surprise. "What's it to you?" he said rudely.

"There's going to be a cloudburst, idiot," Aliena said in her most aristocratic voice. "You can't ask a lady to travel in such weather. Your master will flog you for your stupidity." Aliena turned to Countess Elizabeth. The girl was looking eagerly at Aliena, visibly pleased to see someone standing up to the bullying bodyguard. It started to rain in earnest. Aliena made a snap decision. "Come with me," she said to Elizabeth.

Before the guard could do anything she had taken the girl by the hand and walked away. Countess Elizabeth went willingly, grinning like a child let out of school. Aliena had an inkling that the guard might come after them and snatch her away, but at that moment there was a lightning flash and the shower became a storm. Aliena broke into a run, pulling Elizabeth with her, and they raced through the graveyard to a wooden house that stood beside the church.

The door stood open. They ran inside. Aliena had assumed this was the priest's house, and she was right. A grumpy-looking man in a black tunic, wearing a small cross on a chain around his neck, stood up as they entered. Aliena knew that the duty of hospitality was a burden to many parish priests, especially at present. Anticipating resistance, she said firmly: "My companions and I need shelter."

"You're welcome," the priest said through gritted teeth.

It was a two-room house with a lean-to shed at the side for animals. It was not very clean, even though the animals were kept outside. There was a wine barrel on the table. A small dog yapped at them aggressively as they sat down.

Elizabeth pressed Aliena's arm. "Thank you very much," she said. There were tears of gratitude in her eyes. "Ranulf would have made me go on—he never listens to me."

"It was nothing," Aliena said. "These big strong men are all cowards at heart." She studied Elizabeth, and realized with a sense of horror that the poor girl looked rather like her. It would be bad enough to be William's wife; but to be his second choice must be hell on earth.

Elizabeth said: "I'm Elizabeth of Shiring. Who are you?"

"My name is Aliena. I'm from Kingsbridge." Aliena held her breath, wondering whether Elizabeth would recognize the name and realize that Aliena was the woman who had rejected William Hamleigh.

But Elizabeth was too young to remember that scandal, and all she said was: "What an unusual name."

A slovenly woman with a plain face and meaty bare arms came in from the back room, looking defiant, and offered them a cup of wine. Aliena guessed she was the priest's wife. He would probably call her his housekeeper, since clerical marriage was banned, in theory. Priests' wives caused no end of trouble. To force the man to put her away was cruel, and generally brought shame on the

Church. And although most people would say in general that priests ought to be chaste, they usually took a permissive line in particular cases, because they knew the woman. So the Church still turned a blind eye to liaisons such as this. Aliena thought: Be grateful, woman—at least you're living with your man.

The man-at-arms and the carter came in with their hair wet. The guard, Ranulf, stood in front of Elizabeth and said: "We can't stop here."

To Aliena's surprise, Elizabeth crumbled immediately. "All right," she said, and stood up.

"Sit down," Aliena said, pulling her back. She stood in front of the guard and wagged her finger in his face. "If I hear another word from you I'll call the villagers to come to the rescue of the countess of Shiring. They know how to treat their mistress even if you don't."

She saw Ranulf weighing the odds. If it came to the crunch, he could deal with Elizabeth and Aliena, and the carter and the priest too; but he would be in trouble if any of the villagers joined in.

Eventually he said: "Perhaps the countess would *prefer* to move on." He looked at Elizabeth aggressively.

The girl looked terrified.

Aliena said: "Well, your ladyship—Ranulf humbly begs to know your will."

Elizabeth looked at her.

"Just tell him what you want," Aliena said encouragingly. "His duty is to do your bidding."

Aliena's attitude gave Elizabeth courage. She took a deep breath and said: "We'll rest here. Go and see to the horses, Ranulf."

He grunted acquiescence and went out.

Elizabeth watched him go with an expression of amazement.

The carter said: "It's going to piss down."

The priest frowned at his vulgarity. "I'm sure it will just be the usual rain," he said in a prissy voice. Aliena could not help laughing, and Elizabeth joined in. Aliena had the feeling the girl did not laugh often.

The sound of the rain became a loud drumming. Aliena looked through the open door. The church was only a few yards away but already the rain had obscured it. This was going to be a real squall.

Aliena said to her carter: "Did you put the cart under cover?"

The man nodded. "With the beasts."

"Good. I don't want my yarn felted."

Ranulf came back in, soaking wet.

There was a flash of lightning followed by a long rumble of

thunder. "This will do the crops no good," the priest said lugubriously.

He was right, Aliena thought. What they needed was three weeks of hot sunshine.

There was another flash and a longer crash of thunder, and a gust of wind shook the wooden house. Cold water dropped on Aliena's head, and she looked up to see a drip coming from the thatched roof. She shifted her seat to get out of its way. The rain was blowing in at the door, too, but nobody seemed to want to close it: Aliena preferred to look at the storm, and it seemed the others felt the same.

She looked at Elizabeth. The girl was white-faced. Aliena put an arm around her. She was shivering, although it was not cold. Aliena hugged her.

"I'm frightened," Elizabeth whispered.

"It's only a storm," Aliena said.

It became very dark outside. Aliena thought it must be getting near suppertime; then she realized she had not had dinner yet: it was only noon. She got up and went to the door. The sky was iron gray. She had never known such peculiar weather in summer. The wind was gusting strongly. A lightning flash illuminated numerous loose objects blowing past the doorway: a blanket, a small bush, a wooden bowl, an empty barrel.

She turned back inside, frowning, and sat down. She was getting mildly worried. The house shook again. The central pole that held up the ridge of the roof was vibrating. This was one of the better-built houses in the village, she reflected: if this was unsteady, some of the poorer places must be in danger of collapse. She looked at the priest. "If it gets any worse we may have to round up the villagers and all take shelter in the church," she said.

"I'm not going out in that," the priest said with a short laugh.

Aliena stared at him incredulously. "They're your flock," she said. "You're their shepherd."

The priest looked back at her insolently. "I answer to the bishop of Kingsbridge, not you, and I'm not going to play the fool just because you tell me to."

Aliena said: "At least bring the plow team into shelter." The most precious possession of a village such as this was the team of eight oxen that pulled the plow. Without those beasts the peasants could not cultivate their land. No individual peasant could afford to own a plow team—it was communal property. The priest would surely value the team, for his prosperity depended on it too.

The priest said: "We've no plow team."

Aliena was mystified. "Why?"

"We had to sell four of them to pay rent; then we killed the others for meat in the winter."

That explained the half-sown fields, Aliena thought. They had only been able to cultivate the lighter soils, using horses or manpower to pull the plow. The story angered her. It was foolish as well as hardhearted of William to make these people sell their plow team, for that meant they would have trouble paying their rent this year too, even though the weather had been fair. It made her want to take William by the neck and strangle him.

Another powerful gust shook the wood-framed house. Suddenly one side of the roof seemed to shift; then it lifted several inches, becoming detached from the wall, and through the gap Aliena saw black sky and forked lightning. She leaped to her feet as the gust subsided and the thatched roof crashed back down on its supports. This was now becoming dangerous. She stood up and yelled at the priest over the noise of the weather: "At least go and open the church door!"

He looked resentful but he complied. He took a key from a chest, put on a cloak, and went outside and disappeared into the rain. Aliena began to organize the others. "Carter, take my wagon and oxen into the church. Ranulf, you get the horses. Elizabeth, come with me."

They put on their cloaks and went out. It was hard to walk in a straight line because of the wind, and they held hands for stability. They fought their way across the graveyard. The rain had turned to hail, and big pebbles of ice bounced off the tombstones. In a corner of the cemetery Aliena saw an apple tree as bare as in wintertime: its leaves and fruit had been ripped off the branches by the gale. There won't be many apples in the county this autumn, she thought.

A moment later they reached the church and went inside. The sudden hush was like going deaf. The wind still howled and the rain drummed on the roof, and thunder crashed every few moments, but it was all at one remove. Some of the villagers were here already, their cloaks sodden. They had brought their valuables with them, their chickens in sacks, their pigs trussed, their cows on leads. It was dark in the church, but the scene was illuminated fitfully by lightning. After a few moments the carter drove Aliena's wagon inside, and Ranulf followed with the horses.

Aliena said to the priest: "Let's get the beasts to the west end and the people to the east, before the church starts to look like a stable." Everyone now seemed to have accepted that Aliena was in charge, and he concurred with a nod. The two of them moved off, the priest talking to the men and Aliena to the women. Gradually the people separated from the animals. The women took the children to the little chancel and the men tied the animals to the columns of the nave. The horses were frightened, rolling their eyes and prancing. The cows all lay down. The villagers got into family groups and began to pass food and drink around. They had come prepared for a long stay.

The storm was so violent that Aliena thought it must pass soon, but instead it got worse. She went to a window. The windows were not made of glass, of course, but of fine translucent linen, which now hung in shreds from the window frames. Aliena pulled herself up to the windowsill to look out, but all she could see was rain.

The wind grew stronger, shrieking around the walls of the church, and she began to wonder whether even this was safe. She made a discreet tour of the building. She had spent enough time with Jack to know the difference between good masonry and bad, and she was relieved to see that the stonework here was neat and careful. There were no cracks. The building was made of cut stone blocks, not rubble, and it seemed as solid as a mountain.

The priest's housekeeper lit a candle, and that was when Aliena realized night was falling outside. The day had been so dark that the difference was small. The children tired of running up and down the aisles, and curled up in their cloaks to go to sleep. The chickens put their heads under their wings. Elizabeth and Aliena sat side by side on the floor with their backs to the wall.

Aliena was consumed with curiosity about this poor girl who had taken on the role of William's wife, the role Aliena herself had refused seventeen years ago. Unable to restrain herself, she said: "I used to know William when I was a girl. What's he like now?"

"I loathe him," Elizabeth said with passion.

Aliena felt deeply sorry for her.

Elizabeth said: "How did you know him?"

Aliena realized she had let herself in for this. "To tell you the truth, when I was more or less your age, I was supposed to marry him."

"No! And how come you didn't?"

"I refused, and my father backed me. But there was a dreadful fuss. . . . I caused a lot of bloodshed. However, it's all in the past."

"You refused him!" Elizabeth was thrilled. "You're so courageous. I wish I was like you." Suddenly she looked downcast again. "But I can't even stand up to the servants."

"You could, you know," Aliena said.

"But how? They just don't take any notice of me, because I'm only fourteen."

Aliena considered the question carefully, then answered comprehensively. "To begin with, you must become the carrier of your husband's wishes. In the morning, ask him what he would like to eat today, whom he wants to see, which horse he would like to ride, anything you can think of. Then go to the kitchener, the steward of the hall, and the stableman, and give them the earl's orders. Your husband will be grateful to you, and angry with anyone who ignores you. So people will get used to doing what you say. Then take note of who helps you eagerly and who reluctantly. Make sure that helpful people are favored—give them the jobs they like to do, and make sure the unhelpful ones get all the dirty work. Then people will start to realize that it pays to oblige the countess. They will also love you much more than William, who isn't very lovable anyway. Eventually you will become a power in your own right. Most countesses are."

"You make it sound easy," Elizabeth said wistfully.

"No, it's not easy, but if you're patient, and don't get discouraged too easily, you can do it."

"I think I can," she said determinedly. "I really think I can."

Eventually they began to doze. Every now and again the wind would howl and wake Aliena. Looking around in the fitful candlelight she saw that most of the adults were doing the same, sitting upright, nodding off for a while, then waking up suddenly.

It must have been around midnight that she woke with a start and realized that she had slept for an hour or more this time. Almost everyone around her was fast asleep. She shifted her position, lying flat on the floor, and wrapped her cloak tightly around her. The storm was not letting up, but people's need for sleep had overcome their anxiety. The sound of the rain blowing against the walls of the church was like waves crashing on a beach, and instead of keeping her awake it now lulled her to sleep.

Once again she woke with a start. She wondered what had disturbed her. She listened: silence. The storm had ended. A faint gray light seeped in through the windows. All the villagers were fast asleep.

Aliena got up. Her movement disturbed Elizabeth, who came awake instantly.

They both had the same thought. They went to the church door, opened it, and stepped outside.

The rain had stopped and the wind was no more than a breeze. The sun had not yet risen, but the dawn sky was pearl-gray. Aliena and Elizabeth looked around them in the clear, watery light.

The village was gone.

Other than the church there was not a single building left standing. The entire area had been flattened. A few heavy timbers had come to rest up against the side of the church, but otherwise only the hearthstones dotted around in the sea of mud showed where there had been houses. At the edges of what had been the village, there were five or six mature trees, oaks and chestnuts, still standing, although each of them appeared to have lost several boughs. There were no young trees left at all.

Stunned by the completeness of the devastation, Aliena and Elizabeth walked along what had been the street. The ground was littered with splintered wood and dead birds. They came to the first of the wheat fields. It looked as if a large herd of cattle had been penned there for the night. The ripening stalks of wheat had been flattened, broken, uprooted and washed away. The earth was churned up and waterlogged.

Aliena was horrified. "Oh, God," she muttered. "What will the people eat?"

They struck out across the field. The damage was the same everywhere. They climbed a low hill and surveyed the surrounding countryside from the top. Every way they looked, they saw ruined crops, dead sheep, blasted trees, flooded meadows and flattened houses. The destruction was appalling, and it filled Aliena with a dreadful sense of tragedy. It looked, she thought, as if the hand of God had come down over England and struck the earth, destroying everything men had made except churches.

The devastation had shocked Elizabeth too. "It's terrible," she said. "I can't believe it. There's nothing left."

Aliena nodded grimly. "Nothing," she echoed. "There'll be no harvest this year."

"What will the people do?"

"I don't know." Feeling a mixture of compassion and fear, Aliena said: "It's going to be a bloody winter."

II

One morning four weeks after the great storm, Martha asked Jack for more money. Jack was surprised. He already gave her sixpence a week for housekeeping, and he knew that Aliena gave her the same. On that she had to feed four adults and two children, and supply two houses with firewood and rushes; but there were plenty of big families in Kingsbridge who only had sixpence a week for everything, food and clothing and rent too. He asked her why she needed more.

She looked embarrassed. "All the prices have gone up. The baker wants a penny for a four-pound loaf, and—"

"A penny! For a four-pounder?" Jack was outraged. "We should make an oven and bake our own."

"Well, sometimes I do pan bread."

"That's right." Jack realized they had had pan-baked bread two or three times during the last week or so.

Martha said: "But the price of flour has gone up too, so we don't save much."

"We should buy wheat and grind it ourselves."

"It's not allowed. We're supposed to use the priory mill. Anyway, wheat is expensive also."

"Of course." Jack realized he was being silly. Bread was dear because flour was dear, and flour was dear because wheat was dear, and wheat was dear because the storm had wiped out the harvest, and there was no getting away from it. He saw that Martha looked troubled. She always got very upset if she thought he was displeased. He smiled to show her it was all right, and patted her shoulder. "It's not your fault," he said.

"You sound so cross."

"Not with you." He felt guilty. Martha would rather cut off her hand than cheat him, he knew. He did not really understand why she was so devoted to him. If it was love, he thought, surely she would have got fed up by now, for she and the whole world knew that Aliena was the love of his life. He had once contemplated sending her away, to force her out of her rut: that way perhaps she would fall for a suitable man. But he knew in his heart that it would not work and would only make her desperately unhappy. So he let it be.

He reached inside his tunic for his purse, and took out three silver pennies. "You'd better have twelvepence a week, and see if you can manage on that," he said. It seemed a lot. His pay was only twenty-four pennies a week, although he got perquisites as well, candles and robes and boots.

He swallowed the rest of a mug of beer and went out. It was unusually cold for early autumn. The weather was still strange. He walked briskly along the street and entered the priory close. It was still a little before sunrise and only a handful of craftsmen were here. He walked up the nave, looking at the foundations. They were almost complete, which was fortunate, as the mortar work would probably have to stop early this year because of the cold weather.

He looked up at the new transepts. His pleasure in his own creation was blighted by the cracks. They had reappeared on the day after the great storm. He was terribly disappointed. It had been a phenomenal tempest, of course, but his church was designed to survive a hundred such storms. He shook his head in perplexity, and climbed the turret stairs to the gallery. He wished he could talk to someone who had built a similar church, but nobody in England had, and even in France they had not yet gone this high.

On impulse, he did not go to his tracing floor, but continued up the staircase to the roof. The lead had all been laid, and he saw that the pinnacle that had been blocking the flow of rainwater now had a generous gutter running through its base. It was windy up on the roof, and he tried to keep hold of something whenever he was near the edge: he would not be the first builder to be blown off a roof to his death by a gust of wind. The wind always seemed stronger up here than it did on the ground. In fact, the wind seemed to increase disproportionately as you climbed. . . .

He stood still, staring into space. The wind increased disproportionately as you climbed. That was the answer to his puzzle. It was not the *weight* of his vault that was causing the cracks—it was the *height*. He had built the church strong enough to bear the weight, he was sure; but he had not thought about the wind. These towering walls were constantly buffeted, and because they were so high, the wind was enough to crack them. Standing on the roof, feeling its force, he could just imagine the effect it was having on the tautly balanced structure below him. He knew the building so well that he could almost feel the strain, as if the walls were part of his body. The wind pushed sideways against the church, just as it was pushing against him; and because the church could not bend, it cracked.

He was quite sure he had found the explanation; but what was he going to do about it? He needed to strengthen the clerestory so that it could withstand the wind. But how? To build massive buttresses up against the walls would destroy the stunning effect of lightness and grace that he had achieved so successfully.

But if that was what it took to make the building stand up, he would have to do it.

He went down the stairs again. He felt no more cheerful, even though he had finally understood the problem; for it looked as if the solution would destroy his dream. Perhaps I was arrogant, he thought. I was so sure I could build the most beautiful cathedral in the world. Why did I imagine I could do better than anyone else? What made me think I was special? I should have copied another master's design exactly, and been content.

Philip was waiting for him at the tracing floor. There was a worried frown on the prior's brow, and the fringe of graying hair around his shaved head was untidy. He looked as if he had been up all night.

"We've got to reduce our expenditure," he said without preamble. "We just haven't got the money to carry on building at our present rate."

Jack had been afraid of this. The hurricane had destroyed the harvest throughout most of southern England: it was sure to have an effect on the priory's finances. Talk of cutbacks always made him anxious. In his heart he was afraid that if building slowed down too much he might not live to see his cathedral completed. But he did not let his fear show. "Winter's coming," he said casually. "Work always slows down then anyway. And winter will be early this year."

"Not early enough," Philip said grimly. "I want to cut our outgoings in half, immediately."

"In half!" It sounded impossible.

"The winter layoff begins today."

This was worse than Jack had anticipated. The summer workers normally left around the beginning of December. They spent the winter months building wooden houses or making plows and carts, either for their families or to earn money. This year their families would not be pleased to see them. Jack said: "Do you know you're sending them to homes where people are already starving?"

Philip just stared back at him angrily.

"Of course you know it," Jack said. "Sorry I asked."

Philip said forcefully: "If I don't do this now, then one Saturday in midwinter the entire work force will stand in line for their pay and I will show them an empty chest."

Jack shrugged helplessly. "There's no arguing with that."

"It's not all," Philip warned. "From now on there's to be no hiring, even to replace people who leave."

"We haven't been hiring for months."

"You hired Alfred."

"That was different." Jack was embarrassed. "Anyway, no hiring."

"And no upgrading."

Jack nodded. Every now and again an apprentice or a laborer asked to be upgraded to mason or stonecutter. If the other craftsmen judged that his skills were adequate, the request would be granted, and the priory would have to pay him higher wages. Jack said: "Upgrading is the prerogative of the masons' lodge."

"I'm not trying to alter that," Philip said. "I'm asking the masons to postpone all promotions until the famine is over."

"I'll put it to them," Jack said noncommittally. He had a feeling there could be trouble over that.

Philip pressed on. "From now on there'll be no work on saint's days."

There were too many saint's days. In principle, they were holidays, but whether workers were paid for the holiday was a matter for negotiation. At Kingsbridge the rule was that when two or more saint's days fell in the same week, the first was a paid holiday and the second was an unpaid optional day off. Most people chose to work the second. Now, however, they would not have that option. The second saint's day would be an obligatory unpaid holiday.

Jack was feeling uncomfortable about the prospect of explaining these changes to the lodge. He said: "All this would go down a lot better if I could present it to them as a matter for discussion, rather than as something already settled."

Philip shook his head. "Then they'd think it was open to negotiation, and some of the proposals might be softened. They'd suggest working half the saint's days, and allowing a limited number of upgrades."

He was right, of course. "But isn't that reasonable?" Jack said.

"Of course it's *reasonable*," Philip said irritably. "It's just that there's no room for adjustment. I'm already worried that these measures won't be sufficient—I can't make any concessions."

"All right," Jack said. Philip was clearly in no mood to compromise right now. "Is there anything else?" he said warily.

"Yes. Stop buying supplies. Run down your stocks of stone, iron and timber."

"We get the timber free!" Jack protested.

"But we have to pay for it to be carted here."

"True. All right." Jack went to the window and looked down at the stones and tree trunks stacked in the priory close. It was a reflex action: he already knew how much he had in stock. "That's not a problem," he said after a moment. "With the reduced work force, we've got enough materials to last us until next summer."

Philip sighed wearily. "There's no guarantee we'll be taking on summer workers next year," he said. "It depends on the price of wool. You'd better warn them."

Jack nodded. "It's as bad as that, is it?"

"It's worse than I've ever known it," Philip said. "What this country needs is three years of good weather. And a new king."

"Amen to that," said Jack.

Philip returned to his house. Jack spent the morning wondering how to handle the changes. There were two ways to build a nave: bay by bay, beginning at the crossing and working west; or course by course, laying the base of the entire nave first and then working up. The second way was faster but required more masons. It was the method Jack had intended to use. Now he reconsidered. Building bay by bay was more suited to a reduced work force. It had another advantage, too: any modifications he introduced into his design to take account of wind resistance could be tested in one or two bays before being used throughout the building.

He also brooded over the long-term effect of the financial crisis. Work might slow down more and more, over the years. Gloomily he saw himself growing old and gray and feeble without achieving his life's ambition, and eventually being buried in the priory graveyard in the shadow of a still unfinished cathedral.

When the noon bell rang he went to the masons' lodge. The men were sitting down to their ale and cheese, and he noticed for the first time that many of them had no bread. He asked the masons who normally went home to dinner if they would stay for a moment. "The priory is running short of money," he said.

"I've never known a monastery that didn't, sooner or later," said one of the older men.

Jack looked at him. He was called Edward Twonose because he had a wart on his face almost as big as his nose. He was a good stone carver, with a sharp eye for exact curves, and Jack always used him for shafts and drums. Jack said: "You'd have to admit that this place manages its money better than most. But Prior Philip can't avert storms and bad harvests, and now he needs to reduce his expenditure. I'll tell you about it before you have your dinners. First of all, we're not taking in any more supplies of stone or timber."

The craftsmen from the other lodges were drifting in to listen. One of the old carpenters, Peter, said: "The wood we've got won't last the winter."

"Yes, it will," Jack said. "We'll be building more slowly, because we'll have fewer craftsmen. The winter layoff starts today."

He knew immediately that he had handled the announcement wrongly. There were protests from all sides, several men speaking at once. I should have broken it to them gently, he thought. But he had no experience of this kind of thing. He had been master for seven years, but in that time there had been no financial crises.

The voice that emerged from the hubbub was that of Pierre Paris, one of the masons who had come from Saint-Denis. After six years in Kingsbridge his English was still imperfect, and his anger made his accent thicker, but he was not discouraged. "You cannot dismiss men on a Tuesday," he said.

"That's right," said Jack Blacksmith. "You have to give them until the end of the week, at least."

Jack's stepbrother Alfred chimed in. "I remember when my father was building a house for the earl of Shiring, and Will Hamleigh came and dismissed the whole crew. My father told him he had to give everyone a week's wages, and held his horse's head until he handed over the money."

Thank you for nothing, Alfred, thought Jack. He said doggedly: "You might as well hear the rest. From now on, there's no work on saint's days, and no promotions."

That made them angrier. "Unacceptable," someone said, and several of the others repeated it: "Unacceptable, unacceptable."

Jack found that infuriating. "What are you talking about? If the priory hasn't got the money, you're not going to get paid. What's the point of chanting 'Unacceptable, unacceptable,' like a class of schoolboys learning Latin?"

Edward Twonose spoke up again. "We're not a class of schoolboys, we're a lodge of masons," he said. "The lodge has the right of promotion, and nobody can take it away."

"And if there's no money for the extra pay?" Jack said hotly.

One of the younger masons said: "I don't believe that."

It was Dan Bristol, one of the summer workers. He was not a skillful cutter but he could lay stones very accurately and fast. Jack said to him: "How can you say you don't believe it? What do you know about the priory's finances?"

"I know what I see," Dan said. "Are the monks starving? No. Are there candles in the church? Yes. Is there wine in the stores? Yes. Does the prior go barefoot? No. There's money. He just doesn't want to give it to us."

Several people agreed loudly. In fact, he was wrong about at least one item, and that was the wine; but no one would believe Jack now—he had become the representative of the priory. That was not fair: he was not responsible for Philip's decisions. He said: "Look, I'm only telling you what the prior said to me. I don't guarantee that it's true. But if he tells us there's not enough money, and we don't believe him, what can we do?"

"We can *all* stop work," said Dan. "Immediately."

"That's right," said another voice.

This was getting out of control, Jack realized with a sense of panic. "Wait a moment," he said. Desperately he searched for something to say that would bring down the temperature. "Let's go back to work now, and this afternoon I'll try to persuade Prior Philip to moderate his plans."

"I don't think we should work," Dan said.

Jack could not believe this was happening. He had anticipated many threats to the building of his dream church, but he had not foreseen that the craftsmen would sabotage it. "Why shouldn't we work?" he said incredulously. "What's the point?"

Dan said: "As things stand, half of us aren't even sure we're going to get paid for the rest of the week."

"Which is against all custom and practice," said Pierre Paris. The phrase *custom and practice* was much used in court.

Jack said desperately: "At least work while I'm trying to talk Philip around."

Edward Twonose said: "If we work, can you guarantee that everyone will be paid for the whole week?"

Jack knew he could offer no such guarantee, with Philip in his present mood. It crossed his mind to say yes anyway, and pay the money himself, if necessary; but he realized immediately that his entire savings would not be enough to cover a week's wages here. So he said: "I'll do my level best to persuade him, and I think he'll agree."

"Not good enough for me," said Dan.

"Nor me," said Pierre.

Dan said: "No guarantee, no work."

To Jack's dismay, there was general agreement.

He saw that if he continued to oppose them he would lose what little authority he had left. "The lodge must act as one man," he said, quoting a much-used form of words. "Are we all in favor of a stoppage?"

There was a chorus of assent.

"So be it," said Jack dismally. "I'll tell the prior."

*   *   *

Bishop Waleran rode into Shiring followed by a small army of attendants. Earl William was waiting for him in the porch of the church
on the market square. William frowned in puzzlement: he had been
expecting a site meeting, not a state visit. What was the devious
bishop up to now?

With Waleran was a stranger on a chestnut gelding. The man
was tall and rangy, with heavy black eyebrows and a large curved
nose. He wore a scornful expression that seemed permanent. He
rode beside Waleran, as if they were equals, but he was not wearing
the clothes of a bishop.

When they dismounted, Waleran introduced the stranger. "Earl
William, this is Peter of Wareham, who is an archdeacon in the
service of the archbishop of Canterbury."

No explanation of what Peter is doing here, William thought.
Waleran is definitely up to something.

The archdeacon bowed and said: "Your bishop has told me of
your generosity to Holy Mother Church, Lord William."

Before William could reply, Waleran pointed to the parish
church. "This building will be pulled down to make room for the
new church, Archdeacon," he said.

"Have you appointed a master mason yet?" Peter asked.

William wondered why an archdeacon from Canterbury was so
interested in the parish church of Shiring. But perhaps he was just
being polite.

"No, I haven't found a master yet," Waleran said. "There are
plenty of builders looking for work, but I can't get anyone from
Paris. It seems the whole world wants to build churches like Saint-
Denis, and the masons who know the style are in heavy demand."

"It could be important," said Peter.

"There's a builder who may be able to help waiting to see us
later."

Once again William was a little puzzled. Why did Peter think it
was important to build in the style of Saint-Denis?

Waleran said: "The new church will be much bigger, of course.
It will protrude a good deal farther into the square here."

William did not like the proprietorial air Waleran was assuming.
Now he interjected: "I can't have the church encroaching on the
market square."

Waleran looked irritated, as if William had spoken out of turn.
"Whyever not?" he said.

"Every inch of the square makes money on market days."

Waleran looked as if he was disposed to argue, but Peter said
with a smile: "We mustn't block the silver fountain!"

"That's right," William said. He was paying for this church. Happily, the fourth bad harvest had made little difference to his income. Smaller peasants paid rent in kind, and many of them had given William his sack of grain and brace of geese even though they were living on acorn soup. Furthermore, that sack of grain was worth ten times what it had fetched five years ago, and the increase in the price more than compensated for the tenants who had defaulted and the serfs who had starved to death. He still had the resources to finance the new building.

They walked around to the back of the church. Here was an area of housing that generated minimal income. William said: "We can build out at this end, and knock down all these houses."

"But most of them are clerical residences," Waleran objected.

"We'll find other houses for the clergymen."

Waleran looked dissatisfied, but said no more on that subject.

On the north side of the church a broad-shouldered man of about thirty years bowed to them. By his dress William judged him to be a craftsman. Archdeacon Baldwin, the bishop's close colleague, said: "This is the man I told you about, my lord bishop. His name is Alfred of Kingsbridge."

At first glance the man was not very prepossessing: he was rather ox-like, big and strong and dumb. But on closer examination there was a cunning look about his face, rather like a fox or a sly dog.

Archdeacon Baldwin said: "Alfred is the son of Tom Builder, the first master at Kingsbridge; and was himself master for a while, until he was usurped by his stepbrother."

The son of Tom Builder. This was the man who had married Aliena, William realized. But he had never consummated the marriage. William looked at him with keen interest. He would never have guessed this man to be impotent. He appeared healthy and normal. But Aliena could have a strange effect on a man.

Archdeacon Peter was saying: "Have you worked in Paris, and learned the style of Saint-Denis?"

"No—"

"But we must have a church built in the new style."

"At present I'm working at Kingsbridge, where my brother is master. He brought the new style back from Paris and I've learned it from him."

William wondered how Bishop Waleran had managed to suborn Alfred without arousing suspicion; then he remembered that the Kingsbridge sub-prior, Remigius, was a tool of Waleran. Remigius must have made the initial approach.

He remembered something else about Kingsbridge. He said to Alfred: "But your roof fell down."

"That wasn't my fault," Alfred said. "Prior Philip insisted on a change of design."

"I know Philip," said Peter, and there was venom in his voice. "A stubborn, arrogant man."

"How do you know him?" William asked.

"Many years ago I was a monk at the cell of St-John-in-the-Forest when Philip was in charge there," Peter said bitterly. "I criticized his slack regime, and he made me almoner to get me out of the way." Peter's resentment still burned hot, it was clear. No doubt that was a factor in whatever Waleran was scheming.

William said: "Be that as it may, I don't think I want to hire a builder whose roofs fall down, no matter what excuses there might be."

Alfred said: "I'm the only master builder in England who has worked on a new-style church, apart from Jack Jackson."

William said: "I don't care about Saint-Denis. I believe my poor mother's soul will be served just as well by a traditional design."

Bishop Waleran and Archdeacon Peter exchanged a look. After a moment, Waleran spoke to William in a lowered voice. "One day this church could be Shiring Cathedral," he said.

Everything became clear to William. Many years ago Waleran had schemed to have the seat of the diocese moved from Kingsbridge to Shiring, but Prior Philip had outmaneuvered him. Now Waleran had revived the plan. This time, it seemed, he would go about it more deviously. Last time he had simply asked the archbishop of Canterbury to grant his request. This time he was going to start building a new church, one large and prestigious enough to be a cathedral, and at the same time develop allies such as Peter within the archbishop's circle, before making his application. That was all very well, but William just wanted to build a church in memory of his mother, to ease her soul's passage through the eternal fires; and he resented Waleran's attempt to take over the scheme for his own purposes. On the other hand, it would be a tremendous boost to Shiring to have the cathedral here, and William would profit from that.

Alfred was saying: "There's something else."

Waleran said: "Yes?"

William looked at the two men. Alfred was bigger, stronger and younger than Waleran, and he could have knocked Waleran to the ground with one of his big hands tied behind his back; yet he was acting like the weak man in a confrontation. Years ago it would have made William angry to see a prissy white-skinned priest dominate a strong man, but he no longer got upset about such things: that was the way of the world.

Alfred lowered his voice and said: "I can bring the entire Kingsbridge work force with me."

Suddenly his three listeners were riveted.

"Say that again," said Waleran.

"If you hire me as master builder, I'll bring all the craftsmen from Kingsbridge with me."

Waleran said warily: "How do we know you're telling the truth?"

"I don't ask you to trust me," Alfred said. "Give me the job conditionally. If I don't do what I promise, I'll leave without pay."

For different reasons all three of his listeners hated Prior Philip, and they were immediately gripped by the prospect of striking such a blow at him.

Alfred added: "Several of the masons worked on Saint-Denis."

Waleran said: "But how can you bring them with you?"

"Does it matter? Let's just say they prefer me to Jack."

William thought Alfred was lying about this, and Waleran appeared to think the same, for he tilted back his head and gave Alfred a long look down his pointed nose. However, Alfred had seemed to be telling the truth earlier. Whatever the true reason might be, he seemed convinced that he could bring the Kingsbridge craftsmen with him.

William said: "If they all follow you here, work will come to a complete standstill at Kingsbridge."

"Yes," Alfred said. "It will."

William looked at Waleran and Peter. "We need to talk further about this. He'd better dine with us."

Waleran nodded agreement and said to Alfred: "Follow us to my house. It's at the other end of the market square."

"I know," said Alfred. "I built it."

For two days Prior Philip refused to discuss the strike. He was speechless with rage, and whenever he saw Jack he just turned around and walked the other way.

On the second day three cartloads of flour arrived from one of the priory's outlying mills. The carts were escorted by men-at-arms: flour was as precious as gold nowadays. It was checked in by Brother Jonathan, who was deputy cellarer under old Cuthbert Whitehead. Jack watched Jonathan count the sacks. To Jack there was something oddly familiar about Jonathan's face, as if he resembled someone Jack knew well. Jonathan was tall and gangling, with light brown hair—nothing like Philip, who was short and slight and black-haired; but in every way other than physically Jonathan took after the man who was his surrogate father: the boy was intense, high-principled, determined and ambitious. People liked him despite his rather rigid attitude to morality—which was very much how they felt about Philip.

While Philip was refusing to talk, a word with Jonathan would be the next best thing.

Jack watched while Jonathan paid the men-at-arms and the carters. He was quietly efficient, and when the carters asked for more than they were entitled to, as they always did, he refused them calmly but firmly. It occurred to Jack that a monastic education was a good preparation for leadership.

Leadership. Jack's shortcomings in that area had been revealed rather starkly. He had let a problem become a crisis by maladroit handling of his men. Every time he thought of that meeting he cursed his ineptitude. He was determined to find a way to put matters right.

As the carters left, grumbling, Jack walked casually by and said to Jonathan: "Philip is terribly angry about the strike."

For a moment Jonathan looked as if he was about to say something unpleasant—he was clearly fairly angry himself—but finally his face relaxed and he said: "He seems angry, but underneath he's wounded."

Jack nodded. "He takes it personally."

"Yes. He feels the craftsmen have turned on him in his hour of need."

"I suppose they have, in a way," Jack said. "But Philip made a major error of judgment in trying to alter working practices by fiat."

"What else could he do?" Jonathan retorted.

"He could have discussed the crisis with them first. They might even have been able to suggest some economies themselves. But I'm in no position to blame Philip, because I made the same mistake myself."

That pricked Jonathan's curiosity. "How?"

"I reported the schedule of cuts to the men as bluntly and tactlessly as Philip announced it to me."

Jonathan wanted to be outraged, like Philip, and blame the strike on the perfidy of the men; but he was reluctantly seeing the other side of the coin. Jack decided to say no more. He had planted a seed.

He left Jonathan and returned to his tracing floor. The trouble, he reflected as he picked up his drawing implements, was that the town's peacemaker was Philip. Normally, he was the judge of wrongdoers and the arbiter in disputes. It was disconcerting to find Philip a party in a quarrel, angry and bitter and unrelenting. Someone else was going to have to make peace this time. And the only person Jack could think of to do it was himself. As master builder he was the go-between who could talk to both parties, and his motivation was indisputable—he wanted to continue building.

He spent the rest of the day thinking about how to handle this task, and the question he asked himself again and again was: What would Philip do?

On the following day he felt ready to confront Philip.

It was a cold, wet day. Jack lurked around the deserted building site in the early afternoon, with the hood of his cloak pulled over his head to keep him dry, pretending to study the cracks in the clerestory (a problem that was still unsolved), and waited until he saw Philip hurry across to his own house from the cloisters. When Philip was inside, Jack followed.

Philip's door was always open. Jack tapped on it and went in. Philip was on his knees in front of the small altar in the corner. You'd think he'd get enough praying done, in church most of the day and half the night, without doing it at home too, Jack thought. There was no fire: Philip was economizing. Jack waited silently until Philip rose and turned around. Then Jack said: "This has got to come to an end."

Philip's normally amiable face was set in hard lines. "I see no difficulty about that," he said coldly. "They can come back to work as soon as they like."

"On your terms."

Philip just looked at him.

Jack said: "They won't come back on your terms, and they won't wait forever for you to see reason." He added hastily: "Or what they think is reason."

"Won't wait forever?" Philip said. "Where will they go when they get tired of waiting? They won't find work elsewhere. Do they think this is the only place that is suffering from the famine? It's all over England. Every building site is having to cut back."

"So you're going to wait for them to come crawling back to you, begging forgiveness," Jack said.

Philip looked away. "I won't make anyone crawl," he said. "I don't believe I've ever given you reason to expect such behavior from me."

"No, and that's why I've come to see you," Jack said. "I know you don't really want to humiliate these men—it's not in your nature. And besides, if they returned feeling beaten and resentful, they'd work badly for years to come. So from my point of view as well as yours, we must let them save face. And that means making concessions."

Jack held his breath. That had been his big speech, and this was his make-or-break moment. If Philip remained unmoved now, the future looked bleak.

Philip looked hard at Jack for a long moment. Jack could see reason struggling with emotion in the prior's face. Then at last his expression softened and he said: "We'd better sit down."

Jack suppressed a sigh of relief as he took a seat. He had planned what he was going to say next: he was not going to repeat the spontaneous tactlessness he had shown with the builders. "There's no need to modify your freeze on purchase of supplies," he began. "Similarly, the moratorium on new hiring can stand—no one objects to that. I also think they can be persuaded to accept that there will be no work on saint's days, if they gain concessions in other areas." He paused to let that sink in. So far he was giving everything and asking for nothing.

Philip nodded. "All right. What concessions?"

Jack took a deep breath. "They were highly offended by the proposal to ban promotions. They think you're trying to usurp the ancient prerogative of the lodge."

"I explained to you that that was not my intention," Philip said in an exasperated tone.

"I know, I know," Jack said hastily. "Of course you did. And I believed you, but they didn't." An injured look came over Philip's face. How could anyone disbelieve him? Hastily, Jack said: "But that's in the past. I'm going to propose a compromise that won't cost you anything."

Philip looked interested.

Jack went on: "Let them continue to approve applications for promotion, but postpone the associated pay raise for a year." And he thought: Find something to object to in that, if you can.

"Will they accept that?" Philip said skeptically.

"It's worth a try."

"What if I still can't afford the pay raises a year from now?"

"Cross that bridge when you get to it."

"You mean, renegotiate in a year's time."

Jack shrugged. "If necessary."

"I see," Philip said noncommittally. "Anything else?"

"The biggest stumbling block is the instant dismissal of the summer workers." Jack was being completely candid now. This issue could not be honeyed. "Instant dismissal has never been allowed on any building site in Christendom. The end of the week is the earliest." To help Philip feel less foolish, Jack added: "I ought to have warned you of that."

"So all I have to do is employ them for two more days?"

"I don't think that will be enough, now," Jack said. "If we'd handled it differently from the start we might have got away with that, but now they'll want more of a compromise."

"No doubt you've got something specific in mind."

Jack had, and it was the only real concession he had to ask for. "It's now the beginning of October. We normally dismiss the summer workers at the beginning of December. Let's meet the men halfway, and do it at the beginning of November."

"That only gives me half of what I need."

"It gives you more than half. You still benefit from the rundown of stocks, the postponement of pay raises for promotion, and the saint's days."

"Those things are trimmings."

Jack sat back, feeling gloomy. He had done his best. He had no more arguments to put to Philip, no more resources of persuasion to deploy, nothing left to say. He had shot his arrow. And Philip was still resistant. Jack was ready to concede defeat. He looked at Philip's stony face and waited.

Philip looked over at the altar in the corner for a long, silent moment. Finally he looked back to Jack and said: "I'll have to put this to the chapter."

Jack went limp with relief. It was not a victory, but it was close. Philip would not ask the monks to consider anything he did not himself approve, and more often than not they did what Philip wanted. "I hope they accept," Jack said weakly.

Philip stood up and put a hand on Jack's shoulder. He smiled for the first time. "If I put the case as persuasively as you, they will," he said.

Jack was surprised by this sudden change of mood. He said: "The sooner this is over, the less long-term effect it will have."

"I know. It's made me very angry, but I don't want to quarrel with you." Unexpectedly, he put out his hand.

Jack shook it, and felt good.

Jack said: "Shall I tell the builders to come to the lodge in the morning to hear the chapter's verdict?"

"Yes, please."

"I'll do that now." He turned to go.

Philip said: "Jack."

"Yes?"

"Thank you."

Jack nodded acknowledgment and went out. He walked through the rain without raising his hood. He felt happy.

That afternoon he went to the homes of all the craftsmen and told them there would be a meeting in the morning. Those who were not at home—the unmarried men and the summer workers, mostly—he found in the alehouse. However, they were sober, for the price of ale had gone up along with everything else, and no one could afford to get drunk. The only craftsman he could not find was Alfred, who had not been seen for a couple of days. Eventually he turned up at dusk. He came to the alehouse with an oddly triumphant look on his bovine face. He did not say where he had been, and Jack did not ask him. Jack left him drinking with the other men, and went to have supper with Aliena and the children.

Next morning he started the meeting before Prior Philip came to the lodge. He wanted to lay the groundwork. Once again he had prepared what he had to say very carefully, to be sure he did not damage his case by tactlessness. Once again he tried to handle things as Philip might have.

All the craftsmen were there early. Their livelihoods were at stake. One or two of the younger ones looked red-eyed: Jack guessed the alehouse had stayed open late last night, and some of them had forgotten their poverty for a while. The youngsters and the summer workers were most likely to prove difficult. The older craftsmen took a more long-term view. The small minority of women craftsmen were always cautious and conservative, and would back any kind of settlement.

"Prior Philip is going to ask us to go back to work, and offer us some kind of compromise," Jack began. "Before he comes, we ought to discuss what we might be prepared to accept, what we will definitely reject, and where we might be willing to negotiate. We must show Philip a united front. I hope you all agree."

There were a few nods.

He made himself sound slightly angry, and said: "In my view we should absolutely refuse to accept instant dismissal." He banged his fist on the workbench to emphasize his inflexibility on this point. Several people voiced their agreement loudly. Jack knew this was one demand Philip was certainly not going to make. He wanted the hotheads to get themselves worked up to defend ancient custom and practice on this point, so that when Philip conceded it, the wind would be taken out of their sails.

"Also, we must guard the lodge's right to make promotions, for only craftsmen can judge whether a man is skilled or not." Once again he was being disingenuous. He was focusing their attention on the nonfinancial aspect of promotions, in the hope that when they won that point they would be ready to compromise on payments.

"As for working on saint's days, I'm in two minds. Holidays are normally a matter for negotiation—there's no standard custom and practice, as far as I know." He turned to Edward Twonose and said: "What's your view on that, Edward?"

"Practice varies from site to site," Edward said. He was pleased to be consulted. Jack nodded, encouraging him to go on. Edward began to recall variant methods of dealing with saint's days. The meeting was going just the way Jack wanted. An extended discussion of a point that was not very controversial would bore the men and sap their energy for confrontation.

However, Edward's monologue was interrupted by a voice from the back which said: "This is all irrelevant."

Jack looked over and saw that the speaker was Dan Bristol, a summer worker. Jack said: "One at a time, please. Let Edward have his say."

Dan was not so easily deflected. "Never mind about all that," he said. "What we want is a raise."

"A raise?" Jack was irritated by this ludicrous remark.

To his surprise, however, Dan was supported. Pierre said: "That's right, a raise. Look—a four-pound loaf costs a penny. A hen, which used to be eightpence, is now twenty-four! None of us here has had strong beer for weeks, I bet. Everything is going up, but most of us are still getting the wage we were hired at, which is a twelvepence a week. We've got families to feed on that."

Jack's heart was sinking. He had had everything moving along nicely, but this interruption had ruined his strategy. He restrained himself from opposing Dan and Pierre, however, for he knew he would have more influence if he appeared open-minded. "I agree with you both," he said, to their evident surprise. "The question is, what chance have we got of persuading Philip to give us a raise at a time when the priory is running out of money?"

Nobody responded to that. Instead, Dan said: "We need twenty-four pence a week to stay alive, and even then we'll be worse off than we used to be."

Jack felt dismayed and bewildered: why was the meeting slipping out of his hands? Pierre said: "Twenty-four pence a week," and several others nodded their heads.

It occurred to Jack that he might not be the only person who had come to the meeting with a prepared strategy. Giving Dan a hard look, he said: "Have you discussed this previously?"

"Yes, last night, in the alehouse," Dan said defiantly. "Is there anything wrong with that?"

"Certainly not. But for the benefit of those of us who were not privileged to attend that meeting, would you like to summarize its conclusions?"

"All right." The men who had not been at the alehouse were looking resentful, but Dan was unrepentant. Just as he opened his mouth, Prior Philip walked in. Jack threw a quick, searching look at Philip. The prior looked happy. He caught Jack's eye and gave an almost imperceptible nod. Jack felt jubilant: the monks had accepted the compromise. He opened his mouth to prevent Dan from speaking, but he was an instant too late. "We want twenty-four pence a week for craftsmen," Dan said loudly. "Twelvepence for laborers and forty-eight pence for master craftsmen."

Jack looked again at Philip. The pleased look had gone, and his face had once again set in the hard, angry lines of confrontation. "Just a moment," Jack said. "This is not the view of the lodge. It's a foolish demand cooked up by a drunken faction in the alehouse."

"No, it's not," said a new voice. It was Alfred. "I think you'll find most of the craftsmen support the demand for double pay."

Jack stared at him in fury. "A few months ago you begged me to give you a job," he said. "Now you're demanding double pay. I should have let you starve!"

Prior Philip said: "And that's what will happen to all of you if you don't see sense!"

Jack had wanted desperately to avoid such challenging remarks, but now he saw no alternative: his own strategy had collapsed.

Dan said: "We won't go back to work for less than twenty-four pence, and that's that."

Prior Philip said angrily: "It's out of the question. It's a foolish dream. I'm not even going to discuss it."

"We aren't going to discuss anything else," said Dan. "We won't work for less, under any circumstances."

Jack said: "This is stupid! How can you sit there and say you won't work for less? You won't work at all, you fool. You've got nowhere else to go!"

"Haven't we?" said Dan.

The lodge went quiet.

Oh, God, Jack thought in despair; this is it—they've got an alternative.

"We have got somewhere else to go," Dan said. He stood up. "And as for me, I'm going there now."

"What are you talking about?" Jack said.

Dan looked triumphant. "I've been offered work on a new site, in Shiring. Building the new church. At twenty-four pence a week for craftsmen."

Jack looked around. "Has anyone else been offered the same?"

The whole lodge looked shamefaced.

Dan said: "We all have."

Jack was devastated. This whole thing had been organized. He had been betrayed. He felt foolish as well as wronged. He had completely misread the situation. Hurt turned to anger, and he cast about for someone to blame. "Which of you?" he yelled. "Which of you is the traitor?" He looked around at all of them. Few were able to meet his eye. Their shame gave him no consolation. He felt like a spurned lover. "Who brought you this offer from Shiring?" he shouted. "Who is to be the master builder at Shiring?" His eye raked the assembled company and came to rest on Alfred. Of course. He felt sick with disgust. "Alfred?" he said scornfully. "You're leaving me to work for *Alfred?*"

There was silence. Finally Dan said: "Yes, we are."

Jack saw that he had been defeated. "So be it," he said bitterly. "You know me, and you know my brother; and you've chosen Alfred. You know Prior Philip, and you know Earl William; and you've chosen William. All I have left to say to you is that you deserve everything you're going to get."

Chapter 15

"**T**ELL ME A STORY," Aliena said. "You never tell me stories anymore. Remember how you used to?"

"I remember," Jack said.

They were in their secret glade in the forest. It was late autumn, so instead of sitting in the shade by the stream they had built a fire in the shelter of a rocky outcrop. It was a gray, cold, dark afternoon, but lovemaking had warmed them and the fire crackled cheerfully. They were both naked under their cloaks.

Jack opened Aliena's cloak and touched her breast. She thought her breasts were too big, and she was sad that they were not as high and firm as they had been before she had the children, but he seemed to love them just as much, which was a great relief. He said: "A story about a princess who lived at the top of a high castle." He touched her nipple gently. "And a prince, who lived at the top of another high castle." He touched her other breast. "Every day they gazed at one another from the windows of their prisons, and yearned to cross the valley between." His hand rested in the cleft between her breasts, then suddenly moved down. "But every Sunday afternoon they met in the forest!" She squealed, startled, then laughed at herself.

These Sunday afternoons were the golden moments in a life that was rapidly falling apart.

The bad harvest and the slump in the wool price had brought economic devastation. Merchants were ruined, townspeople were unemployed and peasants were starving. Jack was still earning a wage, fortunately: with a handful of craftsmen he was slowly erecting the first bay of the nave. But Aliena had almost completely closed down her cloth manufacturing enterprise. And things were worse here than in the rest of southern England because of the way William was responding to the famine.

For Aliena this was the most painful aspect of the situation. William was greedy for cash to build his new church in Shiring, the church dedicated to the memory of his vicious, half-mad mother. He had evicted so many of his tenants for rent arrears that some of the best land in the county was now uncultivated, which made the shortage of grain worse. However, he had been stockpiling grain to drive the price up even farther. He had few employees and nobody to feed, so he actually profited from the famine in the short term. But in the long run he was doing irreparable damage to the estate and its ability to feed its people. Aliena remembered the earldom under her father's rule, a rich county of fertile fields and prosperous towns, and it broke her heart.

For a few years she had almost forgotten about the vows she and her brother had made to their dying father. Since William Hamleigh had been made earl, and she had started a family, the idea of Richard winning back the earldom had come to seem a remote fantasy. Richard himself had settled down as Head of the Watch. He had even married a local girl, the daughter of a carpenter; although sadly the poor girl had turned out to have bad health, and had died last year without giving him any children.

Since the famine had started, Aliena had begun to think again about the earldom. She knew that if Richard was earl, with her help he could do a lot to alleviate the suffering caused by the famine. But it was all a dream: William was well favored by King Stephen, who had gained the upper hand in the civil war, and there was no prospect of a change.

However, all these sorry wishes faded away in the secret glade, when Aliena and Jack lay down on the turf to make love. Right from the start they had been greedy for one another's bodies—Aliena would never forget how shocked she had been at her own lust, in the beginning—and even now, when she was thirty-three years old, and childbirth had broadened her rear and made her formerly flat belly sag, still Jack was so consumed with desire for her that they would make love three or four times over every Sunday.

Now his joke about the forest began to turn into a delicious caress, and Aliena pulled his face to hers to kiss him; then she heard a voice.

They both froze. Their glade was some distance from the road, and concealed in a thicket: they were never interrupted except by the occasional unwary deer or bold fox. They held their breaths and listened. The voice came again, and was followed by a different one. As they strained their hearing they picked up an undertone of rustling, as if a large group of men was moving through the forest.

Jack found his boots, which were lying on the ground. Moving silently, he stepped smartly to the stream a few paces away, filled a boot with water, and emptied it on the fire. The flames went out with a hiss and a wisp of smoke. Jack moved noiselessly into the undergrowth, crouching low, and disappeared.

Aliena put on her undershirt, tunic and boots, then wrapped her cloak around her again.

Jack returned as silently as he had left. "Outlaws," he said.

"How many?" she whispered.

"A lot. I couldn't see them all."

"Where are they going?"

"Kingsbridge." He held up a hand. "Listen."

Aliena cocked her head. In the far distance she could hear the bell of Kingsbridge Priory tolling fast and incessantly, warning of danger. Her heart missed a beat. "Oh, Jack—the children!"

"We can get back ahead of the outlaws if we cross Muddy Bottom and wade the river by the chestnut wood."

"Let's go quickly, then!"

Jack put a restraining hand on her arm and listened for a moment. He could always hear things she could not, in the forest. It came of having been brought up in the wild. She waited. At last he said: "I think they've all gone by."

They left the glade. After a few moments they came to the road. There was no one in sight. They crossed the road and cut through the woods, following a barely perceptible track. Aliena had left Tommy and Sally with Martha, playing nine-men's morris in front of a cheerful fire. She was not quite sure what the danger was but she was terrified that something might happen before she reached her children. They ran when they could, but to Aliena's frustration the ground was too rough for most of the way, and the best she could do was jog-trot, while Jack walked with a long-legged stride. This route was harder going than the road, which was why they did not normally use it, but it was much quicker.

They slithered down the steep slope that led to Muddy Bottom. Unwary strangers were occasionally killed in this bog, but there was no danger to those who knew their way across. Nevertheless the waterlogged mud seemed to grasp Aliena's feet, slowing her down, keeping her from Tommy and Sally. At the far side of Muddy

Bottom was a ford across the river. The cold water came up to Aliena's knees and washed the mud from her feet.

From there the route was straightforward. The alarm bell sounded louder as they approached the town. Whatever danger the town faced from the outlaws, at least they had somehow been forewarned, Aliena thought, trying to keep her spirits up. As she and Jack emerged from the forest into the meadow across the river from Kingsbridge, twenty or thirty youngsters who had been playing football in a nearby village arrived at the same time, shouting raucously and perspiring despite the cold.

They hurried across the bridge. The gate was already closed, but the people on the battlements had seen and recognized them, and as they approached, a small sally port was opened. Jack pulled rank and made the boys let him and Aliena in first. They ducked their heads and went through the small doorway. Aliena was deeply relieved to have got back to the town before the outlaws.

Panting with their exertions, they hurried up the main street. The townspeople were taking to the walls with spears, bows, and piles of stones to throw. The children were being rounded up and taken to the priory. Martha would have gone there already with Tommy and Sally, Aliena decided. She and Jack went straight to the priory close.

In the kitchen courtyard Aliena saw—to her astonishment—Jack's mother, Ellen, as lean and brown as ever, but with gray in her long hair and wrinkles around her forty-four-year-old eyes. She was talking animatedly to Richard. Prior Philip was some distance away, directing children into the chapter house. He did not seem to have seen Ellen.

Standing nearby was Martha with Tommy and Sally. Aliena gasped with relief and hugged the two children.

Jack said: "Mother! Why are you here?"

"I came to warn you that a gang of outlaws is on the way. They're going to raid the town."

"We saw them in the forest," Jack said.

Richard's ears pricked up. "You saw them? How many men?"

"I can't be sure, but it sounded like a lot, at least a hundred, maybe more."

"What sort of weapons?"

"Clubs. Knives. A hatchet or two. Mostly clubs."

"What direction?"

"North of here."

"Thanks! I'm going to take a look from the walls."

Aliena said: "Martha, take the children into the chapter house." She followed Richard, as did Jack and Ellen.

As they hurried through the streets, people kept saying to Richard: "What is it?"

"Outlaws," he would say succinctly, without breaking his stride.

Richard was at his best like this, Aliena thought. Ask him to go out and earn his daily bread and he was helpless; but in a military emergency he was cool, level-headed and competent.

They reached the north wall of the city and climbed the ladder to the parapet. There were heaps of stones, for throwing down on attackers, placed at regular intervals. Townsmen with bows and arrows were already taking up positions on the battlements. Some time ago, Richard had persuaded the town guild to hold emergency drills once a year. There had been a lot of resistance to the idea at first, but it had become a ritual, like the midsummer play, and everyone enjoyed it. Now its real benefits were showing as the townspeople reacted quickly and confidently to the sound of the alarm.

Aliena looked fearfully across the fields to the forest. She could see nothing.

Richard said: "You must have got here well ahead of them."

Aliena said: "Why are they coming *here*?"

Ellen said: "The priory storehouses. This is the only place for miles around where there's any food."

"Of course." The outlaws were hungry people, dispossessed of their land by William, with no way to live but theft. In the undefended villages there was little or nothing to steal: the peasants were not much better off than the outlaws. Only in the barns of landowners was there food in quantity.

As she was thinking this, she saw them.

They emerged from the edge of the forest like rats from a burning hayrick. They swarmed across the field toward the town, twenty, thirty, fifty, a hundred of them, a small army. They had probably hoped to catch the town unawares and get in through the gates, but when they heard the bell ringing the alarm they realized they had been forestalled. Nevertheless they came on, with the desperation of the starving. One or two bowmen loosed off premature arrows, and Richard yelled: "Wait! Don't waste your shafts!"

Last time Kingsbridge was attacked, Tommy had been eighteen months old and Aliena was pregnant with Sally. She had taken refuge in the priory then, with the elderly and the children. This time she would stay on the battlements and help to fight off the danger. Most of the other women felt the same way: there were almost as many women as men on the walls.

All the same, Aliena felt torn as the outlaws came closer. She was near the priory, but it was possible that the attackers could break through at some other point and reach the priory before she could get there. Or she might be injured in the fighting and unable to help the children. Jack was here, and so was Ellen: if they should be killed, only Martha would be left to take care of Tommy and Sally. Aliena hesitated, undecided.

The outlaws were almost at the walls. A shower of arrows fell on them, and this time Richard did not tell the archers to wait. The outlaws were decimated. They had no armor to protect them. There was also no organization. No one had planned the attack. They were like stampeding animals, rushing headlong at a blank wall. When they got there they did not know what to do. The townspeople bombarded them with stones from the battlements. Several outlaws attacked the north gate with clubs. Aliena knew the thickness of that ironbound oak door: it would take all night to break through. Meanwhile, Alf Butcher and Arthur Saddler were maneuvering a cauldron of boiling water from someone's kitchen up onto the wall over the gate.

Directly below Aliena, a group of outlaws started to form a human pyramid. Jack and Richard immediately started to throw stones at them. Thinking of her children, Aliena did the same, and Ellen joined in too. The desperate outlaws withstood the hail of rocks for a while, then someone was hit on the head, the pyramid collapsed, and they gave up.

There were screams of pain from the north gate a moment later, as the boiling water poured on the heads of the men attacking the door.

Then some of the outlaws realized that their dead and wounded comrades were easy prey, and they started to strip the bodies. Fights broke out with those who were not so badly wounded, and rival looters quarreled over the possessions of the dead. It was a shambles, Aliena thought; a disgusting, degrading shambles. The townspeople stopped throwing stones as the attack petered out and the attackers fought among themselves like dogs over a bone.

Aliena turned to Richard. "They're too disorganized to be a real threat," she said.

He nodded. "With a little help they could be quite dangerous, because they're desperate. But as it is they've no leadership."

Aliena was struck by a thought. "An army waiting for a leader," she said. Richard did not react, but she was excited by the idea. Richard was a good leader who had no army. The outlaws were an army without a leader. And the earldom was falling apart. . . .

Some of the townspeople continued to throw stones and shoot arrows at the outlaws, and more of the scavengers fell. This was the final discouragement, and they began to retreat, like a pack of dogs with their tails between their legs, looking back over their shoulders regretfully. Then someone opened the north gate, and a crowd of young men charged out, brandishing swords and axes, and went after the stragglers. The outlaws fled, but some were caught and butchered.

Ellen turned away in disgust and said to Richard: "You should have stopped those boys from giving chase."

"Young men need to see some blood, after a set-to such as this," he said. "Besides, the more we kill this time, the fewer we'll have to fight next time."

It was a soldier's philosophy, Aliena thought. In the time when she had felt her life threatened every day she would probably have been like the young men, and chased after outlaws to slaughter them. Now she wanted to wipe out the causes of outlawry, not the outlaws themselves. Besides, she had thought of a way to use those outlaws.

Richard told someone to sound the all-clear on the priory bell and gave instructions for a double watch for the night, with patrolling guards as well as sentries. Aliena went to the priory and collected Martha and the children. They all met again at Jack's house.

It pleased Aliena that they were all together: she and Jack and their children, and Jack's mother, and Aliena's brother, and Martha. It was quite like an ordinary family, and Aliena could almost forget that her father had died in a dungeon, and she was legally married to Jack's stepbrother, and Ellen was an outlaw, and—

She shook her head. It was no use pretending this was a normal family.

Jack drew a jug of ale from the barrel and poured it into large cups. Everyone felt tense and excited after the danger. Ellen built up the fire and Martha sliced turnips into a pot, beginning to make a broth for supper. Once upon a time they would have put half a pig on the fire on a day such as this.

Richard drank his ale in one long swallow, wiped his mouth, and said: "We're going to see more of this kind of thing before the winter's out."

Jack said: "They should attack Earl William's storehouses, not Prior Philip's. It's William who has made most of these people destitute."

"They won't have any more success against William than they did against us, unless they improve their tactics. They're like a pack of dogs."

Aliena said: "They need a leader."

Jack said: "Pray they never get one! They would really be dangerous then."

Aliena said: "A leader might direct them to attack William's property instead of ours."

"I don't follow you," Jack said. "Would a leader do that?"

"He would if he was Richard."

They all went quiet.

The idea had grown in Aliena's mind, and she was now convinced it could work. They could fulfill their vows, Richard could destroy William and become the earl, and the county could be restored to peace and prosperity. . . . The more she thought about it, the more excited she became. She said: "There were more than a hundred men in that rabble today." She turned to Ellen. "How many more are there in the forest?"

"Countless," Ellen said. "Hundreds. Thousands."

Aliena leaned across the kitchen table and locked eyes with Richard. "Be their leader," she said forcefully. "Organize them. Teach them how to fight. Devise plans of attack. Then send them into action—against William."

As she spoke, she realized that she was telling him to put his life in danger, and she was filled with trepidation. Instead of winning back the earldom he could be killed.

But he had no such qualms. "By God, Allie, you could be right," he said. "I could have an army of my own, and lead it against William."

Aliena saw in his face the flush of a hatred long nurtured, and she noticed again the scar on his left ear, where the lobe had been sliced off. She pushed down the vile memory that threatened to surface.

Richard was warming to his theme. "I could raid William's herds," he said with relish. "Steal his sheep, poach his deer, break open his barns, rob his mills. My God, I could make that vermin suffer, if I had an army."

He had always been a soldier, Aliena thought; it was his fate. Despite her fear for his safety, she was thrilled by the prospect that he might have another chance to fulfill his destiny.

He thought of a snag. "But how can I find the outlaws?" he said. "They always hide."

"I can answer that," said Ellen. "Branching off the Winchester road is an overgrown track that leads to a disused quarry. That's their hideout. It used to be known as Sally's Quarry."

Seven-year-old Sally said: "But I haven't got a quarry!"

Everyone laughed.

Then they went quiet again.

Richard looked exuberant and determined. "Very well," he said tightly. "Sally's Quarry."

"We'd been working hard all morning, uprooting a massive tree stump up the hill," said Philip. "When we came back, my brother, Francis, was standing right there, in the goat pen, holding you in his arms. You were a day old."

Jonathan looked grave. This was a solemn moment for him.

Philip surveyed the cell of St-John-in-the-Forest. There was not much forest in sight now: over the years the monks had cleared many acres, and the monastery was surrounded by fields. There were more stone buildings—a chapter house, a refectory and a dormitory—plus a host of smaller wooden barns and dairies. It hardly looked like the place he had left seventeen years ago. The people were different, too. Several of those young monks now occupied positions of responsibility at Kingsbridge. William Beauvis, who had caused trouble by flicking hot candle wax at the novice-master's bald head all those years ago, was now prior here. Some had gone: that troublemaker Peter of Wareham was in Canterbury, working for an ambitious young archdeacon called Thomas Becket.

"I wonder what they were like," said Jonathan. "I mean my parents."

Philip felt a twinge of pain for him. Philip himself had lost his parents, but not until he was six years old, and he could remember them both quite well: his mother calm and loving, his father tall and black-bearded and—to Philip, anyway—brave and strong. Jonathan did not even have that. All he knew about his parents was that they had not wanted him.

"We can guess a lot about them," Philip said.

"Really?" Jonathan said eagerly. "What?"

"They were poor," Philip said. "Wealthy people have no reason to abandon their children. They were friendless: friends know when you're expecting a baby, and ask questions if a child disappears. They were desperate. Only desperate people can bear to lose a child."

Jonathan's face was taut with unshed tears. Philip wanted to weep for him, this boy who—everyone said—was so much like Philip himself. Philip wished he could give him some consolation, tell him something warm and heartening about his parents; but how could he pretend that they had loved the boy, when they had left him to die?

Jonathan said: "But why does God do such things?"

Philip saw his opportunity. "Once you start asking that question, you can end up in confusion. But in this case I think the answer is clear. God wanted you for himself."

"Do you really think so?"

"Have I never told you that before? I've always believed it. I said so to the monks here, on the day you were found. I told them that God had sent you here for a purpose of his own, and it was our duty to raise you in God's service so that you would be fit to perform the task he has assigned you."

"I wonder if my mother knows that."

"If she's with the angels, she does."

"What do you think my task might be?"

"God needs monks to be writers, illuminators, musicians, and farmers. He needs men to take on the demanding jobs, such as cellarer, prior and bishop. He needs men who can trade in wool, heal the sick, educate the schoolboys and build churches."

"It's hard to imagine that he has a role cut out for me."

"I can't think he would have gone to this much trouble with you if he didn't," Philip said with a smile. "However, it might not be a grand or prominent role in worldly terms. He might want you to become one of the quiet monks, a humble man who devotes his life to prayer and contemplation."

Jonathan's face fell. "I suppose he might."

Philip laughed. "But I don't think so. God wouldn't make a knife out of wood, or a lady's chemise of shoe leather. You aren't the right material for a life of quietude, and God knows it. My guess is that he wants you to fight for him, not sing to him."

"I certainly hope so."

"But right now I think he wants you to go and see Brother Leo and find out how many cheeses he has for the cellar at Kingsbridge."

"Right."

"I'm going to talk to my brother in the chapter house. And—remember—if any of the monks speak to you about Francis, say as little as you can."

"I shall say nothing."

"Off you go."

Jonathan walked quickly across the yard. His solemn mood had left him already, and his natural exuberance had returned before he reached the dairy. Philip watched him until he disappeared into the building. I was just like that, except perhaps not so clever, he thought.

He went the opposite way, to the chapter house. Francis had sent a message asking Philip to meet him here discreetly. As far as the Kingsbridge monks were concerned, Philip was making a routine visit to a cell. The meeting could not be kept from the monks here, of course, but they were so isolated they had nobody to tell. Only the prior of the cell ever came to Kingsbridge, and Philip had sworn him to secrecy.

He and Francis had arrived this morning, and although they could not plausibly claim that the meeting was an accident, they were maintaining a pretense that they had organized it only for the pleasure of seeing one another. They had both attended high mass, then taken dinner with the monks. Now was their first chance to talk alone.

Francis was waiting in the chapter house, sitting on a stone bench against the wall. Philip almost never saw his own reflection— there were no looking-glasses in a monastery—so he measured his own aging by the changes in his brother, who was only two years younger. Francis at forty-two had a few threads of silver in his black hair, and a crop of stress lines around his bright blue eyes. He was much heavier around the neck and waist than last time Philip had seen him. I've probably got more gray hair and less surplus fat, Philip thought; but I wonder which of us has more worry lines?

He sat down beside Francis and looked across the empty octagonal room. Francis said: "How are things?"

"The savages are in control again," Philip said. "The priory is running out of money, we've almost stopped building the cathedral, Kingsbridge is on the decline, half the county is starving and it's not safe to travel."

Francis nodded. "It's the same story all over England."

"Perhaps the savages will always be in control," Philip said gloomily. "Perhaps greed will always outweigh wisdom in the councils of the mighty; perhaps fear will always overcome compassion in the mind of a man with a sword in his hand."

"You're not usually so pessimistic."

"We were attacked by outlaws a few weeks ago. It was a pitiable effort: no sooner had the townsmen killed a few than the outlaws started fighting among themselves. But when they retreated, the young men of our town chased after the poor wretches and slaughtered all they could catch. It was sickening."

Francis shook his head. "It's hard to understand."

"I think I do understand it. They'd been frightened, and could only exorcise their fear by shedding the blood of the people who had scared them. I saw that in the eyes of the men who killed our mother and father. They killed because they were scared. But what can take away their fear?"

Francis sighed. "Peace, justice, prosperity . . . Hard things to achieve."

Philip nodded. "Well. What are you up to?"

"I'm working for the son of the Empress Maud. His name is Henry."

Philip had heard talk of this Henry. "What's he like?"

"He's a very clever and determined young man. His father is dead, so he's count of Anjou. He's also duke of Normandy, because he's the eldest grandson of old Henry, who used to be king of England and duke of Normandy. And he's married Eleanor of Aquitaine, so now he's duke of Aquitaine as well."

"He rules over more territory than the king of France."

"Exactly."

"But what's he *like*?"

"Educated, hardworking, fast-moving, restless, strong-willed. He has a fearsome temper."

"I sometimes wish I had a fearsome temper," Philip said. "It keeps people on their toes. But everyone knows I'm always reasonable, so I'm never obeyed with quite the same alacrity as a prior who might explode at any minute."

Francis laughed. "Stay just the way you are," he said. He became serious again. "Henry has made me realize the importance of the king's personality. Look at Stephen: his judgment is poor; he's determined in short bursts, then he gives up; he's courageous to the point of foolishness and he pardons his enemies all the time. People who betray him risk very little: they know they can count on his mercy. Consequently, he's struggled unsuccessfully for eighteen years to rule a land that was a united kingdom when he took it over. Henry already has more control over his collection of previously independent duchies and counties than Stephen has ever had here."

Philip was struck by an idea. "Why did Henry send you to England?" he said.

"To survey the kingdom."

"What have you found?"

"That it is lawless and starving, battered by storms and ravaged by war."

Philip nodded thoughtfully. Young Henry was duke of Normandy because he was the eldest son of Maud, who was the only legitimate child of old King Henry, who had been duke of Normandy and king of England.

By that line of descent young Henry could also claim to be king of England.

His mother had made the same claim, and had been opposed because she was a woman and because her husband was an Angevin. But young Henry was not only male but had the additional merit of being both Norman (on his mother's side) and Angevin (on his father's).

Philip said: "Is Henry going to try for the crown of England?"

"It depends on my report," said Francis.

"And what will you tell him?"

"That there will never be a better time than now."

"Praise God," said Philip.

II

On his way to Bishop Waleran's castle, Earl William stopped at Cowford Mill, which he owned. The miller, a dour middle-aged man called Wulfric, had the right to grind all the grain grown in eleven nearby villages. As his fee he kept two sacks in every twenty: one for himself and one for William.

William went there to collect his dues. He did not normally do this personally, but these were not normal times. Nowadays he had to provide an armed escort for every cart carrying flour or anything else edible. In order to use his people in the most economical way he was in the habit of taking a wagon or two with him, whenever he moved around with his entourage of knights, and collecting whatever he could.

The surge in outlaw crime was an unfortunate side effect of his firm policy on bad tenants. Landless people often turned to theft. Generally, they were no more efficient as thieves than they had been as farmers, and William had expected most of them to die off during the winter. At first his expectations had been borne out: the outlaws either went for lone travelers who had little to be stolen, or they carried out ill-organized raids on well-defended targets. Lately, however, the outlaws' tactics had improved. Now they always attacked with at least double the numbers of the defending force. They came when barns were full, a sign that they were reconnoitering carefully. Their attacks were sudden and swift, and they had the courage of desperation. However, they did not stay to fight, but each man fled as soon as he had got his hands on a sheep, a ham, a cheese, a sack of flour or a bag of silver. There was no point in pursuing them, for they melted into the forest, dividing up and running all ways. Someone was commanding them, and he was doing it just the way William would have.

The outlaws' success humiliated William. It made him look like a buffoon who could not police his own earldom. To make matters worse, the outlaws rarely stole from anyone else. It looked as if they were deliberately defying him. William hated nothing more than the feeling that people were laughing at him behind their hands. He had spent his life forcing people to respect him and his family, and this band of outlaws was undoing all his work.

Especially galling for William was what people were saying behind his back: that it served him right, he had treated his tenants harshly and now they were taking their revenge, he had brought this on himself. Such talk made him apoplectic with rage.

The villagers of Cowford looked startled and fearful as William and his knights rode in. William scowled at the thin, apprehensive faces that looked out from the doorways and quickly disappeared again. These people had sent their priest to plead for them to be allowed to grind their own grain this year, saying that they could not afford to give the miller a tenth. William had been tempted to pull out the priest's tongue for insolence.

The weather was cold, and there was ice around the rim of the millpond. The waterwheel was still and the grindstone silent. A woman came out of the house beside the mill. William felt a spasm of desire when he looked at her. She was about twenty years old, with a pretty face and a cloud of dark curls. Despite the famine she had big breasts and strong thighs. She had a saucy look when she first appeared, but the sight of William's knights wiped it off her face, and she ducked back inside.

"She didn't fancy us," Walter said. "She must have seen Gervase." It was an old joke, but they laughed anyway.

They tied up their horses. It was not exactly the same group that William had gathered around him when the civil war began. Walter was still with him, of course, and Ugly Gervase, and Hugh Axe; but Gilbert had died in the unexpectedly bloody battle with the quarrymen, and had been replaced by Guillaume; and Miles had lost an arm in a sword fight over dice at an alehouse in Norwich, and Louis had joined the group. They were not boys anymore, but they talked and acted just the same, laughing and drinking, gambling and whoring. William had lost count of the alehouses they had wrecked, the Jews they had tormented and the virgins they had deflowered.

The miller came out. No doubt his sour expression was due to the perennial unpopularity of millers. His grouchy look was overlaid by anxiety. That was all right: William liked people to be anxious when he turned up.

"I didn't know you had a daughter, Wulfric," William said, leering. "You've been hiding her from me."

"That's Maggie, my wife," he said.

"Cow shit. Your wife's a raddled old crone, I remember her."

"My May died last year, lord. I've married again."

"You dirty old dog!" William said, grinning. "This one must be thirty years younger than you!"

"Twenty-five—"

"Enough of that. Where's my flour? One sack in twenty!"

"All here, lord. If you please to come in."

The way into the mill was through the house. William and the knights followed Wulfric into the single room. The miller's new young wife was kneeling in front of the fire, putting logs on. As she bent down, her tunic stretched tight across her rear. She had meaty haunches, William observed. A miller's wife was one of the last to go hungry in a famine, of course.

William stopped, looking at her bottom. The knights grinned and the miller fidgeted. The girl looked around, realized they were staring at her, and stood up, covered in confusion.

William winked at her and said: "Bring us some ale, Maggie— we're thirsty men."

They went through a doorway to the mill. The flour was in sacks piled around the outside of the circular threshing floor. There was not much of it. Normally the stacks were higher than a man. "Is this all?" William said.

"It was such a poor harvest, lord," Wulfric said nervously.

"Where's mine?"

"Here, lord." He pointed to a pile of eight or nine sacks.

"What?" William felt his face flush. "That's mine? I've got two wagons outside, and you offer me that?"

Wulfric's face became even more doleful. "I'm sorry, lord."

William counted them. "It's only nine sacks!"

"That's all there is," Wulfric said. He was almost in tears. "You see mine next to yours, and it's the same—"

"You lying dog," William said angrily. "You've sold it—"

"No, lord," Wulfric insisted. "That's all there ever was."

Maggie came to the doorway with six pottery tumblers of ale on a tray. She offered the tray to each of the knights. They took a mug each and drank thirstily. William ignored her. He was too wound up to drink. She stood waiting with the one remaining tumbler on the tray.

"What's all this?" William said to Wulfric, pointing to the rest of the sacks, another twenty-five or thirty piled around the walls.

"Awaiting collection, lord—you see the owner's mark on the sacks. . . ."

It was true: each sack was marked with a letter or symbol. That might be a trick, of course, but there was no way William could establish the truth. He found it maddening. But it was not his way to accept this kind of situation. "I don't believe you," he said. "You've been robbing me."

Wulfric was respectfully insistent, even though his voice was shaking. "I'm honest, lord."

"There's never been an honest miller yet."

"Lord—" Wulfric swallowed hard. "Lord, I've never cheated you by so much as a grain of wheat—"

"I'll bet you've been robbing me blind."

Sweat ran down Wulfric's face despite the cold weather. He wiped his forehead with his sleeve. "I'm ready to swear by Jesus and the saints—"

"Shut your mouth."

Wulfric was silent.

William was letting himself get madder and madder but he still had not decided what to do. He wanted to give Wulfric a bad scare, perhaps let Walter beat him up with the chain-mail gloves, possibly take some or all of Wulfric's own flour. . . . Then his eye fell on Maggie, holding the tray with one cup of ale on it, her pretty face rigid with fear, her big young breasts swelling under the floury tunic; and he thought of the perfect punishment for Wulfric. "Grab the wife," he said to Walter out of the corner of his mouth. To Wulfric he said: "I'm going to teach you a lesson."

Maggie saw Walter moving toward her but she was too late to escape. As she turned away, Walter grabbed her arm and pulled. The tray fell with a crash and beer spilled on the floor as Maggie was jerked back. Walter twisted her arm behind her back and held her. She was shaking with fear.

Wulfric said: "No, leave her, please!" in a panicky voice.

William gave a satisfied nod. Wulfric was going to see his young wife raped by several men and he would be powerless to save her. Another time he would make sure to have enough grain to satisfy his lord.

William said: "Your wife's getting plump on bread made from stolen flour, Wulfric, while the rest of us are tightening our belts. Let's see just how fat she is, shall we?" He nodded to Walter.

Walter grasped the neck of Maggie's tunic and pulled sharply down. The garment ripped and fell away. Underneath she wore a linen shirt that reached her knees. Her ample breasts rose and fell as she panted with fear. William stood in front of her. Walter twisted her arm harder, so that she arched her back in pain, and her breasts stuck out even more. William looked at Wulfric, then put his hands on her breasts and kneaded them. They were soft and heavy in his hands.

Wulfric took a step forward and said: "You devil—"

"Hold him," William snapped, and Louis grabbed the miller by both arms and held him still.

William ripped off the girl's undershirt.

His throat went dry as he stared at her voluptuous white body.

Wulfric said: "No, please—"

William felt his desire rising. "Hold her down," he said.

Maggie began to scream.

William unbuckled his sword belt and dropped it on the floor as the knights took Maggie by the arms and legs. She had no hope of resisting four strong men, but all the same she kept writhing and screaming. William liked that. Her breasts jiggled as she moved, and her thighs opened and closed, alternately hiding and revealing her sex. The four knights pinned her down on the threshing floor.

William knelt between her legs and lifted the skirt of his tunic. He looked up at her husband. Wulfric was distraught. He was staring in horror and mumbling pleas for mercy which could not be heard over the screaming. William savored the moment: the terrified woman, the knights holding her down, the husband looking on.

Then Wulfric's eyes flickered away.

William sensed danger. Everyone in the room was staring at him and the girl. The only thing that could conceivably divert Wulfric's attention was the possibility of rescue. William turned his head and looked toward the doorway.

At that moment something heavy and hard hit him on the head.

He roared with pain and collapsed on top of the girl. His face banged against hers. Suddenly he could hear men shouting, lots of them. Out of the corner of his eye he saw Walter fall as if he, too, had been clubbed. The knights released their hold on Maggie. William looked at her face and read shock and relief there. She started to wriggle out from under him. He let her go and rolled away fast.

The first thing he saw above him was a wild-looking man with a woodsman's ax, and he thought: For God's sake, who is it? The father of the girl? He saw Guillaume rise and turn, and in the next instant the ax came down hard on Guillaume's unprotected neck, its sharp blade cutting deep into his flesh. Guillaume fell on William, dead. His blood spurted all over William's tunic.

William pushed the corpse off him. When he was able to look up again he saw that the mill had been invaded by a crowd of ragged, wild-haired, unwashed men armed with clubs and axes. There were a lot of them. He realized he was in trouble. Had the villagers come to the rescue of Maggie? How dare they! There would be some hangings in this village before the end of the day. Enraged, he scrambled to his feet and reached for his sword.

He did not have it. He had dropped his belt in order to rape the girl.

Hugh Axe, Ugly Gervase and Louis were fighting fiercely against what looked like a huge mob of beggars. There were several dead peasants on the ground, but nevertheless the three knights were slowly being driven back across the threshing floor. William saw the naked Maggie, still screaming, forcing her way frantically through the melee toward the door, and even in his confusion and fear he felt a spasm of regretful desire for that round white backside. Then he saw that Wulfric was fighting hand to hand with some of the attackers. Why was the miller fighting the men who had rescued his wife? What the devil was going on?

Bewildered, William looked around for his sword belt. It was lying on the floor almost at his feet. He picked it up and drew the sword, then took three steps back to stay clear of the fighting a moment longer. Looking past the fracas, he saw that most of the attackers were not fighting at all—they were picking up sacks of flour and running out with them. William began to understand. This was *not* a rescue operation by outraged villagers. This was a raiding party from outside. They were not interested in Maggie, and they had not known that William and his knights were inside the mill. All they wanted to do was rob the mill and steal William's flour.

It was obvious who the raiders must be: outlaws.

He felt a surge of heat. This was his chance to strike back at the rabid pack who had been terrorizing the county and emptying his barns.

His knights were overwhelmingly outnumbered. There were at least twenty attackers. William was astonished at the courage of the outlaws. Peasants would normally scatter like chickens before a band of knights, whether they outnumbered the knights by two to one or ten to one. But these people fought hard, and were not discouraged when one of their number fell. They seemed ready to die if necessary. Perhaps that was because they were going to die anyway, of starvation, unless they could steal this flour.

Louis was fighting two men at the same time when a third came up behind him and clubbed him with an ironheaded carpenter's hammer. Louis fell down and stayed down. The man dropped the hammer and picked up Louis's sword. Now there were two knights against twenty outlaws. But Walter was recovering from the blow to his head, and he now drew his sword and entered the melee. William raised his weapon and joined in.

The four of them made a formidable fighting team. The outlaws were driven back, desperately parrying the flashing swords with their clubs and axes. William began to think their morale might crack and they might flee in disorder. Then one of them shouted: "The rightful earl!"

It was some kind of rallying cry. Others took it up, and the outlaws fought more fiercely. The repeated cry, "The rightful earl— the rightful earl!," struck a chill into William's heart even as he was fighting for his life. It meant that whoever was commanding this army of outlaws had set his sights on William's title. William fought harder, as if this skirmish might determine the future of the earl- dom.

Only half the outlaws were actually fighting the knights, William realized. The rest were moving the flour. The combat settled into a steady exchange of thrust and parry, swipe and dodge. Like soldiers who know that the retreat must be sounded soon, the outlaws had begun to fight in a cautious, defensive style.

Behind the fighting outlaws, the others were carrying the last of the flour sacks out of the mill. The outlaws began to retreat, backing through the doorway that led from the threshing floor into the house. William realized that whatever happened now, the outlaws had got away with most of the flour. In no time at all the whole county would know that they had stolen it from under his nose. He was going to be a laughingstock. The thought enraged him so much that he pressed a fierce attack on his opponent and stabbed the man through the heart with a classic thrust.

Then an outlaw caught Hugh with a lucky jab and stabbed his right shoulder, putting him out of action. Now there were two outlaws in the doorway holding off the three surviving knights. That in itself was humiliating enough; but then, with monumental arrogance, one of the outlaws waved the other away. The man dis- appeared, and the last outlaw stepped back a pace, into the single room of the miller's house.

Only one of the knights could stand in the doorway and fight the outlaw. William pushed forward, shouldering Walter and Gervase aside: he wanted this man for himself. As their swords clashed, William realized immediately that this man was no dis- possessed peasant: he was a hardened fighting man like William himself. For the first time he looked into the outlaw's face; and the shock was so great he almost dropped his sword.

His opponent was Richard of Kingsbridge.

Richard's face blazed with hatred. William could see the scar on his mutilated ear. The force of Richard's rancor frightened William more than his flashing sword. William had thought he had crushed Richard finally, but now Richard was back, at the head of a ragamuffin army that had made a fool of William.

Richard came at William hard, taking advantage of his momentary shock. William sidestepped a thrust, raised his sword, parried a slash and stepped back. Richard pressed forward, but now William was partly shielded by the doorway, which restricted Richard's attack to stabbing strokes. Nevertheless Richard drove William farther back, until William was on the threshing floor of the mill and Richard was in the doorway. Now, however, Walter and Gervase went at Richard. Under pressure from the three of them he retreated again. As soon as he backed through the doorway, Walter and Gervase were squeezed out, and it was William against Richard.

William realized that Richard was in a nasty position. As soon as he gained ground he found himself fighting three men. When William tired he could give place to Walter. It was almost impossible for Richard to hold all three of them off indefinitely. He was fighting a losing battle. Perhaps today would not end in humiliation for William after all. Perhaps he would kill his oldest enemy.

Richard must have been thinking along the same lines and presumably he had come to the same conclusion. However, there was no apparent loss of energy or determination. He looked at William with a savage grin that William found unnerving, and leaped forward with a long thrust. William dodged it and stumbled. Walter lunged forward to defend William from the coup de grâce—but instead of coming on, Richard turned on his heel and fled.

William stood up and Walter bumped into him, while Gervase tried to squeeze past them. It took a moment for the three to disentangle themselves, but in that moment Richard crossed the little room, slipped out and banged the door shut. William went after him and threw the door open. The outlaws were making their escape—and, in a final humiliating stroke, they were riding off on the horses of William's knights. As William burst out of the house he saw his own mount, a superb war-horse that had cost him a king's ransom, with Richard in the saddle. The horse had obviously been untied and held ready. William was struck by the mortifying thought that this was the second time Richard had stolen his war-horse. Richard kicked its sides, and it reared up—it was not kind to strangers—but Richard was a good horseman and he stayed on. He sawed on the reins and got the horse's head down. In that moment William darted forward and lunged at Richard with his sword; but the horse was bucking, and William missed, sticking the point of his blade into the wood of the saddle. Then the horse took off, bolting down the village street after the other fleeing outlaws.

William watched them go with murder in his heart.

The rightful earl, he thought. The rightful earl.

He turned around. Walter and Gervase stood behind him. Hugh and Louis were wounded, he did not know how badly, and Guillaume was dead, his blood all over the front of William's tunic. William was completely humiliated. He could hardly hold up his head.

Fortunately the village was deserted: the peasants had fled, not waiting to see William's wrath. The miller and his wife had also vanished, of course. The outlaws had taken all the knights' horses, leaving only the two carts and their oxen.

William looked at Walter. "Did you see who that was, that last one?"

"Yes."

Walter was in the habit of using as few words as possible when his master was in a rage.

William said: "It was Richard of Kingsbridge."

Walter nodded.

"And they called him the rightful earl," William finished.

Walter said nothing.

William went back through the house and into the mill.

Hugh was sitting up, his left hand pressed to his right shoulder. He looked pale.

William said: "How does it feel?"

"This is nothing," Hugh said. "Who *were* those people?"

"Outlaws," William said shortly. He looked around. There were seven or eight outlaws lying dead or wounded on the floor. He spotted Louis flat on his back with his eyes open. At first he thought the man was dead; then Louis blinked.

William said: "Louis."

Louis raised his head, but he looked confused. He had not yet recovered.

William said: "Hugh, help Louis into one of the carts. Walter, put Guillaume's body into the other." He left them to it and went outside.

None of the villagers would have horses, but the miller did, a dappled cob grazing the sparse grass on the riverbank. William found the miller's saddle and put it on the cob.

A little while later he rode away from Cowford with Walter and Gervase driving the ox carts.

His fury did not abate on the journey to Bishop Waleran's castle. In fact, as he brooded over what he had learned he got angrier. It was bad enough that the outlaws had been able to defy him; it was worse that they were led by his old enemy Richard; and it was intolerable that they should call Richard the rightful earl. If they were not put down decisively, very soon Richard would use them to launch a direct attack on William. It would be totally illegal for Richard to take over the earldom that way, of course; but William had a feeling that complaints of illegal attack, coming from him, might not get a sympathetic hearing. The fact that William had been ambushed, overcome by outlaws, and robbed, and that the whole county would shortly be laughing at his humiliation, was not the worst of his problems. Suddenly his hold over his earldom was seriously threatened.

He had to kill Richard, of course. The question was how to find him. He brooded over the problem all the way to the castle; and by the time he arrived he had figured out that Bishop Waleran probably held the key.

They rode into Waleran's castle like a comic procession at a fair, the earl on a dappled cob and his knights driving ox carts. William roared peremptory orders at the bishop's men, sending one to fetch an infirmarer for Hugh and Louis and another to get a priest to pray for the soul of Guillaume. Gervase and Walter went to the kitchen for beer, and William entered the keep and was admitted to Waleran's private quarters. William hated to have to ask Waleran for anything, but he needed Waleran's help in locating Richard.

The bishop was reading an accounts roll, an endless list of numbers. He looked up and saw the rage on William's face. "What happened?" he said, in a tone of mild amusement that always infuriated William.

William gritted his teeth. "I've discovered who is organizing and leading these damned outlaws."

Waleran raised an eyebrow.

"It's Richard of Kingsbridge."

"Ah." Waleran nodded understanding. "Of course. It makes sense."

"It makes danger," William said angrily. He hated it when Waleran was cool and reflective about things. "They call him 'the rightful earl.'" He pointed a finger at Waleran. "You certainly don't want that family back in charge of this earldom—they hate you, and they're friends with Prior Philip, your old enemy."

"All right, calm down," Waleran said condescendingly. "You're quite right, I can't have Richard of Kingsbridge taking over the earldom."

William sat down. His body was beginning to ache. These days he felt the aftereffects of a fight in a way he never used to. He had strained muscles, sore hands, and bruises where he had been struck or had fallen. I'm only thirty-seven, he thought; is this when old age begins? He said: "I have to kill Richard. Once he's gone, the outlaws will degenerate into a helpless rabble."

"I agree."

"Killing him will be easy. The problem is finding him. But you can help me with that."

Waleran rubbed his sharp nose with his thumb. "I don't see how."

"Listen. If they're organized, they must *be* somewhere."

"I don't know what you mean. They're in the forest."

"You can't find outlaws in the forest, normally, because they're scattered all over the place. Most of them don't spend two nights running in the same spot. They make a fire anywhere, and sleep in trees. But if you want to organize such people, you have to gather them all together in one place. You have to have a permanent hideout."

"So we have to discover the location of Richard's hideout."

"Exactly."

"How do you propose to do that?"

"That's where you come in."

Waleran looked skeptical.

William said: "I bet half the people in Kingsbridge know where it is."

"But they won't tell us. Everyone in Kingsbridge hates you and me."

"Not everyone," said William. "Not quite."

Sally thought Christmas was wonderful.

The special Christmas food was mostly sweet: gingerbread dolls; frumenty, made with wheat and eggs and honey; perry, the sweet pear wine that made her giggly; and Christmas umbles, tripes boiled for hours, then baked in a sweet pie. There was less of it this year, because of the famine, but Sally enjoyed it just as much.

She liked decorating the house with holly and hanging up the kissing-bush, although the kissing made her giggle even more than the pear wine. The first man across the threshold brought luck, as long as he was black-haired: Sally's father had to stay indoors all Christmas morning, for his red hair would bring people bad luck. She loved the Nativity play in the church. She liked to see the monks dressed up as Eastern kings and angels and shepherds, and she laughed fit to bust when all the false idols fell down as the Holy Family arrived in Egypt.

But best of all was the boy bishop. On the third day of Christmas, the monks dressed the youngest novice in bishop's robes, and everyone had to obey him.

Most of the townspeople waited in the priory close for the boy bishop to come out. Inevitably he would order the older and more dignified citizens to do menial tasks such as fetching firewood and mucking out pigsties. He also put on exaggerated airs and graces and insulted those in authority. Last year he had made the sacrist pluck a chicken: the result was hilarious, for the sacrist had no idea what to do and there were feathers everywhere.

He emerged in great solemnity, a boy of about twelve years with a mischievous grin, dressed in a purple silk robe and carrying a wooden crozier, and riding on the shoulders of two monks, with the rest of the monastery following. Everyone clapped and cheered. The first thing he did was to point to Prior Philip and say: "You, lad! Get over to the stable and groom the donkey!"

Everyone roared with laughter. The old donkey was notoriously bad-tempered and was never brushed. Prior Philip said: "Yes, my lord bishop," with a good-natured grin, and went off to do his task.

"Forward!" the boy bishop commanded. The procession moved out of the priory close, with the townspeople following. Some people hid away and locked their doors, for fear that they would be picked on to perform some unpleasant task; but then they missed the fun. All Sally's family had come: her mother and father, her brother, Tommy, Aunt Martha, and even Uncle Richard, who had returned home unexpectedly last night.

The boy bishop led them first to the alehouse, as was traditional. There he demanded free beer for himself and all the novices. The brewer handed it over with good grace.

Sally found herself sitting on a bench next to Brother Remigius, one of the older monks. He was a tall, unfriendly man and she had never spoken to him before, but now he smiled at her and said: "It's nice that your Uncle Richard came home at Christmas."

Sally said: "He gave me a wooden pussycat that he carved himself with his knife."

"That's nice. Will he stay long, do you think?"

Sally frowned. "I don't know."

"I expect he has to go back soon."

"Yes. He lives in the forest now."

"Do you know where?"

"Yes. It's called Sally's Quarry. That's my name!" She laughed.

"So it is," said Brother Remigius. "How interesting."

When they had drunk, the boy bishop said: "And now—Andrew Sacrist and Brother Remigius will do the Widow Poll's washing."

Sally squealed with laughter and clapped her hands. Widow Poll was a rotund, red-faced woman who took in laundry. The fastidious monks would hate the job of washing the smelly undershirts and stockings that people changed every six months.

The crowd left the alehouse and carried the boy bishop in procession to Poll's one-room house down by the quay. Poll had a laughing fit and turned even redder when they told her who was going to do her laundry.

Andrew and Remigius carried a heavy basket of dirty clothing from the house to the riverbank. Andrew opened the basket and Remigius, with an expression of utter distaste on his face, pulled out the first garment. A young woman called out saucily: "Careful with that one, Brother Remigius, it's my chemise!" Remigius flushed and everyone laughed. The two middle-aged monks put a brave face on it and began to wash the clothes in the river water, with the townspeople calling advice and encouragement. Andrew was thoroughly fed up, Sally could see, but Remigius had a strangely contented look on his face.

A huge iron ball hung by a chain from a wooden scaffold, like a hangman's noose dangling from a gallows. There was also a rope tied to the ball. This rope ran over a pulley on the upright post of the scaffold and hung down to the ground, where two laborers held it. When the laborers hauled on the rope, the ball was pulled up and back until it touched the pulley, and the chain lay horizontally along the arm of the scaffold.

Most of the population of Shiring was watching.

The men let go of the rope. The iron ball dropped and swung, smashing into the wall of the church. There was a terrific thud, the wall shuddered, and William felt the impact in the ground beneath his feet. He thought how he would like to have Richard clamped to the wall in just the place where the ball would hit. He would be squashed like a fly.

The laborers hauled on the rope again. William realized he was holding his breath as the iron ball stopped at the top of its travel. The men let go; the ball swung; and this time it tore a hole in the stone wall. The crowd applauded.

It was an ingenious mechanism.

William was happy to see work progressing on the site where he would build the new church, but he had more urgent matters on his mind today. He looked around for Bishop Waleran, and spotted him standing with Alfred Builder. William approached them and drew the bishop aside. "Is the man here yet?"

"He may be," said Waleran. "Come to my house."

They crossed the market square. Waleran said: "Have you brought your troops?"

"Of course. Two hundred of them. They're waiting in the woods just outside town."

They went into the house. William smelled boiled ham and his mouth watered, despite his urgent haste. Most people were being sparing with food at the moment, but with Waleran it seemed to be a matter of principle not to let the famine change his way of life. The bishop never ate much, but he liked everyone to know that he was far too rich and powerful to be affected by mere harvests.

Waleran's place was a typical narrow-fronted town house, with a hall at the front and a kitchen behind, and a yard at the back with a cesspit, a beehive and a pigsty. William was relieved to see a monk waiting in the hall.

Waleran said: "Good day, Brother Remigius."

Remigius said: "Good day, my lord bishop. Good day, Lord William."

William looked eagerly at the monk. He was a nervous man with an arrogant face and prominent blue eyes. His face was vaguely familiar, as one among many tonsured heads at services in Kingsbridge. William had been hearing about him for years, as Waleran's spy in Prior Philip's camp, but this was the first time he had spoken to the man. "Have you got some information for me?" he said.

"Possibly," Remigius replied.

Waleran threw off his fur-trimmed cloak and went to the fire to warm his hands. A servant brought hot elderberry wine in silver goblets. William took some and drank it, waiting impatiently for the servant to leave.

Waleran sipped his wine and gave Remigius a hard look. As the servant went out Waleran said to the monk: "What excuse did you give for leaving the priory?"

"None," Remigius replied.

Waleran raised an eyebrow.

"I'm not going back," Remigius said defiantly.

"How so?"

Remigius took a deep breath. "You're building a cathedral here."

"It's just a church."

"It's going to be very big. You're planning to make this the cathedral church, eventually."

Waleran hesitated, then said: "Suppose, for the sake of argument, that you're right."

"The cathedral will have to be run by a chapter, either of monks or of canons."

"So?"

"I want to be prior."

That made sense, William thought.

Waleran said tartly: "And you're so confident of getting the job that you've left Kingsbridge without Philip's permission and with no excuse."

Remigius looked uncomfortable. William sympathized with him: Waleran in a scornful mood was enough to make anyone fidget. "I hope I'm not overconfident," Remigius said.

"Presumably you can lead us to Richard."

"Yes."

William interrupted excitedly: "Good man! Where is he?"

Remigius remained silent and looked at Waleran.

William said: "Come on, Waleran, give him the job, for God's sake!"

Still Waleran hesitated. William knew he hated to feel coerced. At last Waleran said: "All right. You shall be prior."

William said: "Now, where's Richard?"

Remigius continued to look at Waleran. "From today?"

"From today."

Remigius now turned to William. "A monastery isn't just a church and a dormitory. It needs lands, farms, churches paying tithes."

"Tell me where Richard is, and I'll give you five villages with their parish churches, just to start you off," William said.

"The foundation will need a proper charter."

Waleran said: "You shall have it, never fear."

William said: "Come on, man, I've got an army waiting outside town. Where's Richard's hideout?"

"It's a place called Sally's Quarry, just off the Winchester road."

"I know it!" William had to restrain himself from giving a whoop of triumph. "It's a disused quarry. Nobody goes there anymore."

"I remember," said Waleran. "It hasn't been worked for years. It's a good hideout—you wouldn't know it was there unless you actually walked into it."

"But it's also a trap," William said with savage glee. "The worked-out walls are sheer on three sides. Nobody will escape. I won't be taking any prisoners, either." His excitement rose as he pictured the scene. "I'll slaughter them all. It will be like killing chickens in a hen house."

The two men of God were looking at him oddly. "Feeling a little squeamish, Brother Remigius?" William said scornfully. "Does the thought of a massacre turn the stomach of my lord bishop?" He was right both times, he could tell by their faces. They were great schemers, these religious men, but when it came to bloodshed they still had to rely on men of action. "I know you'll be praying for me," he said sarcastically; and he left.

His horse was tied up outside, a black stallion that had replaced—but did not equal—the war-horse Richard had stolen. He mounted and rode out of town. He suppressed his excitement and tried to think coolly about tactics.

He wondered how many outlaws would be at Sally's Quarry. They had mounted raids with more than a hundred men at a time. There would be at least two hundred of them, perhaps as many as five hundred. William's force could be outnumbered, so he would need to make the most of his advantages. One was surprise. Another was weaponry: most of the outlaws had clubs, hammers or at best axes, and none had armor. But the most important advantage was that William's men were on horseback. The outlaws had few horses and it was not likely that many of them would be saddled ready just at the moment William attacked. To give himself a further edge he decided to send a few bowmen up the sides of the hill to shoot down into the quarry for a few moments before the main assault.

The most important thing was to prevent any of the outlaws from escaping, at least until he was sure that Richard was captured or dead. He decided to assign a handful of trustworthy men to hang back behind the main assault and sweep up any wily ones who tried to slip out.

Walter was waiting with the knights and men-at-arms where William had left them a couple of hours earlier. They were eager and morale was high: they anticipated an easy victory. A short while later they were trotting along the Winchester road.

Walter rode alongside William, not speaking. One of Walter's greatest assets was his ability to remain silent. William found that most people talked to him constantly, even when there was nothing to say, probably out of nervousness. Walter respected William, but was not nervous of him: they had been together too long.

William felt a familiar mixture of eager anticipation and mortal fear. This was the one thing in the world he did well, and every time he did it he risked his life. But this raid was special. Today he had a chance to destroy the man who had been a thorn in his flesh for fifteen years.

Toward noon they stopped in a village large enough to have an alehouse. William bought the men bread and beer and they watered the horses. Before moving on he briefed the men.

A few miles farther on they turned off the Winchester road. The path they took was barely visible, and William would not have noticed it had he not been looking for it. Once on it, he could follow it by observing the vegetation: there was a strip four or five yards wide with no mature trees.

He sent the archers on ahead and, to give them a start, he slowed the rest of the men for a few moments. It was a clear January day, and the leafless trees hardly dimmed the cold sunlight. William had not been to the quarry for many years and he was now not sure how far away it might be. However, once they were a mile or so from the road he began to see signs that the track was in use: trampled vegetation, broken saplings and churned mud. He was glad to have confirmation of Remigius's report.

He felt as taut as a bowstring. The signs became much more obvious: heavily trampled grass, horse droppings, human refuse. This far into the forest the outlaws had made no attempt to conceal their presence. There was no longer any doubt. The outlaws were here. The battle was about to begin.

The hideout must be very close. William strained his hearing. At any moment his bowmen would begin the attack, and there would be shouts and curses, screams of agony, and the neighing of terrified horses.

The track led into a wide clearing, and William saw, a couple of hundred yards ahead, the entrance to Sally's Quarry. There was no noise. Something was wrong. His bowmen were not shooting. William felt a shiver of apprehension. What had happened? Could his bowmen have been ambushed and silently dispatched by sentries? Not all of them, surely.

But there was no time to ponder: he was almost on top of the outlaws. He spurred his horse into a gallop. His men followed suit, and they thundered toward the hideout. William's fear evaporated in the exhilaration of the charge.

The way into the quarry was like a small twisted ravine, and William could not see inside as he approached. Glancing up, he saw some of his archers standing on top of the bluff, looking in. Why were they not shooting? He had a premonition of disaster, and he would have stopped and turned around, except that the charging horses could not now be stopped. With his sword in his right hand, holding the reins with his left, his shield hanging from his neck, he galloped into the disused quarry.

There was nobody there.

The anticlimax hit him like a blow. He was almost ready to burst into tears. All the signs had been there: he had felt so sure. Now frustration gripped his guts like a pain.

As the horses slowed, he saw that this had been the outlaws hideout not long ago. There were makeshift shelters of branches and reeds, the remains of cooking fires, and a dunghill. A corner of the area had been fenced with a few sticks and used to corral the horses. Here and there William saw the litter of human occupation: chicken bones, empty sacks, a worn-out shoe, a broken pot. One of the fires appeared to be smoking. He had a sudden surge of hope: perhaps they had only just left, and could still be caught! Then he saw a single figure squatting on the ground by the fire. He approached it. The figure stood up. It was a woman.

"Well, well, William Hamleigh," she said. "Too late, as usual."

"Insolent cow, I'll tear out your tongue for that," he said.

"You won't touch me," she replied calmly. "I've cursed better men than you." She put her hand to her face in a three-fingered gesture, like a witch. The knights shrank back, and William crossed himself protectively. The woman looked at him fearlessly with a pair of startling golden eyes. "Don't you know me, William?" she said. "You once tried to buy me for a pound." She laughed. "Lucky for you that you didn't succeed."

William remembered those eyes. This was the widow of Tom Builder, the mother of Jack Jackson, the witch who lived in the forest. He was indeed glad he had not succeeded in buying her. He wanted to get away from her as fast as he could, but he had to question her first. "All right, witch," he said. "Was Richard of Kingsbridge here?"

"Until two days ago."

"And where did he go, can you tell me that?"

"Oh, yes, I can," she said. "He and his outlaws have gone to fight for Henry."

"Henry?" William said. He had a dreadful feeling that he knew which Henry she meant. "The son of Maud?"

"That's right," she said.

William went cold. The energetic young duke of Normandy

might succeed where his mother had failed—and if Stephen was defeated now, William might fall with him. "What's happened?" he said urgently. "What has Henry done?"

"He's crossed the water with thirty-six ships and landed at Wareham," the witch replied. "He's brought an army of three thousand men, they say. We've been invaded."

III

Winchester was crowded, tense and dangerous. Both armies were here: King Stephen's royal forces were garrisoned in the castle, and Duke Henry's rebels—including Richard and his outlaws—were camped outside the city walls, on Saint Giles's Hill where the annual fair was held. The soldiers of both sides were banned from the town itself, but many of them defied the ban, and spent their evenings in the alehouses, cockpits and brothels, where they got drunk and abused women and fought and killed one another over games of dice and nine-men's morris.

All the fight had gone out of Stephen in the summer when his elder son died. Now Stephen was in the royal castle and Duke Henry was staying at the bishop's palace, and peace talks were being conducted by their representatives, Archbishop Theobald of Canterbury speaking for the king, and the old power-broker Bishop Henry of Winchester for Duke Henry. Every morning, Archbishop Theobald and Bishop Henry would confer at the bishop's palace. At noon Duke Henry would walk through the streets of Winchester, with his lieutenants—including Richard—in train, and go to the castle for dinner.

The first time Aliena saw Duke Henry she could not believe that this was the man who ruled an empire the size of England. He was only about twenty years old, with the tanned, freckled complexion of a peasant. He was dressed in a plain dark tunic with no embroidery, and his reddish hair was cut short. He looked like the hardworking son of a prosperous yeoman. However, after a while she realized that he had some kind of aura of power. He was stocky and muscular, with broad shoulders and a large head; but the impression of crude physical strength was modified by keen, watchful gray eyes; and the people around him never got too close to him, but treated him with wary familiarity, as if they were afraid he might lash out at any moment.

Aliena thought the dinners at the castle must have been unpleasantly tense, with the leaders of opposing armies around the same table. She wondered how Richard could bear to sit down with Earl William. She would have taken the carving knife to William instead of to the venison. She herself saw William only from a distance, and briefly. He looked anxious and bad-tempered, which was a good sign.

While the earls and bishops and abbots met in the keep, the lesser nobility gathered in the castle courtyard: the knights and sheriffs, minor barons, justiciars and castellans; people who could not stay away from the capital city while their future and the future of the kingdom were being decided. Aliena met Prior Philip there most mornings. Every day there were a dozen different rumors. One day all the earls who supported Stephen were to be degraded (which would mean the end of William); next day, all of them were to retain their positions, which would dash Richard's hopes. All Stephen's castles were to be pulled down, then all the rebels' castles, then everyone's castles, then none. One rumor said that every one of Henry's supporters would get a knighthood and a hundred acres. Richard did not want that, he wanted the earldom.

Richard had no idea which rumors were true, if any. Although he was one of Henry's trusted battlefield lieutenants, he was not consulted about the details of political negotiations. Philip, however, seemed to know what was going on. He would not say where he was getting his information, but Aliena recalled that he had a brother, who had visited Kingsbridge now and again, and who had worked for Robert of Gloucester and the Empress Maud: now perhaps he worked for Duke Henry.

Philip reported that the negotiators were close to agreement. The deal was that Stephen would continue as king until he died, but Henry would be his successor. This made Aliena anxious. Stephen could live for another ten years. What would happen in the interim? Stephen's earls would surely not be deposed while he continued to rule. So how would Henry's supporters—such as Richard—gain their rewards? Would they be expected to wait?

Philip learned the answer late one afternoon, when they had all been in Winchester a week. He sent a novice messenger to bring Aliena and Richard to him. As they walked through the busy streets to the cathedral close, Richard was full of savage eagerness, but Aliena was possessed by trepidation.

Philip was waiting for them in the graveyard, and they talked among the tombstones as the sun went down. "They've reached agreement," Philip said without preamble. "But it's a bit of a muddle."

Aliena could not bear the tension. "Will Richard be earl?" she said urgently.

Philip rocked his hand from side to side in the gesture that meant maybe yes, maybe no. "It's complicated. They've made a compromise. Lands that have been taken away by usurpers shall be restored to the people who owned them in the time of old King Henry."

"That's all I need!" Richard said immediately. "My father was earl in King Henry's time."

"Shut up, Richard," Aliena snapped. She turned to Philip. "So what's the complication?"

Philip said: "There's nothing in the agreement that says Stephen has to enforce it. There probably won't be any changes until he dies and Henry becomes king."

Richard was crestfallen. "But that cancels it out!"

"Not quite," Philip said. "It means that you are the rightful earl."

"But I have to live as an outlaw until Stephen dies—while that animal William occupies my castle," Richard said angrily.

"Not so loud," Philip protested as a priest walked by. "All this is still secret."

Aliena was seething. "I don't accept this," she said. "I'm not prepared to wait for Stephen to die. I've been waiting seventeen years and I've had enough."

Philip said: "But what can you do?"

Aliena addressed Richard. "Most of the country acclaims you as the rightful earl. Stephen and Henry have now acknowledged that you are the rightful earl. You should seize the castle and *rule* as the rightful earl."

"I can't seize the castle. William is sure to have left it guarded."

"You've got an army, haven't you?" she said, becoming carried away by the force of her own anger and frustration. "You've got the right to the castle and you've got the power to take it."

Richard shook his head. "In fifteen years of civil war, do you know how many times I've seen a castle taken by frontal attack? None." As always, he seemed to gain authority and maturity as soon as he began to talk about military matters. "It almost never happens. A town, sometimes, but not a castle. They may surrender after a siege, or be relieved by reinforcements; and I've seen them taken through cowardice or trickery or treachery; but not by main force."

Aliena was still not ready to accept this. It seemed to her a counsel of despair. She could not resign herself to more years of waiting and hoping. She said: "So what would happen if you took your army to William's castle?"

"They would raise the drawbridge and close the gates before we could get inside. We would camp outside. Then William would come to the rescue with his army and attack our camp. But even if we beat him off, we still wouldn't have the castle. Castles are hard to attack and easy to defend—that's the point of them."

As he spoke, the seed of an idea was germinating in Aliena's agitated mind. "Cowardice, trickery or treachery," she said.

"What?"

"You've seen castles taken by cowardice, trickery or treachery."

"Oh. Yes."

"Which did William use, when he took the castle from us, all those years ago?"

Philip interrupted: "Times were different. The country had had peace, under the old King Henry, for thirty-five years. William took your father by surprise."

Richard said: "He used trickery. He got inside the castle surreptitiously, with a few men, before the alarm was raised. But Prior Philip is right: you couldn't get away with that nowadays. People are much more wary."

"I could get in," Aliena said confidently, although as she spoke the words her heart raced with fear.

"Of course you could—you're a woman," Richard said. "But you couldn't do anything once you were inside. That's how come they'd let you in. You're harmless."

"Don't be so damned arrogant," she flared. "I've killed to protect you, and that's more than you've ever done for me, you ungrateful pig, so don't you dare call me harmless."

"All right, you're not harmless," he said angrily. "What would you do, once inside the castle?"

Aliena's anger evaporated. What would I do? she thought fearfully. To hell with it, I've got at least as much courage and resourcefulness as that pig William. "What did William do?"

"Kept the drawbridge down and the gate open long enough for the main attacking force to get inside."

"Then that's what I'll do," Aliena said with her heart in her mouth.

"But how?" Richard said skeptically.

Aliena remembered giving comfort to a fourteen-year-old girl who was frightened of a storm. "The countess owes me a favor," she said. "And she hates her husband."

They rode through the night, Aliena and Richard and fifty of his best men, and reached the vicinity of Earlscastle at dawn. They halted in the forest across the fields from the castle. Aliena dismounted, took off her cloak of Flanders wool and her soft leather

boots, and put on a coarse peasant blanket and a pair of clogs. One
of the men handed her a basket of fresh eggs packed in straw,
which she slung over her arm.

Richard looked her up and down and said: "Perfect. A peasant
girl bringing produce for the castle kitchen."

Aliena swallowed hard. Yesterday she had been full of fire and
boldness, but now that she was about to carry out her plan she was
scared.

Richard kissed her cheek. He said: "When I hear the bell, I'll
say the Paternoster slowly once, then the advance party will start
out. All you have to do is lull the guards into a false sense of
security, so that ten of my men can get across the fields and into the
castle without causing alarm."

Aliena nodded. "Just make sure the main group doesn't break
cover until the advance party is across the drawbridge."

He smiled. "I'll be leading the main group. Don't worry. Good
luck."

"You too."

She walked away.

She emerged from the woodland and set out across the open
fields toward the castle she had left on that awful day sixteen years
ago. Seeing the place again, she had a vivid, terrifying memory of
that other morning, the air damp after the storm, and the two horses
charging out of the gate across the rain-sodden fields; Richard on the
war-horse and she on the smaller mount, both mortally afraid. She
had been denying what had happened, deliberately forgetting, chanting to herself in time with the horse's hoofbeats: "I can't re*member* I
can't re*member* I *can't* I *can't* I *can't*." It had worked: for a long time
afterward she had been unable to recall the rape, remembering that
something terrible had happened but never recollecting the details.
Not until she fell in love with Jack had it come back to her; and then
the memory had so terrified her that she had been unable to respond
to his love. Thank God he had been so patient. That was how she
knew his love was strong; because he had put up with so much and
still loved her.

As she came closer to the castle she conjured up some good
memories, to calm her nerves. She had lived here as a child, with
her father and Richard. They had been wealthy and secure. She had
played on the castle ramparts with Richard, hung around in the
kitchen and scrounged bits of sweet pastry, and sat beside her father at dinner in the great hall. I didn't know I was happy, she
thought. I had no idea how fortunate I was to have nothing to be
afraid of.

Those good times will begin again today, she said to herself, if only I can do this right.

She had confidently said *The countess owes me a favor, and she hates her husband,* but as they rode through the night she had thought of all the things that could go wrong. First, she might not get into the castle at all: something might have happened to put the garrison on the alert, the guards might be suspicious, or she might just be unlucky enough to come across an obstructive sentry. Second, when she was inside she might not be able to persuade Elizabeth to betray her husband. It was a year and a half since Aliena had met Elizabeth in the storm: women could get used to the most vicious men, in time, and Elizabeth might be reconciled to her fate by now. Third, even if Elizabeth was willing, she might not have the authority or the nerve to do what Aliena wanted. She had been a frightened little girl last time they met, and it could be that the castle guard would refuse to obey her.

Aliena felt unnaturally alert as she crossed the drawbridge: she could see and hear everything with abnormal clarity. The garrison was just waking up. A few bleary-eyed guards were lounging on the ramparts, yawning and coughing, and an old dog sat in the gateway scratching itself. She pulled her hood forward to hide her face, in case anyone should recognize her, and passed under the arch.

There was a slovenly sentry on duty at the gatehouse, sitting on a bench eating a huge hunk of bread. His clothing was disarrayed and his sword belt was hanging from a hook at the back of the room. With her heart in her mouth, and a smile that belied her fear, Aliena showed him her basket of eggs.

He waved her in with an impatient gesture.

She had passed the first obstacle.

Discipline was slack. It was understandable: this was a token force, left behind while the best men went to war. All the excitement was elsewhere.

Until today.

So far, so good. Aliena crossed the lower courtyard with her nerves on edge. It was very odd to be a stranger walking into the place that had been her home, to be an infiltrator where once she had had the right to go anywhere she pleased. She looked around, careful not to be too blatantly curious. Most of the wooden buildings had changed: the stables were bigger, the kitchen had been moved and there was a new stone-built armory. The place seemed dirtier than it used to be. But the chapel was still there, the chapel where she and Richard had sat out that awful storm, shocked and numb and freezing cold. A handful of castle servants were beginning their morning chores. One or two men-at-arms moved about the compound. They looked menacing, but perhaps that was because she was aware that they would have killed her if they had known what she was going to do.

If her plan worked, by tonight she would once again be mistress of this castle. The thought was thrilling but unreal, like a marvelous, impossible dream.

She went into the kitchen. A boy was stoking the fire and a young girl was slicing carrots. Aliena smiled brightly at them and said: "Twenty-four fresh eggs." She put her basket on the table.

The boy said: "Cook's not up yet. You'll have to wait for your money."

"Can I get a bite of bread for my breakfast?"

"In the great hall."

"Thank you." She left her basket and went out again.

She crossed the second drawbridge to the upper compound. She smiled at the guard in the second gateway. He had uncombed hair and bloodshot eyes. He looked her up and down and said: "And where are you going?" His voice was playfully challenging.

"To get some breakfast," she said without stopping.

He leered. "I've got something for you to eat," he called after her.

"I might bite it off, though," she said over her shoulder.

They did not suspect her for a moment. It did not occur to them that a woman could be dangerous. How foolish they were. Women could do most of the things men did. Who was left in charge when the men were fighting wars, or going on crusades? There were women carpenters, dyers, tanners, bakers and brewers. Aliena herself was one of the most important merchants in the county. The duties of an abbess, running a nunnery, were exactly the same as those of an abbot. Why, it had been a woman, the Empress Maud, who caused the civil war that had gone on for fifteen years! Yet these wooden-headed men-at-arms did not expect a woman to be an enemy agent because it was not the normal thing.

She ran up the steps of the keep and entered the hall. There was no steward at the door. That was presumably because the master was away. In future I will make sure there is always a steward at the door, Aliena thought, whether the master is at home or not.

Fifteen or twenty people were eating breakfast around a small table. One or two of them glanced up at her, but nobody took any notice. The hall was quite clean, she observed, and there were one or two feminine touches: freshly whitewashed walls, and sweet-smelling herbs mixed with the rushes on the floor. Elizabeth had made her mark in a small way. That was a hopeful sign.

Without speaking to the people around the table, Aliena walked across the hall to the staircase in the corner, trying to look as if she had every right to be there, but expecting at any moment to be stopped. She got to the foot of the stairs without attracting attention. Then, as she ran up toward the private apartments on the top floor, she heard someone say: "You can't go up there—hey, you!" She ignored the voice. She heard someone come after her.

She reached the top, panting. Would Elizabeth sleep in the main bedroom, the one Aliena's father had occupied? Or would she have a bed of her own in the room that had been Aliena's? She hesitated for an instant, her heart pounding. She guessed that by now William had tired of having Elizabeth sleep with him every night, and probably allowed her a room of her own. Aliena knocked at the smaller room and opened the door.

She had been right. Elizabeth was sitting by the fire, wearing a nightshirt, brushing her hair. She looked up, frowned, and then recognized Aliena. "It's you!" she said. "What a surprise!" She seemed pleased.

Aliena heard heavy footsteps on the stairs behind her. "May I come in?" she said.

"Of course—and welcome!"

Aliena stepped inside and closed the door quickly. She crossed the room to where Elizabeth sat. A man burst in, saying, "Hey, you, who do you think you are?" and came after Aliena as if to seize her.

"Stay where you are!" she said in her most commanding voice. He hesitated. She said: "I come to see the countess, with a message from Earl William, and you would have learned that earlier if you had been guarding the door instead of stuffing your face with horse-bread."

He looked guilty.

Elizabeth said: "It's all right, Edgar, I know this lady."

"Very well, countess," he said. He went out and closed the door.

I made it, Aliena thought. I got in.

She looked around while her heartbeat returned to normal. The room was not very different from when it had been hers. There were dried petals in a bowl, a pretty tapestry on the wall, some books, and a trunk for clothes. The bed was in the same place—in fact it was the same bed—and on the pillow was a rag doll just like the one Aliena had had. It made her feel old.

"This used to be my room," she said.

"I know," said Elizabeth.

Aliena was surprised. She had not told Elizabeth about her past.

"I've found out all about you since that terrible storm," Elizabeth explained. She added: "I admire you so much." She had the gleam of hero-worship in her eyes.

That was a good sign.

"And William?" Aliena said. "Are you any happier, living with him?"

Elizabeth looked away. "Well," she said, "I have my own room now, and he's been away a lot. In fact everything's much better." Then she began to cry.

Aliena sat on the bed and put her arms around the girl. Elizabeth cried with deep, wrenching sobs, and tears flooded down her cheeks. In between sobs she gasped: "I—hate—him! I—wish—I—could—die!"

Her anguish was so pitiful, and she was so young, that Aliena was close to tears herself. She was painfully aware that Elizabeth's fate could easily have been her own. She patted Elizabeth's back as she would have done with Sally.

Eventually Elizabeth became calmer. She wiped her wet face with the sleeve of her nightshirt. "I'm so afraid of having a baby," she said miserably. "I'm terrified because I know how he would mistreat the child."

"I understand," Aliena said. She had once been terrified by the thought that she might be pregnant with William's child.

Elizabeth looked at her wide-eyed. "Is it true what they say, about . . . what he did to you?"

"Yes, it's true. I was your age when it happened."

For a moment they looked into one another's eyes, brought close by a shared loathing. Suddenly Elizabeth did not look like a child anymore.

Aliena said: "You could get free of him, if you want. Today."

Elizabeth stared at her. "Is it true?" she said with pitiable eagerness. "Is it true?"

Aliena nodded. "That's why I'm here."

"I could go home?" Elizabeth said, her eyes filling with fresh tears. "I could go home to Weymouth, to my mother? *Today?*"

"Yes. But you'll have to be brave."

"I'll do anything," she said. "Anything! Just tell me."

Aliena remembered explaining how she could acquire authority with her husband's employees, and she wondered whether Elizabeth had been able to put the principles into practice. "Do the servants still push you around?" she asked candidly.

"They try."

"But you don't let them."

She looked embarrassed. "Well, sometimes I do. But I'm sixteen now, and I've been countess for nearly two years . . . and I've been trying to follow your advice, and it really works!"

"Let me explain," Aliena began. "King Stephen has made a pact with Duke Henry. All lands are to be returned to the people who held them in the time of the old King Henry. That means my brother Richard will become earl of Shiring—sometime. But he wants it now."

Elizabeth was wide-eyed. "Is Richard going to make war on William?"

"Richard is very close right now, with a small company of men. If he can take over the castle today, he will be recognized as earl, and William will be finished."

"I can't believe it," Elizabeth said. "I can't believe it's really true." Her sudden optimism was even more heartrending than her abject misery had been.

"All you have to do is let Richard in peacefully," Aliena said. "Then, when it's all over, we'll take you home."

Elizabeth looked fearful again. "I'm not sure the men will do what I say."

That was Aliena's worry. "Who is the captain of the guard?"

"Michael Armstrong. I don't like him."

"Send for him."

"Right." Elizabeth wiped her nose, stood up, and went to the door. "Madge!" she called out in a piercing voice. Aliena heard a distant reply. "Go and fetch Michael. Tell him to come here right away—I want to see him urgently. Hurry, please."

She came back in and began to dress quickly, throwing a tunic over her nightdress and lacing up her boots. Aliena briefed her rapidly. "Tell Michael to ring the big bell to summon everyone to the courtyard. Say you've received a message from Earl William and you want to speak to the entire garrison, men-at-arms and servants and everyone. You want three or four men to stand guard while everyone else gathers in the lower courtyard. Also tell him you're expecting a group of ten or twelve horsemen to arrive at any moment with a further message, and they must be brought to you as soon as they arrive."

"I hope I can remember it all," Elizabeth said nervously.

"Don't worry—if you forget, I'll prompt you."

"That makes me feel better."

"What's Michael Armstrong like?"

"Smelly and surly and built like an ox."

"Intelligent?"

"No."

"So much the better."

A moment later the man came in. He had a grumpy expression, a short neck and massive shoulders, and he brought with him the odor of the pigsty. He looked inquiringly at Elizabeth, giving the impression that he resented being disturbed.

"I've received a message from the earl," Elizabeth began.

Michael held out his hand.

Aliena was horrified to realize that she had not taken the precaution of providing Elizabeth with a letter. The whole deception could collapse right at the outset because of a silly mistake. Elizabeth threw her a despairing look. Aliena cast about frantically for something to say. Finally she was inspired. "Can you read, Michael?"

He looked resentful. "The priest will read it to me."

"Your lady can read."

Elizabeth looked scared, but she said: "I shall give the message to the whole garrison myself, Michael. Ring the bell and get everyone assembled in the courtyard. But make sure to leave three or four men on guard on the ramparts."

As Aliena had feared, Michael did not like Elizabeth taking command like this. He looked rebellious. "Why not let me address them?"

Aliena realized anxiously that she might not be able to persuade this man: he could be too stupid to listen to reason. She said: "I have brought the countess momentous news from Winchester. She wants to tell her people herself."

"Well, what *is* the news?" he said.

Aliena said nothing and looked at Elizabeth. Once again Elizabeth looked scared. However, Aliena had not told her what was supposed to be in the fictitious message, so Elizabeth could not possibly accede to Michael's request. In the end she simply went on as if Michael had not spoken. "Tell the guards to look out for a group of ten or twelve horsemen. Their leader will have fresh news from Earl William, and he must be brought to me immediately. Now ring the bell."

Michael was clearly disposed to argue. He stood still, frowning, while Aliena held her breath. "More messengers," he said, as if it were something very difficult to understand. "This lady with one message, and twelve horsemen with another."

"Yes—now would you please go and ring the bell?" Elizabeth said. Aliena could hear the quaver in her voice.

Michael looked defeated. He could not understand what was happening, but he saw nothing to object to either. Finally he said a grudging "Very well, lady," and went out.

Aliena breathed again.

Elizabeth said: "What's going to happen?"

"When they're gathered in the courtyard, you'll tell them about the peace between King Stephen and Duke Henry," Aliena said. "That will distract everyone. While you're speaking, Richard will send out an advance party of ten men. However, the guards will think they are the messengers we are expecting from Earl William, so they won't immediately panic and raise the drawbridge. You have to try to keep everyone interested in what you're saying while the advance party approaches the castle. All right?"

Elizabeth looked nervous. She said: "And then what?"

"When I give you the word, say you have surrendered the castle to the rightful earl, Richard. Then Richard's army will break cover and charge the castle. At that point Michael will realize what's happening. But his men will be in doubt about their loyalty—because you have told them to surrender, and called Richard the rightful earl—and the advance party will be inside to prevent anyone from closing the gates." The bell began to ring. Aliena's stomach knotted in fear. "We've run out of time. How do you feel?"

"Scared."

"Me too. Let's go."

They went down the stairs. The bell on the gatehouse tower was ringing as it had when Aliena was a carefree girl. Same bell, same sound, different Aliena, she thought. She knew it could be heard all across the fields, as far away as the edge of the forest. Richard would by now be saying the Paternoster slowly under his breath, to measure the time he had to wait before sending his advance party.

Aliena and Elizabeth walked from the keep across the internal drawbridge to the lower courtyard. Elizabeth was pale with fear, but her mouth was set in a determined line. Aliena smiled at her to give her courage, then pulled up her hood again. So far she had not seen anyone familiar, but she was a well-known face all over the county, and someone was sure to recognize her sooner or later. If Michael Armstrong were to find out who she was he might smell a rat, dimwitted though he undoubtedly was. Several people gave her curious glances, but no one spoke to her.

She and Elizabeth went to the middle of the lower courtyard. Because the ground sloped somewhat, Aliena could see over the heads of the crowd and through the main gate to the fields outside. The advance party should be breaking cover about now, but she could see no sign of them. Oh, God, I hope there's no snag, she thought fearfully.

Elizabeth would need something to stand on while she addressed the people. Aliena told a manservant to fetch a mounting block from the stable. While they were waiting, an elderly woman looked at Aliena and said: "Why, it's the Lady Aliena! How nice to see you!"

Aliena's heart sank. She recognized the woman as a cook who had worked at the castle before the coming of the Hamleighs. She forced a smile and said: "Hello, Tilly, how are you?"

Tilly nudged her neighbor. "Hey, it's the Lady Aliena come back after all these years. Are you going to be mistress again, lady?"

Aliena did not want that thought to occur to Michael Armstrong. She looked around anxiously. Happily, Michael was not within earshot. However, one of his men-at-arms had heard the exchange and was staring at Aliena with a furrowed brow. Aliena looked back at him with a simulated expression of unconcern. The man only had one eye—which no doubt was why he had been left behind here instead of going off to war with William—and it suddenly seemed funny to Aliena to be stared at by a man with one eye, and she had to choke back a laugh. She realized she was slightly hysterical.

The manservant came back with the mounting block. The bell ceased to toll. Aliena made herself calm as Elizabeth stood on the block and the crowd went quiet.

Elizabeth said: "King Stephen and Duke Henry have made peace."

She paused, and a cheer went up. Aliena was looking through the gateway. Now, Richard, she thought; now is the time, don't leave it too late!

Elizabeth smiled and let the people cheer for a while, then she went on: "Stephen is to remain king until he dies, then Henry will succeed him."

Aliena scrutinized the guards on the towers and over the gatehouse. They looked relaxed. Where was Richard?

Elizabeth said: "The peace treaty will bring many changes in our lives."

Aliena saw the guards stiffen. One of them raised his hand to shade his eyes and peered out over the fields, while another turned and looked down into the courtyard as if hoping to catch the eye of the captain. But Michael Armstrong was listening intently to Elizabeth.

"The present and future kings have agreed that all lands shall be returned to those who possessed them in the time of the old King Henry."

That caused a buzz of comment in the crowd, as people speculated whether this change would affect the earldom of Shiring. Aliena noticed Michael Armstrong looking thoughtful. Through the gateway she at last saw the horses of Richard's advance party. Hurry, she thought, hurry! But they were coming at a steady trot, so as not to alarm the guards.

Elizabeth was saying: "We must all give thanks to God for this peace treaty. We should pray that King Stephen will rule wisely in his declining years, and that the young duke will keep his peace until God takes Stephen away. . . ." She was doing magnificently, but she was beginning to look troubled, as if she might be about to run out of things to say.

All the guards were looking outward, examining the approaching party. They had been told to expect such a group, and instructed to bring the leader to the countess immediately, so no action was required of them, but they were curious.

The one-eyed man turned around and looked through the gate, then turned back and stared at Aliena again, and she guessed he was frowning over the significance of her presence here and the approach of a troop of horsemen.

One of the guards on the battlements appeared to make a decision, and disappeared down a staircase.

The crowd was getting a little restless. Elizabeth was meandering magnificently, but they were impatient for hard news. She said: "This war started within a year of my birth, and like many young people up and down the kingdom I am looking forward to finding out what peace is like."

The guard from the battlements emerged from the base of a tower, walked briskly across the compound, and spoke to Michael Armstrong.

Through the gateway, Aliena could see that the horsemen were still a couple of hundred yards away. It was not close enough. She could have screamed in frustration. She would not be able to contain this situation much longer.

Michael Armstrong turned and looked through the gate, frowning. Then the one-eyed man pulled Michael's sleeve and said something, pointing at Aliena.

Aliena was afraid Michael would close the gates and raise the drawbridge before Richard could get in, but she did not know what she could do to prevent him. She wondered whether she had the nerve to throw herself at him before he could give the order. She still wore her dagger strapped to her left arm: she could even kill him. He turned away decisively. Aliena reached up and touched Elizabeth's elbow. "Stop Michael!" she hissed.

Elizabeth opened her mouth to speak, but no sound came out. She looked petrified by fear. Then her expression changed. She took a deep breath, tilted her head up, and spoke in a voice ringing with authority. "Michael Armstrong!"

Michael turned back.

This was the point of no return, Aliena realized. Richard was not quite close enough but she had run out of time. She said to Elizabeth: "Now! Tell them now!"

Elizabeth said: "I have surrendered this castle to the rightful earl of Shiring, Richard of Kingsbridge."

Michael stared unbelievingly at Elizabeth. "You can't do that!" he shouted.

Elizabeth said: "I command you all to lay down your weapons. There is to be no bloodshed."

Michael turned around and yelled: "Raise the drawbridge! Shut the gates!"

The men-at-arms rushed to do his bidding, but he had hesitated a moment too long. As the men reached the massive ironbound doors that would close the entrance arch, Richard's advance party clattered over the drawbridge and entered the compound. Most of Michael's men were not wearing armor and some of them did not even have their swords, and they scattered in front of the horsemen.

Elizabeth shouted: "Everyone keep calm. These messengers will confirm my orders."

There was a shout from the battlements: one of the guards cupped his hands around his mouth and yelled down: "Michael! Attack! We're being attacked! Scores of them!"

"Treachery!" Michael roared, and drew his sword. But two of Richard's men were on him instantly, their blades flashing. Blood gushed and he went down. Aliena looked away.

Some of Richard's men had taken possession of the gatehouse and the winding room. Two of them made it to the battlements, and Michael's guards surrendered to them.

Through the gateway Aliena saw the main force galloping across the fields toward the castle, and her spirits rose like the sun.

Elizabeth shouted at the top of her voice: "This is a peaceful surrender. No one is going to be hurt, I promise you. Just stay where you are."

Everyone stood stock-still, listening to the thunder as Richard's army pounded closer. Michael's men-at-arms looked confused and uncertain, but none of them did anything: their leader had fallen, and their countess had told them to surrender. The castle servants were paralyzed by the rapidity of events.

Then Richard came through the gateway on his war-horse.

It was a great moment, and Aliena's heart swelled with pride. Richard was handsome, smiling, and triumphant. Aliena shouted: "The rightful earl!" The men entering the castle behind Richard took up the cry, and it was repeated by some of the crowd in the court-yard—most of them had no love for William. Richard rode around the compound at a slow walk, waving and acknowledging the cheers.

Aliena thought about all she had gone through for the sake of this moment. She was thirty-four years old and she had spent half of those years fighting for this. The whole of my adult life, she thought; that's what I gave. She remembered stuffing wool into sacks until her hands were red and swollen and bleeding. She recalled the faces she had seen on the road, greedy and cruel and lascivious faces of men who would have killed her if she had given the least sign of weakness. She thought of how she had hardened her heart against dear Jack, and married Alfred instead; and she thought of the months during which she had slept on the floor at the foot of his bed like a dog; and all because he had promised to pay for weapons and armor so that Richard could fight to win back this castle. "There it is, Father," she said aloud. Nobody heard her: they were cheering too loud. "This is what you wanted," she said to her dead father, and there was bitterness as well as triumph in her heart. "I promised you this, and I kept my promise. I took care of Richard, and he fought all these years, and now we're home again at last, and Richard is the earl. Now . . ." Her voice rose to a shout, but everyone was shouting, and no one noticed the tears rolling down her cheeks. "Now, Father, I've done with you, so go to your grave, and let me live in peace!"

Chapter 16

REMIGIUS WAS ARROGANT, even in penury. He entered the wooden manor house at Hamleigh village with his head held high, and looked down his long nose at the huge, roughhewn wooden crucks supporting the roof, the wattle-and-daub walls, and the chimneyless open fire in the middle of the beaten-earth floor.

William watched him walk in. I may be down on my luck, but I'm not as far down as you, he thought, noting the monk's much-repaired sandals, the grubby robe, the unshaven chin and the unkempt hair. Remigius had never been a fat man but now he was thinner than ever. The haughty expression fixed on his face failed to conceal the lines of exhaustion or the purplish folds of defeat under his eyes. Remigius was not yet bowed, but he was very badly beaten.

"Bless you, my son," he said to William.

William was not having any of that. "What do you want, Remigius?" he said, deliberately insulting the monk by not calling him "Father" or "Brother."

Remigius flinched as if he had been struck. William guessed he had received a few taunts of that kind since he came down in the world. Remigius said: "The lands you gave to me as dean of the chapter at Shiring have been repossessed by Earl Richard."

"I'm not surprised," William replied. "Everything is to be returned to those who possessed it in the time of the old King Henry."

"But that leaves me with no means of support."

"You and a lot of other people," William said carelessly. "You'll have to go back to Kingsbridge."

Remigius's face paled with anger. "I can't do that," he said in a low voice.

"Why not?" said William, tormenting him.

"You know why not."

"Would Philip say you shouldn't prise secrets out of little girls? Does he think you betrayed him, by telling me where the outlaws' hideout was? Would he be angry with you for becoming the dean of a church that was to take the place of his own cathedral? Well, then I suppose you can't go back."

"Give me *something*," Remigius pleaded. "One village. A farm. A little church!"

"There are no rewards for losing, monk," William said harshly. He was enjoying this. "In the world outside the monastery, nobody looks after you. The ducks swallow the worms, and the foxes kill the ducks, and the men shoot the foxes, and the devil hunts the men."

Remigius's voice sank to a whisper. "What am I to do?"

William smiled and said: "Beg."

Remigius turned on his heel and left the house.

Still proud, William thought, but not for long. You'll beg.

It pleased him to see someone who had fallen harder than he himself. He would never forget the excruciating agony of standing outside the gate of his own castle and being refused admittance. He had been suspicious when he heard that Richard and some of his men had left Winchester; then when the peace pact was announced his unease had turned to alarm, and he had taken his knights and men and ridden hard to Earlscastle. There was a skeleton force guarding the castle, so he expected to find Richard camped in the fields, laying siege. When all appeared peaceful he had been relieved, and berated himself for overreacting to Richard's sudden disappearance.

When he got closer he saw that the drawbridge was up. He had reined in at the edge of the moat and shouted: "Open up for the earl!"

That was when Richard had appeared on the battlements and said: "The earl is inside."

It was like the ground falling away from under William's feet. He had always been afraid of Richard, always aware of him as a dangerous rival, but he had not felt himself especially vulnerable at this moment in time. He had thought the real danger would come when Stephen died and Henry came to the throne, which might be ten years away. Now, as he sat in a mean manor house brooding over his mistakes, he realized bitterly that Richard had in fact been very clever. He had slipped through a narrow gap. He could not be accused of breaching the king's peace, as the war was still on. His claim to the earldom had been legitimized by the terms of the peace treaty. And Stephen, aging and tired and defeated, had no energy left for further battles.

Richard had magnanimously released those of William's men-at-arms who wanted to continue in William's service. Waldo One-eye had told William how the castle had been taken. The treachery of Elizabeth was maddening, but for William it was the part played by Aliena that was most humiliating. The helpless little girl he had raped and tormented and thrown out of her home all those years ago had come back and taken her revenge. Every time he thought of that his stomach burned with bitterness as if he had drunk vinegar.

His first inclination had been to fight Richard. William could have kept his army, lived off the countryside, and extorted taxes and supplies from the peasants, fighting a running battle with his rival. But Richard held the castle, and he had time on his side, for William's supporter Stephen was old and beaten, and Richard was backed by the young Duke Henry, who would eventually become the second King Henry.

So William had decided to cut his losses. He had retired to the village of Hamleigh and moved back into the manor house where he had been brought up. Hamleigh, and the villages surrounding it, had been granted to his father thirty years ago. It was a holding that had never been part of the earldom, so Richard had no claim to it.

William hoped that if he kept his head down Richard would be satisfied with the revenge he had already taken, and would leave him alone. So far it had worked. However, William hated the village of Hamleigh. He hated the small neat houses, the excitable ducks on the pond, the pale gray stone church, the apple-cheeked children, the broad-hipped women and the strong, resentful men. He hated it for being humble, plain and poor, and he hated it because it symbolized his family's fall from power. He watched the plodding peasants begin the spring plowing, and estimated what his share of their crop would be that summer, and he found it meager. He went hunting in his few acres of forest and failed to start a single deer, and the forester said to him: "The boar is all you can hunt now, lord—the outlaws had the deer in the famine." He held court in the great hall of the manor house, with the wind whistling through the holes in its wattle-and-daub walls; and he gave harsh judgments and imposed large fines and ruled according to his whim; but it brought him little satisfaction.

He had abandoned the building of the grand new church at Shiring, of course. He could not afford to build a stone house for himself, let alone a church. The builders had stopped work when he had stopped paying them, and what had happened to them he did not know: perhaps they had all gone back to Kingsbridge to work for Prior Philip.

But now he was having nightmares.

They were all the same. He saw his mother in the place of the dead. She was bleeding from her ears and eyes, and when she opened her mouth to speak, more blood came out. The sight filled him with mortal terror. In broad daylight he could not say what it was about the dream that he feared, for she did not threaten him in any way. But at night, when she came to him, the fear possessed him totally, an irrational, hysterical, blind panic. Once as a boy he had waded into a pond that suddenly got deeper, and he had found himself below the surface and unable to breathe; and the over-powering need for air that had possessed him then was one of the indelible memories of his childhood; but this was ten times as bad. Trying to get away from his mother's bloody face was like trying to sprint in quicksand. He would come awake as if he had been thrown across the room, violently shocked, sweating and moaning, his body taut with agony from the racked-up tension. Walter would be at his bedside with a candle—William slept in the hall, separated from the men by a screen, for there was no bedroom here. "You cried out, lord," Walter would murmur. William would breathe hard, staring at the real bed and the real wall and the real Walter, while the power of the nightmare slowly faded to the point where he was no longer afraid; and then he would say: "It was nothing, a dream, go away." But he would be frightened to go back to sleep. And the next day the men would look at him as if he were bewitched.

A few days after his conversation with Remigius, he was sitting in the same hard chair, by the same smoky fire, when Bishop Waleran walked in.

William was startled. He had heard horses, but he had assumed it was Walter, coming back from the mill. He did not know what to do when he saw the bishop. Waleran had always been arrogant and superior, and time and time again he had made William feel foolish, clumsy and coarse. It was humiliating that Waleran should see the humble surroundings in which he now lived.

William did not get up to greet his visitor. "What do you want?" he said curtly. He had no reason to be polite: he wanted Waleran to get out as soon as possible.

The bishop ignored his rudeness. "The sheriff is dead," he said.

At first William did not see what he was getting at. "What's that to me?"

"There will be a new sheriff."

William was about to say *So what?* but he stopped himself. Waleran was concerned about who would be the new sheriff. And he had come to talk to William about it. That could only mean one thing, couldn't it? Hope rose in his breast, but he suppressed it fiercely: where Waleran was involved, high hopes often ended in frustration and disappointment. He said: "Who have you got in mind?"

"You."

It was the answer William had not dared to hope for. He wished he could believe in it. A clever and ruthless sheriff could be almost as important and influential as an earl or a bishop. This could be his way back to wealth and power. He forced himself to consider the snags. "Why would King Stephen appoint me?"

"You supported him against Duke Henry, and as a result you lost your earldom. I imagine he would like to recompense you."

"Nobody ever does anything out of gratitude," William said, repeating a saying of his mother's.

Waleran said: "Stephen can't be happy that the earl of Shiring is a man who fought against him. He might want his sheriff to be a countervailing force against Richard."

Now that made more sense. William felt excited against his will. He began to believe that he might actually get out of this hole in the ground called Hamleigh village. He would have a respectable force of knights and men-at-arms again, instead of the pitiful handful he now supported. He would preside over the county court at Shiring, and frustrate Richard's will. "The sheriff lives at Shiring Castle," he said longingly.

"You'd be rich again," Waleran added.

"Yes." Properly exploited, the sheriff's post could be hugely profitable. William would make almost as much money as he had when he was earl. But he wondered why Waleran had mentioned it.

A moment later Waleran answered the question. "You would be able to finance the new church, after all."

So that was it. Waleran never did anything without an ulterior motive. He wanted William to be sheriff so that William could build him a church. But William was willing to go along with the plan. If he could finish the church in memory of his mother, perhaps the nightmares would stop. "Do you really think it can be done?" he said eagerly.

Waleran nodded. "It will cost money, of course, but I think it can be done."

"Money?" William said with sudden anxiety. "How much?"

"It's hard to say. In somewhere like Lincoln or Bristol, the shrievalty would cost you five or six hundred pounds; but the sheriffs of those towns are richer than cardinals. For a little place such as Shiring, if you're the candidate the king wants—which I can take care of—you can probably get it for a hundred pounds."

"A hundred pounds!" William's hopes collapsed. He had been afraid of disappointment, right from the start. "If I had a hundred pounds I wouldn't be living like this!" he said bitterly.

"You can get it," Waleran said lightly.

"Who from?" William was struck by a thought. "Will you give it to me?"

"Don't be stupid," Waleran said with infuriating condescension. "That's what Jews are for."

William realized, with a familiar mixture of hope and resentment, that once again the bishop was right.

It was two years since the first cracks had appeared, and Jack had not found a solution to the problem. Worse still, identical cracks had appeared in the first bay of the nave. There was something crucially wrong with his design. The structure was strong enough to support the weight of the vault, but not to resist the winds that blew so hard against the high walls.

He stood on the scaffolding far above the ground, staring close-range at the new cracks, brooding. He needed to think of a way of bracing the upper part of the wall so that it would not move with the wind.

He reflected on the way the lower part of the wall was strengthened. In the outer wall of the aisle were strong, thick piers which were connected to the nave wall by half-arches hidden in the aisle roof. The half-arches and the piers propped up the wall at a distance, like remote buttresses. Because the props were hidden, the nave looked light and graceful.

He needed to devise a similar system for the upper part of the wall. He could make a two-story side aisle, and simply repeat the remote buttressing; but that would block the light coming in through the clerestory—and the whole idea of the new style of building was to bring more light into the church.

Of course, it was not the aisle as such that did the work: the support came from the heavy piers in the side wall and the connecting half-arches. The aisle concealed these structural elements. If only he could build piers and half-arches to support the clerestory *without* incorporating them into an aisle, he could solve the problem at a stroke.

A voice called him from the ground.

He frowned. He had been on to something before he was interrupted, he felt, but now it had gone. He looked down. Prior Philip was calling him.

He went into the turret and descended the spiral staircase. Philip was waiting for him at the bottom. The prior was so angry he was steaming. "Richard has betrayed me!" he said without preamble.

Jack was surprised. "How?"

Philip did not answer the question at first. "After all I've done for him," he raged. "I bought Aliena's wool when everyone else was bent on cheating her—if it hadn't been for me she might never have got started. Then when that fell apart I got him a job as Head of the Watch. And last November I tipped him off about the peace treaty, and that enabled him to seize Earlscastle. And now that he's won back the earldom, and he's ruling in splendor, he has turned his back on me."

Jack had never seen Philip quite so livid. The prior's shaved head was red with indignation and he was spluttering as he spoke. "In what way has Richard betrayed you?" Jack said.

Once again Philip ignored the question. "I always knew Richard was a weak character. He gave Aliena very little support, over the years—just took from her what he wanted and never considered her needs. But I didn't think he was an out-and-out villain."

"What exactly has he done?"

At last Philip told him. "He has refused to give us access to the quarry."

Jack was shocked. That was an act of astonishing ingratitude. "But how does he justify himself?"

"Everything is supposed to revert to those who possessed it in the time of the first King Henry. And the quarry was granted to us by King Stephen."

Richard's greed was remarkable, but Jack could not get as angry as Philip. They had built half the cathedral now, mostly with stone they had had to pay for, and they would continue to get by somehow. "Well, I suppose Richard is in the right, strictly speaking," he said argumentatively.

Philip was outraged. "How can you say such a thing?"

"It's a bit like what you did to me," Jack said. "After I brought you the Weeping Madonna, and produced a wonderful design for your new cathedral, and built a town wall to protect you from William, you announced that I couldn't live with the woman who is the mother of my children. There's ingratitude."

Philip was shocked by this parallel. "That's completely different!" he protested. "I don't want you to live apart. It's Waleran who has blocked the annulment. But God's law says you must not commit adultery."

"I'm sure Richard would say something similar," Jack persisted. "It's not Richard who has ordered the reversion of property. He is just enforcing the law."

The noon bell rang.

"There's a difference between God's laws and men's laws," Philip said.

"But we must live by both," Jack countered. "And now I'm going to have dinner with the mother of my children."

He walked away and left Philip standing there looking upset. He did not really think Philip was as ungrateful as Richard, but it had relieved his feelings to pretend that he did. He decided he would ask Aliena about the quarry. It might be that Richard could be persuaded to hand it over after all. She would know.

He left the priory close and walked through the streets to the house where he lived with Martha. Aliena and the children were in the kitchen, as usual. The famine had ended with a good harvest last year, and food was no longer desperately scarce: there was wheat bread and roast mutton on the table.

Jack kissed the children. Sally gave him a soft childish kiss, but Tommy, now eleven years old and impatient to grow up, offered his cheek and looked embarrassed. Jack smiled but said nothing: he remembered when he had thought kissing was silly.

Aliena looked troubled. Jack sat on the bench beside her and said: "Philip's in a rage because Richard won't give him the quarry."

"That's terrible," Aliena said mildly. "How ungrateful of Richard."

"Do you think he might be persuaded to change his mind?"

"I really don't know," she said. She had a distracted air.

Jack said: "You don't seem very interested in the problem."

She looked at him challengingly. "No, I'm not."

He knew this mood. "You'd better tell me what's on your mind."

She stood up. "Let's go into the back room."

With a regretful look at the leg of mutton, Jack left the table and followed her into the bedroom. They left the door open, as usual, to avoid suspicion if someone should come into the house. Aliena sat on the bed and folded her arms across her chest. "I've made an important decision," she began.

She looked so grave that Jack wondered what on earth it could be.

"I've lived most of my adult life under two shadows," she began. "One was the vow I made to my father when he was dying. The other is my relationship with you."

Jack said: "But now you've fulfilled your vow to your father."

"Yes. And I want to be free of the other burden, too. I've decided to leave you."

Jack's heart seemed to stop. He knew she did not say such things lightly: she was serious. He stared at her, speechless. He was disoriented by the announcement: he had never dreamed she could leave him. How had this dreadful thing crept up on him? He said the first thing that came into his head: "Is there someone else?"

"Don't be daft."

"Then why?"

"Because I can't take it anymore," she said, and her eyes brimmed with tears. "We've been waiting ten years for this annulment. It's never going to come, Jack. We're doomed to live this way forever—unless we part."

"But . . ." He cast around for something to say. Her announcement was so devastating that arguing with it seemed hopeless, like trying to walk away from a hurricane. Nevertheless he tried. "Isn't this better than nothing, better than separation?"

"In the end, no."

"But how will it change anything if you move away?"

"I might meet someone else, and fall in love again, and live a normal life," she said, but she was crying.

"You'll still be married to Alfred."

"But nobody will know or care. I could be married by a parish priest who has never heard of Alfred Builder and who wouldn't consider the marriage valid if he knew of it."

"I don't believe you're saying this. I can't take it in."

"Ten years, Jack. I've been waiting ten years to have a normal life with you. I won't wait any longer."

The words fell on him like blows. She carried on talking, but he no longer understood her. All he could think about was life without her. He interrupted her: "I've never loved anyone else, you see."

She winced, as if she was in pain, but she went on with what she was saying. "I need a few weeks to arrange everything. I'll get a house in Winchester. I want the children to get used to the idea before their new life begins—"

"You're going to take my children," he said stupidly.

She nodded. "I'm sorry," she said. For the first time her resolve seemed to waver. "I know they'll miss you. But they need a normal life too."

Jack could not take any more. He turned away.

Aliena said: "Don't walk out on me. We ought to talk some more. Jack—"

He went out without replying.

He heard her cry out after him: "Jack!"

He walked through the living room, not looking at the children, and left the house. In a daze he walked back to the cathedral, not knowing where else to go. The builders were still at lunch. He was unable to weep: this was too bad for mere tears. Without thinking, he climbed the staircase in the north transept, all the way up to the top, and stepped out onto the roof.

There was a stiff breeze up here, although at ground level it had hardly been noticeable. Jack looked down. If he fell from here he would land on the lean-to roof of the aisle alongside the transept. He would probably die, but it was not certain. He walked to the crossing and stood where the roof suddenly ended in a sheer drop. If the new-style cathedral was not structurally sound, and Aliena was leaving him, he had nothing left to live for.

Her decision was not as sudden as it seemed, of course. She had been discontented for years—they both had. But they had got accustomed to unhappiness. Winning back Earlscastle had shaken Aliena's torpor, and reminded her that she was in charge of her own life. It had destabilized a situation that was already unsteady; rather in the way that the storm had caused cracks in the cathedral walls.

He looked at the wall of the transept and the roof of the side aisle. He could see the heavy buttresses jutting out from the wall of the side aisle, and he could visualize the half-arch, under the roof of the aisle, connecting the buttress to the foot of the clerestory. What would solve the problem, he had thought just before Philip had distracted him this morning, was a taller buttress, perhaps another twenty feet high, with a second half-arch leaping across the gap to the point on the wall where the cracks were appearing. The arch and the tall buttress would brace the top half of the church and keep the wall rigid when the wind blew.

That would probably solve the problem. The trouble was, if he built a two-story aisle to hide the extended buttress and the secondary half-arch, he would lose light; and if he did not . . .

If I don't, he thought, so what?

He was possessed by a feeling that nothing mattered very much, since his life was falling apart; and in that mood he could not see anything wrong with the idea of naked buttressing. Standing up here on the roof, he could easily picture what it would look like. A line of sturdy stone columns would rise up from the side wall of the aisle. From the top of each column, a half-arch would spring across empty space to the clerestory. Perhaps he would put a decorative pinnacle on top of each column, above the springing of the arch. Yes, that would look better.

It was a revolutionary idea, to build big strengthening members in a position where they would be starkly visible. But it was part of the new style to show how the building was being held up.

Anyway, his instinct said this was right.

The more he thought about it, the better he liked it. He visualized the church from the west. The half-arches would look like the wings of a flight of birds, all in a line, just about to take off. They need not be massive. As long as they were well made they could be slender and elegant, light yet strong, just like a bird's wing. Winged buttresses, he thought, for a church so light it could fly.

I wonder, he thought. I wonder if it would work.

A gust of wind suddenly unbalanced him. He teetered on the edge of the roof. For a moment he thought he was going to fall to his death. Then he regained his balance and stepped back from the edge, his heart pounding.

Slowly and carefully, he made his way back along the roof to the turret door, and went down.

Work had stopped completely on the church at Shiring. Prior Philip caught himself gloating a little over that. After all the times he had looked out disconsolately onto a deserted building site, he could not help feeling pleased that the same thing had now happened to his enemies. Alfred Builder had only had time to demolish the old church and lay the foundations for the new chancel before William had been deposed and the money had dried up. Philip told himself that it was sinful to be glad about the ruin of a church. However, it was obviously God's will that the cathedral should be built in Kingsbridge, not Shiring—the bad fortune that had dogged Waleran's project seemed a very clear sign of divine intentions.

Now that the town's biggest church had been knocked down, the county court was held in the great hall at the castle. Philip rode up the hill with Jonathan by his side. He had made Jonathan his personal assistant, in the shake-up that had followed the defection of Remigius. Philip had been shocked by Remigius's perfidy, but he had been glad to see the back of him. Ever since Philip had beaten Remigius in the election, Remigius had been a thorn in his flesh. The priory was a nicer place to live now that he had gone.

Milius was the new sub-prior. However, he continued to fulfill the role of treasurer, and had a staff of three under him in the treasury. Since Remigius had gone, nobody could figure out what he used to do all day.

Philip got deep satisfaction out of working with Jonathan. He enjoyed explaining to him how the monastery was run, educating him in the ways of the world, and showing him how best to deal with people. The lad was generally well liked, but he could sometimes be abrasive, and he could easily raise the hackles of unselfconfident people. He had to learn that those who treated him in a hostile way did so out of weakness. He saw the hostility and reacted angrily, instead of seeing the weakness and giving reassurance.

Jonathan had a quick brain, and often surprised Philip by the rapidity with which he picked things up. Philip sometimes caught himself in the sin of pride, thinking how like himself Jonathan was.

He had brought Jonathan with him today to learn how the

county court operated. Philip was going to ask the sheriff to order Richard to open the quarry to the priory. He was quite sure Richard was in the wrong legally. The new law about the restoration of property to those who had possessed it in the time of the old King Henry did not affect the priory's rights. Its object was to allow Duke Henry to replace Stephen's earls with his own, and thus reward people who had supported him. It was obviously not meant to apply to monasteries. Philip was confident of winning the case, but there was an unknown factor: the old sheriff had died and his replacement would be announced today. No one knew who it would be, but everyone assumed the job would go to one of the three or four leading citizens of Shiring: David Merchant the silk seller; Rees Welsh, a priest who had worked at the king's court; Giles Lionheart, a knight with landholdings just outside the town; or Hugh the Bastard, the illegitimate son of the bishop of Salisbury. Philip hoped it would be Rees, not because the man was a countryman of his, but because he was likely to favor the church. But Philip was not overly worried: any of the four would rule in his favor, he thought.

They rode into the castle. It was not very heavily fortified. Because the earl of Shiring had a separate castle outside town, Shiring had escaped battle for several generations. The castle was more of an administrative center, with offices and quarters for the sheriff and his men, and dungeons for offenders. Philip and Jonathan stabled their horses and went into the largest building, the great hall.

The trestle tables that normally formed a T-shape had been rearranged. The top of the T remained, raised above the level of the rest of the hall by a dais; and the other tables were ranged down the sides of the hall, so that opposing plaintiffs could sit well apart and avoid the temptation to physical violence.

The hall was already full. Bishop Waleran was there, up on the dais, looking malevolent. To Philip's surprise, William Hamleigh was sitting with him, talking to the bishop out of the corner of his mouth as they watched people coming in. What was William doing here? For nine months he had been lying low, hardly moving from his village, and Philip—together with many other people in the county—had entertained the hope that he might stay there forever. But here he was, sitting on the bench as if he were still the earl. Philip wondered what mean-minded, ruthless, greedy little scheme had brought him to the county court today.

Philip and Jonathan sat down at the side of the room and waited for the proceedings to begin. There was a busy, optimistic air to the court. Now that the war had come to an end, the elite of the country had turned their attention back to the business of creating wealth. It was a fertile land and it quickly repaid their efforts: a bumper harvest was expected this year. The price of wool was up. Philip had reemployed almost all the builders who had left at the height of the famine. Everywhere the people who had survived were the younger, stronger, healthier individuals, and now they were full of hope, and here in the great hall of Shiring Castle it showed in the tilt of their heads, the pitch of their voices, the men's new boots and the women's fancy headgear, and the fact that they were prosperous enough to own something worth arguing in court about.

They stood up as the sheriff's deputy walked in with Earl Richard. The two men mounted the dais and then, still standing, the deputy began to read the royal writ appointing the new sheriff. As he went through the initial verbiage, Philip looked around at the four presumed candidates. He hoped the winner had courage: he would need it, to stand up for the law in the presence of such powerful local barons as Bishop Waleran, Earl Richard and Lord William. The successful candidate presumably knew he had been appointed—there was no reason to keep it secret—but none of the four looked very animated. Normally the appointee would stand beside the deputy as the proclamation was read, but the only people up there with him were Richard, Waleran and William. The appalling thought crossed Philip's mind that Waleran might have been made sheriff. Then he was even more horrified as he heard: ". . . appoint as sheriff of Shiring my servant William of Hamleigh, and I order all men to assist him . . ."

Philip looked at Jonathan and said: "William!"

There were sounds of surprise and disapproval from the townspeople.

Jonathan said: "How did he do it?"

"He must have paid for it."

"Where did he get the money?"

"Borrowed it, I suppose."

William moved to the wooden throne in the middle of the top table, smiling. He had once been a handsome young man, Philip remembered. He was still under forty, just, but he looked older. His body was too heavy, and his complexion was flushed with wine; and the lively strength and optimism that makes young faces attractive had gone, to be replaced by a look of dissipation.

As William sat down, Philip stood up.

Jonathan got up too and whispered: "Are we leaving?"

"Follow me," Philip hissed.

The room fell silent. All eyes were on them as they walked across the courtroom. The public crowd parted for them to pass through. They reached the door and went out. A buzz of comment broke out as the door closed behind them.

Jonathan said: "We had no chance of success with William in the chair."

"Worse than that," Philip said. "If we had pressed our case we might have lost other rights."

"My soul, I never thought of that."

Philip nodded grimly. "With William as sheriff, Waleran as bishop, and the faithless Richard as earl, it is now completely impossible for Kingsbridge Priory to get justice in this county. They can do anything they like to us."

While a stableboy saddled their mounts, Philip said: "I'm going to petition the king to make Kingsbridge a borough. That way we'd have our own court, and we'd pay our taxes directly to the king. In effect, we would be out of the jurisdiction of the sheriff."

"You've always been against that, in the past," Jonathan said.

"I've been against it because it makes the town as powerful as the priory. But now I think we may have to accept that as the price of independence. The alternative is William."

"Will King Stephen give us borough status?"

"He might, at a price. But if he doesn't, perhaps Henry will when he becomes king."

They mounted their horses and rode dejectedly through the town.

They went out through the gate and passed the rubbish dump on the waste ground just outside. A few decrepit people were picking over the refuse, looking for anything they could eat, wear or burn for fuel. Philip glanced at them without interest, but one of them caught his eye. A familiar tall figure was stooping over a heap of rags, sorting through them. Philip reined in his horse. Jonathan pulled up beside him.

"Look," Philip said.

Jonathan followed his gaze. After a moment he said quietly: "Remigius."

Philip watched. Waleran and William had obviously thrown Remigius out some time ago, when funds for the new church dried up. They had no further need of him. Remigius had betrayed Philip, betrayed the priory, and betrayed Kingsbridge, all in the hope of becoming dean of Shiring; but his prize had turned to ashes.

Philip turned his horse off the road and crossed the waste ground to where Remigius stood. Jonathan followed. There was a bad smell that seemed to rise from the ground like fog. As he approached, he saw that Remigius was skeletally thin. His habit was filthy and he was barefoot. He was sixty years old, and he had been at Kingsbridge Priory all his adult life: no one had ever taught him how to live rough. Philip saw him pull a pair of leather shoes out of the trash. There were huge holes in the soles, but Remigius looked at them with the expression of a man who has found buried treasure. As he was about to try them on, he saw Philip.

He straightened up. His face evidenced the struggle between shame and defiance in his heart. After a moment he said: "Well, have you come to gloat?"

"No," Philip said softly. His old enemy was such a pitiful sight that Philip felt nothing but compassion for him. He got off his horse and took a flask out of his saddlebag. "I've come to offer you a drink of wine."

Remigius did not want to accept it but he was too starved to resist. He hesitated only for a moment, then snatched the flask. He sniffed the wine suspiciously, then put the flask to his mouth. Once he had begun drinking, he could not stop. There was only half a pint left and he drained it in a few moments. He lowered the flask and staggered a little.

Philip took it from him and put it back into his saddlebag. "You'd better have something to eat, as well," he said. He brought out a small loaf.

Remigius took the proffered bread and began to stuff it into his mouth. He obviously had not eaten for days, and he probably had not had a decent meal for weeks. He could die soon, Philip thought sadly; if not of starvation, then of shame.

The bread went down fast. Philip said: "Do you want to come back?"

He heard a sharp intake of breath from Jonathan. Like a good many of the monks, Jonathan had hoped never to see Remigius again. He probably thought Philip was mad to offer to take him back.

A hint of the old Remigius showed for a moment, and he said: "Come back? In what position?"

Philip shook his head sorrowfully. "You'll never hold a position of any kind in my priory, Remigius. Come back as a plain, humble monk. Ask God to forgive your sins, and live the rest of your days in prayer and contemplation, preparing your soul for heaven."

Remigius tilted his head back, and Philip expected a scornful refusal; but it never came. Remigius opened his mouth to speak and then closed it again and looked down. Philip stood still and quiet, watching, wondering what would happen. There was a long moment of silence. Philip was holding his breath. When Remigius looked up again, his face was wet with tears. "Yes, please, father," he said. "I want to come home."

Philip felt a glow of joy. "Come on, then," he said. "Get on my horse."

Remigius looked flabbergasted.

Jonathan said: "Father! What are you doing?"

Philip said to Remigius: "Go on, do as I say."

Jonathan was horrified. "But, father, how will you travel?"

"I'll walk," Philip said happily. "One of us must."

"Let Remigius walk!" Jonathan said in a tone of outrage.

"Let him ride," Philip said. "He's pleased God today."

"What about you? Haven't you pleased God more than Remigius?"

"Jesus said there's more joy in heaven over one sinner who repents than over ninety-nine righteous people," Philip countered. "Don't you remember the parable of the prodigal son? When he came home, his father killed the fatted calf. The angels are rejoicing over Remigius's tears. The least I can do is give him my horse."

He took the bridle and led the way over the waste ground to the road. Jonathan followed. When they reached the road, Jonathan dismounted and said: "Please, father, take my horse, then, and let me walk!"

Philip turned to him and spoke a little sternly. "Now get back on your horse, stop arguing with me, and just *think* about what is being done and why."

Jonathan looked puzzled, but he mounted again, and said no more.

They turned toward Kingsbridge. It was twenty miles away. Philip began to walk. He felt wonderful. The return of Remigius more than compensated for the quarry. I lost in court, he thought, but that was only about stones. What I gained was something infinitely more valuable.

Today I won a man's soul.

III

New ripe apples floated in the barrel, shining red and yellow while the sun glinted off the water. Sally, nine years old and excitable, leaned over the rim of the barrel with her hands clasped behind her back and tried to pick up an apple in her teeth. The apple bobbed away, her face plunged into the water, and she came away spluttering and squealing with laughter. Aliena smiled thinly and wiped her little girl's face.

It was a warm afternoon in late summer, a saint's day and a holiday, and most of the town had gathered in the meadow across the river for the apple bobbing. This was the kind of occasion that Aliena had always enjoyed, but the fact that it would be her last saint's day in Kingsbridge was constantly on her mind, weighing down her spirits. She was still determined to leave Jack, but since she had made the decision she had begun to feel, in advance, the pain of loss.

Tommy was hovering near the barrel, and Jack called out: "Go on, Tommy—have a go!"

"Not just yet," he replied.

At the age of eleven Tommy knew he was smarter than his sister and he thought he was ahead of most other people too. He watched for a while, studying the technique of those who were successful at apple bobbing. Aliena watched him watching. She loved him specially. Jack had been about this age when she had first met him, and Tommy was so like Jack as a boy. Looking at him made her nostalgic for childhood. Jack wanted Tommy to be a builder, but Tommy had not yet shown any interest in construction. However, there was plenty of time.

Eventually he stepped up to the barrel. He bent over it and put his head down slowly, mouth wide open. He pushed his chosen apple under the surface, submerging his whole face, and then came up triumphantly with the apple between his teeth.

Tommy would be successful at whatever he put his mind to. There was a little of his grandfather, Earl Bartholomew, in his makeup. He had a very strong will and a somewhat inflexible sense of right and wrong.

It was Sally who had inherited Jack's easygoing nature and contempt for man-made rules. When Jack told the children stories, Sally always sympathized with the underdog, whereas Tommy was more likely to pronounce judgment on him. Each child had the personality of one parent and the appearance of the other: happy-go-lucky Sally had Aliena's regular features and dark tangled curls, and determined Tommy had Jack's carrot-colored hair, white skin and blue eyes.

Now Tommy cried: "Here comes Uncle Richard!"

Aliena spun around and followed his gaze. Sure enough, her brother the earl was riding into the meadow with a handful of knights and squires. Aliena was horrified. How did he have the nerve to show his face here after what he had done to Philip over the quarry?

He came over to the barrel, smiling at everyone and shaking hands. "Try to bob an apple, Uncle Richard," said Tommy. "You could do it!"

Richard dipped his head into the barrel and came up with an apple in his strong white teeth and his blond beard soaking wet. He had always been better at games than at real life, Aliena thought.

She was not going to let him carry on as if he had done nothing wrong. Others might be afraid to say anything because he was the earl, but to her he was just her foolish little brother. He came over to kiss her, but she pushed him away and said: "How could you steal the quarry from the priory?"

Jack, seeing a quarrel coming, took the children's hands and moved away.

Richard looked stung. "All property has reverted to those who possessed it—"

"Don't give me that, Aliena interrupted. "After all Philip has done for you!"

"The quarry is part of my birthright," he said. He took her aside and began to speak in low tones so that no one else could hear. "Besides, I need the money I get by selling the stones, Allie."

"That's because you go hunting and hawking all the time!"

"But what should I do?"

"You should make the land produce wealth! There's so much to be done—repairing the damage caused by the war and the famine, bringing in new farming methods, clearing woodland and draining swamps—that's how to increase your wealth! Not by stealing the quarry that King Stephen gave to Kingsbridge Priory."

"I've never taken anything that wasn't mine."

"You've never done anything else!" Aliena flared. She was

angry enough now to say things that were better left unsaid. "You've never worked for anything. You took my money for your stupid weapons, you took the job Philip gave you, you took the earldom when it was handed to you on a plate by me. Now you can't even run it without *taking* things that don't belong to you!" She turned away and stormed off.

Richard came after her, but someone waylaid him, bowing and asking him how he was. Aliena heard him make a polite reply, then get embroiled in a conversation. So much the better: she had said her piece and did not want to argue with him any further. She reached the bridge and looked back. Someone else was talking to him now. He waved at her, indicating that he still wanted to speak to her, but he was stuck. She saw Jack, Tommy and Sally beginning a game with a stick and a ball. She stared at them, playing together in the sunshine, and she felt she could not bear to separate them. But how else, she thought, can I lead a normal life?

She crossed the bridge and entered the town. She wanted to be alone for a while.

She had taken a house in Winchester, a big place with a shop on the ground floor, a living room upstairs, a separate bedchamber, and a large storeroom at the end of the yard for her cloth. But the closer she got to moving, the less she wanted to do it.

The streets of Kingsbridge were hot and dusty, and the air was full of the flies that bred on the innumerable dunghills. All the shops were closed and the houses were locked up. The town was deserted. Everyone was in the meadow.

She went to Jack's house. That was where the others would come when the apple bobbing was over. The door of the house stood open. She frowned in annoyance. Who had left it like that? Too many people had keys: herself, Jack, Richard and Martha. There was nothing much to steal. Aliena certainly did not have her money there: for years now Philip had let her keep it in the priory treasury. But the place would be full of flies.

She stepped inside. It was dark and cool. Flies danced in the air in the middle of the room, bluebottles crawled over the linen and a pair of wasps disputed angrily around the stopper of the honeypot.

And Alfred was sitting at the table.

Aliena gave a small scream of fright, then recovered herself and said: "How did you get in?"

"I've got a key."

He had kept it a long time, Aliena thought. She looked at him. His broad shoulders were bony and his face had a shrunken look. She said: "What are you doing here?"

"I came to see you."

She found she was trembling, not from fear but from anger. "I don't want to see you, now or ever again," she spat. "You treated me like a dog, and then when Jack took pity on you and hired you, you betrayed his trust and took all his craftsmen to Shiring."

"I need money," he said, with a mixture of pleading and defiance in his voice.

"Then work."

"Building has stopped at Shiring. I can't get a job here at Kingsbridge."

"Then go to London—go to Paris!"

He persisted with ox-like stubbornness. "I thought you would help me out."

"There's nothing for you here. You'd better go away."

"Have you no pity?" he said, and now the defiance was gone and the tone was all pleading.

She leaned on the table to steady herself. "Alfred, don't you understand that I *hate* you?"

"Why?" he said. He looked injured, as if it came as a surprise to him.

Dear God, he's stupid, she thought; it's the nearest he's got to an excuse. "Go to the monastery if you want charity," she said wearily. "Prior Philip's capacity for forgiveness is superhuman. Mine isn't."

"But you're my *wife*," Alfred said.

That was rich. "I'm not your wife," she hissed. "You're not my husband. You never were. Now get out of this house."

To her surprise he grabbed her by the hair. "You are my wife," he said. He pulled her to him over the table, and with his free hand he grasped her breast and squeezed hard.

Aliena was taken completely by surprise. This was the last thing she had expected from a man who had slept in the same room as her for nine months without ever managing to perform the sexual act. Automatically she screamed and pulled away from him, but he had a firm grip on her hair and he jerked her back. "There's nobody to hear you scream," he said. "They're all across the river."

She was suddenly terribly afraid. They were alone, and he was very strong. After all the miles she had covered on the roads, all the years she had risked her neck traveling, she was being attacked at home by the man she had married!

He saw the fear in her eyes and said: "Scared, are you? Perhaps you'd better be nice." Then he kissed her mouth. She bit his lip as hard as she could. He gave a roar of pain.

She did not see the punch coming. It exploded on her cheek with such force that she had the terrified thought that he must have smashed her bones. For a moment she lost her vision and her balance. She reeled away from the table and felt herself falling. The rushes on the floor softened the impact as she hit the ground. She shook her head to clear it and reached for the knife strapped to her left arm. Before she could draw it, both her wrists were seized, and she heard Alfred say: "I know about that little dagger. I've seen you undress, remember?" He released her hands, punched her face again, and grabbed the dagger himself.

Aliena tried to wriggle away. He sat on her legs and put his left hand to her throat. She thrashed her arms. Suddenly the point of the dagger was an inch from her eyeball. "Be still, or I'll put out your eyes," he said.

She froze. The idea of being blind terrified her. She had seen men who had been blinded as a punishment. They walked the streets begging, their empty sockets staring horribly at passersby. Small boys tormented them, pinching them and tripping them until they gave in to rage and tried in vain to catch hold of their tormentors, which made the game even better. They generally died within a year or two.

"I thought that would calm you down," Alfred said.

Why was he doing this? He had never had any lust for her. Was it just that he was defeated and angry, and she was vulnerable? Did she stand for the world that had rejected him?

He leaned forward, straddling her, with his knees either side of her hips, keeping the knife at her eye. Once again he put his face close to hers. "Now," he said. "Be nice." He kissed her again.

His unshaven face scratched her skin. His breath smelled of beer and onions. She kept her mouth closed tight.

"That's not nice," he said. "Kiss me back."

He kissed her again, and brought the knife point even closer. When it touched her eyelid she moved her lips. The taste of his mouth sickened her. He thrust his rough tongue between her lips. She felt as if she might throw up, and tried desperately to suppress the feeling, for fear he would kill her.

He pulled away from her again, but kept the knife at her face. "Now," he said. "Feel this." He took her hand and pulled it under the skirt of his tunic. She touched his organ. "Hold it," he said. She grasped it. "Now rub it gently."

She obeyed him. It occurred to her that if she could pleasure him this way she might avoid being penetrated. She looked fearfully at his face. He was flushed and his eyes were hooded. She stroked him all the way down to the root, remembering that Jack was driven wild by that.

She was afraid she would never be able to enjoy this again, and tears came to her eyes.

He jerked the knife dangerously. "Not so hard!" he said.

She concentrated.

Then the door opened.

Her heart leaped with hope. A wedge of bright sunlight fell across the room and shone dazzlingly through her tears. Alfred froze. She pulled her hand away.

They both looked toward the door. Who was it? Aliena could not see. Not one of the children, please, God, she prayed; I would feel so ashamed. She heard a roar of rage. It was a man's voice. She blinked away her tears and recognized her brother Richard.

Poor Richard: it was almost worse than if it had been Tommy. Richard, who had a scar instead of a lobe on his left ear to remind him of the terrible scene he had witnessed when he was fourteen years old. Now he was witnessing another. How would he ever bear it?

Alfred started to get to his feet, but Richard was too quick for him. Aliena saw Richard cross the little room in a blur and lash out with his booted foot, catching Alfred full on the jaw. Alfred crashed back against the table. Richard went after him, trampling on Aliena without noticing, lashing out at Alfred with his feet and fists. Aliena scrambled out of the way. Richard's face was a mask of ungovernable fury. He did not look at Aliena. He did not care about her, she understood. He was enraged, not about what Alfred had done to Aliena today, but because of what William and Walter had done to him, Richard, eighteen years ago. He had been young and weak and helpless then, but now he was a big strong man and a seasoned fighter, and he had at last found a target for the mad rage he had nursed inside for all those years. He hit Alfred again and again, with both fists. Alfred staggered back around the table, trying feebly to defend himself with his raised arms. Richard caught him on the chin with a powerful swing, and Alfred fell backward.

He lay on the rushes, looking up, terrified. Aliena was frightened by her brother's violence, and said: "That's enough, Richard!" Richard ignored her and stepped forward to kick Alfred. Then Alfred suddenly realized that he still had Aliena's knife in his hand. He dodged, came swiftly to his feet and lashed out with the knife. Taken by surprise, Richard jumped back. Alfred lunged at him again, driving him back across the room. The two men were the same height and build, Aliena saw. Richard was a fighting man but

Alfred was armed: they were now unnervingly well matched. Aliena was suddenly afraid for her brother. What would happen if Alfred overcame him? She would have to fight Alfred herself, then.

She looked around for a weapon. Her eyes lit on the pile of firewood beside the hearth. She snatched up a heavy log.

Alfred lunged at Richard again. Richard dodged; then, when Alfred's arm was at full stretch, Richard grabbed his wrist and pulled. Alfred staggered forward, off balance. Richard hit him several times, very fast, with both fists, punching his face and body. There was a savage grin on Richard's face, the smile of a man who is taking revenge. Alfred began to whimper, and raised his arms to protect himself again.

Richard hesitated, breathing hard. Aliena thought it would end then. But suddenly Alfred struck again, with surprising speed, and this time the point of the knife grazed Richard's cheek. Richard jumped back, stung. Alfred moved in with the knife raised high. Aliena saw that Alfred would kill Richard. She ran at Alfred, swinging the log with all her might. She missed his head but struck his right elbow. She heard the crack as wood connected with bone. The blow numbed Alfred's hand and the knife fell from his fingers.

The way it ended was dreadfully quick.

Richard bent, swept up Aliena's knife, and with the same motion brought it up under Alfred's guard and stabbed him in the chest with terrific force.

The dagger sank in up to the hilt.

Aliena stared, horrified. It was a terrible blow. Alfred screamed like a stuck pig. Richard pulled the knife out, and Alfred's blood squirted out of the hole in his chest. Alfred opened his mouth to scream again, but no sound came. His face turned white and then gray, his eyes closed, and he fell to the ground. Blood soaked into the rushes.

Aliena knelt beside him. His eyelids fluttered. He was still breathing, but his life was draining from him. She looked up at Richard, standing over them both, breathing hard. "He's dying," she said.

Richard nodded. He was not much moved. "I've seen better men die," he said. "I've killed men who deserved it less."

Aliena was shocked at his harshness, but she did not say anything. She had just remembered the first time Richard killed a man. It was after William had taken over the castle, and she and Richard had been on the road to Winchester, and two thieves had attacked them. Aliena had stabbed one of the thieves, but she had forced

Richard, who was only fifteen, to deliver the coup de grâce. If he's heartless, she thought guiltily, who made him so?

She looked at Alfred again. He opened his eyes and looked back at her. She almost felt ashamed of how little compassion she had for this dying man. She thought, as she looked into his eyes, that he had never been compassionate himself, nor forgiving, nor generous. He had nursed his resentments and hatreds all his life, and had taken his pleasure from acts of malice and revenge. Your life *could* have been different, Alfred, she thought. You could have been kind to your sister, and forgiven your stepbrother for being cleverer than you. You could have married for love instead of for revenge. You could have been loyal to Prior Philip. You could have been happy.

His eyes widened suddenly and he said: "God, it *hurts*."

She wished he would just hurry up and *die*.

His eyes closed.

"That's it," Richard said.

Alfred stopped breathing.

Aliena stood up. "I'm a widow," she said.

Alfred was buried in the graveyard at Kingsbridge Priory. It was his sister Martha's wish, and she was the only surviving blood relative. She was also the only person who was sad. Alfred had never been good to her, and she had always turned to Jack, her stepbrother, for love and protection; but nevertheless she wanted him buried somewhere close so that she could visit the grave. When they lowered the coffin into the ground, only Martha cried.

Jack looked grimly relieved that Alfred was no more. Tommy, standing with Aliena, was keenly interested in everything—this was his first family funeral and the rituals of death were all new to him. Sally was white-faced and frightened, holding Martha's hand.

Richard was there. He told Aliena, during the service, that he had come to ask God's forgiveness for killing his brother-in-law. Not that he felt he had done wrong, he hastened to add: he just wanted to be safe.

Aliena, whose face was still bruised and swollen from Alfred's last punch, recalled the dead man as he had been when she first met him. He had come to Earlscastle with his father, Tom Builder, and Martha and Ellen and Jack. Already Alfred had been the bully of the family, big and strong and bovine, with a sly cunning and a streak of nastiness. If Aliena had thought then that she would end up married to him she would have been tempted to throw herself off the battlements. She had not imagined she would ever see the family again after they left the castle; but both she and they had ended up living in Kingsbridge. She and Alfred had started the parish guild which was now such an important institution in the life of the town. That was when Alfred had proposed to her. She had not dreamed that he might be motivated more by rivalry with his stepbrother than by desire for her. She had refused him then, but later he had discovered how to manipulate her, and had persuaded her to marry him by promising support for her brother. Looking back on that, she felt that Alfred had deserved the frustration and humiliation of their marriage. His motives had been heartless and his reward had been lovelessness.

Aliena could not help feeling happy. There was no question of her leaving and going to live in Winchester now, of course: she and Jack would be married immediately. She was putting on a solemn face for the funeral, and even thinking some solemn thoughts, but her heart was bursting for joy.

Philip, with his apparently limitless capacity for pardoning people who had betrayed him, consented to bury Alfred.

As the five adults and two children were standing around the open grave, Ellen arrived.

Philip was cross. Ellen had cursed a Christian wedding, and she was not welcome in the priory close; but he could hardly turn her away from her stepson's funeral. The rites were over, anyway, so Philip just walked away.

Aliena was sorry. Philip and Ellen were both good people, and it was a shame they were enemies. But they were good in different ways, and they were both intolerant of rival ethics.

Ellen was looking older, with extra lines on her face and more gray in her hair, but her golden eyes were still beautiful. She was wearing a rough-sewn leather tunic and nothing else, not even shoes. Her arms and legs were tanned and muscular. Tommy and Sally ran to kiss her. Jack followed and embraced her, hugging her hard.

Ellen lifted her cheek for Richard to kiss her, and said: "You did the right thing. Don't feel guilty."

She stood at the edge of the grave, looking in, and said: "I was his stepmother. I wish I had known how to make him happy."

When she turned from the grave, Aliena hugged her.

They all walked slowly away. Aliena said to Ellen: "Will you stay a while, and have dinner?"

"Gladly." She ruffled Tommy's red hair. "I'd like to talk to my grandchildren. They grow so fast. When I first met Tom Builder, Jack was the age Tommy is now." They were approaching the priory gate. "As you get older, the years seem to go faster. I believe—" She broke off in midsentence, and stopped walking.

"What is it?" said Aliena.

Ellen was staring at the priory gateway. The wooden gates were open. The street outside was empty but for a handful of small children on the far side, standing in a knot, staring at something out of sight.

"Richard!" Ellen said sharply. "Don't go out!"

Everyone stopped. Aliena could see what had alarmed Ellen. The children looked as if they might be watching something or someone who was waiting just outside the gate, concealed by the wall.

Richard reacted fast. "It's a trap!" he said, and without further ado he turned around and ran.

A moment later a helmeted head looked around the gatepost. It belonged to a large man-at-arms. The man saw Richard running toward the church, shouted in alarm, and dashed into the close. He was followed by three, four, five more men.

The funeral party scattered. The men-at-arms ignored them and went after Richard. Aliena was scared and mystified: who would dare to attack the earl of Shiring openly and in a priory? She held her breath as she watched them chase Richard across the close. He leaped over the low wall that the masons were building. His pursuers jumped over it behind him, unmindful that they were entering a church. The craftsmen froze in position, trowels and hammers raised, as first Richard, then his pursuers, charged by. One of the younger and more quick-thinking apprentices stuck out a shovel and tripped a man-at-arms, who went flying; but no one else intervened. Richard reached the door that led to the cloisters. The man closest behind him raised his sword above his head. For a terrible moment Aliena thought the door was locked and Richard could not get in. The man-at-arms struck at Richard with his sword. Richard got the door open and slipped inside, and the sword bit into the wood as the door slammed.

Aliena breathed again.

The men-at-arms gathered around the cloister door, then began to look about uncertainly. They seemed to realize, all of a sudden, where they were. The craftsmen gave them hostile stares and hefted their hammers and axes. There were close to a hundred builders and only five men-at-arms.

Jack said angrily: "Who the hell are those people?"

He was answered by a voice from behind. "They are the sheriff's men."

Aliena turned around, aghast. She knew that voice horribly well. There at the gate, on a nervous black stallion, armed and wearing chain mail, was William Hamleigh. The sight of him sent a chill through her.

Jack said: "Get out of here, you loathsome insect."

William flushed at the insult, but he did not move. "I've come to make an arrest."

"Go ahead. Richard's men will tear you apart."

"He won't have any men when he's in jail."

"Who do you think you are? A sheriff can't put an earl in jail!"

"He can for murder."

Aliena gasped. She saw immediately how William's devious mind was working. "There was no murder!" she burst out.

"There was," William said. "Earl Richard murdered Alfred Builder. And now I must explain to Prior Philip that he is harboring a killer."

William kicked his horse and rode past them, across the west end of the unbuilt nave, to the kitchen courtyard which was where laymen were received. Aliena watched him with incredulity. He was so evil it was hard to believe. Poor Alfred, whom they had just buried, had done much wrong through small-mindedness and weakness of character: his badness was more tragic than anything else. But William was a real servant of the devil. Aliena thought: When will we be rid of this monster?

The men-at-arms joined William in the kitchen courtyard and one of them hammered on the kitchen door with the hilt of his sword. The builders left the site and stood in a crowd, glaring at the intruders, looking dangerous with their heavy hammers and sharp chisels. Aliena told Martha to take the children home; then she and Jack stood with the builders.

Prior Philip came to the kitchen door. He was shorter than William, and in his light summer habit he appeared very small by comparison with the beefy man on horseback in chain mail; but there was a look of righteous anger on Philip's face that made him seem more formidable than William.

William said: "You are harboring a fugitive—"

Philip interrupted him with a roar. "Leave this place!"

William tried again. "There has been a murder—"

"Get out of my priory!" Philip yelled.

"I am the sheriff—"

"Not even the king may bring men of violence into the precincts of a monastery! Get out! Get out!"

The builders began to murmur angrily among themselves. The

men-at-arms looked at them nervously. William said: "Even the prior of Kingsbridge must answer to the sheriff."

"Not on these terms! Get your men off the premises. Leave your weapons in the stable. When you're ready to act like a humble sinner in the house of God, you may enter the priory; and *then* the prior will answer your questions."

Philip stepped back inside and slammed the door.

The builders cheered.

Aliena found herself cheering too. William had been a figure of power and dread all her life, and it lifted her heart to see him defied by Prior Philip.

But William was not yet ready to concede defeat. He got off his horse. Slowly he unbuckled his sword belt and handed it to one of his men. He said a few quiet words to the men, and they retreated across the priory close, taking his sword. William watched them until they reached the gate; then he turned back and faced the kitchen door once again.

He shouted: "Open up to the sheriff!"

After a pause the kitchen door opened, and Philip came out again. He looked down at William, now standing unarmed in the courtyard; then he looked at the men-at-arms clustered around the gateway on the far side of the close; and finally he looked back at William and said: "Well?"

"You are harboring a murderer in the priory. Release him to me."

Philip said: "There has been no murder in Kingsbridge."

"The earl of Shiring murdered Alfred Builder four days ago."

"Wrong," Philip said. "Richard killed Alfred, but it wasn't murder. Alfred was caught in the act of attempted rape."

Aliena shuddered.

"Rape?" William said. "Who was he attempting to rape?"

"Aliena."

"But she is his wife!" William said triumphantly. "How can a man *rape* his wife?"

Aliena saw the direction of William's argument, and fury bubbled up inside her.

Philip said: "That marriage has never been consummated, and she has applied for an annulment."

"Which has never been granted. They were married in church. They are still married, according to the law. There was no rape. On the contrary." William turned suddenly and pointed a finger at Aliena. "She has been wanting to get rid of her husband for years, and she finally persuaded her brother to help her get him out of the way—by stabbing him to death with *her* dagger!"

The cold hand of fear gripped Aliena's heart. The tale he told was an outrageous lie, but for someone who had not actually seen what happened it fitted the facts as plausibly as the real story. Richard was in trouble.

Philip said: "The sheriff cannot arrest the earl."

That was true, Aliena realized. She had been forgetting.

William pulled out a scroll. "I have a royal writ. I am arresting him on behalf of the king."

Aliena was devastated. William had thought of everything. "How did William manage that?" she muttered.

"He was very quick," Jack replied. "He must have ridden to Winchester and seen the king as soon as he heard the news."

Philip held out his hand. "Show me the writ."

William held it out. They were several yards apart. There was a momentary standoff, when neither of them would move; then William gave in and walked up the steps to hand the writ to Philip.

Philip read it and gave it back. "This doesn't give you the right to attack a monastery."

"It gives me the right to arrest Richard."

"He has asked for sanctuary."

"Ah." William did not look surprised. He nodded as if he had heard confirmation of something inevitable, and took two or three steps back. When he spoke again his voice was raised so that everyone could hear clearly. "Let him know that he will be arrested the moment he leaves the priory. My deputies will be stationed in the town and outside his castle. Remember—" He looked around at the assembled crowd. "Remember that anyone who harms a sheriff's deputy harms a servant of the king." He turned back to Philip. "Tell him that he may stay within the sanctuary as long as he likes, but if he wants to leave, he will have to face justice."

There was silence. William walked slowly down the steps and across the kitchen courtyard. His words had sounded to Aliena like a sentence of imprisonment. The crowd parted for him. He threw a smug look at Aliena as he passed her. They all watched him walk to the gate and mount his horse. He gave an order and trotted away, leaving two of his men standing at the gate, looking in.

When Aliena turned around, Philip was standing beside her and Jack. "Go to my house," he said quietly. "We must discuss this." He went back into the kitchen.

Aliena had the impression that he was secretly pleased about something.

The excitement was over. The builders returned to work, talking animatedly. Ellen went to the house to be with the grandchildren. Aliena and Jack walked through the graveyard, skirting the building site, and went into Philip's house. He was not yet there. They sat on a bench to wait. Jack sensed Aliena's anxiety for her brother, and gave her a comforting hug.

Looking around, Aliena realized that year by year Philip's house was slowly becoming more comfortable. It was still bare by the standards of an earl's private quarters in a castle, say, but it was not as austere as it had once been. In front of the little altar in the corner there was now a small rug, to save the prior's knees during the long nights of prayer; and on the wall behind the altar hung a jeweled silver crucifix that must have been a costly gift. It would do Philip no harm to be easier on himself as he got older, Aliena thought. Perhaps he would be a little easier on others too.

A few moments later Philip came in, with a flustered-looking Richard in tow. Richard began speaking immediately. "William can't do this, it's mad! I found Alfred trying to rape my sister—he had a knife in his hand—he almost killed me!"

"Calm down," Philip said. "Let's talk about this quietly, and try calmly to determine what the dangers are, if any. Why don't we all take a seat?"

Richard sat down, but he went on talking. "Dangers? There are no dangers. A sheriff can't imprison an earl for anything, even murder."

"He's going to try," Philip said. "He'll have men waiting outside the priory."

Richard made a dismissive gesture. "I can get past William's men blindfold. They're no problem. Jack can be waiting for me outside the town wall with a horse."

"And when you reach Earlscastle?" said Philip.

"Same thing. I can sneak past William's men. Or have my own men come out to meet me."

"That sounds satisfactory," said Philip. "And what then?"

"Then nothing," said Richard. "What can William do?"

"Well, he still has a royal writ that summons you to answer a charge of murder. He'll try to arrest you anytime you leave the castle."

"I'll go everywhere escorted."

"And when you hold court, in Shiring and other places?"

"Same thing."

"But will anyone abide by your decisions, knowing that you yourself are a fugitive from the law?"

"They'd better," Richard said darkly. "They should remember how William enforced his decisions when he was the earl."

"They may not be as frightened of you as they were of William.

They may think you're not as bloodthirsty and evil. I hope they would be right."

"Don't count on it."

Aliena frowned. It was not like Philip to be so pessimistic—unless he had an ulterior motive. She suspected that he was laying the groundwork for some scheme he had up his sleeve. I'd bet money, she thought, that the quarry will come into this somehow.

"My main worry is the king," Philip was saying. "In refusing to answer the charge, you're defying the crown. A year ago I would have said go ahead and defy it. But now that the war is over, it won't be so easy for earls to do as they please."

Jack said: "It looks as if you'll have to answer the charge, Richard."

"He can't do that," Aliena said. "He's got no hope of justice."

"She's right," Philip said. "The case would be heard in the royal court. The facts are already known: Alfred tried to force himself upon Aliena, Richard came in, they fought, and Richard killed Alfred. Everything depends on the interpretation. And with William, a loyal supporter of King Stephen, making the complaint, and Richard being one of Duke Henry's greatest allies, the verdict will probably be guilty. Why did King Stephen sign the writ? Presumably because he's decided to take revenge on Richard for fighting against him. The death of Alfred provides him with a perfect excuse."

Aliena said: "We must appeal to Duke Henry to intervene."

It was Richard who looked dubious now. "I wouldn't like to rely on him. He's in Normandy. He might write a letter of protest, but what else could he do? Conceivably he could cross the channel with an army, but then he would be in breach of the peace pact, and I don't think he'd risk that for me."

Aliena felt miserable and frightened. "Oh, Richard, you're caught in a terrible web, and it's all because you saved me."

He gave her his most charming grin. "I'd do it again, too, Allie."

"I know." He meant it. For all his faults, he was brave. It seemed unfair that he should be confronted with such an intractable problem so soon after he succeeded to the earldom. As earl he was a disappointment to Aliena—a terrible disappointment—but he did not deserve this.

"Well, what a choice," he said. "I can stay here in the priory until Duke Henry becomes king, or hang for murder. I'd become a monk if you monks didn't eat so much fish."

"There might be another way out," said Philip.

Aliena looked at him eagerly. She had suspected that he was hatching a plot, and she would be grateful to him if he could resolve Richard's dilemma.

"You could do penance for the killing," Philip went on.

"Would it involve eating fish?" Richard said flippantly.

"I'm thinking about the Holy Land," Philip said.

They all went quiet. Palestine was ruled by the king of Jerusalem, Baldwin III, a Christian of French origin. It was constantly under attack by neighboring Muslim countries, especially Egypt to the south and Damascus to the east. To go there, a journey of six months or a year, and join the armies fighting to defend the Christian kingdom, was indeed the kind of penance a man might do to purge his soul of a killing. Aliena felt a qualm of anxiety: not everybody came back from the Holy Land. But she had been worrying about Richard in wars for years, and the Holy Land was probably no more dangerous than England. She would just have to fret. She was used to it.

"The king of Jerusalem always needs men," Richard said. Every few years emissaries from the pope would tour the country, telling tales of battle and glory in the defense of Christendom, trying to inspire young men to go and fight in the Holy Land. "But I've only just come into my earldom," he said. "And who would be in charge of my lands while I was away?"

"Aliena," said Philip.

Aliena suddenly felt breathless. Philip was proposing that she should take the place of the earl, and rule as her father had done. . . . The proposal stunned her for a moment, but as soon as she recovered her senses she knew it was right. When a man went to the Holy Land his domains were normally looked after by his wife. There was no reason why a sister should not fulfill the same role for an unmarried earl. And she would run the earldom the way she had always known it ought to be run, with justice and vision and imagination. She would do all the things Richard had so dismally failed to do. Her heart raced as she thought the idea through. She would try out new ideas, plowing with horses instead of oxen, and planting spring crops of oats and peas on fallow land. She would clear new lands for planting, establish new markets, and open the quarry to Philip after all this time—

He had thought of that, of course. Of all the clever schemes Philip had dreamed up over the years, this was probably the most ingenious. At one stroke he solved three problems: he got Richard off the hook, he put a competent ruler in charge of the earldom, and he got his quarry at last.

Philip said: "I've no doubt that King Baldwin would welcome you—especially if you went with such of your knights and men who feel inspired to join you. It would be your own small crusade." He paused a moment to let that thought sink in. "William couldn't touch you over there, of course," he went on. "And you would return a hero. Nobody would dare try to hang you then."

"The Holy Land," Richard said, and there was a death-or-glory light in his eyes. It was the right thing for him, Aliena thought. He was no good at governing the earldom. He was a soldier, and he wanted to fight. She saw the faraway look on his face. In his mind he was there already, defending a sandy redoubt, sword in hand, a red cross on his shield, fighting off a heathen horde under the baking sun.

He was happy.

IV

The whole town came to the wedding.

Aliena was surprised. Most people treated her and Jack as more or less married already, and she had thought they would consider the wedding a mere formality. She had expected a small group of friends, mostly people of her own age and Jack's fellow master craftsmen. But every man, woman and child in Kingsbridge turned out. She was touched by their presence. And they all looked so *happy* for her. She realized that they had sympathized with her predicament all these years, even though they had tactfully refrained from mentioning it to her; and now they shared her joy in finally marrying the man she had loved for so long. She walked through the streets on her brother Richard's arm, dazzled by the smiles that followed her, drunk with happiness.

Richard was leaving for the Holy Land tomorrow. King Stephen had accepted this solution—indeed, he seemed relieved to be rid of Richard so easily. Sheriff William was furious, of course, for his aim had been to dispossess Richard of the earldom, and now he had lost all chance of doing that. Richard himself still had that faraway look in his eyes: he could hardly wait to be gone.

This was not the way her father had intended things to turn out, she thought as she entered the priory close: Richard fighting in a distant land and Aliena herself playing the role of earl. However, she no longer felt obliged to run her life according to her father's wishes. He had been dead for seventeen years, and anyway, she knew something that he had not understood: that she would be a far better earl than Richard.

She had already taken the reins of power. The castle servants were lazy after years of slack management and she had smartened them up. She had reorganized the stores, had the great hall painted, and cleaned out the bakehouse and the brewery. The kitchen had been so filthy that she had burned it down and built a new one. She had started to pay out the weekly wages herself, as a sign that she was in charge; and she had dismissed three men-at-arms for persistent drunkenness.

She had also ordered a new castle to be built an hour's ride from Kingsbridge. Earlscastle was too far from the cathedral. Jack had drawn a design for the new place. They would move in as soon as the keep was built. Meanwhile, they would split their time between Earlscastle and Kingsbridge.

They had already spent several nights together in Aliena's old room at Earlscastle, far from Philip's disapproving gaze. They had been like honeymooners, swamped by insatiable physical passion. Perhaps it was because for the first time ever they had a bedroom with a door they could lock. Privacy was an extravagance of lords: everyone else slept and made love downstairs in the communal hall. Even couples who lived in a house were always liable to be seen by their children, or relatives, or neighbors dropping by: people locked their doors when they were out, not when they were in. Aliena had never been dissatisfied with that, but now she had discovered the special thrill of knowing you could do anything you liked without the risk of being seen. She thought of some of the things she and Jack had done in the past two weeks, and she blushed.

Jack was waiting for her in the partly built nave of the cathedral, with Martha and Tommy and Sally. At weddings, the couple normally exchanged vows in the church porch, then went inside for the mass. Today the first bay of the nave would serve as porch. Aliena was glad they were getting married in the church Jack was building. It was as much a part of Jack as the clothes he wore or the way he made love. His cathedral was going to be like him: graceful, inventive, cheerful, and totally unlike anything that had gone before.

She looked lovingly at him. He was thirty years old. He was such a handsome man, with his mane of red hair and his sparkling blue eyes. He had been a very ugly boy, she remembered: she had thought him somewhat beneath her notice. But he had fallen in love with her at the very start, he said; and he still winced when he remembered how they had all laughed at him because he said he had never had a father. It was nearly twenty years ago. Twenty years . . .

She might never have seen Jack again had it not been for Prior Philip, who now entered the church from the cloisters and came smiling into the nave. He looked genuinely thrilled to be marrying them at last. She thought of her first meeting with him. She recalled vividly the despair she had felt when the wool merchant tried to cheat her, after all the effort and heartbreak that had gone into amassing that sack of fleeces; and her overwhelming gratitude to the young black-haired monk who had saved her and said: "I'll buy your wool any time. . . ." His hair was gray now.

He had saved her, then he had almost destroyed her, by forcing Jack to choose between her and the cathedral. He was a hard man on questions of right and wrong; a bit like her father. However, he had wanted to perform the marriage service.

Ellen had cursed Aliena's first wedding, and the curse had worked. Aliena was glad. If her marriage to Alfred had not been completely insupportable she might be living with him still. It was odd to reflect on what might have been: it gave her chills, like bad dreams and dreadful imaginings. She recalled the pretty, sexy Arab girl in Toledo who had fallen in love with Jack: what if he had married her? Aliena would have arrived in Toledo, with her baby in her arms, to find Jack in the lap of domesticity, sharing his body and his mind with someone else. The thought was horrifying.

She listened to him mumbling the Paternoster. It seemed amazing, now, to think that when she came to live in Kingsbridge she had paid no more attention to him than to the grain merchant's cat. But he had noticed her: he had loved her secretly all those years. How patient he had been! He had watched as the younger sons of the county gentry came to court her, one by one, and went away again disappointed or offended or defiant. He had seen—clever, clever boy that he was—that she could not be won by wooing; and he had approached her sidelong, as a friend rather than a lover, meeting her in the woods and telling her stories and making her love him without her noticing. She remembered that first kiss, so light and casual, except that it had burned her lips for weeks afterward. She remembered the second kiss even more vividly. Every time she heard the rumble of the fulling mill she remembered the dark, unfamiliar, unwelcome surge of lust that she had felt.

One of the abiding regrets of her life was the way she had turned cold after that. Jack had loved her totally and honestly, and she had been so frightened that she had turned away, pretending she did not care for him. It had hurt him deeply; and although he had continued to love her, and the wound had healed, it left a scar, as deep wounds do; and sometimes she saw that scar, in the way he looked at her when they quarreled and she spoke coldly to him, and his eyes seemed to say: Yes, I know you, you can be cold, you can hurt me, I must be on my guard.

Was there a wary look in his eyes now, as he vowed to be loving and faithful to her all the rest of his life? He's got reason enough to doubt me, she thought. I married Alfred, and what greater betrayal could there be than that? But then I made up for it, by searching half of Christendom to find Jack.

Such disappointments, betrayals and reconciliations were the stuff of married life, but she and Jack had gone through them before the wedding. Now, at least, she felt confident that she knew him. Nothing was likely to surprise her. It was a funny way to do things, but it might be better than making your vows first and getting to know your spouse afterward. The priests would not agree, of course; indeed, Philip would be apoplectic if he knew what was going through her mind; but then again, priests knew less about love than anyone.

She made her vows, repeating the words after Philip, thinking to herself how beautiful was the promise *With my body I worship you.* Philip would never understand that.

Jack put a ring on her finger. I've been waiting for this all my life, she thought. They looked into one another's eyes. Something had changed in him, she could tell. She realized that until this moment he had never really been sure of her. Now he looked deeply content.

"I love you," he said. "I always will."

That was his vow. The rest was religion, but now he had made his own promise; and Aliena realized that she, too, had been unsure of him until now. In a moment they would walk forward into the crossing for the mass; and after that they would accept the congratulations and good wishes of the townspeople, and take them home and give them food and ale and make merry; but this small instant was just for them. Jack's look said *You and me, together, always;* and Aliena thought *At last.*

It felt very peaceful.

PART SIX

1170-1174

Chapter 17

KINGSBRIDGE WAS STILL GROWING. It had long ago overflowed its original walls, which now enclosed fewer than half the houses. About five years ago the guild had built a new wall, taking in the suburbs that had grown up outside the old town; and now there were more suburbs outside the new wall. The meadow on the other side of the river, where the townspeople had traditionally held Lammas Day and Midsummer Eve festivities, was now a small village, called Newport.

On a cold Easter Sunday, Sheriff William Hamleigh rode through Newport and crossed the stone bridge that led into what was now called the old town of Kingsbridge. Today the newly completed Kingsbridge Cathedral would be consecrated. He passed through the formidable city gate and went up the main street, which had recently been paved. The dwellings on either side were all stone houses with shops in the undercrofts and living quarters above. Kingsbridge was bigger, busier and wealthier than Shiring had ever been, William thought bitterly.

He reached the top of the street and turned into the priory close; and there, before his eyes, was the reason for the rise of Kingsbridge and the decline of Shiring: the cathedral.

It was breathtaking.

The immensely tall nave was supported by a row of graceful flying buttresses. The west end had three huge porticos, like giants' doorways, and rows of tall, slender, pointed windows above, flanked by slim towers. The concept had been heralded in the transepts, finished eighteen years ago, but this was the astonishing consummation of the idea. There had never been a building like this anywhere in England.

The market still took place here every Sunday, and the green in front of the church door was packed with stalls. William dismounted and left Walter to take care of the horses. He limped across the green to the church: he was fifty-four years old, and heavy, and he suffered constant pain from gout in his legs and feet. Because of the pain he was more or less permanently angry.

The church was even more impressive inside. The nave followed the style of the transepts, but the master builder had refined his design, making the columns even more slender and the windows larger. But there was yet another innovation. William had heard people talk of the colored glass made by craftsmen Jack Jackson had brought over from Paris. He had wondered why there was such a fuss about it, for he imagined that a colored window would be just like a tapestry or a painting. Now he saw what they meant. The light from outside shone through the colored glass, making it glow, and the effect was quite magical. The church was full of people craning their necks to stare up at the windows. The pictures showed Bible stories, Heaven and Hell, saints and prophets, disciples, and some of the Kingsbridge citizens who had presumably paid for the windows in which they appeared—a baker carrying his tray of loaves, a tanner and his hides, a mason with his compasses and level. I bet Philip made a fat profit out of those windows, William thought sourly.

The church was packed for the Easter service. The market was spreading into the interior of the building, as always happened, and walking up the nave William was offered cold beer, hot gingerbread and a quick fuck up against the wall for threepence. The clergy were forever trying to ban peddlers from churches but it was an impossible task. William exchanged greetings with the more important citizens of the county. But despite the social and commercial distractions William found his eye and his thoughts constantly drawn upward by the sweeping lines of the arcade. The arches and the windows, the piers with their clustered shafts, and the ribs and segments of the vaulted ceiling all seemed to point toward heaven in an inescapable reminder of what the building was for.

The floor was paved, the pillars were painted, and every window was glazed: Kingsbridge and its priory were rich, and the cathedral proclaimed their prosperity. In the small chapels of the transepts were gold candlesticks and jeweled crosses. The citizens also displayed their wealth, with richly colored tunics, silver brooches and buckles, and gold rings.

His eye fell on Aliena.

As always, his heart missed a beat. She was as beautiful as ever, although she had to be over fifty years old now. She still had a mass of curly hair, but it was cut shorter, and seemed to be a lighter shade of brown, as if it had faded a little. She had attractive crinkles at the corners of her eyes. She was a little wider than she used to be, but she was no less desirable. She wore a blue cloak with a red silk lining, and red leather shoes. There was a deferential crowd around her. Although she was not even a countess, merely the sister of an earl, her brother had settled in the Holy Land, and everyone treated her as the earl. She carried herself like a queen.

The sight of her brewed hatred like bile in William's belly. He had ruined her father, raped her, taken her castle, burned her wool and exiled her brother, but every time he thought he had crushed her she came back again, rising from defeat to new heights of power and wealth. Now William was aging and gouty and fat and he realized that he had spent his life in the power of a terrible enchantment.

Beside her was a tall red-haired man whom William at first took for Jack. However, on closer examination the man was obviously too young, and William realized it must be the son of Jack. The boy was dressed as a knight, and carried a sword. Jack himself stood next to his son, an inch or two shorter, his red hair receding at the temples. He was younger than Aliena, of course, by about five years, if William's memory was right, but he, too, had lines around his eyes. He was talking animatedly to a young woman who was surely his daughter. She resembled Aliena, and was just as pretty, but her abundant hair was pulled severely back and plaited, and she was quite plainly dressed. If there was a voluptuous body under that earth-brown tunic she did not want anyone to know it.

Resentment burned in his stomach as he regarded Aliena's prosperous, dignified, happy family. Everything they had should have been his. But he had not given up the hope of revenge.

The voices of several hundred monks were raised in song, drowning the conversations and the cries of the hawkers, and Prior Philip entered the church at the head of a procession. There never used to be this many monks, William thought. The priory had grown along with the town. Philip, now over sixty years old, was almost completely bald, and rather stout, so that his formerly thin face had become quite round. Not surprisingly, he looked pleased with himself: the dedication of this cathedral was the aim he had conceived when he first came to Kingsbridge, thirty-four years ago.

There was a murmur of comment when Bishop Waleran came

in, clad in his most gorgeous robes. His pale, angular face was frozen in a stiffly neutral expression, but William knew he was seething inside. This cathedral was the triumphant symbol of Philip's victory over Waleran. William hated Philip too, but all the same he secretly enjoyed seeing the supercilious Bishop Waleran humbled for a change.

Waleran was rarely seen here. A new church had finally been built in Shiring—with a special chapel dedicated to the memory of William's mother—and although it was nowhere near as large or impressive as this cathedral, nevertheless Waleran had made the Shiring church his headquarters.

However, Kingsbridge was still the cathedral church, despite all Waleran's efforts. In a war that had raged over three decades, Waleran had done everything he could to destroy Philip, but in the end Philip had triumphed. They were a bit like William and Aliena. In both cases, weakness and scruples had defeated strength and ruthlessness. William felt he would never understand it.

The bishop had been obliged to come here today, for the dedication ceremony: it would have looked very peculiar if he had not been here to welcome all the celebrity guests. Several bishops from neighboring dioceses were here, as well as a number of distinguished abbots and priors.

The archbishop of Canterbury, Thomas Becket, would not be here. He was in the throes of a quarrel with his old friend, King Henry; a quarrel so bitter and fierce that the archbishop had been forced to flee the country, and had taken refuge in France. They were in conflict over a whole list of legal issues, but the heart of the dispute was simple: Could the king do as he pleased, or was he constrained? It was the dispute William himself had had with Prior Philip. William took the view that the earl could do anything—that was what it meant to be earl. Henry felt the same about kingship. Prior Philip and Thomas Becket were both bent on restricting the power of rulers.

Bishop Waleran was a clergyman who sided with the rulers. For him, power was meant to be used. The defeats of three decades had not shaken his belief that he was the instrument of God's will, nor his ruthless determination to do his holy duty. William felt sure that even while he conducted the consecration service for Kingsbridge Cathedral, he was casting about for some way to spoil Philip's moment of glory.

William moved about throughout the service. Standing was worse for his legs than walking. When he went to Shiring church, Walter carried a chair for him. Then he could doze off for a while.

Here, though, there were people to talk to, and much of the congregation used the time to conduct business. William went around ingratiating himself with the powerful, intimidating the weak, and gathering information on all and sundry. He no longer struck terror into the hearts of the population, as he had in the good old days, but as sheriff he was still feared and deferred to.

The service went on interminably. There was a long interval during which the monks went around the outside of the church sprinkling the walls with holy water. Near the end, Prior Philip announced the appointment of a new sub-prior: it was to be Brother Jonathan, the priory orphan. Jonathan, now in his middle thirties and unusually tall, reminded William of old Tom Builder: he too had been something of a giant.

When the service finally ended, the distinguished guests lingered in the south transept, and the minor gentry of the county crowded around to meet them. William limped over to join them. Once upon a time he had treated bishops as his equals, but now he had to bow and scrape with the knights and small landowners. Bishop Waleran drew William aside and said: "Who is that new sub-prior?"

"The priory orphan," William replied. "He's always been a favorite of Philip's."

"He seems young to be made sub-prior."

"He's older than Philip was when Philip became prior."

Waleran looked thoughtful. "The priory orphan. Remind me of the details."

"When Philip came here he brought a baby with him."

Waleran's face cleared as he remembered. "By the cross, yes! I'd forgotten Philip's baby. How could I have let something like that slip my mind?"

"It is thirty years. And who cares?"

Waleran gave William the scornful look that William hated so much, the look that said *You dumb ox, can't you figure out something that simple?* Pain stabbed his foot, and he shifted his weight in a vain attempt to ease it. Waleran said: "Well, where did the baby come from?"

William swallowed his resentment. "It was found abandoned near his old cell in the forest, if I remember rightly."

"Better and better," Waleran said eagerly.

William still did not see what he was getting at. "So what?" he said sullenly.

"Would you say that Philip has brought the child up as if it was his own son?"

"Yes."

"And now he's made him sub-prior."

"He was elected by the monks, presumably. I believe he's very popular."

"Anyone who is sub-prior at thirty-five must be in line for the post of prior eventually."

William was not going to say *So what?* again so he just waited, feeling like a stupid schoolboy, for Waleran to explain.

At last Waleran said: "Jonathan is obviously Philip's own child."

William burst out laughing. He had been expecting a profound thought, and Waleran had come up with a notion that was totally ludicrous. To William's satisfaction, his scorn brought a slight flush to Waleran's waxy complexion. William said: "No one who knows Philip would believe such a thing. He was born a dried-up old stick. The idea!" He laughed again. Waleran might think he was ever so clever, but this time he had lost his sense of reality.

Waleran's hauteur was icy. "I say Philip used to have a mistress, when he ran that little priory out in the forest. Then he became prior of Kingsbridge and had to leave the woman behind. She didn't want the baby if she couldn't have the father, so she dumped the child on him. Philip, being a sentimental soul, felt obliged to take care of it, so he passed it off as a foundling."

William shook his head. "Unbelievable. Anyone else, yes. Philip, no."

Waleran persisted: "If the baby was abandoned, how can he prove where it came from?"

"He can't," William acknowledged. He looked across the south transept to where Philip and Jonathan stood together, talking to the bishop of Hereford. "But they don't even look alike."

"You don't look like your mother," Waleran said. "Thank God."

"What good is all this?" William said. "What are you going to do about it?"

"Accuse him before an ecclesiastical court," Waleran replied.

That made a difference. No one who knew Philip would credit Waleran's accusation for a moment, but a judge who was a stranger to Kingsbridge might find it more plausible. William saw reluctantly that Waleran's idea was not so stupid after all. As usual, Waleran was shrewder than William. Waleran was looking irritatingly smug, of course. But William was enthused by the prospect of bringing Philip down. "By God," he said eagerly. "Do you think it could be done?"

"It depends who the judge is. But I may be able to arrange something there. I wonder . . ."

William looked across the transept at Philip, triumphant and smiling, with his tall protégé beside him. The vast stained-glass windows threw an enchanted light over them, and they were like figures in a dream. "Fornication and nepotism," William said gleefully. "My God."

"If we can make it stick," Waleran said with relish, "it will be the finish of that damned prior."

No reasonable judge could possibly find Philip guilty.

The truth was that he had never had to try very hard to resist the temptation of fornication. He knew, from hearing confession, that some monks struggled desperately with fleshly lust, but he was not like that. There had been a time, at the age of about eighteen, when he had suffered impure dreams, but that phase had not lasted long. For most of his life chastity had come easily to him. He had never performed the sexual act and he was now probably too old for it.

However, the Church was taking the accusation very seriously. Philip was to be tried by an ecclesiastical court. An archdeacon from Canterbury would be present. Waleran had wanted the trial to be held at Shiring, but Philip had fought against that, successfully, and it would now be held at Kingsbridge, which was, after all, the cathedral city. Now Philip was clearing his personal possessions out of the prior's house to make way for the archdeacon, who would be staying here.

Philip knew he was innocent of fornication, and it followed logically that he could not be guilty of nepotism, for a man cannot favor his sons if he has none. Nevertheless he searched his heart to see whether he had done wrong in promoting Jonathan. Just as impure thoughts were a kind of shadow of a graver sin, perhaps favoritism toward a loved orphan was the shadow of nepotism. Monks were supposed to forgo the consolations of family life, yet Jonathan had been like a son to Philip. Philip had made Jonathan cellarer at a young age, and had now promoted him to sub-prior. Did I do that for my own pride and pleasure? he asked himself.

Well, yes, he thought.

He had taken enormous satisfaction from teaching Jonathan, watching him grow, and seeing him learn how to manage priory affairs. But even if these things had not given Philip such intense pleasure, Jonathan would still have been the ablest young administrator in the priory. He was intelligent, devout, imaginative and conscientious. Brought up in the monastery, he knew no other life, and he never hankered after freedom. Philip himself had been raised in an abbey. We monastery orphans make the best monks, he thought.

He put a book into a satchel: Luke's Gospel, so wise. He had treated Jonathan like a son, but he had not committed any sins worth taking before an ecclesiastical court. The charge was absurd.

Unfortunately, the mere accusation would be damaging. It diminished his moral authority. There would be people who would remember the charge and forget the verdict. Next time Philip stood up and said: "The commandment forbids a man to covet his neighbor's wife," some of the congregation would be thinking *But you had your fun when you were young.*

Jonathan burst in, breathing hard. Philip frowned. The subprior ought not to burst into rooms panting. Philip was about to launch into a homily on the dignity of monastic officers, when Jonathan said: "Archdeacon Peter is here already!"

"All right, all right," Philip soothed. "I've just about finished, anyway." He handed Jonathan the satchel. "Take this to the dormitory, and don't rush everywhere: a monastery is a place of peace and quiet."

Jonathan accepted the satchel and the rebuke, but he said: "I don't like the look of the archdeacon."

"I'm sure he'll be a just judge, and that's all we want," Philip said.

The door opened again, and the archdeacon came in. He was a tall, rangy man of about Philip's age, with thinning gray hair and a rather superior look on his face. He seemed vaguely familiar.

Philip offered a handshake, saying: "I'm Prior Philip."

"I know you," the archdeacon said sourly. "Don't you remember me?"

The gravelly voice did it. Philip's heart sank. This was his oldest enemy. "Archdeacon Peter," he said grimly. "Peter of Wareham."

"He was a troublemaker," Philip explained to Jonathan a few minutes later, when they had left the archdeacon to make himself comfortable in the prior's house. "He would complain that we didn't work hard enough, or we ate too well, or the services were too short. He said I was indulgent. He wanted to be prior himself, I'm sure. He would have been a disaster, of course. I made him almoner, so that he had to spend half his time away. I did it just to get rid of him. It was best for the priory and best for him, but I'm sure he still hates me for it, even after thirty-five years." He sighed.

"I heard, when you and I visited St.-John-in-the-Forest after the great famine, that Peter had gone to Canterbury. And now he's going to sit in judgment on me."

They were in the cloisters. The weather was mild and the sun was warm. Fifty boys in three different classes were learning to read and write in the north walk, and the subdued murmur of their lessons floated across the quadrangle. Philip remembered when the school had consisted of five boys and a senile novice-master. He thought of all he had done here: the building of the cathedral; the transformation of the impoverished, run-down priory into a wealthy, busy, influential institution; the enlargement of the town of Kingsbridge. In the church, more than a hundred monks were singing mass. From where he sat he could see the astonishingly beautiful stained-glass windows in the clerestory. At his back, off the east walk, was a stone-built library containing hundreds of books on theology, astronomy, ethics, mathematics, indeed, every branch of knowledge. In the outside world the priory's lands, managed with enlightened self-interest by monastic officers, fed not just the monks but hundreds of farm workers. Was all that to be taken from him by a lie? Would the prosperous and God-fearing priory be handed over to someone else, a pawn of Bishop Waleran's such as the slimy Archdeacon Baldwin, or a self-righteous fool such as Peter of Wareham, to be run down to penury and depravity as quickly as Philip had built it up? Would the vast flocks of sheep shrink to a handful of scrawny ewes, the farms return to weed-grown inefficiency, the library become dusty with disuse, the beautiful cathedral sink into damp and disrepair? God helped me to achieve so much, he thought; I can't believe he intended it to come to nothing.

Jonathan said: "All the same, Archdeacon Peter can't possibly find you guilty."

"I think he will," Philip said heavily.

"In all conscience, how can he?"

"I think he's been nursing a grievance against me all his life, and this is his chance to prove that I was the sinner and he was the righteous man all along. Somehow Waleran found out about that and made sure Peter was appointed to judge this case."

"But there's no proof!"

"He doesn't need proof. He'll hear the accusation, and the defense; then he'll pray for guidance, and he'll announce his verdict."

"God may guide him aright."

"Peter won't listen to God. He's never been a listener."

"What will happen?"

"I'll be deposed," Philip said grimly. "They may let me continue here as an ordinary monk, to do penance for my sin, but it's not likely. More probably they will expel me from the order, to prevent my having any further influence here."

"What would happen then?"

"There would have to be an election, of course. Unfortunately, royal politics enter into the picture now. King Henry is in dispute with the archbishop of Canterbury, Thomas Becket, and Archbishop Thomas is in exile in France. Half his archdeacons are with him. The other half, the ones who stayed behind, have sided with the king against their archbishop. Peter obviously belongs to that crowd. Bishop Waleran has also taken the king's side. Waleran will recommend his choice of prior, backed by the Canterbury archdeacons and the king. It will be hard for the monks here to oppose him."

"Who do you think it might be?"

"Waleran has someone in mind, rest assured. It could be Archdeacon Baldwin. It might even be Peter of Wareham."

"We *must* do something to prevent this!" Jonathan said.

Philip nodded. "But everything is against us. There's nothing we can do to alter the political situation. The only possibility . . ."

"What?" Jonathan said impatiently.

The case seemed so hopeless that Philip felt there was no point in toying with desperate ideas: it would excite Jonathan's optimism only to disappoint him. "Nothing," Philip said.

"What were you going to say?"

Philip was still working it out. "If there was a way to prove my innocence beyond doubt, it would be impossible for Peter to find me guilty."

"But what would count as proof?"

"Exactly. You can't prove a negative. We would have to find your real father."

Jonathan was instantly enthusiastic. "Yes! That's it! That's what we'll do!"

"Slow down," Philip said. "I tried at the time. It's not likely to be any easier so many years later."

Jonathan was not to be discouraged. "Were there no clues at all to where I might have come from?"

"Nothing, I'm afraid." Philip was now worried that he had raised hopes in Jonathan which could not be fulfilled. Although the boy had no memories of his parents, the fact that they had abandoned him had always troubled him. Now he thought he might solve the mystery and find some explanation which proved they had loved him really. Philip felt sure this could only lead to frustration.

"Did you question people living nearby?" Jonathan said.

"There was nobody living nearby. That cell is deep in the forest. Your parents probably came from miles away, Winchester perhaps. I've been over all this ground already."

Jonathan persisted. "You didn't see any travelers in the forest around that time?"

"No." Philip frowned. Was that true? A stray thought tugged at his memory. The day the baby was found, Philip had left the priory to go to the bishop's palace, and on his way he had spoken to some people. Suddenly it came back to him. "Well, yes, as a matter of fact, Tom Builder and his family were passing through."

Jonathan was astonished. "You never told me that!"

"It never seemed important. It still doesn't. I met them a day or two later. I questioned them, and they said they hadn't seen anyone who might have been the mother or father of an abandoned baby."

Jonathan was crestfallen. Philip was afraid this whole line of inquiry was going to prove doubly disappointing to him: he would not find out about his parents and he would fail to prove Philip's innocence. But there was no stopping him now. "What were they doing in the forest, anyway?" he persisted.

"Tom was on his way to the bishop's palace. He was looking for work. That's how they ended up here."

"I want to question them again."

"Well, Tom and Alfred are dead. Ellen is living in the forest, and only God knows when she will reappear. But you could talk to Jack or Martha."

"It's worth a try."

Perhaps Jonathan was right. He had the energy of youth. Philip had been pessimistic and discouraging. "Go ahead," he said to Jonathan. "I'm getting old and tired; otherwise I would have thought of it myself. Talk to Jack. It's a slender thread to hang on to. But it's our only hope."

The design of the window had been drawn, full size, and painted, on a huge wooden table which had been washed with ale to prevent the colors from running. The drawing showed the Tree of Jesse, a genealogy of Christ in picture form. Sally picked up a small piece of thick ruby-colored glass and placed it on the design over the body of one of the kings of Israel—Jack was not sure which king: he had never been able to remember the convoluted symbolism of theological pictures. Sally dipped a fine brush in a bowl of chalk ground up in water, and painted the shape of the body onto the glass: shoulders, arms, and the skirt of the robe.

In the fire on the ground beside her table was an iron rod with a wooden handle. She took the rod out of the fire and then, quickly but carefully, she ran the red-hot end of the rod around the outline she had painted. The grass cracked neatly along the line. Her apprentice picked up the piece of glass and began to smooth its edges with a grozing iron.

Jack loved to watch his daughter work. She was quick and precise, her movements economical. As a little girl she had been fascinated by the work of the glaziers Jack had brought over from Paris, and she always said that was what she wanted to do when she grew up. She had stuck by that choice. When people came to Kingsbridge Cathedral for the first time, they were more struck by Sally's glass than her father's architecture, Jack thought ruefully.

The apprentice handed the smoothed glass to her, and she began to paint the folds of the robe onto the surface, using a paint made of iron ore, urine, and gum arabic for adhesion. The flat glass suddenly began to look like soft, carelessly draped cloth. She was very skillful. She finished it quickly, then put the painted glass alongside several others in an iron pan, the bottom of which was covered with lime. When the pan was full it would go into an oven. The heat would fuse the paint to the glass.

She looked up at Jack, gave him a brief, dazzling smile, then picked up another piece of glass.

He moved away. He could watch her all day, but he had work to do. He was, as Aliena would say, daft about his daughter. When he looked at her it was often with a kind of amazement that he was responsible for the existence of this clever, independent, mature young woman. He was thrilled that she was such a good craftswoman.

Ironically, he had always pressured Tommy to be a builder. He had actually forced the boy to work on the site for a couple of years. But Tommy was interested in farming, horsemanship, hunting and swordplay, all the things that left Jack cold. In the end Jack had conceded defeat. Tommy had served as a squire to one of the local lords and had eventually been knighted. Aliena had granted him a small estate of five villages. And Sally had turned out to be the talented one. Tommy was married now, to a younger daughter of the earl of Bedford, and they had three children. Jack was a grandfather. But Sally was still single at the age of twenty-five. There was a lot of her grandmother Ellen in her. She was aggressively self-reliant.

Jack walked around to the west end of the cathedral and looked up at the twin towers. They were almost complete, and a huge bronze bell was on its way here from the foundry in London. There was not much for Jack to do nowadays. Where he had once controlled an army of muscular stonecutters and carpenters, laying rows of square stones and building scaffolding, he now had a handful of carvers and painters doing precise and painstaking work on a small scale, making statues for niches, building ornamental pinnacles, and gilding the wings of stone angels. There was not much to design, apart from the occasional new building for the priory—a library, a chapter house, more accommodation for pilgrims, new laundry and dairy buildings. In between petty jobs Jack was doing some stone carving himself, for the first time in many years. He was impatient to pull down Tom Builder's old chancel and put up a new east end to his own design, but Prior Philip wanted to enjoy the finished church for a year before beginning another building campaign. Philip was feeling his age. Jack was afraid the old boy might not live to see the chancel rebuilt.

However, the work would be continued after Philip's death, Jack thought as he saw the enormously tall figure of Brother Jonathan striding toward him from the direction of the kitchen courtyard. Jonathan would make a good prior, perhaps even as good as Philip himself. Jack was glad the succession was assured: it enabled him to plan for the future.

"I'm worried about this ecclesiastical court, Jack," said Jonathan without preamble.

Jack said: "I thought that was all a big fuss about nothing."

"So did I—but the archdeacon turns out to be an old enemy of Prior Philip's."

"Hell. But even so, surely he can't find him guilty."

"He can do anything he wants."

Jack shook his head in disgust. He sometimes wondered how men such as Jonathan could continue to believe in the Church when it was so shamelessly corrupt. "What are you going to do?"

"The only way we can prove his innocence is to find out who my parents were."

"It's a bit late for that!"

"It's our only hope."

Jack was somewhat shaken. They were quite desperate. "Where are you going to start?"

"With you. You were in the area of St-John-in-the-Forest at the time I was born."

"Was I?" Jack did not see what Jonathan was getting at. "I lived there until I was eleven, and I must be about eleven years older than you. . . ."

"Father Philip says he met you, with your mother and Tom Builder and Tom's children, the day after I was found."

"I remember that. We ate all Philip's food. We were starving."

"Think hard. Did you see anyone with a baby, or a young woman who might have been pregnant, anywhere near that area?"

"Wait a minute." Jack was puzzled. "Are you telling me that you were found near St-John-in-the-Forest?"

"Yes—didn't you know that?"

Jack could hardly believe his ears. "No, I didn't know that," he said slowly. His mind was reeling with the implications of the revelation. "When we arrived in Kingsbridge, you were already here, and I naturally assumed you had been found in the forest near here." He suddenly felt the need to sit down. There was a pile of building rubble nearby, and he lowered himself onto it.

Jonathan said impatiently: "Well, anyway, did you see anyone in the forest?"

"Oh, yes," Jack said. "I don't know how to tell you this, Jonathan."

Jonathan paled. "You know something about this, don't you? What did you see?"

"I saw you, Jonathan; that's what I saw."

Jonathan's mouth dropped open. "What . . . How?"

"It was dawn. I was on a duck-hunting expedition. I heard a cry. I found a newborn baby, wrapped in a cut-up old cloak, lying beside the embers of a dying fire."

Jonathan stared at him. "Anything else?"

Jack nodded slowly. "The baby was lying on a new grave."

Jonathan swallowed. "My mother?"

Jack nodded.

Jonathan began to weep, but he kept asking questions. "What did you do?"

"I fetched my mother. But while we were returning to the spot, we saw a priest, riding a palfrey, carrying the baby."

"Francis," Jonathan said in a choked voice.

"What?"

He swallowed hard. "I was found by Father Philip's brother, Francis, the priest."

"What was he doing there?"

"He was on his way to see Philip at St-John-in-the-Forest. That's where he took me."

"My God." Jack stared at the tall monk with tears streaming down his cheeks. You haven't heard it all yet, Jonathan, he thought.

Jonathan said: "Did you see anyone who might have been my father?"

"Yes," Jack said solemnly. "I know who he was."

"Tell me!" Jonathan whispered.

"Tom Builder."

"Tom Builder?" Jonathan sat down heavily on the ground. *"Tom Builder was my father?"*

"Yes." Jack shook his head in wonderment. "Now I know who you remind me of. You and he are the tallest people I ever met."

"He was always good to me when I was a child," Jonathan said in a dazed tone. "He used to play with me. He was fond of me. I saw as much of him as I did of Prior Philip." His tears flowed freely. "That was my father. My father." He looked up at Jack. "Why did he abandon me?"

"They thought you were going to die anyway. They had no milk to give you. They were starving themselves, I know. They were miles from anywhere. They didn't know the priory was nearby. They had no food except turnips, and turnips would have killed you."

"They did love me, after all."

Jack saw the scene as if it were yesterday: the dying fire, the freshly turned earth of the new grave, and the tiny pink baby kicking its arms and legs inside the old gray cloak. That little scrap of humanity had grown into the tall man who sat weeping on the ground in front of him. "Oh, yes, they loved you."

"How come nobody ever spoke of it?"

"Tom was ashamed, of course," Jack said. "My mother must have known that, and we children sensed it, I suppose. Anyway, it was an unmentionable topic. And we never connected *that* baby with *you*, of course."

"Tom must have made the connection," Jonathan said.

"Yes."

"I wonder why he never took me back?"

"My mother left him quite soon after we came here," Jack said. He smiled ruefully. "She was hard to please, like Sally. Anyway, that meant Tom would have had to hire a nursemaid to look after you. So I suppose he thought: Why not leave the baby at the monastery? You were well cared for there."

Jonathan nodded. "By dear old Johnny Eightpence, God rest his soul."

"Tom probably spent more time with you that way. You were running around the priory close all day and every day, and he was working there. If he'd taken you away from the priory and left you at home with a nursemaid, he'd actually have seen less of you. And I imagine as the years went by, and you grew up as the priory orphan, and seemed happy that way, it felt more and more natural to leave you there. People often give a child to God, anyway."

"All these years I've wondered about my parents," Jonathan said. Jack's heart ached for him. "I've tried to imagine what they were like, asked God to let me meet them, wondered whether they loved me, questioned why they left me. Now I know that my mother died giving birth to me and my father was close to me all the rest of his life." He smiled through his tears. "I can't tell you how happy I am."

Jack felt close to tears himself. To cover his embarrassment he said: "You look like Tom."

"Do I?" Jonathan was pleased.

"Don't you remember how tall he was?"

"All adults were tall then."

"He had good features, like you. Well-carved. If ever you'd grown a beard, people would have guessed."

"I remember the day he died," Jonathan said. "He took me around the fair. We watched the bearbaiting. Then I climbed the wall of the chancel. I was too frightened to come down, so he had to come up and carry me down. Then he saw William's men coming. He put me in the cloisters. That was the last time I saw him alive."

"I remember that," Jack said. "I watched him climb down with you in his arms."

"He made sure I was safe," Jonathan said wonderingly.

"Then he took care of the others," Jack said.

"He really loved me."

Jack was struck by a thought. "This will make a difference to Philip's trial, won't it?"

"I'd forgotten that," Jonathan said. "Yes, it will. My goodness."

"Have we got irrefutable proof?" Jack wondered. "I saw the baby, and the priest, but I never actually saw the baby delivered to the little priory."

"Francis did. But Francis is Philip's brother, so his evidence is tainted."

"My mother and Tom went off together that morning," Jack said, straining his memory. "They said they were going to look for the priest. I bet they went to the priory to make sure the baby was all right."

"If she would say so in court, that would really sew it up," Jonathan said eagerly.

"Philip thinks she's a witch," Jack pointed out. "Would he let her testify?"

"We could spring it on him. But she hates him, too. Will she testify?"

"I don't know," said Jack. "Let's ask her."

*   *   *

"Fornication and nepotism?" Jack's mother cried. "Philip?" She started to laugh. "It's too absurd!"

"Mother, this is serious," Jack said.

"Philip couldn't fornicate if you put him in a barrel with three whores," she said. "He wouldn't know what to do!"

Jonathan was looking embarrassed. "Prior Philip is in real trouble, even if the charge is absurd," he said.

"And why would I help Philip?" she said. "He's caused me nothing but heartache."

Jack had been afraid of this. His mother had never forgiven Philip for splitting her and Tom. "Philip did the same to me as he did to you—if I can forgive him, you can."

"I'm not the forgiving type," she said.

"Don't do it for Philip, then—do it for me. I want to continue building at Kingsbridge."

"Why? The church is finished."

"I'd like to pull down Tom's chancel and rebuild it in the new style."

"Oh, for God's sake—"

"Mother. Philip is a good prior, and when he goes Jonathan will take over—if you come to Kingsbridge and tell the truth at the trial."

"I hate courts," she said. "No good ever comes out of them."

It was maddening. She held the key to Philip's trial: she could ensure that he was cleared. But she was a stubborn old woman. Jack was seriously afraid he would not be able to talk her into it.

He decided to try stinging her into consenting. "I suppose it's a long way to travel, for someone of your age," he said slyly. "How old are you now—sixty-eight?"

"Sixty-two, and don't try to provoke me," she snapped. "I'm fitter than you, my boy."

It could be true, Jack thought. Her hair was white as snow, and her face was deeply lined, but her startling golden eyes saw just as much as ever they had: as soon as she looked at Jonathan she had known who he was, and she had said: "Well, I've no need to ask why you're here. You've found out where you come from, have you? By God, you're as tall as your father and nearly as broad." She was also as independent and self-willed as ever.

"Sally is like you," Jack said.

She was pleased. "Is she?" She smiled. "In what way?"

"In her mulish obstinacy."

"Huh." Mother looked cross. "She'll be all right then."

Jack decided he might as well beg. "Mother, please—come to Kingsbridge with us and tell the truth."

"I don't know," she said.

Jonathan said: "I have something else to ask you."

Jack wondered what was coming. He was afraid Jonathan might say something to antagonize his mother: it was easily done, especially by clergymen. He held his breath.

Jonathan said: "Could you show me where my mother is buried?"

Jack let his breath out silently. There was nothing wrong with *that*. Indeed, Jonathan could hardly have thought of anything more likely to soften her.

She dropped her scornful manner immediately. "Of course I'll show you," she said. "I'm pretty sure I could find it."

Jack was reluctant to spend the time. The trial would start in the morning and they had a long way to go. But he sensed that he should let fate take its course.

Mother said to Jonathan: "Do you want to go there now?"

"Yes, please, if it's possible."

"All right." She stood up. She picked up a short cape of rabbit fur and slung it across her shoulders. Jack was about to tell her she would be too warm in that, but he held back: old people always felt colder.

They left the cave, with its smell of stored apples and wood smoke, and pushed through the concealing vegetation around its mouth to emerge into the spring sunshine. Mother set off without hesitation. Jack and Jonathan untied their horses and followed. They had to lead their mounts, for the terrain was too overgrown for riding. Jack noticed that his mother walked more slowly than she used to. She was not as fit as she pretended.

Jack could not have found the site on his own. There had been a time when he could find his way around this forest as easily as he could now move around Kingsbridge. But one clearing looked very much like another to him these days, just as the houses of Kingsbridge would all look the same to a stranger. Mother followed a chain of animal trails through the dense woodland. Now and again Jack would recognize a landmark associated with some childhood memory: an enormous old oak where he had once taken refuge from a wild boar; a rabbit warren that had provided many a dinner; a trout stream where, it seemed in retrospect, he had been able to catch fat fish in no time. For a while he would know where he was, then he would be lost again. It was amazing to think he had once felt totally at home in what was now an alien place, its brooks and thickets as meaningless to him as his voussoirs and templates were to peasants. If he had ever wondered, in those days, how his life would turn out, his best guess would have been nowhere near the truth.

They walked several miles. It was a warm spring day, and Jack found himself sweating, but Mother kept the rabbit fur on. Toward midafternoon she came to a halt in a shady clearing. Jack noticed she was breathing hard and looking a little gray. It was definitely time she left the forest, and came to live with him and Aliena. He resolved that he would make a big effort to persuade her.

"Are you all right?" he said.

"Of course I'm all right," she snapped. "We're there."

Jack looked around. He did not recognize it.

Jonathan said: "Is this it?"

"Yes," Mother said.

Jack said: "Where's the road?"

"Over there."

When Jack had oriented himself with the road, the clearing began to look familiar, and he was flooded with a powerful sense of the past. There was the big horse-chestnut tree: it had been bare of leaves, then, and there had been conkers all over the forest floor, but now the tree was in blossom, with big white flowers like candles all over it. The blossom had started to fall already, and every few moments a cloud of petals drifted down.

"Martha told me what had happened," Jack said. "They stopped here because your mother could go no farther. Tom made a fire and boiled some turnips for supper: there was no meat. Your mother gave birth to you right here, on the ground. You were perfectly healthy, but something went wrong, and she died." There was a slight rise in the ground a few feet from the base of the tree. "Look," Jack said. "See the mound?"

Jonathan nodded, his face taut with suppressed emotion.

"That's the grave." As Jack spoke, a drift of blossom fell from the tree and settled over the mound like a carpet of petals.

Jonathan knelt beside the grave and began to pray.

Jack stood silent. He remembered when he had discovered his relatives in Cherbourg: it had been a devastating experience. What Jonathan was going through must be even more intense.

Eventually Jonathan stood up. "When I'm prior," he said solemnly, "I'm going to build a little monastery just here, with a chapel and a hostel, so that in future no traveler on this stretch of road will ever have to spend a cold winter's night sleeping in the open air. I'll dedicate the hostel to the memory of my mother." He looked at Jack. "I don't suppose you ever knew her name, did you?"

"It was Agnes," Ellen said softly. "Your mother's name was Agnes."

Bishop Waleran made a persuasive case.

He began by telling the court about Philip's precocious development: cellarer of his monastery when he was only twenty-one, prior of the cell of St-John-in-the-Forest at twenty-three; prior of Kingsbridge at the remarkably young age of twenty-eight. He constantly emphasized Philip's youth and managed to suggest there was something arrogant about anyone who accepted responsibility early. Then he described St.-John-in-the-Forest, its remoteness and isolation, and spoke of the freedom and independence of whoever was its prior. "Who can be surprised," he said, "that after five years as virtually his own master, with only the lightest and most distant kind of supervision, this inexperienced, warm-blooded young man had a child?" It sounded almost inevitable. Waleran was infuriatingly credible. Philip wanted to strangle him.

Waleran went on to say how Philip had brought Jonathan and Johnny Eightpence with him when he came to Kingsbridge. The monks had been startled, Waleran said, when their new prior arrived with a baby and a nurse. That was true. For a moment Philip forgot his tension, and had to suppress a nostalgic smile.

Philip had played with Jonathan as a youngster, taught him lessons, and later made the lad his personal assistant, Waleran went on, just as any man would do with his own son, except that monks were not supposed to have sons. "Jonathan was precocious, just like Philip," Waleran said. "When Cuthbert Whitehead died, Philip made Jonathan cellarer, even though Jonathan was only twenty-one. Was there really no one else who could be cellarer, in this monastery of more than a hundred monks; no one but a boy of twenty-one? Or was Philip giving preference to his own flesh and blood? When Milius went off to be prior at Glastonbury, Philip made Jonathan treasurer. He is thirty-four years old. Is he the wisest and most devout of all the monks here? Or is he simply Philip's favorite?"

Philip looked around at the court. It was being held in the south transept of Kingsbridge Cathedral. Archdeacon Peter sat on a large, ornately carved chair like a throne. All of Waleran's staff were present, as were most of the monks of Kingsbridge. There would be little work done in the monastery while the prior was on trial. Every important churchman in the county was here, even some of the humble parish priests. There were also representatives from neighboring dioceses. The entire ecclesiastical community of southern England was waiting for the verdict of this court. They were not very interested in Philip's virtue, or lack of it, of course: they were following the final trial of strength between Prior Philip and Bishop Waleran.

When Waleran sat down Philip took the oath, then began to tell the story of that winter morning so long ago. He started with the upset caused by Peter of Wareham: he wanted everyone to know that Peter was prejudiced against him. Then he called Francis to tell how the baby was found.

Jonathan had gone off, leaving a message to say that he was on the track of new information about his parentage. Jack had disappeared too, from which Philip had concluded that the trip had something to do with Jack's mother, the witch Ellen, and that Jonathan had been afraid that if he stayed to explain, Philip would have forbidden the journey. They had been due back this morning, but had not yet arrived. Philip did not think Ellen would have anything to add to the story Francis was telling.

When Francis had done, Philip began to speak. "That baby was not mine," he said simply. "I swear it was not mine, in peril of my immortal soul I swear it. I have never had carnal knowledge of a woman, and I remain to this day in that state of chastity commended to us by the Apostle Paul. So why, the lord bishop asks, did I treat the babe as if it were my own?"

He looked around at the listeners. He had decided that his only chance was to tell the truth and hope that God would speak loud enough to overcome Peter's spiritual deafness. "When I was six years old, my father and mother died. They were killed by soldiers of the old King Henry, in Wales. My brother and I were saved by the abbot of a nearby monastery, and from that day onward we were cared for by monks. I was a monastery orphan. I know what it's like. I understand how the orphan yearns for a mother's touch, even though he loves the brothers who care for him. I knew that Jonathan would feel abnormal, peculiar, illegitimate. I have felt that feeling of isolation, the sense that I am different from everyone else because they all have a father and a mother and I do not. Like him, I have felt ashamed of myself for being a burden on the charity of others; have wondered what was wrong with me, that I should have been deprived of what others took for granted. I knew that he would dream, in the night, of the warm, fragrant bosom and soft voice of a mother he never knew, someone who loved him utterly and completely."

Archdeacon Peter's face was like stone. He was the worst kind of Christian, Philip realized: he embraced all of the negatives, enforced every proscription, insisted on all forms of denial, and demanded strict punishment for every offense; yet he ignored all the compassion of Christianity, denied its mercy, flagrantly disobeyed its ethic of love, and openly flouted the gentle laws of Jesus. That's what the Pharisees were like, Philip thought; no wonder the Lord preferred to eat with publicans and sinners.

He went on, although he understood, with a sinking heart, that nothing he could say would penetrate the armor of Peter's righteousness. "Nobody could care for that boy as I could, unless it were his own parents; and those we never could find. What clearer indication of God's will. . . ." He tailed off. Jonathan had just come into the church, with Jack; and between them was the witch, Jack's mother.

She had aged: her hair was snow-white, and her face was deeply lined. But she walked in like a queen, her head held high, her strange golden eyes blazing with defiance. Philip was too surprised to protest.

The court was silent as she entered the transept and stood facing Archdeacon Peter. She spoke in a voice that rang like a trumpet, and echoed from the clerestory of her son's church. "I swear by all that is holy that Jonathan is the son of Tom Builder, my dead husband, and his first wife."

There was an astonished clamor from the crowd of clergy. For a while nobody could be heard. Philip was completely bowled over. He stared openmouthed at Ellen. Tom Builder? Jonathan was the son of Tom Builder? When he looked at Jonathan he knew immediately that it was true: they were alike, not just in their height, but facially. If Jonathan had had a beard it would have been obvious.

His first reaction was a sense of loss. Until now, he had been the nearest Jonathan had to a father. But Tom was Jonathan's real father, and although Tom was dead, the discovery changed everything. Philip could no longer secretly think of himself as a father; Jonathan would no longer feel like his son. Jonathan was Tom's son now. Philip had lost him.

Philip sat down heavily. When the crowd began to quiet down, Ellen told the story of Jack hearing a cry and finding a newborn baby. Philip listened, dazed, as she told how she and Tom had hidden in the bushes, watching, as Philip and the monks came back from their morning's work to find Francis waiting for them with a newborn baby, and Johnny Eightpence trying to feed it with a rag dipped into a bucket of goat's milk.

Philip remembered very clearly how interested the young Tom

had been, a day or so later, when they had met by accident and Philip had told him about the abandoned baby. Philip had assumed his interest was that of any compassionate man in a touching story, but in fact Tom had been learning the fate of his own child.

Then Philip recalled how fond Tom had been of Jonathan in later years, as the baby turned into a toddler and then a mischievous boy. Nobody had remarked on it: the whole monastery had treated Jonathan as a pet in those days and Tom spent all his time in the priory close, so his behavior was completely unremarkable; but now, in retrospect, Philip could see that the attention Tom paid to Jonathan was special.

As Ellen sat down, Philip realized that he had been proved innocent. Ellen's revelations had been so devastating that he had almost forgotten he was on trial. Her story of childbirth and death, desperation and hope, ancient secrets and enduring love, made the question of Philip's chastity seem trivial. It was not trivial, of course; the future of the priory hung on it; and Ellen had now answered the question so dramatically that it seemed impossible the trial should continue. Even Peter of Wareham can't find me guilty after evidence like this, Philip thought. Waleran had lost again.

Waleran was not quite ready to concede defeat, however. He pointed an accusing finger at Ellen. "You say Tom Builder told you that the baby brought to the cell was his."

"Yes," Ellen said warily.

"But the other two people who might have been able to confirm this—the children Alfred and Martha—did not accompany you to the monastery."

"No."

"And Tom is dead. So we only have your word for it that Tom said this to you. Your story cannot be verified."

"How much verification do you want?" she said spiritedly. "Jack saw the abandoned baby. Francis picked it up. Jack and I met Tom and Alfred and Martha. Francis took the baby to the priory. Tom and I spied on the priory. How many witnesses would satisfy you?"

"I don't believe you," Waleran said.

"You don't believe me?" Ellen said, and suddenly Philip could see she was angry, deeply and passionately angry. "*You* don't believe me? You, Waleran Bigod, whom I know to be a perjurer?"

What on earth was coming now? Philip had a premonition of cataclysm. Waleran had blanched. There's something more here, Philip thought; something Waleran is afraid of. He felt an excited fluttering in his belly. Waleran had a vulnerable look all of a sudden.

Philip said to Ellen: "How do you know the bishop to be a perjurer?"

"Forty-seven years ago, in this very priory, there was a prisoner called Jack Shareburg," Ellen said.

Waleran interrupted her. "This court isn't interested in events that took place so long ago."

Philip said: "Yes it is. The accusation against me refers to an alleged act of fornication thirty-five years ago, my lord bishop. You have demanded that I prove my innocence. The court will now expect no less of you." He turned to Ellen. "Continue."

"No one knew why he was a prisoner, least of all himself; but the time came when he was set free, and given a jeweled cup, perhaps as recompense for the years he had been unjustly confined. He didn't want a jeweled cup, of course: he had no use for it, and it was too precious to be sold at a market. He left it behind, in the old cathedral here at Kingsbridge. Soon afterward he was arrested—by Waleran Bigod, who was then a plain country priest, humble but ambitious—and the cup mysteriously reappeared in Jack's bag. Jack Shareburg was falsely accused of stealing the cup. He was convicted on the oaths of three people: Waleran Bigod, Percy Hamleigh, and Prior James of Kingsbridge. And he was hanged."

There was a moment's stunned silence, then Philip said: "How do you know all this?"

"I was Jack Shareburg's only friend, and he was the father of my son, Jack Jackson, the master builder of this cathedral."

There was uproar. Waleran and Peter were both trying to speak at the same time but neither could be heard over the astonished hubbub of the assembled clergymen. They came to see a show-down, Philip thought, but they never expected this.

Eventually Peter made himself heard. "Why would three law-abiding citizens conspire to falsely accuse an innocent stranger?" he said skeptically.

"For gain," Ellen said. "Waleran Bigod was made an arch-deacon. Percy was given the manor of Hamleigh and several other villages, and became a man of property. I don't know what reward was received by Prior James."

"I can answer that," said a new voice.

Philip looked around, startled: the speaker was Remigius. He was well past his seventieth year, white-haired and inclined to ramble when he talked; but now, as he stood up with the help of a walking stick, his eyes were bright and his expression alert. It was rare to hear him speak publicly: since his downfall and return to the monastery he had lived a quiet and humble life. Philip wondered what was coming. Whose side was Remigius going to take? Would he seize a last opportunity to stab his old enemy Philip in the back?

"I can tell you what reward Prior James received," Remigius said. "The priory was given the villages of Northwold, Southwold and Hundredacre, plus the forest of Oldean."

Philip was aghast. Could it be true that the old prior had given false testimony, under oath, for the sake of a few villages?

"Prior James was never a good manager," Remigius went on. "The priory was in difficulty, and he thought the extra income would help us out." Remigius paused, then said incisively: "It did little good and much harm. The income was useful for a while, but Prior James never recovered his self-respect."

Listening to Remigius, Philip recalled the stooped, defeated air of the old prior, and at last understood it.

Remigius said: "James had not actually perjured himself, for he swore only that the cup belonged to the priory; but he knew Jack Shareburg was innocent, yet he remained silent. He regretted that silence for the rest of his life."

He would, Philip thought; it was such a venal sin for a monk. Remigius's testimony confirmed Ellen's story—and condemned Waleran.

Remigius was still speaking. "A few of the older ones here today will remember what the priory was like forty years ago: run-down, penniless, decrepit, demoralized. That was because of the weight of guilt hanging over the prior. When he was dying, he finally confessed his sin to me. I wanted—" Remigius broke off. The church was silent, waiting. The old man sighed and resumed. "I wanted to take over his position and repair the damage. But God chose another man for that task." He paused again, and his old face worked painfully as he struggled to finish. "I should say: God chose a better man." He sat down abruptly.

Philip was shocked, bemused and grateful. Two old enemies, Ellen and Remigius, had rescued him. The revelation of these ancient secrets made him feel as if he had been living with one eye closed. Bishop Waleran was livid with rage. He must have felt sure he was safe after all these years. He was leaning over Peter, speaking into the archdeacon's ear, while a buzz of comment rose from the audience.

Peter stood up and shouted: "Silence!" The church went quiet. "This court is closed!" he said.

"Wait a minute!" It was Jack Jackson. "That's not good enough!" he said passionately. "I want to know *why*."

Ignoring Jack, Peter walked toward the door that led into the cloisters, and Waleran followed him.

Jack went after them. "Why did you do it?" he shouted at Waleran. "You lied on oath, and a man died—are you going to walk out of here without another word?"

Waleran looked straight ahead, white-faced, tight-lipped, his expression a mask of suppressed rage. As he went through the door Jack yelled: "Answer me, you lying corrupt worthless coward! Why did you kill my father?"

Waleran walked out of the church and the door slammed behind him.

Chapter 18

THE LETTER FROM KING HENRY arrived while the monks were in chapter.

Jack had built a big new chapter house to accommodate the one hundred and fifty monks—the largest number in a single monastery in all England. The round building had a stone vaulted ceiling and tiers of steps for the monks to sit on. Monastic officers sat on stone benches around the walls, a little above the level of the rest; and Philip and Jonathan had carved stone thrones against the wall opposite the door.

A young monk was reading the seventh chapter of the Rule of Saint Benedict. "The sixth step of humility is reached when a monk is content with all that is mean and vile. . . ." Philip realized he did not know the name of the monk who was reading. Was that because he was getting old, or because the monastery was so big? "The seventh step of humility is reached when a man not only confesses with his tongue that he is most lowly and inferior to others, but in his inmost heart believes so." Philip knew he had not yet reached that stage of humility. He had achieved a great deal in his sixty-two years, and he had achieved it through courage and determination and the use of his brain; and he needed to remind himself constantly that the real reason for his success was that he had enjoyed the help of God, without which all his efforts would have come to nothing.

Beside him, Jonathan shifted restlessly. Jonathan had even more trouble with the virtue of humility than Philip did. Arrogance was the vice of good leaders. Jonathan was ready to take over the priory now, and he was impatient. He had been talking to Aliena, and he was eager to try out her farming techniques, such as plowing with horses, and planting spring crops of peas and oats on part of the fallow land. I was just the same about raising sheep for wool, thirty-five years ago, Philip thought.

He knew he should step down and let Jonathan take over as prior. He himself should spend his declining years in prayer and meditation. It was a course he had often prescribed for others. But now that he was old enough to retire, the prospect appalled him. His constitution was as sound as a bell and his mind was as lively as ever. A life of prayer and meditation would drive him mad.

However, Jonathan would not wait forever. God had given him the skills to run a major monastery, and he was not planning to waste his talents. He had visited numerous abbeys over the years, and made a good impression wherever he went. One of these days, when an abbot died, the monks would ask Jonathan to stand for election, and it would be hard for Philip to refuse permission.

The young monk whose name Philip could not remember was just finishing the chapter when there was a knock on the door and the gatekeeper came in. Brother Steven, the circuitor, frowned at him: he was not supposed to disturb the monks in chapter. The circuitor was responsible for discipline, and like all such men Steven was a stickler for the rules.

The gatekeeper said in a loud whisper: "There's a messenger from the king!"

Philip said to Jonathan: "See to it, would you?" The messenger would insist on handing his letter to a senior monastic officer. Jonathan went out. The monks were all whispering to one another. Philip said firmly: "We will continue with the necrology."

As the prayers for the dead began, he wondered what the second King Henry had to say to Kingsbridge Priory. It was not likely to be good news. Henry had been at loggerheads with the Church for six long years. The quarrel had started over the jurisdiction of ecclesiastical courts, but the willfulness of the king and the zeal of the archbishop of Canterbury, Thomas Becket, had prevented compromise, and a dispute had grown into a crisis. Becket had been forced into exile.

Sadly, the English Church was not unanimous in supporting him. Bishops such as Waleran Bigod took the king's side in order to gain royal favor. However, the pope was putting pressure on Henry to make peace with Becket. Perhaps the worst consequence of the whole dispute was that Henry's need for support within the English

Church gave power-hungry bishops such as Waleran greater influence at court. That was why a letter from the king was even more ominous than usual to Philip.

Jonathan returned and handed Philip a roll of vellum fastened with wax, the wax impressed with the mark of an enormous royal seal. All the monks were looking. Philip decided it was too much to ask them to concentrate on praying for dead people when he had such a letter in his hand. "All right," he said. "We'll continue the prayers later." He broke the seal and opened the letter. He glanced at the salutation, then handed the letter to Jonathan, whose young eyes were better. "Read it to us, please."

After the usual greetings, the king wrote: "As the new Bishop of Lincoln, I have nominated Waleran Bigod, currently Bishop of Kingsbridge. . . ." Jonathan's voice was drowned by the buzz of comment. Philip shook his head disgustedly. Waleran had lost all credibility locally since the revelations at the trial of Philip: there was no way he could continue as bishop. So he had persuaded the king to nominate him bishop of Lincoln—one of the richest bishoprics in the world. Lincoln was the third most important diocese in the kingdom, after Canterbury and York. From there it was only a short step to an archbishopric. Henry might even be grooming Waleran to take over from Thomas Becket. The thought of Waleran as archbishop of Canterbury, leader of the English Church, was so appalling that Philip felt sick with fear.

When the monks calmed down Jonathan resumed: ". . . and I have recommended the Dean and Chapter of Lincoln to elect him." Well, that was easier said than done, Philip thought. A royal recommendation was almost an order, but not quite: if the chapter at Lincoln took against Waleran, or if they had a candidate of their own, they would give the king trouble. The king would probably get his way in the end but it was not a foregone conclusion.

Jonathan went on: "I order you, the Chapter of the Priory of Kingsbridge, to hold an election for the new Bishop of Kingsbridge; and I recommend you to elect as Bishop my servant Peter of Wareham, Archdeacon of Canterbury."

A collective shout of protest went up from the assembled monks. Philip went cold with horror. The arrogant, resentful, self-righteous Archdeacon Peter was the king's choice as the new bishop of Kingsbridge! Peter was exactly the same type as Waleran. Both men were genuinely pious and God-fearing, but had no sense of their own fallibility, so they saw their own wishes as God's will, and pursued their aims with utter ruthlessness in consequence. With Peter as bishop, Jonathan would spend his life as prior battling for

justice and decency in a county ruled with an iron fist by a man with
no heart. And if Waleran became archbishop there would be no
prospect of relief.

Philip saw a long dark age ahead, like the worst period of the
civil war, when earls of William's type did as they pleased while
arrogant priests neglected their people and the priory shrank once
again to an impoverished and enfeebled shadow of its former self.
The thought angered him.

He was not the only angry one. Steven Circuitor stood up, red-
faced, and shouted, "It shall not be!," at the top of his voice, despite
Philip's rule that in chapter everyone must speak calmly and
quietly.

The monks cheered, but Jonathan proved his wisdom by asking
the crucial question: "What can we do?"

Bernard Kitchener, fat as ever, said: "We must refuse the king's
request!"

Several monks voiced their agreement.

Steven said: "We should write to the king saying we will elect
whom we please!" After a moment he added sheepishly: "With
God's guidance, of course."

Jonathan said: "I don't agree that we should refuse point-blank.
The quicker we are to defy the king, the sooner we will bring his
wrath down on our heads."

Philip said: "Jonathan is right. A man who loses a battle with
his king may be forgiven, but a man who wins such a battle is
doomed."

Steven burst out: "But you're just giving in!"

Philip was as worried and fearful as all the others, but he had to
appear calm. "Steven, be temperate, please," he said. "We must
fight against this awful appointment, of course. But we will do it
carefully and cleverly, always avoiding open confrontation."

Steven said: "But what are you going to *do*?"

"I'm not sure," Philip said. He had been despondent at first,
but now he was beginning to feel aggressive. He had fought this
battle over and over again, all his life. He had fought it here in the
priory, when he defeated Remigius and became prior; he had fought
it in the county, against William Hamleigh and Waleran Bigod; and
now he was going to fight it nationally. He was going to take on the
king.

"I think I'll have to go to France," he said. "To see Archbishop
Thomas Becket."

In every other crisis, throughout his life, Philip had been able to
come up with a plan. Whenever he or his priory or his town had

been threatened by the forces of lawlessness and savagery, he had thought of some form of defense or counterattack. He had not always been sure of success but he had never been at a loss to know what to do—until now.

He was still baffled when he arrived at the city of Sens, southeast of Paris in the Kingdom of France.

The cathedral at Sens was the widest building he had ever seen. The nave had to be fifty feet across. By comparison with Kingsbridge Cathedral, Sens gave an impression of space rather than light.

Traveling through France, for the first time in his life he had realized there were more varieties of church in the world than he had previously imagined, and he understood the revolutionary effect travel had had on Jack Jackson's thinking. Philip made sure to visit the abbey church of Saint-Denis when he passed through Paris, and he had seen where Jack got some of his ideas. He had also seen two churches with flying buttresses like those at Kingsbridge: obviously other master masons had been confronted with the problem Jack had faced, and had come up with the same solution.

Philip went to pay his respects to the archbishop of Sens, William Whitehands, a brilliant young clergyman who was the nephew of the late King Stephen. Archbishop William invited Philip to dinner. Philip was flattered, but he declined the invitation: he had come a long way to see Thomas Becket and now that he was so close he was impatient. After attending mass in the cathedral he followed the River Yonne northward out of the town.

He was traveling light, for the prior of one of the wealthiest monasteries in England: he had with him only two men-at-arms for protection, a young monk called Michael of Bristol as his aide, and a packhorse loaded with holy books, copied and beautifully illustrated in the scriptorium at Kingsbridge, to use as gifts for the abbots and bishops he called on during the journey. The costly books made impressive presents and contrasted sharply with the modesty of Philip's entourage. This was deliberate: he wanted people to respect the priory, not the prior.

Just outside the north gate of Sens, in a sunny meadow by the river, he found the venerable abbey of Sainte-Colombe, where Archbishop Thomas had been living for the past three years. One of Thomas's priests greeted him warmly, called servants to take care of his horses and baggage, and ushered him into the guesthouse where the archbishop was staying. It occurred to Philip that the exiles must be glad to receive visitors from home, not just for sentimental reasons, but because it was a sign of support.

Philip and his aide were given food and wine and introduced to

Thomas's household. His men were all priests, mostly young and—Philip thought—rather clever. Within a short while Michael was arguing with one of them about transubstantiation. Philip sipped a cup of wine and listened without taking part. Eventually one of the priests said to him: "What's your view, Father Philip? You haven't said anything yet."

Philip smiled. "Knotty theological questions are the least worrying of problems, to me."

"Why?"

"Because they will all be resolved in the hereafter, and meanwhile they can safely be shelved."

"Well spoken!" said a new voice, and Philip looked up to see Archbishop Thomas of Canterbury.

He was immediately aware of being in the presence of a remarkable man. Thomas was tall, slender and exceptionally handsome, with a wide forehead, bright eyes, fair skin and dark hair. He was about ten years younger than Philip, around fifty or fifty-one. Despite his misfortunes he had a lively, cheerful expression. He was, Philip saw instantly, a very *attractive* man; and this partly explained his remarkable rise from humble beginnings.

Philip knelt and kissed his hand.

Thomas said: "I'm so glad to make your acquaintance! I've always wanted to visit Kingsbridge—I've heard so much about your priory and the marvelous new cathedral."

Philip was charmed and flattered. He said: "I've come to see you because everything we've achieved has been put in peril by the king."

"I want to hear all about it, right away," Thomas said. "Come into my chamber." He turned around and swept out.

Philip followed, feeling at once pleased and apprehensive.

Thomas led him into a smaller room. There was a costly leather-and-wood bed covered with fine linen sheets and an embroidered quilt, but Philip also saw a thin mattress rolled up in a corner, and he recalled stories that Thomas never used the luxurious furniture provided by his hosts. Remembering his own comfortable bed in Kingsbridge, Philip suffered a pang of guilt to think that he snored in comfort while the primate of all England slept on the floor.

"Speaking of cathedrals," said Thomas, "what did you think of Sens?"

"Amazing," Philip said. "Who's the master builder?"

"William of Sens. I'm hoping to lure him to Canterbury one day. Sit down. Tell me what's happening in Kingsbridge."

Philip told Thomas about Bishop Waleran and Archdeacon

Peter. Thomas appeared deeply interested in everything Philip said, and asked several perceptive questions. As well as charm, he had brains. He had needed both, to rise to a position from which he could frustrate the will of one of the strongest kings England had ever had. Underneath his archbishop's robes, it was rumored, Thomas wore a hair shirt; and beneath that charming exterior, Philip reminded himself, there was a will of iron.

When Philip had finished his story, Thomas looked grave. "This must not be allowed to happen," he said.

"Indeed," Philip said. Thomas's firm tone was encouraging. "Can you stop it?"

"Only if I'm restored to Canterbury."

That was not the answer Philip had been hoping for. "But can't you write to the pope, even now?"

"I will," Thomas said. "Today. The pope will not recognize Peter as bishop of Kingsbridge, I promise you. But we can't stop him from sitting in the bishop's palace. And we can't appoint another man."

Philip was shocked and demoralized by the decisiveness of Thomas's negative. All the way here he had nursed the hope that Thomas would do what he had failed to do, and come up with a way to frustrate Waleran's scheme. But the brilliant Thomas was also stumped. All he could offer was the hope that he would be reinstated at Canterbury. Then, of course, he would have the power to veto episcopal appointments. Philip said dejectedly: "Is there any hope you'll come back soon?"

"Some hope, if you're an optimist," Thomas replied. "The pope has devised a peace treaty which he urges me and Henry to agree to. The terms are acceptable to me: the treaty gives me what I've been campaigning for. Henry says it is acceptable to him. I have insisted that he demonstrate his sincerity by giving me the kiss of peace. He refuses." As he spoke, Thomas's voice changed. The natural rise and fall of conversation flattened out and became an insistent monotone. All the vivacity went out of his face, and he took on the look of a priest delivering a sermon on self-denial to a heedless congregation. Philip saw in his expression the stubbornness and pride that had kept him fighting all these years. "The refusal of the kiss is a sign that he plans to lure me back to England and then renege on the terms of the agreement."

Philip nodded. The kiss of peace, which was part of the ritual of the mass, was the symbol of trust, and no contract, from a wedding to a truce, was complete without it. "What can I do?" he said, as much to himself as to Thomas.

"Go back to England and campaign for me," Thomas said. "Write letters to your fellow priors and abbots. Send a delegation from Kingsbridge to the pope. Petition the king. Preach sermons in your famous cathedral, telling the people of the county that their most senior priest has been spurned by their king."

Philip nodded. He was going to do nothing of the kind. Thomas was telling him to line up with the opposition to the king. That might do Thomas's morale some good but it would achieve nothing for Kingsbridge.

Philip had a better idea. If Henry and Thomas were this close it might not take much to push them together. Perhaps, Philip thought hopefully, there was something he could do. The idea excited his optimism. It was a long shot, but he had nothing to lose.

After all, they were only arguing about a kiss.

Philip was shocked to see how his brother had aged.

Francis's hair was gray, there were leathery bags under his eyes, and the skin of his face looked desiccated. However, he was sixty years old, so perhaps it was not surprising. And he was bright-eyed and sprightly.

Philip realized that what was bothering him was his own age. As always, seeing his brother made him aware of how he himself must have aged. He had not looked in a mirror for years. He wondered if he had bags under his eyes. He touched his face. It was hard to tell.

"What's Henry like to work for?" Philip asked, curious, as everyone was, to know what kings were like in private.

"Better than Maud," Francis said. "She was cleverer, but too devious. Henry is very open. You always know what he's thinking."

They were sitting in the cloisters of a monastery at Bayeux, where Philip was staying. King Henry's court was billeted nearby. Francis was still working for Henry, as he had for the last twenty years. He was now head of the chancery, the office that wrote out all the royal letters and charters. It was an important and powerful post.

Philip said: "Open? Henry? Archbishop Thomas doesn't think so."

"Yet another major error of judgment on Thomas's part," Francis said scornfully.

Philip thought Francis ought not to be so contemptuous of the archbishop. "Thomas is a great man," he said.

"Thomas wants to be king," Francis snapped.

"And Henry seems to want to be archbishop," Philip rejoined.

They glared at one another for a moment. If we're having a row already, Philip thought, it's no surprise that Henry and Thomas are fighting so fiercely. He smiled and said: "Well, you and I shouldn't quarrel about it, anyway."

Francis's face softened. "No, of course not. Remember, this dispute has been the plague of my life for six years now. I can't be as detached about it as you."

Philip nodded. "But why won't Henry accept the pope's peace plan?"

"He will," Francis said. "We're a whisker away from reconciliation. But Thomas wants more. He's insisting on the kiss of peace."

"But if the king is sincere, surely he should give the kiss of peace as a surety?"

Francis raised his voice. "It's not in the plan!" he said in an exasperated tone.

"But why not give it anyway?" Philip argued.

Francis sighed. "He would gladly. But he once swore an oath, in public, never to give Thomas the kiss of peace."

"Plenty of kings have broken oaths," Philip argued.

"Weak kings. Henry won't go back on a public oath. That's the kind of thing that makes him different from the wretched King Stephen."

"Then the Church probably shouldn't try to persuade him otherwise," Philip conceded reluctantly.

"So why is Thomas so insistent on the kiss?" Francis said in an exasperated tone.

"Because he doesn't trust Henry. What is to stop Henry from reneging on the deal? What could Thomas do about it? Go into exile again? His supporters have been staunch, but they're weary. Thomas can't go through all this again. So, before he yields, he must have iron guarantees."

Francis shook his head sadly. "It's become a question of pride, now, though," he said. "I know Henry has no intention of double-crossing Thomas. But he won't be compelled. He hates to feel coerced."

"It's the same with Thomas, I think," Philip said. "He's asked for this token, and he can't back down." He shook his head wearily. He had thought that Francis might be able to suggest a way to bring the two men together, but the task looked impossible.

"The irony of the whole thing is that Henry would gladly kiss Thomas *after* they're reconciled," Francis said. "He just won't accept it as a precondition."

"Did he say that?" said Philip.

"Yes."

"But that changes everything!" Philip said excitedly. "What did he say, exactly?"

"He said: 'I'll kiss his mouth, I'll kiss his feet, and I'll hear him say mass—after he comes back.' I heard him myself."

"I'm going to tell Thomas this."

"Do you think he might accept that?" Francis said eagerly.

"I don't know." Philip hardly dared to hope. "It seems such a small climb-down. He gets the kiss—it's just a little later than he wanted it."

"And for Henry, a similar small climb-down," Francis said with rising excitement. "He gives the kiss, but voluntarily, rather than under compulsion. By God, it might work."

"They could have a reconciliation at Canterbury. The whole agreement could be announced in advance, so that neither of them could change things at the last minute. Thomas could say mass and Henry could give him the kiss, there in the cathedral." And then, he thought, Thomas could block Waleran's evil plans.

"I'm going to propose this to the king," Francis said.

"And I to Thomas."

The monastery bell rang. The two brothers stood up.

"Be persuasive," Philip said. "If this works, Thomas can return to Canterbury—and if Thomas comes back, Waleran Bigod is finished."

They met in a pretty meadow on the bank of a river at the frontier between Normandy and the Kingdom of France, near the towns of Fréteval and Vievy-le-Raye. King Henry was already there, with his entourage, when Thomas arrived with Archbishop William of Sens. Philip, in Thomas's party, spotted his brother, Francis, with the king, on the far side of the field.

Henry and Thomas had reached agreement—in theory.

Both had accepted the compromise, whereby the kiss of peace would be given at a reconciliation mass after Becket returned to England. However, the deal was not done until the two of them had met.

Thomas rode out to the middle of the field, leaving his people behind, and Henry did the same, while everyone looked on with bated breath.

They talked for hours.

Nobody else could hear what was being said, but everyone could guess. They were talking about Henry's offenses against the Church, the way the English bishops had disobeyed Thomas, the controversial Constitutions of Clarendon, Thomas's exile, the role of the pope. . . . Initially Philip was afraid they would quarrel bitterly and part worse enemies. They had been close to agreement before, and had met like this, and then something had come up, some point that touched the pride of one or both, so that they had exchanged harsh words and then stormed off, each blaming the intransigence of the other. But the longer they talked, the more optimistic Philip became. If one of them had been ready to storm off, it would surely have happened early on, he felt.

The hot summer afternoon began to cool, and the shadows of the elms lengthened across the river. The tension was unbearable.

Then at last something happened. Thomas moved.

Was he going to ride away? No. He was dismounting. What did it mean? Philip watched breathlessly. Thomas got off his horse, approached Henry, and knelt at the king's feet.

The king dismounted and embraced Thomas.

The courtiers on both sides cheered and threw their hats into the air.

Philip felt tears come to his eyes. The conflict had been resolved—by reason and goodwill. This was how things ought to be.

Perhaps it was an omen for the future.

II

It was Christmas Day, and the king was in a rage.

William Hamleigh was frightened. He had known only one person with a temper like King Henry's, and that was his mother. Henry was almost as terrifying as she. He was an intimidating man anyway, with his broad shoulders and deep chest and huge head; but when he was angry his blue-gray eyes became bloodshot, his freckled face went red, and his customary restlessness turned into the furious pacing of a captive bear.

They were at Bur-le-Roi, a hunting lodge of Henry's, in a park near the Normandy coast. Henry should have been happy. He liked to hunt better than anything else in the world, and this was one of his favorite places. But he was furious. And the reason was Archbishop Thomas of Canterbury.

"Thomas, Thomas, Thomas! That's all I hear from you pestilential prelates! Thomas is doing this—Thomas is doing that—Thomas insulted you—Thomas was unjust to you. I'm sick of Thomas!"

William furtively scrutinized the faces of the earls, bishops and other dignitaries around the Christmas dinner table in the great hall. Most of them looked nervous. Only one had a look of contentment: Waleran Bigod.

Waleran had predicted that Henry would soon quarrel with Thomas again. Thomas had won too decisively, he said; the pope's peace plan forced the king to yield too much, and there would be further rows as Thomas tried to collect on the royal promises. But Waleran had not simply sat back to wait and see what would happen: he had worked hard to make his prediction come true. With William's help, Waleran constantly brought Henry complaints about what Thomas had been doing since he returned to England: riding around the countryside with an army of knights, visiting his cronies and cooking up any number of treacherous schemes, and punishing clergymen who had supported the king during the exile. Waleran embroidered these reports before passing them on to the king, but there was some truth in everything he said. However, he was fanning the flames of a fire that was already burning well. All those who had deserted Thomas during the six years of the quarrel, and were now living in fear of retribution, were keen to vilify him to the king.

So Waleran looked happy while Henry raged. And well he might. He stood to suffer more than most from the return of Thomas. The archbishop had refused to endorse the nomination of Waleran as bishop of Lincoln. Nevertheless, Thomas had come up with his own nominee as bishop of Kingsbridge: Prior Philip. If Thomas had his way, Waleran would lose Kingsbridge but would not gain Lincoln. He would be ruined.

William's own position would suffer too. With Aliena acting as earl, Waleran gone, Philip as bishop, and no doubt Jonathan as prior of Kingsbridge, William would be isolated, without a single ally in the county. That was why he had joined Waleran at the royal court, to collaborate in the undermining of the shaky concord between King Henry and Archbishop Thomas.

Nobody had eaten much of the swans, geese, peacocks and ducks on the table. William, who normally ate and drank heartily, was nibbling bread and sipping posset, a drink made with milk, beer, eggs and nutmeg, to calm his bilious stomach.

Henry had been driven into his current fury by the news that Thomas had sent a delegation to Tours—where Pope Alexander was—to complain that Henry had not kept his part of the peace treaty. One of the king's older counselors, Enjuger de Bohun, said: "There will be no peace until you have Thomas executed."

William was shocked.

Henry roared: "That's right!"

It was clear to William that Henry had taken the remark as an expression of pessimism, rather than as a serious proposal. However, William had a feeling that Enjuger had not said it lightly.

William Malvoisin said idly: "When I was in Rome, on my way back from Jerusalem, I heard tell of a pope that had been executed, for insupportable insolence. Damned if I can think of his name, now."

The archbishop of York said: "It looks as if there's nothing *else* to be done with Thomas. While he's alive he will foment sedition, at home and abroad."

To William those three statements sounded orchestrated. He looked at Waleran. At that moment Waleran spoke. "There is certainly no point in appealing to Thomas's sense of decency—"

"Be quiet, the lot of you!" the king roared. "I've heard enough! All you do is complain—when will you get off your backsides and do something about it?" He took a gulp of ale from his goblet. "This beer tastes like piss!" he shouted furiously. He pushed back his chair and, as everyone hastened to stand, he got up and stormed out of the room.

In the anxious silence that followed, Waleran said: "The message could hardly be clearer, my lords. We are to get up off our seats and do something about Thomas."

William Mandeville, the earl of Essex, said: "I think a delegation of us should go to see Thomas and set him straight."

"And what will you do if he refuses to listen to reason?" said Waleran.

"I think we should then arrest him in the name of the king."

Several people started to speak at once. The assembly broke up into smaller groups. Those around the earl of Essex began to plan their deputation to Canterbury. William saw Waleran talking to two or three younger knights. Waleran caught his eye and beckoned him over.

Waleran said: "William Mandeville's delegation will do no good. Thomas can handle them with one hand tied behind his back."

Reginald Fitzurse gave William a hard look and said: "Some of us think the time has come for sterner measures."

"What do you mean?" William said.

"You heard what Enjuger said."

Richard le Bret, a boy of about eighteen, blurted out: "Execution."

The word chilled William's heart. It was serious, then. He stared at Waleran. "Will you ask for the king's blessing?"

Reginald answered. "Impossible. He can't sanction something like this in advance." He grinned evilly. "But he can reward his faithful servants afterward."

Young Richard said: "Well, William—are you with us?"

"I'm not sure," William said. He felt both excited and scared. "I'll have to think about it."

Reginald said: "There's no time to think. We'll have to go now. We must get to Canterbury before William Mandeville, otherwise his lot will get in the way."

Waleran addressed William. "They need an older man with them, to guide them and plan the operation."

William was desperately keen to agree. Not only would this solve all his problems: the king would probably give him an earldom for it. "But to kill an archbishop must be a terrible sin!" he said.

"Don't worry about that," Waleran said. "I'll give you absolution."

*   *   *

The enormity of what they were going to do hung over William like a thundercloud as the group of assassins traveled to England. He could think of nothing else; he could neither eat nor sleep; he acted confused and spoke distractedly. By the time the ship reached Dover he was ready to abandon the project.

They reached Saltwood Castle, in Kent, three days after Christmas, on a Monday evening. The castle belonged to the archbishop of Canterbury, but during the exile it had been occupied by Ranulf de Broc, who had refused to give it back. Indeed, one of Thomas's complaints to the pope was that King Henry had failed to restore the castle to him.

Ranulf put new heart into William.

Ranulf had ravaged Kent in the absence of the archbishop, relishing the lack of authority rather in the way William had in years gone by, and he was willing to do anything to retain the freedom to do as he pleased. He was enthusiastic about the assassination plan and welcomed the chance of taking part, and he immediately began to discuss the details with gusto. His matter-of-fact approach dispelled the fog of superstitious dread that had clouded William's vision. William began once again to imagine how it would be if he were an earl again, with no one to tell him what to do.

They stayed up most of the night planning the operation. Ranulf drew a plan of the cathedral close and the archbishop's palace, scratching it on the table with a knife. The monastic buildings were on the north side of the church, which was unusual— they were normally to the south, as at Kingsbridge. The archbishop's palace was attached to the northwest corner of the church. It was entered from the kitchen courtyard. While they worked on the plan, Ranulf sent riders to his garrisons at Dover, Rochester and Bletchingley, ordering his knights to meet him on the road to Canterbury in the morning. Toward dawn the conspirators went to bed to catch an hour or two of sleep.

William's legs hurt like fire after the long journey. He hoped this was the last military operation he would ever do. He would be fifty-five soon, if his calculations were right, and he was getting too old for it.

Despite his weariness, and the heartening influence of Ranulf, he still could not sleep. The idea of killing an archbishop was too terrifying, even though he had already been absolved of his sin. He was afraid that if he went to sleep he would have nightmares.

They had figured out a good plan of attack. It would go wrong, of course: there was always *something* that went wrong. The important thing was to be flexible enough to cope with the unexpected. But whatever happened, it would not be very difficult for a group of professional fighting men to overpower a handful of effeminate monks.

The dim light of a gray winter morning leaked into the room through the arrow-slit windows. After a while William got up. He tried to say his prayers, but he could not.

The others were up early too. They had breakfast together in the hall. As well as William and Ranulf, there were Reginald Fitzurse, whom William had made leader of the attack group; Richard le Bret, the youngster of the group; William Tracy, the oldest; and Hugh Morville, the highest-ranking.

They put on their armor and set out on Ranulf's horses. It was a bitterly cold day, and the sky was dark with low gray clouds, as if it might snow. They followed the old road called Stone Street. On the two-and-a-half-hour journey they picked up several more knights.

Their main rendezvous was at Saint Augustine's Abbey, outside the city. The abbot was an old enemy of Thomas's, Ranulf had assured William, but nevertheless William decided to tell him that they had come to arrest Thomas, not to kill him. That was a pretense they would keep up until the last moment: no one was to know the true aim of the operation except for William himself, Ranulf, and the four knights who had crossed from France.

They reached the abbey at noon. The men Ranulf had summoned were waiting. The abbot gave them dinner. His wine was very good and they all drank plenty. Ranulf briefed the men-at-arms who would surround the cathedral close and prevent anyone from escaping.

William kept shivering, even when he stood beside the fire in the guesthouse. It should be a simple operation, but the penalty for failure would probably be death. The king would find a way to justify the murder of Thomas, but he could never support the *attempted* murder: he would have to deny all knowledge of it and hang the perpetrators. William had hanged many people, as sheriff of Shiring, but the thought of his own body dangling at the end of a rope still made him shake.

He turned his mind to the thought of the earldom he could expect as a reward for success. It would be nice to be an earl again in his old age, respected and deferred to and obeyed without question. Perhaps Aliena's brother, Richard, would die in the Holy Land and King Henry would give William his old estates again. The thought warmed him more than the fire.

When they left the abbey they were a small army. Nevertheless they had no trouble getting into Canterbury. Ranulf had controlled this part of the country for six years and he had not yet relinquished his authority. He held more sway than Thomas, which was no doubt why Thomas had complained so bitterly to the pope. As soon as they were inside, the men-at-arms spread out around the cathedral close and blocked all the exits.

The operation had begun. Until this moment it had been theoretically possible to call the whole thing off, with no harm done; but now, William thought with a shiver of dread, the die was cast.

He left Ranulf in charge of the blockade, keeping a small group of knights and men for himself. He installed most of the knights in a house opposite the main gateway to the cathedral close. Then he went through the gate with the remainder. Reginald Fitzurse and the other three conspirators rode into the kitchen courtyard as if they were official visitors, rather than armed intruders. But William ran into the gatehouse and held the terrified porter at sword point.

The attack was under way.

With his heart in his mouth, William ordered a man-at-arms to tie up the porter, then summoned the rest of his men into the gatehouse and closed the gate. Now no one could enter or leave. He had taken armed control of a monastery.

He followed the four conspirators into the kitchen courtyard. There were stables to the north of the yard, but the four had tied their horses to a mulberry tree in the middle. They took off their sword belts and helmets: they would keep up the facade of a peaceful visit a little longer.

William caught up with them and dropped his weapons under the tree. Reginald looked inquiringly at him. "All's well," William said. "The place is isolated."

They crossed the courtyard to the palace and went into the porch. William assigned a local knight called Richard to stay in the porch on guard. The others entered the great hall.

The palace servants were sitting down to dinner. That meant they had already served Thomas and the priests and monks who were with him. One of the servants stood up. Reginald said: "We are the king's men."

The room went quiet, but the servant who had stood up said: "Welcome, my lords. I'm the steward of the hall, William Fitzneal. Please come in. Would you like some dinner?"

He was remarkably friendly, William thought, considering that his master was at loggerheads with the king. He could probably be suborned.

"No dinner, thank you," said Reginald.

"A cup of wine, after your journey?"

"We have a message for your master from the king," Reginald said impatiently. "Please announce us right away."

"Very good." The steward bowed. They were unarmed, so he had no reason to refuse them. He left the table and walked to the far end of the hall.

William and the four knights followed. The eyes of the silent servants went with them. William was trembling the way he used to before a battle, and he wished the fighting would start, for he knew he would be all right then.

They all went up a staircase to the upper floor.

They emerged in a roomy attendance chamber with benches around the sides. There was a large throne in the middle of one wall. Several black-robed priests and monks were sitting on the benches, but the throne was empty.

The steward crossed the room to an open door. "Messengers from the king, my lord archbishop," he said in a loud voice.

There was no audible reply, but the archbishop must have nodded, for the steward waved them in.

The monks and priests stared wide-eyed as the knights marched across the room and went into the inner chamber.

Thomas Becket was sitting on the edge of the bed, dressed in his archbishop's robes. There was only one other person in the room: a monk, sitting at Thomas's feet, listening. William caught the monk's eye, and was jolted to recognize Prior Philip of Kingsbridge. What was he doing here? Currying favor, no doubt. Philip had been elected bishop of Kingsbridge, but had not yet been confirmed. Now, William thought with savage glee, he never would be.

Philip was equally startled to see William. However, Thomas carried on speaking, pretending not to notice the knights. This was a piece of calculated discourtesy, William thought. The knights sat down on the low stools and benches around the bed. William wished they had not: it made the visit seem social, and he felt they had lost impetus somehow. Perhaps that was what Thomas had intended.

Finally Thomas looked at them. He did not rise to greet them. He knew them all, except William, and his eye came to rest on Hugh Morville, the highest-ranking. "Ah, Hugh," he said.

William had put Reginald in charge of this part of the operation, and so it was Reginald, not Hugh, who spoke to the archbishop. "We come from the king in Normandy. Do you want to hear his message in public or in private?"

Thomas looked irritably from Reginald to Hugh and back again, as if he resented dealing with a junior member of the delegation. He sighed, then said: "Leave me, Philip."

Philip stood up and walked past the knights, looking worried.

"But don't close the door," Thomas called after him.

When Philip had gone out, Reginald said: "I require you in the name of the king to go to Winchester to answer charges against you."

William had the satisfaction of seeing Thomas go pale. "So that's how it is," the archbishop said quietly. He looked up. The steward was hovering at the door. "Send everyone in," Thomas said to him. "I want them all to hear this."

The monks and priests filed in, Prior Philip among them. Some sat down and others stood around the walls. William had no objection: on the contrary, the more people who were present, the better; for the object of this unarmed encounter was to establish before witnesses that Thomas refused to comply with a royal command.

When they were all settled, Thomas looked at Reginald. "Again?" he said.

"I require you in the name of the king to go to Winchester to answer charges against you," Reginald repeated.

"What charges?" Thomas said quietly.

"Treason!"

Thomas shook his head. "I will not be put on trial by Henry," he said calmly. "I've committed no crime, God knows."

"You've excommunicated royal servants."

"It was not I, but the pope, who did that."

"You've suspended other bishops."

"I've offered to reinstate them on merciful terms. They have refused. My offer remains open."

"You've threatened the succession to the throne by disparaging the coronation of the king's son."

"I did no such thing. The archbishop of York has no right to crown anyone, and the pope has reprimanded him for his effrontery. But no one has suggested that the coronation is invalid."

Reginald said exasperatedly: "The one thing follows from the other, you damn fool."

"I've had enough!" Thomas said.

"And we've had enough of you, Thomas Becket," Reginald shouted. "By God's wounds, we've had enough of you, and your arrogance and troublemaking and treason!"

Thomas stood up. "The archbishop's castles are occupied by the king's men," he shouted. "The archbishop's rents have been collected by the king. The archbishop has been ordered not to leave the city of Canterbury. And you tell me that *you* have had enough?"

One of the priests tried to intervene, saying to Thomas: "My lord, let's discuss the matter in private—"

"To what end?" Thomas snapped. "They demand something I must not do and will not do."

The shouting had attracted everyone in the palace, and the doorway to the chamber was crowded with wide-eyed listeners, William saw. The argument had gone on long enough: nobody could now deny that Thomas had refused a royal command. William made a signal to Reginald. It was a discreet gesture, but Prior Philip noticed it and raised his eyebrows in surprise, realizing that the leader of the group was not Reginald but William.

Reginald said formally: "Archbishop Thomas, you are no longer under the king's peace and protection." He turned around and addressed the onlookers. "Clear this room," he ordered.

Nobody moved.

Reginald said: "You monks, I order you in the name of the king to guard the archbishop and prevent his escape."

They would do no such thing, of course. Nor did William want them to: on the contrary, he wanted Thomas to attempt an escape, for that would make it easier to kill him.

Reginald turned to the steward, William Fitzneal, who was technically the archbishop's bodyguard. "I arrest you," he said. He grabbed the steward's arm and marched him out of the room. The man did not resist. William and the other knights followed them out.

They ran down the stairs and through the hall. The local knight, Richard, was still on guard in the porch. William wondered what to do with the steward. He asked him: "Are you with us?"

The man was terrified. He said: "Yes, if you're with the king!"

He was too frightened to be any danger, whatever side he was on, William decided. He said to Richard: "Keep an eye on him. Let no one leave the building. Keep the porch door closed."

With the others he ran across the courtyard to the mulberry tree. Hastily they began to put on their helmets and swords. We're going to do it now, William thought fearfully; we're going to go back in there and kill the archbishop of Canterbury, oh my God. It was a long time since William had worn a helmet, and the fringe of chain mail that protected the neck and shoulders kept getting in the way. He cursed his clumsy fingers. He did not have time to fumble anything just now. He spotted a boy watching him openmouthed and shouted to him: "Hey! You! What's your name?"

The boy looked back toward the kitchen, unsure whether to answer William or flee. "Robert, lord," he said after a moment. "They call me Robert Pipe."

"Come here, Robert Pipe, and help me with this."

The boy hesitated again.

William's patience ran out. "Come here, or I swear by the blood of Jesus I'll chop off your hand with this sword!"

Reluctantly the boy came forward. William showed him how to hold up the chain mail while he put on the helmet. He got it on at last, and Robert Pipe fled. He'll tell his grandchildren about this, William thought fleetingly.

The helmet had a ventail, a mouth flap that could be pulled across and fastened with a strap. The others had closed theirs, so that their faces were hidden and they could no longer be recognized. William left his open a moment longer. Each of them had a sword in one hand and an ax in the other.

"Ready?" William said.

They all nodded.

There would be little talk from now on. No more orders were necessary, no further decisions had to be made. They were simply going to go back in there and kill Thomas.

William put two fingers in his mouth and gave a shrill whistle.

Then he fastened his ventail.

A man-at-arms came running out of the gatehouse and threw open the main gate.

The knights William had stationed in the house across the road came out and poured into the courtyard, shouting, as they had been instructed, "King's men! King's men!"

William ran back to the palace.

The knight Richard and the steward William Fitzneal threw open the porch door for him.

As he entered, two of the archbishop's servants took advantage of the fact that Richard and William Fitzneal were distracted, and slammed the door between the porch and the hall.

William threw his weight against the door but he was too late: they had secured it with a bar. He cursed. A setback, and so soon! The knights began to hack at the door with their axes, but they made little headway: it had been made to withstand attack. William felt control slipping away from him. Fighting back the beginnings of a panic, he ran out of the porch and looked around for another door. Reginald went with him.

There was nothing on this side of the building. They ran around the west end of the palace, past the detached kitchen, into the orchard on the south side. William grunted with satisfaction: there on the south wall of the palace was a staircase leading to the upper floor. It looked like a private entrance to the archbishop's chambers. The feeling of panic went away.

William and Reginald ran to the foot of the staircase. It was damaged halfway up, and there were a few workmen's tools and a ladder nearby, as if the stairs were being repaired. Reginald leaned the ladder against the side of the staircase and climbed up, bypassing the broken steps. He reached the top. There was a door leading to an oriel, a little enclosed balcony. William watched him try the door. It was locked. Beside it was a shuttered window. Reginald smashed the shutter with one blow of his ax. He reached inside, fumbled, then opened the door and went in.

William started to climb the ladder.

Philip was scared from the moment he saw William Hamleigh, but the priests and monks in Thomas's entourage were at first complacent. Then, when they heard the hammering on the hall door, they became frightened, and several of them proposed taking refuge in the cathedral.

Thomas was scornful. "Take refuge?" he said. "From what? Those knights? An archbishop can't run from a few hotheads."

Philip thought he was right, up to a point: the title of archbishop was meaningless if you could be frightened by knights. The man of God, secure in the knowledge that his sins are forgiven, regards death as a happy transfer to a better place, and has no fear of swords. However, even an archbishop ought not to be so careless of his safety as to invite attack. Furthermore, Philip had firsthand knowledge of the viciousness and brutality of William Hamleigh. So when they heard the smashing of the oriel shutter, Philip decided to take a lead.

He could see, through the windows, that the palace was surrounded by knights. The sight of them scared him more. This was clearly a carefully planned attack, and the perpetrators were prepared to commit violence. He hastily closed the bedroom door and pulled the bar across. The others watched him, content to let someone decisive take charge. Archbishop Thomas continued to look scornful but he did not try to stop Philip.

Philip stood by the door and listened. He heard a man come through the oriel and enter the audience chamber. He wondered how strong the bedroom door was. However, the man did not attack the door, but crossed the audience chamber and started down the stairs. Philip guessed he was going to open the hall door from the inside and let the rest of the knights in that way.

That gave Thomas a few moments' reprieve.

There was another door in the opposite corner of the bedroom, partly concealed by the bed. Philip pointed at it and said urgently: "Where does that lead?"

"To the cloisters," someone said. "But it's locked shut."

Philip crossed the room and tried the door. It was locked. "Have you got a key?" he said to Thomas, adding as an after-thought, "My lord archbishop."

Thomas shook his head. "That passage has never been used in my memory," he said with infuriating calm.

The door did not look very stout, but Philip was sixty-three years old and brute force had never been his metier. He stood back and gave the door a kick. It hurt his foot. The door rattled flimsily. Philip gritted his teeth and kicked it harder. It flew open.

Philip looked at Thomas. Thomas still seemed reluctant to flee. Perhaps it had not dawned on him, as it had on Philip, that the number of knights and the well-organized nature of their operation indicated a deadly serious intention to do him harm. But Philip knew instinctively that it would be fruitless to try to scare Thomas into fleeing. Instead he said: "It's time for vespers. We ought not to let a few hotheads disrupt the routine of worship."

Thomas smiled, seeing that his own argument had been used against him. "Very well," he said, and he got to his feet.

Philip led the way, feeling relief that he had got Thomas moving and fear that the archbishop still might not move fast enough. The passage led down a long flight of steps. There was no light except what came through the archbishop's bedroom. At the end of the passage was another door. Philip gave it the same treat-ment as he had given the first door, but this one was stronger and it did not open. He began to hammer on it, shouting: "Help! Open the door! Hurry, hurry!" He heard the note of panic in his own voice, and made an effort to stay calm, but his heart was racing and he knew that William's knights must be close behind.

The others caught up with him. He continued to bang the door and shout. He heard Thomas say: "Dignity, Philip, please," but he took no notice. He wanted to preserve the archbishop's dignity—his own was of no account.

Before Thomas could protest again, there was the sound of a bar being drawn and a key turning in the lock, and the door was opened. Philip grunted with relief. Two startled cellarers stood there. One said: "I didn't know this door led anywhere."

Philip pushed past them impatiently. He found himself in the cellarer's stores. He negotiated the barrels and sacks to reach another door, and passed through that into the open air.

It was getting dark. He was in the south walk of the cloisters. At the far end of the walk he saw, to his immense relief, the door that led into the north transept of Canterbury Cathedral.

They were almost safe.

He had to get Thomas into the cathedral before William and his knights could catch up. The rest of the party emerged from the stores. Philip said: "Into the church, quickly!"

Thomas said: "No, Philip; not quickly. We will enter my cathedral with dignity."

Philip wanted to scream, but he said: "Of course, my lord." He could hear the ominous sound of heavy feet in the disused passage: the knights had broken into the bedroom and had found the bolthole. He knew the archbishop's best protection was his dignity, but there was no harm in getting out of the way of trouble.

"Where is the archbishop's cross?" Thomas said. "I can't enter the church without my cross."

Philip groaned in despair.

Then one of the priests said: "I brought the cross. Here it is."

Thomas said: "Carry it before me in the usual way, please."

The priest held it up and walked with restrained haste toward the church door.

Thomas followed him.

The archbishop's entourage preceded him into the cathedral, as etiquette demanded. Philip went last and held the door for him. Just as Thomas entered, two knights burst out of the cellarer's stores and sprinted down the south walk.

Philip closed the transept door. There was a bar located in a hole in the wall beside the doorpost. Philip grabbed the bar and pulled it across the door.

He turned around, sagging with relief, and leaned back against the door.

Thomas was crossing the narrow transept toward the steps that led up to the north aisle of the chancel, but when he heard the bar slam into place he stopped suddenly and turned around.

"No, Philip," he said.

Philip's heart sank. "My lord archbishop—"

"This is a church, not a castle. Unbar the door."

The door shook violently as the knights tried to open it. Philip said: "I'm afraid they want to kill you!"

"Then they will probably succeed, whether you bar the door or not. Do you know how many other doors there are to this church? Open it."

There was a series of loud bangs, as if the knights were attack-

ing the door with axes. "You could hide," Philip said desperately.
"There are dozens of places—the entrance to the crypt is just
there—it's getting dark—"

"Hide, Philip? In my own church? Would you?"

Philip stared at Thomas for a long moment. At last he said:
"No, I wouldn't."

"Open the door."

With a heavy heart, Philip slid back the bar.

The knights burst in. There were five of them. Their faces were
hidden behind helmets. They carried swords and axes. They looked
like emissaries from hell.

Philip knew he should not be afraid, but the sharp edges of
their weapons made him shiver with fear.

One of them shouted: "Where is Thomas Becket, a traitor to the
king and to the kingdom?"

The others shouted: "Where is the traitor? Where is the archbishop?"

It was quite dark now, and the big church was only dimly lit by
candles. All the monks were in black, and the knights' vision was
somewhat limited by their faceplates. Philip had a sudden surge of
hope: perhaps they would miss Thomas in the darkness. But
Thomas immediately dashed that hope by walking down the steps
toward the knights, saying: "Here I am—no traitor to the king, but
a priest of God. What do you want?"

As the archbishop stood confronting the five men with their
drawn swords, Philip suddenly knew with certainty that Thomas
was going to die here today.

The people in the archbishop's entourage must have had the
same feeling, for suddenly most of them fled. Some disappeared
into the gloom of the chancel, a few scattered into the nave among
the townspeople waiting for the service, and one opened a small
door and ran up a spiral staircase. Philip was disgusted. "You
should pray, not run!" he shouted after them.

It occurred to Philip that he, too, might be killed if he did not
run. But he could not tear himself away from the side of the archbishop.

One of the knights said to Thomas: "Renounce your treachery!"
Philip recognized the voice of Reginald Fitzurse, who had done the
talking earlier.

"I have nothing to renounce," Thomas replied. "I have
committed no treachery." He was deadly calm, but his face was
white, and Philip realized that Thomas, like everyone else, had realized that he was going to die.

Reginald shouted at Thomas: "Run away, you're a dead man!"

Thomas stood still.

They *want* him to run, Philip thought; they can't bring themselves to kill him in cold blood.

Perhaps Thomas had understood that too, for he stood unflinching in front of them, defying them to touch him. For a long moment they were all frozen in a murderous tableau, the knights unwilling to make the first move, the priest too proud to run.

It was Thomas who fatally broke the spell. He said: "I am ready to die, but you are not to touch any of my men, priests or monks or laymen."

Reginald moved first. He waved his sword at Thomas, pushing its point closer and closer to his face, as if daring himself to let the blade touch the priest. Thomas stood like stone, his eyes focused on the knight, not the sword. Suddenly, with a quick twist of the wrist, Reginald knocked Thomas's cap off.

Philip was suddenly filled with hope again. They can't bring themselves to do it, he thought; they're afraid to touch him.

But he was wrong. The knights' resolution seemed to be strengthened by the silly gesture of knocking off the archbishop's cap; as if, perhaps, they had half expected to be struck down by the hand of God, and the fact that they had got away with it gave them courage to do worse. Reginald said: "Carry him out of here."

The other knights sheathed their swords and approached the archbishop.

One of them grasped Thomas about the waist and tried to lift him.

Philip despaired. They had touched him at last. They were, after all, willing to lay hands on a man of God. Philip had a stomach-lurching sense of the depths of their evil, like looking over the edge of a bottomless pit. They must know, in their hearts, that they would go to hell for this; yet still they did it.

Thomas lost his balance, flailed his arms, and began to struggle. The other knights joined in trying to lift him up and carry him. The only people left from Thomas's entourage were Philip and a priest called Edward Grim. They both rushed forward to help Thomas. Edward grabbed Thomas's mantle and clung on tight. One of the knights turned and lashed out at Philip with a mailed fist. The blow struck the side of Philip's head, and he went down, dazed.

When he recovered, the knights had released Thomas, who was standing with his head bowed and his hands together in an attitude of prayer. One of the knights raised his sword.

Philip, still on the floor, gave a long, helpless yell of protest: "Noooo!"

Edward Grim held out his arm to ward off the blow.

Thomas said: "I commend myself to Go—"

The sword fell.

It struck both Thomas and Edward. Philip heard himself scream. The sword cut into the archbishop's skull and sliced the priest's arm. As blood spurted from Edward's arm, Thomas fell to his knees.

Philip stared aghast at the appalling wound to Thomas's head.

The archbishop fell slowly forward onto his hands, supported himself only for an instant, then crashed onto his face on the stone floor.

Another knight lifted his sword and struck. Philip gave an involuntary howl of grief. The second blow landed in the same place as the first, and sliced off the top of Thomas's skull. It was such a forceful swing that the sword struck the pavement and snapped in two. The knight dropped the stump.

A third knight committed an act which would burn in Philip's memory for the rest of his life: he stuck the point of his sword into the opened head of the archbishop and spilled the brains out onto the floor.

Philip's legs felt weak and he sank to his knees, overcome with horror.

The knight said: "He won't get up again—let's be off!"

They all turned and ran.

Philip watched them go down the nave, laying about them with their swords to scatter the townspeople.

When the killers had gone there was a moment of frozen silence. The corpse of the archbishop lay facedown on the floor, and the severed skull, with its hair, lay beside the head like the lid of a pot. Philip buried his face in his hands. This was the end of all hope. The savages have won, he kept thinking; the savages have won. He had a giddy, weightless sensation, as if he were sinking slowly in a deep lake, drowning in despair. There was nothing to hold on to anymore; everything that had seemed fixed was suddenly unstable.

He had spent his life fighting the arbitrary power of wicked men, and now, in the ultimate contest, he had been defeated. He remembered when William Hamleigh had come to set fire to Kingsbridge the second time, and the townspeople had built a wall in a day. What a victory that had been! The peaceful strength of hundreds of ordinary people had defeated the naked cruelty of Earl William. He recalled the time Waleran Bigod had tried to have the cathedral built at Shiring so that he could control it for his own ends. Philip had mobilized the people of the whole county.

Hundreds of them, more than a thousand, had flocked to Kingsbridge on that marvelous Whitsunday thirty-three years ago, and the sheer force of their zeal had defeated Waleran. But there was no hope now. All the ordinary folk in Canterbury, even the entire population of Christendom, would not be enough to bring Thomas back to life.

Kneeling on the flagstones in the north transept of Canterbury Cathedral, he saw again the men who had burst into his home and slaughtered his mother and father before his eyes, fifty-six years ago. The emotion that came to him now, from that six-year-old child, was not fear, not even grief. It was *rage*. Powerless to stop those huge, red-faced, bloodthirsty men, he had conceived a blazing ambition to shackle all such swordsmen, to blunt their swords and hobble their war-horses and force them to submit to another authority, one higher than the monarchy of violence. And moments later, as his parents lay dead on the floor, Abbot Peter had come in to show him the way. Unarmed and defenseless, the abbot had instantly stopped the bloodshed, with nothing but the authority of his Church and the force of his goodness. That scene had inspired Philip all his life.

Until this moment he had believed that he and people like him were winning. They had achieved some notable victories in the past half century. But now, at the end of his life, his enemies had proved that nothing had changed. His triumphs had been temporary, his progress illusory. He had won some battles, but the cause was ultimately hopeless. Men just like the ones who killed his mother and father had now murdered an archbishop in a cathedral, as if to prove, beyond all possibility of doubt, that there was no authority that could prevail against the tyranny of a man with a sword.

He had never thought they would dare to kill Archbishop Thomas, especially in a church. But he had never thought anyone could kill his father, and the same bloodthirsty men with swords and helmets had shown him the grisly truth in both cases. And now, at the age of sixty-two, as he looked at the grisly corpse of Thomas Becket, he was possessed by the childish, unreasoning, all-encompassing fury of a six-year-old boy whose father is dead.

He stood up. The atmosphere in the church was thick with emotion as the people gathered around the corpse of the archbishop. Priests, monks and townspeople came slowly nearer, stunned and full of dread. Philip sensed that behind their shocked expressions there was a rage like his own. One or two of them were muttering prayers, or just moaning half audibly. A woman bent down swiftly and touched the dead body, as if for luck. Several other people followed suit. Then Philip saw the first woman furtively collecting some of the blood in a tiny flask, as if Thomas were a martyr.

The clergy began to come to their senses. The archbishop's chamberlain, Osbert, with tears streaming down his face, took out a knife and cut a strip from his own shirt, then bent down by the body and clumsily, gruesomely tied Thomas's skull back on to his head, in a pathetic attempt to restore a modicum of dignity to the horribly violated person of the archbishop. As he did so, a low collective groan went up from the crowd all around.

Some monks brought a stretcher. They lifted Thomas onto it gently. Many hands reached out to help them. Philip saw that the archbishop's handsome face was peaceful, the only sign of violence being a thin line of blood running from the right temple, across the nose, to the left cheek.

As they lifted the stretcher, Philip picked up the broken stump of the sword that had killed Thomas. He kept thinking of the woman who had collected the archbishop's blood in a bottle, as if he were a saint. There was a massive significance to that small act of hers, but Philip was not yet sure exactly what it was.

The people followed the stretcher, drawn by an invisible force. Philip went with the crowd, feeling the weird compulsion that gripped them all. The monks carried the body through the chancel and lowered it gently to the ground in front of the high altar. The crowd, many of them praying aloud, watched as a priest brought a clean cloth and bandaged the head neatly, then covered most of the bandage with a new cap.

A monk cut through the black archbishop's mantle, which was soiled with blood, and removed it. The man seemed unsure what to do with the bloody garment, and turned as if to throw it to one side. A citizen stepped forward quickly and took it from him as if it were a precious object.

The thought that had been hovering uncertainly in the back of Philip's mind now came to the foreground in an inspirational flash. The citizens were treating Thomas like a martyr, eagerly collecting his blood and his clothes as if they had the supernatural powers of saints' relics. Philip had been regarding the murder as a political defeat for the Church, but the people here did not see it that way: they saw a martyrdom. And the death of a martyr, while it might look like a defeat, never failed to provide inspiration and strength to the Church in the end.

Philip thought again of the hundreds of people who had flocked to Kingsbridge to build the cathedral, and of the men, women and children who had worked together half the night to put up the town wall. If such people could be mobilized now, he thought with a mounting sense of excitement, they might raise a cry of outrage so loud it would be heard all over the world.

Looking at the men and women gathered around the body, their faces suffused with grief and horror, Philip realized that they only wanted a leader.

Was it possible?

There was something familiar about this situation, he realized. A mutilated corpse, a crowd of onlookers, and some soldiers in the distance: where had he seen this before? What should happen next, he felt, was that a small group of followers of the dead man would range themselves against all the power and authority of a mighty empire.

Of course. That was how Christianity started.

And when he understood that, he knew what he had to do next.

He moved in front of the altar and turned to face the crowd. He still had the broken sword in his hand. Everyone stared at him. He suffered a moment of self-doubt. Can I do it? he thought. Can I start a movement, here and now, that will shake the throne of England? He looked at their faces. As well as grief and rage, he saw, in one or two expressions, a hint of hope.

He lifted the sword on high.

"This sword killed a saint," he began.

There was a murmur of agreement.

Encouraged, Philip said: "Here tonight we have witnessed a martyrdom."

The priests and monks looked surprised. Like Philip, they had not immediately seen the real significance of the murder they had witnessed. But the townspeople had, and they voiced their approval.

"Each one of us must go from this place and tell what he has seen." Several people nodded vigorously. They were listening—but Philip wanted more. He wanted to inspire them. Preaching had never been his forte. He was not one of those men who could hold a crowd rapt, make them laugh and cry, and persuade them to follow him anywhere. He did not know how to put a tremor in his voice and make the light of glory shine from his eyes. He was a practical, earthbound man; and right now he needed to speak like an angel.

"Soon every man, woman and child in Canterbury will know that the king's men murdered Archbishop Thomas in the cathedral. But that's just the start. The news will spread all over England, and then all over Christendom."

He was losing them, he could tell. There was dissatisfaction and disappointment on some of the faces. A man called out: "But what shall we *do*?"

Philip realized they needed to take some kind of concrete action immediately. It was not possible to call for a crusade and then send people to bed.

A crusade, he thought. That was an idea.

He said: "Tomorrow, I will take this sword to Rochester. The day after tomorrow, London. Will you come with me?"

Most of them looked blank, but someone at the back called out: "Yes!" Then one or two others voiced their agreement.

Philip raised his voice a little. "We'll tell our story in every town and village in England. We'll show people the sword that killed Saint Thomas. We'll let them see the bloodstains on his priestly garments." He warmed to his theme, and let his anger show a little. "We'll raise an outcry that will spread throughout Christendom, yes, even as far as Rome. We'll turn the whole of the civilized world against the savages who perpetrated this horrible, blasphemous crime!"

This time most of them called out their assent. They had been waiting for some way of expressing their emotions, and now he was giving it to them.

"This crime," he said slowly, his voice rising to a shout, "will never—never—be—forgotten!"

They roared their approval.

Suddenly he knew where to go from here. "Let us begin our crusade now!" he said.

"Yes!"

"We'll carry this sword along every street in Canterbury!"

"Yes!"

"And we'll tell every citizen within the walls what we have witnessed here tonight!"

"Yes!"

"Bring candles, and follow me!"

Holding the sword high, he marched straight down the middle of the cathedral.

They followed him.

Feeling exultant, he went through the chancel, over the crossing, and down the nave. Some of the monks and priests walked beside him. He did not need to look back: he could hear the footsteps of a hundred people marching behind him. He went out of the main door.

There he had a moment of anxiety. Across the dark orchard he could see men-at-arms ransacking the archbishop's palace. If his followers confronted them, the crusade might turn into a brawl when it had hardly got started. Suddenly afraid, he turned sharply away and led the crowd through the nearest gate into the street.

One of the monks started a hymn. There were lamps and firelight behind the shutters of the houses, but as the procession passed by, people opened their doors to see what was going on. Some of them questioned the marchers. Some joined in.

Philip turned a corner and saw William Hamleigh.

William was standing outside a stable, and looked as if he had just taken off his chain mail prior to mounting a horse and leaving the city. He had a handful of men with him. They were all looking up expectantly, presumably having heard the singing and wondered what was going on.

As the candlelit procession approached, William at first looked mystified. Then he saw the broken sword in Philip's hand, and comprehension dawned. He stared in awestruck silence for a moment more, then he spoke. "Stop this!" he shouted. "I command you to disperse!"

Nobody took any notice. The men with William looked anxious: even with their swords they were vulnerable to a mob of more than a hundred fervent mourners.

William addressed Philip directly. "In the name of the king, I order you to stop this!"

Philip swept past him, borne forward by the press of the crowd. "Too late, William!" he cried over his shoulder. "Too late!"

III

The small boys came early to the hanging.

They were already there, in the market square at Shiring, throwing stones at cats and abusing beggars and fighting one another, when Aliena arrived, alone and on foot, wearing a cheap cloak with a hood to hide her identity.

She stood at a distance, looking at the scaffold. She had not intended to come. She had witnessed too many hangings during the years when she had played the role of earl. Now that she no longer had that responsibility, she had thought she would be happy if she never saw another man hanged for the rest of her life. But this one was different.

She was no longer acting as earl because her brother, Richard, had been killed in Syria—not in battle, ironically, but in an earthquake. The news had taken six months to reach her. She had not seen him for fifteen years, and now she would never see him again.

Up the hill, the castle gates opened, and the prisoner came out with his escort, followed by the new earl of Shiring, Aliena's son, Tommy.

Richard had never had children, so his heir was his nephew. The king, stunned and enfeebled by the Becket scandal, had taken the line of least resistance and rapidly confirmed Tommy as earl. Aliena had handed over to the younger generation readily. She had achieved what she wanted to with the earldom. It was once again a rich, thriving county, a land of fat sheep and green fields and sturdy mills. Some of the larger and more progressive landowners had followed her lead in switching to horse plowing, feeding the horses on oats grown under the three-field system of crop rotation. In consequence the land could feed even more people than it had under her father's enlightened rule.

Tommy would be a good earl. It was what he was born to do. Jack had refused to see it for a long time, wanting his son to be a builder; but eventually he had been forced to admit the truth. Tommy had never been able to cut a stone in a straight line, but he was a natural leader, and at twenty-eight years of age he was decisive, determined, intelligent and fair-minded. He was usually called Thomas now.

When he took over, people expected Aliena to stay at the castle, nag her daughter-in-law and play with her grandchildren. She had laughed at them. She liked Tommy's wife—a pretty girl, one of the younger daughters of the earl of Bedford—and she adored her three grandchildren, but at the age of fifty-two she was not ready to retire. She and Jack had taken a big stone house near the Kingsbridge Priory—in what had once been the poor quarter, although it was no longer—and she had gone back into the wool business, buying and selling, negotiating with all her old energy, and making money hand over fist.

The hanging party came into the square, and Aliena emerged from her reverie. She looked closely at the prisoner, stumbling along at the end of a rope, his hands tied behind his back. It was William Hamleigh.

Someone in the front spat at him. The crowd in the square was large, for a lot of people were happy to see the last of William, and even for those who had no grudge against him it was quite something to see a former sheriff hanged. But William had been involved in the most notorious murder anybody could remember.

Aliena had never known or imagined anything like the reaction to the killing of Archbishop Thomas. The news had spread like wildfire through the whole of Christendom, from Dublin to Jerusalem and from Toledo to Oslo. The pope had gone into mourning. The continental half of King Henry's empire had been placed under interdict, which meant the churches were closed and there were no services except baptism. In England, people had started making a pilgrimage to Canterbury, just as if it were a shrine like Santiago de Compostela. And there had been miracles. Water tinctured with the martyr's blood, and shreds of the mantle he had been wearing when he was killed, cured sick people not just in Canterbury but all over England.

William's men had tried to steal the corpse from the cathedral, but the monks had been forewarned and had hidden it; and now it was secure within a stone vault, and pilgrims had to put their heads through a hole in the wall to kiss the marble coffin.

It was William's last crime. He had come scurrying back to Shiring, but Tommy had arrested him, and accused him of sacrilege, and he had been found guilty by Bishop Philip's court. Normally no one would dare to sentence a sheriff, for he was an officer of the Crown, but in this case the reverse was true: no one, not even the king, would dare to defend one of Becket's killers.

William was going to make a bad end.

His eyes were wild and staring, his mouth was open and drooling, he was moaning incoherently, and there was a stain on the front of his tunic where he had wet himself.

Aliena watched her old enemy stagger blindly toward the gallows. She remembered the young, arrogant, heartless lad who had raped her thirty-five years ago. It was hard to believe he had become the moaning, terrified subhuman she saw now. Even the fat, gouty, disappointed old knight he had been in later life was nothing like this. He began to struggle and scream as he got closer to the scaffold. The men-at-arms pulled him along like a pig going to the slaughterhouse. Aliena found no pity in her heart: all she could feel was relief. William would never terrorize anyone again.

He kicked and screamed as he was lifted up onto the ox cart. He looked like an animal, red-faced, wild and filthy; but he sounded like a child as he gibbered and moaned and cried. It took four men to hold him while a fifth put the noose around his neck. He struggled so much that the knot tightened before he dropped, and he began to strangle by his own efforts. The men-at-arms stepped back. William writhed, choking, his fat face turning purple.

Aliena stared aghast. Even at the height of her rage and hatred she had not wished a death like this on him.

There was no noise, now that he was choking; and the crowd stood still. Even the small boys were silenced by the horrible sight.

Someone struck the ox's flank with a switch and the beast moved forward. At last William fell, but the fall did not break his neck, and he dangled at the end of the rope, slowly suffocating. His eyes remained open. Aliena felt he was looking at her. The grimace on his face as he hung there writhing in agony was familiar to Aliena, and she realized that he had looked like that when he was raping her, just before he reached his climax. The memory stabbed her like a knife, but she would not let herself look away.

It took a long time but the crowd remained quiet throughout. His face turned darker and darker. His agonized writhing became a mere twitching. At last his eyes rolled up into his head, his eyelids closed, he became still, and then, gruesomely, his tongue stuck out, black and swollen, between his teeth.

He was dead.

Aliena felt drained. William had changed her life—at one time she would have said he had ruined her life—and now he was dead, powerless to hurt her or anyone else ever again.

The crowd began to move away. The small boys mimicked the death throes to one another, rolling up their eyes and poking out their tongues. A man-at-arms climbed up on the scaffold and cut William down.

Aliena caught her son's eye. He looked surprised to see her. He came over immediately, and bent down to kiss her. My son, she thought; my big son. Jack's son. She remembered how terrified she had been that she might have William's child. Well, some things had turned out right.

"I thought you didn't want to come here today," Tommy said.

"I had to," she said. "I had to see him dead."

He looked startled. He did not understand, not really. She was glad. She hoped he would never have to understand such things.

He put his arm around her and they walked out of the square together.

Aliena did not look back.

On a hot day in high summer, Jack ate dinner with Aliena and Sally in the cool of the north transept, up in the gallery, sitting on the scratched plaster of his tracing floor. The sound of the monks chanting the service of sext in the chancel was a low murmur like the rushing of a distant waterfall. They had cold lamb chops with fresh wheat bread and a stone jug of golden beer. Jack had spent the morning sketching the layout of the new chancel which he would begin building next year. Sally was looking at his drawing while she tore into a chop with her pretty white teeth. In a moment she would say something critical about it, he knew. He glanced at Aliena. She too had read Sally's face and knew what was coming. They exchanged a knowing parental look, and smiled.

"Why do you want the east end to be rounded?" Sally said.

"I based it on the design of Saint-Denis," Jack said.

"But is there any advantage?"

"Yes. You can keep the pilgrims moving."

"So you just have this row of little windows."

Jack had thought windows would come up soon, for Sally was a glazier. "*Little* windows?" he said, pretending to be indignant. "Those windows are huge! When I first put windows that size into this church the people thought the whole building would fall down for lack of structural support."

"If the chancel were square-ended, you would have an enormous flat wall," Sally persisted. "You could put in *really* big windows."

She had a point, Jack thought. With the round-ended layout the entire chancel had to have the same continuous elevation, divided into the traditional three layers of arcade, gallery and clerestory, all the way around. A square end offered the chance to change the design. "There might be another way to keep the pilgrims moving," he said thoughtfully.

"And the rising sun would shine through the big windows," Sally said.

Jack could imagine it. "There could be a row of tall lancets, like spears in a rack."

Sally said: "Or one big round window like a rose."

That was a stunning idea. To someone standing in the nave, looking down the length of the church toward the east, the round window would seem like a huge sun exploding into innumerable shards of gorgeous color. Jack could just see it. "I wonder what theme the monks would want."

"The Law and the Prophets," Sally said.

He raised his eyebrows at her. "You sly vixen, you've already discussed this idea with Prior Jonathan, haven't you?"

She looked guilty, but she was saved from answering by the arrival of Peter Chisel, a young stone carver. He was a shy, awkward man with fair hair that fell over his eyes, but his carvings were beautiful, and Jack was glad to have him. "What can I do for you, Peter?" he said.

"Actually, I was looking for Sally," Peter said.

"Well, you've found her."

Sally was getting to her feet, brushing bread crumbs off the front of her tunic. "I'll see you later," she said, and then she and Peter went through the low doorway and down the spiral staircase.

Jack and Aliena looked at one another.

"Was she blushing?" Jack said.

"I hope so," said Aliena. "My goodness, it's about time she fell for someone. She's twenty-six years old!"

"Well, well. I'd given up hope. I thought she was planning to be an old maid."

Aliena shook her head. "Not Sally. She's as lusty as anyone. She's just choosy."

"Is she?" Jack said. "The girls of the county aren't queueing up to marry Peter Chisel."

"The girls of the county fall for big handsome men like Tommy, who can cut a dash on horseback and have their cloaks lined with red silk. Sally's different. She wants someone clever and sensitive. Peter is just right for her."

Jack nodded. He had never thought of it that way but he felt intuitively that Aliena was right. "She's like her grandmother," he said. "My mother fell in love with an oddity."

"Sally's like your mother, and Tommy is like my father," Aliena said.

Jack smiled at her. She was more beautiful than ever. Her hair was streaked with gray, and the skin of her throat was not as marble-smooth as it used to be, but as she got older, and lost the roundness of motherhood, the fine bones of her lovely face became more prominent, and she took on a spare, almost structural beauty. Jack reached out and traced the line of her jaw. "Like my flying buttresses," he said.

She smiled.

He ran his hand down her neck and across her bosom. Her breasts had changed, too. He remembered when they had stuck out from her chest as if they were weightless, the nipples pointing up. Then, when she was pregnant, they had become even bigger, and the nipples had grown larger. Now they were lower and softer, and they swung delightfully from side to side when she walked. He had loved them through all their changes. He wondered what they would be like when she was old. Would they become shriveled and wrinkled? I'll probably love them even then, he thought. He felt her nipple harden under his touch. He leaned forward to kiss her lips.

"Jack, you're in church," she murmured.

"Never mind," he said, and he ran his hand over her belly to her groin.

There was a footstep on the stair.

He pulled away guiltily.

She grinned at his discomfiture. "That's God's judgment on you," she said irreverently.

"I'll see to you later," he whispered in a mock-threatening tone.

The footsteps reached the top of the stair and Prior Jonathan emerged. He greeted them both solemnly. He looked grave. "There's something I want you to hear, Jack," he said. "Will you come to the cloisters?"

"Of course." Jack got to his feet.

Jonathan went back down the spiral staircase.

Jack paused at the doorway and pointed a threatening finger at Aliena. "Later," he said.

"Promise?" she said with a grin.

Jack followed Jonathan down the stairs and through the church to the door in the south transept that led into the cloisters. They went along the north walk, past the schoolboys with their wax tablets, and stopped at the corner. With an inclination of his head Jonathan directed Jack's attention to a monk sitting alone on a stone ledge halfway down the west walk. The monk's hood was up, covering his face, but as they paused, the man turned, looked up, and then quickly averted his gaze.

Jack took an involuntary step back.

The monk was Waleran Bigod.

Jack said angrily: "What's that devil doing here?"

"Preparing to meet his Maker," Jonathan said.

Jack frowned. "I don't understand."

"He's a broken man," Jonathan said. "He's got no position, no power and no friends. He's realized that God doesn't want him to be a great and powerful bishop. He's seen the error of his ways. He came here, on foot, and begged to be admitted as a humble monk, to spend the rest of his days asking God's forgiveness for his sins."

"I find that hard to believe," said Jack.

"So did I, at first," said Jonathan. "But in the end I realized that he has always been a genuinely God-fearing man."

Jack looked skeptical.

"I really think he was devout. He just made one crucial mistake: he believed that the end justifies the means in the service of God. That permitted him to do anything."

"Including conspiring to murder an archbishop!"

Jonathan held up his hands in a defensive gesture. "God must punish him for that—not I."

Jack shrugged. It was the kind of thing Philip would have said. Jack saw no reason to let Waleran live in the priory. However, that was the way of monks. "Why did you want me to see him?"

"He wants to tell you why they hanged your father."

Jack suddenly felt cold.

Waleran was sitting as still as a stone, gazing into space. He was barefoot. The fragile white ankles of an old man were visible below the hem of his homespun habit. Jack realized that Waleran was no longer frightening. He was feeble, defeated and sad.

Jack walked slowly forward and sat down on the bench a yard away from Waleran.

"The old King Henry was too strong," Waleran said without preamble. "Some of the barons didn't like it—they were too restricted. They wanted a weaker king next time. But Henry had a son, William."

All this was ancient history. "That was before I was born," Jack said.

"Your father died before you were born," Waleran said, with just a hint of his old superciliousness.

Jack nodded. "Go on, then."

"A group of barons decided to kill Henry's son, William. Their thinking was that if the succession was in doubt, they would have more influence over the choice of the new king."

Jack studied Waleran's pale, thin face, searching for evidence of guile. The old man just looked weary, beaten and remorseful. If he was up to something, Jack could see no sign of it. "But William died in the wreck of the White Ship," Jack said.

"That shipwreck was no accident," Waleran said.

Jack was jolted. Could this be true? The heir to the throne, murdered just because a group of barons wanted a weak monarchy? But it was no more shocking than the murder of an archbishop. "Go on," he said.

"The barons' men scuttled the ship and escaped in a boat. Everybody else drowned, except for one man who clung to a spar and floated ashore."

"That was my father," Jack said. He was beginning to see where this was leading.

Waleran's face was white and his lips were bloodless. He spoke without emotion, and did not meet Jack's eyes. "He was beached near a castle that belonged to one of the conspirators, and they caught him. The man had no interest in exposing them. Indeed, he never realized that the ship had been scuttled. But he had seen things which would have revealed the truth to others, if he had been allowed to go free and talk about his experience. So they kidnapped him, brought him to England, and put him in the care of some people they could trust."

Jack felt profoundly sad. All his father had ever wanted to do was entertain people, Mother said. But there was something strange about Waleran's story. "Why didn't they kill him right away?" Jack said.

"They should have," Waleran said unemotionally. "But he was an innocent man, a jongleur, someone who gave everyone pleasure. They couldn't bring themselves to do it." He gave a mirthless smile. "Even the most ruthless people have some scruples, ultimately."

"Then why did they change their minds?"

"Because eventually he became dangerous, even here. At first he threatened no one—he couldn't even speak English. But he learned, of course, and he began to make friends. So they locked him in the prison cell below the dormitory. Then people began to ask why he was locked away. He became an embarrassment. They realized they would never rest easy while he was alive. So in the end they told us to kill him."

So easy, thought Jack. "But why did you obey them?"

"We were ambitious, all three of us," Waleran said, and for the first time his face showed emotion, as his mouth twisted in a grimace of remorse. "Percy Hamleigh, Prior James, and me. Your mother told the truth—we all were rewarded. I became an archdeacon, and my career in the church was off to a splendid start. Percy Hamleigh became a substantial landowner. Prior James got a useful addition to the priory property."

"And the barons?"

"After the shipwreck, Henry was attacked, in the following three years, by Fulk of Anjou, William Clito in Normandy, and the king of France. For a while he looked very vulnerable. But he defeated his enemies and ruled for another ten years. However, the anarchy the barons wanted did come in the end, when Henry died without a male heir, and Stephen came to the throne. While the civil war raged for the next two decades, the barons ruled like kings in their own territories, with no central authority to curb them."

"And my father died for that."

"Even that turned sour. Most of those barons died in the fighting, and some of their sons did too. And the little lies we had told in this part of the country, to get your father killed, eventually came back to haunt us. Your mother cursed us, after the hanging, and she cursed us well. Prior James was destroyed by the knowledge of what he had done, as Remigius said at the nepotism trial. Percy Hamleigh died before the truth came out, but his son was hanged. And look at me: my act of perjury was thrown back at me almost fifty years later, and it ended my career." Waleran was looking gray-faced and exhausted, as if his rigid self-control was a terrible strain. "We were all afraid of your mother, because we weren't sure what she knew. In the end it wasn't much at all, but it was enough."

Jack felt as drained as Waleran appeared. At last he had learned the truth about his father, something he had wanted all his life. Now he could not feel angry or vengeful. He had never known his real father, but he had had Tom, who had given him the love of buildings which had been the second greatest passion of his life.

Jack stood up. The events were all too far in the past to make him weep. So much had happened since then, and most of it had been good.

He looked down at the old, sorry man sitting on the bench. Ironically, it was Waleran who was now suffering the bitterness of regret. Jack pitied him. How terrible, Jack thought, to be old and know that your life has been wasted. Waleran looked up, and their eyes met for the first time. Waleran flinched and turned away, as if his face had been slapped. For a moment Jack could read the other man's mind, and he realized that Waleran had seen the pity in his eyes.

And for Waleran, the pity of his enemies was the worst humiliation of all.

IV

Philip stood at the West Gate of the ancient Christian city of Canterbury, wearing the full, gorgeously-colored regalia of an English bishop, and carrying a jeweled crozier worth a king's ransom. It was pouring with rain.

He was sixty-six years of age, and the rain chilled his old bones. This was the last time he would venture so far from home. But he would not have missed this day for all the world. In a way, today's ceremony would crown his life's work.

It was three and a half years after the historic murder of Archbishop Thomas. In that short span of time the mystical cult of Thomas Becket had swept the world. Philip had had no idea of what he was starting when he led that small candlelit procession through the streets of Canterbury. The pope had made Thomas a saint with almost indecent speed. There was even a new order of monk-knights in the Holy Land called the Knights of Saint Thomas of Acre. King Henry had not been able to fight such a powerful popular movement. It was far too strong for any one individual to withstand.

For Philip, the importance of the whole phenomenon lay in what it demonstrated about the power of the State. The death of Thomas had shown that, in a conflict between the Church and the Crown, the monarch could always prevail by the use of brute force. But the cult of Saint Thomas proved that such a victory would always be a hollow one. The power of a king was not absolute, after all: it could be restrained by the will of the people. This change had taken place within Philip's lifetime. He had not merely witnessed it, he had helped to bring it about. And today's ceremony would commemorate that.

A stocky man with a large head was walking toward the city out of the mist of rain. He wore no boots or hat. At some distance behind him followed a large group of people on horseback.

The man was King Henry.

The crowd was as quiet as a funeral while the rain-drenched king walked through the mud to the city gate.

Philip stepped into the road, according to the prearranged plan, and walked in front of the barefoot king, leading the way to the cathedral. Henry followed with head bowed, his normally jaunty gait rigidly controlled, his posture a picture of penitence. Awestruck townspeople gazed on in silence as the king of England humbled himself before their eyes. The king's entourage followed at a distance.

Philip led him slowly through the cathedral gate. The mighty doors of the splendid church were open wide. They went in, a solemn procession of two people that was the culmination of the political crisis of the century. The nave was packed. The crowd parted to let them through. People spoke in whispers, stunned by the sight of the proudest king in Christendom, soaking wet, walking into church like a beggar.

They went slowly along the nave and down the steps into the crypt. There, beside the new tomb of the martyr, the monks of Canterbury were waiting, along with the greatest and most powerful bishops and abbots of the realm.

The king knelt on the floor.

His courtiers came into the crypt behind him. In front of everyone, Henry of England, second of that name, confessed his sins, and said he had been the unwitting cause of the murder of Saint Thomas.

When he had confessed he took off his cloak. Beneath it he wore a green tunic and a hair shirt. He knelt down again, bending his back.

The bishop of London flexed a cane.

The king was to be whipped.

He would get five strokes from each priest and three from each monk present. The strokes would be symbolic, of course: since there were eighty monks present a real beating from each of them would have killed him.

The bishop of London touched the king's back five times lightly with the cane. Then he turned and handed the cane to Philip, bishop of Kingsbridge.

Philip stepped forward to whip the king. He was glad he had lived to see this. After today, he thought, the world will never be quite the same.

I owe special thanks to
Jean Gimpel, Geoffrey Hindley,
Warren Hollister, and
Margaret Wade Labarge
for giving me the benefit
of their encyclopedic knowledge
of the Middle Ages.

I also thank Ian and Marjory Chapman
for patience, encouragement,
and inspiration.